The Heart of What Was Lost

TAD
WILLIAMS

THE HEART
OF WHAT WAS
LOST

A Novel of Osten Ard

DAW BOOKS, INC.

DONALD A. WOLLHEIM, FOUNDER

375 Hudson Street, New York, NY 10014

ELIZABETH R. WOLLHEIM

SHEILA E. GILBERT

PUBLISHERS

www.dawbooks.com

Dedication

The Osten Ard books have been incredibly important to me and also to lots of readers, so writing a sequel to the original story after so many years away has been a daunting and even occasionally terrifying project; but it has also been a joy.

This book, *The Heart of What Was Lost*, starts the journey back to Osten Ard by filling in an important piece of history left out of the last volume of "Memory, Sorrow, and Thorn"—namely, the tale of the Norns after the Storm King's War ended in their defeat.

I honestly never planned to return to Osten Ard, at least not in any major way, and it wouldn't have happened had it not been for all the kind people who asked me over the years, "But are you ever going to go back to Osten Ard?" and "What about those twins and their birth prophecy? Come on, you can't tell me that wasn't setting up a sequel!"

After enough readers asked, I started to think about it. A story finally came to me that I wanted to tell; so now, with this small volume and much more to come, I return to those lands I thought I'd left behind. Thus:

This book is dedicated to the readers who always wanted to know more about Osten Ard, about Simon and Miriamele and Binabik and the Sithi and the Norns, who wanted to know more of the history of Osten Ard before the first books began and also the history that followed the More-or-Less-Happily-Ever-After of the first story's ending. Your love for the characters and the place was something I never expected. I finally gave in, and I'm glad I did. Thank you all for your support and kindness. I'm doing my best to make you glad you encouraged me.

Welcome back! And for those of you who are new to Osten Ard, I paraphrase one of our heroes, Simon Snowlock, as he greeted an ally at the end of the first story: *Come and join us. You have a world full of friends—some of them you don't even know yet!*

Acknowledgments

Getting back to the land of Osten Ard after all these years and exploring old and new parts of it has been a huge and sometimes daunting task. I couldn't have managed without the help of many people.

My wife and partner, Deborah Beale, worked hard to make all the good things happen. Thanks, Deb!

My publishers, Sheila Gilbert and Betsy Wollheim, who are also my award-winning editors, also worked diligently to make this the best book possible, as they have with the whole of my return to Osten Ard. Josh Starr of DAW has also done a great deal to make this book possible. Thanks, Betsy and Sheila! Thanks, Josh!

Copyeditor Marylou Capes-Platt always brings the smarts and has improved every book of mine she's worked with. This book is no different. Thanks, Marylou!

My excellent agent Matt Bialer worked his own magic over the project as well, for which I am always grateful. Thanks, Matt!

Lisa Tveit has been a rock of support for a long time now with her work on the TW webpage and in many other ways. Thanks, Lisa!

I owe special debt of gratitude for this book to Ron Hyde and Ylva von Löhneysen, who have been titans of fact-checking and priceless sources of Osten-Ard-iana, not to mention being such enthusiastic fans of the original books that it makes me feel like I have done something useful with my working life. That alone is a gift beyond thanks, but they've given me much more. Thanks, Ron and Ylva!

And of course, I want to acknowledge the support I've had from so many of the people associated with the *tadwilliams.com* website, including Eva Maderbacher, who offered some very useful opinions on the first draft of *Heart*. The other early readers of the series will be thanked properly and personally in the opening volume of the new trilogy, *The Witchwood Crown*, which many of them read in manuscript. But for now, I just wanted to say: Thanks, friends! Because no author has ever had nicer or more supportive readers.

Author's Note

You can find a cast of characters and an index of other names at the end of this book. You will also find a short essay (by one of the characters) titled *An Explanation of the Fairy People Known as Sithi and their Cousins the Norns*, which those new to the land of Osten Ard might find helpful and might want to read before starting the book.

Tad Williams
October, 2016

Nakkiga   Urmsheim

THE *Hikehikayo* MORNFELLS   *Tungoldyr*

DIMMERSKOG   *Sikkihoq*

Elvritshalla   *Kaldskryke*   *Skoggey*   YIQANUC

RIMMERSGARD

Naarved

Vestvennby

Saegard   THE FROST-MARCH

THE CIRCOILLE   *Naglimund*   *Da'ai Chikiza*

◇*Mezutu'a*   ALDHEORTE

Hernysadharc   THE WEALDHELM

HERNYSTIR   *Nad Mullach*   *Enki-e-Shao'saye*

◇*Sesuad'ra*

Crannhyr   *Abaingeat*   *Erchester*   ERKYNLAND   *Hayholt*   (*Asu'a*)   *Falshire*   HIGH THRITHING

Grenefod

THE SILVER SEA   *Meremund*   *Wentmouth*   MEADOW THRITHING

Kementari

WARINSTEN   LAKE THRITHING

PERDRUIN

Ansis Pelippe

BAY OF EMETTIN

Nabban   NABBAN

N

Kwanitupul

THE WRAN

BAY OF FIRANNOS

NARAXI   HARCHA

NASCADU

OSTEN ARD

Part
One

The Ruined Fortress

At first, in the flurrying snow, he thought the soldier stumbling in front of him, through the icy mud of the Frostmarch Road, had been wounded, that the man's neck and shoulders were spattered with blood. As he steered his horse around the hobbling figure he saw that the blobs of red had a regular shape and pattern, like waves. He reined up until the soldier was limping beside him.

"Where did you get that?" Porto asked. "That scarf?"

The soldier, thin and several years younger than Porto, only stared up at him and shook his head.

"I asked you a question. Where did you get it?"

"My mother wove it for me. Piss off."

Porto settled back in his saddle, amused. "Are you really a Harborsider, or is your mother a bit blind?"

The younger soldier looked up at him with a blend of confusion and irritation: he thought he was being insulted but wasn't sure. "What do you know about it?"

"More than you do, as it turns out, because I'm from the Rocks and we've been drubbing you lot at town-ball for centuries."

"You're a Shoro—a Geyser?"

"And you're a Dogfish, dim as can be. What's your name?"

The young foot soldier looked him over carefully. The two waterfront neighborhoods—*setros,* as they were called in Ansis Pelippé, the largest city on Perdruin—were ancient rivals, and even here, hundreds of leagues north of that island's shores, it was obvious that his first impulse was to brace for a beating. "Tell me yours."

The man on the horse laughed. "Porto of Shoro Bay. Owner of one horse and most of a suit of armor. And you?"

"Endri. Baker's son."

At last, and as if he had been holding it back, the youth smiled. He still had most of his teeth and it made him seem even younger, like one of the boys who had run beside Porto's horse waving and shouting as he made his way through Nabban, all those months ago.

"By the love of Usires, you're a tall one, aren't you!" Endri looked him up and down. "What are you doing so far away from home, my lord?"

"No lord, me, just a man lucky enough to have a horse. And you're freezing to death because you can't walk fast enough. What happened to your foot?"

The younger soldier shrugged. "Horse stepped on it. Not your horse. I don't think it was, anyway."

"It wasn't. I'd have remembered you, with your Harborside scarf."

"I wish I had another. I'd even wear one in damned Shoro blue. It's so bloody cold here I'm dying. Are we in Rimmersgard yet?"

"Crossed the border two days back. But they all live like mountain trolls up here. Houses built of snow and nothing to eat but pine needles. Climb up."

"What?"

"Climb up. First time I ever helped a Dogfish, but you won't even make it to the border fort like that. Here, take my hand and I'll pull you up to the saddle."

When Endri had settled behind him, Porto gave him a sip from his drinking horn. "It was terrible, by the way."

"What was terrible?"

"The beating we gave you lot this year on St. Tunato's Day. Your Dogfish were weeping in the streets like women."

"Liar. Nobody wept."

"Only because they were too busy begging for mercy."

"You know what my father always says? 'Go to the palace for justice, go to the church for mercy, but go to the Rocks for liars and thieves.'"

Porto laughed. "For a sniveling Harborsider, your father is a wise man."

"This is a true story, if words can be true. If not, then these are only words.

"Once upon the past, during the preserve of the queen's sixteenth High Celebrant, in the era of the Wars of Return, our people, the Cloud Children, were defeated by a coalition of mortals and the Zida'ya, our own treacherous kin, at the Battle for Asu'a. The Storm King Ineluki returned to death, his plans in ruins. Our great Queen Utuk'ku survived, but fell into the keta-yi'indra, a healing sleep nearly as profound as death. It seemed to some of our people that the end of all stories had arrived, that the Great Song itself was coming to an end so that the universe could take its next age-long breath.

"Many, many of our folk who had fought for their queen in a losing cause now departed from the southern lands with thought only of returning to their home in the north ahead of the vengeance of the mortals, who would not be content with their victory, but would strive to overthrow our mountain home and extinguish the last of the Cloud Children.

"This was the moment when the People were nearly destroyed. But it was also a moment of extraordinary grace, of courage beyond the proudest demands we make upon ourselves. And as things have always been in the song of the People, in this, too, even the moments of greatest beauty were perfumed with destruction and loss.

"Thus it was for many warriors of the Order of Sacrifice when the Storm King fell, as well as those of other orders who had accompanied them to the enemy's lands. The war was ended. Home was far. And the mortals were close behind, vermin from the filthiest streets of their cities, mercenaries and madmen who killed, not as we do, regretfully, but for the sheer, savage joy of killing."

—Lady Miga seyt-Jinnata of the Order of Chroniclers

"I had hoped you might be exaggerating," said Duke Isgrimnur. "But it is worse than I could have guessed."

"An entire village," said Sludig. "No sense to it." He scowled and made the sign of the Holy Tree. Like the duke himself, the young warrior had seen terrible things during the war just ended, things neither of them would forget. Now another dozen bodies lay sprawled before the tithing-barn in a chaos of mud and bloody snow, mostly old men and a few woman, along with the hacked carcasses of several sheep. "Women and children," lamented Sludig. "Even animals."

At Isgrimnur's feet the body of a child had been half-buried by snow, the blue-gray fingers still reaching for something, the arm stretched like a trampled flower. How terrible it must have been for these villagers to wake in the night and find themselves surrounded by the deathly white faces and soulless eyes of the Norns, creatures out of old and terrifying tales. Duke Isgrimnur could only shake his head, but his hands were trembling. It was one thing to see the mortal ruin of a battle, to see his men dead and dying, but at least his soldiers had swords and axes; at least they could fight back. This . . . this was something else. It made his gut ache.

He turned to look at Ayaminu. The Sitha-woman had been standing a little apart from the duke's men, gazing at the muddle of footprints and hoofprints beginning now to disappear beneath a fresh sifting of white. The steep, golden planes of her face and her long, narrow eyes were alien and unreadable as she examined the ugly work of her people's Norn kindred, different from her only in the color of their skin. "Well?" he demanded. "What do you see? I see only murder. Your fairy cousins are monsters."

Ayaminu's inspection continued for a long moment. She seemed to make little distinction between disturbed snow and tumbled bodies. "The Hikeda'ya were stealing food," she said. "I doubt they would have bothered to harm anyone, but they were discovered."

"What of it?" Sludig was barely containing his anger. "Do you make an excuse for them because they are your kin? I don't care what you call them—Norns, White Foxes, or Hiki . . . what you said. Name them as you like, they are monsters! Look at these poor people! The war is over, but your immortal fairy cousins are still killing."

Ayaminu shook her head. "My kind are *not* immortal, only long-lived. And as recent battles have shown, both my folk and our Hikeda'ya cousins can die. Thousands of them have done so in the past year, many at the hands of mortals like you." She turned to stare at Sludig, but her face was all but expressionless. "Do I excuse this murder? No. But if the Hikeda'ya were hungry enough to steal from a mortal settlement, they must have been very hungry indeed—to the point of madness. Like my own folk, they can survive on very little. But the north has suffered from the Storm King's frosts a long time."

"We Rimmersmen have suffered from this endless winter too, without needing to destroy entire villages!"

Ayaminu gave the young warrior a bemused look. "You Rimmersmen who came out of the west a mere few centuries ago and killed thousands of my people? And just this year brought death to so many of your Hernystiri neighbors?"

"Damn it, that was not us!" Sludig was trembling. "That was other Rimmersmen under Skali of Kaldskryke—Duke Isgrimnur's sworn enemy!"

The duke put his hand on Sludig's arm. "Quiet, man. That argument has no ending." But at this moment, with his insides knotted by the sight of the dead villagers—*his* dead villagers, the people God had given him to protect—Isgrimnur could not look on the Sitha-woman with any kindness. But for the golden hue of her skin, the fairy-woman could have been one of the Norns, the corpse-white creatures whose murderous work lay all around him. "Remember that our memories are not as long as yours, Lady Ayaminu," he said as evenly as he could manage, "and neither are our lives. I gave you leave to come along with us at the request of your Lord Jiriki, friend of our king and queen—but not to pick fights with my men." In fact, it had only been the strong urgings of the newly crowned Simon and Miriamele that had convinced Isgrimnur to let the Sitha woman accompany them at all, and he was still not certain he had made the right decision.

He looked down the hill, where his men waited in disordered ranks stretching half a league back down the Frostmarch Road. They were Rimmersmen for the greatest part, along with a few hundred soldiers from other nations who had missed most of the fighting in Erchester but had been hired to reopen the empty forts along the northernmost borders between the lands of the royal High Ward and the defeated Norns. If any of them had expected the White Foxes simply to slip harmlessly back across the border, they were now learning otherwise.

"This village was Finnbogi's." Bulky, shaggy-bearded Brindur, brother of the thane of Skoggey and an important thane in his own right, had survived the final battle at the Hayholt but had left a great deal of blood and most of one of his ears behind. His helmet sat oddly over the bandages. "I saw him die just outside the castle gate, Your Grace. Had his head torn off by a giant who threw it over the Hayholt wall."

"Enough. And enough of this place, too." Isgrimnur waved his hand in angry disgust. "God preserve me, I can still smell the foul creatures even through all this blood—as though they were here only a moment ago."

"It is not likely . . ." began Ayaminu, but fell silent at the duke's violent gesture.

"We should have rounded up all the White Foxes when the battle ended," Isgrimnur said. "We should have taken their heads, prisoners or no, like Crexis when Harcha fell." He looked to the Sitha. "That works for fairies as well as for ordinary men, doesn't it? Cutting their heads off?"

Ayaminu stared at him but did not answer. Isgrimnur turned his back on her and crunched away through the drifts, back to his waiting soldiers.

"Your Grace, a rider is coming. He bears Jarl Vigri's banner!"

Isgrimnur blinked and looked up from his map to scowl at the messenger. "Why do you shout so, man? There is nothing strange in that."

The young Rimmersman colored, though it was hard to see against his burned-red cheeks. "Because he does not come along the eastern fork of the road, from Elvritshalla, but the western fork."

"Impossible," said Sludig.

"Do you mean from Naarved?" demanded the duke. "What nonsense is that?" He stood, bumping the makeshift tabletop with his belly so that the stones meant to represent armies jiggled and jumped. "Why would Vigri be in Naarved when he's supposed to be protecting Elvritshalla?" Vigri was one of the most powerful Rimmersmen lords after Isgrimnur himself. He and his father before him had been some of the duke's most steadfast supporters. It was impossible to believe that the jarl, as earls were called here in the north, would wander away from his sworn duty. Isgrimnur shook his head as he pulled on his fur-lined gloves. "Thank the Ransomer my Gutrun is still safe with our friends in the south. Has everyone in these lands run mad?" He pushed his way out of the tent with Sludig close behind. The Sitha-woman Ayaminu followed, quiet as a shadow slipping along the ground.

The messenger and his horse were wreathed in the plumes of their frosty breath. Beyond them the immensity of the Dimmerskog forest covered the eastern side of the road in snow-blanketed green, the trees silent as sentries frozen at their posts, rank upon rank until they disappeared into white mist.

"What do you have for me, fellow?" the duke demanded. "Is it truly from Vigri? Why is he not at Elvritshalla, defending the city?"

The dismounted rider did his best to bend a knee, but he was clearly almost too cold and weary to stand. "Here, Your Grace," he said, holding out a folded parchment. "I am but the messenger—let the jarl himself speak."

Isgrimnur frowned as he read, then waved to his carls. "Give this man something to eat and to drink. Sludig, Brindur, Floki—we must have words. My tent."

Inside, the men crowded around the duke, anxious but silent. Ayaminu had come in as well, but she stayed to the shadows as ever, still and watchful.

"Vigri says that the White Foxes have been returning north through our lands for over a month, mostly in scattered handfuls that stayed far from our towns and villages," Isgrimnur began. "But one large group, well-armed, and many of them mounted, were too big to ignore. This one traveled slowly. Vigri says they are carrying the body of a great Norn leader back to *Sturmrspeik*—perhaps even the queen of the Norns herself."

"A body?" said Ayaminu from her place near the doorway. "Perhaps, but it is not the queen's. Utuk'ku Silvermask is not dead. She has suffered a terrible defeat but we would have known if she had perished. And although her spirit was present at Asu'a—the place you call the Hayholt—her bodily form never left Nakkiga. She still waits inside the great mountain."

Isgrimnur frowned. "Well, it is some other notable of the White Foxes whose body they carry, then. It doesn't matter. Vigri says this group have kept together in a small army, and because of that they plunder broadly as they go. They did great damage along the outskirts of Elvritshalla, so Vigri came out to challenge them with much of the city's strength, several thousand men. The Norns fought fiercely, but at last he drove them away into the wilderness. Once he had done that, though, he did not feel he could simply let them escape." He glanced down at the letter, frowned again. "Merciful Aedon grant us good luck, he says he has trapped all those White Foxes—hundreds of them—in a tumbledown Norn border fort on the very outskirts of their land, at Skuggi Pass."

"Their old Castle Tangleroot," said Ayaminu. "It can be no other."

"Vigri left most of his soldiers to protect Elvritshalla," Isgrimnur went on. "He says the men he has are too few to press a siege in such an open place and he fears the Norns will escape again. He asks us to bring our forces and hurry to his aid."

"The castle may be falling down," said Ayaminu, "but the passages beneath it are deep and vast. The Hikeda'ya could hold it for a long time."

"Not if we drive them out like rats," said young Floki, "with fire and black iron." His broad face told how greatly that idea cheered him.

"Let the corpse-skins hide there until Doomsday," Brindur said. "Our men have fought hard and long. Many of them have been away from Rimmersgard for more than a year, and many who came with us now lie buried in Erkynland and foreign lands even farther south. What does it matter what a few hundred Norns do? Their power is broken."

"Their power is never broken while their murdering queen still lives." Sludig bore no title yet, but was certainly due for advancement: he had been one of Isgrimnur's most trusted housecarls even before the war, and had done great deeds in the struggle against the Storm King. "This might be the last of their generals and nobles, trapped in a ruin far from their home. I think Floki has the right of it, Thane Brindur. This is our chance to stamp on the whiteskins like baby snakes found under a rock."

Isgrimnur did not much like either choice. "There are no words for the hatred I feel for those monsters," he said slowly. "For what they did to my son Isorn alone I would kill every last one of them, man, woman, and child." He shook his head, as though it were almost too heavy for his neck to bear. "But Brindur is right, our people are weary. I do not want to see any more good men die fighting the fairies."

"Fight them today or fight them again soon," Sludig said, slapping at one of the axes on his belt. The young Rimmersman had taken the death of the duke's son Isorn almost as hard as Isgrimnur himself. Even now, Sludig's hatred of the Norns ran hot and strong through his blood. "When they have recovered enough to attack our lands again, my lord, we will surely wish we had dealt with them once and for all in their time of weakness."

Isgrimnur sighed. "Let me think, then. We have already made camp so we have this evening, at least. Leave me alone for a while."

As the men went out, Ayaminu stopped at the tent's doorway, her eyes gleaming like golden coins in the reflected light. "Do you wish me to stay, Duke Isgrimnur?"

He snorted. "You wished to come along to listen and watch, and since that was the will of our new king and queen, I said yes. Never did I say that I would let you give me advice."

"That is no surprise, I suppose. Elvrit's race was always stubborn and bloody-minded. Perhaps the days of Fingil Red-Hand are not as far in the past as you would like to think."

"Perhaps not," said Isgrimnur sourly.

"Already slowed by the coffin containing the body of their great warrior, High Marshal Ekisuno, one of the largest troops of the People was soon joined by more Hikeda'ya fleeing the southern defeat. Their swelling numbers now impeded their progress even more.

"Duke Isgrimnur of Elvritshalla, the leader of the Northern mortals, pursued them with a great army of his race, but the People were also harried by one of the duke's strongest allies, Jarl Vigri of Enggidal. Caught between these two cruel enemies, a mixed party of Cloud Children, most of them from the Order of Builders, along with a few Sacrifice warriors and those of other orders, were forced to take refuge in the abandoned fortress of Tangleroot Castle, where it seemed certain that the only conclusion would be their honorable and inevitable deaths."

—Lady Miga seyt-Jinnata of the Order of Chroniclers

Although the roof and most of the upper floors had long ago collapsed, the great hall beneath *Ogu Minurato*, the Fortress with Tangled Roots, was the least damaged part of the ancient, tumbledown castle. It was here that the rubble had been cleared to make room for the great funeral wagon, whose wheels were almost as tall as Viyeki himself. They had to be, because Ekisuno's mighty witchwood sarcophagus was too heavy to be carried by any smaller cart: the various Celebrants now praying around it seemed no larger than children.

Viyeki was disturbed to see how quickly things had fallen apart here outside the sacred protective walls of Nakkiga. Only a few mortal centuries gone and the natural world had all but swallowed Ogu Minurato, eating away at its walls and foundations, replacing them with its own substance, so that a sea of roots now covered the stone floors where the queen's Sacrifices had once drilled. It was a reminder that the greater world lived at the same hurried pace as the mortals—that it was Viyeki and the rest of his Hikeda'ya kind who were forever out of place.

This world knows its own, he decided. After all, the Cloud Children were exiles from the sublime Lost Garden and could not expect any other place to fit them as well.

"We live too much in the past," said a voice behind him, as if contradicting his thoughts.

Caught by surprise, Viyeki turned to see his master Yaarike watching the scene. Viyeki made a gesture of respect. "All praise to the queen, all praise to her Hamakha Clan," he said in ritual greeting. "But I beg your pardon, High Magister. I do not understand what you mean."

"Our love of the past impedes us, at least in this situation," Yaarike said.

By looks alone, Viyeki and his mentor could almost have been brothers. The skin of the High Magister of the Order of Builders was smooth, his face as refined as his noble ancestry, but subtle, almost imperceptible tremors in his hands and his voice revealed his age. Yaarike was one of the oldest of the surviving Hikeda'ya, one who had been born even before the fabled Parting from their Zida'ya cousins—the ones the mortals called Sithi.

"How can we live too much in the past, Magister?" Viyeki asked. "The past is the Garden. The past is our heritage—that for which so many of us have fought and died."

Yaarike frowned slightly. His hair was down; it hung beside his face on either side like fine white curtains. "Yes, of course, the past defines us, but the simplicity of your response disappoints me." He made a flicking gesture with his long fingers that was halfway between irritation and fondness.

"I am shamed, lord."

"You are the cleverest of my host foremen—I should not have to explain myself. But I meant that we are suffering here and now because of our own overconfidence, Viyeki-*tza*." In such moods, his master's endearments often sounded like belittlement. Viyeki waited silently.

"Remember what you first learned when you entered the Order of Builders so long ago? When you discover a flaw in stone, do not examine only the flaw, but how it formed, what it will do if left alone, and how the stone around it has responded. Do not neglect what beauty may have been created—if there were no flaws in order, life would be immeasurably poorer."

Viyeki nodded, uncertain of what this had to do with overconfidence. "Please help me see how to examine this flaw, Master."

"That is a better response." Yaarike nodded. "Ask first how many centuries have we planned this campaign against the mortals? The answer is, for almost eight Great Years—five centuries, as our enemies reckon it, since the Northmen first took mighty Asu'a from our kind. On that day Asu'a and its Zida'ya king, Ineluki, both fell to the enemy, and the precious witchwood groves were burned. So many mourning banners were flown when the news came that all Nakkiga was draped in white."

"I remember, Master."

"Mad with grief," the magister continued, "the people cried, 'Never such loss again!' But now we have been defeated once more."

"Surely not all this could have been foreseen, Master."

Yaarike shook his head. "I do not criticize our Sacrifices, who gave their all, and of course I could never find fault with the Mother of the People—to criticize the queen is to doubt the most sacred of truths. No, it is not our plan of battle I criticize, but our overconfidence. And here we see one perfect example." He gestured to the immense coffin atop the wagon. "I cannot help but think that an army, even one with so distinguished a leader as High Marshal Ekisuno, should not be carrying such impediments as the marshal's casket along with them when they go into battle. If we had won, then whether Ekisuno had lived or not, it would not have been an issue. But since we lost, we are now forced to carry him with us—and as you no doubt noticed, we have been somewhat slowed by the great warrior's corpse in its monstrous, weighty coffin."

In the hush of the ruined great hall, the only noise beside the murmur of the funeral Celebrants repeating their death-prayers was that of the wind keening in the broken ramparts above. Viyeki wondered why his master would say such a thing, especially about a personage as important as the late Ekisuno. It seemed almost a sardonic joke, but it was never possible to be certain with the order's high magister, who was deep as the innermost chasms of Nakkiga. All Viyeki could do was nod and hope that he did not offend.

"Ah. I am glad you agree, Viyeki-*tza*," Yaarike said. "And here is Commander Hayyano and his men, no doubt come to discuss how we may all sell our lives to protect Marshal Ekisuno's lifeless body."

Now Viyeki was almost certain that his master was speaking in some satirical fashion, although he still could not understand why: Ekisuno had not only been the supreme leader of the queen's armies, he was also a descendant of the great Ekimeniso, the queen's long-dead husband. If there was anyone whose corpse should be protected from profane mortals, surely it was Ekisuno.

Hayyano stopped before them and briskly made the several appropriate signs. He had been one of the less effective league commanders of the Order of Sacrifice during the battle for Asu'a, which may have been a reason he had survived, but he had learned the trick of looking busy and important. "How many of your Builders do we have, High Magister?" he demanded before he had even reached them. "We will have need of their engineering skills to defend this place."

Yaarike was silent for several moments, long enough to remind Hayyano that he was outranked not just by Yaarike himself, but even by Host Foreman Viyeki. When Yaarike saw the realization finally cross the commander's face—a subtle but unmistakable flash of unease—he waited a moment longer, then said, "We have enough Builders to make this place secure for a while, perhaps, League Commander, but not enough to defend it against a long and serious siege."

"But there are many tunnels beneath us, Magister!" Hayyano said with poorly hidden surprise. "That is why this place is called Tangleroot! They will never be able to drive us out. And we will kill ten for every one we lose."

"I was aware of the reason for the castle's name, Commander." Yaarike's words were dry as dust. "And if we have no other choice, then yes, each of us can sell his or her life very dearly. But even if we kill twenty for every one of our fallen, we still will not survive long, and we will be little help to those who await us back at Nakkiga. Is that not our greater duty?"

Hayyano drew himself up. He may not have been one of the queen's most successful officers, but he was a handsome, powerful figure and Viyeki knew him to be brave. Talk of duty had brought back his confidence. "My men and I are of the Order of Sacrifice, Lord Yaarike," the commander said. "Our death-songs are already sung. Whatever the outcome, we will make the queen proud of us."

"Certainly. If the queen lives, that is—as we all so dearly pray she will."

Viyeki saw the Sacrifice commander react in shock to old Yaarike's words. "May the Garden preserve her from harm—of course she will survive!"

"As we all pray." Yaarike made the familiar sign that meant *May the queen live forever.* "But in the meantime, we ourselves have two great responsibilities."

"Protecting the body of Ekisuno, the queen's most noble general," said Hayyano promptly.

Yaarike's nod was perfunctory. "Yes, of course. But also the lives of the queen's living servants—my hundred and more Builders, and your three dozen or so Sacrifices, as well as the mixed two or three dozen from other orders, most of whom will be little use in a real fight."

"You would not expect the Celebrants to fight beside Sacrifices, would you?" said Hayyano, looking uneasily at the funeral priests gathered around Ekisuno's coffin. "In any case, they have their own work to do."

"If the choice is between all of us dying like rats and the Celebrants taking a moment between prayers to swing a sword or throw a large rock, then yes, I think they should fight." Yaarike's face was emotionless, but Viyeki knew the magister well enough to hear the anger in his voice. "And as the highest noble within this refuge, I expect my word to be obeyed."

"Of course, High Magister," said Hayyano quickly, but his face suggested he was suppressing more argument. Viyeki thought the commander seemed helplessly transparent. Small wonder that despite high birth, he still held only middling rank.

"Good. Then I want you and your soldiers to make a survey of how we may best defend this place, Commander. We will put my Builders to work shoring up the most needful spots. The mortals who have besieged us—what are they doing?"

"At the moment, not much of anything," said Hayyano. "They seem to think Ogu Minurato is already theirs and that all they have to do is wait."

"They are not entirely wrong," said Yaarike. "We have little to eat and the well is full of rocks. That at least is a task my Builders can begin now. Go, League Commander Hayyano. We will meet again when the First Lantern appears in the sky."

"Yes, Lord Magister." Hayyano crossed his forearms over his breast in ritual acknowledgment, then led his Sacrifices out again.

When he was gone, Yaarike shook his head. "I am glad that the Singers here with us have a field commander like Tzayin-Kha," he said. "She at least is clever and thinks before speaking. What is the Order of Song doing at this moment?"

Viyeki did not like the Singers. Like most servants of the other orders, he distrusted the spell-wielders and was terrified of their great master, Akhenabi, Lord of Song, the most powerful person in Nakkiga but for Queen Utuk'ku herself. "Tzayin-Kha said she would send her followers out in false skins to look upon the enemy's numbers and disposition. And that they would light the fires of unease among the mortals."

"Good. I am glad to hear they are occupied."

For a moment, Viyeki thought he could see the weariness behind his master's immobile face. "I will occupy our Builders as well, Master," he said. "With your permission, I will go and see that the well is cleared of stones."

Yaarike nodded. "Yes, do so, Viyeki-*tza*. Shoring up the defenses of this place will be thirsty work."

He bowed. "It will be done before the Lantern is on the horizon."

"So if you don't want to spend the rest of your life soldiering, what *are* you doing here in the coldest part of the north, little Dogfish?" They were sharing Porto's horse, and the older man was trying to keep Endri distracted. The young man had gone pale when the Northern thane in charge of the mercenaries had given them their orders, and in the two days' riding since then Endri's thoughts had been spinning again and again through the same dismal eddy. "Why aren't you home helping your father make seed cakes?"

"I wanted to see something of the world."

Porto laughed. "And you succeeded! This is certainly something."

"Something dreadful." The youth suppressed a shudder. "Honestly, it's an old story, Porto—too foolish to tell. It was a girl."

"Ah. Her stomach grew large and you began to feel the urge to travel."

"No!" But the young man seemed almost pleased by the idea. "No, not like that. She chose another man. Didn't want to be wed to a baker's son. Didn't want her pretty hands to turn red and sore kneading bread all day, I suppose. I couldn't . . . I didn't want to see her. Her family lived just across from us. So I followed Lord Halawe to Erkynland—to the fighting at the Hayholt."

"Where Lord Halawe was eaten by dirt-goblins, if I remember correctly."

Endri winced. "I didn't see it, but I heard about it." He made the sign of the Holy Tree. "God rest him. He was a good man."

"I've heard that."

"And God preserve us all." Endri made the Tree again.

Porto made the Tree as well. "So all this is just to avoid seeing a girl who threw you over?"

"I didn't think I would end up here, that's certain." A moment later he brightened. "But you, Porto? Do you have a girl back home?"

Porto nodded. "My wife, Sida, may the Aedon bless her and keep her. And our little son who was but a babe in arms. The Lord only knows when I'll see either of them again."

"You'll see them again." When his mood shifted, Endri could be as cheerful and confident as a child. It reminded Porto of his younger brother Andoro, dead ten years or more, and gave him a pang in his chest. "We will come out of this," the youth said, as though Porto had been the worried one. "You'll see."

His attempt at distraction successful, Porto smiled. "I'm sure you're right." But he knew that the deep silent woods and the gray sky would drag the young man back into worry again before too long. "*Heá*, do you know any songs?" he asked.

Endri laughed. "*The Gallant Men of Harborside*, of course. I know all the words, even the part about laying the Dogfish low."

"And me stuck in the saddle in front of you, unable to escape." Porto rolled his eyes. "Go ahead, then, you ungrateful wretch. Make me regret all my kindness."

Endri's singing had ended hours earlier, and conversation had ended not long afterward. As they rode deep between brooding hills, the cold grew and silence settled like a fog over the ancient road.

They first saw the ruins of the castle from the base of the pass, a dark tumble of oblong shapes nestling close to the snow-flecked summit. As they drew nearer, hour by struggling hour, and as the walls of the pass rose higher and higher on either side, plunging them into mist and deep shadow, Porto began to feel he was being dragged helplessly toward the ancient fortress, as if it were some great mill whose stones would grind him to powder.

"I don't understand," said Endri suddenly, his voice startling Porto out of the long quiet. He made the sign of the Tree for perhaps the dozenth time in the last hour. "Sweet Elysia, why did we have to come to this dreadful place? Look at that! Why would Duke Isgrimnur bring us here? He said we were going to a border fort."

"Stop your sniveling, Southerner," called a young Rimmersman riding near them. "You shame us all." The rider was thick as an ox, with a bristling reddish beard that covered much of his broad face; on his shield was painted a red eagle, which told Porto this must be Floki, Thane Brindur's son.

"That *is* a border fort," Floki said. "It just happens to be one of the enemy's, that's all."

"Very clever," said Porto. "But my friend's right. We didn't join for this. We came for a post on the Rimmersgard border."

"Six coppers and food every month," said Endri.

"One silver, four coppers for me," Porto said. "Because I have my own horse."

"But I never said I'd fight the Norns!"

Porto could feel Endri shivering against his back, and knew it was from more than the cold.

"I want to go back," Endri said.

"You didn't think you'd fight the Norns?" brayed Floki, his laugh loud and harsh. "What did you think you'd be doing in a border fort at the edge of the Nornfells?"

"I didn't know we'd go so far," said Endri. "—that we'd . . . that they would . . ." He trailed off into silence.

"Don't let this one discourage you—we'll get back home again," Porto told his young friend, but he was not as confident as he tried to sound. "I'll take you with me, Endri. You'll like the Rocks. My wife's father is a dyer, a wealthy man. He'll give you a place, you'll see."

"He certainly won't give that one a place as a soldier," said the Rimmersman. "Not the way he moans."

"Shut your mouth, Northman," said Porto. "I'm beginning to hate the sound of your voice."

Brindur's son brought his horse closer, and for a moment Porto was afraid he'd have to fight him, but the Northman seemed to have noticed Porto's unusual height. "You'll feel differently about me when the White Foxes are at you, you southern milksop." The bearded youth put his heels to his horse's ribs and raced ahead of them. "Then you'll be crying out for *me*, not your little catamite here," he called back over his shoulder. "'Floki, come save me from the *Vit Refar*!' That's what you'll say."

"I pray that I lose my voice before my tongue ever shames me." It was an old Perdruinese saying which Porto had uttered many times, but he had never meant it more.

"He's right, though," said Endri. "I am no soldier. I'm frightened."

"I fought beside the great Sir Camaris himself when he led Josua

Lackhand's army in Nabban. I was afraid then, I'm afraid now. There is no shame in that."

"I don't care about shame, Porto. In all truth, I just want to go home."

Isgrimnur's men reached Skuggi Pass and made camp on the slopes beneath the ruined castle, beside the army Vigri had brought from Elvritshalla. The meetings of men who had not seen each other for many long months gave the gathering an air of festival, despite the cold and the flurrying white flakes.

Although the addition of the jarl's soldiers had more than doubled their numbers, Duke Isgrimnur still did not feel entirely at ease. Again and again his gaze was drawn to the broken walls at the top of the pass and the eyes he knew were watching there. He had more experience with the White Foxes than any of his men. Even a small troop of Norns could create chaos in opposing armies, and they were harder to kill than angry bees.

He looked over to Vigri's large campfire, where short, stocky Vigri sat surrounded by his thanes, all drinking and laughing. Vigri saw Isgrimnur and waved for him to join them. The duke raised his hand to say, *soon*. He was not quite ready to take his leisure.

Best to follow the hunt while the trail is new, as my father always said. He turned his attention back to the Sitha-woman Ayaminu, who sat across from him. She was carving a walking stick out of a long ash tree branch and seemed as composed and heedless of the falling snow as a statue.

"Why is it still so bloody cold here in late Yuven-month?" he growled. "I thought the Storm King was gone for good."

Ayaminu did not look up. "Ineluki sang up many great storms. They will not go away again so quickly simply because his influence is ended. Besides, it is always cold here."

Isgrimnur brought his hands close to the fire again. "We have a large troop of the Norns that attacked Erkynland trapped in these ruins," he said more quietly. "If you sent your people a message, Ayaminu, would they come? Would they help us to finish this once and for all?"

She returned a look that he could not interpret. It was always difficult with the Sithi, whose emotions and even ages were largely a mystery to mortals. He knew Ayaminu was venerable among her kind, perhaps even ancient, but to look at her she seemed scarcely different than one of the younger Sithi women like Jiriki's sister Aditu. Perhaps her skin was thinner, her movements less robust—there were times when she almost seemed fragile, like a woman once considered a beauty but recently recovered from a long illness. Her golden eyes, though, were as bright as his wife Gutrun's angriest stare, fierce as a hunting hawk's.

"No," the Sitha said at last. "As I told you before, Duke Isgrimnur, my people will not come. The Zida'ya fought as allies to you Sudhoda'ya—you mortals—but that does not mean our paths will always lead the same way from now on. We will not help you destroy our kin."

"Then why are you here? Why travel all this way simply to watch?"

She turned the long staff she was working on this way and that to examine it in the firelight before putting blade to wood again. "You speak as though watching and learning have no value in themselves."

Isgrimnur shook his head. Talking to the Sithi often felt like arguing with drunkards or children—not that they spoke foolishly, but the conversation always went around in circles until he forgot where it had begun. Perhaps she meant what she said—that she was only here to observe—but the duke did not trust it. *Do Simon and Miriamele understand how unlikely it is that we will be able to live comfortably beside such strange creatures as these fairies? We will sooner make partnership with the birds of the air, I think. They are just too different from us—nor do they think we are worth the trouble of honest explanations.* "Please do not muddle me with tail-swallowing words, Mistress Ayaminu," he said. "Of course learning has value, but so does fighting to protect ourselves."

"The Hikeda'ya are retreating to their own land." The Sitha's voice was mild, as though she merely proposed another interpretation.

The duke struggled to keep his temper. "Yes, after pillaging and murdering all over the north—and through Erkynland too. After trying to throw down the mortal kingdoms and set their dead master over all of us."

She might have been amused, but he could not be sure. "So you will teach them not to do that by doing the same thing. Blood for blood."

Isgrimnur shook his head. "Simon and Miriamele, the new king and queen in the Hayholt, bade me only make sure the retreating Norns can do no further harm. But without help from your people, I think I have no other choice but to ensure their good behavior by ending their race completely—that is what I think, more and more."

"And you wonder why my people will not help you."

"I wonder less, now that I have spent time with you, Lady Ayaminu." Despite his best efforts, the duke was finding it hard to keep anger at bay. "It's clear that you think nothing your Norn cousins do is worth punishment."

"No, that is not true. But that is because I know the Hikeda'ya will punish themselves—are already punishing themselves—more deeply than you can understand."

"Enough." Isgrimnur rose in disgust. "Where I come from, we do not let murderers choose their own sentences." He left Ayaminu to her carving and headed to the larger fire where Jarl Vigri and his thanes were passing a skin bag. The sun was down, and the crags behind the White Foxes' castle gleamed like crooked teeth in the last light.

"You are back, my lord!" shouted Vigri. "The ale-feast has its guest of honor!" Vigri of Enggidal was a short man about whom it was an old joke to suggest there might be trolls in his family tree, but he was burly and strong. More than a few arguments at the jarl's own supper table had ended when, offended by something, Vigri had picked up one end of the great oak trestle and flipped everything on it to the floor of the dining hall, often tumbling a few guests into the straw at the same time. Isgrimnur was glad to have Vigri beside him again. He was a steadier, more trustworthy lieutenant than Brindur, who blew hot and cold, or Brindur's son Floki, who blew only hot.

Vigri and his carls seemed surprisingly drunk for so early in the evening, but the duke and his men had only just arrived and Isgrimnur knew it must have been difficult for Vigri's soldiers to wait for reinforcements in an enemy land, especially a spot as gloomy as this, a place so ill-omened that Rimmersmen never ventured here, though the Norns had deserted the crumbling fortress centuries earlier. Vigri and his men would likely have spent the last several days praying for the arrival of Isgrimnur's troop and hearing and seeing evil spirits in every shadow. Small wonder if they celebrated now. "I had to see to a few things. My men are not happy. Most of them expected to be at home in Elvritshalla by now."

"My men feel the same, my lord," said Vigri. "They heard a fortnight ago that the war was over, and not much before that, they learned that Skali Sharp-Nose is dead. We have won, so why are we still fighting?"

"It is one thing to win," said the duke. "It is another to convince your enemies that they have lost."

Vigri grinned. "Killing them is a good way to do that."

Isgrimnur made a sour face. "Killing Norns is never as easy as it sounds. How many of them are here, and how are they disposed?"

"It is hard to say, Your Grace. They move in and out of the shadows like cats. Also, they look so much alike that it might be one Norn soldier seen in a dozen different places."

"Then give me your best guess."

"Perhaps as few as four score or so, perhaps as many as three hundred. But we have seen no giants among them."

"That's something to thank the good God for, at least." Isgrimnur looked around the fire. "And what of us? Most especially, how many archers do we have? I know the White Foxes too well to charge in. We will pick off as many as we can."

"I have a troop of Tungoldyr bordermen who can do what is needed with a yew bow," Vigri said, and waved for the skin once more. "I would put them against any archers in the south, even the Thrithings-men."

Isgrimnur nodded. "And I have my crossbowmen who were with me in Erkynland—those that survived, God save the rest. Those bolts will put a pretty hole even in that damnable witchwood armor." The duke leaned and began to scratch with a stick on the snow-spattered ground. "So what does that make it? I brought a company of paid men for the forts, most of them foot soldiers, but a few lances as well. Most of them are untried, though, and new to the north. I also have a company out of Hringholt, as well as Tonnrud's brother Brindur and their Skoggeymen. What does that make?" He scratched a few more times, frowned. He had not brought anywhere near as many men back from Erkynland alive as he would have hoped, and it pained him deeply. "With yours and mine we must have twelve hundred soldiers altogether, Vigri." He felt a little better, and this time he reached out his hand for the skin as it went around. After a long swallow, he wiped his beard with the back of his hand, then took a second sizable gulp—he had given Vigri and the others a long head start on the drinking, after all. "And the siege machinery we passed on the road?"

"That is what I ordered sent from Elvritshalla, a few stone-flingers and a great iron battering ram to knock down gates and walls—the biggest one we've got."

"Is it the Big Bear?" asked the duke with a smile. "I haven't seen that snarling monstrosity for years. No wonder there were so many horses hitched to the wagon—that thing is heavy as a mountain!"

"Yes, it's the bear. But if we want to use it, we will have to find a tree trunk big enough and strong to mount the head on."

"We will not need the ram here, I think," Isgrimnur said. "There is hardly wall joined to wall in that tumbledown place."

"Better safe than sorry," Vigri said. "Especially with the White Foxes. They are tricksy as weasels."

Isgrimnur nodded. "By all that is holy, you are right about that. I wish we fought men. God grant that at least it all goes quickly. Damn me, where has that sack of ale gone?"

"Why is it always so bloody cold these days?" Endri asked sadly. "It's supposed to be summer!" A tattered rag, dropped by some other soldier, had joined his woolen scarf; with both wrapped around his skinny neck, Porto thought the young Harborsider looked like a turtle. *But,* he thought, *a turtle would be better protected.* Endri's aged chain-link armor had more than a few links missing.

"It's the north," Porto explained.

Endri shivered again. He stared up the hill at the ruined castle, then made the sign of the Tree. "I just wanted to earn a few coppers."

Porto could not help pitying this young man, so far from all that was familiar. "Have you never fought before?"

"In an army? Not really. By the time I joined the prince and Camaris, we were on our way to Erkynland. We were some of the last onto the field at the Hayholt."

"Even the last onto the field must have seen some fierce fighting. I was there."

Endri shrugged, but he looked shamed. "I was near the back. No one ever tried to kill me. I swung my sword at a few of the Norns as they ran past after the tower fell, but I didn't hit any. Too fast. Like swinging at shadows. Or at flying bats. And that was the only fighting I've seen."

"I killed a Norn at the Hayholt," said Porto, and in that moment, beneath dark skies and battered by the wind, it might have just happened. "Or rather I was fighting him when he died. It was when the tower fell, Angel Tower or whatever it was called—were you close when it happened? All around the storms were raging and thundering, but there was fire in the sky, too. The world seemed upside down." He fell silent for a moment, uncertain how much he wanted to remember. "Where I stood," he said at last, "the tower went down with a great groan and roar, like a living thing. The ground jumped beneath me and knocked me down. Snow, dirt, water, all thrown into the air in a great spout, like a whalefish's breath, then they began to fall back to the earth. For a moment I could not see anything at all, mud and stones tumbling down all around me, then something rushed out of the flurry and knocked me over again. Before I even had a chance to make the holy Tree, something swished past my head and a hand grabbed at my arm. Someone was trying to kill me—that was all I knew—and I pulled out my dagger and jabbed and jabbed. I was lucky. I hit something and it collapsed on top of me. As we fought I realized that blood was splashing on me—not dripping, Endri, splashing, as though I lay in the course of a stream. Whatever was on me sagged off then, and I got to my feet. It was one of the White Foxes, and my knife had cut deeply into its belly, but it was also missing part of its head."

"What do you mean?" Endri's eyes were wide, like Porto's younger brother when he had told him ghostly stories in their childhood bed.

Porto shook his head at the memory. He did not like remembering that bloodied, death-pale creature, here, so close to those ruins at the top of the pass. "Perhaps a part of the tower had fallen on him, lad. I can't say. But his helmet was gone and part of his head was dinted in. His one good eye was filming over. I do not know how he fought with me even for those few moments. No mortal could have done it with all his brains out that way."

"Do they not die?" Endri sounded terrified.

Porto silently cursed himself for making things worse. "Nay, nay, of course they do. This one had already died by the time he fell off me. For the love of the Aedon, man, most of his blood was out! The White Foxes are canny fighters, strong and crafty, but when people call them immortals they mean only that they have long lives. They may go on for centuries, as it's said, but with a yard of steel in their guts they will die like anyone else, trust me."

Still, his tale did not seem to make the younger man feel better about the upcoming struggle. Porto decided he would be more careful telling stories in the future.

"While the Order of Echoes sent their calls out upon the dreamwinds, Lord Yaarike the Magister of the Builders employed the Singers led by Tzayin-Kha, who would become one of the revered martyrs of those final battles. Her Singers went secretly among the enemy, traveling on mirrorcourses. Undetected, they spread fear among the mortals, but they were too small a force and too weak after the destruction of Ineluki Storm King to do more than sow confusion and bring back knowledge of the enemy.

"The stories they carried gave Yaarike and his lieutenants no solace. The People were greatly outnumbered, and Isgrimnur of Elvritshalla and most of his mortal troops were battle-hardened.

"Lord Yaarike Kijada and his advisors knew that without the protection of Tangleroot Castle, however degraded that fortress had become, their forces would be quickly overcome. Many of the defenders under him believed that the only choice left was to sell their lives as dearly as they could, but others believed just as strongly that they should abandon the stronghold by night, when the mortals were hampered by darkness, and hope that at least a few of the People might make their way back to Nakkiga, where a proper defense could be mounted.

"But Lord Yaarike knew that to abandon Tangleroot Castle in secrecy and haste would mean not only a shameful retreat, but an even more shameful desertion of the body of the martyred hero, High Marshal Ekisuno . . ."

As Viyeki made his way into the interior of the ancient ruin, the echoes of the funerary priests chanting prayers for General Ekisuno's voyage back to the Garden made the place seem almost homelike. Back in Nakkiga, their city in the mountain, the air of the public places was usually sonorous with the voices of Celebrants, and in the great martyr-temples of the queen's family and other noble dead, the chanting for the departed never ceased.

Only the walls of the old keep still stood intact, though its roofbeams were long gone and the stars now its only ceiling. Viyeki made a ritual obeisance as he skirted the huge casket and its circle of murmuring clerics, then discovered his master standing by himself near the wall in an attitude of meditative contemplation. As always, Magister Yaarike looked to be the very essence of calm, but Viyeki had served the lord of the Builders for more than three Great Years, through times both bad and good, and he had learned that his master was never as unmoved as he appeared. Viyeki treasured the fact that he knew his master so well, but considered such insight to be his secret trust. *We owe correct outward behavior to our inferiors,* his mother had always told him, *but even more to ourselves. When we* think *of what is right, we can* be *what is right.* Warmed by the memory of her, Viyeki sat beside his master and waited.

No little time passed before Yaarike finally spoke to him. "I am beginning to think that the only acceptable tactic is to try to break through the ring of black iron with which the mortals have surrounded us. Not tonight, when they would be expecting us to do so. Tomorrow when the sun comes back they will attack this hill and these inadequate walls. We will have to hold them off at any cost, then be prepared to try our escape when darkness returns—when the mortals will be tending their wounds and expecting us to do the same."

Viyeki was more than a little surprised, but he knew better than to think Yaarike simply wished to run from a fight. "Will you share your reasons, High Magister?"

His master made a small gesture of annoyance. "Have you given up thinking for yourself, Viyeki-*tza*?"

The idea that he had failed his master even in such a small thing burned like fire. "Forgive me, my lord. I understand that you believe our deaths can achieve more somewhere else. But I cannot see that it makes any difference whether we fall here or farther up the pass, or even fleeing toward the outer walls of our city. It is not as though we will be close enough when the mortals catch us for any in Nakkiga to see us die."

"Ah. I sense the misunderstanding." Yaarike nodded. "You are think-ing of only where our deaths will be most appropriate or most useful. But I have another puzzle for you to consider, just as I used to set you problems of engineering when you were an apprentice. What if we do not die?"

"I don't understand, Magister."

"It is too early to start considering an honorable death, Host Foreman Viyeki. In fact, an honorable death is only a suitable alternative when death cannot be avoided. But even the most fanatical of the Queen's Teeth or the Sacrifice Elite know that their first responsibility is to stay alive and perform their duties as long as possible. Did you see the great iron ram the mortals brought? The one lashed to a wagon bigger even than Ekisuno's caisson, pulled by three teams of oxen?"

"Yes. It is made of black iron and shaped like a bear's head." Viyeki frowned. "I think it is foolish. Like a child's toy, however huge it may be."

"You would not say that if you saw it knocking down the walls around our innermost preserve—or even Nakkiga's great gates themselves."

"Impossible!"

"Why?" The magister's eyes were bright, his face unusually animated. "What do you think will happen after we are dead here, our lives tidily but honorably laid down in a hopeless fight?" Viyeki had never seen his master like this, showing what looked like actual anger. "I will tell you. With us gone, the Northmen will proceed through the pass and march across our lands. Soon they will reach our outer walls, the very walls that Akhenabi and the rest convinced the Queen—may she live forever—not to repair. We would need ten thousand Sacrifices to defend that ruined barrier now against even a small army like this. We have not a tenth of that number of warriors left in all Nakkiga, I feel sure. Do you hear my song, Host Foreman? Do you apprehend its melody?"

"I'm . . . I'm not certain."

"The Northmen will be at the very doors of our mountain. And the few of our troops that are not scattered across the south trying to struggle home, or have not already bravely and foolishly given their lives here with you and me, will be all that stands between Nakkiga and the revenge of the mortals. Do you know who waits at the base of the hill right now, staring up at us this very moment? Isgrimnur, the Duke of Elvritshalla, descendant of the same Fingil Red-Hand who slaughtered our kind all over the north, who threw down the holy stones of Asu'a itself and burned a thousand prisoners as demons. What do you think will happen when that great, black iron bear-head knocks down the Nakkiga Gates and Isgrimnur and his savages storm into the city?"

That was impossible, surely. Viyeki found that for a long moment he could not even speak. "But they couldn't—!"

"Couldn't they? Who would stop them? The leaders of the Order of Sacrifice are dead and rotting in the meadows of the south. Our queen has fallen into the *keta-yi'indra*—that deep, deathlike sleep of preservation and recovery. You felt her fall just as I did, just as every single Hikeda'ya felt it. We call it 'the dangerous sleep' because our people are leaderless while she slumbers." He leaned closer. "Who will rule in her absence, Host Foreman Viyeki? The Order of Song, that is who. Akhenabi and Jikkyo and the rest of that bloodless fellowship. And if the gates of Nakkiga will not hold, the Order of Song will take the survivors and flee deeper into the mountain, to places the mortals cannot follow." Yaarike shook his head. "And that is what our people will become—creatures ruled by sorcerers, slaves who never see the light of day, who hide in darkness and can be said to live only in that they have not yet died. The Garden that was our home will not even be a story anymore—or, if the tales still exist, Akhenabi and his order will teach that our people lived in darkness there, too, surrounded by stone and ruled by the masters of Song." The magister paused, as if he had realized how strange and desperate his words had become. He looked around quickly, but they were still alone except for the silent guards and the even more silent coffin. "So tell me, Host Foreman, do you still want only to sell your life as honorably as possible here?"

Before Viyeki could answer—although he had no idea of how to reply—Yaarike waved him away as if he had failed some test.

"Go now, Viyeki-*tza,*" the high magister said. "If your engineers have finished clearing the well of stones, find some other useful task to keep them and yourself occupied. Let me think. It is nearly the only weapon that has been left to me. But remember what I have said, and remember your family and clan who wait for us back home. Most of all, remember that what is an honorable death for you might mean the destruction of your people."

Porto barely slept. The night was full of odd shadows and the wilderness rang with cries that might have been wolves or the ghosts of weeping children, but there was more to his unease than fearsome sounds. He could not shake off the feeling that though the duke's forces far outnumbered their enemy, and their troops were fresh where the Norns were hungry and exhausted, somehow they did not have the upper hand. Lying beneath the distant, uncaring stars, he felt as though he and all the other mortals were in a brightly lit room in the middle of great darkness, being watched by countless unseen eyes.

From time to time his gaze was drawn to the broken walls of Tangleroot Castle and the lights he sometimes saw flickering there. They were nothing wholesome, not the familiar glow of candles, rushlights, or oil lamps, but shimmers of ghostly fire in foul colors, marshy green or a cadaverous yellow that nevertheless caught his eye and seemed to pull him closer, though his body never moved. At last he rolled over to face away from the top of the pass, hoping to find better rest, but then was presented the sight of young Endri trapped in evil dreams, moaning and twitching through his own shallow slumbers, shivering in a cold that no scarf or cloak could keep out.

Dawn finally came, but the morning sun barely made its presence felt. As Porto and Endri and the rest broke their fast on what flatbread the field kitchens managed to turn out, the mists rose as high as the surrounding hills but then stopped and hung, so it seemed as if a great, gray cloud had drifted down from the heavens and fallen across the pass. Although the wind had eased, a river of cold air still flowed down from the heights, making all the men feel heavy and old in their bones, paining the southern soldiers even worse than the Rimmersmen.

"I feel like I will die today," Endri said.

"Don't be foolish." Porto gave him a shove, but the younger man only took it as though it were his due, as a slave might take a beating. "I won't let you."

"You're a good friend, Porto. How did you manage to get born in the Rocks with all the thieves and beggars?"

"Don't ask me, ask my mother. And don't be so fearful. You and I are not even supposed to go up the hill toward the castle. We'll be protecting the donkey—the arbalest. That's what the commander told me."

He and Endri were in position before the sun made its way above the eastern side of the pass. The engineers they guarded made sure the stone-throwing machine was ready, talking warmly and confidently of how soon they would knock down this wall of ancient stone or that one, as though the battle were no more than a tournament, some sort of contest with prizes for the winning troop.

"Like town-ball," said Porto.

"What?" Endri's eyes had a haunted look.

"Town-ball. This, the waiting before it starts. You know that feeling."

"I never played."

"A strapping, strong fellow like you? Why not?"

Endri looked shamefaced. "Too slow." His face brightened a little. "Did you?"

"Play at the proper game, on festival days? Once or twice, before I went to soldiering. It is good to have long legs when you're running, not so much when people are kicking your shins."

Endri smiled. "At least being tall like that keeps your ballocks up high in the air where people aren't as likely to kick them."

Porto shook his head, glad to see the youth's spirits lift a bit. "Don't forget, there's only a small difference between them being too high to kick and them being low enough to punch. I swear by all the saints, it hurts just as much."

Somebody blew a horn. It echoed along the hillside like a sudden shriek. The color drained from Endri's face. "What's that?"

"It's only the stand-ready," Porto told him. "Don't fear. We'll come through this all right."

It is always dreadful, waiting for the fighting to begin, Isgrimnur thought. But it was much worse when the enemy was as unknowable as the Norns.

As he stood watching sunrise color the sky above the pass, Isgrimnur remembered the first time he had waited for a battle to start, long ago—so long ago! Could so many years truly have passed? His father Isbeorn had led a company of dalesmen against Fanngrun, King Jormgrun's rebellious cousin. Isbeorn had not wanted to fight, but Fanngrun had chosen to march through the thane's family lands in the Hargres Dale on his way to attack the king in Elvritshalla, and the king had made it very clear that if Isbeorn and his carls did not dispute Fanngrun's passage across their lands, then they were traitors, too.

As they had stood waiting, on a morning not much brighter or more pleasant than this one, Isgrimnur's father had seen his young son's look of poorly hidden fear.

"Do you know what the worst thing about fighting is?" Isbeorn asked.

"What, sire?"

"There's a good chance we'll live."

Isgrimnur, all of thirteen summers old, though a good size for his age, hadn't known how to answer to that. His father was not a man given to jests, even grim ones. At last, he said, "You say we'll live?"

"The odds are good. It is not our job to stop Fanngrun's army, merely to show ourselves willing—to prove to the king that we are his men. That is best done not by fighting Fanngrun's Vattinlanders face to face, but by harrying them through our land as quickly as possible. They outnumber us greatly."

"I still don't understand. You said we'll probably live. Why is that the worst thing?"

His father grinned, teeth gleaming in his grayshot beard. "Because if we're killed, we go straight to Heaven, don't we? Doing our king's bidding and defending our home in the name of the True God against unbelievers."

This was far beyond Isgrimnur's youthful understanding. "But our King Jormgrun is an unbeliever, too. So are most of his court!"

"God only cares about His soldiers and what they do. So if someone happens to put a spear through me, don't worry—I'll be on my way to Heaven like a stone out of a sling. They can only kill your body, son. Your soul is beyond any mortal harm. If we survive this day, it means we may have to wait another sixty years or more before we can stand before the Lord's great throne."

Isgrimnur had never felt as reassured by the explanation as his bluff, pious father likely meant him to, but it had set things in a different light.

I wish it were true now, he thought. *I wish we had nothing to fear but death.* But fighting the Norns was different: thinking of their dark, empty eyes and their ghostly faces, the duke could not help feeling that his soul *was* in danger—that there were powers that could not just keep him from Heaven but also drag him away to wander in darkness forever. And Isgrimnur was by no means the only one who felt that way: a few enterprising Rimmersgard soldiers had emptied the font at an abandoned church they had passed weeks ago, in their march north, and were now selling the holy water at a brutally high price. Soldiers were rubbing it on their faces and other exposed skin, even drinking it, in the hope of somehow protecting themselves not only from the blades of the White Foxes, but even from the immortals' very existence.

The dawn light was strong enough now to touch the weathered gray stones at the top of the ruined castle's highest tower, a building whose odd, thorny shape and unfamiliar construction whispered that its makers had not been human. The air was chilly but not as bitter as it had been. That was something. Too much cold sapped the strength from a man's limbs.

Isgrimnur ignored the pounding of his heart and the sourness of his stomach as he looked to his captains, then turned and pointed to the catapult men.

"Let fly," he called. "Knock down those walls. Push the whiteskinned bastards' faces into the mud." He turned back to his captains. "With your men, now. We will soften them up a bit, first with stones, then with arrows. Then it will be fieldwork, men—all hard graft until we drive them out."

The first catapult arm leaped forward with a hum and a loud clack. A stone flew through the air and knocked an edge off one of the freestanding walls.

"Soon!" Isgrimnur shouted. "Captains, keep your men at the ready. Soon we will pay them back for Naglimund and the Hayholt!"

Except for a few Sacrifice sentries and the chanting Celebrant priests around Ekisuno's coffin, most of the Hikeda'ya survivors who crowded now into the root-tapestried hall were of Viyeki's own Order of Builders, several score of battle-trained engineers resting quietly or moving like shadows in that ancient place, illuminated by gray morning sky, the ruin's only roof. They could all hear the battle noises from the hill outside the tower, but could do nothing except wait to see if the Order of Sacrifice's defense failed. If it did fail—and Viyeki thought that likely—they would all have to retreat to the tunnels, then sell their lives down in the dark in hopeless resistance against the victorious mortals. Viyeki should have been frightened at what lay before him, at the thought of never seeing his wife or home again, but he was too angry. The more he thought of it, the more he felt certain that Yaarike was right: the Order of Sacrifice as well as Akhenabi and his Singers had been foolishly overconfident, with no plan made for retreat and no attention given to any outcome except victory.

As if he had guessed what his host-foreman was thinking, Magister Yaarike made a gesture of summoning. Viyeki went to him.

"Yes, Master?"

"Let us walk a little ways apart. What I have to say—and show—is not for these others."

Viyeki followed him to the emptiest section of the great hall. The broken spiral columns in each angle of the sixteen-sided room showed him that the tower had been built back in the era of either the fourth or fifth Royal Celebrants. He knew that even now, so many years after Viyeki had left the academy behind, Yaarike would be annoyed with him for not remembering which.

Even in his despair and fury at their situation, Viyeki could not help being excited that his master had so often singled him out on the retreat from the south, treating him almost as an equal. Magister Yaarike was more than the head of an order, although that would have been honor enough to assure a place among the tombs of the greatest; he was also the oldest member of Clan Kijada, a family that had been powerful long before the Hikeda'ya and their kin had fled the Garden and come to these lands. Viyeki's own parents were distinguished enough, a justiciar and an admired court artist, but his Enduya clan had never been of much importance—a middling noble house whose children mostly became palace clerics or low-ranking Sacrifice officers.

But Magister Yaarike had always looked beyond Viyeki's indifferent family heritage, and for that the host foreman was extremely grateful. He doubted any other magister of the Builders would even have given one of such middling birth a position of importance: Yaarike was one of Nakki-ga's few leaders for whom "unconventional" did not always mean "untrustworthy."

"I wish to ask you a favor, Viyeki-*tza*," Yaarike said when they were far enough from the others for private speech.

"Anything, Master."

A slight frown. "Do not make broad promises without knowing what you are promising, Host Foreman, or what may happen in the Song of Fate after you have sworn. Remember the old saying, 'When one finger bends, none of the others can stay perfectly straight.'"

Viyeki bowed. "Apologies, High Magister. I should have said, 'Tell me and I will do all that I can.'"

"Better." Yaarike turned his back on the rest of the room, shielding the two of them from view with the wide expanse of his magisterial robes, then reached into his tunic at the neck and carefully drew out something that gleamed even through his cupped hands, as though he held a live coal. "See." Yaarike raised the object, still keeping it close to his body, and lifted away his upper hand. What he held seemed not just to reflect the sparse light but to contain some inner fire of its own: the magister's pale face was warmed to a ruddy sunset color by its glow.

Viyeki half-closed his eyes as he leaned toward it, the object's beauty too much to take in all at once. "It is magnificent," he said at last. "What is it, Master? Something very unusual indeed, I think. And very old."

Yaarike nodded. "Your eye is good, Host Foreman. It is indeed a thing of great age. Here, take it. Feel its weight."

Viyeki accepted the chain and its dangling pendant, shielding its glow as he had seen his master do. It was surprisingly heavy, but it was typical of the high magister that he should have worn it so long without a word of complaint. The chain was thick and plain, and even in the poor light of the hall Viyeki could see it was made of some strange metal too pale to be copper but too pink to be gold or anything more ordinary. The pendant was the size of his palm, shaped like a rounded triangle hanging point-down. At its otherwise featureless center glimmered a large oval stone of a sublime red-orange color.

"What am I holding?" Viyeki asked at last.

"It is called The Heart of What Was Lost," the magister said. "My forefather Yaaro-Mon brought it from our people's ancient home in Venga Do'tzae when we left that place."

"This truly came from . . . from the Garden, Master?" He had heard of such artifacts, but other than those that Queen Utuk'ku wore for festivals, he did not think he had ever seen one, let alone held it in his hands.

"The gem did, yes. You know the tales of Hamakho Wormslayer, of course."

Viyeki nodded. He could not imagine any of their people who did not know Hamakho, the ancient hero and founder of the queen's clan.

"When Hamakho was dying," the magister said, "he drove his great sword Grayflame into the stone threshold of the Gatherer's Temple in the very heart of the Garden. But when the time came to board the ships, no one could pull Hamakho's blade from the threshold, so it was left behind, another sacrifice to the Unbeing that claimed our homeland. But my forefather Yaaro-Mon prised this gem from the sword's pommel. Here, hold it up and I will show you something marvelous." So saying, Yaarike reached into the sleeve of his robe and produced a small crystal sphere known as a "cleric's lamp." With a brief stroke of his fingers it smoldered into light. "Come closer—I do not want to make too bright a glare and attract attention. Look through the gem with the light behind it."

Viyeki had to turn the heavy pendant on its back and look through it sideways to see what Yaarike meant, then could not help making a small sound of astonishment. For the first time in days their situation, the fighting outside and the implacable mortal enemy, slipped from his thoughts. "It is beautiful, Master! Someone has carved the interior!" Inside the hemispheric gem some careful hand had delineated a city of tall, graceful towers standing upon the cliffs above a great ocean. With Yaarike's lamp behind it, the whole artful scene was colored by the gem itself, so the miniature city seemed to bask under bright vermillion skies. "Who made such a wonderful thing?"

"Yaaro-Mon himself. The carving depicts great Tzo, our beloved city on the shores of the Dreaming Sea, lost with all the rest to Unbeing when the Garden fell. Like your own father, Viyeki-*tza*, my great-grandfather was an artist, and the voyage from the Garden to these lands was a long one. But now it serves as a reminder of all that the People left behind—all that makes us who we are." He nodded gravely, as if in answer to some question, but Viyeki had not asked one. "I will take it back now, before one of the others notices my light and comes to intrude on us." Yaarike accepted the heavy pendant and hung the chain around his neck again, sliding the necklace down into his tunic until it was invisible.

"I am honored that you showed it to me, Master."

"I do nothing without reason, Host Foreman. I showed this to you because I want you to make me a promise about it, but also because I want to make a promise to you." Yaarike shook out his robes until they hung correctly again. Even in such terrible circumstances the magister was correctly dressed at all times: despite months of hardship and bloody battle, he looked as composed as if he stood in his own home. "If I should fall here or somewhere else before we reach Nakkiga, Host Foreman Viyeki, I wish you to take the Heart of What Was Lost and carry it back to my family. It will belong to one of my children or grandchildren if they return from our defeat in the South, may the queen's eye watch over them. It is Clan Kijada's most precious heirloom. Will you accept this charge?"

"With pride and gratitude, Master. Your trust is an honor to my whole family."

"Do not let it go too much to your head," said Yaarike, amused. "If the Heart becomes your responsibility, that will be because I am dead."

Viyeki's face almost went slack with dismay, but he managed to conceal it. "I spoke without thinking, Master. I beg your forgiveness."

Yaarike showed him a thin smile. "Granted. And now my promise to you. I have watched you a long time, Viyeki sey-Enduya. Over the years I have been impressed by your skills with tools and plans but even more with the way you think for yourself, which it grieves me to say is rare among our people in these fallen days. Thus, it is my wish that one day you will follow me as High Magister of the Order of Builders, and I have written a letter to the Queen's Celebrants to say so. That letter is among my effects. If I do not survive this adventure of ours, when you take the Heart, take that letter and others you will find in my possession as well and carry them all to Nakkiga."

Viyeki stood as if thunderstruck, unable for a moment to find his voice. "Truly, Magister? You wish me to be your successor?"

The magister showed a hint of a mocking frown. "If I did not, this would be an oddly complicated and impractical jest, Host Foreman."

Viyeki dropped to his knees. "I will struggle all my life to live up to the honors you have heaped on me."

"And may that life be a long and useful one, Viyeki-*tza*." But before Yaarike could say more, hoarse shouts echoed from somewhere nearby, clearly the triumphant cries of Northmen. The crowd of Builders in the ruined hall murmured uneasily and pressed closer together facing the doorway, weapons raised.

"Well, it seems that the time to make dispensations for the future is over." Yaarike took Viyeki's elbow, and for a moment seemed to need the support. "Let us stand with the others and be ready to fight. The present is all we have—or whatever remains of it."

Isgrimnur had done his best in just a few days to instill some kind of wider discipline into Vigri's men. Unlike the soldiers Isgrimnur had brought back from the south, they still liked to fight in the chaotic Northern style, attacking and falling back individually or in small groups, as the mood struck them. Even with a huge advantage of numbers, this kind of brawling was a bad idea against an enemy as crafty and patient as the Norns, and the duke had set Sludig and several other trusted lieutenants to work trying to teach the rudiments of the more ordered fighting style of the Erkynguard, but within moments of the attack beginning it was clear that the lessons had not really taken. Eager for glory, young Floki and a dozen of his father's bondsmen did not stop at the first set of broken walls to wait for the rest of their comrades, but hammered through the first Norn defenses and rushed uphill toward the round tower where the Norn commanders were presumed to be. Immediately afterward a shower of arrows sealed the way behind them.

It was impossible to know whether Floki and his followers still survived or had been cut down. Isgrimnur could only be grateful that Brindur was on the far side of the field and had not seen what happened to his son: He would have taken his best men and charged after Floki, compounding the mistake.

So this is what it comes to. I do not tell Brindur what has happened to his son for fear of something worse happening. Usires save me, command is more often a curse than a blessing. Isgrimnur certainly understood Floki and the rest—just the sight of the enemy's rigid, corpse-pale faces was enough to raise a red mist of hate before his own eyes—but he could not concern himself with the fate of one mere man or even a dozen, not when the fate of thousands hung on his decisions.

No matter, he told himself, and waved another line of men up the hill. *There will be time for regrets later. There is always time for regret.*

As the day went on the sun should have burned through the fog, or at least so it seemed to Porto on the slopes below the ruins. Instead the mists grew thicker, swirling on the cold breeze until it was almost impossible to see the valley walls or even the old castle. He and Endri hung back to defend the catapult-gunners from counterattack. Black arrows whistled down from the hillside, and occasionally, when the mists cleared for a moment, Norns could be seen peering from the shadows like the unburied dead, but the White Foxes never left the cover of the ancient walls.

The catapult men kept busy, flinging stone after stone at the great tower near the top of the hill, but although they struck it time and again they could not bring it down. As the day lengthened, mists began to swallow up the scarce afternoon light entirely, so that it seemed that night would arrive long before sunset. Determined to break the resistance before dark fell, Duke Isgrimnur and his captains led a troop carrying siege ladders in an attack on the central tower, the last whole piece of the age-old castle. Now the Norns finally came out, and although Porto and Endri were not part of the struggle, it was clear that the fighting was terrible and bloody.

Then, in the middle of the assault, a great braying sound came echoing down from the ridgetop above the castle. Recognizing the horns that had blown at the commencement of battle in the morning, Porto thought a second force of Rimmersmen had made their way up into the valley heights and now meant to attack the castle from above, and his heart filled with hope.

But the blare of horns came instead from a party of scouts hurrying back from farther down the valley. The Northmen up on the ridge were shouting and waving their arms, and in only a few moments Porto went from cheering to mouth-gaping silence as he listened to the growing thunder of something rushing toward them along the valley floor.

The mists began to boil, then a host of armored riders appeared out of the tatters of gray fog at the bottom of the pass, thundering up the valley toward them. The newcomers were all in white or black, riding horses and even stranger creatures.

"Good God!" Endri cried. "What are they?"

"More Norns." Porto had been worried already, fearful of the battle and of this strange place, but now he felt his insides turning to ice. The oncoming Norn troop seemed big enough to roll through the entire valley like a floodtide, sweeping them all to death or worse.

Porto pushed past fleeing catapult engineers to grab Endri and drag him away from the great machine. All around the base of the hill Rimmersmen broke their lines and scattered, many scrambling upslope to join with their fellows who had surrounded the tower, but the Norn riders were among them in mere moments, stabbing and slashing with weird, angular blades. Some of them rode goats tall as horses, unnatural creatures with eyes yellow as sulfur; but the rider who caught Porto's attention was the leader, a horned figure with a terrible, inhuman face. The apparition wore white plate armor and rode a huge white horse.

At his first panicked glance, as the newcomer dealt death with a long, silver-gray sword to any mortal unlucky enough to be caught within its reach, Porto thought the horned figure some kind of demon summoned by the fairies, a creature straight from Hell. But as he dragged Endri out of the path of the oncoming troop and the leader galloped by, he realized that the demonic face was only a helmet in the shape of an owl's head.

It was all Porto could do to fend off the blows smashing down on him from above, but he held his shield up and managed to keep Endri behind him as he backed out of the path of charging Norns. He took a hard swipe to his helmet, and although it almost knocked him down, he stayed on his feet; a moment later the greater part of the Norn troop had ridden past him and up the hill into the ruins. A quick look showed him that Endri seemed to be unhurt.

To Porto's astonishment, the Norn reinforcements barely engaged with Isgrimnur's besieging force at all but crashed through, killing a few of them and losing a handful of their own. Then they continued upslope where they met reserves from inside the tower who helped to protect the entrance until the Norn riders could get inside. After what seemed only a few dozen racing heartbeats after Porto had first seen them appear from the mists, the new troop of Norn soldiers had disappeared into the tower.

The hilltop was strewn with bodies, but most of the Rimmersmen who had fought were still standing, faces sagging with surprise, as the Norns forced the gates closed behind them, sealing the tower once more.

The general lifted off her helmet. Her braided white hair had come undone in the charge and hung across her face until she swept it aside. She had the long chin and narrow nose of the oldest Hikeda'ya families and an expression as stern as some ancient tomb effigy. "Who is the master here?"

"That would be me, General Suno'ku—Yaarike sey-Kijada, High Magister of the Builders." Viyeki's master made a carefully calibrated gesture of welcome. "You arrive hoped-for but unlooked-for. We had thought ourselves beyond the reach of any reinforcements. Our Echoes received no reply to their calls."

"It could not be helped," she said, offering the scantest of ritual salutes in return. "The mortals have one of the Zida'ya with them, and she carries a Witness. We could not risk breaking silence."

Viyeki stared at this savior that had arrived seemingly from nowhere, like a hero out of the oldest tales of the Garden. He knew of General Suno'ku, of course—most Hikeda'ya did. She might be no higher in the Order of Sacrifice than Viyeki was among the Builders—a subordinate of the ordinal leader—but because of her family blood she moved in much higher circles than Viyeki could ever dream of joining.

As he watched her, fascinated, Suno'ku turned to one of her lieutenants. "See to the wounded. Make them well enough that they can ride."

"What about those who are too badly injured?" the Sacrifice asked.

She only stared at him, her expression flat as a frozen pond, then turned back to Yaarike. "How many are you here?"

"Perhaps two hundred left, more than half of them Builders," the High Magister said. "We also have the Celebrants you see with the general's body, half a dozen Singers under Tzayin-Kha, and a few Echoes. The rest are Sacrifices and now fall under your command."

"But you stand over us all, High Magister," the general said. "I would not flout the Queen's sacred ranks." Which was only barely true, Viyeki knew. Suno'ku was of the Iyora, the Owl Clan, in the male line of the legendary Ekimeniso himself, Queen Utuk'ku's long-dead husband. The Iyora were all but co-equal with the queen's own Hamakha clan, and both of them were as far above even Yaarike's noble family as the uppermost peak of the great mountain stood above the squares and public markets of the Nakkiga floor. Among the noblest clans, family blood always outweighed the hierarchy of the orders, even the most powerful, like Sacrifice and Song.

Viyeki's thoughts and Suno'ku's quiet conversation with Yaarike were both interrupted by the arrival of League Commander Hayyano and a troop of his warriors leading three mortal prisoners, all with their arms bound behind them. The largest of the captives, a young, muscular, yellow-bearded Northman, was bellowing in his crude tongue. Like most Builders, Viyeki did not speak a word of any mortal language, and he thought the hairy one sounded more like a bear than any thinking creature.

Suno'ku's lips twisted a little at one edge. "How I hate the sound of their barbaric yapping. Magister Yaarike, may I kill them all so we can have some quiet?"

Yaarike shook his head. "No, General, not yet. Hayyano brought them at my request. Will you question them about their numbers? I do not have the skill to do it myself."

Viyeki could not help wondering at this, since his scholarly master spoke the mortals' common tongue better than almost anyone in Nakkiga. He assumed Yaarike was testing the Sacrifice general in some way.

Suno'ku repeated Yaarike's questions in the mortal's own speech, then shared the answers. "He says that he is Floki, son of the great thane Brindur Golden-Hair," she explained. "He says that if some of his men had not turned coward and fled, he would already have taken all our heads by now and the fighting would be over." But the prisoner would not tell them anything else, not the numbers of the Northmen waiting outside nor any other useful information.

When she had tried several times and could get nothing further from the red-faced mortal or his brutish companions, the general unsheathed her sword, a slender span of silvery witchwood that seemed almost too long for her. The mortals could not look away from it, their eyes so wide the whites showed all around. "I suggest it is time to use more direct methods, Magister," Suno'ku said. "I scarcely blooded Cold Root today, and it still yearns to drink mortal ichor." She then produced her poniard, long and wickedly sharp, and held both blades before the Northmen. "Or if my lord Yaarike wants the conversation to pass more slowly, I can use Cold Leaf, which will remove smaller pieces." She leaned close until she was only a hands-breadth from the prisoners' faces. "Either way, I will make the enjoyment last as long as I can."

The mortal who called himself Floki began bellowing again, but this time there was a tone of terror in his voice that had not been there before.

"Your famous weapons will not teach them what they do not know, General," said Yaarike in a tone of regret. "I fear we have learned all we can from these."

Suno'ku kicked out, knocking the one called Floki to the stone floor. Viyeki heard what sounded like the mortal's shin breaking. The bearded soldier clutched his leg, rolling back and forth, gasping in pain

"Whether they had told us more or not," Suno'ku said, sheathing her weapons once more, "it would not have changed the nature of our problem. You have two hundred here, Magister. I have scarcely twice those numbers myself. I mustered every last able Sacrifice in Nakkiga and could find and mount less than four hundred to bring with me. But it matters not. What we must do now is prepare to escape."

"Escape?" Yaarike was clearly surprised, something Viyeki had seldom seen. "How? The tunnels below us lead nowhere."

She shook her head. "Tunnels? No. We shall ride from here—smash our way free if we have to. I did not come so far and so fast to die here in an obscure border fort. I have a more important task."

Yaarike nodded. "You came for Marshal Ekisuno's body, of course. Your foreparent—your ancestor."

Suno'ku showed him a harsh smile. "No, High Magister. I came for you and your Builders. Because without you, Nakkiga will be overthrown by the mortals. Your clan, my clan, they will all be slaughtered in dark holes, like rabbits."

Unsure of what was happening, the yellow-bearded mortal began to shout again, bellowing threats. Suno'ku gave a sign and one of her Sacrifices drew his sword and struck him hard on the head with the pommel. He did not make another sound, but lay on the floor twitching and drizzling blood from his scalp.

"I will kill that one myself in a moment and enjoy it like a good meal," Suno'ku said. "But our time is short, so first we must make our plans."

As the general conferred with Magister Yaarike and the plainly overwhelmed Hayyano, who could only gaze at Suno'ku in awe, Viyeki watched with an interest that almost made him forget their terrible situation. He had never seen Suno'ku before, but of course he knew of her. The general was famous for her bravery, and although a few other female officers held equally high rank in the Order of Sacrifice, none of those commanded either the loyalty or the fascination that the ordinary Sacrifices felt for Suno'ku.

The general had weirdly light eyes, so pale and gray-shot that they seemed like twilight skies compared to the purplish midnight of most Hikeda'ya. She was tall for her sex, but not unusually so—both Yaarike and Hayyano were taller—and her movements were swift and almost impossibly graceful. She was like a bright flame, Viyeki thought, drawing the eye each time she moved.

"But only a few of the mortals were destroyed during your arrival," Hayyano said. "They vastly outnumber us still. Surely we should wait and let them wear themselves down. They are far from home and their supply lines are vulnerable."

"And what if there are more of them coming, Commander?" asked Suno'ku. Hayyano blinked; he might as well have flinched. "While we are pinned here in the wreckage of Tangleroot Castle, the outer walls of Nakkiga are in ruins and the mountain gate in the City Walls at Three Ravens is all but undefended. Did you not see that great ram of black iron the mortals have brought? Where do you think that is to be used?

Not on these old, decrepit stones. That is for knocking on the very door of our home. They will be breaking into the queen's own chamber before the summer months have ended, may the Garden preserve her always." She shook her head. "No. We must break out of this ring now and make our way north as quickly as we can. High Magister Yaarike, do you agree?"

He looked at her for a moment. "Yes. If it must be so, then let it be sooner rather than later."

"Good." Suno'ku put her helmet down on a broken stone pillar rounded by centuries of rain. "Then call all the chieftains and their troops here, leaving only sentries. If a chieftain has died during today's fighting, Commander Hayyano, appoint one who will do what he or she is told. Do you understand?"

"But what of your ancestor's body and its coffin?" asked Yaarike. He pointed to the massive wagon where the chanting Celebrants still knelt. "How will we manage to carry that away while still putting distance between ourselves and the mortals?"

"We won't," said General Suno'ku flatly. "Leave it behind."

Yaarike was clearly astonished. "You will desert your great-great-grandfather's body?"

She shook her head. "No. That weighs but little. It can be carried on the back of someone's saddle, and I will offer prayers of regret and penitence to my foreparent for the dishonor. But the sarcophagus itself—that is useless. We will not be weighed down by it. Break it to pieces to keep it from the grubby paws of the mortals."

Viyeki was watching the yellow-bearded mortal still writhing in pain between the other two staring prisoners. The murderous invaders showed no bravado now, Viyeki thought. Beneath their hairy pelts these Northmen seemed to hide the hearts of terrified children.

A thought came to him then, but he waited until both Yaarike and Suno'ku had paused before lifting his hand in submissive request. "If my master and the general will permit me . . ."

Yaarike turned to look at him. "Yes, Host Foreman Viyeki?"

"Did I hear you say that Host Singer Tzayin-Kha survived the battle?"

"Yes," said his master. "I have seen her. What of it?"

"If I do not offend by putting myself forward," Viyeki said, "I may have an idea."

The campfires of the duke's army had been kept small, especially those closest to the ruins. Porto and Endri had been left to guard the catapult, which loomed above them in the flickering light like a watchful dragon.

"But where did all those White Foxes *come* from?" Endri asked for perhaps the dozenth time.

Porto had given up trying to answer him. He poked the fire and then pushed his hands as close as he could without burning them.

"Are they ghosts? How could they get so close without our scouts hearing them?"

"Oh, sweet Aedon, they are *Norns*, not ghosts!" Porto felt as though something inside him wanted to escape, but if it did it might tear the world to pieces with its teeth. This hellish place was driving him into madness. "Fairies can be killed. Did you not see the bodies lying in the snow? Did you not see the blood? Red, the same as ours. And when it runs out of them, they *die*."

"You heard that soldier! He put three arrows in one not an hour ago, but the creature took no hurt from it! Just vanished away. If that is not a ghost, what is?"

"God's Blood, man, will you stop this? They are tricky, the Norns. Everybody who was at the Hayholt knows that. They make shadows and cast their voices—but shadows cannot hurt us."

"But, still . . ." Endri was almost breathless and could not let it go. "Where did they all—?"

The fire before them suddenly blazed as if a strong wind had fanned the coals. But instead of the flames bending they grew upward until they danced higher than men's heads. All around the other campfires were also erupting into wavering pillars of flame. Startled Northmen scrambled on their hands and knees. Porto, who had tumbled backward at the first fiery billow, sat sprawled on the freezing ground while Endri stared in bulge-eyed terror. Some of the soldiers were so frightened that they cried out for God or their mothers, or let out simple, incoherent cries of terror.

And then a face appeared in the flames in front of Porto—and not just in his campfire, but in every single one throughout the sprawling camp. This fiery mask rippled and billowed like something seen in deep water; the face was female but also not entirely real. Where the eyes should be and in the open mouth, nothing showed but flames.

"It's the queen!" someone shouted in fright. "The queen of the White Foxes! She has come back!" Men scrambled away from the fires and began to run in all directions, like animals.

"Mortals!" The voice rolled out from every fire, from every circle of men, as chill as the ice that had crystallized on the tent ropes. *"You will die in these lands! We will take back what is ours!"*

Porto could not tell if the dreadful voice was in the air all around or came somehow from inside his own skull. He saw Endri stumble to his feet and managed to grab at the younger man's leg as he lurched past, bringing him down heavily into the snowy mud. Porto had no idea what was happening, but he knew if he let him go Endri would run like a maddened beast into the freezing night, never to return. Endri fought back like a terrified child but Porto hung on, even as the apparition in the fire melted and the flames fell back to what they had been. A moment later the fires sputtered and went out entirely, plunging the camp into darkness.

With that horrible voice still ringing in his thoughts, Porto did not understand at first what else he was hearing, but then he heard men shouting in pain and surprise—brief cries, swiftly ended—and felt rather than saw a flock of swiftly moving shadows sweeping down toward the camp from the ruins atop the hill. Men were suddenly dying all around him at the hands of near-invisible enemies, but Porto could not get free of struggling Endri to unsheathe his blade.

"They are here!" he hissed into his friend's ear. "The Norns are here, trying to kill us all! Damn you, man, get up and fight!"

Endri suddenly stopped struggling, and for an instant Porto thought one of the invisible attackers had stabbed and killed the youth right in Porto's arms. Then a glare of red from the top of the hill revealed Endri's face staring up toward the ruins, mouth stretched in a gape of tortured disbelief. Porto turned to find where this new light came from and saw a great blaze at the edge of the ruins, a pillar of flame higher even than the bespelled campfires, almost to the height of the surrounding trees. Now the burning object began to roll down the hill toward the camp, slowly at first, bucking and jouncing over the stony slope, but picking up speed with every one of Porto's racing heartbeats. Its wheels were as tall as a man.

It's a wagon, was his first, confused thought, *some kind of giant war-wagon*, and that was true enough, but there was also something more. Atop the wain's vast bed lay a sarcophagus, a huge thing, but its lid was partway off and the insides were aflame so that a tail of fire streamed behind it, marking its hastening career down the hill. And even as Porto stared in astonishment, a screaming figure lurched up out of the monstrous, burning box, knocking the lid aside. The writhing figure wore a mask and was itself aflame. Burning bandages turned the thing in the casket into a wildly gyrating torch that flailed the air and shrieked and shrieked—the most inhuman noise Porto had ever heard, an unending, whistling scream without words. Any men who had held their ground during the first onslaught of shadow-warriors from the ruins now turned and ran stumbling downhill from the blazing, howling corpse atop its battle wagon.

The besiegers made no pretense of resistance, but fled the apparition as though one thought controlled them all, raw southern recruits and battle-hardened Rimmersmen alike. Many were struck down by arrows Porto could not see, or surrounded in the darkness by deeper shadows, after which they lay silent in the snow with throats slit or guts spilled.

Something crashed against Porto's face, stunning him. It was Endri, who had lashed out in his desperation to escape and was now half-crawling, half-staggering down the slope away from the ruins, mad with fear.

Porto did not know what to do. The camp was overrun with shadows, and already dozens of his comrades were dead, the rest scattered—he could hear some of them lost in the trees, shouting for God to save them. It had all happened so fast, as if a great wind had blown their army to pieces in an instant.

He crawled to his feet and ran after Endri. He could do nothing else. He had no one else to save.

Her song completed, the Host-Singer Tzayin-Kha fell to the uneven floor stones in the central hall of the ruined fortress where she lay gasping like a landed fish, her starvation-shrunken limbs twitching. Viyeki moved to help her.

"No! Do not touch her!" Yaarike cried. "The fire spirit still flows in her. Look."

As Viyeki watched, several more of the red-robed Order of Song moved toward Tzayin-Kha as cautiously as if she were a sleeping dragon. One put a stick beneath her and rolled her over. Viyeki recoiled. The Singer's face and hands, the only parts of her flesh he could see, smoldered with light beneath the skin, as though she herself had no more substance than a wax candle.

"Will she live?" Viyeki asked his master quietly. "She is the best of her order that we have."

"And she was the only one who could have made the fire speak," said Yaarike, shaking his head. "That was a magister's trick, but she managed it. I am impressed that she still lives, although that may not be true for long. Still, even if she recovers she will be useless to us until she can be healed from this effort back in Nakkiga." He turned to the Singers now lifting Tzayin-Kha's body and wrapping it in a heavy blanket. Viyeki could feel the heat still coming off her at several paces' distance. "Go, now, all of you," Yaarike told them. "Get her away while the mortals are still in confusion. Thanks to Tzayin-Kha's efforts, General Suno'ku has carved us an escape route, but it will close very quickly."

As the Singers hurried out, carrying the steaming body of their leader like a holy relic, Yaarike nodded to Viyeki. "Now that all our Builders are out, we must go, too," he said.

As they made their way up the narrow stairs toward the ground level of the roofless hall, Viyeki marveled at his master's balance. Neither of them had eaten at all, or slept for more than a few moments in days, and Yaarike was old enough to have been alive when the Hikeda'ya first took Nakkiga Mountain for their own, but he climbed like a youth. Viyeki could only hope to have half his master's vigor when he reached the same age. If he reached a greater age at all, which had seemed unlikely for some time now.

"Your idea was clever, Viyeki-*tza*," Yaarike said from the near darkness above, his voice pitched low. "I thought Suno'ku would balk at it, but she is rare for her order, and even more for her age. I admit she surprises me—I was impressed that she would abandon that cumbersome wagon and her ancestor's coffin." He laughed quietly. "Even better, though, your idea amused me."

Yaarike rarely handed out praise. Even though they were now only a few paces away from angry mortals with arrows and axes, Viyeki was full of pride. "Thank you, High Magister." Still, he was puzzled, too. "I only meant to frighten the Northmen. You say it amused you?"

"It is one thing to win a battle that you should lose. It is another to pour salt in the wounds you inflict. It is scant compensation for the Storm King's failure, but I wish I could have seen the mortals' faces as the sarcophagus came down on them. Do you think they thought it was General Ekisuno himself, come to burn them all—?"

Viyeki heard the soft rustle of the magister's garments suddenly cease. He reached out a hand to touch his master's elbow, letting him know he was behind him.

The magister turned and took his hand. He made the finger-sign "*Silence*" against Viyeki's palm, then the brushing symbol that meant "*Wait.*"

A moment later Yaarike said, "They have gone out of the castle again. By the Garden, those mortals are as noisy as cattle. How did they ever defeat us in the past?" He led Viyeki up the crumbling steps and into the night air, his tread slow and cautious.

"Should we not hurry, Magister?"

"There will be no escape at all if we are caught. Save your haste until we need it." Yaarike struck out toward the far side of the ruins, heading at an angle toward the hilltop that towered over the Tangleroot Castle ruins.

Viyeki could hear the shrieks of wounded mortals from the slopes below and was filled with contempt. Foul brutes. Could they not even bear their injuries with dignity? "Do we know where to join Suno'ku and the rest?" he asked.

Yaarike did not turn around, already leaning into the rising slope. His voice fluttered back to Viyeki, soft as a moth in flight. "It will be easy enough, Host Foreman. Suno'ku is her ancestor's heir, and more. We need only follow the trail of dead mortals."

"By Dror and Aedon and all the rest, *what is happening*?" Isgrimnur stamped toward the group of men standing around the wreckage of the fiery wagon that had killed more than a dozen of his soldiers in its downward progress and had terrified at least ten score more into running headlong into the blind night. He feared that many who fled had already been killed by the Norns, but prayed that he would be able to find and bring back any survivors when the sun was up. The night had been a disaster, and now the Norns had escaped the ruins and were heading north again.

Isgrimnur sniffed the air and felt his stomach turn over at the tang of burned flesh. As he neared the gathering, he raised his voice again. "I said, what is happening? Why are you men huddled here? Sludig, is that you? I see Brindur's horse—where is he? I told him to follow those damned, sneaking creatures. We must not let them get away. We must hound them through the wilderness until every last one of them is slaughtered."

"Jarl Vigri went after them with his bowmen," said Sludig from the darkness, but his voice sounded hoarse and strange. "Brindur is . . . he is . . ."

Isgrimnur felt his heart and innards go cold. He hurried forward, ignoring the pain of several bleeding wounds. "Oh, sweet Usires, is it Brindur? Is he . . . ?"

It was only as he reached the circle of men that Isgrimnur could see faces. One was Sludig's long, mournful countenance, and the rest seemed to be Brindur's Skoggeymen. But the man who was kneeling next to the smoking wreckage of the cart and the huge, upended coffin, Isgrimnur was surprised and relieved to see, was Thane Brindur himself.

A black, charred shape lay half in and half out of the scorched sarcophagus. Here and there a bit of pale flesh, a few grinning teeth, or a spot of unburnt bandage gleamed through the ash. Only a single arm protruding from the blackened, shriveled mass remained whole. Around its wrist was a thick gold bracelet.

Brindur glanced up, his eyes red in the torchlight and his face suddenly looking decades older. "It is his." Brindur lifted the arm so that the bracelet caught the light. "He won it at Kraki's Field against the remnants of Skali's army just half a year ago." Isgrimnur must have looked like he still did not understand, because Brindur blinked and said, "This is Floki. My son. They burned him alive and rolled him down the hill to frighten us

like children." Brindur shook his head slowly. "God curse them. God
curse them!" When he spoke again, it was more quietly. "Telling his
mother—that will be the foulest part."

"There is nothing worse," said Isgrimnur. "As I know myself." Sludig
leaned over and touched the duke's arm, reminding him that there was
much to do. "You stay here for now, Brindur," Isgrimnur said. "Bury your
son—and the others. Break camp and follow us when you can."

"And so it goes on," said Brindur.

Isgrimnur didn't like the sound of that, and was almost glad he was
leaving the thane behind for now. Brindur was a good man, but perhaps
this had been one blow too many. Still, Isgrimnur understood the man's
pain. "We will all remember your son," he said. "May God take him
swiftly to His bosom in Heaven. Their tricks, the form of his death, they
mean nothing—just more cruelty in the cruel war these bastard fairies
have forced on us. Floki was captured in battle and died a hero. It is as
simple as that."

"If you say so, Your Grace." Brindur let go of his son's arm.

Isgrimnur did not want to see the burned body any longer: it looked
as though something ancient and inhuman was trying to will itself into
human shape. "It is the truth, Brindur."

The thane of Norskog's face was as still and empty as stagnant water,
but his voice had something ragged in it that Isgrimnur had never heard.
"I don't doubt it. But are you not tired of seeing so many of our sons
turned into heroes before their time, Isgrimnur? I would rather have seen
him live and make sons of his own."

The duke had nothing left to say. He could not even let himself feel
true sadness now, because he knew it would make him weak when he
needed to be strong and move swiftly. He and Vigri had to catch the
Norns in the open before they could find another bolt-hole—or, worse,
slip back to the safety of their city under Stormspike Mountain. He let his
hand fall on Brindur's shoulder, then nodded to Sludig to follow him as he
left the thane to grieve.

Part
Two

Three Ravens Tower

"As all Hikeda'ya know, when the children of our nobility reach the proper age, they are submitted to Yedade's Box, and the way in which they escape the box or the way that they fail determines their path in life.

"When she was put to her test, the young Suno'ku seyt-Iyora broke free so swiftly that none present could remember any other child who had performed the feat so well.

"Thus it was later for Suno'ku as general: When no one else could have broken the siege at Tangleroot Castle, she led a small force there to save those trapped in the ruins and then fought her way out again, scattering the Northmen before her like chaff before a reaper's blade. The rest of the besieged followed her, awed by her courage and skill, and when the trap was behind them she led them all north toward the shelter of the City Walls.

"The walls had been built during the time of our greatest power, when the Zida'ya still held Asu'a, when much of Nakkiga still existed outside the great mountain and the North was ours.

"But as our numbers diminished and the Northmen came across the cold sea and began their career of destruction through the lands of the Keida'ya, at our great queen's order we fell back into the sheltering fastness of the mountain and eventually Nakkiga-That-Was stood deserted. Slowly the trees and grasses and the fierce winds began to take back the outer city. The great walls, a vast ring of stone that stretched for leagues around our mountain, fared little better. In the time of Sulen, the

Thirteenth Celebrant, the Order of Sacrifice removed the last guards from the walls, calling them back to the city to better protect Nakkiga itself and the irreplaceable person of Queen Utuk'ku.

"*So it was that Suno'ku and the rest of her charges, fleeing ahead of the mortal invaders, came at last to the Tower of Three Ravens and found it in a pitiable state, the tower itself gutted and long empty, the great walls it guarded now perilously weak. Although Lord Yaarike, Magister of the Builders, was with her, there was little his small number of workers could do to make repairs with the Northmen so close behind. Still, the Hikeda'ya were determined to make a stand there, trusting in Suno'ku's generalship to keep the mortals from the mountain and from Nakkiga itself as long as could be managed.*

"*In the city, nothing was yet known of General Suno'ku's mission, and after she took the largest part of the surviving warriors with her, the caverns of Nakkiga were silent with foreboding, the queen's subjects fearful of what might come next if the invaders continued unchecked.*

"*They were right to fear.*"

Overburdened with the duke's own considerable weight, his horse nearly lost its footing on the steep track, sliding back a short distance in a flurry of gravel and scree. Isgrimnur reined up, eyeing the looming cliffs on either side with distaste.

"Tell me again how you know they are not lying in ambush for us," the duke said.

The scout nodded. "There has been no movement that we've seen, Your Grace. I think the fairies are too few now—they're all hiding in the tower, I'd say. Come, my lord, it's just a little way more to the spot where we will make camp."

Isgrimnur snorted. "Too few fairies? Don't ever assume that, lad. Especially when we've followed them into their own lands."

"My men and I found high ground to keep watch, my lord; we can see beyond this wall, all the way to their cursed mountain. This time, we would see any reinforcements long before they arrived. Just a little farther, my lord."

Isgrimnur looked back on the line of mounted men making their slow way up the pass behind him, Sludig nearest, following like a faithful hound, then Brindur and his Skoggeymen, with Vigri and the Elvritshalla men close behind leading a train of foot soldiers. Two thousand able-bodied men left, at most. Could he really take such a small force into the forbidden lands of the Norns and hope to come out again in one piece?

But that doesn't matter, does it? Isgrimnur thought. *What matters is that we leave none of the fairies alive to threaten our lands again. If we can manage that, whatever befalls us, it would be a sacrifice worth making.* He thought of his wife Gutrun, waiting for him not at Elvritshalla but far to the south, in the devastation of the Hayholt. She would be busy, he knew, with wounded men and women to care for and the new king and queen in need of her counsel and wisdom. At least she would have something to distract her from their lost son. Isgrimnur himself had spent too many nights under these cold, starry northern skies too pained to sleep, trying to think of ways things could have been different, that they could have beaten back the enemy without losing his son Isorn.

Wars don't end, he thought suddenly. *They become stories, told to children. They become causes that are taken up by those who were not even born when the war started. But they don't end.*

We are a fierce race, we men. We will give up even our short, precious lives for revenge— no, for justice. No wonder the immortals fear us.

The steep track angled to one side, following the line of the pass. As they came out from behind a massive cliff wall, Isgrimnur could suddenly see all the way to the top, to the darkening sky and the great, dark wall that girdled all of the Norn lands. It stretched thirty ells high across the top of the pass, a thing of monstrous black slabs laid flush one on another as though by the work of some gigantic mason.

In the middle of the pass, squarely above the climbing road and a gate that had long since been filled in with even more stone, a tower bulged out from the wall. The entire structure seemed oddly proportioned to Isgrimnur's eye, but the tower's crown was one of the strangest things he had ever seen, with three beak-like projections, the middle pointing forward and the others angled to either side, each one hanging out ten cubits or more beyond the wall. He thought the tower looked more like some huge weapon than a mere building, a battle mace for a sky-tall giant.

"Sweet Elysia, Mother of Mercy," he said.

Sludig had reined up beside Isgrimnur; he looked as though he had bitten into an apple and discovered half a squirming worm. "This is an evil place."

Another voice said, "Evil is in what mortals—and immortals—do. The place itself is but a place." Ayaminu the Sitha-woman rode up beside them on her own horse, which despite its fine-boned slenderness seemed to have less trouble with the cold and the steep climbs than the Rimmersmen's mounts, bred in cold northern lands. "Once it was a point upon the teeming earth like any other."

"Does this abomination have a name?" asked Isgrimnur.

"That?" She made one of the barely perceptible gestures that passed for a shrug among her kind. "It is called Three Ravens Tower. You see the beaks, of course. They allowed the defenders to drop stones, or hot oil, or other even less pleasant things upon anyone trying to take the wall."

Isgrimnur had not come to like the Sitha-woman's company any better during the sennight they had pursued the Norns from Tangleroot Castle. He had found all the Sithi he met difficult to understand and even more difficult to parley with, and he found their reluctance to engage with their murderous cousins even more frustrating; but if the immortals Jiriki and Aditu had been frustrating, and their mother Likimeya close to maddening, Ayaminu made those three seem easy company. Despite accompanying the duke's troop and offering an occasional bit of information, Ayaminu seemed otherwise unconcerned by the doings of the mortals or even their deaths, and did not seem to care at all whether they ever caught the Norns who had brought so much ruin to her own people as well as Isgrimnur's. Many times he had wondered whether they harbored some kind of spy in their midst, though the men he had set to watch her had seen no evidence of any treachery.

"Do you think the Norns are guarding it?" he asked now. "Or are they hurrying back to Stormspike Mountain?"

"They will defend this pass," she said. "They have no choice. Do you see what has happened to the wall on the right side of the tower?"

Isgrimnur squinted, but in the fading twilight it was hard to make out much beyond the high wall's shadowy, massive presence. "No. My eyes are not like a Sithi's. Speak plainly."

"A very few years ago, just before the beginning of the Storm King's war, the earth shook here—a great writhing of the ground that threw down many parts of the wall around Nakkiga-That-Was, including that section beside the tower. If you look closely, you can see that the tower itself tilts slightly to one side."

"I see no sign of the wall having collapsed."

"Because repairs were done—but they were hasty. My people sent a number of our families to help them. This was before the Hikeda'ya moved openly against us, but Queen Utuk'ku still refused our offer. We know, though, that the repairs were over-swift, most likely because the queen's eye was turned southward to the lands of men."

"Over-swift? What do you mean?" This was Brindur, who had joined the impromptu council. "I may not have your damnable fairy eyes, but they look solid enough to me."

As always, Ayaminu seemed unperturbed by insults. "Yes, the stones were piled up once more with as much skill as could be rendered, but not all the rituals were observed or the proper things done. The queen was keeping her holy Singers busy then, preparing the way for the Storm King's return. We can all be grateful they failed at that, but also that they were so gravely occupied by it, because the Words of Binding and other necessary cantrips were not sung here. The wall is weak. It can be breached with nothing but force."

"What else would we use?" Brindur demanded. "Trickery, like your accursed breed?"

Isgrimnur spurred his mount between the furious Rimmersman and Ayaminu. An argument with their one source of knowledge was a bad idea, and the Sitha-woman had seldom offered this much help before. "Please, explain," Isgrimnur said to her. "What do you mean?"

"Just what I said. You have force. You have implements of war and siegecraft like your great battering ram. The wall is weak there, and the rituals that would have made it all but impervious have not been performed. The tower itself was damaged by the shaking earth and the wall was badly weakened." She looked up the pass to the spiky shape of Three Ravens Tower. "You will lose men. The Hikeda'ya will fight fiercely.

But if you wish to pass the walls of their lands, this is the place it can be done."

"And why should we trust you?" Brindur snarled. "You have not seen fit to offer such useful advice before. Why now? And why could you not have told us that another Norn army was coming down upon us at the ruins?"

Ayaminu only looked at him blandly. "I knew nothing of that army. The Hikeda'ya are aware of my presence, I promise you, Northman. They take pains to keep their plans hidden."

Isgrimnur was not to be distracted from the matter at hand. "But are you certain now? Could they be keeping something else from you?"

"Of course. But what I tell you is true—you could ride along this wall until the season changed and not find a more vulnerable spot."

"You see my dilemma, don't you?" Isgrimnur frowned. "I have the safety of several thousand men in my hands. Can you promise me success?"

Now the Sitha showed emotion for the first time, a faint twisting of the lips. "I can promise you nothing, Duke Isgrimnur. Many men will die. So will many Hikeda'ya. Any one of us may suffer that fate at any time, and a battle between desperate enemies will not make the chances less. But if you wish to pass the wall and enter the lands around Nakkiga—if you truly mean to take the city itself—then you can find no better spot. That is all I have to say. The decision is yours."

"Look, we have reached the camp. Endri, did you hear me? We are here." The younger soldier had not been badly hurt during the Norns' escape, but like Porto himself he had been overwhelmed with a terrible, pressing weariness afterward and had spent most of his time on the back of Porto's horse sliding in and out of troubled sleep. "Endri?"

"Can we stop now?"

"Yes, that's what I said. See, the fires are lit—in fact, I smell food cooking." The sun, unnaturally late in the sky this far north, had only just disappeared, although midnight was surely not far away. The camps, set up well out of range of even the strongest bowshot from the looming walls, nestled in the shelter of the thick, snow-mantled pines on either side of the steep canyon. As Porto reined up he took a brief look at the beaked tower, which squatted against the purple-blue sky like some horrid heathen idol from the primeval days before the Ransomer was sent to Mankind. "Come on, lad," he told his companion, deliberately turning his back on the tower. "We don't want to miss whatever supper is left—I am famished." For the last stretch of the climb Porto had been forced to watch the tower loom larger with each moment, and despite his words to Endri, he found that the thing he wanted just now more than food or even drink was to find a spot where he could not see the tower at all until night finally hid it from view completely. It seemed to be watching them. He could almost imagine that their puniness, their mortal insignificance, actually amused it.

When they had found a fire, and were scooping the last congealing bits of stew out of the cooking pot, Endri suddenly looked up. "Porto?"

"What, lad?"

"I can't remember the way home."

"What do you mean?"

"I can't remember the roads we took, or how we got here. I couldn't find my way back again. Don't leave me."

Porto looked at the other men around the fire, mercenaries from Nabban and Perdruin and a scrawny, hard-muscled veteran of Josua's Erkynlandish army, wondering what they would make of the young man's neediness. Not one of them even looked up from their bowls. "What do you mean?" Porto asked him quietly. "I'm not going to leave you, lad. I promise."

"I can't even remember the road to my own house. You remember it, don't you? You've been to Harborside. I know you have."

Porto shook his head. "Been there? I've been trying to rid myself of that memory for years," he said, hoping to jolly the younger man out of his mood. "You should thank the saints to have lost it. Dreadful place. Not a patch on the Rocks."

"No jokes, Porto." Endri was staring intently at him now, his eyes showing a touch of panicked white around the edges, made all the more eerie by the flickering firelight. "I don't want jokes. Promise me that when it's over you will show me the way home."

"We will go together." Porto did his best to keep his voice light, though he was almost as beaten down by these dark, frightening lands as Endri. He sometimes thought that if he did not have the boy to watch over he might already have deserted to head back south, risking wolves and wild giants and all the other dangers. "We'll all go home then—you, me, these fellows here, and old Duke Isgrimnur leading the way. People will line up along the roads to cheer us—'*The men who finally defeated the Norns!*' they'll shout. And you won't need anyone to show you the way because your people, my people—my wife and son—they'll all be waiting to welcome us home."

Endri stared at him for a long moment without saying anything, his face still wild. Around his neck was his red and white Harborside scarf, grimy now with mud and matted with pine needles. The young soldier reached up and touched it and his expression softened, his eyes blinked. "Of course," he said. "Of course. Thank you. You are a good friend."

"If I am a good friend, then why are you letting the wineskin sit by your knee while I die of thirst? Pass it here."

Endri handed it over, and Porto took a long draught. It was sour and tasted strongly of oak, from one of the last and smallest of the barrels the army had carted north from the Yistrian Brothers' vineyards, but at the moment it was all he wanted. It tasted like salvation. It tasted like home.

A feeling of something close to security had stolen over Viyeki since he and the rest of the Hikeda'ya had reached Three Ravens Tower. He knew it was foolish—in truth, the danger grew greater by the moment, not just to themselves but to their entire race. If some miracle beyond foresight did not occur, the mortal army outside would follow them to Nakkiga if it could, take their race's last city, and destroy Viyeki's people, murdering every last man, woman, and child as though they were vermin. But even with the knowledge of the horrors that were surely to come, he felt better than he had since the terrible moment when the Storm King had been defeated and the great tower had fallen in Erkynland, crashing down in smoke and dust and the last flickers of magical flames, taking with it all the People's hope of making the land theirs once again.

In fact, at this instant Viyeki felt almost ordinary, as though the last

horrible months had not happened. It was largely the sturdy stone of Three
Ravens Tower that reassured him, the way it wrapped around them like
the protective mantle of the mountain Ur-Nakkiga itself. The ruins of
Tangleroot had never felt like more than a broken place, suitable only for
a desperate, doomed resistance to the inevitable. Resistance here was no
less doomed, Viyeki knew, but unlike Tangleroot Castle, this tower still
had a roof. Just sheltering in the starless dark beneath it reminded him of
his mountain home. It had been a long time since the Hikeda'ya had felt
safe beneath open sky.

But there was another factor of reassurance, one that he was only beginning to understand, and she stood before him now, conversing with
his master Yaarike. General Suno'ku still wore her battle-stained armor,
but despite the fierce fighting she had sustained only a small cut on her
neck; the line of dried blood made a wandering stripe down her throat
and disappeared into her breastplate like a road on an antique map. Her
pale eyes showed no trace of the exhausting week passed, the numerous
skirmishes fought with Northmen scouts as she led the survivors to Three
Ravens Tower. Viyeki had a beautiful, clever wife back in Nakkiga, but
he had never felt anything quite like the fascination that Suno'ku evoked
in him. Just listening to her firm, quiet voice he felt as though half their
problems were already solved. Viyeki's master, however, seemed less convinced.

"But we still have most of my Builders," Yaarike told the general. "It
is true we cannot perform the spells of Binding—not with the strongest of
our Singers in such condition." He gestured to Host-Singer Tzayin-Kha,
who lay senseless on a makeshift pallet a short distance away, tended by
two of her acolytes. Her pale skin had darkened into bruised shadows
around her eyes, temples, and throat, and her every ragged breath sounded
like it came with terrible effort. "But what Tzayin-Kha and her order
cannot do by songs of Binding, mine can do by skill and application."

"No. It is pointless trying to defend this place for long," said Suno'ku.
"We must return to Nakkiga as quickly as we can."

"Nakkiga?" Yaarike allowed himself a tone of measured irritation.
"You said there were no Sacrifices or other fighters left in Nakkiga, General. That means our only choice is to hold this part of the wall until the
mortals give up and go home. A few months at most. The winter will

drive them out, even with the Storm King banished to the lands beyond the veil of death."

Viyeki wondered how they would feed themselves. The fields between the Wall and the mountain were empty, burned by years of frost and neglect. Some of their people had not eaten in weeks. But he said nothing aloud.

"The problem remains," Yaarike continued. "You command the last of our warriors, General. There is no defense for the innocents in Nakkiga if we fail or falter."

"I said there were no fighters in Nakkiga when I left, High Magister," Suno'ku said. "But they were trickling back. The survivors were scattered widely after the Storm King failed and are returning by many routes, some very long and arduous. I myself took three hundred Sacrifices and members of other orders out of Erkynland and back through the coastal hills of Hernystir, fighting angry mortals all the way. Others are doing the same." She smiled, but it was no more than a slash in her pale skin, a bloodless wound. "No, we must return to Nakkiga. Word of our defeat in the south has given the human creatures courage. These Rimmersmen may be the first to come against us, but they will not be the last." She made a gesture of negation. "Now, attend me closely. If we try to hold this wall, we will fail. But at the same time, we *must* hold it, at least for a little while."

Viyeki did not understand her. Neither did his master, it seemed; the magister narrowed his eyes but spread his fingers in the sign that meant, *"I am listening."*

"We must hold this wall long enough for most of those with us now to return to Nakkiga," she said. "Nakkiga is where we must make our stand, with whatever forces and weapons we can assemble. Even though the queen slumbers in the grip of the *keta-yi'indra* and cannot defend us, you know as well as I that we have not entirely exhausted our resources. There are things in the lower levels—dreadful things . . ."

Yaarike cut her short with another gesture. "How can we accomplish it, General Suno'ku? I admire your Order of Sacrifice, but this tower is meant to be held by a garrison of a hundred, at least. In time of desperation we might halve that—it is said that the great Ruzayo held Midwinter Sun Tower and the wall against an army of giants with but two dozen

Sacrifices—but with all due respect, none of us here are Ruzayo Falcon's-Eye, nor even the mettle of his Twenty-Four."

"I will task each Sacrifice I leave behind with remaining alive until they have taken the lives of at least ten mortals," the general said. "With the help of a dozen or more of your Builders, I think this tower can be held until the rest—"

A strange, croaking sound interrupted her. Suno'ku turned, as did Viyeki and his master Yaarike. Tzayin-Kha, the Host-Singer who had given her all to make the fires speak at Tangleroot Castle, was now struggling to sit up.

"Mistress, no!" cried one of the Singers who had been tending her. He bent to help Tzayin-Kha lie back again, but the Host Singer grasped his arm and flung him away with such astounding force that he spun halfway across the tower chamber, hit the wall with a terrible, muffled crack, then lay still.

Tzayin-Kha slowly rose, clumsy, tottering, her limbs as stiff as alder branches, but it was her face that drew Viyeki's startled attention: her eyes had rolled up until only a crescent moon of white showed in each, and her jaw was working up and down soundlessly, chewing at the empty air.

"I will bring help!" shouted the other Singer. "She is having a fit."

"You . . . will . . . do . . . nothing," were the words that came from Tzayin-Kha's gnashing mouth, each syllable thick and misshapen. Viyeki recognized that grating, deep voice. It did not belong to the dying Host Singer at all, but to someone far more frightening.

Suno'ku drew her great sword, Cold Root, and leveled it at the thing's breast. The blind, upturned eyes could not possibly see the gray blade, but Tzayin-Kha's slack lips suddenly curled in a smile that made Viyeki feel ill.

"My, but we have grown important and impressive," said the scraping voice. *"I always knew you had the seed of greatness in you, Suno'ku seyt-Iyora."*

"Speak your piece, thing of the outer darkness." The general raised her witchwood blade as if to keep the stumbling, loose-limbed Singer at bay. "Then be gone. You sully the body of one who gave her all for her people."

Viyeki was astonished. Despite his master's favor, Viyeki was still an outsider compared to a high noble like Suno'ku, but even he knew the voice of Akhenabi, Lord of Song when he heard it—Akhenabi, second in power only to Queen Utuk'ku herself. How could the general not recognize it?

"Upstart! I speak for the queen!" rasped the voice out of Tzayin-Kha's slack mouth. *"You and the others are to hold your position! Under no circumstance are you to return to Nakkiga! You will defend Three Ravens Tower to your last breath!"*

Suno'ku lifted Cold Root high, took a sudden step forward, and crashed the pommel of her famous sword against Tzayin-Kha's forehead. The Singer's knees buckled, then she dropped like a sack of winter meal.

In the shocked silence that followed the acolyte who had been tending Tzayin-Kha scuttled forward with a look of helplessness on his face, as if all his training had been burned away in an instant. He turned the Host Singer over, but whatever had animated her had now fled. The center of her forehead was pushed in like a broken eggshell.

"You . . . you have killed my mistress!" he said in wonder and horror. "Tzayin-Kha is dead!"

"A regrettable result." General Suno'ku sheathed her sword and bent to examine the body. "I used more force than I intended. But perhaps it is a blessing. The thing that possessed her could not have been driven from her dying body any other way."

"What *thing*?" The acolyte Singer had lost more than his discipline, Viyeki decided—he had all but lost his mind if he thought he could defy an armed superior. "Did you not hear the voice of our master? Of Lord Akhenabi himself?"

Suno'ku gave a pitying shake of her head. "You were fooled by a dark spirit, Singer. Look at your comrade." She gestured to the Singer Tzayin-Kha had flung away, still lying in an awkward, broken-necked sprawl at the base of the chamber's stone wall. "Do you mean to tell me that Lord Akhenabi murdered one of his own Singers for no reason?"

The acolyte's mouth worked, but for a moment nothing came out. Viyeki was fearful that this one too would begin speaking with that terrible, scraping voice, but at last he managed to mutter, "I do not know what to say, General Suno'ku."

She turned to Yaarike and Viyeki. "Do you think it a coincidence that moments after I revealed my strategy, something slipped into the body of Tzayin-Kha to demand we not return? High Magister Yaarike, am I wrong?"

Yaarike again wore a strange expression—Viyeki could almost imagine his master was hiding amusement—but all the magister said was, "I can see no fault in your reasoning, General."

Commander Hayyano and several of his Sacrifices now hurried into the room. All but Hayyano stopped short, staring at the body of Tzayin-Kha. "What has happened here, General?" he asked.

"A deadly trick," she announced. "Perhaps the work of the Zida'ya traitor who travels with the mortal army. But it has failed. Assemble all of your men except the sentries and those on active patrol. With High Magister's Yaarike's permission, I will speak to them."

Hayyano looked to Yaarike. He was better at masking his confusion and doubt than the acolyte Singer had been, but his hesitation was clear to all.

"You heard your general," said Yaarike at last, all surface now, his private thoughts once more hidden behind a wall that needed no sentries to keep it inviolate. "Of course you must follow your orders."

More than two hundred Sacrifices from almost a dozen different troops had crowded into the great, high-raftered hall of Three Ravens Tower. They stood straight, ignoring their many wounds, faces set in masks of resolve. Two torches at either end of Marshal Ekisuno's makeshift bier cast the only light except for the summer star Reniku, burning in the center of the hall's high window like a diamond shining from the ashes of a fire.

"My foreparent Ekisuno lies before you," Suno'ku began, pointing to the marshal's shrouded, unmoving form. Though the general's voice seemed soft, it carried to all parts of the chamber. "He was of the blood of great Ekimeniso himself, our queen's consort, and like his ancestor, Ekisuno was a mighty warrior. He spent his long life fighting the queen's enemies before he died at the fall of the tower of Asu'a, as did so many others. You know what happened. All of you were there."

The torches reflected the gleam of hundreds of pairs of dark eyes, watching her.

"Less than one hundred Great Years ago the first mortals came into our lands, savage, dangerous creatures in numbers ever swelling. But when we would have scoured them from our soil, our cousins the Zida'ya prevented us, saying, 'They are but few, and the land is big enough for all.' You know the tragedy that came from their foolish forbearance. You know how mortals killed Drukhi, the son of our great queen. And that was only the first of the outrages they have visited upon us. They were the wedge that split the two kindreds of the Keida'ya, and although, for a time, we both lived in uneasy peace with the newcomers, it did not last.

"During the lifetimes of most of you here, the first of the bearded ones came over the sea with weapons of black iron and hearts full of hate. Like locusts they devoured all that they touched, destroying even their own kind in their bloodlust and fury. Then the Zida'ya learned to their sorrow the folly of their patience with these short-lived, swift-breeding animals. The last of our people's great cities fell when Ineluki of the Zida'ya was destroyed trying to defend Asu'a against the invaders. Only mortal kings, their hands red with blood—*our* people's blood—have sat on Asu'a's throne ever since."

Here the general suddenly stopped and fell silent, as if some new thought had occurred to her. The assembled Sacrifices, their myriad gazes following her as one, stared raptly at the slender, bright shape in silver-white armor. "Did I say the last city of our people?" Suno'ku asked. "That is not true. One great city remains—one refuge of the People of the Garden. And that city is Nakkiga, our home.

"Beyond this tower, just outside the boundary walls of our land, waits an army of mortals. And not just any mortals, but the very same bearded Northerners who destroyed Ineluki and Asu'a, who laid waste to Hike-hikayo and drove out the last of our people there, who left a trail of our blood across all the lands that once belonged to us. Now they mean to bring down these walls, too. They will swarm in their thousands all the way to Nakkiga itself, now all but undefended after our defeat in the southern lands."

The Sacrifices were stirring, still following Suno'ku's every word and gesture. It felt to Viyeki as though he stood in the middle of a hornets' nest and someone had begun to shake it.

"Will we hold the wall?" she asked. "The answer is, we must, if only for a short while. But we cannot hold it for long. The shaking earth of a few seasons back has weakened it, and if every single one of us laid down our lives here, still we would hold back the mortals for only a short time. In a few days or weeks, a changing of the moon's face at most, our defense would fail before their numbers and they would sweep past us to great

Nakkiga itself. And what would they do there?" Suno'ku's voice became quieter but no less forceful. "When they took Asu'a the first time, a horror that is within the memory of most here today, the mortals killed every living thing within its walls. Nor were those deaths swift and merciful. Do you think they will do any different if they take Nakkiga?"

Now the Sacrifices were openly murmuring, some clenching and unclenching their fists. Viyeki was astounded—the discipline of the fighting order was legendary, and General Suno'ku had broken it in moments. For the first time in his life, Viyeki wondered if his people's eagerness to be ruled by a greater power than themselves might in truth be a sort of weakness, in the same way that over-hardened witchwood lacked flexibility and thus was more easily broken.

"Make no mistake," Suno'ku continued, her noble face as grim as her words. "The mortals will rage through our city like a giant in the Field of Stone Flowers, smashing everything. They will destroy every monument to the Lost Garden, every precious memorial to our sacred martyrs. But what they do to the living will be worse. Your families and clans will fall before them like sheep caught by a pack of raving wolves. Your daughters and wives will be raped and then murdered. No one will be spared. When they have finished, Nakkiga will be a fit place only for bats, beetles, and helpless ghosts." She spoke slowly, each word a painful spite. "They will pull the queen herself from the *keta-yi'indra*, where she lies helpless after the last battle in the south, and they will take her and burn her. The mother of us all will die in agony, and the last living memory of the Garden will disappear from the earth. Because we cannot hold this wall. We are not strong enough. The fortifications are not strong enough. And there is no help coming from Nakkiga. We are alone." And slowly, deliberately, Suno'ku turned her back on the warriors and hung her head as if in final defeat.

The murmuring died away, but for a few noises that might have been strangled sobs. Then, out of the silence, a single voice spoke. It was Hayyano, and the rage and pain in his words made even Viyeki, who thought little of the commander, ache inside. "Is there nothing we can do, then?" Hayyano demanded. "Nothing at all? Why do you tell us this, General? Why do you set our hearts afire and then leave them to burn?"

A moment—a long moment—and then Suno'ku made the gesture for attention. It was only for effect, Viyeki knew: all eyes were already on her. "Yes, there is one chance. One unlikely chance."

"Tell us!" cried Hayyano, and although no one echoed him, it was clear from the shuffling and hand-signs of agreement that he spoke for all the Sacrifices gathered. Viyeki could feel their desperate fury—a rage that now made the very air tremble as if a storm was imminent.

"We cannot in any case hold this wall or this tower for long," she said. "But if enough of us can make it back to Nakkiga, especially the Builders here, it is possible we can shore up the mountain's defenses sufficiently to keep the mortals from victory. The great gates of Nakkiga have never been breached by mortal or immortal—even the queen herself could not take it by force when she first came there, but had to be welcomed in by its citizens. The gates of Nakkiga are strong and we can make them stronger still. But we need time. Can you do that?"

"For our queen, for the Garden, we can do anything!" Hayyano shouted, and at last a chorus of agreement broke from the ranks. "Tell us, General! Tell us what we must do!"

She stared at the eager throng for a moment as if considering. Moved despite his moments of doubt, Viyeki found himself leaning forward, half-hoping she would ask him to join the warriors in sacrificing themselves to save their queen and city. "High Magister Yaarike," the general said at last. "Will you choose a dozen of your engineers to remain behind and help with the defense? They will not return to Nakkiga, but they will be promised a place of glory in the tales of this time—and I promise this time will be remembered as long as the Garden itself is remembered."

Yaarike wore his most solemn face. "I will ask for volunteers, General Suno'ku, but one way or another, you will have your dozen."

"Thank you, High Magister." Suno'ku looked to the assembled Sacrifices, who had grown almost downcast when she turned away, but who were now all attention once more. "And what of you, my warriors? Which of you will offer your lives here and now for the chance that Nakkiga may live? I need a hundred volunteers to stay, and each must give me his or her sworn vow to send at least ten mortals into the darkness before the end comes. How many will do this? Which of your names will be told and retold until the sun itself is consumed by the black emptiness at the end of time and the great song finally ends? *Show me your swords!*"

More than two hundred blades leaped from their scabbards as one, a chiming scrape of witchwood and bronze so harsh and loud that Viyeki nearly put his fingers in his ears. Every Sacrifice had lifted his sword.

"I expected no less," Suno'ku said, nodding. "The queen, were she here, would smile to see her brave children." She turned to Hayyano. "League Commander, you will take charge of the garrison. Choose one hundred Sacrifices, favoring those who are older or without families. And do not insult those now standing guard upon the walls by excluding them from the chance to fight this glorious fight."

"I hear you, General," said Hayyano, his narrow face flushed at cheek-bones and temples as if he had run a long distance through the cold. "We will hold this wall to our last beating heart. We will make you proud."

"You already have," she said. "Your death-songs were sung long ago. The Celebrants have already written down all your names. Now you can give those deaths in perfect glory, for our queen and our race. And I promise you in return that those of us who must go to defend Nakkiga will give every last breath we have to honor your sacrifice and save our people. For the Garden!"

"*For the Garden!*" echoed hundreds of voices, including Viyeki's own. He was surprised to discover that his eyes were brimming. He did not even know when the tears had begun.

Frost made the roof sag, and the wind kept the sides of the big tent rippling. The cold seemed to creep in and bite Isgrimnur with sharp little teeth that pierced even his clothing. The duke thought he had never, not even through the worst of the fighting at the Hayholt or even in the foul, brackish Wran, longed so deeply for a chair before a warm fire in a warm room in a stern, safe castle.

Elysia, Mother of Mercy, I am weary of cold, he thought, then dragged his attention back to the matter at hand.

"So what you are saying, man, is that we are winning," growled Brindur. "That in a matter of a day or two we will have the wall down and our hands on the throats of those corpse-skinned creatures." But as he talked, Brindur did not even look up from the sharpening of his sword. Since his son's terrible death it seemed the only thing he did. Isgrimnur knew that look of disinterest and feared it, for he had seen it on other men and they had never lived long. *"Already looking to the next world,"* his father had said of another battle-mad warrior. What they had lost here in the Norn lands already was bad enough. Brindur was a man Isgrimnur relied on, had always been one of the most dependable of his thanes: but he did not know this Brindur at all.

"No, that is not what I'm saying!" Sludig's voice was tight-strung with anger, but after receiving a pointed look from the duke, he took a breath and tried again, this time speaking directly to Isgrimnur as though Brindur and the others were not inside the tent with them. "What I am trying to say, my lord, is that we should not be winning *this way*. Yes, the Bear has all but knocked down the wall. Yes, the Norn archers in the tower have killed or wounded only a few of the men wielding the ram. But there were several hundred Norn fighters in the group that escaped from us at the ruins. Why do they not fight back as we knock down their wall? Such mildness does not signify. Nothing lies beyond these walls but their stronghold in Stormspike itself!"

"Nothing that we know about," said Isgrimnur. "But our ignorance is as big as my belly. Is he right, Ayaminu? Is there nothing else between us and the Norn mountains? And is my man right to suspect that something else is going on that we do not see?"

"It depends first on what you mean by 'nothing,'" she said. "The lands between the wall and the mountain you call Stormspike are no longer inhabited, and most of the city that was built there long ago is in ruins now. But that does not warrant they will not be waiting in ambush, or that forces from Nakkiga itself will not meet you before you reach the gates."

"We will have more talk about these gates later," said Isgrimnur. "But now we must consider what is immediately in front of us. Sludig, could it be that the Norns simply have no arrows left, no weapons they can hurt us with until we close with them in actual combat?"

"I await that hour," said Brindur, still sharpening. "I wait for nothing else."

"You will have a sword that is little more than a dagger if you keep scraping away at it like that," the duke told him. "But that isn't my chief concern. Is there anything else that makes you worry, Sludig?"

The younger man shook his head, his forehead and brows drawn together in frustration. "Only feelings, my lord—the smell of the thing. We have fought them many times now and the Norns are nothing if not subtle. They brought many strange weapons against us at Naglimund, both during the siege and later, and just as many tricks in the last battle at the Hayholt. Poison powders. False gates. The dead made to walk. Giants summoned like tame hounds, crushing and rending everything they could reach. But where are these things now? Since their escape from the ruined fort they have managed only noises and shadows, which the men have grown used to, which no longer strike fear in any heart. As for actual fighting, we have seen only a few stones and a few arrows from the tower's three beaks and that weak spot on the wall, aimed at the siege engines and the ram. A few of our men have been downed—by chance as much as anything else." Sludig's frown deepened. "And so I must ask myself—are they truly so weak?"

One of Brindur's Skoggeymen, an older warrior with gray-shot whiskers, spoke up. "The fairies are few now, Duke Isgrimnur, whatever Sludig may think. They have lost the war and we carry it to their own land, as we should. Soon we will destroy them all so they cannot trouble us again. Why make a mystery out of weakness?"

Sludig scowled. "Because when you suppose that an enemy is weak, Marri Ironbeard, you only realize you were wrong when they've killed you."

"Perhaps you have lost your taste for this kind of fighting," Brindur said, briefly raising his eyes to give Sludig a hard look. "Or perhaps your friendship with trolls and fairies—yes, I have heard about you, Sludig Two Axes—has made you reluctant to pursue them. Or even afraid."

Sludig's hand dropped to one of the bearded hand-axes in his broad belt. His eyes narrowed. "My lord, did you not grieve the loss of your son, as we all do, I would demand you to prove that charge with your own hand, man to man."

"Enough!" shouted Isgrimnur. "No accusations. Brindur, you insult Sludig for no reason. His loyalty is beyond doubt. I too have conversed with, and even fought beside, trolls and fairies. If you question his loyalty, you question mine!"

Brindur shrugged. "I take nothing back, but I did not say he was guilty of treason, merely asked him if he had the heart for this fight."

"This is only what our enemies would wish, to have us arguing and biting each other's backs. Enough!" Isgrimnur was furious. "I asked Sludig a question, Brindur, and he answered me—before you needlessly insulted him. I ask you the same question. Do you believe that the Norns are as weak now as they appear?"

Brindur tested the edge of his blade with his finger, then sucked the blood from his fingertip and spat onto the packed, icy ground in a place the rugs didn't cover. Outside the wind had risen again, rattling the duke's tent so that the cloth hummed like the wings of a monstrous insect. "Yes, the White Foxes are fierce fighters. Hard to kill. I do not make the mistake of thinking otherwise. They surprised us with reinforcements at the ruined fort, but we have seen no signs of any more coming. We killed enough of them there that I doubt more than ten score or so of those reinforcements survive, and they had scarce enough fighters in the first group. So I think they are spent and have but little strength left. Our own men are hungry enough in this blighted, frozen place, and we have brought food for ourselves out of Rimmersgard. The Norns were already hungry weeks ago, and whatever tricks they have, I doubt they can feed themselves on air or they would not have attacked so many villages for grain and other supplies. So my wits tell me Two-Axes is only jumping at the same shadows and strange noises that he himself talked about."

Another petty, pointless sting. Before Isgrimnur could shape a reply, a figure, half-obscured by a crust of snowflakes, pushed in past the quivering fabric of the tent door.

"I crave pardon, Your Grace, my lords," the soldier said. "I bring a message from Jarl Vigri. He says there are pieces falling from the wall after the last blow of the great Bear. He thinks it is about to come down."

Brindur's dour mood dropped away in an instant. "Ha! By God," the thane said, climbing to his feet, "If the wall is coming down, I will not be the last to paint my blade with fairy blood!" He turned to one of the younger Skoggeymen. "Fani, you fool, where is my helmet?"

Isgrimnur still had things he needed to discuss with Brindur and the rest, including the letter that a messenger had brought him only this morning, but he would never keep their attention now. As he watched the thane and his Skoggeymen scrambling for their weapons, he thought briefly of trying to make their rush toward the wall more orderly, then decided it would be better to bow to the inevitable. Even if the wall was badly damaged it might not fall for many more swings of the battering ram, and even the most anxious Rimmersgard warrior could not come to grips with the enemy until that moment. In the meantime, letting Brindur and the rest vent their impatience on an immense weight of black stone might just be a good idea. His other news could wait.

Two of Isgrimnur's house carls were standing outside the tent, one with his battle-helmet and his White Bear and Stars standard, the other holding the duke's large and patient horse. Isgrimnur heaved himself into the saddle, not without help, then spurred upward after the others.

The battering ram, close against the wall but well to one side of the three-beaked tower, was just about to make another stroke as Brindur and the rest reached it. Like Vigri's soldiers who were already crouched on either side of the massive device, they held their shields above their heads to ward off arrows from the tower or wall, waiting for their chance to attack.

The ram's sloping roof, which protected the men beneath it from defenders' arrows, was the length of a tithing barn, though much narrower, and so large that it had to be assembled in sections like the bear-headed ram itself. Snow had been piled high atop the ram's roof as a protection against flaming arrows, but Isgrimnur saw no sign of Norns now and little evidence of defense or defenders at all.

The ram's overseers chanted loudly and beat their drums, competing with the war-cries of Brindur and his party. The sweating, grunting ram-handlers drew the great log back as far as its heavy chains would allow; then, at the chief overseer's command, let it go. The Big Bear's grinning iron muzzle swung forward and smashed into the already weakened wall with a loud crunch. The wall still did not collapse, but it shifted and bowed inward where the ram had struck, causing a shower of stone chips when cracks between the unmortared stones widened.

"One more time!" shouted Brindur hoarsely. "One more time and they're ours!"

Isgrimnur rode closer, but still held his distance, keeping his eyes on more than that one spot: Brindur and even the usually cautious Vigri seemed blind to anything but the stretch of wall before them. Isgrimnur looked up to the three protruding beaks of the tower as a few arrows came hissing down from the battlements. Although some of these shots found their way between the soldiers' upturned shields, the rest of the ramparts were still all but empty of defenders. Surely the Norns realized that their damaged wall could not hold much longer. Had they turned from their defensive positions and fled toward Stormspike? Or was something else going on?

The ram was pulled back again, the groans of its handlers and the pounding drums mixed with the battle-chants of the waiting Rimmersmen, but the bloodthirsty excitement of his countrymen no longer touched Isgrimnur. Something truly did seem wrong. His men had driven hundreds of Norns to this spot, and although a few of them had been killed on the walls by Vigri's Tungoldyr archers, Isgrimnur knew those had only been a fraction of the enemies that should be fighting to keep mortals from crossing into their lands. *By the Holy Ransomer,* the duke thought, *if Sludig is right, what are they planning?*

The chains creaked as the ram reached its farthest backward point. A moment later the drum fell silent, then the overseer cried, *"Now!"* The ram swung forward and the bear took another crunching bite.

A goodly chunk fell from the middle of the wall where the iron head of the ram had struck; a moment later another piece fell from above it. Then, with a rumble like thunder directly overhead, the great stones began to tip and slide. The troops around the ram, arrested in mid-cheer, scrambled back—some of the stones were bigger than a man.

Once it began, the cascade of black stone could not be stopped. The whole center of the wall before the ram tottered and then fell in on itself with a grinding crash. Huge stones began to cascade on either side, throwing flurries of snow and mud into the air, scattering men in all directions. A moment later the collapse was over: all but the bottom few cubits in the wall's center had toppled, leaving a gaping wound in the great structure like an upturned horseshoe. The Rimmersmen quickly reformed their ranks and began to surge through this opening, climbing over the remaining stones like ants swarming a fallen loaf of bread, screeching and bellowing in their gleeful frenzy to get at the enemy who had evaded them so long.

A moment later the attackers discovered that another wall stood behind the first. It was only barely taller than a man, obviously hasty work by the defenders behind the great wall's weakest spot, but as the first Rimmersmen made their way over the rubble, they found themselves climbing into a hornet's nest of arrows: most of the rest of the castle's defenders were hidden there, waiting patiently for the chance to fight back that had now arrived.

"No fear! They are only a few!" shouted Vigri, his short legs straight in the stirrups as he waved to his troops. "On, now, Northmen! Show them what iron tastes like!"

But even as the jarl's Enggidalers and Brindur's Skoggeymen forged into the gap, Isgrimnur heard another cry. It was only another voice in the chaos of many, but this one caught his attention because it came from a different direction.

To his left and behind him, a good distance back from the breach, stood the catapults that had been pelting the walls with large stones to divert any remaining defenders from the ram. These siege engines were mostly guarded by the mercenaries from the south, men of unknown quality that Isgrimnur had not trusted in his front lines, and now he saw one of these southerners waving his arms and shouting, trying to get the attention of the Rimmersmen fighting near the ram. Isgrimnur could not make out what the man was saying through the noise of the assault, but he followed his wild hand gestures and looked up to the high peaks that framed the wall on either side of the pass. His heart lurched. About halfway up the slope on Isgrimnur's left hand a huge boulder had somehow worked its way loose from the soil and was beginning to move ponderously downward. The massive chunk of stone seemed to be alternately skidding and rolling right toward the Rimmersmen as they fought to get over the collapsed wall through the flurry of Norn arrows.

Isgrimnur shouted a warning, but of course no one could hear him. High above, the irregular boulder slowed for a moment, its flattest side down, and the duke felt a moment of hope that it had stopped; an instant later the great chunk of stone slid over the small level spot that had slowed it and began to roll, big as a three story house in the wealthy merchant's quarter of Elvritshalla, careening toward the base of the hill.

Isgrimnur spurred his horse forward, shouting a warning as he headed toward the hole in the wall the ram had made.

"Forward!" he bellowed with all the strength he had in his great lungs, trying to drive the rest of the waiting troops through the gap. "Forward or be crushed! 'Ware! 'Ware!"

The huge stone smashed the corner of the wall as it scraped past, sending monstrous black shards flying like pebbles but slowing the stone not at all.

The collapsed section of wall lay before him, then his horse was leaping and sliding on the piled stones as men threw themselves out of his way.

"No, forward!" he cried. *"Forward if you want to live!"*

And then a powerful wind nearly blew the duke out of his saddle as the great boulder struck just behind him, grinding men and stones and the mighty bear-headed ram itself into an unrecognizable clutter, with a noise like the end of the world.

Porto, from his position beside the catapult known as the Donkey, had been watching the Rimmersmen waiting to attack with a mixture of admiration and disbelief. As the wall wavered he thought they looked like a pack of dogs, their beards bristling, teeth bared, howling and even singing as they waited, and all he could think was, *Are they really going to charge through that hole into the teeth of whatever defenders are left?* Because surely the Norns were aware of the widening cracks spreading between the great stones. Even a blind man could hear the shifting of tons of rock as the wall slowly began to give way.

Although the catapult had been loaded and wound again, it had not been fired: two of its crewmen lay on the snowy ground with Norn arrows in them and their hammers lying beside them, one man already dead and the other shrieking for God to help him. Several of the long iron stakes that held down the front of the war engine had worked their way loose on its last shot, but Hjortur the catapult master did not seem to have noticed in the confusion of battle. Porto knew that if the front was not anchored the release would not just miss the target, but might throw its stone into the Rimmersmen's own ranks, so he hurried around the wooden frame. As he lifted the heavy maul the dead man had dropped, he heard a sharp, excited cry from the soldiers at the wall as the great Bear was released again and crashed into the heavy stones.

"Endri!" he shouted. "Damn it, man, grab the other hammer and help me knock these stakes in!" Even as he said it, Porto lifted his own maul and swung it, but as he brought it down he was almost knocked from his feet by a tremendous rumbling impact as the great wall that sealed the valley finally collapsed.

He turned and saw the Rimmersgard soldiers scrambling forward over the tumbled stones of the wall. They were bellowing like wild things, and he was so taken by the sound of it, the way it murmured in his bones and made his heart race even faster, that for long instants he did not hear Endri's warning. The young man was leaping up and down, shouting at him and pointing upward; Porto saw a movement at the corner of his eye and turned away from the spectacle of Isgrimnur's soldiers charging the gap just as the first of them began to fall back, sprouting arrows.

Something was tumbling toward him down the slope at the side of the valley. Something very big.

For a brief instant, as Porto tried to understand the size of the shadowy mass skidding downward toward them, he thought, "Dragon!" his mind ready for any kind of madness the Norns might be able to summon. Then he saw it for what it was, a slab of rock the size of a village church. Even as he watched, it tipped and began to tumble.

Porto dropped his heavy maul to run, but because he was still looking back at the huge stone as it grew bigger by the instant, he tripped over the dead man he'd taken the hammer from. The man's face was right below him, mouth sagging open, and for an instant as Porto fell it looked as though the corpse was warning him. Or perhaps taunting him: *You think staying alive is easy?*

Porto hit the icy ground hard, felt a brief spray of cold snow, then struck his head so roughly that his thoughts shrank to a narrow tunnel of light in a field of black emptiness. Even the boulder that was about to crush him seemed far away, without meaning, though its thunderous approach seemed to drown all other noise. *No matter,* he thought absently. Everything was over. Over.

And then he was yanked away, scraped face-first across the rough, stony soil and its layer of snow, heat and chill and bright white pain all battling for his attention—but Porto had no attention to give.

It had not been the great stone that had hit him he realized an instant later, floating in dreamy detachment. He saw its shadow slide past and heard it smash the Donkey into splinters, then he watched the great catapult arm bounce away, end over end like a spoon thrown by an ogre's child, until it finally stopped, leaning upright against the base of Three Ravens Tower.

Endri stood over him now, the sky a swirl of pearl bright light and dark clouds. Porto could only stare up at his friend in wonder. He knew something had happened, but his thoughts seemed to be at the end of a long string, and although he pulled at it, all he was doing was reeling in more and more string.

"The catapult is gone!" Endri cried, as if that should mean something.

The young man's eyes were so wide Porto thought it must be painful.

"Now the ram, too. I think the Norns found a way to push that rock down on . . ." Endri paused with a look of confusion. Still puzzled, he turned to look behind him, as though someone had tapped him on the shoulder while he stood in a deserted place. A moment later the youth dropped to his knees, far more slowly than the great stone had traveled down the mountain. Then, equally slowly, he toppled forward onto his face. His chain mail gave a single soft clash as he hit the ground, then Endri lay still and silent, a black arrow quivering in his back.

Duke Isgrimnur did not want to look back at the damage the monstrous stone had caused in its fall, but he could not help himself. The head of the iron ram was intact beneath the rubble but the great log, a single trimmed pine trunk more than thirty paces long, had been crushed to splinters, and he could see broken bodies in the pile of shattered stone and wood. Then an arrow whickered past his helmet, and he hurriedly turned back to what lay before him.

Fewer Norns had been lying in wait behind the small, hastily built second wall than Isgrimnur had feared at first; the fairies had saved their arrows and put them to deadly use, although most of his men had been shot in the first instants of surprise. Though many Rimmersmen fell in the first charge, their comrades had pushed forward after them, climbing over the dead to reach the second wall. Brindur himself had led his Skoggey kinsmen over the top, shouting the name of his dead son Floki, and within moments was among the Norns on the other side, howling with mad glee as he hacked at his enemies. Vigri's men quickly followed. The Norns were deadly fighters, but they were outnumbered by more than a dozen to one, swarmed as though beset by hunting hounds. Within an hour Isgrimnur's forces had taken control of the wall.

A few more White Foxes tried to hold the tower, but its portals had not been fairy-magicked and Rimmersgard axes soon splintered the doors and knocked them from their hinges. Terrible fights took place in the darkened stairwells and in the uppermost chamber between the great beaks, but at last the final Norn died, pinned against a wall by several spears. The besiegers dragged the pale creature's body to the hole in the bottom of the beak and shoved it through. It spun slowly down the long drop to the ground and bounced when it struck, like a discarded fish head.

Thane Brindur had sustained many wounds but none of them were mortal. He licked his lips and grinned as one of the barber-surgeons cleaned and stitched the worst of them. "I told you," he growled. "Fairies can die like anyone else once you shove a yard of iron into them."

Isgrimnur, who in his time had killed more than his share of Norns, did not bother to reply to Brindur's comment. "The rest of the White Foxes are gone. That was but a token force. I counted only a few score corpses. The rest have fled back to their city."

"So?" Brindur rubbed his finger along a freshly sewn cut that extended from his wrist to beyond his elbow, then he examined the blood. "That is only another hundred that we will kill later rather than sooner."

Jarl Vigri approached with several of his thanes. "The scouts are back from atop the cliffs, Your Grace. Yes, that boulder was the Norns' work—the tools are still there where they dropped them. But looking out across the lands beyond the wall, the scouts say it is still several days' march to Stormspike from here. Those who escaped may be waiting for us in ambush along the way."

Brindur wiped his bloody finger on his already muddy, blood-spattered surcoat. "Slaughter them in droves like the beasts they are or kill them one by one—it makes no difference to me as long as we destroy that foul nest in the mountain."

Isgrimnur frowned and tugged at his beard. "We are already in territory that no mortal armies have entered in centuries. We have lost a quarter of our army in two or three small skirmishes on the outskirts of the enemy's lands—what makes you think they will not fight even harder to defend their home? The Bear is smashed, as well as two of our catapults, so how do you propose we enter Stormspike, Brindur, even if the Norns are too few to defend it? Which is by no damn means certain."

"It is certain," Brindur said. "If they had reinforcements a day or two away, do you think they would have let us break down their wall and walk into the Nornfells without a fight?"

"I do not call it 'without a fight' when more than a hundred of my men are killed," Isgrimnur growled.

Brindur spat on the floor. "This is war, not the squabbling politics of court. If we do not destroy these creatures in their final hole we have wasted those dead."

Vigri cleared his throat. "I do not say that Brindur is right, my lord, but I do not say he is wrong, either. We came to finish with these corpse-skins once and for all. If you set out to burn the wasp's nest, you must finish the job or they will just make more wasps."

Isgrimnur snorted. "These are not wasps. These are not beasts. These are ancient creatures more cunning than we are, and they are certainly not cowards. Do you think we have seen all their tricks?"

"They are running out of feints," Brindur said as flatly as he might have said "the sky is blue," or "blood is red." "We saw no faces in the fires this time, no shadows or ghostly voices. Just arrows and stone walls."

"And a very large rock which destroyed our catapults and our ram," said Isgrimnur. "As well as killing a dozen or more of our men. But we will miss the ram more than any of the rest."

"The Bear is not dead," Brindur declared. "His iron head still wants to bite. There are plenty of trees here. We will build him a new body and knock down the fairies' front door."

Isgrimnur turned to Vigri, since it seemed as if the jarl and Sludig were the only sane voices left. "What do you think?"

Vigri looked weary. His armor was almost as bloody as Brindur's. "What do I think? That this is a dreadful chore, my lord. But we have taken it on and we cannot leave off yet. That is what I think."

Isgrimnur sighed. "I suppose you are right." He reached for the bowl of ale one of his carls had set out on top of a wooden chest and felt the letter that he had thrust into his belt earlier, now scratching against his belly. "Ah! Of course! I have some news that slipped my mind in the clamor. Good news, at that."

"Praise Usires!" said the jarl. "Pray do not keep it to yourself, my lord. That is something we need more than food or drink."

Isgrimnur nodded. "When first I heard from you, Vigri, telling of the siege you had begun, I sent out messengers to the nearest thanes, Alfwer of Heitskeld, Helgrimnur Stonehand, and several others, asking help from everyone within a fortnight's march."

"*Alfwer,*" said Brindur, and although he did not spit again, he might as well have.

"Never mind Alfwer," said Isgrimnur with a tight smile. "I have not heard back from him anyway—doubtless he is busy counting his cattle. But the messenger to Helgrimnur came back just this morning." He paused to take a drink.

"Please, Your Grace!" said Vigri. "What good news? You are torment-ing me."

Isgrimnur could manage only the weariest of smiles. "I beg your par-don, my friend. Helgrimnur writes to say that he had already mustered men to send to Erkynland, but when they were not called for, he released them for the spring planting—or such as it was this year, with the fields all frozen." He opened the letter, smoothing it on his knee. "Yes, here. But when the Norns began to make their way through the nearby lands, he summoned his warriors back, clever fellow. He has half a thousand men under arms, ten score of them experienced fighters. Now, the happiest part—he is sending them with his sister-son, Helvnur, who also leads nearly a hundred mounted men. The messenger said Helvnur and his men are only a few days behind him. They did not expect to find us already so far north."

Vigri clapped his hands together. "Aedon be praised—that is excellent news indeed!"

"I would rather it were ten times that many, but it will surely help." The duke smiled again and raised his ale bowl in a toast. "By my beard, Helgrimnur is a good man, and I will not forget it!"

"Is there a chance that we may hear back from any others?" Vigri asked.

Isgrimnur shook his head. "Not before we cross into the Norn lands, I think. But Helgrimnur's muster makes up for the numbers we have lost so far."

"As long as these new folk don't get between me and the creatures I'll be killing, they are welcome," said Brindur. "I have a mind to lay my hands on the queen of the fairies herself. Maybe she'll grant me a wish before I strangle her."

Isgrimnur hurriedly made the sign of the Tree. "Trust me, Brindur, you don't know what you're talking about. She would freeze the marrow in your bones if you met her."

"We'll see," said Brindur. "In any case, my sword needs sharpening again. Fairy armor makes a blade dull, and fairy bones are worse."

"Even with more fighters, the next part will not be easy," Isgrimnur warned. "God save me, none of this has been easy."

"You think too much, my lord," said Brindur, and it was hard to tell whether he meant sarcasm or honest reproof. "See the enemy. Kill the enemy. That is the whole of our task."

"Ah, such simple bloodlust reminds me of an old friend," Isgrimnur said, half-amused, but a moment later the memory turned sour. "The White Foxes killed him in Aldheorte Forest."

"I hate to disagree with you, Thane Brindur," said Vigri. "But I would like to add another task to your list: Return alive."

"I hold to an older tradition, my lord," said Brindur. "I would like to live, but I would rather see our enemies dead. I will look down happily from the feasting halls of our ancestors if I take enough of the whiteskins with me."

Isgrimnur had heard enough. He had men to bury, if the living had managed by now to make a big enough hole in such icy ground. He reached for the ale and took a long draught, then took another before wiping his mouth with the back of his hand. "God grant us victory," was all he said.

Endri was not dead, but there were moments now that Porto could almost wish the Norn arrow had killed him outright.

One of the Rimmersgard surgeons had cut deep into the young man's back to remove the black dart, and sluiced the wound with strong spirits. At first it seemed that Endri would recover, because the arrow itself had stuck in his shoulder blade instead of slicing through to his lungs and heart, but whether because of the foul airs of the Nornfells or some poison on the arrowhead, the wound did not heal. At first it was only obvious by the fevers that shook his body and the pains that made him cry out as he slipped in and out of restless sleep. But by the time a full day had passed Porto could see a black stain beneath the skin that had spread outward from the original arrow wound into a blotch bigger than his hand. It was hot to the touch, and the skin seemed almost lifeless beneath Porto's fingers.

"Can you feel my touch here?" he asked as he probed at the lumpy area around the wound.

"Yes. But it's no worse . . . than any other part of me. I hurt all over. God help me, Porto, it feels like my blood is on fire in my veins!"

"You should not have risked your life for me," he said, then regretted it.

Endri tried to sit up but failed, slumping back. The light of the campfire made the whites of his eyes seem as yellow as a wolf's. "No!" He struggled to take a deeper breath. "You are my only friend. Don't . . . don't be foolish. You would have done the same . . . the same for me." The effort of speaking had exhausted him, and he closed his eyes again. His chest moved up and down in little jerks.

What are we doing here? Porto wondered. *What are we doing in this cold, empty place, out at the arse-end of nowhere? It would be different if we were fighting for Ansis Pellppé, to protect our own folk*

As if he had heard Porto's thoughts of home, Endri opened his eyes. For a moment he looked around wildly, as if he did not know where he was, but when he saw Porto's face he calmed. "I want to go back," was what he said. "Back to Harborside."

"You will, I promise. Just rest. Here, drink a little of this." He lifted the cup of melted snow to Endri's lips and steadied it while the young man sipped. "You will be well again. We will go back to Perdruin together in triumph." He looked at Endri's dull, listless face and added, "And who knows what booty we will bring? Gold from out of Stormspike itself, maybe, or jewels from some fairy princess's wardrobe. Even a Norn sword or battle helm will bring a pretty price in Ansis Pelippé, you can be sure of that. We will be rich men. Famous, too—the heroes who fought the Norns."

Endri shook his head, eyes closed again, but this time he smiled. "That is why you are my friend, Porto. You tell such pretty lies. And the Geysers and the Dogfish will celebrate together too, and no one will fight."

"Quiet now. Sleep is the best cure."

Endri's smile shrank but did not entirely disappear. When he spoke again, he seemed to be a long distance away. "Don't worry about me, my friend. I will have plenty of time to sleep soon."

Porto pulled the youth's cloak up beneath his chin to keep out the chill. Now that they were on the far side of the pass, there was nothing to block the icy wind that knifed down from the heights. Finished, he turned away from Endri and pretended to stoke the fire, because it was becoming obvious that the freezing drops that stung Porto's cheeks were nothing to do with the fluttering snow.

Part
Three

The Nakkiga Gate

It was hard to see anything except the great cone of Nakkiga; it dominated the center of the uneven plateau like a brooding, robed figure.

To Viyeki, their sacred peak had always meant many things—a refuge, a parent, a stern and disappointed teacher. Now, as it grew larger before them, hour by hour, he felt his sense of shame grow as well, knowing that he and the other children of the Garden were returning to the mountain in such disarray, not as saviors and barely as survivors; drowning men washed up on a beach only after they had given up hope.

General Suno'ku led the procession, riding ahead of the catafalque bearing the makeshift wooden coffin of her foreparent, Ekisuno the Great, hero of a dozen battles but now only one more corpse, another victim of the mortals' hatred. Viyeki could not help thinking of The Heart of What Was Lost, the ancient jewel that hung around his master Yaarike's neck, hidden inside the magister's garments.

Is that all our people have to show in the end? Viyeki wondered. *More losses? Is this tattered army we bring back, a few hundred out of all the thousands who went south, just another display of our ultimate fate, as pointless as a gem commemorating the vanished Garden? Is all we have—all we are—only a memorial of what we failed to save?*

Viyeki could see nothing else ahead for his people, even if they survived this terrible failure. *We retreat. We hide. We diminish. Eventually we will disappear except in old stories. And they will not be our stories.* Alone among her peers, only General Suno'ku seemed to believe differently. Only Suno'ku had given him anything like hope. But now they were home again, and the only real truths were failure, regret, and loss.

He looked to his master, wondering if Yaarike was thinking similar thoughts, but as usual the magister's face was as enigmatic as a stone weathered smooth by centuries of wind and rain. Viyeki could only wonder how he could hope, one day, to replace a leader of such depth and subtlety.

I am not enough, my great queen, he thought. *You need heroes not mere Builders. I am not enough.*

The small procession wound through the ruins of the abandoned city of Nakkiga-That-Was, picking its way across the pocked and uneven surfaces of a road that had once been the Royal Way. Only a few stones remained from a thoroughfare so wide that a dozen riders could make their way along it side by side without touching. The rest of the paving had been plundered long ago for the city inside the mountain when the Hikeda'ya had turned inward, withdrawing from the hostile world the mortals had created.

But the old city still remained in the tumbled ruins and rings of stones that showed where the great buildings had once stood. The high Gyrfalcon Castles that had once clung to the side of the mountain itself were gone, but their telltales remained, at least to Viyeki's practiced eye. The Sky Palace was only a field of rubble and dead frozen grass, but once, its open dome had framed the night sky in glory for the observers below. Here the Moon Festival Canal and its tributaries had wound through the city like rivers of quicksilver. Delicate boats had carried soldiers, courtiers, spies, and lovers to their various destinies.

For a moment it seemed as though Viyeki could see these pathetic remnants and also the glorious city that had rivaled Asu'a itself—both the arches of the solemn Queen's Gallery as it once stood and the long-collapsed pillars of today; the graceful curves of the Bridge of Exodus and the trample of icy mud that marked all that was left. Where the delicate, high houses of lords and ladies had stood, poems in stone and sky, only a few protruding rocks still remained, broken teeth in a skeletal jaw, the mansions' owners long gone into the Elder Halls in the Silent Palace beneath Nakkiga. The only thing that remained of all that glory was the mountain itself, and the tall gates that offered darkness and safety to those they welcomed.

We come out into the sun only to fight now, Viyeki suddenly realized. It was an idea that, once it entered his mind, would not go away. *We call darkness our friend, but when the elders tell us stories of the Garden, they talk of the holy, unending light that was there. How did shadows become our only dwelling?*

As they crossed the rocky, frozen mire at the mountain's foot that had once been the Field of Banners, the great marshaling ground of the Sacrifice order, Viyeki saw that Nakkiga's tall gates stood open. For an instant, all his thoughts fled away in fear that they had come home too late—that the mortals had somehow beat them here, that nothing would be left to greet them but blood and death. Then he saw the thin line of armored Sacrifices drawn up on either side of the massive witchwood doors and his heart slowed. The mortals had not yet come. The people of Nakkiga were waiting to welcome them home.

As they rode up the slope between the waiting Sacrifices, Viyeki could not help noticing that most of these warriors were too young or too old for proper service. Mortals might not be able to tell the difference between one Hikeda'ya and another, but Viyeki saw the tight-stretched skin of the old and weary and the over-straight backs and gleaming eyes of the young, who did not understand yet how many defeated armies had returned through these gates over the years, each time in smaller and smaller numbers.

As General Suno'ku steered her mount between the honor guard, a crowd of Singers stepped out of the great gate, led by a rider on a great black horse. The rider raised his palm in salute, and even from a distance Viyeki could see that his face was covered with a mask of translucent dried flesh.

Viyeki felt his heart grow cold. It was Akhenabi, the Lord of Song. He had returned from the south before them. Viyeki knew he should have been overjoyed that such a powerful figure still lived, but instead he remembered the possession of Tzayin-Kha at Three Ravens Tower and felt instead a choking fear. General Suno'ku had ignored Akhenabi's orders and then killed the Lord of Song's minion, Tzayin-Kha. What would come from that—and would it come only to Suno'ku, or were the rest of them tainted by her disobedience, too? Viyeki had heard enough stories of the Cold, Slow Halls to know that he would rather face the executioner's cord and rod a hundred times than be handed over to the pain-masters of Akhenabi's order.

Although his voice was as harsh and commanding as ever, the Lord of Song offered only pleasantries: "You return to us, General Suno'ku. I see you bring back the remains of your glorious ancestor Marshal Ekisuno as well. He will lie in state in Black Water Field before he goes to the Silent Palace, so that the people may thank him for his sacrifice."

But to Viyeki's astonishment, Suno'ku said, "No. You are kind, High Magister Akhenabi, but my foreparent's body will lie in the dooryard of the Iyora clan-house instead, as is our custom."

Akhenabi was surprised by this refusal, as evidenced by a moment of stillness before he spoke again. "Ah, but such things should not be discussed here, as if you were strangers on the doorstep. I come on the queen's behalf to welcome you home. There is much to discuss."

"Is the queen awake?" asked Suno'ku. "After her valiant efforts were undone by the mortals, I thought she would still be deep in the *keta-yi'indra.*"

"Yes, of course," said Akhenabi with just the faintest trace of stiffness; nobody any farther from the conversation than Viyeki and the other surviving nobles would have recognized it. "The mother of us all still sleeps the *yi'indra*, regaining her strength. I speak on her behalf, only. We have suffered a great catastrophe and Nakkiga was in disarray. Someone had to take the reins of governance." He stopped abruptly, aware that he had been connived into defending himself. Viyeki thought that even where he stood, several paces away, he could feel the Lord of Song's cold rage.

"And, as always, Nakkiga is grateful to you, Magister Akhenabi." Suno'ku turned to the Sacrifice soldiers still waiting in their silent lines. "And to you, true Sacrifices all. We have fought the more bravely because we knew you were here, protecting those we hold dearest." She turned back to Akhenabi and his crimson-robed flock of Singers. "Let us enter now, my lord. We fly just before the storm, and there is little time to waste."

Akhenabi waved his hand and the Singers cleared the doorway; but as Suno'ku rode through, the Lord of Song tugged on the black horse's reins and turned so that he rode beside her. Viyeki felt a moment of helpless envy: Like the Lord of Song and the general, High Magister Yaarike was entering Nakkiga mounted on a fine horse, the property of a Sacrifice who had died at Three Ravens Tower. He and Yaarike had been almost equals while they were on the run in mortal lands, but Viyeki was still on foot, and it would be a long, weary walk to the center of the city for him and the rest of the returning Hikeda'ya.

Did I put too much stock in the favor Yaarike showed me while we were in danger together? He did say I would be his successor. He said it so clearly I could not be mistaken.

As they moved into Nakkiga, Viyeki discovered to his surprise that the city's broad Glinting Passage was lined with hundreds of their people, mostly ordinary Hikeda'ya from the lowest castes. Like the guard of Sacrifices, they seemed mostly very young or very old. All were ragged and hunger-thin, but when they saw Suno'ku they cheered as though she were the queen herself. Nor was it only the lower castes that had come to see the spectacle of their return: other Nakkigai were watching the procession from the balconies of noble dwellings far above them, and many of these were also cheering Suno'ku and her Sacrifices.

Viyeki hurried forward until he caught up to Yaarike, who rode last in the line of returning nobles. "Lord Akhenabi looks unhappy, Master," he said quietly. "*He* has never been celebrated this way."

"Nor does he wish to be." Yaarike sounded out of sorts. "The Lord of Song works best in darkness and quiet. It is not the trappings of power he desires, but power itself."

"But he cannot be happy with how the people cheer for Suno'ku."

"Neither am I." Yaarike made a gesture to forestall his underling's question. "Remember what I tell you now, Host Foreman Viyeki—the enemy of your enemy is not always your friend." He said no more, but spurred his horse ahead. Viyeki was left to wonder at his master's words.

At last they reached Black Water Field, the vast common square at the foot of the cascading Tearfall, where the great stairs led from the main part of the city up to the dwellings of the nobility on the second tier and beyond that to the houses of the dead and the queen's palace on the third tier. The crowds had followed them but the cheering quieted as they moved deeper into the city, where the gaunt faces of the citizens watched as though waiting for some revelation. Suno'ku directed the bearers to carry General Ekisuno's body up onto the great stone platform, a monument commonly known as Drukhi's Altar in honor of the queen's dead son, although in truth it had been built as a memorial to all the martyrs of Nakkiga's wars.

When the catafalque was set down, Suno'ku stood over the simple coffin for a moment, as if in silent conversation with her foreparent, then turned and walked to the front of the platform to face the gathered throng, her silver owl helmet under her arm, her pale hair shining in the torchlight. When she stopped at the edge of the platform it was impossible to miss that she had placed herself between Lord Akhenabi and the people gathered below.

"Hikeda'yei!" she said, her voice loud and clear and tuneful as a battle-trumpet. "Go to your orders now, all you of noble castes—there is much to do to prepare for this coming siege. The rest of you, fear not! You will have work to do as well in the days to come, and your share of the glory will be no less. We will triumph *together*, first against the army that comes to destroy us, later against a mortal world that no longer fears us. Because we will change that. We will *triumph*. For the Garden!"

The general did not wait for the cheers to die down this time but signaled for the bearers to lift her foreparent's catafalque and follow her back down into the square. Viyeki, like many of the other nobles, could only watch in amazement as she and her guards made their way through the throng, so close to the people that many on either side reached out, trying to touch her as she passed. Some even threw flowers, and not just onto Ekisuno's coffin but onto Suno'ku herself, pale blooms of snowsun and everwhite stolen from the offering-vases of long-dead heroes. Others called out her name and begged her to save them. Viyeki had never seen the lower castes so moved by anyone but the queen herself.

The general and her closest followers moved like a wave through the gathered Hikeda'ya until they left the common square and mounted the stair to the second tier, to the great clan compounds and the order houses where the common people could not follow her. A trail of flowers lay on the steps behind them.

After Suno'ku had gone the people finally began to disperse, but they left slowly, reluctantly, as if someone had awakened them from a happy dream they did not want to relinquish.

Despite the great age and degraded condition of the Norn road, the journey from Three Ravens Tower into the Norn lands was the least of Porto's problems. Endri, weak and feverish, could no longer ride behind him, so Porto set him on the front of the saddle as though he were a child and rode with one arm holding the wounded man upright.

The snow continued to flurry, and what was left of the old road quickly became a roil of icy mud as Duke Isgrimnur's army wound its way between the lesser peaks of the Nornfells, headed always toward the ominous, upright bulk of the great mountain that mortals called Stormspike. Nobody was singing now, and the soldiers kept even their speaking voices low, awed to be trespassing in a land that had for so long been the stuff of tales to frighten unruly children. The cloudy, slate-gray sky hung low, like the ceiling of a humble crofter's hut. Porto, like many others, felt as though he was being watched from above, as though tall Stormspike itself had eyes.

Can they see us yet? he wondered. *With their magic tricks? What are they thinking?*

"Is that you, Porto?" Endri asked, each word an effort.

"I'm here, lad."

"I want to go home now, I'm cold."

"I know. We all want to go home." He could feel the younger man shivering, although the day was warmer than most had been since they crossed the Rimmersgard frontier. "We have one more thing to see to, that's all. Then I'll help you get back to Ansis Pelippé—back to Harborside."

"Is it still summer?"

Porto was heartened. Endri hadn't talked this much in days. He hoped it meant that the blackened place in his back was actually beginning to heal, but every time the wind changed direction he could smell the corruption of the young man's wound. "Yes. Still summer."

Endri was silent for a while. "They'll be having the race, the harbor race," he said at last. "My uncle . . . won it once. He had the biggest arms I've ever seen. Like a wrestler. He drowned."

"How could he win the race if he drowned?" Porto leaned forward, hoping to see a smile, but the gape-mouthed emptiness of Endri's face was like that of a dead man. *And God save me, I've seen too many dead men,* Porto thought. *I want to see people I know again. I want to see my Sida, alive and smiling and far, far away from this cursed, freezing place. Thank the Holy Ransomer for Count Streáwe, who kept Perdruin out of the worst of this dreadful war.*

"Uncle didn't . . . drown then. That was another time." Endri sighed, but it turned into a cough that Porto could feel rattling the frail chest through both their armor. "It was all another time," he said when he had his breath back, so softly that Porto had to lean forward again to hear him.

Endri did not say any more and soon his head sagged in sleep as the horse continued to pick its way over the bumpy track that had once been a road as large and as magnificent as the Avenue of Triumph leading to the Sancellan Mahistrevis palace in Nabban. Porto did not know enough about the Norns to guess how long the road had lain like this, all but unused, nor had he heard of a time when the white-skinned northern fairies did anything but lurk in their snowy wastes and plot vengeance against mankind. For a moment the depth of what he did not know, the incomprehensible vastness of history, almost made him dizzy. He looked to the other riders nearby, some Rimmersmen, some southerners like himself, and wondered if the rest thought like he did. By their faces, whatever thoughts they had were just as grim.

Isgrimnur had already grown weary of staring at the mountain, but it had become hard to look at anything else. The great dark cone of Stormspike seemed to swell and spread as they approached until it covered most of the horizon and threatened to pierce the low sky with its sharp peak. Wispy clouds of steam drifted up from crevices in the mountain's flank, then twined upward until the winds of the upper heights snatched them away, leaving only a few faint wisps to wreathe Stormspike's head.

Despite the white wisps at its brow, the mountain was not enfeebled; it towered over the smaller peaks nearby like a great thane among his

kneeling housecarls. The stripes of snow trailing down from the mountain's white cap only made its black stone immensity loom larger, as
though Nature had sought to restrain it and failed. Yet Isgrimnur and a
few thousand mortals planned to bring it under their sway.

"We are fools," said Sludig from just behind him.

Isgrimnur turned and looked at him. "Fools? Why?"

"Why? By the good God, my lord, look at that. That is no tower or
crumbling wall. That is the Lord's own work, set down in the first days of
Creation and still burning with His fires. How can we think to conquer it?"

Isgrimnur was disquieted by how closely Sludig's doubts echoed his
own, but he only said, "If we do God's work, we need not fear God's
creations, however mighty. Besides, we do not seek to conquer the mountain, old friend, just the creatures hiding within it. All that holds us back
is a gate, made by the work of hands, not God."

"Fairy hands," said Sludig glumly. "Fairy magic."

Isgrimnur spotted the Sitha-woman on her white horse just a short
distance behind them, her soft gray garments fluttering in the wind. Unlike the rest of the riders, huddled deep in their saddles with hoods pulled
close against the flying snow, she seemed utterly unconcerned about such
trivialities as wind and weather. "Ho, Lady Ayaminu!" he called. "Will
you talk with me?"

She made no discernible movement but her horse sped its pace until
she was riding between Isgrimnur and Sludig. "I am here," she said.

"What of the gate?" He did not trust her forbearance toward the
Norns, but she had not yet told him anything false and was the best resource they had until they could send out scouts. "Is it as strong as stories
tell? Are there spells or some other Norn trickery protecting it?"

She gave him a look that had a small edge of amusement. "You do not
really understand the ways of our people, Duke Isgrimnur. The two great
doors of the gate were forged of bronze and witchwood long ago. What
you call 'spells,' the tools used in making them, are a *part* of them, not
something that has been put on like a coat of whitewash on a mud hut."

"Are you saying that we cannot knock them down, even if we rebuild
the great Bear? Our weapons are iron—we can smash through any bronze.
But this witchwood . . ." He shook his head. "That is something I do not
understand, a magical wood as strong as forged metal."

Ayaminu made a swift gesture with one hand, as though catching a bird in mid-flight and then letting it go. "Anything can be knocked down. And even witchwood can be broken. Surely you have shattered a few Hikeda'ya swords in battle, so you know that it can be destroyed. But the older it is—the closer it is to its roots in the Garden and the purer its preparation—the more difficult it is to destroy. The gates are old. They have stood for thousands of years. Can you defeat them with a single iron ram? Only the Dance will tell."

"The dance?" Isgrimnur saw that Sludig was glaring. His liegeman did not like talk of spells and magic even in the context of preparing for a fight.

"The Dance of Time," the Sitha said, weaving her fingers in a swift pattern the duke could not follow. "The Dance of What Will Be. It is going on all around us and inside us. It seems to follow a set course of steps, but in truth there is no fixed pattern."

Isgrimnur scowled. "In other words, you don't know if we can knock the gate down."

"Of course not." This time she actually smiled. "But the tide seems to be with you. If there is ever a time when the gates might fall, that time is now. But many things still remain to be seen, and many steps must still be danced." Before Isgrimnur could protest the uselessness of her answers, Ayaminu pointed to a tall ring of standing rocks at the nearest edge of the ruined outer city. "There," she said. "Do you see that vast jumble of unroofed stone? That was once the great Sky Palace, the observatory where the Queen's Celebrants watched the stars."

"What happened to it? And why do you point it out?"

"What happened was that it was abandoned when men became too many and too fierce, as was all the rest of Nakkiga-That-Was, the city outside the mountain we are approaching. The reason I show it to you is because it would make a good place for camp. You do not wish to get too close to the mountain before you are ready, I think."

"Of course not. We will need to send out our scouts."

"Then I think the Sky Palace will make a good camp. There are still some cells that have roofs, where men and horses can sleep out of the cold, and it is far from Stormspike itself and spying eyes."

"This tumbledown Sky Palace of yours looks more like a trap than a refuge," Isgrimnur said, "or at least like a spot where I would plan an ambush if I were the White Foxes."

"I do not think you need fear an ambush. The Hikeda'ya are down to only a few fighters. They have not tried to stop you since you crossed into their lands because the mountain itself is their greatest defense. Their mistress Queen Utuk'ku is deep in what is called 'the dangerous sleep'—the Hikeda'ya have never been so weak as at this moment. As to camping in the Sky Palace, Isgrimnur, though you may not understand me, I promise you the ancient observatory has a . . . spirit of its own. That is the best I can explain it, and that spirit is not at all warlike, which is why it became a spot to contemplate the mysteries of the Sky Dance. I think your army will be safe there. The true danger is farther ahead, at the foot of the mountain itself. At the gates."

Isgrimnur looked from Ayaminu to Sludig, then at the array of titan stones before them, a few still suggesting the vague shapes of walls and arches and other structures, but far more of them toppled. The summer days were cold in these northern reaches but very long, and the men had been riding and marching for at least an hour or two longer than they normally would have.

"Well, then, I will take your advice," the duke said at last. "Sludig, ride to Jarl Vigri and tell him we will make camp in the Sky Palace there, as the lady names it."

Sludig, chewing on unspoken words, gave him a look that Isgrimnur thought bordered on insubordination; Sludig did not like magic, and he had good reason to fear it. Isgrimnur thought he might say something, but instead he only nodded and rode off to find Vigri.

Isgrimnur turned back to the great shadow of Stormspike, a spearhead jutting from the rocky ground and aimed at Heaven, a mute threat that could not be ignored however much he might have wished to turn back toward the lands he understood.

This is a lonely place, he thought. *This is a cold, lonely place we've come to.*

"Husband, come back to bed," said Khimabu. "The bell has not yet sounded."

It was true, the great stone bell in the Temple of the Martyrs had not rung the first hour of morning, but Viyeki had been awake for some time, sleepless and full of buzzing thoughts. "I must go, my wife. There is a meeting of the War Council."

She threw a slender arm across her eyes as he lit a taper. "You are not a member of the War Council, husband. Why must you go? Will you leave me to stand outside the council hall with the commoners and slaves, waiting for news? Yaarike will name you as his successor, will he not?"

"That is not for me to say. All I know is that he wants me there."

Khimabu sat up, the cover falling away. For a moment, as always, Viyeki was stunned by his wife's beauty, her graceful limbs and perfect, narrow face. His mouth dried as he looked at her. How much more astounding that she, a member of venerable Clan Daesa, should have let herself be joined to him. "You have been gone for months. Surely you will not desert me so soon?" She swung her long legs out of the bed and stood up, as unconcerned with her nakedness as a forest creature.

Looking at her—staring at her—as she began to dress, Viyeki was seized by contrasting moods. He was astonished to realize that this flawless scion of one of the oldest Nakkiga clans was his, but that was quickly followed, as it usually was, with the nagging question of why her parents and clansfolk had chosen him as the recipient of this great gift. Certainly few others except High Magister Yaarike had seen much potential in him, and Viyeki had labored long in thankless, middling obscurity for the Order of Builders before being lifted up.

"My wife," he said, and hesitated. She turned and saw him looking at her.

"Ah," she said. "Is there something else on your mind beyond the honor the old man is giving you? Would you perhaps like to see if this is the day we create an heir?" Her morning gown was not yet fastened, and she let it fall open to reveal her body of shadowed ivory. "I would not be unwilling . . ."

"My wife, we cannot celebrate, and we cannot make an heir—not this morning." He was surprised at how little he wanted her at this moment, when he should have been feeling triumphant and powerful. "This is the War Council. We are besieged. I cannot let my own selfish concerns keep me from attending Magister Yaarike. Leaders of all the orders will be there. How could I be the last to enter the Council Hall?"

In an instant the cold look that he so dreaded swept over her like a sudden storm around the mountain's peak. "No, how could you? And do you think you alone have tasks to do, husband? It is war, after all, as you said." She stared at him now as though he were not her mate but only a lowly servant. "I have my own work maintaining this household that you have so seldom visited lately, but I have also to feed and find places for all our workers and slaves whose homes near the gates have been sealed off at your own magister's orders."

"So that it can be better defended," he said with a calmness he did not feel. His wife's sudden angers always left him surprised and unprepared. "What else can be done? We are at war and that is where the enemy will attack."

"Of course, husband. But apparently your beloved master will not even allow you and your household the simple pleasure of celebrating your return and your long-deserved advancement."

"Khimabu, this is not the way . . ."

"I understand." She turned from him with a definite air of dismissal. "Your wife can wait. Making an heir can wait. Do you even *desire* an heir, Viyeki sey-Enduya, or have the mortals at our doorstep changed your mind about that, too?"

"Don't be foolish," he said, but seeing her expression he softened his tone. "You know that I do. If the Garden desires it and fate permits it, yes, my wife, of course I wish to make an heir with you." But after many Great Years without one, he wondered whether they would ever succeed, war or no.

"Then go to your council," she said as if that were something of little import, an amusement. "I will do my own work and think of how best to announce your rise to my kin and your underlings."

"No word of that can be spoken yet, Khimabu! Until my master informs the Celebrants, he still might change his mind."

"Is old Yaarike a fool?"

Even in the privacy of their bedchamber, such talk worried him. "No, of course he is not a fool."

"Then he will not change his mind. He will give my husband what my husband so richly deserves. And if my husband remembers what is important, so will I." She had banished the fury from her face, and now moved toward him, stopping just short. She took his hand and placed it on her breast through the thin fabric of the morning gown. He could feel her heart beating slowly and steadily. "So will I."

Outside the Council Hall, the Martyrs' Temple bell tolled again to mark the middle hour of morning, a deep, flat sound that always made Viyeki think of a heavy door falling shut. It was time for the council to begin.

He was surprised at how sparsely attended it was, how empty the huge, columned hall. Looking across the archaic witchwood table and its centerpiece, an arrangement of stones and living plants meant to symbolize the Garden that had birthed their race, Viyeki could not help wondering why so many of the other orders were not present—not Luk'kaya, High Gatherer of the Order of Harvesters, nor any representatives of other powerful orders like the Echoes.

Zuniyabe, chief of the Celebrants, was of course at the table with several lesser nobles of his order, but it could not have been a Queen's War Council without him, since he was the ultimate authority on tradition and the governing principles of the people.

Lord Akhenabi was absent, but his chief lieutenant Jikkyo, whose blind, white eyes belied his knowledge of all that concerned the Singers' order, had come in his master's place with underlings of his own, explaining that the Lord of Song was busy tending the slumbers of Queen Utuk'ku.

The Order of Sacrifice was doubly represented, both by General Suno'ku and the order's leader, Muyare, who had replaced dead Ekisuno as high marshal. Broad, stern-faced Muyare was Suno'ku's distant cousin, her senior, and—despite her fame and growing popularity among the lesser castes of Nakkiga—her commander.

When High Celebrant Zuniyabe indicated that they could start, Viyeki's master Yaarike extended his fingers in a gesture of polite inquiry. "What of the Harvesters, the Summoners, and the Echoes?" he asked. "I do not see any of them. Have they nothing to say to this council?"

"We thought it best to keep this small, so that we might talk as openly as possible." Suno'ku spoke before Zuniyabe or her superior had even opened their mouths. Viyeki thought Marshal Muyare looked a little regretful when he finally spoke.

"General Suno'ku is correct," he said. "We need only the orders who are already present to discuss the things that must occupy us today. And of course, that which concerns us most are the mortals who even now gather outside our door."

"And thus we strike the most important vein," said Zuniyabe. "Magister Yaarike, what news do you have on your order's preparations?"

Yaarike took a moment to consider the string of tally-beads before him. "Forgive me. In my age, I do not remember every detail as I should. That is why I have brought Host Foreman Viyeki. You all know him, I think."

The others nodded. The Singer Jikkyo turned a bland smile in Viyeki's direction. "We have not met, but I have heard his name. You are welcome to our deliberations, Host Foreman." Viyeki made a ritual gesture of gratitude, but he felt as though he had been greeted by a serpent who had not yet warmed enough to bite, but might soon feel up to it.

Formalities finished, Magister Yaarike went on to detail the various works in which the Order of Builders was occupied—shoring up defenses around and above the gate, clearing old tunnels which had fallen out of use but might be important in the days to come, and a dozen other such unsurprising tasks. Viyeki prompted him once or twice, but he doubted that his master had truly forgotten anything: it was Yaarike's way to seem more distracted and forgetful than he truly was, at least in public meetings.

"And our brave Sacrifices?" Zuniyabe asked when Yaarike had finished. "How do your preparations go, Marshal?"

Muyare made a sign of acceptance, acknowledging the question. High Celebrant Zuniyabe held no more power than the leader of any other order, and certainly was not as feared as Akhenabi, but as keepers of tradition the Celebrants gave shape to gatherings like these.

"As well as can be expected." Muyare glanced briefly at the scroll he had unrolled on the tabletop. "We suffered terrible losses in the south, as all know. Barely half a thousand trained Sacrifices remain here in Nakkiga, and even if others are still trying to return, they will not be able to pass the ring of mortals and their siege. We are desperately outnumbered."

The moment of silence that followed this did not last long. "Our danger is great, but we cannot only dwell on this present struggle," said General Suno'ku. "We need to think also of the future." Even though she did not speak loudly, the strong, clear tones of her voice drew their attention away from the marshal as if he had suddenly disappeared.

"And what does that mean, General?" asked Jikkyo. The blind Singer's hands were folded before him, his face toward the table as though in deep meditation, but it was impossible to ignore the sharpness in his voice. "If we do not succeed in the present, there *is* no future—or am I being unduly pessimistic?"

"I wish you were, Lord Jikkyo," said Suno'ku. "But the problems of tomorrow must not be ignored even in the midst of today's terrors."

"Enlighten us, then, please," said Yaarike, and anyone who did not know the man would have thought him brusque, but Viyeki recognized a hidden edge of mischief in his master's words. Surrounded by such venerable and powerful nobles, there were currents too deep for Viyeki to understand; he could not help admiring the way Suno'ku waded without hesitation into the dangerous waters.

"Yes, I will speak," she said, "but first my master Muyare would finish telling you of the preparations the Order of Sacrifice has made." She turned to him. "High Marshal?"

Suno'ku, despite her youth and rank, was all but giving orders to her superior, her own clansman. But instead of the cold indignation Viyeki expected, the marshal only nodded and then calmly outlined the various efforts his order was making to spread their thin troops over as many potential danger spots as possible. He answered the questions from the other councillors with a sort of numb honesty, as if he could not be bothered at this late date to pretend that their position was anything but hopeless.

"And the gate itself, Lord Jikkyo, Lord Yaarike?" Muyare asked when he had finished his recitation. "How long can it hold?"

Jikkyo unfolded his fingers and made a complicated sign that Viyeki did not understand, part of the Singers' own private language, never shared with other orders. "The gate, as well as many of our other most important measures of defense, has always been guarded by the queen's will. As she grew stronger, she was determined to keep her people safe. Health and long life to the Mother of All!"

The rest dutifully repeated it.

"But that is our greatest problem," Jikkyo continued in his soft voice. He seemed so much the gentle old man that it was hard to reconcile his appearance and manner with the dark tales Viyeki had heard about him, of disturbing exhibitions behind the closed doors of his ancient mansion and the terrifying fates of several of his rivals. But Viyeki did not doubt those rumors: only a creature of unbreakable will and great power could ever rise so high in the Order of Song.

"As you know," said Jikkyo, "after the disaster at Asu'a, the queen sleeps so deeply that it may be a long time until she awakens. We at this table are not children or slaves to be fed reassuring tales, so let us not chop our words too fine—our defeat in the south was terrible, and the queen suffered greatly from it. My master Akhenabi says that she will return to us, but even he in his awesome wisdom cannot say when, and we all doubt it will be soon. So the gate is weak. Yes, it is still a thing of stout witch-wood wound with the powerful songs of its making, but without the will of the waking queen behind it, it is but a *thing*. A mighty thing, but a thing nonetheless, and things can be broken."

Finished, he folded his fingers again and turned his sightless eyes toward the ceiling, as if in contemplation of something above and beyond the mountain itself.

"I can only echo what Lord Jikkyo has told us," Yaarike said. "My Builders will give their all to strengthen the mountain's defenses, including the gates, but our resources and time are limited."

A melancholy silence fell over the Council Hall.

"And the thing *you* wished to discuss, General Suno'ku?" asked Zuniyabe. "It seems it is now time to hear your idea. May the Garden grant it brings us some hope."

"I cannot speak to hope, which is an elusive and often false friend," she said. "What I suggest is simply this. If the gate is breached, then every dweller in our city must be armed, high caste or low, because there are not enough Sacrifices left to defend Nakkiga should the mortals enter."

Several voices spoke at once, but the High Celebrant gestured for silence. "Arm our slaves?" Zuniyabe asked, his legendary calm clearly taxed to its limit. "Are you truly suggesting we arm the lower castes and the slaves, General? To what point? If the Sacrifices fall and the high houses and orders are undefended, then even if the mortals were driven out again what would be left? A disorderly, armed rabble finally able to give vent to their mindless rage?"

"Better the chance of reestablishing order, I would think," said Suno'ku, "than the mortals left to murder, rape, and enslave as they wish."

All the nobles present had questions, although some of the remarks were closer to denunciations, and the argument quickly grew heated. It soon became clear that Marshal Muyare was not entirely in favor of such a scheme himself but seemed resigned to his younger relative having her way. "If we arm them, then they will be fighting the mortals alongside the Order of Sacrifice," Muyare said. "They will be commanded by trained warriors of our order. It will be up to us to maintain discipline. And as General Suno'ku says, we do not have the numbers otherwise to resist an invasion if the gates fail."

Zuniyabe spread his hands in a gesture of frustration. "I do not understand this. Like Lord Jikkyo, I see only evil coming from such a wild, unprecedented action."

"These are wild, unprecedented times," Suno'ku responded. "And before you finish expressing your disgust with my plan, there is more—as I said, we must think not just for today but for the future."

Yaarike, silent through most of the argument, now smiled. "It seems it is our day to entertain interesting ideas, General. Please do not stop now."

She looked at him hard for a moment, as though trying to decide where the Magister of Builders stood in the pantheon of allies and enemies gathered around the great witchwood table. "Very well. I suggest something that was mooted in the past, in the season when our queen sent the great nobles Sutekhi and Ommu and the others to the aid of Ineluki, the king in Asu'a, several Great Years ago. We must breed with the mortals."

Her words fell into utter silence. Even Muyare looked ashamed, though he did not gainsay her, and Viyeki could not help wondering what strange negotiations between the marshal and his younger relative had preceded the council.

"I cannot believe that I heard you correctly, General," said Zuniyabe. "Mortals? Breed with mortals? What blasphemy . . . ?"

"Please, High Celebrant, do not confuse exigency with blasphemy." Suno'ku had clearly come to the part of the gathering she had been anticipating since the start, and Viyeki watched as she began to assert control both over herself and the gathering by sheer force of will. Again, he was astonished that such a prodigy should have appeared at such a time, as if war and chaos were indeed the foundry of change. "As I said, this was spoken of before, in the days of High Celebrant Hikhi, good Zuniyabe's predecessor."

"And roundly rejected!" said Zuniyabe. "The queen herself said it would not be—could not be."

"Of course our queen is always correct," said Suno'ku. "But I think that if she were awake now, she would see that what was bad then has become worse. Think, fellow nobles, think! Our numbers were already dwindling. Long ago we began using mortal slaves to oversee other mortal slaves, and low-caste Hikeda'ya to keep peace among their fellows, because we nobles were too few and our children born too infrequently. But the mortals, both inside and outside our mountain, breed swiftly. If we do not change we will perish, if not by mortals storming our gates then by rebellion here in Nakkiga. All of us—your spouses and children and clansfolk, too—will die in our beds, or be paraded like the scorned losers of the mortals' wars before being torn to pieces by a baying mob." She leaned forward, and her voice became lower, less demanding. "Think on what I say. Only five hundred blooded, death-sung Sacrifices remain! And after the siege, even if we survive it, how many will still live then? Half that number? Fewer? My lords, we feed more than ten thousand peasants and mortal slaves here in Nakkiga. We of the ruling orders are already so few that, after two costly, failed wars, if our underlings did not fear the mortals beyond our mountain more than their own rulers, we nobles would all be in terrible danger."

Again, silence fell, although Viyeki thought it felt like the agitated air just before a storm. But before Zuniyabe could walk out of the council, or someone else say something that would turn the talk from argument into deadly insult, Yaarike let out a strange sound—a whistle, a snatch of melody that Viyeki recognized as an old song from Tumet'ai called "The Musician and the Soldier." The others in the room turned to him, as surprised as Viyeki.

Instead of explaining, Yaarike continued the tune until he had finished the refrain, then said, "I am curious, General Suno'ku, how such matings would be regulated. Would all the noble houses descend to the streets and rut with the lower creatures, or would there be fairs or games of honor so that we could choose the least disgusting?"

Suno'ku did a poor job of hiding her irritation. "Please, High Magister, give me some credit for sense. You know as well as I that many of our high nobility, male and female, already take mortals for lovers, and that sometimes children are born of these unions, however distasteful you find that fact."

Yaarike smiled again. "I find nothing distasteful but death, General, and even that has begun to look more friendly in recent days. But the children of slaves have always been slaves. You would change that?"

Suno'ku shook her head. "Unusual and unprecedented as it may seem, I suggest that noble parents must adopt those children, despite their mongrel blood. They will grow more swiftly than our own children—much more swiftly, as we know from watching the mortals increase through all the lands we once ruled. If these halfblood children are raised by the noble caste and schooled in the orders, who is to say that they will not be just as loyal subjects of the queen as any others?"

"You claimed that *I* confused blasphemy with exigency," said High Celebrant Zuniyabe, sounding more astonished now than angry. "But I think it is you who are confused, General. How can halfbloods feel what true Hikeda'ya feel?"

She shrugged, a very broad gesture for one of her caste and rank. "Test them. Like all entrants into the orders, they will enter into Yedade's Box. Nothing says we must take them all. In fact, the harder they must work to achieve what the true-born receive as their due, I think the more they will value it. And we will birth thousands of Sacrifices for the Queen."

"Tell me what you think of this madness, Jikkyo?" Zuniyabe demanded. "I am astonished beyond reply. What will Lord Akhenabi make of it?"

Jikkyo took a long time to speak. "I do not know. My master is subtle, and there may be branches and twigs to this plan that I cannot see, although I am much of your mind, Zuniyabe. I could not make such a decision on my own. I will let you know his thought."

Across the table, Suno'ku made a gesture of "patience agreed." It was as clear to Viyeki as it was to the rest that even if the Order of Sacrifice and all the others present supported it, no such policy was possible without the agreement of the Lord of Song.

"One last question," said Yaarike. "Marshal Muyare, even if we all agree to consider such an unprecedented and perilous change of policy, many questions remain. What would we do with so many new Hikeda'ya? If we breed halfbloods anywhere near as fast as mortals breed more mortals, surely the time will come when our sacred mountain is too small to shelter us all."

Muyare spread his hands; he still seemed reluctant to argue on his relative's behalf. "Perhaps. But it would be good to have our order at strength again."

"Esteemed Magister Yaarike, you forget something," said Suno'ku. "With the ranks of Sacrifices replenished and our other orders strengthened, we could again turn our hearts to what we all desire—taking back the lands the mortals have stolen from us. Then we would have as much room as we need."

"Another war?" asked Yaarike, but mildly.

"Our enemies' final destruction," said Suno'ku, and for a moment Viyeki saw the hard stone of which she was made, the unbending determination of her blood and upbringing. "We cannot share this land with them—surely we all agree on that. Eventually, one of our races must perish. On my oath as a Queen's Sacrifice, I will make sure it is the mortals."

Porto's father, dead these nine years, had been a carpenter. Porto spent much of his childhood in the Rocks, scrambling up and down ladders, fetching tools, and holding boards in place, so he volunteered to shore up the ranks of army carpenters in cutting and preparing a new pole to hold up the head of the great Bear.

The ram's iron head was immense, but Isgrimnur's men had found an ancient grove of trees at one end of the abandoned city before the mountain, and some of the older trunks there were almost unbelievably large. The leader of the duke's carpenters, a quiet but short-tempered man named Brenyar, chose a peppered birch over sixty cubits tall, a fit size to use for the battering ram's shaft. The wood was very hard, but Porto and a dozen others ax-wielders brought it down in less than a day and began to trim away the largest branches while other workers chopped down smaller trees to make rollers, which would let the great ram smash against the gates at greater speed.

Porto liked the work, but he had asked to join the carpenters in large part because he so badly needed to get away from Endri, at least for a short time. Since arriving at the mountain he had spent much of every day taking care of the younger man, cleaning his wound, giving him water, and trying to keep him warm and fed. He also had listened, and listened, and listened, because despite his weakness, Endri almost never stopped talking. Half the time he was inaudible, his speech little more than murmured sighs, but other times he wept with pain and begged his mother to come and take him home. After days of this, Porto was beginning to feel as though it might turn him mad.

Before leaving to help the woodcutters and carpenters with the day's work, he had managed to get Endri to take a little broth from their thin morning stew, made from a few tiny potatoes and an even smaller handful of soft-footed mushrooms he had gathered. The boy had not only eaten some but also managed to keep it down as well. That had heartened Porto, and as he wrapped Endri up in his own cloak, thinking that the active work in the ancient grove would be enough to keep himself warm, Porto promised the youth he would find something better for their pot that evening. But as it turned out, by the time his work was finished he had little strength left to hunt rabbits or squirrels, so he traded a tiny handful of potatoes to one of the other woodcutters for a bit of salt beef. It would take a while for the dried meat to soften and flavor the stew, Porto knew, but what else did he have here at the cold, gray end of the earth but time?

Endri was asleep when Porto got back to the camp. He made no attempt to wake him but added wood to the fire and put the dented pot on it to boil, which took much longer here than at home. He had chosen a spot separate from the rest of Duke Isgrimnur's troops so that Endri's moaning and mumbling would not keep the other soldiers awake, and now he scoured his tiny fiefdom in search of herbs for the pot. He found something that looked like white onion grass, and when he cautiously nibbled it he found to his delight that it tasted like the stuff as well. He pulled up a large handful and returned. The pot was just beginning to bubble.

"Ah, you'll like tonight's meal," he said as he squatted beside the fire. "Endri, are you awake yet? You won't taste a finer one even in the duke's tent."

Endri said nothing, so Porto leaned over and gave him a gentle shake. "Come on, lad. If you don't get up, you'll miss the feast." But something felt wrong, as though someone had stolen Endri away and replaced him with something solid and immobile.

Porto turned the youth over. Endri's face was slack; his eyes were open, but already they had filmed over. He did not look peaceful, but he did not look pained, either, and that was a small solace. He had been dead for hours.

The meal forgotten and the water boiling away to nothing, Porto slumped down beside the body and wept until the wind made his cold, wet cheeks burn.

He did not want to bury his friend in direct sight of the looming mountain, so he dragged the body to a clearing in a stand of young evergreens at the outer edge of the grove where he had been working. As the long northern twilight waned he scraped and hacked at the hard ground with his axe until he had made a trench deep enough to keep Endri safe from scavengers. Porto reluctantly took back his cloak but felt like a robber for doing it, so he made a bed of pine branches and then cut more branches to make a blanket to cover the body. He briefly considered taking the young man's prized Harborside scarf to return it to the lad's mother, but in the end he could not do it. Never once had Endri taken it off, and his pride in his old *setro* had been one of the most notable things about him. Buried in this bleak, foreign land, without a tombstone, he could at least go into the next life with something he prized, something that had reminded him of his home.

As it grew darker and the stars, like shy children, came out to watch him, Porto laid his friend in the grave and covered him over with fragrant pine boughs, then carefully filled the hole with earth. As he piled heavy stones on top to protect Endri's resting place he could hear other soldiers camped just a short way from him, their quiet conversations beyond his hearing but their voices murmurous as a river, and he wondered in a strange, empty way how many of them would also lie cold beneath these skies before all was done. At last, as night settled onto the north, he kneeled beside the mound and recited the few prayers he could remember.

"So began the Siege of Nakkiga.

"The mortals in their thousands swarmed across the plain at the mountain's foot, making their camp in the fallen houses of our ancestors like snakes in an ancient wall, bringing their great ram and other engines to attack our city's gates. At first the queen's Sacrifices and other orders were in disarray, but Marshal Muyare of the Iyora clan and his descendant-cousin General Suno'ku took the remnants of the Sacrifice army and began to train all Hikeda'ya, male and female, old and young, for a desperate defense of Nakkiga.

"Nor were the other orders idle, and many deeds of unsung heroism were done by the Builders of Lord Yaarike to shore up the city's defenses, and by the Harvesters of Lady Luk'kaya, who labored long and hard in the mountain's deep gardens to feed the people after a long era of war and its hardships.

"The Celebrants and the Echoes bound the other orders together in a web of shared thought. In the midst of all these measures, Akhenabi, the Lord of Song, prepared his order for a great strike against the mortal enemy, to weaken their hearts and turn the taste of their presumed triumph to ashes in their mouths.

"At first all that our people could do to fight the invaders was to attack them from above the gate, tunnels, and emplacements dug in centuries past by the Builders of old. Hikeda'ya struck from secret places along the mountainside, which had long fallen out of use and had to be cleared anew. From these hidden places the finest archers of the Order of Sacrifice rained death on the Northmen, killing many more than they lost.

"Yaarike's Builders, working with the masters of both the Singers

and the Caster engineers, created machines which could throw fire and flaming bolts down on the attackers from these high places, and at first these new engines found great success. Three times did the Northmen try to bring their great ram to the mountain's gates, and three times were they driven back, their hoardings in flame, and many of the ram's wielders dead or terribly burned.

"But the Northmen were determined not to lose their chance to destroy the Hikeda'ya, and so they chose the best climbers from their ranks and set them to scale our great mountain and silence its defenders. Terrible battles took place along the steep mountain tracks, in its darker places, even before the steaming vents that gave forth from Nakkiga's flaming heart. And though our Sacrifices fought bravely, they were greatly outnumbered by the mortals, who could spend men like cheap coins, and at last the Northmen were able to bring their great war engine to the gates. Soon the Northmen had found nearly all of our tunnels along the mountainside, and many pitched battles were fought where the mountain's precious interior touched the outer air. Those passages that had been secret but now were found out were quickly sealed by the queen's Order of Builders, sometimes even as those defending it still remained on the far side, so that the mortals could not come at Nakkiga from those ways. Then the Northerners in turn buried the outside of those passages beneath stone so that we could not use them again even if we chose, and began to find and destroy the few hidden passages still left to us from which our Sacrifices could harry the mortals. The ways into and out of the mountain now nearly all made useless, the battle narrowed to the ground around the great gates themselves.

"The mortals' rebuilt ram was covered with plates of hammered black iron to repel arrows and spears, and its body was the trunk of a great birch tree, the oldest that had stood in the old city's Sacred Grove, which had once been our Garden on this faulty earth, the hallowed spot where traitors and unruly slaves had been sacrificed at the turning of every Great Year, until the Well of Eternity was discovered in the depths of the mountain.

"The gates of Nakkiga themselves had been set up before the days of the Parting, even before the queen first came into possession of the city, and they were strongly built and full of old songs. Even the mortals' mighty ram with its iron head in the shape of a savage bear could not cast it down, but the Northmen had the scent of blood in their nostrils and would not turn away from their purpose.

"Hour after hour, day after day, the ram crashed against the gate's witchwood timbers, and each blow echoed through Nakkiga's squares and across the houses of the city like the tread of some fearsome creature. It seemed that even the gate must fall at last if the Northmen could not be driven back.

"In that terrible hour, one of our nobles took it upon himself to save the city. General Nekhaneyo of Clan Shudra, the greatest warrior of his illustrious family, gathered three score of brave Sacrifices, each one a hero many times over in the Wars of Return, and after consulting with the Celebrants and other loremasters, led his troop into perhaps the last passage still hidden from the mortals, a secret track through the roots of the mountain, untraveled since the days of Ur-Nakkiga's first conquest by our people.

"We will never know what horrors they found there, or what terrors they faced, but when the brave ones emerged once more into the light of day from a forgotten cavern at the mountain's base near the shores of Lake Rumiya, their numbers had been almost halved, and many of those who remained bore dreadful wounds and burns.

"But with the hourly battering of the mighty gates bringing disaster ever nearer, their leader would not give them rest. Nekhaneyo told his warriors, "We are already dead and our ends sung! Let what we have already lost bring freedom to those we loved! For the Queen and the Garden!"

"Their heroic charge will be talked of as long as the Hikeda'ya live and as long as our Garden is remembered. Nekhaneyo led his survivors by cover of darkness around the mountain's foot, riding so fast that it is said their horses' hooves struck sparks from the stones in their path. They came upon the Northmen at the gate just before dawn. With surprise on their side, they slaughtered the sleeping mortals by the hundreds, and would have laid fire to the ram itself had not the mortals' leader, Duke

Isgrimnur of Elvritshalla, rallied his startled troops and led them in counterattack.

"The mortals swarmed like rats, and though Nekhaneyo fought his way through their unending numbers until he had almost reached the Northmen's leader, he fell at last, hacked and almost bloodless, a few scant steps from the mortal duke. The rest of his brave Sacrifices were soon surrounded and pulled down. So ended Nekhaneyo's Ride, and it seemed at that moment that Nakkiga's doom was sealed.

"When they heard of Nekhaneyo's fall the people surrounded the Council Hall, crying out that all was lost and demanding that the sleeping queen be taken down into the mountain's depths so that at least the Mother of All would be saved. But Host General Suno'ku, a great favorite of the people, stood on the steps of the hall and called them all cowards, shaming them, and asking how Nakkiga could fail when so many of them yet lived.

" 'Are there no stones to be cast?' " she demanded. " 'Are there no sticks to be sharpened into spears, no ancient witchwood blades of our ancestors hanging on walls to be taken down and given the chance once more to drink mortal blood? Have all the Hikeda'ya been destroyed already, leaving only ghosts who wail and lament?'

"When she had silenced them, Suno'ku gave them heart again, saying that it was better to die standing than to kneel to a conqueror and still receive death, or worse, to be made a slave. She reminded them of great Hamakho himself, who had walked all the way through Tzo with a dozen fatal arrows in him, and she called out the names of her own ancestors, including Ehimeniso himself.

" 'Do you think when we meet someday in the Garden that I could face the shade of my great foreparent, our queen's consort, if I laid down my arms and let the mortals have their way? Do you think I could bear his gaze if I knew that I had let fear make me a weak thing? Eight hundred seasons gone I killed a mortal slave in combat to win my rank in the Order of Sacrifice. Why should I not rejoice to think that I may yet kill dozens more in defense of my homeland?'

"Their spirit restored by her words, the people dispersed back to their houses and living quarters, determined to fight to their last breath and last

*drop of blood. And some said that in that hour Suno'ku became as great
a hero as her legendary foreparent, Ekimeniso of the Brooding Eye."*

—Lady Miga seyt-Jinnata of the Order of Chroniclers

Aerling Surefoot was a wiry, dark-bearded Rimmersman with hands that
looked too big for his arms. When Porto offered his services, the frowning
man asked only two questions.

"Can you climb?"

"I was raised on housetops. My father was a carpenter."

"Not quite the same, falling off a house and falling off a mountain. But
we'll see. Can you follow orders?"

"Yes, sir."

Aerling looked him up and down. "You're a bit tall for scrambling in
some of the small spaces we have to use, but at least you're thin. 'Twill help."
He narrowed his eyes. "You're not scared of these whiteskins, are you?"

"No. I hate them." Endri's empty face still came to him every night in
his dreams, his friend's ghost silent and sad. "I want to see them all dead."

"You'll get no argument here." Aerling finished sharpening his knife,
wiped the whetstone on his breeks and slid it into his pack. "Just remember, they may look like dead 'uns but they're as alive as you or me. Full of
tricks, yes, but when you cut them, the same red blood comes out. When
you kill them, they're as dead as any ordinary man."

"Did you fight them at the Hayholt?"

Aerling shook his head. "Not me. I was here in the north, where we
had battles of our own. When Skali Sharp-Nose fell in Hernystir we
marched on Kaldskryke to take it back for Duke Isgrimnur. The people
opened the gates for us—they'd had enough of Sharp-Nose long before—
but Skali's son Geli, that scheming little coward, wouldn't surrender. He
took his remaining men and climbed up to the top of St. Asla's church
tower. Sealed the stairs with rubble, they did, then sat up there shooting
arrows at any of the duke's men who dared to show themselves in the
center of town. Thane Unnar sent me and a number of my men up there."

"I thought you said the stairway was blocked."

"We didn't take the stairs, you tall lummox, we climbed it the way we climb the cliffs back home in Ostheim. Ropes, man, ropes. And if you don't know your knots, you'd better learn quick, because you don't want to be fumbling with an overhand bend while someone's trying to put an arrow in your eye." He stared at Porto for another long moment, then reached into his pack and pulled out a looped coil of strong cord. "Here. See that man with half his beard burned off? No, don't ask him why or he'll tell you the whole bloody, boring story. That's Old Dragi. Tell him I said he should show you how to tie an overhand bend and a few other useful things—and how to *untie* them, too, for that's sometimes just as important. Come back to me tomorrow evening and show me what you've learned."

"What happened in the tower?"

"What's that?"

"The tower of St. Asla's. You said you climbed it."

"Of course we bloody well climbed it."

"Well . . . what happened?"

Aerling snorted. "Put it this way. Being Skali's son, young Geli may have had a beak on him like a bird, but he couldn't fly like one."

It was becoming very clear to Viyeki that the informality he had enjoyed with Lord Yaarike during their flight from the southern lands was now truly gone. He had to wait in the antechamber for his master's time just like any other high official of the Builders' order.

Viyeki noticed other high officials looking at him more than they generally did, some curiously, some with scarcely hidden resentment. He wondered whether Yaarike had already told some of them about his plan to make Viyeki his successor. Whatever the case, the magister seemed in no hurry to see him; Viyeki spent a long time waiting in the antechamber.

At last the door to the inner sanctum swung open and several figures emerged. General Suno'ku was in the lead, her pale hair bound in tight military braids, her owl helmet under her arm. As she and the other Sacrifices walked past, faces resolutely empty, she saw Viyeki and slowed long enough to nod formally to him.

"Try and talk sense into your high magister," she said quietly as she passed, and in that instant he suddenly perceived the force of her contained anger and had to resist the urge to step back, as if from an open flame.

Yaarike sat behind the wide table in the middle of his sanctum, almost hidden behind mounds of maps and building plans. Viyeki's first thought was that his master had aged tremendously in the last months. Yaarike's back was as straight as ever, and the hands holding the documents were steady, but there was something in his eyes and face that Viyeki had not seen before, a suggestion of weakness that he could not quite identify but could not ignore. Was it despair, or something more complicated? The continual pounding of the Northmen at the gates had become a drumbeat of approaching doom, and the entire city seemed to shuffle to its rhythm. Only the rigorous training of their orders—or the active threat of over-seers with whips—kept both the high and low castes at their work.

"Come in, Viyeki-*tza*," Yaarike said when he saw him. "Close the door. Have you been to the Singers' order-house?"

"I have been there, yes, but that is all. I told my name and my commission to the speakstone in the courtyard but they did not open the doors or even answer." Scorned and ignored, Viyeki had felt like a mere messenger instead of a magister's heir.

Yaarike slowly shook his head. "Lord Akhenabi is determined to win the war by himself."

"But why, Master? Why will he not work with you?"

"Oh, he sends his minions when it is necessary. And it is not me he resists, but cooperation with the Order of Sacrifice."

Yaarike seemed to be doing Viyeki the honor of speaking to him as an equal again, or nearly, and that eased the host-foreman's mind. "It is a bad time for rivalry," was all he said. "The mortals are at our door."

"The queen is asleep," said the high magister, shaking his head. He lifted an ornament from the table, the skull of a *witiko'ya*, one of the long-toothed, wolflike creatures who had made the lands around Ur-Nakkiga their home before the Hikeda'ya came. Carvings all over the city por-trayed the great hunts of yore, of Ekimeniso and even Queen Utuk'ku herself riding in pursuit of the deadly beasts, carrying no weapon but hunting spears. "The queen is asleep and the mortals, as you correctly observe, are at the door. Now is *precisely* the time for rivalry. When our revered Utuk'ku is awake, all of the ambitious lords and ladies are bottled in a jar like flies and can only buzz in circles, gaining small advantages here or there. No, now is the time for those who want it to grab for power." Yaarike laughed sourly. "In fact, there may never be another chance like this, Host Foreman. They are playing for high stakes in the very shadow of destruction."

"I saw General Suno'ku in the antechamber," Viyeki said. "She told me, 'Try and talk sense into your master.' If I may be so bold, Magister, what did she mean?"

Yaarike set down the long-toothed skull and flicked a bit of dust from its low crown. "She wants my help to force Lord Akhenabi into line, because I am one of the eldest of the order-magisters—almost as august as Akhenabi himself." He showed a wry smile that had little warmth. "She thinks the Lord of Song unwilling to bend himself to the greater good."

"And is she right?"

"Of course she is, as she defines it. But Akhenabi has always considered the greater good to mean what is best for the Order of Song. And for himself."

"So there is nothing you can do."

"Oh, there are things I may yet accomplish before I leave this world. Important things for the survival of our race. But these are not your concerns, Viyeki-*tza*. You will follow me to the magister's chair, if I have my way. But you will not *be me*, nor should you. There may yet be some great calamity in my future, and I wish you to remain separate from me in the thoughts of those outside our order. We will have to stop meeting, at least in the open."

Viyeki felt something like a blow against his heart. "Stop meeting . . . ?"

"I have my reasons."

"Magister, surely nothing you could do . . ."

"I have my reasons."

Viyeki had not heard his master's voice so stern and unyielding toward him since his earliest time in the order. His hands moved rapidly: *I am admonished*, followed by a second sign that meant *silent as the stone*.

In a flat tone Yaarike said, "And yet I can see you still have questions."

It was true, Viyeki's heart was full of pain that he had thought was hidden. He was unhappy to know he had revealed himself so easily. "Yes,

High Magister, I fear that I do. Why is Host Foreman Naji appointed to the greatest task?"

Yaarike eyed him expressionlessly. "What greatest task is that?"

"The work around the mountain's gates, Magister. The work to improve our only protection against the Northmen." Viyeki looked down at the stone flags instead of at his master and tried to find an appropriate composure.

"Ah," said Yaarike after a long moment. "I wondered what was troubling you. I could see it behind your movements." The High Magister pushed his chair back from the table and stood, showing his age in the deliberate way he did it. For a moment Viyeki spotted a bright flash of firelight at Yaarike's throat, or so it seemed. Seeing the Heart of What Was Lost again, even for a brief instant, made him think of the proud moment when Yaarike had trusted him with the safety of his family treasure. But the news of Naji's appointment had made that triumph seem hollow.

"I will walk you to the door," the magister said. "Yes, it is time for you to go, Host Foreman. Learn to measure yourself. Excess of anything is hard to hide—joy, anger, sorrow. And when you reveal yourself, you reveal yourself to your enemies as well as your allies."

"Yes, Master. But I still do not fully understand."

"That may change."

Viyeki took a deep breath. "I beg pardon, High Magister, but even if you cast me from the order, I cannot be silent. The work at the gates is by far the most important task we have. All our lives rest on it. Host Foreman Naji is not up to this challenge. He is a solid workman, but he has not the skill for such a task."

The older man looked at him for a long time, long enough that Viyeki could feel his own heart beat more swiftly at the length of his master's silence. It generally augured either fury or amusement, but little in between.

"I have met no finer Builder's sensibility than yours in all my years in the order," Yaarike finally said. "Your grasp of figures and your imagination, which has startled even me—" He broke off. "But I must take more into account than simply skill, Host Foreman. Or ambition. I must make the decisions I think best for all. And this is my decision. Do your work in the deep tunnels, and do it well. If you fear Naji's abilities are not sufficient, all the more reason for you to prepare a final refuge for our queen and people."

Viyeki did not speak until he felt himself in strict control once more. "If that is your desire, High Magister, of course I will do as you wish."

"Learn to mask your feelings better, Viyeki." Yaarike came forward and took his arm as if in companionship, though it might also have been a sign of the magister's weakness. "In that at least you are definitely Naji's inferior—he is as stolid as the stones he piles. Do not let your emotions blow you like the wind. And do not brood. This is not your fault, but mine. I should not have told you so soon that I wanted you as my successor."

"You have changed your mind, then."

"Young fool!" said Yaarike. "It was not necessary for anyone else to know it yet, and it has made you an object of interest. We must do our best to quell that interest."

"But if you have not informed the Celebrants, how does anyone know? I saw how the others looked at me."

Yaarike ignored the question. "From now on, you will come to me only when summoned, Viyeki. You will confine your correspondence with me to the facts of your work in the deeps. You will answer all questions about your future role in this order with polite evasion. Do you understand?"

"I do." But still his heart was beating wildly.

His master seemed remote now. "The days ahead will be difficult and dangerous, not just for the Order of Builders but for all the Hikeda'ya. General Suno'ku is on the rise. Akhenabi will not give in, although he may make a show of doing so. The dance is barely begun, yet already disaster waits at every step, every turn. And if the mortals break down the gates, nothing else will matter anyway. We will disappear like one of those stars that lights the whole sky and then burns to a cinder and is forgotten. Now you are dismissed."

As Viyeki turned for the doorway, Yaarike reached out and touched his sleeve. "One last thing."

Startled by even such a small, informal contact, Viyeki stopped short. "Yes, Master?"

"I do not wish to interfere in the domain of your home, Viyeki-*tza*, but I strongly advise you to stop your wife from crowing to her relatives in the orders of Sacrifice and Song about your good fortune. No good will come of it. Is that clear?"

Something cold settled in the pit of his stomach. Khimabu, despite his warnings, had told her family. "Yes, Master. Very clear."

The door swung shut. Viyeki had just enough time as he turned to compose his face into a mask of perfect placidity before he walked out past the other supplicants gathered in the high magister's antechamber.

Porto's days merged into what seemed an endless succession of climbing and huddling out of the wind interspersed with moments of sheer terror. He did his best not to think about his home and his wife and child, because what good would that do? He was stuck here at the end of the world, in the most foreign of foreign lands, and he had no more control over whether he would ever return to Perdruin than he did over the stars wheeling through the night sky.

He had plenty of time to watch those stars because, despite exhaustion, most nights he could not easily fall asleep, haunted by ghosts old and new. And since a few of their tunnels still lay undiscovered, the mountainside belonged to the Norns after dark; any mortal rash enough to tread in their domain, or even make himself unnecessarily visible, would usually be found dead in the morning with a single black arrow lodged in a vital spot.

But during the daytime the mortals' greater numbers gave the Mountain Goats, as Porto's troop dubbed itself, an advantage that they pressed as hard as they could, overwhelming the small groups of Norn bowmen they encountered on the mountain's rocky sides—although seldom without a pitched and often deadly struggle. The fairies seemed to have run out of magical tricks, but that only meant they fought more fiercely; one of the White Foxes, already disarmed and all but dismembered, had still managed to drag a comrade of Porto's to the ground and sink teeth into the man's neck before any of the others could help him. Porto and the others had pulled the Norn off him and stabbed the pale creature until it stopped moving, but the man it had attacked bled to death.

Porto could not have hated the White Foxes more, their unnatural quickness, their near-identical faces, their utter refusal to surrender, but he also recognized their bravery. Outnumbered and driven to ground like badly wounded animals, they fought to the last breath for their land. He hated these things that had killed Endri, Brindur's son, Floki, and so many others, but he also had to respect their courage.

Would I do the same, if it were my home and my wife in danger—my sweet Sida? Or little Tinio? He believed he would. He prayed that he would, but only God knew with certainty what a man would do when such a time came.

Hours became days, each day with its mountainside patrol, and virtually every patrol with its ration of sudden danger and death. Days became sennights, and the grave trenches the Northmen had dug were filled and covered over and more trenches started, but still the Nakkiga Gates held—still the mountain would not yield. The air, always cold, began to turn colder. The sleet that blew into their faces as the Mountain Goats clambered over the treacherous high slopes felt as hard and sharp as daggers.

Summer was waning and autumn was coming down across the north. The winter—the true, deadly winter that even the hardiest Rimmersmen feared—was on the way. And Porto and his fellows were trapped in its path like beetles exposed in a shattered log.

Troop Governor Ruho'o looked up from his position of supplication as though ready for execution. He held up his hands in the gesture commonly called *release to the parent*, something taught to children that apparently still remained even after all the training the Builders' order gave its officers.

"They will not go farther, Host Foreman," the governor said without meeting Viyeki's eye. "The shame is on me and my house. I should execute them all, but I cannot."

Viyeki generally did not believe in executing balky workers, especially at a time when trained Builders were in short supply, but he was tempted to make an exception now, starting with the Troop Governor himself.

"Do they not understand their people's need?" Viyeki added an appropriate edge of contempt to his words. "We are preparing a place for our folk to shelter if the gates fall. If there is no water close to that shelter, not even the Order of Song can save us—they cannot sing it up out of pure stone. Our people will all die gasping from thirst, like the proud walking fish in the ancient stories. Like animals. Even the queen herself!" He narrowed his eyes. "I should have these shirkers dig a pit and cast themselves in. You too, though live burial is better than you deserve."

The governor fell forward, sprawled on his face at Viyeki's feet, and moaned. "Take the head from my shoulders, Host Foreman!" he begged. "I have failed you, the Garden, and the Mother of All."

"And what good would your head do me?" Viyeki fought to keep his peevishness in check. "It is too ugly to make much of a trophy. Get up and tell me why your charges are willing to die instead of obeying orders that come not just from me, but from High Magister Yaarike himself."

Ruho'o backed slowly into a crouching position. "The workers are frightened, Lord Viyeki. Nobody but the Order of Song ever goes into those depths by choice, and only the Singers ever come back out again. The workers say . . . they say they cannot help themselves. They take a few steps into the downward tunnels and their hearts squeeze like a fist in their chests until they almost swoon. Something is down there."

"Of course something is down there. Many things are down there. The mountain is ours, though, and nothing down there is to be feared. We have Lord Akhenabi's word."

"All the same, there are still four of our engineers missing, Lord, the ones you sent first into the lower tunnels. They did not return. But some of the men say they heard those engineers' voices. Pleading for someone . . ." The foreman hesitated. "Pleading for someone to come and wake them. That is what I have heard."

"But you did not hear this yourself." Viyeki scowled. Perhaps a few executions would be necessary after all.

"No. But one of them, old Sasigi, appeared to me in a dream. I swear it is true! He said that they were all lost in the darkness. A darkness that *breathed*. And that he feared if he did not find his way out again, it would find him and chew him and swallow him down, and he would never awaken again."

"Superstition," said Viyeki, but that did not keep superstitious fear from tickling the nape of his own neck. "A dream, only. I expect more of you than to spread this kind of thing, Governor Ruho'o." He composed himself. "How many of the men are refusing to do their duty?"

The governor looked at him with something like wonder. "Why, all of them, Lord. I would not trouble you otherwise."

It was an impossible situation. Viyeki could not help imagining what his master Yaarike would think when he failed at even this less glorious task after complaining about Naji being given the work around the great gates. But short of killing enough valuable workers to frighten the rest into compliance, what could he do? The caverns known as the Forbidden Deeps cut right across the path of the new canal, and it seemed impossible to dig around them swiftly enough to make a refuge ready before the Northmen broke down the gates. Nor was Viyeki such a fool as to completely discount the men's fears. He knew they had good reasons to dislike the deepest places.

Even after the Hikeda'ya had held Nakkiga for close to fifty Great Years—three long millennia as mortals would reckon it—the mountain still held many secrets. The Order of Song knew some of them, which was part of what gave them such power in the queen's city, but the mountain had hidden depths that even Akhenabi and perhaps even Queen Utuk'ku herself might hesitate to plumb. Viyeki had felt the terror of those deep places himself in his early years, the freezing claw that gripped the heart and turned all one's thoughts into leaves swept up in a howling gale. He had even once seen Yaarike himself turn back from a place that he said was "too dark to enter," though the high magister had held a brightly burning torch. How to force mere laborers?

He could see no other choice. "Go back and keep the men quiet, Troop Governor Ruho'o. Occupy them with some of the finishing work in the tunnels that are already completed. I will devise a solution. And spread no more tales, nor let others spread them!"

"Go back?" For an instant the governor, who had come prepared to be executed for his failure, did not look overwhelmingly grateful that he was being sent back, but he quickly smoothed his expression into blankness. "Yes, my lord. You are very wise. I will do just as you say."

Though he could hear the sounds of hammers striking stone in many other parts of the city, Viyeki thought the Street of Eight Ships, usually bustling with workers and their overseers, was strangely quiet today. It made the constant shuddering boom of the mortals' mighty ram even more dreadful. The Builders' order-house was all but empty, and the functionary outside the High Magister's sanctum told him that Yaarike was out somewhere, supervising one of the many sites where the Builders were laboring to protect the city. Viyeki was frustrated, but since the functionary could not or would not tell him precisely where Yaarike was, Viyeki had already turned to leave when he met High Foreman Naji in the doorway.

Naji, always correctly courteous, made the appropriate gesture of greeting to an approximate equal, reminding Viyeki that whatever he might have been promised, at this point he was only one among several Host Foremen that Yaarike commanded.

"Is the old man in a good mood?" Naji asked.

"He is not here." Viyeki was suddenly curious. "Is he not at your site at the gates?"

"He has scarcely been there—not for days. Perhaps we have earned his confidence, and so he chooses to spend his time elsewhere." Naji was an unemotional type, generally uninterested in things he had not already learned, but he was no fool, as his look of deliberately bland inquiry demonstrated. "Why do you seek him?"

The last thing Viyeki wished to do was to talk about his unruly workers—it would have been hard enough to admit it to the high magister. "Nothing—a trifle. How goes your work on the gate?"

Naji made a gesture of sufficiency. "It still stands. But the great bolts are slowly shaking free of the surrounding stone, of course. With all the weight above it, if the gate is not flush, that will put great strain on the lintel." For a moment he seemed ready to talk about their shared profession, but a sudden look of distrust flashed across his face, and his posture became more rigid. "But are you not in charge of the refuge down in the deeps? What brings you back up to the city?"

"As I said, a trifle—just an idea I wished to discuss with the High Magister." Viyeki wanted to end this conversation. If word of his troubles with his workers filtered back up to the city, the other High Foremen would see his visit to the order-house for what it truly was—desperation. "If you see our master, tell him I will find him another time."

Naji looked mollified and his posture became less formal. "As I said, I scarcely see him—he is here, then he is there, as swift and hard to track as a rumor. He communicates with us mostly by messenger. The High Magister complains about his years, but should I ever reach such an age I pray I have even a fraction of his vigor."

Age does not always weaken its victims, Viyeki thought. Sometimes, as with Lord Akhenabi, it made them more cruel, more dangerous, and more powerful. "These are deadly times," was what he said to Naji. "Our master gives his all. We can do no less." Viyeki felt the hypocrisy of his words even as he uttered them and abruptly changed the subject. "And what of the fighting outside the mountain? What do you hear from the Order of Sacrifice?"

Naji shook his head. "Grim things, I fear. The Marshal and General Suno'ku must conserve their forces in case we fail and the gate is breached. So the numbers of those fighting the Northmen are small, yet more of them fall every day, though we can ill-afford to lose even one Sacrifice. But Suno'ku inspires them to keep fighting, and the gates have held for far longer than most thought they would."

"What do you think of her? Of the general?"

For the first time, Naji's mask of formality slipped entirely. "I think she is the greatest of us—saving only the Mother of All, of course. We are blessed by the Garden to have her in this dark time. Such courage! But even more, it is a courage that she can lend to others when their own has fled."

"She is brave, yes. And fierce. I saw her at Tangleroot Castle. And at Three Ravens Tower." There were moments when Viyeki remembered the bright-haired warrior as he had first seen her there, and he could almost believe that she *could* save them all. But they were only moments. "I must go now. I dare not leave my governors in charge too long."

"I know what you mean," said Naji. "The unsaddled goat quickly begins to bite." And then he did a strange thing, extending his arm and hand for the other to clasp. "May we both bring credit on our order in this evil time, Host Foreman Viyeki. Who knows when we will see each other again?"

And Viyeki, who had spoken truthfully but spitefully about Naji's shortcomings many times of late, was shamed. He put out his own hand

and clasped Naji's arm just below the elbow. "Yes, order-brother. May we
both make our master proud. And if we do not see each other again in this
world, we will meet in the Garden."

They parted, Naji to his other business, Viyeki back to the depths and
his workmen who would not work. And if the High Magister's wisdom
was not available to him, he knew he must solve the problem himself. He
owed it to his queen and his people.

As he walked down the front steps of the order-house, the iron ram
crashed against the outside of the gates once more, shaking all that was not
solid bedrock. Even the bells of the temple towers swayed from the shock
and uttered softly, like the moans of frightened children.

Isgrimnur never slept well in the field. Part of it was the absence of Gutrun, of course, of his wife's familiar, soothing shape in the bed next to
him, of her voice that calmed him in the night and reminded him that
there was more to life than his worries. On this night he had been slipping in and out of thin sleep for hours, and also in and out of a dream in
which Isorn his eldest son—his dead son—rushed at a gate that broke and
gave way. Behind it lay the darkness of an endless pit. As Isorn struggled
at the edge of this terrible fall, his father tried to call to him but could
not make any kind of warning cry. Then, as his dream-self flailed,
speechless and helpless, something hit the side of Isgrimnur's tent with a
loud enough noise to send him tumbling out of the dream and onto the
floor.

He shouted for his house-carls as he scrabbled in the darkness for his
sword. "*Haddi—Kár! To me!*" Again something struck the tent, this time
scratching and clawing so that the wall bulged first in one place, then
another. Some heavy shape was trying to rip its way in—a bear, perhaps,
or worse, a troop of murderous, white-skinned Norns. "To me!" he
shouted. "Where are you all?" At last he found Kvalnir. His fingers closed
on the sword's hilt, and in a moment, he had worked it out of the scabbard.

"*Duke Isgrimnur!*" Haddi was just outside the tent. He sounded like a
terrified child. "*We are . . . there are . . . !*"

Isgrimnur kicked off the blankets still tangling his legs and staggered upright, then pushed his way out the tent flap. He had only a moment to stare at Haddi, a trained killer who looked like a terrified child, then the bustling, thumping noise started again behind him, but this time the tent yawed and then collapsed beneath the assault. Isgrimnur could see only the dim outlines of something struggling in the midst of the poles and bunched hides. "What in the Holy Name of the Aedon is happening?" the duke bellowed.

Haddi, bizarrely, had fallen to his knees on the snowy ground and was now praying. All around, other shapes moved between the tents of the duke's commanders, some running, others limping or even crawling. Isgrimnur could make no sense of what had happened, only that it must be some terrible disaster. Had the earth shaken? Had a great tree fallen?

A muted noise of something being torn dragged his attention back to his fallen tent, where a dark shape rose from the wreckage. For a brief moment the duke thought he had been right in his first guess, that it was a bear or some other large animal: the thing was crouched and hard to make out except for a gleam of broken teeth. Then it struggled upright and he could see it full in the starlight. It was man-shaped, draped in rags dusted with snow and tattered until they were little more than cobwebs, but the eyes above the grinning jaws were empty black holes.

Duke Isgrimnur had only a moment to gape at this incomprehensible apparition before it lurched toward him, muddy hand grabbing at the empty air. The duke lifted Kvalnir and moved crabways, keeping the great blade between him and the dismal thing. The night was full of despairing cries, but when Isgrimnur called he heard no answering shouts, and he felt a moment of utter terror thinking all his men might have been attacked and killed in their sleep.

The thing with no eyes stumbled toward him like a drunkard, head wagging, jaws snapping loosely. Only as Isgrimnur drew back his sword to ward it off did he see and recognize the bracelet on the thing's clawing hand. It was gold that Isgrimnur himself had given out as war-booty after the battle for the Hayholt, a reward to his brave soldiers. This dead thing had been one of his own men.

The creature moved as crookedly as a wagon with a broken wheel but showed little fear of his sword, so instead of poking at it Isgrimnur strode forward, swinging Kvalnir in a broad arc to take the thing high in the neck. He felt the blow land, felt the bones beneath the rags snap, then the thing staggered to one side and toppled.

"Haddi! To me, curse you!" Isgrimnur called, but before he could find Haddi or any of his other liegemen, the thing the duke had just killed dragged itself back onto its feet.

"Damnation," was all Isgrimnur could say.

With its neck cut mostly through, the dead man's head hung limply to one side, bobbing and swinging as it staggered toward him. The duke cursed again and kept cursing as he lifted his sword and shoved it into the thing's guts, or at least where its guts should be, then put all his weight into it so he could drive the living corpse back into the wreckage of the tent.

Even tangled in the tent's hides, the eyeless thing still did not stop trying to get up, but by luck the duke had sliced through its backbone with his last thrust; now the struggling figure looked like two men huddled in a single costume for some holiday merriment, neither half able to get the other to cooperate. Isgrimnur swore again and hacked with broad Kvalnir until the head finally came off and the dead thing stopped moving.

Haddi had vanished, and none of Isgrimnur's other servants were close by. The camp was in chaos, and now that his eyes had adjusted to the dark, the duke was unsettled to see how many of the shadowy shapes around him were not his living soldiers but corpses animated by witchcraft. He began shouting again for his men, but before any of them reached him he had to kill two more of the terrible things, including one that had only one leg but still hopped slowly after him with intent to murder. Using Kvalnir more like an axe than a sword, he managed to take off the heads of both revenants while sustaining only a few scratches, but already he was winded and seeing sparks at the edge of his vision. Terror was stealing his breath, making him feel as though he fought uphill at a fierce angle. Some terrible Norn magicks were at work, that seemed certain. How many of these creatures were there?

How many have we buried? he thought bleakly. *That's the answer.*

Some of the duke's men finally found him, their eyes bulging with horror as they begged him for answers he could not give. He took a moment to look up to the slope above the camp where they had buried most of the dead, a spot that received more sun than most, which had made the frozen ground easier to dig. A swarm of clumsy shapes were clambering from the burial trenches there, slipping and tumbling but always moving downhill toward the living.

"Take their heads off," he told his men. "Without a head they fall and stay down. Take their heads!"

He was relieved to see a bulky shape he felt sure was Brindur gathering men of his own, and beyond that, like a single tree still standing after a great windstorm, Vigri's banner had been raised and someone was waving it in the air, drawing more survivors.

As Duke Isgrimnur's own small troop set about cutting down the dead that surrounded them, he saw others doing the same. The rout was halted, the men recovering, and the tide of battle finally seemed to be turning, or at least he hoped so. But many of the Rimmersmen had realized what they fought and were weeping even as they cut and hacked at the clumsy dead things.

More cursed Norn tricks, Isgrimnur thought, *and this one the foulest of all. Still, they could not hope to defeat our greater numbers with such slow-moving foes, even if they are our dead comrades.* Something tugged at his thoughts, something beyond the moment's struggle. *But wait, what followed the last time they created such a horror? The White Foxes always have more than one purpose—*

His mind suddenly clear, Isgrimnur began to bellow, *"'Ware the gate, men! 'Ware the mountain! All eyes watch for the White Foxes!"*

Other voices picked up the duke's call and added their own, lifting their warnings above the shouts and curses of those fighting the dead. As Isgrimnur hacked the head from a stumbling thing that would have pulled down one of his soldiers from behind, a sentry's horn sounded raggedly from the base of the mountain near the gates. He heard some of his men shouting, "The gate!" and "The mountain!" and "The gates are open!" Another screamed, "The whiteskins are coming!"

Isgrimnur cursed himself for being right, and also for not being right swiftly enough. "That is the real danger!" he bellowed. "Men, close up. Fight your way toward the Nakkiga Gate. We are attacked! The Norns are trying to flee the mountain!"

But that did not make sense, he realized even as he shouted it. Where would the Norns flee *to?* The mountain was surely their last refuge. Still, it was clear now from the eddying shapes moonlight made of the battling men that those nearest the gate, the sentries and the engineers tending the siege weapons, were bearing the main brunt of a wave of attackers.

"It's the ram, damn it!" the duke cried out as he finally understood. "Hurry to the ram! Vigri! Brindur! They mean to destroy the ram!"

His men could replace the great tree that was its body, he knew, but if the Norns managed to ruin or make off with the mighty iron head of the bear, it could not be replaced before winter came. There was not enough iron left in the camp to forge another without leaving the army weaponless.

"Leave the dead where they are and cut your way toward the gates!" he shouted. It was like a dream, like his dream, like falling helplessly into darkness. "By all that is holy, does no one hear me? *Protect the ram!*"

Porto would never forget that night—the night the dead woke up. He and the rest of Aerling Surefoot's men had found a new tunnel on the mountain, killed its single guard after an exchange of arrows, then blocked the passage at the end of the cavern with heavy stones and logs. With so much to do, they had not returned from the mountainside until after dark. It had been a fearful task, clambering down those icy, treacherous slopes when they did not dare light a torch for fear of lurking Norn bowmen, so by the time they reached the bottom the Mountain Goats had collapsed into sleep in a great huddle without bothering to find their way back to their designated fires.

Porto woke at the first shouts, but in his weariness he took the cries for something less fearful—men brawling among themselves perhaps, a common thing during this long, bone-chilling siege. It was only when he heard the great, creaking noise of the Nakkiga gates swinging open and the nearest sentries shouting their alarms, that Porto realized something dire was happening.

Mounted shadows swept outward from the gate, cutting down all before them in an unnatural near-silence. Even the cries of their victims were louder than the muffled hooves of the attackers' mounts. Then, as Porto hurried forward, trying to find one of the scattered groups of soldiers to join, he saw that the duke's camp was being attacked not just from the front, but from the rear as well, creating terrible confusion.

A man-shaped figure came staggering toward him out of the dark. At first he thought it was some hideously wounded Northman—which, in a way, it was, although this one's wounds had killed him days or weeks earlier. The thing barely had eyes, just gleaming wetness deep in the sockets, and its rotting shroud exposed gaping, bloodless wounds in its face and chest.

The dead, he realized, terrified but also strangely unsurprised. *The Norns have raised the dead. Our dead.*

He dodged the thing's clumsy reach but was almost caught by a swipe from the rusting knife clutched in its other hand. The thing did not even seem to realize it was armed, swinging both arms aimlessly, and Porto thanked God and all the saints that the things were slow as he leaped past it and brought his sword around hard enough to slice the dead man's neck to the bone. The corpse stumbled, then slowly turned toward him as if its head were not half severed. Porto dragged his sword free and this time hacked at the corpse's legs until he smashed its shin into a ragged white pulp of bone and unbleeding flesh and the thing finally toppled. Meanwhile he could hear the cries of his fellows as the shadowy White Foxes from the gate darted in and out among the Northmen, dealing death and terrible wounds, seemingly at will.

Porto finally severed the corpse's head from its shoulders, stilling its movements, but he had been driven away from the nearest group of his fellow soldiers and now stood by himself in a swirling chaos of men and shadows. Some of the dark shapes seemed impossibly swift, others slow as dying insects. He called out for Aerling and the rest of the Mountain Goats but he might as well have been shouting in an empty forest.

Something careened toward him, a huge dark shape that, only at the last instant, he saw was a horse and rider. He had only time to throw himself flat on the snowy ground before he felt the wind of the rider's stroke pass just above him. When he rolled over the Norn had vanished into the dark again.

Porto did not know how long he had been fighting, or even whether many of his fellows still lived. His greatest fear, though, had not come to pass: he had destroyed half a dozen walking corpses and crippled several others, but none of the dead faces had been Endri's. He hoped that if the demon-spell had roused the dead boy, the stones piled on his grave had kept him in the ground.

As he stood for a moment, head bowed, fighting for breath, he heard a shout of something like triumph. It didn't sound like the poisonous cry of one of the Norns but like that of a good, hoarse mortal man, and he felt a sudden hope. What had happened?

The greatest knot of fighting was down by the gates, where Porto could see a large number of living men surrounding a single pale rider, who was slashing away on all sides with a blade that was invisible in the darkness but clearly swift and deadly. Then one of the mortal spearmen got in a lucky thrust and knocked off the rider's helmet. The Norn's horse reared, and Porto saw a gleam of moon-pale hair. It was the female Norn-warrior he had seen at Tangleroot Castle, he felt certain, the woman who had brought reinforcements to save her kin trapped in the ruins. Half a dozen Northmen's bodies lay beneath her horse's hooves, but she was fighting defensively, and even as he admired her speed and skill, Porto headed toward the fight to help his fellows. Thane Brindur and a few of his men were still trying to bring her down with hand-axes, swords, and jabbing spears, but the Norn woman made her horse spin so swiftly it seemed like magic, and each time her arm swung a man reeled back with a fountaining wound or collapsed where he stood.

Somebody called from the gate. This time it was no mortal voice, but a high, birdlike screech, and the Norn woman immediately wheeled her mount toward the sound, her sword cutting the air so swiftly that the soldiers she had been keeping at bay could only throw themselves on the ground and then crawl away to avoid being trampled or decapitated. The pale-haired warrior galloped back toward the gate and the shadows waiting for her there. The Northmen got to their feet and chased her, shouting in triumph.

We've driven them back, Porto realized. He had never really thought he would survive this storm of death and madness, but the Norn horde was retreating into the open gate, fleeing back into the mountain. Brindur led the chase, but he was on foot and the Norns moved like wind itself, seeming to glide across the uneven ground. The Northmen could not catch them.

Porto slumped to his knees. The massive sally-gate groaned as it began to swing inward, then slammed thunderously shut behind the last of the Norns. A dozen or so Northmen leaped and shouted and pounded on the gates with their weapons, still seized by battle madness, as if they could conquer the entire mountain by themselves if only they might pass the threshold.

Porto could feel all his new wounds, the sharp cuts the shadowy Norns had dealt him and the scrapes and bloody weals left by dead fingernails. He was so tired that he almost lay down among his dead and wounded comrades to sleep, but feared he would be buried by mistake.

As he stood trying to get his breath back, his legs shaky as a newborn colt's, he saw something crawling toward him. It was so low to the ground he wanted to believe it some scavenging animal that had crept out onto the field in search of human flesh, but it did not move like any natural thing.

He lifted his sword. The blade felt heavy as a chestnut-wood beam.

His terror that the dead thing would prove to be Endri, or some other comrade, ended when the crawling shape lifted its face to the starlight. He did not recognize its agonized mouth or staring eyes, but there was something strange about it that still caught his attention. He stood all but unmoving as the thing kept crawling toward his feet, his blade quivering with the effort of his aching arms to keep it upright. The slick wetness of the blood trail left on the snowy earth behind it caught his eye. As it drew near, it raised a wavering hand toward him; then, when the effort was apparently too much, it let its pale hand drop onto Porto's boot.

"Help . . . me," it gasped.

The terrible thing was not a moving corpse, Porto realized in shock, but a living man. This was one of his fellow soldiers, a mortally wounded Rimmersman leaving his blood smeared behind him.

Then, as if merely saying those two words had exhausted his last strength, the dying man collapsed to the churned earth. Porto shouted out for help, his voice cracking, but nobody came. In the gray before dawn, the mountainside looked like some mad artist's depiction of Hell itself—a cold hell, not a lake of fire but a place of corpses and near-corpses slowly whitening beneath drifting snow. The man who had collapsed at his feet let out a last, rattling wheeze of breath, then lay still.

Porto crawled a little way off from the dead soldier and sank into a crouch, rocking himself back and forth. The rising sun was just beginning to warm the sky but the new light only made the charnel wreckage around him more horrible, the bodies more pitiful. At last, strengthless and exhausted, he fell back onto the cold ground and wept.

"Before discussing this fateful hour of the siege, when Akhenabi and his Singers raised the mortal dead and General Suno'ku led a sally out of the gates in an effort to destroy the Northmen's great ram, your chronicler must speak with her own voice for a moment, to tell something of the difficulties our order faces when trying to relate the tales of such times.

"It is not for poetry alone that we name our queen's restorative slumbers the keta-yi'indra—"dangerous sleep." The word keta's origins date back to the Garden itself, and it contains in its meaning not just the idea of "dangerous" but also "chaotic" and "unknowable."

We Cloud Children do not use keta to describe other perils. A wounded giant or thousands of Northmen besieging Nakkiga are both dangerous to our folk, but they are not unknowable. But our queen's sleep of recovery brings a special kind of threat to our race—chaos and the unknown—simply because she is not present to guide us. The order of things is compromised, as if the stars themselves left their celestial tracks and made for themselves new and random ways across the sky. When the queen sleeps, instead of her loved and trusted voice, many voices speak to us, and many hands strive for mastery of the People's fate. Nothing is in its proper place.

" 'In the season of keta-yi'indra,' Kusayu the Fourth Celebrant once declared, 'the sky and earth change places and the mountain stands on its peak.' It was in Kusayu's day that Drukhi the Martyr, the queen's son, was murdered by mortals. In her grief, Utuk'ku slept even longer than she has in our present time, and during that sleep many things changed in Nakkiga. The people were lost as though in a great darkness and all was uncertain.

"And so it was on that more recent day we speak of here, during the Northmen's siege of Nakkiga, when sudden victory and sudden defeat were both in our reach at the same moment. But in the end, both possibilities vanished.

"The risk of opening the gates for General Suno'ku's attack on the black iron ram did not end in disaster, as some feared, but neither was the weapon destroyed before the general and her surviving Sacrifices were forced to retreat.

"And Lord Akhenabi sang a song of such power that hundreds upon hundreds of mortal corpses rose from their burial places and walked beneath the sky, slaying many of our enemy and striking terror into them all. But it was not enough to drive the Northmen out of our lands again.

"The uncertainty of those days also spawned many tales and rumors that are still told, and which make the work of a humble chronicler much more difficult. In such times, truth is always elusive. Some might even say that when the queen sleeps there are suddenly many truths, precisely because it is our great queen herself in her wisdom, power, and ubiquity who determines the order of all things. In her absence, facts are no longer trustworthy. In her absence, authority is diffused or even lost entirely. How can we know what is real? And how can a mere chronicler discern the truth of such moments after the fact, even less than a Great Year later?

"All that seems to be certain about that night is that Lord Akhenabi raised the mortal dead and General Suno'ku did her best to cripple the mortals' siege engine. One succeeded and one failed, but still the siege dragged on. Even today many tales are told about that hour of the open gates, of folk slipping out of Nakkiga in the confusion, or (as some claim) spies from outside sneaking into the city itself, but these are whispers from a time when what was real was not fixed, when our queen slept and nothing was certain except chaos and the unknown. No one can say precisely what happened, least of all a mere chronicler, because truth itself was sleeping."

—Lady Miga seyt-Jinnata of the Order of Chroniclers

Isgrimnur was so tired he could barely put one foot in front of the other, but the long day was not quite over yet. He thanked almighty God that at least the risen dead seemed to be staying dead now that the sun had come up. Now the bodies that had risen would have to be burned after appropriate prayers. The duke decided on his way back to his tent that he would let the army's chief priest lead the ritual this time. Wasn't that the fellow's calling, anyway? Isgrimnur had run out of things to say.

Someone was waiting for him inside his tent, silent and unmoving in the shadows. Isgrimnur snatched at his dagger, raging at himself for his inattention, but when he took a menacing step forward, the figure made no move to resist.

"Send your carls away, Duke Isgrimnur. I would speak for your ears only."

"Ayaminu?" Isgrimnur's heart was pounding. "By the Aedon, woman, what are you doing waiting in the dark like that? I might have killed you!"

The Sitha inclined her head. "You might." She did not sound as if she thought it likely.

"Where have you been?" he demanded, the shock making him bluster louder than he might have otherwise. "I called for you many times during the rising of the dead, but you did not answer."

"No," she said. "I did not. And that is all I can safely tell you."

Isgrimnur could not help wondering whether she had done something to betray him but could not imagine a reason why she would. "What is it you want, fairy woman?" he asked at last. "I have dead men to burn and a siege to finish."

Ayaminu nodded. "I told you before, that you could not understand the deeps inside the mountain and the veins of what you might call madness among the Hikeda'ya. Before you plan the rest of your battle, I believe there are other deeps you must plumb. One of them is the history of our folk, which extends far beyond the arrival of mortal men in these lands."

Isgrimnur poured himself a bowl of ale from a pitcher. It was colder than he liked, but he had cursed the weather enough already. He offered some to the Sitha-woman but she shook her head. "So speak," he told her.

"I think you know a little of what is called The Parting, when the Hikeda'ya and my clan, the Zida'ya, went their separate ways," Ayaminu told him. "The Hikeda'ya—the Norns or White Foxes, as you call them— have long declared that it was you mortals who drove our two tribes apart, the Hikeda'ya wanting revenge for the death of Queen Utuk'ku's son but the Zida'ya unwilling to join them in destroying another race."

Isgrimnur had heard something of this from young Simon, but he could remember very little of what their young king had told him of fairy history. Isgrimnur's father had converted from the old faith to the Church of Usires Aedon when Isgrimnur was young, and it had been hard enough to learn all the new Usirean lore. He still swore by the wrong gods sometimes: he had scant room to carry around Sithi stories as well. "Treat me like an ignorant mortal," he suggested.

Ayaminu actually smiled, a sight so rare Isgrimnur was a little startled. He generally thought of her as old, in part because of her snowy white hair and her slow, cautious speech, but by any mortal standard she was quite beautiful, and at this moment he felt almost captivated by her. *Fairy glamours*, he told himself. *Don't ever tell Gutrun or she'll make you regret it.*

"I am not the oldest of my people," Ayaminu said, "but I am by no means the youngest. I was born well before the Parting, and lived the first part of my life in Hikehikayo, in the snowy Whitefells far to the west of here. I see the look in your eyes, Duke—do not be impatient. I have been patient with you, and even though my work here is finished, I have remained to tell you things you need to know."

"What do you mean, your work is finished?"

"What I say. I never claimed my people wanted the same thing yours do. I have done all that was asked of me."

"And what was that work?"

She gave him a solemn stare. "It is possible you will never know—these are strange times, and they have spawned many strange enmities and alliances which cannot yet be divulged. And it may come to nothing in any case—only the Dance of Years will tell. But I have done what I came to do, and I promise I have not interfered in your war."

"*Our* war?" He felt a rising surge of anger. "You call it ours?"

She raised a hand. "Peace, Duke Isgrimnur. I have things to tell you, and we are wasting time. War is like a skein of wool. Does the wool begin with the skein, or the sheep from which it came, or even from the person who first conceived of weaving with it? Does it end when the skein is finished, or when the garment is woven, or does it exist until the garment itself finally falls to tatters? What about those who remember that garment? It is still alive in their memory."

"I don't understand you. This seems like scholar-talk to little point!"

"Perhaps. But whoever's war this is, I have done what was asked of me, and now it is finished. It is time for me to return to my people. If a day comes when I am allowed to speak of my part in things, I promise I will tell you. But before I go, I will speak to you from my own heart and tell you something that I think you should know, so heed me, Duke. There are some inside the mountain—some Norns, as you call them—who wish to end the fighting."

Isgrimnur felt himself turning red. "Are you mad? Did you see what they did? Did your work, as you call it, whatever it was, prevent you from seeing how our own dead were summoned out of their graves and set against us?"

"That was by the hand of Akhenabi, Lord of Song. But he is not the only one defending the mountain, and while the queen of the Hikeda'ya sleeps, he is not the only voice and hand that matters."

The duke shook his head in angry confusion. "What are you suggesting? That we bargain to lift the siege? Even if I believed you, why would I do such a thing? My men want blood for blood and death for death."

"Of course they do. That is the nature of anger, of pain. But both your people and mine choose the most clear-headed among them to consider all possibilities when the rest are mad for destruction. Your people have chosen you, Duke Isgrimnur."

"Tell me straightly what you're saying, Ayaminu. I am tired, and my heart is cursed heavy with all that's happened." He poured himself more ale, drank it off this time in a swallow. "What are you telling me?"

"I did not finish my own history, Duke Isgrimnur," she said, still standing in shadow. "Be patient with me yet a while. As I said, I was born in Hikehikayo before the Parting. In that city in those days there was no great separation between the Norns and the Sithi. All lived together and were much alike, and all gave their loyalty to the whole people. But that changed, and not just because of the death of the queen's son. Long before Prince Drukhi's death, a certain envy had already crept into Utuk'ku's heart. I will not muddle you with the tangled details, but when Utuk'ku and her husband left my folk to lead their loyal clans on a different road, it was more to do with past grievances and perceived slights than anything else. The death of Drukhi was only the excuse."

"I am already muddled."

"Then I will make it simpler, Duke Isgrimnur. Just as there are Sithi who do not love mortals, there are a few Norns who do not entirely hate mortals. I grew up in Hikehikayo when those you call Norns and those you call Sithi, like me, still lived together in peace. And despite all the seasons that have swirled by since that time, I still know some among the Hikeda'ya, and know their hearts."

"Are you saying you could convince them to surrender?"

She made a noise he couldn't unpuzzle, a little burst of breath. "Me? No. As long as the queen lives, they will not surrender, especially the Order of Sacrifice. But that does not mean that the end of this struggle cannot be made less bloody, less vicious."

Isgrimnur groaned. "For the love of the Lord God, no more clans, orders, or history, I beg you! Just tell me what you mean!"

"Only this. Speak to them, as you would any besieged mortal enemy. Give them your terms and let the less bloody-minded of Nakkiga hope for something other than complete destruction. It could be that the results will be better than you can now foresee."

"How do you know? Perhaps like Brindur I have come to feel that only destroying every last one of those murdering creatures will satisfy me."

"I know little of mortals, although I have long studied them, Isgrimnur—but I think I know something about you. I will say no more. I cannot say more. And this suggestion of mine may come to nothing, but I would not rest easily when my own song finally ends if I had not made the attempt."

He did not like the implication that this strange, ageless female creature might know him better than he did himself. "A parley, then? All of this is to get me to parley with our enemies? The same white-skinned beasts who butchered my son Isorn and thousands upon thousands more?"

"To consider it, Duke, yes. To consider what such a parley might bring. To think about other ways of solving this problem. And it is a problem, Isgrimnur—mark me well. Even when you knock down the ancient gates, your work will only have begun. Do you think Akhenabi's tricks were the worst thing you will ever see? I promise you, there are things waiting for you in the darkness of Ur-Nakkiga that will make you wish yourself deaf and blind from birth." Her voice had risen a little, and although it was still not loud, it was all he could do not to step away from her. "Utuk'ku did not conquer an empty mountain. And the Norns have not stayed free for so long without learning something of their conquest and its secrets."

"Is that a warning or a threat?"

"What warning does not contain some threat in it? But I promise I do not threaten you on the Hikeda'ya's behalf. I say these things because, though I still find your people as dangerous as wild animals—but, sadly, without the innocence of beasts—I think there is more to you. The end of every battle is the beginning of something else, often something too large to understand at that moment, inside the Dance of Time." Ayaminu now did something even more surprising than her smile: she bowed. "I must take my leave. I doubt we will see each other again, Isgrimnur, or that I will ever have the chance to explain more of what I have done here, and why. The world does not spin that way yet, and may never do so. But I wish you well."

She slipped out of the tent while the duke was still trying to make sense of her last words, and by the time he pushed out through the door a few moments later he saw no sign of her, but only the frozen, muddy camp and the soldiers dragging bodies in the flurrying snow.

Part
Four

The Fatal Mountain

After long hours studying old charts and making his own painful and occasionally dangerous explorations, Viyeki had found a course for his men that would allow them to skirt the Forbidden Deeps in their continued excavation of a refuge. Still, solving that problem did not much improve his mood: even the most blinkered foreman in the order would have recognized the doom that hung over them, which might render even a completed refuge pointless. And that grim knowledge was not limited to the nobility. Every Hikeda'ya in Nakkiga knew what was coming, although some, by reason of their responsibilities or simple stubbornness, would not admit it.

Viyeki had long ago given up his family litter so that its parts could be used in repairs to the gate and other important things. Thus, on this day of the council meeting that might determine the fate of his entire race, the host foreman walked to the great Council Palace. His sacrifice was a minor one, he knew, compared to most—the sight of so many starving folk in the streets made that clear. Many of the slaves and lower-caste Hikeda'ya seemed to have simply run out of strength even to finish their errands or return home, and sat slumped in the streets wherever they had stopped. But although Viyeki's household still had food enough to maintain life, they did not have enough to share, especially with so many sufferers. More than half of the houses in Nakkiga's lowest tier were now shuttered and dark, some because the residents had not returned from the war in the south, or had died from illness or starvation, but in many others the occupants were alive but staying almost motionless, hour after hour, to preserve their dying strength.

In the low-caste district close to the foot of the thundering Tearfall something had corrupted a warehouse full of black rye, sickening many of the already hungry residents and driving them to acts of madness so disturbing that the Queen's Teeth, Utuk'ku's private guard, had been dispatched by the War Council to close off the entire neighborhood. The queen's elite guard sealed many houses with the howling tenants still inside; even after the noises finally ceased, nobody went near them. Viyeki had passed through the district once after the madness struck. Now he went no small distance out of his way to avoid it.

But even on the second tier, site of Viyeki's own house and the mansions of other noble families, the distress of his people had become all too evident. Even the privileged clerics and Celebrant officials employed in the queen's palace were growing emaciated, the skin of their faces almost transparent over the bones. Fear was everywhere, hanging over the city like smoke. Akhenabi's great casting and Suno'ku's raid had failed. The Northmen had not fled, the queen slept on, and the Order of Sacrifice had dwindled to a few hundred. And hour after hour, the pounding of the great ram thundered through Nakkiga's silent streets.

But for the Tearfall and the temple bells, the city has gone completely silent, Viyeki noted. *But that is our nature.* He felt both despair and a kind of helpless love for his people. *When we are threatened, we turn inward. We close ourselves in, we sink into the dark. We survive. But when survival is the only goal, what do the survivors become?*

This city of Nakkiga, he reflected, was like one of the cave-borers—blind, cattle-sized crustaceans that made their home in the deepest, dark parts of the mountain, seldom seeing any light. As with all their kind, the cave-borers carried their skeletons on the outsides of their bodies, and even when they were dying they gave no outward sign: the many-legged things would stagger onward, still acting out the patterns of life, until they simply stopped in place, like a wagon with a broken axle, and never moved again—apparently whole on the outside, but utterly dead within.

Is that to be the fate of our city, the lights going out one by one, never to be lit again? The fate of our entire people? To stumble blindly forward, dying with every step, until at last we simply cease to move?

Viyeki made his way across Nakkiga's third tier, toward the arching entrance of the Maze and the dark facade of the Council Hall behind it, as lost in his grim thoughts as a man wandering in heavy mist.

The last guard finished examining Viyeki's summoning-stone, then bowed and ushered him into the great chamber of the Council Hall. Once inside, he was surprised to discover several newcomers around the witchwood table, including several nobles from the Order of Echoes and their partners from the Maze Palace, the Queen's Whisperers.

The new face beside Lord Jikkyo of the Singers was a female member of his order too young to wear the mask of one of the Eldest, those born in the first years after the escape from the Garden. Her face was marked all over with strange runes, so that from a distance her skin looked almost black.

As Viyeki entered the vast, high-ceilinged room and seated himself, Magister Yaarike gave him a brief glance and nod but otherwise showed him no particular attention. As if to underscore this new distance between them, two other high foremen were seated on the magister's far side. One of them was Viyeki's rival, Naji. Viyeki put on a face as expressionless as a bowl of still water, but it was painful to have his diminished importance displayed to all in the War Council, even if it was, as Yaarike had suggested, only for show.

I am dying but still walking like a thing alive, he thought, then chided himself for such self-indulgent brooding. He was the scion of Clan Enduya, his family old in the service to the queen, even if not as exalted as some of the other clans represented around the table. Viyeki too was Hikeda'ya nobility: he would be true to his blood.

"So," said High Celebrant Zuniyabe after the Invocation of the Garden and other preliminaries had been finished, "for today's gathering, we welcome Magister Kuju-Vayo of the Echoes and Lord Mimiti of the Queen's Whisperers to our number. And, unless I miss my guess, you have brought someone new to our deliberations as well, Lord Jikkyo."

The blind Singer nodded. "Our great master Akhenabi, like our revered queen, has exhausted himself in defense of the Hikeda'ya. Like her, he is also deep in the slumber of renewal. As acting leader of the Order of Singers, I have brought Host Singer Nijika to be my second."

The younger Singer looked around the council table, her wide, dark eyes almost indistinguishable from the black runes tattooed on her face, but she gave no other sign of greeting or even acknowledgement. The others at the table exchanged grim looks at the loss of Akhenabi, the most powerful of their number.

"I am sorry to hear Lord Akhenabi is unable to join us," Yaarike said. "There are many questions he might have answered. As it is, we must examine the failure of our efforts outside the gates without his wisdom to guide us."

General Suno'ku spoke up, and Viyeki thought he heard a tremble of anger in her voice. "My Sacrifices and I did what we could, High Magister. We were informed of what was happening only a bell-hour before Akhenabi's resurrection song began, and also the distraction of the dead rising did not serve as well as we had hoped—the mortals regrouped quickly." Her relative the High Marshal now made a sign and Suno'ku fell silent, but it was clear she would have said more.

"I hope I am not hearing people blaming my master, who nearly gave his life to sing that song." Jikkyo spoke with deceptive mildness. "Such great shapings are not conjured from nowhere. They take time and they take strength—nearly all the strength the Lord of Song possessed, as it happened. He only narrowly escaped death. Also, the hour of the song's effect cannot always be accurately anticipated. Tell me, please, does the Order of Sacrifice truly blame Lord Akhenabi for the failure of the sortie?"

Before the disagreement worsened, High Celebrant Zuniyabe raised his hand, demanding the council's attention. His ivory mask did not hide the narrowing of his eyes. "I pray that at such a moment we will remember that dissension among us only serves our enemies. We have more important matters to talk about than affixing blame. The mortal commander has asked to parley."

For those who had not heard this request—a number that most definitely included Viyeki—the revelation was like a lightning strike. Faces turned as members of the council tried to ascertain who was surprised and who was not. The first to ask the question that was on most tongues was Kuju-Vayo, the immensely tall and slender master of the Order of Echoes.

"How did this come about?" he demanded. "And why would the mortals want such a thing in the first place? They have overwhelming numbers on their side. It is a trap or a trick."

It would be strange indeed, Viyeki thought, if Kuju-Vayo and his officers had in truth been unaware of the request for parley, since their task was to pass the thoughts and demands of Nakkiga's ruling elite to the other royal orders by use of the sacred objects called "Witnesses," mirrors said to have been fashioned from dragon's scales. It was axiomatic that the Echoes knew their people's great secrets before anyone else, yet the Lord of Echoes seemed to have been caught by surprise.

"Perhaps my master's Song of the Dancing Dead has shocked the mortals more than all of you suspected," said Jikkyo. "Perhaps they are frightened and this King Isgrimnur wants only a face-saving excuse to retreat."

"He is not a king," said Yaarike. "He is the leader of his own nation, Rimmersgard, but he is not the king of all the mortal lands. Those are his masters in Erkynland, and this Northman duke can only speak with them by sending written messages." He nodded slowly. "But it could still be a trick, of course."

"One of the Zida'ya accompanies them," said Suno'ku. "We have seen her. She carries a Witness."

"But that one is gone," Jikkyo countered. "She left their camp days ago and has departed our lands entirely. We know this beyond doubt."

"Perhaps a falling-out between allies," said Marshal Muyare, all heavy satisfaction. "They could never understand each other, the Year-Dancers and the mortals. It is another proof that the Zida'ya have chosen the wrong side, and another reason our weakling kin must go the same way as the mortals."

"I will slit the throats of every member of Year-Dancing House myself," said Suno'ku in perfect seriousness. "They have been traitors to the Keida'ya race since before the Parting."

Zuniyabe held up his hand for attention. The great hall did not become quiet as swiftly as it had the first time he had done it. "The Song has become muddled between many voices, as the old saying goes," he said when the gathering had finally gone silent. "No, we must speak now about what *is*, not what we believe or guess. The facts are that a message from the mortals stamped with this Duke Isgrimnur's seal was left in our last spy-tunnel on the mountainside—a tunnel we thought was still undiscovered." His gaze darted briefly to Muyare and Suno'ku. "Clearly, we were wrong."

"If it was found by one of my Sacrifices, I should have seen it first," protested Muyare. "This is a breach of our oldest traditions—!"

"Nevertheless, it came to me." Zuniyabe lowered his voice, which for a moment had become loud. "Let us worry about protocol and tradition another day, High Marshal. This secret was too great to risk until it could be revealed to you all, in this room." He looked around. "The message asked for one of our number to come out of the gate unarmed to speak with their commander, who swears he will also come open-handed. His troops will be withdrawn far enough from the gate that we can see there is no treachery intended."

"This is nonsense," declared Kuju-Vayo of the Echoes. "Who could we send to speak for all? Only the queen, and she sleeps!"

"This is not meant to be a negotiation, I suspect, but only the presentation of demands," said Zuniyabe. "And there is another thing. The mortals have asked particularly that we send General Suno'ku—or, as they put it, 'the great she-warrior with the war-braided hair.'"

Now several spoke at once, in tones that ranged from questioning to open fury.

"No," said Viyeki's colleague Naji, and seemed surprised to discover he had spoken. "That is, surely it is a trick. They wish to take our beloved general from us. The people will not stand for it."

"Ha! Let the people do what they please—I will go, yes!" said Suno'ku, and slammed her fist against the tabletop. "By the sacred walls of Tzo, I will go to the gates, then before the mortal chieftain speaks a word I will pull out his heart with my bare hand and show it to him. Let his liegemen kill me then. It will not matter. We will have given the only answer we can give!"

Competing voices rose louder and louder, until Zuniyabe reached out his hand in the gesture demanding immediate silence.

Even the Chief Celebrant cannot make us behave well, thought Viyeki in something like despair. *With the queen gone and Akhenabi now sleeping too, we are a hair's breadth from chaos. It would take only a mistake, a single hot word, to have the orders at swords-point with one another.*

"You will not harm the mortal leader, Suno'ku," said Zuniyabe, making a sign of displeasure. "At parley, it would be beneath us. We will hear their demands." The High Celebrant turned to Muyare. "Marshal? Will you make certain your cousin-descendant understands?"

For long moments Muyare stared back at him, his handsome face un-readable. "I will vouch for the general's understanding," he said at last. "And, if need be, her willingness to do what the council decides."

"Good. We want to know what the mortals think and plan. There must be no attack from us during the parley, unless they show treachery." Zuniyabe now turned to Jikkyo the Singer. "I do not think even so illus-trious a hero as General Suno'ku should go by herself, however. What do you think, Host Singer?"

Jikkyo also waited long moments before replying. "I agree. Some of the other orders should also be represented, that we may all feel comfort-able we have heard the mortals' demands correctly."

"Do you doubt my honesty?" Suno'ku asked him. "Or my loyalty to our queen?"

"Neither, but I do admit to doubting your restraint, General." Jikkyo folded his long hands, which—like his subordinate Nijika's face—were covered with intricate black designs. "I think one of each of the orders who make up this war council should accompany General Suno'ku. Since there is to be no negotiating during this parley, Host Singer Nijika is ca-pable of representing our order on my behalf."

The masters of the other orders agreed and also chose subordinates to attend the parley, promising that nothing would be decided until the news of the Northman's words had been brought back to Nakkiga.

Viyeki's master Yaarike was the last to speak. "I agree that my order should be represented as well," he said. "But I have an urge to see these mortal creatures face to face. Sadly, I was only able to show them my back as we returned from the South. I myself will go to the parley on behalf of the Order of Builders."

This seemed to cause only a little surprise among the other orders—Yaarike was known for his unconventional ideas and general stubbornness—but it startled Viyeki, and the words were out of his mouth before he realized. "Master, you cannot go! Please forgive my forwardness, but short of only the leaders of the Sacrifices, you are crucial to the defense of the city. What if it is a trick by the mortals, as some fear? Bad enough we lose important leaders from the other orders, but at least their magisters remain behind. We cannot afford to risk you on such a dangerous task, my lord."

Yaarike turned toward Viyeki, an uncharacteristic anger pulling at the magister's lean face, but General Suno'ku spoke up from the far side of the table. "I think the Host Foreman is right. At best, the mortal vermin will honor their promise, and we will hear their terms for our surrender—a demand that the Order of Sacrifice will never accept. At worst, it is a trap, and the city will still need to protect itself and prepare to deal with the mortals should they breach the gate. Send your second-in-command, High Magister Yaarike."

Viyeki's master tried to argue, but it was clear that with Akhenabi still recovering, the possibility of losing the lord of the Builders as well, worried everyone present. Viyeki could sense the fear behind the array of careful faces. At last Yaarike appealed to Zuniyabe, but the High Celebrant only shook his head. "Your whims cannot win out this time, caste-brother. You have heard the will of the entire Council of War. Host-Singer Viyeki will go in your stead."

There was still much to discuss, both about the parley and the larger matters of the siege and the city, and so the meeting went on and on until the evening bells finally began ringing in the Temple of the Martyrs.

From the moment Viyeki had gainsaid him before the council, Yaarike would not even look at him. Viyeki did his best to remain outwardly unmoved, but inside he was hollow. *I have ended my career, it seems. But I did it because I knew it was right for our people.* Still, he could not escape the idea that it might have been his own jealousy and hurt as much as fear for his master's safety that had driven him to speak up.

He would have to tell his wife Khimabu that he was going out unarmed to face the enemy. Why did he fear that more than the blades of the Northmen?

I wonder if all of history was as muddled as this? Viyeki was filled with the weary hopelessness of one who had lived for a long time under siege. *The chroniclers of future years, if there are any, will only be able to guess at what a mass of contradictions we were, who lived in such times.* He had a moment of sour amusement. *If the lives and deaths of such small creatures as myself ever reach their notice at all.*

News had spread through Duke Isgrimnur's army that there was to be a parley with the White Foxes. The troops were to withdraw back down the line of the valley before twilight came, but first the duke wanted to make sure no nests of Norn bowmen remained in undiscovered holes on the heights above the gate, and a task like that was work for the Mountain Goats. They had already labored long to find and seal all the Norns' escape routes, but the immortals were as crafty and determined as they were hateful.

As the cold afternoon faded, Aerling Surefoot led Porto and four others on a patrol across the lower slopes. For the first hours of the gray day they found nothing but traces of earlier skirmishes, broken Norn arrows, and remnants of their own camps. The Norns never left the bodies of their fallen behind, so even places where the Mountain Goats had killed some of the mountain's defenders only days before now seemed to have been deserted for years, and the brooding sky seemed to hang low over their heads.

"Make no mistake," said Aerling as they rested on an outcrop and scanned the dark slopes above, "the whiteskins won't give up. As well expect a nest of snakes to surrender. We'll have to kill every cursed one of them."

Porto had already had his fill of tunnel-fighting in the Norn passages which they had found and cleared during the weeks of siege. Even when the Mountain Goats outnumbered the pale things by a dozen to one, the silent, swift Norns were horribly difficult to kill. The idea of trying to clear an entire underground city made him feel sick at his stomach.

When they had all caught their breath Aerling led them farther up the mountain. They followed the faint tracks they had made in earlier forays, and if Porto did not quite have the confidence of some of the veterans, his long legs had become strong, and he could move uphill and leap from one perilous spot to another as well as any of his comrades. Thus it was that he was near the front of their small line, just behind Aerling, when he saw something flash in a thick copse of trees above and a little toward the southern side of the mountain. Porto tugged at the leg of Aerling's breeks to get his attention. The Goats following behind took note and wordlessly crouched to wait.

When Porto whispered to Aerling about what he'd seen, the leader nodded, then motioned to the group to split into two parts. Aerling chose Porto to accompany him, along with a whippet-fast young fellow from

Vestvennby named Kolbjorn, who despite his name—he had proudly informed Porto it meant "black bear"—was so pale and slender that he looked more Norn than Rimmersman. Aerling sent the other two with the old campaigner Dragi, to make their way up behind the trees while Porto and the other two approached from the front.

They climbed toward the copse as slowly and as silently as they could manage, crawling on their bellies through snow and over rocks until they had reached the trees. Unlike his fellows, Porto did not carry a bow—several attempts to teach him to shoot had failed to convinced him it was worth tripping over it—so he unsheathed his sword and stayed as low as he could behind Aerling and Kolbjorn. They paused frequently to listen and look for any sign of movement where Porto had seen something gleaming, but when the wind slowed, the mountainside seemed utterly silent.

At last they reached an overhang of stone just below their target where they sheltered for long moments, waiting for the wind to rise again. When it did, Aerling motioned to them both, then scrambled up over the top and charged into the clearing with Porto and Kolbjorn just behind him.

The open space between the pines was empty, nothing but muddy scrapes on the ground, half covered by snow, to show anyone had ever been there. But something shiny hung from a tree branch about chest-high. Aerling lifted it from the place it had caught, then brought it back to show the other two. It was a necklace of some kind, a piece of pale blue crystal about the size of a finger, carved crudely in the shape of a woman. Its slender chain was broken. Porto guessed that it had caught on the branch as one of the Norns had retreated from a skirmish. He leaned nearer and saw that what had at first appeared plain and even crude was instead beautifully simple: each angle was perfectly shaped, and the closer he looked the less he could make out what it was supposed to be.

Aerling held his hand out, proffering the necklace. "You saw it, Southerner. It's yours."

Porto's first desire was to step back. Although in some ways the thing was beautiful—how brightly it would glimmer against Sida's breast when he brought it home to her!—it was alien, too; just looking at it filled him with a sudden, fierce pain of homesickness.

Someone shouted in alarm from beyond the trees, a ragged, rising cry that ended abruptly. Even as Porto and his two companions turned from side to side, trying to judge the direction it had come from, another voice shrieked out a single word: *"Hunë!"*

It took Porto a moment to understand, but then terror came: it was a Rimmersgard word he had heard before and always to his sorrow. *Giant.* It meant giant.

A terrible crash, loud as thunder but far closer, then suddenly trees were falling everywhere around them. A moment later, even as Kolbjorn turned and dashed out of the clearing, Porto realized that the trees were all falling from one direction, and that Kolbjorn had sensibly, if not bravely, gone the other way. Porto had only a moment to lament his own slow reflexes, then something hurtled out of the mass of broken, sagging trees and landed at Aerling's feet. It was the headless corpse of Dragi, recognizable only by the boots the old soldier always cared for so lovingly.

More trees fell, making the ground jump; one of them nearly crushed Porto, but he threw himself to one side. Then the monster emerged out of the fog, striding over the felled trunks, sweeping smaller trees out of its path as if they were reeds.

Porto had seen giants before, when the troops had crossed over into the Nornfells, and he had watched from a grateful distance as the Rimmersmen had killed them, usually by sheer force of numbers. A dozen or more soldiers would pierce the huge beasts with arrows then keep them at bay with long spears until they finally fell bleeding to the ground, where they could be finished. But he had never seen one so close, and it all but stopped his heart.

The monstrous creature was half again the height of a man, with long arms and a face as ugly and full of rage as a demon's from another world. Its shaggy fur was as white as the snow itself, which meant it was still young, and unlike those Porto had seen in battle, it did not wear the leather harness that the Norns put on those who fought for them. As the giant pulled itself loose from the last fallen tree and advanced on Aerling, it bared its huge, yellow fangs. The stench of rotting flesh made Porto gag even as he stumbled back.

But Aerling was wedged between two fallen trees, branches tangling him from all sides. The Mountain Goat leader tried to work his bow free and could not, so he let go of it and pulled his sword instead. The giant growled, a rumble Porto could feel deep in the bones of his chest, then slapped at Aerling with a hand the size of a serving platter. The Rimmersman lunged at the massive paw and managed to sink his blade into the creature's wrist, but the heavy hand knocked him loose from the trees that had held him. Aerling flew half a dozen steps across the clearing and landed like a mealsack among the broken trunks.

Porto's blood was thundering so loudly in his brain that he could not think. He wanted to pray, wanted to tell his wife goodbye, but all he could see was that red, dripping mouth and the creature's deep-set eyes as it moved toward him, splintering fallen wood beneath its feet. Porto turned and ran. Snagged by branches, stumbling across toppled trees, his retreat seemed impossibly, fatally slow, but he dared not look back. At last he reached the center of the clearing where Aerling lay motionless, only a few steps away from the edge of the outcrop they had climbed. Porto knew that if he jumped off the stony shelf the giant would be on him before he could rise, and that would be the end.

He set his back foot, dodged a swipe from a huge, hairy hand, and swung at the thing's legs, but he caught his sword on the spiky branch of a fallen tree and barely creased the giant's fur. In a heartbeat, the beast had lurched forward and snatched him up into the air. Porto's sword fell from his fingers as the breath whistled out of him.

Yellow teeth grimaced only inches from his face. Tiny eyes peered out at him from under the bony shelf of the monster's brow, and in that moment of ultimate, dreamlike terror, he could see something looking back at him, a mocking intelligence in the giant's inhuman gaze that was almost worse than anything else.

Then the creature's hot, putrid breath blasted him as it let out a sudden, deafening roar. Porto was flung to the side so hard he bounced, the world turning up and down, whirling around him until it seemed almost like a dream. At last he stopped rolling and lay flat. Airless, he gasped and choked, struggling to fill his burning lungs and to rise before the monster seized him again. But the giant was doing some kind of bizarre dance and seemed not even to notice him; instead it whirled in place, flailing its huge arms and roaring so loudly that the branches on the remaining trees shook and rattled.

Something was dangling from the giant's neck, though Porto could make little sense of any of it. His air was out, his sight was going black, and no matter what he did he could not seem to suck anything into his straining chest. Still, he could not help thinking that it looked almost like the giant's throat was pulsing blood.

Another shape joined the dance, tiny, slender, and swift. It was Kolbjorn, and he held a long, crooked spear in his hand. As a little air began to creep back into Porto's starving lungs, and his vision cleared, he saw that the thing wagging in the monster's gorge was also a crude spear. As the monster spun and contorted, trying to dislodge that weapon, Kolbjorn kept stabbing at him with his other spear. The young Vestiman had not run away after all, but had found fallen branches and hastily carved the ends into sharp points.

Porto could not leave Kolbjorn to fight and die alone. He pulled himself up onto his hands and knees but could barely feel his limbs, and still could not breathe deeply enough to snuff the spangles of light floating before his eyes. Something inside him was cracked, broken. He crawled to his sword, narrowly avoiding the giant's ponderous feet as the beast finally dislodged the makeshift spear and turned to face the attacker.

Porto curled his hand around his sword hilt and kept crawling forward. Kolbjorn thrust again, and this time his spear went high into the giant's belly, but was stopped from sinking in too far by a cross-branch left on the shaft. Now Kolbjorn could only hold grimly onto the end of his weapon as the giant tried to reach him, the broken branch like the haft on a boar spear. Then the monster reached down and snapped the spear in half with a twist of its massive hand. Red blood was blooming in the white fur where the spear had entered, but only a trickle compared to the larger wound in its throat.

As the giant lurched toward Kolbjorn, its roars now ragged at the edges with fury and pain, it turned its back on Porto. He heaved himself onto his feet and staggered toward it. His chest seemed to be on fire, but he set his feet as well as he could and swung his sword through a hard, flat arc into the back of the creature's leg just above the knee. The giant staggered, then threw back its head and howled, and in the monster's moment of inattention Kolbjorn snatched up the spear that had first wounded the creature's neck and drove it as hard as he could into the hairy white stomach. The roar changed pitch once more, growing higher and even angrier, but as the creature staggered toward Kolbjorn with arms spread, yet another shape rose from the broken trunks.

Porto had thought Aerling killed by the giant's terrible blow, but now the leader of the Mountain Goats climbed unsteadily onto his feet, supporting himself on a fallen tree, then stepped under the giant's reaching arms to ram his own sword into the creature's groin. The iron blade was yanked from Aerling's hand as the giant staggered backward, but blood now fountained from the monster's inner thigh.

Growling, moaning, the creature raised both arms above its head, as though in its rage it wished to pull down the whole wide sky. It took a single step toward Aerling, spraying blood over the broken trees and snow, then it tottered, took another step, and fell.

Porto crawled toward it, his thoughts so disordered he could not even remember where he was or how such a madness had come to be. As he climbed onto the creature's back he could still feel its hitching breath. The feeling of the huge, warm thing beneath him was so disgusting, so maddening, that Porto plunged his sword into its back, then pulled it out despite the shrieking pain of his own ribs and rammed it into the giant's back over and over until the pain finally took all his senses away.

The afternoon had all but gone by the time they had found what was left of the other Mountain Goats and buried them in the clearing near the blood-matted body of the Hunë. Dragi's head had rolled or been flung a hundred paces down the mountainside. When they found it, the old soldier's face wore an expression closer to surprise than fear.

"A head for a head," said Aerling, and began to hack through the giant's shaggy neck, a butchery that took a long time. Porto knew he would never forget the noise it made. Then the last of the Mountain Goats stumbled back down the mountain as the gray day waned, Aerling carrying the monster's heavy, bloody head cradled against his chest as though it were something precious.

The duke's army had already begun their withdrawal from the gate for the parley, but several sentries rushed toward Porto and the rest when they appeared out of the heights of the mountain. Porto simply stood and stared at the faces around them and the bustle of activity across the camp as though he had never been there before.

The sentries escorted them back to the remains of the camp with no little ceremony, and a crowd soon formed around them. He and Aerling and Kolbjorn could muster only a few words for their comrades, but Aerling's bloody trophy quickly made the main details clear. Porto met his second nearly mythical creature of the day only a short time later, when Duke Isgrimnur himself came to see them. The duke was almost as tall as Porto but twice his girth, and although Isgrimnur was clearly distracted by the approaching parley, he clasped each Mountain Goat's hand and thanked them.

"By God, you have done a hero's work today, each of you," he said. "If that thing had come down from the mountain and caught me and the others unarmed at the parley . . ." He shook his head. "But look at you, wounded and still bleeding! God's Suffering, why hasn't anyone seen to these men?" He called for a surgeon.

Porto watched the duke and the others as though from the bottom of a deep well. He could hear what was said but it seemed mostly nonsense, and his thoughts kept wandering away.

"Why do you stand so, fellow?" Isgrimnur demanded of him. "Oh, aye, you're the Perdruin-man. What is your name—is it Porto? Here, what are you hiding under that cloak?"

"Nothing," said Porto, finding his tongue at last. "My ribs, I think . . . might be broken."

"Can you kneel?" Isgrimnur asked him, but Porto did not understand his meaning, nor much of anything else. "See, Sludig? He's almost dead on his feet, the poor devil," the duke fumed. "Frayja's Garters, where is that surgeon?"

"His Grace wants you to kneel if you can," said Isgrimnur's yellow-bearded lieutenant, not unkindly.

Will they put us to death? Porto wondered, and at that moment it did not seem a strange thing. He felt as though he and Aerling and Kolbjorn were all steeped in blood and destruction, that they had become something apart from all these ordinary soldiers—something terrible.

Young Kolbjorn looked up at the duke. The young man's gaze was distant and almost sleepy, his hands red with dried blood. "It killed Dragi. Tore his head off."

"I heard, lad," said Isgrimnur, "and I am sorrier than you can guess. But you have done a brave thing, the three of you."

"We were six when we went up," said Aerling, still clutching the giant's head like a treasured heirloom.

"And we will say prayers for your brave brothers tonight, I promise," the duke said. "But I have the authority of the king and queen of all the High Ward, and you will be knights for this."

Porto tried to lower himself to his knees, but the pain was so fierce in his chest that he swayed.

"Sludig, help that man," the duke said, and the yellow-bearded one clasped a strong hand around Porto's arm and let him down slowly.

Isgrimnur began to speak words that Porto could only partly hear, because a red noise was rising in his skull that seemed loud as a rushing river. He heard the names of King Seoman and Queen Miriamele and wondered why he did not entirely remember who they were. In his weary mind he imagined them as Isgrimnur's masters, monarchs of the far north sitting on thrones of ice, both swaddled in furs and jewels.

Something touched him. It was Isgrimnur's great sword Kvalnir, and it moved gently from one side of his head to the other, tapping each shoulder. "Then I name you champions of the High Ward," the duke said, "and lay on you the charges of knighthood. Arise, Sir Aerling, Sir Kolbjorn, Sir Porto."

But Porto could not manage to get up until the yellow-bearded one named Sludig helped him. He felt like a newborn colt, his legs shuddering sticks that could barely hold his weight. The duke was already being called away to other duties. A surgeon had arrived, his pack full of linen bandages and salves.

Aerling was still clutching the giant's bloody head and would not let anyone take it from him.

Is it an honor, his wife had demanded, *or does your master mean to see you killed?*

Even now, as he approached the crowd waiting at the ancient gatehouse, Viyeki could not guess at the true answer. He had not admitted to

Khimabu that he had probably destroyed any chance of succeeding Yaarike as magister. Viyeki had the courage to face the Northman hordes—just barely—but not enough to admit his foolishness to his wife. As it was, she had bidden farewell to him at the door of their house stone-faced and dry-eyed, as though she had already been widowed for many seasons.

General Suno'ku was at the gatehouse before them, pacing back and forth, a display of impatience and vigor seldom seen among the impassive Hikeda'ya. She did not wear her white armor, but only what was called a house uniform of the same color, as if she did not fear the barbs of the enemy at all. As usual, Viyeki was torn between his admiration of her spirit and concern for her stubborn, heedless bravery. As the day had worn on and this hour had come ever closer, he had found himself hoping that something would arise to change the plan. It was not a fear of being injured or killed he felt, but a sort of deeper, more formless dread, like a man in the wilderness watching an approaching storm as it turned the skies black.

You're a fool, he told himself. *Nothing will happen today. The Northmen will give their terms, and we will take them back to our masters. There will be no great deeds. Suno'ku has sworn to abide by the council's will, and whatever else she may be—however uncommon she may be in our dark, quiet world—she is no traitor.*

Viyeki joined the other two legates, rune-faced Nijika of the Singers' order and a thin, small-statured Celebrant named Yayano of the Pointing Finger, kin to Zuniyabe and a powerful noble in his own right. Together, they followed Suno'ku through the echoing gatehouse. The general seemed to want to waste no time. Before they had even reached the gates—which were heavily patched and barricaded on the inside, the hasty work of High Foreman Naji's crew of Builders—Suno'ku was already signaling to the guards to open them. As the bars and bolts were drawn from the sally-gate and the Sacrifice guards moved into close order to prevent mortal trickery, Viyeki and the other legates all stood silently. At last the pulleys creaked, the heavy witchwood timbers groaned, and the tall but narrow salley-gate swung open.

Even under dim twilight, it seemed bizarre to see the sky again. Viyeki had been back inside Nakkiga long enough to regain the feeling that stone above his head was the natural order of things. The great gray expanse of clouds outside the mountain seemed almost too vast to bear, as if something monstrous had torn off the top of the world. The rocky slopes on either side of the gate seemed to stretch out forever.

A dozen Northmen waited in the no-man's-land beyond the gates, behind and a bit to the side of their great ram, which had been left in place—as a reminder, Viyeki did not doubt. He turned to look back at the gates and saw the great dints in their stony timbers, as well as all the places the metal bracings had buckled under the repeated pounding. Most of the ornamentation had long since been smashed into fragments. The gates now looked, not like the symbol of power and protection they had always been, but like something old and frail and long forgotten. Seeing the damage made Viyeki's guts churn, and he turned to discover what expression Suno'ku wore. But if she had seen what he had, the general had not stopped to dwell on it; she faced the mortals squarely and began to walk toward them.

"But there are only supposed to be four," said Yayano. "Four of them, four of us!"

"The others are merely guards. They will make sure we have not brought weapons," Suno'ku called sharply over her shoulder. "By the Garden that made you, show the mortals no fear!"

She stopped a few steps away from the bearded Northmen, who stared back at the Hikeda'ya as though they were something entirely unknowable. Suno'ku spread her arms and stood with her feet wide apart; it took a moment before the guards realized she was waiting for them. Half a dozen burly Northmen now came toward her, creatures Viyeki thought more like stubby mountain giants than people. These gross mortals ran their hands over Suno'ku's body and one of them said something to his fellows, which provoked a nervous laugh from a few of the others.

"I speak your tongue well enough," Suno'ku said. "And in any case, you should know that I do not need any weapon to end you. I could do it with my hands alone, and you would be dead before you fell."

The Rimmersmen were war-hardened killers who gave no obvious sign of having heard what she said, but Viyeki's keen eyes saw the tightening of their muscles, the narrowing of their eyes.

When the Hikeda'ya legates had all been searched, the mortal guards retreated to one side. The biggest of the waiting Northmen waved them back even farther. They obeyed him, but with the unhappy look of dogs kept on too short a rope. Viyeki thought the large one must be their leader, Duke Isgrimnur. His beard was not quite so long or full as the others—the shortest of the mortal captains had a trail of whiskers so lengthy it was tucked into his belt—but everything else about the duke seemed over-sized. His chest was broad, his belly even more so, and Viyeki thought he looked like a creature who could not control his appetites. His face was broad too, with a tinge of choleric red, but the man's eyes were shrewd and strangely calm.

"Well, my lady, we meet at last," said the duke in a deep, rumbling voice. "I fear none of us can speak your tongue. Can we trust you to trans-late our words fairly to your people?"

"As I said, I use your tongue well enough for this day," said Suno'ku. "And though I do not know all its twistings and turnings, I do not think in any case that I am anyone's *lady*. I am Suno'ku seyt-Iyora, Host General of the Queen's Sacrifices, and I speak for my lord Muyare, the Queen's High Marshal. Speak your terms so that we may get on with this."

Isgrimnur's mouth curled in what might have been a smile. "Very well. You see that we have come in good faith, as we promised on our love for our God. Neither my companions nor myself are armed. We wish only to talk straightly with you."

"There has already been more than enough talk," she said. "State your terms."

"You are as abrupt in diplomacy as in battle," the duke said almost approvingly. "Very well. You must know that your position is hopeless. We have cleared the mountainside of your soldiers, sealed your burrows, and now you are trapped in this place with your backs against stone. Your people crossed into our lands and attacked us, and aided the Storm King in trying to destroy us. But we are not animals. If you surrender and open your mountain fortress to us, we will not harm any innocent women or children. In fact, they may go freely and we will give them passage, as long as they do not try to cross back into the lands of men."

Several of the duke's men stared open-mouthed, as though this were something they had not heard before. The short one with the long beard said, "Let them go free? Even if it is only women and children, that is madness, my lord!"

"Quiet, Vigri. The king and queen in Erkynland gave me the power to dispose of this struggle as I deem fitting." Isgrimnur had never taken his eyes off General Suno'ku. "Do you understand me?"

Do the rest of us not even exist? Viyeki wondered. *Are we no more than court musicians, while Suno'ku is the dancer who all watch?* But as he looked at the pale-haired warrior standing so straight and unconcerned before the burly mortals, he was content to let her stand for them all.

"Truly?" Suno'ku asked. "I am female, Duke, as you may have noticed. Will you let me walk free? And many of my Sacrifices are women too. Shall they all go free?" She shook her head. "You do not know anything about us, mortal. Children? Even our children are twice your age—thrice, even ten times!—and, I doubt not, many times wiser as well."

The yellow-bearded mortal beside the duke said something quiet but angry into Isgrimnur's ear.

"Peace, Sludig," the duke said. "She is more fighter than diplomat, but we guessed that already. I said 'innocent,' General. I understand your women fight too. I meant those who had not raised arms against us."

"Are those your only terms, then?" Suno'ku demanded, her disgust very plain. "Surrender our home and our females and children can go free?"

The duke shook his head. "Your warriors—Sacrifices, do you call them?—must all lay down their arms. When they do, we will decide their fate, male or female. And your leaders must surrender to us as well. But for the rest, I will be merciful. You have my word as a man and as an Aedonite."

For the first time one of the other legates spoke. "Our leaders?" demanded Yayano of the Celebrants. Viyeki thought his astonishment and fury must have been clear to even the most obtuse of the mortals. "You say we must surrender our leaders? Do you mean the queen herself, too—the Mother of All?"

Isgrimnur looked uncomfortable. "We will treat her with respect, you have my word. But yes, she must surrender to us along with her advisors. Your queen is no innocent. She was a great force behind the Storm King's wrongful war on our people and lands."

Viyeki was as shocked as the rest. He had been curious what the mortals intended to gain from this seemingly pointless meeting, but not in his wildest imaginings had he thought they would ask for the queen to be handed over. He felt as though he were on fire inside, and when Suno'ku raised her hand to forbid Yayano more angry questions, he was relieved. Now the general would curse the mortals and refuse them, then he and the others would return to the mountain so they could all prepare to die in a way that was fitting. If that was all they had left, the decision of how to make a proper end to the great song of their race, it was still better than surrender to this pack of hairy animals.

But to Viyeki's astonishment, Suno'ku merely said, "If you are finished, we will take your words to our leaders. You will have our reply by dawn tomorrow." She turned on her heel and began to march back toward the gates. Viyeki fell in behind her with the rest of the legates, so stunned that his thoughts seemed barren, like a high mountain pass scoured by gale winds.

As the mountain's face loomed above them, Suno'ku abruptly stopped. The salley-gate was opening, but at her sharp order the guards inside let it grind to a halt.

"Wait for me there," she told Viyeki and the others. "I have one last word for the duke."

"Do not throw yourself away," said Yayano. He looked to Nijika, legate from the Order of Song, but it was impossible to tell from her expression whether the tattooed Singer agreed or disagreed with him.

Viyeki felt the ominous mood drop over him again like a chilly fog. "Stay with us, General," he begged. "There is nothing to dispute. Their surrender terms are no terms at all."

"I did not ask you, Builder," Suno'ku said, not even glancing in his direction. "You have the words to take back to our masters. Those shameful words." Her face was like something carved on an old temple, the expression something that no one alive could read and properly understand. "I have now fulfilled my task, and thus am no longer a legate."

"But, General . . . !" Viyeki began.

"Silence." She fixed him with a stare so hard and cold that it almost made him stagger. "Go back to your drawings and tools, although they will avail you little. Mere stones cannot save us now." And so saying, she left them in the shadow of the gate and marched toward the mortals.

Duke Isgrimnur and his men had turned away to return to their lines, but a cry of warning from one of the guards made them face around.

Viyeki could see the duke talking angrily to his men as he tried to get free of them and turn back to meet Suno'ku.

Here is the flaw in the stone, Viyeki thought with sudden apprehension but could not say why. All he knew was that in that instant, as he watched the two walk toward each other, the slender Hikeda'ya and the broad, shaggy mortal, he felt he stood before a weak place in the world and time, a flaw that had been there for countless years but had only now worked its way to the surface. He did not know precisely what had come before or what would come after, but he knew nothing would be the same. Without thinking, he took a few steps after Suno'ku, but the other legates grabbed at him and held him back.

"Damn you, Sludig, I love you like a son, but if you lay your hand on me again you will lose it."

"My lord, Duke Isgrimnur, please—"

"By Heaven's bloody hammer, *I will speak to her!*" Isgrimnur knew it was what his young king and queen back in Erkynland would want. And even though he had to swallow his own hatred to do it, he knew that it was what his God wanted, too, or his faith was all sham.

He turned to face the Norn warrior. Even as a trickle of fear made its way through his innards, he could not help admiring her. Her walk was purposefully martial, yet her every movement was that of a sleek predator, a cat or wolf. The duke was twice her size, but Isgrimnur had seen the Norns fight hand to hand, and he knew that if it abruptly came to blows, he would be hard-pressed to keep himself alive until his men could help him.

"I wait for you, General," he called. "Do you think to kill me? I warn you, Jarl Vigri is small but his heart is that of a giant's. It is also full of hate for your people. And there are others of my nobles I could not even bring to the parley because I could not trust their fury."

"I do not come to kill you, Duke Isgrimnur." She stopped in front of him. "I come to tell you something you should know. The Hikeda'ya will never surrender either our mountain or our queen. Never."

"Then why the hurry to inform me? Tomorrow at dawn would be soon enough. Our task will still be the same."

The fairy woman stared at him for long moments. Isgrimnur did his best to hold her eye calmly, marveling that he should have to steady his knees in the face of a slender woman more than a head shorter than himself.

"I think your kind are little better than animals," she said at last, "But I think you are an honest mortal. That does not mean I would not happily kill you and tie your head to my saddle by that bristling beard."

"Of course not. Is that why you returned—to flatter me?"

She smirked—it could be called nothing else. The duke had never seen a Norn smile. It was an unsettling experience.

"I said before that you do not understand us. I will tell you once more, and then the Garden itself will witness I have behaved honorably. We will not surrender, mortal. Even if you batter down our ancient gates and bring all your numbers into our mountain, still we will not surrender. You said that the women and children could flee, but you understand nothing about us. Not even the lowliest caste-servants or slaves will give in, even if you kill every Sacrifice." She pointed toward the mountain. "Those Hikeda'ya you dismiss as mere women and children will lie in wait for your warriors in every dark place of our home, at every bend in every tunnel, with stones and sharp sticks. And eventually there will come a moment desperate enough that the Order of Singers will call up some of the older, darker inhabitants of our mountain. Those of your brutes who are not slaughtered will stumble in waking nightmare through the dark places until they die. You cannot conceive of the terrors you will face, Duke of Elvritshalla. Victory? That is no word for what the survivors of your army will take away from Nakkiga—those few who escape. Madness will be their reward. Madness and death."

Something rumbled as she finished. Isgrimnur looked up at the sky, but the low gray firmament was so full of darkly knotted clouds that the thunder might have come from any direction.

"I thank you for your honesty, General. I will not make the mistake of calling you 'Lady' again." He folded his arms across his chest. "But do not mistake my troops, either. They are fierce fighters all, hard men. They have faced your kind many times already and do not fear them. And they have many losses to avenge."

Suno'ku looked at him again. The duke thought he could see

something moving behind the bland face, a hint of what almost looked like surprise.

"Losses?" she said, her voice cold as the sky. "Losses, you say? I saw a hundred of my best Sacrifices die before my eyes at Asu'a. I saw my foreparent, our greatest general, pulled down and swarmed by your rabble. I found his body in pieces."

"Asu'a. You mean the Hayholt." Isgrimnur fought down his own anger. "My son and heir died there at your people's hands. *My son.* And Thane Brindur's son was burned alive by your troops only a short time ago, remember? We could hear his screams all over the battlefield." The sky rumbled again, and this time even the ground seemed to shudder. Isgrimnur wondered if the Norns were working some foul new weather-magic. Was he being stalled? What other reason could this hard-faced killer have to trade words with him after their business was plainly finished?

"Then we both have little reason to speak more," she said. Strangely, she seemed almost relieved. "We are finished here."

"I suppose we are," said Isgrimnur. "But I would ask one more question. You are brave, General—maybe even more than the rest of your fierce race. I knew that from the first moment I saw you. I do not expect any pity from you for my kind, but is there no pity in you for your own people? Would your pride condemn every one of them to death?"

"It is not pride, Duke Isgrimnur. My people are everything to me," she said. "I would die for them a thousand times, but they would do the same for their queen and their land without question." She said it so simply that he knew for her it was an utter truth. It also meant that she was right: the time for talk was over.

This time the rumble came not just from the sky but all around. Isgrimnur looked up, surprised. Sludig was running toward him.

"The gate!" he shouted. "The White Foxes are opening the gate! Treachery! The Norns are attacking!"

But the gate was still closed, Isgrimnur saw, nothing open but the salley-port, and that barely, with the other three Norn legates still standing before it, watching. He looked to Suno'ku, but she seemed as puzzled as he was. She stared up into the sky for a long, searching moment before turning toward the great bulk of the mountain.

Sludig reached Isgrimnur, grabbed his arm, and yanked so hard that the duke almost fell. Another guard reached him too, and the two of them began to wrestle him back toward the Rimmersgard lines. "Hurry!" Sludig cried.

But no force of Norns were issuing from the gate; it was still closed, though the noise was growing louder all around, deafeningly loud, like the hooves of ten thousand mounted riders or more.

Stumbling backward as his men pulled at him, Isgrimnur looked up at the mountainside and saw a massive cornice of stone, far above the gate, abruptly break loose from the slope's evening-darkened face with a crack louder than a thunderclap. It began to shudder and slide downward, breaking into pieces as it came.

"The mountain," Isgrimnur cried. "By Dror's Mallet, the mountain itself is falling!"

The first great pieces of stone smashed down around the gate, digging huge gouges in the snowy ground, throwing up splatters of mud. A massive length of stone had come loose from the mountain face directly above the gate, a piece of rock big enough to hold a good-sized Rimmersgard town; it broke into pieces as it shuddered and scraped its way downward. Men were screaming and shouting all around. Isgrimnur himself might have been one of them, but the roar was growing louder by the instant and he could not tell. The rumble became a deep, rasping growl that seemed to shake every bone in his body until he thought they would shatter—and yet, astonishingly, his feet were still under him.

Isgrimnur was half-running, half-staggering toward his troops when suddenly his legs were swept from beneath him and he fell heavily, face down into the mud. Then something shook the ground so brutally that he was bounced up into the air and flipped over onto his back. He saw a black boulder the size of a house cartwheel toward him down the sloping side of the valley, but he could not move because Sludig was clutching his legs.

The great oblong stone bounded past them. It hit the looser soil of the valley floor and teetered up on one end for a moment, then fell back, crashing to the ground in an eruption of snowy earth and small stones just a scant dozen yards from where the duke and his rescuer Sludig lay. Shards of rock as big as Isgrimnur himself rained down around them, but the duke could only cover his head and stare back at the mountain.

As the last and largest chunks of stone tumbled down the steep mountain face, some of them a hundred cubits or more in length, Isgrimnur thought he saw the pale form of the Norn general Suno'ku still standing in the same spot where they had last spoken, facing the mountain, as unmoving as if she had been god-struck. Then the great sliding mass of stone came down where she stood, grinding and crashing, and she was gone.

For long moments afterward the noise echoed along the valley like the groan of a retreating storm. Then, at last, it was silent.

The ancient gate and the entire lower front of the mountain had vanished from view, buried under uncountable tons of black stone, a monstrous mass of ship-sized boulders and crushed and broken rock piled far up the mountain's slope.

Isgrimnur wiped his face. His hand came away bloody, although he felt no pain. Sludig crawled up beside him. The duke could hear screams from the troops who had been crushed beneath the outer edge of the rockfall but had not been lucky enough to die. But from the mountain, from the city of the Norns, there was only the near-silence of settling stone and the occasional patter as a rock bounced down the piled rubble until it found a resting place.

"Duke Isgrimnur," Sludig asked, pulling at his arm. Isgrimnur could barely hear him, his ears still deafened. "Do you live? Are you badly hurt?"

Isgrimnur stared at the blood on his fingers as though it were something he had never seen before, then lifted his eyes to the grave, silent stillness of the mountain, which stood wreathed in stone dust and swirling snow.

"It's over," Isgrimnur said, though his mouth was so choked with dirt he could barely form the words. Despite everything else, he could only think of the pale shape of the warrior Suno'ku, her back straight as a sword blade while she waited for death. He spat to clear his tongue. "God save us all, Sludig, we will never clear that . . . and they will never escape. The war is over."

Part
Five

The Long Way Back

"The thoroughfares of Nakkiga's first tier were hung with snowy mourning banners, and even the poorest of the poor had some white token tied at arm or neck. The general's own Sacrifice host formed an honor guard for their fallen leader, lining up along both sides of the Glinting Passage so that all who came to Black Water Field to honor her walked between them.

"Suno'ku seyt-Iyora's coffin was empty, of course, but the people of Nakkiga still turned out in great numbers to bid the beloved warrior farewell. Despite the loss of such a figure, some even sensed an air of triumph to the ceremony: after all—and against all expectations—the mortals' siege had ended, the enemy was leaving, and Nakkiga still stood.

"Except for the queen herself and Lord Akhenabi, both still under the veil of the yi'indra, all the highest nobles of our race attended Suno'ku's funeral. Prince-Templar Pratiki of the queen's own Hamakha clan placed a sacred witchwood crown upon the empty coffin, and the general's commander and relative, High Marshal Muyare sey-Iyora, honored her with a wreath of yew branches. And as a further tribute to Suno'ku's bravery and the esteem in which she was held by all, High Magister Yaarike of the Builders brought his family's greatest heirloom, a jeweled necklace called The Heart of What Was Lost, and placed it beside the other offerings.

"When the ceremony was ended, the coffin and tributes were carried *in a slow march through the crowds and then deposited in the Iyora clan vault. In a time of great danger to our race, Suno'ku had become the spirit of the Hikeda'ya. The people would never forget her."*

—Lady Miga seyt-Jinnata, the Order of Chroniclers

"Come, husband, why can I not tempt you? The smoked blind-fish is exquisite, the best we have had in an age. Even better, it comes from your lake."

"It is not *my* lake," Viyeki said, but even he thought he sounded unconvincing.

"Of course it is." Khimabu gestured for one of the new servants to take him the platter. "Who else's would it be?"

One of the strangest and most fortuitous things that had happened when the stones fell and sealed off the gates was that the great throbbing and shifting of the mountain's substance had also caused a collapse at the site deep in the mountain where Viyeki's Builder host had begun digging around the Forbidden Deeps. This great rupture of stone had exposed an entrance into another part of the lower depths, revealing a heretofore unknown lake that had lain hidden in the darkness of Nakkiga's roots since Time itself began. The new body of water, which a surprised Viyeki named Dark Garden Lake when he was summoned there by his workers the day after the collapse, proved to be rich with eyeless fish and other edible creatures and mosses, easing at a stroke the city's fears of starvation. Although it seemed certain that public sentiment would rename it Lake Suno'ku, in all other ways Viyeki had received the credit for the momentous discovery. And if he was uncomfortable with his newfound acclaim, his wife was not.

"Why will you not eat?" she asked. "If you will not try the fish, at least have a little porcupine moss. The cook has outdone himself." Porcupine moss was a bristly sort of lichen, hard to find, but when boiled and spiced it was a favorite of the old noble families.

"I cannot help thinking it all too convenient," Viyeki said. "Magister Yaarike knows more of the deep places than anyone else in Nakkiga. He must have known there was a chance we would find a lake there."

"It is of no matter," said Khimabu in frustration. "Yaarike favors you, as he should. Despite all your worries, he has now announced to the Maze that you will be his successor as high magister! Is it so strange or wrong that he might have hoped you would find such a place?"

Viyeki put down his fork with the untasted fish still on it. "Forgive me, wife," he said. "I am troubled by many things. I am poor company."

"You are, it is true," she said. "But I forgive you." She brightened. Her features might have been those of a girl just emerged into womanhood. "My cousin Jasiyo says he thinks the Maze will honor you on the queen's behalf. Think of that!"

He rose, trying not to seem too hasty, but his stomach had suddenly gone sour and the smell of the meal was making him queasy. "Yes, we are honored, of course," he said. "And I am grateful. Please excuse me, my wife. My head is aching, and I feel the need of some air."

It was not air he needed, or even freedom of movement. As he paced the streets of the second tier, Viyeki knew that what he really needed was certainty, or at least understanding. What he needed was for all his painful, confused thoughts to give him some peace.

The Hikeda'ya of Nakkiga had always lived with the shaking and crumbling of the earth. Thus, when the great stones had fallen upon the gates, most of the people had thought it only another example of the mountain's uneasy sleep. But Viyeki had been outside the mountain during the first moments, before the others had dragged him through the sally gate. He had seen the twilight suddenly turn black and the sky turn to falling stone. He had seen dozens of Rimmersmen obliterated beneath the tumbling rocks in an instant. He had watched General Suno'ku wait calmly for death, then saw her snuffed like a candle. He still awoke several times each night, gasping, trying in vain to shield himself from a thundershower of stone.

But his continuing disquiet was not caused simply by what he had experienced when the mountain fell. What was troubling him far more was Yaarike's strange gesture at the general's funeral.

Like the rest of the Hikeda'ya who were present, serfs and nobles, Viyeki had applauded Yaarike's generous tribute to the fallen warrior, his tomb-gift of Clan Kijada's treasured relic, The Heart of What Was Lost; unlike the others, though, Viyeki's approval had not even lasted until the coffin had been slid into its niche. And the more he considered it the less sense it made, until now the question tormented him through all his waking hours.

Why would his master do such a thing? Many of the Hikeda'ya had genuinely loved and admired Suno'ku, but Yaarike had not been one of them. If any other high official had spoken of her so slightingly, then put a magnificent and treasured family heirloom—an heirloom of the Garden itself!—on her coffin, Viyeki would have thought it merely cynical, a political gesture to buy favor with the common herd who had revered the general and almost come to believe that she had fought off the Northmen and saved them single-handedly. But Viyeki's master was famous for his dismissal of mere gestures, of his refusal to court popularity by appeasing either the masses or the powerful elite. In any case, Yaarike had no need to appease anyone. Even after the great rockfall, the work of the Builders during the siege and Viyeki's own discovery made the high magister nearly unassailable.

So why should Lord Yaarike do such a strange thing? Why had Viyeki's unsentimental old master felt moved enough to seal away his family's greatest prize in someone else's grave?

At a moment when his own fortunes were at their height, the puzzle of it would not let him be. And so, churning inside, Viyeki walked the dark streets, barely seeing the other nobles when they saluted him or the servants and low-caste workers who scurried out of his path.

"I have been the besieger and also the besieged," Isgrimnur said as he sipped his bowl of ale. "But I have never seen anything as damnably strange as this."

He was sitting on a wooden chest in front of his tent while his carls cooked supper over the fire. The skies had cleared, and despite the afternoon shadow of the mountain stretching over the valley, it was not terribly cold. Sludig, still done up in his furs, held out his own bowl to be refilled.

"Rocks fall," Sludig said. "Even mountains. God has His own plans."

"It is not that." Isgrimnur wiped his lips with the back of his hand. "It's knowing that the White Foxes are *still there*. It's as if they went into a house

and closed the door and shuttered the windows, leaving us to stand helplessly in the street. The murdering creatures are *there*, only a few steps from
us, but we can do nothing! If I had twice the number of men it still would
take me half a year or more to clear all that stone."

Sludig shrugged. "Let the fairies starve in their hole, my lord. We can't
get in, but they can't get out, either."

"They will not stay in there forever," said Isgrimnur. "I cannot believe
they will be unable to find their way out again. They tunnel like moles,
those Norns."

"Then we will come back and finish the job," said Sludig, and drank
deeply.

Isgrimnur watched his men beginning the long process of breaking
down the camp and preparing for the trip south. They were in no hurry,
nor should they be: many of the wounded were still too weak to walk, and
it would be a long march home to Rimmersgard—even farther for most
of the mercenary troops. He thought for a moment of the tall fellow he
had knighted for helping kill a giant. Nabbanai, was he? Or Perdruinese?
Something southern. That one likely wouldn't reach home until Aedon-
tide, poor devil. But perhaps his new rank would help speed his way. "Did
we give those fellows who killed the giant anything? Some gold?"

"I will see to it, my lord." Sludig stretched. "But not being a knight
myself, I don't know exactly how much to give them."

Isgrimnur showed him a sour grin. "You need not fear I'll forget your
long, hard service, Sludig. In any case, you will be recognized and rewarded by the king and queen, too. So these men—reward them well. It
takes courage as well as luck to kill one of those monsters."

"Courage is always in supply," Sludig said. "Luck, not so often, so let's
offer our thanks to the mountain for coming down on our enemies. The
good Lord alone knows how many men we would have lost if we'd had
to take the city inside it."

"Shall we drink to the mountain? That seems strange, somehow." Isgrimnur looked up at the great jagged cone. Steam and smoke still
wreathed its upper reaches, as if to show that no matter what had happened, a scattering of stones here or there, the great peak still remained
above such mundane things as even a war between mortals and fairies.

"Why not?" Sludig waved his bowl for more and one of the carls dutifully came forward with the jug. "We have drunk to defeated enemies before this, if they were brave or noble. The mountain ended the war, and because of that many of our men will see their homes and families again. That strikes me as noble enough to warrant a salute." He lifted his bowl. "To the mountain! Long may she keep her secrets hidden from God-fearing men. Long may she keep the Norns out of the light and away from our lands."

"Yes, I can drink to that, my friend," said Isgrimnur as he lifted his own. "To the mountain, and to the end of killing."

"And to all our brave dead."

Isgrimnur, thinking of Isorn his son, suddenly could not find words and only nodded.

When they finished their toast Sludig sat silently, regarding the shadow-darkened peak. "At any rate," he said suddenly, "now perhaps we can put our swords away for a time. The war is over. The Storm King and the Norns have been destroyed or driven back into the darkness." He looked at the duke, slightly shamefaced. "In truth, I think I would like to buy a farm."

Isgrimnur laughed so hard he spilled the last of his ale. "By the Ransomer, I wager that never in a thousand, thousand years, will such a thing come to pass—my brave, bloody-handed Sludig turned farmer! But thank you for amusing me when I thought I was beyond it."

Sludig smiled. "Perhaps it will not happen, my lord. I have been wrong erenow, and changed my mind a hundred times about other things. But at this moment, after all we've seen and done, I think it would be nice to watch things grow."

The Order of Builders had repair work underway almost everywhere in Nakkiga; with his noble blood, rank, and especially his new importance, it was easy for Viyeki to go where he pleased, see what he wished, and ask whatever questions he wanted. But the thing he was seeking did not appear on any of the official schemes, so it took some time before he tracked down the gang chief who had led the small crew.

The chief, a slender, older Hikeda'ya with hands so callused they were yellow, led Viyeki into the highest tunnels behind the mountain's face, far above most of the work that had been done to shore up the gates and defend the heights of Ur-Nakkiga, to a place many hundreds of cubits above the starting point of the rockfall.

"Here it is, my lord Host Foreman," said the underling. "The work was done in the very first days of the siege and then abandoned."

Viyeki looked around. The natural cavern had been hastily and crudely enlarged, but that was not what caught his attention. A row of a dozen or more tunnels had been gouged in the cavern's rough floor nearest the outside of the mountain, each tunnel as wide as Viyeki's waist. Somewhat strangely, the rough chamber had its own well.

"Where does this water come from?" he asked, looking down into the blackness. He dropped a pebble, heard it splash not far below.

"From one of the meltwater rivulets that run down from the peak," the chief told him. "All thanks to the Garden, the mountain itself makes certain we will never die of thirst."

"And what was the purpose of your task here? What need was this digging so high above the gates meant to serve?"

"We were never told, Lord Viyeki."

Finished with his inspection of the well, he examined the crude tunnels that had been sunk into the cavern floor. Their endings were beyond what he could see with his torch but they seemed unexceptional. When he had first discovered a passing mention of this place in the order's records chamber, Viyeki had felt sure he had found something important, but now that he was here it was hard to see it as anything more than another abandoned project from the confusion of the siege's early days. "Do you know who ended the digging here?"

The gang foreman looked at him in surprise. Underlings were seldom told much about their work, and they almost never, ever asked. "No, Host Foreman. But the high magister himself came to see it in the beginning. Perhaps he was displeased with the location chosen."

So Yaarike had been here to inspect the digging. "And did he say anything about the project being abandoned?"

Again the look of incomprehension. "No, lord. The order came to us some eight or nine bells later. There was much to do and it was a muddled time. I'm sorry I cannot tell you more."

Viyeki nodded. "No matter. I am only correcting some of our records back at the order-house. Your assistance has been appreciated."

The gang chief looked cautiously pleased, but still maintained his stance of extreme humility. "It is an honor to serve you, Lord Viyeki," he said. "Everyone knows that you saved our people from starvation."

He waved his hand, dismissing the praise. "The spirit of the Garden was watching out for us all."

As he followed his guide back down the steep tunnels to the lower levels of the works, he felt compelled to ask, "Did anyone visit this site during the last days of the siege, after the work was abandoned?"

"I don't think so, Lord Viyeki. Why would they?"

"Of course," Viyeki said. "Why indeed?"

The temple bells rang to mark the passage of the days, and the life of Nak-kiga continued as it had since the siege's end, the city both mourning its dead and rejoicing at its unexpected salvation. But Viyeki found he could not do either with any comfort: the questions of what had happened before the collapse of the mountainside still worried at his thoughts like a canker. Even his wife Khimabu, who was otherwise very contented with the state of affairs, noticed his distraction.

"It would be one thing if you mourned the dead properly, dressing in white and paying the priests for bells to be rung on feast days," she told him. "But instead you go about with a long face and your robes covered in dust like a common laborer. My family wonders what is wrong with you—and so do I."

But on the few occasions he tried to explain, she did not want to hear.

"Why would you act this way? Can you not understand that we have been very fortunate? Why would you wish to trouble your people, who have had enough of suffering, with questions about something that is over and done with?"

Thus, when Viyeki discovered several more similarly abandoned projects above the failure line of the collapse, each one with its own well, all strung along the face of the mountain like gems on a necklace, he told no one. There was only one he wished to speak with about it in any case, and Viyeki was not quite ready for that conversation.

"We come now to the end of this particular tale of the Wars of Return, and to a necessary apology from your chronicler. Because these words were written less than half a Great Year after the events described, and because your scribe lived through the siege of the city and felt the mountain fall it has been more difficult than usual to keep this chronicler's flawed perceptions from affecting the proper recounting of fact.

"The only true history is that which has survived for generations and provided edification to our people, history that gives us an understanding of the past which holds firmly to the eternal truths of who we are—the undeniable truths of our martyrs, our sacred home, and our beloved monarch.

"But since Queen Utuk'ku slept the keta-yi'indra throughout the siege, and even as of this writing has still not returned to us from her healing exile on the Road of Dreams, this telling of our history can only be flawed and incomplete, full of the errors that come when one humble chronicler tries to tell the tale without the necessary perspective of time and the corrections of her superiors. Still, it was this scribe's duty to do so, and she performed it as best she could.

"A great tragedy in the south was nearly followed by an even greater tragedy, the loss of our longtime home and the destruction of our people. But by the virtue of the nobles of our most important orders, the Sacrifices, the Singers, and the Builders, we survived. A lesson is here for all: Do not trust in what seem to be the truths of the moment. Put your faith instead in the things that are eternal. Love our queen and love our mountain, love and remember the Garden That Was Lost, and the song of our race will find its proper melody.

"Here this telling ends. The humble chronicler begs pardon for her failings and hopes that her efforts have brought at least something of use to those who read this."

—Lady Miga seyt-Jinnata, Order of Chroniclers,
in the Eighth Great Year of High Celebrant Zuniyabe,
16th magister of that order

Viyeki's Builders were digging out a blocked main tunnel to the outside. As he returned from an inspection of the workers' progress, making his way down a narrow, nameless alley on the main tier of Nakkiga, he suddenly felt the hairs on his neck rise. It took a moment longer before he heard the muffled sound of soft boots. Instead of waiting to discover whether any of those coming behind him even approached his own rank, Viyeki heeded the warning of his lifted hackles and stepped to the side to allow those behind him to pass.

It was a line of Singers in robes the color of dried blood, a dozen or more, and the four at the back were carrying a litter. As the procession went by, some silent signal was passed. The litter stopped and its curtains parted. Viyeki could see nothing of the face in the deep-shadowed hood that appeared there, but he knew that unmusical voice the instant he heard it.

"Hold, there! I see a face I believe I know. Is that Viyeki sey-Enduya of the Builders?"

Surprised and perhaps even a bit frightened at the unexpected recognition, Viyeki made all the proper gestures of respect as he bowed low. "It is, great Lord Akhenabi, and it is flattering that you remember me. I only heard of your recovery a few bells ago, but I have already lit several candles in the temples in gratitude for your return to us. I'm sure all of Nakkiga feels the same." Despite his fear of the powerful Lord of Song, Viyeki was not exaggerating: the people of Nakkiga might all tremble before the magician, but Akhenabi had been a familiar part of all their lives since before any but the queen and a few of her eldest councilors could remember. The news of his reawakening had been greeted by most as a reassuring return to the way things had been.

As befitted one of his stature, the great Singer gave no sign he had heard the flattering words. "I have been told that Lord Yaarike has named you his successor, Host Foreman. I hope that when you ascend to Yaarike's title you will be as cooperative with the important work of our order as your master has been."

Without another word or any sort of sign, Akhenabi's litter rose back onto the shoulders of his carriers. The hooded procession abruptly moved off down the street, vanishing into the darkness and leaving Viyeki to ponder all the meanings that could lurk in the Lord of Song's words.

Cooperative. He hopes I will be as cooperative as Lord Yaarike. That innocuous phrase, which ordinarily would have seemed only a bit of obvious politicking, seemed in present circumstances something more sinister. *Of course our orders worked together during the siege for the good of all Nakkiga. But does Akhenabi mean some other cooperation with the Order of Song? Something darker and more secret?*

After a long day spent breathing stone-dust in the sweltering depths of the mountain, Viyeki wanted nothing more than to return to his house, to order and quiet. But Akhenabi's cryptic words gnawed at him, and he knew rest would be as elusive as it had been for many nights now. The only thing that might quiet his mind was finding answers to the questions that tormented him, though he knew hearing them might destroy his world.

But even if he could not put off the confrontation any longer, he still had to return to his house first. He had something there that he needed.

"Southerner! Porto! Over here!"

It was Kolbjorn, waving from the other side of a group of men hitching oxen to carts. "Hoy! Over here!" the Northman called.

Porto went to join him, stepping over the quantities of dung that decorated the muddy road. The wind had a freezing bite to it today, and the drovers and others were struggling to work while keeping their backs to the icy breeze.

"I've been looking all over for you," the young Rimmersman said. "One of the duke's men is waiting for us back at the campfire."

Porto pulled his cloak tighter. "Why? By the Good God, they're not going to keep us here any longer, are they? I have five hundred leagues to ride home. I will be fortunate if I am back before the Elysiamansa festival."

"You will be fortunate indeed if snakes don't eat you," said Kolbjorn. "I hear the southern lands are fierce with snakes."

Porto rolled his eyes. The Rimmersmen all seemed to think he had spent his life in a steaming jungle like the swampy Wran instead of a perfectly civilized city. "Oh, yes, the snakes are common as kittens where I come from. They crawl into your bed at night to stay warm and then lick your nose to wake you when they're hungry."

Kolbjorn stared at him for a moment, sensing the other might be having fun at his expense. "Well, I'd rather fight giants every day than have those Devil's creatures under my feet all the time."

Porto laughed. "You are a braver man than I, Kolbjorn, but we already knew that. What does the duke's man want?"

"Ask him. There he stands."

The yellow-bearded Rimmersman was the only figure beside the fire—the one they called Sludig Two-Axes, one of Isgrimnur's fiercest fighters. At the moment he looked distracted but otherwise approachable.

"You were looking for me, my lord?"

Sludig lifted his head. "Ah, yes. Porto of Perdruin, am I right? And don't call me "my lord." You're a knight and I'm not." He showed his teeth in a hard grin. "Yes, I've been looking for you. The duke sent this." He lifted his broad hand. It held a purse.

When he was sure it was really meant for him, Porto reached out. "What is it?" He loosened the string and looked inside. "Sweet Mother of the Aedon, this is for me? Three gold imperators? And look at all this silver!"

Kolbjorn was smirking. "I already got mine. Counted it, too. Five gold's worth all together."

"But why?"

"Because it is traditional when a man has been knighted that he be given land or wealth," Sludig said, grinning. "Duke Isgrimnur asked me to tell you he is short of land these days until all the new king's and queen's business is dealt with, but he can at least give you something to make your homeward trip a little easier. Do you accept it?"

"Accept it? My wife would skin me if I didn't. Please thank the duke—he is very generous."

"More than generous," said Kolbjorn. "Was there one for Aerling as well? The man who led us?"

"He has had it already," said Sludig. "Barely seemed to notice, I have to say. Busy polishing that giant's skull."

Porto shook his head. "He has not been entirely right since . . . the day the mountain fell."

Sludig nodded. "In truth, none of us have been. Now I must be going. There is much to do before we break camp tomorrow and start back. Before your road parts from ours, Southerner, you and this young Vestiman should come and take a cup with me."

"Seems a nice enough fellow," Kolbjorn said when Sludig was gone. "He strangled one of the White Foxes with his bare hands, did you know that?"

Porto shrugged. "We have all done strange things here at the ends of the earth."

The magister's chamber on the highest floor of the order-house was chilly, as Yaarike always kept it, with a small oil lamp on his table providing the only light and heat. They had been working together for hours bringing the master lists up to date on the order's many current tasks, but Viyeki was so full of disquiet he had spoken very little.

"You seem remote, Viyeki-*tza*," Yaarike finally said. "You have scarcely attended to a word I've said, forcing me to repeat myself many times. That is not like you. You were always my most eager student."

Viyeki took a breath, then another. "That is because something is troubling me, High Magister."

Yaarike's sharp eyes watched him closely. "Speak, then. I hope it is not that thing we spoke of before. You deserve all that has come to you from finding the hidden lake. It does not harm your fitting modesty."

"That is not what troubles me now. May I share my thoughts, Master?"

"I think you should."

Now that the time had come he found it hard to speak. The basalt walls of the order-house pressed in on him, their great age a silent reproof. How dare he stand beneath that arched ceiling, which had seen hundreds of foremen like Viyeki come and go, and harbor such thoughts about a high magister, let alone one who had been so generous to him? He felt he stood on sliding ground, being carried toward a precipice.

Better to jump than to fall.

"I have been thinking about how you showed me the Heart of What Was Lost when you thought you might not survive to return to Nakkiga, and wished to make certain it would reach your family. That was a great honor, High Magister."

"I have trusted few who are not my blood as I trust you, Viyeki-*tza*."

"But then you gave your sacred family treasure to be buried with General Suno'ku, to honor her. Putting the happiness of the people above your own desires."

Yaarike looked at him evenly, but his tone had a question in it. "Yes. That is always a magister's duty."

"I do my best to understand all your lessons, Master. Because of that, I have been thinking, and I have decided that I need to show you something of my own family heritage. May I?"

"Of course."

Viyeki withdrew the bundle of cloth from his robe and placed it on the table in front of his master. Then he carefully unwrapped it until the gray thing lay revealed.

For long moments Yaarike only looked down at the witchwood dagger, at its long, thin blade and its pommel in the shape of a flower, the petals made of milky crystal. "It is a beautiful thing," the magister said at last. "How old?"

"Nothing like the Heart of What Was Lost," said Viyeki. "This snow rose dagger did not come from the Lost Garden, but was made here in this land—in our old city of Kementari before it fell. It was given to my foreparent Enduyo in the era of the fifth Celebrant, as a token of gratitude from the queen. In some ways it is the foundation of our clan."

"Your foreparent was greatly honored indeed, if this gift came from the queen's own hand. May I hold it?" Now Yaarike glanced up to meet Viyeki's gaze, his questioning look almost aggressive.

Viyeki spread his hands. "Of course, Master."

Still cradling it in its wrappings, the magister tilted the slender blade to study it more carefully in the unsteady lamplight. *Dark*, thought Viyeki. *It is always so dark inside the mountain and inside the hearts of the Hikeda'ya.* For a moment, with the end of all things familiar pressing on his mind and speeding his heart, he again felt himself to be a creature that lived its life in secret, some sightless, burrowing thing of the dark depths. If the race of Hikeda'ya all died here beneath the mountain, the world outside might never know.

Nor care if they did know, except to breathe a sigh of relief, Viyeki decided, and in that instant nothing seemed to matter at all—not his honor, not his painful, complicated feelings about his master, not his marriage nor his clan nor any of the things that he had thought important.

Suddenly he felt too weak to stand. Without asking permission, he let himself sag into the chair opposite his master's seat. Yaarike glanced up briefly from the snow rose dagger but said nothing. After a moment's more inspection, the magister held out the knife. Viyeki took it back.

"I seem to remember some controversy surrounding Enduyo," said Yaarike, "but I never knew the details."

"Forgive me, Master, but I do not believe you." Viyeki found himself growing bolder, as though he had let go of something that had previously kept him tethered to the known, the comfortable. "No, I cannot believe one of your wisdom would have offered someone like me the chance to succeed you unless you knew every detail of my ancestry back to the Eight Ships—if not all the way back to the Garden itself. And the controversy, as you call it, happened during your lifetime, when you were already a young foreman in this order. Surely you remember? After all, it ended my ancestor's life."

Yaarike actually smiled, a wintry twitch of his thin lips. "Ah, but I am old and have much to recall. Perhaps you could remind me, Viyeki-*tza.*"

"My ancestor Enduyo of Kementari was an official of the palace, a master cleric. He was ordered by the queen's Oathbound to confirm the treachery of two Maze clerics with whom he often worked. He had no personal proof of their guilt, but the palace believed them guilty so he was ordered to testify against them. To refuse would have meant the disgrace and destruction of his entire family. Given no honorable choice, he elected instead to use this dagger and end himself. Like so." Viyeki pulled his robe aside and let the knife slide forward a little until the tip of the narrow gray blade rested against his chest. "Even the clerics he had been ordered to incriminate attended his funeral, out of respect. Of course, they were still found guilty—still went to the executioner." He looked up at his master. "So you see, this blade is schooled at solving difficult problems."

"And is there a reason you brought it here to show me?" the magister asked. "I certainly hope you are not planning to use it to take a life today . . . yours or anyone else's." Yaarike poured himself a cup from the ewer on the table, then without asking filled another cup for Viyeki and pushed it toward him. "Here. This cloudberry wine is a very old vintage. It is said there is a trace of *kei-mi* in every barrel."

Viyeki had never tasted the witchwood extract and knew he might never have another chance. He took the cup and drank deep. The wine was tart, almost too sour, with a taste that lingered on his tongue for long moments, as arresting as a memory both strong and bittersweet. "Thank you, my lord." But he would not let himself be distracted. "So you see, I find myself in a dilemma today, High Magister. Only you of all others can help me to resolve it."

"And this dilemma is . . . ?"

"Two choices. One is to denounce someone who has been my teacher and guide much of my life, one whom I have loved like a grandfather."

"A truly dreadful possibility. And your alternative?"

"To remain silent about a terrible crime—not just the murder of a beloved hero but an attack on truth and history itself. So it seems I am trapped between betraying my mentor or my queen." He touched the dagger lying in his lap. "You can see that following my ancestor's course seems the only honorable alternative to those two unthinkable acts."

His master drank deeply, then carefully wiped his upper lip with the back of his hand. "I think you had better tell me what has led you to this perilous situation, High Foreman."

"The death of General Suno'ku, Magister. And the collapse of the mountainside. I have come to believe that neither were accidents."

Yaarike's eyes narrowed ever so slightly, but he only signaled for Viyeki to continue.

He marveled at the calm in his own voice as he described the row of diggings he had found above the gate inside the mountain, all of them listed in the order's records as abandoned projects, all of them exactly the same.

"And what do you guess the purpose of these diggings, as you call them, to have been?" Yaarike asked.

"To make the mountain fall."

"And how would that be accomplished—and kept secret, no less?" He

sounded as if he was challenging a bright pupil to think harder, not arguing against a foolish impossibility.

Now that he was committed to speaking what he had so long kept
secret and silent, Viyeki felt as though his gut had been tied into a cruel
knot. "The hard part would be the secrecy, because it would not be a
simple or swift task. After all, it took nearly two score of our Builders
working for days to bring down a much smaller weight of stone at Three
Ravens Tower."

"True enough. But who could undertake such a complicated and dangerous task here in Nakkiga without anyone knowing? And why hide it?
The collapse of the mountainside saved our city and our people, after all."

Every word from his master's mouth pulled at the ends of the knot
inside him, tightening it. "The deed was hidden because defense of our
mountain was not its only purpose, I would guess. As to the other question, the person or persons responsible would need both knowledge of
such things and the power make to make it happen and keep it secret from
the people of Nakkiga."

Yaarike nodded slowly. "That makes sense, at least. Please continue,
Host Foreman. Tell me the rest of how this astounding trick could be
accomplished from inside the mountain."

"The set of tunnels in each digging would have been excavated by
workmen who would not know what they were doing—tunnels leading
down to a place where the rock of the mountain's face was weakest. Then
the workers would be sent away and the diggings declared useless. But
each of those places also had a source of water close at hand. Could not
someone repeatedly fill those new tunnels with water, which would then
run down and into the cracks behind that weak spot in the mountain's
face? Even the youngest scholar in our order knows that once such water
reached the end of its journey it would freeze because of the chill of the
outside air. When the ice expanded, pushing the rock outward around it,
more water could be poured in, beginning the process again. Eventually,
enough of such careful, secret work could weaken the entire rock face
until it split loose from the mountain's surface and fell, destroying our
enemies below and sealing the gates off from invaders for a long time. And
only the most skillful of Builders could even hope to make such a thing
happen at the proper time. Even so, it must have been very difficult."

"I hear many interesting ideas in what you say, Viyeki-*tza*, but not much in the way of proof. And although it caused the tragedy of Suno'ku's death, the collapse also saved our city—perhaps our entire race. It would be a hard thing to accuse an official of high family of such a strange and userful crime."

"I know, Master. That is one of many reasons why I brought this." He patted the blade in his lap. "Because with it I can solve that problem without bringing the official's family or my own into disrepute."

"Solve what problem, exactly?"

"The problem of not being able to let it go. I need to *know*, High Magister. I need to know what happened, and the truth about someone I admired beyond any other."

His master looked from the knife in Viyeki's hands to his own hands, graceful and strong, roughened by the handling of innumerable stones. "Let me then hasten you toward your solution." Abruptly, Yaarike pulled open his heavy robes, exposing the thin tunic he wore beneath. "You are right in your suspicions, Viyeki-*tza*—all of them. It was my idea to bring the mountain down. And I also caused Suno'ku's death, although that was not as I wished it. Now strike, then fold my hands around the blade so it will seem I pierced my own heart. Otherwise my clan will hound you, and you should not take the punishment for my mistakes."

Viyeki shook his head. "No. This blade is not for you, Master—it is for me to end my own life. I cannot live in a world where one who means so much to me, who has shaped my being more than my own parents, could do such a thing." His hand closed around the hilt and he lifted the needle-sharp dagger to his breast. "Just tell me why first, Master. Why did you kill the general? She seemed brave and honorable to me. Why did you hate her so?"

Yaarike seemed surprised. "I did not hate her. I said what I believed at her tomb—she was the best of us."

"But you killed her!"

The Lord of Builders sighed. "Not by choice—I for one hoped she would escape to the Northmen's side of the rockfall, but the collapse took longer to begin than I'd guessed. Why do you suppose I tried to take on the role of legate—the role you infuriatingly stole back from me? I did not want to see you killed or made a prisoner of the mortals. If things went awry, I wanted you to replace me as leader of this order."

But Viyeki was fixed on one word. "What do you mean, 'we,' Magister? Did you take Naji into your confidence when you would not trust me?"

Yaarike shook his head. "Ah, Viyeki, how can you be so clever and yet such a fool? Host Foreman Naji is of no importance. He knew nothing of any of this. I gave him the task of supervising the gate only because I wanted no blame to adhere to *you* if my plan went awry."

"But you said *we*, Master. Who else planned this with you?"

"You spoke of the need for secrecy. That is what Lord Akhenabi brought to the conspiracy. Who better to undertake a task like that, to undermine the mountain under the very nose of a hundred Builders, than his Singers? They can walk the between-spaces when they must. They can be all but invisible."

"But . . . Akhenabi was asleep!" The idea that his master had planned this with the Lord of Song was the most disturbing thing he had heard.

"So it was told to all Nakkiga. It made his work—our work—easier. But he was not the only one who took part in the plan. Again, why do you think I pushed you away, made it clear that you were not privy to my inmost counsels? Because that inner circle was myself, Akhenabi, and Marshal Muyare."

"The marshal? Sunoku's own relative conspired against her?" Viyeki let the hand holding the blade fall back into his lap. He had thought himself a cynic, but now was revealed as childishly naive. "Her own clansman wished our greatest general dead?"

"If our people could also be saved, yes," Yaarike said. "Few reach the highest circles in Nakkiga if they are crippled by too much sentiment, and Muyare knew it was only a matter of time until she supplanted him. But Muyare's price for joining the conspiracy was that Akhenabi and I had to agree to support Suno'ku's plan to rebuild our people through interbreeding with slaves. Muyare saw the wisdom in growing a new army, so there will be half-mortals in the houses of our nobles one day soon—half-mortals in the orders themselves."

"So you all joined together to murder her?"

"I did not want to, but it was Akhenabi's price, and if he was willing to gamble with the survival of our people, I was not. As I said, I hoped Suno'ku would only be exiled—that she would become a prisoner of the mortals, along with those who accompanied her. I did not lie when I said she was the best of us. It grieves me still that she was the last casualty of the war against the Northmen."

"This is serpent-talk—truth and lies mixed." Viyeki felt something like a storm boiling inside him now. How simple it would be to end all the confusion, all the disillusionment, with one swift thrust of the knife into his own breast. "Do you tell me you and all the others admired your victim?"

"I cannot speak for Muyare. As for Akhenabi, no. He saw only a rival for power, one who could best his reign of fear with something more genuine—the belief of the people."

"And yet you helped him kill her."

"As I said, I admired her, but I also saw her for what she would become—the end of our race. I did not want her dead, but I did want her gone from Nakkiga."

The tip of the blade had actually pierced the cloth and pricked the skin of his chest; Viyeki could feel the pain like a tiny star burning a mere hand's-breadth from his heart. But as much as he wanted an end to the agony of his thoughts, he wanted answers more. "I do not understand you, Yaarike."

"Suno'ku *was* the heart of what was lost, but made flesh—one who believed the old truths with all her spirit, and could make them real to others by the force of her own belief. But the old truths, I fear, are no longer true, Viyeki-*tza*. That is why the next generation will require different minds, different truths. General Suno'ku, in the burning purity of her heart, would never have given up the struggle against the mortals. She would have waited only until we had bred enough new soldiers to be fit for war again, then led our people into first one disastrous fight against the swarming mortals, then another. Again and again, until nothing of our people and our orginal bloodline was left." Yaarike reached out his hand and gently touched Viyeki's where it held the dagger. "Do you not understand? I have chosen you because you always look at and consider what the others do not, my young pupil. I said once that you could see around corners. Look ahead now. Let your heart tell you if I am wrong or not. Let your heart tell you if what I did was wrong for our people. If your answer is different than mine, then I was wrong about you—wrong about everything—and you must denounce me."

Viyeki closed his eyes. How could the deepest wishes of his people be wrong? How could Suno'ku, that bright, brave flame, have been a danger? One might as easily say that the queen herself had betrayed them. "You are far wiser than I am, Master, but you cannot change me with words. I have already made my peace with death before I came here today," he said. "Like our Sacrifices, I am dead already."

A sudden movement; the magister, moving more quickly than Viyeki could have supposed, knocked the witchwood knife from his hand and sent it clattering to the floor. "By the Garden and all who escaped it, we do not need more Sacrifices!" Yaarike put a hand on him again, his grip surprisingly strong for his great age, holding Viyeki in the chair when he would have scrambled after the fallen blade. "Listen. We have always had Sacrifices and they have always done their duty without question. But in the days and years ahead, we need something different. We need Builders."

Yaarike straightened up, then bent and retrieved the knife, placing it on the table before Viyeki with a deliberateness that was almost like ritual. "Here. It is yours. But do not hasten to end yourself. Think first and think carefully. Suno'ku and Akhenabi and Marshal Muyare—all of them are what we have always been. Even I am too old to change, though I can see the consequences. No, if you choose to live, it will be left to you and those still to come to find a new way, so that our people can survive in this world and still honor the Garden and those who have gone before."

Viyeki could only stare at the knife. His master's voice seemed to come from a long way away.

"I am leaving now," Yaarike said. "Back to my house and my servants and my family, to return here tomorrow and continue with rebuilding our Nakkiga. If you choose to live, you may also choose to denounce me. So be it. My crime is greater than any punishment the palace could devise, so whatever happens, be assured I am already my own torturer. The loss of a family jewel, however precious, is nothing to that. As for you, Viyeki-*tza* . . . what you will become is still an unanswered question." And then, surprisingly, Yaarike bowed with the deep courtesy given from one of high standing to an equal before turning and walking toward the door.

Viyeki sat in the chair, staring at the knife. Enough time passed that it became clear no guards had been summoned, that his master had done just as he had said he would. But Viyeki, his thoughts now weary, dull, and bruised like over-disciplined slaves, did not know what to do next. He had come to the order-house prepared to die. But what if he did not? How could he live each day from now on knowing that all he had thought simple and true was instead as tangled and foul as the roots of a rotting tree?

The lamp burned down until only a flicker lit the room, and still he sat.

When he walked through the front door, his wife and the servants were waiting. When Khimabu saw him she made a gesture of respect that had both fright and anger in it. "Husband! I feared something had happened to you!"

"Nothing has happened to me." He walked past her and placed the wrapped snow rose dagger back in its box upon the fireplace mantel. "Nothing is different. Nothing will change." But as he said it, he knew it was not true. Whatever might follow from this moment, everything had changed.

"I thought you might have been hurt or even killed in some accident," she said, but her tone suggested that she was almost disappointed that nothing had happened to be worth so much worrying.

He shook his head. He had left the house empty, a man who thought himself already dead. Now he was something else—a man who, as his master had said, could see around corners. A man who could think about the days still to come.

"Do not make a few hours of absence sound so dreadful, my wife," he said, and stood patiently while the servants hurried to remove his robes. "What terrible things could happen to me? I will get up tomorrow like all days, and go to work for my master and my people. After all, I am no Sacrifice, am I? No, I am a Builder."

Aerling, busy as always with his grisly task, scarcely looked up when Porto asked permission to leave the camp and bid Endri goodbye. Porto could scarcely remember the last time Aerling had put down the giant's head. He had removed its flesh and cleaned the skull with rock dust and snow until it almost gleamed, even in the dull northern light. It seemed a strange way to honor fallen comrades, but since he had been in the north, Porto had seen the same look Aerling wore on many other faces and had learned not to ask. If he had possessed a mirror, he suspected he would have seen it on his own face as well.

"We won't have time in the morning," Aerling said. "Go and do what you must now." And then he looked up, and there was something else on his face this time beside mere emptiness. "We have to *remember*. We all have to remember. So go and do your remembering."

Porto nodded.

Aerling looked from Porto down to the grinning, fanged skull. "I need to remember, too." He held up the skull with both hands, tilted it, then lowered it to his lap again and began scraping with his knife at a remaining lump of dried flesh where the neck had joined the head. "I'm going to take it home," he said. "I'm going to put it by the fireplace," he said. "That way I'll remember."

"I'll remember the men too, Thane," Porto said after a moment of silence. "Old Dragi and the rest. They died bravely. You can tell their families that."

Aerling shook his head. "No. I'm going to take this home so that when I wake up in the night sweating cold and my heart beating too fast, remembering that creature staring down at me, I'll look at this instead and I'll remember that it's dead. Dead." He nodded, as though he had proved a point, and went back to his scraping.

As Porto walked out of camp and back into the mountain's long shadow he could not help wondering that everything in the valley now looked so ordinary, so harmless. But for the immense tailing of boulders and broken stones that seemed to have been dumped against the mountain's base, there was no sign anything had happened here for centuries. The gate was buried, the monsters inside now invisible. The trees dripped with melting snow. Even the sounds of his comrades readying for departure seemed to fade away.

He made his way through the abandoned grove, past trees so tall he thought they must have grown before men came to Osten Ard. It was even more quiet here, like an empty church. He hoped the winter would remain at bay until he had at least made his way out of cold Rimmersgard. Porto had a fierce longing for the true southern sun, for the sound of the ocean and the smell of the harbor. He might have been knighted by the duke of Elvritshalla, but he had never felt so Perdruinese as he did now, surrounded by Northmen and the great cold mountains. He could not imagine that, once home, he would ever leave Ansis Pelippé again. Not to fight, that was certain. Not to see friends and comrades die.

Porto saw from the edge of the clearing that something was wrong with Endri's grave. As he neared it he made out that it had been torn open and his heart dropped—the stone cairn he had built had clearly not been enough to keep the scavengers away. Then another thought crept into his mind and his innards went icy cold. He stood at the edge of the pit and looked at the way the stones had been pushed outward around the mound and the way the earth itself had fallen in.

He had prayed Endri's grave had been beyond the Norns' terrible spells, but the marks in the earth of hands digging upward like the claws of a mole told him otherwise. The hole had been emptied, but not from outside. The chances were good that if he had risen, Endri had been burned with the others.

Porto was turning to go when he glanced to the southern side of the clearing. In a knot of young trees, none of them much more than twice the height of a man, leaned an upright, unmoving man-shape, sagging like a scarecrow in a Nabbanai field.

"Oh, dear God," Porto moaned softly, and made the sign of the Tree on his breast. "Sweet Usires preserve us."

As he drew closer to the body he saw that the garments did indeed look like Endri's, stained with earth and blotched with melted snow. But when he was only a yard or so away he saw what had stopped the dead man here, so far from everyone else, so far from both the living and the other spell-raised dead. Endri's red Harborside scarf was tangled in low branches and had pulled tight around the corpse's throat like a hangman's noose. The young man's head hung down, hiding his face, but the skin Porto could see was mottled and black.

He reached out toward the body, doing his best to ignore the terrible stench, disgust and pity fighting in his trembling hands. Endri was facing south. He had not been moving toward the Norn summons, or even toward his living fellows, Porto realized, and tears sprang into his eyes as he understood. The dead man had been trying to go home.

Then Endri moved.

Porto jumped back in horror, and when he made the Tree this time it was as though he stabbed at his own breast. The dead fingers twitched and the corpse tried to take a stumbling step, but it was held fast. Porto could not move either, though no scarf held him.

The corpse lifted its head, revealing the full horror of weeks in the ground. Something in the ruined eyes seemed to recognize Porto, because the dead hand rose as though trying to touch him.

"God in His mercy, what did they do to you?" Porto whispered.

He could not stand to look at the corrupted, collapsing face a moment longer. He drew his sword and hacked as hard as he could at the thing's neck, but was unable to swing his blade cleanly among the encroaching trees. After many more clumsy swipes, the head at last parted from the neck and thumped to the ground. The body slipped from the restraining scarf and tumbled down beside it.

"Now you can go home," he said as he stood over the corpse, though it was hard for him to speak. "Go in peace."

Porto carried first the body and then the head back to its grave, fighting down the urge to retch at the ripe smell of death, trying to remember that this was Endri his friend, who deserved better than he had been given. Then he went back for the scarf, untangling it carefully from the branches. At the grave, he placed the head atop the body and then carefully wrapped the scarf around Endri's neck again, the beloved scarf the boy's mother had woven, to hide the raw and ragged wounds Porto's sword had made.

When he had filled in the grave, and had again piled the heavy stones atop it, he kneeled to pray, then said farewell to his friend for the second and last time. When he was done, Porto climbed to his feet and walked slowly back to camp.

Appendices

An Explanation . . .

***An Explanation of the Fairy People Known as Sithi,
and their Cousins the Norns,
as well as their sometime Servants, the Ocean Children.***

Excerpted from *A History of the Erkynlandish People and Their Great Capital,
the Hayholt* by Tiamak of Erchester, Counselor to the High Throne

Despite appearing to be of two quite separate races, the golden-skinned
Sithi and the Norns with their faces and limbs as pale as snow both belong
to a single fairy race which was once called the Keida'ya, which in their
tongue means "Children of the Witchwood Trees."

Long before men recorded history, the ancient Keida'ya lived (or so we
are told and must believe, for no mortal man was there to see it) in a far-
away land called *Venyha Do'sae*, the Garden that was Lost. And although
the reasons for the Keida'ya leaving that place and coming here are mostly
unknown to us, stories told to our own High King Seoman when he lived
among the Sithi, and to ancient travelers like Caias Sterna of Nabban, help
us to know something of those elder days before the immortals came to
Osten Ard. The Keida'ya lived in a city on the shore of a great sea, and by
their own account lived there for a hundred centuries or more in peace
and prosperity. But then something came to break that peace, a foe or
plague known only as Unbeing. The Keida'ya fought against it, but the
power of this Unbeing was too great, and at last they were forced, with
the help of their magical servants the Tinukeda'ya, to build eight great
ships and escape the Garden that they had lost to Unbeing.

So they came to our land of Osten Ard. The immortals claim they came here long before the first of our own ancestors arrived, but since that goes flatly against the teaching of the Aedonite Church, few scholars accept this as truth. Still, it is known from writings that survived the fall of Khand that even in the days of that impossibly remote empire the *Hyan,* or "Immortal Ones" as they were named by the Khandians, had already built great cities across the world, from the distant north Trollfells to the southern islands.

What also is known beyond doubt is that the Keida'ya saw the growth of the Nabbanai Imperium from the earliest confederations of tiny fief-doms to its world-spanning heights. The co-existence of the two empires, mortal and immortal, was not without strife, but the Keida'ya, even after they divided themselves into two great clans, the *Zida'ya* and *Hikeda'ya,* their names for Sithi and Norn, respectively, largely kept their attention fixed upon their own domains and ceded all the lands and mortal men that did not interest them to the expanding Imperium.

Like the long-vanished Khandians, we of the current age call the Keida'ya and their component clans "immortals," but believe from what we have learned that they are merely long-lived, not truly undying. They can be killed, of course, or else the great war just ended would have gone against us, and it seems that at last, after many centuries, a form of old age finally overtakes them. Eventually even these ancient creatures die, although at an age hard for men to believe.

King Seoman met the revered matriarch of the Sithi, Amerasu, called Ship-Born, and the king tells that despite her birth on one of the crafts that brought her people to Osten Ard countless centuries ago, she seemed no older than a woman of handsome and healthy middle age. She died violently, so how long she might have otherwise lived is unknown, but it is agreed by all that Queen Utuk'ku, mistress of the Norns, is older still—she might have been Amerasu's great-grandmother—and that Utuk'ku once lived in the legendary Garden itself before her people fled. The Norn Queen at least does appear to be immortal, or as close to it as any of her kind have yet come . . .

[material excised here]

. . . At some time between the rise of the mortal empire of Khand and the later dominion of the Nabbanai Imperators, some conflict split the immortal Keida'ya into two races, the golden creatures we know as the Sithi, or *Zida'ya*—in their tongue the name means "Dawn Children"—and the pale, deadly *Hikeda'ya*, which seems to translate to "Cloud Children," the enemies men call "Norns" because of their home in the far north.

In the years since the Rimmersmen came across the western oceans with their iron weapons and destroyed the peace of both men and fairies and captured the immortals' palace of Asu'a (which now exists only as ruins beneath the castle called Hayholt in Erkynland) the Sithi deserted their great cities and retreated to the forests and wastelands and other remote places of Osten Ard. The Norns, still ruled by their deathless queen, Utuk'ku, also fled before the violence of the newly-arrived Rimmersmen, and the last of that fairy-clan survives in the hidden fastness of their northern mountain fortress, Nakkiga, the last of the great cities built by the immortals . . .

[material excised here]

. . . One last race must be spoken of, because the Keida'ya did not come to these lands alone, but brought with them their servants and slaves, the Tinukeda'ya, or "Ocean Children," who because of their many forms are sometimes considered together by mortal scholars under the name "Changelings." The Tinukeda'ya, though they share an origin in the Garden with the Sithi and Norns, are not all of one general appearance, as is true with the golden and white clans of the Keida'ya, who are almost uniformly slender and manlike, with large, upturned eyes and narrow faces. But some Tinukeda'ya are as big as mountain giants, and seem to serve only as beasts of burden. Others are small, fitted for work in narrow underground tunnels, as though Heaven itself had crafted them with that purpose in mind. In truth, many of the Tinukeda'ya grew skilled not just in delving but in crafting stone and other arts, and served the Keida'ya by building their great cities. Some even say that the Eight Great Ships that sailed away from the dying Garden and brought the immortals here were largely built by their Tinukeda'ya servitors, but that is not known for certain. However, High King Seoman was told by a noble of the highest Sithi clan that holding the Tinukeda'ya in slavery and bringing them to our lands against their will, was his people's greatest shame. In time many of these "Ocean Children" escaped their masters, and it is said that like the

Sithi and the Norns, many still survive in places remote from mankind. Others live among us, like the Niskies of Nabban, who use their songs to protect the ships they serve.

So it is that three tribes of immortals share this world with mankind, the Hikeda'ya pale as death, the Zida'ya as golden as the sun, and the Tinukeda'ya in all their manifold sizes and shapes. Perhaps someday these fairy-folk will be gone, and remain only as a memory among our kind, a dim, partial tale like The Lion-Fighter of Old Khand. Or perhaps it is too soon to write their epitaph, and they will rise again one day from the shadowed places to contend with us once more. We know little of them for certain, but we do know that none of them love men, and some despise us utterly.

Glossary of Terms

PEOPLE

RIMMERSMEN

Aerling Surefoot—leader of the Mountain Goats

Alfwer—Rimmersgard thane (baron) of Heitskeld

Brenyar—leader of the army's carpenters

Brindur—thane (baron) of Norskog

Dragi—the oldest Mountain Goat

Elvrit—founder of Rimmersgard

Fani—one of Brindur's Skoggeymen

Fanngrun—a Rimmersgard noble of Vattinland, cousin to former King Jormgrun

Fingil Red-Hand—king of Rimmersgard, descendant of Elvrit, conqueror of Asu'a

Finnbogi—a Rimmersgard thane (baron) killed at the Hayholt

Floki—son of Brindur

Isbeorn—thane (baron) of Hatgres Dale, later Duke of Elvritshalla and Isgrimnur's father

Geli—son of Skali Sharpnose of Kaldskryke, late enemy of Isgrimnur

Gutrun—Duchess of Elvritshalla, Isgrimnur's wife

Haddi—one of Isgrimnur's house-carls

Helgrimnur Stonehand—Rimmersgard thane (baron)

Helvnur—nephew of Helgrimnur Stonehand

Hjortur—in charge of the Donkey (catapult)

Isgrimnur—Duke of Elvritshalla, ruler (beneath the High Throne) of all Rimmersgard

Isorn—Isgrimnur's son, killed in the Storm King's War

Jormgrun—King of Rimmersgard, overthrown by John of Erkynland

Kár—one of Isgrimnur's house-carls

Kolbjorn—a Vestiman

Marri Ironbeard—one of Brindur's Skoggeymen

Sludig (aka Sludig Two-Axes)—one of Isgrimnur's most loyal men, a veteran of the Storm King's War

Unnar—a Rimmersgard thane (baron)

Vigri—jarl (earl) of Enggidal

HIKEDA'YA (NORNS)

Ekimeniso of the Brooding Eye—late husband of Queen Utuk'ku, leader of Clan Iyora

Enduyo of Kementari—Viyeki's ancestor, a palace functionary, founder of Clan Enduya

Hamakho Wormslayer—founder of the Hamakha Clan and ancestor of Queen Utuk'ku

Hayyano—League Commander of the Order of Sacrifice

Hiki—High Celebrant, Zuniyabe's predecessor."

Jasiyo—Khimabu's gossipy cousin

Jikkyo, Lord, a high noble of the Order of Song

Khimabu—Viyeki's wife, of Clan Daesa

Kuju-Vayo—an official of the Order of Echoes

Mimiti—one of the Queen's Whisperers

Kusayu—eleventh High Celebrant

Luk'kaya—High Gatherer, Magister of the Harvesters

Miga Seyt-Jinnata, Lady—a High Scribe of the Order of Chroniclers

Muyare—Marshal of Sacrifices, Suno'ku's relative, replaces Ekisuno as leader of armies

Nekhaneyo—a noble of Clan Shudra

Nijika—a Host Singer of the Order of Song

Pratiki—a "prince-templar" of Clan Hamakha, Queen Utuk'ku's clan

Ruho'o—a Governor of the Order of Builders

Ruzayo Falcon's Eye—famous Hikeda'ya hero of the Giant Wars

Sasigi—member of the Order of Builders

Sulen—the thirteenth High Celebrant

Suno'ku, General—an important leader of the Order of Sacrifice, member
   of Clan Iyora
Twenty-Four, The—famous heroes who fought at Ruzayo's side
Tzayin-Kha—a Host Singer of the Order of Song
Viyeki—Host Foreman of the Order of Builders, member of Clan Enduyo
Yaarike—High Magister of the Order of Builders, leader of Clan Kijada
Yaaro-Mon—Yaarike's great-grandfather, a fugitive from the Garden
Yayano of the Pointing Finger—a noble Celebrant, kin to Zuniyabe
Zuniyabe—the sixteenth High Celebrant

OTHERS

Andoro—Porto's brother
Ayaminu—a Sitha, originally from Hikehikayo
Crexis, Imperator—the ruler of Nabban at the time of the execution of
   Usires Aedon
Endri—a soldier from Harborside in Ansis Pelippé in Perdruin
Halawe, Lord—Perdruinese noble who went to fight at the Hayholt, killed
   by bukken. Endri was one of his "recruits
Miriamele, Queen—at the time of this story the High Queen of Osten Ard
Porto—a soldier from The Rocks in Ansis Pelippé
Sida—Porto's wife
Simon, King—aka "Seoman Snowlock," at the time of this story the High
   King of Osten Ard
Tinio (short for "Portinio")—Sida and Porto's son
Usires Aedon—the martyr who was executed on The Holy Tree in Nab-
   han but came back to life, celebrated as the child of God

PLACES, CREATURES, THINGS

Asu'a—the Sithi and Norn name for their ancient city, currently buried
   beneath the mortal's castle called the Hayholt
Avenue of Triumph—a processional road leading to the Sancellan Mahistrevis in Nabban

Black Water Field—a great common square in Nakkiga, at the foot of the Tearfall

Bridge of Exodus—a structure in Nakkiga-That-Was

Cold Root—Suno'ku's sword

Cold Leaf—Suno'ku's dagger

Dirt Goblins—informal name for "Bukken" (Rimmersgard name) or "diggers"—burrowing, manlike creatures

Elder Halls—older cemeteries

Field of Banners—the muster-place of the Hikeda'ya armies outside of the mountain, now a bare spot in Nakkiga-That-Was

Field of Stone Flowers—memorial to Queen Utuk'ku's most beloved dead

Gatherer's Temple—a building at the heart of Tzo, in the Lost Garden

Glittering Passage—the great main boulevard on the first tier of Nakkiga

Grayflame—sword of the Hikeda'ya hero, Hamakho

Green Angel Tower—mortal name for the last Sithi structure at the Hayholt; the tower collapsed at the end of the Storm King's War

Gyrfalcon Castles—fortresses built on the side of Ur-Nakkiga Moon Festival Canal—one of several canals, now dry and obscured, that once crisscrossed Nakkiga-That-Was

"The Musician and the Soldier"—an old Keida'ya song from Tumet'ai

Hall of Sleeping Sacrifices—a tomb

Hikehikayo—once a city inhabited by both Sithi and Norn, now deserted, located in the Whitefell Mountains west of Nakkiga

House of Sleep—places where the dead are prepared for entombment

Hringholt—a province of Rimmersgard

Kei-mi—an extract of witchwood bark

Kementari—a Keida'ya city, now ruined, on the island of Warinsten

keta-yi'indra—a deep, deathlike, rejuvenative sleep utilized by very old, very skilled immortals

Kraki's Field—battle site in Rimmersgard near Hernystiri border

Kvalnir—Isgrimnur's sword

Lake Rumiya—lake on the northeastern side of the mountain Ur-Nakkiga (or Stormspike, as the Rimmersmen call it)

Nakkiga-That-Was—the ruined city outside the mountain, once also inhabited by the Hikeda'ya

Norskog—Brindur's home, next to Skoggey

Ostheim—Aerling's home city in Rimmersgard

Queen's Gallery—a structure in Nakkiga-That-Was

Royal Way—ancient ceremonial road through Nakkiga-That-Was, now ruined

Silent Palace—the complex containing the Elder Halls

Skuggi Pass—near the border of Northern Rimmersgard and the Norn lands

Castle Tangleroot—a ruined Hikeda'ya border fort

Sky Palace—an observatory in Nakkiga-That-Was where the Hikeda'ya once watched the stars

Sky Dance—Hikeda'ya term for the changing constellations

St. Asla's church—Rimmersgard church where Geli, Skali's son, took sanctuary

Street of Eight Ships—a wide avenue in Nakkiga

Temple of the Martyrs.—building at the heart of Nakkiga, famous for its water clock and bells

The Cold, Slow Halls—a place of punishment in the depths of Nakkiga

The Heart of What Was Lost—a gem brought out of the Garden by Yaaro-Mon

Saint Tunato's Day—known in the north as St. Tunath's Day, Decander the 21st

Three Ravens Tower—a fortress built into the wall guarding the inner Norn lands

Well of Eternity—also known as The Well of the Breathing Harp, at the heart of Nakkiga

White Bear and Stars—Duke Isgrimnur's family standard

Witiko'ya—a ferocious, wolflike creature

Yedade's Box—a device by which Hikeda'ya children are sorted

WORDS

Hikeda'yei!—literally, "You Hikeda'ya people!"

Ogu Minurato—Hikeda'ya name for "Tangleroot Castle"

Sturmrspeik—Rimmerspakk name for "Stormspike"

Venga Do'tzae—Hikeda'ya version of Zida'ya name meaning "The Lost Garden" or "The Blessed Garden"—the abandoned ancient home of the Keida'ya (the combined race)

Shu'do-tkzayha—Hikeda'ya version of Zida'ya name for mortals, "Sudhoda'ya," meaning "Sunset-children"

Franchise

The Golden Arches in Black America

MARCIA CHATELAIN

LIVERIGHT PUBLISHING CORPORATION

A Division of W. W. Norton & Company

Independent Publishers Since 1923

New York London

For Mark Yapelli and his mother, Elaine Desow Yapelli

CONTENTS

Franchise

From Sit-In to Drive-Thru

Police and National Guard forces swarmed the McDonald's on Florissant Avenue in Ferguson, Missouri, about one week after police officer Darren Wilson killed Michael Brown, an unarmed teenager, on August 9, 2014. Photo by Scott Olson / Getty Images.

"Hands up . . ."

"Don't shoot!"

Across the streets of Ferguson, Missouri, protesters and mourners shouted the call-and-response dirge in memory of Michael Brown Jr. On August 9, 2014, police officer Darren Wilson shot and killed the teenager while he was walking through an apartment complex with a friend. After six of Wilson's bullets struck the recent high school graduate, his body remained uncollected and uncovered for nearly four hours. Residents captured the morbid scene—with their cellphones and their memories—and shared them across social media. Brown's death and all it represented—police violence and disregard, racism, and poverty—catalyzed the

nascent Movement for Black Lives and sparked a global conversation about American justice. By the next evening, seasoned and first-time protesters joined Ferguson residents on the town's main drag, Florissant Avenue. Some carried signs demanding JUSTICE FOR MICHAEL BROWN! Others linked arms with clergy members, belting out civil-rights-era freedom songs. Savvy political leaders and grief-stricken family members sat for interviews with the reporters who traveled to Missouri searching for new angles on the story. A small group of provocateurs brought Molotov cocktails, glass bottles, and matches to the streets. All of these people were met by local and county police, and later the Missouri National Guard, armed with tear gas, rubber bullets, and tanks. The gear was courtesy of the U.S. Department of Defense's 1033 Program, which outfits domestic police forces with weapons unused in Afghanistan and Iraq.[1]

For weeks, traditional news outlets and amateur digital storytellers broadcast updates on the uprising that disrupted life in the town of 21,000. Ferguson's landmarks became familiar scenes for the millions who followed the crisis on their televisions and smartphones. Newscasters appeared live in front of the QuikTrip gas station that was burned down the day after Brown's death. Facebook and Twitter curated the images of makeshift memorials to Brown in the center and on the edges of Canfield Road where he died. But, of all the places that represented Ferguson in the public eye that summer, the McDonald's restaurant at 9131 West Florissant best symbolized the interplay between racial justice and the marketplace in America, past and present.[2]

The Florissant Avenue McDonald's was both an escape from the uprising and one of its targets. On some days, the McDonald's was a beacon. Reporters found live electrical outlets to charge their computers and Wi-Fi to send emails to their editors. Demonstrators took breaks from marching and ordered cold drinks as the daytime temperature hovered around 80 degrees. Police officers, overheated by their uniforms of domestic war, found air-conditioned relief as they awaited shift changes. In the parking lot, television camera crews arranged tripods. Organizers distrib-

uted leaflets. At the counter, cashiers managed their regular duties while also attending to an increase in requests for bottles of milk, used to relieve the sting from the chemicals launched into the late summer sky. The manager kept a television tuned to the news and watched alongside patrons when President Barack Obama addressed the nation about "the passions and the anger" that had been ignited in Ferguson. The McDonald's was a center of that passion and anger too. One night, two journalists were arrested for trespassing after they questioned why they were being asked to leave an ostensibly open restaurant.[3] On the night of August 17, a crowd broke the front window of the McDonald's; some say they were fleeing another tear gas attack and needed more milk. Others wrote them off as looters. Eventually, calm was restored in Ferguson, and in the recap of what happened in the St. Louis exurb, the Florissant McDonald's was portrayed as a bright spot and an anchor for the community.

The Ferguson moment was not the first time that McDonald's played a major role in a racial crisis. In fact, the Florissant Avenue McDonald's—as a franchise location owned and operated by an African American businessman—is the descendant of a somewhat bizarre but incredibly powerful marriage between a fast-food behemoth and the fight for civil rights. After the assassination of Martin Luther King Jr. in 1968 and the ensuing urban upheavals, the movement for racial justice pivoted its focus toward black business ownership. Hamburger, fried chicken, and taco chains eagerly met the gaze of those interested in using business development as a strategy to quell unrest, and introduced fast-food franchising to inner-city black communities. This book tells the hidden history of the intertwined relationship between the struggle for civil rights and the expansion of the fast-food industry.

The United States is the birthplace of some of the world's most successful fast-food brands, as well as the home of its most enthusiastic eaters. On any given day, an estimated one-third of all American adults is eating something at a fast-food restaurant.[4] Millions of people start their mornings with paper-wrapped English muffin breakfast sandwiches, order burritos hastily secured in foil

for lunch, and end their evenings with extravalue dinners consumed in cars. People of all ages and backgrounds enjoy fast food, but it does not mean the same thing to all people. For African Americans, the history of the development of the fast-food industry and its presence in their communities reveals the complicated ways that race is lived in America. Racism constrains choices and limits opportunities, from how much you earn to how long you live. Race also informs where you can sit comfortably and what foods are available to you. Even after segregation was legally dissolved by the Civil Rights Act of 1964, African Americans were still left with a low ceiling hovering over their social and economic mobility. The restrictions that emerge because of race and class would place African Americans in a close relationship with an industry built on the idea that food could be delivered cheaply, uniformly, and without consideration of a person's social station. Fast food is a prism for understanding race, shifts in the movement for civil rights, the dissemination of black culture, and racial capitalism—the deep connections between the development of modern capitalism and racist subjugation and oppression—since the 1960s.[5] Before fast food became a quotidian fixture of American life in shopping malls, schools, airports, and rest stops, it was an object of curiosity, fascination, and even hope for many black communities.

Today, fast-food restaurants are hyperconcentrated in the places that are the poorest and most racially segregated.[6] Due to its saturation in black America, fast food is often identified as the culprit among the research on high rates of obesity, diabetes, and hypertension among blacks. Since the early 2000s, studies have focused on the relationship between access to healthy foods and the nutrition color line. Researchers have warned that a black child born in the year 2000 has a 53% chance of developing type 2 diabetes; the likelihood of a white child developing the potentially fatal disease is less than 30%.[7] In 2015, nearly 75% of African-American adults and 33% of black adolescents were considered overweight or obese. Blacks were 1.4 times more likely than their white counterparts to

be obese.[8] Economic inequality exacerbates health inequality, and poor and working-class black families often lack access to quality preventative health care. In the year that Ferguson entered the national consciousness, the average white family had the equivalent of one month's income in liquid savings, while a black family could rely on only five days of pay.[9]

In addition to the well-circulated results of health studies, scrutiny of the fast-food industry has come from journalists, documentarians, and even customers. The publication of Eric Schlosser's *Fast Food Nation: The Dark Side of the All-American Meal* in 2001 and the release of the Academy Award–nominated documentary *Super Size Me* four years later helped raise awareness about the fast food industry's impact on the health of people of color.[10] In 2002, two teenagers from the Bronx filed a lawsuit against McDonald's for causing their obesity and diabetes. By 2010, when former First Lady Michelle Obama introduced her Let's Move! initiative to promote improved child nutrition and healthier school lunches, the nation was well versed in the vocabulary of healthy eating: "whole grains," "low fat," and "organic." Racialized health disparities—as well as the dearth of grocery stores in poor communities of color—have inspired a food justice and nutrition education movement. Farmers' markets now occupy empty city lots. Nutritionists visit inner-city schools to teach children the difference between mustard greens and kale. Public service announcements interrupt family-friendly television programs to remind parents to encourage good eating habits at home. The message is clear, but the problems persist.

While health warriors laudably fight an army of trans fats, kids' meals, and splashy advertisements, few have considered how exactly fast food became a staple of black diets. Many of the critiques and responses to the impact of fast food on communities of color focus solely on food and not the infrastructure that surrounds food systems. In a response to the failed lawsuit filed by the Bronx teenagers, the *New York Times* editorial page rehearsed an argument that is often expressed in conversations about race and

health. "That Americans are getting heavier is especially hard to deny the day after Thanksgiving. But America's weight problem has less to do with holiday binges than with everyday choices and circumstances. That's especially true for children, who are gaining weight in epidemic numbers, particularly in minority communities." The editorial concluded that while more data on child obesity are needed, for the time being, children should be encouraged to become more physically active. "In many low-income minority neighborhoods, fried carryout is a cinch to find, but affordable fresh produce and nutritious food are not. Those same neighborhoods often lack many safe public places to play and exercise."[11] At best, these kinds of reflections are simply shortsighted and affirm what we already know about the importance of healthy food and exercise for all people. Unfortunately, this type of analysis ignores history. It presupposes that people of color have a natural affinity for fast food. What are the "everyday choices and circumstances" for black Americans? Why is "fried carryout" so easy to get? Why is "fresh produce" a rarity? What failures have created cities with few "safe public places to play and exercise"? Instead of simply evaluating the fact that so many African Americans patronize fast food today, it is far more instructive to consider what has undergirded the symbiotic relationship between African-American communities and the fast food industry.[12]

For too long, research on race and fast food has placed the onus solely on black palates and parents for the dismal state of black health. Without an understanding of how we got here, the food justice movement will never move beyond the idea of individual choice and continue to ignore structural disequilibrium. Knowing the caloric content and fat grams in a cheeseburger from Krystal is important. Educating the public on how much of the recommended daily allowance of sodium is exceeded by an order of Burger King onion rings is helpful. Promoting healthy lifestyles can improve lives. But understanding how shifts in the priorities of the mid-century civil rights struggle, changes in federal policy on business and urban development, and the boom years of fast food converged in the lives of black America is equally critical.

* * *

Fast food restaurants were, and are, able to expand quickly because of the franchising model, which draws upon an old business practice and adapts it for a modern world. Most business scholars believe that the roots of franchising can be traced to the Catholic Church in the Middle Ages, when tax collectors were allowed to keep a portion of revenues retrieved from citizens. Fast forward several hundred years to the late nineteenth century, when the current practice of franchising began with Coca-Cola. First made in 1888, Coca-Cola (the franchisor) licensed businesses (franchisees) to mix, bottle, and sell their refreshing sugary beverage in drugstores, and later restaurants, across the country. Environmental historian Bart Elmore has called this method Coca-Cola capitalism, in which a company relies on a massive "outsourcing strategy to build a mass marketing giant." This form of commercial development allows corporations to pass on their liabilities to third-party suppliers, franchisees, and to some degree, local governments. Cities eager to attract businesses subsidize business growth through the preparation of land, by providing increased policing, and by offering tax breaks.[13] Franchising is big business in America because it may be the most American idea in the world. An individual with no formal training or education can become a business owner— maybe even a millionaire—with only an owner's manual and sheer will. Franchising was the channel for converting a couple of ice-cream parlors or a few hot dog outfits into multibillion-dollar businesses, with the power to influence supply chains, workers' wages, and global tastes.[14]

The fast food family tree reads like the book of Genesis, with businesses begetting other businesses in rapid succession. Although not the oldest member of the family, McDonald's looms as an ambitious offspring who managed to outpace and outshine its elders. Fast food's mainstay, the hamburger, was once considered a low-quality food product designed to nourish workers and the poor. Cash-strapped laborers could purchase these sandwiches from carts and stands in urban centers, near work sites and bustling

downtowns. White Castle helped popularize, and perhaps dignify, the burger with signature "thin, one-inch-square patties," which came to be known as sliders.[15] In the pioneering era of fast food, corporate marriages reconfigured the blood lines that fueled the franchise race. In 1919, Lodi, California's A&W root beer entered the beverage franchising game, alongside Coca-Cola, and would later try its hand at burgers and other fare.[16] The partnership of Allen and Wright—the A and the W—inspired one of their franchisees, J. Willard Marriott, to strike out on his own and establish a national hotel chain.

Burgers paved the way for the expansion of other brands that started in small towns before setting up shop along highway exits or in newly built suburban plazas. The first national burger chain, Billy Ingram and Walt Anderson's White Castle—inspired by Chicago's iconic Water Tower building—was established in 1921. White Castle innovated many of the practices that would be revolutionized by McDonald's, including streamlining and centralizing their supplies in warehouses, creating assembly-line consistency across its locations, and defending its corporate identity. White Castle's commercial success and ability to convert a public once suspicious of ground beef into fans of the slider inspired copycats, including White Tower and Royal Castle. Royal Castle—an evil twin in the franchising origin story—eventually surpassed White Castle in numbers of location. White Castle is still with us today—and many iconic brands are protected—because of their pursuit of their imitators in court. The outcome of a 1937 Supreme Court case determined that White Tower couldn't copy the design, color scheme, and style of White Castle's offerings. They were also told they couldn't use the derivative slogan "Take Home a Bagful," as long as White Castle urged its customers to "Buy 'Em by the Sack."[17]

Royal Castle was later absorbed by a fried chicken concern promoted by performer Minnie Pearl and gospel standout Mahalia Jackson. Minnie Pearl's and Mahalia Jackson's Glori-Fried formed after their founders took note of the immense popularity of Kentucky Fried Chicken, established when Harland Sanders visited

Pete and Arline Harman in Utah; their bestselling chicken was "made Southern" in Louisville, Kentucky, with a move in 1954. Dave Thomas, an Army veteran in Ohio, worked for the real Colonel Sanders, before he joined two endeavors that were once eponymous and are now largely forgotten, Arthur Treacher's Fish & Chips and Burger Chef.[18] He finally found his stride with his own burger franchise, Wendy's, named for his daughter. In 1954, Ray Kroc entered business with Maurice and Richard McDonald, and he built the foundations of the world's most powerful burger. Glen Bell and Neal Baker, founders of Taco Bell, like the McDonald brothers, were from San Bernardino and turned to their interpretation of Mexican food after a failed attempt to compete with the McDonalds' burgers. Glen's Taco Bell begot Del Taco, which was opened by Ed Hackbarth, a former Taco Bell employee who loved eating at the original San Bernardino McDonald's location.[19] El Pollo Loco was later adopted by the Denny's family, and it produced a child that was one of the first nonfried chicken outlets in the country.[20]

West of San Bernardino, Harry and Esther Snyder sold their hamburgers and French fries in the town of Baldwin Park to workers, and they assured customers they could "get in and get out" quickly. The Snyders established In-N-Out Burger in 1948. They were encouraged to enter the business by their friends Carl and Margaret Karcher. The Karchers turned the hot dog stands they started in 1941 into a barbecue enterprise in 1945, which began offering hamburgers a year later. The family's Carl's Jr. international franchise would always share a special bond with the geographically bound In-N-Out, which never became a franchise.[21]

The founding generation worked hard, made wise decisions, and made the most of every opportunity. For many of the first families of fast food franchising, they were connected not only by place (many of them were Southern Californians), but they were also racially homogenous and privileged in their time. The people who established the franchises that are so easily identified by their logos, their slogans, and the distinct taste of their French fries over a competitors' were all white Americans whose whiteness worked

in their favor. They were able to benefit from a host of financial and social pathways for their businesses to start, expand, rebound from setbacks, and remain within their family networks. Shortly after the federal government declared that their establishments would not be allowed to refuse customers on the basis of race in 1964, their progeny—the franchises—would slowly accept non-white members.

The relationship between franchisor and franchisee is like a distorted parent and child bond, in which the parent sets the rules and the child pays all the household bills. At its heart, franchising is based on expectations set by a parent company (Subway, Hilton Worldwide Holdings Inc., Roto-Rooter Plumbing and Water Cleanup) and an individual entity (Jane Doe, Bob Smith, Doe-Smith Enterprises) to operate an outlet of said business. Franchises do the same thing in different places; they yield fortunes birthed from uniformity. A Dunkin' Donuts store in Rhode Island and Illinois should have the same menu, save a few regional specificities (like the copious packets of sugar and half-and-half that Ocean Staters like in their "plain coffees"). The uniforms at the Chick-fil-A in Oklahoma City are the same ones worn in Manhattan, although the workers wearing the signature red-and-black ensembles most likely earn different wages. Save Alaska and Hawaii, you should be able to get nearly identical deals on Little Caesars pizza in Las Vegas as you would on Long Island. The success of the fast food franchise model has inspired other retail and service categories. Franchise newcomers like boutique exercise studios Orangetheory Fitness and SoulCycle, and speedy beauty service providers Drybar and Massage Envy, may have little in common with their chicken-frying franchise cousins. But they can be just as costly to invest in, requiring fees up to a million dollars or more, and they are governed by the same laws and regulations.

Franchisees can make good money, but the franchising system requires skill at navigating an unequal power relationship. After fees are paid—ranging from tens of thousands to millions of dollars—and documents are signed stating that a franchisee will do business in the ways that the headquarters have determined—

the dream can begin.[22] Jane and Bob must be prepared to assume the liabilities and risks of business ownership that the corporate heads of Taco Bueno in Farmers Branch, Texas, or Domino's in Ann Arbor Charter Township, Michigan, never have to consider. Jane and Bob deal with it all. They have to file a police report after a robbery during the lunchtime rush. They have to determine when to close if a hurricane is coming and then clean up after it hits. They need to know how to respond to upticks in the cost of flour, which leads to hamburger buns cutting deeper into the bottom line. If Jane and Bob are people of color, they are more likely to do business in a community with higher insurance costs or receive less attention from the parent company, despite earning the most profits in their chain's system.

* * *

Among the brands that have emerged in the fast food franchise world, none has eclipsed McDonald's in influence. With more than 14,000 restaurants in the United States, and another 23,000 locations in 100 countries, McDonald's has affected the ways Americans eat, play, and work. Journalists, business historians, economists, and cultural critics have all investigated and written about the chain, which was established as a franchise company in 1955. Yet, despite the wide body of Golden Arches scholarship, few acknowledge, let alone analyze, the way that McDonald's ingratiated itself to black America, and the ways that black America has been integral in McDonald's many feats. Due to its age, size, and footprint, McDonald's looms large in this history of fast food and race in America, and other fast food chains followed McDonald's path as they identified and cultivated a black consumer market and franchisee corps.

The roots of the contemporary conversation about race and fast food begin with the founding of McDonald's in the 1940s. When Maurice and Richard McDonald established their hamburger drive-in, they may have been unconcerned with the racial politics of their age. Yet segregation, racial restrictions on housing, discriminatory financial lending, and the growth of a highway

system that decimated African-American communities allowed the men all the advantages necessary to establish a formidable business. The original McDonald's was able to survive through World War II and thrive in the postwar economic boom. The restaurant's accessible menu coupled with their family-friendly dining experience ensured their marketability and profitability. As the brothers' small business evolved into an industry-defining franchise, McDonald's was also shaping the country's definition of what historian Lizabeth Cohen calls a "consumer republic." Cohen argues that as consumption of goods and services rose in the 1950s, Americans began to see "their nation as the model for the world of a society committed to mass consumption and what were assumed to be its far-reaching benefits." These benefits extended beyond the department store or the local five-and-dime shop. In the consumer republic, Cohen asserts, the marketplace "also dictated most central dimensions of postwar society, including the political economy, as well as the political culture." [23]

African Americans, who were systematically denied citizenship in the consumer republic, used the marketplace to make claims for their rights. Since the dawn of the twentieth century, the National Association for the Advancement of Colored People, the Urban League, the Congress of Racial Equality, and the Southern Christian Leadership Conference all organized mass-movement campaigns to deny businesses their dollars if they operated on a segregated basis or failed to employ members of the communities that supported them. Activists targeted fast food chains, drugstore lunch counters, soda fountains, and diners, in a crusade to end separate but equal dining, especially in the South. Their strategies connected consumer power to citizenship rights and effectively expanded black access to the marketplace. Eventually, the focused and steady activism of great orators, skilled organizers, and the will of everyday people upended segregation. What was to come next? Legally, the state was no longer a party to excluding blacks from the schoolhouse or the snack bar. But equal opportunity and antipoverty legislation, no matter how strongly supported by a president or a Congress, could only do so much. Rather than agi-

tating for more generous social spending or suggesting that elected leaders champion civil and economic rights more vociferously, a cadre of American leaders across the ideological spectrum determined that private business would be the answer to the unfinished business of securing equality for all.

As African-American consumers were gaining rights in the marketplace, the fast food franchise frenzy was underway. *Barron's* reported in the summer of 1969—five years after the federal government banned discrimination in public accommodations—that restaurant franchises rose from a "scant dozen or two in the postwar years to more than 150 by 1967."[24] Two years later, one hundred more franchise businesses were established, from Mr. Rib International to Tennessee Ernie Ford's Steak and Biscuits. An American born in 1945 came into a world with 3,500 fast food outlets; by the time he or she celebrated a thirtieth birthday, there were 44,000 places to pick up lunch on the go, and most of them were franchises.[25] When the sit-in protest—the ultimate symbol of nonviolent resistance to segregation and discrimination—faded out of public view, the march for civil rights changed course. After claiming major legislative victories but witnessing few gains in black economic security, activists sought other avenues to advocacy. Exhausted freedom fighters, who viewed boycotts and pickets as efficacious during the preceding decades, found themselves more and more interested in using the marketplace as a means of securing progress, not just access. As the 1970s approached, they began to run for elective office and to ascend the ranks of the private sector. In their new roles as politicians and business owners, they strategized how to convert their social gains into economic ones. They looked to black business ownership as a viable way forward.[26]

In the 1960s, after a century of protracted growth since the abolition of slavery, Martin Luther King Jr. identified economic justice—not business development—as his fuller, more vivid dream for the nation's future. His death cut short the possibility of a social revolution guided by the needs of the poor, and his absence forced his various successors to search for a strategy to bridge the widening chasm between blacks and whites. The

violent and destructive reactions to King's assassination during the period after his death, dubbed the Holy Week Uprising, sparked a number of efforts to respond to the anger and grief of the poor communities that burned. Governors, city councils, and interracial commissions convened to discover what caused uprisings—and what would future ones. Both discussions tended to converge on the role of business. In report after report, "ghetto businesses" were cited as the reason why poor blacks in urban communities felt overcharged, exploited, and demeaned while shopping. Part of the answer would be a sort of Marshall Plan for black America; a cluster of programs that ensured an infusion of capital for small business development, the opening of new job-training centers, and assistance for youth who did not complete high school. These efforts concentrated on keeping black dollars within black communities and, more important, incorporating black business ownership into the federally funded list of solutions to an array of issues from poverty to marketplace discrimination to emotional despair. In the post-King years, businesses would not simply be targets of protest, they would become the vehicles for the economic prosperity that President Lyndon Johnson's War on Poverty could never deliver.[27]

The disparate ideas and earmarks for building black America after the King uprising all fit under the capacious umbrella of black capitalism. The notion that black liberation can come through black control of the means of production and access to consumption was not created in the late 1960s. Since the late nineteenth century, African-American business clubs, churches, and mutual aid societies have preached that blacks were wise to establish their own economic centers, if only to avoid the indignities of Jim Crow or as a way of proving their suitability to vote and participate in the larger democracy. Regardless of the motivations surrounding the endorsement of black capitalism, the concept enjoyed a revival in the late 1960s and 1970s, as the discourse of social welfare as a response to racism quieted. The new mandate toward marketplace solutions reasoned that capitalism could loosen the grip that racism had over the quality of black life.[28]

Black capitalism united seemingly incongruent organizations and people. President Richard Nixon, who perfected racial dog whistles and oversaw the covert destruction of Black Power organizations, was black capitalism's goodwill ambassador and benefactor. In lieu of supporting critical civil rights protections for fair housing and school desegregation, Nixon promoted legislation that provided business loans, economic development grants, and affirmative action provisions on federally contracted projects as a means of suppressing black rage and securing black endorsements.[29] From former civil rights activist Floyd McKissick to soul singer James Brown and football star Jim Brown, Nixon formed alliances with black notables who all agreed with him: more capitalism would mean less unrest in a nation divided by not only racism, but also war abroad and the demands of domestic feminism, economic justice, and environmental movements.[30]

With so much growth in the franchise sector, the federal government encouraged this type of venture for first-time business owners. Feds promoted franchising to budding black entrepreneurs who wanted to help revitalize neighborhoods ravaged by economic decline and the domestic rebellions of the 1960s that destroyed parts of Watts, Chicago, and Newark. Beginning with Nixon's support for black capitalism, the federal government would prop up and underwrite the expansion of fast food restaurants in black communities for decades. Regardless of political affiliation, the White House, through the Small Business Administration, would be a loyal partner in bringing fast food to black America.[31] This constellation of plans—coupled with the dizzying growth of the franchise—paved the way for the first black franchisees to enter into the thoroughfares of hollowed-out and burned-up black America. Equipped with federal loans and personal commitments to the urban centers in which they would open their little piece of hope, the franchise pioneers believed that business would save the day and the days to come for their people.

Shortly after the first African American took possession of his own franchise, the fast food restaurant—a symbol of American dependence on cheap mass-produced sustenance for economic

efficiency—became a focal point of organized efforts to ride the wave of black capitalism. African Americans have never had an easy time breaking the color barrier in their respective fields, and franchising was no different. Herman Petty, the first African American to franchise a McDonald's restaurant, acquired the keys to a restaurant in one of the many Chicago neighborhoods shaken by the King uprising. Petty relied on a mix of franchise training and street smarts to turn around the location, and he went on to not only own additional restaurants, but also helped to establish the National Black McDonald's Operators Association (NBMOA). The NBMOA, formally established by black operators in 1972, was the first black franchise affinity group and soon became the black voice within the McDonald's corporation. As was the case in Petty's early years, the overwhelming majority of black franchisees operate businesses in majority black locations, and as fast food became the predominant retail food option in many communities, NBMOA outperformed their white counterparts. The rapid success of these locations sparked McDonald's and their competitors to concentrate on black diners, recruit more black franchisees, and commit to developing strategies to cultivate this consumer base.

Petty and other NBMOA founders reasoned that their restaurants' popularity was an outgrowth of the deliciousness of McDonald's burgers, as well as the sweet satisfaction found in supporting a black business. In the 1970s, African Americans gained more opportunities to not only buy black, but also vote black. In urban centers, where blacks had delivered electoral change through city councils and city halls, McDonald's entry into black communities was sometimes met with protest. In Cleveland, locals asserted that they should establish the rules of engagement with McDonald's, and they demanded opportunities for local black entrepreneurs to enter franchising because blacks were shoring up unprecedented profits for the corporation. Operation Black Unity (OBU) formed with the explicit purpose of challenging the presence of white franchisees in black communities and compelling the city's first black mayor, Carl Stokes, into action on the issue.

The standoff between residents of Cleveland's predominately black Hough community and McDonald's reveals the way that fast food was redefining the political culture of black consumer activism. While OBU appealed to Stokes, mainstream civil rights groups, and Black Power collectives to make their case against McDonald's, the limits of black capitalism were being exposed. Black franchise ownership could only do so much for a community that experienced overwhelming rates of poverty and unemployment. But the OBU protest forced McDonald's broadly, and black franchisees specifically, to develop practices and protocols for addressing black consumers who were critical of entities that profited so much from people with so little. In the short but quite dramatic saga of black Cleveland and McDonald's, it became clear that black capitalism not only created friendships of convenience among probusiness enthusiasts, but it also could easily tear apart these same comrades when they were forced to agree upon a definition of victory.

McDonald's survived what newspapers were calling a "burger battle" in Cleveland, but it was not done dealing with community resistance. Throughout the 1970s, the fast food industry had to contend with attacks on its business model, its labor policies, growing concern about its impact on the American diet, and its influence on small children. In black communities, the critiques of fast food rested in its poor citizenship practices and its lack of racial authenticity. Grassroots movements against fast food desired different things, but they were all united in their certainty that African Americans were exploited, manipulated, and taken for granted by the industry they supported. The solutions would range from negation to elimination to imitation. In Portland, Oregon, the local chapter of the political organization the Black Panther Party for Self-Defense demanded that their McDonald's be a good neighbor and support the Party's local efforts, especially their Free Breakfast for School Children program. In Atlanta, future Congressman Julian Bond joined a biracial business partnership to open a Dairy Queen franchise in the inner city. He believed that the enterprise would demonstrate the power of black capitalism. Black

Atlantans had little to say about soft serve treats and much to say about whether the business was authentically black. In Philadelphia, a multiracial coalition gathered to stop the building of a new McDonald's restaurant in the Ogontz neighborhood, a racially mixed, working-class neighborhood that held a long history of supporting school desegregation. They linked their concerns about McDonald's in their backyard to their lack of control over commercial development and the city's prioritization of business over social services. Enterprising African Americans noticed these conflicts, and they rightfully sensed that the black consumer market was often united by a desire to purchase from black businesses as an act of racial solidarity and pride. Black celebrities launched a number of "real" black businesses which catered to a desire to keep dollars in black hands and interest in low-cost franchising opportunities that appealed to individuals as well as community groups. Three short-lived celebrity-backed endeavors—Muhammad Ali's ChampBurger, Mahalia Jackson's Glori-Fried Chicken, and James Brown's Gold Platter Restaurants—exemplified this trend. These restaurants used the language of black capitalism to convince blacks that patronizing their respective establishments would be in the best interest of the black community at large. The conditions that imperiled each of these ideas highlight why this form of black wealth building belied its authenticity claims, and their lack of viability further exposed black capitalism's incompatibility with its own goals of black freedom.

Black Power burger joints and soul-styled chicken shacks did not survive the competition to conquer black America's appetite. This did not mean that the leaders of the fast food industry could ignore black customers entirely. After consumer studies and internal reports assured fast food companies that blacks led among their most frequent customers, they enlisted black franchisees, advertisers, and marketing specialists to grow this reliable base. Chicago-based market research firm ViewPoint, Inc., and advertising agency Burrell Communications facilitated this transition. ViewPoint's studies of black preferences for fast food and Burrell's targeted advertising campaigns worked in concert to keep fast food

companies abreast of what black America wanted. In the race to capture black hearts and minds through targeted marketing and philanthropy, the fast food industry provided a platform for black culture and taste making. Regional and national advertising campaigns, as well as on-the-ground franchisee engagement, brought black dance, art, and history to audiences inside and outside of restaurants. From high-profile philanthropic partnerships with organizations like the United Negro College Fund and the underwriting of gospel music performances and black literary contests, black franchisees became leaders in their communities. The growth of black franchisee networks and direct appeals to black audiences uncovered the way that fast food satiated a hunger for representation and cultural validation.

By the 1980s, most fast food franchises had settled into the landscape of black and, increasingly, Latino neighborhoods. McDonald's continued to lead the way in developing franchisees of color and establishing trust among black eaters, but these gains were still subject to questions about equity and fairness, both outside and inside the corporation. A legal conflict between Charles Griffis, a black McDonald's franchisee in Los Angeles, and McDonald's headquarters uncovered that even among wealthy black operators, black capitalism only went so far in delivering equal access to profits. The dispute included accusations that McDonald's only assigned black franchisees to unstable neighborhoods that generated high profits, but required high overhead costs. McDonald's viewed Griffis as a faulty franchisee and reiterated a claim they first made in the late 1960s that expansion into the inner city was a socially progressive move. As the two sides argued their positions in the pages of major newspapers, the Los Angeles chapter of the NAACP was trying to mediate the conflict, with attention to how Griffis's grievance could translate into support for its own revamped black capitalism style initiatives. After the collapse of the Nixon administration and a retrenchment in funding for black businesses when Ronald Reagan assumed the Oval Office, the language of black capitalism had lost cachet. But the idea that business could "fix" black America did not perish in the 1980s. The

NAACP and its counterparts, including relative newcomer Operation PUSH (People United to Save Humanity), breathed new life into black capitalism under the guise of Fair Share programs, which settled boycotts and protests with agreements to invest in black America. The agreements required corporations to expand access to franchising contracts, therefore encouraging the introduction of more fast food outlets into already crowded black communities.

The dozens of franchise covenants that were inked and celebrated throughout the 1980s and early 1990s required companies to go beyond their traditional recruitment strategy, in which individuals used life savings and relatively small government loans to take possession of one or two stores at a time. Fair Share goals and timetables brought wealthy African Americans and asset-rich development groups into the fold, and many were granted multiunit, multiterritorial rights to expand into some of the most blighted communities in the country. The fast food industry entrusted its expansion to a number of business entities—some wildly successful, others stunningly reckless. Two black franchisees—Ted Holmes, founder of the now-defunct Chicken George chain, and La-Van Hawkins, a fallen franchise entrepreneur, illustrate the ways that black capitalism underdeveloped black America.

A few years after the Los Angeles NAACP toasted its Fair Share deals with McDonald's, Burger King, and other fast food chains, the organization returned to its core issue from the early twentieth century: racial violence. The acquittal of four police officers for the beating of taxi driver Rodney King ignited the 1992 Los Angeles uprising, which mirrored many of the elements of the response to Martin Luther King's assassination twenty-four years earlier. As was the case after King was slain, much of the postrecovery analysis of South Los Angeles focused on the property damage to businesses and the disaffection of black and brown consumers in neighborhoods where few black or brown people owned businesses. This time was a bit different in that a handful of franchisees of color testified to the power of their business's presence in the community, and they claimed little to no damage during an event that destroyed a billion dollars in property. Their anecdotes helped

fuel another round of experimentation with using fast food as a tool of racial justice, and this iteration of federal support was christened black empowerment. Supported by a government's purse of Empowerment Zone programs throughout the 1990s and into the 2000s, fast food was able to more efficiently and economically capitalize on the burned- out lots that had been vacant since 1968, or were leveled in 1992.

The contemporary health crisis among black America—like all of our society's most pressing problems—has a history. By unmasking the process of how fast food "became black," we are able to appreciate the difficult decisions black America has had to make under the stress of racial trauma, political exclusion, and social alienation. This story is about how capitalism can unify cohorts to serve its interests, even as it disassembles communities. By locating the origins of the urban food crisis to the advent of the fast food franchise, we can become more aware of choices—who has them and who creates them. Ultimately, history encourages us to be more compassionate toward individuals navigating few choices, and history cautions us to be far more critical of the institutions and structures that have the power to take choices away.

Fast Food Civil Rights

After Ray Kroc purchased the McDonald's drive-in concept from founders Richard and Maurice McDonald, he concentrated on recruiting franchisees to open new restaurants in growing suburbs across the United States. Photo by Hulton Archive / Getty Images.

San Bernardino, California's stretch of Route 66 has seen better days.

The former "Mother Road" that connected Chicago to Los Angeles was born in 1926. Route 66 has been memorialized in movies, television, and song. Long since replaced by a network of superhighways, freeways, and toll roads, old Route 66 intersects cities and towns across a 2,448-mile expanse. Some Chambers of Commerce and city councils have allocated funds to ensure their Route 66 historical markers remain clean and old neon road signs illuminated. San Bernardino isn't so fortunate. Many of the indicators of its history as part of the "Main Street of America" have been largely neglected, a victim of the city's economic woes: a deflated housing market, a Chapter 9 bankruptcy in 2012, population loss,

and shuttered buildings in the city's central business district. Amid the empty storefronts and vacant houses, one of the remnants of Route 66's golden years draws thousands of visitors to the corner of 14th and E Streets.[1]

On weekends, rental car sedans, motor coaches too large to fit in the parking lot, and muddied motorcycles converge outside of the Original McDonald's Site and Museum, a shrine to mid-century America, fast food, and the route itself. The Site and Museum is carefully named to distinguish it as the first-ever McDonald's, founded by two brothers in 1940. The museum is not affiliated with the behemoth franchise that rewrote its founding story to claim its birthplace as Des Plaines, Illinois, in 1955, after being acquired by franchise pioneer Ray Kroc. Although it is not the official McDonald's Museum sanctioned by the corporate giant based in Chicago, it is no less an overwhelmingly rich tribute to the brand, its founders, and the globalization of all-American tastes and sensibilities.

Local businessman Albert Okura, who created the Southern California rotisserie chicken franchise Juan Pollo in the 1980s, established the museum in 1998. Okura purchased the property from the city after he heard that it was slated for demolition. Okura's love of fast food and his admiration for the industry compelled him to convert the abandoned restaurant and adjoining property into a memorial to Maurice and Richard McDonald's legacy (and Juan Pollo's corporate headquarters). Lovers of kitsch, scholars of all things Americana, and hungry travelers misled by their GPS navigation apps gather on the very spot where the McDonald brothers perfected their million-dollar idea. They changed the American restaurant industry with a simple menu of hamburgers and French fries. The museum tries to narrate this with each photograph, paper cup, and tray liner. Outside of the museum entrance is a replica of an early McDonald's sign boasting the sale of over 1 million hamburgers; that number has since climbed to more than 1 billion.

Okura's ever-expanding collection records seventy years of evolving tastes in food, aesthetics, and children's popular culture in the United States and around the world, all emanating from one

company and the assurance that everyday people can get a hot meal quickly for a low price. Okura and his team receive, catalog, and display hundreds of donated objects each year from site visitors worldwide. Former McDonald's crew members add to the Museum's extensive fashion exhibit of polyester-blend uniforms, standard-issue visors and paper hats, gifted manager's ties with embroidered Golden Arches wrapped in tissue, and commendation pins earned at their first jobs. International visitors offer cardboard pie sleeves for the dessert flavors only found in Asia: taro root, banana, and sweet corn. The museum's assortment of Happy Meal toys and McDonald's commissioned children's activity books range from an educational newsletter promising fun learning the metric system to plastic Chicken McNugget action figures dressed in Halloween costumes.

The museum is like the attic of a family elder with the presence of mind to label each piece of their personal collection of chaos. This corpus of McDonald's history is arranged chronologically in some places, thematically in others, and haphazardly throughout. To the left of a McDonald's Playland carousel that greets visitors when they enter are artifacts of early McDonald's history. There is a collection of steel utensils that were used to cut French fries and flattened shovels that placed the piping hot potato sticks into paper envelopes. The original mustard and "katsup" funnel used to dress hamburgers in rapid succession is identified as the work of the Toman Brothers, "Local Craftsmen." The walls display pictures of employees from the 1940s. Ruth Black, who worked at McDonald's in 1942, is captured in her uniform of a short skirt, starched white blouse, and black sweater. Her coworker, Helen Anderson, is pictured with a "frycook" only identified as Frenchy. The museum's 4,000 square feet can barely contain the collection, so objects from different times and places share whatever space is available. The very first "Orange Juice Machine" used at the location occupies a spot in a corner with a Captain Crook statue. Captain Crook bears an uncanny resemblance to the Captain Cook character that appeared in Disney's 1953 version of *Peter Pan*. Before the Hamburglar became the most wanted criminal in

McDonaldland, Officer Big Mac pursued Crook for stealing Filet-O-Fish sandwiches.

The tour also highlights McDonald's many partnerships, past and present. A commemorative plate from the 1984 Olympic Games featuring three American gold medalists and the silhouette of the Los Angeles Memorial Coliseum reminds visitors of the company's sponsorship of the global competition. A shelf of Happy Meal Beanie Babies and Muppet figurines highlights the fact that McDonald's is the largest distributor of toys in the entire world. The museum's sizable international section, which features cardboard poutine containers, vegetable deluxe sandwich boxes and menus in various languages, showcases the unifying power of a set of Golden Arches.

As versed as Okura and his curatorial team is in the story of the McDonald brothers, the Kroc family, the manufacturers of McDonald's ephemera, and the evolution of McDonaldland characters, there is a gaping hole in the museum's historiographical view of the Golden Arches. There is no recognition of the calamitous meeting between McDonald's and black America and the way this encounter shaped civil rights, transformed the health and wealth of entire communities, and directed sectors from advertising to education to labor policy. This untold history is not articulated in the glass shelves of the McDonald's Museum or told in most of the case studies on McDonald's rise, dominance, and recent missteps.

This is the missing piece of the story of how race, civil rights, and hamburgers converged and changed everything. This is the story of how McDonald's became black.

*　*　*

Maurice McDonald was born in Manchester, New Hampshire, in the fall of 1902; his brother Richard arrived seven years later in February of 1909. In 1902, eighty-five African Americans were reportedly lynched nationwide. Four days before Maurice's birth, the National Association for the Advancement of Colored People (NAACP) was founded by an interracial coalition seek-

ing to eradicate the reign of Jim Crow terror over black America. These historical moments may appear disparate—the birth of two white entrepreneurs in what was then the rural Northeast and the racial violence meted upon blacks, largely in the Deep South, and the activist response to it. Yet everything that shaped their legacy in the fast food industry—their ability to move across the country without fear of racial violence, their access to second and third chances before they were able to strike gold in California with a hamburger stand, and the avenues available for their namesake restaurant to become a global leader—was dependent on systems that denied African Americans routes to social mobility and equal rights. In the early twentieth century, racism dictated that African Americans strategize how to provide for themselves, their families, and their communities without drawing the ire of white power structures that could deprive them of liberty, livelihood, or life. The McDonald's narrative that is captured in books like John F. Love's *McDonald's: Behind the Arches* and the 2016 film *The Founder* center on how innovative thinking, opportunities made possible by a booming wartime economy, and the American desire for expediency and novelty formed the company.[2] These stories are both accurate and deceptive. McDonald's—and its fast food brethren—illuminates the ways that many Americans live and what they enjoy and how they consume. For good or for ill, McDonald's can be a reliable mirror. But like many aspects of American mass culture, the centrality of race, its role in shaping what is possible for some and impossible for others, is obscured in the interests of forgetting what is painful, what is complicated, or what is merely hard to digest.

Maurice and Richard McDonald, having seen the ravages the Depression wreaked on their family, decided to head west in 1930 to seek their fortunes. The twenty-somethings were probably lured to California by Hollywood's images of cosmopolitan nightlife in a voraciously growing Los Angeles or San Francisco. Maybe they saw themselves in Gary Cooper's cowboy roles, conquering the West with a trusty horse and a gun at his hip. The men undoubtedly had an affinity for film, and after working as stagehands

they opened a movie theater in Glendale, a few miles northeast of Hollywood. In addition to Westerns and over-the-top musicals, Hollywood churned out features that delivered the most insidious and harmful images of African Americans, Native Americans, Asians, and Mexican Americans. In 1915, the Los Angeles NAACP joined forces with other local civil rights groups to request the city council ban the screening of Thomas Dixon's film adaptation of his book *The Clansman: A Historical Romance of the Ku Klux Klan.* The film version, *The Birth of a Nation,* was heralded for the cinematic techniques infused into a disturbing, historically inaccurate telling of Reconstruction and the rise of the Ku Klux Klan. Fearful that the film would incite violence against blacks in Los Angeles, NAACP chapter leaders joined their colleagues across the country in pleading for a ban.[3] The city council's prohibition against screening the film was later overturned by the state supreme court, and *Birth of a Nation*—a film that depicted an attempted rape by an African American man on a white teenage girl, a group of bare-footed black congressmen eating fried chicken on the floor of the U.S. House of Representatives, and an image of Jesus superimposed on a scene of a cavalcade of righteous KKK members— was screened for an entire year at L.A.'s Clune Theater.[4] Between 1930 and 1937, before the brothers pivoted from the movie business to a drive-in venture, films such as Fred Astaire's "Swing Time" and Judy Garland's "Everybody Sing" presented the stars in blackface as they danced and sang in the style of African-American folk and jazz culture.[5] Despite the best efforts of the national and local NAACP, Hollywood rarely censored racist content or took seriously the claims that what was seen by white viewers on the screen had real implications for black people on the streets. To be sure, the McDonald brothers were not settling in a region as devoted to Jim Crow as the Deep South or a city as overwhelmed by the rural emigrants of the Great Negro Migration as Chicago or New York, but the West was not a land of racial harmony.[6] The McDonald brothers established themselves in a state built upon a history of Native American conquest and extermination, border wars with Mexico, a dependence upon and vilification of Asian and Middle

Eastern immigrant labor, and a hostility toward blacks likely only tempered by their relatively small population.

In 1937, the brothers and their father, Patrick, opened the Airdrome hot dog stand in Monrovia. Convinced that they needed to move to a place with more car traffic, the trio found a spot in downtown San Bernardino. The McDonald men struck out a few times before they found a bank willing to lend them $5,000 to move to the more populous and diverse town forty-four miles east of Monrovia.[7] In 1940, San Bernardino was well on its way to becoming a utopia for the fast food industry.[8] Its location near a military base, on Route 66, and in the center of growing lower-middle-class suburbs made it the ideal location for a restaurant that you could drive, walk, or ride a bike to, and with only a few coins in your pocket enjoy a full meal. Initially, the brothers departed from the austere menu they offered at the Airdrome and indulged their interest in barbecuing for the new location. Within a few years, patrons could choose from an array of dishes that included hamburgers, peanut-butter-and-jelly sandwiches, tamales, chili, and barbecued beef, ham, and pork sandwiches. The brothers assured diners that their meats were not simply "cooked in a stove" and passed off as barbecue, a sham they accused other restaurants of pulling, and they even welcomed guests to see the barbecue pit for themselves.[9]

The early menu was a hit with locals, and the offerings were versions of European (hamburger), Mexican (tamale), and Caribbean (barbecue) cuisine. Foods from around the world were adjusted and Americanized for mid-century taste buds. The origins and the popularization of the most iconic fast food staple in the United States, the hamburger, are often traced to German immigrants, who developed the idea of sandwiching the thinly pressed Hamburg steak served between slices of bread. Hamburger historian Andrew Smith argues "there are several contenders for the title of 'inventor of the hamburger' . . . [but] no primary evidence has surfaced to support any of their claims."[10] No one has definitively settled the debate about who first made and marketed the hamburger, but it is clear that the advent of the meat grinder and the ability to form, grill, dress, and serve hamburgers rapidly transformed the

American diet. The demonstration of the meat grinder to visitors at the 1876 Philadelphia Centennial Exposition introduced a far more economical way of feeding people than the tradition of butchering cattle into steaks and chops. "The meat grinder was a great asset to butchers, who could now use unsaleable or undesirable scraps and organ meats that might otherwise have been tossed out."[11] Cheaper meat meant that working-class people could incorporate beef—often enriched with additives and pieces of fat and gristle that were previously discarded or fed to animals—into their everyday meals. Soon, the hamburger sandwich was being sold throughout major cities, from carts, roadside stands, and automats.[12]

From the existing historical records of McDonald's businesses in Monrovia and San Bernardino, it is unclear whether the men served up their barbecue and burgers exclusively to white patrons. Both locations were home to African Americans and Mexican Americans. Monrovia's African-American community was founded in the 1880s. These freedmen and descendants of enslaved peoples believed their destinies would be met out West after the end of Reconstruction. Black Monrovians established churches, mutual aid societies, and their own NAACP chapter. Monrovia's shared name with the capital city of Liberia—the African nation colonized by emancipated black Americans—may have made it doubly attractive to blacks who looked west for greater freedoms. Despite Monrovia's vibrant black community and the fact that the city may have been the site of the first all-black jury to hear a case anywhere in the United States, blacks were still subject to the color line.[13] The archives of those that settled in Monrovia, and nearby Pasadena, chronicle separate schools, colored days at the local pool, a segregated cemetery, and battles over access to library cards and representation on the police force.[14] San Bernardino's Mexican-American community members were descendants of ancestors from the days when California was still part of Mexico. Mexican Americans in the twentieth century worked in the Inland Empire's agricultural fields and railroad yards, and they shared similar limitations as blacks in the region. Mexican Americans in San Bernardino also share a similar history with blacks of exclusion in

the town. The extant oral histories and biographies of Mexican-American people and communities in pre-1960s San Bernardino attest to being barred from using public pools and being limited in their housing options. Mexican-American parents also organized antisegregation actions against public schools on behalf of their children.[15] In Okura's collection of photographs from the late 1940s, there are a few images of customers who may have been of Mexican descent visiting the drive-in. If blacks and Mexicans were served, they may have had to patronize the outlet on specific days, during certain hours, or wait for whites to order first before requesting their meals. Although there is no evidence to suggest that McDonald's was segregated in its service delivery or in its customer base, the dynamics that surrounded the building and expansion of McDonald's depended on racial inequality.

Within the confines of the McDonalds' drive-in, there were no reasons to be concerned about color lines, movements organizing against it, or the world outside of San Bernardino. For the first eight years of the brothers' success in their octagonal building, which had been split in two and physically moved from Monrovia to San Bernardino, they only had to focus on the immediate future and maintain their success. McDonald's was averaging $200,000 in sales each year, with the men splitting $50,000 in profits. The cold winters of their New Hampshire youth and the lean years in Glendale were long gone.[16] In 1948, the men began to take stock of the drive-in. They accounted for their unreliable workforce and the revolving door of carhops and cooks they supervised, the demand of replacing pilfered and broken dishware, and the money and time wasted stocking so many different foods and allowing individualized customer orders. The brothers rethought their approach. They wanted to serve families, not rowdy teenagers. The menu was too complicated. Competitors and copycats were beginning to sprout up along Route 66. The founders decided to close their business and spent three months gestating the modern fast-food restaurant that would mature into the McDonald's we know today. Maurice and Richard determined which foods turned the highest profits and were easiest to prepare, and designed or commissioned kitchen

supplies to maximize efficiency. They dispensed with the carhop concept, believing young women were too distracting to customers and distracted as employees. Then, in a move that surprised their competition, they lowered the prices on their scaled-back menu. At the new McDonald's, you could purchase a 15-cent standardized hamburger, a 19-cent cheeseburger, a 19-cent milkshake, and a dime could get you a side of French fries (which ended a short-lived foray into potato chips), a paper cup of milk, root beer from a barrel, a fresh glass of orange juice (or an orange soda, called orange-ade), a Coca-Cola, or a slice of pie. The new McDonald's, outfitted with a fishbowl kitchen staffed exclusively by men, introduced their signature Speedee Service System—an approach to making and delivering food quickly. Speedee came to life with a hamburger bun–faced cartoon chef in motion on neon signs, menus, and stationery.[17] The revamped McDonald's hamburger assembly line resembled the factory floors of the nation's post–World War II manufacturing centers, at a time when U.S.-made products dominated the global marketplace. The "new" McDonald's was so successful that within seven years the brothers had doubled their profits.

McDonald's success wasn't just a response to the menu and staff changes; the lightning-speed dominance over the local restaurant market was delivered by the rise in household incomes. McDonald's catered to the newcomers in town, who were drawn to the Inland Empire by the drivers of mid-century, middle-class prosperity: the military and the manufacturing industries. Each of these institutions were conduits for white families to surpass the class positions of their old-world immigrant, or native-born, working-class parents and become a part of the middle-class consumer republic. Although San Bernardino was not among the most affluent of the Southern California communities born from the suburbanization movements of the late 1940s and 1950s, the town and its beloved hamburger spot was one way an upwardly mobile person could exercise his newly obtained consumer power and spend a little of the discretionary income that came his way.

When military and manufacturing opportunities were opened up to blacks, they were segregated, racially discriminatory, or abusive.

African Americans, despite their long service in the military, trained
and served on a segregated basis until President Harry S. Truman
signed Executive Order 9981 in 1948, nearly a decade after the
U.S. Army acquired the San Bernardino airport for its Air Mate-
riel Command Center, which drew scores of military trainees and
employees to the area.[18] San Bernardino's railroads, and its steel,
metalwork, and machinery plants, created well-paying, union jobs
for white workers.[19] But black workers, excluded from labor unions,
found themselves routinely among the first fired and last hired.
There is no indication that the Speedee system in San Bernardino
refused to deliver to the city's residents of color, but there was no
question that equal opportunity was not in full supply during the
boom years. Even if black working-class families were allowed to
also enjoy trips to McDonald's on weekend evenings, their experiences of job instability and earning lower wages may have prevented
them from exercising this option very often.[20]

The McDonalds were prescient in their projection that highway travel would increase and that their restaurant was the perfect
stop for a hurried and hungry traveler. Cars, car travel, and car
ownership were key ingredients in the formula for growing a fast
food empire. Outside, in the drive-in's congested lot, Henry Ford's
dream of a car priced so that his workers could afford it could be
found in real life. From the comfort of their cars, families waited
for food that the motor company's workers could also afford. Inside
the kitchen, Fordist work principles kept the cooking staff attuned
to the rhythms of the flat-top grill, the Multimixer machine whisk-
ing milk and ice cream, and the deep fat fryers calibrated to render each French fry perfectly cooked and crisped. The revamped
McDonald's was a suitable place for a family, children could run in
and collect the evening meal—each component wrapped in disposable paper—and return to the car, which could double as a dining
room. The prices and the burgers drew in customers, but the car
also made it possible for the roadside eatery to thrive. In 1950, an
estimated 8 million new cars were joining the already 25 million
cars traversing the expanding highway system. By 1960, the number of cars in the United States doubled, and car culture from hot

rod racing to drive-in movies characterized the sense of freedom and independence cars provided anyone seeking a quick escape from everyday life.

Car ownership, however, was not as simple as saving up money and visiting a local dealership to make a purchase. The color line and its extensions—lack of access to capital, racial discrimination in selling, and unsafe driving conditions for black motorists traveling far from home—made driving a fraught, and sometimes terrifying experience.[21] Black car ownership rates lagged behind that of whites, but even if all things were equal, where African Americans could travel to was determined by the "local customs" and their approach to still-legal racial segregation. The uncertainty of safety allowed black-owned restaurants, gas stations, and motels to distinguish themselves in the growing hospitality industry emerging from the creation of the highway and road improvements. Black drivers could rely on Victor H. Green's essential travel guide, *The Negro Motorist Green Book,* which was published between 1936 and 1967 and listed the addresses of hotels, restaurants, resorts, and entertainment venues that did not discriminate.[22] In a 1958 report titled "The Negro Market Potential: The U.S. Negro Market Today, $17.5 Billion in Purchasing Power," researchers described the "basic areas of human activities" for blacks.

> For the Negro of sophistication and poise, as well as for the Negro who is ill-at-ease and insecure, there is always uncertainty as to whether an otherwise pleasant evening will be marred by discourteous employee treatment in public places or whether he will be the victim of insults from the non-Negro patrons.

When McDonald's patrons returned to their cars with a full stomach, some drove to the newly built suburban housing developments that sprouted across the city and country in the late 1940s and 1950s. The opening of an air command center in San Bernardino in 1941 brought 4,000 members of the military and an additional 11,000 family members into a town of 43,000 people.[23] After the end of World War II, military personnel continued to move to the area,

leading to a housing shortage on the base. In 1948, 4,000 more Air Force employees arrived for new roles in the one-year-old branch of the military. As the military scrambled to accommodate newcomers in hotels, campsites, and private homes, returning veterans of color struggled to find a place of their own. The *Los Angeles Sentinel*, an African-American newspaper, reported on the plight of Marvin Spears, a returning veteran who tried for two years to secure the home loan he was entitled to under the Servicemen's Readjustment Act of 1944, known as the GI Bill. The newspaper described his battle with the Veterans Administration as "typical of what Negro and Mexican veterans in Southern California face in trying to substitute homes for the shacks, trailers, and emergency housing in which they still live with their families." The *Sentinel* hoped that in publishing Spears's account of being denied an adequate appraisal for the home he wanted built and being forced to navigate several bureaucracies, "the loan guarantee division of the veterans' administration will get off its dime."[24]

San Bernardino epitomized mid-century America's many contradictions. A world war had been fought overseas to destroy fascism and totalitarianism. While one segment of the population was enjoying the fruits of a postconflict economy, others could only imagine what such prosperity felt like. White San Bernardino families were able to buy homes, purchase cars, and enjoy nights out for the family at McDonald's without fear or intimidation. Blacks and Mexican Americans would have to wait for a plethora of events to unfold before they could do the same.

* * *

As word of the McDonald's magic spread across the region, and national trade publications like *American Restaurant Magazine* featured McDonald's in its pages, businessmen with aspirations of their own began to visit San Bernardino and seek advice. Older franchises like White Castle and Howard Johnson's were doing well, but McDonald's volume and consistency in a relatively small location was a model of distinction. The McDonalds saw no harm in disclosing how they sourced their ingredients, commissioned

specially designed equipment, or managed their crew members. It was a wide-open world, and they were not interested in growing McDonald's beyond a few additional restaurants in California and one franchise deal they inked in Arizona. Some visitors returned to their hometowns and tried to replicate the McDonald's System but realized that it took more than mimicry to make a successful business. The McDonalds possessed the hindsight of past failures, and then they could later afford to shut down and reopen their restaurant in order to make improvements. They forged trusting relationships with suppliers. They went to great lengths to institute and preserve the efficiency of their kitchen by demarcating preparation zones and timing production. But even those who couldn't replicate the McDonald's formula used McDonald's methodology to sell hot dogs, fried chicken, and roast beef sandwiches. Glen Bell, a San Bernardino local, was so inspired by the men he opened a fast food restaurant of his own but added a twist: tacos. Bell regularly patronized the Mitla Café, a Mexican restaurant across the street from his business, and he even visited their kitchen. Later he abandoned burgers altogether and created Taco Bell, the first national chain of Anglicized Mexican food in the United States.[25] By today's standards, it may seem bizarre, if not foolish, that the men with the winning ideas would be so willing to allow others to use and adapt them. But the growth of America's roadsides, especially after the passage of the Federal Aid Highway Act of 1956, convinced fast food pioneers that there was enough market share for everyone.

Highway developments were not only welcomed by the fast food industry. Housing interests that wanted to maintain segregation also used highways to protect the racial boundaries of the nation. Advocates for a national highway system saw it as essential to boosting the attractiveness of racially exclusive suburbs. Highway proposals often claimed that a network of roads could address the problems of overcrowded and dilapidated inner cities, which grew in black population from World War I until the early 1970s. From Harlem to Chicago to Oakland, Negro slums made city leaders anxious, but never so concerned that they took steps to fight the housing discrimination that limited where blacks could live. The building

of highways provided the impetus for slum clearance, the demolition of unsightly, low-quality and dangerous housing, which also served to disrupt black communities, some that had formed before the Great Migration.[26] Seven years before the Federal Highway Act was passed, lobbying organizations like the American Road Builders Association offered that highways could accelerate the process of eliminating "slum and deteriorated areas." The primary target of this dual approach to transportation and urban renewal caused planners to "drive the Interstates through black and poor neighborhoods."[27] Racially segregated public housing replaced some slums; other "cleared out" residents moved into older housing that whites left behind. The targets of slum clearance became the food deserts of the twenty-first century.[28]

Ray Kroc was not troubled about the impact of highways on the nation's racial disharmony when he traveled to San Bernardino in 1954. Highways would help him make a fortune, but as he made the pilgrimage from his office in Illinois to McDonald's for the first time, all he could think about was milkshakes. The Multi-Mixer milkshake machine salesman had seen the piece in *American Restaurant Magazine* praising McDonald's. He knew firsthand that there was something special about this drive-in. McDonald's was among his best customers, having purchased up to ten of the five-spindle milkshake machines from him in a few years. Kroc was accustomed to supplying soda fountains and diners with one or two, and he heard from his West Coast colleague that McDonald's had to be seen to be believed; the customer lines snaked around the front lot, and they could serve thousands of people out of a 600-square-foot restaurant.[29] Soon Kroc was in business with the McDonald brothers. He replaced the McDonald's franchising agent, a position they needed to guarantee some level of uniformity among their handful of franchise owners in California and their one outlet in Arizona.

Kroc's original intention was to help McDonald's expand in order to boost sales of the milkshake mixers, in which he had a financial stake. Yet Kroc realized something bigger was afoot. In the spring of 1955, Kroc established McDonald's System, Inc.,

and set about recruiting new franchisees among his peer groups: fellow salesmen, first-generation suburbanites, and members of his country club that catered to the newly upper-middle-class. Kroc's strategy to entice new franchise owners was to keep the initial investment as low as possible, provide exhaustive detail on how to improve on the already breakneck speed of food preparation, and keep franchise fees at a level that ensured that franchisees could turn profits quickly and sustain their restaurants for the long run.[30] Kroc signed up new franchisees throughout the 1950s, but he did not take full control of McDonald's until 1961, after years of a deteriorating relationship with and tense exchanges between Kroc and the brothers. At the end of a flurry of correspondence between San Bernardino and Des Plaines, a wild goose chase for funding, and hours of meetings among attorneys, company executives, and accountants, Ray Kroc at last became the head of a newly independent McDonald's. Richard and Maurice each received a check for $1 million and dispensation from dealing with the sometimes harsh and impossible Kroc. Kroc lost access to the San Bernardino store in the sale. He exacted his vengeance by opening his own McDonald's one block away from the birthplace of the chain. Confused customers patronized what they believed was a relocated McDonald's. The "old McDonald's" was no longer the brothers' namesake; Kroc prevented the men from using their own surname on their store. Although longtime employees christened it the Big M, they could not compete against the brand name they created. In 1970, the property at 1398 North E Street in San Bernardino closed. Nearly three decades passed until Albert Okura resuscitated the lot where the first McDonald's stood and resurrected it into a fast food memorial.[31]

* * *

Three days after Christmas in 1961, Ray Kroc assumed the leadership of 323 McDonald's restaurants across 44 states.[32] Even before the McDonalds relinquished the business to Kroc, he was developing an aggressive expansion plan. Kroc boarded a single-engine Cessna plane with his trusted advisors and scouted locations for

potential new franchises from the air. He took note of the neatly drawn grids of suburban towns, the highway exits and the vacant lots near schools and churches. As the men searched for places to build McDonald's, and for the franchisees that would implement the Speedee system, they took note of the land below them. McDonald's executive Harry Sonneborn presented the idea of circumventing the negotiation process for land leases and franchise subleases altogether. Sonneborn proposed that McDonald's purchase the real estate on which future restaurants would be built. Kroc liked the way that Sonneborn thought. With the establishment of the Franchise Realty Corporation in 1956, McDonald's acquired new assets and collateral as it fanned out into new territories. One biographer of the company credits the investment in real estate as "the most important reason why McDonald's . . . boasts a financial position" unmatched by other fast food companies.[33]

As Kroc flew over the country evaluating McDonald's next territory, his pilots probably didn't linger over the inner cities, which by 1961 were becoming less white and less affluent. Kroc called suburbia "where McDonald's grew up," and he expressed uncertainty about the urban landscape.[34] Despite his own reservations about the city, some of the early franchises were in fact in neighborhoods transitioning from all white to all black, and local franchisees in the new McDonald's hub of the Midwest advertised in African-American newspapers. In 1957, a location opened near Chicago's South Side Chatham community. Chatham had transitioned from a predominately white, middle-class enclave in 1950 to a mostly black, middle-class neighborhood by 1960. The franchise operator, Joseph Fine, appeared to have a cordial relationship with local black residents; his wife cohosted a community Chamber of Commerce event in 1959. In the pages of one of the most influential African-American dailies, the *Chicago Defender*, the McDonald's location used the image and recommendation of James North, an African American. "For a treat that can't be beat . . . I'll take McDonald's Hamburgers."[35] Another McDonald's franchise opened in the heart of black Chicago in 1961, in the Bronzeville neighborhood, and the outlet promised "plenty of parking, no car hops, no tipping,"

only the "tastiest food in town at prices that please!"[36] Throughout the 1960s, the Bronzeville location purchased *Defender* ads to entice locals to try French fries made from Idaho premium potatoes, sample the new Fish Filet sandwich, and tune in to local stations to see the McDonald's float in the 1965 Macy's Thanksgiving Day Parade. The next year, the newspaper published a story with a headline, "McDonald's Hamburgers Are Just Great," and a profile piece about Samuel Sheriff, a black McDonald's manager, at the helm of the company's fifth-highest-grossing store.[37]

Black Chicagoans with the means and desire to eat at McDonald's, or try to follow in Sheriff's footsteps as a manager, may have read the *Defender* items with interest. For *Defender* readers in the Deep South, the advertisements and stories may have been difficult to relate to. Wherever whites and "others" lived in proximity, a color line could be erected and legislated, but the most virulent application and defense of separation resided in the South. In the years that McDonald's was taking its model national, the struggle against Jim Crow was internationalized as television stations worldwide broadcast the violent responses to nonviolent sit-ins, boycotts, and marches. These protests, brought to homes across the world through television sets, radios, magazines, and newspapers, heightened awareness of the ways that blacks were relegated to second-class consumer citizenship. Black women had to use their imaginations if they spotted the perfect dress at a segregated department store, because they were not allowed to try it on. Black men had to defer to white children while waiting in line to order food to bring home to their families. Black children, including Martin Luther King Jr.'s daughter Yolanda, had to ask their parents why they were not allowed to go to amusement parks.[38] The national enthusiasm for the marketplace, and the local realities of segregation, separated black consumers from the nation's prosperity. Blacks and other people of color were in many ways social aliens in white America, observing a world they could never fully belong to or enjoy.

Public humiliation was commonplace in the Jim Crow era, and restaurants were the setting for a host of embarrassing

experiences. Exclusionary and abusive behavior toward blacks in restaurants often began with a host or a manager ignoring an expectant black customer or simply stating that they do not serve black people at their establishments. Customers who challenged these policies and practices could be physically removed by restaurant staff or be arrested by police. African-American activists and writers have long reflected on the ways that segregation at fine restaurants, casual lunch counters, and even rundown barbecue shacks illustrated their exclusion from the small luxuries that consumer culture offered whites. In Melba Pattillo Beals's autobiography, *Warriors Don't Cry: A Searing Memoir of the Battle to Integrate Little Rock's Central High,* she recalled a family vacation to Cincinnati, where she ate at an integrated restaurant for the first time. She described it as dining in "the promised land." The following fall, as one of nine high-schoolers selected to integrate Little Rock Central High School, she again thought about restaurant segregation. Beals and her eight compatriots were targets of violence and harassment for their acts of bravery, and they were supported by the NAACP's legal defense arm. When NAACP lawyer Thurgood Marshall visited the Arkansas capital to meet with the students, Beals remembered feeling ashamed because the future Supreme Court justice could only "eat a greasy hamburger" for dinner. Little Rock's fine restaurants were closed to blacks, especially ones fighting for civil rights.[39]

Black people from San Bernardino to Selma were usually aware of the rules—spoken and unspoken—about where they could enter and be served. They protected visitors by preparing meals in their homes or listing the places to avoid or consulting a copy of their *Green Book.* Uninitiated travelers passing through racially segregated towns or visiting the United States for the first time were shocked and insulted by these experiences. This was the case when William Henry Fitzjohn, a Sierra Leoncan diplomat, was refused service at a Howard Johnson's restaurant on Maryland's Route 40 while traveling between Washington, D.C., and Pittsburgh. This length of Route 40 was filled with segregated eating establishments and gas stations, and it was a Congress of Racial Equality (CORE)

target of protests due to its policies against blacks. Fitzjohn and his cohort of African diplomats and exchange students who came to the nation's capital in the early 1960s had encountered difficulties renting apartments and being served at restaurants before. Sometimes a phone call from an influential white colleague or the simple clarification that they were African, not African-American, could remedy the situation. But Fitzjohn was far from Washington on Route 40, and he had no one to turn to in the moment. When he later reported on his journey, the State Department was compelled to respond. At the height of the Cold War, when U.S. interests wanted to promote democracy among recently independent African states, they knew that these racist incidents could contribute to the accurate and damning anti-American critiques made by Communist states. For President John F. Kennedy's White House and his brother Robert's Department of Justice, the inability for blacks to be served in restaurants was not only a national injustice, it exacerbated a global crisis.[40]

Many Route 40 businesses, like the Howard Johnson's that refused to seat and serve Fitzjohn, were based on the model of the sit-down dining experience, in which a customer interacted with a host, a waiter or waitress, and if problems arose or the service was particularly excellent, maybe a manager. Fast food in the early 1960s was still based on the drive-in model. With no seats, no wait staff, and a mostly outdoor or car-based dining experience, fast food did not feel as wedded to the machinations of separate and unequal. McDonald's did not begin to incorporate seating into new restaurants until 1963, and Kroc maintained many of the Speedee system elements that discouraged diners from lingering: no silverware, limited seating, and counter workers were told to be friendly, but to avoid small talk with customers. The building of McDonald's was still not race-neutral in its site selection or its reliance on a disparate set of racially informed federal policies and social practices. McDonald's restaurants developed a reputation as ahead of its time in its business processes and models, but when it came to race, especially in the South, franchisees did not rock the boat. While diplomats and foreign affairs officers could appeal

to Kennedy's presidential power to mobilize advisors and cabinet members, everyday people relied on the strength of homegrown, unelected leaders to address the problem of restaurant segregation and other forms of consumer discrimination.

Activists used the sit-in strategy throughout the country to make a case for the end of segregation in libraries, churches, and, most famously, lunch counters. The sit-in, initially called a sit-down, has had a long history as a tool of nonviolence, with the strategy being used in anticolonial struggles and union work strikes. In the 1940s, CORE sat in at a segregated coffeeshop in Chicago.[41] Sit-ins were well-orchestrated, dramatic demonstrations of the injustice of segregation in their simple but precise choreography and staging. Civil rights organizers often instructed protesters to dress in their Sunday best. Women arranged their hair in neat styles, made up their faces modestly, and appeared as ladylike as possible. Men wore suits or their military uniforms to emphasize the reality that their patriotism meant nothing in the eyes of the Jim Crow state. Sitting took courage, patience, and determination. In the best-case scenario, a protester would be told to leave and quit causing trouble. If a mob was present, a favorite sweater could be ruined by a steady stream of mustard poured down a sitter's back. Carefully pinned hair could become coated in maple syrup. Every CORE and NAACP member knew that things could get worse. A member of the mob may strike a protesting student with a bat. A police officer may break a pastor's shoulder while trying to move him off a silver stool seat.[42] Some sit-ins concluded with no violence and quick resolution. Sit-ins in cities like Wichita, Miami, and Oklahoma City in the late 1950s opened up access to lunch counters and drugstores in cities with small black populations. These sit-ins gave advocates of nonviolent protest evidence that the act of remaining unmoved by jeers and threats could actually make a difference. But it would take the February 1, 1960, sit-in at a North Carolina Woolworth & Company lunch counter to inspire a critical mass of people to test its suitability and potency throughout the South.

Four students from the historically black North Carolina Agricultural and Technical College—Ezell Blair (now Jibreel Khazan),

Frank McCain, Joe McNeil, and David Richmond—grew close over the course of the 1959–60 school year by sharing their frustrations over segregation in Greensboro, North Carolina. After deliberating about the decision to challenge Woolworth's segregation and acknowledging that their actions could imperil their families and friends, the four well-dressed men set out for their local Woolworth's. After purchasing a few items from the five-and-dime section of the store, they headed to their target: the whites-only lunch counter.[43] The men remained unmoved after the restaurant staff, and then a hovering police officer, tried to instruct them to leave. The first day, the men stayed at the counters, as white customers began to leave and the lingering ones silently stared at them. The manager closed the store early for the evening, and the men promised to show up again the next day, and the next. The Woolworth sit-ins drew more A&T students, as well as women from the historically black Bennett College and white women from the Woman's College of the University of North Carolina. The sit-in benefited from the men's resolve and the emergence of more civil rights movement reporting in the South. Prior to the murder of fourteen-year-old Emmett Till in the summer of 1955, the black press was the only reliable source of consistent movement coverage. By 1960, civil rights news was more readily available, and organizations knew to alert the press about their planned marches and demonstrations.[44] The Greensboro sit-in was inspirational and generative, and in a day's time, it inspired southern college students to put their bodies on the line to push against segregation in their local communities. The sit-ins also helped define the purpose of the Student Nonviolent Coordinating Committee (SNCC), which was founded on the campus of Shaw University in Raleigh two months to the day that the men entered Woolworth's. The Greensboro Woolworth's—after closing their lunch counters on multiple occasions and becoming tethered to some of the most vitriolic scenes of white mob intimidation and violence—desegregated their store in the summer of 1960. Woolworth's waited for the students to go home for the season, and the first four black customers to be served there were black women who worked at the retailer but could not be served prior to the sit-ins.

Much of the public memory surrounding Greensboro and the invigoration of the southern sit-in movement is associated with national companies and local-level chains that have all but vanished from most American cities: Woolworth's, S. H. Kress & Company, and Rexall drugstores. There are fewer commemorations of the activists who devoted their energies to desegregating the fast food restaurants that are still with us today. After winning concessions with Main Street and central-city business, protesters began to turn an eye toward roadside businesses, which had largely avoided the attention and disruption of the sit-ins. Protesters had to improvise on the sit-in strategies because restaurants like McDonald's and its peers did not provide seating inside of their stores. Drive-ins either refused service to blacks or operated out of separate windows, which would only be tended to after whites had placed orders. Joe McNeil recounted that, at McDonald's in Greensboro, "you were required to go to the rear of a McDonald's and place your order."[45] The fight to end segregation required the same meticulous organizing and dedication as the first round of sit-ins.

Between 1960 and 1963, CORE, SNCC, and the NAACP branches organized protests against segregated McDonald's restaurants. In Memphis, movement leaders had already celebrated the removal of COLORED waiting signs at the Greyhound bus station and were engaged in a lawsuit to desegregate the public libraries when they began a campaign against McDonald's.[46] The group of protesters targeted the city's first McDonald's in March of 1960. The location had been open nearly two years, and as the twentieth franchise in his McDonald's System, Kroc must have been aware of the tensions between the franchisee, Saul Kaplan, and black customers.[47] There is no record of Kroc publicly acknowledging or addressing the sit-in movement. Each franchisee was responsible for QSCV, the shorthand for Kroc's top priorities: quality, service, cleanliness, and value. If protests disrupted the franchise's ability to make sales, keep the stores tidy, or make every hamburger according to the manual, then the franchisee would have to deal with it. Kroc stayed out of civil rights. But civil rights would not ease up on

Kroc's prized possession. Kaplan tried to stand his ground against the protests. But the NAACP won out after an eighteen-month, city-wide campaign against Kaplan and other discriminating restaurants. They not only opened the drive-in to black customers, but they also secured a guarantee to hire black employees.[48]

In the spring of 1963, CORE strengthened campaigns against McDonald's in North Carolina by assisting fed-up black customers in High Point and Asheville. In Greensboro, SNCC and community activists were not resting on their laurels from the 1960 wins. Asheville, North Carolina, native Brandon Lewis took the skills he acquired sitting in at Woolworth's and Kress's to the area McDonald's. Lewis was among a subset of Greensboro activists who set their sights on "attacking the problems with desegregation in the city" outside of the downtown core. In early May of 1963, Greensboro Movement activists gathered outside the McDonald's in a commercial strip at 1101 Summit Avenue, less than two miles from the Woolworth's counter. Armed with signs that said, "Mc—Don't Set America Back—Get on the Right Track," the group of mostly college students demanded that the drive-in that opened the previous year end its segregation practices.[49] On the first night of the protest, Lewis and other demonstrators had rocks thrown at them outside the McDonald's. When they returned to the A&T campus, they were harassed by people throwing glass bottles at their dorms. The protesters returned to McDonald's the next day, but this time Greensboro police were dispatched to deter their action. The arrests drew more supporters to the group, and they were joined on the third day by local high school students and community members. A minister involved in the McDonald's campaign told leaders: "Now, you've got something going here. Keep it going and I'll have a mass meeting at my church and we'll turn out the adult community."[50] Further mobilization would not be necessary. The McDonald's franchisee did not want any more negative publicity and relented within four days of the first protest. Blacks would no longer have to wait until whites had been served before they could order their meals.

While Greensboro was settling its dispute with McDonald's,

Chicago-based CORE members were meeting with the company's executives and explaining the urgent need to end segregation in southern drive-ins. CORE left the gathering with a commitment that McDonald's would order franchisees to "hire [blacks], upgrade, and desegregate all Southern units" by May 15, 1963. On May 25, McDonald's in Durham stopped segregating black customers.

Franchisees were often selected and retained based on their sense of duty to the restaurant's mandates. But some southern operators did not accept the new order, so blacks continued to apply pressure on their local McDonald's.[51] In the winter of 1963, SNCC took on a citywide desegregation effort in Arkansas targeting McDonald's #433. The McDonald's drive-in was in a residential area in Pine Bluff, a town forty miles south of Little Rock. The franchise opened the previous year on July 3, 1962, just in time for Independence Day celebrations.[52] Within six months of the grand opening, members of SNCC's Pine Bluff branch became aware that the McDonald's was barring black customers from service, and they folded the restaurant into its larger plan to transform the city.[53] The Pine Bluff contingent started developing a plan to demand that blacks be served at McDonald's. After exhausting their patience for polite requests and appeals to the city, SNCC mounted a four-day-long demonstration in early August of 1963. Vivian Carroll Jones and other Pine Bluff volunteers entered the restaurant one by one and formed a line in front of the order counter. They were ignored. Jones remembered, "the orders were served over our heads to white customers," while the demonstrators remained in line. As was common across the South, the protesters' passive resistance was met by a crowd's escalating emotions. The white patrons began pushing and cursing at the demonstrators. The protesters drew upon the training that SNCC provided on how to remain calm and unresponsive to the invectives, slurs, insults, threats, shoves, and slaps. The mob persisted. The SNCC team refused to respond. Eventually, their attention shifted to sounds coming from outside the restaurant, where a single-arch neon sign beckoned customers to McDONALD'S HAMBURGERS. Sensible

drivers proceeding down Pine Bluff's Main Street toward the restaurant may have kept on driving when they saw a "mob of about two hundred white youth . . . carrying bats, bottles, and bricks." There were also plenty of people in Pine Bluff who wanted to teach SNCC a lesson. They were the same kind of people who had been harboring their outrage since Beals and her friends in Little Rock had the president of the United States protect their right to attend the crown jewel of southern high schools. Those folks headed to the parking lot or across the street and joined the mob.

Jones felt the temperature rise inside the restaurant; maybe it was stress that was making her sweat. She looked around and noticed that everyone looked flush and overheated as they breathed in the air thick with the smell of hamburgers left too long on grills and the perspiration of the workers, protesters, and customers. Someone had locked them inside of the McDonald's out of concern for their safety. But no one felt secure. A McDonald's employee had disabled the air-conditioning unit in the restaurant, and as the temperatures rose, Jones wondered if she would make it out alive. Anyone involved in SNCC knew that civil rights demonstrations, protests, and mass meetings, as well as car trips through unfamiliar territory, and even talking back to your boss or a storekeeper, could all have deadly consequences. Activism had taken the lives of people demanding the basic rights of American citizenship before—whether you were seeking a ballot or a burger, standing up for yourself could lead to your death. Then, the doors to the McDonald's were unlocked, allowing the group to inhale some desperately needed fresh air. But the respite turned into a brutal reckoning as local police charged for the SNCC members and arrested them for "failure to leave a place of business." The officers did little to protect the arrestees from the rabidity of their canines or the madness of the crowd of Pine Bluff's segregation advocates. Someone in the mob attacked three young women with a makeshift weapon of ammonia.[54] An injured Arkansas Agricultural and Mechanical student hoped that a handkerchief would soothe her burning face, but it would be of no help. Instead, the chemical devoured the cloth.[55]

The visit left protesters traumatized, injured, and with arrest records, but nothing had changed at the Pine Bluff McDonald's.

Nearly a year of strategizing and protesting yielded no changes, and the Pine Bluff freedom workers called for a "nationwide protest" against the hundreds of McDonald's locations coast to coast. Perhaps under advisement from McDonald's headquarters or local businesses, the Pine Bluff franchise operator used the courts in an attempt to dress down the activists and impede further demonstrations. The franchisee saw that SNCC would not back down from "mass arrests, beatings, and the throwing of acid," so he figured that an injunction banning further action at the restaurant may be the solution to his problem. Store owners, school boards, and cities filed injunctions against major civil rights organizations throughout the 1950s and 1960s to suppress boycotts, marches, and demands to enforce the laws equally. Even when judges ruled these injunctions unconstitutional, the process of responding to the orders in court could tie up precious movement time and slow momentum. If activists defied the injunctions, it put them at risk for arrests as they awaited the news if the order was indeed enforceable. In late November, two SNCC field secretaries accompanied Pine Bluff members to a hearing on whether a McDonald's franchise could permanently ban SNCC from protesting at the restaurant. The order was also filed to keep members of the Arkansas chapter of the "NAACP and Black Muslims" from mobilizing in front of the store. McDonald's inflexibility was particularly enervating considering that SNCC found "most lunch counters" in the area were racially integrated.[56] In February of 1964, after a full year of action, the Pine Bluff McDonald's moved to desegregate.[57] Food historian Angela Jill Cooley believes that fast food chains in the South were particularly loyal to the local customs of segregation even when maintaining it was against their own interests or was out of step with other businesses. Cooley discovered that "when McDonald's implemented indoor seating, in the midst of civil rights sit-in activism, many Southern franchisees practiced racial segregation even when other local eateries had abolished the practice."[58] Franchises with ties to profitable corporate brands may have felt less motivated to comply with federal antidiscrimination policies because their parent companies did not demand it, or because they

did not feel as beholden to local community challenges. Regardless of how franchises approached the new law, the sit-ins and the signing of the Civil Rights Act of 1964 would not adjourn the conversation about restaurants and racism.

If Kroc and his associates knew about the Pine Bluff protests—which was highly likely as Kroc was known to be controlling to the point of obsession about his restaurants—then it was either too insignificant or too damning to be included in his biography and other official accounts of McDonald's history. If McDonald's executives remained silent about Pine Bluff because they believed that the racial violence and chaos in Arkansas was an outlier, an issue that had nothing to do with Speedee or his growing dominance in the burger market, then they would soon learn better. Kroc's McDonald's—only ten years old when President Lyndon Johnson signed the Civil Rights Act and made it a violation of federal law to keep people out of McDonald's, a Howard Johnson's, the local swimming pool, or a movie theatre—was maturing in a turbulent decade, and the company would have to grow up fast in unfamiliar territory: America's inner cities.

* * *

The July 2 signing ceremony for the Civil Rights Act was the sort of interracial gathering civil rights organizations hoped could then be replicated in restaurants and diners across the country. The Act made it plain that the federal government would have the authority to ensure that "all persons" would be "entitled to the full and equal enjoyment of the goods, services, facilities, and privileges, advantages, and accommodations . . . without discrimination or segregation on the ground of race, color, religion, or national origin."[59] After the president celebrated with the guests present at the signing—including an ebullient King, Urban League head Roy Wilkins, and the supporters of the bill who waited out a seventy-five-day filibuster against it—the hard work of implementation was still ahead.

The law was only as strong and meaningful as local compliance and enforcement, and a presidential pen could not compel obe-

dience to the Act. Attorney General Robert Kennedy dispatched Department of Justice investigators to monitor adherence, and each month field reports from southern cities charted how much impact the Act was having on the local level. Uncooperative tavern owners and impertinent innkeepers got creative with their strategies of circumvention. Richmond's Emporia Diner offered two sets of menus to black and white customers with varying prices. Whites were offered an "order of southern fried chicken at $1.75 . . . and $5.25" was the price for "undesirable" customers.[60] While the Justice Department concentrated its attention on the South, blacks in northern cities were not sure what to make of it. Jim Crow–style segregation was not as much of a fixture in their lives, and they needed legislation to address their more urgent needs—fair or "open" housing, equal education, and redress for police brutality. Three months after he attended the White House ceremony celebrating the act becoming law, Urban League Executive Director Whitney Young summed up the limits of the public accommodations effort in his "What Negroes Want" column in the *Chicago Defender.* "Negroes are learning that even the passage of a historic Civil Rights Act is not sufficient to wipe out rats . . ." He accused whites of being delusional about the impact of the change in law, arguing that "frivolous inertia" and "conscienceless gentility" was a result of when "a human being tries desperately to believe that, by the removal of old signs and symbols—in this case 'white only'—that a new world has been created . . . the rats are still biting; the children are still in the worst schools; the prenatal care is absent; the landlord won't send up any heat, and the husband is doing the hardest, dirtiest work for the smallest pay and then labeled as 'lazy,' that is, if he's lucky enough to find work."[61] Young's editorial gave voice to the frustrating state of black America as the goodwill and hope engendered by the March on Washington for Jobs and Freedom and the passage of major civil and voting rights legislation between 1963 and 1965 yielded little in terms of employment, health, housing, and educational opportunity.

Young and other activists not only lamented the growing poverty

among black communities devastated by bisecting highways; they were also connecting a growing disillusionment and hopelessness, especially among black youth, with increasing instances of urban uprisings and rebellions. Throughout the twentieth century, African-American communities resisting police violence or mobs of vengeful whites have borne the brunt of lost lives and property damage when their neighborhoods become the battlefields of racial unrest. By 1967, these confrontations were so prevalent and disturbing that the year's summer was christened "the long, hot summer." From June to August, uprisings broke out in Buffalo, Detroit, Atlanta, Cincinnati, and Birmingham. At the close of the season, at least 85 people were dead, more than 2,000 injured, and 11,000 had been arrested. The summer inspired the formation of the National Advisory Commission on Civil Disorders—known colloquially as the Kerner Commission after the committee chairman, Illinois Governor Otto Kerner. The commission was tasked with assessing the causes of the violence and suggesting ways to stave off future devastation.

The Kerner Commission determined that blacks living in the inner cities from Watts, California, to Newark, New Jersey, were partly prone to loot and riot out of retaliation for the abysmal condition of their neighborhood businesses. The commission's investigation asserted that blacks expressed "grievances concerning unfair commercial practices affecting Negro consumers," and they often encountered "inferior quality goods (particularly meats and produce) at higher prices and they were subjected to excessive interest rates and fraudulent commercial practices."[62] The commission advocated a plethora of federal, local, and private-sector funded programs to increase job training, educational opportunities, and better community-police relations. The two-paragraph "Conclusion" section of the report quoted Kenneth B. Clark, the noted black psychologist whose "doll study" poignantly linked the experience of segregation with the internalization of self-hatred among black children. Clark was among the first experts called before the august panel, and his words captured the skepticism of black Americans:

> I read that report . . . of the 1919 riot in Chicago, and it is as if
> I were reading the report of the investigating committee on the
> Harlem riot of 1935, the report of the investigating committee on
> the Harlem riot of 1943, the report of the McCone Commission
> on the Watts Riot. I must again in candor say to you members of
> the Commission—it is a kind of Alice in Wonderland with the
> same moving pictures reshown over and over again, the same
> analysis, the same recommendation, and the same inaction.

Shaped by Clark's words, the Kerner Commission contended that
it was "time now to end the destruction and the violence, not only
in the streets of the ghetto but in the lives of people."[63] Five weeks
after the first printing of the *Report of the National Advisory
Commission on Civil Disorders* by the U.S. Government Printing Office, Clark's reflection about the cycle of racial uprisings and
Kerner's declaration that now was the time, would be read with
even more scrutiny and urgency. Martin Luther King Jr. had been
assassinated in Memphis.

* * *

Martin Luther King's 1968 visit to Memphis was not about the
business community's segregation practices—this time. King
had visited the city throughout his tenure as head of the Southern Christian Leadership Conference, and he knew the contours
of black struggle in Tennessee around equal access to the city's
downtown shops, local colleges, and well-compensated jobs. Some
observers considered Memphis a "racially moderate city" in light
of the police brutality that met civil rights workers in Alabama
and the proliferation of those deemed "missing," actually victims
of racial violence, in Mississippi. In 1957, King joined Arkansas
NAACP chairwoman and Little Rock Nine representative Daisy
Bates to support a slate of black candidates for local office, the Volunteer Ticket, who were competitors for commissioner of public
works, juvenile court judge, and two seats on the city's board of
education. The pamphlet introducing the candidates displayed the
group's slogan: "The Negro Has a Love Affair with Destiny."[64]

He returned again two years later, in 1959, to assist a Volunteer Ticket hopeful, civil rights attorney Benjamin Hooks (who would later play his own role in fast food franchising as the legal representative for Mahalia Jackson's Glori-Fried Chicken).[65] By 1968, locals had witnessed the end of segregation in restaurants, stores, public parks and libraries, and celebrated the first black graduate of Memphis State University. The black vote was also able to secure a victory for A. W. Willis, a member of the state's General Assembly in 1964, a first for a black Tennessean since the Reconstruction era.

Triumphs aside, King descended upon a depressed city, where sanitation workers were on strike. In the spring of 1968, Memphis was an apt illustration for the minister's concern about the next stage in the fight to realize racial progress. The COLORED ONLY signs had disappeared, but the signs of economic inequality were still clearly visible—and seemingly permanent—throughout the city. Black sanitation workers took to the streets to protest the unsafe conditions and poor pay they endured while keeping Memphis communities free from garbage and vermin. After the horrific deaths of Echol Cole and Robert Walker, two black workers who were crushed to death by a malfunctioning trash compactor, their compatriots and community were galvanized to strike. Thirteen hundred workers went on strike. Hundreds of the workers, costumed with sandwich boards covering their torsos that declared I AM A MAN, marched along the main thoroughfares of Memphis protesting the dehumanizing machinery of low-wage work and racism.

"The Negro Has a Love Affair with Destiny." Who still believed that in 1968?

Blacks in Memphis were not living out anything resembling a love affair with the city. The dilapidated housing. The schools that had yet to desegregate. The jobs, if you were lucky to have one, and their insulting wages. With no love lost between them, the city and the sanitation workers remained at an impasse as strikers continued to wear their signs and hold up their placards. As the work stoppage continued and the heightened tensions of the strike led to instances of violence during workers' marches, local organizers reached out to the SCLC and requested that King visit the workers and their support-

ers. King's presence could guarantee stirring and passionate words of encouragement, and the flash of news cameras at the very least.

On his first visit to address the sanitation workers and their supporters, King reminded them how essential the boycott was because black rights meant nothing without economic justice. He asked:

> What does it profit a man to be able to eat at an integrated lunch counter if he doesn't have enough money to buy a hamburger? What does it profit a man to be able to eat at the swankest integrated restaurant when he doesn't even earn enough money to take his wife out to dine? What does it profit one to have access to the hotels of our cities, and the hotels of our highways, when we don't earn enough money to take our family on a vacation?[66]

On his second visit to Memphis in April, King gathered the increasingly weary movement followers for a mass meeting at the Bishop Charles Mason Temple to expound on his meditation about black wealth and black economic power. The audience braved a tornado warning to hear King's electrifying message. The radical reverend spoke for more than forty minutes about the arc of history, from the chosen people's biblical march through the wilderness to the most recent turning points in the civil rights movement—from the sit-ins to the freedom rides to the securing of voting rights in Alabama. King reminded the crowd of their moral power when they practice nonviolence, as well as their economic import. This address—King's final public oration—is often noted for its prophetic declarations, including the haunting statement "I may not get there with you." Yet, the substance of the address also forecasts the ways that economic issues—from ending poverty to strategic boycotting of national companies to business ownership—would become central to civil rights visions in the 1970s.

King, in his fiery style, stood at the podium and said:

> Now the other thing we'll have to do is this: always anchor our external direct action with the power of economic withdrawal.

Now we are poor people, individually we are poor when you compare us with white society in America. We are poor. Never stop and
forget that collectively, that means all of us together, collectively
we are richer than all the nations in the world, with the exception
of nine. Did you ever think about that? After you leave the United
States, Soviet Russia, Great Britain, West Germany, France . . .
the American Negro collectively is richer than most nations of the
world. We have an annual income of more than thirty billion dollars a year, which is more than all of the exports of the United
States and more than the national budget of Canada. Did you
know that? That's power right there, if we know how to pool it.[67]

King spoke about initiating a "bank-in" movement in Memphis
by withdrawing monies from discriminatory banks and moving
accounts to black-owned institutions. He suggested an "insurance-
in" to promote the handful of black insurance companies still in
operation in the late 1960s, and gestured toward a young Jesse Jackson's experience with consumer boycotts.[68] King advised the group
to boycott Coca-Cola, Sealtest Dairy Milk, Wonder and Hart's
Breads. He continued:

> As Jesse Jackson has said, up to now only the garbage men have
> been feeling pain. Now we must kind of redistribute that pain. We
> are choosing these companies because they haven't been fair in
> their hiring policies, and we are choosing them because they can
> begin the process of saying they are going to support the needs
> and the rights of these men who are on strike.[69]

The tragic accident that claimed the lives of Cole and
Walker—eight years to the day that the Greensboro sit-in ignited
a movement—ended a period of King's leadership and guidance
of the nonviolent movement toward integrating explicit calls for
an economic response to racial inequality. The distance between
the Woolworth's counter in Greensboro and the pulpit of Mason
Temple was bridged by the March on Washington's call for *jobs*
and freedom. The route between Greensboro and Memphis was

connected by the SCLC's Northern Campaign to end housing discrimination in Chicago. This ideological road was traveled by the architects of the Poor People's Campaign, King's ambitious second March on Washington to create a tent city in the capital where the poor from every corner of the nation could rally for economic justice.[70] At the close of the Memphis event, King bid farewell to the crowd: "And so I'm happy tonight; I'm not worried about anything; I'm not fearing any man. Mine eyes have seen the glory of the coming of the Lord."[71]

The next evening, an assassin shot and killed Martin Luther King Jr.

That night, the Holy Week Uprising began.

* * *

McDonald's store manager Roland Jones heard the news out of Memphis as he prepared to leave a suburban Washington, D.C., franchise and head into the District. The West Tennessee native moved to Memphis when he was ten years old, and he considered the City of Blues his hometown. He sat behind the wheel of his car and wondered what direction he was going to take. He knew he had to check on his boss's other restaurants, including the New York Avenue location that had always been a little tough because of the neighborhood.[72] As one of the few black people with a supervisory role with McDonald's, Jones had never imagined a career at a fast food chain. He didn't grow up eating in restaurants, and he had never been to a McDonald's drive-in until he became an employee. In Memphis, he learned early to stay on his side of town. The few times he tested the city's color line, he was harassed by police. He was careful in Memphis, and on April 4, 1968, he knew he had to remain vigilant in Washington, D.C.[73] For the time being, he decided to stay put and ignore the part of him that told him to turn around and head back south. Jones called the area franchise owners to see what he could do to keep watch over the McDonald's restaurants in the eye of the storm, as local and federal forces tried to compel order on streets across the country. Chicago's local authorities were not as successful as their municipal peers elsewhere in

restoring order, and McDonald's executives housed in a downtown office building nervously fielded reports on how their city locations were faring during the unrest. Jones's success in keeping restaurants closed immediately after King's death, and later securing and cleaning up vandalized locations, brought him to the attention of McDonald's senior corporate leaders. After a series of phone calls back and forth between Jones and McDonald's executives in downtown Chicago, Jones was offered a promotion into an entirely new role with the company. Jones would travel around the country and search for someone to become the very first black franchise owner in McDonald's history. Jones had a feeling that what he was about to do was going to be important for McDonald's and for the black community that would get their "own" franchise.

Three years earlier, on April 21, 1965, McDonald's became a publicly traded company and the first fast food IPO. While investors on New York's Wall Street watched the offering climb from $22.50 to more than $30.00 a share, Martin Luther King Jr. was delivering a talk to the Bar of the City of New York. He spoke of an economic boycott in Alabama and offered that, in response to Klan violence, "the economic power structure of our nation can do a great deal to stop that kind of terror."[74] These two events—both reported in national newspapers—may have appeared in different sections of the papers and seemed worlds apart to the readers. But within a few years, McDonald's ambitions for its company and King's unrealized dreams for the nation would converge.

But first, Roland Jones had to get to Chicago.

CHAPTER TWO

Burgers in the Age of Black Capitalism

After Martin Luther King Jr.'s assassination in Memphis
on April 4, 1968, cities across the country exploded in violence. Some black business owners tried to reduce property
damage to their stores by indicating that they were "soul
brother" outfits. Photo by Paul Sequeira / Getty Images.

The storefronts that lined the commercial boulevards of
Chicago's black neighborhoods after the Holy Week uprising reflected the mood of a city distraught by a leader's death
and disheartened by its familiarity with the destruction that followed. Along Madison Street and Roosevelt Road, the damage was

incongruous, but the entire neighborhood remained bleak. KING IS DEAD and LONG LIVE THE KING painted on a partially boarded-up store window stood as an unrefined but heartfelt memorial. A burnt-out brick building was marked BLACKSTONE KILLERS, a reference to the Blackstone Rangers street gang that controlled pockets of Chicago's South Side. The gang had actually assisted police in cooling youth anger in their territories during the chaos. Both levels of the Madison-Albany Department store were gutted; the merchandise was likely looted and the windows were blown out in a fire. Eerily, the store's brightly printed sign advertising "Men's and Boy's Ready to Wear Shoes" was still intact. An undisturbed tailor shop or dry cleaner provided a glimmer of hope among the blocks and blocks of devastation. More than two hundred buildings had been destroyed; many of them would never be rebuilt.[1] Roland Jones surveyed all the broken windows, vacant lots, and debris, as he headed to the Woodlawn neighborhood, where a battered but still functional McDonald's waited for a new owner.

The Woodlawn restaurant was the eighth McDonald's location opened after Kroc began his leadership of the chain, and the store initially served mostly white diners. Rapid changes in the surrounding community's racial demographics transformed Woodlawn. In the spring of 1968, it was among the roster of white-owned businesses that attracted the irritation of its black neighbors and clientele during the uprisings. Jones and another Washington, D.C.–based manager, Carl Osborne, drew the notice of McDonald's executives when the men adeptly took control of the area's restaurants after white franchisees and employees fled their stores and were too afraid to return to their positions. Even after calm was restored in cities that were inflamed by King's death and stores could resume normal operating order, some white franchisees wanted out. McDonald's became the fast food market leader by being relentless, and this national crisis would not stop it. The sit-ins across the South were a minor disruption in years in which they continued to outperform their competitors. Why would this moment be any different? The white franchisees would be allowed to walk away. In lieu of retreating from the inner city, McDonald's

would simply find translators. These new McDonald's employees would explain why they could be trusted and why they were different than the merchants that regularly ripped off and disrespected black customers. Although McDonald's corporate offices had previously discussed the possibility of recruiting black franchisees to open new, urban stores, the 1968 unrest hastened the process. King's assassination rendered some of their restaurants targets and they couldn't allow the company to be vulnerable if another event—another assassination, another tragedy, another explosion—like this were to happen.

McDonald's decision to seek black franchisees to replace white ones in predominantly black communities was affirmed by influential voices which suggested that national trends indicated that if the nation did not act, U.S. cities would experience more disturbances. Foundations, think tanks, and riot commissions published a spate of alarming studies on the pervasive economic and social problems that plagued black America. Meanwhile, Madison Avenue and Wall Street were evaluating advertising and marketing reports that advised that companies should capture a lucrative and growing market of upwardly mobile black consumers. The 1968 presidential election, slated for seven months and one day after King's assassination, opened up conversations about the federal government's role in protecting and financing equal opportunity. All of these forces informed McDonald's next steps in Chicago and across the country throughout the 1970s. The knowledge, rhetoric, and insight generated from these experts and industries pointed toward private business as the answer to a myriad of problems. Almost immediately after he was laid to rest in his hometown of Atlanta, King's death became inextricably tied to the advancement of capitalism, which he had believed "failed to meet the needs of the masses," and was on a par with the "evils of militarism and evils of racism."[2]

Jones had King on his mind when he met with Ed Schmitt, Chicago's regional manager of franchises, to accept a special consultant role on black franchising. Jones described Schmitt as "pretty liberal," and applauded his commitment to not only identifying black franchisees, "but also transforming the image of blacks in the

system."[3] McDonald's had little information on its black consumer market, and with few black managerial or executive staff, Schmitt and his colleagues placed a lot of trust in Jones to understand how to best select someone who was willing, able, and determined enough to take on a restaurant that had been insulted, robbed, or even shot at in the past. The seasoned McDonald's manager believed that the right person would possess a mix of characteristics learned inside and outside of school. Jones recalled thinking that McDonald's needed to find someone "who could communicate with the corporate structure, and identify with blacks on the grassroots level." Familiarity with "grassroots" meant being attuned to what was happening on the streets and on the stock market. Grassroots businessmen were regular folk who managed to survive the ins and outs of Chicago's slums and who could command respect from gang members and corporate board members alike.[4] The search ended when he met Herman Petty, a recent visitor to a local franchising fair. Jones liked the way Petty carried himself; Petty could talk to the white managers and executives comfortably, which could be a challenge for men of his generation who grew up under some of the most rigid segregation. The Tennessean tasked with marching McDonald's into a multiracial future had never sat next to a white person or had a substantive conversation with one until he joined the military.[5]

Petty was a military man, too. He was even from Woodlawn and grew up at 65th and Evans, a little more than a mile from the McDonald's. Petty was a true son of the South Side, which was remade by the Great Migration, when nearly a million African Americans moved to Chicago between 1916 and 1970.[6] He was born at Provident Hospital, the historic black training facility founded in 1889 as a nursing school for black women.[7] He attended Roosevelt University, a consciously integrated school in Chicago's downtown. In 1968, he was among a generation of South Siders who tried to eke out opportunity in the Windy City any way he could. Petty made ends meet driving a city bus and running a barber shop. Neither job required a formal education, and both almost certainly underutilized his skills and training. But they were the types of positions that routed blacks into a solidly middle-class

life in the 1960s. The high rates of unemployment on Chicago's South Side and waves of deindustrialization in the 1970s ravaged Woodlawn and surrounding communities. By 1975, Woodlawn's unemployment rate reached 30%, and the joblessness rate for youth was at 50%. Chicago's overall unemployment rate was only 8%. Nearly two-thirds of Woodlawn residents that year reported relying on some form of government assistance. Local activists believed that the numbers were actually higher.[8] Even before Petty attended a 1968 franchising fair, where representatives recruited curious attendees to invest in the next big idea in fried fish made fast or quickie oil changes, he was doing pretty well for himself given the city's economic picture painted by racial discrimination.[9] But solid jobs were just that, jobs, and for African Americans, how hard you worked was an independent variable in the calculus of how much wealth you were able to build.

Petty's work ethic and reputation would compensate for his lack of capital. In the excitement to place a black franchisee, McDonald's exhibited an uncharacteristic flexibility. Petty was already somewhat familiar with the restaurant business, having been previously approached by two white businessmen about opening a new venture. That eatery never materialized, but the men steered Petty toward learning about franchising. After a meeting with Jones and Schmitt, Petty agreed to take over the Woodlawn property and started his franchisee training program at Hamburger University, the intensive preparation program that was housed at McDonald's campus in Oak Brook, a Chicago suburb. Petty later recalled: "One minute I was in Oak Brook finding out more about McDonald's, and the next minute I was on the telephone telling my wife I'm not a barber anymore."[10] In McDonald's enthusiasm to install a black owner, they waived the requirement that a franchisee personally provide 100% of the contract fee. In the late 1960s, a McDonald's franchise license fee could cost up to $150,000 for a "turnkey" quality store.[11] The franchisee operated the restaurant for a fixed period of time, and then the corporate offices either renewed or denied the license. Black franchisees looked for help with the additional costs that came due

each year after they first opened their restaurants. In the 1970s, franchisees paid a rental fee of no less than 8.5%, which was based on a store's annual revenues. McDonald's also collected an annual 3.5% service charge, and eventually franchisees had to contribute to advertising funds to support national and local campaigns.[12]

Petty was also given dispensation to partner with white investors to provide monies, as long as he was the majority owner and the public face of the store in the community. Franchisees were asked to be a presence in their stores, and they could not hold multiple jobs and responsibilities that kept them away from their patrons. Crudely called "zebra" or "salt and pepper" partnerships, these agreements designated white benefactors as silent investors and secondary partners. McDonald's did not stipulate the finance terms between white investors and black franchisees, and the parties with more financial leverage could charge whatever administrative fees, interest rates, and management dues they wanted. After a few years of bringing more blacks to the McDonald's System, Jones fielded complaints about reckless investors removing cash from registers at closing time.[13] Franchisees complained of neglectful silent partners who failed to make payments and settle debts. In the early 1970s, McDonald's eventually intervened and paid out half a million dollars to expel problematic investors.[14]

Petty's partnership with white investors was not the only delicate relationship he had to manage. The Blackstone Rangers, who had proved themselves helpful during the uprising, had claimed the Woodlawn McDonald's as part of their turf. They had intimidated the previous franchisee into hiring some of their members. The Rangers were not the best employees, and the presence of gang members in the restaurant deterred older people and families from dropping by for a milkshake. The Rangers also had a reputation for shaking down neighborhood businesses. White business owners often lamented that Chicago's gang members would threaten them with arson, violence, even death if they failed to pay them for diverting trouble from their stores or determining it untouchable in their robbery sprees. Rangers leader Jeff Fort, who famously applied for and secured a million dollars in federal and private

funds for a combination of real and bogus South Side job training and business initiatives, used a variety of methods to extort businesses. In March of 1969 he formalized the Rangers business protection plan by forcing a Red Rooster grocery store to hire 22 of his members.[15] The Red Rooster was one of the South Side food stores that black residents and local civil rights groups accused of "selling poor quality meat, overcharging and short changing." Operation Breadbasket—the economic justice wing of the Southern Christian Leadership Conference—negotiated with the supermarket to improve the quality of its foods and hire neighborhood people, and the Rangers demanded a share of the jobs. After hiring the gang members, the store reported the Rangers to the police. The employment scandal propelled Red Rooster to write off doing business on the South Side, and in 1970 they closed seven of its stores, which led to the dismissal of 300 black workers.[16] Petty knew that he couldn't be equivocal in his stance with the Rangers. They had to be out. Petty leveraged some of his goodwill from his barber shop to level with the Rangers: The gang members had to leave, they couldn't negotiate any job guarantees, and no more loitering around the property.[17] The Rangers were not looking to fight Petty, and they may have been pleased to see the restaurant change hands from white to black.[18] They agreed to concede the sliver of gang territory to the McDonald's franchisee.

Once Petty resolved the Rangers situation, he had to find reliable employees. Like many African-American firsts, he had to depart from the McDonald's directives that were designed with someone white working in somewhere suburban in mind. Since the McDonalds revamped their San Bernardino restaurant by eliminating the carhop role, many McDonald's franchisees did not employ women. Even after the first woman franchised a Pontiac, Michigan, McDonald's in 1960, it was rare to see women at the grill or the Multi-Mixer station. Petty, having observed their abilities in the community, prioritized hiring black women to work at his restaurant, and he hosted restaurant operations trainings at local churches to prepare them before they applied their lessons in the store. Petty and other black operators are often credited with

bringing women employees back into the restaurant and furrowing entry points into managerial positions and franchise ownership. Next on Petty's employment list were "guys who came out of the service," like he did. [19] Restaurant training often adapts elements of military procedure—formalities regarding neat uniforms, an emphasis on precision and efficiency, and a system of ascending ranks. As a black franchisee, Petty may have felt the pressure for his restaurant to outshine those of his white compatriots, and in selecting workers, he could not leave anything to chance.

Regardless of the strength or might of his crew, Petty confronted problems that were not solvable with street-level negotiations or discerning personnel choices. The physical state of his store, as was the case of all businesses caught in the crosshairs of the uprising, was poor. Jones found that black owners were usually assigned to facilities that were "run down and the equipment mostly broken."[20] This was a common problem for black franchisees; they inherited some of the system's most damaged city properties. As black franchisees' numbers grew, they watched enviously as white operators acquired well-maintained suburban stores with functioning exhaust fans, freezers that could preserve shipments of beef patties, and air-conditioning units that could match unseasonably hot summers. Blacks would wait longer to be paired with newly built restaurants, adapted for the newest trends in fast food: indoor dining, drive-thru windows, and PlayPlaces. For some black franchisees, acquiring a restaurant that a white person no longer wanted may have been reminiscent of how they had always lived their lives. On Chicago's South Side, even upper-middle-class blacks moved into homes that were abandoned by whites who were panicked about the possibility of having them as neighbors. In the South, black schoolchildren would learn from textbooks that had become too outdated or degraded for white children to use, so they were retired to "the colored school." In Great Migration cities, blacks worshiped at churches and synagogues that converted from Episcopalianism and Judaism to Baptist. Blacks were used to making the most out of what whites had cast off and what was left behind. The fast food industry was no different.

On December 21, 1968, Herman Petty opened the first black-franchised McDonald's in the country. As the tumultuous year drew to a close, Chicago was still troubled by the past spring's Holy Week. Compounding the city's springtime distress was the turbulent Democratic National Convention in August, where anti–Vietnam War protests overtook the downtown and convention gathering places. For the second time in one year, the National Guard was called in to assist local police in restoring order. The luxury hotels and restaurants that catered to the Democratic Party's nominees and delegates were a world away from Petty's McDonald's. But in a year in which many black Chicagoans felt ignored or disregarded, something (almost) brand-new, something in the possession of a black person, and something to celebrate may have been a welcomed change of pace. By the first anniversary of King's death, Petty had gained a hold of his business. He figured out how to upgrade the facilities. He was a regular fixture in the kitchen and front counter to oversee operations. At the end of his first year, his restaurant sales had increased by 75%.[21] McDonald's supported his bid for a second South Side property on nearby Vincennes Avenue, and they helped free him from his partnership with outside investors.[22]

Black franchisees' presence alone did not mean that they would automatically attract black customers, although it did make a difference. McDonald's was popular because it was cheap and it was among the few choices left in black neighborhoods eviscerated after civil insurrections. Mom-and-pop diners and catfish shacks, as well as larger outfits like grocery stores and furniture galleries, packed up and left for good in 1968. Even black franchisees were surprised by how well their restaurants performed. Wayne Embry, a professional basketball player–turned–McDonald's franchisee, gained his Milwaukee store in 1969. He was told that his restaurant would earn approximately $750,000 a year; he soon was earning $1.2 million.[23] His store's success reflected the research findings on black people and fast food. By 1972, one study found that "in the poor black neighborhoods, the cheap mass-produced food was more than a snack. It generally constituted an all-purpose meal. Not surprisingly, a disproportionate number of 'ghetto stands' belong to

Hamburger Central's 'million-dollar club,' the restaurants which do over a million dollars a year in business."[24] "Black stores," as they were called, on average grossed 25% more profits than "white stores."[25] Throughout the 1970s, market research reports found that black men displayed a "tendency" to eat at McDonald's more than any other demographic. Blacks were also more likely to be "heavy users," meaning they consumed McDonald's food at least once a week and tended to spend more money than whites on fast food. Although the data indicated that McDonald's was doing well with blacks, their studies cautioned that black customers generally "display more use vulnerability to competition," so they required concentrated efforts to maintain their loyalties.[26] Consultants recommended that McDonald's pursue several paths to expanding black market share through black franchisee induction. The suggestions included setting up "a high priority program to build more stores to serve black customers," increasing their use of "local store marketing programs" for their black-owned franchises, and establishing a Black Store Task Force to streamline the planning process and beat out Burger King, which was close on McDonald's heels in forging black franchising networks. McDonald's was even advised to find ways to make their reliable clown mascot Ronald McDonald more appealing to black children.[27]

Implementation of these ambitious ideas fell on the shoulders of black franchisees and the small number of black executives that joined McDonald's after 1968. Petty made the idea of a black franchisee viable, and McDonald's had a number of cities in mind where they wanted to recreate this model. McDonald's needed more people out in the field to identify black talent, and CEO Fred Turner invited Bob Beavers, a future board member, to talk about a new opportunity with the company. Beavers, a native of Washington, D.C., was initially taken aback by the office's demographics. "When I was being interviewed, I got the tour of our offices, which covered three floors of the building . . . there was not a single person of color in the entire building." The office did not give him a "comforting feeling."[28] Beavers had worked at franchises back home, and he may have heard from Jones and Osborne about McDonald's

heightened seriousness about diversifying the operator corps.[29] Beavers was attuned to the changes in the U.S. business climate in the late 1960s, and he knew that franchise expansion would require McDonald's to capitalize on federal programs and acknowledge the distinct challenges of black franchises. Beavers proposed the 50-2 Program, which set a goal of opening 50 stores by operators of color in a 2-year span. To tackle this ambitious goal, Beavers worked with a black Small Business Administration bureaucrat to teach potential franchisees to tap into the federal agency's programs for minority businesses.[30] He also convinced McDonald's to establish a satellite campus for Hamburger University. With the expansion of black franchisees on Chicago's South Side, who in turn hired more black managers and crew shift leaders, traveling to suburban Chicago was not practical or comfortable. The demand for operator and employee training in Chicago's black centers was high, and improvisation like Petty's use of churches to meet staff was not sustainable. McDonald's opened a permanent classroom building on the South Side, where black operators took crash courses on the ins and outs of franchise management—registers, food handling safety, security measures, and scheduling. Black franchise owners in other cities traveled to the facility to catch up with their friends and learn from each other. Kroc, hardly a racial liberal, supported the idea and even offered the new corps access to a bus and the company's private airplane. Kroc did not quite understand the pressures that black professionals inside of his organization faced, and he may have not cared. But he understood the bottom line, and as long as black franchisees could deliver profits and deliver QSCV—quality, service, cleanliness, and value—he was willing to meet them where they were.[31]

In the three years after Petty assumed control over the Woodlawn location, the roster of stores operated by black McDonald's franchisees grew from four to almost fifty. Despite many successes, black franchisees had to manage a sometimes uncomfortable duality. They were enlisted to engender in the black community trust in a white corporation. Yet, they still struggled with their own feelings of being exploited and misunderstood within the McDonald's fran-

chise system. The operators related to the reasons why throwing a rock at a grocer that never sold fresh meats or produce to your family could feel like a release, a triumph even. They also knew that few blacks had the opportunity they were given as franchisees—to actually own something (in part) and to be able to not just get by, but to really earn money. They were a minority within a minority. In 1968, *Time* magazine estimated that only 1% of the nation's 5 million private businesses were black-owned, and black business comprised mostly "mom-and-pop operations, catering to a ghetto clientele and providing a slim income for their owners and a few jobs for others," and that "a quarter of Negro firms [were] barbershops or beauty salons . . . mortuaries, restaurants, bars, small grocery stores and cleaning establishments," and "few manufacturing or distribution firms."[32] Many of those businesses would close, or they required their owners to have second jobs to stay open. Faced with those damning numbers, black franchisees sought every possible path to continue to succeed with McDonald's.

Black franchisees couldn't talk to very many members of the Oak Brook staff about how they felt, so every time another black operator was handed keys to a store, he joined a community that welcomed him with open arms. The first twelve black franchisees acquired restaurants in Chicago, Kansas City, St. Louis, and Milwaukee. They came from different backgrounds—some had business experience, others did not. Some had actually worked at McDonald's, others had rarely encountered it. But they all relied on each other to talk about the things that would be unfamiliar or unappreciated at Oak Brook. After meeting with each other at the "other" Hamburger University over the years, they decided to formalize their community. In 1972, they formed the National Black McDonald's Operators Association (NBMOA). The operators were well aware of the discomfort that black organizations elicited, regardless of the substance of their work. An early supporter of the group reasoned that McDonald's allowed the black organization to exist "as long as the BMOA was localized to the Midwest, confined to one field consultant, and focused on training and self-improvement, it had been accepted as a positive by the

executives."[33] In the age of the Black Power movement's calls for separatism and a white resistance to efforts to integrate schools and neighborhoods, an all-black anything could raise eyebrows. In his description of the NBMOA, Petty emphasized that "they were not a militant group," which may have been his way of saying that the NBMOA would not challenge McDonald's too much or too quickly about the conditions of their stores or the lack of racial diversity within their headquarters. Gradually, as the organization expanded, they would take on McDonald's on issues of equity and parity among franchisees. By the time Hank Thomas entered franchising in 1982, the former civil rights movement activist described the NBMOA as "both the NAACP and SCLC for us."[34] For black organizations, whether it be a business group, an art league, or a concerned parents club, racism necessitates some engagement with the politics of access or the search to belong. Since its founding, the NBMOA has mitigated slights and oversight from McDonald's toward its members, and they have had to address demands from the communities that have enriched them. With time, they would increase in their capacity and sophistication in finding middle ground between the wishes that divided black politics and Golden Arches.

McDonald's risk of staying in, and expanding in, the inner city had paid off. Instead of closing their doors like their smaller business counterparts, they realized that they could maintain their investments—both in buildings and the real estate they sat upon. In 1967, McDonald's real estate holdings were valued at $100 million, which accounted for 35 to 40 percent of the company's business. Only a year after its debut on the New York Stock Exchange, and a year before it launched its first national advertising campaign, McDonald's was outpacing its competitors.[35] By installing black franchisees, McDonald's was able to tap into a consumer base that was watching the exodus of big and small business in their communities. They were also able to buy up land in the inner city at cheaper prices than in the suburbs. The uprisings had cleared commercial lots, and most business owners preferred to collect an insurance settlement rather than invest in a grand reopening. Between 1968 and 1973, predominately black neighborhoods declined in

land values by 30% on average. It was cheaper to build in the inner cities, and the balance sheets from urban restaurants showed that their profits were increasing.[36]

Fast food franchising attracted the attention of both business and civic leaders in inner cities, because it was moving against the tide of business loss, and the profitability of well-run franchises could not be beat. In 1969, Chicago's Better Boys Foundation partnered with the community-based West Side Organization to franchise a McDonald's in the interest of both groups. Founded by businessman and Lawndale neighborhood native Joe Kellman in 1961 as a boxing gym for neighborhood boys, the Better Boys Foundation evolved throughout the 1960s as a community resource for one of Chicago's poorest areas. When Kellman grew up in the Chicago neighborhood, he was part of a predominately white ethnic enclave that by the early 1960s had become mostly black. Kellman remained a fixture in Lawndale, and he identified franchising as a vehicle for expanding the job-training and uplift functions of the foundation. The team used two franchises to employ teenage men from the West Side, where jobs were difficult to secure for youths, especially those without high school diplomas.[37] The partnership took over an existing franchise, which was grossing about $200,000 a year in 1969; sales more than tripled when it was in the hands of the West Side Organization. By 1973, Westside Hamburger Inc. presided over one of the top ten franchises in the Midwest. Walter Pitchford, a NBMOA founding father, managed the outfit. Pitchford believed that the turnaround required them to change the "bad image that that store had under its previous owner."[38] Warner Saunders, the executive director of Better Boys, was happy to have the McDonald's as a training ground and funding source, but he acknowledged that the needs of West Side youth could not be solved solely with a boxing gym and a burger grill. "We have had a success rate among those with total involvement, but we don't have enough money to hire a large enough staff to reach everyone. We know how to solve social ills, but society has not made a total commitment."[39] The gaps between what was available to the West Side and what was needed grew as the nation's economy left poor, black

America behind, and social spending continued to shrink. McDonald's local-level gains were part of a larger political moment that would carry it into the next decades and affix it to black America.

* * *

Discounted burgers and swift service were integral to McDonald's popularity and brand recognition, but by themselves they were not enough to make an impact in black America. Fast food's entry into the inner city was also contingent on the alignment of federal policy and shifts in the ideological perspective on what black America needed at the precipice of the 1970s. The probusiness tune of Richard Nixon's administration coupled with a chorus of economists, activists, and researchers singing the praises of black capitalism scored the franchise age. If the 1960s was about ensuring each person's political destiny at the voting booth or guaranteeing a seat at the lunch counter, then the 1970s was about making business plans the new freedom papers.

The idea of black capitalism was by no means invented in the 1970s, although black capitalism was heavily debated and discussed during the decade. The principles connecting self-determination, economic sustainability, and black pride have been mainstays in African-American history. Groups like the National Negro Business League, founded in 1900 by black capitalism's great patriarch Booker T. Washington, believed that in the absence of full citizenship, full economic power would more than suffice; it was the quintessential way to escape Jim Crow's indignities.[40] Black capitalism's broad definitions and methods—government loans, coalition building with private industry, community-run business cooperatives—allowed programs under the label to receive support across a wide ideological expanse. In the late 1960s, the nation was still transitioning from the use of the word "Negro" to "black" in everyday parlance and in print media, so the declaration that blacks would be linked to and benefit from capitalism should have aroused anxiety or suspicion among white powerbrokers. "Black," when put next to the word "power," sent ripples of unease through white America. Capitalism, a system predicated on harsh inequali-

ties, paradoxically softened the word "black," because capitalism's rough edges were smoothed by its association with Americanism and patriotism. Cold War anti-Communism made capitalism as comforting as an icebox filled with food and as gentle as a baby blanket purchased from Sears. If black capitalism meant that blacks would live well and earn honestly, apart from whites, then who could object? Perhaps the nation could awake from its racial nightmares without soul-searching, without being distracted by the moral challenges to segregation and exclusion that caused such uproar, especially after 1954. And if black capitalism meant that marginalized people would get a chance to earn more and spend more, what could be the harm in that? Black capitalism inspired black communities, while it united white ideologues. Historian Devin Fergus characterizes the 1970s as encouraging "liberals from Nelson Rockefeller to the editorial board of the *New York Times* [to] put aside initial concerns that black capitalism promoted black segregation and endorsed . . . that federal aid be given to minority enterprises as a means of growing the black middle class."[41]

If realizing separate-but-equal class mobility was more important than King's beloved community, then black capitalism could be directed by anyone, even Richard Nixon. Nixon was not a friend of civil rights, but on the 1968 campaign trail he presented himself as an admirer of black capitalism. A week before King's death, he told a crowd in Milwaukee: "What most of the militants are asking is not for separation, but to be included in—not as supplicants, but as owners, as entrepreneurs—to have a share of the wealth and piece of the action." Black capitalism's appeal to small-state conservatives was that it could ostensibly trickle down to the lower classes of black America as long as it remained segregated. The federal government had to play a part in clearing a way for "more black ownership," and deliver on the remaining demands of the times: "black pride, black jobs, black opportunity, and yes, black power, in the best, the constructive sense of that often misapplied term."[42] The more race-conscious campaigns of Robert Kennedy and Hubert Humphrey offered a black capitalism program that required white business interests to lend a hand. Howard J. Samuels

of the Small Business Administration crafted Project OWN, which encouraged the kinds of transfers that McDonald's engaged in, where white business owners who wanted to leave cities would get special funding to sell their enterprises to blacks. The project failed because, as historian Robert Weems discovered, the program attracted "many existing businesses . . . [that couldn't be] operated profitably regardless of the owners' races."[43] The SBA did not want to appear to be using federal funds to simply give white businesses an easy exit out of black America. Under the cover of programs designed to promote black businesses, federal and local programs protected white business interests by incentivizing business transfers like the ones proposed by Samuels while ignoring racial discrimination in bank lending and the extension of credit. Additionally, federal and state funding subsidized costly public works that helped create suburban shopping malls and office parks.

Black capitalism was not a panacea. But in the aftermath of King's death, while progressive Americans cried for their lost leader and mourned those killed in the uprising violence and saw their neighborhoods in pieces, business renewal felt like self-renewal. Three weeks after King's assassination, Nixon delivered his "Bridges to Human Dignity" radio address to allay concerns that if he were to become the commander-in-chief, he would not leave the inner city behind.

It's no longer enough that white-owned enterprises employ greater numbers of Negroes, whether as laborers or as middle-management personnel. This is needed, yes—but it has to be accompanied by an expansion of black ownership, of black capitalism. We need more black employers, more black businesses . . . We have to get private enterprise into the ghetto. But at the same time, we have to get the people of the ghetto into private enterprise—as workers, as managers, as owners. At a time when so many things seem to be going against us in the relations between the races, let us remember the greatest thing going for us: the emerging pride of the black American. That pride, that demand for dignity, is the driving force that we all can build upon.

The black man's pride is the white man's hope—and we must all, black and white, respond to that pride and that hope. These past few years have been a long night of the American spirit. It's time we let in the sun.[44]

Nixon closed his invitation for black America to step into the sunshine by asking his supporters to let that same sun set on the past goals of the freedom struggle. He signed off by saying: "It's time to move past the old civil rights, and to bridge the gap between freedom and dignity, between promise and fulfillment."[45] Nixon was never a civil rights man, and the urgency of the unfinished business of King's legacy was not going to make him one. Nixon believed that "old civil rights" needed to be dispensed with in order to create that link between "freedom" and "dignity." The option of bartering civil rights for economic opportunity has been presented to African Americans for centuries. In exchange for silence, black communities could acquire a plethora of resources. The colored part of town could get a new high school if the residents didn't fight segregation. Funds for a county hospital was the reward for not registering to vote. A new law school at a historically black college could be offered to suspend a lawsuit against a public university that closed its doors to qualified black applicants. Nixon hinted that a new business may be the reward for abandoning the fight for school busing.[46] Once Nixon was in the White House, he directed federal assistance to black communities for business, and he signed an executive order in the spring of 1969 to open the Office of Minority Business Enterprise. The scale and size of these federal commitments were modest at best, and offices like OMBE were most concerned with hosting black entrepreneurs at White House ceremonies and dispatching positive press releases. Minority set-aside programs could passively enrich white-owned businesses. Minority bank deposit programs fell short. The OMBE's role was that of consultant to federal agencies and private business, rather than co-creator of black business.[47]

The Republican president's actions were weak, but the rhetoric remained powerful. With each photo opportunity or empty dec-

laration about the importance of enterprise, black capitalism was able to gather more allies. Nixon's vision for black business was also energized by support from celebrities like R&B sensation James Brown and Cleveland Browns star Jim Brown. But, Nixon's gospel of black capitalism was most effectively reinforced by civil rights advocates who in one breath criticized his regressive racial politics and in another repeated his ideas about black capitalism chapter and verse. Jesse Jackson began calling for blacks to pursue their "silver rights." Jackson had seen the effectiveness of boycotting in the South to unlock the doors to public accommodations. Sit-ins also allowed for black customers to open up their wallets to spend at movie theaters and motels. Meanwhile in Chicago, Jackson and his associates at Operation Breadbasket, and later Operation PUSH (People United to Save Humanity), facilitated demonstrations, boycotts, and selective buying campaigns that unlocked jobs and put money in black wallets. If Nixon and Jackson disagreed on a million things, they could find common ground on the notion that economic development should be a key component in black visions of freedom.

While black capitalism was forging tenuous alliances with Washington, a circle of critics was gathering to unmask Nixon's cynicism and question how in the world would bank deposits and business loans feed the hungry or shelter the homeless. Scholars and anti–silver rights activists attacked black capitalism from a range of perspectives. Believers in capitalism found the business development dollars and the new businesses established under these plans far too low, and they also knew that a racialized marketplace would not be so easily defeated. Civil rights activists saw the embrace of capitalism among their peers as morally bankrupt, and they reminded organizations about the very inequalities that nurtured capitalism.

The Kerner Commission famously warned that the nation was "moving toward two societies—one black, one white." The consumer market was already there. The 1969 collection of essays *The Ghetto Marketplace* tackled this issue. The book's editor, Frederick Sturdivant, wrote that in suburbia, there was a "bountiful

cornucopia that delivers to the nation the necessities, gadgetry, and playthings associated with its high standard of living" and this disparity reflected "the incongruity in the American economic system." This is where McDonald's imagined it would mature, a world with "huge department stores, ubiquitous supermarkets and gasoline stations, and modern suburban shopping centers." Meanwhile, poor blacks and communities of color were relegated to low-quality retailers with exorbitant layaway fees, vulnerable to predatory contract-leasing programs, and "often the victims of unethical or illegal merchandising practices."[48] Soon, McDonald's discovered that it could actually thrive in that America also.

Sturdivant and his colleagues did not have to wait and see what would happen when the federal government pledged allegiance to black capitalism: nothing large-scale, sustainable, or sufficiently funded emerged to make a difference. Post-riot cities were magnets for acronym-laden policy programs that claimed to be in the interest of rebuilding businesses, seeding manufacturing outfits, and bringing jobs to the jobless. Even Lyndon Johnson's alphabet soup of ambitious programs against poverty adopted probusiness development provisions amid its crusade. The SCLC worried that these black capitalism efforts were made at the expense of youth job and Head Start early education programs.[49] Black economists, scholars, activists, and business owners learned this lesson after the Watts uprising in August of 1965. Sparked by confrontations between residents of the South Los Angeles neighborhood and police officers conducting an arrest, the six-day rebellion claimed 34 victims and $40 million in property damage. Black business owners like Larry Brown painted the words SOUL BROTHER on their storefronts in hopes looters would bypass their location in the spirit of racial solidarity.[50] Sometimes this kind of tactic worked; sometimes it did not. What would stop this the next time people were upset at the police? Former-police-officer-turned-councilman Tom Bradley, who was on a journey to becoming Los Angeles's first black mayor, believed that developing more soul brother businesses would help. "The proper way to stop racism and return Watts to normalcy includes jobs and job training, inducement to business

and industry to return to the stricken communities, federal tax inducements for relocation of firms to Negro areas, and reduction of insurance rates."[51] Federal and state governments could craft and implement enticements like tax relief for new businesses and rebates in exchange for hiring local people. But weary and traumatized business owners found the financial and emotional costs of rebuilding far too taxing, regardless of state support. After a community experienced a riot, the spike in insurance and security costs was often passed on to shoppers in the area, the majority of whom had nothing to do with the disorder. Watts was "caught in a cost-price whirl," reflected one economist.[52] Paying more for lower-quality goods and services was a common experience for blacks across class lines. Additionally, blacks were underwriting their own oppression when they paid taxes for the improvement and maintenance of schools that barred them or funded the salaries of police officers that terrorized them. Bradley's recommendations were contingent on local business owners' willingness to stay and expand in Watts.

The "white flight" of homeowners from central cities to suburbs is a historical phenomenon that has long been recognized and documented, but fewer Americans are aware of how the collapse of business districts created a parallel, racially based process.[53] When white business owners fled black neighborhoods or refused to reopen stores after unrest, the flight of jobs, tax revenue, and services constricted an already limited marketplace. While some whites held on to residential properties in black communities and profited handily from a discriminatory housing market, this form of absentee landlord arrangement was not as lucrative for commercial properties.[54] After collecting an insurance disbursement for a torched store, business owners simply relocated or moved on to a new line of work. Vacant lots remained as a sign of what once was. "Why should I reopen? So, it can happen again?" a white appliance store owner in Watts asked. He decided that he wasn't "going to give 'em another chance," and he started over in a whiter part of Los Angeles. He committed himself to trying "to forget Watts." His conclusion: "To hell with civil rights and all their causes."[55]

Civil rights and civil disorder became one and the same in the shop owner's mind, and reactionary policymakers and voters agreed. In forgetting Watts, Chicago, and Newark, the nation was also forgetting King's message and rewriting his legacy to fit with the desires of corporations, racist politicians, and wealthy people.

Some civil rights activists who had worked with Jackson, and others who pivoted toward black capitalism, refused to bend to the idea that it was the next step in the struggle. Former Student Nonviolent Coordinating Committee member James Forman took a critical stance on black capitalism and was wary of anyone swayed by it. If there was to be talk of money, Forman supported reparations for slavery, real recompense for centuries of subjugation. Grocery stores and drive-ins could never do that. Forman wrote in the spring of 1969:

> We must separate ourselves from those Negroes who go around the country promoting all types of schemes for Black Capitalism. Ironically . . . the most militant Black Nationalists, as they call themselves, have been the first to jump on the bandwagon of black capitalism. They are pimps; Black Power Pimps and fraudulent leaders and the people must be educated to understand that any black man or Negro who is advocating a perpetuation of capitalism inside the United States is in fact seeking not only his ultimate destruction and death, but is contributing to the continuous exploitation of black people around the world.[56]

Three years into Nixon's presidency, critics had more evidence that the movement to put businesses on every inner-city block was a failed one. Economist Frederick Case charted attempts to "attack the root causes of the disturbances and revitalize the economic lives of South Central and East Los Angeles" by "providing more and better jobs and increased opportunities for minority businessmen to enter managerial and entrepreneurial ranks."[57] The strategy yielded little more than an "abundance of publicity . . . of business and government rolling up their sleeves and combining to slay the dragons of discrimination, inadequate education, poverty, and pri-

vation."[58] Like the Nixon White House, local-level governments projected a semblance of economic progress at groundbreaking celebrations and ribbon cuttings. For the constituents, business-inclined and otherwise, new stores offered another choice or opportunity in a place constrained by race and economics. A minority of Angelenos of color drafted business plans and tried to open their own business. The majority exercised the few options they had and figured out how to make the most with less, or they packed up their lives and set out for other cities. Case pointed out that poverty in Los Angeles was not ameliorated by post-Watts investments; it merely migrated to other parts of Los Angeles County and the surrounding area. South Los Angeles's unemployment rate continued to rise after the uprising and didn't abate when business funding came to Watts; between 1965 and 1969, the unemployment rate in the area was nearly triple the national and regional average.[59] Black business owners' attitudes toward black capitalism were also varied. Their position on the local and federal programs was sometimes as much about the size and type of business they owned as about their opinions on Nixon or their ideas about how to fix black America.

Small business owners complained of complicated application forms, lending limits, and bureaucratic mismanagement when they sought help from or enrolled in local business development programs. One black bookstore owner became deeply skeptical of black capitalism fanfare after multiple attempts to navigate a small loans program. The Small Business Administration rejected four separate business proposals from him, and after consulting a "major investment company" about the matter, they were surprised that his plan was not funded.[60] Black capitalism initiatives usually assigned seasoned businesspeople to mentor or advise program participants, and these coaches rarely hailed from the communities they were tasked with guiding. The bookstore owner found his advisor unskilled in interpersonal communication and his unwillingness to "get down in his community and start setting an example for the young" bothered him. The man abandoned all hope that the business program would help him, and he deemed

"minority capitalism . . . one of the biggest frauds ever perpetrated on the aspirations of the black people." The programs didn't serve the people, they catered to political cronies. "They're pork barrels for politicians to use for putting their people in jobs."[61]

Even influential black thinkers, who took no issue with capitalism itself, hesitated to support black capitalism. Save black insurance agencies and banks, black small business concentrated in urban cores had not proven to be an economic boon, and more of them would put more people at risk. Andrew Brimmer, the first African-American Federal Reserve Board governor, cited the high failure rates of small businesses and their inability to employ significant numbers of people as the key reasons why encouraging new business development was a fool's errand. The Harvard-educated economist had broken many racial barriers over the course of his education and career, and he didn't see black capitalism as solely failing the nation financially. Having grown up in a segregated, small town in northeastern Louisiana, Brimmer feared that black capitalism encouraged the separatism that dictated his youth and young adulthood. "In the long run, the pursuit of black capitalism may retard the Negro's economic advancement by discouraging many from the full participation in the national economy with its much broader range of challenges and opportunities."[62] Brimmer advocated for blacks to seek careers in corporate America if they wanted to make a difference in the lives of black people, because affirmative action, minority training programs, and diversity recruitment efforts promised far more stability than small business.[63] Brimmer's concerns about black capitalism increased after the arrival of recession in 1970. The nearly year-long downturn, and subsequent recessions, reduced allocations for OMBE-adjacent projects and initiated social welfare spending freezes, which caused black communities to fall further into the economic depths.

Black capitalism was down, but it wasn't out. Federal black capitalism programs failed to invigorate the barbershops, beauty parlors, barbecue takeouts, and Black Power bookstores that tried to anchor post-uprising business districts. But they boosted a powerful newcomer into the inner city: fast food. With the benefit of

corporate offices staffed with attorneys, lobbyists, and business strategists, and good relationships with the White House, fast food companies encouraged their potential black franchisees to pursue OMBE programs to access loans and business advantages. Professional athlete and Nixon ally Brady Keys's business success exemplified the ways that black capitalism undergirded the expansion of fast food in black communities. His challenges also exposed how little capitalism could actually alleviate the problems of black communities.

Brady Keys was the unofficial spokesperson for Nixon's black capitalism efforts. The former Colorado State University cornerback played football with the Pittsburgh Steelers, garnering All-Pro status during his eight-year stint between 1961 and 1969. After leaving the National Football League, Keys wanted to follow in the footsteps of his teammates and devote himself fully to business. During his football career, Keys tried to franchise a car dealership and had difficulties securing financing. Banks refused him ten times, and he needed to leverage a Steelers connection in order to receive his first business loan. The post-King climate alleviated his credit crunch. Keys intimated that the post-unrest desire to quell tensions through business creation worked in his favor. "At the time, I was a professional athlete, and I had a lot of credibility as a businessman already . . . [but] I had real big problems getting financing—until right after the riots . . ." After Keys retired his Steelers uniform, he devoted himself full-time to his self-referential All-Pro Chicken, a takeout he opened in 1967 with the hopes of turning it into a competitive franchise. Keys was able to take advantage of the lack of fried chicken competitors on his block of Harlem. The low-overhead business was a smash hit, and Keys expanded All-Pro to thirty-five franchises across the country.[64]

National chains took notice of Keys's All-Pro, as they were probably keeping tabs on McDonald's inner-city campaign, and drafted Keys for their team of black franchisees. In 1969 he met with executives from Miami-based Burger King and took possession of his first burger restaurant, an unprofitable and failing location in inner-city Detroit. Like Petty, Keys was tasked with turning around the store,

and after a strong opening year, Keys acquired his second Burger King. Keys, like other black franchisees, used his instincts and revised the company's directives in order to turn the tide for his restaurants. He revived waning Whopper sales in 1969 by selling the iconic burgers in his store on a made-to-order basis, which inspired Burger King's "Have It Your Way" tagline of the 1970s. *Black Enterprise* magazine praised him for developing "the innovations [that] turned his Burger King store into the top selling store in the nation. In just three months, the outlet's sales rocketed to $65,000 a month, up from a meager $25,000." Keys also lowered the average employee turnover rate from the fast food standard of 300% to 100% in a year.[65]

Keys's good ideas were supplemented with cash courtesy of the federal government's black capitalism platform. Between 1969 and 1973, the former NFL defensive back drew upon an estimated $9 million in federal funds for his various businesses.[66] He told *Black Enterprise* in 1974: "All the franchise companies want to go into the inner city now. And since my company has been successful . . . it's fashionable to give franchises to blacks."[67] The appeal of the inner-city market and the reality of it were vastly different, and Keys believed that due to franchise saturation in the suburbs, the industry had to find ways around the fact "that doing business in my area is hell." Keys contended with "cutting, shooting, killing" inside and outside the restaurants, and he believed black franchisees were used as conduits into and buffers from the inner city. The retired athlete realized that black franchised restaurants were extensions of a larger system that would always outprofit and overpower "little guys" like him, no matter how many profitable franchises he operated. Keys figured that franchiser logic reasoned: "Why don't we get this black cat over here and franchise him? It may cost us $100,000 [in aid] to get him in business, but it would put a whole bunch of stores up and we'll make that much in a year from royalties, advertising, and supplies we sell him."[68] The All-Pro founder hoped to earn enough money in the management of other franchises to finance his own businesses, but he knew that it would be a long time coming, as the 1970s economic downturns were exacerbated by oil shortages, rising food

costs, inflation, and growing unemployment. Every dollar Keys earned was hard-earned, and with his stores in poor areas, he had to remain vigilant about price and operations. "We've come off a real bad year," he said. "About 35 percent of the people in the inner city are on some type of welfare. Their income doesn't go up. So where in hell do they find the money to spend on a luxury such as fast food?" Gradually, fast food was transforming from a luxury to a staple of the diets of Keys's target markets, but relying on this market meant responding to their resistance to changes to the menu and the prices of food. He told the magazine:

> And how much can you charge for a hamburger? Eighteen months ago, the meat was 55 cents a pound. Now it's $1.02 a pound, but it's the same hamburger. And you can only charge so much. As the price of all this food increases, you try to raise your price, so that you can keep your level of profit. But this year it seriously reached the point of no return, where you could no longer raise your prices. Because the people rebel. As the costs keep going up, you've got to keep raising your prices accordingly, but then your sales just drop, drop, drop—the people can't afford your food.[69]

The nation's economic crises provided one competitive advantage for Keys, Petty, and the first generation of franchisees of color; their customers were less likely to actually drive to a drive-in. Carless and public-transportation-dependent consumers usually could walk to their favorite fast food spots, unlike suburban diners whose lifestyles were shaped by car travel. Without cars, inner-city customers were also unable to stray too far from home in search of a hot breakfast or a quick snack; therefore, fast food companies did not have to worry too much about oversaturating population-dense cities. This difference between urban and suburban stores was magnified in the fall of 1973, when the United States entered an oil crisis that lasted until the spring.[70] The McDonald's footprint in cities was growing throughout the 1970s, but the company had spent the prior two decades investing in mostly suburban towns and locations proximate to highways. American car owners waited in long lines that snaked out

of gas station parking lots onto the street in hopes they wouldn't be turned away. If drivers were lucky enough to get gas, they could plan on paying nearly double what they were used to and weren't guaranteed they could leave with a full tank. No matter how strong a driver's hankering for a Filet-O-Fish sandwich, they had to think twice about expending precious fuel to get one. Although some of its suburban franchises were hit by the embargo, McDonald's official word was that the Big Mac was stronger than global export conflicts and their spokespeople were coy about acknowledging the crisis. At the close of 1973, McDonald's CEO Fred Turner told the *New York Times* that they were in the process of expanding their "efforts to keep stores near population centers so that people can walk in, rather than drive," and he conceded that "the energy shortage" heightened interest in the new focus. But he remained steadfast in the assertion that oil prices were irrelevant to the bigger picture. "We never have been a roadside chain." Turner claimed that in a year in which McDonald's stock prices dipped, the company actually experienced gains in business during the nationwide Sunday gas holidays, the weekly moratorium on fuel sales. The rise in oil costs also elevated building and construction budgets, and McDonald's had to rethink new store locations in case the nation's oil and economic problems lasted into the following fiscal years. According to Turner, the shift in focus to "moving more into the cities" led the company to discover "black neighborhoods and poorer communities."[71]

Because of the lessons learned from black franchisee success and the memories of the previous decade's uprisings, these new stores would rely heavily on black labor, management, and franchisees to maximize their popularity in black communities and insulate themselves from criticism and harm. Black capitalism did not work for many black businesses, but it was a godsend for players in the fast food race to the top. Massive entities like McDonald's and Burger King could sustain the ups and downs of market changes. New restaurants could be built on cheap land, and old ones could be resuscitated at relatively low cost. Black franchises, even when given internal funding to enter the business, were eligible for federal support, and ultimately, they contended with the high costs of

security and insurance as part of their leasing agreements. More important, by expanding into neighborhoods with few drivers and even fewer choices, McDonald's and Burger King were able to overcome some of the economic challenges of the 1970s by exploiting the financial perils of poor communities.

Since the first McDonald's opened in 1940, the company was able to shapeshift for the times. The McDonald brothers understood the importance of efficiency in the 1940s. In the 1950s, Kroc tapped into the desires of the suburban nuclear family and their fascination with cars and consumption. By the late 1960s, McDonald's was forced to take its cues from a culture in constant conflict with its stated principles and its inability to fulfill them. A burger company does not set policies or elect candidates. But under capitalism, a company's influence is broad and deep, and the most powerful companies synchronize their movements to the beat of social change, without ever acknowledging that it can hear its sounds.

In order to survive and flourish after 1968, McDonald's not only had to learn how to listen to black America; the company would also have to learn how to talk to black America. Black franchises were their interpreters. In April of 1969, Ralph Abernathy, King's successor at the Southern Christian Leadership Conference, visited Chicago as part of a nationwide pilgrimage to honor his friend. Months earlier, Abernathy had announced that a reinvigorated Poor People's Campaign would commence that year. The campaign was part of King's vision to gather a multiracial caravan to travel to Washington, D.C., to amplify the struggles of poor whites, Native Americans, blacks, and veterans. Emboldened by King's final year of life dedicated to critiquing economic inequality, Abernathy declared, "We don't want rich individuals; we want rich communities." Abernathy made it plain: "I don't believe in black capitalism. I believe in black socialism."[72] Despite these declarations, while visiting Chicago, Abernathy accepted a donation of $1,300—the equivalent of one-day profit from Petty's restaurant—to the SCLC. The donation was the first of many that flowed between McDonald's and civil rights organizations, and it further tied King's dream to Kroc's dream, despite the two men's hopes for the world being miles apart.[73]

CHAPTER THREE

The Burger Boycott and the Ballot Box

In 1967, Cleveland's Carl Stokes became the first black mayor of a major city. A conflict over McDonald's profitability in black neighborhoods led to a series of boycotts of the restaurant, and Stokes was called in to mediate the battle. Bettman Archive / Getty Images, 1967.

On the night Martin Luther King Jr. was killed, Cleveland's Mayor Carl Stokes would not let his hometown burn, not again. He was the first black mayor of a major U.S. city, and he knew that he was always under surveillance—by the black Clevelanders who organized to help him eke out a 50.5% victory in 1967, and by whites who were unsure if he would serve their needs at all. Stokes was also a subject of fascination and scrutiny by news media and businessmen. They wondered if the charismatic attorney could prevent a repeat of what happened in the summer of 1966, when the predominately black and overwhelmingly poor Hough neighborhood was nearly leveled in an uprising. That unrest started on

the evening of July 18 after white bar owners allegedly posted a sign on their door's business warning No WATER FOR NIGGERS. Some people said that the barkeep refused to give a black man a glass of water. Others reported that the business owners had thrown a grieving woman out of the establishment for collecting donations for her dead child. Or was it for her friend's child? Like most uprisings, the details of what started the commotion felt less important than the horrors of what unfolded. Fires devoured wood frame houses and the heat's impact exploded windows, hurling glass onto sidewalks and into the streets. The main strip of Hough Avenue drew the reckless, the curious, and the desperate. Hough was home to many hungry families, and when the windows and doors to the Gale's Super Valu market on Superior Avenue were destroyed, they may have seen the event as a mixed blessing. The fires at All-Brite pharmacy and Sav-Mor market may have consumed all the wares in the stores before it was cleared out, so no one would ever benefit from the bottles of medicine, packs of diapers, and assortment of shampoos that were difficult to afford. Hough was ablaze, but for a moment, in a warped twist of fate, Hough was able to provide for the community. Young men who had been hassled by police for years fought back and tussled with the Cleveland Police Department. The mostly white police force was not able to maintain order, and later 1,700 members of the Ohio National Guard were put on alert to contain the chaos within a fifteen-block perimeter inside Hough.[1]

As was the case in many city neighborhoods that became the final destinations for blacks seeking refuge from Jim Crow's chokehold on personal and political freedom during the Great Migration, Hough's racial composition had transformed from upwardly mobile whites to plucky blacks who learned that they had to be careful with each step they made. Carl Stokes must have remembered the scenes from an intact Hough Avenue, one of the neighborhood's main arteries, as he strolled down the numbered side streets with the volunteer cleanup crews that gathered to collect rubble and mourn what had just been there a few days earlier. Swift Dry Cleaners' brick frame sides remained strong, but without a roof. The wire grate that was supposed to shield Al's Cut

Rate Store off of Lexington was no match for the mobs, and the store that offered BEER TO GO was left dry. All that remained of the University Party Roller Rink Hall was the sign that helped mark it, like a headstone. In 1966, Stokes represented Cleveland as the first black Democrat to sit in the Ohio statehouse, and although the rebellion in Hough was devastating, it may have been no surprise that tensions would boil over there. At mid-decade, Hough was nearly 90% black and one of the poorest parts of the city, with residents earning nearly 40% less than the citywide average. The economic disparity in Hough was fueled by double-digit unemployment rates, and families tried to make ends meet with welfare benefits and charitable donations.[2]

On the first day of the Hough uprising, the future mayor asked his brother Louis to travel to Hough with him. The men were greeted by the sight of "flames leaping out of storefronts and billowing up into the darkening sky." They heard gun shots, police sirens, and screams. In his memoir, Congressman Louis Stokes recalled the mood in Hough in the years before the unrest. "The lack of jobs and health care, the absence of essential social services, the ongoing victimization by police, the general perception of black disenfranchisement and white entitlement fed a growing undercurrent of anger."[3]

Hough was not going to happen again. The mayor headed first to a news channel to plead with Clevelanders to "do honor to the memory of MLK by reacting to the tragic loss in the peaceful manner in which he lived." Then he traveled to Cleveland's East Side, walking the streets with other persuasive, civic-minded black leaders to reason with the angry and the frustrated. He asked that the police department deploy black officers onto the streets that night, knowing that the memories of 1966 and the realities of the present would make the appearance of white police officers a barrier to peace. Stokes and his associates spent four long days in Hough pleading for people to "Keep it cool." There were no reports of violence, property damage, or arson in Hough. Clevelanders were saddened by King's death, but Stokes's position as mayor may have kept them from turning their grief into full-on retaliation in the streets.[4] Stokes won over the city, and the nation, in the spring by

keeping Cleveland calm and safe. But the favor curried during Holy Week would dissolve into bitterness over the summer, when a shootout in Glenville, a neighborhood northeast of Hough, claimed seven lives—four African-American civilians and three white police officers—during a two-day uprising.[5] After Glenville, Stokes knew that his reelection bid the following year would be tough, so he strategized how to convince voters that he could ably maintain relationships with a police force that had long antagonized black Clevelanders and appease a powerful white business community that saw uprisings cut into their bottom line. Stokes knew that his position as mayor required more than approving budgets and appearing at ribbon cuttings; as a black mayor, his job required him to juggle black expectations, reduce white apprehension, and tend to his personal ambitions for city politics. What he never could have anticipated as he prepared for his reelection bid in the summer of 1969 was that he would also have to cautiously maneuver a community conflict with McDonald's if he was going to realize a second term in office.

As McDonald's franchising opened up to African-American businessmen in the inner cities, these same cities were undergoing radical shifts in political power. Few blacks were moving into city hall like Stokes or Gary, Indiana's Richard Hatcher in the late 1960s, but African Americans were running for and winning seats on city councils, joining school boards, and securing statehouse seats by mobilizing black coalitions.[6] After President Lyndon Johnson inked the Voting Rights Act of 1965, southern blacks were able to exercise the power of their vote more freely in local and national elections, while experienced black voters in the North were finding avenues to translate voting power into community control of the institutions that were failing them. Blacks organized for more black police officers in hopes of reducing the problem of police brutality. Exasperated parents established alternative schools or petitioned school boards to ensure their children received equal access to public school programs, and to expel the vestiges of segregation-era textbooks and teachers. Blacks in Great Migration cities were for the first time voting for black candidates from their own communities, who were alternative choices

to the same white Democratic machine politicians who had held their votes hostage by making sure that district and ward lines preserved the color line.[7] Black voters electing black politicians did more than externalize their desires to see themselves reflected in positions of power and authority. In electing black candidates, a number of black voters were also explicitly or implicitly supporting black capitalism. Capitalism relies on a political system that supports its interests and protects its excesses. For black political candidates like Stokes, who spoke to black voters about the importance of social revolution through black representation and opportunity expansion, they had to also craft a message to assuage white anxieties. One of the most effective ways to make white voters comfortable, if you were a first black mayor, was to assume a pro-business stance. By talking about black capitalism and economic development in the inner city, black elective leaders were able to secure their position of power without attracting too much opposition. But in the late 1960s and beyond, when there was a conflict between white-owned businesses and the black communities they profited from, black political leaders had to somehow mediate tensions without alienating either group. Stokes was no different in his embrace of private business development as a means of realizing racial justice. Historian Keeanga-Yamahtta Taylor notes in her assessment of black political ascendancy after the passage of the Civil Rights Act that the Stokes campaign became the "focal point of the civil rights establishment, whose leaders worried about the political drift of their organizations after the end of legal discrimination in the South and the urban uprisings in the North."[8] Nothing could be left to chance.

Although Hough residents were only spectators of the drama acted out in other U.S. cities after King's death, they were still in dire straits the year after King. Buildings that had been lost in 1966 had not been rebuilt, and the community understood well its neighbors in Glenville, who took to the streets after suspicions that police were in the area to harass members of the community. The exchange of gunfire between a supposed group of nationalists and police officers set Stokes into action again, and he tried to remove

white officers from the area. The withdrawal did little, and white officers were soon back on Glenville blocks to maintain law and order. Community members were still unable to achieve financial stability and were regularly exploited by business. As one study poignantly described it: "One of the bitterest complaints among Hough residents is that white businessmen raise their prices on 'Mother's Day'—the tenth of each month, when mothers receive aid-to-dependent-children welfare checks."[9]

In the aftermath of the Hough and Glenville uprisings, neighborhood groups and local leadership began the process of rebuilding with even less than they had before. The new business climate not only necessitated physical repairs and cleanups, but also led to a spike in the cost of doing business in areas already plagued with higher security, insurance, and carrying costs. One study found that a Hough pawn brokerage and jewelry store owner faced an increase in his fire insurance after the riots. Although he was able to defend his property with a "shotgun and revolver," his $144 a year fire insurance policy skyrocketed to $621 for the same coverage.[10] In response to these and other challenges, Operation Breadbasket had come to Cleveland to do the type of work it was known for in Chicago, which included pressuring businesses in black communities to commit to improving the quality of customer service, hiring local people, and addressing discriminatory practices. From its offices at 11006 St. Clair Avenue (blocks from the site of a future McDonald's), Breadbasket established itself on Cleveland's East Side. In the winter of 1967, Breadbasket announced that it had entered an agreement with Pick-N-Pay Supermarkets, leading to 300 "new and upgraded jobs" for the community. The positions varied from store managers, department heads, meat cutters and wrappers, and "salaried employees," yielding payroll expenses of more than $1.7 million. The agreement stipulated that the supermarket chain post jobs with black community agencies, advertise in black newspapers, deposit monies in black banks, stock the store with products made by black businesses, and donate to the United Negro College Fund as well as an internal employee scholarship. The statement announcing the negotiation reiterated the goal of Breadbasket:

Any company doing business in the ghetto must radically recon-
struct its employment practices commensurate with the profits
which it is taking out of the community. For any company to receive
sizeable profits from the Negro community while employing only
a small number of community residents, and thus reinvesting only
a small percentage of its profits back into the community is one of
the factors which creates a slum.[11]

Operation Breadbasket did not have an easy time coming into
Cleveland. Some leaders found the organization's tactics too heavy-
handed, like Clarence H. Holmes, director of Cleveland's public-
private employment program named AIM-JOBS, who said that
"Breadbasket activities have had no noticeable effect on . . . efforts
to place hard-core unemployed Negroes." Johnson feared that
Breadbasket inadvertently created negative attitudes toward those
who needed jobs. "Nobody likes to be coerced into action."[12] Some
Clevelanders—black and white—believed that the line between
coercion and community action was a thin one. The question of
how to compel businesses to listen to black consumers lingered as
Hough managed its introduction to McDonald's and the goals of
black franchising. While black Chicago welcomed the arrival of the
Golden Arches with little consternation, McDonald's entry into
the East Side of Cleveland was incredibly difficult. An inexplicable
homicide, a possible con artist, a tense mayoral race, and uncomfortable alliances frame the story of how McDonald's met Hough,
and how Hough exposed what McDonald's meant for black people, possibilities, and protest. Uncertainty and instability blanketed
Hough, and that meant one thing: McDonald's was on its way.

* * *

Toledo was the first home for McDonald's in Ohio, and in 1961,
Ray Kroc saw growth potential in moving to other cities across the
state. By 1965, Cleveland was already home to two McDonald's
restaurants, and due to their popularity, the company committed
to a major expansion in Ohio, bringing the total to ten drive-ins,
second in locations after Kroc's home state of Illinois.[13] In 1969,

Kroc exceeded his earlier goals for Ohio with twenty-four profitable locations in the state. It appears that the white franchisees
of McDonald's locations in black neighborhoods benefited from
the calm Holy Week in 1968 and survived Glenville that summer,
because there were no complaints of unsafe stores or attempts to
leave the neighborhoods. McDonald's in Cleveland was big business, with the restaurants predominately on the East Side, where
Hough was located, regularly ranking among the highest-earning
locations. Three white businessmen profited nearly $2.5 mil-
lion a year from four East Side franchises: referred to as the 83rd
Street, Euclid, St. Clair, and Kinsman locations. Edward Bood,
vice president and director of franchising for McDonald's, estimated that two of the Cleveland restaurants serving the Hough
community alone exceeded the national average of profits each
year. The bustling locations employed many locals and collectively
paid black employees "more than $600,000 a year."[14] With an
estimated 38% of black men in Hough unemployed, McDonald's
offered badly needed jobs. After the loss of so many restaurants in
Hough, McDonald's provided a place to eat. But, as some community leaders—energized by a round of conversations about what
came next for the East Side—watched as the franchise locations
filled cash registers day after day with money from black customers, eyebrows began to raise. Who was getting rich off all these
people? Where did the money go? It didn't go to the public parks,
the schools, or the people, that was for certain.[15] Besides, now that
Cleveland had a black mayor, wasn't it time for a black businessman to have a chance at some of the wealth that had come from
the East Side?

In the winter of 1969, Ernest Hilliard of suburban Warrenville
Heights decided he would try his hand at this new fast food ven-
ture. The native of Uniontown, Pennsylvania, was known by most
in Cleveland, and across the country, as radio evangelist Prophet
Frank Thomas of the First Spiritual Christian Church of America.
Hilliard shepherded his flock by using the airwaves as his staff,
and he was visible in Hough with a religious goods store. After
Hilliard decided that he would try to apply for a McDonald's fran-

chise on St. Clair and 105th Streets, he consulted his friend and fellow religious leader David Hill, who called himself Rabbi Hill of the House of Israel. Black franchisee may have been the role that Hilliard wanted most, but it was Hill who would emerge as the interlocutor in an absorbing exchange between black Cleveland and McDonald's. Hill was part of a long tradition of urban prophets who offered black people an alternative explanation of the world, in which their racial origins could be traced to African nobility and offered a radical vision of their purpose on earth, which challenged salvationist views of Christianity that rationalized suffering as the price one paid for a glorious afterlife.[16] If slavery and Jim Crow were the price of admission for paradise, some black believers questioned the cost and worth of this precious ticket. They flocked to figures like Hill, whose problack ideologies not only instilled pride but also rejected any demands to surrender to the inevitability of suffering at the hands of a white man's racism. Hill's path to establishing the House of Israel wended through correctional facilities in the South and Midwest. Between 1951 and 1966, the native of the western Arkansas town of Nashville, a place vastly different than the similarly named city in Tennessee, had been charged with a host of crimes. He was convicted of forgery, grand larceny, fraud, and writing bad checks, and he spent time in the Lima State Hospital for the Criminally Insane.[17]

Hill's past did not disqualify him from becoming a self-proclaimed leader of black Cleveland. This house that David built rested on an amalgamated foundation of ideologies. The organization was loyal to black nationalism in its dedication to black institution building. They preached a vision of black millennialism, a belief that blacks should invest in the future possibilities of an all-black society within a larger racist one. They expressed their commitments to black radicalism by using protest to disrupt the status quo and demand social change. And when it came to what Hough needed, they embraced black capitalism. Hill was adept at not only preaching all of these belief systems, but he was also skilled in adapting them into political theater. In the fall of 1969, Hill announced that he would execute Santa Claus as part of the

local Black Christmas Committee's attempt to have blacks boycott Christmas. Hill explained that in "typical Western custom,"
Santa would be paraded to the city's Public Square and found
guilty of "exploitation and fostering white racism"; then he would
be hanged. In typical Hill custom, the dramatics were meant to
address the quotidian abuses felt by blacks in Hough and other
parts of Cleveland, particularly reports that police officers intimidated black voters when they turned out to support Stokes on the
most recent Election Day. [18]

Ever attuned to new opportunities for himself, in the summer
of 1969, Hill believed that he and his fellow prophet had discovered something positive and profitable for their section of black
Cleveland. Hilliard began the process to become a franchisee that
year, contacting Mayor Stokes's office for help and arranging meetings with McDonald's regional franchise managers. Like many
interested candidates, McDonald's recommended that Hilliard
gain in-store experience, so he reported for duty to the St. Clair
location. Hilliard discovered that actual McDonald's training
occurred at Hamburger University, to which he never received an
acceptance letter. Hilliard then hired an attorney and again tried
to learn what was required to open a franchise, but the regional
manager told him that he could not give Hilliard a franchise on the
East Side because of territorial rights held by the current franchisees. In its early franchise days, McDonald's allowed franchisees
to lay claim to large geographic regions, but ceased the practice
when it was revealed to undercut their earning potential. Believing
that he was a victim of racial discrimination, Hilliard appealed to
Hill and his associate, activist and House of Israel Director James
Raplin, for assistance.[19] Except for each being led by charismatic
black men, the House of Israel and the mayor's office appeared as
if they existed on different planets. But Stokes won his election by
finding common ground with the more radical elements of black
Cleveland, and as fixtures on the East Side, Hilliard and Hill probably felt at home meeting with McDonald's executives in the Tapestry Room of Cleveland City Hall under a Stokes administration.
What use is a black mayor if the people can't use one of his meeting

rooms? As tensions heightened around the issue of black franchising in Cleveland, the Beaux-Arts style building would serve as a neutral territory between McDonald's and a demanding public.

McDonald's did not come to the meeting prepared to offer anything to the duo, except for a request for names. If Hill and Raplin could generate a list of potential black franchisees who could pay a $2,500 application fee and $2,500 upon acceptance of their bid, then—after some vetting—an African American could possibly join the Golden Arches family in Cleveland. Hill and Raplin claimed to have already compiled a roster of twenty black Clevelanders for this effort, including football star Jim Brown, who patrolled the streets of Cleveland with Stokes that fateful April night that King was assassinated. Other hopefuls included an entire black investment club and a local public school system leader. While Hill and Raplin reported that the meeting was just a discussion of names, one Stokes biographer characterized the event as far more combative. Hill demanded that McDonald's "hand over the keys to all white-owned franchises in Cleveland's inner city."[20] A practiced provocateur, Hill knew that the odds were not in his favor that McDonald's would surrender anything to the men that afternoon. Hill and Raplin still wanted to know why their preferred members of black Cleveland had been denied and explore how and when Hilliard would get an opportunity to command his own franchise.[21] The meeting ended with little but an agreement to reconvene for another confab on July 7. By the time the assigned date and hour arrived, one man would be dead.

Three days before the meeting, when a shot rang out on Hathaway Lane in Warrenville Heights, neighbors may have thought they heard a lone firecracker left over from the Independence Day celebrations that evening. Hilliard's wife, Georgia, thought so too. But when she stepped outside her home to double check, she found her husband in the driveway gasping for air. Ernest had been shot. Georgia was in shock as she scrambled to talk to her dying husband. She started connecting the dots. Georgia later told the press that her husband was a victim of a "professional murder," a targeted killing that could only be tied to one

thing: "the McDonald's deal." After Ernest was pronounced dead, his friends started to tell Georgia things. He had received a phone call from an unknown person who threatened: "We will let you make niggerburgers in hell." His wife remembered him mentioning "receiving threatening telephone calls," but Ernest didn't say much more. Georgia did not know who was behind the threats or just how disturbing the anonymous calls were to her husband, but she knew that the franchise was consuming a lot of time. As Ernest lay dying, Georgia asked, "Who shot you?" His reply: "White folks." Did she hear that correctly? Police later speculated he was actually saying "white Ford," because neighbors told authorities that they saw a white car speed away from the crime scene. But Georgia and Ernest's friends knew better. They were certain that this all circled back to McDonald's. [22] Hill decided that yet another white business—like that bar that put out the sign or the ones that marked up their prices on stale bread and rotting meat or the ones that refused to hire black teenagers—had gone too far. Hilliard's murder was never officially deemed associated with McDonald's or his franchising bid, but grief can activate old wounds. King's death had made some cities burn. Ernest Hilliard's death, at the very least, would make Cleveland change.

In a matter of days, Hill garnered support from an array of Cleveland-based community groups and local chapters of civil rights organizations to sign on to a new group, Operation Black Unity, headquarted at his House of Israel building. Hill and the members of the loosely bound OBU may have thought they would disrupt the flow of McDonald's traffic for a few days, find an avenue to get some blacks into franchising, and take their rightful place in Cleveland history alongside Stokes. Hill's first boycott flyer laid bare the enemy combatants in the war he was waging on fast food: "McDonald's Hamburger Corp versus Black People." On July 10, OBU directed concerned citizens to four McDonald's restaurants on the East Side to participate in staged demonstrations or to stay home and boycott the stores. [23] At one location, a group of young men outfitted in "black jackets and berets" told passersby not to enter a McDonald's. The store's manager claimed that ten carloads

of protesters approached the store, so he threw in the towel and locked the doors of his restaurant at 12:35 P.M., the height of lunchtime service. Another location closed by the late afternoon.[24] The chapeau-clad young men may have been members of Afro Set, a local black nationalist group founded in 1968 that partnered with Stokes's Cleveland: NOW! economic development program. Afro Set advocated for developing the black community through business and social programs, so it could exist apart from the larger white economic power structure. Afro Set and Stokes were often opposed about methods and goals, but they were joined in their desire to see the East Side recover from its injuries. Black politics could bring board coalitions together for a greater good, whether to mourn a death or to seek healing for an ailing city.

McDonald's believed that the worst of doing business in the inner city was behind them. Restaurants in Washington, D.C., Detroit, Chicago, and Los Angeles rebounded from the property damage of April 1968 and the hot summers that followed, and by 1969, McDonald's corporate offices had constructed a well-oiled mechanism for transferring franchises from white to black hands. They were even getting good press for their bold commitment to black wealth building. McDonald's had "sent a directive to all white owners of inner-city franchises asking them to sell to blacks," and reported that the transfers were rapid and efficient. The scheme to shift operators across racial lines led to changes in nineteen existing stores, and two brand-new stores were designated for blacks.[25] The NBMOA expanded out of its midwestern center and included members in Los Angeles and Kansas City.[26] Things were looking good for McDonald's. Until the frantic calls from Cleveland reached their headquarters.

If the Cleveland boycotters wanted to show McDonald's the power of the black dollar, it was working. Five days into the boycott, three of the stores had ceased operations and only one of the restaurants kept its doors open.[27] Accustomed to earning $400 by noon, a manager at Kinsman Road reported $36 in sales.[28] The next day, the newspaper business pages outside of Cleveland were taking notice. Afro Set was performing its signature, choreographed

drills. Dressed in bold print dashikis and necklaces with dangling African-inspired medallions, Afro Set sometimes performed with machetes and nationalist flags, and the sight of the young men heightened the tensions of managers and franchisees who did not care for the news cameras that began to gather around the restaurant. Four stores were "all but closed" by the boycotts. The OBU action was working so well that it was shaping business outside of the East Side. A fifth McDonald's location—which was not originally a target of the protest—also reported a decline in patrons.[29]

McDonald's tried to defend themselves from the accusations and insults leveled by Hill, the OBU's conductor and loudest mouthpiece. Black Cleveland—they argued—simply misunderstood what had happened. Months before Hilliard's death, McDonald's regional representatives claimed, they were trying to find black franchisees as early as March but couldn't find qualified operators. Cleveland's McDonald's outlets were not harmed or abandoned, like Petty's Woodlawn outfit. In fact, they netted more than their average stores, and those high profits contributed to the franchise's value. Cleveland's black business community could not clear the financial hurdle to qualify for a restaurant. Hill countered McDonald's claim by citing his list of twenty potential franchisees, as well as Hilliard's efforts to return the conversation to OBU's central argument: McDonald's wanted to dictate a process that belonged in the community's hands. McDonald's may have laid down the most valuable card in its deck when they strayed from the boycott and focused on its leader. McDonald's spokespeople shared with the *New York Times* and other news sources that Hill had used aliases for decades and had been arrested dozens of times between 1943 and 1960.[30] Hill may have been used to his criminal record becoming an inconvenient truth for him, and he simply reminded the public that McDonald's was no better than a white overseer of a plantation or any other predatory authority that did not respect black self-determination. Hill rested his case in the way he rested all his debates; there was no room for negotiation. "McDonald's people say they want to deal with some responsible and sophisticated colored people. They're looking for some good niggers," he retorted. Hill grandstanded: "If you don't meet with

Rabbi David Hill, then you won't meet with anyone. The black community will tell McDonald's who's qualified to run these things and who's not." [31]

The boycott continued.

McDonald's may have finally found a race-based challenge that they couldn't ignore like the southern sit-ins or capitalize upon like the damages of post-King cities. McDonald's representatives not only had to respond to OBU as boycotts imperiled their businesses, but they also had to address a news media that found the story noteworthy because of what was happening and where it was unfolding. Cleveland was rife with the appearance of racial contradictions. A black mayor was elected in a city that was only 37% black. He was smart enough to prevent a major catastrophe after King, only to have to manage a firestorm a few months later. McDonald's had seamlessly entered other inner cities in places that were larger, more racially polarized, and far more influential, but Cleveland was showing the country something different. If blacks were supposed to select what their freedom would look like off a limited menu of capitulation to capitalism or resistance to capitalism, then OBU was suggesting that they should customize it to fit their tastes. Black Power capitalism, as it emerged in Cleveland, prioritized black ownership, wealth building, and community connectedness.

The OBU boycott quickly revealed that the actions that shut down or disturbed McDonald's business were emblematic of black politics in Cleveland. Complaints about the mayor's cautious ways of talking about the protests—validating the right to protest without interrogating McDonald's responsibility to local communities—highlighted the disappointment with the limits of being governed by a black mayor. Concerns about Hill's suitability to speak for all of black Cleveland emanated from both his criminal history as well as his adoption of black radical ideals. McDonald's assertion that the boycott actually hurt black workers who could not collect paychecks when stores were closed exposed the unequal consequences of black political action in a low-income community. With each day, a new insight became visible or kernel of informa-

tion was revealed about the nature of the boycott and black capital-ism. OBU members and leaders had to wonder if the boycott was the right thing to do, and if a franchise could actually do very much for the East Side. Although OBU was forged out of a sense that McDonald's owed black Cleveland something, identifying the boy-cott's goals was difficult by virtue of the groups that came together over the McDonald's issue. On the whole, black advocacy groups sought the eradication of racism and organized themselves around ideas of racial justice, but there was no uniformity in opinion on how these principles should be manifested in the world, especially in the marketplace. In the ways that the term "black capitalism" could mean so many things to so many people, OBU's boycott expressed their opposition to McDonald's, but depending on each organization's history and political position, what they believed to be the solution varied greatly. The diversity among this group of black freedom seekers served to raise awareness of the boycotts and indicated that McDonald's had a formidable community to deal with, but that same diversity made it difficult to define the parameters of success.

As the boycott passed the two-week mark, an article in the *Cleveland Plain Dealer* captured the divergent ideas of what a black McDonald's meant to black residents. The newspaper reported: "Some members of the unity group want black own-ers of McDonald's franchises. Some want a structure of such a nature that profits will benefit the total black community. Some want McDonald's out of black neighborhoods."[32] A public-private development group founded to revitalize blighted neighborhoods, wanted to see a reduction in franchise fees. Franchise prices were based on annual sales, and there were questions and concerns about how a boycott could artificially depress a store's value. They repeated the claim made by black franchise applicants, who accused white operators of inflating the price tag on the boycotted restaurants. McDonald's accused OBU of using boycotts to "lower sale prices of the franchises" and held that black activists misun-derstood why each franchise was offered at a different price—new stores and existing stores varied in the cost of investment because

of differential profit margins, set volumes, and prior sales.[33] Boy-cotting, in McDonald's estimation, was merely a market manip-ulation trick. McDonald's argued in the court of public opinion that OBU activists were using the pickets to sink the franchises and snap them up for cheap.

Franchise costs were less important to the local Urban League, an organization founded on the principle of fighting racial discrim-ination. Urban League leaders did not get mired in the details of sale prices. An enthusiastic partner on many economic and housing development programs, the Urban League understood the boycott as a matter of blacks and whites being able to access franchises on an equal basis. Their position gestured toward the accusations that perfectly qualified black applicants were rejected out of hand from franchising. Civil rights mainstay CORE, which had been so inte-gral in the sit-ins that desegregated the southern fast food industry, had pivoted toward economic development and black capitalism in the late 1960s. The Cleveland chapter wanted blacks to "define [their] own turf and control it." CORE Cleveland's spin-off proj-ect, Target City, also weighed in on the debate. Target City, which scholar Nishani Frazier has described as espousing "communal capitalism," believed that it was possible for franchising to do more than enrich individuals.[34] Target City's director explained, "We're not talking about making a half-dozen black millionaires . . . CORE is interested in a structure in which profits from the res-taurants will benefit the total black community." Meanwhile, the Southern Christian Leadership Conference, which was still vibrant despite losing King a year earlier, was among the first supporters of the demonstrations, and they hoped that more restaurants and ownership opportunities could lead to better jobs for black peo-ple.[35] Each organization believed that if the boycotts could compel McDonald's to put the restaurants under the auspices of a black owner, some (if not all) of their goals for the community could be met. The fact that a fast food restaurant bore the weight of all these wants elucidates both the desperate state of black Cleveland in finding vehicles to address economic disenfranchisement and the pragmatism of some black leaders in using fast food's expansion as

a way to meet community demands for jobs, as well as avenues to business ownership.

In the hands of the most talented organizer, the competing desires of OBU, McDonald's reticence to negotiate, and the uncertainty of how long the boycott would last would be incredibly difficult to manage. For Hill, whose strength was mostly showmanship, maintaining control of OBU became increasingly difficult. When McDonald's reached out to OBU to schedule a meeting after the first week of boycotting, Hill said that OBU was only willing to negotiate if McDonald's president Fred Turner came to Cleveland. Turner had no intention of boarding a plane to visit Hill or any other member of OBU. But McDonald's finally conceded to OBU demands and sent top-level McDonald's leaders, including a newly hired Bob Beavers, to the offices of the *Call & Post*, black Cleveland's trusted newspaper, to meet. The intensity that enveloped the gathering was on a par with a hostage negotiation or a wartime surrender. Guards stood outside the doors of the meeting room. The McDonald's representatives later revealed that they were advised to arm themselves with a gun in case someone made good on the threats that franchisers and franchisees had received since the boycott opened. The current franchisees had waved the white flag, and they wanted out as soon as possible. The offer to sell the franchises to a black businessman was not going to be accepted so hastily. Hill had been the public face and voice of the boycott for weeks, but McDonald's did not want to acknowledge Hill's leadership in the opening stages of the negotiation. Further, McDonald's refused his request to apologize for the various accusations they made about his character and criminal history in the press. Hill had already warned McDonald's that they had to meet with him and no one else would accommodate a request to talk. The Black community, Hill reminded, was in charge, and there was no question that they would win. McDonald's claimed that throughout the early days of the boycott, the corporation and its franchisees were recipients of threats and harassment. McDonald's executive Edward Bood assured OBU that they were supportive of a potential sale from white operators to black ones but wanted to

avoid appearing as if they were rewarding "threats and intimidation," and he admitted that he didn't want to "deal with Hill" as the lead negotiator of the issue. When given the opportunity to talk to Hill directly, McDonald's representatives declined.

The McDonald's reps headed for the door, and they probably reasoned that any movement organized by Hill would eventually burn out. But as they began to measure the boycott in weeks rather than days, McDonald's grew afraid that if black diners took too long a break from their swiftly prepared burgers and perfectly browned potatoes, they would not return. Internally, McDonald's worried that the boycott was shifting the "eating habits of customers in the area" and making room for competing fast food outlets to enter their territory. They were not far off in their assessment; Mahalia Jackson's Glori-Fried Chicken restaurant visited Cleveland in the summer of 1969 to see if they could benefit from blacks taking a break from burgers.[36] Externally, McDonald's implored OBU to consider the ways they were imperiling black jobs by keeping the restaurant closed. The optics of the boycott may have been amplified because the employees and the boycotters were all black, highlighting the fissures among black community relationships to the burgeoning franchise. OBU supporters who wanted to realize black control of McDonald's in Cleveland could not ignore the fact that boycotts sometimes led to intimidation and violence between picketers and potential customers, as well as picketers and black employees. The consequences of picketing were a contentious issue for a community that often used this form of protest to access a restaurant, not to own it. An Urban League representative remarked:

> The objective is different from that of former picketing . . . it's to make them hurt to the point that they stop playing games and consummate the negotiation that has been going on for some time. I think this form of picketing is just as ethical and just as moral.[37]

McDonald's, of course, did not appreciate the ethical and moral imperatives of protest.

Blacks were welcome to try their hands at franchising, but ulti-

mately the corporation would decide where, when, and how. Bood reiterated that they would do everything to "encourage Negro ownership," but criticized OBU for lacking "a responsible and reasonable approach" to appealing for the franchise. While Petty and others were encouraged to tap into Small Business Administration lending programs and McDonald's was willing to be flexible with other black franchisees unable to gather the requisite funds for stores, McDonald's would not bend in Cleveland. This was not about discrimination, they argued; they were uncertain about the OBU's capacity to cover the franchise's price. In 1969, franchise fees were set at $12,500 for a company-developed property plus 2.2% of profits for a "continuing service fee." Franchisees had to present approximately $45,000 to secure the deal, including up to $15,000 for "security on the leased property and building," in addition to a down payment of $8,000 "for signs and equipment, [and] $7,000 for operational items."[38] The only area in which McDonald's was willing to bend was that it would allow "responsible black community organizations to operate franchises," due to having "difficulty in locating financially qualified individuals." The announcement of the policy change toward allowing organizations to apply for franchises instantly piqued the interest of House of Israel members. Bood said Hill's church did not meet criteria. "The House of Israel in our opinion represents its own interests and objectives and not those of the black community in Cleveland." In McDonald's estimation, anything associated with Hill failed to qualify as responsible. As the boycott story remained on the pages of local and national newspapers, McDonald's may have worried that protests like these would multiply across the very markets they wanted to enter. McDonald's could not afford to have several of these actions dictate the future of their urban expansion.[39]

For the white franchisees in the middle of this fight, they were done with all of it: OBU's obstinance and McDonald's stubbornness. Bood claimed he was actively encouraging "white owners of franchises in black communities to sell to qualified black individuals" and assured that "many such sales have transpired." But Cleveland was not going to be that easy.[40] One white franchisee

of the boycott's first targeted store, Orvin Benson, said that he was "perfectly willing to entertain any legitimate offer." His experience called McDonald's narrative of the boycott into question. Benson claimed that he was terrified by "shots through [his store] window," and for all of McDonald's posturing about supporting franchise sales, he had yet to engage in any "talk about a deal." Prior to the picketing, Benson said he actually tried to sell his franchise to Hilliard, but Hilliard could not get financing. Benson conceded that OBU's suspicions were correct but misunderstood. He did raise the price of his franchise for resale. His accountant valued the restaurant at $250,000 when Hilliard applied to franchise it. His location at 10411 St. Clair Avenue grew by 86% in one year, and Benson presented a letter from McDonald's stating that the St. Clair store witnessed "the biggest increase ever" that year.[41]

While McDonald's negotiated with OBU, the stores remained mostly closed as boycott activity entered its second month in August. McDonald's and OBU agreed to return to the drawing board, on the condition that McDonald's respect the request of the local chapters of the NAACP and Urban League: keep stores closed until after the two parties had a chance to meet. After agreeing to "carefully consider" the request, McDonald's fears of losing another day of sales receipts led them to reopen the stores. To add insult to injury, McDonald's paid for a full-page ad in the *Cleveland Press* announcing that stores were open for business.[42] Two weeks later, the OBU reopened conversations with McDonald's with a revised proposal for how the stalemate could come to an end. OBU ignored McDonald's earlier assessment of Hill and the House of Israel's suitability for franchise leadership, and they strategized how they would raise the capital to make a bid for at least one of the East Side locations.

But if OBU was to do any deals with McDonald's, they were not going to simply acquire a franchise, they were going to change how businesses entered black Cleveland altogether. Hill demanded that in addition to the keys to the properties, McDonald's give $10,000 to the black community of Cleveland for local projects and neighborhood resources. In recognition of their work in arrang-

ing the transfers, OBU also asked for a fee equal to 2% of the franchise sale price. Hill also requested that in order to prevent another instance like the one that frustrated Hilliard's attempt at getting his restaurant, OBU hold the exclusive right to determine Cleveland's future black franchisees. Exhausted and beleaguered white franchisees were willing to accept the 2% provision and turn over their stores, but McDonald's could not stomach the proposal. McDonald's, which had shown itself to be flexible with other black operators, believed that by accepting the OBU terms they would inflict "substantial harm" on other franchise operators, other business interests, and the East Side. By harm, Bood probably meant evidence that boycott was an effective means of challenging businesses and that black consumer power was still real after the sit-in movement had passed. In Bood's estimation, McDonald's "best contribution to the black community is being a good citizen and providing jobs and taxes, and encouraging our operators to support all worthy community programs."[43] OBU was willing to offer a slight compromise. If McDonald's didn't want to make a direct gift to OBU, each franchisee—acting independently of McDonald's—should offer $2,500 and collectively donate $20,000, which amounted to approximately 20% of the sale price of each store.[44] The two sides were approaching a compromise on sales to black franchisees, but McDonald's vice president demanded that no one give in to OBU's request for donations. McDonald's was willing to fund a community swimming pool, playground, or recreation center for east Cleveland, but no direct cash payment would be on the table. Besides, McDonald's argued, their initiative was worth far more than the original donation requests.[45]

The OBU would not be treated this way. Black people could determine their own destiny, and the group probably balked when a McDonald's representative listed its donations to the NAACP, the United Negro College Fund, schools on Native American reservations, and "educational institutions and local civic causes to the tune of $5,000." They would be open to donating to the Cleveland Urban Coalition, but not to OBU or OBU-connected projects.[46] McDonald's unquestionably would need to prioritize philanthropy if they

were to expand in black America, but benevolence didn't mean that the company would acquiesce to every request or protest. The Cleveland crisis was actively shaping how McDonald's was establishing its community relations protocols for the future, and it was enhancing the expectation that black franchisees would function as peacekeepers and bulwarks between the corporate office and the community. The dynamic between OBU and McDonald's also foreshadowed the future of franchises in black areas, as their involvement in subsidizing swimming pools and neighborhood resources blurred the boundaries between company and community trust.

McDonald's rejection of the OBU plan momentarily reignited the fight. The week after Bood elaborated McDonald's good citizenship, OBU drew 500 people to a mass meeting about McDonald's. National CORE leader Roy Innis came to Cleveland to encourage the boycott. Innis was the only national civil rights leader to visit Cleveland during the protest. National Urban League and NAACP heads opted to have locals determine the way forward for themselves. Among the many lines that drew applause from the crowd, Innis said he was glad that Clevelanders did not ask for jobs at their local McDonald's—they wanted power. "The demand is to take over the whole damned instruments," he lectured.[47] White franchise owners were willing to hand over the instruments, but McDonald's was unmoved. Ed Greenwald, an attorney for a white franchisee, recognized that McDonald's would not concede to anyone even as their franchisees searched for an exit. "Big Daddy has final control and Big Daddy said no." The patriarchal will of the franchise over the franchisee was absolute: "If we want to sell our franchises, we gotta look to Big Daddy for the blessing. We can't move without their consent." Whether they were moved by the spirit of social change or collapsed by the stress of the boycotts, white franchisees agreed more than they disagreed with the transfer program, even if they did not initially seek it out. "Our franchise holders, after a lot of thought, have agreed that it makes perfectly good sense that these businesses should be sold to blacks because these are very different times," Greenwald said. "I have no guide for what is right in these times. Nobody has."[48]

The McDonald's franchise manual covered a myriad of topics, but challenges by black nationalists were not one of them. With "no guide" available on engaging groups like OBU, but an awareness that what happened in Cleveland may set a precedent, McDonald's continued to discredit OBU and their requests. Bood asked, with "no trust fund set up, no funds to be administered through any trust fund, no foundation or anything," how could OBU be trusted with thousands of dollars for the community? "Who are to be the officers? Who'll get the benefits of any monies collected from royalties?"[49] OBU was also without much of a blueprint on how to negotiate with a corporate entity like McDonald's. Previous large-scale boycotts among black communities were guided by the leadership of an Operation Breadbasket or an NAACP in solidarity with other groups. OBU imagined the organization to be an equal member of the boycott campaign, but Hill's dominance and the uncertainty of how each entity would intersect with the desired outcomes undermined the movement's strength.

As the summer gave way to a fall election season, the boycott's foundations began to crack. The wide range of OBU member perspectives, growing discomfort with Hill's assertive style, and the enlarging specter of the boycott on Stokes's reelection efforts began to disassemble the group.

Cleveland NAACP members grew outraged by Hill's alleged behavior behind the scenes of the boycott. Initially, his OBU compatriots did not address his criminal record, and he could rely on black establishment types in Cleveland to stand up for him when his character was in question. As an unnamed member of Stokes's inner circle told the press in response to revelations about Hill's past: "The man's not important but the issue of black control is."[50] The *Plain Dealer* summed it up: "OBU members were familiar with Hill's background, but they agreed with his position on black capitalism."[51] The possibilities of black ownership in Hough were too lucrative to let Hill's rap sheet get in the way. But eventually rumors circulated that Hill was asking for money to go into his pockets, not OBU coffers, and he may have been directing rogue boycotters to threaten franchisees. The NAACP wondered how their beloved organization was entangled with an "extortionist attempt."[52]

Urban League members were also becoming targets of criticism for associating with Hill. Leaders issued a joint statement from NAACP and Urban League members disavowing "extortion or blackmail." A member of a local business league offered: "We are opposed to any group trying to force others to sell their businesses. Negro people must build something of their own instead of taking from others."[53] One by one, the "mainstream" or "old-school" groups began to withdraw from OBU. In September of 1969, the Urban League broke from OBU.[54] A week later, Hill was ousted as the chair of the OBU Negotiating Committee. The group that expended significant social capital by supporting him unanimously accepted his reluctant resignation. Hill warned, "I don't share those beliefs, but they will soon learn that I am not the problem, but the enemy is." The final straw for OBU: Hill allegedly held onto $50,000 in franchisee applicant fees, a charge he denied.[55] Black capitalism could bring people together, but it alone was not enough to keep them united. McDonald's resistance to negotiate with OBU became secondary to Hill's reputation or the fear that the coalition would seem undeserving or overly greedy. In the struggle for black organizations to petition for resources—whether from the state or the marketplace—blacks always remained vigilant that they not conform to stereotypes of being idle or insolent, even when they were victims of injustice. Although Hill was a flawed leader in a variety of ways, OBU's defectors shifted their ire from the hamburger stand in their neighborhood to their neighbors who requested that the hamburger stand contribute to community resources.

Soon after Hill's ouster, a grand jury was assembled to determine if OBU violated extortion laws. Any opponent of black nationalism or the House of Israel lined up to make an example of Hill and to tell a black community organizing around boycotts and economic development that they would be watched. While anti-integrationist whites found black capitalism's comfort with separatism appealing, white authorities would not allow black communities to operate unchecked. Whether OBU was the real target, or the mayor heading into an election, the fallout around Hill

and the boycott muffled black voices who took economic exploitation to task. A crusading state representative from the suburbs assured that if no specific laws were violated in this case because the OBU manipulated legal loopholes, then he would propose new extortion laws during the upcoming legislative period. Black Cleveland could agitate all they wanted, but ultimately the state could and would have the last word. In response to the threat of drafting new extortion laws to punish OBU activism, OBU supporter Hilbert Perry retorted that he wanted to impanel a grand jury to investigate racism in the city. "McDonald's can take $2.5 million out of the black community and not have the responsibility to help rebuild the inner city," and in his estimation, "this act of theft warranted some type of inquiry." Why stop there, Perry wondered. He also wanted someone to look into "the lack of fair housing . . . high inner-city unemployment rate, and current welfare programs."[56]

Having managed his own ups and downs with his colleagues in state and city government, Carl Stokes knew that some of his white detractors would rather spend time litigating OBU controversies than funding the construction projects needed in Hough and Glenville. He also knew the boycott was going to remain strong into September, and his primary race was on October 1. And he was aware that he had to stave off Democratic challengers, assure black voters he was still with them, and remind white voters that 1966 was behind them. Mayor Stokes did not have time for the back-and-forth with McDonald's, but he didn't get where he was without understanding that all things were political. He was feeling the pressure from the local party, which met in late August to express concern that Stokes was mum on the McDonald's issue, and the party formed a committee with the explicit purpose of discussing his strategy on managing it.[57] Then there were the newspapers with the embarrassing headlines that seemed to be making fun of the mayor. "Hamburger Hassle Imperils Stokes," cried the *Washington Post*. "Friends and advisers are praying that Mayor Carl B. Stokes won't trip over a hamburger between now and Election Day."[58] His campaign manager tried to keep his official comments strictly on the act of protest, rather than on the target. "They are exercising

a constitutional right to picket. And they are sitting down at the negotiation table trying to settle their grievances with a company regarding what they consider to be an injustice in the community." Stokes called "picketing at McDonald's as American as apple pie."[59] The Stokes campaign's sanitized statement was vaguely supportive without choosing a side.

McDonald's was exposing how black politics, economics, and even identity could converge into high-stakes decision-making. The McDonald's boycott was about more than a business; it was testing the volume of black voices in setting the standard and expectation of their consumer citizenship in Hough and surrounding areas, which set the tone of how they could maintain their electoral power. Stokes's Democratic primary opponent Robert J. Kelly used the issue to blow a dog whistle toward white voters uncertain about a black mayor's ability to effectively control black communities. Kelly seized on the apple pie analogy: "This shows how little he knows about America or apple pie when he tries to compare legitimate picketing with extortion." Kelly asked which of Cleveland's beloved businesses would next fall victim to black irascibility? Would A&P, Pick-N-Pay, Sears, or the Cleveland Trust find themselves targeted by black ire? "Or will it be the little businessman in the neighborhood trying to make a living?"[60] Those closest to Stokes knew that white Clevelanders, maybe even some that voted for the charismatic mayor, had doubts about his ability to improve the city. Meanwhile black voters were perpetually reminded of how little had changed. One observer took blacks to task for believing too deeply in Stokes. "People thought that once a black mayor was elected, money was going to start falling from the sky, and jobs were going to be lying around in the streets."[61] Black Clevelanders were not so naïve as to think everything would change overnight, but how would change come if they didn't fight? Recognizing that there were battles to join across the city, black Cleveland turned out for their mayor in the Democratic primary, helping Stokes collect 60% of the vote to shore up his candidacy for a second term.[62]

The day before Stokes's electoral victory, he celebrated a smaller

win—the end of the McDonald's boycott. With Hill under investigation and a dwindling base of supporters, the mayor may have realized that this was his chance to step in and settle the boycott. The remaining leadership of the OBU accepted Stokes's proposal that in exchange for the end of the boycotts, McDonald's would immediately identify and turn over the stores to black franchisees. OBU was probably unaware that McDonald's already had their future franchisee in mind. In October, DeForest Brown Jr., president of the Hough Area Development Corporation (HADC), contacted what was left of the OBU to submit a bid to franchise two locations. Founded by Brown, a minister and social worker, after the Hough uprising in 1967, the HADC drew upon federal, city, and private dollars to finance community-based projects, including a shopping plaza, affordable housing, and a small factory. The HADC replicated a popular model created in the late 1960s, which brought social service organizations in conversation with private foundations and corporations to underwrite a host of initiatives that matched the enthusiasm for black capitalism with millions of dollars.[63] Brown came prepared to offer $400,000 for the franchises, with assistance from a local bank, more than $50,000 of HADC venture capital, and federal resources from the Office of Economic Opportunity (OEO). Once they acquired the restaurant, the HADC would transfer ownership to the newly formed Ghetto East Enterprises, Inc., a for profit corporation. Then, after a year, they would transfer ownership to the larger Hough community by offering shares in the franchise.[64] Hill and his faction were angered that the HADC was granted a franchise before them and the list of twenty, some of whom believed they were close to entering franchise agreements. The HADC's liquidity and its experience with tapping into federal resources aligned with how McDonald's inner-city expansion plan had worked. Although the HADC was not opposed to using protest to apply pressure to draw investments into Hough, they were able to allay fears that McDonald's would be asked to underwrite pools or parks. From the perspective of the HADC, they would do that themselves by running a profitable business and putting the means of ownership in the hands of the people.[65]

After the deal was finalized, McDonald's revealed in the spring of 1970 that they had reached out to the HADC at the height of the protest that past summer. HADC's interest in McDonald's remained quiet, perhaps causing OBU to feel more confident about its prospects for acquiring the restaurants. McDonald's did not remark on this until a *Plain Dealer* article exposed that the HADC partnership was "part of a move to take over control of two McDonald's outlets in black areas." Fearing the boycotts would become "damaging to race relations in Cleveland" and could impede "acceptance of the restaurants" as truly black franchises, a local attorney admitted that he helped McDonald's contact the HADC. The lawyer also emphasized that Hill actually tried to undermine the deal, and he was grateful to Stokes for discreetly helping broker the process.[66] McDonald's refusals of the OBU were not only about their insistence not to capitulate, but also their awareness that they could find a better partner if they held out. By allowing their franchisees to fret, the community to become more incensed, and the mayor to contemplate if he was going to win reelection, McDonald's sent a clear message about how much community agitation they would tolerate. At the offices of the community development groups that sprouted up in cities across the country after 1968, the HADC McDonald's projects were inspiring them to think about how fast food could fit in their lofty plans to resuscitate the inner city. McDonald's had appeared unkind and unresponsive during the OBU boycotts, but soon after, they partnered with HADC and other community development groups to franchise restaurants in Hough, and McDonald's was able to seal its image as a socially progressive supporter of black capitalism.

McDonald's may have resolved their boycott issues, but for Hill and other OBU members, the final act of the drama was set in the courtroom, not at the counter. There was no grand jury assembled to think about poverty in Hough, as Hilbert Perry sarcastically suggested. A Cuyahoga County grand jury was, however, impaneled, and they called potential franchisees, OBU members, and McDonald's executives to answer questions about whether Hill solicited money for his backing their McDonald's bids. They all

denied giving any money to Hill. Potential franchisee applicants all testified that McDonald's referred them to Hill before the pickets started, suggesting that they saw him as a valuable asset in finding black franchisees or an object of diversion to avoid engaging with the men.[67] The testimonies of Bood and McDonald's spokesman John Devitt probably convinced the jury to move forward with an indictment of four counts of blackmailing. In what was described as an "unprecedented move" by the prosecutor, the charge claimed that by initiating the boycott, Hill threatened to end the profits of the restaurants, which "carried the implicit threat of violence to anyone crossing the picket line," thus supporting a blackmail charge. For black organizations across Cleveland, the indictment may have alerted them to the risks of executing boycotts. James Raplin, Hill's right-hand man, was also charged with blackmail. The prosecutorial strategy was believed by some to be an attack on Stokes, who had lent support to other black boycotts.[68] Despite another court declaring him mentally incompetent, Hill stood trial for blackmail. OBU's attorney emphasized that the label of incompetence would have "no effect whatsoever on David Hill's position in Operation Black Unity," hinting that the gutted and discredited organization would continue on after the trial. Hill's defense attorney called the assessment of his client's faculties a "typical racist reaction to a black radical's efforts to help his people."[69] Hill's mental state aside, the attorney was accurate in describing the justice system's pathologizing of black anger and discord. State prisons and mental institutions housed black men and women who were labeled criminally insane, when in fact they were simply indignant over racist treatment. Protest would not die in Cleveland after a verdict came in Hill's trial, but the sheer power and influence of McDonald's and their ability to control the Cleveland crisis dampened the belief that gaining economic power meant gaining freedom from the racism found in other power structures.

By the start of 1970, the issue of black ownership of Cleveland McDonald's had officially come to an end.[70] The Hough Area Development Corporation was now at the helm of the East 82nd and East 107th Street restaurants. Kinsman Road went to

Charles E. Johnson, the president of CAM, Inc. Johnson had tried for more than a year to acquire a franchise, but he couldn't secure a loan until the OBU boycotts brought the ownership issue to the fore. The community-owned McDonald's locations were unable to maintain their hold on the businesses, especially after cuts to federal economic development programs depleted their financial and political power. In 1982, the HADC struggled to "replace 84% of its operating costs" after the OEO's successor, the Community Services Administration, was obliterated by federal budget cuts. Those locations, as well as more fast-food restaurants in black areas, would be franchised by blacks throughout the following two decades.[71] The *Atlanta Daily World* applauded the protests for showing "the viability of black power and the stability of appetites."[72] Each of these locations also showed the viability of fast food in environments shaped by economic, racial, and social instability.

As for Hill and Raplin, they would not know their fates until the winter of 1972. By then, Stokes had won the 1969 mayoral election, served his second term as mayor, and moved on to a career in broadcasting in New York City. Everyone had seemed to move on, except the pair. The men were found guilty, and then their paths diverged. Hill—who was facing up to forty-five years in prison for nine counts of blackmail—was determined not to serve another day in an institution after spending years in and out of juvenile and adult facilities. The Rabbi fled to Guyana, the South American nation that had long been seen as a promised land for American blacks.[73] In Guyana he established the House of Israel again, and in leaving Cleveland he not only fled the consequences of his McDonald's case, but he also evaded an unrelated legal matter in which he faced four counts of "larceny by trickery."[74] After years in Guyana, Hill found himself in trouble again and in a Guyanese prison for manslaughter. Hill was charged with ordering the murder of a House of Israel member's husband, and he served six years of a twenty-six-year sentence. In 1992, after verifying that he could not be apprehended for the Cleveland charges, and in accordance with his release agreement with Guyanese officials,

Hill returned to the United States. Hill, now calling himself Rabbi Edward Washington, arrived in New York on August 8, nearly a quarter century after initiating the boycott.[75] Hill was happy to leave Guyana, but he was warned that he could not return to Cleveland. A county prosecutor promised, "If he comes back, he's going to jail." In the fall of 1992, Hill returned to Guyana to craft his memoir of leading a congregation of 10,000 devotees, financing his church with Rabbi Chips—a banana snack—and serving Guyana's president Forbes Burnham.[76]

While his friend fled Cleveland to bask in the sun, Raplin set out to do his time for extortion and blackmail. On his first night at the Marion Correctional Institute, a "little disturbance" in the prison caused the kitchen to shut down. The correctional officers ordered McDonald's cheeseburgers to feed Marion's residents. Raplin wondered to himself as he peeled the paper wrapper from his dinner, "How did I get into this?"[77] Raplin was released in August of 1974, and he returned to his activist life in Cleveland. He joined the staff of a new Afro-American Studies program at Case Western Reserve University and organized an affordable and fair housing campaign.[78] In the revised, reconsidered, and reframed story of black franchises in Cleveland, Raplin (and Hill to some degree) were cast in the roles of unsung heroes of a difficult moment. At the seventh annual meeting of the National Black McDonald's Operators Association in Cleveland in 1978, the former mayor acknowledged the two men as playing an integral role in clearing a path for the city's black franchisees and their colleagues that came after them nationwide. Raplin was happy to accept some praise, and in remembering the coalition that formed under OBU, he believed the real feat was getting everybody together. Raplin acknowledged that OBU organized "the militant blacks, the almost militant blacks, the moderate blacks, the almost moderate blacks and even some of the most perennial Uncle Toms."[79] Raplin was accurate that black capitalism could bring a cross section of a population in community, but regardless of business success or failure, maintaining coalitions was difficult. And when groups formed to negotiate or leverage their power with major corpora-

tions, the terms of the negotiation were sometimes far apart from the values of the group.

After the dust had settled from the tense negotiations over franchises in Cleveland, future McDonald's CEO Ed Rensi took his experiences as a field consultant in Cleveland to Chicago, believing that the corporation needed to learn from the debacle with the black community. Franchise recruiter Roland Jones and a fellow black management team member offered a mostly white office a presentation on "what it was like to be black in America." According to McDonald's insiders, the lecture—which some were concerned would be too divisive—proved to be beneficial in not only creating deeper understanding but also forecasting the ways the company was willing to be flexible and open to feedback in growing the "ethnic market." A future McDonald's vice president for diversity believed that the lesson learned was that "a proactive approach to minority licensing was the only way to avoid similar situations in major cities across the country."[80] The corporation hired black consultants to assist in redefining McDonald's corporate culture, from former Freedom Rider, and Southern Christian Leadership Conference member, civil rights legend C. T. Vivian, to future Secretary of Commerce Ron Brown. Brown worked with McDonald's in 1979 to assess how blacks could be part of what was described as a sometimes renegade and "wild and crazy" company.[81]

The Cleveland McDonald's boycotts encapsulated the central questions of how to ensure black economic development post-1968. Was it a matter of not unfairly enriching the already rich individuals Ralph Abernathy and James Forman cautioned against, or could franchises work in the service of creating rich communities? The Cleveland boycotts did not revolve around gaining access to a public accommodation, as was the case in the great sit-ins in Greensboro and Nashville years earlier. Clevelanders were protesting to *own* the accommodation. The Cleveland boycott reflected the convergence of differing political ideologies in black cities, contentions over ownership, the terrains in which the future of black struggle would play out, and the limits of black politicians and black capitalism. By the late 1960s, McDonald's and its close peers

were not formally discriminating against black customers. In fact, from all reports blacks were enjoying spending their time and dollars at the drive-ins, and later drive-thrus. Rather, this boycott was about what was owed to black Cleveland in the form of economic opportunity and whether black capitalism could cover the nation's promises made to blacks, which Martin Luther King Jr. likened to a bad check at the 1963 March on Washington.

For black communities in the 1960s and 1970s, it seemed as if chaos was the only way to coax concern and maybe see change. Slum housing, overcrowded schools, and hungry children were all visible signs of poverty throughout black communities. But these scourges were magnified when buildings were on fire or businesses were looted. Activists who wanted to see improvements in their community's quality of life needed to learn how to capitalize on federal and state urgency to create businesses as a response to inadequate housing or health care. Whether a black leader found black capitalism hopeful or shameful was unimportant. Her ability to tap into the resources that black capitalism endowed made the difference between living in a community with a free meals program for children and the elderly or on a block filled with hungry people. Increasingly, as fast food expanded, the choice between a McDonald's and no McDonald's was actually a choice between a McDonald's or no youth job program. If McDonald's could be convinced to provide, why not find ways for them to become a member of the community? For boosters of black capitalism, the answer was self-evident. But for those skeptical of business, or at the very least invested in making sure that black dollars stay close to black businesses, fast food franchises still had to plead their case.

CHAPTER FOUR

Bending the Golden Arches

A protester outside of a McDonald's in the Albina neighborhood of Portland, Oregon. Albina was the center of black organizing in Portland and home to the local Black Panther Party chapter. City of Portland (OR) Archives, A2004-005.1808.

"Franchises: Boom or Bust for Blacks?"

The question posed on the cover of the inaugural issue of *Black Enterprise* magazine, launched in August of 1970, has been asked in the pages of the monthly for decades in different places and different ways. The bible of black capitalism always declares franchising a boom, and in this opening issue Brady Keys's All-Pro Chicken and McDonald's were presented as shining examples of the business model that seemed to effortlessly capture black dollars. Between the covers of the new publication, article after article reinforced its message to black America: it's time to get down to business. In a statement that ignored the long history of black business creation and wealth accumulation, *Black Enterprise* suggested

that black people were just getting started on a path to economic
success. "As a nation, as a people, we have begun in recent years
to make modest beginnings toward making black people meaningful participants in our economic system. We feel that our people
and our times require that we do more—much more—than settle for these modest beginnings."[1] According to *Black Enterprise,*
fast food franchises were on the lookout for talent of color to open
stores in their communities and help them achieve the Department
of Commerce's 25x2x25 program goals of having 25 franchise
companies offer 25 new franchises to minority applicants over the
following two years.[2] With the private sector working so closely
with federal agencies, fast food companies would meet and exceed
their targets handily. Franchising had created a boom for black
entrepreneurs. But, fast food still had hurdles to clear in some areas
as movements emerged to ask critical questions of the industry and
its representatives. Could a burger stand be a good neighbor? What
did it mean to patronize a black-owned outlet of a white-owned
company? What does it mean to buy black after all?

While the expansion of black-owned McDonald's franchises
was a victory for the community development model in Cleveland
and a coveted opportunity in Chicago, the movement of fast food
into black communities was not uniformly welcomed or its potential problems mediated by the possibility of black financial investment. The presence of fast food franchises in cities from Portland
to Philadelphia gave some black leaders an illustrative example of
the problems of capitalism relative to black self-determination,
while others held fast to the fantasy that the right kind of capitalism could clear the way for true racial liberation. The varied
responses to fast food's encroachment into the inner city throughout the 1970s revealed that organized efforts to influence or altogether stop fast food in black neighborhoods became a proxy for
talking about racial and economic inequality. Critics and activists
believed that a new fast food restaurant in a black neighborhood
wasn't just an addition to the marketplace of goods and services.
Fast food represented larger structural and social problems, and
the actions that some took against franchises demonstrated how

much ground the industry had covered in relatively unfamiliar territory. The 1970s would usher in a decade of continued struggle against economic racism in local contexts, while the popularity of fast food was transforming how people viewed eating, working, and living. Franchise chains depended on their growing cohort of franchisees of color to buffer them from controversy, influence black consumer behavior, and acclimate communities to their foods. In the process, fast food franchises learned that blacks valued the very things—neighborhood control, care for community, or cultural authenticity—that fast food companies could never provide. Every fight wasn't about owning a franchise, in fact, most fights were not. The central question in all these conflicts: could fast food be a good citizen to, neighbor in, or symbol of black America?

*　*　*

The streets of Portland, Oregon, also managed to stay quiet the night that King died, but not very many people outside of the city or state took notice. Places with such small black populations rarely got mentioned in the somber national news stories about what was happening in and to the country in 1968. While Mayor Stokes was gaining nationwide praise for keeping things calm in Hough, the residents of the predominately black Albina neighborhood of Portland were quietly mourning King, too. Many of the residents remembered his Urban League–sponsored tour in 1961, when he visited one of the few black churches in Portland, the Vancouver Avenue First Baptist Church, a stately Gothic Revival building with stained-glass windows from the Povey Brothers Studio, the Tiffany & Co. of the Pacific Northwest. On that fall day, King told an audience at Portland State University, "We have come a long way toward making integration a reality, but we still have a long way to go." Folks in Albina knew that all too well. In the late 1960s, the population of blacks in Portland comprised only 5% of the city, but nearly 90% of them lived in Albina. King's legacy, in addition to recent memories of a 1967 uprising may have given people pause about going out on the streets again.

Albina was a testament, in many ways, to black resilience in a place that didn't want them there. Between 1844 and 1922, Oregon Country and later the State of Oregon (established in 1859) maintained laws that banned blacks from permanent residency.[3] By banning and expelling blacks in its early years, black sojourners were deterred from settling in the state even after they could legally live there. Oregon's cities observed racial, residential segregation, and blacks were mostly relegated to areas west of the Willamette River, which allowed black workers access to the railroad, defense industry, and domestic service jobs available to them.[4] The flooding of the river in the late 1940s, in addition to municipal expansion, highway projects, and the building of industrial centers, pushed black Portlanders across the Willamette into Albina. As the black population grew, white neighborhoods used the trusty mechanism of racially restrictive covenants to ensure their neighbors stayed the right color. Its proximity to the waterfront and expanding downtown also made Albina ripe for slum clearance and urban redevelopment. Where rows of houses once stood, the city of Portland sliced through Albina in 1956 to extend Interstate 5 and build Veterans Memorial Coliseum in 1960.[5] With so much compression, Albina became the only place where blacks who had to follow the employing industries could live.

On the same night that Detroit's 1967 uprising commenced, the Albina neighborhood was also kindled by confrontations between black youth and area police. The evening of July 20 brought a crowd to Irving Park for "Sunday at the Park," an interactive series of musical performances, lectures, and visual art that focused on the themes of Black Power, social revolution, and civil rights. The anticipated featured speaker, the Black Panther Party for Self Defense's Eldridge Cleaver, never appeared, and rumors spread that the Panthers' minister of information had been arrested. Although Irving Park was often busy on weekends, a nervous city leadership deployed police to patrol the park that day and kept the National Guard on standby, which only aided in riling the crowd. By early evening, tensions between the event attendees and the police reached a point of no return. The inexperienced police department

lacked access to sufficient riot gear, so officers brought rifles and shotguns from their homes to reinforce the 200 officers deployed on the streets. Young men—white and black—fought with officers, threw Molotov cocktails at store windows, and spilled onto the streets. Residents locked their doors and prayed that a fire at a tavern or supermarket wouldn't spread to their homes. The uprising lasted two tense nights and claimed no fatalities, but many were injured or arrested, and neighborhood businesses were destroyed. After the $50,000 in property damage was totaled and the nearly 100 people arrested were processed, some Albina leaders hoped the incident could open up conversations about the way forward, as was the case in so many other cities. White Portland leaders chose to speak only about a disproven theory that outside agitators had caused the unrest, and they clung to a myth that Portland was a city for everybody, regardless of race. The Irving Park conflict did not inspire the same kind of large-scale urban investment plans, interracial rap sessions, or black business initiatives that emerged in blacker and more populous cities. In many ways, Portland's small black community was on its own.

The unresolved issues that surfaced at the Irving Park struggle inspired another round of disturbances two years later, on June 13, 1969, when a local member of Albina's National Committee to Combat Fascism (NCCF) noticed a confrontation between police and a group of black youths at Lidio's Drive-In, a hamburger stand.[6] That night, Kent Ford opened the door to a police cruiser and told the detainee—who Ford believed was only ten years old—to run, while he fought with police officers. Ford was then arrested, and officers drove him from the burger joint to another one, a McDonald's on Union Avenue. By the end of the night, officers had beaten the handcuffed Ford and placed him in custody. The five nights of fire bombings that followed Ford's arrest stopped when the weather changed. A rise in the temperature often led to a cool down of anger during riots. The streets of Albina were still by the evening of June 18, while a small group of white demonstrators appeared in front of City Hall to protest the arrest of five members of the Black Panther Party. Local business owners decided

to arm themselves to stave off any bombers or looters, and others told the press that they would "move their businesses out of the fire and assault plagued area as soon as possible."[7] After spending more than two weeks in jail, Ford was welcomed back by his fellow NCCF comrades and friends. On the steps of the police station he gave a speech about police brutality and talked about the platform of the Black Panther Party. The NCCF transitioned into the local Panther Party by 1970, and they brought the signature initiatives of the then-four-year-old group from Oakland to the Rose City with gusto.[8] Even before they were officially chartered by the headquarters in California, the Portland NCCF was leading free breakfast programs, political education classes, and support for black students at the racially hostile Roosevelt High School.

Black Panther organizing illuminated a common theme in black life in America: survival in the face of suppression. The Portland Panthers were not only spreading the movement's message about self-determination and nation building; they were also filling a crucial gap between what blacks contributed to the system and what they were able to receive from it. No matter how hard African Americans worked and how many of their dollars ended up in public treasuries, basic services of the state were distributed in limited quantities, if at all. The Panthers filled voids for the hungry, the unemployed, and in Portland they were especially important to the sick. The 1969 establishment of Albina's People's Free Medical Clinic, part of a network of health care facilities operated and partially staffed by Panther members and a cohort of social-justice-oriented practitioners, transformed the health of black Albina. The clinic was later renamed for magnetic Chicago Panther leader Fred Hampton, who was slain by police alongside Panther Mark Clark in the winter of 1969.[9] In addition to offering routine physicals, the clinic could refer its clients to specialists in everything from dermatology to oncology. The clinic coordinated health education and offered sickle cell anemia screenings, helping African-American Portlanders understand the genetic disease. The clinics accommodated clients by opening on late afternoons and evenings, and trained medical and pharmacy

assistants who were supervised by local medical and dental students. The Portland clinic was the only Panther project to provide dental services, in partnership with the University of Oregon Dental School.[10] Eventually, the Portland Panthers operated three medical centers—the Hampton location, a dental center named for Malcolm X, and the People's Clinic.[11] The clinics relied on donated supplies and volunteer time to ensure that vaccinations were administered and cavities filled.

The Portland Panthers were also dependent on the willingness and generosity of a wide swath of Albina to keep their initiative afloat, especially their signature free breakfast program. The first time Black Panthers served up a hot breakfast for area children was in Oakland in 1969, and they immediately discovered how desperately this meal was needed. The national school breakfast program wouldn't become part of the school day until 1975, so the Black Panthers' morning meal service became the most expansive of their offerings.[12] Free breakfast was highly visible and highly successful in bringing members of the community in contact with the group, and sometimes helped alleviate concerns about the Panthers. Educators appreciated being able to teach children without contending with distracting hunger pangs. While under the NCCF banner, the breakfast program promoted free meals as a means of chiseling away at the edifice of racial inequality in local schools. They critiqued the treatment of black children and the language used to deem them uneducable or ill-suited for school. "The root cause of the problem is not mental incapabilites or 'cultural deprivation,' but HUNGER."[13]

In the fall of 1971, *The Oregonian* reported that the Panther breakfast and clinic countered "the militant Panther image," and characterized Albina as approving of the Panthers' desire to "serve the people, body and soul." Kent Ford was quoted in the article, and he determined that the children who enjoyed the Panthers' meal "wouldn't be getting breakfast at home . . . not all of them are poor, but most come from homes where the mother doesn't have time to get up and cook in the mornings." He countered criticisms by arguing that "when the government steps forward and gives our people

a balanced diet, we'll be glad to stop." The seemingly innocuous act of serving a hot breakfast to a child was a magnet for criticism, as anti-Panther forces believed it was a vehicle for radicalizing youth. Ford addressed the suspicions that the group was "indoctrinating" children. *The Oregonian* wrote that in the previous year teachers at a local school "complained that the breakfast program was making the children more hostile in the classrooms," but the complaints soon subsided. Black children conversant in Black Power ideology may have frightened their white teachers, but they couldn't argue that the children didn't arrive more focused and energetic each morning since the program started. Ford clarified that the children were only learning "by example, that socialism can work," as well as the stories of Panther icons, like the slain prisoner George Jackson, "for whom the meal program [was] named."[14] Decades later, adults recalled the breakfast program's meals and volunteers with fondness, because the organization's daily gathering spared them from the bland corn mush or toast doused in syrup sold at their local public school. The quality of the food, as well as the connection with adults, reassured children in a hypersegregated, and often ignored, community that they were cared for and loved. "The Panthers fed us well . . . pancakes or waffles, juice, and milk. Eggs with sausage was a staple. The Panthers served potatoes. The Panthers had a saying: . . . if a kid is hungry, he isn't thinking about learning."[15] Another frequent guest at breakfast recalled: "I loved going to the breakfast program . . . I remember Mr. Ford used to talk to us about staying in school, doing the right thing, and getting our lives together. I looked forward to seeing the Panthers. They always had something positive to say."[16] Albina's hungry children, their cash-strapped parents, and eventually their schoolteachers all came to appreciate what the breakfast program was doing for the community.

For Ford and the Portland Panthers, the breakfast program was not only rooted in their concern for children's nutrition, but also in their belief in redistributive justice. From their estimations, area businesses owed something to the Albina community that kept their doors open. When local Party members received cash dona-

tions or were gifted supplies, they were overseeing a little justice in a place where justice was in short supply. Ford explained that donating jugs of orange juice, cartons of eggs, and slabs of bacon to the breakfast program was the least that could be done by "the businessmen who take from our community," and the donations were one way they could "leave a little something in return."[17] Albina's businesses, especially the ones owned by whites, may have not fully supported the Black Panthers, but they figured that fortifying breakfast supplies could cultivate some amity with the local radicals, who some found confusing and others inspiring. In order for the program to survive, Kent Ford, and his wife Sandra Ford, had to constantly solicit businesses for support. After the last child was served hot chocolate and griddles were washed and dried, the pair would visit businesses to ask for help to maintain the breakfast, which some mornings drew more than a hundred hungry children. For the Panthers, the impact that the health screenings and hotcakes were having on the neighborhood spoke volumes about the community's rudimentary requirements and their ability to realize them. When the Panthers approached businesses for donations to sustain their programs, they offered business owners tours of the clinics and tallies of the pounds and pounds of food they were serving children each week at the Highland United Church of Christ.[18]

The Albina neighborhood McDonald's, located at 3510 N.E. Union Avenue, was under the charge of Al Laviske, who managed six other drive-ins across the area. Of all his stores, the Albina one may have presented the greatest challenge. The tensions that rose between his McDonald's and the Black Panther Party in the summer of 1970 can be traced back to a meeting that summer between Laviske and the Fords about McDonald's and the breakfast program. From Ford's perspective, he and associate Linda Thornton simply asked Laviske if he would be interested in helping them continue to feed children before school. Laviske claimed that he was the target of extortion, that Ford demanded $300 a month in cash from the restaurant, and they threatened him and the drive-in if he failed to deliver. The divergent origin stories of why the Panthers and McDonald's were at odds were difficult to prove then

and cannot be proven now. What is clear is that Laviske's refusal led the Panthers to stage a boycott of his store, and that in the activists' estimation, it would be unwise to allow another white-owned business to profiteer from Albina without a sense of responsibility to the community. Kent Ford decided it was time to picket McDonald's. A Panther flyer called black Portland to

> Boycott!! Boycott! McDonald's does not support the FREE BREAKFAST FOR SCHOOL CHILDREN PROGRAM or MALCOLM X DENTAL CLINIC or FRED HAMPTON PEOPLE'S CLINIC.

As the protest intensified, McDonald's became a totem of the challenges that black people faced in Albina. The Panthers' protest exposed how the brand was associated with unchecked white domination, police brutality, and exploitative labor practices. The flyer also accused the McDonald's parking lot of doubling as a "base area for PIG attacks."[19] McDonald's, in the Panthers' view, not only refused to be a good citizen, but they also exacerbated the hyper-policing of blacks in Albina by welcoming law enforcement into its parking lots to transfer subjects, as was done with Ford the night the 1969 uprising started. Protesters chanted "No more pigs in our community" outside the restaurant, a critique of police relations in the neighborhood, which was especially on the hearts and minds of concerned residents after the winter of 1970, when a Portland police officer shot nineteen-year-old Albert Wayne Williams at the Portland Panthers headquarters, located a few doors down from McDonald's. Officers claimed they were trying to serve Williams an arrest warrant when he fired at them. Community members organized a "speech in" at a meeting at city hall, demanding that the mayor and city council respond to their suspicions about and anger over the shooting. Williams's shooting and the conflicting reports about it were emblematic of the strained relationships in Albina, powered by the pervasive police and informant surveillance in the community and the decision to send "beefed up patrols" to the neighborhood after Ford was acquitted of a charge of inciting a riot.[20]

The Panther protesters also took issue with the employment practices of the Albina McDonald's, as well as the nature of fast food work broadly. The demonstrators jeered managers for not hiring blacks and demanded that dismissed employees be reinstated. They passed out flyers that accused McDonald's of perpetuating a system of "unfair labor."[21] McDonald's expansion in the 1970s made it a frequent target of activists who believed that the brand suppressed organizing activity and used their business influence to shape labor policy. By the late 1970s, McDonald's employed approximately 150,000 people who had no access to any union representation. An investigative journalism project reported that the company subjected their workers to "arbitrary shift assignments, boring work, pressure from managers and customers, no paid holidays, and no hospital insurance," and they alleged that McDonald's used "sophisticated secret internal anti-labor apparatus effectively [rooting] out pro-union sympathizers from within employee ranks." The article also included accusations that managers regularly bullied crew members by forcing them to take lie detector tests and relied on an "interrogation technique."[22] The Panthers' concentration on labor issues stemmed from the treatment of individual black workers, and it may have been part of larger concerns about unemployment. In 1970, black unemployment nationally was at nearly 9% and would rise throughout the decade. Meanwhile, Ray Kroc tried to manipulate labor laws in his favor, which stood to undermine the earning potential of working youth. Kroc famously donated a quarter of a million dollars to Richard Nixon's reelection campaign, some believe in order to get him to support a proposed "youth differential" clause that exempted minors from the minimum wage bill being debated in Congress. When the donation was discovered and the brand was scrutinized, Kroc realized that he had to tread more carefully in political matters.

The Black Panthers' succinct enumeration of their community-based institutions that McDonald's chose not to support was a testament to Panther-led infrastructure in Albina, as well as a reminder of the many needs not being met by the state in a poor community. The health clinics and the food program were a direct

response to the difficulty in securing quality health care in poor black communities and the continued nutritional challenges and difficulties experienced by black families, especially single women with children. In cities like Las Vegas and Los Angeles, black women—many on welfare assistance—organized campaigns to not only secure basic needs, but also to challenge assumptions about the black family's care for its own children and the political power of the poor.[23] The National Welfare Rights Organization, like the Black Panther Party, organized poor and working-class blacks to strengthen their capacities to provide for each other. They also crafted plans to maximize support from state and federal programs and cultivated relationships with philanthropic sources.

The Panthers picketed the restaurant between eight and ten hours a day, beginning at the lunchtime rush and remaining as late as 10 P.M. The protesters tried to stop customers from entering the McDonald's or cars from pulling into the lot. The protest continued for about a month. The Panthers were exercising their right both to organize and to demand that McDonald's be a good citizen. McDonald's workers and customers disagreed. They accused the Panthers of threatening patrons and scaring employees. At one point an employee asked a protester, "May I help you, please?" and the alleged response was "Be nice to me, I'm going to burn your place down."[24] It is difficult to know now if that exchange was a taunt or an actual threat. The Panthers often displayed their special kind of performative militarism with their unofficial uniform of fitted black leather jackets and berets. The Black Power newspapers they sold were filled with pictures and illustrations of armed revolutionaries. Their chants of black power taking over may have also been more provocative than predictive. Regardless of the intent, in the eyes of racist, fearful, or uninformed whites, the Panthers were always up to trouble.

From the remaining records on the protest, it is clear that the boycott did not hamper the Albina restaurant to the extent the Cleveland boycotts did, but McDonald's executives may have learned not to allow issues like these to fester for too long. The Portland Panthers were in no position to lobby for a franchise,

and although other Panthers were proponents of black capitalism for their own communities, this chapter did not seem interested in investing itself in business like Operation Black Unity. In the investigation documents about the protests and Laviske's extortion accusations, it is clear that McDonald's corporate executives were attentive and aware of a conflict in Portland.[25] At some point in 1970, Laviske claimed that "two black representatives" from McDonald's traveled from Chicago to Portland to look for Ford, perhaps to see if he would ease his protest, but the meeting never materialized. Laviske testified that "they spent the entire day in the Albina area trying to locate Ford without success."[26]

Laviske and Ford were left to their own devices to end the boycott. The McDonald's manager continued complaining that he was being threatened by Panthers and their supporters. Laviske may have been without McDonald's corporate on his side, but as a white Portlander doing business in Albina, he turned to the power of the police and the courts to protect him, in a similar tactic as the Pine Bluff franchisee who sought legal protection against SNCC protesters. Laviske sought a restraining order against Ford; he brought copies of protest leaflets as evidence of his being harassed.[27] Laviske was not granted a protection order, and an ongoing police investigation of Ford for extorting other Albina businesses yielded insufficient evidence. A district attorney suggested that Laviske seek an injunction against three Black Panthers for protesting in front of his store and disturbing his business. While filing the paperwork, his assistant manager called from the McDonald's. Nine picketers were handing out pamphlets again and trying to convince customers not to enter the restaurant. With no injunction in hand yet, and no case against the picketing, the manager decided to close the store nearly six hours early "due to the forcefulness" of the boycott. The next day, Laviske's injunction was delivered, and the protest moved across the street.[28] With the protests now away from the store's entrance and parking lot, Laviske may have believed that it was only a matter of time before the Black Panthers relented, or at the very least, his customers would be able to avoid them and resume enjoying burgers and fries as before.

Then, disaster struck.

Around 2 A.M. the morning of August 22, someone threw four sticks of dynamite through the Albina McDonald's front window. The blast was powerful enough to hurl a metal picnic table eight feet from its perch across the parking lot. Most of the windows on the restaurant's north side combusted and scattered shards and specks of glass across the property.[29] No one was hurt, but the bombing unnerved other local businesses, who had monitored the McDonald's boycott and nervously anticipated an upcoming peace rally outside an American Legion conference. The store managers reported to police that someone made good on threats to "blow the place up."[30] Immediately, the local police—who were collaborating with a covert FBI investigation of Ford and the Panthers—swarmed the McDonald's to collect evidence. After businesses were reopened the next day, detectives fanned across Union Avenue to ask local grocers, pharmacists, and store managers if they were threatened by Ford or any other Panther members. From the investigators notes, it's clear that Albina's business community regularly butted heads with their black neighbors. Black teens were not trusted inside stores. Black residents were overlooked for jobs. The police may have been shaken, but they were not surprised by the bombing, having been tipped off by an undercover report. An agent noted:

> He overheard . . . that they were going to get McDonalds on the 1st or 2nd day of the upcoming Legion conference. Informant believes this to mean that they will bomb or burn out the McDonalds establishment at location at NE Union and Fremont and that they also indicated they might possibly hit other McDonalds establishments.[31]

The police tip may have been about a number of radical groups that had settled in Portland to protest the Vietnam War, take down capitalism, and, most recently, disrupt the upcoming visit by the Legion. Portland was also home to a chapter of the White Panthers, a radical group of antiracist whites who were also subject to FBI watch and a raid in December 1970. The extant investigative

notes about the McDonald's bombing and the Black Panthers are not necessarily conclusive, considering that throughout the period black activist organizations—moderate and radical—were subject to state-generated misinformation, interference, and even assassination campaigns. The files confirm that the Portland Panthers had an adversarial relationship with some business owners, and donations made to them may have been acts of insurance more than generosity. But there was no evidence that Ford and the Panthers bombed McDonald's. The group denied any connection to the bombing. After canvassing the neighborhood, police compiled a suspect list that included "white hippies" who used assumed names to purchase explosives days before the bombing. Similarly, FBI agents, under the auspices of J. Edgar Hoover's COINTELPRO program, were directed to use any means necessary—from drugs to violence—to disrupt Black radical groups, especially the Panthers. In light of this history, it is impossible to rule out agent provocateurs as staging the bombing to discredit Panthers.[32]

With little evidence on Ford or the Panthers, the group was able to proceed with their projects. Within a month of the bombing, the contentions between the Panthers and the McDonald's actually waned. The restaurant eventually began supporting their initiatives with "fifty pounds of meat and five hundred paper cups, weekly."[33] Accounts in the years following the bombing indicate that McDonald's franchises forged a workable peace with the local community. At a sickle cell anemia testing drive organized by the Black Panthers, people who visited the McDonald's parking lot received one of 1,500 donated coupons for a hamburger, fries, and soda courtesy of their local franchisee.[34] After the bombing, Nate Proby, a local civil rights activist and leader of the United Minority Workers organization, was welcome to use McDonald's reinstalled picnic table to register voters. The picket and the bombing were minor disruptions in the much larger context of Albina, where blacks were constantly negotiating with local business owners, police forces, and political figures to have their voice heard. By using the consumer boycott to assert their position about the way that life was managed in Albina, the black population discovered

a means of communicating how racism shaped the conditions and possibilities of the community.

Portland's Black Panther Party and McDonald's represented the pragmatism that allowed black radicalism to survive day to day, especially where blacks were at a population and power disadvantage. Although African Americans were small in number across the entire city, segregation concentrated their influence in mostly one location in Portland, which required them to find ways to challenge and reconcile with existing power structures. Kent Ford denies bombing the McDonald's, which he said was close to fulfilling his request for assistance. His colleague Percy Hampton believed the FBI told businesses not to pitch in for the breakfast program. "They said we were strong-arming businesses for donations. None of that was true . . . [The FBI] stayed one step ahead of us and one step behind."[35] What is most helpful to understand, in hindsight, are the ways that, on the local level, activists knew that critique or conflict didn't foreclose future collaboration. The Portland Black Panther Party, like their friends in Cleveland, used protest to air grievances and injustices about McDonald's, and then found ways to capitalize on their power relative to McDonald's. In prioritizing the breakfast program over his battles against McDonald's, Ford showed that even blacks with the most radical of imaginations could recognize the realities of the few choices black people had under capitalism. Eventually the destabilization of the Black Panther Party's national leadership would undermine the work of local chapters. Between 1975 and 1980, the controversies and transgressions of national Black Panther leadership in Oakland led to rudderless and embroiled chapters. Former Panthers were also subject to continued surveillance, police brutality, and tightening financial resources for the clinic. All these factors contributed to the Party's dissolution by 1980.[36] The McDonald's on Union Avenue (which was renamed Martin Luther King Jr. Boulevard in 1989) didn't make it either. By the early 1990s, the restaurant closed. Depopulation of the commercial strip and a rampant infusion of drugs in the immediate neighborhood drove out people and businesses that were privileged to have the choice to begin again in another place.

* * *

While the Portland Black Panther Party was renegotiating the terms of its relationship to McDonald's, thousands of miles away, the much older city of Philadelphia was on the precipice of its own political action against the Golden Arches. The expansion of McDonald's and other fast food restaurants along highways and beside the shopping malls and plazas that bookended suburban developments was met in most places with excitement and curiosity. A place to eat along a network of interconnecting expressways and toll roads was convenient. An affordable destination for a family's dinner night out meant more special outings for budget-conscious families. A fast food place where teens could get a bite to eat before a school dance seemed like harmless fun to an ever-growing fast food republic. As consumers grew accustomed to picking up buckets of chicken for a picnic or devouring an entire meal kept warm by Styrofoam, the environment's great enemy, the experience of eating outside the home became an everyday activity that required no planning and little thinking about the hands that prepared foods or the planet that provided it. Yet a national wave of environmental activism, movements that questioned the very foundations of capitalism, and citizen efforts to reclaim local policy and decision-making galvanized to halt or at least slow the march toward a fast food future.

Organizations like Cleveland's Operation Black Unity and the Portland chapter of the Black Panther Party believed that there was room for negotiation and mutual agreement with fast food restaurants. Other black-led entities believed that fast food had no place in community life. Some arguments against fast food focused on combating juvenile delinquency and reducing gang activity. Similar to Herman Petty's concern about his restaurant remaining Blackstone Rangers territory, fast food restaurants could be easily claimed by street gangs, especially after the development of dine-in facilities. Truant and troublemaking teenagers could linger in parking lots in the summer, and when temperatures dropped, they could park themselves in a molded plastic booth for hours. Urban

McDonald's locations often kept late hours, and franchisees under pressure to make money may have felt as if they couldn't do anything to alienate problematic, but paying, customers. Some black franchisees were able to win over gangs, like Harlem franchisee Lee Dunham, a former police officer who met with members of the Savage Skulls, the Wild Bunch, and the Saigons to ensure that they didn't disrupt his store, the country's third-busiest outlet in 1972. The first four months after he took hold of the franchise, he developed a rapport with the gang members, who marked his restaurant near the famed Apollo Theater as theirs by wearing their designated gang jackets and even firing guns inside while guests tried to enjoy their Big Macs.[37] Other stores couldn't handle the chaos. In the fall of 1976, at another New York City McDonald's, a group of twenty white teenagers brandishing baseball bats and sticks gathered outside of a McDonald's at West Third Street and Avenue of the Americas before setting out on a series of racist attacks in Washington Square Park. What started as an attempt to avenge a marijuana sale gone wrong turned into the young men screaming, "Get the niggers out of the park," and didn't end until a black teenager suffered a fractured face and eye.[38] News items of this kind were all that concerned parents and critical activists needed to convince their neighbors to join their crusades against hoisting another pair of golden arches or a giant bucket to hover over their neighborhoods.

Anti-fast food campaigns—in both affluent white and poor black communities—converged in the assertion that their neighborhoods warranted protection from the nefarious presence of burger stands and chicken joints. In an era in which racial disparities in quality, and even duration, of life calcified, there were few issues that could unite such defuse populations. Both parties agreed that no matter how profitable, popular, or even publicly altruistic these businesses were or could be, they ultimately undermined the elements of community that residents valued. The Small Business Administration classified fast food franchises as small businesses eligible for minority funding grants, but neighborhoods did not experience them like a mom-and-pop bakery that whipped up a beloved pineapple upside-down cake or a family enterprise

where everyone knew the shopkeeper's name and her children. Fast food restaurants exported dollars outside of their communities with franchise fees and high-volume purchase orders that rarely, if ever, landed on a local business's desk. Researchers at the Institute for Local Self-Reliance estimated that in 1979, for a typical McDonald's restaurant, "only 17 percent of the store's expenditures clearly remains in the community where it is based: 15 percent for local labor (always hired at minimum wage) and 2 percent for local taxes." The remaining 83% went to McDonald's special suppliers, land leases, the national advertising fund, the company's management fees, loan repayments, and taxes. The study suggested that if "buildings were owned locally, management hired from local residents, and supplies purchased locally, some of this leakage could be effectively plugged."[39] While fast food benefited from tax breaks and cheap land, in some cities the franchisee and company contributed to the community at their discretion, not by mandate. Restaurants were known to attract litter, worsen traffic, and perpetuate youth misbehavior. When the tony community of Martha's Vineyard organized locals and the vacation home set against a proposed McDonald's in 1978, they submitted evidence from a Canadian researcher who "determined that an average purchase at McDonald's entails a minimum of ten pieces of trash, much of it nonbiodegradable—plastic straws, plastic covers for the paper cups, Styrofoam burger containers and plastic condiment containers." Opening the restaurant, the anti-McDonald's group argued, would add more than 5 million items to the Martha's Vineyard waste management system.[40] Cohesive, strategic communities believed that they could take steps to hold off McDonald's, but when the communities were black and lacked wealth, the task was far more difficult.

In the summer of 1970, the Ogontz Neighbors Association (ONA) invited residents to "Save Your Community!" The plea was a bit more ambitious than the actual matter at hand, but residents were moved to attend a meeting to discuss an issue that had been lingering for a while: the city of Philadelphia had authorized a permit for McDonald's to open a location at 6100 North Broad Street.

Ogontz in the 1970s was a working-class neighborhood of North Philadelphia that had felt some of the sting of the dual forces of residential and economic white flight in the previous decades. What made Ogontz distinct from other sections of major cities was that the residents went to great lengths to preserve the multicultural nature of the community. Having been particularly vocal in school integration efforts and projects to reduce housing discrimination, the ONA's strong tradition of organizing since the late 1950s would come in handy as they waged a new war on the North Broad Street construction project. The ONA argued against the McDonald's on a number of grounds, and unlike the protests in Cleveland or Portland, the ONA was not concerned about their ability to own a franchise or reap the rewards from its profitability. Rather, the ONA believed that the increasing commercialization of their neighborhood amounted to the city and private sector allowing a business to strip citizens of their power to determine the community's priorities. In their campaign against a new McDonald's, they cited the saturation of existing fast food restaurants in Ogontz, the threats to the historical significance of the area slated for rezoning, the socioenvironmental safety of Ogontz, and the fact that they had no opportunity to weigh in on the proposed restaurant. In a sophisticated, multipronged assault, the ONA used various organizing tools from nonviolent direct action to media outreach to municipal appeals to halt the building of a McDonald's. Campaign leaders also studied the OBU's fight in Cleveland to plan their own fast food resistance movement.

After the McDonald's construction crew first broke ground in 1969, the ONA deployed weekly "picket lines" to attract neighborhood attention to the building and its shift from residential to commercial. HOMES NOT HAMBURGERS! MCDONALD'S MAKES CHOPPED MEAT OUT OF A CHOICE COMMUNITY. If passersby asked about the protest, the ONA demonstrators explained that the McDonald's would "be detrimental to the health, safety and welfare of the residents." The ONA also bristled at the chosen location. The McDonald's would be built near the De Benneville Family Burial Ground, a private cemetery established in the 1750s,

and the final resting place of Christian Universalist Dr. George De Benneville. In a city that prided itself on being older than the actual nation and its founding documents, the ONA believe that it could make a claim about respect for the city's history, as well as its departed notables.

The ONA wasn't expressly anti–fast food, but they were concerned with the proliferation of fast food joints in the area. Ogontz was already home to a Gino's Cheesesteak outlet, the Marriott hotel company's two franchise concepts, the hamburger-and-ice-cream specialist Hot Shoppe, and a Roy Rogers. Adding a McDonald's drive-in to the mix meant "more air pollution, littering, noise, traffic hazards, congestion, crime" they did not "want or need."[41] Anxieties about public safety often followed the opening of new fast food restaurants in the 1970s. The umbrage the McDonald brothers took about flirting and defiant teenagers in post–World War II era San Bernardino seemed insignificant in cities grappling with increased drug sales and substance abuse. Street gangs relied on all-night establishments to serve as a base for their operations, convene their members, and sometimes shake down store owners. In a letter opposing McDonald's, an ONA representative emphasized that Ogontz needed real community resources, not convenient restaurants. "The 24th gang slaying occurred in our area," wrote Kelly Miller, a minister and ONA advocate. "We have sufficient problems with gangs now without adding another hangout for them such as McDonald's . . . our organization has been working on constructive problems for youth for many years. We are opposed to adding to the gang problems."[42] Chicagoans had waged a fight against McDonald's in 1963 based on the same argument that the fast food restaurant would promote gangs and interfere with education because it was a magnet for truants. In a flyer headlined "Hamburgers vs. Education," a group of concerned residents of the West Side made it clear that they had "nothing against McDonald's putting up a hamburger stand in our community," but they believed that the location across the street from Marshall High School would exacerbate "cutting classes . . . gang fights . . . and other serious problems."[43]

The Ogontz collective connected the upcoming McDonald's opening to another form of lawlessness—the Mafia. In a July 1970 letter to the Federal Trade Commission, the ONA requested that the agency investigate the "Mafia penetration into McDonald's." Having noticed that the Commission investigated McDonald's for fraud claims associated with a sweepstakes contest, ONA member Robert Smalls hoped that the chair's office would investigate the ownership of 6100 North Broad Street. The location had been partly owned by a realtor who was also the nephew of a man believed to be a Philadelphia organized crime head. He closed the letter by referring to a current issue of *Reader's Digest,* which published an article about A&P grocery stores and organized crime. Another crusader appealed to the Licenses and Inspections Review Board using the Mafia angle to ask how the site developer was able to get the permit to build; the man had been indicted for perjury and bribery in the act of purchasing the building. [44] The ONA's savvy in attacking McDonald's from multiple angles, from its placement to its financers—reflected the diverse swath of talents that the organization possessed. The ONA believed that local people should have a say, if not the final say, in what their community needed and should look like. In an era in which the destabilization of civil rights groups, slum clearance, and failures in postriot leadership left inner cities voiceless or at the mercy of unethical business development, the ONA offered an example of the strength of racially mixed coalition building.

The ONA's protest provided the greater public with information about the fight. Behind the photographers' flash and away from neighborhood watchers, the ONA drew upon their bureaucratic knowledge to delay the start of construction on the new McDonald's building. The ONA requested that the city's Department of Licenses and Inspections investigate the permit process for the project. Their search uncovered why the McDonald's seemed to materialize out of nowhere; it was initiated by a councilman who did not represent Ogontz. The reclassification of the site was done without consulting the actual councilman from Ogontz. "We have more than enough eating places in the area," the ONA wrote in

their petition. "We desire to maintain high residential standards in our community and oppose increasing . . . commercialization . . ." The ONA did not comprise the wealthiest or most politically connected Philadelphians, but that did not mean that they saw themselves as unworthy to drive municipal matters. When the maneuver was discovered, the ONA was able to halt further development on the site. The city issued a stop-work order, and combined with their picketing, the ONA stalled the construction for so long that the original building permits expired.[45]

For African Americans shaped by the promotion of self-determination found among black nationalist groups, community control in the 1970s was a hot-button issue. In a newspaper feature about why the ONA opposed McDonald's, respondents shared their fears about the deterioration of public services available to residents, as well as a rich pride in their sense of place and collective power. Distance from fast food restaurants was not only a sign of affluence for the Philadelphians, but keeping them at bay was an indicator that communities had the power to determine their own destinies. To be forced to live within the sight lines of arches or under a pungent cloud created by deep-fat fryers was to be without influence. One member of the association offered: "I don't see why these business people who don't live here should keep coming into our neighborhood and destroying the residential nature of it. Something constructive should be done with this land—like building low-cost housing on it." The rector of a neighborhood Episcopal Church highlighted the racial elements of the struggle. "It must be recognized that because a community changes racially, it's still a community to be reckoned with. When a community becomes predominantly black, there seems to be no need to be concerned with the feelings of the people there, but America must realize this is a new day, and this is definitely no longer the case." In a survey of opinions about the McDonald's project, it is clear that the restaurant issue was a vehicle for communicating the ways that Ogontz felt it would be left behind by the forces of urban neglect and overpowered by fast food's dominance. One local woman added that in addition to having to contend with traffic and trash with so many

drive-ins in Ogontz, she added, "I don't see why we can't have a mental health clinic on its land." "Many people moved here to get away from the ghettos," she added. "Now the commercial interests who don't care about the people are coming in here and trying to make this a ghetto too." One resident cited gang concerns and suggested another institution that could actually help the community. "They should build a recreation center here. We don't have one in the whole neighborhood—and we don't have a library either."[46] The ONA was not swayed by arguments that the McDonald's would provide jobs to youth or exist as a partner with the community. They believed that it was not only their right, but their duty, to fight for what Ogontz truly needed.

It was a tough fight, and the ONA ultimately lost the war. The city's zoning decision was upheld in July of 1970, after the Philadelphia planning commission determined that the proposed site was already being used for commercial purposes and would not interfere with the historic cemetery.[47] Eventually, the 6100 Broad Street McDonald's became a black-franchised location, part of a six-store portfolio belonging to businessman Ed Johnson. By the 1980s, there were several McDonald's restaurants dotting the communities around Ogontz, and local attitudes toward them had seemed to shift. In 1983, when McDonald's corporate officials relieved Latino operator Juan Miranda of his franchises citing financial mismanagement, the nearby North Philadelphia Neighborhood Association mounted a boycott to show their gratitude for Miranda's impact on the community.[48] In the intervening years from the start of the ONA boycott to the show of solidarity with a franchisee of color, Ogontz bore the brunt of the wave of issues that made black, low-income neighborhoods less suspicious of fast food as recessions made people poorer and opportunities more scarce.

* * *

The competition was keeping tabs on how McDonald's inner-city campaign was going. For every headache acquired in Cleveland, Portland, or Philadelphia, there were opening day parties, sometimes a few blocks away from a boycotted store in the same city.

Other fast food chains took modest steps to see if opening in predominately black neighborhoods could pay off in the same ways as it had for Ronald McDonald. Recruiting and retaining a trusted member of the community to be the face of the franchise was essential, and in cities with sizable black populations, finding the right person was never as challenging as ensuring potential customers could trust the brand.

In the case of a doomed Dairy Queen franchise effort in Atlanta in the 1970s, the fast food industry slowly learned that the recipe for creating a profitable outlet in the inner city required more than a prominent African-American folded into a black neighborhood with a splash of soul talk. Dairy Queen and McDonald's share a birth year. John Fremont McCullough offered the newly invented soft serve ice cream in Joliet, Illinois, in 1940. McCullough and his business associate, Sherb Noble, were early adopters of the franchise model, and Dairy Queen stands—sometimes operated seasonally and other times year-round—multiplied at an impressive speed more than a decade before Kroc established the McDonald's franchising arm. By its eleventh birthday, Dairy Queen had captured a third of the soft-ice-cream market and reported that you could order a cone at one of their 1,400 franchises in a mix of small towns, suburbs, and cities across the country.[49] In 1957, they introduced the brazier concept, which converted Dairy Queen from a place to get sweet treats to a place to enjoy a full meal of hot dogs and burgers.

Dairy Queen, unlike McDonald's and Burger King, did not appear to have attracted external pressure to open their franchise opportunities to African Americans. Dairy Queen had a history of maintaining white and colored takeout windows in the past, and some black people may have still been apprehensive about the brand after they shifted to equal dine-in restaurants. But if Dairy Queen officials had access to the consumer market data on their peers, they would likely embrace the interest, because black consumers were the heavy users the industry hoped to cultivate and retain. Black consumers—even in a city like Atlanta with some black leadership—still had fewer choices of where to shop and where to eat.

In 1968, Georgia state legislator Julian Bond decided that the time was right for him to do something about this. The son of a black college president and graduate of the esteemed Morehouse College, Bond was born in Tennessee, but he was treated like a native son of Georgia. As a member of the courageous group of activists who tested segregation in interstate travel during the Freedom Rides of 1961, Bond risked his life to challenge the fact that despite the illegality of segregation on buses and in transportation stations, southern facilities still hung signs pointing to colored- and whites-only restrooms, waiting rooms, and seats. Court rulings in *Morgan v. Virginia* (1946) and *Boynton v. Virginia* (1960) should have protected the Riders, but when they stopped in bus depots across the South, the activists were met with screaming mobs, barking dogs, and exploding bombs.[50] Having played a role in establishing the Student Nonviolent Coordinating Committee, Bond was a civil rights notable before his twenty-fifth birthday. In his transition from freedom struggle leader to franchise business operator, Bond was joined by fellow Freedom Rider Hank Thomas and white civil rights advocate and dentist Gerald Reed. While Bond was fighting his expulsion from the Georgia statehouse for opposing the Vietnam War, Thomas was overseas fighting in it.[51] Thomas earned a Purple Heart for his service. Reed continued his work in interracial organizing; while practicing dentistry, he helped establish a branch of Operation Breadbasket in Atlanta. The three men were committed to the principle of nonviolence, and although they each took divergent paths after the Freedom Rides era and their activism changed, their shared experiences within the movement inspired them to use business as a means of continuing their commitments to racial and economic justice.

Bond's state house seat was restored by the time his friend Hank returned to Atlanta after fulfilling his military obligation. The doggedly focused Thomas sought an opportunity to build something of his own, but with little money and rigid barriers for blacks who wanted to join the owner class, Thomas's ambitions were stalled. The Jacksonville, Florida, native settled into a series of jobs that taught him various aspects of business. After work-

ing for the Army, a part-time gig at Sears and tenure as a fire-man, Thomas finally found an opening when he learned about an opportunity to manage apartment laundromats. Drawing on his experience as a protester and an activist, he appeared at banks and began "threatening to go all the way to Washington and demon-strate, if necessary," in front of the Small Business Administration office to show how serious he was about getting a business loan. Reed, who may have known Thomas from movement work in the past, saw a commercial for the army veteran's laundry service and reached out to the budding entrepreneur. Reed believed that part-nering with Thomas was a powerful symbol of interracialism, one of the values he carried with him as a supporter of civil rights. Schools, residential communities, and churches were slow to inte-grate. The men may have hoped that businesses could lead the way. Reed also contacted Bond, who would hold a smaller stake in their efforts. From there, the Reed-Thomas Enterprises was born, and the men set out to find the next big thing to bring to inner-city Atlanta. Reed offered Thomas access to a plot of land that he owned on which the men could build a Dairy Queen franchise. Thomas sold his interest in the laundromat and entered into busi-ness with Reed. For Georgians who wanted to separate the state from its associations with their most racially regressive southern neighbors—namely Alabama and Mississippi—Atlanta was a cru-cial exemplar of what was possible in the New South. In the 1970s, Atlanta—King's birthplace and place of rest—was attracting edu-cated blacks on a reverse migration course out of the North and back to their Southern roots. The excitement about Atlanta's pos-sibility in expanding its black middle class, fortifying its histori-cally black colleges, and opening businesses that could revitalize poor communities motivated civil rights movement alums to pur-sue fast food franchising.[52]

The trio's new Dairy Queen opened in 1970, and it offered the features of the most modern of the chain's brazier concept with an air-conditioned dining room and a parking lot that could accom-modate more than thirty cars. The menu introduced one of the newest fast food concepts, "a kind of a chicken—a chicken pat-

tie," that Thomas assured Georgians, many of whom believed that they perfected fried chicken, was actually "very delicious."[53] In a feature on the Dairy Queen's groundbreaking ceremony, an *Atlanta Journal-Constitution* real estate writer explained that the restaurant on Ashby Street, S.W., near the hub of the city's black colleges, was a mechanism for helping to "finance other Negroes who want to go into business for themselves." The initiative was framed as a matter of investment and business, not white benevolence, and the article captured a great hope in what the newspaper called "Hank Thomas' Black Capitalism." This version of black capitalism placed Reed as the "catalytic agent" in the Negro community, in a "marriage of white capital with black initiative." This was not necessarily a new or novel approach to projects believed to be a realization of black capitalism, but Reed's presence and their desire to broadcast to whites that they could and did have a role to play in building black community wealth would soon become its own liability. Purists were concerned about the way that Reed fit into a black endeavor, and whites unable to see the value in Reed's efforts with Thomas and Bond, saw his actions as an example of white liberalism run amok.[54]

The thrill of the new Dairy Queen—and the subsequent second Dairy Queen and two Wishbone Fried Chicken franchises the men established—was short-lived. The brazier became a magnet for crime and protest, and the partnership became untenable due to the financial inequality among venture investors. By the time temperatures started to rise in Atlanta, and more people were flocking to the cool relief of a Dairy Queen treat, the business was in jeopardy due to community resistance. A headline blared: "Bond's White Associate Forced Out of Business." After a series of terminations of black employees, a group had begun to form a picket line in front of the partnership's restaurant, where a year earlier the men smiled at news cameras as they broke ground. As was the case in other cities, the fast food franchise was the place where communities litigated their frustrations with Atlanta's racial politics. Protesters called Reed a "filthy rich white racist[s] [*sic*] . . . sucking blood out of the black community." Thomas and Bond's partici-

pation in the endeavor was irrelevant; the picketers believed that they were being sold a black business that was actually replicating the way that whites lorded over blacks in Atlanta. Thomas's authority over the store operations was not compelling to the protesters, and vandals constantly targeted the restaurant. The black partners believed that the community had painted them into a corner, and regardless of their feelings of camaraderie with Reed, the business would not be able to survive him. "We told him (Reed) it wouldn't be settled until he got out and he agreed," Bond told the press. "He said pickets raised the issue of whether whites could do business at all in the black community—not if they could help and then withdraw." The beleaguered dentist hoped that the city's four-year-old Community Relations Commission, a community action group, would get involved, but they declined to get in the middle of this skirmish. Reed also used the Dairy Queen to punctuate his laments about what he perceived as a "rising tide of 'anti-white hatred' in the black community." Reed was no longer welcomed at black neighborhood and organizational activities as he was in the 1960s, and as a result, he was no longer sure where he fit. SNCC lost white members in a massive realignment in 1967 in which the organization decided to pivot from integration as a goal and instead encouraged whites to organize among themselves. Black Power and other nationalist movements' calls for black self-governance alienated some white liberals, who felt excluded or betrayed. Although black capitalism was a largely interracial movement in its enmeshment with white bureaucrats and even a racist president, the optics of black ownership were sometimes more important than the realities. Black businesses in black communities created to serve the needs of black people did not support the presence of well-intentioned men like Reed, regardless of their personal commitments to black wealth building. Feelings of white ostracism tested the limits of interracial solidarity politics throughout the period, and it played right into the hands of conservatives who relished the perceived failures of whites who were foolish enough to engage in what they saw as futile attempts to ally with blacks. *New York Times* columnist Jon Nordheimer believed that the partnership's

dissolution proved that there was "a growing concern about the anti-white feeling that has emerged among Southern blacks." Accusations that groups committed to black self-sufficiency were particularly antiwhite could be heard across the country as some observers "discovered" what they believed was a new black radicalism.[55] "The heart of the matter," in the columnist's assessment, was the fact that Reed had secured the $100,000 worth of financing for the businesses, and he was unjustly moved out of the effort. Reed and Bond were no more than "noble jerks," who were hung out to dry by the "moderate black leadership" who refused to defend them in the attacks on the Dairy Queen. As franchises sought minority partners, civil rights organizations and community foundations who had their eyes on establishing their own stores may have been cautious not to rankle the regional franchising managers. Black conservative George Schuyler also seemed to revel in the Dairy Queen misfortune. Schuyler represented a strain of anti–Black Power, anti–Black Is Beautiful thinking that questioned the premise of black nationalism. Once a socialist, Schuyler's opinions of the Atlanta incident were forged after decades of deliberation on what black America should and shouldn't do. He called the Dairy Queen a "pipedream . . . [of] setting up a chain of food stands primarily to give managerial employment to promising young Negroes. A laudable ambition, but scarcely a basis for economic enterprise." Schuyler charged that the men's arrogance, ignorance of business, and misinformation about how capitalism worked led to their undoing. Critical of the activists' second acts as businessmen, Schuyler charged that "Bond and Reed violated about all of the laws of free enterprise . . . they knew nothing about business, and were experts in disturbing the public peace . . . They thought all they had to do to succeed was to get a little capital, yell 'Race,' and hire some blacks."[56]

Reed did not fully disavow black self-help, but he suggested that "the black community destroys its own . . . because the robber feels he'll get better from a white judge if he steals from a black business." Reed may have been attempting to garner sympathy, but he also exposed the pervasive racism that blacks faced in the courts,

as well as on Main Street. Bond maintained his focus on structural issues, but his resentment also came through in his comments:

> Any business needs capital and there's not much of it available in the black community . . . I'm against having white businesses in the black community, but this will mean a black can't get any white help . . . when Gerry and I started out in this I didn't think we had anything to risk . . . we had the mistaken idea that we were performing a service in providing 80 jobs.

Businesses in other cities empathized with the partners. When Washington, D.C.'s T. M. Alexander Jr. entered into a 50-50 arrangement with a white colleague, they were proud to offer "more than average salaries to [their] car wash, liquor store and restaurant employees." But the wrath of the neighborhood soon surfaced and his businesses were targets of "harassment and intimidation from a local black minister and so-called leader of the people." The businesses couldn't survive, and the partners decided that they had no choice but to close their many doors. Alexander predicted that "local financial institutions are going to become more and more dubious of making substantial loans to blacks."[57]

Reed's departure did not immediately solve any problems. Within three days after Reed's exit, Dairy Queen was still contending with pickets during the day and burglars at night. The Dairy Queen had been robbed fifteen times during the winter of 1970. By spring, Bond was breathing a sigh of relief that the "armed bandits" were no longer attacking his restaurants, but the protests were far from resolved.[58] The protesters were organized by the Enterprise's former bookkeeper and five fired employees. The men were fired for "spreading dissension among the other employees" and "mismanagement of funds." Thomas enlisted Atlanta police to supervise their dismissals to stop the employees from taking anything else from the store and hopefully keep cooler heads.[59] The men, perhaps having learned about the elements of demonstration in the civil rights center, mounted a "one hundred percent effective" picket line by targeting the Dairy Queen in two-to-three-hour

blocks twice a day, during its busiest hours. The men then adopted the name Black Unity Association and began organizing other community groups against the Dairy Queen, including men from Bond's alma mater to recruit students to their cause. The pickets began to alarm the men more and more when they learned that the Association was armed, and Thomas believed that the group likely had stolen the gun he kept in his car's glove compartment. The weapons, coupled with the threatening calls he and his wife began receiving at home, heightened their nervousness about the business. The Black Unity Association said that Thomas's business "would not be just another front for white men . . . ," and in an effort to further discredit Bond and Thomas, the group stole "records in its possession to support its contention that Dr. Reed controlled and dominated the business."[60]

At Reed's final meeting as a part of the Enterprises, the three men assessed their debt, which extended across three franchises and was owed to a number of banks across the country. Their total payroll costs were estimated at $100,000. The Ashby Avenue Dairy Queen had $30,000 in debt alone. They were behind on payments for the Dairy Queen on Bankhead Highway. The Gordon Road Wishbone Fried Chicken had an $850 debt due in a few months, and $450 was owed by the Simpson Road chicken shack. A note worth $15,000 was owed to Citizens & Southern National Bank and the Northwest Bank of Minneapolis. They were also paying the Internal Revenue Service $1,000 a week to pay down an $18,000 tax bill. Soon the men would discover they didn't have a clear sense of what was really owed, but what was indisputable was that Reed had underwritten all of these loans.[61] Over the course of the following three years, the men's lawyers would try to settle the matter, with Reed taking the most substantial financial hit. Reed was pensive at the end of the transfers, having expended considerable financial resources with very little to show for it. In an October 1971 letter to Bond hoping to collect some assistance with the efforts' outstanding debts, which Reed figured cost him $160,000, Reed wrote "the nightmare actually happened and the community remains the real loser," and he expressed regret at the collapse of

the enterprise. "Julian," he told his former comrade in struggle and friend in business, "neither of us asked for or deserved what happened . . . the failure of our plan was a keen disappointment to me, for we had such high hopes for helping the community."[62]

Despite the unpleasantness with the Dairy Queen deal, Thomas remained committed to the franchising model. In a segment on the Atlanta University Center's radio show entitled "Economic Literacy," Thomas was celebrating four years at the helm of what was now his own Dairy Queen, which was among those with the "highest volume of service" in the country.[63] Thomas was glad that he stayed the course. Fast food was a sound business, he argued, because "a higher percentage of blacks spend more of their income with fast food services than whites who can better afford the higher tablecloth restaurants." Thomas eventually transitioned to franchising a Burger King, then he took the reins of six McDonald's restaurants throughout the South, including a High Point, North Carolina, location that denied him service as a young man. In the 2000s, he sold his restaurants and became a hotel franchisee.[64]

Bond never returned to the franchise game, but he did lend his voice as the narrator of an official National Black McDonald's Operators Association video that celebrated the organization's history and linked the franchisees' fight to win franchises with Bond's earlier career for fighting for black political and social enfranchisement.

* * *

Franchising and the question of black ownership lingered as new restaurants tried to enter black neighborhoods. Shrewd researchers and marketing experts helped major franchises obscure their corporate ties or the very nature of the franchise arrangement to convince black customers that they were supporting black business in earnest. In the summer of 1981, a new Sisters Chicken and Biscuits restaurant exemplified this approach on Cleveland's East Side, the epicenter of the McDonald's boycotts more than a decade earlier. Residents were concerned that the franchise was pretending to be black-owned, and the allegations led co-owner Tom Henning to

respond in the pages of the *Call & Post*.[65] The newspaper suggested that "with a name like Sisters, and the fact that the stores sells beans and rice as well as chicken, makes it obvious that the chain hopes to attract a large black clientele."[66] Sisters riled concerned community members because of a comment made by advertising account executive Tim Robson: "Church's Chicken is the most profitable fast food operation in black America, because they go into black neighborhoods where they can get cheaper real estate . . ." He continued: "Church's cannot compete in a marginally black or suburban area; they can't compete against a white-oriented fast food market." The executive may have been talking about a number of fast food restaurants, as the cheaper access to purchase or lease land allowed the building of more franchise sites, which could then become available to black operators, who would assume the decidedly high costs of insurance, security, and sometimes repairs if the store was older. The *Call and Post* also challenged why Henning would call the Sisters effort an investment in the black community when ultimately there were no black construction workers on the $300,000 building project. The newspaper concluded that "the only thing left for blacks will be part time, minimum wage jobs that only serve to maintain the status quo." Having been out of jail for nearly a decade, activist James Raplin reminded Clevelanders that they couldn't "retrogress to pre-1969 conditions in which blacks were denied ownership in fast food restaurants in our own neighborhoods."

Sisters was still in the experimentation stage of the restaurant concept in 1981, and they had not established any minority franchising initiative. They did clarify that they were interested in local people operating stores, did not want to franchise to cooperatives or development groups, and they wanted people with significant experience in fast food. Franchising aside, the word "sister" was an issue of contention, whether the name of the restaurant was to reflect black modes of addressing black women or, as a co-owner suggested, "the main concept of the name Sisters has to do with chicken you would eat on your sister's front porch." The editorial concluded:

Whether the name Sisters was chosen because blacks will relate to it is really unimportant. What is important, however, is the message black neighborhoods are trying desperately to communicate to white fast food entrepreneurs. That message simply states: "come on in but, we want a slice of the economic pie not just a piece of your pre-packaged micro-wave oven pie!"

Sisters, a subsidiary of Ohio-based Wendy's, did not expand much after the Cleveland experiment. Wendy's sold the concept in 1987, and by 1994 the company closed the restaurants with the distinctive wrap-around porches and slanted roof.[67]

The various resistance strategies to the growing reach of fast food in the early 1970s all point to the diversity of black communities and leadership models that emerged in the period. Some of the strategies are familiar to us—boycotts, protests, and pickets. But some anti–fast food movements emerged in unlikely places, created new coalitions, and were inspired by concerns over a wide array of agenda items—including fidelity to the letter of the laws of black capitalism and the future of the environment. From Portland to Philadelphia to Atlanta, the fast food resistance movement took many forms, and taken together, it is clear that fast food's attempt to colonize black America was not unchallenged. Opposition to fast food was not solely about the industry itself, but rather who was profiting from it.

In Albina and across the country, fast food, racial politics, and competing demands—separately and together—could ignite the powder keg enflamed by tensions over community control and business citizenship. Even though the bombing in Albina was a foretold event, the responses to it were still revelatory about the economic, social, and political dynamics of the period. The relationship between the fast food restaurant—still in its adolescence—and a small, black community grappling with being infantilized and silenced in an overwhelmingly white city, exposed the tensions that the "urban turn" in fast food franchising would engender in working-class and poor neighborhoods of color throughout the 1970s. As conflicts over race and policing, access to good jobs, and

the rightful role of businesses in communities continued to grow among black America, fast food restaurants could symbolize economic possibility or structural perniciousness and bigotry. This was all a matter of perspective. While McDonald's was able to win over black Chicago with the installation of Herman Petty at the helm of the Woodlawn location and the Cleveland boycotts yielded black franchise ownership, in Portland and other cities, concerns and conflicts over McDonald's were not so easily mediated. Some community groups took their critiques to city councils and municipal planning boards instead of the streets.

The 1970s was every bit as bittersweet as the decade that preceded it. Each year, African Americans were running candidates for mayoral races and city councils in greater numbers, and winning. Yet, federal programs were not addressing black unemployment. Organized parents' groups were battling boards of education, and sometimes teachers' unions, for community leadership of their children's schools. Other parents divested entirely from public schools, and creative parents established alternative, Afrocentric schools to circumvent a system they believed was harming their children. Meanwhile, busing was under attack at the highest levels in Washington.[68] A new generation of black doctors and nurses found greater employment opportunities in newly built community hospitals and clinics, but African Americans were still dying younger than whites. The Black Arts Movement inspired innovative theater, visual arts, and television shows with black audiences in mind, but mainstream entertainment was still fixated on stereotype and caricature. While black America was continuing its fight against the old problems of racism in jobs, schools, housing, and health, its entanglement with the fast food industry was still brandnew. And no one could predict if the drive-thru was a window that looked out onto a new world of possibility, or just provided a view of the same old problem-plagued street.

The Portland drama highlighted the ways that local politics would start to shape how McDonald's corporate would nationally address and cultivate black communities in the face of their own internal research reports that black consumers were key to their

success. As they gingerly navigated opposition, they were devising strategies that would allow them to continue to grow the critical black consumer market. Portland's struggle also helps us understand that black militancy does not mean a total rejection of business influence or largesse, rather a way of being radically pragmatic and manipulating the flow of limited resources.

The transition from civil to silver rights was not seamless. Objection to fast food's desire to dominate the "urban market" was articulated in a number of ways as blacks strengthened and exercised their consumer citizenship. Many communities and organizations decided to play the role of objector, as well as competitors in the market. Both approaches required black people to define themselves in relationship to big business, as equally entitled to a number of explicit, as well as more nebulous, rights—from safe neighborhoods to a clean planet to black economic investment and healthy foods. Black neighborhoods and organizations challenged the presence of fast food and tried to set the terms of engagement on how the fast food industry would treat black communities. What was at stake for black America in the 1970s was whether a generation of citizens testing the strength of civil rights legislation, economic opportunity, federal policy, and corporate responsibility would let fast food become part of their worlds.

Black America, Brought to You by . . .

Contemporary artist Hank Willis Thomas uses images from advertising to capture the complex relationships between the marketplace and race. In *So Glad We Made It, 1979*, Thomas has removed the branding from a vintage McDonald's advertisement targeted toward black consumers. These ads were crucial for McDonald's success in capturing black diners. © Hank Willis Thomas. Courtesy of the artist and Jack Shainman Gallery, New York.

The Spirit of '76 needed some soul. So a group of black McDonald's franchisees offered "Soul of a Nation," a more inclusive history lesson to its customers on the occasion of the nation's 200th birthday. Black History Month received official White House recognition that year, after scholars at Kent State University made a case for Negro History Week's extension in 1970.[1] In the bicentennial year, red-white-and-blue jelly glasses were offered

at gas stations. Uncle Sam top hats and Betsy Ross–style wigs adorned sports mascots and corporate logos.[2] Outside of the burgeoning Afro-American studies programs on campuses scattered across the country and the small black history collectors that turned community centers and trailers into museums, black history was not easy to learn about in the deep, rich ways that would emerge in the late 1980s. Black history had to be learned and enjoyed where it could be found, including McDonald's. A group of franchisees underwrote "Soul of a Nation," described as "an illustrated collection of historical narratives reproduced from McDonald's special Black Bicentennial Radio Series." The radio show, broadcast from stations in Atlanta and Los Angeles, provided an interruption to the dominant, Founding Fathers–heavy celebration of the nation. In an era when slavery was scarcely acknowledged at historical sites and textbooks described the peculiar institution as a benevolent one, a black Bicentennial program proved meaningful to black customers, and the initiative illustrated the relative independence of black franchisees to determine what would work in their markets, as well as the cultural work of the fast food industry in the 1970s.

"Soul of a Nation" brought together scholars from Cleveland State and Wayne State Universities, which established black studies programs in 1969 and 1970, with black artist Carl Owens to create twenty-four historical profiles for the booklet. Comedian Bill Cosby lent star power to the recorded component as the narrator, and music sensation Ray Charles scored the show. The series applauded exceptional individuals and institutions in the nation's history, including Mary McLeod Bethune, "a woman who kept the faith"; George Washington Carver, "a man for all men"; the "unsung hero of the American West," the black cowboy; and "The Black Church," which had been "leading the way for nearly two centuries." The list of notables is, on its surface, inoffensive and may seem mundane, but even suggesting that African Americans deserve a laudatory history was not commonplace thinking in the period. The printed accompaniment to the radio program may have been drafted to quell any concerns about a hidden agenda. White audiences could be particularly sensitive that the word

"soul" was a weapon of exclusion. "Soul of a Nation" wanted everyone to know that this effort was just about including African Americans in the national narrative. Cosby's note in the recording's guidebook clarified that "the word 'soul' means different things to different people. But to Black men and women, 'soul' means something very special. McDonald's Restaurants recognize this, and more importantly they have done something about it."[3] If you missed the "Soul of a Nation" on the radio, you could stop by a participating McDonald's and receive a copy of the program's script. Each profile reminded readers that the nation would not be possible without the diligence, wisdom, and insight of African Americans. There would be no nation's capital if it wasn't for "the good memory of one Black man," Benjamin Banneker. There would be no Will Rogers without the black cowboy Bill Pickett, who taught him "his famous rope tricks." And there would be no bicentennial without the courage of Crispus Attucks. "Soul of a Nation" re-created his fight in the Revolutionary War by making it clear that his battle was not "just another street fight."[4]

"Soul of a Nation" was one of a myriad of locally sponsored forms of outreach financed by franchisees and used to supplement the national advertising campaigns dictated by McDonald's corporate headquarters. Funding national advertising was a contentious issue for black franchisees of McDonald's and Burger King, and it was likely a problem in other franchise systems. Every franchisee contributed a percentage of profits or a fee for ads, but national campaigns that only used white actors and models, or were only played on radio stations that did not explicitly cater to black musical preferences, amounted to black franchisees throwing good money after bad. Brady Keys protested paying his Burger King advertising fees, and he purchased air time in 1978 to broadcast his own commercials on local television.[5] Franchisees with the means to do so could follow suit, but most needed to either create small-scale promotions to reach their target audiences or advocate for the inclusion of special advertising to their markets. Franchisees undertook both approaches, and in doing so—leveraging what was called ethnic advertising and underwriting creative projects—they

were making an impact on the cultivation and dissemination of black culture.

"Soul" was hard to define precisely, but fast food marketers were hopeful that black customers could recognize it when they saw it in their attempts to reach black diners. In the late 1960s, black celebrities lent their names and likenesses to a number of businesses. These franchises suggested that they were truly black-owned and, in their spokesperson's authentic soulfulness, better poised to make black consumers happy and even improve black communities. All of these short-lived efforts failed because the brands were built on unstable foundations. Sometimes insufficient capital and poor planning led to a business closure. A few years after Mahalia Jackson's Glori-Fried Chicken was introduced in 1968, the business folded. The company's masterminds—two white lawyers from Nashville—structured it like a Ponzi scheme. Muhammad Ali's Miami-based ChampBurger, also introduced in 1968, only lasted a couple years. Friend of black capitalism and singer James Brown launched the Gold Platter restaurant franchise in 1969, which later spun off into a convenience store concept. After he convinced his fans that franchising would be his brand-new bag, the restaurant closed its few locations. Each of these companies assured black customers that in choosing the Negro Songbird, the Greatest, or the Godfather of Soul over Ronald, the Colonel, or the Burger King, they were choosing to not only support a black business, but they were also celebrating their own blackness.[6]

The collapse of each of these ventures animated the issue taken up by the Dairy Queen protesters that surrounded Julian Bond's brazier: in America, there were few truly black businesses. Between the time the first business plan was drafted and the moment the first profit collected, one could encounter white financiers, white franchising representatives, white federal agency heads, or white French fry distribution company owners. If one could not buy black authentically, then the very least a black customer could do was look for products tinged with soul. For fast food companies that counted few franchisees of color among their ranks but recognized the power of the black dollar, building the soul market was

a top priority. As the "soul businesses" flopped one by one, white-owned national chains took note of the centrality of amplifying soul in communicating to blacks. The 1970s and 1980s created a vital demand for the work of firms that could provide advertisements, consumer research, and product development focusing on black sensibilities. The line between appealing and offensive was a fine one in the corporate effort to integrate soul style into the selling of fast food. Businesses entrusted this delicate translation to a burgeoning generation of black professionals, who were beneficiaries of the opening of more opportunities to attend college and earn business degrees, ascend career tracks commensurate with their talents, and establish businesses predicated on their desire to improve the representation of blacks in mass media. Fast food's explosion was advantageous for franchisees and in-house professionals, as well as for a rising creative class of blacks looking to share their art, scholars hoping to spread their passion for black history, and black cultural institutions seeking to extend their reach. If black people were indeed the soul of a nation, then the fast food industry was determined to feed it.

McDonald's believed that its marketing strength came from its franchisees. Ostensibly, as members of the community, franchisees could best assess which charities were most worthy of free apple pie coupons or what Kiwanis Club had the most clout in town. Franchisees were better positioned to know which Fourth of July parade float or Little League team to sponsor than any bean counter or consultant in Oak Brook. The autonomy afforded franchisees in developing their community outreach was unusual, considering that every part of the McDonald's operations and business process was scripted by the corporate office. From its very beginning, McDonald's set the bar high for community outreach. Franchisees hosting children's days at the zoo, visiting hospitals, and offering scholarships were ways, according to a biographer of Ray Kroc and his wife Joan, to "counter the negative association with fifteen-cent hamburger joints." Serving up a few trays of free cheeseburgers and presenting oversized novelty checks now and then was also "cheaper than advertising," especially in the years before national television

commercials dominated fast food marketing plans.[7] McDonald's approach to philanthropy has been accurately described as "carefully constructed" and "a master stroke of public relations in an age long before the trendy catchphrase, 'corporate social responsibility.' "[8] These franchisee activities occurred in different contexts. For black operators, their community outreach delved into areas that exposed the power of charitable acts in places where people struggled with profound powerlessness.

From the very beginning of their entry into McDonald's franchising, black franchisees were visible in various social aspects of community life. Black franchisees could be counted on to support the schools near their stores, which were most likely to be majority or entirely black. In Cleveland, franchisees initiated a series of summer events in 1972 in which the operators paid for buses to take neighborhood children on tours of the city, supplementing the field trip experience for low-income students.[9] Wilson Rogers, another Cleveland operator, adopted Paul Revere School after parents asked that the businessman help with litter, vandalism, and behavior problems among their students. Rogers used "a sizeable personal contribution" to organize a coalition of business leaders, elected officials, and parent-teacher association members to intervene in the school's troubles. Students were enticed to participate in antilittering campaigns with gift certificates to McDonald's. The McDonald's partnership with local schools spread, and the "be my guest card" became a standard prize for students with perfect attendance and academic honors.[10] McDonald's encouraged these appeals to children because they knew that youngsters held sway over whether a family would stay in or grab up a few burgers for dinner. One study found that "in three-quarters of the cases where a family decides to eat out the children choose the restaurant," hence much of "McDonald's advertising [appealed] directly to young TV viewers."[11]

Outside of school, McDonald's franchisees were regular funders of extracurricular activities, especially sports. On the local level, franchisees created new sports leagues, subsidized expenses, and hosted victory parties at their restaurants. McDonald's estab-

lished the McDonald's All-American Game in 1977, where the best American and Canadian high school basketball players showcased their talents in tournaments. Being a McDonald's All-American athlete was a valuable distinction on the dossiers of the nation's best African-American high school basketball stars, including Magic Johnson in 1977 and Patrick Ewing in 1981. In a pre-Internet era, the games allowed an array of young black athletes to travel and capture the attention of college recruiters. The majority of these national youth sports opportunities were closed to girls' athletics until the 2000s, but one female-dominated sport made a splash with McDonald's earlier. The American Double Dutch League (ADDL)—conceived by two New York police detectives searching for a youth activity that appealed to girls—highlighted the athleticism and performative strengths of black girls through jump rope. In 1980, a collaboration of franchisees from New York, New Jersey, and Connecticut promoted the McDonald's Dynamos, a quartet of Double Dutchers. The ADDL-McDonald's partnership helped local communities establish rope-jumping leagues at rec centers and parks across the country. Three years later, McDonald's announced their support of the ADDL as a part of their official youth sports program.[12] Between 1979 and 1985, Double Dutchers were featured in McDonald's commercials, singing songs about their favorite items on the McDonald's menu. In one of the first ads featuring girls Double Dutching in New York City, the accompanying music was as much of an affirmation of the targeted black audience as it was a sales pitch. "McDonald's knows your Double Dutch is really hard to beat, cause when you're jumping you do something magic with your feet," crooned the commercial's voiceover. The 1985 "Jump to It" commercial featured the team in a McDonald's parking lot wearing red, white, and yellow uniforms, singing the praises of the Chicken McNugget. "Down at McDonald's where the arches glow, they've got Chicken McNuggets and they're hot to go." The team added cartwheels and complicated hand games to their already intricate choreography as a rap-style vocal described the delicious attributes of the poultry dish. The commercial ends with the jingle, sung in the style of R&B, "It's a

good time for the great taste of McDonald's." For audiences unfamiliar with Double Dutch, the ad was an entertaining introduction to the impressive tradition of black rope-jumping. For black audiences, the ads that portrayed scenes of the Double Dutchers turning rope in front of an elder's house during a family gathering or on a strip of city street suggested that McDonald's also appreciated the ways that rope-jumping was familiar and joyful in black communities. Even activities that didn't necessarily have an exclusive association with African Americans were avenues for McDonald's to connect with black audiences. The McDonald's All-American High School Band, formed in 1967, was part of a cultural diplomacy effort to advertise a then-relatively-new brand. In 1980, when legendary band director William Foster was named the head of the All-American Band, he integrated elements of black marching band style into the competitive corps of 104 high school musicians. Foster, who also led the Florida Agricultural & Mechanical University Rattlers marching band, directed the group at national events like the Macy's Thanksgiving Day Parade, and some of the performers were featured in national commercials. For viewers with little experience of the rich tradition of historically black colleges, the All-American band may have been their first experiences of the moves, motions, and music of this black performance tradition.[13]

School programs and sports tournaments were some of the easier issues for black franchisees to tackle. In addition to offering free Happy Meals to children with straight A's and new goal posts for the local high school football program, black franchisees also responded to the fact that a mass of their clientele were earning low incomes, and sometimes assisted in helping families meet basic needs. In 1972, Cleveland's black franchisees partnered with three neighborhood Opportunity Industrialization Centers— a public-private partnership concept pioneered by Philadelphia's Leon Sullivan—to distribute more than 4,000 pairs of shoes across the East Side.[14] Each year, the franchisees marveled at how quickly the shoes were claimed and how many people were turned away because the demand significantly exceeded the supply. Black franchisees often pointed to their value to communities in not only

providing charity, but also creating jobs for youth. Youth unemployment was, and continues to be, a chronic challenge for black communities. In the 1970s, inner-city youth joblessness rarely migrated below 50%. The teenagers and young adults who couldn't find work were often more susceptible to dropping out of school and finding themselves locked into a cycle of poverty. Federal assistance for youth jobs distributed through state agencies could only provide so many entry-level positions, and corruption in the administration of these programs sometimes diverted opportunities from youth to experienced workers. McDonald's franchises partnered with some of these state programs to staff their stores, and the high employee turnover rate of the fast food industry ensured constant openings. Working at McDonald's could teach youth, especially those who had not completed high school, a variety of skills. Some franchisees, however, noticed that their workers struggled with basic math when a register failed or a customer complained about being shortchanged. In the fall of 1979, at Caesar Burkes's Carnegie Avenue location in Cleveland, the operator invested more than $12,000 to build a training center inside his restaurant. He purchased two computers programed to teach employees how to operate newer models of cash registers.[15] Burkes said that educational deficiencies led to a 300% turnover rate among his crew, and the computers would allow employees to complete modules at their own pace. That year, the U.S. Department of Education reported the black high school dropout rate was 21.1%, compared to 12% for whites.[16] Burkes hoped that the training would not only strengthen their skills, but it would also "have doors open to them that are normally closed."[17]

While black franchisees tried to remedy the problems in inner-city education, there were times they were called upon to respond to immediate crises exacerbated by the lack of attention poor black neighborhoods endured. In the spring of 1974, in Chicago, residents of the Altgeld Gardens Homes public housing development observed a strange cloud lingering over the complex, which housed 2,000 families. Bordered by factories and a landfill, the Altgeld Gardens community had long been exposed to chemical

hazards from neighboring plants. This eerie, gray sight in the sky was the result of a silicon tetrachloride leak from a nearby chemical company. A breach in a 500,000-gallon storage tank caused hydrochloric acid to mix with moisture in the air and gather above the South Side neighborhood. The acid made the residents susceptible to respiratory and gastrointestinal problems, especially children, pregnant women, the elderly, and people with asthma and bronchitis.[18] Many of the Garden residents reported feeling a burning sensation in their throats and used towels, handkerchiefs, and whatever cloth they could find to cover their mouths and noses. Fifty people were taken to the hospital for the day. A University of Illinois toxicologist advised the state's branch of the Environmental Protection Agency to begin evacuating the housing site in the late afternoon, but officials delayed the process for hours. Concerned residents called the police, who had little to offer by way of advice. When one resident called for help, she realized her actions were in vain. "They didn't send anyone. . . . If I'd known what this was, I could have been ready to take my family out of here. They should have told us so we would have been ready."[19] Eventually, the city dispatched public transit buses and police vehicles to Altgeld Gardens to start the evacuation process.[20] Some residents were unsure if they should leave, fearing that their homes would be robbed if they were gone for the night. The mayor dispatched police patrols to watch over the Garden homes. The only thing that the residents could depend on was a meal from McDonald's. A local black franchisee brought more than a thousand hamburgers and drinks for the evacuated Chicagoans, who waited for further instructions at a local high school. At the end of a long day that included being ignored by authorities, evacuated, and then moved to three different shelter sites, black McDonald's franchisees emerged as heroes. In a statement to the press, the National Black McDonald's Operators Association remarked, "We at McDonald's are sincerely interested in community involvement and can always be counted upon in a crisis."[21] Memories of the 1974 leak, which led the city to file a $5.4 million lawsuit against the responsible company, helped Altgeld Gardens resident Hazel Johnson recruit people for her environ-

mental justice group, People for Community Recovery. Johnson, who is credited as the mother of the urban environmental justice movement, devoted her life to holding the city's housing authority, as well as the chemical and industrial plants in the surrounding area, responsible for the high rates of environmental illnesses in her community. Having lost her husband to lung cancer, Johnson later worked with a young community organizer, Barack Obama, to seek justice for the community's long-term health and economic suffering from pollutants and deindustrialization. For blacks in underserved areas, crisis was a constant. When McDonald's managers could be relied on more than school administrators or police officers, then the lines between where leadership and power rested in a city could become so blurred that a fast food restaurant could begin to look like a solution instead of a symptom.

Community outreach was effective advertising, but McDonald's had realized in the late 1960s that in order to remain dominant in the fast food field, they needed to do more. The company could not maintain its prowess in the market without the help of broad-based national advertising efforts, and they debuted their first coast-to-coast commercial in 1967. The spot featured children singing the refrain "McDonald's is our kind of place." The commercial's narrator assured parents that their spillproof cups and full-size bibs prevented stained shirts or messy car interiors. With each year, McDonald's advertising would feature higher production values, sleeker camera shots, clearer narrative structure, and more celebrities. Until actor John Amos (of *Roots* and *Good Times* fame) appeared in a McDonald's commercial in 1971 as part of a singing McDonald's crew, the television and print ads featured white people living in nearly all-white worlds. This did not sit well with the growing number of franchisees of color who were dutifully paying into the advertising fund but seeing few advertisements in the pages of the magazines they read or the radio stations they listened to. As was the case with most issues involving McDonald's, a small group of black operators had to advocate for themselves. This required them to return to where it all started: Chicago.

In addition to being the birthplace of some of the most cele-

brated black periodicals, like the *Chicago Defender, Ebony*, and *Jet*, Chicago was also the home of the very best in black advertising and market research.[22] Founded in 1971, black advertising pioneer Tom Burrell's agency, Burrell Communications, transformed the way the nation's largest retailers talked to black America. After a brief and mixed experience with a Philip Morris campaign to make the Marlboro Man more "soulful," Burrell received its most lucrative and impactful client—McDonald's. Burrell's first independent foray, a partnership named Burrell-McBain, focused on helping companies understand that "black people were culturally distinct enough and profitable enough as a consumer group to be worthy of a separate advertising initiative."[23] Burrell had to overcome the racial biases of the advertising industry that often treated black advertising talent as tokens or failed to take their advice into account. Historian of black advertising Jason Chambers described Burrell's success as a result of his refusal to accept "corporate handouts then used by some companies as a kind of community-relations effort . . . in which they gave money to black-owned companies but required little in the way of professional execution or actual deliverables."[24]

Under the leadership of an NBMOA founder, Columbus, Ohio's Carl Osborne, the black franchisees gathered with Roland Jones to discuss their being shut out of the McDonald's advertising strategy. McDonald's conceded that they should provide some avenue for black-oriented commercials to reach their customers, especially considering the importance of the urban stores to the chain's expansion. As black franchisees were making a case for more advertising, McDonald's was learning a lesson about simply recycling campaigns and pitching them to blacks, when they tried to circulate their popular "You deserve a break today" campaign to black outlets. Tom Burrell personally studied consumer reaction to the slogan, and he believed that black customers were not getting it. Black customers were confused. There were no breaks in their America. Unlike white suburban families that traveled to McDonald's to indulge their children's fancy, black families went to McDonald's to satisfy hunger momentarily before heading back

into the challenges of their work and home lives. A history of Burrell Communications found that "the idea that the restaurants were only useful when one needed or wanted a break was meaningless to blacks."[25] Burrell Communications steered the advertising strategy in a wholly different direction. Burrell crafted the "So get up and get away to McDonald's" tagline, which anchored the first promotional material to feature blacks exclusively. The print advertisement featured an intimate moment between a stylish black couple, both sporting perfectly coiffed Afros. The woman looks directly at the viewer, while her companion is caught in the middle of saying something to her. The advertisement did not merely replace white faces with black ones. The woman's Afrocentric jewelry and the man's patterned shirt reflected popular black clothing styles of the time. Burrell was not holding back, and he struck gold. The ad worked, and from that moment onward, Burrell would set the standard on how to market to black America. Even with a team of black copywriters, photographers, and creative directors, this was no easy task.

Burrell's appeals to McDonald's to learn the language necessary to talk to blacks was supplemented by research from Chicago-based ViewPoint, Inc., which was founded in 1976 by Felix A. Burrows Jr., a Florida native who earned a master's degree in food chemistry in 1967. Burrows took his expertise to the food industry, working on quality control for dairies, and later attempted a Ph.D. in food chemistry, but the racial climate of the academic program led him to leave without a doctorate. His entry into market research came after being hired as a senior chemist by Kraft Foods in suburban Chicago. After executing a survey of housewives' perspectives on Kraft foods in development, he left the company for one of the area's leading consumer analysis firms. A few years later, Burrows decided to hang his own shingle and established ViewPoint, Inc., which grew to employ more than fifty researchers and staff, consulting on "food product acceptance and marketing dynamics" among blacks. ViewPoint broadened its scope to conduct market research for companies as diverse as Amoco, Coors Brewing Company, and Sears.

Agencies like Burrell and ViewPoint were essential in helping companies construct the dream worlds their advertising presented to consumers, who were frustrated with limited representation in commercials and campaigns. This lack of representation was cause for concern for civil rights groups, who recognized mass media as integral to buttressing their vision for a peaceful, integrated society. In 1967, the NAACP Legal Defense and Education Fund reported that "of 351 commercials monitored, 17 included Negroes," and among that group, "only three involved a principal role for a Negro." The New York City Commission on Human Rights conducted a similar watch and discovered that only 4% of commercials created between the fall seasons of 1966 and 1967 included blacks or Puerto Ricans. The study reported "minorities in TV advertising . . . instead of progressively increasing each year [in] integrated advertising, had actually fallen behind."[26] Occasionally, advertisements featured scenes of racially mixed community life, which viewers of all colors found forced and unrealistic. In a focus group about the "Coke Adds Life" campaign for Coca-Cola, one respondent said that interracial commercials were sometimes nonsensical. In reaction to a 1979 ad featuring a doo-wop group on a stoop of a Harlem brownstone, a viewer asked, "When have you ever seen a white dude harmonizing like that?" The resulting report on the study of the advertisement recommended that companies not resort to the "overuse of slang" and recognize that there was "no inherent magic in using black personalities in advertising" when crafting appeals to black consumers. The analysis concluded that "blacks are very skeptical as to whether the business establishment is sincerely interested in black customers."[27] Increasingly, as the experts weighed in about what blacks wanted to see, the few scenes of racial harmony were being replaced with black-only scenarios, perhaps mirroring a move away from interracialism as an aspiration. Although public alarm about separatism or black militancy, as it was called, was exaggerated, the advertising from the period reflected a more accepted idea that black life could evolve and reflect progress independent of the white gaze or approval. By the mid-1970s, African Americans were becom-

ing more visible on network television and in commercials, but the desire for more black representation did not mean that black consumers were confident that their marketplace experiences would be free from the discrimination that was supposed to be socially and legally unacceptable. A president of a marketing consulting firm described the change in attitudes of black consumers as a matter of moving away from white ideals. "A decade ago, the typical successful black adopted the white man's middle-class style. The black from Tuskegee was more Ivy League than the Brahmin from Yale. Blacks are no longer emulating whites. They are expressing their black consciousness."[28]

Black consciousness and what the Burrell firm termed "positive realism" were the dual muses that inspired their oeuvre of ads. Burrell's team believed that they could subtly counter more than a century of racist depictions of black people and racist modes of addressing black consumers by highlighting the aspects of black cultural and social life that made people proud.[29] Burrell followed that first successful ad with the slogan "Get Down with Something Good at McDonald's," which highlighted McDonald's as a place to get something edifying, suggesting that this was a special, if not rare experience in black communities. One advertisement in the series, entitled "Carver Day Camp Gettin' Down," featured black adults and children enjoying McDonald's foods as they participated in the type of urban social programs that by the early 1970s were fading from black life. Clearly referring to black scientist George Washington Carver, the day campers are seated outside of a van as they enjoy their lunch with a camp counselor. The use of "gettin'" and "eatin'" versus "getting" and "eating" in the ad copy were deliberate choices to engage black vernacular. The advertisement's text also used slang, telling customers, "on the real side, kids can really dig" a stop at McDonald's.

The use of black vernacular and slang were risky tactics in advertising, but the presence of attractive, dignified black adults and cute children in the depiction signaled that the dropped g's were gestures of recognition, not ridicule. The ad introduced two of the most prevalent tropes in the Burrell projects of the 1970s: the

importance of male authority in the black community and home life, and blacks living in modest and working-class communities. Burrell's intentions were transparent. He believed in the corrective possibility of advertising. Chambers argues that "beyond changing McDonald's slogan for the black community, Burrell also created ads that conveyed his vision of black life."[30]

Black media professionals concerned with the portrayal of black families were countering negative depictions in popular media, in academia, and in government policy. The Burrell goal of framing the black family as valuable and black men as responsible citizens evoked the generalizations of the oft-referenced government study *The Negro Family: The Case for National Action*, which was colloquially known as the Moynihan Report. Coordinated by then–Assistant Secretary of Labor, sociologist, and future New York Senator Daniel Patrick Moynihan, the Report provided confirmation for those who were inclined to believe that black poverty and rage were the result of family disorganization and a crisis of manhood. Moynihan encouraged a type of commonsense thinking that supported regressive ideas that black women emasculated their male partners, black families invested too much in their daughters at the expense of their sons, and that in order to restore black America, black men should either enlist in the military or receive preference over black women for jobs. The Report, which was supported by policy shapers of all races, led to a sort of Moynihan logic, in which black families were believed to be so deficient that they needed constant instruction on how to be a family.[31] This logic ignored the devastating impact of racism on people and blamed blacks for being unable to stabilize their families, while ignoring the ways that race and poverty truncated possibilities for advancement. Although Burrell disagreed there was anything wrong with black people and families, by presenting ads featuring black men as model fathers, he reflected the intense pressure black cultural producers felt to use advertisement to not only sell products, but to salvage images also. In the agency's focus on "featuring images of strong and capable black men," they inadvertently gave weight to Moynihan logic, which argued that every problem was caused by

and could only be solved by patriarchs. Despite the role of women workers in the service industry or the real experiences of female-headed households, many of Burrell's ads from the 1970s and 1980s focused on black men and the families they ruled over.[32]

The 1971 "She Deserves a Break Today" campaign, a play on "You Deserve a Break Today," portrayed a nuclear family that Burrell hoped could illustrate their efforts to counter stereotypes about black family dysfunction, which was supposedly rooted in black women's dominance and black men's incompetence. The ad featured a middle-class family in a dining room. The father brings home McDonald's so the mother does not have to worry about the family's evening meal. The assumption is that the mother has been home all day, and the father is going above and beyond his patriarchal duties by having worked a full day and "made dinner" by bringing home McDonald's. The convenience of the fast food restaurant allowed this black family to enjoy time together, and in turn, maintain the equilibrium of the father's role as breadwinner and the mother's as homemaker.

Market research in the 1970s recommended that McDonald's advertise more directly to black women, and Burrell eventually created more advertisements that centered black women in the storytelling. A 1979 McDonald's television commercial promoted its breakfast service with an entirely black cast and recognized the value of black matriarchs by featuring a middle class family comprising a professional, working mother, a father, children, and a grandmother. The black grandmother waited for her children to wake up and expected the woman of the house to cook breakfast before church, but the tired and busy family was able to barely make it out the door in their Sunday best. In a time crunch to eat before church, they stopped at McDonald's before services. The commercial was set to the tune of a Gospel-style song that is sung from the mother's perspective: "After working hard all week, I'd like to get some rest." The song speeds up as the family enjoys their breakfast; each member of the family ordered a different offering, from Egg McMuffins to hotcakes. The song closes with the lead singer's vocals accompanied by a clapping, tambourine-shaking gospel

choir: "Since we are going to get to church on time, mama is proud of me," and the campaign tagline "McDonald's, we do it all for you."[33] McDonald's, according to the advertisements, showed how they allowed black families to be their very best. Market research confirmed that their investment in Burrell was a smart one. A market assessment from 1977 outlined that "the image of McDonald's is very positive in the minds of many [blacks surveyed]. McDonald's is seen as a company with quality products at a reasonable price . . . [and people are] aware of McDonald's involvement in the black Community."[34]

An array of classic black McDonald's ads have been pilloried or criticized in recent years as silly or racist. Some of the ads, despite their place in the genre's history, do not age well, and frequently bloggers and writers circulate the now-vintage appeals to castigate either the advertising agency or the corporation itself. A 1979 advertisement that supported McDonald's "We do it all for you" campaign has been relitigated in the pages of *The Atlantic* and on National Public Radio, among other media outlets.[35] The ad copy reads: "Dinnertimin' at McDonald's" and it sells diners on the McDonald's experience by stating: "You don't have to get dressed up" and "there's no tipping." The twenty-first-century commentary on this, and similar ads, immediately registers the absence of the g in "timing" and the presence of racist stereotypes about black diners being poor tippers and unable to understand how to dress for polite society. This analysis offers valid concern about racial affectation in advertising, but if this and other ads are understood from the long view of blacks and dining, then another perspective is possible and essential. In ViewPoint's research, blacks indicated a preference for restaurants that didn't require dressing up, and the ads may have been designed to recognize and confirm that.[36] In light of the conflicts around access to restaurants as physical spaces, as well as their exemplification of sites of resistance and violent, racist intimidation during the civil rights movement, including the early McDonald's drive-ins throughout the South, the advertisement's directives about tipping and dress also recognize and alleviate historical anxieties. The ads speak to a troubled relationship between

the black consumer and private-establishment dining. Another ad reinforces these ideas with the promise that "At McDonald's dinner is a good deal, not a big one." The ad reassures the black family on their way to McDonald's that they can "come as you are, and you don't have to come far, since McDonald's is right in your neighborhood." Years after the passage of the Civil Rights Act, the memory of the way things used to be, as well as the knowledge of the things that still remained after the Act, loomed large over black customers. These were wounds that needed healing. Burrell and his creative team knew about the fears that followed blacks when they took a seat in a booth or made a left turn into their favorite drive-thru.

Due to the importance of individual franchisees in black consumer markets, some advertisements also gestured toward black customers' relationship with franchisees, rather than food. Two 1984 advertisements in *Ebony* magazine attempted to communicate McDonald's proximity to the secondary goals of black capitalism: the elevation of a black managerial, as well as entrepreneurial, class. "At which $8 billion corporation do Black executives help call the shots?" Accompanying the answer was a small photograph that captured a partial image of a man's fist, but it was not the Black Power salute of the Portland Panthers or a hand clenched in anger during an uprising in Chicago. The man's fist rested on a telephone and was outfitted with a McDonald's ring, presumably the type of corporate appreciation gift given to franchise owners. The advertisement, part of the "Good Neighbors . . . Together, McDonald's and You" campaign, claimed that "black executives are helping shape the future of McDonald's." Citing the hiring of black lawyers, accountants, engineers, and marketing directors, McDonald's positioned itself as a socially responsible brand not only because of the way it treated diners, but because it also elevated the black middle class. The advertisement claimed that these leaders within McDonald's corporate structure began "as crew employees and worked their way up."[37] The second *Ebony* advertisement posed another question: "Who's the largest employer of Black youth in America?" The associated photograph depicted a young black man arranging a paper McDonald's hat

atop his head like a soldier with a garrison cap. The ad proudly claimed that "almost 6,000 McDonald's restaurants in neighborhoods across the country employ thousands of Black men and women." Many of these workers earned low wages as they tended griddles and wiped plastic trays, but McDonald's reminded that "since most of the employees live in neighborhoods where they work, their wages have a very positive impact on businesses in their community."[38] The trickle-down reasoning of the advertisements suggested a dollar earned at a fast food joint traveled across the community, but these claims were refuted by researchers. One think tank estimated that a McDonald's in Washington, D.C., that generated "sales of $750,000 a year, and earned $50,000 in profit before taxes," sent more than $500,000 out of the area.[39]

As Burrell's ads continued to evolve and match the type of television programs that featured blacks, McDonald's advertising moved closer to reflecting the ringed executive and away from the young man who took orders at the counter. The growing numbers of upwardly mobile blacks in the 1980s contributed to a move to reflect this change in black marketing, causing a bifurcation of so-called ethnic advertising. Agencies began to devise marketing plans that created content targeting middle-class and lower-income blacks separately. While advertising successfully expanded the markets, television programming like the 1980s hits *The Cosby Show* and spin-off *A Different World* represented aspirational scenarios involving black professionals and middle-class family life.[40] The late-1980s McDonald's commercial entitled "Fraternity Chant" re-created a common scene on college campuses that housed historically black fraternities and sororities. This ad, which resonated with African Americans who attended college, featured a fictional Sigma Delta Phi. A group of black fraternity members lined up at attention awaiting instructions from their pledge master to perform a coordinated routine of step dancing and chanting. "Want to be in my frat? Do the McDonald's menu chant," the pledge master demanded. Actual black fraternities and sororities pair stepping with rapid fire recitations of their Greek organization's history or principles.

In the commercial the men recite the McDonald's menu while performing a synchronized routine featuring precise footwork and clapping. "Fraternity Chant," like the Double Dutch ads of the preceding decade, again brought black dance to a national audience through a McDonald's commercial. Breakdancing, rap music, and hip-hop beats would be added to future campaigns to maintain the brand's requisite level of cool to attract black customers, and as these cultural forms dominated mainstream popularity, these ads engendered familiarity for Americans of all racial and ethnic backgrounds.[41]

By the 1990s, McDonald's continued to find new ways to talk to black America about its preferences and projections in ways that seemed realistic and, more important, would get them to go to McDonald's. Advertisements targeting black customers were shaped around the inedible parts of the fast food experience, from black franchise ownership to the nature of McDonald's work. Two types of work-scenario–based ads emphasized the company's insistence that the person preparing French fries could one day become a franchise owner. Debuting in 1990, the "Calvin" ads were shaped by a synthesis of the two previous periods. Viewers initially met Calvin, a teenager in the inner city, and his appearance was peak cool in his time, with a backward cap, baggy clothes, and high-top sneakers. Soon you learn that Calvin, who passes a basketball court, a group of idle black men hanging out on a street corner, and an elderly woman hauling her groceries home, is on his way to a job at McDonald's. The commercial ends with Calvin flipping his cap and kindly saying, "Welcome to McDonald's. May I help you?" Over the course of the television spot, Calvin is transformed from a stereotype of a menacing black youth to an ambitious and responsible one. The "Calvin" series continued to include his promotion to manager and neighborhood chatter suggesting that Calvin becomes a franchisee, to which he responds "not yet." In a matter of time, the ad suggested, Calvin will join the Cosby class of high-earning black professionals.

Robert Jackson, a consultant on the Calvin ads, said the campaign was as much about getting customers through the doors as

it was about rehabilitating the image of a McDonald's job.[42] In the early days of black advertising, working at the Golden Arches was presented as a stepping-stone, but by the late 1980s the image of a fast food job was far from appealing. The term McJob, coined by sociologist Amitai Etzioni, characterized fast food employment as inherently dead-end work that provided no educational value to youth. With McDonald's expansion still strong at the dawn of the 1990s, the company believed it needed to revamp the perception of their jobs, especially as it boasted that it was one of the largest employers of youth.[43] In his meditation on class politics, scholar Robin Kelley reflected on his own time working at a McDonald's in Pasadena in the late 1970s. As a pre–Calvin era worker, Kelley described the various ways that his McJob was the site of irritation, as well as a place for mischief, pleasure, and everyday acts of rebellion within the workplace. Kelley recalled:

> Like virtually all of my fellow workers, I liberated McDonaldland cookies by the boxful, volunteered to clean "lots and lobbies" in order to talk to my friends, and accidentally cooked too many Quarter Pounders and apple pies near closing time, knowing fully well that we could take home whatever was left over.[44]

The complicated nature of fast food work could never be fully represented in a Burrell Communications ad, but for black viewers who were proximate to the experience of working fast food, Calvin's smile and enthusiasm may have been the subject of skepticism, and for white audiences, the disruption of stereotype may have been instructive. Targeted advertisements are not in the business of selling hard truths even when they are designed to refute ugly vestiges of racism, but the lens through which viewers read them provide a challenge to advertisers who must speak with many voices through a singular mouthpiece. Burrell's advertisements did not shy away from referring to the urgency of black America's need for jobs or pathways to professional careers, but each reminder of the obstacles to black equality led to an assurance that McDonald's was lighting the way.

* * *

McDonald's advertising to black consumers seemed more concerned with the heart and soul than with the stomach, but as more black consumers entered the category the industry calls "super heavy users," McDonald's knew that it was worthwhile and advantageous to develop products that catered specifically to this population. In a 1977 report, the distinctions between a heavy and light fast food user showed how race and class informed market segmentation. Heavy users represented 48% of their customers and tended to be "younger, male and blue collar occupationally," and on the whole heavy users were "non-white, principally black, but also other racial minorities." Light users by contrast were "substantially older, female, white and somewhat better educated."[45] The initial fast food staples of hamburgers, hot dogs, fried chicken, and tacos were bestsellers in the consumer market. But companies knew that in order to increase their market share they needed to continually improve and expand their menus, while still maintaining strong profits and keeping prices low. Although McDonald's was a leader in the fast food space, it was particularly timid in its expansion of its menu. Most of the popular revisions to the menu boards were introduced by franchisees. From the Filet-O-Fish to the Shamrock Shake, local operators used regional tastes to pitch additions to the national roster of selections. This was a point of pride for Kroc, who was not as adept at identifying and cultivating culinary trends for the restaurant as he was at selling billions of burgers.[46] For every successful product or concept, such as the Big Mac and the McMuffin, there were more false starts, including the east European pastry kolache and a roast beef sandwich.[47] When McDonald's unveiled new products, they did so with considerable attention to the customers that would be most drawn to them. As Burrell Communications created vibrant images of "real" black life for McDonald's, ViewPoint helped them strategize on how to please black palates. Creating foods for the black consumer market required insights into how blacks perceived and consumed foods for reasons other than sustenance. In the landmark study

of black consumer behaviors, D. Parke Gibson's *$70 Billion in the Black,* researchers advised the food industry to pay special attention to black women's attitudes on how to properly feed children. In emphasizing the care black mothers took in choosing their children's food, he may have also wanted to counter the growing and pervasive stereotypes of black maternal carelessness and inadequacy. The report advised:

> Black mothers are more concerned about nutrition. They have less faith in the lunches their children get at school. They put more emphasis on breakfast. While proportionately more black mothers work and would seem good prospects for instant or easy-to-prepare foods, there is a counteracting factor. Black mothers will not sacrifice nutrition or taste . . . Black mothers use meals to a much greater extent as a reward system and as a means of keeping the family together. They put more of themselves into food.[48]

In contrast, white mothers were believed to be moving away from time-consuming food preparation and embracing just-add-water cake mixes, mashed potatoes whipped together from powdered flakes and cups of milk, and aluminum-foil–wrapped trays of Salisbury steak. In 1969, trade magazine *Chain Store Age* predicted that "the clamor for convenience" was permanent.[49]

While the manufactured foods market noted this racial difference in black women's cooking habits, the fast food industry also noticed racial disparities in consumption. When black women chose not to cook, they were willing to spend money on fast food. In the late 1970s, blacks spent an average of 13 cents more per visit than whites on McDonald's. A market research firm discovered that between 1970 and 1976, the number of black female-headed households had increased more than 40%. This rapid increase in women out-earning male partners or not having one at all meant that Burrell's ads couldn't speak only to black men and black fathers. In 1977, consultants told McDonald's to focus more on the 36% of black families being led by women. They also recommended that more advertisements target black tweens and black women by pur-

chasing commercial time during the hit music television show *Soul Train*, sponsoring concerts by talents like singer Natalie Cole, and donating to agencies devoted to sickle cell anemia.[50]

When new products were developed, sometimes McDonald's offered something first and collected feedback later, often to their own peril. Two products illustrated the ways that fast food viewed "urban" consumers as crucial targets of new food items: the fried chicken sandwich and the ill-fated Chopped Beefsteak. Both products, McDonald's reasoned, would be appealing to African Americans. ViewPoint conducted ethnographic research, taste tests, surveys, and focus group interviews to assess how blacks thought about and interacted with new and existing products for various fast food restaurants. McDonald's was well aware of the success of fried chicken in the fast food market, and product development conversations about whether to offer it led nowhere. In 1980, the McChicken sandwich and the Beefsteak, which was to be served with a side of Onion Nuggets, were first introduced. The logic behind these products was to create something that black adults would enjoy when they took their children to McDonald's. Although McDonald's performed well with blacks on the whole, their data from the late 1970s suggested that as consumers aged, they were less interested in the menu. By investing in chicken and steak sandwiches, McDonald's believed they could retain black adults as diners long after their children grew up.

The consumer research offers a window into the modern era of race-conscious marketing. These products required carefully crafted messaging due to their histories as well as the way McDonald's wanted to position them. The McChicken, associated with a highly popular and racially laden dish, fried chicken, needed to taste good and be sold without too much regard to race. The Beefsteak, offered as part of a dinner menu available between 4 and 9 P.M., was advertised as an economical treat for a working-class person who could not afford steak. ViewPoint had experience surveying blacks about other parts of the McDonald's menu, having coordinated studies on the Filet-O-Fish and McRib sandwiches. In 1979, ViewPoint reported that "onion nuggets are faring

poorly in black stores" and dispatched in-store surveyors to ask why people were avoiding the product. In the memo instructing field researchers on how to talk to customers, ViewPoint directed them to "probe for purchase of onion nuggets for carry-out purposes"; blacks were more likely to eat fast food at home than in the restaurant. Then, if possible, researchers were to find "a tactful way [to] probe for gas giving nature of product. Try to determine if this is indeed a problem." In a survey of people who had tried the onion side dish, analysts were to "be on the lookout" for the following negatives about the product: "Greasiness, lack of 'real' onion taste, gets cold faster than French Fries," and whether the onion nuggets were delivered "too crisp" or "overdone." [51] It didn't take very long for ViewPoint to realize what the corporation was also discovering from its in-house product development team; the nuggets didn't taste very good. McDonald's lacked a single supplier for the onions, and the lack of consistency flew in the face of what the restaurant prided itself on. The Onion Nugget soon went the way of the McDonald's Hula Burger and strawberry shortcake. [52]

Regardless of race, very few people liked the onion nuggets. But the other products assigned to ViewPoint offered up revelatory insights about what McDonald's was up against if it wanted of maintain its share of urban eaters. ViewPoint sometimes asked interviewees about who they would connect a particular product with, and then assess if these associations were positive or negative. The Filet-O-Fish, created as an alternative for observant Catholics during Lenten Fridays, was a poor performer among blacks. [53] The battered cod sandwich may have seemed like a strange choice for southern-born blacks accustomed to the cornmeal-crusted catfish available at most soul food restaurants. Black diners were less concerned about prohibitions against eating meat before the Easter holiday, and respondents believed the sandwich to be overwhelmingly white in its sensibilities. In one focus group, researchers asked which celebrities, careers, and activities aligned with the Filet-O-Fish. Respondents offered that the sandwich was like comedian Paul Lynde, television sitcom star Mary Tyler Moore, and Secretary of State Henry Kissinger. They believed it to be the meal of choice for

suburban housewives who played tennis, Chinese flower arrangers, and others "who did not embody the boldness of McDonald's beef product."[54] It was clear that the Filet-O-Fish had no soul.

Message received. McDonald's believed there was no product bolder than the new Chopped Beefsteak sandwich, and they asked ViewPoint to provide insight on how to sell an ostensibly more refined sandwich than a hamburger to black consumers. A storyboard for a Beefsteak ad alerted black commercial viewers that consuming fast food was nothing to be ashamed of, and that it could be elevated into an economical, yet pleasant treat. In the illustration for a potential Beefsteak ad, a couple is seen riding a city bus together. The "well-dressed black man and woman" are deciding on dinner. The woman asked, "What'd you want for dinner, honey? Hmm, I've got a taste for something special." The man didn't lose a bit of his confidence when he admitted, "Well, I've got a hamburger wallet, and a beefsteak appetite." The bus driver, ostensibly a trusted member of the community, or at the very least an appropriate commenter, suggests: "Try a chopped beef steak sandwich."

The man's dress belied his financial status, an outward sign of a piece of marketing common sense that often was applied to black people: appearance is everything and overcompensation was critical. Market research designed to tap into the hearts and minds of black America assumed that black consumer self-consciousness was central to how blacks interacted with buying toothpaste, choosing a burger, or signing a lease on a luxury car. An article in *Sales Management* magazine advised, "The black traveler is one example of how wrestling with self-perception shapes consumption habits." Citing the 1971 book *The Black American Travel Guide*, the trade journal noted that while on holiday, blacks were likely to spend 30% more on accommodations and food than their fellow white vacationers. The travel guide reasoned that the black consumer spent more "because he doesn't want others to think he can't afford the best." It also offered that travel—and by extension retail spending—was based on "the need to get away from depressing ghettoes."[55] Market researchers also found that blacks, regardless of their economic station, used their clothing as a means

of garnering respect. The disparity between what the man in the ad wore and the cash in his pocket was one way of marketing an inexpensive dining option as appealing even to those who looked like they could afford better.

The helpful bus driver went on to describe the virtues of the sandwich. "Pure chopped beefsteak, through and through, on a French roll with onions! And steak sauce too!" The commercial spot followed another adage of how to market to blacks; a touch of slang went a long way. The bus driver assures the pair that "the taste is outta sight!" The duo punctuates his description with a hearty "Alright!" After background singers crooned that the "Chopped beefsteak sandwich is served from four to nine," the man was sold on taking his date to McDonald's. "Right on time!" The man finished the statement started by the singers, "Chopped Beefsteak Sandwich, the taste is . . ." with a "mighty fine," and adds that "It's not just another steak sandwich. It's made to please a man." His companion added, "And his lady. Nobody can do it like McDonald's can."[56]

Based on the available archive of McDonald's commercials that promoted the Beefsteak sandwich, this ad may have never taken shape beyond the storyboards. When compared to other advertisements of this product, when whites were sold the Beefsteak, there was no emphasis on its price or its ability to serve as a prelude to a romantic evening. Ads that were broadcast on television featured white leads or an interracial cast, emphasized the Beefsteak's size, ability to quench an adult's hunger, and convenience after a long and frustrating day at work. Beefsteak lovers were upper-class white-collar employees, mailmen, and construction workers of all races who needed to eat something delicious and filling in the evening. McDonald's reasoned that they could combat the lagging sales of the late 1970s by introducing a time-limited product that would, hopefully, boost the numbers of "dinner-hour customers," who would ordinarily patronize McDonald's during the brisk breakfast and lunch times.[57]

ViewPoint's research files indicate that there was far less concern about the black reception of the Beefsteak sandwich because

blacks did not have strong feelings about how steak should taste or look. Perhaps due to the high price of steak, blacks were less likely to consume it on a regular basis. Chicken was an entirely different story. After regional testing of the chicken sandwich, McDonald's made it available to all stores in mid-1980. The chicken sandwich, described in the *Wall Street Journal* as a "sort of chicken burger," was one of the first large-scale commercial attempts to serve what had long been made in the South, a piece of fried chicken between two slices of white bread. Fried chicken, known by some as holy bird or the Gospel bird, was both ubiquitous and special in the African-American communities that would populate the Great Migration destinations of urban America. Often served on Sundays in the South after one's spiritual hunger was satiated, this dish was rendered an everyday food in northern cafés and luncheonettes, which helped popularize southern foods more broadly. Fried chicken and its careful preparation from slaughtering the bird, to sectioning it, to the proper brining or seasoning process, and then the eventual moment when the poultry met the lard or Crisco or oil, is a deceptively difficult dish in that it masks the levels of mastery and care necessary to make it delicious, perfectly crisped, juicy, and appetizing. So to make a chicken patty—a condensed, salty but generally flavorless slab—appealing among the people who perfected the dish in the United States was a formidable challenge.[58] The participants in a McChicken taste test offered an earful for the facilitators. "I never would guess it was chicken . . . you got to have the skin on it." Another offered: "You go there thinking you'll get chicken—you'll get a piece of chicken and . . . when you get there the effect is completely different and it sort of blows your mind . . . expecting chicken dripping or something and it's like . . . looks like a hamburger out there . . . It sort of pulls you apart from . . . what you went there for." One respondent thought the condiments on the sandwich were out of place. "You don't usually eat chicken with mayonnaise . . . you eat chicken with hot sauce."[59]

The taste testers in the ViewPoint study would have probably preferred the Georgia-based Chick-fil-A, which grew from S. Truett Cathy's Dwarf Grill, and began franchising its concept

in 1967. After establishing Dwarf and renaming it to focus on chicken, the franchise specialized in opening in mall food courts over the following two decades. The outlet didn't begin building drive-thru–accessible locations until 1986. Today, Chick-fil-A's signature pressure-cooked breaded-chicken-and-pickle sandwiches have attracted a wide following outside of the South, but the sandwich is as emblematic of southern foodways as it is of race. The fried chicken sandwich was the basis of black women's small-scale business life throughout the late nineteenth and twentieth centuries as "waiter-carriers," who sold food to stopped train passengers along train tracks.[60] The sandwiches were a delicious treat for travelers of all colors, and the sandwiches' golden-fried chicken and fresh-tasting bread could never be fully replicated by a frozen chicken patty and shelf-stable hamburger bun. But changes in travel—from greater highway access to the expansion of airline routes—made long-distance train travel less efficient and less popular. In addition to shifts in black women's employment opportunities and more stringent regulations on the sale of food in public places, fewer black women sold their once sought-after chicken sandwiches. The mass-produced disk of chicken would eventually be understood as a fried-chicken sandwich. That conversion would take some tweaking in the advertising strategy to make it more enticing, as well as in the recipe to make it taste more edible.

"Black consumers are heavy chicken eaters, particularly fried chicken," opened ViewPoint's statement on the McChicken sandwich. "As such, blacks were overwhelmingly disappointed with the McChicken sandwich." A number of factors inhibited immediate acceptance of the product. First of all, despite its status as a sandwich, respondents in the study still associated a chicken with "whole chicken on the bone." ViewPoint concluded that the "product therefore did not meet their expectations given their reference point." The accoutrements couldn't help the sandwich either. "Fried chicken with lettuce and mayonnaise-type sauce appears to be an unfamiliar combination which is not appreciated by these black consumers." As Gibson noted, "A meal without gravy or sauce doesn't look appetizing."[61]

The McChicken sandwich did not have to be a total flop, argued ViewPoint. The new menu item did not need better-tasting chicken or different condiments. Rather, ViewPoint saw the McChicken as a matter of reeducating blacks on how they felt about fried chicken and how they could feel about the sandwich. The research team recommended that McDonald's merely take the "perceived negative product attribute—its boneless feature—and highlighting it in such a way as to develop and encourage a more attractive and alluring product." This could be achieved by describing the sandwich as "a unique and delectable piece of boneless chicken that is served in an enticing, unusual sandwich form." Blacks would forget about "proper" fried chicken by simply associating the sandwich with a different way to consume poultry. ViewPoint's excitement increased with each suggestion in the memo: "The McChicken sandwich would be cast as a new and savory approach to fried chicken designed expressly for ardent chicken lovers. It would be removed from the ordinary fried chicken position and advertised as a boneless chicken delicacy." By framing it as an "easy-to-eat, filling, and economical fried chicken delicacy that was created especially for them," blacks would feel catered to and appreciate McDonald's for "offering them a whole new way to love chicken." The new marketing campaign would just need better "definition," and they suggested that black men could help usher in McChicken success. While black men indicated that they "generally disliked McDonald's food and only went to McDonald's because their families like it," ViewPoint found that the men "felt that the McChicken sandwich would be the least objectionable item to purchase for themselves." In order to prevent a mass exodus of these men from McDonald's—especially when their children outgrew the restaurant—the chicken sandwich had to be "substantially improved," in hopes that they "might become heavy McChicken users and would thus remain within the McDonald's consumer franchise." Another recommendation was just to rechristen the sandwich. The researchers reasoned that "since the respondents associate the name 'McChicken' with real chicken on the bone, some consideration should be given to

toning down the product name to possibly 'McChicken Steak,' or 'McChicken Patty.' By avoiding the words "chicken" and "sandwich" in the same name, they would avoid the "disappointment with the McChicken." They recommended research that would "secure a name that provides a better understanding of this product offering prior to purchase."[62]

The first McChicken did not have enough market, or internal, support to continue on, and the product was pulled soon after its debut. The Chicken Nugget, however, went on to great fame. McDonald's decided to give the chicken sandwich a second life in 1988, nearly a decade after reintroducing a fried chicken product that was cut into boneless chunks and was evocative of, but never fully resembled, proper fried chicken. By the late 1980s, consumers welcomed a chicken sandwich, and despite a temporary retirement of the McChicken, it continues to live on in fast food menus across the industry. The McChicken taught McDonald's that after their food became a staple, familiarity was more important than taste.

* * *

Burrell's advertising and ViewPoint's insights hammered home that McDonald's could use the icons and symbols of black life and culture to their advantage. Considering the ways that Martin Luther King Jr.'s death loomed large in the way McDonald's and the NBMOA described their journey into black communities, black franchisees and McDonald's national office were leaders in celebrating the Martin Luther King Jr. holiday. The utility of King the icon—versus King the iconoclast—is that his diluted characterizations could be manipulated and recalled for an array of purposes. With each year that passed since his death in 1968, King transformed from a radical, Communist threat to democracy to a man who simply wanted all people to be friends. Fast food franchises are not responsible for the accurate accounting of civil rights history, but their reliance on a flattened image of King allowed them to ingratiate themselves to black communities without having to amend a chicken recipe, reconsider their inner-city market saturation strategies, or raise a wage. Black franchisees,

who believed themselves indebted to King's sacrifice, took steps to honor him before it was clear that the nation wanted him remembered as a hero of the people, not as a heretic against democracy. Coretta Scott King hoped that the King holiday would provide workers with a day off and properly commemorate her husband's commitment to labor struggle. Instead, the King holiday became a prime opportunity to sell apolitical ideals like color blindness, which obscures the vicious impacts of racism on people's lives and livelihood.[63] The further the nation moved from King's death and the aftermath, the more King and the movements he led became uncontroversial markers of the past. The profits of the urban market were so high that even Kroc, a staunch conservative, declared himself a supporter of "social change of the late sixties," made evident in his company's recruitment of black franchisees.[64]

Eleven years after King's death, the movement to create a federal holiday to honor the leader took root. Historian David Chappell argues that the concerted four-year effort was one that implicitly conceded that "if substantive gains were no longer feasible, symbols were still important."[65] President Jimmy Carter—at the time desperately trying to stave off Ted Kennedy as the anointed presidential candidate of black America—declared his support for a King national holiday in his 1980 State of the Union address. Carter did not linger on the topic for too long, simply stating:

> Dr. Martin Luther King, Jr. led this Nation's effort to provide all its citizens with civil rights and equal opportunities. His commitment to human rights, peace and non-violence stands as a monument to his humanity and courage. As one of our Nation's most outstanding leaders, it is appropriate that his birthday be commemorated as a national holiday, and I will continue to work with the Congress to enact legislation that will achieve this goal.[66]

While the Congressional Black Caucus, Coretta Scott King, and King's former colleagues were lobbying the halls of Congress, at local McDonald's restaurants the King holiday was being commemorated. Some franchisees ordered tray liners printed with facts

about King. Local stores sponsored essay contests about King's legacy. Other franchises displayed widely circulated photos of King at the 1963 March on Washington for Jobs and Freedom in restaurant lobbies.

The federalization of the holiday in 1983 led McDonald's corporate office to buttress the local franchisee efforts, leading to more public programs and commemorations. In 1986, McDonald's restaurants across the country displayed posters with an image of King looking stoically into the distance. His candlelit visage was accompanied with text that explained, "His Light Still Shines, a celebration of the life and message of Dr. Martin Luther King, Jr." Underneath the description was a pair of Golden Arches. "His Light Still Shines" was then the nation's "largest traveling exhibit highlighting the civil rights movement" and King's work. After it toured twenty-two cities and informed and inspired more than a million visitors, the exhibit became part of the permanent collection of the Atlanta Hartsfield (now Hartsfield-Jackson) Airport. Edward Rensi, then–president and chief operating officer of McDonald's, said "it was created for the world's children. Now it will continue to be viewed by millions."[67] At these events, no speaker ever raised the issue that McDonald's would open the year celebrating a fervent anticapitalist, and close it with more than $4 billion in revenue and $480 million in profits.[68] Perhaps, it was easier to evoke the grief of his loss than the substance of his message. For those who were most challenged by King's declaration that America faced "the inevitable choice between materialism and humanism" and his assertion that "capitalism was built on the exploitation and suffering of black slaves and continues to thrive on the exploitation of the poor—both black and white, both here and abroad," the entanglement of a fast food giant and King's legacy may have felt uncomfortable at the very least.[69] But negotiation was nothing new for black people who supported movements for racial and economic justice. With every showing of "His Light Still Shines," or every time a black franchisee sponsored a Black History Month celebration or donated to a historically black college, McDonald's was writing itself into an accessible, sanitized story

about civil rights, in which the ability to own a franchise was tantamount to leading a movement for racial and economic justice.

The King holiday experienced a slow start in national acceptance and corporate investment, and McDonald's was unique in its hearty show of support for the remembrance in the 1980s. The Hartsfield Airport commemoration may have come as a relief after a disappointing response to the call to support the country's first official King Day celebration in 1986. The Martin Luther King Jr. Federal Holiday Commission, which included such luminaries as former Ambassador to the United Nations Andrew Young and former franchisee Julian Bond, was unable to raise their projected $1.5 million for various events. Their efforts yielded a war chest of $300,000 from private donors and an additional $100,000 in federal and state funds. The City of Atlanta had to bail out the national King Day grand parade after the event was forced to slash its budget and reduce its number of marching bands able to participate. In addition to the exhibit, which included memorabilia and photographs from the King Center for Nonviolent Social Change, McDonald's commissioned black artist Richard Hunt to create a sculpture entitled "The Altar of Freedom," for the King exhibit. Commissions to and patronage of black artists were also part of McDonald's cultural work in the 1980s.[70] The Black McDonald's Operators Association of Chicago and Northwest Indiana underwrote a musical performance to honor King entitled "If I Can Help Somebody," and the show aired on the home of the Chicago Cubs, WGN-TV.[71]

In areas where the King Day activities were less than robust, observers could check their local listings and watch a McDonald's-funded short film entitled *Happy Birthday, Dr. King: A Celebration of His Life and Times*. Burrell Communications helped with the production and content for the twenty-six-minute tribute, which was a decidedly uncomplicated retrospective, but supporting the King holiday was not without concerns for corporate sponsors. Albert Davis, a former Coca-Cola vice president, admitted that he was advised by some that "it was politically unwise to give this [the holiday] major support."[72] McDonald's, with its history of the

franchise transfers and prominent black spokespeople, could not distance itself from the King celebration. In embracing the holiday, they may have made it easier for other corporations to make King work for them.[73] In the decades since the first King holiday, King has been memorialized in volunteer projects, community performances, a thirty-foot granite memorial on an edge of Washington, D.C.'s Tidal Basin, and, in January, inside of fast food restaurants. Although the irony of linking King's message and the practices of the fast food industry remains, the passage of time has further buried these contradictions under piles of advertisements for King Day, buy-one-get-one-free coupons, and circulars promoting sales at shopping malls.

As the National Black McDonald's Operators Association network grew, McDonald's franchisees were able to maintain their enthusiasm for black history and culture beyond the wintertime King activities and Black History Month. Present at the "His Light" ceremony was gospel music star Shirley Caesar. Caesar won a Grammy in 1986 for her tribute to King, and her presence was particularly fitting because of the relationship between black McDonald's franchisees and the spiritual music circuit. Gospel music—the electrification of black, sacred song—and the fast food sector came together previously when Mahalia Jackson debuted Glori-Fried. After her chain closed, fast food companies seeking to connect with black consumers sponsored a series of Gospel music endeavors, from concerts to battle-of-the-choirs performances and songwriting competitions.[74]

Black arts and artists also benefited from the black franchisee turn toward supporting cultural production. The McDonald's Literary Achievement Awards of the 1980s honored poets and essayists who captured the "black experience in America." Under the auspices of the Negro Ensemble Company, a groundbreaking theater troupe based in Harlem, the organization was integral to launching the careers of major black dramatists and actors. Up-and-coming writers could compete for the McDonald's-sponsored Lorraine Hansberry Award, an honor for college students who best portrayed black life on stage. Winners were invited to par-

ticipate in a feedback session in New York, and the revised screenplay was table-read by professional actors. The partnership among McDonald's, the American College Theater Festival, the American Theatre Association, and the Kennedy Center opened doors for young dramatists, and listed actors Denzel Washington and Phylicia Rashad among the program's mentors.[75]

In the 2000s, appeals to black consumers have used hip-hop aesthetics, social media lingo, and continued sponsorship of black organizations to remain relevant and legible to consumers, but now all of their competitors have learned their secret, which has expanded the fast food industry's imprint on black cultural life. Since 2003, McDonald's has used the 365Black.com website as an online portal to cultural content and directed marketing campaigns. The associated recognition and awards program has honored figures as varied as Herman Petty and other NBMOA founders, the Reverend Jesse Jackson, Congresswoman Maxine Waters, and Harvard University scholar Henry Louis Gates Jr.

* * *

Fast food is about more than just food. Consumers make marketplace choices based on a constellation of emotions, past experiences, memories, desires, and actual hunger. At any moment, one of these impulses can dictate whether a person drives south to a Hardee's or north to a Wendy's or home to cook. The fast food industry invests millions upon millions of dollars each year to better understand how this psychology of buying works, to create business models that convince customers that their burritos, chicken tenders, and hot fudge sundaes can meet whatever needs that propel a person to their restaurant. In the case of black consumers in the United States, these motivations are also shaped by racism and its hold over nearly every aspect of life—housing, education, health, wealth, and socialization. Thus, fast food is as much about the spice levels on a fried chicken sandwich as it is about a franchisee paying for your child's cash-strapped school to go to a museum. Fast food marketing promises authentic experiences in places that are designed to be inauthentic. But, knowing the first name of the

owner of your local Burger King and appreciating the touches of black history on her store's wall can mediate the reality that the food sold at that restaurant is no different than the food at the airport terminal or the outlet on the other side of your town. Even if you are skeptical about the fast food industry as a whole, you may appreciate the band of franchisees who contributed to your favorite King exhibit, because you wonder if anyone else would have paid for it. A black college graduate may adopt a vegan diet as an adult but remain grateful for her NBMOA-sponsored tuition scholarship.

The diligence required to cultivate the black McDonald's market in the 1970s and 1980s not only enriched the company and allowed it to wrap itself around so many aspects of black cultural life, but it also provided a model for its competitors to do the same. The industry used similar strategies to enter other communities of color. By the late 1980s, affinity groups for black, Latino, and Asian-American/Pacific Islander franchisees were formed to expand into other market segments. White fast food customers may also know the good works of their local franchisees or read with interest about donations to a Ronald McDonald House— which provides housing for families with children being treated in hospitals—but, on the whole, black consumers' proximity to franchises and franchising is far closer and more dependent because of their distance from economic stability.

The close ties between a black franchisee and the surrounding community is best illustrated in the 1988 film *Coming to America*, and the movie's delightful sight gag, McDowell's, a clear rip-off of a black-franchised McDonald's.[76] The film's protagonist—Eddie Murphy in the role of African royal Akeem Joffer—is a prince who searches for his future queen in the borough of Queens, New York. In an attempt to shield his identity as the heir to the throne of the fictional nation of Zamunda, Murphy goes to work in a regular American job—a fast food restaurant. Owned by the sly Cleo McDowell (played by actor John Amos from the 1971 McDonald's commercial), McDowell's is subject to investigation by McDonald's for trademark infringement and operating a copycat business.

Despite his clear poaching of the burger giant's many concepts, Cleo vehemently defends his business and suggests he came up with the distinctive Golden Arcs and the Big Mic sandwich. Although the McDowell's Restaurant is merely a backdrop for Murphy's budding romance with Lisa, Cleo's daughter, Amos's portrayal of a social-climbing yet community-minded businessman adeptly captures aspects of the culture of black entrepreneurship in the fast food sector in the 1980s. Cleo's presence in his store mirrors the ways that black franchise owners were often present in their restaurants to not only oversee their businesses, but because they also tended to operate fewer restaurants than their white peers. Cleo's sponsorship of a "Black Awareness Rally," a combination beauty pageant and talent show, emceed by a local pastor, was a comedic sendup of the types of community engagements often financed and catered by NBMOA members. Cleo's management of a store constantly being targeted by a neighborhood robber, played by relative newcomer Samuel L. Jackson, also matched the experiences of many franchisees whose businesses were often in areas with high crime. In the film, McDowell's does not have to sort through the challenges and responsibilities of being a black-owned fast food establishment. In real life, frustrated black franchisees could not ignore the inequalities they faced as operators, and as was done in the past, the first step in seeking redress was to call on the civil rights establishment to lend a hand.

CHAPTER SIX

A Fair Share of the Pie

Jesse Jackson's Operation PUSH and Reverend Al Sharpton's National Action Network led national boycotts of corporations throughout the 1980s and 1990s. These boycotts led to aggressive expansion plans that brought more fast food outlets to black neighborhoods across the country. New York Post Archives / Getty Images.

McDONALD'S BLACK OWNERS ARE IMPRISONED IN THE GHETTO!

The protest signs greeted the visitors to the spring 1984 McDonald's national operators' meeting in Los Angeles. The demonstration was sponsored by the city's chapter of the National Association for the Advancement of Colored People, and at seventy-five years old, the NAACP was taking up the cause of a different kind of victim of racial discrimination than it had become accustomed to representing.[1] The protest was not about a miscarriage of justice in which a black defendant was wrongly sentenced to death. Nor did this moment pivot upon the promise of a child seeking access

to a well-funded school district. This action centered on Charles Griffis, a black McDonald's franchisee who had made millions on his Los Angeles locations, and the issue at hand was his access to still greater fortunes in the fast food business. As the signs intimated, the NAACP accused McDonald's of relegating black franchisees to doing business in the most economically depressed, most dangerous, and most expensive-to-insure communities of Los Angeles and other cities. In the fourteen years that lapsed since Herman Petty's grand opening in Woodlawn, McDonald's had franchised restaurants to 137 black, and mostly male, operators. Black women were slowly entering the franchise system as spouses and co-owners of restaurants, and they would grow in numbers over the following decades. With fewer than 150 black franchisees in a system of nearly 8,000 franchise locations across the United States at the time and with many of their white counterparts able to franchise multiple locations, black franchisees wondered why the numbers of black-owned restaurants was still so low. The unquestionable profitability of black-franchised locations, in their view, should have caused McDonald's to clamor for black franchisees to acquire more stores, but expansion was limited. While a McDonald's grand opening happened every seventeen hours in 1984, including an opening in Finland for the first time, few were presided over by a black businessperson.

Experienced black franchisees, as well as franchise applicants, had long appealed to the National Black McDonald's Operators Association to raise this issue with the corporate offices. Some NBMOA members believed that McDonald's was using techniques akin to "redlining," the practice of branding black residential maps with red marks to demarcate them as undesirable. NBMOA members who operated McDonald's in black neighborhoods long maintained that despite profiting from a captive market that wanted to buy affordable food, they shouldered a disproportionate burden because they were presiding over dilapidated stores and protecting employees and patrons from crime. Among those in the know, there were rumors circulating that regional franchising managers maintained black lists and white lists for franchise assignments. These speculations may

have conjured up memories of the racism blacks sometimes encountered when trying to buy homes. Even after the practice was deemed unconstitutional, residential redlining continued to shape black community building and economic opportunities. Similarly, despite their economic prosperity as a group, African-American McDonald's franchisees often found themselves in an uneasy position as both models of racial progress and victims of racial discrimination.

Black franchisees may have been reluctant to speak out about their struggles with McDonald's, knowing well that biting the hand that fed millions of people burgers may do more harm than good. Yet racial disparities among franchisees evolved into an attractive civil rights issue for the NAACP and its peers as these organizations sharpened their focus on aligning with corporations that profited handily from black customers and could not risk public accusations of racism and discrimination. The events leading to the Convention Center protest reveal that the success of black franchisees was not a simple tale of how time, legislation, and activism could eradicate racism. Two racial discrimination lawsuits filed by black franchisees against McDonald's led to a rather public exposure of their discontent. The lawsuits evoked the pervasive racial problem of equal access, and showed that wealth did not provide relief from the impact of racial discrimination. The public exchanges between McDonald's corporate and its black franchisees fueled the redlining accusations, and called into question what racial progress actually looked like in the world of franchising.

Los Angeles was among the first cities after Chicago to debut a black franchisee in the local system. In 1969, Bert Willis and Henry Clark franchised a McDonald's in the Crenshaw neighborhood. The duo branded their restaurants the "Willis-Clark McDonald's" in advertisements in the *Los Angeles Sentinel* newspaper so that readers were clear that their franchise was different than the white-owned locations in other parts of the city.[2] Willis-Clark newspaper advertisements emphasized that their McDonald's provided more than food to local communities—it also provided much-wanted jobs and training. Willis-Clark ads featured teen employees testifying to how much McDonald's prepared them to take on

life's challenges. In one ad, employee Emma Rayfield's "on and off the job" attitude was consistent with the "Willis-Clark customer service motto of enthusiasm, courtesy and friendliness to all customers."[3] In addition to providing teens like Emma their first jobs, Los Angeles black franchisees used their restaurants as part-time community meeting places and senior citizen centers, while also sponsoring youth sports and college scholarships.[4]

For political candidates and others looking to capture the attention of black audiences, McDonald's was the place to initiate outreach. In 1974, a newly elected Mayor Tom Bradley attended the grand reopening of Ed Lewis's Crenshaw-area McDonald's on South La Brea Avenue, and he continued to take calls from black franchisees as their presence and influence grew throughout Los Angeles.[5] Bradley also delivered the opening address of the 1979 annual meeting of the NBMOA, held at the Century Plaza Center.[6] As the NBMOA grew in size and wealth, members could find a friend in the cohort of history-making black elective officeholders. Black mayors provided immeasurable hope for voters who saw local-level leadership as a means to alleviate their day-to-day struggle: earning well-paying jobs, the enforcement of fair housing laws, and access to good public schools for their children. Carl Stokes in Cleveland, Richard Hatcher in Gary, Coleman Young in Detroit, Maynard Jackson in Atlanta, Harold Washington in Chicago, and Bradley formed a far-flung fraternity of city leaders who had to balance the racial allegiances that earned them support with the watchful and critical eyes of white power brokers. These mayors mostly ran campaigns that united black voters and white progressives with a vision of shared governance for the city and the expansion of equal opportunity, but often led with a moderate, probusiness style that did not challenge the status quo in favor of catering to economic interests among wealthier citizens. Therefore, many of the mayors aligned with the concerns of the black franchise community, and they were indebted to their assistance in raising campaign funds, facilitating voter registration at their restaurants, and bridging the gap between candidates and the black business community. Historian Tom Adam Davies described these

mayors' collective leadership strategy as prioritizing "the interests of middle-class whites and blacks and of downtown elites."[7]

Local NAACP chapters were also important actors in helping both franchisees and mayors achieve success through partnerships that could ascribe a civil rights sensibility to any venture or campaign. The Los Angeles chapter of the NAACP, founded in 1914 by two University of Southern California–trained dentists, contributed to the fight for the civil rights agenda that blossomed in mid-century America—ending employment discrimination, litigating school desegregation, and increasing voter rights.[8] The NAACP stepped into new territory when they were approached by two franchisee applicants who believed they were denied restaurants on the basis of race. The first McDonald's case involved the type of person who could have easily been identified as an ideal plaintiff in any civil rights lawsuit, California sheriff's deputy and narcotics specialist James T. Jones, who decided to pursue a franchise in 1971. The celebrated officer had no desire to rock the boat; he simply wanted in on the business after a McDonald's Regional Licensing Manager approached him during a search for potential franchisees of color.[9] By 1975, Jones had graduated from Hamburger University, submitted notice of his retirement from the Sheriff's Office, and prepared to move to Phoenix, where he believed his new store would be located. Jones shortly discovered, however, that the time, energy, and effort he expended studying the required internal temperature of a beef patty and the intricacies of replacing the nitrogen supply on a soda machine had been a waste. McDonald's informed him that he would not receive the Phoenix store. Jones's disappointment with McDonald's turned into indignation when he learned that Paul Gutierrez, a Mexican-American friend he introduced to the McDonald's program, received a franchisee contract in Lancaster, a desert town forty miles north of Los Angeles. Jones then polled the black friends he recommended as potential franchisees, and he learned that not a single one received approval to franchise.[10] The details of Jones's experience are similar to the failed list of twenty that David Hill claimed he provided McDonald's recruiters in Cleveland, to no avail.

Armed with the survey of his peers, Jones contacted the state's equal employment authority for guidance, and in August 1974 the commission determined that Jones "had the right to bring a civil action."[11] Two years later, his lawyers filed a lawsuit on behalf of Jones against McDonald's in Los Angeles Superior Court.[12] Jones's claim against McDonald's included allegations that the company succumbed to pressure from an all-white network of Phoenix operators "who protested Jones's potential appointment by threatening to withhold monies from the Optional Advertising Fund" if he was assigned the Phoenix store.[13] Jones believed that the operators didn't want a black franchisee in the area, and the handful of blacks who later acquired stores in mostly white areas sometimes experienced cold shoulders from fellow operators when they arrived to start their businesses. Along with the lawsuit, Jones submitted letters promising him the Maricopa County restaurant, which was supposedly under construction, a rarity for a black franchisee, a copy of blueprints, and a note that estimated the completion date for the store, January 10, 1974. Jones's lawyer probably knew he would be outmatched by McDonald's legal team, and he advised that Jones seek out additional expertise from civil rights lawyers to pursue his racial discrimination claim against McDonald's.

The Los Angeles NAACP branch president Dr. H. Claude Hudson, a successful banker and cofounder of the Niagara Movement that led to the creation of the NAACP, placed Jones's case on the agenda of their spring 1976 meeting. The executive body agreed that Jones's claim against the leader in fast food was worthy of their time and resources. The chapter's vice president believed that the case could garner publicity for the NAACP, a particular area of interest for the organization as they redefined their role in the era that ushered in the rise of the political right in the state, and concluded with a Republican winning the White House.[14] After making remarkable strides in the fight for school desegregation with the NAACP Legal Defense and Education Fund's masterful work in the 1954 *Brown v. Board of Education of Topeka, Kansas* case, the NAACP's legal wing continued to fight for school desegregation mechanisms, such as redistricting and busing, in an era in which the

backlash against these measures migrated from mob rule to school board manipulation. The 1960s and 1970s brought the NAACP lawyers more cases of protesters denied their freedom of assembly, the racially discriminatory application of the death penalty, and even legal cases that blamed the organization for hurting businesses by supporting boycotting and picketing. By the late 1970s, the NAACP was struggling to get its bearings. The Los Angeles base was in dire straits, and nationwide, local chapters hosted "Save the NAACP events" to help it pay off its debts and reclaim its legitimacy. While Black Power radicals convincingly questioned why integration was a worthy goal, the NAACP did not have an articulate response to a younger generation's probing inquiries into what the organization could do for them.[15] Having survived bankruptcy, and observing the way that Jesse Jackson's Chicago-based Operation PUSH was enriched by its corporate negotiation efforts, the Los Angeles chapter may have seen the McDonald's case as the perfect way to join the conversation about economic development in black communities.

Dr. Hudson's letter to the McDonald's System of California office on Wilshire Boulevard read like Operation Black Unity's pitch to bring black franchisees into Cleveland's East Side. The NAACP leader argued that Jones's case for franchising was inextricably tied to black buying power. Jones's grievance was a matter of economic justice and consumer fairness. "A large volume of McDonald's business is done in the Black Community," he wrote, and it was only reasonable that Jones and other "Black business persons [should be] afforded an opportunity to share in the profits derived from doing business in the Black Community." Hudson's argument that black communities should see a return on investment for their spending was one way that the ties between black franchise contribution and black community went above and beyond the framework of corporations as good neighbors to their customers. McDonald's was likened to a wealthy citizen of black America, and in the same ways that wealthy blacks consolidated their power over poorer black people by leveraging their wealth in exchange for loyalty or access to privilege, McDonald's was expected to do the same.

News of Jones's lawsuit led other Los Angeles black franchi-

sees to weigh in on what they viewed as similar problems with McDonald's, namely having their businesses receive inadequate attention from the parent company. "They do these things [discrimination] to black dealers and then they come back and cover it up. They are some treacherous people . . . They are tricky . . ."[16] The "tricks" that frustrated the operator became a subject of an investigation by the California Assembly's Finance, Insurance, and Commerce Ad Hoc Subcommittee, which opened an investigation of allegations of racial discrimination in the franchising sector. Henry Clark, of the Willis-Clark partnership, corroborated Jones's claims: "We are specifically limited to, in our case, Black operators to Black areas of the city which have the maximum problems, minimum income, [and] minimum opportunity for social-economic growth . . ."[17]

Ultimately, a court ruled in favor of McDonald's in the fall of 1975, but Jones's challenge and the issue of black franchisee dissatisfaction would remain a point of interest for the NAACP in the following decades. The news of the problems on the West Coast traveled to Chicago, where PUSH entered the conversation on black franchisees as early as 1979. In 1982, PUSH sent a letter to McDonald's inquiring about accusations that black operators were "being subjected to a double standard" in their ability to access franchises. The next black franchisee dispute, while far more complicated because it involved a less-than-ideal plaintiff, benefited from a more mature Los Angeles NAACP, which was better equipped to confront racial disparity in corporate America. This racial discrimination challenge attracted the necessary press coverage and public concern to force McDonald's to publicly defend its practices and philosophy on black business.

Los Angeles transplant and franchisee Charles Griffis shared many similarities with Herman Petty and the other NBMOA founders. Griffis saw himself as a "race man," a prosperous African American whose greatest weapon in his personal arsenal to fight racism were his bootstraps and his steely focus. "I was twelve years old before I ever saw the inside of a schoolhouse," he reminisced. The former Tennessee sharecropper eventually graduated high school, and following in the footsteps of many African

Americans of his generation, he enlisted in the military in order to widen his career prospects. After serving in the Air Force, Griffis earned a degree from the Northern Michigan University.[18] The budding entrepreneur was operating a gas station in Detroit when he learned of the opportunities available to African Americans to franchise McDonald's restaurants.[19] In 1977, Griffis enthusiastically accepted an offer to purchase a Santa Barbara McDonald's, which he assumed was located in the posh coastal city north of Los Angeles. Griffis claimed his trek from Michigan to California ended with a shocking discovery: Griffis had actually invested in a McDonald's restaurant "on Santa Barbara Street [Martin Luther King Jr. Boulevard as of 1983]," which he described as "right in the middle of the ghetto." An irritated Griffis proceeded with the deal despite being the new owner of "an old store in real bad shape." He managed the Santa Barbara Street restaurant expertly, generated substantial profits, and expanded his McDonald's portfolio to include three more restaurants in South Los Angeles within four years of his heading West. Griffis was a bona fide McDonald's success story with annual sales receipts "ranging from $1.2 million to $1.7 million." His stores met or exceeded the national sales averages in 1982. The man who survived poverty in the South and military service became a business owner with two Rolls-Royces in the driveway of his home in affluent Bel-Air.[20]

Griffis's relationship with McDonald's may have continued unremarkably well if his wife, Patricia—perhaps inspired by her husband's success and encouraged by efforts devoted to recruit women into franchising—did not set out to become a franchisee also. Instead of burgers, Patricia Griffis decided that her destiny awaited her in chicken; she entered a franchise agreement for two Popeyes Chicken and Biscuit shops in Crenshaw in 1982.[21] As Mr. and Mrs. Griffis prepared to become a franchising power couple, McDonald's promptly sued Charles for breach of contract in 1983, citing his franchise agreement which stipulated that profits from Big Macs and Chicken McNuggets could not be used toward the purchase of a competing franchise. Charles Griffis would not allow McDonald's to have the last word on his wife's forays into franchis-

ing, and he responded with his own legal action. Griffis filed a lawsuit claiming McDonald's engaged in racial discrimination in the assignment of franchises, which ultimately hampered his capacity to acquire more restaurants.[22] By 1984, when Griffis claimed that he was "systematically kept from buying stores in white neighborhoods," the Los Angeles NAACP chapter had become practiced in deliberating with corporations. The NAACP local eagerly joined Griffis in his public divulgence of his problems with McDonald's and provided a survey they conducted of black franchise locations that supported the conclusion that McDonald's purposely kept black operators out of white areas.

McDonald's was also savvier, having survived Operation Black Unity, Black Panthers, the Ogontz Neighbors Association, and other challengers. They justified their franchisee placement strategy by asserting that they were merely respecting black business owners' stated desire to serve their own communities. If black franchisees wanted to cater to black customers and employ black people, then of course they would be in predominately black locations, McDonald's reasoned. But Griffis's position as a wealthy McDonald's man who lived in the predominately white Bel-Air raised an important question about race and social mobility: where was his community exactly?[23]

Soon the fight over local McDonald's franchises became a topic of national debate. The intersecting issues of race, wealth, and the definition of ownership sparked a series of heated and dramatic conversations between Griffis and McDonald's executives and attorneys. Both sides of the conflict used the language of civil rights to litigate their respective cases in the court of public opinion. Griffis, the Los Angeles NAACP, and two Oakland-based lawyers aggressively attacked McDonald's for betraying the stories of limitless black entrepreneurship featured in advertorials purchased in *Black Enterprise* and *Jet* magazines. The Griffis camp declared that McDonald's treatment of black franchisees was akin to the devastatingly unequal employer-employee relationships of the Jim Crow era when the apparatus of white supremacy suppressed black autonomy at home and at work. Los Angeles NAACP head John

T. MacDonald also evoked the language of housing and mortgage loan discrimination. "We are very concerned about what seems to be McDonald's redlining in the Los Angeles area, and we are collecting information nationwide." The legal pair accused McDonald's of engaging in "unreasonable restraint of trade through racial discrimination and other unreasonable measures to deny free access to the marketplace" in violation of the California Fair Dealership Law and the Civil Rights Act of 1964, because black and white franchise candidates were allegedly placed on separate waiting lists for stores.[24] A former Los Angeles franchisee told the *Sentinel* that he also believed McDonald's kept "two lists of available stores . . . one is for blacks and the other list is for non-blacks."[25]

After news of the lawsuit circulated among major news outlets, Griffis used his newly found platform to deflect McDonald's legitimate contract claims against him. Griffis ignored the Popeyes problem and instead focused on the disparity in restaurant quality among the operator community. In direct conflict with the litany of pro-McDonald's testimonials from other black franchisees, Griffis refused to attribute his high earnings to McDonald's over his own business acumen and hard work. He described his four profitable restaurants to the *New York Times* as being located "in hellholes." Griffis continued: "[My stores] get robbed once or twice a month, and I pay $20,000 a month in security services . . . we had a murder in one and we still get the windows smashed and the bathrooms vandalized. I've upgraded my stores a lot and I don't see why I shouldn't have a shot at a store in a good neighborhood."[26] The day after Griffis shared his story with the *Times*, the *Sentinel* reported that his 1800 South Western Avenue store was the stage for a gun battle between a would-be robber and the store manager.[27] Griffis's characterization of doing business in South Los Angeles required that he make a claim about McDonald's limiting his opportunity while stereotyping the predominately black and brown communities that made him so wealthy. Undoubtedly, some of Griffis's customers felt uncomfortable reading his broad generalizations, while also agreeing with the nature of his challenge. Fair was fair, and why shouldn't black people be allowed to profit off of whites?

McDonald's was not interested in indulging any of Griffis's claims and countered that what Griffis called racism was in fact an enlightened attitude toward race. In placing black franchisees in black communities, McDonald's was simply listening to black consumers and black activists. Borrowing the language of Black Power adherents, black capitalism devotees, and probusiness black mayors, McDonald's stated that where some saw redlining, they were actually being "sensitive to black leaders' requests" by placing "black businesspeople into inner-city neighborhoods."[28] A McDonald's attorney argued that it was Griffis who was duplicitous toward a benevolent company that had given the poor southerner the opportunity to amass a fortune.[29]

The Griffis family held fast to the portrayal of McDonald's as the meddling overseer interfering in their family affairs. Griffis's lawyers adroitly drew upon a long history of African-American economic subjugation, familial disruption, and anxieties about the ways that racism emasculated men in their pithy reply to McDonald's challenge to Patricia's franchise dreams. Griffis's attorney argued that McDonald's could not interfere in "what a member of a man's family does in order to make a living." They offered a simple explanation: Patricia saved her own money and sought an opportunity. They balked at McDonald's actions because the franchise did not "have the right to tell a man how his wife . . . must or must not spend their own money." By restricting Patricia's entrepreneurial drive and independence, McDonald's had intervened in a black man's home in order to "create a virtual monopoly on how far a man can go in business if he is a part of the McDonald's chain."[30] The notion that McDonald's impeded Griffis's ability to establish his patriarchal authority at home and be a businessman resonated with anyone sensitive to the black struggle for personal and professional freedom. The Griffis narrative harkened to the days in which blacks were beholden to white authority at every waking hour. Griffis wanted to make it clear that he was a sharecropper no longer.[31] Griffis enjoyed an early victory in his war on Ronald McDonald. A month after Griffis filed his lawsuit in January 1984, a district court judge refused to grant

McDonald's an injunction that would force Griffis to relinquish his McDonald's franchises. The judge did not believe that Griffis caused McDonald's "any great loss" and "that the matter was for another court."[32]

As each legal team waited for their next day in court, the NAACP invited McDonald's to a meeting about franchise redlining; Mayor Bradley agreed to attend. Bradley's intervention in the boycott was consistent with his probusiness, procompromise managerial style. An historian of the "mainstreaming" of Black Power characterizes Bradley as someone who "lamented urban inequality" but "rarely addressed issues affecting the black poor explicitly." When he did speak about economic inequality or more generally about black advancement, it was almost exclusively communicated in terms of community development, minority business support, and affirmative action—approaches that scarcely made a difference and did not threaten to increase either taxes or welfare spending. He was especially keen to enlist business in the effort to solve urban poverty, believing that private enterprise could "teach poverty communities about how the system works, that it can work and to develop a stake in it."[33] The words "black capitalism" were uttered fewer and fewer times by black leaders in the 1980s, but the spirit of the movement was alive and well. Yet Bradley was not entirely compliant in his plans to ensure that city and business resources flowed toward blacks; but his sensibilities about opportunity were often concentrated in the direction of middle-class people. When he asked businesses to sign an affirmative action agreement in order to secure lucrative contracts with the city, local GM, Ford, and Chrysler dealers refused. Using the most powerful weapon in his arsenal—municipal procurement power—Bradley held firm to his provision. Los Angeles found itself without enough cars for police officers, but Bradley remained unmoved, and eventually the companies conceded. This moment probably confirmed Bradley's hunch that economic hardball could yield results, and his thinking was in line with the NAACP chapter's approach to the McDonald's franchisee dispute.[34]

The ghosts of Cleveland may have haunted the meeting as the

parties gathered in Los Angeles City Hall. With the hindsight of fifteen years since the OBU boycott, McDonald's applied a few lessons since learned about black America's complaints about their business. By the early 1980s, the corporation had hired more black management professionals at Oak Brook, had become more fluent in the language of corporate diversity, and now emphasized that their franchisees were a living memorial to their commitments to equity. From the outside, Griffis may have seemed like an outlier, because the majority of news stories and magazine features about blacks in franchising overemphasized the personal wealth, community impact, and contentment of black franchisees. Frequently featured and quoted in the press, happy black franchise owners emphasized their ability to use the qualities of self-reliance and self-discipline to establish their business. They rejected the idea that McDonald's did anything short of providing spectacular, and equal, opportunity.

While the standard narrative surrounding black franchisees recognized challenges in securing financing or confronting gang activity in and near the stores, black franchisees rarely took McDonald's to task for inequities in restaurant conditions. Nor did they raise their concerns about racially divisive moments endured by franchisees, beginning with Ray Kroc's transgressions. An incident at a franchisee gathering in 1972 illuminated the distance between Kroc's conservative values and the positions of its black operators. In a 1976 exposé about McDonald's entitled *Big Mac: The Unauthorized Story of McDonald's*, writers Max Boas and Steve Chain delved into race relations under the Golden Arches. A chapter opens with the 1972 First International McDonald's Convention in Honolulu. The men described the summit as an opulent affair with no hamburgers in sight at the elegantly catered dinners, but filled with "hamburger millionaires" showing off silk suits and accompanied by wives adorned with diamond jewelry, also financed by Big Macs.[35] The convention was like a fast food world's fair, with new inventions and demonstrations dazzling the participants. McDonald's debuted the Quarter Pounder, screened new advertising campaigns from powerhouse agency Needham, Harper & Steers, and

commissioned songs to introduce upgraded store equipment. The convention—and other meetings like it—were designed to unify operators and recommit them to the house that Kroc built. Regardless of where your restaurant was located, you were bound together by your shared interest in providing quality, service, cleanliness, and value. Yet for black operators, these calls for unity were always tempered by the reality that they were superminorities, and often their stores needed more resources than their white counterparts. When Kroc invited newsman Paul Harvey to deliver remarks to the crowd, the fragile unity of the McDonald's System shattered with Harvey's ode to the kind of American myths that extolled meritocracy and ignored discrimination, which easily devolved into racist attacks on communities of color. Boas and Chain described the speech as a "paean to free enterprise mixed with hoary clichés." Harvey decried rioters, those "too lazy to work," and anyone who expected "something for nothing." The speech may have been the final straw for a subset of black operators, who knew that they were running highly profitable, and largely unsupported, restaurants. After the convention, McDonald's executives received a protest letter from black operators in New York, Cleveland, and Chicago; the letter's signatories included the only woman to own a franchise. At least one franchisee claimed that the speech sent him on a path to see what Burger King had to offer.[36]

Big Mac suggested that despite successful endeavors like the Better Boys Foundation partnership and the high grosses of the "ghetto stores," McDonald's corporate failed to take heed of the feedback provided by the early NBMOA. They highlighted missteps like the Ronald McDonald character visiting black neighborhoods; the writers speculated that because of "the new ghetto militancy" the children rejected a white clown. Black labor organizations rallied to get McDonald's to underwrite college scholarships for its workers, an initiative that would later be partially fulfilled by NBMOA partnerships with the United Negro College Fund. During an attempt to counter rumors that McDonald's was selling bad meat at its restaurants in the center of black Chicago, the Oak Brook outfit was unable to maintain a veneer of good public relations to effectively

argue its case. McDonald's invited black news reporters to their headquarters to tour the offices and a local meat-processing plant, and then meet with the man himself, Ray Kroc. Instead of assuaging concerns about the food quality, the famously exacting Kroc instead fixated on Lu Palmer, a radio host and writer for the *Black X-Press* newspaper, and his decision to not wear a tie to the event. Palmer said that Kroc told him, "If you let a guy take his tie off, then next he'll want to take off his shirt, and where do you stop?" As tempers flared in the meeting, Kroc decided to simply depart, confirming or exacerbating reporters' suspicions about McDonald's racism. Palmer wrote about his experience the next day, noting that as he left Oak Brook's "fantastic monument to hamburger power," he thought about the "countless blacks who helped build it with their quarters and dimes and pennies."[37]

McDonald's executives were willing to learn more about franchise concerns, but they would not demur from the fight. Representation did not always build trust. Frustrated black operators resented McDonald's bringing black executives to the confab in order to deflect charges of racism. Black executives, including West Coast regional manager Reginald Webb, believed that his employer was being "unfairly castigated and attacked." Webb defended McDonald's, pointing to the statistic that "eight percent of all McDonald's franchise owners are black." The NAACP rebutted that over the course of twelve years, "out of 137 black franchise operators nationwide, only one is in a white area."[38] Webb evoked ideas of racial pride to match the redlining accusations: "I don't see anything wrong with doing business in a minority area . . . Mr. Griffis seems to think there is something particularly wrong with it . . . Every black community is not a ghetto."[39] This was correct, but most black communities where McDonald's stood were disproportionately affected by higher operation costs, and few of the restaurants were in solid condition. Webb suggested that critics look at the big picture. "There isn't a more successful group of black entrepreneurs in America." Webb took umbrage at Griffis's assault on "the very system that had provided him with seven years of such professional and financial success."[40] Griffis retorted by attack-

ing one of the key advertising angles articulated by McDonald's in its targeted marketing toward blacks—McDonald's as a major source of work for youth. "When McDonald's says it is the largest employer of black youth, who are they kidding? I'm the one that hired the 600 employees who work for me."[41]

In addition to deploying black executives to defend McDonald's, the corporation relied on stories of prosperous black franchisees who claimed they saw nothing unfair or restrictive in McDonald's practices. In a feature on Lonear Heard, a Southern California franchise owner, *Black Enterprise* dubbed her the "McQueen of the Golden Arches." As black women were stereotyped as welfare queens—a racist characterization of lazy and unethical recipients that shaped public opinion and public policy—the coronation of a black woman as the queen of the franchise was a routine flourish in black business publications. These feature stories often used the impressive personal narratives and the sizable financial portfolios of upper-income blacks to contest negative depictions of the race.[42] The black press often highlighted the modest backgrounds of the franchise owners, their role as job creators in black communities, and their proximity to community efforts. Heard, the vice president of the Los Angeles chapter of the NBMOA, and her husband relocated to California to manage a McDonald's restaurant. After his death in 1981, she took the helm of her family's multifranchise business. She operated stores in Compton, Los Angeles, and Long Beach. In 1987, her six outlets grossed $11.9 million. Heard said she didn't "buy the argument that black franchisees are intentionally discriminated against by McDonald's and given unprofitable inner-city franchises." *Black Enterprise* reported that "her inner-city restaurants, where the clientele is 80% black, are more profitable than her suburban outlets where the clientele is 60% white." Perhaps inadvertently, she actually confirmed part of Griffis's claims; the article also mentioned that she hired security guards to stand post at all her restaurants.[43]

The problem of fast food in black communities was one of safety and limited institutional commercial choices as much as it was a symbol of unprecedented black success and economic progress.

Griffis's refusal to present his relationship with McDonald's in this way was novel and revelatory, proving that money and class mobility could not trump racism's deceitfulness. The NAACP leadership left their city hall meeting undeterred by the failure to come to a middle ground on Griffis's case. The group decided to escalate its efforts. At a March 6, 1984, press conference, John T. MacDonald asked black Angelenos to "buy with . . . conscience," and indicated that solutions to McDonald's racial disparity problems had to be resolved and realized in the offices of their corporate headquarters, as well as among the ranks of franchisees. He chastised McDonald's for a lack of black management and business leadership, particularly on its board of directors, as well as its lack of contracts with black manufacturers, contractors, and suppliers. In a press conference outside of one of Griffis's stores nearly a month later, the NAACP president declared the start of a selective buying campaign—essentially, a partial boycott that asked the public to *only* patronize black-owned McDonald's restaurants. The NAACP leader shared the organization's collection of damning statistics on how few blacks were in the operator corps. Between 1977 and 1984, McDonald's built 115 new restaurants, and a black franchisee operated only one of them. Although buttressed by compelling data, the campaign subverted the logic of the boycott as a means of economic starvation and illustrated just how much the franchise model obscured the issue of ownership. Although black consumers were asked to refrain from patronizing white-owned franchises, ultimately, McDonald's still benefited from profits generated at black-owned restaurants. The NAACP did not bother drafting and sharing a list of stores to support and which ones to avoid: "It's really pretty simple. Minorities don't own ones in white neighborhoods."[44]

McDonald's may have thought that they didn't need outsiders telling them how to connect to black America. In addition to employing franchisees who provided jobs in black communities, McDonald's devised a strategy for spreading their wealth on their terms. At the close of 1983, McDonald's announced it would provide more than $108 million in contracts to black insurance firms. The

black insurance business—which grew from black mutual aid societies established as early as the nineteenth century—was far from its apex in the 1980s. Black insurance companies began to decline in the 1960s, when larger companies were able to expand their already dominant role among black consumers.[45] As part of the McDonald's agreement, black-owned companies—Atlanta Life Insurance Company, Los Angeles's Golden State Mutual Life, the North Carolina Mutual company in Raleigh, and the Chicago Metropolitan Mutual Assurance Company—would capture what accounted for 17.5% of McDonald's life insurance business. Yet, as in many matters involving the expansion of black opportunity, there were white powerbrokers involved. This scheme was facilitated by recommendations from insurance giant Travelers Insurance, which McDonald's contacted for the suggestions.[46] These may have been preventive steps for McDonald's as they saw other companies become more vulnerable to PUSH boycotts, especially in major actions against the beer industry.

McDonald's knew it had to remain vigilant after Operation PUSH launched a national boycott of Anheuser-Busch in the fall of 1982. Operation PUSH was reshaping the landscape of boycotts and would influence how the NAACP proceeded in the Griffis matter. In a feat of expertly synchronized organizing, thirty-three PUSH partners announced plans of the beer boycott on the afternoon of September 4. PUSH emphasized that despite the beer company's popularity in the black alcohol-buying market, Anheuser-Busch had only one black-owned distributor, only 2% of its subsidiaries were black, and blacks were often trapped in the lowest-rung jobs in the company. Company head August A. Busch III refused to meet with Jackson about the issue, and Jackson claimed that Anheuser-Busch not only tried to discredit him and his efforts, but offered support to other black organizations as a way to tamp down on the growth of the boycott.[47] The boycott continued into 1983, and PUSH attracted the support of the National Association of Black Promoters, who were also concerned about the lack of black contractors hired to support the popular Bud Fest concert series, which was favored by black audiences with musical headliners Frankie

Beverly, Kool & the Gang, and Ashford & Simpson. The promoters association sought a negotiation with Anheuser-Busch years before the boycott but were unhappy with Anheuser-Busch's offer, which they described as a "sharecropping or 'colonial' arrangement." The events, PUSH claimed, "attract a significant Black audience, using a large number of Black acts," but shut out black contractors and vendors from the festivals. There were no excuses for the poor record of black hiring, considering the festivals were hosted at venues like the Forum in Inglewood, California, and the Omni in Atlanta. Initially, in Jackson's signature style, he called on blacks to participate in a boycott by declaring, "Bud is a dud, don't drink those suds."[48] Busch, the maker of the "dud" beer, realized that Jackson's rhyming directives like "Dump Those Suds in the Mud" and "Demonstration without Hesitation" were persuasive, and it settled with PUSH a year after the first call to boycott.[49] The settlement carried promises to hire blacks and Latinos at rates that would yield employment statistics inside the company that matched the nation's population percentages. The beer producer also agreed to earmark $23 million in supplier contracts for minority-owned businesses, another $10 million to construction companies, and $8 million in business with advertising firms, such as Burrell Communications. In an attempt to infuse capital into the black banks that began disappearing over the preceding decades, Anheuser-Busch devoted $8 million to certificates of deposit and payroll checks. They also looked to recruit more distributors of color to add to the existing six in their network of hundreds.[50]

Operation PUSH was unabashed in its belief that black power was a matter of politics and the purse. At a 1983 commemoration of King's death, Jackson repeated the well-worn phrase at a rally in Anderson, Indiana: "We have our civil rights, now we're fighting for our silver rights." Jackson continued, "We're not fighting for social generosity, we're not marching for welfare, we're marching for jobs."[51] In the 1980s, even a King disciple like Jackson saw social welfare as an enemy, rather than a friend, to the poor. In the span of a few days, Jackson could be found pontificating to white Republicans about breaking bread with black voters, chas-

tising black nationalists to disavow themselves of "ghetto habits" in order to succeed, and pitching a corporate reparations plan to business executives.[52] Regardless of the audience, Jackson's message about economics castigated companies for failing to do right by black America in the form of jobs and wealth-building opportunities, while also blaming black Americans for failing to capitalize on few jobs and even fewer routes to joining the ownership class. The black capitalists of the 1980s linked the inability of blacks to connect civil rights with the pursuit of silver rights to their own pathological failings, even as they sought structural redress from businesses in the form of employment and economic development. This befuddling mix of rhetoric that simultaneously blamed victims and oppressors melded into a vague call for more black-owned businesses and for blacks to ally with the private sector, with no regards to the negative implications of seeking relief in structures built on inequality. While the advice was sometimes confusing, the financial stakes were crystal-clear. Over the course of a decade, PUSH was able to receive corporate donations and consultation fees that exceeded $15 million. The money that flowed into PUSH supported community-based programming for blacks, as well as buttress the organization and its leadership's influence.

The NAACP was taking notes. In early April of 1984, the Los Angeles NAACP ended a successful five-day boycott of the Coors Brewing Company after gaining concessions on minority hiring. The Coors action, spurred by racist remarks made by sales division head Peter Coors about the transatlantic slave trade being a cosmic favor to blacks, yielded promises for minority hiring and contracting.[53] Years of cultivating internal black talent and support for the NBMOA did not, and could not, provide cover for McDonald's. Black organizations, due in large part to Jackson's example, reimagined what a community demand looked like. The community was not the customer or the barber around the corner who may want to one day have a franchise. The community meant the professionals and professional societies with the talents, skills, and social capital to be included in the wealth that was being made off the backs of working and middle-income people. The franchise

dispute highlighted that blacks at every rung of society contended with some form of exclusion and racial barrier to achievement and self-sufficiency. But as the boycott became an extension of securing business for well-positioned blacks, the poor and struggling received programs and coupons instead of substantive work and more choices.

* * *

In May of 1984, a month after the operators' meeting boycott, the NAACP turned up the heat with a message to black Los Angeles via the pages of the *Sentinel*. "You Need to Know!!! The McDonald's Corporation has no respect for Los Angeles Mayor Tom Bradley, the NAACP, or the black community!"[54] At a meeting regarding McDonald's "hiring, franchising and purchasing policies, claims which spoke of overt racial discrimination," McDonald's vice president Richard Starmann, probably cognizant of the Coors concessions, held his ground and he told the NAACP, "We'll be happy to discuss anything . . . but we're not in any way conducting negotiations or bargaining with them."[55] The advertisement made clear that the NAACP would accept nothing less than *negotiations and bargaining*. The ad continued: "The McDonald's Corporation owes the black community through the NAACP a total commitment to reinvest a Fair Share of the $1.6 billion Black people spend on their products to show the proper respect to an organization which has spent over 75 years fighting for full and equal rights for all Americans."[56] The rules and terms of engagement were now in the hands of the NAACP and their vision of economic progress—reinvestment through corporate employment, promotion, and contracts—was going to dictate any further conversation. The presenting issue was expanding black franchising, but focusing on white-collar employment and contracting was grafted onto the call to hold McDonald's accountable to black communities.

By the time a Los Angeles jury finally heard *McDonald's Corp. v. Griffis* in 1984, the melee over burgers had shifted. The NAACP was poised to initiate another action if necessary, and McDonald's abandoned its defensive stance in the charges of franchise redlining.

Instead, spokespeople took a laudatory tone about the special gifts that black franchise owners brought to service counters and drive-thru windows in predominately black neighborhoods. McDonald's gushed about the "exceptional skill of black franchisees" and claimed that they enlisted their talents because it "was a matter of good business" to cultivate an affinity between owners and communities. One spokesperson explained, "The fact that problems of operating certain locations in the inner-city, predominately black areas, require a person with particular abilities and that persons having these abilities have, in many instances, been black, involves no act of racial discrimination."[57] Black franchising began because of white hesitancy in doing business in black neighborhoods, a fact that McDonald's openly discussed in the late 1960s and 1970s. In 1984, McDonald's presented the issue of blacks in black communities as both a concerted effort to respect racial solidarity, and a coincidental fact that blacks tend to have the ability to do business well in black areas. Although the logic wasn't the most cohesive, McDonald's may have believed that it was in their best interest for the suit to resolve itself quickly before Griffis gave another one of his press interviews. Griffis and McDonald's eventually settled the lawsuit in 1985.[58] McDonald's paid Griffis $4.7 million in the settlement, but they stressed that the payment was unrelated to charges of racial discrimination. A McDonald's attorney stated that they had simply offered to "buy back Mr. Griffis's four restaurants." He added that Griffis was not given "15 cents for those bogus racial discrimination claims."[59] Griffis collected his millions and continued in the restaurant business. In 1987, the Griffis family opened a small soul food chain named Chicken Charlie, which specialized in "truly down home style fried chicken." Griffis used his experiences with McDonald's to convince black customers to support a "real" black-owned business. "We've eaten everybody else's food for centuries; indeed, our food is a composite of other ethnic dishes, so why not a chain featuring the improved version of soul?" Griffis rehearsed arguments that echoed the sometime castigating tones of other black capitalism missives suggesting that buying black was a way of expressing racial authenticity and

solidarity. They argued that to not buy black was to betray one's people. Griffis argued, "Every other racial extraction has pride in their heritage and cultural background that includes their food, so why not Black Americans?"[60]

The NAACP was also asking McDonald's "Why not black Americans?" after they settled with Griffis. Fair Share, however, could never address or repair the foundational problems that triggered McDonald's push for black franchising in the first place, including the loss of capital into and within inner cities and commercial white flight, and it did not guarantee employment for more black, low-wage workers. To be sure, the NAACP and its legal branch did not abandon housing, education, and employment justice broadly, but their pivot toward corporations did mean that fewer resources were available to address the economic calamities concentrated in black America. The NAACP became a major beneficiary of lucrative financial sponsorships from McDonald's corporate coffers. Franchise ownership could not and would not effectively expand the power of African Americans within McDonald's, so the Fair Share and hiring approaches to equity would provide another means of turning the tide, if only a bit. While wages and conditions were not focal point issues about people of color and the fast food giant, the distribution of contracts was the closest to a trickling down of any economic benefit from the wealthy, franchisee elite to communities.

Even with Griffis out of the picture, the organization still believed that their relatively small boycott could yield large returns. The issue of franchisee redlining was never sufficiently addressed, but the NAACP did not need Griffis's claims to leverage a Fair Share plan with McDonald's, having already tested the waters with executives in meetings for months. Weeks after the Griffis case was settled, the national NAACP announced a historic agreement with McDonald's that "reaffirmed a commitment to economic development for blacks and other minorities." Bob Beavers, then McDonald's only black senior vice president, called the five-year agreement "good business and . . . good corporate citizenship." McDonald's promised to "employ the same percentage of minorities and females

as the nation's workforce, increase the number of minority suppliers, strengthen its minority insurance program, and hire more minority construction companies."[61] The plan included a provision that McDonald's would "establish 100 new black-owned restaurants" over a four-year period, hire more black managers, and offer more contracts to black businesses—from food suppliers to attorneys.

With an estimated $100 million worth of business on the table, the Los Angeles chapter wanted to make sure that some of those dollars returned home where the campaign began. The NAACP chapter estimated that 10 percent of the contracts and new business generated from the agreement would come to Los Angeles and offered to help McDonald's identify potential black contractors and franchisees.[62] The McDonald's victory represented a key moment in how the franchise operated among African-American communities across a broad spectrum—from the low-income diners who frequented the restaurant multiple times a week to black businesspeople to civil rights establishment leaders. The campaigns deconstructed the layered and enmeshed ways community resources were made available or limited due to race, and it determined what was a "fair share."

In the late 1980s and into the 1990s, the black franchise community multiplied throughout Southern California, and the legacy of the Griffis boycott allowed for more franchisees of color to enter the McDonald's System and black professionals to blaze trails in the McDonald's headquarters. When the NBMOA met in Long Beach in 1989 for its annual convention, executive board members emphasized that the franchisee was a leader in the issue of opening opportunities for black professionals. NBMOA president Kendrick Ross proclaimed that their "restaurants provide business opportunities for numerous minority suppliers, as well as meaningful jobs and career options in the food service industry for Black youth." Like Herman Petty's donation of his profits to Martin Luther King Jr.'s right-hand man twenty years earlier, Ross's speech placed McDonald's franchising squarely in the history of black freedom movements. "After years of marching, protesting and civil rights gains, the next step for many adults is to enter into the economic mainstream." Ross reflected that with 220 black franchise owners

nationwide, the uptick in the black franchisee corps proved "that dreams come true."[63] Not all dreams are found at the end of a lawsuit or part of a Fair Share plan. But, in the 1980s, the expansion of black franchising further placed businesses in the position of not only setting the agenda for individuals in industry, but also setting the priorities of black civil rights organizations.

Silver rights were winning. Black unemployment and poverty in the 1980s were still pervasive reminders of how little had changed since the sweeping legal changes of the 1960s, so fast food may have seemed like a sensible industry to appeal to for the economic opportunities that the government did not care to support. It is difficult to fault organizations like the NAACP and Operation PUSH entirely for being lured by the financial promises of the fast food industry, especially if their respective leaders believed that concessions were the only way to keep civil rights struggles alive. Constrained choices yield constrained possibilities. Yet, it may be also possible that considering the power of the boycott in areas in which fast food was so wildly popular, the NAACP could have brought corporations to the negotiation table with other demands, more in line with the people the organization struggled to reach in the 1970s and '80s. The same strategy of consumer abstinence and business disruption could have been used for the purpose of organizing workers to raise wages, improve scheduling practices, or provide workers with child care facilities or transportation subsidies. Maybe the fast food industry could have bent under the pressure of an Operation PUSH call for health care rights alongside silver rights? Would today's urban landscape have been different if the Griffis case had not only exposed the discrimination franchisees experienced, but also the extent to which black and brown taxpayers subsidized his operations and turned consumer attention on the federal government's corporate welfare to the inner city? It is easy to speculate what could have happened in this moment and others. As the 1990s approached, civil rights organizations, the federal government, and everyday people would continue to turn to the fast food industry to deliver on the very thing it could never prepare, sell, market, or deliver—justice.

The Miracle of the Golden Arches

After the 1992 Los Angeles riots, McDonald's claimed that its restaurants in the epicenter of the violence remained untouched because of the company's deep connection with black consumers. John T. Barr / Getty Images.

G etting back to normal was going to take a while. Los Angeles had been on fire for five days. On April 29, 1992, a not-guilty verdict had been delivered in the Rodney King police brutality case. As it had been in other moments in years past and in places near and far from Los Angeles, the denial of justice for a black

person beaten by the police ignited an uprising. The fury was not only about the King decision. A week earlier, a California Court of Appeals upheld the sentence of no jail time for a Korean convenience store owner who shot and killed black teenager Latasha Harlins. These two moments aggravated the same racial and economic tensions that boiled over in Watts in 1965. Over the course of five days, the city endured at least 58 deaths, 2,400 injuries, and property damage totaling a billion dollars.[1] Media from all over the world swarmed Los Angeles. Each night, photographers risked their safety on the streets to capture scenes of pharmacies and convenience stores on fire. Reporters in helicopters accustomed to covering the snail's pace traffic of Southern California's freeways were suddenly capturing shopkeepers armed with handguns and semiautomatic weapons, hell-bent on protecting their stores. At press conferences held after the trial's conclusion was made public, journalists asked why police officials were so lax in dispatching assistance to the heart of the crisis zone, South Los Angeles. On May 4, Mayor Tom Bradley took the first step toward normalcy when he lifted a citywide curfew. After firefighters extinguished the flames of burning buildings, cleanup crews cleared glass and debris off the streets, and shop owners tallied what had been lost and damaged, Los Angeles's most difficult work was still ahead. What could be learned from this latest uprising? Was there some way to prevent it from happening again? Did Los Angeles really want to return to normal?

Twenty-seven years of hindsight hadn't changed much in the approach to solving the American dilemma of racism; businesses were expected to save the day, again. Although the King beating raised serious concerns about racial violence and the Los Angeles Police Department, businesses also occupied the center of the story of what went awry when the chaos broke. The Korean-owned supermarket—like the one where Harlins was shot and killed because store owner Soon Ja Du saw a bottle of orange juice in the girl's backpack and did not see the money in her hands as she approached the checkout counter—represented the life-or-death tensions in the multiethnic inner city. News pundits provided commentary over live footage of looters carrying everything from loaf-

ers to portable CD players to gallons of milk out of vandalized stores. When Los Angeles finally quieted down, some op-eds in national newspapers and talking heads on cable news programs seemed to mourn the loss of commerce more than the loss of life. On that fragile Monday the curfew ended, when Los Angeles was to ready itself for healing and rebuilding, the city looked to business to lead the effort to get back on track. In future retellings of how Los Angeles made it through the upheaval, McDonald's would emerge as one of the strongest leaders throughout. When a school couldn't get its lunch shipments delivered, black franchisee Harold Patrick donated Happy Meals. When fatigued National Guardsmen and police officers who had been dispatched to the crisis at the height of the unrest needed something to eat, they could take their meal vouchers to McDonald's.[2] When business interests needed to make a case for their role in Los Angeles's recovery, they also looked to McDonald's.

McDonald's provided no comment about state-sanctioned violence or the recklessness of the Los Angeles Police Department, but it had plenty to say about the uprising. McDonald's proudly proclaimed that their South Los Angeles restaurants were spared the ire of the angriest and most disaffected Americans who took to the streets that spring. The fast food chain declared itself inoculated from the virus of urban anger and suggested that its vaccine was injected after the Holy Week uprising in 1968. A business magazine suggested that McDonald's survival was "the vindication of enlightened social policies begun more than three decades ago." McDonald's CEO Edward Rensi theorized: "Our businesses [in Los Angeles] are owned by African-American entrepreneurs who hired African-American managers who hired African-American employees who served everybody in the community." Rensi's claims were the basis of a *Financial Week* article, which quoted Leighton Hull, a black franchisee from Lynwood, a town north of Compton. Hull posited that McDonald's "involvement in the neighborhoods it serves" was a defense mechanism tested but not pierced by the Los Angeles rebellion. *Financial Week* mused, "It has evolved, at least in the inner cities, as a plan for peaceful and prosperous

coexistence between the corporation and its occasionally fractious environment."[3] In the same ways that the spray-painting of SOUL BROTHER or SOUL BUSINESS on the exterior windows of businesses was considered a prophylactic at the height of the 1960s uprisings, the declaration that a business was black-owned was believed to be a survival strategy during the Los Angeles crisis. In addition to this measure, historian Brenda Stevenson found that "some Korean shop owners who were known to have employed blacks found themselves immune from attack or were protected by the employees who lived in the neighborhood."[4] After more than two decades, Ronald McDonald had finally become a naturalized citizen of black America.

Whether McDonald's was protected due to trust, good luck, or the efforts of police to protect its restaurants is hard to assess. There is little mention of activity near McDonald's restaurants in the official accounting of the uprising by the Los Angeles Webster Commission, the body assembled to study what went wrong in the lead-up to and during the event. From the existing records, it is difficult to corroborate Rensi's claim. In some reports, McDonald's only suffered minor damage and was able to reopen quickly. In other tellings, the restaurant was protected by police, community members, and employees. The *Orange County Register* reported that the McDonald's at 18th Street and Western Avenue was spared the ruinous fate of neighboring "restaurants and a supermarket, which was cleaned out by looters," including a Winchell's Donut House and a J. J. Newberry's discount store. The location was operated by African-American franchisee Harold Patrick beginning in 1983, and he reasoned that he was saved because the staff were "close with our customers." "We know them." He told the *Minneapolis Star Tribune* that his patrons saved the day. "Our customers stood outside and talked to those from outside the neighborhood . . . they told them this is their restaurant."[5] He may have also benefited from the National Guardsmen dispatched to the area on the afternoon of April 30.[6] Perhaps in gratitude or out of fear, Patrick later planned to create a police substation inside the restaurant. The *Orlando Sun-Sentinel* published a picture of a

McDonald's with the words BLACK OWNED spray-painted on the window.[7] Another McDonald's location hung a perhaps redundant sign: DUE TO CURRENT PROBLEMS, WE ARE CLOSED.[8] *Time* magazine reported that McDonald's "suffered the least damage," with the loss of a few windows, but "Burger Kings and Taco Bells in the same neighborhood took it on the chin." A franchisee figured that the community believed that "these are the good guys; let's not do this to them."[9] In a National Black McDonald's Operators Association video, franchisee Larry Tripplett reiterated his version of what happened in Los Angeles:

> When they had the Rodney King incident, one of my stores is African American . . . I was there that evening, and this is the Bay Area, not Los Angeles, they burned down . . . and trashed the Kentucky Fried Chicken, it's out of business now, they trashed a post office, they burned down a market . . . My store was open, did not get touched, had nothing but high volume sales that day. Now that was because . . . we had given back to the community, we knew everybody in the community, and quite frankly, that community to this day is very proud of this McDonald's . . .[10]

Whether or not this moment for McDonald's—this Miracle of the Golden Arches—is a fact or a convenient truth is unimportant. That it could be believed and that McDonald's suggested that it was so familiar, important, and precious to communities that had been distanced from institutions, equity, and justice speaks volumes about a process that started decades earlier. McDonald's was a citizen of black Los Angeles, and despite the calamity of 1992, it wasn't going anywhere. The testimonies about the Miracle of the Golden Arches revealed how constrained choices can lead to forgetting, on the local and national level, about the other kinds of conflicts that surrounded all-American meals. The Los Angeles uprising's emergence almost twenty-five years after King's assassination made some reflective about what, if anything, had actually changed over two and a half decades of continued struggle. More blacks were in elected office. Colleges and universities were starting to see the

effects of affirmative action policies that not only diversified student bodies, but also brought well-trained doctors, lawyers, and educators in service to underresourced communities. If fast food franchising was a metric for progress, franchisees were expanding their small empires, donating vast sums of money, and continuing to employ a large swath of black America. But honest accounting cannot allow the most positive stories to hold the most weight, and the issues of continued racial discrimination, poverty, health disparities, and unemployment continued to torment black America. A quarter of a century after the entry of blacks into franchising, the problems of the 1960s continued to plague inner-city America.

While the fast food industry had created growth opportunities for individual franchisees and corporate executives, the success of a few black elites had little impact on the life of those languishing in the very communities that housed and staffed their businesses. As the language of black capitalism transformed into the rhetoric of black empowerment, the fast food industry made more aggressive promises to help rebuild the inner city. No longer pursuing the piecemeal recruitment efforts of the 1960s and 1970s, the Fair Share and voluntary affirmative action agreements of the 1980s and early 1990s pursued corporations with as much gusto as movement activists of the past. Fast food franchises sought powerful holding companies and partnerships to open their restaurants in multiple locations and territories to capture the black dollars that were still up for grabs, as supermarkets and large retailers still ignored pockets of working-class and poor black America. This transitional period was grounded in the certainty that fast food was an accepted and welcomed presence in black communities. Franchisees of color, in their own self-evaluation and in the eyes of government lenders, the hearts of chambers of commerce, and the minds of probusiness politicians, could be trusted to not only feed black America, but also lead black America. For decades, black publications had celebrated franchisees for massing sizable assets and donating generously to black causes, while also staying connected to poor and working-class blacks through their employees, customers, and beneficiaries of their community outreach. After the

Miracle of the Golden Arches was widely distributed in the press, an audience of white business consultants, government aides, and philanthropists learned about the multiple roles that black franchisees played in their communities. So, they thought, more franchises could solve more complex problems.

Initiating conversations about what black America has to do to get better has always been a popular American pastime. Unlike the questions about black opportunity and black economic independence in the previous decades, the conversation in the 1990s did not wonder about the potential of black franchising. The decade's musings on what black America needed began with a sense of certainty that black franchises were viable solutions, it was only a matter of how many and how fast they could open.

Two black franchisees whose businesses were built in the period before and after the Los Angeles uprising capture the transition in franchising from the late 1980s to the 1990s. Ted Holmes's Chicken George was one of the last black franchises that was baptized by the spirit of black capitalism in the 1960s and survived to see the late 1980s. Blacks would establish franchises after the last Chicken George closed its doors, but the ways that Holmes's restaurant venture reshaped the fried chicken market is illustrative of why it was difficult for black capitalism's boosters to implement their own advice after the major fast food companies saturated inner-city markets with black-franchised outlets that could make a case to consumers who wanted to "buy black." Holmes's Baltimore-based Chicken George franchise modeled itself in the ways of Champ-Burger and Mahalia's Glori-Fried in its claim to be authentically black. It was so genuine that it took its name from *Roots*, the book and film fictionalization of author Alex Haley's genealogy. Chicken George's early success pushed major fast food restaurants to think about its appeal to African Americans, and then they were able to use their massive resources to overtake Chicken George.

After Holmes's Chicken George faded into obscurity, La-Van Hawkins became the talk of the fast-food world with aggressive franchising deals that demonstrated the ways that access to franchises provided vast amounts of power to few people in urban

America. Hawkins's story also explains how the policies of the 1990s, as well as the racial tensions of the period, reinforced hope that fast food would pave the way forward for black communities. Hawkins, the P. T. Barnum of black empowerment, was a larger-than-life black franchisee who peddled everything from burgers to chicken to pizza. Supported by a plethora of Fair Share–style initiatives and federal assistance, Hawkins's forays into D.C., Philadelphia, and Detroit epitomized how franchises sought to claim every commercial inch of the food landscape. Hawkins, who had entanglements with a number of major companies, and created his own franchise concepts, provides a cautionary tale about the limits of black capitalism as a sustainable economic investment strategy and pathway to racial reconciliation. In both instances, Hawkins's enterprises and Chicken George illustrated how fast food no longer relied on small-scale franchisees to make their restaurants black, and in the ongoing use of franchises to equalize racial opportunity, black franchisees continued to find themselves at the margins.

Ted Holmes, a Congress of Racial Equality alum from York, Pennsylvania, first entered business in 1969, when he founded a personnel services company. Holmes was well aware of the opportunities available from the Office of Minority Business Enterprise and Small Business Administration, and after handling government contracts, he realized the lucrative nature of food service agreements.[11] Holmes found the post–King-uprising climate for business rife with tokenism, and despite invitations to apply for lucrative financial grants, he did not know if the black capitalism moment was making much of a difference. When asked if segregation was a good thing for black business, he answered, "Yes, but I would qualify that by saying that the word 'segregation' may be a little harsh. I think 'community-minded' might be a better term. There were, all across this country, flourishing black shopping areas prior to desegregation laws in the '50s and '60s. Once we started shopping everywhere those businesses just melted away."[12] In the post–Civil Rights Act world, the question of segregation and integration weighed heavily on black consumers and business owners. If segregation stalled black progress, what did integration do to black com-

munities? In trying to resolve the question, black businesses often overemphasized their authentic blackness, and nothing screamed authenticity like Alex Haley's *Roots*.[13] Chicken George, the restaurant, debuted in 1979 and capitalized on the popularity of the character Chicken George from the 1976 book and the television miniseries that premiered the next year. Portrayed by actor Ben Vereen, Chicken George was the clever grandson of Haley's fictitious patriarch Kunta Kinte. George gets his name after participating in the cockfighting racket on his master's plantation. Costumed with a feathered bowler hat and a green scarf, George's charisma grants him an opportunity to travel to England, secure his freedom, and return to the states on the eve of the Civil War. The eight-part series drew an average of 32 million viewers per evening, and for years after its airing, Haley's representation of black familial bonds and connections to Africa resonated with black America. McDonald's even sponsored a sweepstakes in which winners could travel to West Africa and meet members of the Haley family. Curiously, Haley and broadcaster ABC held no trademark on the name Chicken George, and Holmes cleverly used the moniker to squeeze himself into the fast food chicken market.

As Holmes entered franchising, he studied up on why other black-owned enterprises failed, and he believed that a lack of capital held black people back. He set the restaurant's entry fee at $25,000, a more accessible amount for black businesspeople. Soon he was able to sell restaurants in more than a dozen locations. The entry fee wasn't the only distinction for the restaurant; unlike Mahalia's and ChampBurger, which drew mixed reviews for the quality of its food, Chicken George was known for its outstanding fare. In a feature on the business, the *Baltimore Sun* wrote:

> Unlike other fast-food operators, Chicken George's served up its spicy chicken with the appetites and pocketbooks of middle-class blacks in mind. In an industry conspicuously lacking in minority ownership, this company established itself—setting sales records unequaled by the industry at large—by going to the roots of the black community.[14]

Holmes was particularly proud of his ability to make Chicken George authentic. "No one had collard greens in the fast-food concept . . . Popeyes, that had biscuits and rice, but that was out of the Louisiana experience." Chicken George didn't take its cues from Popeyes, and the restaurant was not afraid of offending the tastes of nonblack consumers.[15] By opening its first location at the Mondawmin Mall, which then served a mostly middle-class area of Baltimore, Holmes prepared and priced his foods for a slightly more discriminating consumer. Market segmentation among racial lines was proving a smart strategy for major retailers and companies in the 1970s, but the secondary segmentation of blacks across class lines was still emerging as a viable avenue to maximize profits. While other chains imagined their black consumers as mostly low-income even as their advertisements signaled their desire to depict black, middle-class life, Chicken George believed it could capture a slightly more affluent market. In its franchise recruitment materials, Chicken George talked about a desire to appeal to the "untapped market" and believed that "the black community was just waiting for a business that wouldn't take them, their tastes or their dollars for granted."[16]

In the model of the traditional black franchises, Chicken George was also seen as a sound investment for community programs. In Camden, New Jersey, the Black People's Unity Movement—a one-time radical collective—had incorporated into a community development group, BPUM Impact Corp., which tried its hand at a Chicken George franchise.[17] Chicken George was a runaway hit. Within four years of opening, it was number 64 on *Black Enterprise*'s annual list of black-owned businesses, with a gross of $13 million.[18] Although Holmes struggled with self-promotion and granting media interviews for the business, the company eventually hired black advertising firm Lockhart & Pettus to create a campaign for them from their new Atlanta branch, and they called upon Image Advertising in Chicago to develop ads in 1984.[19] In the winter of 1983, a Houston real estate development team announced plans to develop up to 600 locations in Texas, Oklahoma, Louisiana, and New Mexico, with a plan for the Chicken George headquarters to add another 300 franchises.[20]

Chicken George's low-budget television commercials captured diners eating their products inside a restaurant and declaring the chicken better than a wife's and a mother's recipe. The tagline of the campaign, "Say good bye to ho hum chicken, say hello to Chicken George" was sung by a throaty blues singer and depicted an interracial customer base. With little money spent on advertising and only eight locations in the 1980s, Chicken George's success was unprecedented for a new restaurant franchise. With average sales per outlet exceeding a million dollars, Chicken George was even able to put a nearby Popeyes restaurant out of business, and a Kentucky Fried Chicken representative conceded that the business was like "a house on fire," with its long line of customers and repeat business. Chicken Georges in Baltimore and Philadelphia lured larger and better-financed Popeyes and Kentucky Fried Chicken to compete in the market more aggressively. With so many failures in the franchise market, Chicken George's resilience shocked the major chicken outlets in the Northeast. Kentucky Fried Chicken, which had yet to make a splash in the region, decided to commit to an extensive market penetration strategy. They began a plan to enter Baltimore and its suburbs with sixty new restaurants over a four-year period between 1984 and 1988.[21]

Chicken George may have had authenticity and flavor on its side, but it could not compete in terms of capital. While its franchise expansion plan was hampered by a lack of headquarters leadership and by sparsely supported franchisees, its competitors could pour more resources into developing products and could bear the losses on failed stores. Chicken George's business model, a news article reported, collapsed when "the competition was realizing the black community is an entity and was going after them with coupons, which effectively lowered the price of their product to the consumer."[22] When the company started to waver due to stronger competition and Big Chicken's ability to provide more product discounts, the founder became more withdrawn from Chicken George and its processes. Few could get ahold of Holmes, who had turned his attention overseas. Holmes befriended African businessmen, who were determining how to leverage "American

corporate assets in South Africa to pass on to black entrepreneurs in that country."[23] Holmes had moved on.

The void left by Chicken George was filled by an amended Kentucky Fried Chicken chain that targeted inner-city locations. In the early 1990s, Kentucky Fried Chicken unveiled twenty-seven "Neighborhood" stores, which appears to have been a code for "black." Diners could decide among the Colonel's traditional recipe chicken and biscuits or "red beans and rice, mean greens, macaroni and cheese," and finish off lunch or dinner with southern favorites "peach cobbler or sweet potato pie." In Detroit, the newly renamed KFC presented restaurants that offered the locally made Mr. FoFo's sweet potato pie. A press release explained that the "new crew uniforms" would include African kufis (hats) and "kente cloth–accented dashikis." KFC explained, "The uniforms evoke the proud heritage of African-Americans to whom Neighborhood KFCs are targeted." While eating Honey BBQ Wings or Hot 'n Spicy Chicken in Baltimore, Atlanta, Boston, Chicago, New York, Detroit, and Philadelphia, customers could listen to "tunes likely to be found on local urban radio stations."[24] The greens were test-marketed in the early 1980s, and some speculated it was a response to the popularity of Chicken George's collards side dish.[25] KFC had traditionally tested well with black consumers, but the Neighborhood concept was the most explicit adoption of foods and reconfiguring of the in-store dining experience in the direction of black customers. Had Holmes decided to use his experiences in business to simply franchise one of Chicken George's competitors, his story may have ended much differently.

In 1986, after filing bankruptcy, Holmes's interest in franchising collapsed and he was now invested in using his strengths in the fight against apartheid. He was still willing to share the hard lessons he learned after the end of Chicken George, a cautionary tale about businesses' missteps for the next generation of entrepreneurs.[26] Chicken George, and Holmes's experiment, could not survive the outgrowths of the very movement, black capitalism, that brought him to the food business. Holmes retreated from the public eye, and another black businessman's attempt to reopen

Chicken George in Baltimore failed. By the 1990s, the fast food industry realized how to be attentive to black consumer preferences and present in black communities, and by relying on franchisees to assume the liabilities of the risky restaurant business, they could stay the course when upstart competitors challenged their positions. In the fast food franchise world, making a good product or simply being black-owned was not enough. The name of the fast food game was capital, and without it, a new restaurant could disappear as quickly as a two-piece chicken meal.

* * *

"Come on La-Van!"

A voiceover's soulful command—a cross between Anita Baker and Gladys Knight—introduced the star of the television commercial: the one and only La-Van Hawkins. "You got to twist and dip," the voice crooned. An all-female dance team comprised of uniformed Pizza Hut employees began a choreographed number. "My new twisted crust pizza is lavish," said the Pizza Hut franchisee, a tall, broad man outfitted with an apron and dark-rimmed glasses. Hawkins, much larger than the dancers and the background performers jamming to the Pizza Hut song, awkwardly bounced to the song. As the identified creator of this innovation that married a pizza with several servings of breadsticks, Hawkins looked straight into the camera and provided a bizarre description of the new dish as both "luscious" and "lusty," in addition to being "crusty." Hawkins's voice boomed: "It's pizza and breadsticks in one hardworking bite!" Throughout the 1990s and early 2000s, Hawkins was also hard at work, having spent the better part of nearly two decades inking deal after deal to franchise hundreds of inner-city fast food restaurants in succession and concurrently.[27] Detroiters in the 1990s craving a Whopper, carrying out a Twisted Crust Pizza, or even dining on a plate of haute-cuisine chicken and waffles, knew Hawkins, fast food's greatest hypeman.

Hawkins's persona and approach was an amalgam of all the black business rhetoric from the late 1960s up to the 2000s; his recipe for success included a bootstraps-heavy personal narrative,

a charismatic presence in urban centers, and friends in high places with access to investment dollars. Hawkins moved from city to city, from franchise to franchise, offering some of the most blighted black and brown corners of America unparalleled opportunities for jobs and advancement in the franchise system. When he would exit those same cities after complications with his businesses emerged, he often left behind broken promises and bad debts. Somehow, although his enterprises often fell short, he managed to find a way to acquire more franchise opportunities. The revival of the myth that black businesses could deliver the black poor from economic isolation had no better representative than Hawkins. Hawkins's run with and through the fast food industry exemplified the limits of fast food as an answer to complex social problems.

A striking man more than six feet tall, Hawkins had a compelling, albeit sometimes hard-to-corroborate rags-to-riches story that began with a childhood in poverty. Hawkins recounted that his father died when he was in high school, compelling him to drop out of private school and go to work to support his mother. The mix of youthful independence and a paycheck may have contributed to his troubled adolescence in a Chicago street gang, and he claimed that he developed a costly drug addiction before his sixteenth birthday. Hawkins credited his working at an uncle's McDonald's franchise as salvific, giving him the requisite knowledge of the industry that would change his life. Determined to make something of himself, Hawkins left behind the vagaries of street life and immersed himself in the whirlwind of fast food. His first stop was Kentucky Fried Chicken, where he rose through the ranks to work with the franchise on its minority recruitment efforts. Kentucky Fried Chicken had long boasted its partnership with All-Pro Chicken founder Brady Keys, who sold his franchise to Kentucky Fried Chicken and acquired his own four locations in 1970.[28] In the late 1980s, Hawkins departed Kentucky Fried Chicken to enter franchising himself. He was part of a financial development group, contracted to build a dozen Bojangles' Famous Chicken 'n Biscuits restaurants in the Northeast. Many of the outlets of the North Carolina–based chicken franchise went under,

but Hawkins exited Bojangles without any major financial losses. He then returned to his roots: burgers.[29]

Between 1991 and 1996, Hawkins introduced Checkers on the East Coast, with locations in Washington, D.C., Baltimore, and Philadelphia. Checkers was a relative newcomer to the fast food family system, and its merger with Rally's, founded a year earlier in 1985, brought the drive-thru concept to cities on both coasts and points in the middle. Hawkins's deal with Checkers was one of the first major moves for the La-Van Hawkins Inner City Foods company. For his goal of making black millionaires via franchising, Hawkins was lauded in the press for establishing Checkers in some of the most economically devastated communities and providing well-paying jobs to local youth. He boasted to *Nation's Restaurant News*: "I'm in the unique position to take people off welfare, give them job training, and educate and motivate them."[30] Taking people off of welfare was an oft-repeated goal of CEOs and politicians. President Bill Clinton's historic Personal Responsibility and Work Opportunity Reconciliation Act of 1996 limited the length of time a person could receive state-funded public assistance and often required workforce participation to receive benefits. This shift funneled many former aid recipients into fast food and other service sector jobs.[31] These efforts definitely employed people, but education and motivation may have been scarce.

Hawkins's promises were in the same vein of the black franchisees who converted gang members into crew members in the early 1970s and brought much-needed jobs to Chicago, Detroit, and Los Angeles after the uprisings of the 1960s. But job creation in black communities in the 1990s was contending with conditions even more vexing than those of 1968. New fast food restaurants were settling in and around neighborhoods devastated by the introduction of crack cocaine into the urban drug market and greater efforts to police and incarcerate blacks in an ongoing War on Drugs. The war created casualties in black America.[32] The urgency of providing relief to neighborhoods eviscerated by decades of poverty may have inspired so much hope and relief that Hawkins's promises did not meet scrutiny from the private investors, public officials, and

community partners who entrusted Hawkins with so many millions and millions of dollars.

While most cities rolled out the red carpet for Hawkins's Checkers, Hawkins's return to Philadelphia was not welcomed. Fresh memories of the abandoned Bojangles experiment from the 1980s summoned more fury than fanfare. When locals learned that Hawkins had leased a location (complete with a sign that alerted: "Another La-Van Hawkins Checkers Coming Soon") at the intersection of Broad and Girard Streets, the community made its feelings clear. Members of the Girard and Broad Business Association repeated some of the concerns voiced by Ogontz decades earlier. In addition to the usual worries about saturation and public safety, Hawkins's involvement was a major point of contention. He didn't meet with the association prior to seeking approval for the Checkers, known for its double drive-thru architecture, making it a greater traffic generator than traditional fast food places. Checkers officials entrusted Hawkins to deal with the opposition without them, and they were unmoved by the arguments against Hawkins's leadership and the neighborhood's existing goals. To add insult to Hawkins's history of injuries, residents initially believed that Checkers was black-owned, a common misconception due to Hawkins's profile and the chain's inner-city locations. The misunderstanding may have also emerged from the way Hawkins indicated, or misrepresented, his franchise leases as ownership. In 1993, Hawkins's actual ownership stake was 25% of three Atlanta locations and another 25% claim on five locations in Philadelphia.[33] Hawkins opened a Washington, D.C., location with a far warmer welcome, but his promise to add ten more stores to the area never materialized. His investments were not the only issue that raised eyebrows. With every interview he granted to the press, and every contact he made in the industry, Hawkins's backstory changed ever so slightly. Was he really the youngest McDonald's manager ever? Was he 16 or 11 when he started working at McDonald's? Hawkins's claims were inconsistent at best, but the most important question was, would he really help black America as much as he said he would?

At the start of 1996, Hawkins was preparing to move again,

this time leaving behind a sinking Checkers brand and selling his franchises back to the parent company and whoever wanted the dozens of store locations Hawkins acquired in the South and the East. Hawkins was on to higher climes with a new fast food company, and he was making friends. Hawkins was meeting with fellow fast food enthusiast President Bill Clinton. In a ceremony celebrating Clinton's rendition of the federal Empowerment Zone program, a collection of initiatives to fight unemployment, business loss, and other critical needs in blighted areas. Cities—via economic development councils and community-development corporations—submitted proposals based on the neediness of sections of their cities and towns, and "winners" could offer tax breaks, job-training programs, and other enticements to business to move into the zone. Competitions in 1994, 1998, and 2001 brought hundreds of millions of dollars into the cities, and a later program extension allowed for additional funding schemes until the program formally ended in 2013.[34] Hawkins joined the CEO of Burger King to announce their commitment to open 25 outlets in black neighborhoods, which would be the start of something even bigger for Hawkins. Hawkins claimed that he would eventually build 225 restaurants in the inner city. For the second-largest fast food burger chain, the ceremony was part of a *mea culpa* of sorts, forced from the corporation as part of an Operation PUSH settlement to bring more business to black suppliers and contractors, as well as boost the number of minority franchisees.

While Clinton offered the nation a series of programs aimed at reducing the number of welfare recipients, he presented the private sector with an expanse of tax breaks and subsidies.

> The solutions to America's real challenges, economic and social challenges, have got to be community driven. The private sector has got to be an integral part. The Government—it's not like the Depression—the Government is broke. We have some money to invest in education and training, to invest in environmental protection, to invest in new technologies, to invest in infrastructure, but we got to get rid of this deficit. So we can't go out and just hire

everybody that doesn't have a job. The private sector has got to do that. And we have to have the right kind of partnership to get them involved . . . [35]

The Empowerment Zones included the same geographic areas that were studied by riot commissions in 1968, received Fair Share–brokered businesses in 1984, and became the new magnets for federal dollars and tax breaks under the Empowerment Zone program, which resided in the Department of Housing and Urban Development (HUD). As historian Chin Jou has noted in her research on the relationship between the federal government and the fast food industry, the Empowerment Zones "were a recycled initiative under a new name."[36] The 1994 "winners" included economically depressed areas of Atlanta, Baltimore, Chicago, Detroit, New York, and the Philadelphia-Camden metro area as well as rural locales such as the Kentucky Highlands, the Mid-Delta in Mississippi, and the Rio Grande Valley. The secondary competition program offered funds to Los Angeles and Cleveland.[37] A 2005 yearbook of successful Empowerment Zone projects included a roster of fast food favorites. The report heralded a grant of more than $230,000 for a Popeyes franchise's rehabilitation project and tax subsidies for the thirty-five local people employed at the restaurant. A black-franchised Wendy's in Columbus, Ohio, also enjoyed the tax credit provision for employing local people. The list of franchises benefiting from additional funding included a Cold Stone Creamery, a Moe's Southwest Grill, a Pizzeria Uno, a Chili's Bar & Grill in the "economically distressed" Overtown neighborhood of Miami, and a Gary, Indiana, Bennigan's pub.[38] Fast food seized on the moment and focused on building its own power rather than changing the features of its industry. Taxpayer subsidies helped establish and maintain fast food restaurants, and welfare reform helped supply applicants for low-wage jobs. Communities, in theory, would be able to determine what they needed and wanted, but in practice the investments were determined by the types of businesses that saw the poor, urban community as a viable consumer market.

At the White House ceremony featuring Hawkins and announcing his partnership with Burger King, Clinton complimented HUD Secretary Henry Cisneros for making ends meet with a shrinking budget and then pledged $3.5 billion in federal monies and tax breaks to the private sector. In a statement about the event, Burger King called the partnership a renewal of its "commitment to minority development."[39] The Burger King deal drew an even brighter spotlight onto Hawkins. A *Newsweek* profile highlighted his "half-million-dollar grants to church foundations and school programs" and his appearance on the dais of the Million Man March, where he "preached his personal gospel of black self-help." Hawkins believed himself to be modern-day black America's great benefactor and statesman in the mold of Booker T. Washington. He underwrote Cirque du Soul, the popular black circus that toured throughout the country in the late 1990s and early 2000s. His wealth made him a minor celebrity and he socialized with a higher-profile crowd each year. In the spring of 1997, he joined Louis Farrakhan to assist in negotiating a ceasefire after the murder of rapper Biggie Smalls in Los Angeles.[40] La-Van Hawkins was indeed everywhere.

Burger King gave Hawkins critical latitude with his locations and his business development company, allowing him to make changes as he saw fit and acquire other franchises while holding the leases on more than two dozen Burger King locations. Burger King said nothing about Hawkins displaying a portrait of himself on his outdoor drive-thru menus. Or perhaps Hawkins merely acted first and asked permission later. What was clear was that a Hawkins-franchised restaurant was different, and it resonated with black customers. The Hawkins touch on a Burger King was the embodiment of decades of fast food's investment on how to reach black consumers. At Hawkins's franchises you could think you were buying authentically black, you were supporting jobs in your community, and you were eating food tailored for you. Hawkins introduced Cajun fries and banana milkshakes to his Burger King menus and got rid of onion rings and salads. Burger King later amended his changes, but they claimed only "to improve the ideas." Over the

course of a year between 1996 and 1997, Hawkins built 25 Burger Kings, many of them Express locations designed to do only drive-thru business, a measure believed to protect staff from crime and serve areas where residents relied on cars. He was making changes at his other places, too. For the 60 Perkins Family Restaurants he claimed he would bring into his portfolio, Hawkins wanted to infuse a little soul into the chain founded in Cincinnati in 1958 to serve up hot pancakes and coffee. Hawkins promised to add "ribs, pork chops, Southern-fried chicken, macaroni-and-cheese, and black-eyed peas" to the menu.[41] In 1998, Hawkins established Wolverine Pizza, LLC, and moved his operation from Baltimore to Detroit so that he could take possession of 8 Pizza Huts, in a deal that was the beginning of his acquisition of 89 Pizza Hut restaurants across the state of Michigan. In typical Hawkins fashion he left the Charm City with no fewer than 12 lawsuits for "unpaid services and breach of contract . . . in monetary claims from $31,000 to $14 million."[42]

While Hawkins was presiding over grand openings and reopenings across Detroit, the question of equity in the fast food industry persisted among potential franchisee and civil rights groups. Although the NAACP, PUSH, and other organizations that facilitated the recruitment of black franchisees were sometimes on retainer as consultants, the process was not seamless. Questions remained across the franchise industry. In the summer of 1997, a group of black franchisees took their concerns public and asked why, among the more than 5,000 KFC stores in the United States, did only 70 belong to African Americans? After Popeyes acquired Church's Chicken, why did the parent company put more resources into promoting Church's at the expense of its black Popeyes franchisees? While racial discrimination issues regarding Denny's, where Secret Service members were refused service, captured most headlines, the franchise world was embroiled in a less public debate.[43] Kentucky Fried Chicken's Office of Minority and Governmental Affairs claimed that it was difficult to convince people to invest in the inner city. He pointed to "an African American owner in Detroit" who cashed out and reestablished his business elsewhere.

In Detroit, the Wayne County executive said companies such as KFC used crime statistics as a smoke screen. Businesses were doing just fine. "According to the FBI reports, crime is down in Detroit. But all you have to do is look at La-Van Hawkins Burger Kings and McDonald's and you can see that fast food franchises are operating well."[44]

While large-scale programs were able to help franchise companies meet their aggressive goals sooner, they still needed the traditional franchise recruitment and development that helped build their consumer base in the urban market. In the 1990s, the Kentucky Fried Chicken minority financing program offered "95% of the total cost of the franchise" and exempted applicants from the personal finance requirement of possessing a net worth of $400,000 and $150,000 of liquid cash. Applicants of color only needed to prove that they could front 10% of the fees, between $65,000 and $75,000.[45] Twelve years after the Fair Share agreement, KFC was still struggling to make good on its promises. A national boycott was planned for late November 1994. Louis Coleman Jr., a leader with the Justice Resource Center of Kentucky, listed the issues he heard from franchisees: rundown restaurants, pay disparities between blacks and whites, repercussions for hiring too many employees of color, few store managers of color, and problems with PepsiCo, the owner of KFC. Employees accused a manager of telling them that suburban stores paid their employees more for the same work because "kids in the suburbs don't have to work."

On the other side of the issue were members of the Executive Leadership Council, an organization of senior-level executives from different corporations, who sided with PepsiCo. Coleman's earlier negotiation with KFC indicated that food quality and nutrition were slowly entering the conversation about the industry's responsibilities to communities. "We met with Walt Simon (KFC's vice president–minority business development) and he made a commitment that 35% African Americans would be placed in management positions in inner city stores in Louisville and promised salad bars in inner city stores," stated Reverend Coleman. "Nothing has been done." He also said that the minority franchising schemes

ensnared optimistic franchisees and they were often "set up to fail." Attorneys for a group of KFC franchisees in Yuba City, California, who filed a grievance against the chicken chain argued that "the whole thing could have been resolved at the cost of the chicken they throw out every week."[46]

While Kentucky Fried Chicken was struggling to use franchising as an inroad into the inner city, Hawkins was working his magic in Detroit. With the Checkers issue behind him, Hawkins became a local hero with his Burger King outlets. His connections to the city's mayors, religious leaders, and business communities could have protected him from questions about what happened in Philadelphia, Baltimore, Washington, D.C., Atlanta, where the loathed name La-Van Hawkins was associated with checks bounced, drive-thrus closed suddenly, or entire staffs left unemployed. Locals didn't care what happened on the East Coast, they knew what was happening in Detroit, and the promise of two hundred more La-Van Hawkins stores coupled with his Pizza Hut franchises made Hawkins a top employer of black youth in a city that had suffered the worst of deindustrialization and depopulation. In true Hawkins fashion, his relationship with Burger King eventually began to sour. Bills weren't being paid, and Burger King wanted their stores back. Burger King argued that Hawkins had falsely represented their expansion agreement and refuted his claim that they had entrusted him with developing hundreds of new stores. Citing the expiration of his franchise leases due to failure to pay rent, Burger King announced that Hawkins was in violation of trademark laws in continuing the operation of his locations. Burger King was in the process of seeking new franchisees for his locations, and they had to figure out how to take care of the hundreds of employees still working at his stores.[47] This was a matter of money.

Hawkins was not accustomed to backing down without a spectacular fight, and he matched Burger King's lawsuit with his own. Hawkins countersued for nearly $2 billion, claiming that Burger King had used him "as a pawn to make them look good to black people and black leaders," and then retaliated when he became too successful.[48] The allegations hurled from the two camps read like

fodder more suited for a gossip column than for the business pages. Hawkins had shored up the urban market for Burger King, and they didn't appreciate that he did the very thing that they had asked him to do: connect with his consumer base, a loyal base for the fast food industry. The customizations may have been "too ethnic" for Burger King, but they resonated with black Detroiters. He flew black, green, and red black-liberation flags over American flags at the store. He hired Nation of Islam members—decked in their signature black sunglasses and shirts advertising that they were F.O.I. or Fruit of Islam—as security. The R&B hits that replaced the Muzak in the restaurant was sometimes piped outside and inside. What was wrong with that? He charged that Burger King's racially discriminatory practices were limiting his ability to expand his own franchise kingdom.[49] Unlike Charles Griffis and the other franchisees before him, Hawkins's claims to be on his way to building hundreds of more franchises made his argument unconvincing. Yet, Hawkins's case provided the opening for civil rights groups to insert themselves in a dispute with Burger King again, which cemented more opportunity for their members and associates to enter franchising.

Boycott and protest are critical actions to expanding opportunities for marginalized groups. Yet, by the 2000s, the fast food industry knew that these measures would yield concessions that ultimately benefited them in that they brought more franchisees of color into the parts of the country that were the riskiest and most profitable. If fast food companies could withstand the sting of a little bad press, agreements like the ones that brought Hawkins to Burger King franchising were not too bad after all. It was as if there were two keys that opened the door to opportunity for blacks. One of them was the uprising and the other, the national boycott. On the other side of that door, however, was a plethora of low-wage jobs and a few people able to get rich.

With the lawsuits filed and the accusations flying, Hawkins made himself available for press interviews so he could take his case to the American public. A 2000 profile on Hawkins's struggle with Burger King described him as a "folk hero in the inner cities," who

treated his customers to "thumping hip hop and Motown music, inside and out." He added: "I've proven I know how to create jobs and opportunities for them," he said. "They trust me."[50] Hawkins may have had questionable business acumen, but there was no uncertainty that he was a consummate entertainer. When Burger King filed suit against Hawkins, he enlisted the equally charismatic and verbose attorney Johnnie Cochran, of the O. J. Simpson murder trial, and National Action Network's Al Sharpton for assistance. Sharpton's siding with Hawkins may have initially seemed a low-stakes gesture considering the good Reverend had long been involved in boycotts of corporations, police departments, and U.S. government policy. Boycott was second nature to the New Yorker, whose reputation loomed large over organizations nervous about their record on minority hiring or embroiled in racial scandal. Evoking Sharpton conjured up an image of picketing, followed by dealmaking. Corporations did not want to have to give into Sharpton, but they knew he had a platform, and so did he. Sharpton called for a regional boycott of Burger King in September of 2000 based on Hawkins's claims, and he organized pickets of New York franchise locations that October.[51]

The Burger King issue actually put Sharpton at odds with his friend and colleague Jesse Jackson, who had negotiated a Fair Share plan with Burger King in the 1980s. Jackson argued that Hawkins was the one who had acted in bad faith, and even if that Reverend saw merits in Hawkins's case, he could not betray Burger King. The path of corporate negotiation for civil rights groups may have expanded the field of possibilities for black businesspeople, banks, insurance companies, and advertising agencies, as well as minimumwage employees, but it ultimately bound up the ways that these organizations deployed their activism while settlements and deals were being implemented. The rift not only put Hawkins at odds with Burger King, but it also triangulated black America's Three Kings of Black Empowerment: La-Van Hawkins, Jesse Jackson, and Al Sharpton. The fight, intensified by their own feelings about how much access they had to the Clinton White House, led both Jackson and Sharpton to spend a year taking jabs at each other.

Sharpton believed this was a matter of where they existed in the civil rights leadership orbit. "Our conflict is also definitely generational," Sharpton, who is thirteen years Jackson's junior, said. "There is a younger voter that Jesse can't reach, that I can. Poor folks in the projects. The hip-hop generation . . . Jesse doesn't have the defiance I have."[52]

Sharpton's defiance-fueled boycott, supported by the Nation of Islam, didn't get too far, nor did Hawkins's lawsuit. A few months after talk of a boycott, a judge dismissed Hawkins's $1.9 billion lawsuit against Burger King. In the winter of 2000, the New York State Supreme Court had the final say, ruling that Hawkins and his business entities owed Burger King's affiliated entity, Franchise Acceptance Corporation, the company's lending arm, $8.4 million.[53] At the start of the new year in 2001, Burger King settled with Hawkins, who initially estimated his debts at $6.5 million in unpaid fees, rent, and supplier invoices. Burger King agreed to take back twenty-three of his twenty-five franchise locations. Apologies were also exchanged between the two clergymen that year. Burger King's battle with Hawkins exemplified the way that franchising had become so imbricated in black life and culture that his defenders ranged from Sharpton to fruitarian Dick Gregory and other black leaders beholden to Hawkins's commitment to black charities, especially for children and education.[54] After agreeing to an undisclosed payout, an only slightly chastened Hawkins told the press, "Burger King and I have shaken hands, and I wish them all the best of luck. I'm still spending their money and enjoying my luck."[55] But Hawkins's luck ran out rather quickly, and he eventually lost his Pizza Hut franchises, fine-dining restaurants in downtown Detroit, and his jazz club.

In the years following the Burger King debacle, Hawkins was inexplicably able to acquire more franchises, and each came with higher risk, few community rewards, and more legal trouble. As he did in the Motor City, Hawkins promised that his ventures would bring jobs and dollars to black communities, and with each agreement executed, he reified the idea that fast food not only had a special place in black America, but could do the work of

transformation. In 2004, he returned to court to respond to corruption charges stemming from serving as a go-between for fraudulent activity between a Philadelphia attorney and Detroit's city treasurer. The indictment revealed that Hawkins was part of a scheme to purchase one hundred Church's Chicken locations, then resell them back to the parent company.[56] For his role in the plot, Hawkins received a sentence of nearly three years in jail and was ordered to pay $25,000 in restitution. As he arranged to report to a Duluth, Minnesota, correctional facility, he was served a separate set of papers from a Chicago-based Italian beef and pizza franchise for bouncing checks and failing to pay vendors.[57] After serving eighteen months of his jail term, Hawkins was embroiled in yet another municipal scandal; this time it involved Detroit's "hip-hop mayor," Kwame Kilpatrick, who was forced to resign from office after pleading guilty to obstruction-of-justice charges.[58] In August of 2007, Hawkins was found guilty of wire fraud and perjury and received a twenty-two-month prison sentence for his role in a Detroit bribery and conspiracy case involving local businessmen.[59]

After disappointing and imperiling his employees and charities, serving multiple prison sentences for fraud, and having been exposed as untrustworthy, Hawkins maintained that ultimately black indifference sunk his enterprises. Hawkins traded in the specious, but well-worn, claim that the economic problems of black America stemmed from its failure to invest in itself. When newspapers interviewed black business owners who could not match the high discounts that major retailers could offer, they blamed black customers for not supporting their own. Rarely did these reports explore why black customers had to be so price-conscious. If a black business was destroyed in an uprising, then the conclusion was that blacks don't value their own people's businesses. Few of the conversations lingered on why people were so upset. When La-Van Hawkins deceived scores of people in the nation's most vulnerable neighborhoods, few asked how in the world he had the power to do this. When times were good and cash was flush, Hawkins had the solution to what afflicted black America—jobs at his franchise restaurants. But, after he was held accountable for the

financial mismanagement of his stores, he argued that it was franchising itself that was the problem, and that blacks on the whole did not know how to achieve financial freedom because they were tethered to the white benevolence of the industry. In a postprison interview with a local Detroit television show *American Entrepreneur*, Hawkins claimed that he had finally seen the light. From his telling, his newfound independence from franchising represented his greater commitment to empowering black communities. "We give away 95 cents of every dollar . . . the shackles have been put on our mind . . . We allow every dollar . . . to leave our community."[60] Hawkins hinted that he had spent his prison term dreaming up new franchise concepts that could ensure that the black dollar didn't go anywhere. Using this "common sense" diagnosis of the black condition and echoing the sentiments expressed by Charles Griffis after he left McDonald's franchising, Hawkins offered that his new franchise concept, Sweet Georgia Brown restaurants, was not only going to provide black economic freedom, but would also decolonize the black consumer mind. The critiques of these franchises as falling short of authentically allowing customers to "buy black" still swirled, but those voices were dampened by the praise for the industry from civil rights organizations, local economic development councils, and the White House. Soon after he did the interview on liberating black consciousness, Hawkins was convicted of tax evasion, and the court gave him a ten-month sentence and an order to pay back $5.7 million.[61] Despite the jail time and the declining reputation, Hawkins—the king of reinvention—hadn't turned his back on franchising entirely.[62] In 2018, a company associated with Hawkins had applied to bring twenty Habit Burger Grill franchises to the Midwest. Hawkins did not live to see the plan emerge; he died on April 6, 2019. *Crain's Detroit Business* described him as "a one-time fast food franchise mogul, restaurateur and controversial figure."[63]

Decades of failed attempts to use capitalism as a balm, a shield, or an antidote to the sting, force, and toxicity of racism has failed to change the narrative that what ailing communities need most are fast-food restaurants. On the whole, black franchisees have

tried to provide stop-gap measures to employ people, provide them with peripheral community programs, and leverage their influence for broader black achievement. There is no doubt that some difference has been made. For black women like Janice Baker, a McDonald's manager in Dallas, Texas, her time working for a former NBMOA chairman allowed her to create a stable, middle-class life after her husband died. Baker takes pride in hiring people who would not otherwise have access to employment because of prior felony convictions or a lack of experience. The longtime McDonald's manager also appreciates the opportunity to work for a black boss, franchisee Roland Parrish, after experiencing racism in the workplace. Parrish has given generously to Fisk University and his alma mater Purdue University, local youth sports programs, and has employed thousands at his more than twenty McDonald's restaurants. To ignore the positive impacts of franchise networks among communities of color that appreciate their contributions would be shortsighted. It is equally shortsighted to ignore the government subsidies, civil rights organization endorsements, limited community resources, and economic desperation that supports the dubious idea that fast food—and business on the whole—can solely, or even substantively or singularly, breathe life into an underdeveloped community.

If the fast food industry was concerned that hucksters like La-Van Hawkins would endanger their rapid-growth strategies and the fulfillment of lingering Fair Share–style deals, then they may have elevated the vetting process for new franchisees, or simply returned to their roots in recruiting high-profile, and ostensibly cash-rich, celebrities to enter multiunit franchising contracts. Founded by the Los Angeles Lakers star in 1987, Magic Johnson Enterprises began after he made relatively modest investments in retail stores and a couple of radio stations. A few years later, he partnered with *Black Enterprise* founder Earl G. Graves to acquire a Pepsi-Cola distribution outfit, a franchise opportunity that was slower to expand to African Americans than fast food. Graves and Johnson's purchase of a Washington, D.C., area bottler in 1990 was believed to be a first for investors of color for Pepsi. The men

were receiving a more lucrative financial opportunity than a franchisee.[64] Johnson Enterprises expanded over the following decades
with cobranded outlets of movie theatres created by the Johnson
Development Corporation, hundreds of Starbucks coffee stores,
TGI Fridays restaurants, dozens of Burger Kings, and Fatburger
locations.[65] Johnson's franchises were located in diverse communities from South Los Angeles to Harlem, but whether he was selling
movie tickets or milkshakes, the promise of bringing jobs to where
they were needed made these massive, and often Empowerment
Zone–funded, projects welcomed additions to blocks that may
have already had more than their fill of fast-food joints but where
jobs were always needed. Yet, like the business owners who bristled at the Small Business Administration programs that promised to rebuild Watts in the 1960s and failed to even communicate
with Watts, not every community felt these initiatives were indeed
magic. Johnson argued he was bringing "retail justice" to people
long denied the opportunity to keep their black dollars inside of
black neighborhoods, but one observer believed that in South
Los Angeles—and by extension all the places that Johnson set up
shop and sometimes closed the shops when they were deemed too
difficult to operate or not as profitable as he had hoped—people
wanted "real justice."[66]

While some people wondered if retail justice was a worthy
goal, growing concerns about food justice were also emerging
among public conversations about the wealth and health of black
America. By the time Hawkins was singing the praises of a pizza
and breadstick combo and Magic Johnson's name was on everything from fries to Frappuccinos in the inner city, the nation was
well aware of the long-term impacts of a diet filled with food rich
in fats. In 1988, Surgeon General of the United States C. Everett
Koop published the results of his office's first study of the relationship between diet and chronic disease. The report highlighted that "Black Americans, for example, have higher rates of
high blood pressure, strokes, diabetes, and other diseases associated with obesity . . . than the general population."[67] Subsequent
research studies and surgeons general would discourage overin-

dulgence in fast food, and public health practitioners would provide suggestions on modifying fast food–dependent diets. These interventions were important in helping the nation to make more discerning choices about what to eat. In the constant evaluation of black health as jeopardized, many public health advocates fixated on food choices and acknowledged the disproportionate numbers of fast food locations in black neighborhoods. But, few made the connection with the federal government's concentrated, sustained efforts to bring more and more fast food into the inner city, nor did they see the handiwork of the civil rights authorities in sanctioning the process.

While accusations that racist, corporate greed fueled fast food's proliferation in the inner city were not inaccurate, the other actors that could be appealed to for catalyzing the corporation were rarely made visible. Rallying against fast food companies for endangering black health was a start. The campaigns organized on behalf of fast food workers that materialized as the Fight for $15 to raise the minimum wage were another way of taking up the problems created by fast food in poor communities. In 2012, the same year that Fight for $15 commenced, the National Labor Relations Board determined that fast food companies are coemployers with fast food franchisees, and therefore they share the responsibility in adjudicating wage disputes. This decision came after labor activists in the Fight for $15 movement alleged workers were fired and intimidated for their organizing activities. Six years later, in 2018, the NLRB allowed McDonald's to settle the issue and the company admitted no wrongdoing. Overseas, McDonald's workers have organized unions, but the fast food industry relied on the franchise issue to keep collective groups out of their restaurants. The transition from a Democrat to a Republican in the White House endangered the ruling, and activists are concerned that settlements further obscure the problem of wages and workers' rights.[68]

Perhaps the most vexing work may come in reconciling fast food's nonfood, nonwork properties, namely its very association with feelings of black pride, belief in community investment, and response in times of crisis. As historian Bethany Moreton has dis-

covered in her research on Wal-Mart and its ability to fuse fervent Christianity with ferocious, free-market capitalism, Wal-Mart does not explicitly call itself a Christian company. Rather, Moreton effectively proves, Wal-Mart provided the terrain in which a "particular strain of "family values" Christianity . . . met mass consumption . . ."[69] By no means is McDonald's a "black" company per se, but its ability to use the tropes of blackness skillfully and to leverage its black franchisees in the service of proximity to black communities provides a worthy, and insightful, entry point into thinking about racialized health disparities in the service of eradicating them. The affective is effective, and there is no way of staving off the influence of fast food in vulnerable communities without recognizing this poignant and unsettling fact.

* * *

Twenty years after the Los Angeles uprising, residents near South Van Ness Avenue celebrated the opening of a Food 4 Less. The store opened less than a mile from the intersection where truck driver Reginal Denny was beaten by a group of young men. The crowds that gathered to check out the discount grocer may have thought about Denny that day before they perused the produce section or evaluated the bakery's offerings. One appreciative shopper said the store and the accompanying projects in the Chesterfield Square Plaza "provided jobs, a lot of jobs, for our youngsters to keep them off the street . . . Some of them are minimum wage, but that's better than nothing."[70] At present, there are two McDonald's restaurants within a mile of the grocery store, as well as a Wingstop, Pizza Hut, Taco Bell, and KFC. This was not what was promised in 1992, but it was appreciated in 2012. South Los Angeles, like the other sections of U.S. cities of the 1960s and '70s that were noticed only after their businesses and community centers disappeared, had waited and waited for change to come. In its wake, they got more fast food and fewer options.

Below the surface of the energetic conversations about rebuilding Los Angeles and the swelling of the Miracle of the Golden Arches, there were doubts and questions. A former Korean busi-

ness owner who left Los Angeles after the uprising believed that the focus of the recovery was misguided. The head of the Korean American Grocers Association observed: "The rich and poor gap is getting bigger. That is the reason for riots. The job is not done with getting a McDonald's there. It is the unemployment."[71] Even the restaurant industry was willing to concede that it was a fallacy to rely on service sector jobs to lead the way forward. *Nation's Restaurant News* warned: "No one expects the restaurant industry to pioneer an economic renaissance of our inner cities. After all, only so many service businesses can hope to exist in locales where disposable income so often consists of welfare checks, food stamps and the limited rewards of dead-end jobs." One of Los Angeles's few independent black restaurant owners agreed. Multigenerational poverty would only be solved through "jobs for the upcoming generation that will be meaningful, so that they can educate their kids properly."

Despite the critiques, the magazine also presented its own version of the Golden Arches miracle with an anecdote about "the survival of a franchised Denny's under construction in Watts" that was "protected from looters and arsonists by residents who recognized the restaurant and its surrounding shopping center as a nucleus of opportunity for the long-blighted neighborhood."[72] No matter how many times the Miracle was repeated and amplified as the perfect case study in why corporate community investment could pay off, the notion that fast food would save communities was a leap of faith some were unwilling to take. Integral to the post–Los Angeles rebuilding process was a gang truce supplemented with greater economic opportunities, but a new generation of South Los Angeles residents knew that prosperity after peace would require serious investment in an expansion of good employment. As one former gang member put it, "Now that the killing has stopped, there are no jobs." He added: "People are standing around wondering what is next. We have to support our families . . . We need some long-term jobs, not McDonald's," he said.[73] Rebuild L.A., the organization tasked with redeveloping the battered city, fell short of its own lofty goals. Bernard Kinsey, the cochair of Rebuild

L.A., characterized the inner city as littered with "liquor stores and funeral homes," and "every other retail establishment is looking at a potential gold mine in the neglected areas."[74] Another publication put it more simply: "The Crips and Bloods held up their part of the bargain, Rebuild LA did not hold up theirs."[75]

In addition to jobs, the issue of supermarkets became less and less avoidable. The Crenshaw neighborhood mourned the loss of beauty shops in their community after the uprising but hoped the new development plans would not only rebuild the salons, but also bring in badly needed grocers and affordable retailers. "It's not that there's anything wrong with the beauty shops themselves," explained the executive director of the Crenshaw Chamber of Commerce. "What we have is not enough supermarkets."[76] The supermarkets eventually came, in small numbers and of varying quality, to South Los Angeles. They also came to Chicago's South Side, Washington, D.C.'s U Street corridor, and the other centers that were obliterated in the 1960s, and, in some cases, the 1990s. The new supermarkets were at times a sign of gentrification, and in other cases actual attempts to serve the local market. Regardless of the motivations and circumstances surrounding their arrivals, supermarkets could not adequately address the myriad problems that led to the development of retail at the exclusion of public housing and services, the distribution of low-wage jobs, and the subsidizing of tax breaks for business. But at the very least they provided an avenue to improve nutritional choice in communities flooded with fast food restaurants.

With the benefit of more research on fast food, race, and nutrition, as well as the addition of words like "food desert" in the national lexicon of inequality, Los Angeles political and business leaders tried to find creative solutions to health disparities that had worsened since the uprising. In 2007, Los Angeles City Councilwoman Jan Perry proposed a moratorium on new fast food restaurants in South Los Angeles for two years in order to promote better health in the area. Perry framed the issue in terms of the rising health care costs among her residents, who she claimed had "higher incidence of diseases that doctors link to

obesity than the rest of the city and the county." Nearly half of all restaurants serving the 700,000 residents of South Los Angeles were fast food outlets. On Los Angeles's richer and whiter West Side, only 12% of dining options fell under the fast food category. The initiative challenged the long-held notion that any business was good business in low-income communities, and while a two-year halt would not eliminate existing restaurants, the failed proposal revealed how much of the fast food problem was linked to individuals with limited choices. An opponent of the plan argued that this was not a matter of market saturation, but of overcoming nutritional ignorance. "We have to teach inner-city kids how to eat or they will find the less healthy foods even at the better restaurants," reifying the notion that better nutritional information could disrupt the deep bonds that the industry had forged with black consumers. In the press coverage of the proposal, newspapers also noted that the dilemma of fast food was also a matter of failed attempts to mediate the problems of the uprising. "After the Rodney King riots in 1992 devastated these neighborhoods," the *Christian Science Monitor* reported, "officials promised more supermarkets and restaurants . . . But for a variety of reasons, that has not happened."[77]

Black capitalism's progeny—public-private partnership and economic empowerment—was welcomed into black communities with the same mix of hopefulness and skepticism as its ancestors. An array of researchers and scholars have examined whether Empowerment Zone (EZ) initiatives paid off in terms of rates of poverty, economic growth, and unemployment. In one of the more sanguine assessments, urban studies scholars found that although "several EZ cities produced improvements in their distressed neighborhoods . . . The gains were modest." They concluded that "none of the local EZ programs fundamentally transformed distressed urban neighborhoods."[78] With varied levels of funding, the federal Empowerment Zone program was geared to engage the private sector and was one of a number of supposedly race-neutral, lean-government, bi-sector ideas that captured the attention of post-1968 political leaders. The language and rhetoric of black capitalism became the framework

of empowerment. With the departure from black capitalism came a resounding endorsement of the Empowerment Zone idea. Imported from the United Kingdom in the era of Thatcherism, conservatives from Ronald Reagan to Jack Kemp welcomed this free market solution. "Those who view poverty and unemployment as permanent afflictions of our cities fail to understand how rapidly the poor can move up the ladder of success in our economy," Reagan said during his bid for the White House, "but to move up the ladder, they must first get on it. And this is the concept behind the enterprise zones."[79] As nebulous as black capitalism was as a goal for an earlier generation, empowerment was just as hard to capture. Who was to be empowered? And could power be held by many, not just one? These were the questions that remained unanswered, if uttered at all, as Hawkins and his cadre in fast food found a new way to link federal investment in business with black people's investment in seeing blacks succeed in their communities, sometimes without meditating on the consequences for too long.

The idea of financially sound black institutions is alluring across the ideological spectrum because it allows white conservatives and liberals alike to claim plausible deniability in their role in supporting systems and policies that maintain racial capitalism. Whether it's called black capitalism or empowerment, the politics of black business can serve many interests, except for those of blacks most susceptible to the extremes of capitalism and racism. Historian of black banks Mehrsa Baradaran describes the pull of supporting black economic empowerment as binding unlikely partners. "On the right, the myth that capitalism can fix what racist state policy created . . . on the left, it's the idea that microcredit can fix macro injustices."[80] The label "black-owned" obscures the multiple systems that are not only outside of the hands of people of color, but will never be truly accessible under capitalism.

In some rare instances, chefs and entrepreneurs have tried to "hack" the fast food formula and make healthy fast food.[81] LocoL, the experiment in low-cost, healthy food by Roy Choi, the Korean-American food truck king of Southern California, and double Michelin star holder Daniel Patterson has been lauded for its creative

foods and desire to address the challenge of affordability and nutrition. LocoL offered tofu burgers, whole-wheat tortilla sandwiches, and juices alongside quesadillas and burgers, made from carefully sourced ingredients sold by local vendors. Meals were priced to compete with the extra-value-meal crowd. People from the neighborhood were hired.[82] LocoL's multiple locations experienced challenges. The downtown Oakland restaurant closed after thirteen months in business, and the Watts location and a scaled- back Oakland outpost required several tweaks to address the lack of profitability.[83] Choi and Patterson have emphasized that the goal of the initiative is not to make money, but to create a community resource.[84] In a departure from the methods of the Empowerment Zone, LocoL relied on a mix of private investment and crowdfunding, a twenty-first-century way of funneling the public's funds directly to projects (in addition to the tax breaks and incentives still enjoyed by businesses that move to poor areas). LocoL's debut was held on the 2016 celebration of Martin Luther King Jr. Day. Black capitalism's indefatigable advocate Jim Brown was on hand to cut the ribbon. The event's soundtrack featured King's "I Have a Dream" speech and the Black Lives Matter movement's informal anthem, Kendrick Lamar's "Alright." The past was the present. A newspaper report described the grand opening in Watts this way: "Like other economically depressed communities without access to fresh food, its citizens are at increased risk of obesity and its attendant ailments: heart disease, stroke, high-blood pressure, diabetes, cancer." Like other economically depressed communities without access to choices, the people of Watts, still hoping to dissociate their neighborhood's name from racial chaos, held their breaths and hoped that this time, things would be different. The restaurant closed in August of 2018, but some are hopeful that the adjacent catering company will make it.[85]

CONCLUSION

Bigger than a Hamburger

The Fight for $15 movement has targeted McDonald's and other fast food restaurants for low wages and bad working conditions, including inconsistent scheduling practices and sexual harassment of workers. A protest in Chicago used elements of the civil rights struggles of the 1950s. Photo by Scott Olson / Getty Images.

Eventually, the news cameras, the protesters, and the National Guard cleared out of Ferguson, Missouri. In their place came a few new community programs and some more businesses. The QuikTrip that burned after Michael Brown was killed has been converted into an Urban League Community Empowerment Center and a Salvation Army mission. The Boys and Girls Club of Greater St. Louis broke ground for a new youth center on the former site of a Ponderosa Steakhouse. Over the course of four years, nearly $40 million in investments for new businesses and municipal improvements have flowed into Ferguson; most of it has enriched the historic downtown and predominantly white sections of town.

In 2016, Starbucks CEO Howard Schultz made good on his pledge to open a Ferguson branch of the coffeehouse. Unlike most of the new businesses, the Starbucks is located on West Florissant, across the street from the now-repaired and still-bustling black-franchised McDonald's. Poor and working-class black residents of the apartments and single-family homes near West Florissant Avenue have yet to realize much of the economic benefits of the renewed interest in Ferguson.[1]

This book is concerned with the reasons that places like Ferguson are more likely to get a fast food restaurant rather than direct cash aid to the poor, oversight over the police department, or jobs that pay more than $8.60 per hour after an uprising. This story also explains how fast food became black and why it came to mean so many things to black communities. In order to fully appreciate the origins of our contemporary health crisis, we cannot fixate solely on the food. We have to tell stories about the many functions of capitalism, and its ability to satisfy some of our most personal needs while starving our collective present and future. Government support for fast food franchising has imperiled black health, but our societal vigilance should take us beyond that. In addition to government assistance, the fast food industry relies on indefinable, but palpable, emotional appeals to black consumer citizenship, the extension of the mid-century march for civil rights toward the marketplace, and calls for racial solidarity under the expansive umbrellas of "black capitalism," and later "black empowerment." The origins of the urban food crisis reveal the ways that various actors—politicians, civil rights activists, business executives, advertising agencies, community organizers, and market researchers—aligned to use the symbols, language, and strategies of black freedom movements to sell scores of hamburgers, myriad buckets of fried chicken, and gallons of soda. Studying the hidden history of how fast food and civil rights aligned to change black America, and the ways that black America changed fast food, can lead to more nuanced understandings of our concerns about ensuring that communities that have the least receive the most support to create choices for themselves and for their future generations.

A public that decries fast food as a matter of bad choices is a public that is ignorant to the fact that the meeting of racism and capitalism can only produce demeaning and uncomfortable options.[2] In the ongoing, yet still superficial, public conversation about fast food, race, and health, we have to remember that our catastrophic disparities are a result of a structural indifference to the depth of black hunger for everything from nutritious foods to well-compensated jobs to racial justice. This hunger makes communities without wealth or power vulnerable to the excesses of government and corporate impulses that seek to deprive or overfeed rather than nourish. Social critic Naomi Klein's 2007 book *The Shock Doctrine: The Rise of Disaster Capitalism* is a helpful guide to interrogate the concern about fast food and health. In tracing the ways that natural and political disaster facilitate the arrival of sweeping, and disastrous, market-based policies and processes that exploit the vulnerable and destabilize the distribution of public resources, Klein's framework is instructive for all invested in food justice. Whether it be the reinvigoration of the service-based tourism economy after an earthquake or the elimination of public schools in favor of charter schools after a hurricane, disaster capitalism feeds on destitution and chaos. In Klein's view, the disasters are sometimes dramatic, like a civil war, and in other times, the disaster comes with a seemingly peaceful election of a probusiness politician or a promise to reform public entitlements. Regardless of how rapidly or quickly the shock to citizens is delivered, there are commonalities in its effect. Klein notes: "All these incarnations share a commitment to the policy trinity—the elimination of the public sphere, total liberation for corporations, and skeletal social spending . . ."[3] Since the late 1960s, the fast food industry has similarly capitalized on racial unrest to infiltrate black communities, ingratiate itself with the community's most influential figures, and evoke a complicated set of emotions about the industry by contributing to black cultural and social life but never fully enriching it.

Attempts to legislate food choices, or to provide "healthy alternatives" to food that has been labeled junk, can also confuse and distort the difference between real food and highly processed

food. This gesture can also distract us from which people are most subject to eating what is offered rather than choosing what is desired. Although states like California have been successful in banning soft drinks and junk food from school vending machines, food in schools is not necessarily fresh or healthy. Considering black children attend public schools at a rate of more than 90%, their schools also play a role in developing food habits and preferences. Bans on fast food in schools do not mean that children are not consuming products that mimic the taste level, preparation style or nutritional emptiness of fast food. Chicken fingers—the close cousin of the McNugget—and crispy shelled tacos of the kind Glen Bell popularized in the United States are pervasive on school lunch menus. Even if McDonald's or Chick-fil-A is not in a specific school cafeteria, the palates of students are still being set by the fast food industry. Fast food's multivalent definitions—as social scourge, evidence of family decline, a marker of blackness—are contingent upon who is eating it, where they are eating it, and how often. The fare at an earth-toned Panera franchise or a sleekly designed Starbucks are both fast food products, but due to their price points, their claims about sourcing and the locations of these establishments, they are not marked as places where parents should not take their children frequently, nor are they targets of criticism about nutrition.[4]

The castigation of the eating habits of poor people, or the choices they make for their children's meals, obscures the origins of those choices. Judging food selections and indulgences assumes that what we eat only has to do with food. In tackling the problems borne from a faulty food environment for poor African Americans, it is also essential to dispense with romanticized notions of a healthier food past, as this nostalgic rhetoric can often be used to excoriate women for failing to cook healthy meals for their families, or to suggest that there was a time that black communities easily provided food for themselves without need of capital investment. There was a time in the pre–Great Migration era that blacks—concentrated largely in the South—subsisted on a diet that derived from the land they toiled. But often blacks did

not own the land they worked, and it is misleading to assert that race did not overdetermine the quality of the black diet in the era before fast food became a fixture in largely black neighborhoods. Blacks may have eaten more freshly harvested vegetables and fewer Whoppers or chicken tenders, for sure, but the quantity and consistency of food has always been a challenge for black people and families in America.

Food writer Michael Pollan has observed that fast food "obscures the histories of the foods it produces by processing them to such an extent that they appear as pure products of culture rather than nature—things made from plants and animals."[5] Similarly, the mainstream discussion about fast food and health in communities of color disguises the intertwined histories of capitalism, racism, and violence that undergirds every part of the nation's existence, and therefore foodways and dining are no exception. The history of blacks in fast food franchising—when integrated into the historical analysis of black capitalism—yields a story of troubling success. The meeting of burgers and black capitalism worked. In fact, one of black capitalism's greatest experiments—to bring fast food within the reach of black communities—went so well that its origins have been underresearched, its impacts masked, and its history largely ignored.

For most Americans, it may be hard to imagine a world without McDonald's or Kentucky Fried Chicken or Taco Bell. Now, in the early adulthood of the twenty-first century, we may not be able to conceive of the United States without some form of cheap and easy food source. The sit-in's descendants—the Black Lives Matter die-in at a mall food court or a Starbucks picket line after a racist incident happens inside the coffee shop or a petition against a restaurant's practices that gets circulated among social media channels—have revealed themselves as of late. They remind us of the effectiveness of litigating social wrongs by taking to the streets, including Main Street. Yet the market cannot dictate opportunity or solely guarantee the well-being of communities. In our contemporary fight to ensure the health and wealth of people relegated to the margins, all does not begin and end with the presence of

the drive-thru. In order to combat the outsize, and possibly harmful, impact of that very drive-thru, we must assess the lack shaped by the racist commitments of the state. When resources that create steady infrastructure for well-paying jobs, a multitude of food options, and safe spaces for children and senior citizens to build community are absent, then fast food is able to present itself as capable of providing sustenance rather than simply feeding. Moving forward, food justice movements must interrogate the racist suppositions about poor people's nutritional ignorance of the dangers of fast food and question the assumptions that black people are innately attracted to it.

Attempts to revolutionize the food system must begin with the history of the ways communities have been sold the idea of fast food as a practical solution. We all must remain vigilant in the places that the industry appears: where students go to school, where families worship, where young athletes demonstrate their talents, where the elderly monitor their blood glucose levels, where high school students proudly collect their scholarship checks, where a formerly incarcerated person is able to work, where Martin Luther King Jr.'s legacy is commemorated, and where children play on weekends. In each of these spaces where the funds from the industry flows, food justice activists must imagine a world in which public funds, community investment dollars, and collective energies sustain them. Before another garden bed is prepared or a vegan recipe is shared and demonstrated in the name of food justice, the concerned must have a thorough and deep deliberation on racial capitalism. When McDonald's, or any other corporation, supplants the state in neighborhoods forced to scramble to acquire necessities for life, then we must adjust our focus to understand how this happened and continues to happen. Fortunately, an emergent generation of food justice advocates, based in communities of color, are linking the fight for healthy and nutritious food options to radical critiques of capitalism that are patient and compassionate toward the people they choose to serve.[6]

Activist Ella Baker was especially prescient and prophetic when

she argued that the sit-in movement's goal of ending discrimination at lunch counters and other public accommodations was only half of the battle, and that economic justice needed to match the fight for access. In matters of race and capitalism, Baker argued, the struggle is "something much bigger than a hamburger."[7]

ACKNOWLEDGMENTS

If I had to sum up the origins of this project, I'd say it began with my participation in a black-history–themed quiz bowl, *Know Your Heritage*, in my sophomore year at St. Ignatius College Prep in Chicago. Broadcast on a local TV station and hosted by ABC-7 news anchor Jim Rose, *Know Your Heritage* was aired during Black History Month. Each year the competition revolved around a central theme, and watching the show on Saturday mornings always introduced me to something new about African-American life and culture. *Know Your Heritage* led to my first experience of reading about Chicago's Great Migration, my area of study in graduate school and the topic of my first book. Although our team was outmatched by better-prepared squads from across the city, I appreciated the chance to visit a television studio, spend time with the other students on the team, and, more important, travel to the DuSable Museum of African American History for the awards ceremony. The show and our consolation prizes were underwritten by the Black McDonald's Operators Association of Chicago and Northwest Indiana.

Growing up, McDonald's was everywhere. We ate at McDonald's before or after church on Sundays. I hosted my friends at birthday parties there, and no matter how many high-end pastries I sample, the chocolate-banana birthday cake offered at the McDonald's on Western Avenue in Chicago's Rogers Park is my favorite of all time. My friends and I would pool our orders of French fries on the brown trays after school and chat as we enjoyed our growing

freedom. In high school, I would go to a McDonald's in downtown Chicago that was decorated with portraits of black history makers and prints from black painters and visual artists before I took an hour-long train-and-bus commute home. In my financially lean days of college and graduate school, McDonald's was a staple of my diet when I was scrambling to finish term papers and dissertation chapters. I frequented other fast food restaurants over the years, but McDonald's was where I grew up, and for most of my life, I have eaten there and enjoyed it. As I have aged and studied, my feelings about fast food have changed, but my gratitude remains for the many memories I have collected over the years sitting in swivel chairs or smashed into a booth catching up with my mom, Mecthilde Boyer, in between her shifts of work. My appreciation for her love and care can never be fully articulated, and it has never been unfelt. My mother's membership among the army of women who work without the protection of unions, the promise of fair compensation, or the possibility of stable retirement has taught me volumes about injustice. My siblings, Regine, Lupita, and Ronald Rousseau have provided me with the support integral to taking risks and charting one's own path. My niece and nephew Emmanuel and Anastasia have brought our family closer together, and I strive to be an aunt that can fill them with pride.

The nourishment I cannot receive from food comes to me through love. My network of aunts, uncles, cousins, kinfolk, fictive kin, and family members in the making have nurtured my ambitions since I was a little girl. My in-laws, Elaine and Fred Yapelli, supported and cared for me from our first introduction in the summer of 2006. Their encouragement—and the love of my now-departed grandmother-in-law Valerie Yapelli—has made me feel like I have always been a member of their family. I am saddened that Elaine passed away five months before the publication of this book. But I am grateful that she was able to receive an advanced copy before she was hospitalized and that she held it in her hands before she was too weak to do so. A great lover of books and a teacher of reading, she appreciated having what she called "such a valuable copy."

This book is as much dedicated to every stranger who has worked to feed me as it is to the people I know and love. When I am eating a plate of Haitian fried pork and plantains at an aunt's house, grabbing a premade salad at an airport concessions kiosk, or on the rare occasions I actually cook in my home, I try to remember the hands—coerced and free—who toil in fields, farms, and factories so others can eat. I'm also grateful to the scores of hotel workers who prepared my rooms, made my breakfasts, retrieved my rental cars, and asked me how my day was going when this book project took me to Los Angeles, Portland, Chicago, Dallas, Charlottesville, New York, Atlanta, and all points in between. In addition to archival research, this book was strengthened by conversations with members of the National Black McDonald's Operators Association and former McDonald's executives, including Roland Parrish, who spent some of his precious time away from his more than twenty franchises to talk to me about history. Roland Jones, Wayne Embry, Albert Okura, Robert Jackson, Janice Baker, Leroy Walker, and Eugene Morris provided me with interviews about their years with and feelings about McDonald's. I am also grateful to Myaisha Hayes for her insights about the work outside of fast food franchises, namely in the Fight for $15 movement, to give me a window into the complexity of worker concerns and worker constraints.

Writing a book is a daunting and often intimidating task, and with each sentence you write, you expose something about yourself and how you look at the world. In turn, the process also invites feedback about how the world looks at you. This process is grueling and can be infuriating without the love and support of friends and community. I'm fortunate to have people in my life who care about my ideas and who help me bear the weight of my internal criticism and fears. While completing this book, I celebrated twenty years of friendship with Elizabeth Pickens, whose book *Your Art Will Save Your Life* did just that for me when I was too overwhelmed and afraid to write and to believe that I had something of value to say. Her care and love for art and artists has changed so many people's creative trajectories, and her humility masks her tremen-

dous impact on arts and activist communities. Writer and artist Ali Liebegott was a virtual companion on many of my research trips, where I could count on her to read my text messages about what true crime television show I was watching, while I decided what I would eat for dinner.

I developed my passion for writing in college at the Missouri School of Journalism and as a student in the Department of Religious Studies. My Missouri family has remained close more than two decades after I showed up for new student orientation with no sense of what I was doing. My mentors Jill Raitt, Laura Hacquard, and Sue Crowley guided my scholarly and activist paths, and their examples are why I decided to pursue the professoriate and a career in higher education. My friends Jamila Wilson, Mark Powell, Michael Watters, Andrew Allan, Brad Paul, Nikole Potulsky, and Michael Lockner supplied the humor and compassion I relied on for years after we graduated to get through my twenties (and thirties, for that matter). Without my selection as a Harry S. Truman Scholar in my junior year of college, I can't imagine how I would have realized my career goals as an academic committed to public service. Fortunately, I had the excellent mentorship and guidance of Andrew Rich, Tara Yglesias, Tonji Wade, the late Diana Aubourg-Millner, and scores of Truman Scholars whose commitment to the greater good always inspires me. I am especially indebted to my Truman Scholar friends Matthew Baugh, Wendi Adelson, Rebecca Buckwalter-Poza, Monica Bell, Nate Watson, and Alex Tyson.

In my graduate school days, I doubted whether I could actually complete a dissertation, let alone two whole books, but my mentors constantly pushed me to sharpen my focus and remember the impact scholarship can have on not only commemorating the past, but also on reimagining the future. My dissertation committee chair Mari Jo Buhle continues to be a model of scholarly discipline and productivity in my transition to a new phase of my career. When I see James Campbell at events, we are now colleagues, but I still remain a student of his flourishes in storytelling on the page and in person. My friendship with Matthew Garcia has steadied me during some of the most difficult and disappointing inflec-

tion points in my career. With every twist and turn, I know that I can call Matt and he will remind me that the track is long, and my voice is necessary. I've loved growing up with my friends from those years at Brown, and every time we meet, we are able to mentor each other on our academic paths, as well as provide advice on managing the sometimes crushing realities of aging, parenting, and caring for aging parents. Thank you to Matthew Delmont, Mireya Loza, Mario Sifuentez, Sarah Wald, Angela Mazaris, Angela Howell, Ricardo Howell and the members of my Brown community for getting older with me. And, my "young friends" from Brown, Hentyle Yapp and Izetta Autumn Mobley, thank you for your constant light when I am afraid to venture outside of my head.

My career has taught me that the smartest people are often the kindest ones. The generosity of my colleagues at the University of Oklahoma and Georgetown University can never be repaid, but I will always try to match it when I'm in the world. Julia Ehrhardt, Maurice Jackson, Katherine Benton-Cohen, John Tutino, Chandra Manning, Carol Benedict, Bryan McCann, Judith Tucker, John McNeill, Jim Collins, Michael Kazin, Aviel Roshwald, Ananya Chakravarti, and Joseph McCartin have been incredible advocates for me, and I wish every academic experienced their level of commitment and concern as they navigate their careers. Georgetown has brought incredible people into my life, and by way of my work with Georgetown University's Working Group on Slavery, Memory, and Reconciliation, I was able to see the integrity and intellectual leadership of David Collins, Kevin O'Brien, and Adam Rothman. The generosity of Adam, and the students who have organized the Georgetown Slavery Archive, in helping families stitch together the narrative fibers of their ancestry has inspired me to fight the cynicism that can obscure my perspectives. My friendship with and spiritual guidance from Kevin O'Brien has been a gift, and his introducing me to Ignatian exercises has centered so many parts of my life. My Georgetown community—especially Greg Schenden, Madeline Vitek, Ben Shaw, Colleen Roberts, Aya Waller-Bey, Missy Foy, Corey Stewart, Jason Low, Sarah Johnson, Terrence Johnson, James Benton, and Olivia Lane—has always shown me such grace and

appreciation. I am also especially appreciative of the support I have received from Georgetown University's president, John D. DeGioia. At every opportunity, he introduced me as a scholar working on a very important book. Thank you for your vote of confidence, Jack!

Over the years, I have received invaluable funding and research support that allowed me to travel to archives, hire lifesaving assistants, and take the necessary time away from the classroom to finish this book. I owe everything to the librarians and archivists at the various libraries and museums where I collected my research, including libraries at the University of California–Los Angeles, Portland State University, the University of Virginia, Duke University, the University of Southern California, and the Chicago Public Library, the New York Public Library, the Western Reserve Historical Society, the Chicago History Museum, and the Library of Congress. I am thankful for grants from the Ford Foundation Diversity Postdoctoral Fellowship, the New America Eric and Wendy Schmidt Fellowship, the National Endowment for the Humanities Faculty Fellowship, and small research grants from Duke University Libraries and the Summersell Center for the Study of the South, as well as internal Georgetown University faculty grants. I wish I knew all the names of the program officers, reviewers, and office support staff who made sure my applications were logged in, reviewed, and my monies disbursed. Research assistance from Yongle Xue, Khadijah Davis, Esther Olowobi, Cheynee Napier, Alex Vicas, and Sade Bruce were godsends when my office was overrun by photocopies and magazine clippings. I owe special gratitude to Julian St. Reiman who contacted me out of the blue and asked if I needed research help. Without him, I would have never been able to write my proposal. Photographer Francis Shad helped me to look my very best on this book jacket, and I thank him for his creativity. At the eleventh hour when I needed those last few bits of research done, permissions secured, and facts checked, doctoral student Emily Norweg stepped up with such precision and speed. Last but not least, I would have not survived the years between 2015 and 2017 without Nicolette S. Thompson's work as my assistant when there were way too many flights to book, appointments

to manage, and urgent emails that needed responses. Nikki's drive and work ethic will be known by many soon enough.

This book has been nurtured by so many brilliant readers and listeners. I presented on this project for the first time in 2013, at the Dark Room Symposium on Race and Visual Culture, and over the past seven years, each audience question and feedback session has challenged and strengthened my ideas. I am deeply indebted to Kimberly Juanita Brown's organization of the Dark Room, as well as her friendship and modeling of how to be a generous academic. Early meetings about this project with editors from other presses helped form the work, and I appreciate the comments that Susan Ferber of Oxford University Press and Mark Simpson-Vos of the University of North Carolina Press offered. Their passion for good historical scholarship has been helpful to so many. I am thankful to the Georgetown University Americas Initiative Seminar, the Johns Hopkins University History Seminar and Center for Medical Humanities and Social Medicine, the University of California-Santa Barbara's Seminar on Work and Labor, the College of William & Mary's Law School, Lewis & Clark College, the University of California-Los Angeles Black Feminist Visions Symposium, the University of Georgia's Dirty History Workshop, the Washington, D.C., Area African American Studies Works-in-Progress Seminar, the Smithsonian National Museum of American History Seminar, the Woodrow Wilson Center for Scholars History Seminar, Princeton Food Studies Conference, New America Fellows Lunch Series, and Yale University's departments of history and African American studies for invitations to share my research and for all of the great advice on improving it. Fellow historians Robert Weems and Carol Anderson were invaluable sounding boards for this book and career matters as I navigated the tenure track. My colleagues at New America—Ted Johnson, Nikole Hannah-Jones, Robin Harris, Janell Ross, Awista Ayub, Veronica Mooney, and Samieleen Lawson—made my time on fellowship there rewarding and welcoming. There were many days I was certain I couldn't read one more newspaper article or sort through one more box of documents, when text messages, phone

calls, emails, and happy-hour excursions with Sheyda Jahanbani, Nathan Connolly, Sam Pinto, Nicole Ivy, Christian Hosam, Amira Rose Davis, and Sherie Randolph lifted my spirits and helped lead me back to my computer. A research presentation on this paper led to a friendship with Brandi Thompson Summers, and that made it all worth it.

This book would not exist without Carole Sargent's encouragement. Carole saw me through the publication of my first book, and she was the first person who celebrated when I signed the contract for this one. Carole connected me to Michelle Tessler, who represented me after I overcame my fears and decided to pitch my book with a trade press. Michelle has an uncanny way of investing in an author's project while respecting the author's vision and expertise. As I waited to hear about press interest in my book, I kept my fingers crossed that this project would land with Katie Adams of Liveright Publishing. Katie's warmth toward and encouragement of her writers parallels her intelligence and wit. From our very first conversation, I knew that working with a person of such integrity and one who valued the many dimensions of who I am was exactly what I, and this book, needed. When Katie left her post with Liveright, I was able to transition to the incredibly talented and enthusiastic agenda of Marie Pantojan. And editor Dan Gerstle and associate editor Gina Iaquinta's inheritance of the book after Marie left Liveright was seamless. The patience, dedication, and professionalism of the Liveright and Norton teams allowed my years of research to transform into a book that I can be proud of; for this, I am deeply grateful and humbled. Steve Attardo's beautiful cover design captured the complexity and the sensitivity I hoped to convey with this project. Production manager Julia Druskin and assistant project editor Amy Medeiros made this project's release stress free. Copyeditor Fred Wiemer's diligent review of my manuscript may have cured me of my addiction to commas. Proofreader Susan Goarke and compositors Joe Lops and Ken Hansen carefully managed my many changes during the proofing process, and JoAnne Metsch elegantly designed the interior of the book. Finally, I'm grateful to the marketing and publicity team—Golda Rademacher,

Peter Miller, Cordelia Calvert, and Nick Curley—at Liveright for their hard work promoting my book.

My most ebullient thanks go to my spouse, Mark Yapelli, for living with this project in the best and worst ways. I know that my work does not make our lives easy, but I hope it is always worth it. Even though this journey has ended, I will still point out converted Pizza Huts to you while we are on road trips, and I will still light up when you mention Arthur Treacher's Fish & Chips.

After the 2016 election, I found myself with a heightened sense of despair about the direction of the nation, the future of my students, and the safety of the people I love most. At the end of the academic year, a student asked me, "What's going to happen next?" As a historian, I love pretending that I can actually predict the future because I believe myself to have a grasp on the past. But, I am not so arrogant as to believe that I could do this in such troubling times. So, I told my students the one thing I find myself repeating constantly, because it is not a prediction, but rather a truth I've discovered over the years. "I do not know what will happen, but I know we have each other, and that is worth a lot." The future is uncertain, indeed, but if the present is any indicator, I know I will not face it alone.

NOTES

Introduction: From Sit-In to Drive-Thru

1. Radley Balko, *Rise of the Warrior Cop: The Militarization of America's Police Forces* (New York: PublicAffairs, 2014). In a *Newsweek* article from the summer of 2014, Taylor Wofford reported that small towns acquired grenade launchers, Humvees, and mine-resistant, ambush-protected (MRAP) vehicles through this program. Taylor Wofford, "How America's Police Became an Army: The 1033 Program," *Newsweek*, August 13, 2014.

2. Ferguson, Missouri, and St. Louis County have been the topic of a number of scholarly examinations on racial divides among municipalities, as well as the ways that city-county separation has exacerbated social problems. See Colin Gordon, *Mapping Decline: St. Louis and the Fate of the American City* (Philadelphia: University of Pennsylvania Press, 2009), and *Citizen Brown: Race, Democracy, and Inequality in the St. Louis Suburbs* (Chicago: University of Chicago Press, 2019). Keona K. Ervin's *Gateway to Equality: Black Women and the Struggle for Economic Justice in St. Louis* (Lexington: University Press of Kentucky, 2017) explores the role of black women in fighting for improved working and living conditions in the city.

3. On Wednesday, August 13, 2014, *Washington Post* reporter Wesley Lowery and the *Huffington Post*'s Ryan Reilly were arrested by Ferguson police for "trespassing in a McDonald's." St. Louis County later dropped the charges against the journalists. Wesley Lowery, "In Ferguson, Washington Post Reporter Wesley Lowrey Gives Account of His Arrest," *Washington Post*, August 14, 2014, and Niraj Chokshi, "Ferguson-Related Charges Dropped Against *Washington Post* and *Huffington Post* Reporters," *Washington Post*, May 19, 2016.

4. Centers for Disease Control, National Health and Nutrition Examination Survey, 2018, https://www.cdc.gov/nchs/nhanes/index.htm.

5. Cedric Robinson, *Black Marxism: The Making of the Black Radical Tradition* (Chapel Hill: University of North Carolina Press, 1983).

6. Angela Hilmers, David C. Hilmers, and Jayna Dave, "Neighborhood Disparities in Access to Healthy Foods and Their Effect on Environmental Justice," *American Journal of Public Health* 101, no. 9 (September 2012): 1644–54.

7. National Institutes of Health, "Rates of New Diagnosed Cases of Type 1 and Type 2 Diabetes on the Rise Among Children, Teens," April 13, 2017.

8. "Table 58: Normal Weight, Overweight, and Obesity Among Adults Aged 20 and Over, by Selected Characteristics: United States, Selected Years 1998–1994 through 2011–2014," National Center for Health Statistics, With Chartbook on Long-term Trends in Health, Hyattsville, MD, 2017.

9. Pew Charitable Trusts, "The Role of Emergency Savings in Family Financial Security: What Resources Do Families Have for Financial Emergencies?" November 2015, 8.

10. Eric Schlosser, *Fast Food Nation: The Dark Side of the All-American Meal* (New York: Mariner's Press, 2013). Schlosser's text is one of the most important pieces of research about the fast food industry. In *Super Size Me*, filmmaker Morgan Spurlock embarked on a thirty-day diet of only products purchased at McDonald's. During the course of his experiment, Spurlock gained more than twenty pounds, and his doctor reported that his cholesterol levels were significantly raised. Morgan Spurlock, director, *Super Size Me*, Samuel Goldwyn Films, 2004.

11. "America's Epidemic of Youth Obesity," *New York Times*, November 29, 2002. Accessed December, 2018.

12. The research and scholarship on food justice, health equity, and the fast food industry is vast. A few texts have gained considerable attention in their analysis of these issues, but they often fail to take on how race and history intersect with their concerns. Vegan and environmental activist John Robbins, who spurned his family's Baskin-Robbins Ice Cream inheritance, approaches the issue of food justice by challenging the consumption of meat from a moral-ethical as well as a health perspective. John Robbins, *Diet for a New America: How Your Food Choices Affect Your Health, Happiness, and the Future of Life on Earth*, 2nd ed. (San Francisco: HJ Kramer/New World Library, 2012). Nutritionist Marion Nestle's research on food and politics exposes the way that the food industry not only establishes what people want to eat, but she indicts its leaders for using bad science to influence how the federal government sets standards for nutrition and deems products "healthy." Marion Nestle, *Unsavory Truth: How Food Companies Skew the Science of What We Eat* (New York: Basic Books, 2018); *Soda Politics: Taking on Big Soda (and Winning)* (New York: Oxford University Press, 2015); *Food Politics: How the Food Industry Influences Nutrition and Health* (Berkeley: University of California Press, 2013); and *Safe Food: The Politics of Food Safety* (Berkeley: University of California Press, 2010). Michael Pollan's writing on the nature of food, cooking, and advice on what to eat has been quite popular, and his suggestion that people need to "eat food, not too much, mostly plants," emerges from several studies that distinguish between real food and fake food. Michael Pollan, *Cooked: A Natural History of Transformation* (New York: Penguin, 2013); *Food Rules: An Eater's Manual* (New York: Penguin, 2009); *In Defense of Food: An Eater's Manifesto* (New York: Penguin, 2008); and *The Omnivore's Dilemma: A Natural History of Four Meals* (New York: Penguin, 2006). African-American food studies have provided critical interventions into the food studies field to highlight the importance that race

plays in what people cook, consume, and contend with under oppressive systems, from slavery to the era of segregation to contemporary struggles. Jennifer Jensen Wallach's *Every Nation Has Its Dish: Black Bodies and Black Food in Twentieth-Century America* (Chapel Hill: University of North Carolina Press, 2019) emphasizes the way food is an expression of black identity and politics. Jessica B. Harris, *High on the Hog: A Culinary Journey from Africa to America* (New York: Bloomsbury, 2012), provides a wide overview of black foodways. *Black Hunger: Soul Food and America* (Minneapolis: University of Minnesota Press, 2004) by Doris Witt is an excellent exploration of the meaning of food to the black cultural experience. Toni Tipton-Martin, *The Jemima Code: Two Centuries of African American Cookbooks* (Austin: University of Texas Press, 2015), examines the ways that black food writing has been used as a tool of cultural self-fashioning and self-preservation. Similarly, the essays in Rafia Zafar, *Recipes for Respect: African American Meals and Meaning* (Athens: University of Georgia Press, 2019), uncover how black food writing serves as a lens for understanding black politics and cultural life. Most recently, anthropologist Ashanté M. Reese directs attention to the bigger picture of food justice and race in her study of the ways that African Americans in a Washington, D.C., neighborhood navigate food access restraints in a gentrifying city. Ashanté M. Reese, *Black Geographies: Race, Self-Reliance, and Food Access in Washington, D.C.* (Chapel Hill: University of North Carolina Press, 2019).

13. Bart Elmore, *Citizen Coke: The Making of Coca-Cola Capitalism* (New York: W. W. Norton, 2014), 10. Also see Peter M. Birkeland, *Franchising Dreams: The Lure of Entrepreneurship in America* (Chicago: University of Chicago Press, 2002).

14. In James Watson's *Golden Arches East: McDonald's in East Asia*, 2nd ed. (Stanford, CA: Stanford University Press, 2006), he demonstrates how McDonald's has had an influence on how affluent people in Hong Kong, China, Taiwan, South Korea, and Japan relate to a business that is both associated with the United States and adjusted for local consumer market preferences. This process leads to a form of naturalization in which McDonald's is simultaneously foreign and familiar.

15. Andrew Smith, *Hamburger: A Global History* (London: Reaktion Books, 2008), 25.

16. Smith, 31.

17. Smith, 31. Also *White Tower System, Inc. v. White Castle System of Eating Houses Corporation*, May 4, 1937.

18. Burger Chef was founded by Frank and Donald Thomas as an Indianapolis-based franchise restaurant. The men had designed the first flame broiler, which would be used to distinguish Burger King's burger from its competitor McDonald's. Burger Chef expanded throughout the 1960s and 1970s, after General Foods acquired the chain. Often credited with developing a children's meal and toy combination that inspired the McDonald's Happy Meal, Burger Chef mostly disappeared by the early 1980s. See Eric Dodds, "*Mad Men*: A Brief History of the Real-World Burger Chef," *Newsweek*, May 19, 2014.

19. Albert Okura, *Albert Okura: The Chicken Man with a 50 Year Plan* (Author House, 2014), 51.

20. Okura, 60.

21. Stacy Perman, *In-N-Out Burger: A Behind-the-Counter Look at the Fast-Food Chain That Breaks All the Rules* (New York: Harper Business, 2010).

22. Schlosser's *Fast Food Nation* pays particular attention to the stresses felt by franchisees who must meet royalty, advertising, and leasing requirements before they can make any profits.

23. Lizabeth Cohen, *A Consumers' Republic: The Politics of Mass Consumption in Postwar America* (New York: Vintage Books, 2003), 7. See also Traci Parker, *Department Stores and the Black Freedom Movement: Workers, Consumers, and Civil Rights from the 1930s to the 1980s* (Chapel Hill: University of North Carolina Press, 2019).

24. "Speculative Bellyache: Fast Food Franchisers Are Risking a Bout of Indigestion," *Barron's*, August 25, 1969.

25. "Speculative Bellyache."

26. The history of black business illustrates the ways that African-American ingenuity has led to more than just the selling of goods or the opening of stores. African-American businesses secured the freedom of the enslaved, supported institutions in the era of segregation, and funded critical social movements. See Juliet K. Walker, *Free Frank: A Black Pioneer on the Antebellum Frontier* (Lexington: University Press of Kentucky, 1983), and *The History of Black Business in America: Capitalism, Race, Entrepreneurship*, vol. 1, *To 1865* (Chapel Hill: University of North Carolina Press, 2015). John Sibley Butler, *Entrepreneurship and Self-Help Among Black Americans: A Reconsideration of Race and Economics* (Buffalo: SUNY Press, 2005), emphasizes the civic role of black businesses. Some studies look at African-American leadership in specific industries. Quincy T. Mills, *Cutting Along the Color Line: Black Barbers and Barber Shops in America* (Philadelphia: University of Pennsylvania Press, 2013), and Douglas Bristol Jr., *Knights of the Razor: Black Barbers in Slavery and Freedom* (Baltimore: Johns Hopkins University Press, 2015), explore the importance of black barber shops. Tiffany Gill, *Beauty Shop Politics: African American Activism in the Beauty Industry* (Urbana: University of Illinois Press, 2010), and Susannah Walker, *Style and Status: Selling Beauty to African American Women, 1920–1975* (Lexington: University Press of Kentucky, 2007), highlight the ways that beauty salons and the beauty industry at large allowed black women to voice their political concerns, assert their financial independence, and circumvent working for whites. In Shomari Will's profiles of black millionaires, the journalist highlights economic success across sectors, and he highlights the economic gains collected in all-black towns. Shomari Wills, *Black Fortunes: The Story of the First Six African Americans who Escaped Slavery and Became Millionaires* (New York: Amistad, 2018). African-American banks played a critical role in helping businesses grow. See Shennette Garrett-Scott, *Banking on Freedom: Black Women in U.S. Finance Before the New Deal* (New York: Columbia University Press, 2019).

27. For more on the War on Poverty, see Jill Quadagno, *The Color of Welfare: How Racism Undermined the War on Poverty* (Oxford: Oxford University Press, 1996), and Marissa Chappell, *The War on Welfare: Family, Poverty, and Politics in Modern America* (Philadelphia: University of Pennsylvania Press, 2011).

28. Laura Warren Hill and Julia Rabig, "Introduction," in Laura Warren Hill and Julia Rabig, eds., *The Business of Black Power: Community Development, Capitalism, and Corporate Responsibility in Postwar America* (Rochester, NY: University of Rochester Press, 2012), 2.

29. Leah Wright Rigeur, *The Loneliness of the Black Republican: Pragmatic Politics and the Pursuit of Power* (Princeton: Princeton University Press, 2015), is an excellent analysis of black support and critique of Richard Nixon, as well as conservatives broadly, and it presents a nuanced look at how economic issues shaped racial politics for black and white Republicans from 1968 to the 1980s.

30. For more on black capitalism, see Robert L. Allen, *Black Awakening in Capitalist America: An Analytic History* (Trenton, NJ: Africa World Press, 1990).

31. Chin Jou, "Donald Trump Isn't the First President to Give Fast Food His Seal of Approval," *Washington Post*, January 18, 2019.

Chapter One: Fast Food Civil Rights

1. Keeley Webster, "San Bernardino Faces Its Post-Bankruptcy Future," *Bond Buyer*, December 30, 2016, https://www.bondbuyer.com/news/san-bernardino-faces-its-post-bankruptcy-future. Also, Joe Mozingo, "San Bernardino: Broken City," *Los Angeles Times*, June 14, 2015.

2. John F. Love, *McDonald's: Behind the Arches* (New York: Bantam Press, 1995), and *The Founder*, directed by John Lee Hancock (New York: Weinstein Co., 2016), Netflix Streaming.

3. Douglas Flamming, *Bound for Freedom: Black Los Angeles in Jim Crow America* (Berkeley: University of California Press, 2005).

4. Flamming, 88.

5. See Stephen Johnson, *Burnt Cork: Traditions and Legacies of Blackface Minstrelsy* (Amherst: University of Massachusetts Press, 2012), and John Strausbaugh, *Black Like You: Blackface, Whiteface, Insult, and Imitation in American Popular Culture* (New York: Penguin Press, 2006).

6. The literature on race and western United States history has contributed significantly to understanding the African-American experience outside of the confines of the South and the industrial North. Josh Kun and Laura Pulido, eds., *Black and Brown in Los Angeles: Beyond Conflict and Coalition* (Berkeley: University of California Press, 2013); Shana Bernstein, *Bridges of Reform: Interracial Civil Rights Activism in Twentieth-Century Los Angeles* (Oxford: Oxford University Press, 2011); and Kenneth W. Mack, *Representing the Race: The Creation of the Civil Rights Lawyer* (Cambridge: Harvard University Press, 2010), provide an excellent analysis of the Los Angeles NAACP and their leader, attorney Loren Miller.

7. Lisa Napoli, "The Story of How McDonald's First Got Its Start," Smithsonian.com, November 1, 2016.

8. "New Utopia for Negroes," *Los Angeles Times*, December 19, 1904.

9. Jason Kottke, "Early McDonald's Menus," last modified March 18, 2013, https://kottke.org/13/03/early-mcdonalds-menus, and Donna Scanlon, "McDonald's Bar-B-Que," *Library of Congress* (blog), May 15, 2010, https://blogs.loc.gov/inside_adams/2010/05/mcdonald%E2%80%99s-bar-b-que/.

10. Andrew Smith, *Hamburger: A Global History* (London: Reaktion Books, 2008), 10. Smith debunks the urban legend that Delmonico's restaurant in New York City invented the hamburger, as well as the claim that the hamburger debuted in 1904 at the Louisiana Purchase Exposition in St. Louis.

11. Smith, 15.

12. Smith, 20–24.

13. "All-Colored Jury Hears Man's Case in California," *Pittsburgh Courier*, March 27, 1926.

14. See "Guide to the Black History Collection, 1984–1999," Pasadena History Museum, http://pdf.oac.cdlib.org/pdf/phm/blackhis.pdf.

15. Lisa Morehouse, "So Much More than Tacos: San Bernardino's Mitla Café," Eater.com, July 25, 2018. The owners of the Mitla Café claim that Glen Bell, founder of Taco Bell, learned about Mexican food from them. Bell's hot dog stand was located across the street from their café. Opened in 1937, it was a place for Mexicans and Mexican-Americans in San Bernardino to not only eat familiar foods, but to organize politically against segregation and discrimination. See also Gustavo Arellano, *Taco USA: How Fast Food Conquered America* (New York: Simon & Schuster, 2012). For more on Mexican Americans and segregation in California, see Vicki L. Ruiz, "South by Southwest: Mexican Americans and Segregated Schooling, 1900–1950," *OAH Magazine of History* 15, no. 2 (Winter 2001): 23–27.

16. Love, 12.

17. Love, 15, and George Harrison, "Anyone for a Tempting Cheeseburger? This is What the Original McDonald's Menu Looked Like," *The Sun*, December 2, 2016.

18. The Air Material Command Center, later renamed for World War II casualty Leland Francis Norton, became known as Norton Air Force Base. Norton was where a young Morgan Freeman discovered he did not want to become a fighter pilot; rather, he wanted to play the role of a pilot in the movies. See Henry Louis Gates Jr., *In Search of Our Roots: How 19 Extraordinary African Americans Reclaimed Their Past* (New York: Crown, 2009).

19. A. J. Scott, "The Technopoles of Southern California," *Environment and Planning* 22 (1990): 1575–1605.

20. "FEPC Hearing Opens on Railman's Charge," *Los Angeles Times*, January 10, 1961.

21. Thomas J. Sugrue, "Automobile in American Life and Society, Driving While Black: The Car and Race Relations in Modern America," http://www.autolife.umd.umich.edu/.

22. For more on the *Negro Traveler's Green Book*, see Michael Ra-Shon Hall, "The Negro Traveller's Guide to a Jim Crow South: Negotiating Racialized Landscapes

During a Dark Period in United States Cultural History, 1936–1967," *Postcolonial Studies* 19 (January 2015): 1–13, and Erin Krutko Devlin, "Navigating the Green Book (The Negro Travelers' Green Book)," *Journal of American History* 104, no. 1 (2017): 312–13.

23. Ryan Hagen, "Norton Air Force Base Marks 20 Years Since Closure," *San Bernardino Sun*, March 22, 2014.

24. Jean Simon, "San Bernardino Vet Tells Story of Two-Year House Hunt," *Los Angeles Sentinel*, January 15, 1948.

25. Love, 25–26.

26. Raymond Mohl, "Planned Destruction: The Interstates and Central City Housing," in John F. Bauman, Roger Biles, and Kristin Sylvian, eds., *From Tenements to the Taylor Homes: In Search of an Urban Housing Policy in Twentieth Century America* (State College: Pennsylvania State University Press, 2000), 226–45.

27. Mohl, 233–34.

28. The term "food desert" was first used by researchers Steven Cummins and Sally Macintrye in relationship to a study of residents in a Scottish public housing community. Other researchers and food justice activists argue for different terminology to describe the phenomenon of people being unable to access healthy foods close to where they live. Karen Washington offers the term "food apartheid" because it signals a concern about inequality broadly. See Steven Cummins and Sally Macintyre, "Food Deserts—Evidence and Assumption in Health Policy Making," *The BMJ* 325, no. 7631 (August 24, 2002), 436–38, and Karen Washington, "It's Not a Food Desert, It's Food Apartheid," *Guernica*, May 7, 2018.

29. Love, 27–28.

30. Love, 41–44.

31. Love, 192–201. Love estimated in 1995: "If McDonald had not sold his right to the 0.5% of McDonald's sales that was due him and Mac under their ninety-nine-year contract with Kroc, he would have become one of the country's wealthiest men, almost as wealthy as Ray Kroc. Since the brothers sold their rights for $2.7 million in late 1961, McDonald's restaurants have rung up a total of $198 billion in sales. The royalty payments that would have been due the McDonald brothers had they not sold out come to a total of $990 million. Today, the McDonalds would be earning more than $109 million a year." Love, 201.

32. Love, 201.

33. Love, 153.

34. Ray Kroc, *Grinding It Out: The Making of McDonald's* (New York: Bedford/St. Martin's, 1992), 203.

35. "Other People's Business," *Chicago Defender,* June 13, 1959, and "Other People's Business," *Chicago Defender,* April 8, 1957.

36. Untitled display ad, *Chicago Defender*, September 9, 1961.

37. "A Great Decade," *Chicago Defender*, February 24, 1966, and "Opportunity Awaits at McDonald's," *Chicago Defender*, March 12, 1966.

38. Victoria W. Wolcott addresses the struggle for racial integration and places of amusement. Victoria W. Wolcott, *Race, Riots, and Roller Coasters: The Strug-*

gle over Segregated Recreation in America (Philadelphia: University of Pennsylvania Press, 2014).

39. Anne Moody, *Coming of Age in Mississippi* (New York: Dell, 1992), and Melba Patillo-Beals, *Warriors Don't Cry: A Searing Memoir of the Battle to Integrate Little Rock's Central High* (New York: Simon & Schuster, 2007), 21, 66.

40. Renee Romano, "No Diplomatic Immunity: African Diplomats, the State Department, and Civil Rights, 1961–1964," *Journal of American History* 87, no. 2 (September 2000): 546–79.

41. August Meier and Elliot Rudwick, "How CORE Began," *Social Science Quarterly* 49, no. 4 (1969): 789–99.

42. For more on fashion, hair, and protest during the civil rights movement, see Tanisha C. Ford, *Liberated Threads: Black Women, Style, and the Global Politics of Soul* (Chapel Hill: University of North Carolina Press, 2015), and Tiffany Gill, *Beauty Shop Politics: African-American Women's Activism in the Beauty Industry* (Urbana: University of Illinois Press, 2010).

43. Rebecca Cerese and Steven Channing, *February One*, distributed by California Newsreel, aired 2004 on *Independent Lens*, PBS.

44. Aniko Bodroghkozy, *Equal Time: Television and the Civil Rights Movement* (Urbana: University of Illinois Press, 2013).

45. Melissa Clark, "Other People's Food and the Greensboro Four," *Splendid Table*, August 16, 2016. William Henry Chafe, *Civilities and Civil Rights: Greensboro, North Carolina, and the Black Struggle for Freedom* (Oxford: Oxford University Press, 1981).

46. "August 15, 1958 Complaint," Library Integration Collection, Digital Archive of Memphis Public Library, https://memphislibrary.contentdm.oclc.org/digital/collection/p15342coll4/id/88.

47. Wayne Risher, "Golden Arches Paved Way for Memphis Entrepreneur Saul Kaplan," *Memphis Commercial Appeal*, February 26, 2016.

48. "List of Memphis Businesses Willing to Desegregate," Maxine A. Smith NAACP Collection, Box 4, Folder 2, Civil Rights Digital Library, http://crdl.usg.edu/export/html/tnmpl/smithnaacp/crdl_tnmpl_smithnaacp_000210.html?Welcome

49. Jerry Bledsoe, "The Story of Hardees," May 27, 2011, https://www.ourstate.com/hardees/. See also "Greensboro, North Carolina, 1963," Assistant Director's File, 1942–1965, Box 3, Folder 12, Congress of Racial Equality (CORE) Records, 1941–1967, Wisconsin Historical Society, Madison, Wisconsin. The arrival of the thrifty meal had been a hit, and the restaurant would later inspire Navy veteran-turned-restaurateur-and-innkeeper Wilber Hardee to create his namesake burger franchise a year later in Greenville.

50. Eugene F. Pfaff Jr., oral history interview with Brandon A. Lewis III, Greensboro Voices/Greensboro Public Library Oral History Project, Tape 1 transcript, http://libcdm1.uncg.edu/cdm/ref/collection/CivilRights/id/807.

51. "Memorandum," dated May 10, 1963, Departments and Related Organizations Memoranda, 1963–1965, Box 48, Folder 9, CORE Records, 1941–1967, Wisconsin Historical Society.

52. "McDonald's Store #433 Sign," National Register of Historic Places Registration

Form, http://www.arkansaspreservation.com/national-register-listings/mcdonald-39-s-store-433-sign. Accessed January 26, 2018.

53. Randy Findley, "Crossing the White Line: SNCC in Three Delta Towns, 1963–1967," in Jennifer Jensen Wallach and John A. Kirk, eds., *Arsnick: The Student Nonviolent Coordinating Committee in Arkansas* (Fayetteville: University of Arkansas Press, 2011), 68, and Vivian Carroll Jones, "The Civil Rights Movement in Pine Bluff" in Wallach and Kirk, eds., 170–71. "Students Attacked with Ammonia Acid in Pine Bluff, Ark.," *Atlanta Daily World,* August 4, 1963.

54. "Students Attacked with Ammonia."

55. "Students Attacked with Ammonia."

56. "In Arkansas: McDonald's Boycott Called; Helena Police Arrest Three," *Student Voice,* December 9, 1963.

57. "SNCC Annual Report, 1964," in Jensen et al., *Arsnick.*

58. Angela Jill Cooley, "A Helping of Gravy: Golden Arches & White Spaces," *Gravy* 53, (December 3, 2014), and *To Live and Dine in Dixie: The Evolution of Urban Food Culture in the Jim Crow South* (Athens: University of Georgia Press, 2015).

59. United States, *Civil Rights Acts of 1964* (Washington, D.C.: U.S. Government Printing Office, 1969). For more on the journey to the passage of the Civil Rights Act, see Todd S. Purdum, *An Idea Whose Time Has Come: Two Presidents, Two Parties, and the Battle for the Civil Rights Act of 1964* (New York: Henry Holt & Co., 2014), and Clay Risen, *The Bill of The Century: The Epic Battle for the Civil Rights Act* (New York: Bloomsbury, 2014).

60. "Fried Chicken: Whites, $1.75 Negroes $5.25," *Chicago Defender,* September 24, 1964.

61. Whitney Young, "To Be Equal," *Chicago Defender,* October 24, 1964.

62. United States National Advisory Commission on Civil Disorders, *The Kerner Report: The 1968 Report on the National Advisory Commission on Civil Disorders* (New York: Pantheon Books, 1968), 82. See also Thomas J. Hrach, *The Riot Report and the News: How the Kerner Commission Changed Media Coverage of Black America* (Amherst: University of Massachusetts Press, 2016), and Steve Gillon, *Separate and Unequal: The Kerner Commission and the Unraveling of American Liberalism* (New York: Basic Books, 2018).

63. United States National Advisory Commission on Civil Disorders, Report of the National Advisory Commission on Civil Disorders: Summary of Report (Washington, DC: United States Government Printing Office, 1968), 26.

64. "Civil Rights Timeline, August 21, 1959," Civil Rights Collection, Digital Memphis.

65. "Campaign Flyer for Sugarmon, Hooks, Bunton, and Love," George W. Lee Collection, Digital Memphis, https://memphislibrary.contentdm.oclc.org/digital/collection/p13039coll2/id/170/rec/2. For more on black civil rights in Memphis, see Shirletta Kinchen, *Black Power in the Bluff City: African American Activism in Memphis, 1965–1975* (Knoxville: University of Tennessee Press, 2016); Aram Goudsouzian and Charles W. McKinney Jr., *An Unseen Light: Black Struggles for Freedom in Memphis, Tennessee* (Lexington: University Press of Kentucky, 2018); and Jonathan Chism, *Saints in the Struggle: Church of God in Christ*

Activists in the Memphis Civil Rights Movement, 1954–1968 (New York: Lexington Books, 2019).

66. Martin Luther King Jr., "All Labor Has Dignity," American Federation of State, County, and Municipal Employees (AFSCME) mass meeting, Memphis Sanitation Strike, Bishop Charles Mason Temple, Church of God in Christ, Memphis, Tennessee, March 18, 1968, in Cornel West, *The Radical King* (Boston: Beacon Press, 2015).

67. Martin Luther King Jr., "I've Been to the Mountaintop," April 3, 1968, Memphis, TN, http://kingencyclopedia.stanford.edu/encyclopedia/documentsentry/ive_been_to_the_mountaintop/.

68. Black insurance companies provided life insurance and burial policies to African Americans, and sometimes played the role of lender and investor for blacks unable to access bank services. Walter B. Weare, *Black Business in the New South: A Social History of the North Carolina Mutual Life Insurance Company* (Durham: Duke University Press, 1993).

69. "I've Been to the Mountaintop."

70. For more on the Poor People's Campaign, see Charles Fager, *Uncertain Resurrection: The Poor People's Washington Campaign* (Grand Rapids: Eerdmans, 1969); Hilliard Lawrence Lackey, *Marks, Martin, and the Mule Train: Marks, Mississippi—Martin Luther King, Jr. and the Origin of the 1968 Poor People's Campaign* (Xlibris, 2014); Sylvie Laurent, *King and the Other America: The Poor People's Campaign and the Quest for Economic Equality* (Oakland: University of California Press, 2018); and Gerald D. McKnight, *The Last Crusade: Martin Luther King, Jr., The FBI, and the Poor People's Campaign* (Boulder, CO: Westview Press, 1998).

71. "I've Been to the Mountaintop."

72. "McDonald's Buys Gee Gee Holdings," *Washington Post*, October 25, 1967.

73. Author interview with Roland Jones (former McDonald's executive), March 2018.

74. Martin Luther King Jr., "The Civil Rights Struggle in the United States Today," *Record of the Association of the Bar of the City of New York* 20, no. 5 (April 21, 1965): 20.

Chapter Two: Burgers in the Age of Black Capitalism

1. "Mayor Daley Orders Chicago's Policemen to Shoot Arsonists and Looters," *New York Times*, April 16, 1968.

2. Vincent Harding, *Martin Luther King: The Inconvenient Hero* (Maryknoll, NY: Orbis Books, 2000), 78.

3. Author interview with Roland Jones.

4. Author interview with Roland Jones.

5. Author interview with Roland Jones.

6. The Great Migration radically transformed the racial politics, economic systems, and cultural production of northern and western cities, from New York to Los Angeles. For more on the Great Migration, see James N. Gregory, *The Southern Diaspora: How the Great Migrations of Black and White Southerners Trans-*

formed America (Chapel Hill: University of North Carolina Press, 2005); Isabel Wilkerson, *The Warmth of Other Suns: The Epic Story of America's Great Migration* (New York: Vintage, 2011); and James Grossman, *Land of Hope: Chicago, Black Southerners, and the Great Migration* (Chicago: University of Chicago Press, 1991).

7. For more on black hospitals, see Vanessa Northington Gamble, *Making a Place for Ourselves: The Black Hospital Movement, 1920–1945* (Oxford: Oxford University Press, 1995).

8. Robert McClory, "Unemployment at 30% in Woodlawn," *Chicago Defender*, May 20, 1975.

9. "McLegends in Spotlight: NBMOA Celebrates 25 Years of Progress," *Atlanta Daily World*, October 16, 1997.

10. Herman Petty, Transcript from National Black McDonald's Operators Anniversary Film.

11. Patricia Sowell Harris, *None of Us Is as Good as All of Us: How McDonald's Prospers by Embracing Inclusion and Diversity* (Hoboken, NJ: Wiley, 2009), 31.

12. "Hamburger's Last Stand: Hidden Costs of Fast Food," *East West Journal*, June 1979, 30.

13. Jones, 169–75, and Harris, 33.

14. Perri Small, "City's Black McDonald's Owner Reflects on Career," *Chicago Weekend,* November 13, 1997, and "Black Owners Meet," *Chicago Tribune*, August 25, 1980. Harris, 33.

15. "Rangers to Open Restaurant," *Chicago Tribune*, November 11, 1968, A18.

16. William Jones, "How Blackstone Rangers Helped Scuttle Red Rooster Food Chain," *Chicago Defender*, March 8, 1970.

17. Harris, 32.

18. Tom Brune and James Yliselany, "The Making of Jeff Fort," *Chicago Magazine*, November 1988. Jeff Fort, who migrated to Chicago from Mississippi as a child, was a proponent of black capitalism, so much so that he famously received an invitation to President Richard Nixon's 1968 inauguration. Fort organized his gang into a political group, the Grassroots Independent Voters of Illinois, and received a million dollars in grants and donations, including monies from the Office of Equal Opportunity, to open businesses and provide job training. A month before Petty's McDonald's store opened, in November of 1968, the Rangers debuted their own non-profit, twenty-four-hour restaurant on the site of a former coffeehouse. Funded by a $3,000 loan from the Kenwood-Oakland Community Organization—a local body that drew the funds from another program named Toward Responsible Freedom—the restaurant was supposed to provide job training to local youth. But the restaurant's greatest challenge was Fort's federal indictment over how he secured so much funding for his projects, which provided him with a salary.

19. Harris, 32.

20. Harris, 33.

21. Harris, 33.

22. For more on the 1968 Democratic National Convention, see Michael Schumacher, *The Contest: The 1968 Election and the War for America's Soul* (Minneapolis: University of Minnesota Press, 2018); John Schultz, *No One Was Killed: The Democratic National Convention, August 1968* (Chicago: University of Chicago Press, 2009): and Jan Weiner, *Conspiracy in the Streets: The Extraordinary Trial of the Chicago Eight* (New York: New Press, 2006).

23. Author interview with Wayne Embry.

24. Max Boas and Steve Chain, *Big Mac: The Unauthorized Story of McDonald's* (New York: E.P. Dutton & Co., 1976), 167.

25. ViewPoint, Inc. 1994/04, Subject Files, Box 90-5, SF, Corporate Files, McDonald's, 1975–1977, 90-5, ViewPoint, Virginia G. Harsh Research Collection, Carter G. Woodson Regional Library, Chicago Public Library.

26. ViewPoint, Inc. 1994/04, Subject Files, Box 90-5, SF Corporate Files, McDonald's, 1975–1977, ViewPoint.

27. ViewPoint, Inc. 1994/04, Subject Files, Box 90-5, SF Corporate Files, McDonald's, 1975–1977, ViewPoint.

28. Harris, 39.

29. Graydon Megan, "Robert Beavers, Former McDonald's Executive, Dies at 71," *Chicago Tribune*, June 27, 2018.

30. Harris, 40.

31. Harris, 42.

32. "Birth Pangs of Black Capitalism," *Time*, October 18, 1968, 124–27.

33. Harris, 45.

34. Petty, Transcript, 4. The first efforts to recruit minority franchisees mostly focused on African-Americans but would soon pivot toward Latinos, Asian Americans, and Pacific Islanders. This new interest in being supportive of people of color was embraced by some but for others made the question of racial identity rise to an uncomfortable surface. Outside of McDonald's, the franchising rush was also consuming the thoughts of potential businesspeople. For some, franchising was not as fulfilling as the potential of starting one's own business, and the issue of opening opportunities to minorities drew some people to questions about their own identities. "I always considered myself a normal American," Albert Okura wrote in his self-published autobiography about his life in the chicken business with his small California franchise, Juan Pollo. He said the franchise race led him to think: "But now I am considered a minority. By the time I entered the management ranks of Burger King I was the only non-Anglo manager in the meetings." His survival strategy, as a second-generation American and son of Japanese internees, was to "go with the flow." Okura concluded, "I can tell people I'm a minority when it is convenient and I can tell others I am a red-blooded American when it is convenient." As a manager in the Burger King system in the 1970s, Okura noticed the dizzying pace of store openings and franchise recruitment. "Burger King owned by the deep pockets of Pillsbury Foods was competing with McDonald's to become the largest chain in America . . . Areas and territories were being snapped up left and right. Corporate executives were jumping ship to buy a franchise." See Albert Okura, *Albert Okura: The Chicken Man with a 50 Year Plan* (Author House, 2014), 28.

35. Carol Kramer, "McDonald's Plans TV Specials," *Chicago Tribune*, August 4, 1967.

36. "Most Chicago Land Values Found Higher," *Chicago Tribune*, June 5, 1973.

37. Yla Eason, "They Invest in Themselves for Fun and Profit," *Chicago Tribune*, June 21, 1973.

38. "Better Boys' Burgers, McDonald's Franchise Nets Profits for Chicago Boys Club," *Ebony*, March 1972.

39. "Better Boys' Burgers."

40. For an excellent treatment on business and gender, which looks at the National Negro Business League and other black organizations, see Tiffany Gill, *Beauty Shop Politics: African American Women's Activism in the Beauty Industry* (Urbana: University of Illinois Press, 2010), and Kevern J. Verney, *The Art of the Possible: Booker T. Washington and Black Leadership in the United States, 1881–1925* (New York: Routledge, 2014).

41. Devin Fergus, *Liberalism, Black Power, and the Making of American Politics, 1965–1980* (Athens: University of Georgia Press, 2009), 200.

42. Robert E. Weems Jr. with Lewis A. Randolph, *Business in Black and White: American Presidents and Black Entrepreneurs in the Twentieth Century* (New York: New York University Press, 2009), 115.

43. Weems, 98.

44. Richard Nixon, Remarks on the CBS Radio Network: "Bridges to Human Dignity, The Concept," April 25, 1968, *The American Presidency Project*, http://www.presidency.ucsb.edu/ws/?pid=123905.

45. "Bridges to Human Dignity."

46. Rachel Devlin, *A Girl Stands at the Door: The Generation of Young Women Who Desegregated America's Schools* (New York: Basic Books, 2018). In Devlin's analysis of school desegregation cases, she notes the ways that legal challenges to segregation masked attempts to draw funding to segregated schools. Megan Ming Francis has traced the relationship between donors and the agenda of the NAACP, and she argues that pressure from funders shifted the civil rights organization's attention from racial violence to education in the early twentieth century. Megan Ming Francis, "The Price of Civil Rights: Black Lives, White Funding, and Movement Capture," *Law & Society Review* 53, no. 1 (2019): 275–309.

47. Mehrsa Baradaran, "A Bad Check for Black America," *Boston Review*, November 9, 2017.

48. Frederick Sturdivant, *The Ghetto Marketplace* (New York: Free Press, 1969), ix–x. See also Anne Fleming, *A City of Debtors: A Century of Fringe Finance* (Cambridge: Harvard University Press, 2018).

49. Under the Economic Opportunity Act of 1964's Title IV, the federal government encouraged low-income citizens to "create or expand" businesses. The Office of Economic Opportunity established thirty-nine centers to work with the Small Business Administration to allocate small loans at modest interest rates. With grants up to $25,000 available, the program also provided guidance and mentorship for the aspiring businesspeople. The Southern Christian Leadership Conference (SCLC) criticized the Johnson administration for favoring investment in

business over people. In a document entitled "A Supplemental Appropriation for the Office of Economic Opportunity, Facts, and a Proposal," the SCLC accused Johnson of steering funding toward business efforts at the expense of "urban programs to fight poverty." The White House decided to support a National Alliance of Businessmen (NAB) program, with use of Office of Economic Opportunity funds that ended supplemental funding for a summer jobs programs for youth. The NAB appropriation also stripped $100 million from the Head Start early-education program, the Neighborhood Youth Corps, and the Job Corps. Supporters of the move said it would help reduce unemployment. But, the SCLC said the proposal was foolhardy in that it would imperil 16 Job Corps Centers, would bar 6,800 people from access to job training, and remove 170,000 low-income youths from Neighborhood Youth Corps programs. Head Start also lost 13,000 slots. "A Supplemental Appropriation for the Office of Economic Opportunity, Facts and a Proposal," undated, King Center Online Archive, http://www.thekingcenter.org/archive/document/supplemental-appropriation-office-economic-opportunity.

50. Sturdivant, xv.
51. Sturdivant, xvii.
52. Sturdivant, 130.
53. Urban historians have chronicled the impact of race on shaping and remaking cities: Arnold Hirsch, *Making the Second Ghetto: Race and Housing in Chicago 1940–1960* (Chicago: University of Chicago Press, 1998); Thomas Sugrue, *The Origins of the Urban Crisis: Race and Inequality in Postwar Detroit* (Princeton: Princeton University Press, 2005); Robert Self, *American Babylon: Race and the Struggle for Postwar Oakland* (Princeton: Princeton University Press, 2003); Becky M. Nicolaides, *My Blue Heaven: Life and Politics in the Working-Class Suburbs of Los Angeles, 1920–1965* (Chicago: University of Chicago Press, 2002); and Richard Rothstein, *The Color of Law: A Forgotten History of How Our Federal Government Segregated America* (New York: Liveright, 2017).
54. For more on white real estate interests and the manipulation of markets, see Nathan Connolly, *A World More Concrete: Real Estate and the Remaking of Jim Crow South Florida* (Chicago: University of Chicago Press, 2014).
55. Sturdivant, xvi.
56. James Forman, "Black Manifesto, To the White Christian Churches and the Jewish Synagogues in the United States of America and All other Racist Institutions," Presentation by James Forman Delivered and Adopted by the National Black Economic Development Conference in Detroit, Michigan, on April 26, 1969, Herzog Race Relations Collection, Box 17, Duke University Library, Durham, NC.
57. Frederick Case, *Black Capitalism: Problems in Development, A Case Study of Los Angeles* (New York: Praeger Publishers, 1972), 5.
58. Case, 9.
59. Case, 9.
60. Case, 47.
61. Case, 50.

62. Andrew F. Brimmer, "The Economic Potential of Black Capitalism," a Paper Presented before the 82nd Annual Meeting of the American Economic Association, New York Hilton Hotel, New York, New York, December 29, 1969, Board of Governors of the Federal Reserve System (U.S.), https://fraser.stlouisfed.org/title/463/item/10372. Accessed on January 6, 2019.

63. Robert Dowling, "Negro Business Leaders Charge Brimmer Is out of Touch with Changing Black Climate," *American Banker*, January 7, 1970. "Ownership Favored, Black Businessmen Hit Brimmer View," untitled newspaper, undated, Dempsey Travis Papers, Box 14, Chicago History Museum Archives Center.

64. Eric Wheelwright, director, *The Brady Keys, Jr. Story*, 2014.

65. *The Brady Keys, Jr. Story.*

66. Max Holleran, "How Fast Food Chains Supersized Inequality," *New Republic*, August 2, 2017.

67. Brady Keys Jr., "I Recommend Blacks Go into Business via the Franchise Route," *Black Enterprise*, May 1974, 28.

68. "I Recommend Blacks Go Into Business via the Franchise Route."

69. "I Recommend Blacks Go Into Business via the Franchise Route." By 1988, Keys held the contracts on 13 Burger Kings in Detroit and 11 Kentucky Fried Chickens in Albany, Georgia, and other parts of the state. Keys expanded his business interests into video games, a computer- and telephone-based educational tutoring service, real estate, and energy production.

70. See Meg Jacobs, *Panic at the Pump: The Energy Crisis and the Transformation of American Politics in the 1970s* (New York: Hill & Wang, 2016).

71. Ernest Holsendolph, "Keeping McDonald's Out in Front," *New York Times*, December 30, 1973.

72. Robert Gordon, "Abernathy Advocates 'Black Socialism': Wants Rich Communities, Not People," *Chicago Defender*, January 9, 1969.

73. Caption to photo of Ralph Abernathy, *Chicago Defender*, April 29, 1969.

Chapter Three: The Burger Boycott and the Ballot Box

1. For more on Cleveland's racial demographics, see Kenneth Kusmer, *A Ghetto Takes Shape: Black Cleveland, 1870–1930* (Urbana: University of Illinois Press, 1978), and Bessie House-Soremekun, *Confronting the Odds: African American Entrepreneurship in Cleveland, Ohio* (Kent, OH: Kent State University Press, 2011).

2. Leonard Moore, *Carl B. Stokes and the Rise of Black Political Power* (Urbana: University of Illinois Press, 2003), 45. See also David Stradling, *Where the River Burned: Carl Stokes and the Struggle to Save Cleveland* (Ithaca: Cornell University Press, 2018).

3. "White Withdrawal: Ghetto Merchants Shy Away from Civic Ties in Areas They Serve," *Wall Street Journal*, August 16, 1977, 1.

4. Kyle Swenson, "How a Mayor's Bold Action Helped Save His City from Burning After MLK's Assassination," *Washington Post*, April 4, 2018, and "Cleveland Mayor Takes to Streets: Stokes Praises His City for Avoiding Racial Disorder," *New York Times*, April 12, 1968.

5. James Robenalt, *Ballots and Bullets: Black Power Politics and Urban Guerilla Warfare in 1968 Cleveland* (Chicago: Chicago Review Press, 2018).

6. John Kramer, "The Election of Blacks to City Councils: A 1970 Status Report and Prolegomenon," *Journal of Black Studies* 1, no. 4 (June 1971): 443–76, and Jon C. Teaford, "'King Richard' Hatcher: Mayor of Gary," *Journal of Negro History* 77, no. 3 (Summer 1992): 126–40.

7. For two examples on local control movements in policing and education, see Tera Agyepong, "In the Belly of the Beast: Black Policemen Combat Police Brutality in Chicago, 1968–1983," *Journal of African American History* 98, no. 2 (2013): 253–76, and Heather Lewis, *New York City Public Schools from Brownsville to Bloomberg: Community Control and Its Legacy* (New York: Teachers College Press, 2013).

8. Keeanga-Yamahtta Taylor, *From #BlackLivesMatter to Black Liberation* (Chicago: Haymarket Press, 2016), 85.

9. "White Withdrawal: Ghetto Merchants Shy Away from Civic Ties in Areas They Serve."

10. Frederick Sturdivant, *The Ghetto Marketplace* (New York: Free Press, 1969), 134.

11. "Operation Breadbasket memo, dated December 12, 1967, Statement by Dr. Martin Luther King, Jr.," Alvin Pitcher Papers, Box 1, Folder 4, University of Chicago Special Collections Research Center.

12. "Breadbasket Technique Called Passé in Cleveland," *Chicago Defender*, February 10, 1968.

13. "Restaurant Chain Will Expand Here," *Cleveland Plain Dealer*, June 12, 1961.

14. "Blacks Picket McDonald's, Demand Negro Ownership," *Cleveland Plain Dealer*, July 11, 1969.

15. "A Minister Finds His Work in the Slum," *Wall Street Journal*, April 10, 1967.

16. For more on the Black Israelites movement and other groups that formed to offer black religious alternatives to Christianity, see Jacob S. Dorman, *Chosen People: The Rise of American Black Israelite Religions* (Oxford: Oxford University Press, 2016).

17. Moore, 120.

18. "Rabbi David Hill Plans Black Xmas," *Call & Post*, November 29, 1969.

19. "In McDonald's Boycott, Leaders Plead Innocent," *Daily Kent Stater*, October 9, 1969.

20. Moore, 121.

21. "The Price of Equality," *Call & Post*, March 30, 1989.

22. "Don't Buy at McDonald's Flyer," undated, Operation Black Unity Records, Box 1, Folder 3, Western Reserve Historical Society, Cleveland, Ohio.

23. "Don't Buy at McDonald's" Flyer.

24. Moore, 123.

25. "McDonald's Moves Franchisees as Fast as Hamburgers," undated press clipping, OBU Papers, Box 1, Folder 4, Western Reserve Historical Society.

26. "Blacks Picket McDonald's, Demand Negro Ownership."

27. "Protestors Request Parley with Head of McDonald's," *Cleveland Plain Dealer*, July 20, 1969.

28. "Two McDonald's Outlets Stay Open Despite Protest," *Cleveland Plain Dealer*, July 16, 1969.

29. Anthony Ripley, "Negroes Continue a Boycott in Ohio: Protest All but Closes Four McDonald's," *New York Times*, July 16, 1969, and Toni Berry, "The Afro Set," *Cleveland Historical*, accessed March 7, 2019, https://clevelandhistorical .org/items/show/777.

30. "Negroes Continue a Boycott in Ohio."

31. "Negroes Continue a Boycott in Ohio."

32. "Unity Group, McDonald's to Parley on Picketing," *Cleveland Plain Dealer*, July 26, 1969.

33. "Unity Group, McDonald's to Parley on Picketing," and "Two McDonald's Outlets Stay Open Despite Protests."

34. Nishani Frazier, *Harambee City: The Congress of Racial Equality in Cleveland and the Rise of Black Power Populism* (Fayetteville: University of Arkansas Press, 2017), 160.

35. "Unity Group, McDonald's to Parley on Picketing," and "Two McDonald's Outlets Stay Open Despite Protests."

36. "Memo Regarding OBU Protests," undated, OBU Papers, Western Reserve Historical Society.

37. "Two McDonald's Outlets Stay Open Despite Protests."

38. "McDonald's to Open in Face of Boycott," *Cleveland Press*, July 11, 1969.

39. "Negroes Continue a Boycott in Ohio: Protest All but Closes Four McDonald's."

40. "Search for Blacks Told by McDonald's," *Cleveland Press*, July 14, 1969.

41. "Search for Blacks Told by McDonald's."

42. "NAACP, Urban League Ask McDonald's to Delay Opening," *Cleveland Press*, August 8, 1969.

43. "McDonald's Rejects Plan for Negro Profit Sharing," *Washington Post*, August 23, 1969.

44. "Gift Question Delays Sale of 4 McDonald's," *Cleveland Press*, August 22, 1969.

45. "McDonald's Offers Swim Pool Aid," *Cleveland Press*, August 28, 1969.

46. "Memorandum from Walker Williams to Philip Mason," dated August 12, 1969, Box 23, Folder 440, Hough Area Development Corporation Papers, Western Reserve Historical Collection, Cleveland, Ohio.

47. Carlotta Washington, "500 at Antioch Meet, Black Unity to Expand Boycott of McDonald's," *Call & Post*, August 30, 1969.

48. "A Negro Protest in Cleveland Ends on Primary Eve," *New York Times*, September 30, 1969.

49. "NAACP, Urban League Ask McDonald's to Delay Opening."

50. "Negroes Continue a Boycott in Ohio: Protest All but Closes Four McDonald's."

51. "McDonald's Is Reopening Four Outlets in Inner City," *Cleveland Plain Dealer*, August 8, 1969.

52. "500 Meet at Antioch."

53. "McDonald's Is Reopening Four Outlets in Inner City."

54. "Black Unity Hit by Urban League," *Cleveland Press*, September 2, 1969.

55. "Hill Ousted as Leader of Black Unity Negotiators," *Cleveland Plain Dealer*, September 9, 1969.

56. "Probes by Jury Urged in McDonald's Dispute," *Cleveland Plain Dealer*, August 23, 1969.

57. "Accord Seen in McDonald's Dispute," *Cleveland Plain Dealer*, August 21, 1969.

58. "Racism Charge Stirs Boycott of McDonald's: Hamburger Hassle Imperils Stokes," *Washington Post*, August 25, 1969.

59. "Kelly Rips Boycott of McDonald's," *Cleveland Press*, September 8, 1969.

60. "Kelly Rips Boycott of McDonald's."

61. "Racism Charge Stirs Boycott of McDonald's."

62. "Stokes Nominated for Second Term in Cleveland Vote: Stokes Nominated for 2d Term as Cleveland Mayor," *New York Times*, October 1, 1969.

63. For more on the HADC and the sale of the McDonald's franchises, see Nishani Frazier, "A McDonald's that Reflects the Soul of the People," in Laura Warren Hill and Julia Rabig, eds., *The Business of Black Power: Community Development, Capitalism, and Corporate Responsibility in Postwar America* (Rochester, NY: University of Rochester Press, 2012).

64. Letter from DeForest Brown to James DiGilio, dated October 27, 1969, Hough Area Development Corporation Records, Box 23, Folder 440.

65. The HADC used a sophisticated mix of financing strategies by accessing federal urban development funds to enter franchising. This model was used to transfer ownership of all the East Side McDonald's locations throughout the 1960s and into the early 1970s. These deals also expanded the portfolio of McDonald's in black neighborhoods from four to six. In the winter of 1969, the Office of Economic Opportunity approved the HADC's acquisition of the East 107th Street McDonald's, but made clear that the OEO was not "the guarantor of the total purchase price," and approved their use of $62,500 from the agency's Venture Capital Fund to acquire the franchise. Letter from Geoffrey Faux to DeForest Brown, dated December 10, 1969, Hough Area Development Corporation Records, Box 23, Folder 440. The remaining funds were secured by a loan of $100,000 to the HADC from Union Commerce Bank. See also "Action of Directors Without a Meeting," undated, Hough Area Development Corporation Records, Box 23, Folder 440. HADC later borrowed $225,000 to acquire the 83rd Street store. McDonald's was happy to allow HADC to franchise the two locations but required that each store install a manager who could hold a 25% stake in the business. See Certification, Hough Area Development Corporation Records, Box 23, Folder 440. In the case of the 107th Street location, the HADC proposed loaning $11,000 to Harry Sykes to manage the restaurant. Using a second mortgage on his house as collateral, Sykes had already invested $12,500 in the 107th Street Corporation. Sykes could not secure traditional bank financing because he had too little of his own money and was a credit risk due to his assuming the franchise and the lease, and he could not find a loan at rates "he could reasonably be expected to meet." HADC decided to provide the loan because they deemed Sykes "uniquely qualified to run the new restaurant." Sykes was

from Cleveland and he had worked at McDonald's for years, climbing his way up from a "$1.50 an hour . . . hamburger dispenser," to a manager at the 83rd Street store. He was so successful in the McDonald's System that he was given a salary of $15,000 per year, a considerable wage by the area's standards. Sykes demonstrated his enthusiasm by enrolling in special training courses and was attending a local college part-time to study business administration. Letter from DeForest Brown to James DiGilio. A short-lived Kinsman Development Corporation took over the franchise agreement of a sixth location in 1971. Headed by Wilson Rogers, a die maker at National Screw and Manufacturing Company, Rogers later owned the Kinsman restaurant outright, but the development company probably helped him secure the $232,500 loan for the store, which was guaranteed by General Motors, the SBA, and a local Cleveland community trust. See "Kinsman Businessmen Buy Area McDonald's," *Call & Post*, November 13, 1971.

66. "McDonald's Says It Asked Hough Corp. to Buy In," *Cleveland Press*, April 7, 1970.

67. "3 Franchise Seekers Say They Paid Nothing to Hill," *Cleveland Press*, September 23, 1969.

68. "Jail Boycott Leader on Blackmail; Pickets Gone but McD Biz Slow," *Restaurant News*, October 27, 1969.

69. "Hill Lost Rights as Incompetent, Judge Declares," *Cleveland Press*, August 11, 1969. See Jonathan Metzl, *The Protest Psychosis: How Schizophrenia Became a Black Disease* (Boston: Beacon Press, 2010), which links the development of antipsychotic drugs, the criminalization and medicalization of black anger, and the development of schizophrenia as a diagnosis commonplace among blacks in Detroit.

70. "Cleveland Negro Wins a Franchise," *New York Times*, January 25, 1970.

71. Robert Morris, "Funds Sought to Save HADC," *Call & Post*, July 24, 1982.

72. "Cleveland Negroes Boycott White-Owned Businesses," *Atlanta Daily World*, March 31, 1970.

73. See Gaiutra Bahadur, "The Jonestown We Don't Know," *New York Review of Books*, December 21, 2018.

74. "Black Boycott's Leader Ends Exile," *Cleveland Plain Dealer*, August 14, 1992; "Cult Leader Awaits Word on Old Blackmail Charges," *Cleveland Plain Dealer*, August 7, 1992; and "Cleveland Fugitive to Leave Guyana Prison," *Cleveland Plain Dealer*, February 9, 1992.

75. "Man Who Fled Cleveland in '71 Returning to the U.S.," *Cleveland Plain Dealer*, August 8, 1992.

76. "Cult Ex-Leader Hill in Guyana for Book," *Cleveland Plain Dealer*, November 1, 1992.

77. "Raplin Honored for Boycott Role," *Cleveland Plain Dealer*, September 25, 1993.

78. "Jim Raplin Remembers His Search for a Pot of Gold for Blacks Behind McDonald's Golden Arches," *Call & Post*, August 23, 1975.

79. "Jim Raplin Remembers His Search for a Pot of Gold for Blacks."

80. Patricia Harris Sowell, *None of Us Is as Good as All of Us: How McDonald's Prospers by Embracing Diversity and Inclusion* (Hoboken, NJ: Wiley, 2009), 44.
81. Harris, 50.

Chapter Four: Bending the Golden Arches

1. "Why Black Enterprise?" *Black Enterprise*, August 1970, 4.
2. "Minority Franchising: Boom or Bust?" *Black Enterprise*, August 1970, 51.
3. Peggy Pascoe, *What Comes Naturally: Miscegenation Law and the Making of Race in America* (New York: Oxford University, 2015).
4. DeNeen L. Brown, "When Portland Banned Blacks: Oregon's Shameful History as an All-White State," *Washington Post*, June 7, 2017.
5. Karen J. Gibson, "Bleeding Albina: A History of Community Disinvestment, 1940–2000," *Transforming Anthropology* 15, no. 1: 3–25.
6. Ethan Johnson and Felicia Williams, "Desegregation and Multiculturalism in the Portland Public Schools," *Oregon Historical Quarterly* 11, no. 1 (Spring 2010): 6–37.
7. "Calm Returns to Fire-Raked Albina District," *Oregonian*, June 19, 1969.
8. Lucas N. N. Burke and Judson L. Jeffries, *The Portland Black Panthers: Empowering Albina, Remaking a City* (Seattle: University of Washington Press, 2016), 60–89.
9. Jakobi Williams, *From the Bullet to the Ballot: The Illinois Chapter of the Black Panther Party and Racial Coalition Politics in Chicago* (Chapel Hill: University of North Carolina Press, 2015).
10. Alondra Nelson, *Body and Soul: The Black Panther Party and the Fight Against Medical Discrimination* (Minneapolis: University of Minnesota Press, 2013), 9.
11. Nelson, 111.
12. The Black Panther Party for Self-Defense was founded in Oakland in 1966 by Bobby Seale and Huey Newton. Donna Murch, "The Campus and the Street: Race, Migration, and the Origins of the Black Panther Party in Oakland," *Souls: A Critical Journal of Black Politics, Culture, and Society* 9, no. 4 (2007): 333–45, and Donna Murch, *Living for the City: Migration, Education, and the Rise of the Black Panther Party in Oakland, California* (Chapel Hill: University of North Carolina Press, 2010). For more on the history of school lunches, see Susan Levin, *School Lunch Politics: The Surprising History of America's Favorite Welfare Program* (Princeton: Princeton University Press, 2010), and A. R. Ruis, *Eating to Learn, Learning to Eat: The Origins of School Lunch in the United States* (Newark: Rutgers University Press, 2017).
13. "Breakfast for School Children Programs Flyer," National Committee to Combat Fascism, Folder 3/5, Black Panther Party Police Records, City of Portland Archives.
14. "Breakfast Clinic Programs Belie Militant Panther Image," *Oregonian*, November 12, 1971.
15. As quoted in Burke and Jeffries, 110.
16. As quoted in Burke and Jeffries, 108.
17. "Breakfast Clinic Programs Belie Militant Panther Image."

18. "Breakfast Clinic Programs Belie Militant Panther Image."

19. "Boycott Flyer," Folder 2/5, Black Panther Party Police Records, City of Portland Archives.

20. "Crowd Storms City Hall to Protest Shooting," *Oregonian*, February 20, 1970.

21. "Intelligence Division Report," dated September 13, 1970, Folder 3/5, Black Panther Party Police Records, City of Portland Archives.

22. "Hamburger's Last Stand: Hidden Costs of Fast Food," *East West Journal*, June 1979, 36.

23. Annelise Orelick, *Storming Caesar's Palace: How Black Mothers Fought Their Own War on Poverty* (Boston: Beacon Press, 2006).

24. "McDonald's Field Report," Folder 2/5, Black Panther Party Police Records, City of Portland Archives.

25. "Officers Report, re: McDonald's Hamburger," dated August 12, 1970, Folder 2/5, Black Panther Party Police Records, City of Portland Archives.

26. "Officers Report."

27. "Officers Report."

28. "Officers Report."

29. "Narrative," dated August 8, 22, 1970, Folder 2/5, Black Panther Party Police Records.

30. "Report of Crime Against Property," dated September 14, 1970, Folder 2/5, Black Panther Party Police Records.

31. "Confidential Detective Division Report, Confidential Informant Note," dated August 18, 1970, Folder 2/5, Black Panther Party Police Records, City of Portland Archives.

32. The Counterintelligence Program was an official FBI initiative between 1956 and 1971 with the explicit intention of keeping tabs on and undermining the work of activist groups. Although COINTELPRO has ceased, state surveillance of activists continues. Betty L. Medsger, *The Burglary: The Discovery of J. Edgar Hoover's Secret FBI* (New York: Vintage, 2014), and David J. Garrow, *The FBI and Martin Luther King, Jr.: From "Solo" to Memphis* (New York: W. W. Norton, 1981).

33. Burke and Jeffries, 131.

34. Nelson, 122.

35. Polina Olse, *Portland in the 1960s: Stories from the Counterculture* (Mount Pleasant, SC: History Press and Arcadia Publishing, 2012).

36. Burke and Jeffries, 181–223.

37. C. Gerald Fraser, "Burger Shop in Harlem Shows It Can Cut the Mustard," *New York Times*, November 11, 1972.

38. Joseph B. Treaster, "White Youths Attack Blacks in Washington Square," *New York Times*, September 9, 1976.

39. "Hamburger's Last Stand," 35.

40. "Hamburger's Last Stand," 35.

41. "Ogontz Neighbors Association Flyer," 1969, and "Philly Black Community Battles to Keep Out McDonald's Unit," undated press clipping, Ogontz Area Neigh-

bors Association Records, Box 3, Folder 5, Temple University Special Collections Research Center, Philadelphia, Pennsylvania.

42. Letter from Kelly E. Miller to Edmund N. Bacon, dated June 27, 1969, Ogontz Neighbors Association Records, Box 3, Folder 6.

43. "Hamburgers vs. Education Flyer," 1963, CORE Chicago Chapter, Congress of Racial Equality Papers (CORE), 1941–1967, Wisconsin Historical Society, Madison, Wisconsin.

44. Letter from Robert Smalls to Paul Rand Dixon, dated July 21, 1970, Ogontz Neighbors Association Records, Box 3, Folder 7.

45. "Petition to Councilman Paul D'Ortona," President of City Council, Ogontz Neighbors Association Records, Box 3, Folder 6.

46. "Residents' Outcry: 'Too Many,'" undated article, Ogontz Neighbors Association Records, Box 3, Folder 6.

47. Letter from Edmund Bacon to Kelly Miller, dated June 23, 1969, Ogontz Neighbors Association Records, Box 3, Folder 5.

48. Maurice White, "McDonald's Restaurant Owner Pushing His Way Up Business Ladder," *Philadelphia Tribune*, December 5, 1978, and "McDonald's Cites Financial Reasons for Ouster of Owner," *Philadelphia Tribune*, October 28, 1983.

49. "Soft Ice Cream Sales Soar as Demand Dips for Regular Variety," *Wall Street Journal*, January 8, 1951.

50. For more on the Freedom Rides, see Raymond Arsenault, *Freedom Rides: 1961 and the Struggle for Racial Justice* (Oxford: Oxford University Press, 2007).

51. U.S. Supreme Court, *Bond v. Floyd*, 385 U.S. 116 (1966).

52. For more on Atlanta and the New South, see Maurice J. Hobson, *The Legend of the Black Mecca: Politics and Class in the Making of Modern Atlanta* (Chapel Hill: University of North Carolina Press, 2017); Jessica Ann Levy, "Selling Atlanta: Black Mayoral Politics from Protest to Entrepreneurism, 1973 to 1990," *Journal of Urban History* 41, no. 3 (May 2015): 420–43; and Beverly Hendrix Wright, "Atlanta: Mecca of the Southeast," in Robert D. Bullard, ed., *In Search of the New South: The Black Urban Experience in the 1970s and 1980s* (Tuscaloosa: University of Alabama Press, 1989). "Blacks Played Major Role in City's Economic Development," *Atlanta Daily World*, August 13, 1978. Clark Rozell, "Auburn's 'Sweet' History," *Atlanta Daily World*, June 17, 1979.

53. "Vet Says He'll Make Good in Business," undated, unsourced article, Julian Bond Papers, Box 116, MSS 13346, University of Virginia Albert and Shirley Small Special Collections Library, University of Virginia.

54. "It's Business—Not Charity," undated article, Julian Bond Papers, Box 116, University of Virginia Special Collections Library.

55. Jon Nordheimer, "Black Atlanta Venture Backfires on Liberals," *New York Times*, June 15, 1970.

56. George S. Schuyler, "Atlanta's Sorcerer's Apprentices," *Macon Herald*, news clipping, Julian Bond Papers, University of Virginia Special Collections Library.

57. T. M. Alexander, "Nothing New," undated clipping, Julian Bond Papers, University of Virginia Special Collections Library.

58. "Bond's Fast Food Business Robbed 15 Times," *Jet*, June 4, 1970, and David Halberstam, *The Children* (New York: Fawcett Books, 1999), 690–94.
59. "Minutes of Special Meeting of Directors," dated June 1, 1970, Julian Bond Papers, University of Virginia Special Collections Library.
60. "Minutes of Special Meeting of Directors."
61. "Minutes of Special Meeting of Directors."
62. Letter from Charles M. Kidd to Julian Bond, Julian Bond Papers, University of Virginia Special Collections Library.
63. "Franchise Route Looks Good for Blacks—Thomas," *Atlanta Inquirer*, February 24, 1973.
64. William Reed, "Saluting a Champion—Businessman Henry Thomas," *Smithsonian*, November 29, 2017.
65. "Sisters Chicken and Biscuits a Hot Item in East Cleveland," *Call & Post*, June 6, 1981, and "Sisters Chicken and Biscuits Coming, Controversy Started," *Call & Post*, May 30, 198.
66. "Sisters Chicken and Biscuits Coming, Controversy Started."
67. Garth Bishop, "Repast from the Past," *City Scene*, October 29, 2013, http://www.cityscenecolumbus.com/eat-and-drink/eat/repast-from-the-past/.
68. For more on the politics of schools in the 1970s, especially community control over education, see Matthew Delmont, *Why Busing Failed: Race, Media, and the National Resistance to School Desegregation* (Oakland: University of California Press, 2016), and for more on the community development movement in the 1970s, see Tom Adam Davies, *Mainstreaming Black Power* (Berkeley: University of California Press, 2017).

Chapter Five: Black America, Brought to You by . . .

1. Gerald R. Ford: "Message on the Observance of Black History Month, February 1976," February 10, 1976. Online by Gerhard Peters and John T. Woolley, *The American Presidency Project*, http://www.presidency.ucsb.edu/ws/?pid=6288.
2. For more on the Bicentennial and public history in the 1970s, see M. J. Rymsza-Pawlowska, *History Comes Alive: Public History and Popular Culture in the 1970s* (Chapel Hill: North Carolina University Press, 2017).
3. "Soul of a Nation: An Illustrated Collection of Historical Narratives Reproduced from McDonald's Special Black Bicentennial Radio Series," 1976, booklet, Andrew J. Young Papers, Box 33, Folder 19, Auburn Avenue Research Library, Atlanta, Georgia.
4. "McDonald's Soul of a Nation."
5. Eric Wheelwright, director, *The Brady Keys, Jr. Story*, 2014.
6. For more on Mahalia Jackson's Glori-Fried Chicken, see Bill Carey, "Failed Fortunes," *Nashville Scene*, September 28, 2000, https://www.nashvillescene.com/news/article/13004920/failed-fortunes, and Bill Carey, *Fortunes, Fiddles, and Fried Chicken: A Business History of Nashville* (Franklin, TN: Hillsboro Press, 2000). ChampBurger's short life was chronicled in many African-American newspapers. See also "Sports of the Times: Foodstuffs," *New York Times*, November

21, 1968, 57; "Ali an Owner of New Negro Drive-In Chain," *Washington Post*, November 21, 1968, H10; "Ali Has $1 Million Hamburger-Stand Deal Grilling: Firm Hops to Franchise Drive-Ins for $10,000," *Philadelphia Tribune*, December 28, 1968; and "Muhammad's Ali's ChampBurgers," *Chicago Defender*, December 21, 1968, 1. James Brown's Gold Platter, despite receiving an investment of $1 million, could not survive. "James Brown Announces 'Gold Platter' Chain of Restaurants," *New York Amsterdam News*, January 18, 1969; "Soul Singer Forms Fast Food Restaurant Chain," *New Pittsburgh Courier*, January 15, 1969; "Soul Singer James Brown Opens 2 Restaurants in His Home Town," *Philadelphia Tribune*, September 2, 1969; and "Jim Brown's Chain Fading," *Baltimore Afro-American*, February 21, 1970.

7. Lisa Napoli, *Ray and Joan: The Man Who Made the McDonald's Fortune and the Woman Who Gave it Away* (New York: Dutton Press, 2016), 10. Mrs. Kroc became known for her contributions to a wide array of liberal and left-leaning causes after Ray's death, and it seemed like her donations were done as much in the spirit of actual generosity as they were declarations of independence from her husband's notable conservativism.

8. Napoli, 10.

9. "McDonald's Hosts Tour," *Call & Post*, July 8, 1972.

10. "Wilson Rogers Has Personal Plan for Affirmative Action," *Call & Post*, June 16, 1973, and "Ground Breaking for McDonald's on Miles," *Call & Post* December 27, 1975.

11. "Hamburger's Last Stand: Hidden Costs of Fast Food," *East West Journal*, June 1979, 30.

12. "McDonald's to Sponsor Double Dutch League," *Atlanta Daily World*, June 14, 1983. For more on the Double Dutch and hand game traditions, see Kyra D. Gaunt, *The Games Black Girls Play: Learning Ropes from Double-Dutch to Hip-Hop* (New York: New York University Press, 2006).

13. "102 Youngsters March in McDonald's Band," *Atlanta Daily World*, December 2, 1979.

14. "Area Youngsters Fitted with Fancy Footwear," *Call & Post*, December 16, 1972.

15. Shuara Wilson, "Inner City McDonald's Restaurant Gets Computer Training Terminal," *Call & Post*, September 15, 1979.

16. U.S. Department of Commerce, Census Bureau, Current Population Survey (CPS), October 1967 through October 2006.

17. "Inner City McDonald's Restaurant Gets Computer Training Terminal."

18. "Chemical Peril Eased in Chicago," *New York Times*, April 28, 1974.

19. Jon Van, "Gas Victims Help Each Other; Kept in Dark, They Assert," *Chicago Daily Tribune*, April 28, 1974; Frank Zahour, "Fume Victims Still Feeling Symptoms," *Chicago Daily Tribune*, May 5, 1974, 22; and "$5.4 million Suit Filed in Gas Leak," *Chicago Tribune*, May 24, 1974.

20. David Smallwood, "Gas Peril Continues," and Lorac Lawas, "Gas Fumes Invade Community," *South End Review*, May 2, 1974.

21. "Big Mac Helped Big Leak Victims," *Chicago Daily Defender*, June 1, 1974.

22. Jason P. Chambers, "A Master Strategist: John H. Johnson and the Develop-

ment of Chicago as a Center for Black Business Enterprise," in Robert E. Weems and Jason P. Chambers, eds., *Building the Black Metropolis: African American Entrepreneurship in Chicago* (Urbana: University of Illinois Press), 191.

23. Chambers, 198, in Weems and Chambers, *Building the Black Metropolis*.

24. Chambers, 198, in Weems and Chambers, *Building the Black Metropolis*.

25. Jason Chambers, *Madison Avenue and the Color Line* (Philadelphia: University of Pennsylvania Press, 2008), 246. See also David Green, "How McDonald's Learned Specific Target Marketing; Ads Show 'They Understand Me; They Get It,'" *Advertising Age*, June 3, 1996.

26. D. Parke Gibson, *$70 Billion in the Black: America's Black Consumers* (New York: Macmillan, 1978), 82.

27. "Commercial Evaluation of Racial Integration, 1977," 5-14, ViewPoint, letter dated November 6, 1977, From ViewPoint, Inc. to Sharon Ray, Needham, Harper and Steers Advertising, Inc, ViewPoint, Inc. Archives, Vivian Harsh Collection, Carter G. Woodson Regional Library, Chicago Public Library.

28. Kelvin Wall, "Positioning Your Brand in the Black Market," *Advertising Age*, June 18, 1973.

29. Chambers, 192, in Weems and Chambers, *Building the Black Metropolis*.

30. Chambers, *Madison Avenue and the Color Line*, 246.

31. *The Negro Family: The Case for National Action*, United States Department of Labor Office of Policy Planning and Research, U.S. Department of Labor, 1965.

32. Chambers, 204, in Weems and Chambers, *Building the Black Metropolis*.

33. "Breakfast: We Do It All for You," McDonald's Advertisement, YouTube, 1978. Accessed January 10, 2019.

34. "Commercial Evaluation of Racial Integration, 1977," letter dated November 6, 1977, from ViewPoint, Inc to Sharon Ray, Needham, Harper and Steers Advertising, Inc, ViewPoint, Inc. Archives, Box 5, Folder 14.

35. Lenika Cruz, "'Dinnertimin' and 'No Tipping': How Advertisers Targeted Black Consumers," *The Atlantic*, June 7, 2015, https://www.theatlantic.com/entertainment/archive/2015/06/casual-racism-and-greater-diversity-in-70s-advertising/394958/; Chris Bodenner, "When Do Multicultural Ads Become Offensive? Your Thoughts," *The Atlantic*, June 22, 2015, https://www.theatlantic.com/entertainment/archive/2015/06/advertising-race-1970s-stereotypes-offensive/395624/; and Code Switch, "Black People Are Not Dark-Skinned White People," National Public Radio, September 5, 2017.

36. "Analysis of McDonald's National Baseline Study for 1974 and for 1977 As It Relates to Black Consumers, 1978," Box 62, Folder 3, Project Reports, Other, Burrell Advertising Analysis of McDonald's National Baseline Study for 1974 and for 1977 as it Relates to Black Consumers, 1978, 62-3, ViewPoint, Inc.

37. McDonald's Advertisement, *Ebony*, November 1984.

38. McDonald's Advertisement, *Ebony*, May 1984.

39. "Hamburger's Last Stand: Hidden Costs of Fast Food," *East West Journal*, June 1979, 35.

40. For more on African Americans on television, see David J. Leonard and Lisa A. Guerrero, eds., *African Americans on Television: Race-ing for Ratings* (New

York: Praeger Press, 2013); Darnell Hunt, *Channeling Blackness: Studies on Television and Race in America* (New York: Oxford University Press, 2004); and Donald Bogle, *Primetime Blues: African Americans on Network Television* (New York: Farrar, Straus & Giroux, 2002).

41. "Good Time, Great Taste," McDonald's Advertisement, YouTube. Accessed January 9, 2019.

42. Author interview with Robert Jackson, March 20, 2017.

43. Amitai Etzioni, "The Fast-Food Factories: McJobs Are Bad for Kids," *Washington Post,* August 24, 1986.

44. Robin Kelley, *Race Rebels: Culture, Politics, and the Black Working Class* (New York: Free Press, 1994), 1–3.

45. "McDonald's, National Baseline Study, 1977, Project Reports, Other, Market Facts, Inc., (13) 63-9" Box 29, ViewPoint, Inc. Archives.

46. John F. Love, *McDonald's: Behind the Arches* (New York: Bantam Press), 204.

47. Love, 295–96.

48. Gibson, 63.

49. Fran Zell, "How Women Shop: Why You Buy What You Buy—and What it All Means," *Chicago Tribune,* September 6, 1970.

50. "McDonald's, National Baseline Study, 1977," and "KFC/Brown's Chicken Taste Test, 1981, Project Reports, Other, Market Facts, Inc., (1) 63-7," Box 29, Folder, ViewPoint, Inc. Archives.

51. "Probe on McDonald's Onion Nuggets," Box 15, Folder 12, ViewPoint, Inc. Archives.

52. Love, 204.

53. Love, 226.

54. "Probe on McDonald's Fish Filet," Box 15, Folder 12, ViewPoint, Inc. Archives.

55. Robert Hayes, *The Black American Travel Guide* (San Francisco: Straight Arrow Books, 1971).

56. "Storyboard for McBeefsteak Ad," Box 22, Folder 12, ViewPoint, Inc. Archives.

57. Paul Ingrassia and David Garino, "Burger Battle: After Their Slow Year, Fast-Food Chains Use Ploys to Speed Up Sales," *Wall Street Journal,* April 4, 1980.

58. Frederick Douglass Opie, *Hog and Hominy: Soul Food from Africa to America* (New York: Columbia University Press, 2010), 86–90, and Psyche Forson-Williams, *Building Houses Out of Chicken Legs: Black Women, Food, and Power* (Chapel Hill: University of North Carolina Press, 2006). For more on soul food, see Adrian Miller, *Soul Food: The Surprising Story of an American Cuisine: One Plate at a Time* (Chapel Hill: University of North Carolina Press, 2013).

59. "A Qualitative Exploration of Black Consumer Attitudes Relative to the McDonald's McChicken Sandwich," prepared for Burrell Advertising, by ViewPoint, Inc., August 1979, Box 16, Folder 12, ViewPoint, Inc. Archives.

60. Forson-Williams, *Building Houses Out of Chicken Legs,* 32.

61. Forson-Williams, 64.

62. "A Qualitative Exploration of Black Consumer Attitudes Relative to the McDonald's McChicken Sandwich," prepared for Burrell Advertising. Naming foods was a delicate issue for other ViewPoint clients. Throughout the late 1970s and

early 1980s, ViewPoint consulted with the three chicken chains on the quality of their side dishes, their advertising campaigns, and the quality of the store experience. Church's lackluster French-frying techniques sunk it with blacks. KFC had to work on the size of their chicken pieces, and Popeyes—despite winning high marks on market testing—had to contend with its attempt to mark itself as a Cajun creation. The use of the word Cajun for Popeyes was a lightning rod for consumers in Louisiana, who were protective of the word's rootedness in their experiences in the South. The participants in a ViewPoint study explained that Popeyes was among their favorite fast food outlets, but they got a few things wrong about what it meant to be Cajun. "Chicken doesn't have anything to do with Cajun." "I like Popeyes identifying with New Orleans but not with Cajun." "It's not right. My mother-in-law is Cajun and she makes fried chicken but it's not Cajun fried chicken." In Popeyes' case, founder Al Copeland was an asset to the black consumer base, because of his popular annual Christmas lights display at his home. Copeland's refusal to bend to pressures from neighbors to stop sharing his home with the throngs of viewers made him a hero in the study. "Church's Fried Chicken, Focus Group II, 1986 (1)," Box 5, Folder 18, ViewPoint Inc. Archives, "Focused Group Interviews with Popeyes Users, Prepared for: Fitzgerald Advertising, New Orleans, La., November, 1984," and "A Qualitative Exploration of Black Consumer Attitudes Toward Popeyes Famous Fried Chicken and Biscuits, November 1984," Box 90, Folder 5, View Point, Inc. Archives.

63. David Chappell, *Waking from the Dream: The Struggle for Civil Rights in the Shadow of Martin Luther King, Jr.* (Durham: Duke University Press, 2016), 92. See also Jacquelyn Dowd Hall, "The Long Civil Rights Movement and the Political Uses of the Past," *Journal of American History,* 91, no. 4: 1233–63.

64. Ray Kroc with Robert Anderson, *Grinding It Out: The Making of McDonald's* (New York: St. Martin's Press, 1977).

65. Chappell, 101.

66. Jimmy Carter, "The State of the Union Annual Message to the Congress, January 21, 1980," The American Presidency Project, University of California–Santa Barbara, http://www.presidency.ucsb.edu/ws/index.php?pid=33062. Accessed January 4, 2019.

67. "Atlanta Airport Home for Dr. King Exhibit," *New York Amsterdam News,* January 31, 1987. For more on the battle to equalize opportunities associated with Hartsfield-Jackson Airport, see Maurice J. Hobson, *The Legend of Black Mecca: Politics and Class in the Making of Modern Atlanta* (Chapel Hill: University of North Carolina Press, 2017).

68. Ben Fiber, "McDonald's Corp. Is Still Eating Up Its Fast Food Rivals," *Globe and Mail,* April 27, 1987.

69. Martin Luther King Jr., "The Three Evils of Society, Address at the National Conference for New Politics, August 31, 1967," Martin Luther King, Jr. Research and Education Institute, Stanford University.

70. "Atlanta Airport Home for Dr. King Exhibit."

71. "Martin Luther King Day Advertisement," *Chicago Weekend,* January 10–13, 1985.

72. Kathy Sawyer, "Atlanta Commemoration Limited by Tight Budget: But Enthusiasm Plentiful for Grand Parade," *Washington Post*, January 12, 1986.

73. "Atlanta Commemoration Limited by Tight Budget."

74. "Atlanta Airport Home for Dr. King Exhibit" and "McDonald's Gears Up for King Celebration," *New York Amsterdam News*, November 2, 1985.

75. "McDonald's to Sponsor Lorraine Hansberry Awards," *Atlanta Daily World*, December 8, 1983.

76. In *Double Negative: The Black Image and Popular Culture* (Durham: Duke University Press, 2018), Raquel J. Gates offers a clever read of the cultural politics of *Coming to America*.

Chapter Six: A Fair Share of the Pie

1. "NAACP Boycotts McDonald's on Coast," *New York Times*, April 11, 1984.

2. Advertisement, *Los Angeles Sentinel*, October 9, 1969. Keith Jones was the first black operator in Los Angeles.

3. Advertisement, *Los Angeles Sentinel*.

4. Don't Give Up Your Right to Vote!" *Los Angeles Sentinel*, October 5, 1978. In 1987, NBMOA members donated to Jesse Jackson's presidential campaign in recognition of his service to them. Thirty NBMOA members bundled $22,500 for Jackson's presidential campaign after his appearance at their annual meeting, held in Dallas. Jackson's campaign said that this donation was in support of his efforts "through Operation PUSH to promote economic advancement for minorities." "Black Businessmen Donate $22,500 to Jackson," *New York Times*, December 6, 1987.

5. "Business and People," *Los Angeles Sentinel*, July 4, 1974.

6. "NBMOA Annual Conference Program Booklet, 1984," Records of the National Association for the Advancement of Colored People (NAACP), Part VIII, Folder 338, Library of Congress, Washington, D.C.

7. Tom Adam Davies, *Mainstreaming Black Power* (Berkeley: University of California Press, 2017), 172.

8. In Josh Kun and Laura Pulido, eds., *Black and Brown in Los Angeles: Beyond Conflict and Coalition* (Berkeley: University of California Press, 2013), several of the essays in the volume highlight the Los Angeles chapter of the NAACP's advocacy for Mexican-American interests. Shana Bernstein's *Bridges of Reform: Interracial Civil Rights Activism in Twentieth-Century Los Angeles* (Oxford: Oxford University Press, 2011) emphasizes the branch's role in the 1948 *Shelley v. Kramer* case, in which the Supreme Court ruled that restrictive covenants were unconstitutional. For more on Loren Miller, the branch lawyer who was active in the *Shelley* case among other housing cases, see Kenneth W. Mack, *Representing the Race: The Creation of the Civil Rights Lawyer* (Cambridge: Harvard University Press, 2010). For a general view of Los Angeles and the NAACP, see Douglas Flamming, *Bound for Freedom: Black Los Angeles in Jim Crow America* (Berkeley: University of California Press, 2005).

9. Letter from James T. Jones to Los Angeles Chapter of the NAACP, dated February 11, 1975, Part V: Legal Department, Box 2691, Folder 9, NAACP Records.

10. Letter from James T. Jones to Los Angeles Branch of the NAACP regarding "Violation of Civil Rights."

11. Summons in *Jones v. McDonald's System of California*, dated January 2, 1976, Part V: Legal Department, Box 2691, Folder 9, NAACP Records.

12. Summons in *Jones v. McDonald's System of California*.

13. Judgment in *Jones v. McDonald's System of California*, dated September 24, 1975, Part V: Legal Department, Box 2691, Folder 9, NAACP Records.

14. Letter to Nathaniel Jones from Joseph E. Grimmett, dated March 8, 1976, Part V: Legal Department, Box 2691, Folder 9, NAACP Records.

15. Brad Pye, Jr. "Mayor Joins NAACP Miss. Fund Drive—Save the NAACP!" *Los Angeles Sentinel*, September 23, 1976.

16. "Business and People," *Los Angeles Sentinel*, July 4, 1974.

17. "Jesse Jackson Asked McDonald's for Parity," *Los Angeles Sentinel*, January 26, 1984.

18. "Charles Griffis Appointed to Shorter College Board," *Los Angeles Sentinel*, February 25, 1988.

19. Don Forney opened the first black-owned McDonald's in Detroit in 1969. "Black McDonald's Operators' Association Commemorates 25 Years," *Michigan Chronicle*, November 5, 1997.

20. "Discrimination Charge Hurled, Denied: Black Franchise Owner's Relationship with McDonald's Turns Sour," *Los Angeles Times*, August 12, 1984. "Big Mac Attack: Black Franchisee Charges Bias," *ABA Journal* 70, no. 12 (December 1984): 32. The Santa Barbara Avenue store opened in 1969 and advertised to black readers of the *Los Angeles Sentinel*. "Grand Opening Held for New McDonald's," *Los Angeles Sentinel,* January 30, 1969.

21. Al Copeland established Popeyes in 1972 in a New Orleans suburb. The distinctive, spicy chicken and Cajun style offerings distinguished it from competitors Kentucky Fried Chicken and Church's Chicken. Popeyes began contracting franchises in 1976.

22. "Big Mac Attack: Black Franchisee Charges Bias," 32.

23. "McDonald's Is Battling with Black Franchisee," *New York Times*, March 12, 1984.

24. "Minority Operator Sues McDonald's, Former Trainee Joins In," *Los Angeles Sentinel*, January 12, 1984. Around the same time Griffis initiated his countersuit, Herman V. Christopher Jr. also filed a claim that McDonald's misrepresented the terms of the franchise by charging him twice the agreed upon amount for franchising fees.

25. "McDonald's Faces Contract Fight," *Los Angeles Sentinel*, March 8, 1984.

26. "McDonald's Is Battling with Black Franchisee."

27. "Shootout Rocks McDonald's: Gunfire Rocks Area McDonald's Franchise," *Los Angeles Sentinel*, March 15, 1984.

28. "McDonald's Is Battling with Black Franchisee." Black mayors and mayoral candidates in Cleveland, Los Angeles, New York, and Memphis have all been entangled with McDonald's issues, and they have all paid close attention to local BMOA chapters and their demands. For more on black mayors, see J.

Phillip Thompson, *Double Trouble: Black Mayors, Black Communities and the Call for a Deep Democracy* (Oxford: Oxford University Press, 2005).

29. "McDonald's Faces Contract Fight."
30. "McDonald's Faces Contract Fight."
31. For an analysis of the transition from slave labor to free labor and the gendered ramifications of this process see Tera W. Hunter, *To Joy My Freedom: Southern Black Women's Labor and Lives After the Civil War* (Cambridge: Harvard University Press, 1998), and Amy Dru Stanley, *From Bondage to Contract: Wage Labor, Marriage, and the Market in the Age of Slave Emancipation* (Cambridge: Cambridge University Press, 1998).
32. "McDonald's Loses First Round," *Los Angeles Sentinel*, February 16, 1984.
33. Davies, 183.
34. Davies, 210.
35. Max Boas and Steve Chain, *Big Mac: The Unauthorized Story of McDonald's* (New York: E. P. Dutton, 1976), 159–60.
36. Boas and Chain, 161.
37. Boas and Chain, 70.
38. "McDonald's Is Battling with Black Franchisee."
39. Jube Shiver, Jr., "Discrimination Charge Hurled, Denied: Black Franchise Owner's Relationship with McDonald's Turns Sour," *Los Angeles Times*, August 12, 1984, E3.
40. "Black Boycott Unfair, McDonald's Says," *Montreal Gazette,* April 12, 1984.
41. "Discrimination Charge Hurled, Denied."
42. Ange-Marie Hancock, *The Politics of Disgust: The Public Identity of the Welfare Queen* (New York: New York University Press, 2004).
43. "McQueen of the Golden Arches," *Black Enterprise*, September 1987, 64–69.
44. "NAACP Boycotts McDonald's on Coast," *New York Times*, April 11, 1984.
45. "A Crumbling Legacy: The Decline of African American Insurance Companies in Contemporary America," *Review of Black Political Economy* 23, no. 2 (Fall 1994): 25.
46. "3 Firms to Get Major McDonald's Contracts," *New York Amsterdam News*, December 17, 1983.
47. "PUSH Announces Anheuser-Busch Boycott," *Pittsburgh Courier*, October 2, 1982.
48. "Black Promoters Join Bud Boycott," *Chicago Independent Bulletin*, February 17, 1983, Harold Washington Archives and Collections, Development Sub-Cabinet, Box 20, Folder 3, Harold Washington Library Center Special Collections, Chicago Public Library, and "Promoters Join Brewery Boycott," *New York Amsterdam News*, February 26, 1983.
49. "Jackson: Busch Using King's Dream," *Philadelphia Tribune*, February 18, 1982.
50. "Operation PUSH Calls Off Boycott of Anheuser-Busch," *Afro-American*, September 17, 1983.
51. "Turnout Small at King Memorial," *Chicago Sun-Times*, April 15, 1983.
52. David Chappell, *Waking from the Dream: The Struggle for Civil Rights in the Shadow of Martin Luther King, Jr.* (New York: Random House, 2014), 125–27.

53. "NAACP, Coors Set Plan," *Los Angeles Sentinel*, April 10, 1984.

54. "Advertisement," *Los Angeles Sentinel*, May 10, 1984.

55. "NAACP Halts 3-Day McDonald's Boycott," *Los Angeles Times*, April 14, 1984.

56. "Advertisement," May 10, 1984.

57. "Big Mac Attack: Black Franchisee Charges Bias."

58. "McBias Case Over: Burger Chain, Operator Settle," *ABA Journal* 71, no. 1 (January 1985): 25.

59. Tamar Lewin, "McDonald's Dispute on Coast," *New York Times*, November 9, 1984.

60. "Chicken Charlie's Coupon Special, Great Food Bargain," *Los Angeles Sentinel*, January 28, 1988.

61. "NAACP Bids Reagan Meet with its Leaders," *New York Times*, February 17, 1985.

62. "NAACP Works for L.A. Gains at McDonald's," *New York Times*, February 19, 1985.

63. "Black McDonald's Franchisees Address Economic Development," *Los Angeles Sentinel*, October 26, 1989. The Griffis case was not the last claim about racial discrimination and franchisees in the fast food world. Throughout the ensuing decades, McDonald's franchisees of color have continued to call into question how McDonald's manages potential franchise locations. A 2000 case involving Deborah Sonnenschein also involved a local chapter of the NAACP. Sonnenschein, who stated she had worked for McDonald's her entire adult life, claimed that McDonald's opened several competing stores near her four outlets, and that this move was emblematic of discriminatory practices toward black franchisees. The case was originally a lawsuit based on unfair market practices, but evolved into a racial one after Sonneschein's attorneys collected data about similar problems felt by other black franchisees. "Black Owner Spars with McDonald's," *Chicago Tribune*, December 28, 2002.

Chapter Seven: The Miracle of the Golden Arches

1. "The Multiracial Nature of Los Angeles Unrest in 1992," in Kwang Chung Kim, ed., *Koreans in the Hood: Conflict with African Americans* (Baltimore: Johns Hopkins University Press, 1999), 24–26.

2. "McDonald's," *PR Newswire*, May 1, 1992.

3. Patricia Sowell Harris, *None of Us Is as Good as All of Us: How McDonald's Prospers by Embracing Diversity and Inclusion* (Hoboken, NJ: Wiley, 2009), 72.

4. Brenda Stevenson, *The Contested Murder of Latasha Harlins: Justice, Gender, and the Origins of the LA Riots* (Oxford: Oxford University Press, 2013), 299.

5. Carol Byrne, untitled article, *Star Tribune*, March 21, 1993.

6. James V. Grimaldi, "Cleanup, Outsiders Turn Out to Pitch in," *Orange County Register*, May 3, 1992, and Jenna Chandler, Adrian Glick Kudler, and Bianca Barragan, "Mapping the 1992 L.A. Uprising," April 30, 2018, LaCurbed.com, https://la.curbed.com/maps/1992-los-angeles-riots-rodney-king-map.

7. "Rainbow of Anger, Decades of Rage at the Root of Tumult in South-Central Los Angeles," *Fort Lauderdale Sun Sentinel*, May 3, 1992.

8. David Leon Moore and Maria Goodavage, "Crisis in L.A," *USA Today*, May 1, 1992.

9. Susan Campbell, "Untitled," *Hartford Courant*, July 7, 1992.

10. National Black McDonald's Operators Association, "NBMOA Video," Larry Tripplett interview transcript, 15–16.

11. Jacques Kelly, "Theodore Holmes, Founder of Chicken George Restaurant Chain," *Washington Post*, December 8, 2011.

12. "Guts, Spice, and Integration: A Recipe for One Man's Success," *Washington Post*, April 3, 1983.

13. For more on *Roots*, see Matthew F. Delmont, *Making Roots: A Nation Captivated* (Oakland: University of California Press, 2016), and Erica L. Ball and Kellie Carter Jackson, eds., *Reconsidering Roots: Race, Politics, and Memory* (University of Georgia Press, 2017).

14. "Chicken George: Triumph and Disappointment," *Baltimore Sun*, March 1, 1987.

15. "Guts, Spice, and Integration: A Recipe for One Man's Success."

16. Sam Fulwood III, "Running off Power of One Man's Charisma, Food Empire Falters," *Baltimore Sun*, March 2, 1987.

17. Eric Harrison, "Once-Radical Group Now Is the System," *Philadelphia Inquirer*, June 23, 1985.

18. "Chicken George's D.C. Roots," *Black Enterprise*, February 1982, 28.

19. "Advertising Accounts," *Daily Oklahoman*, March 5, 1984.

20. Tim Chavez, "Chicken George Picks Oklahoma to Expand Chain," *Daily Oklahoman*, January 4, 1983.

21. "Chicken George's D.C. Roots." See also "Theodore Holmes," *Ebony*, August 1983, 162.

22. "Running off Power of One Man's Charisma, Food Empire Falters."

23. "Running off Power of One Man's Charisma, Food Empire Falters."

24. "Kentucky Fried Chicken Launches Hip New Restaurants in D.C. and Baltimore," *PR Newswire*, April 8, 1993.

25. Jennifer Lin, "Pecking Order—Fried Chicken Outlets Staking Out Turf," *Philadelphia Inquirer*, April 19, 1984; and "Chicken George: Triumph and Disappointment."

26. "Theodore Holmes, Founder of Chicken George Restaurant Chain."

27. Pizza Hut Commercial, undated, YouTube. Accessed January 11, 2019.

28. Trudy Gallant-Stokes, "Franchisee of the Year: Brady Keys Does Franchising Right," *Black Enterprise*, September 1988, 56.

29. Marc Rice, "A Taste of Life Outside the Ghetto," *Chicago Sun-Times*, September 6, 1994.

30. "La-Van Hawkins' Future Plans Will Still Involve Lots of Food: The Checkers Man," *Afro-American Red Star*, February 17, 1997.

31. Robert A. Mofitt, "From Welfare to Work: What the Evidence Shows" (Washington, D.C.: Brookings Institution), January 2, 2002. See also Barbara Ehrenreich, *Nickel and Dimed: On (Not) Getting By in America* (New York: Picador, 2011); Katherine Newman, *No Shame in My Game: The Working Poor in the Inner City* (New York: Vintage, 2000); and Joseph Shapiro and Barbara Murray,

"Fast Food and Welfare Reform: Success of the Effort May Hinge on 'Dead-End Burger' Flipping-Jobs," *U.S. News & World Report*, August 18–25, 1997.

32. For more on the War on Drugs, see Michelle Alexander, *The New Jim Crow: Mass Incarceration in the Age of Colorblindness* (New York: New Press, 2010), and Elizabeth Hinton, *From the War on Poverty to the War on Crime: The Making of Mass Incarceration in America* (Cambridge: Harvard University Press, 2016).

33. Larry Copeland, "Foes: Checkers Should Check Out: The Chain Disrespected the Girard Avenue District, Critics Say," *Philadelphia Inquirer,* December 31, 1993.

34. United States Department of Housing and Urban Development, "List of Current Empowerment Zones and Updated Contact Information," 2013.

35. William J. Clinton: "Remarks to the White House Conference on Empowerment Zones," *Public Papers of the Presidents of the United States*, January 1 to June 30, 1996.

36. Chin Jou, *Supersizing Urban America: How the Federal Government Created the Obesity Crisis* (Chicago: University of Chicago Press, 2017), 139.

37. "Clinton: $3.5 for Empowerment Zones," *Time*, December 21, 1994.

38. United States Department of Housing and Urban Development, *Spotlight on Results: Capturing Successes in Renewal Communities and Empowerment Zones* (U.S. Department of Housing and Urban Development, 2015), 40, 68.

39. T. Trent Gegax, "Burger King Plans Inner-City Venture," *Washington Post*, February 22, 1996, and Peter Behr, "Fast Food Tracker," *Newsweek*, May 25, 1997.

40. "Fast Food Tracker."

41. "Keeping the Faith," *Christian Science Monitor*, November 2, 1998.

42. Donna DeMarco, "Hawkins Leaving Town," *Baltimore Business Journal,* November 23, 1998.

43. "Black Agents Sue Denny's," *New York Times*, May 25, 1993.

44. "KFC About to Be Skinned?" *Michigan Chronicle*, July 16, 1997.

45. Alexei Barrionuevo, "Franchising Hope: Chain Outlets Offer Promise as Seeds for Inner-City Development," *Los Angeles Times*, February 3, 1993.

46. Staci Bush, "Bias in the Chicken? Former Kentucky Fried Chicken (KFC) African American Employees Along with Franchise Holders," *Sacramento Observer*, November 23, 1994.

47. "Burger King Corporation Announces Update on Legal Proceedings with La-Van Hawkins, Urban City Foods," *PR Newswire*, May 2000.

48. "Restaurateur on Way to Prison Is Sued by Franchiser," *Chicago Tribune*, December 22, 2007.

49. "Ex-BK Franchisee Gets 'Sweet New Start,'" *Nation's Restaurant News*, July 8, 2002.

50. Nichole M. Christian, "A Model Partnership for Inner-City Renewal, Derailed," *New York Times*, May 14, 2000.

51. Adrian Sanz, "Sharpton Calls for Burger King Boycott," *Philadelphia Tribune*, September 12, 2000.

52. Jack Newfield, "Rev. vs. Rev.," *New York Magazine*, January 7, 2002.

53. "Franchise Acceptance Corporation, $8.4 Million," *PR Newswire*, New York, December 2000.

54. "Burger King Loses Round One in $1.9 Billion Lawsuit, Announces Attorney Willie Gray," *PR Newswire*, New York, September 27, 2000.

55. "Ex-BK Franchisee Gets 'Sweet New Start.' "

56. "La-Van Hawkins Linked to Philadelphia Corruption Probe," *Black Enterprise*, September 1, 2004.

57. "Local Restaurateur Serving Time for Fraud Accused of Fraud," *Chicagoist*, January 8, 2008, http://chicagoist.com/2008/01/08/local_restaurat.php.

58. Susan Saluny, "Detroit Mayor Pleads Guilty and Resigns," *New York Times*, September 4, 2008.

59. "Convictions of Corey Kemp, Four Others Upheld," *Bond Buyer*, August 29, 2007.

60. La-Van Hawkins, "LaVan Hawkins on *American Entrepreneur*," interview by Ed Foxworth, *American Entrepreneur*, YouTube video, at 4:03–5:02, https://youtu.be/xcH0z7tLJ94.

61. "Chicago Chicken and Waffles Owners Sue Former Partner," *Austin Weekly News*, December 14, 2011.

62. In the late 2010s, Hawkins produced another local advertisement for his new venture, a Krispy Krunchy Chicken in Detroit. The ad reminded viewers that they were probably familiar with Hawkins from his "hundreds" of Burger Kings and Pizza Huts, "as well as Georgia Brown's." In 2017, Hawkins was part of a new effort, the Boaz Group, and tried to make a move toward purchasing the Ruby Tuesday restaurant, which chose a private equity group instead. "Ruby Tuesday Publicly Rejects, Criticizes New Offer for Company," *USA Today*, December 18, 2017.

63. Annalise Frank, "Onetime Metro Detroit Fast Food Mogul, Restaurateur La-Van Hawkins Dies," *Crain's Detroit Business*, April 10, 2019.

64. Margaret K. Webb, " 'Magic Johnson' to Buy Stakes in Pepsi's D.C.-Area Bottler," *Washington Post*, July 21, 1990.

65. "Our History," Magic Johnson Enterprises, http://www.magicjohnson.com/company.

66. Bryant Simon, " 'A Down Brother': Earvin 'Magic' Johnson and the Quest for Retail Justice in Los Angeles," *Boom: A Journal of California* 1, no. 2 (Summer 2011): 43–58.

67. United States Public Health Service, *Surgeon General's Health and Nutrition Report*, 1988.

68. Nancy Luna, "McDonald's and NLRB Reach Settlement in Joint-Employer Case," *Nation's Restaurant News*, March 20, 2018. Michelle Chen, "Trump's Labor Board Is Making It Even More Difficult to Unionize Fast-Food Workers," *The Nation*, February 9, 2018.

69. Bethany Moreton, *To Serve God and Wal-Mart: The Making of Christian Free Enterprise* (Cambridge: Harvard University Press, 2009), 99.

70. "Commercial Real Estate: Seeking Customers in a Blighted Area," *New York Times*, February 12, 2013.

71. William Booth and Jeff Adler, "Los Angeles Looks Back at Riots," *Washington Post*, April 28, 2002.
72. "In Wake of LA Riots, Industry Must Do Its Part for Inner Cities," *Nation's Restaurant News,* May 25, 1992.
73. Dean E. Murphy, "Former Gang Members, Minister Call for Jobs to Keep Post-Riot Truce," *Los Angeles Times*, August 9, 1995.
74. "Franchising Hope: Chain Outlets Offer Promise as Seeds for Inner-City Development."
75. Melissa Chadburn, "The Destructive Force of Rebuild LA," *Curbed Los Angeles*, April 27, 2018, https://la.curbed.com/2017/4/27/15442350/1992-los-angeles-riots-rebuild-la.
76. Andrea Maier, "Black-Owned Beauty Salons Hurt by Riots," *Los Angeles Times*, July 2, 1992.
77. Daniel Wood, "Diet-Conscious Los Angeles Eyes Moratorium on Fast-Food Outlets," *Christian Science Monitor*, September 13, 2007.
78. Timothy Weaver, "Elite Empowerment," *Jacobin* 29 (Spring 2018).
79. William Yardley, "Peter Hall, Who Devised the Enterprise Zone, Dies at 82," *New York Times*, August 6, 2014.
80. "Black Banks Can't Fix Racial Capitalism," *Public Books*, June 8, 2018. For more on racial capitalism, see Donna Murch, ed., *Racial Capitalism in the Age of Trump* (Cambridge: Massachusetts Institute of Technology Press, 2019), and Cedric Robinson, *Black Marxism: The Making of the Black Radical Tradition* (Chapel Hill: University of North Carolina Press, 1983).
81. Chris Ying, "The Los Angeles Fast Food Revolution," *The Guardian*, February 21, 2016.
82. "The Los Angeles Fast Food Revolution."
83. Justin Phillips, "LocoL Closes Uptown Oakland Location," *San Francisco Chronicle*, June 25, 2017.
84. Monica Burton, "LocoL Isn't Making a Lot of Money—but Roy Choi Says That's Okay," Eater.com, September 29, 2017, https://www.eater.com/2017/9/29/16384706/locol-business-model-roy-choi.
85. "The Los Angeles Fast Food Revolution," and Hillary Dixler Canavan, "The LocoL Revolution Is on Hold," Eater.com, August 24, 2018, https://www.eater.com/2018/8/24/17770792/locol-roy-choi-daniel-patterson-closing-watts-san-jose-rip.

Conclusion: Bigger than a Hamburger

1. Tracy Jan, "Four Years After Michael Brown Was Shot by Police, the Neighborhood Where He Was Killed Still Feels Left Behind," *Washington Post*, June 21, 2018.
2. Carol Anderson, *White Rage: The Unspoken Truth of Our Racial Divide* (New York: Bloomsbury, 2015), 3.
3. Naomi Klein, *The Shock Doctrine: The Rise of Disaster Capitalism* (New York: Metropolitan Books, 2007), 14–15.
4. Food studies scholar Kyla Tompkins makes the point: "No matter how many kale salads Starbucks puts in their case, Starbucks is a fast-food purveyor." The

latte, she argued, "is a high-calorie food that's being pushed in an industrialized way largely to working-class people." And, she added, "it's important to think about the explosion of all of these industrialized lattes, all these frozen lattes, all the Frappuccinos, as links to a larger problem of creating cheap, high-calorie, low-nutrition food for working-class people." She continued, "How does the symbolism of a thing get dislodged from the ways in which it's actually used and actually consumed? What is that except another way in which we're stopped from really looking at what problems actually exist?" Anna North, "If You Read This, You Might Never Drink a Latte Again," *New York Times*, July 10, 2014. Jonathan Metzl's research on whites and health argues that despite imperiling white health and life expectancy, some white voters still support detrimental policies in order to maintain their sense of racial superiority and power. Jonathan Metzl, *Dying of Whiteness: How the Politics of Racial Resentment Is Killing America's Heartland* (New York: Basic Books, 2019).

5. Michael Pollan, *The Omnivore's Dilemma: A Natural History of Four Meals* (New York: Penguin, 2007), 113.
6. Alison Alkon and Julie Guthman, eds., *The New Food Activism: Opposition, Cooperation, and Collective Action* (Oakland: University of California Press, 2017).
7. Ella J. Baker, "Bigger than a Hamburger," *Southern Patriot* 18 (1960).

INDEX

Page numbers in *italics* indicate photographs. Page numbers followed by *n* indicate notes.

and Speedee system, 41
support for black franchisees, 68

labor unions, McDonald's opposition to, 131, 252
Lamar, Kendrick, 258
Laviske, Al, 129, 130, 133
Let's Move initiative, 5
Lewis, Brandon, 45
Lewis, Ed, 200
Lidio's Drive-In (Portland, Ore.), 125
Lima State Hospital for the Criminally Insane, 95
Little Rock, Arkansas, 40
Lockhart & Pettus, 232
LocoL, 257–58
Lorraine Hansberry Award, 193
Los Angeles, California, 19, 27
and black franchisees, 199–210, 220–21
food issues in 2012, 253–56
Charles Griffis case, 204–10, 212–15
Rodney King riots, 20–21, *223*, 223–27
Watts uprising (1965), 77–80
Los Angeles Police Department, 225
Los Angeles Sentinel, 199, 207
Love, John F., 26
Lowery, Wesley, 275*n*

McCain, Frank, 44
McChicken sandwich, 182, 186–89
McCullough, John Fremont, 145
MacDonald, John T., 206–7
McDonald, Maurice and Richard, 22
and Airdrome hot dog stand, 28–30
birth of, 25
business methods imitated by other restaurants, 34–35
early changes in strategy, 30–31
and efficiency, 86
and origins of McDonald's, 11, 26–27
McDonald, Patrick, 28
McDonald's: Behind the Arches (Love), 26
McDonald's All-American Game, 164
McDonald's All-American High School Band, 165
McDonald's Corp. v. Griffis, 218–20
McDonald's Dynamos, 164
McDonald's Literary Achievement Awards, 193–94

McDonald's origins
and Airdrome hot dog stand, 28–30
business methods imitated by other restaurants, 34–35
early changes in strategy, 30–31
and early history of franchising, 7
first restaurant, 22–25, 28–30
founding, 11–12
IPO, 57
in 1980s, 19
McDonald's System, 35–37
McJob, 179
McKissick, Floyd, 15
McNeil, Joe, 44
Madison-Albany Department Store (Chicago), 59
Mafia, 142
Magic Johnson Enterprises, 250–51
March on Washington for Jobs and Freedom (1963), 50, 55, 120, 191
Marion Correctional Institute, 118
marketing, 158–62, 177–78; *See also* advertising campaigns
market research, 18–19, 177–78; *See also* ViewPoint, Inc.
Marriott, J. Willard, 8
Marshall, Thurgood, 40
Martin Luther King Jr. Day, 189–93, 258
Martin Luther King Jr. Federal Holiday Commission, 192
mayors, 200–201
Memphis, Tennessee, 44, 52–56
Memphis State University, 53
Mexican Americans, 29–30
Miller, Kelly, 141
Million Man March, 241
Milwaukee, Wisconsin, 66
Miranda, Juan, 144
Missouri National Guard, 2
Mitla Café (San Bernardino), 35, 280*n*
Monrovia, California, 28, 29
Moreton, Bethany, 252–53
Morgan v. Virginia, 146
Movement for Black Lives, 2
movies, racism in, 27
Moynihan, Daniel Patrick, 173
Moynihan Report, 173–74
Murphy, Eddie, 195–96

Franchise

a new name, and stripped bare of fictions.[82] In Massachusetts, in the seventeenth century, litigants used the action of "case," a residual action, not used for this purpose at all in England.[83] In the eighteenth century, all the old actions disappeared, and a single, all-embracing form replaced them, called a plea of ejectment, or a plea of entry, or, most simply, a plea of land. This plea avoided all the old technicalities and led to an ordinary civil suit.[84]

SUCCESSION AT DEATH

When a person died in England, the property left behind was under the regime of two quite different sets of rules. Common-law rules and courts governed the land; church law and courts the personal property. If the deceased left no will, the common law gave the land to the eldest son; the church courts divided money and goods in equal shares among the children. The colonies either had no church courts or fused, as in early Massachusetts, the laws of Caesar and God. Probate power was given to regular courts or to special (but secular) branches of these courts. The courts also handled closely related matters—guardianship of minors, for example.[85] In general, the probate process, including the filing of inventories, was carried over into the colonies. But there was considerable innovation in the *substance* of succession.

The colonies greatly modified the law of descent of lands. In standard English law, primogeniture was the rule; lands descended to the eldest son. But "standard English law" meant the law of the landed gentry; and for this elite class, it was important to keep "estates" together, rather than to split them among the children. Even in England, primogeniture was not universal; local customs superseded it in some parts of the kingdom. In Kent, there was so-called gavelkind tenure; land descended to all sons in equal shares. The New England colonies, remote from upper-class English law and upper-class English society, had little use for primogeniture. Except for Rhode Island, all of New England rejected the rule. The seventeenth-century Massachusetts codes gave the eldest son "a double portion" of the "whole estate reall, and personall."[86] This special birthright was apparently a gesture to the Bible, not to English law. The double portion was also a feature of the law of Pennsylvania. In New York, the Duke's laws provided that property, after the widow's share, was to be divided "amongst the Children, provided the oldest Sonne shall have a double portion, and where their are no Sonnes the daughters shall inherit as Copartners."[87] This double share was found in other colonies, too, for example,

---

[82] John T. Farrell, ed., *The Supreme Court Diary of William Samuel Johnson, 1772–1773* (1942), xxxiii–xxxv.

[83] David T. Konig, *Law and Society in Puritan Massachusetts*, pp. 60–62.

[84] William F. Nelson, *Americanization of the Common Laws*, p. 74.

[85] See Lois Green Carr, "The Development of the Maryland Orphans' Court," in Aubrey C. Land, Lois Green Carr, and Edward C. Papenfuse, eds., *Laws, Society, and Politics in Early Maryland* (1977), p. 41.

[86] *Laws and Liberties of Massachusetts, 1648* (1929 ed.), p. 53.

[87] See David E. Narrett, "Preparation for Death and Provision for the Living: Notes on New York Wills (1665–1760)," 57 N.Y. Hist. 417, 420 (1976).

Connecticut and New Hampshire.[88] But primogeniture was a feature of the law in the southern colonies—Maryland, Virginia, and the Carolinas—until Revolutionary times.[89]

Scholars do not agree on the origins of New England's system of partible descent (that is, division of land among children). Some suspect direct borrowing from local English custom. Many colonial charters granted lands to be held of the king "as of his manor of East Greenwich." East Greenwich was located in Kent. Was it the purpose or effect of these charters to bring in gavelkind tenure? The evidence is confusing, inconclusive, and probably irrelevant. Partible descent was the practice in New England, from a very early date—probably long before anyone thought of arguments based on the charters. Primogeniture and the fee tail survived in the South, partly because of their system of land use. Southern planters used slave labor and grew sugar, rice, and tobacco on large estates. English land tenure, and the English way of life—the habits and legal institutions of the landed gentry—were more suitable to the southern social order than to the social order in the North.

Primogeniture and its substitutes were rules about *intestacy;* a property-owner could make some other disposition, if he went to the trouble to make out a *will.* This basic document for gifts at death—the last will and testament—came over as part of the colonists' cultural heritage. The English middle class used wills widely. Form was regulated by such laws as the Statute of Wills (1540). But the statutes presupposed, and modified, customs already in existence. And the content of wills tended to follow, in a rough and ready way, what was in the intestacy laws. A study of Virginia wills (seventeenth century) showed that property owners were anxious to keep their property within the bloodline. Few men left more than a life interest to their wives; and sons were much preferred over daughters, since land left to daughters would fall out of the bloodline when the daughter married.[90] The traditional (English) form of the will appeared early in the colonies. The formal written will, signed by the decedent and attested by witnesses, was part of the general legal culture. So was the oral (nuncupative) will. The Provincial Court of Maryland, for example, heard oral testimony of two witnesses that John Smithson, in 1638, "lying then very sick," had promised, "in case God should call him," to leave his estate to his wife; upon "these depositions . . . the judge did approve the said last will and testament."[91]

The essential patterns of the will were part of English folk law. These patterns recurred in the colonies, preserved in the memories of men and women far from home. Wills from Maine to Georgia strikingly resembled English wills and each other, particularly in their use of singsong, almost balladlike phrases. Shakespeare's will begins with the words: "In the name of God Amen . . . I commend my soul into the hands of God my Creator . . . and my body to the earth

---

[88] Carole Shammas, Marylynn Salmon, and Michel Dahlin, *Inheritance in America: From Colonial Times to the Present* (1987), pp. 32–33.

[89] On the subject of colonial land law, especially primogeniture and fee tail, see Richard B. Morris, *Studies in the History of American Law* (2nd ed., 1959), pp. 69–125.

[90] James W. Deen Jr., "Patterns of Testation: Four Tidewater Counties in Colonial Virginia," 16 Am. J. Legal Hist. 154, 160–61 (1972).

[91] *Archives of Maryland,* vol. IV (1887), pp. 45–46. For another vivid example of a nuncupative will, see Narrett, "Preparation for Death," p. 429.

whereof it is made."[92] The will of Henry Simpson, written in Maine in 1648, begins as follows: "In the name of God Amen, I, Henry Simpson . . . Doe make this my last will and testament First commending my soule to God that gave it. . . . And my body to Christian buriall."[93]

Thousands of colonial wills have survived. They shed a great deal of light on colonial society. Some were drawn up by important people and disposed of substantial estates. Slaves, servants, and the very poor stood outside the property system and left no wills to speak of. Many ordinary people probably left so little behind that nothing went through probate. Others died intestate, that is, without wills. Between 1690 and 1760, New York City recorded 1,600 estates with wills, and only 535 estates without.[94] Wills were by no means only for the rich, at least in the early years of the colonies, when the local law and the local courts were at the fingertips of every man and woman. Many wills in this period disposed of nothing but a few household goods and other odds and ends. Bethia Cartwright of Salem, Massachusetts, who died in 1640, disposed by will of her bedding and bed, pewter platters, a "double saltseller . . . half a dozen spoones and a porrenger," and a "box of linning, with a payre of shetes."[95] In Bucks County, Pennsylvania, in 1751, 43 percent of the men who died (but only 2 percent of the women) left a will. Men in this county tended to leave their land to their sons, and to give less to their daughters. They tended, too, to leave more to their wives than the law required—but with restrictions; for example, many men provided in their wills that the widow would lose her share, if she remarried.[96]

In the early days, probate administration was quite loose by English or later American standards. In classic English law, the widow's share of her husband's estate—called dower—was a life interest in one-third of her husband's lands Colonial law, particularly in New England, was apparently less rigid. In Massachusetts, magistrates had discretion to modify the wife's share, according to her needs and local social and ethical standards. Rules were not hard and fast: even the eldest son's double portion was not an absolute right; the general court "upon just cause alledged" could "judge otherwise." The rules got stiffer and more absolute over time. The small face-to-face communities grew larger and became societies of strangers. At this point, the demands of economic rationality and the need for predictability and certainty asserted their claims. This meant more formality; and more hard-and-fast rules. But the gulf between rules about land and rules about goods was never so great as in England. And some colonial innovations—particularly partible inheritance—survived every attack.

CRIMINAL LAW

The earliest criminal codes mirrored the nasty, precarious life of pioneer settlements. Dale's laws in Virginia (1611) were a special case. They were almost

---

[92] Quoted in Virgil M. Harris, *Ancient, Curious and Famous Wills* (1911), pp. 305–6.

[93] *Province and Court Records of Maine*, vol. I (1928), p. 126.

[94] David Narrett, "Preparation for Death," p. 430.

[95] *Records and Files of the Quarterly Courts of Essex County, Massachusetts, 1636–1656*, vol. I (1911), p. 18.

[96] The data on Bucks County is from Shammas et al., *Inheritance in America*, ch. 2.

martial law—draconian rules for a small, imperiled community. Once the colony became more secure, Virginia's criminal procedure shed most of the harshest aspects of Dale's laws.

Criminal justice in the colonies, like colonial law in general, was "on the whole less formal and more direct" than English law; though here too, as time went on, there was a certain amount of "conformity to the English practice."[97] In Massachusetts, early political struggles weakened the power of the oligarchy; and the colony embarked on an extraordinary course of drafting codes. Behind this creative urge was a simple penal philosophy: no one should be punished for crimes not clearly and openly labeled. In a just society, the rules of the criminal law had to be written down, and known to one and all. *The Laws and Liberties of Massachusetts* (1648) was an early product of this movement. It was a general code; but it included much material on criminal law: the standard crimes— murder, arson, and theft—were included, as well as more exotic and specialized offenses. The aim of the code was to correct and teach the weak and to cut off from the community, as a last resort, those people who were incorrigibly harmful. In many ways, the code was an "extraordinary achievement." even a "radical" one, in that it aimed to set out the law in simple, practical terms, both to restrain authority, and to express the laws for all to see and understand.[98]

That the law should be known and accessible was a fundamental concept in colonial law. Punishment too was open and public: whipping in the town square, the pillory, and the stocks. These were small, inbred, gossipy communities. Public opinion and shame were important instruments of punishment. This was true in Massachusetts Bay, and also in Quaker Pennsylvania; there, a good deal of the work of discipline was carried on at Quaker meetings, where men and women were punished for such things as "disorderly walking" (sexual offenses), swearing, missing meetings, and "disorderly marriages" (marrying a non-Quaker). The goal was repentance, men and women were expected to humble themselves; those who were resistant could be "disowned."[99]

The use of shaming techniques was particularly striking in Massachusetts Bay. Under its code, if a man forged legal documents, so as to "pervert equities and justice," he was to "stand in the *Pillory* three several lecture days and render double damages to the party wronged." Shaming was for people who were not totally beyond redemption. Thus, Anabaptists were liable to be "sentenced to Banishment"; they were presumably incurable (and perhaps infectious). Witches, of course, could be put to death. For community punishment to work, it had to be visible and public; and punishment often left physical marks on

---

[97] Arthur P. Scott, *Criminal Law in Colonial Virginia* (1930), p. 136; on Dale's laws, see David T. Konig, "'Dale's Laws' and the Non-Common Law Origins of Criminal Justice in Virginia," 26 Am. J. Legal Hist. 354 (1982).

There is a sizable literature on colonial criminal justice. See Douglas Greenberg, "Crime, Law Enforcement, and Social Control in Colonial America," 26 Am. J. Legal Hist. 293 (1982); Kathryn Preyer, "Penal Measures in the American Colonies: An Overview," ibid., at 326; Donna J. Spindel, *Crime and Society in North Carolina, 1673–1776* (1989); N. E. H. Hull, *Female Felons: Women and Serious Crime in Colonial Massachusetts* (1987).

[98] Daniel R. Coquillette, "Radical Lawmakers in Colonial Massachusetts: The 'Countenance of Authoritie' and the *Lawes and Libertyes*," 67 New England Quarterly 179 (1994).

[99] See William M. Offutt Jr., *Of "Good Laws" and "Good Men": Law and Society in the Delaware Valley, 1680–1710* (1995), ch. 6.

the condemned. So, burglars, for the first offense, were to be "branded on the forehead with the letter (B)," for the second offense, whipped—in public, of course—and only if there was a third offense was the burglar to be "put to death, as being incorrigible." A burglar who committed his crime on the "Lords day" lost an ear as additional penalty. If he did it again, he lost his other ear. The crime of "fornication with any single woman" was punishable by fine, by corporal punishment, or "by enjoyning to marriage." "Inhumane, barbarous or cruel" punishments were forbidden; and though the *Body of Liberties* (1641) and later codes had accepted torture as a legitimate device, its use was, on paper at least, severely limited:

> No man shall be forced by Torture to confesse any Crime against himselfe nor any other unless it be in some Capitall case where he is first fullie convicted by cleare and suffitient evidence to be guilty. After which if the cause be of that nature, That it is very apparent there be other conspiratours, or confederates with him, Then he may be tortured, yet not with such Tortures as be Barbarous and inhumane.[100]

Particularly interesting was a small subcode of "Capital Lawes," imbedded in the early Massachusetts lawbooks, and copied by other New England and Middle Atlantic colonies. Some scholars used this subcode as prime evidence that the basic stuff of Bay law was biblical, not English common law. The capital laws did have a strong Mosaic flavor; in print, each of them was buttressed by a biblical citation: "If any man or woman be a WITCH, that is, hath or consulteth with a familiar spirit, they shall be put to death. *Exod.* 22.18 *Levit.* 20.27 *Deut.* 18.10.11." But certainly not all biblical crimes were Massachusetts crimes, and not all Massachusetts crimes were Biblical. The Puritan mind filtered out of the Bible what they wanted to use, and what they thought was God's plan for their community. For many of these crimes, English law could have been cited as easily as Exodus or Leviticus. Some of the laws were dead letters. A "stubborn or REBELLIOUS son," sixteen or over, who did not "obey the voice of his Father, or the Voice of his Mother," was supposed to be put to death (nothing was said about daughters). But nobody was in fact ever executed for this crime.[101] And the capital laws were only a small part of the criminal law, which was itself a small part of the law as a whole.

Neither in theory nor in practice was colonial law very bloodthirsty. There were fewer capital crimes on the books than in England. In England, death was a possible punishment for many thieves; in Massachusetts, only for repeaters. The Quaker laws of West New Jersey substituted restitution of property or hard labor for hanging. The death penalty was not carried out very frequently in the colonies. One study found a total of forty executions in the colonies, before 1660. The figure is perhaps a bit understated; but it does not suggest wholesale carnage. There were fifteen executions in Massachusetts in this period: four for murder, two for infanticide, two for adultery, two for witchcraft, one for "buggery"; four Quakers were also put to death.[102] But later on, nobody was

---

[100] *Colonial Laws of Massachusetts, 1660–1672* (1889), pp. 43, 187. *General Laws and Liberties of Massachusetts, 1672,* p. 129.

[101] Lawrence M. Friedman, *Crime and Punishment in American History* (1993), p. 41.

[102] Bradley Chapin, *Criminal Justice in Colonial America, 1606–1660* (1983), p. 58.

executed for adultery or for the crime of being a Quaker. The Quakers themselves, in their strongholds, were loath to execute anyone, except for murder or
treason. The southern colonies were more bloodthirsty than the northern
ones; and they were particularly liable to kill black slaves. In North Carolina, at
least a hundred slaves were executed in the period between 1748 and 1772—
more than the total number of whites executed in that colony during its entire
colonial history.[103]

Some of the southern colonies recognized a peculiar English practice
called benefit of clergy. Benefit of clergy was a privilege originally (as the
name suggests) for clergymen only. Later it came to cover anybody who knew
how to read. A person condemned to death, who claimed the privilege, would
be presented with a Bible. The book was opened to the so-called "neck" verse,
a line from Psalm 51: "Have mercy upon me, O God, according to thy loving
kindness; according unto the multitude of thy tender mercies blot out my
transgressions." He would read the verse—even illiterates could memorize it,
of course. The death penalty was avoided, and a lesser penalty (branding with
a hot iron) was then carried out. Thus, Edward Reddish of Virginia, convicted
of manslaughter in 1671, "did read and by the Governor's clemency and mercy
was acquitted from burning."[104] In 1732, Virginia passed an "Act for settling
some doubts and differences of opinion in relation to the benefit of Clergy; for
allowing the same to Women; and taking away of Reading." This law abolished
the reading test completely.[105] Despite "clergy," colonies reimposed the death
penalty for crimes that seemed particularly heinous. In Maryland, where tobacco was king, a statute of 1737 decreed "Death as a Felon . . . without Benefit of Clergy" for anyone who broke into and robbed a tobacco house.

Famous periods of hysteria, such as the notorious Salem episode, beginning
in 1692, have unduly blackened the colonial reputation.[106] Blood-letting also followed incidents of real or imagined revolts and conspiracies on the part of
slaves; this did not happen only in the South. After a supposed conspiracy was
uncovered in New York, in 1741, over 150 men and women, mostly black, were
put on trial; and dozens were executed.[107] In the "terrible assize" in Salem, nineteen persons were put to death on charges of witchcraft; fifty or so were tortured
or terrified into confessions. On September 22, 1692, eight persons were led to
the gallows. The hysteria at Salem has made "witch hunt" a permanent part of
the language. County courts in eighteenth-century Virginia sometimes used

[103]Stuart Banner, *The Death Penalty: An American History* (2002), p. 9.

[104] George W. Dalzell, *Benefit of Clergy in America and Related Matters* (1955), p. 98; see
also Bradley Chapin, *Criminal Justice in Colonial America*, pp. 48–50.

[105] Dalzell, *op. cit.*, pp. 103–4.

[106] There is a large literature, of course, on the Salem witch trials. See Kai T. Erikson,
Wayward Puritans (1966); David T. Konig, *Law and Society in Puritan Massachusetts*, ch. 7;
Paul Boyer and Stephen Nissenbaum, *Salem Possessed: The Social Origins of Witchcraft* (1974);
a succinct and able account is Peter C. Hoffer, *The Salem Witchcraft Trials: A Legal History*
(1997); see also, for an interesting interpretation, Mary Beth Norton, *In the Devil's Snare:
The Salem Witchcraft Crisis of 1692* (2002).

[107] See Peter C. Hoffer, *The Great New York Conspiracy of 1741: Slavery, Crime, and Colonial
Law* (2003). See also Thomas J. Davis, introduction to Daniel Horsmanden, *The New York
Conspiracy* (1971).

castration as a punishment for slaves convicted of rape.[108] In Richmond County, Virginia, a slave owner, in 1745, got permission to cut off a slave's toes, in order to make him more obedient. Two years later, the court allowed a slave owner to cut off the ears of one of his slaves.[109] In Massachusetts, the death penalty was imposed on those who particularly outraged the morals of society. In 1673, Benjamin Goad, "being instigated by the Divill," committed the "unnatural & horrid act of Bestiallitie on a mare in the highway or field." This was in the afternoon, "the sun being two howers high." The Court of Assistants sentenced him to hang; and the court also ordered "that the mare you abused before your execution in your sight shall be knockt on the head."[110]

The colonial laws punishing gaming, idleness, drunkenness, lying, and disobedient children are famous. A New Hampshire law of 1693—of a common type—punished those who "on the Lords day" were found to "doe any unnecessary Servall Labour, Travell, Sports," or to frequent taverns, or "Idly Stragle abroad."[111] Especially in the seventeenth century, these moral laws were by no means empty words. They were taken quite seriously. Rules about personal conduct, and about sexual morality, according to the evidence of county court records, fell most heavily on the lower social orders—on servants, on the poor, and on slaves. Early colonial law was strongly paternal. Trials were, in Garfinkel's striking phrase, status degradation ceremonies.[112] Punishment was frequently open and corporal; its goal was to reteach and retouch the erring soul, and it used, as means to this end, confession, public humiliation, and infamy. One Pennsylvania law of 1700 (disallowed by the British five years later), was aimed at persons "clamorous with their tongues"; it gave the magistrate discretion to sentence the offender to be "gagged and stand in some public place."[113] Stocks and pillory were in common use. In 1673, Sarah Scott, in Suffolk County, had to stand on a stool in the marketplace, in Boston, with a sign that told of her "undutiful, abusive and reviling" conduct toward her mother. In 1641, a servant, Teagu Ocrimi, was made to stand on the gallows, in Boston, a rope around his neck, for a "foul and devilish attempt to bugger a cow."[114]

Crime and punishment meant shame, and beyond that, reform. The codes and their enforcers never abandoned this aim; and the goal of enforcing moral laws. The most commonly punished crimes in seventeenth-century Massachusetts were fornication and drunkenness. Both continued to be punished in the eighteenth century. Taverns (inns, or "ordinaries") had to be licensed; and the

[108] Hugh F. Rankin, *Criminal Trial Proceedings in the General Court of Colonial Virginia* (1965), p. 221.

[109] Gwenda Morgan, *The Hegemony of the Law, Richmond County, Virginia, 1692–1776* (1989).

[110] *Records of the Court of Assistants of the Colony of the Massachusetts Bay: 1630–1692*, vol. 1 (1901), pp. 10–11. Punishing or forfeiting the thing or animal that had done wrong was an old English institution, called *deodand*. In Maryland in 1637, a tree that caused the death of one John Bryant was "forfeited to the Lord Proprietor," Archives of Maryland, vol. IV (1887), p. 10.

[111] *Laws of New Hampshire, Province Period, 1679–1702* (1904), p. 564.

[112] Harold Garfinkel, "Conditions of Successful Degradation Ceremonies," 61 Am. J. Sociol. 420 (1956).

[113] *Statutes at Large of Pennsylvania, 1682–1801*, vol. II (1896), p. 85.

[114] Edgar J. McManus, *Law and Liberty in Early New England: Criminal Justice and Due Process, 1620–1692* (1993).

colonies, at least in theory, insisted that owners of taverns had to be sober, respectable men and women.[115] As to fornication, the eighteenth-century situation was a bit more complicated. This continued to be the most common crime: fornication accounted for 53 percent of all criminal prosecutions in Essex County, Massachusetts, between 1700 and 1785; and an amazing 69 percent of the prosecutions in New Haven's county court between 1710 and 1750.[116] William E. Nelson analyzed all the prosecutions in seven Massachusetts counties between 1760 and 1774. There were 2,784 in all; 1,074 of these— 38 percent—were for sexual offenses, almost always fornication. Even at this late period, the connection between crime and sin was still close; and the typical criminal, in Nelson's view, was an ordinary person who had strayed from the righteous path. Thirteen percent of the cases, 359 in all, were for religious offenses: blasphemy, profanity, nonattendance at church.[117] But change was in the air. The fornication actions, by this time, were mostly directed at cases where women had given birth to bastards. The real question was: Who will support this child? Over time, then—say, between 1650 and the 1760s—the point of the fornication actions changed. The element of pure punishment for sin declined; the economic point increased.[118]

Control of sin had certainly been a factor in all of the blue laws of the seventeenth century. Servant codes and slave law were aimed at sin, too; and also had the job of keeping social lines distinct, maintaining order in the lower ranks. If an indentured servant refused to serve out his term, he was punished with extra years of service. This, too, was the usual fate of servant girls who gave birth to bastards. Fines were useless against the poor; imprisonment would have punished the master as well as the servant. Extra service was the most effective sanction; and it was freely and frequently used. In a typical example, in Kent County, Delaware, in 1704, John Mahon brought a mulatto servant, Charles, to court. Charles had been a runaway for twenty-six days; it cost his master three pounds, three shillings, and sixpence to bring him back. The court ordered the boy to serve "for his Runaway time. . . . One Hundred and thirty days and for the said sume of three Pounds three Shillings and Six pence soe Expended . . . he shall serve the said John Mahon or his Assigns the time and terme of six Monts," all this to begin *after* his regular term of service had expired.[119]

In cases of fornication, idleness, and the like, defendants were overwhelmingly servants and the poor. Few clergymen or merchants or substantial landowners were whipped or put in the stocks for fornication. Yet, prominent people *were* punished in Puritan Massachusetts for religious infractions

[115] Sharon V. Salinger, *Taverns and Drinking in Early America* (2002).

[116] Richard Godbeer, *Sexual Revolution in Early America* (2002), p. 230.

[117] Nelson, *Americanization of the Common Law*, p. 39.

[118] See Hendrik Hartog, "The Public Law of a County Court: Judicial Government in Eighteenth-Century Massachusetts," 20 Am. J. Legal Hist. 282, 299–308 (1976); Richard Gaskins, "Changes in the Criminal Law in Eighteenth-Century Connecticut," 25 Am. J. Legal Hist. 309, 317–18 (1981). In New York, "morals issues were never very important." Douglas Greenberg, "Crime, Law Enforcement, and Social Control in America," 26 Am. J. Legal Hist. 293, 307 (1982).

[119] Leon de Valinger Jr., ed., *Court Records of Kent County, Delaware, 1680–1705* (1959), pp. 283–84.

(heresy, for example); or for contempt of authority.[120] And the general theory of crime as sin led to a certain amount of leniency in practice. Sinners, after all, can become repentant; and a whipped or punished child can mend its ways. Eli Faber's study of Puritan criminal justice turned up the fact that, in some towns, offenders punished by the courts later became prominent citizens, holding elective or appointive offices. Concord named Abraham Wood a town clerk and selectman in 1701; he had been found guilty of fornication in 1684. The policy of the law, after all, was "reabsorption" into the community.[121]

In criminal justice, as in other aspects of colonial legal experience, it is sometimes treacherous to generalize. Place and period made a significant difference. The picture one gets of early Massachusetts is a picture of a pervasive, intrusive, but *effective* system of social control. Yet Douglas Greenberg has painted a contrasting picture for eighteenth-century New York: erratic, chaotic, and on the whole ineffective. He finds a general "failure of institutional arrangements to keep pace with social change."[122] No doubt many features of New York's history and society were special. But his evidence is consistent with a more general thesis, too. As the colonies grew in size, as economic and social life became more complex, as mobility (of all sorts) increased, the techniques and mental habits that worked in the early days lost a good deal of their bite and their magic. Criminal justice was ripe for reform and for change.

A crime is, in theory, a public wrong: a wrong against some victim, to be sure, but also something that hurts society—which is why society takes over the job of punishing it. This was the case, at any rate in the colonies. In England, there was no such thing as a district attorney—no public prosecutor. People were supposed to do their own prosecuting—and pay for it themselves. Very early, this system was rejected in the colonies; crime was too serious and important a business to leave to individuals. Also, in a less stratified society, criminal justice was more popular—more the duty and task of the whole community.[123] Crime, then, was a public duty. And criminal law, as it always does, expressed more than current standards of morality, although that was extremely significant. It was also a vehicle for economic and social planning and an index to the division of power in the community.

Thus, economic crimes were as much part of criminal law as murder, rape, theft, and crimes against morality. Of course, the lines between economic control, control of morality and status, and suppression of dangerous behavior are quite artificial; the laws governing servants and slaves had all of these objectives. The organization of economic life explains many peculiarities of the criminal codes. In Virginia, hogs were more vital than sheep; stealing hogs, then, was a

[120] Eli Faber, "Puritan Criminals: The Economic, Social, and Intellectual Background to Crime in Seventeenth-Century Massachusetts," in 11 Perspectives in Am. Hist. 81 (1977–1978).

[121] Faber, *op. cit.*, pp. 138–43. Quite naturally, then, as the colonies grew in size, and the theories and practices appropriate to the small, tight settlements became impractical, one would expect a shift away from leniency. This is perhaps why, in New York, after 1750, whipping as the punishment of choice for convicted thieves dropped off (from 70 to 25 percent); the death penalty and branding rose substantially. Douglas Greenberg, *Crime and Law Enforcement in the Colony of New York, 1691–1776* (1976), p 223.

[122] Greenberg, *Crime and Law Enforcement*, p. 213.

[123] Lawrence Friedman, *Crime and Punishment*, pp. 29–30.

more serious crime than stealing sheep.[124] In 1715, New York made it unlawful "from & after the first day of May, until the first day of September Annually to gather, Rake, take up, or bring to the Market, any Oysters whatsoever, under the penalty of Twenty shillings for every Offence"; or for "any Negro, Indian or Maletto [sic] Slave to Sell any Oysters in the City of New York at any time whatsoever."[125] Criminal laws naturally expressed economic policy in societies with a strong sense of authority and few special agencies of economic control. In Puritan New England, civil obedience and respect for authority were the essence of social order; proprietary and crown colonies had a somewhat different definition of authority, but the same habits of command.

In other words, even though concepts of sin suffused the criminal codes, they also carried a heavy dose of politics and economic policy. The codes also expressed power: who governed, who had the final say. The colonists had their own interests, and these were not at all the interests of the mother country. The laws against smuggling, or the opposition to the Stamp Act, and the Acts of Trade, in the middle of the eighteenth century, were at the boiling center of controversy. The war of 1776 was a war for independence. But independence did not mean the right to be free from law; it meant, not a ship without a captain, but a ship whose captain could be trusted, a captain of native heart and mind.

GOVERNMENT, LAW, AND THE ECONOMY

The colonies began long before Adam Smith published *The Wealth of Nations.* Free enterprise was no part of the ethos of the colonies. Each colony tried to regulate, control, and monitor the economy. Regulation of business was primitive by modern standards. Yet in some ways, it was fairly pervasive. The settlements depended on roads, ferries, bridges, and gristmills for transport, communication, and the basic food supply. These businesses were privately owned; but the public had a deep interest in how they were run; and there were rules and regulations that expressed colonial policy. In a typical grant, East Haven, Connecticut, gave to a certain Heminway in 1681 an old dam, some land, timber, and stone, and exempted him from tax; in exchange, Heminway agreed to erect and maintain a gristmill, to attend to the mill one day a fortnight, to grind all the corn brought that day, and to limit his toll to the legal rate.[126] Throughout the colonial period, colonies regulated and fixed the miller's rate of toll. In New Hampshire, for example, an act in 1718 set up "the Toll for grinding all Sorts of Grain" at "one Sixteenth part, and no more," except for "Indian Corn, for which the Mill shall take One Twelfth."[127] Government also regulated markets, road building, and the quality of essential commodities. As in England, local authorities controlled the inns and taverns along the roads; these were regulated both because they served liquor, and also because they were the restaurants and motels of the day. But "control" may be too strong a word. Innkeepers had to be

---

[124] Arthur P. Scott, *Criminal Law in Colonial Virginia* (1930), pp. 225–27.

[125] *Colonial Laws of New York,* vol. I (1894), p. 845 (law of May 19, 1715).

[126] Henry Farnam, *Chapters in the History of Social Legislation in the United States to 1860* (1938), p. 96.

[127] *Laws of New Hampshire, Province Period, 1702–1745,* vol. 2 (1913), p. 265.

licensed; and there were many decent, comfortable inns. But just as many were filthy, disreputable, full of drunks and infested with vermin. One Maryland traveler complained that he had "For my company . . . Bugs in every part of my Bed—& in the next Room several noisy Fellows playing at Billiards." Privacy was nonexistent. The traveler was expected to share room and bed. Alexander Hamilton was once put up at a house where his "landlord, his wife, daughters, and I lay all in one room."[128]

Public business needs taxes to fuel the public machine. Money was scarce in the colonies. To build roads, a labor tax was commonly used. Every adult man was obligated to pay the tax, either in money, produce, or the sweat of his brow. A New York law of 1713, "for Mending and keeping in Repair the Post-Road from New York to Kings-Bridge," began by deploring the "ruinous" and "very dangerous" condition of the road. The act then provided for surveyors, to plan out the necessary repairs, and directed the people who lived in the affected wards to "meet and convene with Carts and Carriages, Shovels, Spades, Pick-axes, Mattocks, and other Tools," either to do the work themselves or to provide "sufficient working hands."[129]

In these days, long before anybody had heard of "free enterprise," the proprietors, squires, and magistrates of America certainly did not hold to the mantra that the best government was the one that governed least. On the other hand, the people who ran the colonies had very little in the way of tax money, or staff, at their disposal. Regulation tended to be local, and as cheap in money and men as possible. When a government wished, therefore, to make sure bread was baked and priced correctly, it insisted that each baker brand his bread. Under a Pennsylvania law of 1700, every baker had to have "a distinct mark to be set on all the bread he shall bake."[130] For many commodities, the laws provided for "viewers," "searchers," and "inspectors." These men were generally paid through users' fees, not out of tax funds. In general, fees, not salaries, supported public officials. There were other ways to put the burden on private citizens, in money or otherwise, in order to achieve certain public ends. To light its dark streets, the town fathers of New York ordered householders to hang lights on a pole, from the upper windows of houses, "in the Darke time of the moon." Philadelphia ordered citizens in 1700 to plant shade trees in front of their doors, "pines, unbearing mulberries, water poplars, lime or other shady and wholesome trees," so that the town might be "well shaded from the violence of the sun in the heat of the summer and thereby be rendered more healthy."[131]

From England, the colonies copied laws about public markets. These laws laid down rules about where and when key products could be sold. A scattered market is difficult to control or to regulate. When all sellers of wood, or hay, or grain meet at one place and time, regulation can be cheap and effective. A South Carolina law, passed in 1739, set up a public market for the sale of meat

---

[128]Sharon v. Salinger, *Taverns and Drinking in Early America* (2002), pp. 211, 214.

[129] *Colonial Laws of New York*, vol. I (1894), pp. 792–95 (act of Oct. 23, 1713). The act provided that "no person shall be compellable to work above Eight Days in the year, nor at any time in seed-time, Hay or Corn Harvest."

[130] *Statutes at Large, Pennsylvania*, vol. II (1896), pp. 61–62 (act of Nov. 17, 1700).

[131] Carl Bridenbaugh, *Cities in the Wilderness* (1938), p. 169.

and "other butchery wares" in Charleston. No meat could be sold except at the market, and during proper hours.[132]

As in England, too, local—county and city—courts held much of the power to run the economy. This arrangement had a drawback—at least from the standpoint of the mother country. It meant that local gentry, and local magistrates, could make or break imperial policy. Local rule is efficient, from the standpoint of the center, only if local people can be trusted. American squires and American merchants had fallen out with their English overlords long before 1776—over the Stamp Act, the Acts of Trade, and other aspects of British rule.[133] Enforcement became, frankly, impossible.

Colonial government made a constant effort, not always effective, to keep its staple crops under some kind of quality control. In Virginia and Maryland, tobacco was the major crop. A long series of laws dealt with this crucial commodity.[134] Very early, Virginia tried to reduce the dependence of the colony on a single cash crop and to improve the quality and price of tobacco. In 1619, the Virginia House of Burgesses set up a system of tobacco inspection. Any tobacco which might "not proove vendible" was liable to be burned. In 1621, settlers were restricted to one hundred plants per person, and nine leaves to a stalk. The purpose of this act was to draw people away "from excessive plantinge of Tobacco." Maryland enacted its first inspection law in 1640. In 1657, second crops were outlawed, to prevent a glut on the market, and to cut down the flow of substandard tobacco, which depressed prices and ruined the reputation of Maryland tobacco.

Twentieth-century farm schemes were foreshadowed in old Maryland and Virginia: quality control, inspection laws, regulation of the size of containers, subsidies for planting preferred kinds of crop, public warehousing, export controls. In the 1660s, the tobacco colonies were fearful of a radical oversupply. Maryland in 1666 ordered a complete stop to tobacco cultivation, between February 1667 and 1668, if Virginia and Carolina followed suit (they did). (Lord Baltimore voided this act; he felt it was harmful to Great Britain.) Tobacco regulation was, if anything, more pervasive in the eighteenth century. Maryland, in 1747, enacted its most comprehensive statute, modeled on an equally elaborate Virginia law of 1730. The law required all tobacco to be brought to public warehouses and forbade the export of bulk tobacco. Inspectors at each warehouse would inspect, weigh, and repack the tobacco, branding each cask with the name of the warehouse, the tare, and the net amount of leaf. There were to be some eighty warehouses in all. Unacceptable tobacco was to be burned or repacked by the owners. Inspectors were to give out tobacco notes, transferable and redeemable, for all tobacco brought to the warehouse in payment of debts. These notes were legal tender—a kind of money. A later form of the act, passed in 1773, was in force when the Revolution came.

Virginia and Maryland were not the only colonies that regulated their staple crop. Connecticut grew tobacco, too, and passed an inspection law in 1753. A Pennsylvania law of 1724 forbade the export of any flour not submitted to an

[132] James W. Ely Jr., "Patterns of Statutory enactment in South Carolina, 1720–1770," in Herbert A. Johnson, ed., *South Carolina Legal History* (1980), pp. 67, 69.

[133] See, for example, on the Stamp Act resistance, Edmund S. Morgan and Helen M. Morgan, *The Stamp Act Crisis* (1953).

[134] See, in general, Vertrees J. Wyckoff, *Tobacco Regulation in Colonial Maryland* (1936).

inspecting officer, "who shall search and try the same in order to judge of its goodness." Merchantable export flour had to be branded with the "provincial brand-mark, . . . sufficient and capable to impress in a fair and distinguishable manner the arms of the province of Pennsylvania with the letter P on each side"; for his trouble, the officer was to have from the shipper "one penny per cask and no more."[135] Flour for domestic consumption was also to be inspected and branded, though with less stringent controls. A statute of the same session continued in effect a bounty of a penny a pound for hemp "to the end that the people of this province may be further encouraged in the raising of good and merchantable hemp." Georgia began colonial life as a planned economy, with public sawmills, farms, and herds of livestock. Even after Georgia became a crown colony (1752), lumber inspection laws were passed (1760), followed by laws setting up grades and specifications for beef, pork, pitch, tar, and turpentine. Later, special legislation dealt with leather and tobacco.[136] Massachusetts Bay had had a leather statute for more than a century. Under the *Laws and Liberties* of 1648, towns were empowered to "choose one or two persons of the most honest and skilfull" to act as "searchers" of leather. The law limited the tanning trade, and gave directions for the proper manufacture of leather. Searchers had power to seize all leather made contrary to the dictates of the law:

> Nor shall any person or persons using or occupying the mysterie of tanning, set any their Fats [vats] in tan-hills or other places, where the woozes or leather put to tan in the same shall or may take any unkinde heats; nor shall put any leather into any hot or warm woozes whatsoever on pain of twenty pounds for everie such offence.[137]

COMMERCE AND LABOR

When the colonies were first settled, the *law merchant*—the rules and practices of commercial law—had not yet been fully "received" into common law, that is, the royal courts of England did not yet recognize these rules and practices. (Special merchants' courts in England filled the gap.) Yet, on both sides of the Atlantic merchants followed much the same commercial habits. This was only natural. The law merchant was, in theory, international. More to the point, colonial merchants did business with English merchants; their ties with each other became even tighter in the eighteenth century. Negotiable instruments were known and used in all the colonies. In the eighteenth century, many colonies experimented with paper currency. In some, chattel notes were common; tobacco notes were ubiquitous in Maryland and Virginia. By mercantile custom, commercial paper circulated freely, from hand to hand; a holder in due course—a person who got possession in the ordinary course of business—had full rights to use, sue, and collect on the note or the bill. The old common

---

[135] *Statutes at Large, Pennsylvania, 1682–1801,* vol. IV (1897), p. 5 (act of Mar. 20, 1724–1725).

[136] Milton S. Heath, *Constructive Liberalism: The Role of the State in Economic Development in Georgia to 1860* (1954), pp. 55–56.

[137] *Laws and Liberties of Massachusetts, 1648* (1929 ed.), p. 33. "Wooze" is a variant of "ooze," and refers to the liquid in the tanning vats.

law had been quite stiff and stubborn on this point; it refused to honor the rights of a person to whom an intangible had been transferred. Here colonial law ran far ahead of English law. As early as 1647, Massachusetts provided by statute that "any debt, or debts due upon bill, or other specialtie assigned to another; shall be as good a debt & estate to the Assignee as it was to the Assigner at the time of its assignation . . . provided the said assignement be made upon the backside of the bill or specialtie." A similar statute appeared in Connecticut (1650), Pennsylvania (1676), New York (1684), and in Delaware, New Jersey, and colonies to the South.

The colonies depended on ocean commerce. In England, common law and commercial law were, as we said, not yet unified. The colonies were free from—and indeed, sometimes ignorant of—many of the technicalities and rigidities of the mother country. Hard currency was in short supply in America. This meant that merchants were very much dependent on commercial paper for carrying on trade. In the eighteenth century, commercial law, like other branches of law, crept closer to the practices that prevailed in England. Colonial society became more mature, commercially speaking—more tied to the great world of international trade. Many variations and innovations on this side of the Atlantic were useful, and became permanent parts of the living law.[138] But the system of commercial law, in general, became more formal, more formalistic. Small town disputes between neighbors are one thing; commercial transactions in biggish towns quite another. When friends or relatives or neighbors go to law (or arbitration), the context becomes relevant: the world they live in, their families, and the way they had interacted with each other. When merchants sue, what is important are standard ways of behaving, mercantile custom—and law.[139]

Labor was as essential and problematic a factor of production as money. The colonies drew up codes of labor law, and constantly tinkered with them. These codes were not totally indigenous; they owed a good deal to mercantilist theory, and of course to English law. As always, these codes had a special character, based on specific colonial needs and conditions. There was no such thing as slavery in England. Its law of apprenticeship was the nearest thing to the law of indentured service. The colonies, by grim necessity, had to attract and hold a population, organize a workforce, and keep it in place. Families worked together on the farm, and in stores and inns. There was also hired labor; but the part of the workforce that was bound, not free, was of enormous importance. There were two types of bound labor: indentured servitude, a kind of temporary slavery; and slavery itself. Indentured servitude, for all its abuses and inequities, held open a promise of freedom and a decent living at the end of the road. It gave way, in the end, to free labor.[140] The law—and practice—of slavery, on the other hand, led downward into cruelty and grief and to political turmoil as well.

---

[138] Frederick Beutel, "Colonial Sources of the Negotiable Instruments Law of the United States," 34 Ill. L. Rev. 137, 141–42 (1939).

[139] See, on the increasing sophistication of modes of handling and evidencing debt, and commercial law in general, Bruce H. Mann, *Neighbors and Strangers: Law and Community in Early Connecticut* (1987); Deborah A. Rosen, *Courts and Commerce: Gender, Law, and the Market Economy in Colonial New York* (1997).

[140] On indentured servitude and labor conditions in general, there is a classic study by Richard B. Morris, *Government and Labor in Early America* (1946).

In the early days of colonial life, it was a common rule, both North and South, that every able-bodied man had a duty to work. Idleness was a punishable offense. No person, said the *Laws and Liberties of Massachusetts* (1648) shall "spend his time idly or unprofittably under pain of such punishment as the Court of Assistants or County Court shall think meet to inflict." This principle was never formally abandoned. But in time, it became a matter of caste and class. The magistrates of early New England had to work hard with their hands, just as their servants did. In the eighteenth century there was a definite leisure class, the families of rich merchants and planters. Only the poor were impressed into work gangs; only the poor paid their road taxes in personal sweat.

Some colonies tried to control the cost of labor. Scarcity tends to push up the price of the workingman's efforts. John Winthrop reported that in Massachusetts in 1633 "the scarcity of workmen had caused them to raise their wages to an excessive rate, so as a carpenter would have three shillings the day, a laborer two shillings and sixpence." As a result, commodity prices were "sometimes double to that they cost in England." The general court took action; they "made an order, that carpenters, masons, etc. should take but two shillings the day, and laborers but eighteen pence, and that no commodity should be sold at above four pence in the shilling more than it cost for ready money in England." Oil, wine, and cheese were excepted, "in regard of the hazard of bringing."[141] Massachusetts Bay later provided that "the freemen of every Town may from time to time as occasion shall require, agree amongst themselves about the prizes and rates of all workmens Labour and servants wages."[142] Particularly vital occupations, like draymen and ferrymen, were most prone to be regulated. Price regulation, in turn, fell on those who supplied vital commodities, such as bakers. Wage-price regulation was virtually abandoned by 1700. It was briefly and ineffectively revived during the Revolutionary War, as an emergency measure. But the shortage of labor probably frustrated every attempt to control prices and wages.

Throughout the colonial period, colonies were anxious to attract and keep skilled workmen. South Carolina, in 1741, prohibited artisans from keeping taverns, a less essential occupation. Skilled laborers tried, in some instances, to control entry into their trades and keep prices high. These attempts were no more successful than wage controls. New York and other colonial cities at one time restricted crafts to men who enjoyed the "freedom" of the city. By the middle of the eighteenth century, this system too was dead; the "freedom of the city" was available to all, practically for the asking.

Up and down the coast, indentured servants acted as farm and household workers, hewers of wood, drawers of water—the laboring hands and feet of the colonies. Indentured servants were the personal property of their masters. "Indentures" were written documents, somewhat similar to English articles of apprenticeship. In the early seventeenth century, many servants, with or without indentures, were Indians or blacks. Many white immigrants (probably more than one-half) arrived either as "redemptioners" or became redemptioners on arrival. This meant that they sold their labor, for a definite period of time, to pay for the price of passage. Some signed indentures in England, before sailing.

---

[141] John Winthrop, *The History of New England from 1630–1649*, vol. 1 (1853), p. 116.
[142] *Colonial Laws in Massachusetts, 1660–1672*, vol. I (1889), p. 174.

They signed themselves over to the master of the ship; when ship and passenger landed, a New World broker would sell the indenture in the market, to raise the price of passage. Indentured servitude usually lasted from four to seven years. Those who came without indenture, and without money to pay the captain, had to serve "according to the custom of the country." This "custom" depended on the age and condition of the servant. Often, young immigrants and orphans were brought into court for a decision (or guess) about their age. Court records are full of such proceedings. In Kent County, Delaware, in 1699,

> Mr. John Walker brought into Court a Servant boy named Richard Cundon, to be Judged, he cominge in without Indentures, which being Considered, the Court doe deeme him the said Richard Cundon to be about Twelve years of age, and doe order that he shall serve the said John Walker or his Assignes, Untill he shall arrive to one and twenty years of age, and that at the Expiration thereof, the said John Walker or his assignes shall pay him his Corne, Cloaths and Tolls, accordinge to Law.[143]

At the end of his term, the servant went free, and in addition, recovered by right certain "freedom dues." In early Maryland, servants, whether indentured or not, had the right to an outfit of clothes, a hat, ax, hoe, three barrels of corn, and (until 1663) fifty acres of land, at the end of the term.[144] In later times, clothing, food, and a sum of money were more typical dues (the "Corne, Cloaths and Tolls" of the example).

By no means all indentured servants were "free-willers." England dumped a certain number of convicts onto the colonies as indentured servants, to the distaste of the residents, who attempted (futilely) to legislate against "jail birds." Some unlucky people were kidnapped in England and sold into servitude. For others, servitude was the punishment for crime. But most people sentenced to a term of labor were already servants; they had no goods or lands to satisfy debts or pay fines. They paid their debt to society by adding on to their term of service. Even more than England, colonial society used indentures of apprenticeship to handle poor orphans and abandoned children. This shifted a social problem to private masters. Masters and mistresses gained extra hands; in exchange, masters were supposed to teach boys to read and write, and to introduce them to some useful trade. Girls learned to cook and sew and do household work. The indenture system fulfilled a great many functions. It was a method of organizing labor, of financing immigration, a penal sanction, a way to train the young, a kind of welfare institution, and a crude instrument of credit. Court records show surprising uses of this protean device. In 1703, in Delaware, a "poor Aged lame Man," Leviticus John Wassell, "did bind himselfe a Servant to One Edward Starkie . . . for the time and terme of foure years In Consideration that the said Starkies Wife Would cure the said Leviticus John Wassell his sore leg." And Joseph Groves "bound himselfe to serve Thomas Bedwell" for two years "In consideration Whereof the said Thomas Bedwell being here present in Court did Promise to learn the said Joseph to write and

---

[143] Leon de Valinger Jr., ed., *Court Records of Kent County, Delaware, 1680–1705* (1959), p. 152.

[144] *Archives of Maryland*, vol. 53 (1936), xxxii.

Cypher soe far as the said Joseph should be capable of receaving during the said time."[145]

Some men of wealth or position began their careers as servants or apprentices. Roger Sherman, for example, was apprenticed as a boy to a shoemaker. Daniel Dulany came to Maryland in 1703 as an indentured servant; he had the good fortune to be sold to Colonel George Plater, who needed a clerk in his law office. Ten years later, Dulany was a lawyer and a landowner.[146] These success stories were not rare; but neither were they typical. More commonly, former servants continued to work at their trades, only now as free men. So, Abraham Daphne, a carpenter, advertised in 1753 that he was "now acquitted and discharged" from servitude, and ready "to undertake any work in his business."[147] Many more no doubt never made it very far up the ladder. A study of indentured servants, in late seventeenth-century Maryland (Charles County), underscores this point. The servants in the county mostly died or disappeared from the records; many apparently simply left the county. Of those that finished out their term, and became free, 58 percent remained laborers or, at best, tenant farmers. About a third became smallholders. About 17 percent ended up with more than average holdings (250 to 600 acres); some 5 percent achieved substantial wealth. Servitude was not a dead end, by any means; but true success stories were certainly not the general rule.[148]

The lot of the servant, during his term, was rarely a bed of roses. Many Englishmen or Germans, enticed into servitude by glittering propaganda, found they had chosen a life of hardship and tyranny. The servant, by law, had the right of redress against a cruel or incompetent master. In the court records, we find a long litany of complaints by servants, about beatings, bad food, nakedness, cold, and general misery. Often, they found justice: a study of Maryland came to the conclusion that servants there "understood their legal rights, sought relief for their grievances, and succeeded in their efforts." Some women servants complained of rape or sexual abuse—Anne Gould, for example, of Kent County, whose master (she said), threw her on a bed, forced her to have sex, and left her infected with the pox.[149] Still, no doubt, many ill-used servants were too ignorant or frightened to complain. Thousands of servants ran away. And servants, even when they were treated decently, were subject to many legal disabilities. They could not marry without their master's consent. They could not vote or engage in trade. Masters could buy and sell their labor; could trade them to other masters. They were, in short, slaves for the time being.[150]

Yet servants eventually turned into ordinary laborers. Indentured servants were part of the household: They earned no wages, but they could not be fired,

[145] Valinger, op. cit., pp. 274–76.

[146] Louis B. Wright, *The Cultural Life of the American Colonies, 1607–1763* (1957), p. 14.

[147] Warren B. Smith, *White Servitude in Colonial South Carolina* (1961), p. 88.

[148] Lorena S. Walsh, "Servitude and Opportunity in Charles County, Maryland, 1658–1705," in Aubrey C. Land, Lois Green Carr, and Edward C. Papenfuse, *Law, Society, and Politics in Early Maryland* (1977), pp. 111, 115–18.

[149] Christine Daniels, "'Liberty to Complaine': Servant Petitions in Maryland, 1652–1797," in Christopher L. Tomlins and Bruce H. Mann, *The Many Legalities of Early America* (2001), pp. 219, 225, 238.

[150] See, in general, Abbott E. Smith, *Colonists in Bondage, White Servitude and Convict Labor in America, 1607–1776* (1947).

and if they got sick and unable to work, the master was supposed to take care of them. The system became obsolete in a modernizing economy, where bosses hired and fired, and where workers were free to move about, and change jobs, and where workers were out of the household, working for money wages. In the early years of the colonial period, indentured servants were everywhere in colonial America. By the middle of the eighteenth century, servitude was concentrated in Pennsylvania and the Chesapeake area. Servants were imported until about 1820, but by the time of the revolution, they were no longer a significant part of the workforce; and in the nineteenth century, servitude totally disappeared.[151]

SLAVERY[152]

Indentured servants were a vital part of the labor system in the North, in southern towns, and in frontier regions, as we have seen. But in the tobacco, rice, and sugar colonies, black slavery more and more replaced white servitude. The first blacks were apparently servants, not slaves; perhaps they had more or less the same status as white servants or Indian captives. But blacks were pagans, and their skin was a different color. A special sentiment crystallized around the black Africans in the workforce. The rancid poison of racism goes very far back in American history. A peculiar mixture of bigotry, dread, and sexual envy went into the brew. And racism in turn created an ideology that helped justify and legitimate the cruelty of chattel slavery.

The precise legal origins of slavery are obscure. Clearly, there was a kind of custom of enslaving blacks, before law explicitly recognized the status of the slave. There was no such thing as slavery in England. In the colonies, the earliest references to Africans had a certain vagueness and ambiguity. Yet, before the end of the seventeenth century, slavery had become a definite legal status in both North and South; it was peculiarly associated with the blacks; it had become a terrible, lifetime condition. Piece by piece, a slave code was gradually built up.[153] In Virginia, insofar as these developments can be dated, the evidence points to the years between 1660 and 1680 as the time when the status hardened into formal law. A Virginia law of 1662 asserted that the children of slave mothers would themselves be slaves, and never mind the status of the father.[154] Would conversion to Christianity free a slave? As early as a Maryland

---

[151] Robert J. Steinfeld, *The Invention of Free Labor: The Employment Relation in English and American Law and Culture, 1350–1870* (1991), pp. 10–11.

[152] The literature on slavery is large, and keeps growing. The most general treatment of the law of slavery is Thomas D. Morris, *Southern Slavery and the Law, 1619–1860* (1996); the most comprehensive study of the criminal law of slavery is Philip J. Schwarz, *Twice Condemned: Slaves and the Criminal Laws of Virginia, 1705–1865* (1988).

[153] Carl N. Degler, *Out of Our Past: The Forces that Shaped Modern America* (1959), p. 30; Winthrop D. Jordan, *White over Black: American Attitudes Toward the Negro, 1550–1812* (1968), pp. 91–98. On the colonial slave codes, see William M. Wiecek, "The Statutory Law of Slavery and Race in the Thirteen Mainland Colonies of British America," 34 William and Mary Q. (3rd ser.) 258 (1977).

[154] John H. Russell, *The Free Negro in Virginia, 1619–1865* (1913), p. 37.

law of 1671, the clear answer was: No. Baptism brought no escape from slavery.[155] Converted slaves would wait for their freedom in another world.

Once the law established the fundamentals, the colonies carried the logic of slavery to its grim outer limits. The slave was property, a capital asset of his master. White people could buy slaves and sell them, mortgage them, lend them and borrow them, leave them to their heirs in their wills, or give them away as gifts. The slave could be seized for his master's debts, and was taxed like other property. Virginia, in 1705, declared the slave to be real estate, the same as houses, trees, or land. (Elsewhere, slaves were simply chattels.) The strange Virginia law had a certain inner logic: it meant that the slaves were part of the "estate," as integral an aspect of the plantations as the soil, the houses, and the growing crops.[156]

Slaves themselves had few legal rights. They could not testify in court against whites. Slaves could not vote, own property, or (legally) marry. The master was supposed to treat slaves fairly, to feed them and clothe them, and to punish them no more severely than the situation demanded. These rights were occasionally enforced in court—but only occasionally. Slaves had neither the power nor the support in public opinion to translate paper rights into living law. Masters were, in fact, specifically allowed to "correct" their slaves—punish them, usually by whipping. Of course, slaves were valuable assets; the rational slave owner would want his property sound, alive, in good health and good working condition. But the system had no real protection against masters who made mistakes or who were cruel, drunk, or irrational. No account was taken, in law at least, of the feelings, hopes, and desires of the slaves themselves.

Slaveholders, North and South, had many fantasies about blacks—about their intelligence, strength, and sensibilities. They were capable of believing, and saying, that blacks were best off as slaves; that nature intended them for this role, and not for civilized life. Yet, white southerners never quite convinced themselves that the slaves were content with their lot. They never really trusted their slaves. On the contrary, the white population was haunted by a fear of slave violence, and possible rebellion. They complained constantly about the "insolence" of slaves, and about the need for firm control. Some slaves indeed dared to raise a hand against their masters; or even to commit murder—a constant source of dread. In South Carolina, in 1749, two slaves were convicted of poisoning their master; and in 1754, slaves were executed for murdering Charles Purry, whose body was found "in the River, with Bags of Shot tied to each of his wrists and feet, a Stab in his breast, and one of his eyes thrusted out of his head."[157] According to one account, 266 slaves were convicted of killing whites in Virginia in the period from 1706 to 1864.[158]

[155] James M. Wright, *The Free Negro in Maryland, 1634–1860* (1921), p. 22.

[156] In South Carolina, too, after 1690, slaves were considered "freehold property" in most respects. M. Eugene Sirmans, "The Legal Status of the Slave in South Carolina, 1670–1740," in Stanley N. Katz, ed., *Colonial America: Essays in Politics and Social Development* (1971), pp. 404, 408.

[157] Robert Olwell, *Masters, Slaves, and Subjects: The Culture of Power in the South Carolina Low Country, 1740–1790* (1998), p. 91.

[158] Philip J. Schwarz, "Forging the Shackles: The Development of Virginia's Criminal Code for Slaves," in David J. Bodenhamer and James W. Ely Jr., eds., *Ambivalent Legacy: A Legal History of the South* (1984), pp. 125, 133.

The threat of slave revolt was also serious. This too was not sheer paranoia. There were any number of actual disturbances—all futile, all put down with barbarous severity.[159] Even so, fear of uprising verged at times on hysteria. Slave codes grew steadily more repressive. In North Carolina, for example, the Fundamental Constitutions codified the custom that slave owners had "absolute power and authority over negro slaves."[160] The statutes were revised in 1715, restricting free whites from trading with slaves, and forbidding intermarriage of blacks and whites. A master could be fined for permitting blacks to build a "house under pretence of a meeting house upon account of worship." This was presumably to avoid risks of paganism and conspiracy. Emancipated slaves, under the law, had to leave the colony within six months. Those who did not could be sold to whomever might promise to get them out of the state. An act of 1729 prohibited slaves from hunting with dog or gun on any but the master's land. In 1741, the right to carry a gun and hunt, even on the master's land, was limited to slaves who carried a certificate, signed by the master and countersigned by the chairman of the county court. Only slaves who had performed "meritorious services," certified by the local courts, could be set free. A 1753 law set up a system of "viewers" to deal with slave problems. Courts were authorized to divide their counties into districts and appoint such "viewers," who could search slave quarters and seize any weapons found. Slave owners insisted that slaves were well treated and were content with their lot. But, in many places and, in many regards, the plantation world lived inside a ghastly fog of fear.

The master himself was law, judge, and jury in his household; this was inherent in the system of slavery. The master could whip his slave or otherwise punish him; and if the slave was injured or died, this was usually no crime at all, but an unfortunate accident. A Virginia statute of 1669 made this explicit; and a law of 1723 provided that there was to be no punishment if a slave died "by reason of any stroke or blow given, during his or her correction."[161] But in North Carolina, at least as early as 1715, there were special courts for slaves who disobeyed the law. Whipping was the common mode of punishment. Serious crimes called for the death penalty; but when a slave was put to death, the master was paid for him out of public funds. Slaves, after all, were valuable property; and the law did not want the master to have an incentive to hide or protect slaves who broke the law. For serious crimes, castration was a possible punishment, though this was eliminated in 1764. But in 1773, a black was burned alive for murdering a white man.

Few of the North Carolina provisions were original or unique. They were typical of the law of slavery in the southern colonies. Each jurisdiction added or subtracted a detail here or there. A Georgia statute of 1770, fearful that blacks might wish to "plot and confederate together," forbade slaves to "buy, sell, trade, traffic, deal, or barter for any goods or commodities," except under special circumstances. Slaves could not own or keep "any boat, perriagua, or canoe" or breed cattle. To avoid "ill consequences," groups of seven or more slaves were forbidden to go on the highway, unless accompanied by a white man; violators

---

[159] Edward Franklin Frazier, *The Negro in the United States* (1957), pp. 86–87.

[160] For the following discussion, see John Spencer Bassett, *Slavery and Servitude in the Colony of North Carolina* (1896).

[161] Morris, *Slavery and the Law*, pp. 163–64.

could be whipped. Since "inconveniences" might arise from book learning, any-one who taught a slave to read or write was liable to be fined. Under a Virginia act of 1748, slaves who, "under pretense of practising physic, have prepared and exhibited poisonous medicines" were to suffer "death without benefit of clergy."

There were slaves in every colony, not just in the South. But there were fewer of them outside the South; and the New England slave codes were relatively mild. Only Massachusetts had a statute against intermarriage; and Northern blacks were allowed to testify in court. But where blacks lived in sizable num-bers (in Rhode Island, for example), or during times of panic over possible black unrest, Northern communities were capable of great severity and sav-agery, as we have seen.[162] Boston, in 1723, afraid of black firebugs, enacted emergency regulations to punish all blacks caught near a fire. Under an ordi-nance of South Kingston, Rhode Island (1718), if a slave was found in the house of a free black, both slave and host were liable to be whipped. In the 1750s, no black in South Kingston might own a pig or cow or livestock of any kind. No cider could be sold to a slave. Indians and blacks could not hold out-door gatherings. In New York, after 1705, a slave found traveling alone forty miles from Albany could, on conviction, be put to death.[163]

Not all blacks in the colonies were slaves, especially in the eighteenth cen-tury. Some of these free blacks were emancipated slaves; some were descended from black servants who had never been slaves. As the racist element in the slave codes increased, the legal position of free blacks deteriorated. One fear was that blacks as a group might conspire against whites. The law discrimi-nated against free blacks and hounded them from colony to colony. Law and society debased this class of people, treated them like pariahs, then used their low status as an excuse for further debasement. By 1776, the free black was a kind of half slave in many parts of the country.

THE POOR LAWS

In 1647, a Rhode Island statute enjoined the towns to "provide carefully for the reliefe of the poore, to maintayne the impotent . . . and [to] appoint an over-seer for the same purpose." The law then cited "43 Eliz. C.2."[164] This was a ref-erence to the poor laws passed in the forty-third year (1601) of the reign of Elizabeth I. These famous laws were part of the legal background of the colonists, and indeed part of their legal culture. The New England colonies copied the general features of these poor laws. One of their chief features was local rule. Each town maintained its own poor—those who were "settled" in the town. Some poor people were placed in private homes, to be cared for at public expense. Sometimes this meant auctioning off the poor person; who went to the lowest bidder.[165] On the other hand, the law of "settlement," hammered out in

---

[162] See p. 56, n. 107, *supra*.

[163] Lorenzo J. Greene, *The Negro in Colonial New England, 1620–1776* (1942), pp. 142, 161.

[164] Quoted in Margaret Creech, *Three Centuries of Poor Law Administration: A Study of Leg-islation in Rhode Island* (1936), p. 8.

[165] Walter I. Trattner, *From Poor Law to Welfare State: A History of Social Welfare in America* (6th ed., 1999), p. 18.

the case law, proved to be highly technical, and tricky. Towns were eager to dodge the problems and costs of paupers, especially if they were relative newcomers; they frequently sued some other town, trying to palm a pauper off, and using the law of settlement as the basis for their suit. By the Plymouth laws of 1671, any person who had been "received and entertained" in a town became the responsibility of that town, if he later became destitute. The town escaped this duty if the new settler was "warned by the Constable, or some one or more of the Select men of that Town, not there to abide without leave first obtained of the Town."[166] Out of this kind of law grew the custom of "warning out." Between 1737 and 1788, 6,764 persons were "warned out" in Worcester County alone.[167] "Warning out" was not a sentence of banishment, but a disclaimer of responsibility; some towns "warned out" practically every new arrival. "Warning out" threw the burden of support back on the former place of settlement. The system, in other words, discriminated against unfortunate strangers. No doubt, people were willing to help out friends and neighbors who had fallen on evil day. But their sympathy went no further.

The poor laws were only part of what we might call the welfare system of the colonies. Orphans became apprentices. Adults who were poor but could work, turned themselves into indentured servants; an indenture was their ticket to food, work, and a roof over their heads. Poor laws were used, then, for a helpless residue of society. For all others, poverty and want meant an adjustment of status, not a draft on the public purse.

STATUTE AND COMMON LAW IN THE COLONIAL PERIOD

The colonies, to a striking extent, drafted and enacted "codes"—more or less systematic bodies of written law. Yet, these were common-law jurisdictions, after all; and common law was essentially uncodified. There was certainly nothing in England even remotely resembling codification. Why then were there American codes, even in the earliest days and in the earliest colonies?

In one sense, codification is natural in a colony. A new settlement cannot sit back and wait for the slow evolution of its legal system. England could make do with an unwritten constitution; the United States could not. Any fresh start demands codification. When Japan and other countries decided to adopt a "modern" legal system, they turned to the European codes. The common law was not a realistic alternative; it seemed too shapeless, too complex. There were too many books. The law was simply not packaged for export. It could never be restated authoritatively. A code may be a behavioral mirage; it may not mean what it says; it may be "interpreted" totally out of shape. But at least it has an authoritative text. It can be copied in the letter, if not in the spirit. The first codes of the colonies were fresh-start codes. Later ones were often borrowed from the earlier codes.

---

[166] Josiah H. Benton, *Warning Out in New England* (1911), p. 54; see also Douglas L. Jones, "The Strolling Poor: Transiency in Eighteenth-Century Massachusetts," 8 J. Social Hist. 28 (1975).

[167] Benton, *loc. cit.*, p. 59.

Each code had its own unique history. The first Massachusetts codes rose out of political struggle in the colony. The desire for a code was, among other things, a desire to limit autocracy.[168] The codes were reactions to the power and discretion of the magistrates in Massachusetts Bay. It was a delicate issue: those who supported putting the law into a clear, definite book—a code—felt that it was bad to concentrate power in a few hands. The earliest code, of a rather crude sort, was in New Plymouth, in 1636; it lay down rules of procedure, and put limits on the power of the magistrates. This same urge, to control and limit the power of the elites of the colony, lay behind the *Body of Liberties,* drafted by Nathaniel Ward and adopted by the Massachusetts General Court in 1641. In 1648, a more comprehensive code was drafted, the *Laws and Liberties of Massachusetts.* This was not a code in the modern European sense—a logical, systematic arrangement of the law. Rather, it was a collection of important legal rules, listed alphabetically by subject. The code began with a noble paragraph: "no mans life shall be taken away," or his "honour or good name . . . stayned, or his person arrested, or his goods taken, except by the vertue or equity of some expresse law of the Country, or in defect of a law in any particular case by the word of God." Then came a provision on "Abilitie" (persons over 21 may make out wills and dispose of property), then "Actions," "Age," and "Ana-Baptists," ending (except for some "Presidents and Forms of things frequently used") with "Wrecks of the Sea." The code had material on the general framework of government, the court system, and a miscellaneous group of legal subjects. Once these laws had been printed, the colonists could proudly assert that their laws were "now to be seen by all men, to the end that none may plead ignorance, and that all who intend to transport themselves hither may know that this is no place of licentious liberty."[169]

The code also reflected, as Professor Haskins has put it, the "traditional Puritan belief in the importance of the written word," evidenced by "literal use of the Bible as authority and by Puritan demand for explicit church canons which would leave no doubt as to what the law was."[170] Precise, knowable law is law that a citizen can easily follow (at least in theory). It is also law that rulers must also follow. If they do not, the citizens can plainly see their defaults.

Case law—court decisions—did not easily pass from colony to colony. There were no printed reports at all, though in the eighteenth century some manuscript materials did circulate among lawyers. These could hardly have been very influential. No doubt custom and case law slowly seeped from colony to colony. Travelers and word of mouth must have spread some knowledge of living law. It is hard to say how much; thus, it is hard to tell to what degree a common legal culture developed in the colonies.

To borrow statutes (even whole codes) was easier to do. Partly for this reason, some colonies had great apparent influence on other colonies. Legal skill

---

[168]On the codification movement in the early colonies, see Edgar J. McManus, *Law and Liberty in Early New England,* pp. 3–10.

[169]Edward Johnson, *Wonder-Working Providence* (Jameson, ed., 1910), p. 244.

[170]George L. Haskins, "Codification of the Law in Colonial Massachusetts: A Study in Comparative Law," 30 Ind. L.J. 1, 7 (1954). On the code-making impulse, see also G. B. Warden, "Law Reform in England and New England, 1620–1660," 35 William and Mary Q. (3rd ser.) 668 (1978).

was a rare commodity. Newer settlements found it convenient to borrow laws from older neighbors, who had similar outlooks, goals, experiences, and problems. Virginia, in the South, and Massachusetts Bay, in the North, were major exporters of laws.

The Massachusetts example is the most striking. The *Laws and Liberties of 1648* were widely emulated.[171] Of 78 provisions in Robert Ludlow's Connecticut code of 1650, 22 were copied, almost verbatim, from the Massachusetts code, 36 were adopted with certain deletions or amendments, 6 came from other Massachusetts sources; only 14 (chiefly on local matters) were "original."[172] The New Haven code of 1656 was also much indebted to Massachusetts. Before the code was drafted, the general court charged the governor to "send for one of the new booke of lawes in the Massachusetts colony, and to view over a small booke of lawes newly come from England, which is said to be Mr. Cottons, and to add to what is already done as he shall thinke fitt."[173] New Hampshire drew most of its code of 1680 (the so-called Cutt code) from laws of Massachusetts and Plymouth. The famous Duke's laws of 1664, in force in New York, Pennsylvania, and Delaware, were "Collected out of the Severall Laws now in force in his Majesties American Colonyes and Plantations."[174] Massachusetts Bay was the source of many of these laws; Virginia also made a contribution. The criminal code of East New Jersey (1668–1675) borrowed provisions from the Duke's laws, and also from the laws of the Northern colonies. Like the *Laws and Liberties,* the Duke of York's laws were arranged alphabetically by subject headings; this code contained organic law, matters of procedure, and matters of substance. It was hardly a slavish imitation of Massachusetts; it rejected as much as it accepted. In Pennsylvania, too, the colony borrowed from the Duke's laws, and from the New England codes; but the borrowing was always selective and eclectic; never random or blind.[175]

By the eighteenth century, the period of wholesale borrowing of codes had largely ended. The colonies, as they developed bodies of statutory law, worked within three distinct traditions: their own, that of their neighbors, and that of the mother country. Incipient nationalism operated to sustain, deepen, and enhance the local element in all these laws; commercial ties, and the efforts of the English government, pulled law in the direction of English sources. Statutes of the eighteenth century were better drafted than the earlier ones. The Privy Council, as we mentioned, reviewed colonial statutes; the Council had a certain influence on substance and style. There were new codes in New Jersey and Pennsylvania, which were at the same time closer to English models, and yet more original, than the Duke's laws. The influence of Massachusetts faded. Trott's laws, compiled by Nicholas Trott and formally adopted by South Carolina in 1712, merely declared which English statutes were in force in the colony. Many laws of England, Trott conceded, were "altogether useless" in

---

[171] Stefan Riesenfeld, "Law-Making and Legislative Precedent in American Legal History," 33 Minn. L. Rev. 103, 132 (1949).

[172] George L. Haskins and Samuel E. Ewing, "The Spread of Massachusetts Law in the Seventeenth Century," 106 U. Pa. L. Rev. 413, 414–15 (1958).

[173] Quoted in Haskins and Ewing, *op. cit.,* p. 416. The Cotton code had never been adopted in the Bay colony.

[174] *Charter to William Penn and Laws of the Province of Pennsylvania* (1879), p. 3.

[175] George L. Haskins, "Influences of New England Law on the Middle Colonies," 1 Law and Hist. Rev. 238 (1983).

South Carolina, "by reason of the different way of agriculture and the differing productions of the earth of this Province from that of England"; others were "impracticable" because of differences in institutions.[176] That left 150 relevant statutes; the code reprinted these and declared them to be law.

THE LEGAL PROFESSION

The early colonial years were not friendly years for lawyers. There were few lawyers among the settlers. In some colonies, lawyers were distinctly unwelcome. In Massachusetts Bay, the *Body of Liberties* (1641) prohibited pleading for hire. The "attorneys" in the early Virginia records were not trained lawyers, but attorneys-in-fact, laymen helping out their friends in court. In 1645, Virginia excluded lawyers from the courts; there had been a ban in Connecticut, too. The Fundamental Constitutions of the Carolinas (1669) were also hostile; it was considered "a base and vile thing to plead for money or reward." Apparently, no lawyers practiced law in South Carolina until Nicholas Trott arrived in 1699.[177] The Quaker colony at Burlington, West New Jersey, made do with a single lawyer until the end of the seventeenth century.[178] In Pennsylvania, it was said, "They have no lawyers. Everyone is to tell his own case, or some friend for him . . . 'Tis a happy country."[179]

There is some evidence to back Daniel Boorstin's comment that "ancient English prejudice against lawyers secured new strength in America. . . . [D]istrust of lawyers became an institution."[180] Thomas Morton, who arrived in Plymouth about 1624 or 1625, has been called the first Massachusetts lawyer. He was jailed and expelled for scandalous behavior. Thomas Lechford, who had some legal training, arrived in 1638. He practiced in the colony as a courtroom attorney and as a draftsman of documents. Lechford had unorthodox religious views, which won him no friends among the magistrates, nor did the fact that he meddled with a jury by "pleading with them out of the Court." Lechford eventually sailed back to England.[181]

Distrust of lawyers arose from various sources. The Puritan leaders of Massachusetts Bay had an image of the ideal state. Revolutionary or Utopian regimes tend to be hostile to lawyers, at least at first. Lawyers of the old regime have to be controlled or removed; a new, revolutionary commonwealth must start with new law and new habits. Some colonists, oppressed in England, carried with them a strong dislike for all servants of government. Merchants and planters

---

[176] *Statutes at Large of South Carolina*, vol. II (1837), p. 401. Trott's laws were not actually published until 1736. See Beverly Scafidel, "The Bibliography and Significance of Trott's Laws," in Herbert Johnson, ed., *South Carolina Legal History* (1980), p. 53.

[177] Anton-Hermann Chroust, *The Rise of the Legal Profession in America*, vol. I, p. 297.

[178] H. Clay Reed and George J. Miller, eds., *The Burlington Court Book: A Record of Quaker Jurisprudence in West New Jersey: 1680–1709* (1944), xlii.

[179] Quoted in Francis R. Aumann, *The Changing American Legal System: Some Selected Phases* (1940), p. 13.

[180] Daniel J. Boorstin, *The Americans: The Colonial Experience* (1958), p. 197.

[181] In England, he published *Plaine Dealing, or Newes from New England*, and warned, "Take heede my brethren, despise not learning nor the worthy lawyers . . . lest you repent too late" (1867 ed.), p. 68.

wished to run their affairs without intermediaries. The theocratic colonies believed in a certain kind of social order, closely directed from the top. The legal profession, with its special privileges and principles, its private, esoteric language, seemed out of place in a government that aimed to be both efficient and godly. The Quakers of the Middle Atlantic were opposed to the adversary system in principle. They wanted harmony and peace. Their ideal was the "Common Peacemaker," and simple, nontechnical justice. They looked on lawyers as sharp, contentious—and unnecessary—people. For all these reasons, the lawyer was unloved in the seventeenth century.

In the eighteenth century, too, there was sentiment against lawyers. The lower classes came to identify lawyers with the upper class. Governors and the royalists, on the other hand, were not sure of the loyalty of lawyers, and were sometimes afraid of their influence and power. In 1765, Cadwallader Colden, lieutenant governor of New York, told the Board of Trade in England that the "Gentlemen of the Law" had grown overmighty. They ranked just below the large landowners, and just above the merchants in society. Lawyers and judges, said Colden, had such power that "every Man is affraid of offending them"; their "domination" was "carried on by the same wicked artifices that the Domination of Priests formerly was in the times of ignorance."[182] Lay judges, too, may have resented the lawyers' threats to their competence and prestige. And as law became more "rational" and "professional," it became more confusing and remote to merchants and businessmen.

How strong the resentment against lawyers was, how deep it went, is hard to say. The evidence is partly literary; pamphlets and speeches are notoriously unreliable as measures of actual feeling among a diverse population. Some hatred was surely there; there is hard evidence of riots and disorders against lawyers and judges. Lawyers, like shopkeepers, moneylenders, and lower bureaucrats, are social middlemen; they are lightning rods that draw rage during storms in the polity. In eighteenth-century New Jersey, the "table of the Assembly groaned beneath the weight of petitions . . . invoking vengeance on the heads of the attorneys." The "Regulators," in late colonial North Carolina—a kind of vigilante group—rose up to smash corrupt and incompetent government. Lawyers were in the camp of the enemy. They perverted justice; they were "cursed hungry Caterpillars," whose fees "eat out the very Bowels of our Common-wealth."[183] In Monmouth and Essex counties (New Jersey), in 1769 and 1770, mobs rioted against the lawyers.[184]

But the lawyers were, in the end, a necessary evil. When all is said and done, no colony could even try to make do without lawyers. The makeshift alternatives worked in the early days; but when society became more complex—and more commercial—the lawyers became essential. To be sure, lay judges knew enough English law to run their local courts; and a few practical books of English law circulated in the colonies. In Maryland in 1663, a layman, Dr. Luke Barber, accused of slandering a woman by calling her a whore ("taken . . . with

---

[182] *Colden Letter Books, 1765–1775,* vol. II (Collections of the New York Historical Society, 1877), pp. 68, 70, 71.

[183] H. T. Lefler, ed., *North Carolina History as Told by Contemporaries* (1956), p. 87.

[184] Richard S. Field, *The Provincial Courts of New Jersey, with Sketches of the Bench and Bar* (1849), pp. 171ff.

her coates up," and with a "rogue" with "his Breeches downe") argued his own
case and cited, in his own behalf, a recent English law book, "Shephard, and his
authorities."[185] The magistrates of Massachusetts Bay, who struggled to keep
out lawyers, made use of their own legal knowledge in drafting legislation and
in governing. John Winthrop was one such magistrate. Nathaniel Ward, who
drafted the *Body of Liberties* (1641), had had some legal training in England.
Richard Bellingham, former town recorder of Boston, England, was governor of
the Bay Colony in 1641; according to a contemporary, this "much honored"
man worked to "further civill Government of this wandering people, he being
learned in the Lawes of England, and experimentally fitted for the worke."[186]

As soon as a settled society posed problems for which lawyers had an answer
or at least a skill, lawyers began to make their way, and to thrive, despite any lingering hostility. Courts were in session; merchants were involved in litigation;
documents about land and other matters had to be drawn up; and the skill of
the lawyer had a definite market value. Men trained in law in England, who
came over, found their services in demand; so did laymen with a smattering of
law. There were semiprofessionals, too, with experience for sale. In the late seventeenth century, justices of the peace, sheriffs, and clerks, acted as attorneys
in New Jersey.[187] Many of the early lawyers in Maryland were planters, who acted
as part-time lawyers. An unauthorized or underground bar has been common in
many societies; it crops up when the need for legal services outstrips the supply
of legitimate lawyers. But by the eighteenth century, professional lawyers dominated the practice—Alan Day has counted 146 of these men in Maryland,
though not that many were in full-time practice at any one time.[188]

In the literature, there are constant complaints against unauthorized lawyers,
pettifoggers, shysters, and lowlifes—unprincipled men who stirred up unnecessary lawsuits. All these lawyers cared about (people said) was money. One man
wrote to a Maryland newspaper, in the eighteenth century, that the "gentlemen"
who professed law "can't hear you, can't see your papers without first feeling
your cash"; and if the cash was insufficient, "they remain both deaf and
blind."[189] Complaints about negligence, greed, and incompetence were in the
air, like the later complaints against crooked lawyers, ambulance chasers, and
others who disgraced the profession. These complaints were sometimes inconsistent. The lawyers were too technical, but also too careless; too sloppy, but also
too zealous.

The truth was, a competent, professional bar, dominated by brilliant and
successful lawyers—Daniel Dulany of Maryland, Benjamin Chew of Philadelphia, and many others—existed in all major communities by 1750. Many of
these men were deeply learned in the law. Yet there was no such thing as a law
school in the colonies. Particularly in the South, where there were no colleges
at all, some young men went to England for training, and attended the Inns of

---

[185] *Archives of Maryland*, vol. 49 (1932), p. 116. The reference is to William Sheppard, *The Faithful Councellor, or the Marrow of the Law in English;* a second edition of this book was published in 1653.

[186] Edward Johnson, *Wonder-Working Providence* (Jameson, ed., 1910), p. 97.

[187] Anton-Hermann Chroust, *op. cit.*, p. 198.

[188] Alan F. Day, *A Social Study of Lawyers in Maryland, 1660–1775* (1989), pp. 28–29.

[189] Quoted in Day, *A Social Study of Lawyers*, at p. 126.

Court in London. Many of the leading Maryland lawyers had this kind of experience. The Inns were not law schools as such; they had "ceased to perform educational functions of a serious nature," and were little more than living and eating clubs. Theoretically, a man could become a counselor-at-law in England without reading "a single page of any law book."[190] But the Inns were educational in another sense. They were part of English legal culture; Americans could absorb the atmosphere of English law at the Inns; they could read books, but also look around them and see English law in practice, as a living system.

For all lawyers, the road to the bar went through some form of clerkship or apprenticeship. A young man who wanted to be a lawyer usually entered into a contract with a lawyer already in practice. The student paid a fee; in exchange, the lawyer promised to train him in the law; sometimes, too, the lawyer would provide food and lodging.[191] Apprenticeship was a control device as well as a way of learning the trade. It kept the bar small; and older lawyers were in firm command. How much the apprentice learned depended greatly on his master. At worst, an apprentice toiled away at drudgery and copywork, with a few glances, catch-as-catch-can, at the law books. William Livingstone, who was clerking in the office of a New York lawyer, denounced the system in a letter to the *New York Weekly Post-Boy* (August 19, 1745). The system was an "Outrage upon common Honesty . . . scandalous, horrid, base, and infamous to the last degree!" No one could "attain to a competent Knowlege in the Law . . . by gazing on a Number of Books, which he has neither Time nor Opportunity to read; or . . . be metamorphos'd into an Attorney by virtue of a *Hocus-Pocus.*" A young clerk "trifle[d] away the Bloom of his Age . . . in a servile Drudgery nothing to the Purpose, and fit only for a Slave."[192] But this was not everybody's experience. There were others who found the clerkship a valuable experience. Some senior lawyers were good teachers and good men. Some famous lawyers trained or attracted clerks, who themselves became famous. Thomas Jefferson was a student of George Wythe. James Wilson studied with John Dickinson, paying Dickinson a fee from the sale of a farm.[193] The first law schools, as we shall see, grew out of law offices that became so good at teaching that they gave up practice entirely.

From the seventeenth century on, the British exported some lawyers to help them govern their colonies. This was another fountainhead of the American bar. Nicholas Trott, an English lawyer, arrived in Charleston in 1699 as attorney general. He came to dominate the judicial life of South Carolina. In 1703, he was chief justice; he was also a member of the court of chancery, judge of the vice-admiralty court, the court of common pleas, and of the king's bench; he also compiled the *Laws of the Province of South Carolina.* Contemporaries complained that "the sole Judicial Power [was] lodg'd" in his hands, "a Trust

---

[190] Paul M. Hamlin, *Legal Education in Colonial New York* (1939), p. 16.

[191] Charles R. McKirdy, "The Lawyer as Apprentice: Legal Education in Eighteenth Century Massachusetts," 28 J. Legal Educ. 124 (1976); Hoyt P. Canady, "Legal Education in Colonial South Carolina," in Herbert Johnson, ed., *South Carolina Legal History* (1980), p. 101.

[192] Reprinted in Paul M. Hamlin, *op. cit.*, pp. 167–68.

[193] Charles P. Smith, *James Wilson, Founding Father, 1742–1798* (1956), p. 24.

never repos'd in any one Man before in the World."[194] In 1719, when proprietary government was overthrown, he lost his power. Mathias Nicolls came to
New York in 1664. He had been a barrister of Lincoln's Inn and Inner Temple;
he had fifteen years' practice in London. In 1683, Governor Dongan appointed him a judge of the court of oyer and terminer.[195] In Massachusetts,
too, most good lawyers in the generation after 1690 at one time or another
held appointive office.[196]

Each colony had its own standards for admission to the bar. New Jersey tried
to set up a graded profession, on the English plan. By a rule of 1755, the
colony's supreme court established the order of *serjeants-at-law,* a rank higher
than ordinary "counselors." Only the court could appoint to the higher rank;
and the court later restricted the number of serjeants to twelve. The serjeants
had the power and duty to conduct examinations for admission to the bar.[197] In
Virginia, a law of 1748 gave its high court control over licensing and admission
to the bar. In Massachusetts, in the eighteenth century, each court admitted its
own lawyers. In 1762, the chief justice of the Superior Court, Thomas Hutchi-
son, instituted the rank of barrister; twenty-five lawyers were called to this
rank.[198] In Rhode Island, any court could admit; but admission to one was admission to all. In many colonies, the requirements for admission included a
long period of apprenticeship, though in some colonies, if a man was a college
graduate, the term was a year or two less.

The legal profession was one road to money and success in the eighteenth
century. Wealthy lawyers tried to keep up their prices and prestige and keep
down the supply of practitioners. They never quite succeeded. The lower levels
of the bar were hard to control. Law, in that period, was something like acting
or painting: there were many who did it part time, and quite a few amateurs.
In seventeenth-century Maryland, most lawyers were planters, who spent part
of their time in the practice. It was only in the eighteenth century that it was
possible to speak of lawyers in Maryland as "professional" at all. Of 207 attorneys in Maryland, between 1660 and 1715, 79 were planters; others were clerks
or merchants; only 48 could be described as professional lawyers.[199] The situation in Maryland, as we have seen, changed later in the eighteenth century. In

---

[194] Anne K. Gregorie, ed., *Records of the Court of Chancery of South Carolina, 1661–1779*
(1950), pp. 6, 53. On Trott, see Herbert Johnson, ed., *South Carolina Legal History* (1980),
pp. 23–64.

[195] Paul M. Hamlin and Charles E. Baker, *Supreme Court of Judicature of the Province of New
York, 1691–1704,* vol. I (1959), p. 19.

[196] John M. Murrin, "The Legal Transformation: The Bench and Bar of Eighteenth-
Century Massachusetts," in Stanley N. Katz, ed., *Colonial America: Essays in Politics and Social
Development* (1971), pp. 415, 423.

[197] Anton-Hermann Chroust, *op. cit.,* p. 200.

[198] Gerard W. Gawalt, *The Promise of Power: The Emergence of the Legal Profession in Massachusetts, 1760–1840* (1979), pp. 16–17.

[199] Alan F. Day, "Lawyers in Colonial Maryland, 1660–1715," 17 Am. J. Legal Hist. 145,
164 (1973). For 33 lawyers, there was no information; for the latter situation in Maryland,
see Day, *op. cit. supra,* n. 188. On the increasing sophistication of the profession in the eighteenth century, see also Stephen Botein, "The Legal Profession in Colonial North America," in Wilfrid Prest, ed., *Lawyers in Early Modern Europe and America* (1981), p. 129.

Connecticut, part-time lawyers made up a sizable part of the bar, up to the time of the Revolution. Joseph Adams of New Haven "combined the duties of attorney and innkeeper"; he "did not do very well at either, for his estate proved insolvent when he died in 1782." Another Connecticut lawyer in the 1750s, Peletiah Mills of Windsor, doubled as "principal taverner of his home town." Still other Connecticut lawyers were cloth merchants, clergymen, or soldiers.[200]

In the eighteenth century, the demand for lawyers' skilled services increased; the bar became much more professional; yet in many colonies, the bar was extremely, and artificially, small. There were only 15 lawyers in Massachusetts in 1740—one for every 10,000 inhabitants. Even in 1775 there were only 71.[201] So few trained lawyers were qualified to practice before the New York Supreme Court, that an act of 1695 ordered litigants not to hire more than two "Attorneys at Law" to handle a case "in any of the Courts of Record Within this Province." Apparently, it was possible to "fee" all the attorneys, that is, hire the whole New York bar, leaving one's opponent high and dry.[202] As of 1700, only about a dozen men practiced before the New York high court. Between 1700 and 1720, six attorneys had the lion's share of practice in New York's mayor's court. In 1731, the New York City charter gave seven attorneys (mentioned by name) a monopoly of this practice. Two years before, a group of New York lawyers had formed an "association" to supervise legal education, regulate practice, and control admission to the bar. In 1756, these "gentlemen of the law" agreed to take on no clerks, except their own sons, for the next fourteen years.[203]

There were similar guildlike movements in other colonies. In Rhode Island, eight lawyers signed a "Compact" in 1745 to make sure fees would always be "sufficient for our support and subsistence." No case was to be pleaded at Superior Court for less than a three pound fee; only a "standing client" was "to be trusted without his note." Attorneys were not to sign "blank writs and disperse them about the colony, which practice . . . would make the law cheap." They agreed not to defend any client whose lawyer was suing for his fee unless three or more "brethren" determined that the lawyer's demand was "unreasonable."[204] In Virginia, when Thomas Jefferson was admitted to practice before the General Court in Williamsburg, in 1766, only six or seven lawyers were active before that Court.[205]

The struggle for control of the trade went on incessantly. John Adams complained, in 1759, that the "practice of Law [was] grasped into the hands of deputy sheriffs, pettifoggers, and even constables who filled all the writs upon bonds, promissory notes, and accounts, received the fees established for

---

[200] John T. Farrell, ed., *The Superior Court Diary of William Samuel Johnson, 1772–1773* (1942), l-li. On part-time and self-trained lawyers in Massachusetts, see Gawalt, *op. cit.*, pp. 24–25.

[201] Gawalt, *op. cit.*, p. 14.

[202] Paul M. Hamlin and Charles E. Baker, *op. cit.*, pp. 99–101.

[203] Richard B. Morris, ed., *Select Cases of the Mayor's Court of New York City, 1674–1784* (1935), pp. 52ff.

[204] Quoted in Wilkins Updike, *Memoirs of the Rhode Island Bar* (1842), pp. 294–95. For the situation in Maryland, see Day, *op. cit.*, n. 199, at 150.

[205] Frank L. Dewey, *Thomas Jefferson, Lawyer* (1986), p. 2. There were other lawyers, however, who practiced in the lower courts.

lawyers, and stirred up many unnecessary suits." No doubt he saw it that way. There were upper and lower lawyers, rich and poor, exclusive lawyers and lawyers hungry for clients, just as there are today. Many lawyers had to struggle for their daily bread. The "professionals," on the other hand, were often rich— or got rich. The rich lawyers resented the poor ones, who threatened and disgusted them; and they also despised the amateurs and the quacks, who were trying to grab a share of the trade. Many aristocrats, of mind and money, were lawyers. Politically, too, many lawyers were conservatives. But lawyers, or men who called themselves, lawyers, were among the founders of the Republic. John Marshall, John Adams, Thomas Jefferson, James Wilson, John Jay of New York. George Wythe of Virginia, Francis Hopkinson of Pennsylvania—all these were lawyers. Some leading lawyers—Anthony Stokes of Georgia and William Smith of New York—chose the losing side in the Revolution and left the country. Smith later became chief justice of the province of Quebec. It is possible that more lawyers were loyalists than were backers of the Revolution. Yet 25 of the 56 signers of the Declaration of Independence were lawyers, and 31 of the 55 delegates to the Constitutional Convention were lawyers. What these facts show, according to Professor Boorstin, is "the pervasiveness of legal competence among American men of affairs and the vagueness of the boundary between legal and all other knowledge in a fluid America."[206] Still, these men identified themselves as lawyers, not as doctors, politicians, or historians. The line between lawyer and laymen was not as indistinct as it had been in earlier years. There was a pride of profession among these men, who thought of themselves as attorneys, and a common fund of experience and training, whether or not they had ever replevied a cow or drawn up a chancery bill.

THE LITERATURE OF THE LAW

In one sense, colonial legal literature is quickly disposed of. No such thing worthy of the name existed before 1776. Law libraries were scarce, small, and scattered. In the seventeenth century, few people who called themselves lawyers owned many law books at all. Law books were more common in the eighteenth century. But a lawyer's library was not full of books about *American* law; the books were English law books, with perhaps a few local statutes thrown in. Most popular were English practice manuals.[207] Native law books were few and utterly insignificant. There were no printed collections of cases. When Blackstone's *Commentaries* were published (1765–1769), Americans were among his most avid customers. At last there was an up-to-date shortcut to the basic themes of English law. An American edition was printed in 1771–1772, on a subscription basis, for $16 a set; 840 American subscribers ordered 1,557

---

[206] Daniel J. Boorstin, *The Americans: The Colonial Experience* (1958), p. 205. John M. Murrin, commenting on the "signs of creeping respectability" in the eighteenth-century bar in Massachusetts, remarks that "Before 1730, many gentlemen felt qualified to practice law on the side without bothering to study it. A generation later, gentlemen were beginning to study it with no intention of practicing it." Murrin, *op. cit.,* p. 432.

[207] See Herbert A. Johnson, *Imported Eighteenth-Century Law Treatises in American Libraries, 1700–1799* (1978).

sets—an astounding response. Not all subscribers were lawyers and judges, but many were; and Blackstone's text became ubiquitous on the American legal scene.[208]

Literature is a conscious creation; but it is also recorded life. In this sense, the toiling scribes of colonial courts made literature. A few of their records were printed in the nineteenth century. Slowly, more have been unearthed; some have been edited and published. Most of the material is useful, but dreary, as formal legal prose tends to be. Yet, among the reports are flashes of extraordinary vividness and color. These records, like no others, lift the veil that hides the face of daily life. They paint a rich and marvelous picture. To be sure, the picture is a bit distorted—after all, the matters that got into court tended to be disputes, crimes, and disorders, large and small. No one reading these records can cling to the view that Puritan life, for example, was uniformly solemn, dour, and high-minded gray. Joseph Warrinar and Peter Swinck swore, in the Pynchon Court Record, for June 20, 1661,

> that in the forenoone last Sabbath in sermone tyme they saw Samuell Harmon thrust and tickle Jonathan Morgan and Pluckt him of [off] his seate .3. tymes and squeased him and made him cry.[209]

The cruelty of life is recorded, and the lust, sin, hatreds, and conflicts of human existence. William Myers, testifying in West New Jersey in 1686, shows us slavery bare and unadorned:

> Hee heard at a Considerable distance many blowes or stripes . . . hee thought hee heard a Negro Cry out many tymes . . . he supposed it to be James Wills beating his Negro woman, and heard still many Lashes more and Crying out, until hee was greevd and went into his owne house and shut the dore, and said to his wife oh! yond cruell man.[210]

Even in the pleadings and the formal speech-ways of law we can hear the echoes of actual voices, the words of living human beings. Bits of popular speech peep out among the legal phrases. So, for example, in the papers of South Carolina's chancery court (1721), where Mrs. Elisabeth Weekley, the "Relict" and "Executrix" of Richard Weekley, "Planter," told how she was induced to intrust her share of the estate to Mrs. Sarah Rhett:

> the said Mrs. Sarah Rhett did advise your Oratrix That it was not safe for your Oratrix being a Widow and an Ancient Woman and living on the Broad Path to keep soe much moneys in here own House least she should be robbed thereof by her Negroes or otherwise and offered to take charge thereof. . . . Your Oratrix . . . delivered over to the said Mrs. Sarah Rhett the said four hundred and Eighty pounds in Bills of Credit who took the same out of a paper Wrapper . . . and the said Mrs. Sarah Rhett then counted the said Bills into her lap . . . and cryed Lord Bless me Woman here's five hundred pounds wanting twenty pounds I did not think you had soe much money . . . then taking your Oratrix by the hand put her

[208] Paul M. Hamlin, op. cit., pp. 64–65.

[209] Joseph Smith, ed., Colonial Justice in Western Massachusetts, 1639–1702: The Pynchon Court Record (1961), p. 253.

[210] H. Clay Reed and George J. Miller, eds., The Burlington Court Book: A Record of Quaker Jurisprudence in West New Jersey 1680–1709 (1944), p. 57.

other hand upon her own Breast and told your Oratrix that the said mon-
eys should be as safe as if it were in her . . . own hands and that as she was
a Christian she would never wrong Your Oratrix of a Farthing.[211]

Court records are full of these flashes of life, these vignettes, as if we were
peeking through an old window, into the heart of colonial society. Hence the
living law is in some ways more knowable in this obscure period of American
law, than for later periods that one might have imagined as more accessible. An
avalanche of papers and forms smothered the minds and the mouths of ordinary litigants in the nineteenth and twentieth centuries. But the sound of
American law, in its lusty youth, clear as a bell, speaks from the pages of colonial county courts.

[211] Anne K. Gregorie, ed., *Records of the Court of Chancery of South Carolina, 1661–1779*
(1950), p. 272.

PART II

From the Revolution to the
Middle of the Nineteenth Century:
1776–1850

CHAPTER 1

THE REPUBLIC OF BEES

REVOLUTIONARY ARDOR

In 1776, the colonies declared themselves independent. The bitter war that followed ended in an American victory. Peace, of course, raised as many questions of government as it answered. A plan of government is a plan for distribution of the power and wealth of a society. The choice of system is no idle exercise in political theory. How to plan the new American government was the major policy issue of the late eighteenth century. The first grand scheme was embodied in the Articles of Confederation. It proved unsatisfactory to powerful circles in the country. After the failure of the Articles, a federal Constitution was drawn up and ratified in 1787. It is still in force—it has been amended from time to time, to be sure; but the basic text is essentially the same.

Each colony, too, underwent its own revolution. Colonies became states, and embarked on new courses of action with new problems and new programs. First, they had to fight a war and patch up domestic disruptions. All this called for a major outburst of lawmaking. In Pennsylvania, for example, a constitutional convention, in 1776, declared a general amnesty and established a new form of government. Colonial officials were replaced by men loyal to the Revolution. The usual business of Pennsylvania would continue, where possible; but the emergencies of war had to be coped with. In October 1777, British troops "penetrated into [the] state, and after much devastation and great cruelty in their progress," seized Philadelphia; the state government then created a "council of safety," with vast and summary powers "to promote and provide for the preservation of the Commonwealth." It had power to seize goods "for the army and for the inhabitants," punish traitors, and "regulate the prices of such articles as they may think necessary." Still, the "ordinary course of justice" was, as far as feasible, not to be interrupted. In the same year, the legislature passed a bill of attainder against a number of men who had "traitorously and wickedly" gone over to the king. The state redefined and punished treason, made legal tender out of the bills of credit of the Continental Congress and the state,[1] and, inevitably, legislated about the militia, army supplies, taxes, and the policy of war.

When the war ended, debates over law continued. The colonists had overthrown the King of England and his government. Should the king's law also be

---

[1] *Statutes at Large, Pa., 1682–1801,* vol. IX (1903), p. 149 (act of Oct. 13, 1777); p. 201 (act of Mar. 6, 1778); p. 34 (act of Jan. 29, 1777).

overthrown? Should ordinary private law be radically altered? The first generation seriously argued the question. The common law was badly tarnished; so was the reputation of the lawyers, many of whom had been Tories. Some people thought that new democratic states needed new institutions, from top to bottom, including fresh, democratic law. A pamphleteer, who called himself Honestus, asked, in 1786: "Can the monarchical and aristocratical institutions of England be consistent with . . . republican principles?" He thought it "melancholy" when the "numerous volumes" of English law were "brought into our Courts, arranged in formidable order, as the grand artillery to batter down every plain, rational principle of law."[2] Thomas Paine, a true firebrand, spoke for at least some zealots when he denounced, in 1805, the "chicanery of law and lawyers." He complained that Pennsylvania courts, even at that late date, had "not yet arrived at the dignity of independence." The courts, he said, still "hobble along by the stilts and crutches of English and antiquated precedents," which were often not democratic at all, but "tyrannical."[3] During Shay's Rebellion, in Massachusetts (1786), mobs stopped the courts from sitting, and forcibly kept the courts from executing judgments against debtors. It was easy for people to feel that the courts were biased, and easy to assume that the bias came from an oppressive, old-fashioned system of law.

Were there any alternatives to the stilts and crutches? The common law could be replaced by some other system. Or it could be replaced by natural principles of justice. The first alternative was, in theory, not impossible. There *were* other systems of law. There was, for example, French civil law, which, particularly after the French revolution, had a certain attraction for American liberals. In the early nineteenth century, the Napoleonic Code was a model of clarity and order. A few civil-law books were translated into English during this period: *"A Treatise on Obligations, Considered in a Moral and Legal View,* translated from the French of [Robert] Pothier," appeared in New Bern, North Carolina, in 1802. Common law, to some jurists, seemed feudal, barbaric, uncouth, at least in comparison to the neatness of some features of civil law.

In hindsight, the common law had little to fear. It was as safe as the English language itself. The courts continued to operate, continued to do business; they used the only law that they knew. Few lawyers had any grasp of French or any other language or system. James Kent of New York was of the few who did; another exception was Joseph Story, the Supreme Court justice, a tower of erudition. These men cited and used bits of foreign law in their works and opinions. But they were hardly revolutionaries. They wanted to purify and improve the common law, not overthrow it. They were willing to snatch doctrines and ideas from the civil law countries; but even English law did that. One of the culture heroes of the American legal elite was England's Lord Mansfield, who died in 1793. Mansfield was Scottish by birth and an ardent admirer of Roman-flavored civil law. But all this was the exception, not the rule. The fact was, English authorities flooded the country.

---

[2] The strictures of Honestus were ultimately published in Boston, in 1819, under the title *Observations on the Pernicious Practice of the Law;* and have been reprinted in 13 Am. J. Legal Hist. 244, 257 (1969).

[3] Philip S. Foner, ed., *Complete Writings of Thomas Paine,* vol. II (1945), p. 1003.

And of course the common law had defenders. Not everybody denounced it as old, despotic, and chaotic. It was also romanticized, as the birthright of free men. It was a precious heritage—perverted, to be sure, by the British under George III, but nonetheless a precious heritage. Many jurists argued that the common law was the foundation of their freedoms; that it embodied fundamental norms of natural law. The first Continental Congress, in 1776, adopted a Declaration of Rights; it declared that the colonies were "entitled to the common law of England," in particular the right of trial by jury. Americans were also entitled to the benefit of those English statutes that "existed at the time of colonization; and which they have, by experience, respectively found to be applicable to their several local and other circumstances."[4]

Common-law lawyers were among the heroes of the Republic. John Adams was one; Thomas Jefferson, for all his ambivalence toward common law and its judges, another. Lawyers mostly drafted the state and federal constitutions. Courts were increasingly manned by lawyers, who listened to the arguments of other lawyers. Lawyers moved west with the line of settlement; they swarmed into state capitals and county seats. Wherever one looked in political life—in town, city, county, state, and national government—the lawyers were there. Unlike some later revolutions and some earlier colonial Utopias, the new republic did not try to do business without lawyers. Old lawyers continued to function, training new lawyers in their image, who, like their teachers, turned almost instinctively to common law. The common law was also a weapon of integration. The Northwest Ordinance imposed common law on the lands of the American frontier. In the prairies and forests, where French settlers lived and worked in the path of the American onrush, the common law was an agent of American imperialism.

The common law would have to be Americanized, of course. Now that the states had freedom to choose, what parts of English law would remain in force? This was a difficult question. Many states passed statutes to define the limits of the law in force. A Virginia law of 1776 declared that the "common law of England, all statutes or acts of Parliament made in aid of the common law prior to the fourth year of the reign of King James the first, and which are of a general nature, not local to that kingdom . . . shall be considered as in full force."[5] The Delaware Constitution of 1776 (art. 25) provided that "The common law of England as well as so much of the statute law as has been heretofore adopted in practice in this State, shall remain in force," except for those parts which were "repugnant to the rights and privileges" expressed in the constitution and in the "declaration of rights."

The New York experience was particularly complex. A 1786 law declared the common law in force, and such English statutes as were in effect in the colony on April 19, 1775. Later, New York specifically re-enacted some British laws—the Statute of Frauds, for example, a law first passed in 1677, which had virtually become a part of the common law. In 1788, a New York law, "for the Amendment of the Law, and the better Advancement of Justice," declared that

---

[4] Quoted in Elizabeth G. Brown, *British Statutes in American Law, 1776–1836* (1964), p. 21.

[5] William Walter Henning, *Statutes at Large . . . of Virginia*, vol. 9 (1821), p. 127.

"after the *first* day of *May* next," no British statutes "shall operate or be considered as Laws" in the state.[6] The New York Constitution of 1821 (art. VII, sec. 13) stated that "Such parts of the common law, and of the acts of the legislature of the colony of New York, as together did form the law of the said colony" on April 19, 1775, and the resolutions of the colonial Congress, "and of the convention of the State of New York," in force on April 20, 1777, would continue to be law, unless altered or repealed, and unless they were "repugnant" to the constitution. No mention was made of British statutes; for good measure, an act of 1828 specifically pronounced the British statutes dead.

Yet, even this flock of New York laws fell short of solving the problem. A New York court later held that some English statutes had become part of the "common law" of the colony.[7] If so, an indefinable, unknowable cluster of old laws had a more or less ghostly presence in the state. They survived only insofar as they were not "repugnant" to the Constitution or not suitable to New York conditions—whatever that meant. New York was not the only state where nobody could tell precisely which English laws were dead and which were alive. For a long time, cases occasionally turned on whether some statute or doctrine had been "received" as common law in this or that state. In a broader sense, the question of "reception" is endemic to the common law. Judges must always consider how much old law still has value, and how much deserves to be thrown on the ash-heap, once and for all.

Reception statutes dealt with *older* English law. Did new English law count for much? To Jesse Root of Connecticut, writing in 1798, courts of a free country should not allow themselves to be governed by foreign law. His ideal was "the republic of bees," whose members "resist all foreign influence with their lives," and whose honey, "though extracted from innumerable flowers,"[8] was indisputably their own. In pursuit of the republic of bees, New Jersey passed a law, in 1799, that

> no adjudication, decision, or opinion, made, had, or given, in any court of law or equity in Great Britain [after July 4, 1776] . . . nor any printed or written report or statement thereof, nor any compilation, commentary, digest, lecture, treatise, or other explanation or exposition of the common law, . . . shall be received or read in any court of law or equity in this state, as law or evidence of the law, or elucidation or explanation thereof.[9]

Kentucky prohibited the mere mention of recent British law. Its statute, passed in 1807, declared that "reports and books containing adjudged cases in . . . Great Britain . . . since the 4th day of July 1776, shall not be read or considered as authority in . . . the courts of this Commonwealth."[10] During the spring term, 1808, Henry Clay, appearing before the court of appeals of Kentucky, "offered to read" a "part of Lord Ellenborough's opinion" in Volume 3 of East's reports; the "chief justice stopped him." Clay's co-counsel argued that

---

[6] On the New York reception laws, see E. G. Brown, *op. cit.*, pp. 69–75.

[7] *Bogardus v. Trinity Church*, 4 Paige 178, 198–99 (1833), discussed in E. G. Brown, *op. cit.*, pp. 72–73.

[8] I. Root's Reports (Connecticut), xlii, xliii (1798).

[9] Quoted in E. G. Brown, *op. cit.*, p. 82.

[10] Quoted in E. G. Brown, *op. cit.*, p. 132.

the legislature "had no more power to pass" such a law than to "prohibit a judge the use of his spectacles." The court decided, however, that "the book must not be used at all in court."[11] But it was not so easy to get rid of Lord Ellenborough and his colleagues, even in New Jersey or Kentucky. The New Jersey statute was repealed in 1819. As a practical matter, courts and lawyers continued to refer to English law throughout the period and throughout the country. It was impossible to throw over the habits of a lifetime. Indigenous legal literature was weak and derivative. There was no general habit of publishing American decisions; American case reports were not common until a generation or more after Independence. To common-law lawyers, the shortage of cases was crippling. English materials, English reports, and English authorities filled the gap. In the first generation, more English than American cases were cited in American reports. Ordinary lawyers, too, were constantly referring to Blackstone. They used his book as a shortcut to the law; and Blackstone was English to the core. Sometimes curiously old-fashioned bits of law—phrases, old doctrines, old writs—turned up in odd places (for example, on the American frontier); these antiques came from Blackstone, for the most part, whose book was the Bible even in far-off jurisdictions.

American law continued, in short, to borrow. The English overlay was obvious, pervasive—but also selective. The country invited in only those English doctrines that were needed and wanted. Between 1776, and the middle of the nineteenth century, there were sweeping changes in American law. During that time, there developed a true republic of bees, whose flowers were the social and economic institutions that developed in their own way in the country. They, not Lord Ellenborough and Lord Kenyon, were the lawmakers that made American law a distinctive system: a separate language of law within the family founded in England.

The second apparent alternative to the common law was also a mirage. To get rid of the tyranny of lawyers, to reduce legal gibberish to common sense, and to frame rules of simple, "natural" justice that anybody could understand—this was an age-old dream but it flared up with special vigor after 1776. As one citizen of Kentucky put it, the state needed "a simple and concise code of laws . . . adopted to the weakest capacity."[12]

There was a certain radical element in this antilaw movement. There were those who thought the law was remote from the needs of ordinary people and was biased toward the rich. Others condemned the law as archaic, inflexible, and irrelevent—as out of step with the needs of merchants or business people as it was for the needs of plain folk. Lawyer's law suited nobody but the lawyers themselves. There was, then, a general interest in reform that rich and poor, radical and conservative could share. But in fact, it was Utopian to imagine that society could overthrow lawyers' law and replace it with natural justice, whatever that might mean. Society was too complicated for that. In fact, what society seemed to need, as time went on, and what it got, was not less but more rules, of more and more definite shape. The reform urge, as we shall see, did

[11] *Hickman v. Boffman,* Hardin 356, 372–73 (Kentucky, 1808). L vol. III of East's Reports contains cases from the court of king's bench for the years 1802 and 1803.

[12] Quoted in Charles M. Cook, *The American Codification Movement: A Study of Antebellum Legal Reform* (1981), p. 16.

not abate; but it came to mean, not artlessness, but adaptation to the needs of a market economy.

One basic, critical fact of nineteenth-century law was that the official legal system penetrated, and had to penetrate, deeper and deeper into society. Medieval common law was not the law everywhere in England; nor was it everybody's law. It was the law of the gentry; local customs were the living law for ordinary folks. American law was more popular in a profound sense. It had no archaic or provincial rivals. It had no competitive substratum. Paradoxically, American law, divided into as many subsystems as there were states, was less disjointed than the one "common law" of older England.

Millions, to be sure, were beyond the reach of formal law and indifferent to it. But comparatively speaking, American law had an enormous range. It drew its strength from the work and wealth of millions, and it affected the work and wealth of millions more. In sixteenth- or eighteenth-century England, few people owned or dealt in land. Only a small percentage were inside the market economy. Only a few were potential customers for family law, commercial law, land law, or the law of corporations. There was surely less oligarchy in the United States than in the old kingdoms of Europe. In colonial America, there was a great deal of hierarchy and deference; but there was also widespread ownership of land. And by the time of the Revolution, and after the Revolution, even the hierarchy and deference had diminished. More men voted; more men *counted* in society.[13] That a far greater percentage of families owned land, compared to England, was a crucial fact. Thus, a law for the millions, and for the middle class, had to develop. And this law, to survive, had to be more pliant and accessible than a law for the wealthy few.

In short, law had to suit the needs of its customers; it had to be easy to use—or at least easy for ordinary lawyers to use, as brokers of legal information. What happened to American law in the nineteenth century, basically, was that it changed dramatically, fundamentally, to conform to the needs, wants, and pressures coming from the vast increase in the numbers of consumers of law. It is dangerous to sum up long periods and great movements in a sentence. But if colonial law had been, in the first place, colonial, and in the second place, paternal, emphasizing community, order, and the struggle against sin, then, gradually, a new set of attitudes developed, in which the primary function of law was not suppression and uniformity, but economic growth and service to its users. In this period, after the Revolution, the people who mattered came to see law, more and more, as a utilitarian tool: a way to protect property and the established order, of course, but beyond that, a way to further the interests of the middle-class *mass*, to foster growth, to release and harness the energy latent in the commonwealth: "Dynamic rather than static property, property in motion or at risk rather than property secure and at rest."[14]

[13] On this general theme, of course, one has to cite Gordon Wood's seminal work, *The Radicalism of the American Revolution* (1991).

[14] J. Willard Hurst, *Law and the Conditions of Freedom in the Nineteenth Century United States* (1956), p. 24; on the general issue of the extent to which the Revolution itself was a great watershed, see Hendrik Hartog, "Distancing Oneself from the Eighteenth Century: A Commentary on Changing Pictures of American Legal History," in Hendrik Hartog, ed., *Law in the American Revolution and the Revolution in the Law* (1981), p. 229.

It was not only property to which the word dynamic seemed more and more apt. These two polar words—dynamic and static—aptly describe a fundamental change in the concept of law. The source of the change lay not so much in the Revolution as in revolution: the transformation of economy and society that occurred in the machine age and the age of rational thought. A dynamic law is a manmade law. The Constitution talked about natural rights, and meant what it said; but these rights served as a framework for the fulfillment of people's needs and desires. Every society has a theory of law—a popular theory, not something philosophers dreamt up. What came bubbling up from society was an *instrumental* theory, a relativistic theory. It was the idea that law was something people used to further their ends, and when ends changed, so did means. Such a theory implied a more creative view of precedent. It meant asking, whether a rule or a doctrine made sense, and whether it met the needs of the here and the now.

At one time, law was conceived essentially in static terms. Any change was considered exceptional; and treated almost apologetically. But in the nineteenth century, legislatures made law wholesale, without any sense of shame. Judges made law, too, in the course of deciding cases—whether they admitted it or not. Society was changing rapidly; and legislatures and courts both worked creatively, building and rebuilding the house of the common law.

CONSTITUTIONS: FEDERAL AND STATE

The Revolutionary period was, by necessity, an age of innovation in fundamental law. The old ties with England had been snapped. The states and the general government began to draft written constitutions. Some states had started life as chartered colonies; they had gotten into the habit of living under the umbrella of a charter and had even learned to love and honor their charters, which guaranteed their liberties. Political leaders tended to look on a written constitution as a kind of social compact—a basic agreement among citizens, and between citizens and state, setting out their mutual rights and duties, and in a permanent form.

The Articles of Confederation (1777) envisioned a loose, low-key group of highly sovereign states. It did not provide for a strong executive. It had no provision for a federal judiciary. Congress, however, got some judicial power; it was "the last resort on appeal in all disputes and differences . . . between two or more states concerning boundary jurisdiction or any other cause whatever." Congress also had admiralty power, with "sole and exclusive right" to establish "rules for deciding, in all cases, what captures on land or water shall be legal," and how prizes might be "divided or appropriated." Congress had sole right to set up "courts for the trial of piracies and felonies committed on the high seas," and courts "for receiving and determining, finally, appeals in all cases of captures" (art. IX).

The Articles of Confederation, by common consent, were something of a failure; the Constitution of 1787 was a stronger, more centralizing document. The Northwest Ordinance (1787), which set up a scheme of government for the Western lands, and which was enacted shortly before the Constitution, took it for granted that all future states would have a "permanent constitution," and a "republican" one at that, consistent with federal law (Northwest Ordinance, 1787, art. V).

The original states had in theory the option to write or not write constitutions. But most of them quickly chose to write. Within a short time after the war broke out, eleven states had drafted and adopted new constitutions. Constitution-making was a fairly broad-based enterprise. In most of the states, special congresses or conventions were elected to do the work of writing constitutions.[15] Among other things, a constitution was a rallying point, a symbol of unity during war. The New Jersey Constitution (1776) put it this way:

> in the present deplorable situation of these colonies, exposed to the fury of a cruel and relentless enemy, some form of government is absolutely necessary, not only for the preservation of good order, but also the more effectually to unite the people, and enable them to exert their whole force in their own necessary defense.

A few states chose to rest upon their original charters. But these, too, were eventually replaced by new documents—constitutions. Connecticut discarded its charter and adopted a constitution in 1818. Eventually, every state in the union had its own constitution. All, in short, embarked on careers of making, unmaking, and remaking the texts of their basic rights and principles.

Constitutionalism responded to a deep-seated need among members of the articulate public—a need for formal, outward signs of political legitimacy. This urge had driven tiny, isolated colonies in what is now Rhode Island or Massachusetts to express the structure and principles of government through a written agreement—a visible, legible bulwark against the lonely disorder of life outside the reach of the mother country. Much later, but driven by the same instinct, the remote Oregon pioneers, in a no-man's land disputed among nations, drew up a frame of government and called it a constitution. So did the residents of the "lost state of Franklin" in the 1780s, in what is now part of eastern Tennessee. So did the handful of citizens of the "Indian Stream Republic," in disputed territory near the border of New Hampshire and Canada. And so did the Mormons of the "State of Deseret." These "constitutions," to be sure, were mostly copycats; they borrowed provisions from existing constitutions, taking a phrase here, a clause there, and making whatever changes were considered appropriate. They were short-lived and of dubious legality. But they illustrate how strong the *idea* of the written constitution had become in American life.

There have been dozens of state constitutions. Their texts, style, and substance vary considerably. Some of the earliest ones, written before the 1780s, were quite bold and forward-looking for their times. The New Jersey Constitution gave the right to vote to "all inhabitants" who were worth fifty pounds; this gave some single women and widows the right to vote, a daring move (perhaps inadvertent) that was snuffed out in 1807.[16] The first Pennsylvania Constitution (1776) represented a sharp victory for the liberals of the state; and was considered rather radical. The federal bill of rights—and the Constitution could not have been ratified, without the promise of such an addition, which

---

[15] Marc W. Kruman, *Between Authority and Liberty: State Constitution-Making in Revolutionary America* (1997), p. 20.

[16] Marc W. Kruman, *Between Authority and Liberty*, pp. 105–6.

took the form of ten amendments—was modeled largely after provisions already in state constitutions.[17] Virginia, in particular, was a pioneer, with its Declaration of Rights (1776). The Declaration began with the ringing words: "that all Men are born equally free and independent"; and that power to govern was in the people; officers of government were their "Trustees and Servants, and at all times amenable to them."[18] Today, such a statement seems banal, obvious, boring. But not in the eighteenth century. The idea that the people ruled, not the King or the King in Parliament, was a fairly radical idea, though it did not come completely out of the blue—intellectually, it rested on progressive English thinkers; socially, it rested on colonial experience, and the colonial condition. Virginia talked about "men" as born equal; and this was no accident; moreover, Virginians certainly did not mean to include people who happened not to be white. Again, these omissions seem to us, in contemporary times, to be hypocritical, or blind, or both; but in the context of the eighteenth century, even male liberation was dramatic and different.

The Virginia declaration of rights was influential. It was copied, more or less, in North Carolina, for example. Massachusetts had a declaration of rights in its 1780 constitution, including long, explicit clauses on freedom of religion.[19] Indeed, the states were, as Jack Rakove has put it, "the great political laboratory" whose work the framers drew on as they labored at the Constitutional convention.[20] After 1787, the language and organization of the federal Constitution became in turn a powerful model for state constitutions. One feature, however, was not easily transferred to the states: durability. There has been only one federal Constitution. It has been amended from time to time—actually not very frequently—but has never been superseded. It has become a symbol, an icon, a part of American culture. In this regard it is unique among American constitutions.[21] The state constitutions are hardly icons. Very few people know much about them, except for a handful of specialists. And these constitutions have not been particularly long lasting. A few states (for example, Wisconsin) have made do with one constitution. Other states have had a more chaotic constitutional history. Louisiana has had nine constitutions, perhaps ten, depending on how you count. Georgia has had at least six.

The federal Constitution was marvelously supple, put together with great political skill. The main reason why it has lasted so long is that the country—aside from the Civil War crisis—has been remarkably stable. The first revolution was

---

[17] On state constitutions and their Bills of Rights, see, in general, Robert Allen Rutland, *The Birth of the Bill of Rights, 1775–1791* (1962); Willi Paul Adams, *The First American Constitutions: Republican Ideology and the Making of the State Constitutions in the Revolutionary Era* (1980); Patrick J. Conley and John P. Kaminski, eds., *The Bill of Rights and the States: The Colonial and Revolutionary Origins of American Liberty* (1992).

[18] See Warren M. Billings, " 'That All Men Are Born Equally Free and Independent:' Virginians and the Origins of the Bill of Rights," in Conley and Kaminski, eds., *The Bill of Rights and the States*, p. 336.

[19] John M. Murrin, "Massachusetts: From Liberties to Rights: the Struggle in Colonial Massachusetts," in *The Bill of Rights and the States*, pp. 63, 93–94.

[20] Jack N. Rakove, *Original Meanings: Politics and Ideas in the Making of the Constitution* (1996), p. 31.

[21] On this subject, see, in general, Michael Kammen, *A Machine that Would Go of Itself: The Constitution in American Culture* (1986).

the last. But the Constitution itself deserves at least a bit of the credit. It was neither too tight nor too loose. It was in essence a frame, a skeleton, an outline of the form of government; on specifics, it mostly held its tongue. The earlier state constitutions, before 1787 and for some decades after, also guarded themselves against saying too much. There were some idiosyncratic features, even before 1787, in state constitutions. New Hampshire (1784), in the spirit of Yankee thrift, solemnly declared that "economy" was a "most essential virtue in all states, especially in a young one; no pension shall be granted, but in consideration of actual services, and . . . with great caution, . . . and never for more than one year at a time."[22] There was interesting material in all the early state constitutions. But most of them began with a bill of rights, described the general frame of government, and were fairly content to leave it at that.

A constitution is different from ordinary statute law. It has two crucial functions. First, it sets up and sets out the structure of government—its permanent shape, its organs or parts, and their rights, duties, boundaries, and limits. Second, it can list the essential rights of the citizen; this list is supposed to limit what government is allowed to do—it is a list, in other words, of rights that the state must not and cannot infringe. These, then, are rules of higher law, which are meant to be permanent and unassailable, protected against the winds of temporary change. But this second function has no obvious boundary lines. Different ages and different people have different ideas about what is and what is not a fundamental right. And even the federal Constitution was more than a mere framework. Imbedded in it were fragments of a code of law. Trial by jury, for example, was guaranteed (art. III, sec. 2, par. 3). The Constitution defined the crime of treason (art. III, sec. 3), and set out minimum requirements for convicting any person of this crime. The Bill of Rights contained, in a way, a minicode of criminal procedure—rules about warrants, searches and seizures, forms of punishment, the privilege against self-incrimination, and so on.

What existed in embryo, and in reasonable proportions in the federal Constitution, was carried to much greater lengths in the states. Constitutions began to inflate. This process reached its high (or low) point after the Civil War. But the process began long before that. Even the bills of rights became bloated. The federal Bill of Rights had ten sections; Kentucky's, in 1792, had twenty-eight. Some of these were quite vague: "elections shall be free and equal" (art. XII, sec. 5); others seemed hardly to deserve their exalted position—for example, that estates of "such persons as shall destroy their own lives shall descend or vest as in case of natural death."[23]

The Delaware Constitution of 1792 was another offender. It was full of details of court organization and procedure; for example, "No writ of error shall be brought upon any judgment . . . confessed, entered, or rendered, but within five years after the confessing, entering or rendering thereof."[24] This constitution also specified minutely how courts should handle accounts of executors, administrators, and guardians. The Alabama Constitution of 1819 provided

---

[22] New Hampshire Const., 1784, art. XXXVI.

[23] Art. XII sec. 21. This was not by any means a unique clause. See Alabama Const., 1819, art. I, sec. 21; Mississippi Const. 1817, art. I, sec. 21; Tennessee Const. 1796, art. XI, sec. 12; Delaware Const., 1792, art. I, sec. 15.

[24] Delaware Const., 1792, art. VI, sec. 13; Const. 1831, art. VI, sec. 20.

that "A competent number of justices of the peace shall be appointed in and for each county, in such mode and for such term of office, as the general assembly may direct." Their civil jurisdiction, however, "shall be limited to causes in which the amount in controversy shall not exceed fifty dollars."[25] Clearly, the fifty-dollar limit was no immutable right of man. The Tennessee constitution of 1796 set a ceiling on the governor's salary ($750 a year) and this figure was not to be changed before 1804.[26] No one could deduce these numbers from principles of universal justice.

There was a point to every clause in these inflated constitutions. Each one reflected the wishes of some faction or interest group, which tried to make its policies permanent by freezing them into the charter. Constitutions, like treaties, preserved the terms of compromise between warring groups. Sometimes, this took the form of a clause that postponed the power of the state to enact a given kind of law. The federal Constitution left the slave trade untouchable until 1808; until that year "the Migration or Importation of such Persons as any of the States now existing shall think proper to admit, shall not be prohibited by the Congress" (art. I, sec. 9, par. I). Ohio (1802) made Chillicothe the "seat of government" until 1808; the legislature was not to build itself any buildings until 1809.[27] On some delicate issues, there was a strategic reason to load it into the constitution. Otherwise, a shift in the political wind could upset a careful compromise. One legislature can easily undo what an earlier legislature did. But a constitution is comparatively tough and unyielding.

Between 1790 and 1847, state constitutions became more diverse and diffuse. Some developments, like some problems, were peculiar to one state, or to one group of states; some were common to the country as a whole. The most general problems were apportionment and suffrage. Any change in the electoral map or in the right to vote meant a reallocation of political power. Who voted determined who ruled; hence suffrage was a crucial bottleneck of law. The right to vote was precious   after all, taxation without representation was one of the slogans that underlay the revolution itself. But *who* was entitled to vote? Perhaps only people with a real stake in the polity. That meant property owners. John Adams, among others, warned against broadening the franchise. What if "every Man, who has not a Farthing," demanded a voice? "Women will demand a vote. Lads from 12 to 21 will think their Rights not enough attended to"; the result might be to "confound and destroy all Distinctions, and prostrate all Ranks, to one Common level."[28]

Many disagreed with this assessment. Sometimes, constitutional disputes over suffrage and apportionment turned bitter. In Rhode Island, the franchise was narrow, and the apportionment scheme outdated. Only those men who owned real estate worth $134 were entitled to vote; this excluded perhaps nine out of ten even of white males over twenty-one. Conservatives stubbornly resisted any change. The so-called "rebellion" of Thomas Dorr (1842) was an

---

[25] Alabama Const., 1819, art. V, sec. 10.

[26] Tennessee Const., 1796, art. I, sec. 20.

[27] Ohio Const., 1802, art. VII, sec. 4.

[28] Quoted in Marc W Krumin, *Between Authority and Liberty: State Constitution Making in Revolutionary America* (1997), p. 89.

unsuccessful, mildly violent attempt to force a change. A new constitution, which went into effect in 1843, finally brought about some measure of reform.[29]

This was an extreme case. But it had once been almost universal that the right to vote belonged only to men who owned land or paid taxes. Under the Connecticut Constitution of 1818 (Art. 6, sec. 2), voters had to be "white male citizens," twenty-one or older, with a "freehold estate of the yearly value of seven dollars" in the state, or someone who had done militia service, or paid a state tax (he also was supposed to have a "good moral character"). Some states specifically excluded "paupers." Those who entered the poor house in these states lost not only their self-respect and their place in society; they also lost their vote.[30] But in the decades after the revolution, state after state got rid of the property qualification—Delaware in 1792, Massachusetts and New York in 1821 (though not for African Americans!); Virginia and North Carolina, the laggards, did not abolish all property qualifications until 1850.[31] Unlike Rhode Island, these were mostly bloodless revolutions. The defenders of the system, men like James Kent, were fighting a losing battle.

Everywhere, the search for permanence was constant, but permanence escaped the people's grasp. The Pennsylvania Constitution of 1776, a product of advanced eighteenth-century liberalism, was replaced in 1790 by a much more conservative constitution; and in 1838 by a moderate one. Statute books were supple; new governments changed them as they wished. Constitutions were brittle. They could be patched up at times; but when they were drenched too thoroughly in the policies and interests of an old or lost cause, they had to be completely redone. Inflexibility was the vice of constitutions, as well as the virtue.

An observer with nothing in front of him but the texts of these state constitutions could learn a great deal about state politics, state laws, and about social life in America. The Southern constitutions gave more and more attention, over time, to ways to buttress the institution of slavery and to repress free blacks. Legislatures were forbidden to emancipate slaves, unless the master agreed and was compensated. In Pennsylvania (1838) any person who fought a duel, or sent a challenge, or aided or abetted in fighting a duel, was "deprived of the right of holding any office of honor or profit in this State."[32] The Connecticut Constitution of 1818, though it paid lip service to freedom of worship, froze every resident into his "congregation, church or religious association." A man might withdraw only by leaving a "written notice thereof with the clerk of such [religious] society."[33] Constitutions often dealt with the state militia, a matter of considerable interest to the Revolutionary generation. In Ohio (1802), brigadiers-general were to be "elected by the commissioned officers of

---

[29] Peter J. Coleman, *The Transformation of Rhode Island, 1790–1860* (1963), pp. 254–94. Rich material on suffrage questions is contained in Merrill D. Peterson, ed., *Democracy, Liberty and Property: The State Constitutional Conventions of the 1820s* (1966); Adams, *The First Constitutions*, pp. 197–217.

[30] See Alexander Keyssar, *The Right to Vote: The Contested History of Democracy in the United States* (2000), pp. 60–61.

[31] Alexander Keyssar, *The Right to Vote*, p. 29.

[32] Pennsylvania Const., 1838, Art. VI, sec. 10. Many states had similar clauses.

[33] Connecticut Const., 1818, art. VII, sec. 2.

their respective brigades."[34] Some states barred practicing clergymen from public office. The Tennessee Constitution of 1796 testily remarked that "ministers of the gospel are, by their professions, dedicated to God and the care of souls, and ought not to be diverted from the great duties of their functions."[35] The draft constitution of "Franklin," in 1784, would have extended this ban to lawyers and "doctors of physic." The Georgia Constitution of 1777 declared that "Estates shall not be entailed; and when a person dies intestate, his or her estate shall be divided equally among their children; the widow shall have a child's share, or her dower, at her option."[36] As early as 1776, North Carolina provided that "the person of a debtor, where there is not a strong presumption of fraud, shall not be confined in prison, after delivering up, *bona fide*, all his estate real and personal, for the use of his creditors, in such manner as shall be hereafter regulated by law."[37] Imprisonment for debt, or its abolition, was a subject many nineteenth-century constitutions touched on.

State constitutions reflected the theories of the day on separation of powers, and on checks and balances. The earlier the constitution, however, the weaker the executive branch. Eighteenth-century constitutions usually gave only feeble powers to the chief executive (called a governor, like his colonial antecedent). His term of official life was typically brief. The Maryland Constitution of 1776 solemnly asserted that "a long continuance" in "executive departments" was "dangerous to liberty"; "rotation" was "one of the best securities of permanent freedom." This constitution practiced what it preached. The governor—a "person of wisdom, experience, and virtue"—was to be chosen each year, on the second Monday of November, for a one-year term, by joint ballot of the two houses of the legislature. Despite his "wisdom, experience, and virtue," he was not to continue in office "longer than three years successively, nor be eligible as Governor, until expiration of four years after he shall have been out of that office."[38]

The Pennsylvania Constitution of 1776 showed a similar bias. It too called for rotation in office. In England, office tended to depend on the crown or on powerful members of the nobility. Public office was essentially a nice warm udder to be milked. Patronage and connections were the keys to office. This had been also, to a large degree, colonial practice. American constitutions firmly rejected this notion. According to the Pennsylvania Constitution of 1776, "offices of profit" were not to be established; such offices led officeholders to a state of "dependence and servility unbecoming freemen," and created "faction, contention, corruption, and disorder" in public life (sec. 36). The modern notion of politics as a specific career was foreign to the Republican mind. Rather, politics was a duty, a form of public service, open to the

---

[34] Ohio Const., 1802, art. VIII, sec. 4.

[35] Tennesse Const., 1796, art. VIII, sec. 1.

[36] Georgia Const., 1777, art. LI.

[37] North Carolina Const., 1776, art. XXXIX. This was also a feature of the Pennsylvania Constitution of 1776.

[38] Maryland Const., 1776, declaration of rights, art. XXXI, const., arts. XXV, XXXI. The governor had to be rich as well as wise. Only residents above twenty-five years of age, "and having in the State real and personal property above the value of five thousand pounds, current money (one thousand pounds whereof, at least, to be freehold estate) shall be eligible as governor" (art. XXX).

virtuous amateur, something like jury service today. Hence the emphasis on rotation in office. This noble concept of office did not, alas, survive very long.

Early constitutions, as was mentioned, slighted the executive; they preferred
to give the lion's share of power to the legislature. In the light of American political history, this was only natural. The colonial governor—and the judiciary,
to a certain extent—represented foreign domination. The assemblies, on the
other hand, were the voice of influential local people. The Pennsylvania Constitution of 1776 gave "supreme legislative power" to a single house of representatives. No upper house or governor's veto checked its power.[39] As the years
went by, however, the states became somewhat disillusioned with legislative supremacy. The governor was one beneficiary of this tendency. Typically, he
gained a longer term of office, and the power to veto bills. In the federal government, the president had this power from the start. Judicial power, too, increased at the expense of the legislature. The most striking example was what
came to be called judicial review. This was the right and power of courts, in a
proper case, to monitor and control the acts of other branches of government.
Courts assumed, indeed, the right to declare these acts—including statutes
solemnly passed by the legislature—to be absolutely null and void, if, in the
judges' opinion, the acts violated the constitution. The more clauses there
were in the constitution, the more occasion for judicial review.

In the first generations of the new Republic, this mighty power was rarely
used—and its very existence was a matter of controversy. The most famous instance was the great case of *Marbury v. Madison* (1803). Here, for the first time,
John Marshall and the U.S. Supreme Court dared to declare an act of Congress
unconstitutional.[40] But the Court made no clear use of this power, against Congress, for over fifty years. The weapon was used more frequently against *state*
statutes. State supreme courts, too, began to exercise judicial review. It was an
uncommon technique; it was hated by Jeffersonians; some judges resisted it; it
made little impact on the ordinary working of government. But when its occasion arose, it was an instrument of unparalleled power.

Why did legislatures lose some of their power? Influential people, for one
thing, tended to be more afraid of too much law than of not enough. In some
states, scandals blackened the name of the legislature: bribery, corruption,
general malfeasance. Blocs of voters became afraid that landlords, "moneyed
corporations," and other wealthy and powerful forces were too strong in state
lobbies. Rules to control legislation were written into one constitution after
another. The process began modestly enough. Georgia's Constitution (1798)
outlawed the practice of legislative divorce, except if the parties had gone to
"fair trial before the superior Court," and obtained a verdict upon "legal principles." Even then, it took a "two-thirds vote of each branch of the legislature"
to grant a divorce.[41] Indiana, in 1816, forbade the establishment by statute of

---

[39] J. Paul Selsam, *The Pennsylvania Constitution of 1776* (1936), pp. 183–84.

[40] *Marbury v. Madison* is 1 Cranch (5 U.S.) 137 (1803). There is a large literature on this
famous case. See Robert Lowry Clinton, *Marbury v. Madison and Judicial Review* (1989),
which also deals with the later reputation and history of the case; William Nelson, *Marbury
v. Madison: the Origins and Legacy of Judicial Review* (2000); see also Larry D. Kramer, *The People Themselves: Popular Constitutionalism and Judicial Review* (2004), ch. 2.

[41] Georgia Const. 1789, art. III, sec. 9.

any "bank or banking company, or monied institution for the purpose of issuing bills of credit, or bills payable to order or bearer."[42]

The Louisiana Constitution of 1845 was something of a turning point. More than those that came before, this constitution was a charter of economic rights and obligations, and a code of legislative procedure, as well as a plain frame of government, in which matters of economic policy remained implicit. The constitution sharply restricted the state's power to pledge its credit or to lend its money. The state was not to "become subscriber to the stock of any corporation or joint-stock company." Lotteries, legislative divorces, and special corporate charters were forbidden. Every law was to "embrace but one subject, and that shall be expressed in the title." No new exclusive privileges or monopolies were to be granted for more than twenty years. No banks of any sort were to be chartered.[43] These were not random ideas. And they were not, in the eyes of contemporaries, extreme. Louisiana was trying to rein in the legislature, and it was doing this by antilegislation, that is, by foreclosing whole areas of law to statutory change. Other states jumped on this particular bandwagon. Yet, in the history of state constitutions, tides often turned; public opinion would shift, and what had been done came to seem wrong or an obstacle to progress. At that point, constitutional provisions would be amended—or evaded—or, often, it would seem time to make a whole new constitution.

No two state constitutions were ever exactly alike. Nor was any constitution pure innovation. States copied each other; there was what might even be called a kind of constitutional *stare decisis*.[44] Popular clauses or provisions tended to spread far and wide. New states borrowed clusters of clauses and sections from old states. Neighboring states, or the home state of the settlers, were often the favorite source. The New York Constitution of 1846 left a deep mark on Michigan, and later on Wisconsin. The first California Constitution was heavily indebted to Iowa; Oregon was indebted to Indiana.

Borrowing and influence are not, of course, the same. The states shared a common political culture. Michigan was not a legal satellite of New York; the people in the two states were Americans of the period, and, for the most part, thought alike on political and legal issues. The New York Constitution was a recent model; this is why people in Michigan used it. Why draft something from scratch, when you can borrow from materials right at hand. Borrowing was always selective. No constitution was swallowed whole. On the big issues, there was always conscious choice. States borrowed, then, out of expedience and fashion—but in a limited way.

THE JUDGES

In a common-law system, judges make at least some of the law, even though legal theory has often been coy about admitting this fact. American statesmen were not naive; they knew that what judges believed, and who they were, made a difference. How judges were to be chosen and how they were supposed to behave

---

[42] Indiana Const., 1816, art. X, sec. 1. But a state bank was allowed.
[43] Louisiana Const., 1845, arts, 113, 114, 116, 117, 118, 121, 122, 123, 124, 125.
[44] J. Willard Hurst, *The Growth of American Law: The Law Makers* (1950), p. 224.

was a political issue in the Revolutionary generation, an issue whose intensity has rarely been reached since that time. State after state—and the federal government—fought political battles over issues of selection and control of the judges. The bench was not homogeneous. Judges varied in quality and qualification, from place to place, and according to their position in the judicial pyramid. Local justices of the peace were judges; so were the justices of the U.S. Supreme Court. English and colonial tradition had allowed for lay judges, as well as for judges learned in law. There were lay judges both at the top and the bottom of the pyramid. In the colonies, the governor frequently served, *ex officio*, as chancellor. New Jersey continued this system, in its constitution of 1776. This constitution also made the governor and council "the court of appeals in the last resort in all causes of law as heretofore."[45] Since governor and council were or might be laymen, this meant that nonlawyers had final control over the conduct of trials and the administration of justice. In the New York system, too, laymen shared power at the apex of the hierarchy of courts. The constitution of 1777 set up a court "for the trial of impeachments, and the correction of errors," consisting of senators as well as judges.[46] This system lasted well into the nineteenth century. The lay judges were usually but not always politicians. But they were invariably prominent local men. And they were often related to each other by blood or marriage. William E. Nelson studied the background and careers of the eleven men who served as justices of the superior court of Massachusetts between 1760 and 1774, on the eve, that is, of the Revolution. Nine had never practiced law; six had never even studied law. All, however, of these lay judges had "either been born into prominent families or become men of substance." Stephen Sewall, chief justice in 1760, was the nephew of a former chief justice; he had served thirteen years as a tutor at Harvard College.[47]

Laymen were even more dominant at the base of the pyramid. Lay justice did not necessarily mean popular or unlettered justice at the trial court level. The English squires were laymen, but hardly men of the people. Lay justice in America had a certain resemblance to the English system of rule by local squires. Lay justice was not necessarily informal. A lay justice, sitting on the bench for years, tended to soak up at least something of the lawyer's jargon, tone, and lore. After all, the difference between lawyers and nonlawyers was not that sharp. Law was not as much of a career or a profession as it is today. A man frequently came to the bar after the briefest of clerkships and with little more than a smattering of Blackstone. The way judges absorbed law was not so different from the way a young lawyer did, on his journey to a legal career.

Many anecdotes in print label lay judges as coarse and stupid, especially the lay judges of the West and South. Old lawyers, writing years later, and historians of bench and bar, repeat these stories. Were the pioneer judges really so raw and vulgar? The truth is both elusive and ambiguous. People did complain about the courts; but the complaints had nothing to do with whether judges were laymen or not. The complaints were about bias, in favor of creditors, or the rich.

---

[45] New Jersey Const., 1776, art. IX.

[46] New York Const., 1777, art. XXXII. In England, too, the highest court, the House of Lords, included laymen as well as judges.

[47] William E. Nelson, *Americanization of the Common Law: The Impact of Legal Change on Massachusetts Society, 1760–1830* (1975), pp. 32–33.

In any event, the lay judge was slowly passing from the scene. First, the lay judge disappeared entirely from the upper courts. The first lawyer on Vermont's supreme court was Nathaniel Chipman (1752–1843). He took office, in 1787, as an assistant judge of the court. Not one of the other four judges was an attorney.[48] Chapman more or less took the lead. He later became chief justice, and edited law reports for Vermont. In other states, professionalization came even earlier. All five of the judges of the Virginia Court of Appeals, established in 1788, were lawyers; Edmund Pendleton headed the court.[49]

Historically, judges had been appointed from above. But American democracy put strong emphasis on controls from below. This implied giving the voter a say in the choice of judges. Under the Vermont Constitution of 1777, the "freemen in each county" had the "liberty of choosing the judges of inferior courts of common pleas, sheriff, justices of the peace, and judges of probates."[50] Under the Ohio Constitution of 1802, "judges of the supreme court, the presidents and the associate judges of the courts of common pleas" were to be "appointed by a joint ballot of both houses of the general assembly, and shall hold their offices for the term of seven years, if so long they behave well."[51] This gave the electorate at least an indirect voice in judicial selection. Georgia in 1812, and Indiana in 1816, provided for popular election of some judges;[52] Mississippi in 1832 adopted popular election for all. New York followed in 1846, and the rush was on.

The movement, according to Willard Hurst, was "one phase of the general swing toward broadened suffrage and broader popular control of public office which Jacksonian Democracy built on the foundations laid by Jefferson." It was a movement, however, "based on emotion rather than on a deliberate evaluation of experience under the appointive system."[53] There is no easy way to compare the work of elected and appointed judges. But elected judges at least *seemed* more responsive to the will of the people.

The elective principle, thus, was one way to solve the problem of judicial power. Judges were supposed to be impartial and neutral, mere servants of the law. Once upon a time, they seemed to be servants of the crown. In a common law system, the judges invent or modify many of the working legal rules. Judges

[48] Daniel Chipman, *The Life of the Hon. Nathaniel Chipman, Ll.D.* (1836), p. 69.
[49] See S. S. Patterson, "The Supreme Court of Appeals of Virginia," 5 Green Bag 310, 313–18ff. (1893).
[50] Vermont Const., 1777, ch. II, sec. 27. See, in general, Evan Haynes, *The Selection and Tenure of Judges* (1944).
[51] Ohio Const., 1802, art. III, sec. 8.
[52] In Georgia, the "justices of the Inferior Courts" were to be elected for four year terms, Georgia Const., 1798, art. III, sec. 4 (amendment, ratified 1812); in Indiana, the supreme court was appointed by the governor, the president of the circuit court by "joint ballot of both branches of the General Assembly"; associate judges of the circuit courts were to be "elected by the qualified electors in the respective counties." Indiana Const., 1816, art. V, sec. 7.
[53] J. Willard Hurst, *The Growth of American Law: The Law Makers* (1950), p. 140. Jacksonian democracy did not mean, necessarily, that every man could or should be a judge. Jackson himself, for example, did not appoint the common man to the bench. His appointments were men of high status, by background or achievement, just as Adams's were. But the Jacksonian *attitude* differed from the earlier one; this may have led to change in the long run. See Sidney H. Aronson, *Status and Kinship in the Higher Civil Service* (1964), p. 170.

clearly exercised power. They were part of the system of checks and balances; but who was going to check and balance *them?* One obvious answer was: the voters.

There was good evidence that judges could be biased, partisan, and factional. Thomas Jefferson and his party were convinced of this. Federal judges were appointed for life. Before Jefferson came to power, they were naturally Federalists. Some of them acted in a way that could not help but be controversial. They seemed, to the Jeffersonians, "partial, vindictive, and cruel," men who "obeyed the President rather than the law, and made their reason subservient to their passion."[54] As John Adams was leaving office, in 1801, Congress passed a Judiciary Act.[55] The act created a flock of new judgeships, among other things. Adams nominated judges to fill these new posts; they were confirmed by the Senate in the last moments of the Adams regime. Jefferson's party raged at these "midnight judges." It was a final attempt, Jefferson thought, to stock the bench forever with his political enemies.

The law that created the "midnight judges" was repealed; the judges lost their jobs; but other Federalist judges stayed on serenely in office. There was no easy way to be rid of them. As Jefferson put it, "Few die and none resign." The new president wanted to limit their power; he wanted to make them more responsive to national policy—as embodied, of course, in Jefferson and his party. John Marshall, the Chief Justice of the United States, was particularly obnoxious to Jefferson. He was a man of enormous talents, and (as luck would have it) enjoyed good health and long life. He outlived a score of would-be heirs to the office, including Spencer Roane of Virginia, and cheated a whole line of presidents of the pleasure of replacing him. Equally annoying to Jefferson and his successors was the fact that some justices they appointed seemed to fall under Marshall's spell, once they were safely on the bench. Madison appointed Joseph Story, who was at least a lukewarm Democrat. But Story became a rabid fan of the Chief Justice. Roger Brooke Taney, who finally replaced John Marshall, had been a favorite of Andrew Jackson, and a member of his cabinet. But Taney, too, became living proof of the perils of lifetime tenure. He outlived his popularity. He wrote the main opinion in the infamous *Dred Scott* case. He tottered on in office until 1864, almost to the end of the Civil War, to the vast annoyance of Abraham Lincoln.

The prestige of federal courts stands high today, especially, but not exclusively, with liberals and intellectuals. An independent court system is (at least potentially) a tower of strength for the poor, for the downtrodden, for the average person who is trying to fight big institutions or big government. It did not seem that way in the early nineteenth century. Jefferson's famous fight against Federalist judges is one aspect of his administration that has not done so well in the court of history. But it was true that some federal judges behaved in ways that we would consider disgraceful today. Federal judges did not run

---

[54] Quoted in Charles Warren, *The Supreme Court in United States History,* vol. I (1923), p. 191.

[55] 2 Stats. 89 (act of Feb. 13, 1801); repealed, 2 Stats. 132 (act of March 8, 1802). See Erwin C. Surrency, "The Judiciary Act of 1801," 2 Am. J. Legal Hist. 53 (1958).

for reelection; but they played a more active political role in the courtroom than judges today are allowed to do. Some Federalists made what were in effect election speeches from the bench. They harangued grand juries in a very partisan way. This gave some point to Jefferson's attacks. Other judges were more discreet, but (in Jefferson's view) equally partisan. On the other hand, John Marshall was a tower of strength. His opinions were cautious, yet solemn; his language was mellifluous, grand, sometimes even pompous. His principles purported to be timeless and nonpolitical. He appealed to fundamentals or to the Constitutional texts themselves. His tone, and the rigorous logic of his opinions, implied that the law itself impelled his decisions; that he himself was an impartial instrument of the law, whose conclusions followed from iron and unassailable logic. This attitude irritated Jefferson, who saw in it nothing but a subtle, maddening hypocrisy. But Marshall's work was effective, not least as political theater.

Jefferson's attacks on the judges were not a total failure. The president lost a battle but won the war. This happened again, much later, when Franklin D. Roosevelt tried to pack the court in 1937. In both cases, Congress rejected an extreme tactic. But in both cases, perhaps, the tactics *may* have worked: as deterrence, as a way to frighten the judges (although in both cases this is a hotly disputed notion).

The Constitution gave federal judges tenure for life. There was only one way to get rid of judges: to smite them with the terrible sword of impeachment. Federal judges could be impeached for "Treason, Bribery, or other high Crimes and Misdemeanors" (art. II, sec. 4). The South Carolina Constitution of 1790 permitted impeachment for "misdemeanor in office" (art. V, sec. 3). Literally interpreted, then, constitutional law allowed impeachment only in rare and extreme situations.[56] But there were a few notable cases, in the early nineteenth century, where impeachment was used to drive enemies of party and state out of office. In 1803, Alexander Addison, presiding judge of the fifth judicial district in Pennsylvania, was impeached and removed from office. He was a bitter-end Federalist; as a lower-court judge, he harangued grand juries on political subjects. On one occasion, he refused to let an associate judge speak to the grand jury in rebuttal; impeachment was grounded on this incident. A straight party vote removed Addison from the bench. Eighteen Republicans in the Pennsylvania senate voted him guilty; four Federalists voted for acquittal.[57]

On the federal level, the purge drew first blood in 1804. It was a rather shabby victory. Impeachment ended the career of John Pickering, a Federalist judge. He had committed no "high crimes and misdemeanors"; but he was an old man, a drunk, and seriously deranged. It was understandable to want him off the bench; but it was far from clear that the words of the Constitution were meant to apply to this kind of judge. Pickering's removal was, in fact, a stroke of politics,

---

[56] In some states, the wording of the constitution was much less emphatic. So, in New Hampshire, under the constitution of 1792, the governor, with the consent of the council, might "remove" judges "upon the address of both houses of the legislature" (part II, sec. 73).

[57] S. W. Higginbotham, *The Keystone in the Democratic Arch: Pennsylvania Politics, 1800–1816* (1952), pp. 53–55.

a dress rehearsal for a far more important assault, the impeachment of Samuel Chase.[58]

This celebrated affair took place soon after Pickering's trial. Chase was a Justice of the U.S. Supreme Court. He had a long and distinguished career, but he was an uncompromising partisan, and a man with a terrible temper. He was also notorious for his grand-jury charges; these were savage attacks on the party in power. President Jefferson stayed in the background; but his close associates moved articles of impeachment against Chase. There were a number of specific charges of misconduct: One of them was the accusation that, at a circuit court, in Baltimore, in May 1803, he did "pervert his official right and duty to address the grand jury" by delivering "an intemperate and inflammatory political harangue," behavior which was "highly indecent, extra-judicial and tending to prostitute the high judicial character with which he was invested to the low purpose of an electioneering partizan."[59]

But the anti-Chase faction overplayed its hand. In a frank private conversation, Senator Giles of Virginia admitted what was really at stake:

> a removal by impeachment [is] nothing more than a declaration by Congress to this effect: You hold dangerous opinions, and if you are suffered to carry them into effect you will work the destruction of the nation. We *want your offices,* for the purpose of giving them to men who will fill them better.[60]

The trial was long, bitter, and sensational. Republicans defected in enough numbers so that Chase was acquitted, on all the counts brought against him. John Marshall and his court were thenceforward "secure." It was the end of what Albert Beveridge claimed was "one of the few really great crises in American history."[61] Some of the more rabid Federalists suspected Chase was only the beginning; the real target was Marshall and his court. But there is no evidence to support this point of view.[62] In January 1805, an attempt was made to impeach all but one of the judges on Pennsylvania's highest court; it failed by a narrow vote.[63] Impeachment was not a serious threat after these years. There were sporadic attempts to use this device—for example, against James Hawkins Peck, the federal district judge in Missouri. Peck, temperamental and controversial, made many enemies. The House of Representatives voted articles of impeachment in 1830; there was a six-week impeachment trial in the Senate, on the charge of "abuse of judicial authority"; but the Senate failed to convict, and

---

[58] Lynn W. Turner, "The Impeachment of John Pickering," 54 Am. Hist. Rev. 485 (1949). The actual meaning of the constitutional provision on impeachment is not as clear as one might suppose. See Raoul Berger, "Impeachment of Judges and 'Good Behavior' Tenure," 79 Yale L.J. 1475 (1970).

[59] *Report of the Trial of the Hon. Samuel Chase* (1805); Appendix, pp. 5–6; see also Richard B. Lillich, "The Chase Impeachment," 4 Am. J. Legal Hist. 49 (1960).

[60] Quoted in J. Willard Hurst, *The Growth of American Law*, p. 136.

[61] Albert Beveridge, *The Life of John Marshall*, vol. III (1919), p. 220.

[62] Jean Edward Smith, *John Marshall, Definer of a Nation* (1996), p. 347.

[63] S. W. Higginbotham, *The Keystone in the Democratic Arch*, p. 79.

Peck stayed on the bench.[64] Impeachment was and is rare—and used only for flagrant cases.

Another radical plan to get rid of bad judges was to abolish their offices. Of course, Jefferson could not do away with the Supreme Court, even had he wanted to; that would have meant amending the Constitution; and this was clearly impossible. But his administration repealed the Judiciary Act of 1801; that at least put the midnight judges out of business. An ingenious method for removing unpopular judges was tried out in Kentucky. In 1823, the Kentucky court of appeals struck down certain laws for relief of debtors; this act aroused a storm of protest. Under Kentucky law, the legislature could remove judges by a two-thirds vote; the "relief party" could not muster that percentage. Instead, the legislature abolished the court of appeals and created a new court of four judges, to be appointed by the governor. The old court did not quietly give up its power. For a time, two courts of appeal tried to function in the state, and state politics was dominated by the dispute between "old court" and "new court" factions. Most lower courts obeyed the old court; a few followed the new court; a few tried to recognize both. Ultimately, the "old court" party won control of the legislature, and abolished the new court (over the governor's veto). The old court was awarded back pay; the new court was treated as if it had never existed at all.[65]

As these crises died down, it seemed as if the forces of light had triumphed over darkness—that this country was to have a free-wheeling, independent judiciary rather than judges who were servile mouthpieces of the government. The Chase impeachment failed (it is said) because in the end both parties believed in a strong judiciary that did not have to curry executive favor. Both parties believed in the separation of powers. Many politicians did in fact have qualms about impeachment; it smacked of overkill. Some of Jefferson's men shared these qualms. It was not right, they felt, to replace a sitting judge for political reasons. But the failure of impeachment was not a clear-cut victory for either side. It was rather a kind of social compromise. The judges won independence, but at a price. They became more cautious—Chase himself was more restrained after his trial. Ultimately, the states turned to the elective principle. There would be no more impeachments, but also no more judges like Chase. What carried the day, in a sense, was the John Marshall solution. The judges would take refuge in professional decorum. They would still make policy—how could they help it? But policy would be divorced from overt, partisan politics. They would use principles and policies that were always dressed in the somber clothes of the formal law. Justice would be blind; and it would wear a poker face. This

---

[64] Lawrence H. Larsen, *Federal Justice in Western Missouri: The Judges, the Cases, the Times* (1994), pp. 17–20.

[65] On this controversy, see George DuRelle, "John Boyle," in *Great American Lawyers*, vol II (1907), pp. 221–59. There were cleaner ways than impeachment or abolition of courts to get rid of old and inconvenient judges. Under the New York constitution of 1821 (art. V, sec. 3), the chancellor and justices of the supreme court had to retire at the age of sixty. (A similar provision, art. 24, had been part of the New York Constitution of 1777.) The clause ended the judicial career of James Kent, who left office in 1823 and took a kind of revenge by writing his famous *Commentaries*.

ideal had enough hypnotic force to bring some peace and consensus to issues of tenure, selection, behavior, and removal of judges. Perhaps it even affected the way judges actually played their roles.

As we said, courts had no way to avoid the minefields of American law. High courts faced sensitive issues, burning political issues, every term. Sometimes the veil of objectivity fell or was torn from the judges' faces. *Dred Scott,* in 1857, was an instance where the court overreached itself. The case was a blatant political act, and more significantly, a wrong-headed one.[66] There were many minor *Dred Scott* cases at lower levels of decision. Prejudice and arrogance were less overt, harder to document; but they were there. American history is full of political trials—trials of unpopular people; or dissenters. In 1845, Circuit Judge Amasa J. Parker presided at the trial of the anti-rent rioters of upstate New York; his behavior was as partisan and prejudiced as any Federalist judge of the early 1800s.[67] But more and more, the judges took on a posture of propriety. Meanwhile, the actual power of judges, as makers of doctrine and framers of rules, may have actually grown somewhat after 1800. The courts had to hammer out legal propositions to run the business of the country, to sift what was viable from what was not in the common-law tradition, to handle disputes and problems that bubbled to the surface, in a period of rapid political, social, and technological change. The legal generation of 1776 had been a generation of political thinkers and statesmen. The U.S. Constitution was their greatest legal monument. In the next generation, the great state papers, in a sense, were cases like *Marbury v. Madison,* or the *Dartmouth College Case.* The best of the early nineteenth-century judges had a subtle, accurate political sense, and an intelligent set of economic and social opinions. They molded the law, in particular, with regard to basic aspects of life in America: rules and doctrines about land, houses, husbands and wives, buying and selling. They built scaffolding to support (as they saw it) the architecture of human affairs.

Perhaps the greatest of the judges was John Marshall, Chief Justice of the United States.[68] He, more than anyone else, gave federal judgeship its meaning. The judiciary was, of course, a co-ordinate branch of government. The branches were separate; but were they equal? As the Federalist papers put it, the courts were the "least dangerous branch." And the weakest. But less so after Marshall had done his work. In *Marbury v. Madison* (1803), as we mentioned, John Marshall invented or affirmed the power of the court to review even acts of Congress. But the *Marbury* decision was only one dramatic instance of Marshall's work. His doctrines made constitutional law. He personally transformed the function and meaning of the Supreme Court. When he came on the bench, in 1801, the Supreme Court was a frail and fledgling institution. In 1789, Robert

[66] The definitive treatment of the case in Don E. Fehrenbacher's book, *The Dred Scott Case: Its Significance in American Law and Politics* (1978).

[67] Described in Henry Christman, *Tin Horns and Calico* (1945), pp. 220–41; on the background, see Charles W. McCurdy, *The Anti-Rent Era in New York Law and Politics, 1839–1865* (2001).

[68] There is an enormous literature on John Marshall. See, for example, Jean Edward Smith, *John Marshall: Definer of a Nation* (1996). On the work of the Marshall court, an especially good source is G. Edward White, *The Marshall Court and Cultural Change, 1815–1835* (Vol's III and IV of the Holmes Devise, History of the Supreme Court of the United States, 1988); see also Herbert A. Johnson, *The Chief Justiceship of John Marshall, 1802–1835* (1997).

Hanson Harrison turned down a position on the Court to become chancellor of Maryland. John Jay resigned in 1795 to run for governor of New York.[69] In the first years, the Court heard only a handful of cases. It did not make much of a stir in the country. By the time Marshall died, the Court was fateful and great.

Marshall had a sure touch for institutional solidity. Before he became chief justice, the judges delivered seriatim (separate) opinions, one after another, in the English style. Marshall, however, put an end to this practice. The habit of "caucusing opinions," and delivering up one unanimous opinion only, as the "opinion of the Court" had been tried by Lord Mansfield in England. It was abandoned there; but Marshall revived the practice. Unanimity was the rule on the Court; for a while, until William Johnson (1777–1834) was appointed by Jefferson, in 1804, the unanimity was absolute, with not a single dissenting opinion. Johnson broke this surface consensus.[70] Yet, neither Johnson nor any later justices could or would undo Marshall's work. He was the dominant figure. The Court handed down forty-one decisions during the 1809 term. Marshall wrote thirty of these. Seven were *per curiam;* the rest of the Court was responsible for a mere four opinions. Johnson wrote two dissents. The rest of the cases were unanimous.[71] Marshall was on the court for thirty-four years; he wrote 574 opinions. Justice Todd, on the court for eighteen years, wrote exactly fourteen.[72]

Over the years, doctrines changed; personalities and blocs clashed on the court; power contended with power; but these struggles all took place within the fortress that Marshall had built. The court remained strong and surprisingly independent. Jefferson hoped that Johnson would enter the lists against Marshall. Yet, Johnson more than once sided with Marshall, in opposition to Jefferson, his leader and friend. The nature and environment of the court—life tenure, the influence of colleagues—loosened his other allegiances. Even the fact that the justices lived together, in boarding-houses in Washington, during the (relatively short) period they spent in Washington, militated against dissent, and buttressed Marshall's dominance.[73] Presidents throughout American history have been disappointed in the way Justices whom they appointed turned out. Joseph Story betrayed Madison; Oliver Wendell Holmes let down Theodore Roosevelt; Eisenhower disliked what Earl Warren did to the Supreme Court; the Warren Burger court slapped Richard Nixon in the face; Frankfurter deserted the liberals, Souter and Blackmun deserted the conservatives.

There were strong leaders and builders in the state courts, too. James Kent dominated his court in New York, in the early nineteenth century. As he remembered it, "The first practice was for each judge to give his portion of opinions,

---

[69] The election for governor of New York was held in April 1795, and Jay's opponent happened to be Abraham Yates, chief justice of the New York supreme court; in short, no matter who won, it was inevitable that a judge would desert the bench for a governorship.

[70] Donald G. Morgan, *Justice William Johnson: The First Dissenter* (1954), pp. 168–89; the phrase about "caucusing opinions" is from a letter written by Jefferson. See also Karl M. Zo-Bell, "Division of Opinion in the Supreme Court: A History of Judicial Disintegration," 44 Cornell L.Q. 186 (1959).

[71] Jean Smith, *John Marshall,* p. 386.

[72] White, *The Marshall Court,* p. 191.

[73] White, *The Marshall Court,* p. 190.

when we all agreed, but that gradually fell off, and, for the last two or three years before I left the Bench, I gave the most of them. I remember that in eighth Johnson[74] all the opinions for one term are 'per curiam.' The fact is I wrote them all . . ."[75] Kent's pride in his work was justified. But the opportunity was there. The judges were independent in two senses: free from England, but also free, for the moment, from stifling partisan control. Also, they were published. The colonial judges, who left no monuments behind, are forgotten men. From 1800 on, strong-minded American judges, whose work was recorded, influenced their courts and the law. In New York there was, as we mentioned, Chancellor Kent (1776–1847); in Massachusetts, Theophilus Parsons (1750–1813) and Lemuel Shaw (1781–1861); in Pennsylvania, John B. Gibson (1780–1853); in Ohio, Peter Hitchcock (1781–1853). In the South, there was Francis Xavier Martin of Louisiana (1762–1846); Thomas Ruffin of North Carolina (1787–1870), and Joseph Henry Lumpkin (1799–1867) of Georgia, among others.[76]

These state judges worked on a more modest scale and in smaller ponds than the Supreme Court in its greater moments. Their work had less national significance. But in their home states, and in the common law world, they made a definite impact. Some of them were fine stylists. Many of them wrote in what Karl Llewellyn has called the Grand Style:[77] their opinions were sometimes little treatises, moving from elegant premise to elaborate conclusion, ranging far and wide over subject matter that was boldly defined. They were, at their best, far-sighted men, impatient with narrow legal logic. Marshall, Gibson, and Shaw could write for pages without citing a shred of "authority." Precedent was important, but not crucial. They chiseled law out of the hard rock of basic principle. Past cases were only evidence of principle, and rebuttable at that. They firmly believed in *law,* and law, they believed rested on the same base of concepts and ideas that a good society was based on. The needs of a living society, as they saw these, were critical elements in their work. Some were conservative men, passionate about tradition; but they honored tradition, not for its own sake, but for the values that inhered in it. They were political animals, and they believed in politics; on the other hand, as G. Edward White has argued, they separated politics in its noble sense from politics in the sense of dirty, partisan wrangling.[78] They were important not because they stuck to the past, but because they lived in the present, shaping and reworking the living law. Many of the great judges were scholarly men; a few were very erudite, like Joseph Story, who could stud his opinions with learned citation—a thing Marshall tended to avoid. The great judges were creative, self-aware, and willing to make changes. James Kent described his work in New York as chancellor as follows:

---

[74] That is, the eighth volume of Johnson's *Reports* of New York cases. Kent is referring to the October term, 1811, of the New York Supreme Court. 8 Johns 361–492. *Per curiam* means "by the court," that is, the opinion is not signed by any particular or specific judge.

[75] Quoted in William Kent, *Memoirs and Letters of James Kent* (1898), p. 118.

[76] On Lumpkin and Ruffin, see Timothy S. Huebner, *The Southern Judicial Tradition: State Judges and Sectional Distinctiveness, 1790–1890* (1999), chs 3 and 5.

[77] Karl N. Llewellyn, "Remarks on the Theory of Appellate Decision and the Rules or Canons about How Statutes Are to Be Construed," 3 Vanderbilt L. Rev. 395, 396 (1950).

[78] White, *The Marshall Court,* pp. 196–98.

> I took the court as if it had been a new institution, and never before known in the United States. I had nothing to guide me, and was left at liberty to assume all such English Chancery power and jurisdiction as I thought applicable. . . . This gave me grand scope, and I was checked only by the revision of the Senate, or Court of Error. . . .
>
> My practice was, first, to make myself perfectly and accurately . . . master of the facts. . . . I saw where justice lay, and the moral sense decided the court half the time; and I then sat down to search the authorities until I had examined my books. I might once in a while be embarrassed by a technical rule, but I most always found principles suited to my views of the case. . . .[79]

Nobody cited his predecessors—as Kent immediatcly noticed. Their opinions, unpublished, were gone with the wind. He made sure his work would have a different fate. He worked closely with William Johnson (1769–1848), who reported his cases. Other judges did this job themselves. F. X. Martin compiled Louisiana decisions from 1811 to 1830; during much of this time, he was himself one of the judges. Some judges were active in collecting, revising, or digesting the statutes of their states, and in writing or rewriting treatises. Joseph Story wrote a series of treatises on various branches of law. James Kent, after retiring from the bench, wrote his monumental *Commentaries*. John F. Grimke (1753–1819) published the laws of South Carolina, wrote a treatise on the "Duty of Executors and Administration," and the inevitable "South Carolina Justice of the Peace" (1788). Harry Toulmin (1766–1823) edited the statutes of Kentucky; then, as judge of Mississippi Territory, he edited the territorial statutes. Still later, in Alabama Territory, he edited the statutes there, too.

Many appellate judges were versatile and highly educated. George Wythe of Virginia (1726–1806), chancellor of the state from 1788 to 1801, was perhaps the foremost classical scholar in the state; as "professor of law and policy" at William and Mary (1779–1790), he occupied the first chair of law at an American college. Augustus B. Woodward (1774–1827), judge of Michigan Territory from 1805, prepared a plan for the city of Detroit, wrote on political subjects, and published a book called *A System of Universal Science*.[80] Some judges were well versed in Latin and Greek, had gifts for science or language, or, like Story, wrote bad poetry. Theophilus Parsons of Massachusetts published a paper on astronomy, and dabbled in mathematics. His "Formula for Extracting the Roots of Adjected Equations" appears as an appendix to the memoir of his life, which his son published in 1859. Parsons was also a Greek scholar and wrote a Greek grammar that was never published. John Gibson of Pennsylvania was a devotee of French and Italian literature, a student of Shakespeare and an excellent violinist. He was probably the only major judge who designed his own false teeth. William Johnson, while a Supreme Court justice, wrote and published a life of Nathanael Greene, in two volumes, nearly 1,000 pages long.[81] He was also an active member of the Charleston, South Carolina, horticultural

---

[79] Quoted in William Kent, *Memoirs and Letters of James Kent* (1898), pp. 158–59.

[80] On Woodward, see Frank B. Woodford, *Mr. Jefferson's Disciple: A Life of Justice Woodward* (1953).

[81] Donald G. Morgan, *Justice William Johnson: The First Dissenter* (1954), pp. 148–49.

society, and wrote a "Memoire on the Strawberry" in 1832.[82] John Marshall himself wrote a life of George Washington, first published in 1805, in five volumes; it was a success; was translated into French, German, and Dutch; and went through many editions. Marshall even prepared an abridgement (in two volumes) for schoolchildren.[83] Very often, judges were men who had political careers before they became judges, although most of them willingly "put aside ambition" when they "donned the ermine." On the frontier, judging was only one aspect of a politician's busy life. Harry Toulmin, in the Old Southwest, was "also postmaster, preached and officiated at funerals and marriages, made Fourth of July orations, practiced medicine gratuitously and in general was the head of the settlements."[84] Before his arrival in the territory, he had been secretary of state in Kentucky. John Boyle (1774–1835), chief justice of Kentucky, was a member of Congress before he became a judge. Joseph Story was speaker of the Massachusetts House when he was appointed to the Supreme Court. For some judges—John Jay, for example—judgeship was an interlude between other political posts.

Judgeship, then, was not a lifetime career for all judges. It was a stepping-stone, or a refuge from politics, or a political reward. It was not a distinctive career, with its own distinctive pattern of training and background, as in many Continental countries. Judgeship was a matter of luck and opportunity, not special skill, background, or aspiration. It was and is an offshoot of the bar—of that part of the bar active in political affairs. Kermit Hall studied the men appointed to the federal bench between 1829 and 1861. An astonishing 78 percent of the judges had held prior elective public office. This was the Jacksonian era; but it was also true (though to a slightly lesser degree) of the pre-Jacksonians—65 percent of those federal judges had served in elective office.[85]

A successful lawyer usually suffered a drop in income, if he became a judge. The salaries of judges, like those of public officials in general, were not generous. Judges continually complained that they were pinched for money. By statute in 1827, New Jersey fixed the salary of the justices of the state supreme court at $1,100. The chief justice earned $1,200. The governor earned $2,000.[86] Lemuel Shaw became chief justice of Massachusetts in 1830, at a salary of $3,000. The low salary, in fact, was the only source of reluctance for Shaw. For trial judges, the fee system was common. A New York law of 1786 awarded fees to the judge of the court of probates: "For filing every petition, one shilling; for making and-entering every order, six shillings; for every citation, under seal, to witnesses, or for any other purposes, six shillings . . . for copies of all records and proceedings, when required, for each sheet consisting of one hundred and twenty-eight words, one shilling and six-pence."[87] Under the fee

[82] Irwin F. Greenberg, "Justice William Johnson: South Carolina Unionist, 1823–1830," 36 Pa. Hist. 307, 331n (1969).

[83] Jean Smith, *John Marshall,* p. 331.

[84] Dunbar Rowland, *Courts, Judges and Lawyers of Mississippi, 1798–1935,* vol. 1 (1935), p. 21.

[85] Kermit L. Hall, *The Politics of Justice: Lower Federal Judicial Selection and the Second Party System, 1829–61* (1979), pp. 166–67.

[86] Acts N.J. 1827, p. 9.

[87] Laws N.Y. 1778–92, vol. 1 (1792), p. 240.

system, some lower-court judges got rich. Still, a seat on a state supreme court paid off in the coin of high status.

THE ORGANIZATION OF COURTS

The Constitution of 1787 created a new system of federal courts. Like the privy council before 1776, the federal courts had power to review the work of state courts. The extent of that power was and still is a matter under constant definition and redefinition. The Constitution severely limited the scope of review. Yet, in its sphere, it was more potent than colonial review by the British government. Federal courts were relatively close at hand; no ocean intervened; federal judges were often familiar with local problems and how to handle them. The Constitution gave the federal courts jurisdiction over admiralty cases. On matters of federal law, litigants could appeal from state to federal courts. Unless there was a real federal question, the state courts had the last and only word.

The text of the Constitution concerning judges was the start of an evolutionary process; and a way of marking off some obvious limits. No one even dreamt of the great forests of law that would grow from these eighteenth-century seeds. In the late eighteenth century, and in the first half of the nineteenth, the federal courts were clearly subordinate. They outranked state courts, but in a rather narrow ambit. Not much is known about the way the lower federal courts functioned. A pioneer study, by Mary K. Tachau, examined the records of the federal court in Kentucky, between 1789 and 1816. She found a surprisingly active, useful, and competent court, handling a large volume of casework, in a place that was at the very edge of American civilization.[88]

The federal Constitution, as is well known, was drenched with ideas about separation of powers and checks and balances. The state constitutions were part of the same intellectual tradition, on the whole. But separation of powers was not always as separate then as it was later understood. It was traditional to mix branches of government at the highest level. After all, in England, the highest court was the House of Lords (although, in good English fashion, it evolved into a court quite distinct from the actual House of Lords). In Connecticut, the governor, lieutenant governor, and council constituted a "Supreme Court of Errors." At one time, the legislature itself had acted as the court of last resort.[89] Under the New Jersey Constitution of 1776, the governor held the office of chancellor; and together with his council, constituted "the court of appeals in the last resort." In New York, the court for the "trial of impeachments and the correction of errors"—the highest court, under the constitutions of 1777 and 1821—consisted of the president of the senate, the senators, the chancellor, and the justices of the supreme court.[90]

Once by one, however, states began to give their highest court final judicial authority. The New Jersey Constitution of 1844 and the New York Constitution

[88] Mary K. Bonsteel Tachau, *Federal Courts in the Early Republic: Kentucky, 1789–1816* (1978).

[89] Roscoe Pound, *Organization of Courts* (1940), p. 95.

[90] New Jersey Const., 1776, art. IX; New York Const., 1777, art. XXXII; New York Const., 1821, art. V, sec. 1; see Peter J. Galie, *Ordered Liberty: A Constitutional History of New York* (1996), p. 82.

of 1846 put the seal on this change. Rhode Island was the last state to join the movement. As late as the 1850s, the legislature passed an act which in effect granted a new trial in a pending case. The Rhode Island court, in 1856, interposed itself, labeled the practice intolerable, and appealed to the concept of separation of powers.[91] By that time, political opinion, almost universally, rejected this kind of legislative action. On the other hand, throughout the period legislatures passed private acts that did things we would now consider purely judicial or executive. They granted charters for beginning corporations, and divorces for ending marriages. They quieted title to property, declared heirships, and legalized changes of name. As in colonial days, in most states the division between trial and appellate courts was hardly clear-cut. High-court judges often doubled as trial or circuit judges. Appellate terms of court were held in the capital at fixed times of the year. In between, judges spent part of the year on coach or horseback, traveling circuit.

Circuit duty was a considerable hardship. The country was huge, parts of it were sparsely settled, the interior was pretty much a wilderness. Mud or dust, depending on the season, made the roads a torture. Often, the judges rode circuit in their own home districts, which made the burden somewhat lighter. Still, many judges complained bitterly about their gypsy life. The system did have some virtues. It brought justice close to home; it conserved judicial manpower. Circuit duty gave the appellate judge actual trial experience. This gave him exposure to real litigants, and this (some felt) was good for his soul.

Trial work also cemented relations between bench and bar. Around 1800, in York County, in what later became the state of Maine, judges and lawyers traveled together, argued together, joked together, drank and lived together; this traveling "collection of lawyers, jurors, suitors, and witnesses filled up the small villages in which the courts were held." Often there was literally no room at the inn. "It was quite a privilege, enjoyed by few, to obtain a separate bed." The members of the bar "were no ascetics. The gravity and dignity of the bar . . . were very apt to be left in the courtroom—they were seldom seen in the bar room."[92] On the frontier, the circuit system made or demanded a fairly rugged type of judge. In Missouri, around 1840, Charles H. Allen, appointed to one of the Missouri circuits, traveled "on horseback from Palmyra," his home, about two hundred miles; then "around the circuit, about eight hundred more. This he did three times a year, spending nearly his whole time in the saddle. He was, however, a strong, robust man, and capable of the greatest endurance. He always traveled with a holster of large pistols in front of his saddle, and a knife with a blade at least a foot long. But for his dress, a stranger might have readily taken him for a cavalry officer."[93]

As the states grew in wealth and population, they tended to sharpen the distinction between trial courts and courts of appeal. In some states, there were general trial courts, often called circuit courts, superior courts, or courts of common pleas. These courts also heard appeals, or retried matters, which began in the lowest courts—courts of justices of the peace, for example. Above

[91] *Taylor & Co. v. Place,* 4 R.I. 324 (1856).
[92] William Willis, *A History of the Law, the Courts, and the Lawyers of Maine,* p. 278.
[93] W. V. N. Bay, *Reminiscences of the Bench and Bar of Missouri* (1878), p. 211.

the trial courts was the state supreme court. This, more and more, was purely a court of appeal, even if its members sometimes rode circuit.

Most of the historical research has concentrated on the U.S. Supreme Court. The judges of the Supreme Court wore robes, stood heir to a great tradition, and heard cases of far-reaching importance. The further down one goes in the pyramid of courts, state or federal, the thinner the trickle of research. Yet the humble, everyday courts churned out thousands of decisions on questions of debt, crime, family affairs, and title to land. Each particular case meant very little, except to the litigants; but in the aggregate, this work was tremendously important. Who were the trial court judges? And what sorts of people served as justices of the peace? What was their background and influence? The justice of the peace was "arch symbol of our emphasis on local autonomy in the organization of courts," reflecting the "practical need, in a time of poor and costly communications, to bring justice close to each man's door."[94] In Philadelphia, the aldermen acted as justices of the peace after 1789; among them, we find craftsmen, shopkeepers, a druggist, a flour inspector, a keeper of a prison, and a sea captain.[95] We know very little about the actual quality of justice in these bottom courts. Probably their role and function changed greatly between 1790 and 1840; and there were no doubt differences between East and West and North and South. State courts tended more toward specialization than the federal courts. Some states, for example, used separate courts for wills and probate matters. Others, as is the practice today, gave these problems over to courts of general jurisdiction. In New Jersey, the "ordinary" probated wills, and granted letters of administration and guardianship in his "prerogative court." Other estate matters were handled in New Jersey by the oddly named orphans' court.[96] This tribunal was made up of judges who also served on the court of common pleas in the New Jersey counties.[97] Some states had separate courts of equity. Georgia's Constitution of 1789 (art. III, sec. 3) declared that "Courts-merchant shall be held as heretofore"; but the constitution of 1798 deleted the clause. In Delaware, there were courts of oyer and terminer, and courts of general sessions and jail delivery. Memphis, Cairo, and Chattanooga had their own municipal courts, New York, its mayor's court; Richmond's hustings court preserved an ancient, honorable name. The St. Louis Land Court (1855) was an unusual example of specialization.

Unlike the state constitutions, which often discussed the structure of courts in some detail, the federal Constitution was quite laconic on the subject. Judicial power was to be vested in a "Supreme Court" and such "inferior courts" as "the Congress may from time to time ordain and establish." For a few types of cases, the Supreme Court was to have "original" jurisdiction, meaning that these cases begin in the Court and do not work their way up the ladder of

---

[94] J. Willard Hurst, *The Growth of American Law: The Law Makers* (1950), p. 148. For a rare study of the lower courts in a state, see Robert M. Ireland, *The County Courts in Antebellum Kentucky* (1972).

[95] Allen Steinberg, *The Transformation of Criminal Justice: Philadelphia, 1800–1880* (1989), pp. 39–40.

[96] Pennsylvania, too, had a court with this name. An "ordinary," in England, had been an official in the church courts

[97] Stats. N.J. 1847, p. 205.

appeals. This was true for cases involving ambassadors, and those in which a state itself was a party. Congress had power to decide how much appellate jurisdiction, and of what sort, the Supreme Court would enjoy. The president had power to appoint justices, subject to Senate confirmation. The Senate proved to be no rubber stamp. George Washington appointed John Rutledge of South Carolina to succeed Chief Justice Jay. Rutledge, however, made the mistake of bitterly denouncing the treaty Jay had made with Great Britain. This set off a firestorm of vituperation, on the part of a bloc of Federalists. Rutledge served a few months on an interim basis, and wrote a few opinions. But criticism, poor health, deaths in the family, and financial disaster, drove him to depression and despair. He even tried twice to drown himself. On December 28, 1795, he resigned. Ironically, this was unnecessary: although he did not know it, the Senate had voted him down already on a straight party-line vote.[98]

Under the U.S. Constitution, Congress could have dispensed with any lower federal courts. State courts would then have had original jurisdiction over all but a few federal issues. The famous Judiciary Act of 1789 provided otherwise.[99] It divided the country into districts. Each district was generally coextensive with a state; each had a Federal district court, and a district judge. The districts, in turn, were grouped into three circuits. In each circuit, a circuit court, made up of two Supreme Court justices and one district judge, sat twice a year. In general, the circuit courts handled cases of diversity of citizenship— cases in which citizens of different states were on opposite sides of the case. The district courts heard admiralty matters. In certain limited situations, the circuit courts heard appeals. One defect of the system was that it forced the justices to climb into carriages and travel to their circuits. At first, the justices were on circuit twice a year. Later, the burden was lightened to once a year. Additional judges were added to the court, and new circuits were created as the country grew. But these changes helped only a little. In 1838, Justice McKinley traveled 10,000 miles in and to his circuit (Alabama, Louisiana, Mississippi, Arkansas). Five other justices traveled between 2,000 and 3,500 miles each.[100] As was true of state courts, there were those who argued that circuit duty was beneficial. It brought the judges closer to the people; it subjected them to the discipline of trial work. But as Govenor Morris pointed out, no one could argue that

> riding rapidly from one end of this country to another is the best way to study law. . . . Knowledge may be more conveniently acquired in the closet than in the high road.[101]

Reform proved politically impossible. In Congress, a strong states-rights bloc was hostile to the federal courts. This bloc saw no reason to cater to the convenience of the judges. The Judiciary Act of 1801 abolished circuit riding for Supreme Court justices. Unhappily, this was the famous act of the midnight

---

[98] James Haw, "John Rutledge: Distinction and Declension," in Scott Douglas Gerber, ed., *Seriatim: The Supreme Court before John Marshall* (1998), pp. 70, 85–88.

[99] For the early history of federal jurisdiction, see Felix Frankfurter and James Landis, *The Business of the Supreme Court* (1928), pp. 4–52.

[100] Frankfurter and Landis, *op. cit.*, pp. 49–50.

[101] Quoted, *ibid.*, p. 17.

judges. It was an admirable law in the technical sense, but its political origins doomed it. The Jefferson administration promptly repealed it. Again and again, reform proposals were entangled in sectional battles or battles between Congress and the president, and so went down to defeat. As was so often the case, more powerful values and interests won out over notions of technical efficiency.

CIVIL PROCEDURE

Left to themselves, the colonies might have developed modes of procedure more rational and streamlined than anything in England. The increasing influence of English law in the eighteenth century retarded the process. Many lawyers and judges were English trained; English legal texts were in use. Imperial rule, English prestige, and the growth of a professional bar led to a reaction against the "crudities" of colonial procedure. The colonial systems became compromises between English law and native experiment. By the time of the Revolution, colonial procedure was a jumble of contradictions.

There was no chance that classical English pleading would be established after Independence. For one thing, the American bar was simply not equipped to handle this dismal science. It was in nobody's interests to introduce the weird complexities of English pleading—certainly not the interests of business people. It was one thing for a system of this kind to evolve over the centuries, which is what happened in England; it was quite another to bring it in from outside. But at first English lawbooks were pretty much all that lawyers and judges had to look at. This was particularly true of lawyers in the first generation after independence. There were a few pleading and practice manuals, written in America, which stressed local forms and procedures. Joseph Story published *A Selection of Pleadings in Civil Actions* (1805); he took some of his forms from Massachusetts lawyers; and he justified the book on the basis of differences in "customs, statutes, and common law" between England and Massachusetts. But basically the book was a book about English pleadings, some of it of fairly ancient vintage. He merely adapted these pleadings for Americans, thus avoiding "the high price of foreign books." James Gould's *Treatise on the Principles of Pleading in Civil Actions*, published in Boston in 1832, made the rather grandiose claim of setting out principles of pleading as a "science." It paid scant attention to American law as such:

> As the English system of pleading is, in general, the basis of that of our country; the former has, in the following treatise, been followed exclusively, without regard to any peculiarities in the latter; excepting a very few references to those, which exist in the law of my native State.[102]

In fact, certain popular English manuals circulated freely in the United States. In some cases, American editions of these manuals and treatises were prepared. Joseph Chitty's treatise on pleading was so well received that an eighth American edition was published in 1840. Chapter 9 of this dreary book bore the following title: "Of Rejoinders and the Subsequent Pleadings;

[102] Preface, ix.

of Issues, Repleaders, Judgments non Obstante Veredicto, and Pleas Puis Dar-
rein Continuance, or now Pending Action; and of Demurrers and Joinders in
Demurrer." An American lawyer, reading this book, could absorb such strictures as the following:

> A traverse may be *too extensive*, and therefore defective, by being taken in
> the *conjunctive* instead of the *disjunctive*, where proof of the allegation in
> the conjunctive is not essential. Thus, in an action on a policy on ship and
> tackle, the defendant should not deny that the ship and tackle were lost,
> but that *neither* was lost.[103]

English common-law pleading was an elaborate contest of lawyerly arts, and
winning a case did not always depend on who was in the right or who had the
law on their side. The winner might be the better pleader. There were too
many rules, and they were too tricky and inconsistent. The idea behind English
pleading was not ridiculous in itself. Pleading was supposed to distill, out of
the amorphousness of fact and fancy, one precious, narrow issue on which trial
could be joined. Principles of pleading were, in theory, principles of economy
and order. But in reality, mastering this business took great technical skill.
Those who had the skill—highly trained lawyers and judges—saw no reason to
abandon the system. But the United States was not run by lawyers. It was run by
merchants, bankers, landowners—and voters. To these people, the "science of
pleading" was nothing but empty hocus-pocus, a lawyer's plot to avoid real justice, or to frustrate the expectations of ordinary people of affairs. It is pretty
obvious what Chitty's ship-merchant would have thought of disjunctive and
conjunctive traverses.

English procedure, in other words, was too medieval for the modem world.
(One wonders why it was not too medieval for the Middle Ages.) Reform of civil
procedure, at any rate, found fertile soil in the United States. Pleading reform
was one of the changes the explosion in legal consumers made necessary. This
was a middle-class country—in the sense that ordinary families, especially in
the north, owned a piece of land. They sometimes needed legal help. But legal
skill was a scarce resource. It had to be husbanded. Shrewdness in pleading
was not cheap and universal enough to pay its way in American society. Popular
democracy, the colonial tradition, the demands of business and the land market for a rational, predictable system—all of these were allies, in a sense, in the
war against the "science of pleading." The few troops of bench and bar, a rag-
tag army, defended the "science," if at all, in a half-hearted way. Educated
judges who knew French found the common law contemptuous. Rank-and-file
lawyers were too untrained to be able to cope with Chitty. English procedure
had become like a drafty old house. Those born to it and raised in it loved it;
but no outsider could tolerate its secret panels, broken windows, and on-again,
off-again plumbing.

Reform did not come in one great burst. The actual practice of courts, particularly trial courts, was freer and easier than one might assume from reading
manuals of procedure. As more research is done, more variance between book
learning and reality comes to light. Alexander Hamilton prepared a manuscript manual of practice in 1782, probably for his own use in cramming for

---

[103] Joseph Chitty, *Treatise on Pleading*, p. 645.

the bar. In it, he noted a decline in "nice Learning" about pleas of abatement. These pleas, he said, are seldom used; and are always "discountenanced by the Court, which having lately acquired a more liberal Cast begin to have some faint Idea that the end of Suits at Law is to Investigate the Merits of the Cause, and not to entangle in the Nets of technical Terms."[104]

New York was, relatively speaking, quite conservative in legal affairs. Hamilton's manual of New York pleading, if it can be trusted, shows deep dependence on English formalities and forms. Yet, even here we see many cracks in the armor, many defections in favor of "the Merits of the Cause." Other jurisdictions departed even further from English propriety. Georgia, in the eighteenth century, passed a series of laws that went a long way toward rationalizing its civil procedure. The climax was the Judiciary Act of 1799. Under Georgia's laws, a plaintiff might begin civil actions simply by filing a *petition*, setting out the case "plainly, fully and substantially"; the defendant would file his answer, stating whatever was necessary to constitute "the cause of his defense."[105] Georgia's law was, among other things, a courageous attempt to join together equity and common-law pleading. It also got rid of the forms of action, those ancient pigeonholes of procedure (or straitjackets) into which pleaders were forced to fit their pleas, or else. Supposedly, conservative Georgia courts, outraged at all this boldness, undermined the Georgia reforms. But the evidence for this charge rests on nothing more than scraps of talk from appellate courts. The reform may have made a real difference to trial court behavior in Georgia.

By the 1830s, reform of procedure was in the air—even in England itself, the native habitat of the common law. Jeremy Bentham cast a long shadow. Lord Brougham, in Parliament in 1828, urged thorough reform. He and others like him began a process that had consequences for the whole world of the common law. England was also a modernizing society; it was far ahead of America in industrial development, even though far behind on the road to democratic equality. During the nineteenth century, the two countries traveled roughly parallel routes of change. But as far as civil procedure is concerned, most of the key developments took place only toward the middle of the century, or even later.[106]

In the Middle Ages, equity courts had been in a way a source of reform. Equity boasted a flexible collection of remedies; it had often prodded and pushed the more lethargic common law in more rational (and just) directions. But equity had itself become hidebound; by 1800, it needed procedural reform even more desperately than the common law; it was equity, not law, that Dickens flayed and excoriated in his masterpiece, *Bleak House*. By then, the very existence of equity was an anomaly: a separate and contradictory jurisprudence, living uneasily beside the "law." In the United States, many states simply handed over the powers and tools of equity to ordinary courts of common law. The same judges decided both kinds of case. They simply alternated roles. North Carolina, for example, in 1782, empowered "each superior court of law"

---

[104] Quoted in Julius Goebel Jr., ed., *The Law Practice of Alexander Hamilton, 1757–1804*, vol. 1, *Documents and Commentary* (1964), p. 81.

[105] Robert W. Millar, *Civil Procedure of the Trial Court in Historical Perspective* (1952), p. 40.

[106] See part III, ch. 3.

to "be and act as a court of equity for the same district."[107] In a few states (Mississippi, Delaware, New Jersey), there were distinct courts of law and equity, with different judges presiding. This was true of New York until the 1820s, when the circuit judges were made "vice-chancellors," and given full equity powers within their circuits. But a loser could not appeal from these "vice-chancellors" to ordinary appellate courts; instead, he had to appeal to the chancellor.[108] Some states had no equity or equity courts at all. Louisiana was one of these, because of its civil-law heritage. Massachusetts and Pennsylvania were outstanding common-law examples. Before 1848, however, only Georgia (and Texas, whose history was deviant) had actually abolished the distinction.

States that lacked "equity" had developed a rough union of law and equity on their own. Statutes made equitable defenses available in cases at "law." In Massachusetts, the supreme judicial court had "power to hear and determine in equity all cases . . . when the parties have not a plain, adequate and complete remedy at the common law." The statute listed what these "cases" were, for example, "All suits for the specific performance of any written contract."[109] In Pennsylvania, "Common law actions were used to enforce purely equitable claims; purely equitable defenses were permitted in common law actions; and, at rare times, purely equitable reliefs were obtained by means of actions at law."[110] Throughout the period, Pennsylvania legislatures, by private laws, gave individuals permission to do things which, in other states, were within the scope of equity power. For example, Pennsylvania sometimes allowed an executor to sell parcels of land to pay the debts of a deceased.[111] In 1836, on the advice of a law-revision commission, Pennsylvania gave broad equity powers to some of its state-courts. Thus, Pennsylvania (and Massachusetts), by a piecemeal process, attained a "curious anticipation of future general reforms."[112]

In general, "law" was bent to suit "equity"; but not all the change was in one direction. The common law courts loved the spoken word—testimony, cross-examination—all in open court. Equity loved documents, papers, written evidence, and classically tolerated nothing else. But the Judiciary Act of 1789 provided for oral testimony in federal equity cases. Georgia allowed trial by jury in some kinds of lawsuit which, traditionally, belonged on the equity side of the bench. North Carolina, in a statute of 1782, did the same. And a North Carolina law of 1801 provided a simple way to continue equity actions after the death of a party on either side. This replaced the "bill of revivor," one of the prime procedural culprits, a device so slow and technical that it gave rise to the suspicion that a chancery bill, once begun, would never come to an end.[113]

In English law, there were countless kinds of "appeal," calling for different pleadings and forms, full of dark mysteries, tripping and trapping the unwary. The word *appeal*, strictly speaking, applied only to review by higher equity

[107] Laws N. Car. 1782, ch. 11.
[108] Rev. Stats. N.Y. 1829, vol. II, part III, ch. 1, title II, sections 2, 59.
[109] Rev. Stats. Mass. 1836, ch. 81, sec. 8.
[110] Spencer R. Liverant and Walter H. Hitchler, "A History of Equity in Pennsylvania," 37 Dickinson L. Rev. 156, 166 (1933).
[111] Thomas A. Cowan, "Legislative Equity in Pennsylvania," 4 U. Pitt. L. Rev. 1, 12 (1937).
[112] Millar, *op. cit.*, p. 40. The Pennsylvania law of 1836, incidentally, did not put an end to private acts of "legislative equity"; these lasted for almost forty more years.
[113] Laws N. Car. 1782, ch. 11; 1801, ch. 10.

courts. The states, continuing a trend that began in the colonial period, fixed on and emphasized two kinds of review by higher courts: the equity *appeal* and, for common-law actions, proceedings by writ of *error* or the equivalent. Local variations were frequent. In North Carolina, instead of writs of error, *writs of certiorari* were used. This was a form of review which, in England, could only be used to review noncommon-law courts.[114] In Connecticut the writ of error reviewed decisions in equity, taking over the role of the "appeal."

The basic problem of review or appeal is how to avoid doing everything over again—which would be a tremendous waste—but at the same time make sure that there is a way to correct mistakes in the lower courts. In essence, writs of error corrected only some kinds of errors, those that appeared on the face of the formal record. These were pleading errors mostly, except insofar as a party, in a bill of exceptions, preserved the right to complain about other kinds of "error"—if the judge, for example, let in evidence that was improper or prejudicial. But these various kinds of "errors" rarely went to the heart of the matter. The appeal system suffered from what Roscoe Pound has called "record worship"—"an excessive regard for the formal record at the expense of the case, a strict scrutiny of that record for 'errors of law' at the expense of scrutiny of the case to insure the consonance of the result to the demands of the substantive law."[115]

This system was not completely irrational. It could be defended as a reasonable way to divide powers and functions between high and low courts. High courts were concerned with the law itself—the rules, the doctrines, the principles. Low courts actually held trials and decided cases. By correcting errors of record, high courts were able to adjust any kinks in formal doctrine. But at the same time, they left the day-to-day work of the trial courts alone. Still, record worship meant that many mistakes and injustices could never be reviewed by a higher court; at the same time, high courts sometimes reversed perfectly proper decisions on highly technical grounds. In fact, we have to confess that we know very little—and *can* know very little—about how effectively upper courts actually controlled trial courts, in the first half of the nineteenth century. And the impact of "record worship" is similarly unknown. We have to bear in mind that in all periods only a small minority of cases were ever appealed. Most ended where they began, in the ordinary trial courts.

Record worship was a disease that probably did not randomly infect every type of case. Courts are stickier, for example, about small errors in cases where life or liberty is at stake. It would be no surprise, then, to find that the law of criminal procedure outdid civil procedure in record worship and technical artifice. This branch of law had a special place in American jurisprudence. The Bill of Rights contained what amounted to a miniature code of criminal procedure. Warrants were not to be issued "but upon probable cause, supported by Oath or affirmation, and particularly describing the place to be searched, and the persons or things to be seized" (art. IV). No person "shall be held to answer for a capital, or otherwise infamous crime" without presentment or indictment by grand jury (art. V). No one "shall be compelled in any Criminal Case to be a witness against himself" or be "deprived of life, liberty, or property, without due

---

[114] Roscoe Pound, *Appellate Procedures in Civil Cases* (1941), p. 288.
[115] Roscoe Pound, *Criminal Justice in America* (1930), p. 161.

process of law" (art. V). The accused "shall enjoy" the right to a "speedy and public trial," by an "impartial" jury of the vicinage; the accused must be told the nature of his crime; must be able to confront the witnesses; must "have compulsory process for obtaining witnesses in his favor" and the "Assistance of Counsel for his defense" (art. VI). "Excessive bail" was not to be required (art. VIII). Many states adopted their own bills of rights even before the federal government did, as we have seen; other states copied or modified the federal version. Criminal procedure was a major part of all of these bills of rights. The basic rights of man turned out, in large part, to be rights to fair criminal trial. These rights were thought of as a way to guard the citizen against the tyranny of kings, rulers, governments. Abuse of power by Federalist judges only strengthened the ideas that underlay the Bill of Rights. Criminal procedure, on paper, gave a whole battery of protections to persons accused of crime. The defendant had the right to appeal a conviction; the state had no right to appeal an acquittal.[116] In a number of cases, it seemed as if the high court searched the record with a fine-tooth comb, looking for faulty instructions, improper evidence, error in formal pleadings, or prejudicial actions by the judge. Sometimes the upper court quashed an indictment for a tiny slip of the pen or set aside a verdict for some microscopic error at the trial. In *State v. Owen*, a North Carolina case of 1810, the grand jurors of Wake County had presented John Owen, a cabinetmaker, for murder. According to the indictment, Owen, in Raleigh, on April 21, 1809,

> not having the fear of God before his eyes, but being moved and seduced by the instigations of the Devil . . . with force and arms, at the city of Raleigh . . . in and upon one Patrick Conway . . . feloniously, wilfully, and of his malice aforethought, did make an assault . . . with a certain stick, of no value, which he the said John Owen in both his hands then and there had and held . . . in and upon the head and face of him the said Patrick Conway . . . did strike and beat . . . giving to the said Patrick Conway, then and there with the pine stick aforesaid, in and upon the head and face of him the said Patrick Conway, several mortal wounds, of which said mortal wounds, the said Patrick Conway then and there instantly died.

Owen was found guilty and appealed. His attorney argued that the indictment was defective, in that it did not "set forth the length and depth of the mortal wounds." A majority of the supreme court of North Carolina regretfully agreed: "It appears from the books, that wounds capable of description must be described, that the Court may judge whether it be probable, that death might have been produced by them." Since the indictment did not allege that the wounds were two inches long and four inches deep, or the like, the case had to be overturned, and Owen won a new trial.[117]

Roscoe Pound has called this kind of case the "hypertrophy of procedure."[118] This hypertrophy, he felt, was nineteenth century run riot. The criminal law tolerated "hypertrophy" because this fit in with the self-image of the

---

[116] *State v. Jones*, 5 N. Car. 257 (1809).

[117] *State v. Owen*, 5 N. Car. 452 (1810). The North Carolina legislature promptly passed an act (1811) to remedy such excesses. See also the provisions of the New York revised statutes of 1828 dealing with indictments.

[118] Pound, *Criminal Justice in America* (1930), p. 161.

American male: the pioneer man, self-reliant, supremely confident of his own judgment, but jealous of the power of the state. Court and prosecutors should be tied down, roped in, fettered by technical rules; better to let a few guilty people free, than to allow courts and prosecutors any real power, any genuine discretion.

But it is doubtful if Pound's description fits the working law. Cases like *State v. Owen* were aberrations. Pound's picture was based on a tiny group of instances, mutations preserved in appellate records like flies in amber. Who took advantage of procedural rights and of record worship? Only the few people that appealed. Slaves, ordinary farmers, the dependent poor, urban workers—certainly not these. There is not enough systematic information on what the *average* trial was like. American law, we know, has had its dark undersides—vigilantism, lynching, mob rule, police brutality. In some communities, for some sorts of cases, the mass of the people did not want or even tolerate the niceties of procedural justice. Even the *formal* rights were, by the standards of the early twenty-first century, not what they should be. Thousands were arrested, tried, and sentenced without lawyers. But only a lawyer could make the Bill of Rights effective—let alone cash in on record worship and "hypertrophy." What we do know is that the average trial was simple, short, and relatively informal. And even some major trials—trials with political overtones—were by later standards unfair.

THE LAW OF EVIDENCE

The law of evidence seemed to tighten up considerably in the first generations after the Revolution. Surviving transcripts of criminal trials suggest rather loose attitudes toward evidence around 1800. In the trial of the so-called Manhattan Well Mystery—the transcript was found among Alexander Hamilton's papers—hearsay was freely admitted; and "some of the most important testimony was not elicited by questions" from the attorney, but rather "by allowing the witnesses to give a consecutive and uninterrupted account."[119] Opposing counsel did not meekly wait their turn to cross-examine. Rather, they broke in with questions whenever they wished.

When a field of law suddenly becomes cancerously complicated, some fundamental conflict of interest, some basic tension between opposing values must be at the root of the problem. The American political public has always resisted strong, central authority. Power tends rather to be fragmented, balkanized, dispersed. This attitude found expression in the theory of checks and balances; but it stained the law of evidence deeply as well. The modern European law of evidence is fairly simple and rational; the law lets most everything in, and trusts the judge to separate good evidence from bad. But American legal culture tends to distrust the judge; and, of course, American law has the jury. The jury has power to find the facts, and it has, in criminal cases, the final word on innocence or guilt. Yet, the system obviously trusts the jury even less than it trusts the judge. The rules of evidence grew up as some sort of countervailing force. The jury only hears bits and pieces of the story—it hears

---

[119] Julius Goebel Jr., ed., *The Law Practice of Alexander Hamilton: Documents and Commentary*, vol. 1 (1964), p. 701.

only that part which the law of evidence allows. The judge's hands are also tied. If he lets in improper testimony, he runs the risk that a higher court will reverse his decision. The strict and complicated rules of evidence bind and control both jury and judge.

In medieval times, the jury had been a panel of neighbors—knowing busybodies, who might even have personal knowledge of the facts or the people involved in a case. Slowly, over time, the jury changed function. It became an impartial panel of listeners. They had to be outsiders, unaware of the facts and unacquainted with the people—twelve strangers, twelve virgins, as it were. As this concept of the jury deepened, the law of evidence underwent explosive growth. The point of the rules was to keep out everything shaky, improper, or second-hand. Only the most tested, predigested matter was fit for the jury's consumption. In the nineteenth century, for example, courts developed and elaborated the so-called *hearsay rule*. This was a vast and bizarre body of doctrine. At the base of it was one simple, if somewhat Utopian idea, along with a puzzle box of exceptions. The jury was not to hear second-hand stories. They should listen to Smith's story out of his own mouth, and not Jones's account of what Smith had to say. Smith should testify himself—and on the stand, alive, under oath, and available for vigorous cross-examination. That was the general principle. But in many situations, the ban on "hearsay" was impractical, or unjust; and all sorts of exceptions to the rules were carved out. These ranged from involuntary utterances ("ouch!"), to shopbooks, to the dying words of a murder victim, naming his killer.

Hearsay rules grew luxuriantly, on both sides of the Atlantic. Most of the doctrines appeared first in England; but not all. The business-entry rule admits records made in the ordinary course of business, even though these are, strictly speaking, hearsay. This particular doctrine seems to have appeared in America around 1820.[120] In general, the American law of evidence outstripped English law in complexity, perhaps because the American fear of concentration of power ran deeper than in England.

The rules relating to witnesses were as complicated as rules about the kind of evidence that juries could hear; and perhaps for similar reasons. In 1800, husbands and wives could testify neither for nor against each other. No person could testify as a witness if he had a financial stake in the outcome of the case. This meant that neither the plaintiff nor the defendant, in most cases, was competent to testify on his own behalf; their mouths were shut in their very own lawsuits. This rule may have had a major impact on certain types of litigation—a personal injury suit, for example. It was hard to win such a case, if the victim had no right to tell his story.[121] During the period, some fresh restrictions on evidence were added. The doctor-patient privilege, for example, prevents a doctor from giving medical testimony without his patient's consent. A New York law of 1828, it seems, was the first appearance of this privilege. Missouri passed a similar law in 1835.[122]

---

[120] *Two Centuries' Growth of American Law 1701–1901* (1901), pp. 324–25.

[121] See John Fabian Witt, "Toward a New History of American Accident Law: Classical Tort Law and the Cooperative First-Party Insurance Movement," 114 Harv. L. Rev. 692, 754 (2001).

[122] John H. Wigmore, *A Treatise on the System of Evidence in Trials at Common Law*, vol. IV (1905), sec. 2380, pp. 3347–48.

In theory, the rules of evidence were meant to be rational rules of legal proof. Trials were to be orderly, businesslike, and fair. Each rule had its reason. But the rules as a whole, in their sheer complexity, tended to defeat the rationale. They seemed bewildering and even senseless, as liable to cheat justice as to fulfill it. Exclusionary rules, said Jeremy Bentham, had the perverse effect of shutting the door against the truth; the rules gave "license to oppression by all imaginable wrongs." For example, since Quakers refused to take an oath, for religious reasons, their testimony was excluded. Such a rule, he felt,

> in a case of rape . . . includes a license to the whole army to storm every quakers' meeting-house, and violate the persons of all the female part of the congregation, in the presence of fathers, husbands, and brothers.[123]

It is unlikely that a gang rape of this sort ever took place. But there was enough real and potential abuse, in the law of evidence, to feed the appetite for reform. And indeed, at the very point that courts were putting more building blocks in place, constructing the modern law of evidence, some of these very rules were showing signs of decay. But major change came only later in the century.

At the close of a trial, the judge instructs the jury—tells them about the applicable law. In the twentieth century, lawyers write these instructions themselves, or (far more often) copy them from form-books. The instructions tend to be dry, dreary, stereotyped—antiseptic statements of abstract rules. They are couched in cautious lawyer-talk. Often, it is hard to see how lay juries can make heads or tails of these "instructions." Yet the lawyers argue endlessly about wording; and they base appeals on alleged "errors" in the instructions the judges may have given. In 1776 or 1800, judges tended to talk more freely to the jury. They summarized and commented on the trial; they explained the law in simple, nontechnical language. Instructions were clear, informative summaries of the state of the law. Chief Justice Richard Bassett, of Delaware, explaining adverse possession to a jury, in 1794, remarked: "If you are in possession of a corner of my land for twenty years by adverse possession, you may snap your fingers at me."[124] All this changed in the nineteenth century; there was to be no more finger snapping, no more vivid language, no more clarity, no metaphors. As early as 1796, a statute in North Carolina made it unlawful, "in delivering a charge to the petit-jury, to give an opinion whether a fact is fully or sufficiently proved," since that was "the true office and province of the jury."[125] In the nineteenth century, a number of state statutes took away the judge's right to comment on evidence. This, to be sure, made it harder for the judge to dominate the jury. Bland, stereotyped instructions may confuse the jury; but they

---

[123] Jeremy Bentham, *Rationale of Judicial Evidence*, vol. IV (1827), pp. 491–92. This particular horrible example could not occur in the United States. Quakers were, in general, competent witnesses in the United States. They were allowed to make "affirmations" instead of taking oaths.

[124] Daniel Boorstin, ed., *Delaware Cases, 1792–1830*, vol. I (1943), p. 39.

[125] Laws N. Car. 1796, ch. 4. See the comments on this statute by Ruffin, in *State v. Moses*, 13 N. Car. 452 (1830).

help maintain its autonomy. The judge under this regime is more careful, more rulebound—hamstrung, one might even say.

In the early years of the nineteenth century, the roles of judge and jury were subtly altered and redefined. Up to that point, both judge and jury had been relatively free to act, each within its sphere. According to William Nelson, the jury "ceased to be an adjunct of local communities which articulated into positive law the ethical standards of those communities." It was rather an "adjunct" of the court, whose main job was to handle "facts," not "law." Nelson traces to the first decade of the nineteenth century, in Massachusetts, the articulation and definition of what became a classic definition of powers and roles: that the judge was master of "law," the jury of "fact."[126] The result, in theory at least, was a better balance of power. This division of function, it was hoped, made a more rational, predictable system of justice possible, especially in commercial cases.

Other changes were on the way. The witness disqualification rule began to weaken, even before the middle of the century.[127] Within the little world of the courtroom, the two major powers, judge and jury, were locked into tighter roles, more carefully defined. Checks and balances were more than constitutional concepts; they pervaded the whole of the law.

[126] William E. Nelson, *Americanization of the Common Law: The Impact of Legal Change on Massachusetts Society, 1760–1830* (1975), pp. 170–71; Note, "The Changing Role of the Jury in the Nineteenth Century," 74 Yale L.J. 170 (1964). Very little is known, however, about the actual behavior of jurors. See David J. Bodenhamer, "The Democratic Impulse and Legal Change in the Age of Jackson: The Example of Criminal Juries in Antebellum Indiana," 45 The Historian 206 (1982).

[127] See Part III, ch. 3.

CHAPTER 2

OUTPOSTS OF THE LAW: THE FRONTIER
AND THE CIVIL LAW FRINGE

Colonial America was a coastal country. But even before achieving independence, the line of settlement had crept far inland. The colonies claimed vast tracts of inner wilderness. The Louisiana Purchase added another immense and largely unsettled area. Throughout the period, population flowed into the West and Southwest. These lands of forest and plain, great gushing rivers, fertile soil, and sweeping distances captured and held the American imagination. In 1800, the American frontier represented an empire of the future. By 1900, the frontier was an empire of the past. People talked about the death of the frontier, the closing of the frontier, the end of an era. In literature, the frontier was always described as a land of heroes. Life on the edge was vibrant, novel, rough, and ready. The democratic spirit burned there like a flame, free from the defects, troubles, and exhaustion of the older East. The heady eye of modern scholarship has reduced the frontier to a more human, and reasonable, scale. The law of the frontier, too, has been gradually stripped of its husk of legend.

After independence, the states faced the problem of what to do with the western lands. The new republic, a collection of former colonies, itself became a kind of colonial power once the decision was made to treat the western lands as common property of the nation. The Ordinance of 1787—the so-called Northwest Ordinance—prescribed basic law for that huge area of forest and plain that later became Ohio, Indiana, Illinois, Michigan, and Wisconsin. The Ordinance of 1798 extended the influence of the Northwest Ordinance into the Southwestern territories—to Alabama and Mississippi.

The Ordinance of 1787 is one of the most important documents in American legal history. It adopted a bold policy of decolonization. Everyone expected that the territories would gradually fill with settlers. As soon as there were enough people living there, the territories were to take their place in the Union as full, free, sovereign states. First, however, came a period of tutelage. Until there were "five thousand free male inhabitants, of full age," living in the territory, the governor and three judges had power to make laws. The three judges had to live in the district. Any two of them could "form a court." They were to exercise "a common-law jurisdiction."[1] They were supposed to be substantial people;

---

[1] The term "common law" was ambiguous. Probably—but by no means certainly—the term was meant to exclude equity jurisdiction.

105

people who, "while in the exercise of their offices," owned a "freehold estate" of at least five hundred acres of land. The governor and a majority of the judges had power to "adopt and publish in the district such laws of the original States, criminal and civil, as may be necessary, and best suited to the circumstances of the district."[2] Congress had the power to disallow these laws. This was a striking—and by no means accidental—parallel to the British power of review over colonial laws.

The phrase "adopt and publish" was troublesome, and confusing, from the start. It seemed to imply that the territories had no right to make law on their own. They had only the power to rummage around in the statute books of older states, picking and choosing what they wanted or needed. Of course, this provision could not be carried out literally. At the very least, dates and place names in borrowed statutes had to be changed. In practice, the territories avoided and evaded the "adopt and publish" rule. Some territories adopted laws from states like Kentucky, which was not an "original" state. Some statutes were patched together from more than one statute in the older states. One critic charged that:

> They parade the laws of the original states before them, on the table, and cull letters from the laws of Maryland, syllables from the laws of Virginia, words from the laws of New York, sentences from the laws of Pennsylvania, verses from the laws of Kentucky, and chapters from the laws of Connecticut—jumble the whole into such form as they conceive the most suitable to facilitate their schemes . . . and then call it a law.[3]

This was a gross exaggeration; still, many territorial statutes were in fact a product of scissors and paste.

However odd the "adopt and publish" rule may seem, it only expressed, in a rather unusual form and as a binding rule, a procedure that new states in the West followed in making up their laws, even *without* compulsion. A new state, an Idaho or Montana, had no time to invent a whole statute book. It made more sense to take texts from older states, adding a patch of novelty here and there. Policy choices were made by choosing among old models, not by drafting fresh laws. In the old Northwest, settlers tended to borrow from states they knew best—the states they came from. From 1795 on, the governor and judges of Northwest Territory listed the source of each law they adopted for the territory. From 1795 to 1798, twenty-seven out of forty-nine laws came from Pennsylvania, the home state of the governor, Arthur St. Clair. Michigan Territory, between 1814 and 1823, adopted 168 laws from thirteen states; 134 of these were from Ohio, while Tennessee supplied only one.[4] In 1795, Michigan adopted from Virginia its general statute receiving the common law. In theory at least, this imported the whole body of the common law, and some unknown number of statutes of Parliament, into the wilds of early Michigan.

[2] This provision was not applicable to Louisiana and Arkansas territories. On territorial government in general, see Jack E. Eblen, *The First and Second United States Empires: Governors and Territorial Government,* 1784–1912 (1968).

[3] Quoted in William W. Blume, ed., *Transactions of the Supreme Court of the Territory of Michigan,* vol. I (1935), p. xxiii.

[4] William W. Blume, "Legislation on the American Frontier," 60 Mich. L. Rev. 317, 334 (1962).

Under the Ordinance of 1787, when the threshold number of "five thousand free male inhabitants, of full age" was reached, the territory entered the second stage. Now the governor and judges had to share lawmaking power with a body of elected representatives. Owners of property chose one representative "for every five hundred free male inhabitants," up to twenty-five; beyond this, "the number and portion of representatives" was to be "regulated by the legislature." The elected assembly would nominate ten persons to serve on the governor's council. Every nominee had to be a resident; and each had to be "possessed of a freehold in five hundred acres of land." Congress would select five councilmen from these ten nominees. The governor, council, and house had authority "to make laws," so long as the laws were "not repugnant" to the ordinance—again, somewhat like Parliament's former power over the colonies. When sixty thousand free inhabitants lived in the territory, the territory was eligible for the third stage—statehood.

The pattern set by the Ordinance was both durable and workable. It guided the territories of the old Northwest and Southwest smoothly along a road that led to statehood.[5] There was none of the usual colonial unrest. The Wisconsin Territorial Act of 1836 established a somewhat different model.[6] It eliminated the first stage of territorial life. This act also junked property qualifications; and (male) voters elected the legislature directly. The new model also paid more attention to details of court organization. Wisconsin's law, for example, specified "a supreme court, district courts, probate courts, and . . . justices of the peace."[7] But even in this, and later territorial laws, there were strong echoes of the Northwest Ordinance. Residents of Wisconsin Territory were guaranteed "all the similar rights, privileges, and advantages granted and secured to the people of the territory of the United States northwest of the river Ohio, by the articles of the compact, contained in the ordinance for the government of the said territory, passed on the thirteenth day of July, one thousand seven hundred and eighty-seven."

These laws are a kind of outer skin; they tell us very little about the living law of the American frontier. Research has dispelled some myths and legends about frontier law and added to the stock of new knowledge. Civilization advanced in undulating waves, generally along river valleys. Law followed the ax. Of course, the land was not empty before the Americans came. There were native tribes scattered throughout the area. In the Mississippi Valley, a cluster of Frenchmen lived in villages along the Mississippi, governed by the kind of rough mixture of Spanish and French law that prevailed in Louisiana. The Americans, by sheer force of numbers, overwhelmed this alien system (more on this later).

Frontier law has a reputation for crudity—rough men of the forest administering rough justice, at least until the settlers (and the opportunists) arrived. If we can believe some of the tales of the pioneers, there were early courts in which justice was drunken, corrupt, and intensely idiosyncratic. At Green Bay, in 1816, two decades before Wisconsin Territory was established, an "old

---

[5] Louisiana and Florida territories were handled differently.

[6] See Joseph A. Ranney, *Trusting Nothing to Providence: A History of Wisconsin's Legal System* (1999), pp. 27–31.

[7] Act Establishing the Terr. Govt. of Wisconsin (1836), sec. 9.

Frenchman" named Charles Reaume, who "could read and write a little," acted as justice of the peace. In his court, it was said, "a bottle of spirits was the best witness that could be introduced." Once, when the losing party scraped up some whiskey for the judge, Reaume ordered a new trial and reversed his prior decision, on the strength of this "witness." Reaume's "court" was a long, difficult journey from the county seat. His word, in effect, was final. He took care not to decide cases against those traders who were "able to bear the expense of an appeal"; hence, his incompetence was not exposed to a wider public. At Prairie du Chien, at the same period, Nicholas Boilvin, a French-Canadian, was "clothed with the dignified office . . . of Justice of the Peace." Boilvin was as uneducated as Reaume. He owned a library of exactly three law books: the statutes of Northwest, Missouri, and Illinois territories. But in deciding a case, "he paid no attention to the statute"; he merely "decided according to his own idea of right and wrong."[8]

Polish and legal skill were in short supply, too, in the Illinois country. A small group of amateur lawyers, merchants, and political adventurers ran the government. The staple business of the courts was litigation on land claims and grants. The judges were speculators themselves, and judged their own claims. A federal board of land commissioners was appointed in 1804 to investigate land claims in the Illinois country. The board uncovered "incredible forgeries, fraud, subornation and perjuries," the "very mire and filth of corruption."[9] A certain Robert Reynolds had rushed to file claims with the commissioners, which was an act of great "effrontery," since Reynolds "forged the names of witnesses, deponents and grantors . . . gave depositions under an assumed name, and appeared before a magistrate with deponents who deposed under false names for his benefit. He forged a grant to himself from a slave woman."[10] Yet, Reynolds had once been a judge. He had been appointed a county court judge in 1801 and "attended very regularly to his duties."

Reynolds was not the only forging judge. He was, however, probably the only one ever indicted for fraud; and his indictment, it was said, owed more to his political enemies than to public outrage. Even after Illinois became a state, "a great rascal" named William P. Foster served on the state supreme court. According to Governor Thomas Ford, Foster was "no lawyer, never having either studied or practised law; but . . . a man of winning, polished manners, and . . . withal a very gentlemanly swindler." Foster was assigned to hold courts "in the circuit on the Wabash; but being fearful of exposing his utter incompetency, he never went near any of them." After a year he resigned, pocketed his salary, and left the state to become a "noted swindler, moving from city to city, and living by swindling strangers, and prostituting his daughters, who were very beautiful."[11]

Life was undeniably violent and crude in parts of the frontier. Henry Marie Brackenridge visited Missouri in 1810–1811. He saw lawyers and judges who

---

[8] James H. Lockwood, "Early Times and Events in Wisconsin," Second Annual Report and Collections of the State Historical Society of Wisconsin, vol. II (1856), pp. 98, 105, 106, 126.

[9] Francis S. Philbrick, ed., The Laws of Indiana Territory, 1801–9 (1930), lxxxvii.

[10] Ibid., lxxxix–xc.

[11] Governor Thomas Ford, A History of Illinois from Its Commencement as a State in 1818 to 1847 (1854), p. 29.

went about armed with pistols and knives. Duels were an everyday affair.[12] Governor Ford of Illinois has given us a graphic description of a trial court at work in Illinois around 1818:

> The judges . . . held their courts mostly in log-houses, or in the barrooms of taverns, fitted up with a temporary bench for the judge and chairs or benches for the lawyers and jurors. At the first circuit court in Washington county, held by Judge John Reynolds, the sheriff, on opening the court, went out into the court-yard and said to the people: "Boys, come in, our John is going to hold court." This was the proclamation for opening the court. In general, the judges were averse to deciding questions of law if they could possibly avoid doing so. They did not like the responsibility of offending one or the other of the parties, and preferred to submit everything they could to be decided by the jury. They never gave instructions to a jury unless expressly called for; and then only upon the points of law raised by counsel in asking for them. They never commented upon the evidence, or undertook to show the jury what inferences and presumptions might be drawn from it; for which reason they delivered their instructions hypothetically, stating them thus: "If the jury believe from the evidence that such a matter is proved, then the law is so and so." This was a clear departure from the practice of the judges in England and most of the United States; but the new practice suited the circumstances of the country. It undoubtedly requires the highest order of talent in a judge to "sum up" the evidence rightly to a jury, so as to do justice to the case, and injustice to neither party. Such talent did not exist to be put on the bench in these early times; or at least the judges must have modestly believed that they did not possess it.[13]

Still, Ford felt that the judges were "gentlemen of considerable learning and much good sense." In Eastern trial courts, too, judges were losing their power to comment on evidence, for reasons already explored. The diffidence of the judges, then, like a lot of other behavior labeled as "frontier" behavior, was part of the mainstream of American legal life. Reynold's court was lax and informal; but so are traffic courts and municipal courts today.

People liked to tell these entertaining stories about the early years of the territories and the frontier states. But there was also trained legal talent on the frontier, along with the fraud and the animal cunning. The level of legal sophistication in a community depended on its size, on its economic base, and on whether it was close to the centers of government. Men like Reaume and Foster were perhaps distortions or exceptions. After territorial government was organized, the "primitive" stage of frontier justice usually ended for good. Samuel Holden Parsons and James Mitchell Varnum, solid lawyers with good reputations, were among the first judges of Northwest Territory. In Michigan Territory, Augustus Brevoort Woodward, a versatile, cultured lawyer with a

---

[12] William F. Keller, *The Nation's Advocate: Henry Marie Brackenridge and Young America* (1956), pp. 101, 104. It may be worth mentioning, however, that the most famous duel among lawyers was the duel in which Aaron Burr killed Alexander Hamilton, who was (among other things) a successful commercial lawyer at New York. The duel took place, not on the frontier, but in Weehawken, New Jersey. Dueling was also common in the South, frontier or not, as an aspect of the Southern code of honor. See Edward L. Ayers, *Vengeance and Justice: Crime and Punishment in the Nineteenth-Century American South* (1984), ch. 1.

[13] Ford, *op. cit.*, pp. 82–83.

college education, compiled the Woodward Code, a collection of thirty-four laws adopted in 1805. The governor of Michigan was also a lawyer, and another Michigan judge had studied law, though he had never practiced.[14] Woodward later became a territorial judge in Florida; and the judges in that territory were said to be men of learning, and in general, "excellent." William Marvin, one of these judges, became an expert on the law of the sea and published a *Treatise on Wreck and Salvage* in 1858.[15]

In time, a mobile, vigorous bar flourished in the West: a bar made up of quick-witted, adventurous young operators. Law practice required their full cunning. Joseph G. Baldwin (1815–1864) described them, with frontier hyperbole, as they were during the "flush times" of Alabama and Mississippi. In those days:

> many land titles were defective; property was brought from other States clogged with trusts, limitations, and uses . . . universal indebtedness . . . made it impossible for many men to pay, and desirable for all to escape paying . . . a general looseness, ignorance and carelessness in the public officers . . . new statutes to be construed . . . an elegant assortment of frauds constructive and actual . . . in short, all the flood-gates of litigation were opened, and the pent-up tide let loose upon the country. And such a criminal docket! What country could boast more largely of its crimes? What more splendid role of felonies! What more terrific murders! What more gorgeous bank robberies! What more magnificent operations in the land offices! . . . Such superb forays on the treasuries, State and National! . . . And in INDIAN affairs! . . . the romance of a wild and weird larceny! . . . Swindling Indians by the nation! . . . Stealing their land by the township! . . . Many members of the bar, of standing and character, from the other States, flocked in to put their sickles into this abundant harvest.[16]

There were fortunes to be made. The new states and territories were ripe for the plucking, ripe with careers for ambitious young men. The economic base was land: town land and country land. Who had the skill to decipher titles to land? Who could master the maze of rules on land grants, or on the sale and transfer of land? Only the lawyers. Government jobs were another rich plum. The territories at first were net importers of the taxpayer's money. Judgeships and clerkships were patronage jobs, to be given out in Washington. Local jobs became available by the thousands in courts, in legislatures, and in the executive branch, and in territory, state, county, and town. The lawyer, again, was peculiarly suited for these jobs. He scrambled for public office. He also collected debts for Eastern creditors; he dabbled in land speculation and townsite booming. He scrounged around for any niche that took skill and know-how. He was a jack-of-all-trades. He did whatever his nose sniffed out as promising and lucrative. Not every young lawyer made it. Many of them failed and moved on to other jobs or places. Others stayed the course; some became rich and prominent.

[14] William W. Blume, "Legislation on the American Frontier," 60 Mich. L Rev. S17 (1962).

[15] James M. Denham, *"A Rogue's Paradise"; Crime and Punishment in Antebellum Florida, 1821–1861* (1997), pp. 27–28.

[16] Joseph G. Baldwin, *The Flush Times of Alabama and Mississippi: A Series of Sketches* (1957 ed.), pp. 173–74. See also Elizabeth G. Brown, "The Bar on a Frontier: Wayne County, 1796–1836," 14 Am. J. Legal Hist. 136 (1970).

The lawyers of the West were a mixed lot. If we can believe Baldwin, at the bar of the old Southwest there were "no seniors: the bar is all Young America. If the old fogies come in, they must stand in the class with the rest."[17] Some of these young lawyers had gone West after college and clerkship. Others learned their law as they went along. In any case, frontier law was not book law in the usual sense. There were no libraries, and books were expensive. The practice put no premium on erudition. The best trial lawyers used and enjoyed good tricks, jokes, a neat technicality or two. The poverty of source materials left a vacuum, filled in by Blackstone, local statutes, and native wit. Few lawyers were well enough trained to be able to distinguish the fossils in Blackstone from the living law back East. For this reason, court law was, simultaneously, free-wheeling and curiously archaic. The papers of Thomas Rodney, judge in the old Southwest (1803–1811), preserve such museum pieces as the writ of account and *de homine replegiando*.[18] Rodney wrote that "Special Pleading is adhered to in our Courts with as much Strictness Elegance and propriety as in any of the States, so that Even the young Lawyers are obliged to read their books and be very attentive to their business or want bread."[19] In one equity proceeding, when a litigant objected that "the practice in G[reat] B[ritain] does not apply here," the judges replied:

> We Shall be guided by The practice in England So far as it is admissible here because there is no Other Safe and Regular guide, for there it has been brought to perfection by long Experience and the practice of the ablest Judges, and being Contained in their books of practice They can always be resorted to—without which the practice here would be always irregular and Uncertain.[20]

Professor William W. Blume studied the work of the court of common pleas of Wayne County, Michigan (1796–1805). He saw

> almost no evidence of the informality often supposed to be a characteristic of frontier justice. Instead, we find a strict compliance with applicable statutes, and, where the procedure was not governed by statute, with the English common law.[21]

Though most territorial statutes had been passed or adopted to solve real problems of legal behavior or the organization of the legal system, a few of these, too, had the musty air of museum pieces. The laws of Michigan mentioned essoins and wager of law, no doubt needlessly; most lawyers would have been just as bewildered by these medieval rags and tatters as the layman. The first Illinois legislature "imported [laws] . . . for the inspection of hemp and tobacco, when there was neither hemp nor tobacco raised in the country."[22]

---

[17] Baldwin, *op. cit.*, p. 171.

[18] The writ, literally "for replevying a man," was a means of procuring the release of a prisoner—an earlier equivalent of the writ of *habeas corpus*.

[19] William Baskerville Hamilton, *Anglo-American Law of the Frontier: Thomas Rodney and His Territorial Cases* (1953), pp. 137–38.

[20] Hamilton, *op. cit.*, p. 197.

[21] William W. Blume, "Civil Procedure on the American Frontier," 56 Mich. L. Rev. 161, 209 (1957); to the same effect, Cornelia Anne Clark, "Justice on the Tennessee Frontier: The Williamson County Circuit Court, 1810–1820," 32 Vanderbilt L. Rev. 413 (1979).

[22] Ford, *op. cit.*, p. 34.

Blume and Elizabeth Brown found in frontier law "two general attitudes and resultant influences attributable to frontier life." The first was a "strong desire to have all statute law published locally so that reliance on laws not available on the frontier would be unnecessary—codes were welcome." The second was a "lack of 'superstitious respect' for old laws and legal institutions; in other words—a readiness to make changes to suit new conditions."[23] These attributes of frontier law—archaism and hypertechnicality on the one hand, crudity, rough-hewn justice, and frontier impatience with form on the other—were not as inconsistent as they might seem. They flowed from the need to make law work in a transplanted setting. The Western communities swallowed batches of old law whole. This was not because of some sentimental attachment to tradition, but because this course of action was, under the circumstances, the most efficient way to get on with the job. There was neither time nor skill to make it all up anew; to use borrowed law was like buying clothes off the rack, or renting a whole suite of furniture at once.

Once a territory became a state, it had complete power to make and unmake its own laws, and to do exactly as it (or its electorate) liked. There was, in fact, a great deal of continuity, just as there was in the thirteen original states after they broke away from England. The common law survived everywhere. Governor Ford thought that Western legislatures passed too many laws, that they overturned too much too soon: "A session of the legislature was like a great fire in the boundless prairies of the State; it consumed everything. And again, it was like the genial breath of spring, making all things new."[24] But this was almost certainly a gross exaggeration. The statute books of the Northwest states were, by modern standards, skimpy and undernourished. New states and territories had no time, skill, or inclination to make up law all over again. They were faithful, on the whole, to what they inherited. Ohio, even after it became a state, kept the statutes left over from its days as part of the Northwest Territory. The territorial laws were handed on to Indiana Territory (1800); Indiana passed them to Michigan and Illinois territories (1809); Michigan Territory was the source of the earliest laws of Wisconsin Territory (1836), which in turn delivered them to Iowa (1838) and Minnesota (1849). In the Southwest, the line went from Louisiana to Missouri Territory (1812), from there to Arkansas (1819), and from Mississippi to Alabama (1817).

In most cases, the basic process was simple: The old territory divided, like an amoeba, into two pieces; and the laws of the original territory now governed in both parts.[25] Without particular thought or debate, a bundle of well-worn statutes traveled on to new jurisdictions. The old "statute of frauds" (a law that required certain types of contract to be in writing) and the statutes of limitations (laws cutting off lawsuits that become too stale) traveled cross-country without major change. In 1799, Northwest Territory enacted a statute "making Promissory Notes and Inland Bills of Exchange negotiable"—another standard

[23] William W. Blume and Elizabeth G. Brown, "Territorial Courts and Law: Unifying Factors in the Development of American Legal Institutions," Part II, 61 Mich. L. Rev. 467, 535 (1963).

[24] Ford, *op. cit.*, p. 32.

[25] William W. Blume and Elizabeth G. Brown, "Territorial Courts and the Law," Part II, 61 Mich. L. Rev. 467, 474–75 (1963).

American law. Such statutes became part of the basic legal framework. Town laws, election laws, laws about the militia, tax laws, laws on court process: All were freely borrowed and passed along from jurisdiction to jurisdiction.

In time, some of the new states repaid their legal debt. They trained new legal and political leaders. Henry Clay (born and educated in Virginia), Thomas Hart Benton, and Abraham Lincoln were all Western lawyers. The West was mobile, fluid; like the colonies in comparison to Britain, it was freer from the dead hand of the past, freer from the friction and inertia of tradition. Out of the West, then, came legal innovations that became enduring features of the law. The homestead exemption began in Texas; from there, it spread to the North and the East. The first Married Women's Property Act, oddly enough, was passed in Mississippi. A number of important legal institutions began life in experimental milieus, on the outskirts of American society.

THE CIVIL LAW FRINGE

In the first generation of independence, the civil law domain, vast but sparsely settled, encircled the domain of the common law. Civil law—French and Spanish—governed along the Mississippi and the river bottoms of its tributaries; in Kaskaskia, St. Louis, New Madrid, and St. Charles; in the bustling port of New Orleans; in the Floridas; and in Texas. When this empire became American property, it fell subject to American government and law.

A massive invasion of settlers doomed the civil law everywhere, except in Louisiana. The new judges and lawyers were trained in the common law tradition. They supplanted judges of French and Spanish background. The United States did not disturb, in general, rights of property that had vested under civil law. In fact, American courts had to wrestle for years with civil law problems of land law, family law, laws of descent and inheritance. Among Thomas Rodney's papers, from the Natchez district, are case records in which points at issue were resolved by reference to Spanish law or jurisprudence, translated for the benefit of jury and court.[26] The Northwest Ordinance, after prescribing its own rules about wills and inheritance, promised to preserve, for "the French and Canadian inhabitants, and other settlers of the Kaskaskies, Saint Vincents, and the neighboring villages," the benefit of "their laws and customs now in force among them, relative to the descent and conveyance of property."

But it was American policy to Americanize the law, thoroughly, and as quickly as possible. The area that later became the state of Missouri had a small population, mostly French speaking. But within a year of the Louisiana purchase, American lawyers flocked into the old river town of St. Louis, where Spanish law was technically in force, supplemented by French customs. These lawyers entered what they thought of as almost a legal void; they and the judges had to deal with "Laws of which we know nothing."[27] This situation did not last very long. From the very first, American officials aimed "to assimilate by insensible means, the habits and customs of the American and French inhabitants; by

---

[26] E.g., Hamilton, *op. cit.*, p. 176.

[27] Stuart Banner, *Legal Systems in Conflict: Property and Sovereignty in Missouri, 1750–1860* (2000), pp. 96–98.

interweaving some of the regulations of the latter into our Laws, we procure a ready obedience, without violence or complaint."[28] As the American population increased, more direct action supplemented these gentle and "insensible means." A statute of 1807, applicable to what became Missouri Territory, repealed the civil law on wills and inheritance and introduced American intestacy laws and laws about wills. American lawyers lobbied successfully for a law that made the common law of England the basis of law in Missouri Territory (1816). Crowds of Anglos soon outnumbered the speakers of French. For a while, on issues of land law and the like, Spanish law remained relevant. But by the time it entered the Union, Missouri had little left of its civil law past, except for some tangled land titles and a passion for procedural simplicity.

The French in Illinois were similarly doomed to lose their legal inheritance. The guarantee of the Ordinance applied only to laws of succession. The French were immediately subjected to an elaborate county and township organization, on the model developed in the British colonies, despite the fact that they had "retained in their isolation . . . the political and economic traditions of the France of Louis XIV, of common fields and manorial organization."[29] American officials had no particular sympathy for the culture of French settlers. Judge John C. Symmes, who came to Vincennes in 1790, reacted to the French with chauvinistic disgust. They "will not relish a free government," he wrote. "They say our laws are too complex, not to be understood, and tedious in their operation—the command or order of the Military commandant is better law and speedier justice for them and what they prefer to all the legal systems found in Littleton and Blackstone. It is a language which they say they can understand, it is cheap and expeditious and they wish for no other."[30] Traces of French *coutumes* lingered on briefly in family law. Gradually, French law and language disappeared.

An indigenous law, without prestige and in a minority status, can hardly survive. The sheer mass of American settlers easily conquered Spanish law in Florida; the original population was sparse. In 1821, Andrew Jackson imposed, by proclamation, common-law procedure in criminal cases, including the right to trial by jury. But Spanish law had gained only a temporary reprieve even in civil cases. In 1829, a statute established the common law, and English statutes passed before 1776, as norms of decision in the territory. The Spanish period left behind, in the end, only a few archeological traces in the law of Florida.

Spanish-Mexican law left a much greater imprint on Texas. Partly, this was because Texas was rather fully formed, as a polity, before it passed into American hands. Here, too, however, trial by jury was an early import. The constitution of Coahuila and Texas (1827), during the Mexican period, exhorted the legislature, as one of its "principal subjects," to enact legislation "to establish, in criminal cases, the trial by jury, extending it gradually, and even adopting it in civil cases, in proportion as the advantages of this precious institution may be practically developed."[31] American settlers probably pressed

---

[28] Judge John Coburn to Secretary of State James Madison, 1807, quoted in William F. English, *The Pioneer Lawyer and Jurist in Missouri* (1947), p. 56.

[29] Francis S. Philbrick, *The Laws of Indiana Territory, 1801–1809* (1930), ccxviii.

[30] Quoted in Philbrick, *op. cit.*, ccxvi–ccxvii.

[31] Coahuila and Texas Const., 1827. sec. 192.

for this enactment. The Texas government later enacted a form of trial by jury, but not exactly in the American mold.[32] The constitution of the republic of Texas (1836), in its declaration of rights, affirmed the right of an accused "to a speedy and public trial, by an impartial jury. . . . And the right of trial by jury shall remain inviolate."

The Texas Constitution also contemplated wholesale adoption of the common law. "Congress," it said, "shall, as early as practicable, introduce, by statute, the common law of England, with such modifications as our circumstances, in their judgment, may require" (art. IV, sec. 13). But Texas never really "received" English law in any literal or classical sense. Rather, the republic adopted a Texas subdialect of the American dialect of law. There was thoroughgoing acceptance of trial by jury, "that ever-to-be prized system of jurisprudence," as the supreme court of Texas called it in 1840.[33] From the very start, however, court organization and procedure merged law and equity. The constitution of 1845 specifically gave to the district courts jurisdiction "of all suits . . . without regard to any distinction between law and equity."[34] In 1840, the civil law was formally abolished; but Texas never fell under the yoke of common-law pleading in all its rigor. Rather, Texas retained "as heretofore" the civil law system of "petition and answer." Procedure was, in short, a kind of hybrid system. Judges and lawyers, in the early years, seemed genuinely ambivalent about which of the two rival systems had the edge. On the one hand, civil law was strange and unfamiliar to most lawyers. The law of 1840, since it kept some aspects of civil law pleading, put courts in the position (as one judge said) of searching for "principles and criteria in a language generally unknown to us." This brought about "constant perplexities," which annoyed and delayed the courts "at each step."[35] Yet another Texas judge condemned common-law pleading as "Bold, crafty, and unscrupulous."[36] Still, a third judge took a middle view:

> The object of our statutes on the subject of pleading is to simplify as much as possible that branch of the proceedings in courts, which by the ingenuity and learning of both common and civil law lawyers and judges had become so refined in its subtleties as to substitute in many instances the shadow for the substance.[37]

In the long run, the common law was bound to win. The civil law tradition was too alien and inaccessible to survive. But the practice in Texas did undermine the idea that strict common law pleading was either natural or desirable. What resulted was a procedure that used common law terms and some common law attitudes, but in a more streamlined and rational way. Peripheral Texas was, in short, free to do what other states could do only by breaking with habit and tradition. But in Texas, divergences from the common law did not

---

[32] Edward L. Markham Jr., "The Reception of the Common Law of England in Texas and the Judicial Attitude Toward That Reception, 1840–1859," 29 Texas L. Rev. 904 (1951).

[33] *Edwards v. Peoples,* Dallam 359, 360 (Tex., 1840).

[34] Texas Const., 1845, art. IV, sec. 10. On Texas procedure, see Joseph W. McKnight, "The Spanish Legacy to Texas Law," 3 Am. J. Legal Hist. 222, 299 (1959).

[35] *Whiting v. Turley,* Dallam 453, 454 (Tex., 1842).

[36] *Long v. Anderson,* 4 Tex. 422, 424 (1849).

[37] *Hamilton v. Black,* Dallam 586, 587 (Tex., 1844).

look like reforms; they looked like civil law survivals. In a sense they were; what survived, however, survived because it suited the needs and wants of Texas jurists.

Chunks of civil law also remained imbedded in the substantive law of Texas as well. Texas recognizes the holographic will—an unwitnessed will in the dead person's handwriting. Texas has also kept the community property system; indeed, Texas gave the system constitutional recognition.[38] Texas shares these "survivals" with Louisiana, and with a number of states carved out of Mexican territory, notably California. That these institutions lived on, despite the terrific pressure for common law, indicates either that they were tightly sewn into the social fabric, or that they fulfilled some unique social function. The holographic will, for example, invited ordinary people to make wills by themselves, without consulting lawyers. The community property system, too, may have suited the facts of family life better than common law rules of marital property. In fact, the common law rules were themselves in process of change.

Louisiana was the only solid, durable enclave of civil law. Here America swallowed up a territory with a sizeable population, a population centered in New Orleans, that was used to civil law forms. But Louisiana itself was in a state of great confusion. Its brand of civil law was a far cry from the elegance and system we associate with the civil law in nineteenth century Europe. At the time of the Louisiana Purchase, Louisiana law was an arcane, bewildering hodgepodge of French and Spanish law, a melange of codes, customs, and doctrines of various ages. The French had settled Louisiana, but the Spanish had governed it from 1766 to 1803. Louisiana law was as baffling as the common law at its worst. Its "babel" of legislation, according to Edward Livingston, was only equaled by the "Dissonances" of the Court of Pleas, "where American Shop keepers, French planters and Spanish clerks sit on the same bench," listening to "American Attorneys, French procureurs and Castillian Abogados," each speaking his own language.[39]

In Louisiana, too, the usual conflict developed between the native population and incoming lawyers and judges.[40] Jefferson was anxious to Americanize the government and law. He appointed the governor and the territorial judges. But the Creole population was a continuing problem. The territorial legislature, in 1806, under some pressure to move toward common law, was willing to accept trial by jury in criminal cases, along with the writ of *habeas corpus,* but otherwise declared the civil law in force, that is, the "Roman Civil code . . . which is composed of the institutes, digest and code of the emperor Justinian, aided by the authority of the commentators of the civil law. . . . The Spanish law, consisting of the books of the *recopilación de Castilla* and *autos acordados* . . . the seven parts or *partidas* of the King Don Alphonse the learned [and others] . . . the ordinances

[38] Texas Const., 1845, art. VII, sec. 19.

[39] Quoted in George Dargo, *Jefferson's Louisiana: Politics and the Clash of Legal Traditions* (1975), p. 112.

[40] See, in general, Elizabeth G. Brown, "Legal Systems in Conflict: Orleans Territory, 1804–1812," 1 Am. J. Legal Hist. 35 (1957); further, on the "intricate task of fusing alien French and Spanish legal customs with Anglo-American precepts of law and justice," see Mark F. Fernandez, "Local Justice in the Territory of Orleans," in Warren M. Billings and Mark F. Fernandez, eds., *A Law unto Itself? Essays in the New Louisiana Legal History* (2001), p. 79. The quote is from *ibid.,* at 84.

and royal orders and decrees [applicable to] . . . the colony of Louisiana"; and "in matters of commerce," the "ordinance of Bilbao," supplemented by "Roman laws," a number of named English and civil law treatises, "the commentaries of Valin," and "the respectable authors consulted in the United States." Governor William Charles Claiborne vetoed the law. The legislature was under the control of the Creole population; and Claiborne felt the law of 1806 was particularly dangerous.[41]

The matter did not end there. The leading Creole residents of Louisiana clamored for a code, to clarify the law and to ensure them against sudden, disruptive change in their social and economic status. They wanted familiar law in a workable form. The Digest of 1808, designed to bring order out of chaos, was influenced by drafts of the new French code, the Code Napoleon. This Louisiana code, then, was a civil law code to the core; but it remains a question whether the law of Louisiana was more French than Spanish or more Spanish than French. People in Louisiana actually *spoke* French; but Louisiana judges often drew on elements of the older Spanish tradition.[42] According to a careful student of the period in Louisiana, the civil code adopted in 1808 ultimately "was the political compromise on the basis of which the settled population of Lower Louisiana finally accepted permanent American rule." Essentially, the Jefferson administration accepted the code, and thereby gave up the chance of completely Americanizing Louisiana, in return for a speedier and less bumpy absorption of "what was essentially a colonial possession."[43] The compromise worked, and outlasted the code itself. The supreme court of Louisiana later held (in 1817) that the code of 1808 had not driven out all of the old Spanish law. "Our civil code," said the court, "is a digest of the civil laws, which were in force in this country, when it was adopted"; those laws "must be considered as untouched," wherever the "alterations and amendments, introduced in the digest, do not reach them."[44] This decision brought back a certain amount of confusion, as in the days before the code, when the civil law of Louisiana was "an indigested mass of ancient edicts and Statutes . . . the whole rendered more obscure by the

[41] Dargo, *op. cit.*, p. 136.

[42] On this issue, see Richard Holcombe Kilbourne Jr., *A History of the Louisiana Civil Code: The Formative Years, 1803–1839* (1987); Mark F. Fernandez, *From Chaos to Continuity: The Evolution of Louisiana's Judicial System, 1712–1862* (2001).

[43] Dargo, *op cit*, p. 173. The actual sources of the code of 1808 are far from clear; basically, the code seemed to be French, with a certain Spanish element, but there is great doubt, and much arguing among scholars, as to the precise weighting of the two. On this point, see Dargo, *op. cit.*, pp. 155–64. Whatever the facts about the code itself, there is evidence that the courts cited Spanish authorities almost as much as they cited French ones. See Raphael J. Rabalais, "The Influence of Spanish Laws and Treatises on the Jurisprudence of Louisiana, 1762–1828," 42 La. L. Rev. 1485 (1982).

The living law of the territory, the actual legal customs of the people, is still another matter. Hans Baade has examined marriage contracts in French and Spanish Louisiana and concluded that French "legal folkways" with regard to marital property were dominant before Spanish rule; that they continued in some parts of the territory during Spanish rule; and that they popped back into full vigor throughout the colony when Spanish rule ended in 1803. Hans W. Baade, "Marriage Contracts in French and Spanish Louisiana: A Study in 'Notarial' Jurisprudence," 53 Tulane L. Rev. 3 (1978).

[44] *Cottin v. Cottin,* 5 Mart. (O.S.), 93, 94 (1817).

heavy attempts of commentators to explain them."[45] At legislative request, Louis Moreau Lislet and Henry Carleton translated and published "The Laws of Las Siete Partidas which are still in force in the State of Louisiana" in 1820. The legislature also moved to recodify the basic law of Louisiana. They appointed three commissioners for this purpose. These commissioners drafted what became the famous Civil Code of 1825. The leading figure in drafting this code was Edward Livingston. He was a New Yorker, devoted to law reform, who found fertile soil for his talents in Louisiana. About 80 percent of the code's provisions were drawn directly from the Code Napoleon. French legal commentary was another important source. The common law had some influence, particularly on the law of obligations. The special needs of Louisiana were only one factor in the minds of the commissioners. They also wanted to prove that a pure, rational system of law was attainable in America:

> They rejected the undefined and undefinable common law. . . . [In England] the Judge drew his own rule, sometimes with Lord Mansfield, from the pure fountain of the Civil Code, sometimes from the turbid stream of doubtful usage, often from no better source than his own caprice. . . . [In Louisiana] our Code . . . will be progressing toward perfection. . . . the Legislature will not judge, nor the Judiciary make laws. . . . [W]e may hope to have the rare and inestimable blessing of written Codes, containing intelligible and certain rules to govern the ordinary relations and occurrences of life, the operations of commerce and the pursuit of remedies by action.[46]

As the quotation shows, the commissioners expected that the civil code would be only the first of a series. By 1825, a code of practice was adopted as well. It was one of the most original of the codes. It blended French, Spanish, and common-law forms into a skillful, efficient whole. The code of 1805 had asserted that common-law writs had to "pursue the forms, and be conducted according to the rules and regulations prescribed by the common law"; no such provision appeared in the new code. Louisiana, then, basically came to use a tripartite system of procedure, vaguely similar to the compromise in Texas. The court structure was American. Some aspects of the common law were preserved, notably trial by jury in criminal cases. The rest of the system joined together two civil-law streams. In Texas, common law had the upper hand, in Louisiana civil law. In both cases, the blend was more streamlined and efficient than the common law, at least in its nineteenth-century version. Other states, less free to innovate, took more time to shake off the shackles of old common law forms.

Once the legislature in Louisiana had enacted a civil code and a code of procedure, it seem to lose its zest for novelties. A proposed code of commerce was never adopted.[47] Livingston's codes of evidence and criminal law were too advanced for the legislature to swallow. The age of innovation passed. French language and French customs also slowly lost their grip. The civil law substrate remained solid, but in translation. The constitution of 1812 expressly

---

[45] Quoted in William B. Hatcher, *Edward Livingston* (1940), p. 247. For Livingston's role in the making of the civil code of 1825, see ch. 11, "The Codifier," pp. 245–88.

[46] Louisiana Legal Archives, vol. 1 (1937), xcii.

[47] The civil code already covered some aspects of commercial law.

provided that the legislature "shall never adopt any system or code of laws, by a general reference to the said system or code, but in all cases, shall specify the several provisions of the laws it may enact" (art. IV, sec. 2). This was meant to rule out a general statute purporting to "receive" the common law. The gesture was probably unnecessary. The civil law, like the right to trial by "an impartial jury of the vicinage"[48] (also preserved by the constitution), was too important to the people who mattered in New Orleans. They were used to it; they did business by it. The codes survived the destruction of a distinctive French culture. They became an element of Louisiana's legal culture—part of the learning and lore of lawyers, part of the life and experience of consumers of law. Because of this, the costs of changing the system—social and educational costs—seemed much greater than any possible gains from matching the law of the neighboring states. The goal of the codes was clear, concise, and useful law, law that a man could count on and do business by, law that could be easily mastered. To the old-line residents, the common-law system was a weird and foreign chaos. What is clear is that, in the main, Louisiana's codes, like the pleading system in Texas, cannot be shrugged off as some sort of accident, some sort of survival or accident of evolution, like the vermiform appendix in the human body. Rather, the codes reworked and refined an inherited legal culture, along paths of reform—paths that ran parallel to those the common law itself would ultimately follow.[49]

In Louisiana, the distinctive legal tradition has become a matter of local pride. Jurists treasure their membership in the great civil law family. Stanley Kowalski, hardly a jurist, in Tennessee William's *Streetcar Named Desire*, mentions the Napoleonic Code. It is natural, and easy, to overstate differences between Louisiana's legal culture and that of (say) Arkansas or Texas. Louisiana is part of a federal system and is subject to federal law. That was significant even in the early nineteenth century. It has grown more so with the passage of time. Louisiana shares a common economic system with its neighbors, and a common culture. The political system is somewhat flamboyant, but not much more so than in Mississippi or Alabama. American settlers streamed in and out across the border, neither noticing nor caring, by and large, that they crossed a frontier between civil and common law. Attitudes toward law and expectations about law, one guesses, are more or less the same in Shreveport as in Little Rock or Natchez. The cultural elements of Louisiana law were and are closer to Mississippi and Texas than to Ecuador or France. Whole raw pieces of common law—such as the trust—were eventually absorbed by Louisiana. Much new law that was added during the nineteenth century was not noticeably "civil law" in its content: business law, railroad law, and the law of slaves. The civil law lives on in Louisiana, but mostly as lawyers' law and lawyers' process. In most other essential regards, Louisiana law has long since joined the Union.

---

[48] Louisiana Const., 1812, art. VI, sec. 18.

[49] The same 1812 constitution, which forbade a change to the common-law system, declared that all laws and public records had to be in "the language in which the constitution of the United States is written" and the same for "judicial and legislative . . . proceedings," Louisiana Const., 1812, art. VI, sec. 15. For those who did not speak French, French was a nuisance. This callous attitude toward the historic tongue of the settlers suggests obliquely that the preservation of the civil law in Louisiana owed precious little to sentiment.

CHAPTER 3

LAW AND THE ECONOMY: 1776–1850

LAISSEZ-FAIRE AND ITS LIMITS

By reputation, the nineteenth century was the high noon of *laissez-faire*. Government, by habit and design, supposedly kept its heavy hands off the economy. But when we actually burrow into the past, what we find is much more complicated. Yes, it is true that, for much of the century, opinion leaders and official policy strongly supported business, growth, and production. In particular, the first half of the century was a period of promotion of enterprise. Policy aimed—in Willard Hurst's phrase—at the release of creative energy; and that meant economic energy, enterprise energy. Government reflected what its constituents wanted. It did what it could to help the economy grow. Where this meant subsidy or intervention, theories and dogmas rarely held government back. This puts the case somewhat negatively. In fact, as William Novak has argued, people in the nineteenth century believed that government had a positive obligation to "further the welfare of the whole people and community."[1]

If we talk about government intervention, or government regulation, in the first half of the nineteenth century, we are talking primarily about the states, not the federal government. We are so used to a big central government that we forget that the country was local, fragmented, disjointed, in 1800 or 1830. We forget that the federal government was tiny; we forget how little it actually did. Legal literature never has given the states their due. National events seemed so much more important than what happened in the towns and localities. Dramatic and striking events, acted out on a national stage—the growing storm over slavery and the slave trade; or the delicate relationship between state and federal governments; or the debates over tariff policy, a national banking system, and internal improvements—these captured the attention of most scholars. This left little room for a Vermont statute on the licensing of peddlers. But to draw an accurate picture of law and the economy, we have to look closely at what went on in states and counties and townships and towns.

The federal government was not totally passive. There was some pressure to build big works of internal improvement; this actually bore some fruit in the National Road. The federal effort was not frustrated by a *laissez-faire* philosophy;

---

[1] William N. Novak, *The People's Welfare: Law and Regulation in Nineteenth-Century America* (1996), p. 9.

the "real issue," rather, was "between national and state action."[2] Generally speaking, the states carried the day. The federal government owned no railroads and acts of Congress showed little awareness of railroads before the Civil War. But this did not mean that the effort to build railroads was essentially, as in England, private. There was feverish activity in the states. The Pennsylvania Railroad was once quite literally the railroad of the state of Pennsylvania. The state of Georgia built a railroad, too—the Western and Atlantic Railroad. Other states bought stock in railroads, or authorized local governments to do so. Some states gave tax breaks, or exemptions, to railroads.[3] State governments, furthermore, turned to railroad building after years of intimate involvement with turnpikes, plank roads, ferries, and bridges.

In the first half of the century, to be sure, laws and doctrines did not, on the whole, try to regulate, meaning monitor and control. The thrust of the law was promotional. The aim was to stimulate and encourage. There were cycles of up and down. The depression of 1837 left states with debts and bad investments. This led to a reaction against direct investment in railroads. The Michigan Constitution of 1850 told the state it could not own stock in any corporation; and most northern states, by 1860, had something similar in their fundamental law.[4]

Public opinion strongly supported the general idea of building railroads and other public improvements. But routes, terms and conditions, and other details were the stuff of intense political battle. And canals, turnpikes, and railroads were often at battle with each other. In each state, pressure groups tried to gain advantages. Harry Scheiber studied the Ohio canal era; he found that strong political forces not only demanded state intervention to provide a general basis for economic growth, but demanded "equal distribution of costs and benefits among all members of the polity as well." This meant, in essence, giving every identifiable interest group (geographical ones included) its cut of the pie—its canal, railroad, turnpike, bank, bridge, patronage, county seat, or whatever.[5] If there was a golden age of *laissez-faire* at all, in its pure, libertarian sense, it came later in the century; and even then, it was never clean and unadulterated. Government promoted and encouraged the building of the Western railroads, and there was a constant stream of state laws that affected the economy in one way or another.

In the first half of the century, *franchise* was a key legal concept. The franchise was a grant to the private sector, out of the inexhaustible reservoir of

[2] Carter Goodrich, *Government Promotion of American Canals and Railroads, 1800–1890* (1960), p. 44.

[3] See, in general, James W. Ely Jr., *Railroads and American Law* (2001), ch. 1.

[4] Ely, *op. cit.*, at 20.

[5] Harry N. Scheiber, *Ohio Canal Era: A Case Study of Government and the Economy, 1820–1861* (1969). See also Scheiber's essay, "The Transportation Revolution and American Law: Constitutionalism and Public Policy," in *Transportation and the Early Nation* (1982), p. 1; on the general question of the relationship between law and the economy, the pioneer work of J. Willard Hurst is still a fundamental starting point, especially *Law and the Conditions of Freedom in the Nineteenth Century United States* (1956); *Law and Economic Growth: The Legal History of the Lumber Industry in Wisconsin, 1836–1915* (1964); and *Law and Markets in United States History: Different Modes of Bargaining among Interests* (1982).

state power. Historically, it meant a freedom, a release from restraint. But it also carried with it the flavor of monopoly. This meant that franchise and franchises were bound to be controversial, either in general, or in particular cases. Before 1850, there was more emphasis on how to unlock the door of enterprise than on whether enterprise should be given exclusive rights. It was not uncommon for railroad charters to confer monopoly status—New Jersey, for example, gave the Camden and Amboy railroad, in 1832, the sole franchise to haul people and goods across the state, between New York City and Philadelphia.[6]

There was a public right—indeed, a public duty—to help foster growth, production, and enterprise. This meant that government must provide public goods, especially transport, but also currency and credit. The monetary system was one of the irritants that led to Shays's Rebellion. This bitter struggle between debtors and creditors raged in the background at the very time that the men in Philadelphia were debating the Constitution of 1787. This background noise profoundly affected the debate. The Constitution itself clearly showed a "strong distrust of allowing state legislatures to set money-supply policy"; rather, control of the money supply had to be "a matter of national policy."[7] Thus, the Constitution federalized the coinage of money; the states could not "emit Bills of Credit"; they could not "make any Thing but gold and silver Coin a Tender in Payment of Debts."[8]

Banking policy was always a subject of controversy. Early banks, in the 1780s for example, were really clubs of merchants—a kind of credit union for merchants.[9] But they soon became important sources of notes—of currency, in short. Should the federal government play a role? Twice, the federal government chartered a national bank. President Andrew Jackson was the sworn enemy of the second bank; and he succeeded in killing it. Both before and after this event, there was far more banking activity in the states. The states tried to ensure sound money and credit by creating their own banks or by encouraging private banking.[10] Pennsylvania owned one-third of the capital of the Bank of Pennsylvania, chartered in 1793. The Bank of the State of South Carolina, chartered in 1812, acted as the state's depository and fiscal agent; it was in effect the banking arm of the state itself.[11] Later on, it was not so common for states to own an outright share of banks. Instead, they enacted programs of regulation, which on paper were often quite heavy. In either case, the banks, public and private, were deeply enmeshed in politics. The currency and credit problem seemed central to the life of the community. An unsound bank—and there were many of these— threatened its community with financial ruin.

---

[6] Ely, *op. cit.*, pp. 11–12.

[7] J. Willard Hurst, *A Legal History of Money in the United States, 1774–1970* (1973), p. 8.

[8] U.S. Const., art. I, sec. 10.

[9] Joseph H. Sommer, "The Birth of the American Business Corporation: Of Banks, Corporate Governance, and Social Responsibility," 49 Buffalo Law Review 1011 (2001).

[10] The subject is exhaustively treated in Bray Hammond, *Banks and Politics in America, from the Revolution to the Civil War* (1957); see also J. Willard Hurst, *A Legal History of Money in the United States, 1774–1970* (1973). There is interesting material on bank litigation in Alfred S. Konefsky and Andrew J. King, eds., *The Papers of Daniel Webster: Legal Papers*, vol. 2, *The Boston Practice* (1983), pp. 527–37.

[11] Hammond, *op. cit.* p. 168.

States chartered their banks one by one. The chartering process was therefore a rite de passage in the life of every bank; at this crucial point, the state could (in theory) exert critical control over the bank, simply by inserting clauses into the charter. There was a good deal of variation in bank charters; and many of them had provisions designed to tie the hands of the bank in this or that way. For example, a Vermont law of 1833 chartering a bank to be known as The Farmer's Bank, limited interest on loans to 6 percent, required every director to post bond with the state treasurer, and kept for the state of Vermont the option of acquiring 10 percent of the shares.[12]

In practice, the special charter system was not a convenient or effective way to control the behavior of banks. The states began instead to adopt general banking laws—laws that would apply to any and every bank. In 1829, New York passed a safety fund law. Under this law, banks had to contribute a portion of their capital to a general fund, to insure payment of the notes of insolvent banks.[13] In 1837, Michigan passed the first free banking law. This dispensed with the need for a special charter. Any group of incorporators could start up a bank, so long as they followed the statutory formula. New York passed a similar law in 1838.[14]

The banks of New England were, in the period before the Civil War, typically small and closely held. Their customers were local people. In fact, they did a great deal of their business with "insiders," that is, their own directors and stockholders, and their families. A new group of insiders would form its own bank, to give themselves a supply of credit. By 1960, there were 91 banks in little Rhode Island; there were 178 in Massachusetts. Other states followed different patterns. There were branch banks in Pennsylvania and Virginia. In some states, there was more direct government involvement: the Bank of the State of South Carolina was wholly owned by the state, and lent money to planters and farmers, who felt they could not get credit from the other banks. Tennessee and Illinois also chartered banks.[15] Meanwhile, the "free banking" law made a difference, ultimately, in the nature of banking. By 1860, eighteen states had free banking laws; and a few others had variants of the law. As we shall see, corporation law went through the same cycle of development, from special charter to general laws: from narrow, one-at-a-time acts of the legislature, to a general business form, open to all budding entrepreneurs.

Transport, like money, was part of the economic infrastructure, the skeletal frame of economic life. The federal government was clearly not going to play a big role. So the states and cities moved into the vacuum. After 1820, a tremendous amount of statutory law dealt with bridges, roads, ferries, and canals. Much of the work of the legislatures, in the first half of the nineteenth century,

---

[12] Acts of Vt., 1833, ch. 34, pp. 60–67.

[13] Ronald E. Seavoy, *The Origins of the American Business Corporation, 1784–1855* (1982), pp. 117–48.

[14] For a study of one such bank, see Howard Bodenhorn, "Free Banking and Financial Entrepreneurship in Nineteenth Century New York: The Black River Bank of Watertown," 27 Business and Economic History 102 (1998). See also J. T. W. Hubbard, *For Each, the Strength of All: A History of Banking in the State of New York* (1995), pp. 94–96.

[15] Howard Bodenhorn, *A History of Banking in Antebellum America: Financial Markets and Economic Development in an Era of Nation-Building* (2000), pp. 31–44.

consisted of chartering transport companies, and amending these charters. Taking the Maryland laws of 1835–1836 as an example, we find in the first pages an amendment to "an act for building a bridge over the Little North-East, in Cecil County, near McCauley's mill" (ch. 23), three more bridge laws, and an amendment to "the act incorporating the Annapolis and Potomac Canal Company" (ch. 37), all in January 1836; many other laws in the same session incorporated or amended the charters of road or turnpike companies, or authorized road building, for example, "An Act to lay out and open a road through a part of Frederick and Baltimore Counties," which was passed March 2, 1836 (ch. 121). Chartering, however, was only one of the ways in which the government played a role in stimulating transport, as we have already noted. The states and cities supported internal improvements with money, credits, and favorable laws. They did some of the building work themselves. New York dug the great Erie Canal between 1817 and 1825—363 miles long—at a cost of a little more than $7 million. It was a tremendous financial success. The tolls surpassed all expectations. Even more important, the canal stimulated commerce and served as a "great channel of westward migration." Its opening "may be regarded as the most decisive single event in the history of American transportation."[16] The success of the Erie Canal invited emulation. In the peak year of 1840, an estimated $14.19 million was invested in canals in the United States.[17]

By this time, the railroad was already moving toward the center of the stage. The full flowering of the railroad era came later. But both the Pennsylvania Railroad and the Baltimore and Ohio (B&O) were founded in this period; and both were supported if not controlled by government. The city of Baltimore supplied the money for the B&O. Other states chose one or the other path of support for their railroads during the early, flush period of enthusiasm. In 1837, Ohio passed a general law—the "Loan Law"—promising support in the form of matching funds, to *any* internal improvement company (railroad, canal, or turnpike) that met certain standards. The law was repealed in 1842; but more than a hundred special laws, between 1836 and 1850, authorized local aid to the promoters of railroads.[18]

The states granted charters; sometimes they contributed money. They also used their lawmaking power to make rules and give instructions to legal institutions, in ways that would help the entrepreneur. For example, the state had the power of eminent domain (the power to seize property for public use). If it did so, the state had to pay fair value for any property it took. This requirement of "just compensation" was written into federal and state constitutions. More often than not, in the first half of the nineteenth century, it was not the state itself that used the power. Rather, the power was rather freely lent to private businesses that served "public" purposes—canal or turnpike companies, very notably. The companies could then take what land they chose. This was itself a

---

[16] Carter Goodrich, *Government Promotion of American Canals and Railroads, 1800–1890*, pp. 52–55.

[17] Carter Goodrich et al., *Canals and American Economic Development* (1961), p. 209; see also the excellent study by Harry N. Scheiber, *Ohio Canal Era: A Case Study of Government and the Economy, 1820–1861* (1969).

[18] Carter Goodrich, *Government Promotion of American Canals and Railroads*, pp. 136–37; Harry Scheiber, *Ohio Canal Era*, pp. 110–11, 152.

kind of subsidy, but there was more. Judicial doctrine tilted very substantially toward the companies, and not the landowners. In many places, for example, the doctrine of "offsetting" values was in effect. This meant that if a canal company took my land, worth $5,000, it did not necessarily have to pay me $5,000. It was entitled to take account of the benefits I would get from the canal. If the canal would raise the value of the *rest* of my land by $3,000, this could be subtracted from my compensation. The result was "no doubt a very large involuntary private subsidy" for public undertakings.[19]

On the surface, such policies favored business, especially transport business, and disfavored the ordinary farmer and landowner, the backbone of the country. But this is somewhat misleading. These policies were, no doubt, genuinely popular. A few unlucky people suffered; but the great bulk of farmer-settlers had a desperate hunger for transport: bridges, ferries, canals, turnpikes, and later, railroads. They needed these things to carry their goods to market, to bring settlers to their region, to stimulate business, to raise the overall value of their lands. In general, the subsidies were welcomed, and so was the orgy of bond-floating and shaky investment, which the states and cities indulged in like drunken sailors. The national hangover came somewhat later.

Outside of transport and finance, state regulation was rather random and planless. Not that a massive ideology dictated limits. The country was underdeveloped; most Americans no doubt felt that the state should encourage development, though perhaps they also felt that the state, like the Lord, helped those who helped themselves. Economic law was practical and promotional. Trade laws were tailored to specific needs. The states continued colonial programs of quality control over export commodities. Georgia law (1791) required tobacco to be "packed in hogsheads or casks" and "stamped by some inspector legally thereunto appointed";[20] unstamped tobacco could not be legally exported. In Connecticut, by a law of 1794, bar iron could not be sold unless "stamped with the name of the manufacturer thereof, and of the town where such iron is manufactured."[21] In New York, salt was to be packed "in barrels, casks or boxes" and inspected to make sure that the salt was "free from dirt, filth and stones, and from admixtures of lime . . . and fully drained from pickle."[22] The New York revised statutes of 1827–1828 included laws to regulate sales by auctioneers, hawkers and peddlers, and provisions for the inspection of flour, meal, beef, pork, "pot and pearl ashes," fish, "fish or liver oil," lumber, staves, flaxseed, sole leather, leaf tobacco, butter, and pressed hay. Not all of these were export commodities. Some were merely staple goods.

It was an established task of government to regulate weights and measures and to provide standard measures for commodities. Massachusetts, for example, prescribed standard measures by statute for potatoes, onions, salt, and

[19] Harry N. Scheiber, "The Road to *Munn:* Eminent Domain and the Concept of Public Purpose in the State Courts," in Donald Fleming and Bernard Bailyn, eds., *Law in American History* (1971), pp. 329, 364. On eminent domain in this period, see also Tony A. Freyer, *Producers versus Capitalists: Constitutional Conflict in Antebellum America* (1994), ch. 4.

[20] Oliver H. Prince, comp., *Digest of the Laws of the State of Georgia* (2nd ed., 1837), p. 817 (act of Dec. 23, 1791).

[21] Stats. Conn. 1808, pp. 421–22 (act of May, 1794).

[22] Rev. Stats. N.Y. 1829, vol. I, p. 270.

wood. There were also state laws that aimed at protecting consumers against false labeling and adulteration. In Massachusetts (1833), only "pure sperma-ceti oil"[23] could be "sold under the names of sperm, spermaceti, lamp, summer, fall, winter and second winter oils." A seller who sold "adulterated" oils under one of these names had to pay double the difference between the value of pure and adulterated oil. No statutory machinery was set up to enforce this law. Per-haps it was hoped that the crude penalties would be enough of an incentive for aggrieved merchants or consumers to enforce the law on their own.

The age of conservation was a long way off; nonetheless, there were some small moves to protect natural resources. Massachusetts in 1819 made it un-lawful to take pickerel "with spears, in the night time," or to shoot these fish "at any time." This act attached a money penalty of fifty cents per unlawful fish, payable "to and for the use of the person who shall sue for the same."[24] The usual motive for such laws was economic, not the love of Mother Nature. Massachusetts (1818) prohibited indiscriminate killing of birds that were "use-ful and profitable to the citizens, either as articles of food or as instruments in the hands of Providence to destroy various noxious insects, grubs, and caterpil-lars."[25] New Jersey, in 1789, restricted the picking of cranberries between June 1 and October 10, because "cranberries, if suffered to remain on the vines until sufficiently ripened, would be a valuable article of exportation."[26] By a protec-tionist act of 1822, Massachusetts forbade nonresidents to "take any lobsters, tautog, bass or other fish, within the harbors, streams, or waters of the towns of Fairhaven, New Bedford, Dartmouth, and Westport," and transport the catch "in smacks or vessels" of over fifteen tons, or in those of any size owned outside the Commonwealth.[27]

Public health was also a matter of some state concern, though the tools were primitive and the scope of regulation rather narrow. Quarantine laws were common, however. New York had an elaborate law in the 1820s directing ships to anchor near "the marine hospital on Staten-Island," dividing ships into classes depending on the perceived danger, and prescribing rules for clearing quarantine, including whitewashing and fumigation "with mineral acid gas" and the washing and airing of clothing and bedding. The rules were especially strict for ships coming from places where "yellow, bilious, malignant, or other pestilential or infectious fever" had existed, or if disease had broken out on board the ship.[28] State laws allowed "nuisances" to be "abated" when they were a danger to health. Land-use controls were in their infancy; but Michigan, for example, in the 1830s, authorized township boards, village governments, and the mayors and aldermen of cities to "assign certain places for the exercising of any trade or employment offensive to the inhabitants, or dangerous to the public health." Any such "assignment" could be revoked if the place or build-ing became a "nuisance" because of "offensive smells or exhalations," or was

---

[23] Laws Mass. 1833, ch. 215.
[24] Laws Mass. 1819, ch. 45. A later act subjected the operation of this law to local option.
[25] Laws Mass. 1818, ch. 103.
[26] Rev. Stats. N.J. 1821, p. 89 (act of Nov. 10, 1789).
[27] Laws Mass. 1822, ch. 97.
[28] Rev. Stats. N.Y. 1829, vol. I, pp. 425ff. On quarantine laws, see William Novak, *The Peo-ple's Welfare*, pp. 204–17.

"otherwise hurtful or dangerous."[29] Fire was a constant threat to cities; hence, New York City, by 1813, had rather elaborate regulations to prevent and handle fires: bans on fireworks or the shooting of guns in the city, for example; and the mayor had the power, if two aldermen agreed, to destroy buildings when necessary, to prevent a fire from spreading.[30]

When food products were regulated, the primary goals were usually economic; but sometimes public health or the protection of consumers was at least a secondary goal.[31] Some states gave local medical societies the power to examine and license prospective doctors. Unlicensed doctors were not allowed to collect fees through regular court process. Other laws made unauthorized practice subject to fines.[32] Lastly, laws on gaming, drinking, and gambling aimed to protect public morality. In New York, no "puppet-show . . . wire or rope-dance, or . . . other idle shows" could be exhibited for profit.[33] These regulations of morality were also, in a way, economic; they defined the permissible limits of earning a living. In a way, too, much of the penal code aimed to protect property and the economy—laws against theft, to take the simplest example.

Novak's point about the nature of nineteenth-century government, and its commitment to public welfare, is thus a good one, as these examples show. But we have to remember that nineteenth-century government was certainly in no way a leviathan. Even the bigger states had only a weak hold over the economy. Some programs probably existed only on paper. Many inspection laws, licensing laws, and laws about weights and measures were probably weakly enforced. Two pillars of the modern state were missing: a strong tax base and a trained civil service. Without these, the state could do only so much to master and control. State government depended chiefly on the property tax. This tax was locally assessed and locally collected. It was supplemented by excise taxes—on slaves, on carriages, or on personal property in general. Hard money was scarce, and the voting public was not used to the idea of handing over to the state any appreciable part of their income or wealth. John Marshall, in one of his most famous lines, said that the power to tax was the power to destroy.[34] Power to destroy was not given away lightly in the nineteenth century.[35] Taxing and spending were, by the standards of later times, laughably small. The state of Massachusetts

---

[29] Rev. Stats. Michigan 1838, p. 171.

[30] William Novak, *The People's Welfare,* p. 57.

[31] Oscar and Mary Handlin, *Commonwealth: A Study of the Role of Government in the American Economy: Massachusetts, 1744–1861* (rev. ed., 1969), p. 206.

[32] Laws N.Y. 1806, ch. 138; Laws Mass. 1819, ch. 113; Laws N.Y. 1830, ch. 126; unauthorized doctors were liable to forfeit "a sum not exceeding twenty-five dollars." See, in general, Richard H. Shryock, *Medical Licensing in America, 1650–1965* (1967).

[33] Rev. Stats. N.Y. 1829, vol. 1, p. 660.

[34] The case was *McCulloch v. Maryland,* Wheat. 316 (1819).

[35] There was some concern about fairness in tax policy. A clause in the Arkansas Constitution of 1836 declared that "no one species of property . . . shall be taxed higher than another species of property, of equal value," excepting taxes on "merchants, hawkers, peddlers, and privileges" (art. VII, Revenue, sec. 2). Citing this clause, the state supreme court declared void a special tax on billiard tables, and a tax on "the privilege of keeping each stallion or jack." The right to own a billiard table or to keep a stallion was a "property right" not a "privilege"; it was unlawful, therefore, to tax these rights specially. *Stevens v. State,* 2 Ark. 291 (1840); *Gibson v. County of Pulaski,* 2 Ark. 309 (1840).

spent $215,200, all told, in 1794. More than half of this was interest on debt.[36] Dollars went a lot further in those days; still, the puniest sewer district today could better that mark.

State action, then, was pinched for pennies. It had to find substitutes for the tax dollars it simply did not have. Hence there was heavy use of the fee system. Wherever possible, the costs of state services were shifted to users. Litigants paid judges for their lawsuits; brides and grooms paid for their marriage licenses. Local users had to pay assessments for local roads; if they were cash-poor themselves, they could pay off this tax in labor or sweat. In Mississippi, under a law of 1831, free adult males who paid less than six dollars of taxes a year had to "perform not exceeding four days labour on the roads in each year," along with "all free persons of colour, male and female, over eighteen and under forty-five years of age." Under some conditions, a man could substitute by providing horses, oxen, and plows.[37] Under a Virginia act of 1818, staves could not be exported before an inspector general and "cullers" had inspected them. The inspector general was "entitled to demand and receive" a fee of ten cents "on every thousand merchantable staves"; cullers too had to be paid their fee.[38] An elaborate Pennsylvania act of 1835 set up a similar system for meat. For "inspecting, examining and branding each tierce, barrel and half barrel of salted beef or pork," the inspectors could demand eight cents.[39]

There was no trained civil service in the modern sense. Government was not run by experts, even experts in running a government. Politics was a way to make money or use power. It was sometimes an occupation, less frequently a calling. Many politicians were amateurs, or lawyers who were amateurs except at law. That every man could aspire to high office was part of the democratic faith; as we saw, the principle of rotation was written into some of the early constitutions. Men like Jefferson and Jackson considered high turnover a positive virtue in government. Jackson, especially, felt that government jobs called for basic, fungible skills; any man of intelligence and honor could hold office. In fact, Jefferson and Jackson tended to appoint men of elite background and standing to higher offices, despite their egalitarian ideologies—men who were not experts, but were skilled, and educated. If there was any lack of trained men in government, the lawyers filled the gap. Lawyers had some education, some grasp of the machinery of government, some insight into state ways.[40]

In general, then, administration was weak and limited. Regulation tended to be local, self-sustaining—as in the fee system—and conservative in the use of staff. Often administrative jobs went to existing officeholders. If, for example, a state set up an insurance commission, it might appoint the state treasurer commissioner. Laws often required private citizens to stamp, mark, label, or post, to make for easier oversight. Every ferry keeper in Illinois had to maintain "a post or board, on which shall be written the rates of ferriage . . . by law allowed."[41] Private citizens usually had to enforce what regulation there was. If

---

[36] Handlin and Handlin, *op. cit.,* p. 62.
[37] Laws Miss. 1831, p. 364 (act of December 16, 1831).
[38] Va. Rev. Code 1819, vol. II, pp. 197, 200.
[39] Laws Pa. 1834–35, sec. 82, p. 405.
[40] See, in general, Sidney H. Aronson, *Status and Kinship in the Higher Civil Service* (1964).
[41] Francis S. Philbrick, ed., *Pope's Ill. Digest, 1815,* vol. 1 (1938), p. 264.

no one brought a lawsuit, or complained to the district attorney about some violation, nothing was done.

Some types of social control, which worked better in tight, narrow, seabound colonies, were strained to the breaking point in a huge, sprawling country, with a scattered population. In the Western states and territories, there were laws, borrowed from the East, that mentioned public markets and commodity inspection. Probably these were dead words on paper. Weak government, in general, opened a door to the private sector. Traditionally, money and credit were public functions; and the state built and ran highways, ferries, bridges, and canals. In the nineteenth century, farmers and merchants had a great hunger for these improvements. They wanted infrastructure. At a critical point, the state could not meet the demand; and the market took over. *Laissez-faire*, it may turn out, was more powerful as practice than as theory, even in the nineteenth century.

THE BUSINESS CORPORATION

A corporation, in the jargon of law books, is an artificial person. This means that it is a legal entity, which, like a person, can sue and be sued, own property, and transact business. Unlike natural persons, the corporation can dream of immortality. Officers and shareholders die, but the corporation lives on. The life of a corporation begins with a charter; and it ends if and when the charter runs out or is done away with. But the charter can provide for perpetual life; and this, in fact, is the normal case for corporations of the twentieth and twenty-first centuries.

The charter is a grant of authority from the sovereign. It specifies the powers, rights, and duties of the corporation. In an American state in the beginning of the twenty-first century, anybody who fills out a simple form and pays a small fee can get articles of incorporation and embark on corporate life. In the early nineteenth century, however, charters were statutes. They were doled out one by one. Every charter was in theory tailor-made to the case at hand.

In the colonial period, this was a perfectly appropriate system. Corporations were uncommon before 1800. And few of these were business corporations. Almost all of the colonial corporations were churches, charities, or cities or boroughs.[42] New York City was a chartered corporation.[43] In all of the eighteenth century, charters were issued to only 335 businesses. There were only seven in

---

[42] In England, only the crown had the right to incorporate. In the colonies, royal governors, proprietors, and in some cases legislative bodies issued charters. Actually, not many colonial cities and towns were technically corporations at all. It did not seem to make much difference in the way these municipalities behaved. In 1778, Governor Livingston of New Jersey tried to issue a charter himself without legislative approval, but that was an isolated incident. It was generally recognized after the Revolution that the legislature was the branch of government that made corporations. John W. Cadman Jr., *The Corporation in New Jersey: Business and Politics, 1791–1875* (1949), p. 4.

On the colonial corporation in general, see Joseph S. Davis, *Essays in the Earlier History of American Corporations* (1917).

[43] See, in general, Hendrik Hartog, *Public Property and Private Power: The Corporation of the City of New York in American Law, 1730–1870* (1983).

the whole colonial period; another 181 were granted between 1796 and 1800.[44] Banks, insurance companies, water companies, and companies organized to build or run canals, turnpikes, and bridges made up the overwhelming majority of these early corporations. A mere handful, notably the New Jersey Society for Establishing Useful Manufactures (1791), were established for manufacturing purposes.

In the nineteenth century, the situation began to change. In the first place, more and more charters were issued each year. Most charters, in the first half of the century, were still connected with finance and transport. A small but growing minority had more general commercial or industrial purposes. In Pennsylvania, 2,333 special charters were granted to business corporations between 1790 and 1860. Of these about 1,500 were transportation companies; less than two hundred were for manufacturing.[45] Joseph S. Davis has pointed out that:

> The English tradition that corporate powers were to be granted only in rare instances, never deeply intrenched here, was opposed by a strong and growing prejudice in favor of equality—a prejudice which led almost at once to the enactment of general incorporation acts for ecclesiastical, educational, and literary corporations. Partiality in according such powers was to be expected of the English crown, but it was a serious charge to lay at the door of democratic legislatures. . . . Not least important, the physical ease of securing charters was far greater in the new states than in England. . . . Legislatures were not overworked and did business free of charge and with reasonable promptness. . . . Finally, the practice in creating corporations for non-business purposes, though it did not lead promptly to granting freedom of incorporation to business corporations, undoubtedly smoothed the way for special acts incorporating business associations.[46]

Until about the middle of the century, the corporation was by no means the dominant form of business organization. Most commercial enterprises were partnerships. They consisted of two or three partners, often related by blood or marriage. The partnership was "used by all types of business, from the small country storekeepers to the great merchant bankers."[47] But as the economy developed, entrepreneurs made more and more use of the corporation, especially for transport ventures. The corporate form was a more efficient way to structure and finance their ventures. The special charter system, though, was clumsy and cumbersome. It was a waste of the legislature's time as well—or would have been, if in fact the legislature scrutinized each charter, and cut its clauses to order for the particular case. In fact, except for projects of special importance, charters became stylized, standardized, matters of rote. They were finally replaced, as we shall see, by general incorporation laws.[48]

[44] Joseph S. Davis, *Essays in the Earlier History of American Corporations*, vol. II (1917), p. 24.

[45] Louis Hartz, *Economic Policy and Democratic Thought: Pennsylvania, 1776–1860* (1948), p. 38.

[46] Davis, *op. cit.*, vol. 11, pp. 7–8.

[47] Alfred D. Chandler Jr., *The Visible Hand: The Managerial Revolution in American Business* (1977), pp. 36–37.

[48] The movement from special charter to general incorporation laws in New York is treated in Ronald E. Seavoy, *The Origins of the American Business Corporation, 1784–1855* (1982).

Early charters had many features that, from the standpoint of the corporation law of recent times, appear odd or idiosyncratic. Eternal life was not the rule. In the early nineteenth century, charter terms of five, twenty, or thirty years' duration were quite common. In New Jersey, every manufacturing company (except one) had a limited term of life before 1823; perpetual duration remained rare before the Civil War.[49] In Maryland, a general law of 1839 limited corporate life (for mining or manufacturing companies) to a maximum of thirty years.[50] Early charters also often departed from the principle of one vote for each share of stock. It was not the rule in Maryland, for example, until after 1819. In New Hampshire, under the charter of the Souhegan Nail and Cotton Factory (1812), each of the fifty shares of capital stock was entitled to a vote, but no member was entitled to more than ten votes, no matter how many shares he owned.[51] The 1836 charter of a Maryland company, incorporated to build a turnpike from Hagerstown to the Pennsylvania border, allocated votes as follows: "for every share . . . not exceeding three, one vote each; for any number of shares greater than three and not exceeding ten, five votes; for any number of shares greater than ten, and not exceeding fifty, seven votes; for any number of shares greater than fifty, and not exceeding one hundred, ten votes; and for every additional hundred shares above one hundred, ten votes"; thirty votes was the maximum for any shareholder.[52] Some charters restricted the number of shares any individual might hold in any one corporation. In Pennsylvania, after 1810, bank charters usually prohibited the transfer of bank stock to "foreigners."[53] In 1822, a bank charter in New Jersey required the new corporation to use some of its capital to aid the fisheries at Amboy.[54] Limited liability is the doctrine that shareholders are liable for corporate debts only up to the value of their shares, but nothing more; once their investment is wiped out, they cannot be made to pay for corporate debts. Limited liability is now considered one of the main reasons to choose the corporate form, and it is one of the basic features of corporation law. Limited liability had been part of English law, but in the United States, there was a reaction against it, in the early years of the century. Bank stock did not possess this great boon in New York, for example. In Connecticut, limited liability was common for manufacturing companies before the 1830s; but in some charters—for example, that of the Mystic Manufacturing Company of 1814—the stockholders were to be "responsible in their private capacity," if the corporation became insolvent. Massachusetts's law briefly provided for unlimited liability. But limited liability, by the 1830s or so, was clearly dominant.[55]

The main line of development in corporation law seems fairly clear. Variations were leveled out, and the practice moved in the direction of a kind of common law of corporations; business custom and the needs of entrepreneurs fixed its basic contours. Between 1800 and 1850, the essential nature of the corporation changed. The corporation was, originally, a kind of monopoly. It

[49] John W. Cadman, *The Corporation in New Jersey, 1791–1875* (1949), p. 366.

[50] Joseph G. Blandi, *Maryland Business Corporations, 1783–1852* (1934), p. 56.

[51] Laws N.H., vol. 8, 1811–20 (1920), p. 149.

[52] Laws Md. 1835–36, ch. 321, sec. 4.

[53] Hartz, *op. cit.,* p. 255.

[54] Cadman, *op. cit.,* p. 68.

[55] *Resolves and Private Laws, Conn., 1789–1836,* vol. II (1837), p. 851; Herbert Hovenkamp, *Enterprise and American Law, 1836–1937* (1991), pp. 49–55.

was a unique, ad hoc creation; it tended to vest exclusive control over a public asset, a natural resource, or a business opportunity in one group of favorites or investors. This was the essence of a charter to a town, a hospital—or a turnpike, a bank, or a bridge company. As such, it was odious to many people, especially those of the Jeffersonian persuasion. But now the corporation began to become a general form for organizing a business, legally open to all, and with few real restrictions on entry, duration, and management. The law moved, in a sense, to democratize the corporation, to make it available to everybody.[56] Business practice led the way, in many regards. The living law on proxy voting, general and special meetings, inspection of books, and the transfer of stock, gradually created demands (which were met) for standard clauses in corporate charters; and ultimately these norms found their way into the statute and case law of corporations.

There were many detours along the way before the law arrived at the position that access to the corporate form should be simple and open to everybody. Something must be said about state partnership in corporate affairs, about the anti-corporation movement, and about the fate of rival forms of business organization.

It seemed only natural, in the early nineteenth century, for the state to act in partnership with corporations, for a number of reasons. In the first place, many corporations were chartered to do work that was traditionally public: road building, banking, digging canals, and so on. Secondly, since each franchise was a privilege and favor, the state had the right to exact a price,[57] which might include strict controls or even profit sharing. Thirdly, state participation was a good way to help out an enterprise. It was a way of priming the pump, a way of supporting enterprise that would in turn enrich the economy. Fourth, public participation increased public control: if the state owned stock, and its men sat on the board, they could make sure the company acted in the public interest. And fifth, state investment could bring money into the treasury. If the dreams of the enterprise came true, big dividends would flow into public coffers. Thus Pennsylvania, for example, not only owned stock in its banks, but, after 1806, invested in turnpikes, bridge companies, canal companies, and finally in railroads. States and cities both engaged in railroad boosting. Initially, there was an orgy of chartering. Ohio granted forty-seven charters for railroads between 1830 and 1859; Illinois in 1857 incorporated fifty-five railroad companies.[58] Then there was outright aid: Between 1827 and 1878, New York State lent, leased, or donated $10,308,844.77 for construction of sixteen railroads.[59] Some of these loans turned very sour in the aftermath of the panic of 1837. The New York constitution of 1846 severely restricted state aid to private corporations. The railroads then turned to the cities and towns with "astonishing success."

---

[56] Hovenkamp, *op. cit.*, p. 2. Hovenkamp calls this a "distinctively Jacksonian" development.

[57] Sometimes quite literally. The charter of the Bank of Philadelphia (1803) required the bank to pay a bonus of $135,000 to the state. The bonus practice was not abolished in Pennsylvania until 1842. Hartz, *op. cit.*, pp. 54–56.

[58] James W. Ely Jr., *Railroads and American Law* (2001), p. 18. On financial aid to the railroads, *ibid.*, pp. 19–23.

[59] Harry H. Pierce, *Railroads of New York: A Study of Government Aid* (1953), p. 15.

Cities and towns were passionately eager to get railroad routes that connected them to the rest of the world. A railroad meant access to markets, rising land values, and general prosperity. Most commonly, the cities bought stock in the railroads. The city of Buffalo, for example, subscribed $1,000,000 for stock in the Buffalo & Jamestown Railroad. A few towns bought bonds; a few donated money outright; and in 1842, the city of Albany guaranteed, by endorsement, $100,000 worth of bonds of the Mohawk & Hudson.[60]

Pennsylvania also experimented with mixed public and private enterprises. At one stage in the state's marriage with its railroads, in the 1830s, Pennsylvania furnished locomotives; private companies supplied the other cars. Before 1842, the state of Maryland chose ten of the thirty directors of the B&O; the city of Baltimore chose eight. In New Jersey, the "monopoly bill" of 1832 granted exclusive transport franchises in exchange for gifts of stock to the state. The state's shares carried a higher priority for dividends than other shares—one of the earliest instances of preferred stock. For years, New Jersey profited nicely from its railroad investments; the income helped lower the taxes that New Jersey levied on its residents.

State participation in enterprise, as it turned out, was only a passing phase. There were always people who felt that the state should not go into business. The business cycle made this argument compelling. During periods of crashes, panics, and depressions, states lost money on their investments. The whole idea of state participation turned sour. States and cities, nearly bankrupted in the years after 1837, were tempted to sell off their assets for cash. In 1844, a referendum in Pennsylvania approved sale of the Main Line to private interests. As it happened, the sale was not consummated until 1857. The Pennsylvania Railroad then bought the line for cash and railroad bonds. In exchange, the state gave the railroad all tracks and equipment of the line, and exempted it "forever, from the payment of taxes upon tonnage or freight carried over the said railroads; and . . . on its capital stock, bonds, dividends or property, except for city, borough, county, township, and school purposes." This extraordinary boon was declared unconstitutional one year later, in the great case of *Mott v. Pennsylvania Railroad*.[61] Pennsylvania's Chief Justice Ellis Lewis wrote a strong opinion denying that the state had any right to commit "political suicide" by giving up the power to tax. Legislative authority was not for sale. Lewis also felt that the public had to exert some control over the legislature, to keep it from pawning its sovereignty. Alas, faith in the "fidelity of the legislature" was often misplaced:

> Limitations of power, established by written constitutions, have their origin in a distrust of the infirmity of man. That distrust is fully justified by the history of the rise and fall of nations.[62]

The system of checks and balances fed on this very American fear. It was a fear of unbridled power—mostly, government power, but also the power of large landholders and dynastic wealth. Politically active members of the public

[60] Pierce, *op. cit.*, pp. 18–19.
[61] 30 Penn. State 9 (1858); see James W. Ely Jr., *Railroads and American Law* (2001), pp. 8–9.
[62] 30 Penn. State at 28.

were willing to try all sorts of techniques to keep authorities in check, and to offset the corrosive effects of money. Corruption was a problem from the start; legislatures that had power to grant franchises and to charter corporations, could also be bribed with money and stock.

The story of the business corporation is a story of triumph and success. But the process was neither painless nor noiseless. There was much controversy over corporations in the first half of the nineteenth century. People tended to associate them, not illogically, with franchises and monopolies. They were entities the state created, to hold some power or right that no one else could lay claim to. Most corporations were transportation monopolies, banks, insurance companies—aggregations of "capital," representing the "few" against the "many." Unlike farms and industrial enterprise, they did not *produce* anything real—at least this is what people thought. They were in a sense parasitic, and unduly powerful. The more corporations, the more danger to the body politic. James Sullivan, attorney general of Massachusetts, warned in 1802 that "The creation of a great variety of corporate interests . . . must have a direct tendency to weaken the power of government."[63]

The word "soulless" constantly recurs in debates over corporations. Everyone knew that corporations were really run by human beings. Yet, the word was not completely inappropriate. Corporations did not die, and there was no real limit to their size, or their greed. Corporations might aggregate the worst urges of whole groups of men. No considerations of family, friendship, or morality, would temper their powers. People hated and distrusted corporations, the way some people came to fear the soulless computer—machines that can join together the wit, skill, power, and malevolence of infinite numbers of minds.

In theory, the special charter system was a good way to control corporations. But the demand for charters, in the end, got to be too heavy. By the 1840s and 1850s, it would have swamped the legislatures, if the process had not become so routine. Even so, state session laws bulged with special charters. Time was wasted in the drudge work of issuing, amending, and extending hundreds of charters. In the rush, there was little time to supervise those charters that perhaps needed supervision.

Legislatures then took the next logical step—they passed general corporation acts. The legislature could save itself time, and could effectively make rules for all corporations, by passing one carefully considered law. They could also turn the corporate form into a right which any person or group could make use of, rather than a privilege of the few.

Even in the late eighteenth century a few general laws were passed, which applied to churches, academies, and library societies. A New York law of 1811, "relative to incorporations for Manufacturing purposes," is usually credited as the first general law for *business* corporations. Under this law, "any five or more persons who shall be desirous to form a company for the purpose of manufacturing woollen, cotton, or linen goods, or for the purpose of making glass, or for the purpose of making from ore bar-iron, anchors, millirons, steel, nail-rods, hoop-iron and ironmongery, sheet copper, sheet lead, shot, white lead and red lead," and who filed a certificate with some standard information in the office of the secretary of state, became, for "the term of twenty

---

[63]Quoted in Handlin and Handlin, *op. cit.,* p. 260.

years next after the day of filing such certificate," a "body corporate and politic, in fact and in name."[64]

Other corporation acts picked up the New York plan. These laws were general in the sense that they applied to all corporations in a particular field— manufacturing, banking, or insurance. Typically, too, the laws did not provide an exclusive method of starting a corporation. They left the door open for private charters, if the incorporators preferred. In fact, the early general laws were not particularly effective. When they imposed rules with any bite at all, the business community ignored them and took the private-charter route. Some entrepreneurs incorporated temporarily under a general law, and then tried to extract a private charter from the legislature. To put teeth into the general laws, the New York Constitution of 1846 took a somewhat more drastic step. It restricted special charters to "cases where in the judgment of the Legislature, the objects of the corporation cannot be attained under general laws."[65] As it turned out, the legislature was quite accommodating in making such judgments. At the close of the period, then, the special charter was still dominant. But the handwriting was on the wall. The Louisiana Constitution of 1845, a bellwether in many ways, contained a much stronger clause: "Corporations shall not be created in this State by special laws except for political or municipal purposes."[66]

The fight against corruption was one of the reasons for these constitutional revisions. There were unscrupulous incorporators, and there were recurrent bribery scandals. These scandals weakened public confidence in elected officials. To win the war against evil corporations, the legislatures had to be put under restraint. Under the New York Constitution of 1821, the "assent of two-thirds of the members elected to each branch of the legislature" was needed for passage of any bill "creating, continuing, altering, or renewing any body politic or corporate."[67] A similar provision appeared in the Delaware Constitution of 1831. Delaware would one day be a snug harbor for out-of-state corporations; but this was still far off in 1831. Under the Delaware Constitution, no act of incorporation "shall continue in force for a longer period than twenty years, without the re-enactment of the Legislature, unless it be an incorporation for public improvement."[68]

There were two sides to the debate. When a two-thirds provision, like New York's, was proposed in the New Jersey convention of 1844, one delegate remarked he was "a friend to corporations. They have done more to increase the prosperity of our State than anything else. Let the legislature grant all that may apply, if the object is to benefit the community." The two-third rules was a way for people to "show their teeth at these little monsters, but if they believe them to be such dangerous creatures as they have represented them to be, they had better come manfully up to the work and strangle them at once, than to keep up this continued snapping at their heels."[69] The proposal was defeated.

---

[64] Laws N.Y. 1811, ch. 47.

[65] New York. Const., 1846, art. 8, sec. 1. See Seavoy, op. cit., pp. 177–88.

[66] Louisiana Const., 1845, art. 123. This provision was copied in Iowa the following year. Iowa Const., 1846, art. 8, sec. 2.

[67] New York Const., 1821, art. 7, sec. 9.

[68] Delaware Const., 1831, art. 2, sec. 17.

[69] Proceedings of the New Jersey State Constitutional Convention of 1844 (1942), pp. 537–38, 539.

In fact, the anti-corporation movement never succeeded in doing more than snapping at heels; strangulation was simply not in the cards.

But the issue of *control* over corporations was a persistent one, in the first half of the nineteenth century. It was a period that made distinctions between the productive use of capital, and wasteful, parasitic, nonproductive use. Money-lenders were parasites; and people who played the stock market were little better than gamblers. These attitudes weakened over time, but slowly and somewhat painfully. Some states passed laws against speculation in stocks. A Pennsylvania law of 1841, for example, made contracts for the sale of securities void, if the delivery was to be done more than five days in the future. New York in 1837 prohibited people who bought stock in banks from selling the stock, until three months after all the stock had been paid for. Mississippi in 1840 made it illegal for a bank to deal in "stocks of any kind." Virginia and other states licensed stockbrokers. None of these laws was particularly effective; but they illustrate how queasy many people felt about those who bought, sold, and dealt in corporate securities.[70]

In the famous case of *Dartmouth College v. Woodward* (1819),[71] the U.S. Supreme Court faced squarely the issue of control over corporations. By the terms of the federal Constitution, no state could impair the obligation of a contract. But what was a "contract"? Dartmouth College was a corporation, with a charter from New Hampshire. The state enacted a law changing the terms of that charter. The Supreme Court held that this was beyond the power of the state. A corporate charter was "a contract made on a valuable consideration," a "contract for the security and disposition of property." It followed that the legislature could not change the terms of a charter. To do so would "impair" the charter, that is, the contract between the state and the corporation.[72]

Dartmouth College was no business corporation; but the court, and the newspaper-reading public, well understood that the decision went beyond any question of a small college and its charter from the state. News of the decision evoked a great howl of protest. Many contemporaries felt that the case was a blow to popular sovereignty; it took away from "the people and their elected representatives" a "large part of the control over social and economic affairs." That was one way of looking at the case. The court and its defenders saw it differently. This decision, and others like it, protected investments and property interests. It shielded them from shifting, temporary winds of public opinion.

---

[70] Stuart Banner, *Anglo-American Securities Regulation: Cultural and Political Roots, 1690–1860* (1998), pp. 222–36.

[71] 4 Wheat. 518 (1819). An important precursor was *Fletcher v. Peck*, 6 Cranch 87 (1810). This case came out of the so-called Yazoo land scandals in Georgia. The Georgia legislature entered into a corrupt land-grant deal. The next legislature repealed the grant; but, meanwhile, some of the land had passed into the hands of out-of-state investors who were not part of the original tainted deal. The United States Supreme Court, under John Marshall, sided with the buyers of the land. The grant of land by the legislature, said Marshall, was a "contract"; what one legislature gave, the next could not take back. See C. Peter Magrath, *Yazoo, Law and Politics in the New Republic: The Case of Fletcher v. Peck* (1966).

[72] On Marshall's opinion in *Dartmouth College*, and the other contract-clause cases, see Charles F. Hobson, *The Great Chief Justice: John Marshall and the Rule of Law* (1996), pp. 78–110.

The doctrine, guaranteed a level of legal stability. In this way, it promoted economic growth. It encouraged risk-taking in business.

Dartmouth College had a far less sweeping effect on the law of corporations than one might have guessed. In a concurring opinion, Justice Joseph Story hinted, perhaps deliberately, at a simple way to get around the new rule. If the legislature, Story said, really wanted to alter corporate charters, it ought to reserve the right to do so when it issued such charters. Then the right to change the terms of the charter would be, legally speaking, part of the "contract" between the state and the corporation; and when the legislature passed a law amending the charter, there would be no "impairment." In later years, it was routine for the legislature to insert in every charter a clause reserving to the state the right to alter, amend, and repeal. This right was also a common feature of general incorporation laws. Finally, the right was inserted in state constitutions. The New York Constitution of 1846 provided that "all general laws and special acts" about corporations "may be altered from time to time or repealed" (art. 8, sec. 1).

Corporations were rare before 1800; hence the case law on corporations was thin before the nineteenth century. As corporations multiplied, so did litigation over rights and duties. For all practical purposes, the courts created a body of corporation law out of next to nothing. Old decisions and doctrines, from the time when most corporations were academies, churches, charities, and cities, had little to say about managers and directors that was germane to the world of business corporations.

At first, the courts treated corporate powers rather gingerly. They adhered to the "general and well settled principle, that a corporation had no other powers than such as are specifically granted; or, such as are necessary for the purpose of carrying into effect the powers expressly granted."[73] This "principle" followed from the idea of a corporation as a single venture, or a mass of capital to be used for a single purpose—a bridge, a factory, a bank. Chief Justice Roger Taney built on this principle in the famous case of the Charles River Bridge (1837).[74] Massachusetts had chartered a company to build a bridge over the Charles River, in the late eighteenth century. It was to be a toll bridge. Many years later, the state granted another charter, to a new group of entrepreneurs. The second bridge, to be built very close to the first one, would eventually be entirely free. This would destroy the investment in the original bridge. The owners of this bridge sued, claiming the second charter violated the constitution: it impaired the obligation of a contract (their charter). The Supreme Court held against them. A charter had to be strictly construed. The state had never promised not to charter a competing bridge. The case can be read narrowly, to mean only that the powers of corporations, like those of government, had to be kept within narrow boundaries; and its charter had to be read in that light. But the case also stood for "progress," for impatience with vested rights;

---

[73] Joseph K. Angell and Samuel Ames, *A Treatise on the Law of Private Corporations Aggregate* (2nd ed., 1843), p. 66.

[74] *Proprietors of the Charles River Bridge v. Proprietors of the Warren Bridge,* 11 Pet. 420 (1837). On the background and meaning of the case, see Stanley I. Kutler, *Privilege and Creative Destruction: The Charles River Bridge Case* (1971).

it stood for the idea that you can't make an economic omelette without breaking eggs. The old bridge, like the old turnpikes, had to give way to what was more dynamic, more modern, and more progressive.

This was the lasting message of the Charles River Bridge. In the long run, the creative draftsmanship of private citizens—the people who actually wrote the texts of the charters—helped to bury the idea of strict construction. Business practice led the way. The charters came to reflect what was fact: enterprise was growing in scope and flexibility. The logic of economic growth, invisible to most contemporaries, was drawing up law for itself. What the draftsmen devised, the courts accepted, and legislatures only weakly resisted. The old controls on corporations, meant to reduce their power or their economic role, either disappeared or became innocuous.

But while one kind of restriction faded, others were beginning to develop. The business corporation was an economic animal. It existed to make profits. It was managed by officers and directors; and it had stockholders, who were in theory the people who owned the company. Then there were the corporation's creditors. What rights and duties did all these people have, with regard to each other? The case-law tried to answer these questions. There was, for example, the so-called trust-fund doctrine, which Joseph Story gets credit for inventing. The leading case was *Wood v. Drummer* (1824).[75] Stockholders of the Hallowell and Augusta Bank, of Maine, which was winding up its corporate existence, declared dividends amounting to 75 percent of the capital stock of $200,000. The bank thus became a hollow shell, especially since not all of the capital stock had actually been paid in. The plaintiffs held bank notes that became worthless. Story held that it was wrong for the stockholders to distribute the capital to themselves in such a way as to defraud the bank's creditors, that is, the holders of the bank notes. The capital stock of banks was "to be deemed a pledge or trust fund for the payment of the debts contracted by the bank." Creditors could "follow" the funds "into the hands of any persons, who are not innocent purchasers," and recover it from them. This gave the plaintiffs a right to recover from the stockholders, who had lined their pockets with the money from the bank. Later cases picked up this doctrine, and applied it to other situations. Meanwhile, the courts slowly built up a body of rules about the internal life of corporations, and the relationships between corporations and the outside world.

The triumph of enterprise was probably inevitable; but the corporate form was not the only possibility. A New York statute of 1822, widely copied later on, introduced the limited partnership into American law. This was based, in part, on a French business form, the *société en commandite*. In a limited partnership, some members ("general partners") were fully responsible for partnership debts. Limited (or "special") partners, however, were liable "no further than the fund which he or they have furnished to the partnership stock."[76] A limited partnership (with its "one or more sleeping partners") was "supposed to be well calculated to bring dormant capital into active and useful employment."[77] (The words are Chancellor Kent's.) Most commercial

---

[75] 3 Mason C.C. Rpts. 308, Fed. Cas. No. 17,944 (1824).

[76] See Edward H. Warren, *Corporate Advantages without Incorporation* (1929), pp. 302ff.

[77] James Kent, *Commentaries on American Law* [cited hereafter as Kent, *Commentaries*], vol. III (2nd ed., 1832), p. 35.

enterprises were partnerships of one form or another before the middle of the nineteenth century.

Another kind of business association was the Massachusetts or business trust. This was an unincorporated association, which used the structure of a trust. Managers (trustees) held title to the property of the trust. Instead of stockholders, there were "beneficiaries"; instead of capital stock, the owners held certificates of beneficial interest. A "trust government," something like a charter, spelled out the powers and duties of the managers.

The joint-stock company was another type of business association, in common use. It was something like a partnership; but its capital, unlike that of a partnership, was divided into transferable shares.

It was by no means certain that a corporation, as that term was understood in 1800 or 1820, was the best way to raise and manage money for a new enterprise. Shaw Livermore studied early American land companies. They made use of a broad menu of business forms. Speculative land companies, even before 1800, showed "all the various states of complexity in modern business organization beyond the partnership"; yet they were not incorporated. Livermore has argued that these associations were the "true progenitors of the modern business corporation."[78] The argument, in other words, is that the modern corporation is not really the direct descendant of the special charter system, but rather an evolution from a rich palette of business practices and business forms.

Words, forms, and slogans did come from the old law of corporations; and these were used, like rubble from which a new bridge is built. The architecture and the plans came from business practice, and from the marketplace. That the final, triumphant form was a "corporation," not some mutation of the partnership or Massachusetts trust might be due to almost random factors, which tipped the balance one way or another. Similarly, in the twentieth century, before the Uniform Commercial Code was adopted by the states, the legal form used for goods sold on the installment plan differed in *form* from state to state. In some states, the form was called a conditional sale; in some, a chattel mortgage; in Pennsylvania, a bailment lease; in England, a hire-purchase contract. If some annoying or technical case, doctrine, or statute blocked one type of arrangement, the practice flowed freely into another channel, like water when it is dammed. This was the case with the triumph of the corporate form. What the growing market needed was an efficient, trouble-free device to aggregate capital and manage it in business, with limited liability and transferable shares.

The argument over origins—this is often the case—is mostly an argument over words. French law was not the "progenitor" of the limited partnership; charters of towns, colleges, and hospitals were not the "progenitors" of railroad charters; land syndicates were not the "progenitors" of general corporation laws. All these were merely models and occasions. The theory of legal history is that contemporary fact is always the architect of contemporary law. History does not supply decisions—only raw materials and plans.

---

[78] Shaw Livermore, *Early American Land Companies: Their Influence on Corporate Development* (1939), p. 216.

CHAPTER 4

THE LAW OF PERSONAL STATUS:
WIVES, PAUPERS, AND SLAVES

MARRIAGE AND DIVORCE

In England, ecclesiastical courts had jurisdiction over marriage and divorce, and the church had an important role in family law. The United States had no such courts and, after the early nineteenth century, no established churches. Family law was thoroughly secular in the United States. Marriage, in legal theory, was a contract—an agreement between a man and a woman. The law did not forbid or even discourage religious ceremonies. And moral and religious ideas were, as always, powerful influences on the law of marriage and divorce. But American law recognized two secular forms of marriage: the civil ceremony, which had been well known during the colonial period, and the so-called common-law marriage, which may have been an American innovation.

The concept of a common-law marriage is often misunderstood. People today sometimes use this phrase to mean a man and woman who live together without the slightest pretense of marriage. The legal meaning is very different. If a state recognizes common-law marriage, then that marriage is as valid as any other kind—as valid as a formal marriage, complete with minister, witnesses, and the usual ceremony. A common-law marriage is completely informal. No need for a license, minister, judge, witnesses, or anything else. It is a "verbal contract," that is, an agreement by a man and a woman to consider themselves husband and wife. Once they say this to each other, they are fully and completely married. That is the core idea of a common-law marriage.[1]

The origins of this form of marriage in the United States are fairly murky. There were customary forms of marriage in England and in the colonies; but English law, from 1753 on, definitely outlawed all nonceremonial forms of marriage; and this, of course, was before the American revolution. Yet, Chancellor Kent and other American jurists expressed the view that the common law did not require any "peculiar ceremonies" in order for a marriage to be

---

[1] On the common law marriage in general, see the material in Michael Grossberg, *Governing the Hearth: Law and the Family in Nineteenth-Century America* (1985); Ariela Dubler, "Wifely Behavior: A Legal History of Acting Married," 100 Columbia L. Rev. 957 (2000); Lawrence M. Friedman, *Private Lives: Families, Individuals and the Law* (2005), pp. 17–26, 44–46.

valid. The presence of a clergyman, though a "very becoming practice," was unnecessary; the "consent of the parties is all that is required."[2]

Kent and other judges of the early nineteenth century perhaps misread the English authorities. But mistakes in reading old cases cannot really explain the rise of this institution. It had a more solid basis in the social context—the intellectual climate and the felt needs of the population. Joel Bishop, writing in 1852, advanced this explanation: In England, only Episcopalian clergymen were authorized to perform marriages. The Puritan dissenters had "fled to these western wilds for the single purpose of escaping from what they regarded as oppression and moral contagion flowing from those churches." They would not have tolerated any requirement that they import an "Episcopal ecclesiastic . . . paying him tithes, simply that he might become an invited guest at their weddings. Though the American colonies were not all settled by puritans, the spirit of this suggestion will apply to most of them."[3]

To be sure, there was a shortage of clergymen of every faith in some parts of the United States. Much of the population lived outside the cities; and parts of the country were thinly populated. Charles Woodmason, an Anglican minister, traveled to the back country of South Carolina, in 1766, to bring religion to this benighted area (and perform marriages). He complained that "thro' want of Ministers to marry and thro' the licentiousness of the People, many hundreds live in Concubinage—swopping their Wives as Cattel, and living in a State of Nature, more irregularly and unchastely than the Indians."[4] In Texas, we hear about a custom called "bond marriage." Man and woman signed a written agreement; and this agreement (which was witnessed) was considered the basis of a real marriage—at least for the people involved, and their community.[5]

More to the point, large numbers of ordinary people owned houses and farms and had a real stake in the economy. There were, apparently, couples who lived together after makeshift ceremonies, or no ceremony at all. These couples raised flocks of children. The doctrine of common-law marriage allowed the law to treat these "marriages" as holy and valid. If a man and a woman in fact lived together, raised children, and *acted* married, then they were presumed to *be* married—that is, the law assumed they had a common-law marriage. Why was this important? Because if the husband died, the woman he left behind was a real, actual widow, with the rights of a widow; and the children were legitimate and could inherit the land. Questions of title, inheritance, and so on, are irrelevant to people who own nothing. But this was a country where land was widely held, especially in the north and middle west. In the United States, unlike Great Britain, land law and inheritance law were not just for the rich.

Bishop, a shrewd observer of law and morals, felt that the early settlers were inclined to make a virtue of necessity, or at least come to terms with it. Despite their "pure morals and stern habits," the settlers could not or would not go along with the strict English marriage laws, or their American counterparts.

---

[2] Kent, *Commentaries*, vol. II (2nd ed., 1832), pp. 86–87.

[3] Joel Bishop, *Commentaries on the Law of Marriage and Divorce* (1852), p. 130.

[4] Quoted in Nancy F. Cott, *Public Vows: A History of Marriage and the Nation* (2000), p. 32.

[5] Mark M. Carroll, *Homesteads Ungovernable: Families, Sex, Race, and the Law in Frontier Texas, 1823–1860* (2001), p. 113.

The strict marriage laws of Pennsylvania, for example, were "ill adapted to the habits and customs of society"; a "rigid execution of them," remarked Chief Justice John Bannister Gibson in 1833, "would bastardize a vast majority of the children which have been born within the state for half a century."[6] This was not just a matter of social stigma: It was a question of who got the farm, the house, the country acreage, the lot in town.

Still, there was opposition to the common-law marriage. It was, after all, extremely loose. To some people, it seemed a "strange and monstrous crossbreed between a concubinage and a marriage." Common-law marriage helped straighten out questions of property rights. But it could also complicate these rights; and it could lead to public scandal. Some states rejected the doctrine outright. In *Grisham v. State* (1831),[7] the highest court of Tennessee refused to accept the idea of a common-law marriage. John Grisham, a widower, and Jane Ligan, a widow, had agreed to cohabit as man and wife; they swore an oath, before witnesses, to that effect. They were indicted and convicted of "lewd acts of fornication and adultery . . . to the great scandal of the . . . good and worthy citizens." The court upheld the conviction. Law, said this court, was the "guardian of the morals of the people." But in most states, this "guardian" bowed to the inevitable and accepted the validity of informal marriage. Common-law marriage was simply too useful a tool.

England had been a "divorceless society," and remained that way until 1857. Henry VIII had gotten a divorce; but ordinary Englishmen had no such privilege. The very wealthy might squeeze a rare private bill of divorce out of Parliament. Between 1800 and 1836 there were, on the average, three of these a year. For the rest, unhappy husbands and wives had to be satisfied with annulment (no easy matter) or divorce from bed and board (*a mensa et thoro*), a form of legal separation. Separated couples had no right to remarry. No court before 1857 had authority to grant a divorce. The most common "solutions" when a marriage broke down were adultery and desertion.[8]

In the colonial period, the South was generally faithful to English tradition. Absolute divorce was unknown, divorce from bed and board very rare. In New England, however, courts and legislatures occasionally granted a divorce. In Pennsylvania, Penn's laws of 1682 gave the right to a "Bill of Divorcement" to a spouse whose partner was convicted of adultery. Later, the governor or lieutenant governor was empowered to dissolve marriages on grounds of incest, adultery, bigamy, or homosexuality. There is, however, no evidence that the governor ever used this power. Still later, the general assembly took divorce into its own hands. The English privy council disapproved of this practice and, in the 1770s, disallowed legislative divorces in Pennsylvania, New Jersey, and New Hampshire. The Revolution put an end to the privy council's power.[9]

---

[6] C. J. Gibson, in *Rodebaugh v. Sanks,* 2 Watts 9, 11 (Pa., 1833).

[7] 10 Tenn. 588 (1831).

[8] See Gerhard O. W. Mueller, "Inquiry into the State of a Divorceless Society: Domestic Relations Law and Morals in England from 1660 to 1857," 18 U. Pitt. L. Rev. 545 (1957); Stephen Cretney, *Family Law in the Twentieth Century: A History* (2003), pp. 161–95.

[9] Nelson M. Blake, *The Road to Reno: A History of Divorce in the United States* (1962), pp. 34–47. There is a growing literature on the history of divorce. See, especially, Norma

After Independence, the law and practice of divorce began to change; but regional differences remained quite strong. In the South, divorce continued to be unusual. The extreme case was South Carolina. Henry William Desaussure, writing in 1817, stated flatly that South Carolina had never granted a single divorce.[10] He was right. There was no such thing as absolute divorce in South Carolina throughout the nineteenth century. In other southern states, legislatures dissolved marriages by passing private divorce laws. The Georgia constitution of 1798 allowed legislative divorce on a two-thirds vote of each branch of the legislature—and after a "fair trial" and a divorce decree in the superior court. This left the judges unsure of their exact role in the process.[11] The legislature later resolved these doubts; it passed a law reserving to itself the exclusive right to grant divorces. Between 1798 and 1835, there were 291 legislative divorces in Georgia. The frequency curve rose toward the end of the period. Twenty-seven couples were divorced legislatively in 1833—for example, Green Fuller and Susannah Fuller, whose "matrimonial connection, or civil contract of marriage," was "completely annulled, set aside, and dissolved"; so that the two would "in future be held as distinct and separate persons, altogether unconnected by any mystical union or civil contract whatever."[12] The legislatures were certainly not rubber stamps. In Virginia, for example, Olympia Meridith was married to a scoundrel with the marvelous name of Moody Blood. She was left with two children (Fleming Blood and Friendless Blood) when Moody, who had abused her, was sent to jail for receiving stolen property. She asked the legislation in 1841 for a divorce. The answer was no. Two years later, she tried again. Again, she was turned down.[13] In Virginia, overall, only one petitioner out of three succeeded in getting a divorce.

North of the Mason-Dixon line, courtroom divorce replaced legislative divorce. Pennsylvania passed a general divorce law in 1785, Massachusetts one year later. Every New England state had a divorce law before 1800, along with New York, New Jersey, and Tennessee. In these states, divorce took the form of an ordinary lawsuit. An innocent spouse sued for divorce, which had to be based on legally acceptable "grounds." Grounds for divorce varied somewhat from state to state. New York's law of 1787 permitted absolute divorce only for adultery. Vermont, on the other hand, allowed divorce for impotence, adultery, intolerable severity, three years' willful desertion, and long absence with presumption of death (1798). Rhode Island allowed divorce for "gross misbehaviour and wickedness in either of the parties, repugnant to and in violation of the marriage covenant."[14] In New Hampshire, it was grounds for divorce if a

Basch, *Framing American Divorce: From the Revolutionary Generation to the Victorians* (1999); Glenda Riley, *Divorce: An American Tradition* (1991).

[10] Henry W. Desaussure, *South Carolina Eq. Rpts.*, vol. I. p. liv; vol. II, p. 644.

[11] See Oliver H. Prince, comp., *A Digest of the Laws of the State of Georgia*, vol. II (2nd ed., 1837), p. 187. In Mississippi, during the territorial period, judicial divorces were the norm; but the legislature also passed some private bills of divorce. Donna Elizabeth Sedevie, "The Prospect of Happiness: Women, Divorce and Property in the Mississippi Territory, 1798–1817," 57 Journal of Mississippi History 189 (1995).

[12] Laws Ga. 1835, pp. 82–83.

[13] Thomas E. Buckley, S.J., *The Great Catastrophe of My Life: Divorce in the Old Dominion* (2002), pp. 96–97.

[14] Blake, *op. cit.*, p. 50.

spouse joined the Shaker sect—not an unreasonable rule, since the Shakers did not believe in sexual intercourse.[15]

This outbreak of divorce laws surely represented a real increase in the demand for legal divorce. More marriages seemed to be cracking under the strains of nineteenth-century life. This increased the demand for divorce—or for legal separation.[16] As the demand for divorce grew, private divorce bills became a nuisance—a pointless drain on the legislature's time. At the end of the period, some states still granted legislative divorce; but others had abolished them. Maryland passed a general divorce law in 1841; but for years, women still petitioned the legislature to set them free from odious or abusive husbands.[17] Still, by the end of the century, private divorce laws had become extinct. The only road to divorce ran through the courtroom.

So much was structural. Where did this growing demand for easy (or at least easier) divorce come from? The rate of divorce in the nineteenth century was the merest trickle compared to rates in later times. But it was noticeable. To many devout and respectable people, it was an alarming fire bell in the night, a symptom of moral dry rot and a cause in itself of further moral decay. President Timothy Dwight of Yale, in 1816, called the rise in divorces "dreadful beyond conception." It was a form of "stalking, barefaced pollution"; if things went on as they appeared to be going, Connecticut would become "one vast Brothel; one great province of the World of Perdition." The "whole community," he warned, could be thrown "into a general prostitution."[18]

This apocalyptic vision never really came to pass. The family, in any event, was not breaking down as badly as Dwight thought. Yes, the family was changing. There was a slow but real revolution in the way men and women related to each other. William O'Neill put it this way: "when families are large and loose, arouse few expectations, and make few demands, there is no need for divorce." That need arises when "families become the center of social organization." At this point, "their intimacy can become suffocating, their demands unbearable, and their expectations too high to be easily realizable. Divorce then becomes the safety valve that makes the system workable."[19] Moreover, a divorceless state is not necessarily a state without adultery, prostitution, and fornication. It is certainly not a place where there are no drunken, abusive husbands. What it may be—or rather, what it became later in the century—was a place where the official law and the world of real life were sharply different.

A country with rare or expensive divorce—like England—may well be a country with two kinds of family law, one for the rich and one for the poor. The United States had its rich and its poor; but, unlike England, enormous numbers of people owned property and had some stake in society. Easy divorce laws reflected changes in the nature of marriage; but they also grew out of the needs of the middle-class mass. The smallholder had to have some way to stabilize and

---

[15] See *Dyer* v. *Dyer.* 5 N.H. 271 (1830).

[16] For rich material on some nineteenth century separation disputes, see Hendrik Hartog, *Man and Wife in America: A History* (2000).

[17] Richard H. Chused, *Private Acts in Public Places: A Social History of Divorce in the Formative Era of American Family Law* (1994), p. 142.

[18] Quoted in Blake, *op. cit.,* p. 59.

[19] William L. O'Neill, *Divorce in the Progressive Era* (1967), pp. 6–7.

legitimize relationships, to settle doubts about ownership of family property. It was the same general impulse that lay behind the common-law marriage. Divorce was simplest to obtain and divorce laws most advanced in those parts of the country—the West especially—least stratified by class. Divorce had other functions, too. In 1812, the legislature of Maryland granted a divorce to Anne Hoskyns. Her husband, John, was a criminal, a forger, who had absconded, leaving behind a mountain of debts and three children. But legally, as long as they were married, John was in control of her property—and his creditors could reach it, too. The solution was divorce.[20] And, in the restless, mobile society of nineteenth-century America, absconding husbands were far from rare.

Divorce, then, had genuinely popular roots. Even in Timothy Dwight's day, there were plenty of writers and jurists who did not agree with his fire-eating words. Zephaniah Swift, who wrote at the end of the eighteenth century, thought it morally wholesome for Connecticut to recognize absolute divorce. The alternative was divorce from bed and board—legal separation. This, he felt, was an "irresistible temptation to the commission of adultery," suitable only to those with "more frigidity or more virtue than usually falls to the share of human beings." Liberal divorce laws, on the other hand, were "favourable . . . to the virtue, and the happiness of mankind."[21] Divorce, after all, was the gateway to remarriage. And through remarriage a man or woman could create a new and respectable family. The children, for example, would be legitimate. And the wife would have her share of her husband's land and goods if he died.

Since there was strong opinion on both sides, it was only natural that neither side got its way completely. Divorce laws were a kind of compromise. In general, the law never recognized full, free consensual divorce. It became simpler to get a divorce than in the past; but divorce was not routine or automatic. As we said, divorce was in form an adversary proceeding. An innocent and virtuous spouse sued an evil or neglectful partner. The defendant had to be at fault; there had to be "grounds" for the divorce. Otherwise, divorce was legally impossible. Later, the collusive or friendly divorce came to dominate the field. What went on in court was a show, a charade, an afterthought. The real issues were hammered out long beforehand. The law insisted that divorce by mutual consent was wrongful and impossible. But that was what in fact occurred.

The collusive divorce did not become pervasive until later in the century. But it was not unknown in 1840. Collusion was probably most common in states with strict divorce laws, like New York, where adultery was the only practical grounds. Chancellor Kent observed, from his experience as a trial judge, that the sin of adultery "was sometimes committed on the part of the husband, for the very purpose of the divorce."[22] How common this was, is hard to tell. Probably not very common. In fact, since a little white lie—even when it is technically perjury—no doubt bothers people much less than actual adultery, collusion is probably what Kent really had in mind.

---

[20] Richard Chused, *Private Acts in Public Places,* p. 44.

[21] Zephaniah Swift, *A System of the Laws of the State of Connecticut* (1795), vol. I, pp. 192–93. Bishop called the divorce a *mensa et thoro* "a carbuncle on the face of civilized society," a "demoralizing mock-remedy for matrimonial ills." Bishop, *op. cit.,* pp. 217–18.

[22] Kent, *Commentaries,* vol. II (2nd ed., 1832), p. 106.

FAMILY PROPERTY

At common law, there were elaborate rules about the property rights (and duties) of married women. These rules, however, were mainly deducible from one grand "principle of the Common Law, by which the husband and wife are regarded as one person, and her legal existence and authority in a degree lost or suspended, during the continuance of the matrimonial union."[23] Essentially, husband and wife were one flesh; but the man was the owner of that flesh:

> The husband, by marriage, acquires a right to the use of the real estate of his wife, during her life; and if they have a child born alive, then, if he survives, during his life, as tenant by the curtesy. He acquires an absolute right to her chattels real, and may dispose of them. . . . He acquires an absolute property in her chattels personal in possession. . . . As to the property of the wife accruing during coverture, the same rule is applicable.[24]

Actually, customs and practices—and legal doctrine—were more complex than appears from this quotation. There were ways around this dictatorial doctrine. A father could, for example, set up a trust for his daughter, or make some sort of settlement, before marriage; he would thus create a separate estate that courts of equity would recognize. In England, these arrangements were common. Marriage settlements were accepted as valid by the courts, and a rich body of law grew up about them. They were technical and expensive and were, practically speaking, confined to the wealthy, landed classes.

In the United States, these English doctrines and practice had been recognized and, to some extent, followed. Not every colony or state had courts of equity; this was a complication. The status of married women in colonial times is a matter of some dispute. It was once widely assumed that colonial law, compared to English law, was quite liberal; it tended to treat married women much more as free souls. This began a tradition that perhaps never quite died out. Other scholars have questioned the picture of an enlightened colonial past. The issue remains in some doubt.[25]

Essentially, the English system was tolerable, in its home territory, only for upper-class landowners, and even then only because of elaborate tricks and bypasses, which softened its impact. Plantation owners of the South, and other members of the elite, were also able to adapt to the law of settlements and trusts. But these devices were far too intricate for the average person to handle, or the average farmer, or small merchant; perhaps they were too intricate even for the average lawyer. Reform, in the beginning, was modest. In 1787, Massachusetts, recognizing that "sometimes . . . husbands absent themselves from this Commonwealth, and abandon their wives . . . who may be thereby reduced to great distress," enacted a statute that gave the deserted wife authority to petition a court for the right to sell land, "as if she was sole and unmarried."[26]

---

[23] *Ibid.*, p. 129.

[24] Chief Justice Sephaniah Swift, in *Griswold* v. *Penniman*, 2 Conn. 564 (1818). A lease is an example of a "chattel real." The term "coverture" basically refers to marriage.

[25] The issue is dealt with in detail in Marylynn Salmon, *Women and the Law of Property in Early America* (1986), chs. 5 and 6.

[26] *The Perpetual Laws of the Commonwealth of Massachusetts* (1788), p. 362 (act of Nov. 21, 1787).

There were other piecemeal reforms, and also private acts, to take care of particular situations—the legislature could give "feme sole" status to a married woman whose husband had abandoned her, making it possible for her to sell or mortgage her land.[27]

Major reform came with passage of so-called married women's property acts. The first of these, a crude and somewhat tentative version, was enacted in 1839 in Mississippi (another example of reform that began on the legal periphery).[28] The early statutes on married women's property did not give married women full legal equality; they attacked the problem bit by bit. Four of the five sections of the Mississippi act regulated the rights of married women to own and dispose of slaves (the husband retained "control and management of all such slaves, the direction of their labor, and the receipt of the productions thereof").[29] In Michigan, for example, a statute of 1844 merely exempted the wife's earned or inherited property from liability for her husband's "debts and engagements." Still, there was a strong trend at work—though not without opposition. In a speech in Wisconsin in 1847, Marshall Strong denounced the laws: They would take a woman away from her "domestic sphere," and from her children, and thrust her into a world where her "finer sensibilities" would be "blunted . . . and every trait of loveliness blotted out." The husband would be "degraded, the wife unsexed, the children uncared for." And when a husband would come home at night "perplexed with care, dejected with anxiety, depressed in hope," Strong asked, would he find "the same nice and delicate appreciation of his feelings he has heretofore found?" Obviously not. Moreover, this was a civil law idea: "It exists in France, and . . . more than one-fourth of the children annually born in Paris are illegitimate."[30]

Despite such jeremiads, Wisconsin, like other states, followed the general trend. New York passed its first law in 1848; and by 1850, about seventeen states had granted to married women some legal capacity to deal with their property.[31] Real changes had occurred in the social and economic position of women between 1800 and 1845. A few bold and militant women spoke out for women's rights; they made themselves heard, for example, during the debates on the New York law of 1848. But the real fulcrum of change was outside the family and outside the women's movement. There were different forces at work in different states. In New York, the law reacted to property law "reforms" that drastically reduced the ambit of trusts; this made it more difficult, technically,

[27] See Richard H. Chused, "Married Women's Property Law: 1800–1850," 71 Georgetown L.J. 1359, 1370 (1983), for examples in Alabama.

[28] On the possible origins of the Mississippi statute, see the interesting study by Megan Benson, "*Fisher v. Allen:* The Southern Origins of the Married Women's Property Acts," 6 J. Southern Legal History 97 (1998).

[29] Laws Miss. 1839, ch. 46.

[30] Quoted in Catherine B. Cleary, "Married Women's Property Rights in Wisconsin, 1846–1872," 78 Wisconsin Magazine of History 110, 119 (1995).

[31] There is a growing literature on these statutes, stimulated by the new interest in women's history. Two books deal with New York: Peggy Rabkin, *Fathers to Daughters: The Legal Foundations of Female Emancipation* (1980); Norma Basch, *In the Eyes of the Law: Women, Marriage, and Property in Nineteenth-Century New York* (1982). The study by Richard H. Chused, "Married Women's Property Law," cited previously, has material from Maryland; on Wisconsin, see Catherine Cleary, n. 30, supra.

to get around the doctrine of coverture.[32] But everywhere, perhaps, what was most significant was the mass ownership of property, perhaps also the increased activity of women in managing property, and certainly the felt needs of an active land market. The number of women with a stake in the economy had increased dramatically. As we stressed before, the number of *men* with a stake in the economy had increased even more dramatically. This was an extremely important social fact. The ancient disabilities of the married woman were anomalies in the market society that had emerged in the United States. In that society, the dominant actors were smallholders. Land was a commodity to be bought and sold freely.

A key factor, then, was the breakdown in the United States of the specific brand of legal pluralism that was so prominent a feature of English law. In England, the classic common law was geared primarily toward the needs of a tiny minority, the landed gentry. In the United States, the middle-class family was at the core of the law—the Illinois farmer and his family; or the shopkeeper in Boston and *his* family. These men were deeply engaged in the ordinary, working legal system. English land-law practices were too cumbersome, technical, and expensive for this class to use or to tolerate. Moreover (and this was critical), the tangle of rules and practices interfered, potentially, with an efficient, speedy market in land. The statutes spoke about the rights of husbands and wives, as if the main issue was marital intimacy. The nascent women's movement pressed hard for reform. But the main point of the statutes was more modest. They did not aim at revolution inside the little kingdom of the family. They "aimed mainly to keep ordinary families solvent" in parlous economic times.[33] They were meant to rationalize more mundane, even cold-blooded matters, such as the rights of a creditor to collect debts out of land owned by husbands, wives, or both. Most litigation over married women's property was not litigation between spouses, or within the family at all. In almost no case were husbands and wives on opposite sides. The typical cases, both before and after the married women's property acts, therefore, were about the family's external relations, not its internal life. Passage of these laws did not signal a revolution in the status of women; rather, they *ratified* and adjusted a silent revolution. Even though the statutes were about the family, as basic an institution as there is, and seemed to work an important change, still the debates were only modest and fitful. Newspapers made almost no mention of the laws. Little agitation preceded them; great silence followed them. It was the silence of a *fait accompli*.[34]

ADOPTION

Another innovation in family property law was the passage of laws permitting the adoption of children. England was not only a divorceless society; it was a

---

[32] See Gregory S. Alexander, *Commodity and Propriety: Competing Visions of Property in American Legal Thought, 1776–1970* (1997), pp. 158–84.

[33] Nancy F. Cott, *Public Vows*, at 53.

[34] No doubt many and complex forces lay behind the new laws. See Linda E. Speth, "The Married Women's Property Acts, 1839–1865: Reform, Reaction, or Revolution?" in D. Kelly Weisberg, ed., *Women and the Law: The Social Historical Perspective*, vol. 2 (1982), p. 69.

society without adoption laws as well. A child was natural-born or nothing. Not until 1926 did Parliament pass a general adoption law. The United States, as a common-law country, also had no formal provisions for adoption. The first general adoption law, it is usually said, was a Massachusetts law passed in 1851.

In point of fact, there were precursors; adoption laws, or something similar, tucked away in the pages of the statute books. It was a time when many parents died young, when women died in childbirth by the thousands. Large numbers of children were raised by relatives or neighbors. As David Dudley Field put it, "Thousands of children are actually, though not legally, adopted every year."[35] Private acts helped fill this gap; they often took the form of name-change statutes, statutes creating heirship, or the like. In 1846, Mississippi gave local courts power to change names; and, on request, to legitimate a person's "offspring, not born in wedlock"; and also to make any such "offspring" the lawful heir of the petitioner. The court also had power to make "any other person" an heir, that is, not just bastard children. This was an adoption statute in everything but name.[36] The wave of general laws, which started in the 1850s, replaced the rather clumsy system of private acts. It spread like wildfire; and by the end of the century, almost every state had some sort of adoption law. Moreover, the laws tended to put the child, not the adopting parent, in center stage; a judge had to find that the adoptive parents were fit and able to bring up the child properly.[37]

The historical literature on American adoption law lays stress on changes in the nature of family life, in the role of children and their parents, and their relationships to each other.[38] But the point of adoption, as a *legal* device, was not love, but land and money. Nobody needs formal adoption papers or a court decree to love a child deeply, to raise a child, and care for a child; and thousands of people had done this for centuries. Inheritance of property from a "father" or a "mother" is another matter. Most of the statutes stressed the rights of the new son or daughter to inherit. New York's statute, for a while, refused to allow the adopted child to inherit; but this was an exception. To put it another way, the landless poor do not need an adoption law. The passage of these adoption laws may be yet another reflection of the master fact of American law and life: In this society, an enormous mass of ordinary people owned land and other types of property.

POOR LAWS AND SOCIAL WELFARE

In every period, society makes some attempt to care for its weaker members. Legal or social devices try to insure at least some people against some social risks. Law and order are themselves a kind of social insurance. The criminal

---

[35] Quoted in Grossberg, *Governing the Hearth*, p. 272.

[36] Laws Miss. 1846, ch. 60, p. 231. See E. Wayne Carp, *Family Matters: Secrecy and Disclosure in the History of Adoption* (1998), p. 11.

[37] E. Wayne Carp, *op. cit.*, pp. 11–12.

[38] See, for example, Jamil Zainaldin, "The Emergence of a Modern American Family Law: Child Custody, Adoption, and the Courts, 1796–1851," 73 Northwestern U.L. Rev. 1038 (1979); Michael Grossberg, *Governing the Hearth* (1985), pp. 268–80; E. Wayne Carp, *op. cit., supra*, n. 36; Lawrence M. Friedman, *Private Lives*, ch. 4.

law tries to guard people's property against thieves and robbers. Debtor protection laws keep merchants and landowners from falling too far and too fast in the social scale. The family takes care of small children until they can care for themselves. Church groups, the extended family, and the web of personal friendships provide relief for many more of the helpless.

In the nineteenth century, society relied much more on private institutions, to be sure, than on government. The so-called poor laws were the basic welfare laws. The people at the absolute bottom of the social ladder, those who had nowhere to go and no one but government to turn to were labeled "paupers." They were the subjects—perhaps victims is the better word—of the poor laws. These laws probably worked best in small towns and rural areas. The failures of the system were most glaring when its creaking institutions faced a large class of transients or the urban landless poor.

Few scholars have had a kind word to say about nineteenth-century poor laws. But their weaknesses have to be understood in context. Respectable people were hard put to think of real alternatives. Private charity was best; but it never quite filled the need. Some people wanted to abolish poor relief completely, arguing that it did more harm than good. It encouraged idleness and gave money to the "sturdy beggar," one of the (mostly mythical) bogeymen of the nineteenth century. But this extreme view did not win out. For want of anything better, the colonial poor laws stumbled on, after 1776, at first without much change. The basic principle was local rule. As expressed in the New York law of 1788: "Every city and town shall support and maintain their own poor."[39] The administrative unit was the city, town, township, county, or some combination of these.[40] Centralized state administration was a century away.

A fortiori, in a system of this sort, the federal government had nothing to do with the poor laws. It played a minute role in social welfare. The exceptions were few and revealing. On February 17, 1815, after the great earthquake in New Madrid, Missouri, Congress passed an act to help those whose lands had "been materially injured by earthquakes." These sufferers were allowed to locate "the like quantity of land" in other parts of the public domain in Missouri Territory.[41] This act, one notes, did not extract a cent of hard cash from the treasury. The federal government was short of money, but long on land. It gave away geese, not golden eggs.

Even at that, there were few federal land grants for welfare purposes. Only after long and bitter debate did the federal government assign land to the Kentucky Deaf and Dumb Asylum (1826). Dorothea Dix lobbied vigorously for land grants to aid the insane. Yet, President Franklin Pierce vetoed such a bill in 1854, partly because he felt it was inappropriate for the federal government to act as "the great almoner of public charity, throughout the United States."

In some instances, the federal government was more lavish, and states' righters did not question its authority. A law of 1798 imposed a payroll tax on the wages of sailors. The money was to be used to support hospitals for sick and

---

[39] Quoted in David M. Schneider, *The History of Public Welfare in New York State, 1609–1866* (1938), p. 112.

[40] Fern Boan, *A History of Poor Relief Legislation and Administration in Missouri* (1941), pp. 22–23.

[41] 3 Stats. 211 (act of Feb. 17, 1815).

disabled seamen.[42] Veterans of national wars were entitled to pensions and bonuses of land. Neither veterans nor sailors, of course, were pariahs. They were in the same category as the victims of the New Madrid earthquake: Their deprivations, people felt, were in no way their own doing. These beneficiaries were respectable people, voters, the family that lived next door. Veterans' benefits, indeed, had a double meaning. After all, men would be more likely to enlist if they thought a grateful nation would take care of them when they became old and sick and poor. And, although the federal government avoided anything that smacked of poor relief, there was in fact a tradition of federal disaster relief. It was at times controversial; but it was consistent throughout American history. Money, for example, went to victims of a fire in Alexandria, Virginia; to people who suffered damage in the War of 1812; and to people who suffered from various raids of native tribes.[43]

The general public, like Congress, tended to be relatively generous to sufferers who were socially defined as blameless—the sick, the old, the deaf and dumb, the insane. Kentucky established a state home in the 1820s for those "who, by the mysterious dispensation of Providence, are born deaf and of course dumb." The law called on all "philanthropic citizens" to "promote an object so benevolent and humane," and backed up its words with a cash appropriation. Kentucky also established a public asylum for the insane. Massachusetts set up a state reform school in 1847 for young offenders.[44] This was an early example of special treatment for the young, of a kind which became more prominent later on.

The township pauper, on the other hand, particularly when he was a stranger in town, had no such claim on public sympathy. The pauper was condemned as an idler, a profligate, a weakling, a drunk. Communities bitterly resented the money they had to pay for support of this sort of person. The people who wanted to discard the whole system of relief pointed to these people; they argued that "distress and poverty multiply in proportion to the funds created to relieve them." The dole, in other words, was counterproductive; it tended to "impair that anxiety for a livelihood which is almost instinctive"; giving out money could "relax individual exertion by unnerving the arm of industry." These are quotes from an influential New York report published in 1824.[45] Poor relief was not, in

---

[42] Henry W. Farnam, *Chapters in the History of Social Legislation in the United States to 1860* (1938), pp. 232–34.

[43] Michele L. Landis, "Let Me Next Time Be 'Tried by Fire'": Disaster Relief and the Origins of the American Welfare State, 1789–1874," 92 Northwestern U. Law Rev. 967 (1998).

[44] Sophonisba P. Breckinridge, *Public Welfare Administration in the United States* (2nd ed., 1938), pp. 98, 99, 101, 113. The treatment of dependent children, however, seems by modern standards barbaric. Orphans were liable to be sold as apprentices. But there was little else to be done with homeless boys and girls. A master was at least supposed to teach his apprentice to read and write. Girls learned to cook and sew. Boys worked, and learned a trade, in exchange for meals and a home. In 1794, for example, ten New York boys from the almshouse were "bound to Andrew Stockholm & Co. at the Cotton Manufactury." Schneider, *op. cit.,* p. 181. On the founding of houses of refuge for wayward children, in the 1820s, see Robert M. Mennel, *Thorns and Thistles: Juvenile Delinquents in the United States, 1825–1940* (1973), p. 50.

[45] *Report of the Secretary of State on the Relief and Settlement of the Poor,* New York Assembly Journal, Feb. 9, 1824.

fact, abolished; but many people felt the laws should be punitive, even harsh. These laws were supposed to deter, to make poverty unpalatable, to make relief come bitter and dear.

How the laws actually worked is not always easy to tell. No doubt there were acts of kindness, empathy, humanity. But there were abuses, too, which scream from the record. The law itself had a certain callousness. Case after case bore on the question of whether a pauper was "settled" in this or that county or town. "Settlement" fixed responsibility for the upkeep of a pauper. Under a New Hampshire law of 1809, which was not atypical, a town might support a pauper even if he was not technically "settled" there. But the creditor town could then sue the town of settlement to recover its costs.[46] There are many such cases reported, in which towns and counties sued each other, over the issue of "settlement."

A legal concept begins its career as smooth and as perfect as an egg. But if the concept has economic or social consequences and leads to controversy and contention between interest groups, litigation can batter and bruise it out of shape; or turn it into a rat's nest of complexity. This happened to the concept of "settlement." In one volume alone of the *Connecticut Reports* (volume VII, for 1828–1829), four cases on poor relief were reported. The town of Litchfield sued the town of Farmington over support of a pauper named Asabel Moss and his family. The town of Reading sued the town of Weston "for supplies furnished to *Harriet,* the wife, and *Sally* and *Lucinda,* the minor children, of Samuel Darling." The keeper of the county jail in Norwich sued the town of Norwich "to recover for support furnished by the plaintiff, to *James Hazard* and *John Blake,* prisoners in such gaol." In the same volume, the town of Plainfield sued a putative father, one Hopkins, "for the maintenance of a bastard child." And these were appellate cases only—the visible tip of the iceberg. Decades of litigation made the whole concept incredibly complex and intricate.

Since one township could get money back from the township where the pauper was (legally) settled, a misplaced pauper, in theory, was not going to starve. But lawsuits cost money. Towns could hardly predict how difficult cases would come out. Lawsuits were a last resort. It was better not to have paupers to begin with. Besides, if a pauper stayed around long enough, he just might gain a valid settlement. In many states, it was a crime to bring a pauper into a new county. By an old custom, newcomers who looked dubious were "warned out" to prevent them from gaining a settlement. This was the opposite of the welcome wagon: It was a threat to get going—or else. If the pauper did not leave, he and his family could be taken to the county or township line and dumped over the border. In extreme cases, paupers were passed on from place to place, "sent backwards and forwards . . . like a shuttlecock, without end."[47]

Local authorities were constantly trying to keep down the costs of relief. Under a law of Indiana Territory (1807), by no means unique, overseers of the poor in each township had the duty "to cause all poor persons, who have, or shall become a public charge to be farmed out at public vendue, or out-cry, to wit; On the first Monday in May, yearly and every year, at some public

---

[46] Laws N.H. 1809, ch. 36.
[47] Quoted in Martha Branscombe, *The Courts and the Poor Laws in New York State, 1784–1929* (1943), p. 102.

place . . . to the person or persons, who shall appear to be the lowest bidder or bidders."[48] In 1845, Emaley Wiley bought all of the paupers of Fulton County, Illinois, for $594.[49] Obviously, farming out the poor to the lowest bidder had a perverse effect; it drove the level of care down to the very bottom; it encouraged the worst penny-pinching, if not outright starvation tactics. It was an engine of exploitation as well.

Many contemporaries agreed that the system was cruel and inhuman. Many felt it failed to get at the roots of the problem. The medicine was harsh; but it was not working. Paupers seemed to be multiplying in the land. Josiah Quincy's report of 1821, on the pauper laws of Massachusetts, issued blunt words of warning. "Outdoor relief"—providing money and other help to people in their own homes—was of all methods of relief "the most wasteful, the most expensive, and the most injurious to their morals and destructive to their industrious habits."[50] The whole system had to be restructured. Outdoor relief had to go. The auction system was also bad. The report strongly urged adoption of what came to be called *indoor* (that is, institutional) relief. The New York report on the welfare laws, which was quoted earlier, and which was published in 1824, agreed with Quincy; indoor relief was the better way. The right method was the almshouse, poorhouse, or poor farm: more efficient, and a way to provide moral education, not to mention putting the poor to work. Best of all, the government would save money:

> It is believed that with proper care and attention, and under favorable circumstances, the average annual expense *in* an almshouse, having a convenient farm attached to it, will not exceed from 20 to 35 dollars for the support of each pauper, exclusive of the amount of labour he may perform; while *out* of an almshouse, it will not be less than from 33 to 65 dollars, and in many instances where the pauper is old and infirm, or diseased, from 80 to 100 dollars, and even more.[51]

The poor farm was not a new invention; but these two reports helped give the idea fresh popularity.[52] In 1824, New York passed a comprehensive act "to provide for the establishment of county poorhouses." This act, a "historic step," established the "principle of indoor relief"; it made the county poorhouse "the center of the public relief system." It also introduced some wholesome reforms; it "advanced the principle of county responsibility for all poor persons lacking settlement," and prohibited "removals of indigent persons across county lines."[53] Of course, this law could not and did not guarantee that poor farms would be efficient or humane, despite the hopes of its sponsors. As was true of prison reform, well-meant changes sometimes merely centralized the horror. By 1838, some county homes were reported to be in a state of inhuman squalor.[54]

---

[48] Francis S. Philbrick, ed., *The Laws of Indiana Territory, 1801–1809* (1930), pp. 308–9.

[49] Sophonisba P. Breckinridge, *The Illinois Poor Law and Its Administration* (1939), p. 63.

[50] Quoted in Walter I. Trattner, *From Poor Law to Welfare State* (6th ed., 1999), p. 56.

[51] *Ibid.*, p. 43.

[52] See Michael B. Katz, *In the Shadow of the Poorhouse: A Social History of Welfare in America* (rev. ed., 1996), Part I.

[53] Schneider, *op. cit.*, p. 236.

[54] *Ibid.*, pp. 244–45.

The root of the problem was not structural. It lay in society's indifference. The mass of the public feared and distrusted vagrants. Even men of good will were blinded by the fantasy of "sturdy beggars," that is, the able-bodied poor, men unwilling to earn an honest living. Reform movements fed on a few noisy scandals, emphasized the failures of the old system, and called for fresh approaches. But reformers lacked the will to follow through, and no concrete interest group had any reason to gain from a thorough reform of the welfare system. So, even when reforms succeeded in changing formal law, the new programs did not work as they were supposed to; old evil habits soon reappeared. From poor laws to poor farms to AFDC, to the "end of welfare as we know it" under President Clinton, it is all a single sad lesson on what powerlessness and pariah status can mean in the United States.

SLAVERY AND AFRICAN AMERICANS

The most visible American pariah, before the Civil War, was the black slave. As we have seen, an indigenous system of law grew up to govern the "peculiar institution" of slavery.[55] What was at first a law for the servant class developed deeper and deeper overtones of color. The slave laws then became laws about the fate of a race.

No feature of American life has been so marked with blood and failure as the confrontation of white and black. Yet in 1776, liberals had some reason to be optimistic. The air rang with hopeful speeches on the inherent rights of man. Were these rights for black men as well as white men? (Women, of course, were another question). There was, in fact, widespread agreement that the slave trade was an abomination; that it had to be ended. A society was formed in Pennsylvania in 1784 "for promoting the abolition of slavery, and the relief of free negroes, unlawfully held in Bondage, and for Improving the Condition of the African Race." In New York in 1785, John Jay and Alexander Hamilton helped organize a "Society for the Promotion of the Manumission of Slaves and Protecting such of them that have been or may be Liberated."[56] Before the end of that century, northern states took definite steps to rid themselves of slavery. A Pennsylvania law of 1780, "for the gradual abolition of slavery," recited its belief that all "inhabitants of the . . . earth," were "the work of an Almighty Hand," even though different "in feature or complexion." The statute promised to "add one more step to universal civilization by removing as much as possible the sorrows of those who have lived in undeserved bondage, and from which by the assumed authority of the Kings of Britain, no effectual legal relief

[55] The literature on slavery is immense, and growing all the time. See, in general, Kenneth M. Stampp, *The "Peculiar" Institution: Slavery in the Antebellum South* (1956); Ira Berlin, *Many Thousands Gone: The First Two Centuries of Slavery in North America* (1998). There is a good deal of material too in John Hope Franklin and Alfred A. Moss Jr., *From Slavery to Freedom: A History of African Americans* (8th ed., 2002). Specifically on the law of slavery, see Thomas D. Morris, *Southern Slavery and the Law, 1619–1860* (1996).

[56] Merrill Jensen, *The New Nation* (1950), pp. 135–36.

could be obtained."[57] All slaves held in Pennsylvania were to be registered; and there were to be no new slaves. The statute also took steps to assimilate the legal condition of black slaves to that of white indentured servants. Other northern states also provided for an end to slavery—but never at once; it was always a gradual process.[58] New Jersey was the last of the northern states to get rid of slavery. Children of slaves born after July 4, 1804 were to be servants, not slaves, and at 25 (21 for females) were to go free.[59]

Even the South felt some of this moral fervor. Quaker and Methodist leaders were dead set against slavery. A distinguished and respected minority in the South, including such political leaders as Jefferson, Washington, and Madison, were disturbed by the "peculiar institution," and hoped it would disappear. St. George Tucker, one of the most eminent of Virginia lawyers, wrote a *Dissertation on Slavery; with a Proposal for the Gradual Abolition of It, in the State of Virginia* (1796). "Abolition" was not yet a curse word in the South. Some slave owners actually set their slaves free. Southern legislatures had for some time passed a number of private acts of manumission. In 1782, Virginia passed a general and permissive law, allowing owners to set slaves free. Maryland, in 1790, gave slave owners the right to manumit slaves in their last wills and testaments.

It was, for the blacks, a false dawn only. Slavery was not destined to wither away. The Constitution of 1787 never mentioned the word "slavery," but slavery was an issue in the Constitutional debates; and the final document tried to deal with slavery in a way that would offend neither North nor South. On the question of fugitive slaves, the Constitution was relatively firm. A fugitive slave "shall be delivered upon Claim of the Party to whom [his] Service or Labour may be due" (art. IV, sec. 2). A similar provision appeared in the Ordinance of 1787, though slavery itself was outlawed in the Northwest Territory. In the South, it became clearer and clearer as the years went on that the legal rights of man stopped at the color line. The cleavage between North and South did not dissolve; on the slavery question, it deepened and darkened.

On paper at least, the law of slavery grew more severe between the Revolution and the Civil War. The slave-owning South dug in its heels. Slavery had become an essential pillar of the labor system, particularly in the plantation South; it was a pillar of the southern social system too. Slaves were the hands and the bodies that picked the cotton and other crops. They were the cooks and the nannies and the gardeners and the servants that took care of white people with money. There were also thousands of urban slaves. They were the porters, luggage-haulers, and maids in the hotels. They were also workers in factories and mills. In Richmond, Virginia, by the time of the civil war, slaves

[57] *Statutes at Large of Pennsylvania from 1682 to 1801*, vol. X, 1779–81 (1904), pp. 67–68; see, in general, Arthur Zilversmit, *The First Emancipation: The Abolition of Slavery in the North* (1967).

[58] Joanne Pope Melish, *Disowning Slavery: Gradual Emancipation and "Race" in New England, 1780–1860* (1998), ch. 3.

[59] Daniel R. Ernst, "Legal Positivism, Abolitionist Litigation and the New Jersey Slave Case of 1845," 4 Law and History Review 337, 339 (1986). As late as 1840, however, there were still 674 slaves in New Jersey, though most of them were (of course) over 55 (ibid., at 340).

made up almost half the city's workforce. They processed iron and tobacco; they built the railroads.[60]

The South needed its slaves. It profited from their labor. Yet in some ways, economic motives seem too flaccid to explain the southern passion about race. The slave system was a way of life. It was a social system, a culture. And slave owners, in the course of time, felt more and more threatened, more beleaguered. The South became, in a way, a kingdom of fear—fear of the influence of free blacks, fear of the North, fear of abolitionists. But above all, race war was the fear. Race war, said de Tocqueville, "is a nightmare constantly haunting the American imagination," both North and South.[61] Sometimes the nightmare became a reality. There were conspiracies in Virginia, in 1800 and 1802; these were crushed, and the slaves involved, including Gabriel, one of the leaders of the first of these, were hanged.[62] There were other plots, conspiracies, and rebellions: Denmark Vesey's in South Carolina, and the most famous of all, Nat Turner's attempt, in 1831, to "lead his people out of bondage." In the small war that followed, some 60 whites were killed. But this was a hopeless struggle; Turner's revolt was put down savagely, and he and some of his followers swung from the gallows.[63]

The southern states passed laws to crush any possible slave revolt, and to punish disobedience and rebellion with brute force. The best tactic was prevention. Slaves could not legally own guns. Actual insurrection led to absolute, certain death. Free persons who incited rebellion were not spared. Incitement to insurrection by free persons became a capital crime in Alabama in 1812; in 1832, the state authorized the death penalty even for those who published or distributed literature which might tend to arouse slave rebellion.[64]

Rebellion is a collective act; more frequently, slaves fought back against the system in other ways—disobedience, petty theft, and especially, by running away. It is not easy to know how many slaves deserted their masters. Perhaps it was on the order of a thousand a year. A study of newspaper ads for runaways in Virginia found more than 600 in the decade of the 1850s.[65] The runaway issue was a constant irritant in North-South relations, as we will see. Southern states moved, too, to tighten the law of manumission. They did not want a growing population of free blacks. Yet there were slave owners who set slaves free; and some slaves, too, who earned money somehow, and bought their freedom. The number of freed slaves varied from state to state. Manumission was more common in Virginia than in South Carolina. In some states, the law required freed slaves to get out of the state. After 1805, any freed slave who stayed on in Virginia, for more than a year after manumission, might legally be "apprehended and sold by the

---

[60] Midori Takagi, *"Rearing Wolves to Our Own Destruction": Slavery in Richmond, Virginia, 1782–1865* (1999), pp. 73–77.

[61] Alexis de Tocqueville, *Democracy in America* (J. P. Mayer and Max Lerner, eds., 1966), p. 329.

[62] On this episode, see Douglas R. Egerton, *Gabriel's Rebellion: The Virginia Slave Conspiracies of 1800 and 1802* (1993).

[63] John Hope Franklin and Alfred A. Moss Jr., *From Slavery to Freedom: A History of African Americans* (8th ed., 2002), pp. 162–66.

[64] Farnam, *op. cit.,* p. 187.

[65] William A. Link, *Roots of Secession: Slavery and Politics in Antebellum Virginia* (2003), p. 99.

overseers of the poor of any county . . . in which he or she shall be found."[66] Two slaves, Patty Green and Betty, of Charles City County, Virginia, found guilty of staying in the state more than a year, were re-enslaved in 1834, by court order.[67] Private statutes sometimes softened this harsh law. In 1814, for example, a special act allowed an old black, George Butler, to remain in Virginia with his family, who were still slaves. By the 1830s, petitions for this sort of private act were common enough to warrant a general law on the subject. In the new law (1837), the legislature washed its hands of the matter and referred individual cases to the courts.[68] On the whole, however, white opinion was hostile to African Americans who were at least nominally free. They were a cancer, an "evil and . . . moral danger." Virginia passed a law in 1856 to encourage "voluntary enslavement."[69]

It was fortunate that exile laws were not strictly enforced. Free blacks had nowhere to go. Northern states did not greet them with open arms, to put it mildly. By an Illinois statute of 1829, any "black or mulatto person" who wanted to settle in Illinois had to show the county court where he lived "a certificate of his or her freedom;" and had to post a thousand-dollar bond "conditioned that such person will not, at any time, become a charge to said county, or any other county of this state, as a poor person, and . . . shall . . . demean himself, or herself, in strict conformity with the laws of this state, that now are or hereafter may be enacted."[70] A Tennessee law put it bluntly: "No free person of color shall remove from any other State or territory of the Union into this State to reside here and remain in the State twenty days."[71] The city of Cincinnati tried to enforce a law requiring blacks to post a five-hundred-dollar bond (1829). Blacks petitioned for relief; white mobs took to the streets; riots ensued; afterwards, more than a thousand blacks moved to Canada.[72]

There was, as always, another side to this picture. In the North, there was a growing abolition movement. And northern states were stubborn and hostile, at times, with regard to the fugitive slave laws. The Constitution called for returning such fugitives; Congress passed a law to flush out this mandate in 1793. It allowed a slave owner, or his agent, to take a fugitive, and bring him before a judge; if the case was made out, the judge was to issue a warrant to return the slave to the place he came from.[73] As the years went by, important segments of opinion in northern states found the professional "slave-catchers," and the whole business of finding and seizing runaway slaves, more and more obnoxious. Some states passed "antikidnapping" laws. Cases under the fugitive slaves laws generated enormous heat. One of the most noted was *Prigg v. Pennsylvania*.[74] Edward Prigg was one of a group of men from Maryland who seized

---

[66] Laws Va. 1805, ch. 63, sec. 10.

[67] Thomas D. Morris, *Southern Slavery and the Law*, p. 372.

[68] Laws Va. 1836–37, ch. 70.

[69] Link, *Roots of Secession*, pp 156, 158; on voluntary enslavement in New Orleans, see Judith Kelleher Schafer, *Becoming Free, Remaining Free, Manumission and Enslavement in New Orleans, 1846–1862* (2003), ch. 9.

[70] Rev. Laws Ill. 1829, p. 109.

[71] Tenn. Code 1858, sec. 2726.

[72] Leon F. Litwack, *North of Slavery: The Negro in the Free States, 1790–1860* (1961), p. 72–73.

[73] Don E. Fehrenbacher, *The Slaveholding Republic* (2001), p. 219.

[74] 16 Pet. (41 U.S.) 539 (1842).

Margaret Morgan, a runaway slave, who was living in Pennsylvania. Prigg asked for a certificate, under the 1793 law; the local judge refused to grant it. Prigg took Morgan and her children anyway. He was indicted under the local anti-kidnapping law. The Supreme Court reversed the conviction. State laws that interfered with enforcement of the fugitive slave law were unconstitutional.[75] The 1850 fugitive-slave law, passed during the administration of Millard Fillmore, basically increased the federal role in bringing back fugitive slaves. The law was at least somewhat effective; in a few years, about 70 fugitives were dragged back to bondage.[76] But by this time the situation was, in a way, politically hopeless. This was the period of *Uncle Tom's Cabin;* the fugitive-slave law only added fuel to the antislavery fire. The Fugitive Slave Law of 1850 was supposed to make it easy, indeed, almost automatic, for a slave to be ordered back to the owner. But attempts to do this met with bitter, sometimes violent resistance in a number of northern cities. A Virginia slave owner was able to get his runaway slave, Anthony Burns, back from Boston in 1854, but only after a long, bitter trial, and horrendous controversy that threatened to rip the city apart.[77] In 1856, Kentucky slave owners recovered seven runaways, caught near Cincinnati, but there was violence, and one of the slaves, Margaret Garner, tried to kill her children rather than see them returned to slavery.[78] Free blacks in the north felt threatened by the fugitive slave law. Nefarious gangs like the "Black Birds" of New York, or the "Gap Gang" in Lancaster County, Pennsylvania, brought terror to black communities.[79] The Underground Railway, spiriting fugitives to Canada, increased its efforts during this period. The split between slave and free states was turning into a jagged chasm. A course of legal wrangling had begun that reached its climax in the *Dred Scott* case.[80] The majority opinion in this notorious decision (1857), written by Chief Justice Taney, was an attempt to put the slavery issue beyond the reach of Congress—or of anybody. What the case actually decided was that Dred Scott was still a slave, even though he had once lived in free territory. (Arguably, a slave became automatically free once

[75] Paul Finkelman argues that Joseph Story, who wrote the opinion in the Prigg case, had as his "primary goal" enhancing the power of the federal government in this area. Paul Finkelman, "Story Telling on the Supreme Court: Prigg v. Pennsylvania and Justice Joseph Story's Judicial Nationalism," 1994 Supreme Court Review 247, 249.

[76] Fehrenbacher, *Slaveholding Republic,* p. 235.

[77] See Albert J. Von Frank, *The Trials of Anthony Burns: Freedom and Slavery in Emerson's Boston* (1998).

[78] Fehrenbacher, *Slaveholding Republic,* p. 238.

[79] James Oliver Horton and Lois E. Horton, "A Federal Assault: African Americans and the Impact of the Fugitive Slave Law of 1850," in Paul Finkelman, ed., *Slavery and the Law* (1997), pp. 143, 152.

[80] Russel B. Nye, *Fettered Freedom: Civil Liberties and the Slavery Controversy, 1830–1860* (1963), pp. 257–78. On the enforcement issues under the fugitive-slave laws, see Robert Cover, *Justice Accused: Anti-Slavery and the Judicial Process* (1975); Paul Finkelman, *An Imperfect Union: Slavery, Federalism, and Comity* (1981), deals with the tangled issues of the extraterritorial effects of slavery in a federal union that was half slave and half free. The full meaning of the *Dred Scott* case is explored in Don E. Fehrenbacher, *The Dred Scott Case: Its Significance in American Law and Politics* (1978).

There had been enforcement problems under the laws against the slave trade as well. See Warren S. Howard, *American Slavers and the Federal Laws, 1837–1862* (1963).

he was living in free territory.)[81] But Taney went far beyond this point. He argued that the Missouri Compromise was unconstitutional, that Congress had no power to abolish slavery in the territories, and that blacks were not and could not be citizens of the United States. The decision, as William Wiecek has put it, relegated "black people in America to some extraconstitutional limbo where they were to remain perpetually, as something less than citizens."[82] Taney perhaps thought this decision would settle matters. He was badly mistaken. It only added fuel to the raging fire.

The southern states, for their part, defended their institution with great vigor. Southern propaganda lauded slavery. Southern legislatures passed laws against abolitionist propaganda. When antislavery petitions flooded into Congress, in the 1830s, southern legislators shoved through a "gag rule" that kept the issue of slavery off the agenda; the "gag rule" was finally eliminated after a long struggle, led by John Quincy Adams.[83] Southern intellectuals wrote books in defense of the "peculiar institution." And southern law put more and more restraints on manumission. Blacks were destined to be, and always be, slaves.

Some control over manumission was, in context, understandable. Otherwise, an owner might be tempted to set free slaves who were old or sick, and shift the cost of food, medicine, and clothes to the state. An insolvent master might maliciously manumit his slaves, to spite or thwart his creditors. Still, the *political* sins of emancipation no doubt stood uppermost in southern minds. The South did not want the free black mass to grow. As early as 1800, South Carolina law declared it an abuse to set free any depraved or dependent slaves. A slave could only be emancipated if "five indifferent freeholders living in the neighborhood" certified that the slave had good character and could support himself. By 1820, South Carolina cut off all emancipations except by will, and only as a reward for meritorious service. The final step, outlawing *all* manumissions, occurred reluctantly and late: in 1858 in Arkansas; in 1860 in Maryland and Alabama.[84] Soon afterwards, the civil war dealt with the issue once and for all.

Dominant southern opinion insisted on keeping blacks firmly in their place. Slaves were not supposed to work for wages or to own anything. A few slaves, however, were only nominally slaves. Their owners let them do as they pleased. In Vicksburg, Mississippi, in 1857, a black barber, Oliver Garrett, earned enough money to buy his freedom; a few slaves even started their own businesses.[85] In general, the free black population was not inconsiderable. All northern blacks were free. In 1860, there were 488,000 free blacks in the United States. There

[81] This was, for example, established doctrine in Louisiana, though the United States Supreme Court had held otherwise. In 1846, Louisiana tried to close this loophole, by passing a law that said that no slave was entitled to freedom "under the pretense that he or she has been . . . in a country where slavery does not exist, or in [a state] . . . where slavery is prohibited." Louisiana Acts 1846, p. 163, quoted in Judith Schafer, *Becoming Free, Remaining Free* (2003), p. 16.

[82] William M. Wiecek, *Liberty under Law: The Supreme Court in American Life* (1988), p. 78.

[83] William Lee Miller, *Arguing about Slavery: The Great Battle in the United States Congress* (1996).

[84] Farnam, *op. cit.*, pp. 199–200.

[85] Christopher Waldrep, *Roots of Disorder: Race and Criminal Justice in the American South, 1817–80* (1998), p. 30.

were 83,900 in Maryland. There were over 25,000 in Baltimore alone, over 10,000 in New Orleans.[86] In Virginia, there were almost 60,000 free blacks. Free blacks were a negligible part of the population only in the newer slave states, such as Mississippi. Legally, free blacks lived in a kind of modified slavery. Nowhere were they treated as the equal of the white man. As of 1830, only four states, all in New England, allowed free blacks the same right to vote as free whites. Many northern states—for example, Illinois—did not allow inter-marriage between black and white. As we saw, free blacks were unwelcome as im-migrants in many northern states. Many people in the North—perhaps most people—despised the institution of slavery; and soldiers were willing to die in a war that was at least in some measure a war against slavery. But this did not mean these same people believed in racial equality, or that all men were brothers (let alone women as sisters). They most assuredly did not, and the treatment of free blacks is part of the evidence.

In slave states, there were extreme disabilities against free blacks. In Mary-land (1806), a free black could not own a dog. In Georgia, free blacks could not own, use, or carry firearms, dispense medicine, set type, or make contracts for repairing buildings. They could not deal in agricultural commodities without permission. They could not acquire land or slaves in Savannah and Augusta; in some Georgia cities, they could not operate restaurants and inns. Under some criminal laws, there were special punishments for free black offenders, more se-vere than those imposed on whites who committed the same crime.[87] Free blacks, as a Virginia legislator said, had "many *legal* rights but no constitutional ones."[88] They had some formal rights, in other words, but what these were worth is another question. The free black, in the words of a notorious Georgia case, "resides among us, and yet is a stranger. A *native* even, and yet not a citizen. Though not a *slave*, yet is he not free. . . . His fancied freedom is all a delu-sion. . . . [S]ociety suffers, and the negro suffers by manumission."[89]

Even the formal rights were subject to constant attrition. In southern eyes, black was black. Whether the person was slave or free was almost incidental. The free black was a dangerous person. The free black threatened the whole caste system. He was an anomaly. As we saw, newly freed slaves were often told to leave the state; and immigration of free blacks was outlawed—in Virginia as early as 1793. Later, Virginia appropriated money to help send free blacks to Africa. After 1830, law often frowned on giving an education to blacks, free or slave. The Georgia penal code made it a crime to "teach any slave, negro, or free per-son of color, to read or write, either written or printed characters."[90] In South Carolina, it was already unlawful in 1800 for "any number of slaves, free negroes, mulattoes, or mestizoes, even in company of white persons, to meet together for the purpose of mental instruction or religious worship, either before the rising of the sun or after the going down of the sun." White fraternizers were highly unwelcome, too. By an 1834 law in South Carolina, a white man who gambled with a black, slave or free, was liable to be whipped "not exceeding thirty-nine

[86] Franklin and Moss, *From Slavery to Freedom* (8th ed., 2002), p. 169.

[87] W. McDowell Rogers, "Free Negro Legislation in Georgia before 1865," 16 Ga. Hist. Q. 27 (1932).

[88] Quoted in John H. Russell, *The Free Negro in Virginia, 1619–1865* (1913), p. 122.

[89] J. Lumpkin in *Bryan* v. *Walton*, 14 Ga. 185, 202, 205 (1853).

[90] Laws Ga. 1833, p. 202.

lashes." In New Orleans, in 1835, the city council adopted an ordinance that allocated the city's cemeteries one-half to whites, one-fourth to slaves, one-fourth to free blacks. In 1841, an ordinance required separate burial registration lists for whites and blacks.[91]

William Goodell, an antislavery writer, stated wryly that American slavery might be added "to the list of the strict sciences. From a single fundamental axiom, all the parts of the system are logically and scientifically deduced." The axiom was that the slave was property, that he had "no rights."[92] To be sure, the slave was a "person," for purposes of the criminal law, and indeed, criminal law was much harsher for blacks than for whites. But in other regards, the slave was a commodity. No slave could vote or hold office, enter into contracts, own property. Slaves were bought and sold like so many bales of cotton. The case reports of slave states are full of wrangles about sales, gifts, mortgages, and bequests of slaves. In a case from Kentucky, one of the parties took "a negro boy" to the races at New Orleans, and bet him on the horse Lucy Dashwood.[93] There were frequent lawsuits arising out of the sale of slaves—cases where buyers complained that the slave was sick, or mentally ill, or a runaway, and that the owner had known about this fact, and cheated the buyer. In one case in Louisiana, for example, the buyer of a nineteen-year-old woman, Ellen Dorn, complained that the slave had epilepsy and "other fits," that she had seizures and foamed at the mouth. The buyer got his money back.[94] These cases were, in fact, the most common of all civil cases involving slaves, throughout the South.[95]

Although slaves were not allowed to marry, there were slave "marriages"— stable and lasting unions; strong, well-knit family groups.[96] But they were never recognized by law. The family could be, and often was, broken up by sale, gift, or transfer of a parent, spouse, or child. This happened out of sheer callousness at times; at other times, it was forced on slave owners, who were in debt, or on the occasion of a slave owner's death, or the liquidation of his estate. In South Carolina, in fact (and no doubt in other states), the state itself, through tax sales and the like, was the "largest slave auctioneering firm."[97] Moreover, these sales often disrupted families. Most of the slaves were sold as individuals, not as families or groups. When an estate in Texas was divided among the heirs in 1848, a blacksmith, Armystead was sold in one lot; and his wife and three children were sold in another lot. This was not an isolated case.[98] A few states

---

[91] Roger A. Fischer, "Racial Segregation in Antebellum New Orleans," 74 Am. Hist. Rev. 926, 933 (1969).

[92] William Goodell, *The American Slave Code in Theory and Practice* (1853), p. 105.

[93] *Thomas v. Davis*, 7 B. Mon 227 (Ky,, 1846). The horse won the race.

[94] Judith Shafer, *Slavery, the Civil Law, and the Supreme Court of Louisiana*, p. 135.

[95] Ariela Gross, *Double Character: Slavery and Mastery in the Antebellum Southern Courtroom* (2000), ch. 5.

[96] See Herbert G. Gutman, *The Black Family in Slavery and Freedom, 1750–1925* (1976), pp. 9–17. These marriages, moreover, often began with a ceremony. On the plantation of James Henry Hammond, in South Carolina, the master conducted weddings, gave gifts to the bride and groom, and punished slaves who were unfaithful to their husbands or wives. Drew Gilpin Faust, *James Henry Hammond and the Old South: A Design for Mastery* (1982), p. 85.

[97] Thomas D. Russell, "South Carolina's Largest Slave Auctioneering Firm," 68 Chicago-Kent Law Review 1241 (1993)

[98] Randolph B. Campbell, *An Empire for Slavery: The Peculiar Institution in Texas, 1821–1865* (1989), pp. 165–66.

had laws that prohibited selling little children apart from their mothers; but even these statutes had exceptions; and in countless sales husbands and wives were sold away from each other, brothers were separated from brothers and sisters from sisters; and older children from their parents and loved ones.[99]

Some scholars have argued that slavery in the United States was completely different from slavery in Latin America. The Latin American slave was allowed to marry. To the Church, he was a soul, to be treated as a soul; he was not quite so dehumanized as were the slaves in the states.[100] American law was on the surface harsher, more rigorous. In this regard, the law may have reflected something real in social attitudes, underlying the law: a more deep-seated race-consciousness, a more profound rejection of any notion of equality, and, perhaps, a greater sense of danger to the social order.

Slavery was essential to the southern economy. This was particularly true of the plantation economy. Slaves were a capital asset; they were as much a part of the estate as the good earth itself. A law of colonial Virginia (1705), as we have seen, declared slaves to be real estate, not personal property. There were similar laws in Kentucky in 1798, and in Louisiana Territory in 1806.[101] In those jurisdictions, this meant that, in essence, one single cluster of rules applied to transfer and inheritance of the whole "estate." That is, the same rules covered both the plantation and farm, and the slaves who worked in the fields and in the house. In these jurisdictions, for example, widows had dower rights in their husbands' slaves. Virginia repealed its law in 1792, perhaps because it was technically cumbersome. Nonetheless, the law remained sensitive to connections between slaves and the land. A Virginia statute of 1794, for example, prohibited the sale of slaves to satisfy the master's debts, unless all other personal property had been exhausted. Legally, land could not be levied on until *all* the personal property had been sold to pay debts. Under this statute, then, the legal status of the slave was somewhere in the middle, between the legal status of land, and the legal status of personal property, at least with regard to creditors' rights. And after 1823, slaves owned by a child, who died before twenty-one, were treated as if real estate, for purposes of settling the dead child's estate.

Slaves themselves had little claim on the law for protection. A South Carolina judge, in 1847, put the case bluntly. A slave, he said, "can invoke neither *magna carta* nor common law. . . . In the very nature of things, he is subject to despotism. Law as to him is only a compact between his rulers."[102] The Louisiana Black Code of 1806 (sec. 18) declared that a slave "owes to his master, and to all his family, a respect without bounds, and an absolute obedience, and . . . is . . . to execute all . . . orders." The Texas penal code of 1856 recognized the power of

[99] Thomas D. Russell, "Articles Sell Best Singly: The Disruption of Slave Families at Court Sales," 1996 Utah L. Rev. 1161 (1996).

[100] For this thesis, much discussed and much criticized, see Stanley M. Elkins, *Slavery: A Problem in American Institutional and Intellectual Life* (1959); Herbert S. Klein, *Slavery in the Americas: A Comparative Study of Virginia and Cuba* (1967).

[101] Farnam, *op. cit.*, p. 183. The study of the slave as property (in the technical, legal sense) has been much neglected. But see Thomas D. Morris, *Southern Slavery and the Law, 1619–1860* (1996), chapters 3–6 try to fill in some of the gaps. And see also the work of Thomas Russell, nn. 97, 99 *supra*.

[102] J. Wardlaw in *Ex Parte Boylston*, 2 Strob. 41, 43 (S. Car., 1847).

the master "to inflict any punishment upon the slave not affecting life or limb . . . which he may consider necessary for the purpose of keeping him in . . . submission."[103]

On the other hand, some slave rights were written into law. Ten southern codes made it a crime to mistreat a slave. The law of six states required the master to provide suitable food and clothing for his slaves. The Black Code of Louisiana of 1806 made "cruel punishment" a crime (except "flogging, or striking with a whip, leather thong, switch or small stock, or putting in irons, or confining such slave"). Under the Louisiana Civil Code of 1825 (art. 192), if a master was "convicted of cruel treatment," the judge could order the sale of the mistreated slave, presumably to a better master.[104] And a black who was held as a slave, illegally, had the right to sue for his freedom.

How real were these rights? Did they mean much in practice? There is evidence that at least some southern courts honestly enforced the law in cases on the rights of slaves that came before them. There are decisions on record in which courts punished slave owners for acts of cruelty that were so awful that they shocked the conscience of the South. The highest state court of Alabama, in 1843, upheld the conviction of William H. Jones, indicted for murdering a slave girl, Isabel. Jones, it was charged, "did . . . feloniously, wilfully and of his malice aforethought, cruelly, barbarously and inhumanly beat and whip" the girl to death.[105] There are a few other cases, too, in which men were convicted of killing slaves with incredible, inhuman brutality. In a Louisiana case, the defendant had beaten his slave to death; the "immediate cause of death" was a hole in the abdomen, "the size of a dollar and appearing to have been 'gouged out.' "[106]

But it is important not to make too much of these cases. Reported cases, appealed cases, were quite exceptional. The Louisiana Supreme Court heard only three civil cases on abuse of slaves during the entire antebellum period. They heard *no* criminal cases at all on this subject until 1846, and very few thereafter.[107] Life and death on the plantation, day by day, however brutal, never got

---

[103] Quoted in Farnam, *op. cit.*, p. 184.

[104] But in an interesting case, *Markham* v. *Close*, 2 La. 581 (1831), the Louisiana court refused to allow a third party to bring a civil suit to compel the sale of a mistreated slave. A certain D. K. Markham, probably out of the kindness of his heart, alleged that the defendant had acted cruelly toward his slave. The slave, Augustin, had run away and been recaptured. There was testimony that he was then lashed "severely," his "back and hips were much cut and skinned. The weather being warm, the wounds smelled badly"; the slave was so severely hurt that he could not sit or lie. But because the master had not been actually *convicted* of cruelty, the court held it was powerless to order Augustin to be sold.

[105] *State* v. *Jones*, 5 Ala. 666 (1843). Between 1830 and 1860, there were thirteen reported appellate cases in which a master's conviction for homicide or attempted homicide of a slave was upheld. A. E. Keir Nash, "A More Equitable Past? Southern Supreme Courts and the Protection of the Antebellum Negro," 48 N. Car. L. Rev. 197, 215 (1970). Nash's work has been criticized for depending solely on appellate cases; see Michael S. Hindus, *Prison and Plantation: Crime, Justice and Authority in Massachusetts and South Carolina, 1767–1878* (1980), pp. 130, 135. Nash defended his work in "Reason of Slavery: Understanding the Judicial Role in the Peculiar Institution," 32 Vanderbilt L. Rev. 7 (1979). What is clear is that cases were few and far between; and the everyday reality was basically one of frequent brutality.

[106] See Judith Kelleher Schafer, *Slavery, the Civil Law, and the Supreme Court of Louisiana* (1994), pp. 31–32.

[107] *Ibid.*, pp. 55–57.

to court. What did get to court often ended with an acquittal. White juries were reluctant to convict for these offenses. And only especially blatant incidents got to court, and perhaps only such situations where the black slave had some white man to champion the cause. After all, the law clearly allowed masters to whip and punish slaves, and harshly; and slaves were not supposed to resist. And there were plenty of brutal, unfeeling owners and overseers; some were even cruel to the point of psychopathic behavior. In Florida, a study of advertisements for runaways noted that almost a third of the notices "described individuals as having flogging scars"; some had "iron clogs, chains, iron collars, or pot hooks around their necks"; some had had toes removed or ears cropped; one had even been castrated.[108] No matter how vicious the punishment of a slave, or how inhuman the treatment, a slave that lifted a hand against a master or an overseer stood little chance of getting off; the duty of obedience trumped the laws that "allegedly protected slaves from the cruelty of their owners."[109] And the law clearly recognized the right of the master to "correct" his slave, to punish his slave, even with extreme methods; the physical power of the master was, indeed, a pillar of the southern slave system.[110]

Thus the rights of slaves were narrowly defined, often violated, and hard to turn into reality. Yet these rights, as they appeared on the books, and in the few cases that invoked them, gave southern law at least an appearance of justice, an appearance of fairness—appearances that the slaveholding class valued greatly. At the same time, there was no way the enforcement of rights could threaten the real social order. Had these rights been widely used, or used beyond the limits of southern toleration, they would not have survived, even on paper.

As it was, a slave who wanted his day in court faced formidable barriers. No slave could testify against his master. In some states, no black could testify against a white man at all. In "free" Indiana Territory, for example, by a law of 1803:

> No negro, mulatto or Indian shall be a witness except in the pleas of the United States [i.e., criminal cases] against negroes, mulattoes, or Indians, or in civil pleas where negroes, mulattoes or Indians alone shall be parties.[111]

Forty-three years later, in 1846, the law was still on the books. This fact drew caustic remarks from a select committee of the Indiana Assembly:

> The track of the foot, the nail of the shoe, the bark of the dog, or the bray of the donkey, may be given in evidence to ferret out villainies; but the negro . . . though acquainted with the villain, and cognizant to the villainy, for no reason than because he is a negro, is not even permitted to develope corroborating circumstances.[112]

---

[108] Larry Eugene Rivers, *Slavery in Florida: Territorial Days to Emancipation* (2000), p. 142.

[109] Morris, *Southern Slavery and the Law*, p. 283.

[110] Andrew Fede, "Legitimized Violent Slave Abuse in the American South, 1619–1865: A Case Study of Law and Social Change in Six Southern States," 29 Am. J. Legal History 93 (1985).

[111] Francis S. Philbrick, ed., *Laws of Indiana Territory, 1801–1809* (1930), p. 40. A mulatto was defined as a person with "one fourth part or more of negro blood."

[112] Quoted in Emma Lou Thornbrough, *The Negro in Indiana* (1957), p. 122.

On countless occasions, the rule must have frustrated justice. In 1806, the chancellor of Virginia, George Wythe, together with a black servant, died after drinking from a pot of coffee. The coffee had been laced with arsenic. The finger of suspicion pointed toward Wythe's great-nephew; he was arrested for murder. A black cook could have given evidence against him. But the court was unable to hear this testimony; and the nephew went free.[113]

On the other hand, when it came to controlling the slave population, society and law were willing to dispense with all the niceties. The black criminal codes were clear and severe. Slave punishment was largely corporal. Fines and imprisonment meant nothing—slaves were penniless, and were already unfree. Slaves who transgressed were whipped—thoroughly, soundly, and often. In the local courts of South Carolina, convicted blacks were whipped in 94.7 percent of the cases; only 10 percent were jailed (most of these, of course, were also whipped). One out of twelve received more than 100 lashes.[114]

Some laws authorized even stronger bodily penalties. Under a Mississippi law of 1822, if any "Negro or mulatto" gave "false testimony," he was to be nailed by the ear to the pillory for one hour; then the ear was to be cut off; then "the other ear to be nailed in like manner," and after one hour cut off.[115] For serious crimes, the codes often imposed the death penalty. Burning grain or stealing goods were capital crimes for slaves in Georgia (1806). Under the codes, arson by slaves was frequently a capital crime. Attempted rape of a white woman was punishable by death in Georgia and Louisiana in 1806, in Kentucky in 1811, in Mississippi in 1814 and 1822, Tennessee in 1833, Texas in 1837, South Carolina in 1843.[116] As we noted, the law looked very severely on slave insurrection. Under the North Carolina Code of 1854, any slave "found in a state of rebellion or insurrection," or who agreed to "join any conspiracy or insurrection," or who persuaded others to join, or who "knowingly and wilfully" helped or encouraged slaves in a "state of rebellion," was liable to the death penalty. Slaves could be convicted, too, of the usual crimes for which white men were liable; and slaves were probably punished with special severity, even when the law did not specifically so provide. Between 1800 and 1855, 296 slaves were executed in South Carolina.[117]

A dead slave was a capital loss for his master. This put at least *some* natural check on the cruelty of masters. It was irrational, economically speaking, to harm a slave. Unfortunately, not everybody is rational. (It is also irrational to wreck a car, or beat a wife in a drunken rage, but people do it nonetheless.) Economic rationality also had its dangers. A master was tempted to hide the crimes his slaves committed, to keep them from dying on the gallows. To avoid this collusion, states gave compensation to owners of slaves put to death. A law of Alabama of 1824 provided that the jury, trying a slave for a capital offense, should also "assess the value of the slave"; the owner was entitled to claim up to

---

[113] See William Draper Lewis, ed., *Great American Lawyers*, vol. I (1907), pp. 84–85.

[114] Michael S. Hindus, *Prison and Plantation,* p. 145.

[115] Laws Miss. Adj. Sess. 1822, p. 194 (act of June 18, 1822, sec. 59). In addition, there would be thirty-nine lashes on the "bare back, well laid on." Note that the punishment applied to free blacks as well as to slaves.

[116] Farnam, *op. cit.,* pp. 184–85.

[117] Hindus, *op. cit.,* p. 103. The number of whites executed is unknown; but almost surely the rate of execution was far less.

one half this amount.[118] Virginia appropriated $12,000 in 1839 to pay owners "for slaves executed and transported."[119] A law of Mississippi, of 1846, called for a special panel of five slave holders, to assess the value of any slave who had been sentenced to death; the owner would get half of this amount as compensation.[120]

Court records in the South reveal a good deal about social control of the slave population. In the day-to-day cases, nobody paid much attention to due process, although this was probably true of routine cases where whites were prosecuted, too. For special problems, the South evolved special procedures. In some states, there were "slave patrols," which roamed the countryside, looking for slaves who could not give good accounts of themselves.[121] If a stray black in Georgia could not show a pass (or "free papers") the patrol might "correct" him on the spot, "by whipping with a switch, whip, or cowskin, not exceeding twenty lashes."[122] Patrols also searched the cabins and huts where slaves lived, looking for guns and knives—and sometimes for such lethal and forbidden weapons as books, paper, and writings.[123]

Equally important, if not more so, was what Michael Hindus has called plantation justice.[124] Basically, the master's will, uncontrolled by formal rules, was law for the slave. He was judge and jury; he tried "cases," passed sentences, and had them carried out in his little world. From the slave-owner's law there was no appeal, except in the most desperate, deviant cases—and only rarely then, as we pointed out. Anyone who argues that at least in the formal courts southerners dispensed justice for slaves, has to bear in mind the overwhelming reality of justice on the plantation.

Slave law, in short, had its own inner logic. Its object was repression and control. Everything tended toward that end. The South shut every door that could lead to black advancement or success—slave or free. The South deprived and degraded its blacks, then despised them for what they were; at the same time, the South was desperately afraid of the monster it had created. Slavery was a coiled spring. In the end, it was a trap for whites as well. The whites, of course, had the upper hand; but even *they* paid the price in the long run. Slavery was a raw, open wound, afflicting the country. It helped bring on the great Civil War. Hundreds of thousands died, North and South; families were wiped out; men lost arms, legs, and eyes; large areas of the country were laid waste. In a sense, all of these grieving families, these young lives sent to early graves, were victims of the South's "peculiar institution."

---

[118] Laws Ala. 1824, p. 41. The law also levied a tax—"one cent on all negroes under ten years, and two cents on all negroes over ten and under sixty"—to provide a compensation fund. The slaveowner had to employ "good and sufficient counsel" to defend the slave, and was forbidden from concealing a slave "so that he or she cannot be brought to condign punishment."

[119] Laws Va. 1839, ch. 3.

[120] Laws Miss. 1846, ch. 31, p. 193.

[121] The subject is treated in Sally E. Hadden, *Slave Patrols: Law and Violence in Virginia and the Carolinas* (2001).

[122] Prince, *Digest of the Laws of Georgia* (2nd ed., 1837), p. 775 (law of 1765).

[123] Sally Hadden, *Slave Patrols*, p. 106.

[124] Hindus, *op. cit.*, p. 117.

CHAPTER 5

AN AMERICAN LAW OF PROPERTY

THE LAND: A NATIONAL TREASURE

Land law was the kernel and core of common law. More exactly, real-property law was the core. Real property meant more than land; the term applied to that cluster of privileges and rights that centered on land, or on the exercise of power that depended on its location in space. In medieval England, rights to real property meant more than "ownership"; such rights conferred jurisdiction. The lord of the manor was a little sovereign in his domain, as well as the person who had title to houses, fields, and growing crops. Only people with land or land rights really mattered: the gentry, the nobles, the upper clergy. Land was the source of their wealth and the source and seat of their power. Well into modern times, power and wealth were concentrated in the hands of great landlords. The social system of the kingdom turned on rights in land.

Clearly, American conditions were quite different. There was no landed gentry. The land was widely held. But in America, too, land was the basic form of wealth.[1] This was especially true in the new lands to the west of the Atlantic strip—fertile land, abundant land, and land that was there for the taking, once the native tribes could be dispossessed, by treaty or otherwise. After 1787, the vast stock of public land was at once a problem and a great opportunity. The newly independent states ceded millions and millions of acres to the national government. The Louisiana Purchase brought in millions more. As the frontier

---

[1] Nor did ownership of land have the same relationship to power that it did in England. It was not irrelevant. Ownership of land was or was thought to be, the proper foundation stone of a republic. Certainly, Jefferson thought so. And the right to vote, in the early Republic, depended on ownership of property. But, after all, most adult white males *did* own land; property qualifications apparently nowhere excluded even half the potential voters; and in some states—South Carolina, Virginia, perhaps New York—very few men were affected at all. See Willi Paul Adams, *The First American Constitutions* (1980), pp. 198–207; on the property qualification and the right to vote, see Alexander Keyssar, *The Right to Vote: The Contested History of Democracy in the United States* (2000), pp. 42–52, and the table, pp. 328ff. on constitutional provisions in the states. The property qualification was gradually eliminated; by 1850, it was practically gone. It had had its defenders. Chancellor Kent argued in 1821 that New York needed it, for the Senate at least, as a "security against the caprice of the motley assemblage of paupers, emigrants, journeymen manufacturers, and those undefinable classes of inhabitants which a state and city like ours is calculated to invite." L. H. Clarke, *Report of the Debates and Proceedings of the Convention of the State of New York.* (1821), p. 115. But this was a rear-guard, losing struggle.

moved toward the West, American society faced a central issue: how to measure, map, settle, and distribute, this almost limitless treasure of land.

The disposition of the public domain is a story of staggering detail.[2] The issue was as persistent in the first half of the nineteenth century as issues of war, slavery, and the tariff. The public-land question touched every other item on the national agenda—fiscal policy, veterans' benefits, the spread or containment of slavery, population diffusion, and the political strength of factions and regions. Federal law determined the very shape of the land. Ways of measuring and surveying were a subject of active discussion; and men with sextants, chains, pegs, and axes worked at turning the land into rectangles that could be described, located, and sold.[3] The act of May 18, 1796, "for the Sale of the Lands of the United States, in the territory northwest of the river Ohio, and above the mouth of [the] Kentucky river,"[4] created the office of surveyor general. Public lands were to be surveyed "without delay" and divided into townships of six miles square. Half of the townships were to be further divided into sections. Each section contained one square mile, that is, 640 acres. Under later acts, sections were further divided into half-sections, and tracts of 160, 80, and 40 acres. In any event, the land had to be surveyed before it was sold, and the units of sale were strict rectangular plots. No chain of title could escape federal land policy, any more than the lots and farms could ignore the merciless, invisible grids stretched over the land at government order. The law of 1796, and its later versions, made us a nation of squares.

Once land was surveyed, the idea was to dispose of it. Public land law flowed from a few basic ideas and a few basic choices. The land was a commodity, an asset, something to be bought and sold, and the squares and grids were ways of turning land into a commodity. The land was not, on the whole, to be treated as a capital asset of government. On the contrary, the point was to transfer it to private citizens, in an orderly, fruitful way. The United States, in essence, gave away a continent: to veterans, settlers, squatters, railroads, states, colleges, speculators, and land companies. On the surface, the policy seems to reflect the powerful influence of free enterprise and *laissez-faire*. Washington, D.C., possessed a resource of incalculable value; but the goal was to privatize it, as soon as was humanly possible. True, the land was often sold for cash; and the government wanted the money. But not to make itself powerful or to increase the size and scale of the public sector.

Public land law was complex and full of angles and technicalities. But underlying everything was the ferocious hunger of the citizens for land. Selling or giving away the land was not so much the reflex of an ideology (weak government), as a way to get land into the hands of the ravenous public. It was a way to shore up the dominant form of land tenure—not the English way, but

²See, in general, Benjamin H. Hibbard, *A History of the Public Land Policies* (1939); Paul W. Gates, *History of Public Land Law Development* (1968); Everett N. Dick, *The Lure of the Land* (1970); Paul W. Gates, "An Overview of American Land Policy," 50 Agricultural History 213 (1976); and on the colonial and early Republican background, Edward T. Price, *Dividing the Land: Early American Beginnings of our Private Property Mosaic* (1995).

³Andro Linklater, *Measuring America* (2002), pp. 74, 75; this book in general has material on surveying and the division of the land into grids.

⁴1 Stats. 464 (act of May 18, 1796).

the American way, that is, small-holders, families sitting each on their own little farm. This was the idea: free (white) citizens, independent, unbeholden to any landlord. Nothing was to stand in the way—certainly not the native tribes; and not the government itself. The government, to be sure, was more than a passive umpire; it did more than chop the land into units and market it. It had its own interests and needs. And the land was its main asset—in some ways, its only major asset. How it handled the land was not merely a question of economic philosophy, but a response to concrete interests, demands, and needs, pressing in politically on Washington.

The federal government was not totally supine, spending its wealth (land) without any checks and controls. The government, for example, fought stubbornly to keep mineral rights out of private hands, dreaming of the gold and silver that might be hiding in the ground out West. The Ordinance of 1785 reserved to the government "one-third part of all gold, silver, lead and copper mines." The law of 1796 held back from sale "every . . . salt spring which may be discovered."[5] In 1807, Congress provided that lead-bearing lands should be leased, not sold.[6] Land grants in general were gifts on condition. They had a purpose: to encourage states to build colleges, or to get railroads constructed, or to provide incentives for the draining of swamps; or simply to give new states a kind of dowry. Unfortunately, national land programs never worked as they were meant to work on paper. Field administration was the weak point: feeble, incompetent, corrupt.[7] Where national policy was more or less consistent with the economic self-interest of local residents, the policy worked more or less well. But when policy collided with self-interest, Washington's arm was never long enough or steady enough to carry through.

Land grants for special purposes aside, the basic theme was *divestment*. When land was given to a state, as a dowry, or for other purposes, the point was not to encourage the state to guard the land jealously. No, the state was expected, in turn, to give away or sell the land. And the states, in turn, used their lands for the same purposes as the federal government: to raise money (sometimes), but more often, to further some policy. During the Revolution, southern states offered land to soldiers: 50 acres to a private in Maryland, 650 acres in North Carolina; for a captain, 200 acres in Maryland, 3,840 in North Carolina.[8] But the constant theme was divestment and disposal. And this hardly varied, throughout the nineteenth century.

All along, however, subsidiary decisions had to be made. Should the public domain be sold in great blocks to wholesalers, or in small pieces to actual settlers? How important was it to raise money from land sales? Should farmers or veterans be given some preference, or should the person with cash on hand always call the tune? On all these points, the federal government vacillated—pushed and pulled in this or that direction, by political pressures, especially from the West.

[5] 1 Stats. 464, 466, sec. 3 (act of May 18, 1796).
[6] 2 Stats. 445, 446, sec. 2 (act of March 3, 1807).
[7] See, in general, Malcolm J. Rohrbough, *The Land Office Business; The Settlement and Administration of American Public Lands, 1789–1837* (1968).
[8] Edward Price, *Dividing the Land*, pp. 186–7.

The act of 1796 clearly called for sales of large tracts of land. This policy favored land companies, and big speculators (including some of the Founding Fathers). Politically, however, the policy ran into trouble. It raised the bogeyman of land monopoly. It was never popular to favor dealers and speculators over simple farmers. In any event, the land sold badly. To encourage sales, the government sharply reduced the minimum unit of sale to half-sections, quarter-sections, eighty-acre tracts, and then finally (in 1832) to forty-acre tracts.[9] The price of public land weakened, too. The 1796 act had fixed a minimum price of two dollars an acre—much higher than the price at which huge blocks had earlier been sold. For a while, the price held firm. Between 1800 and 1820, public land sold at or near the two dollar price; during sieges of speculative fever, the price went even higher. Yet the Western states and territories insisted all along that the price must come down.

An important law of 1820 tried to meet these Western demands, while reforming the methods of sale. Under earlier acts, the government had sold its land on credit. By 1820, settlers owed the federal government about $21 million. Periodically, Congress passed laws giving its debtors some relief; an act in 1816, for example, gave land claimants in Mississippi Territory two years and eight months more to pay what they owed.[10] Still, many settlers could not pay; they had to forfeit their lands. The 1820 act reduced the minimum price to $1.25. At the same time, it put an end to sales on credit. Every buyer had to make "complete payment" at the time he bought his land.[11]

The point of the law was to vest land and power in the hands of smallholders, without giving up the hope of making money from the sale of public land. But the settlers, actual and potential, never really subscribed to government policy. Settlers (and speculators) streamed west far ahead of the formal date of sale, sometimes even ahead of the official survey. Theoretically, no one could gain a good title to the land until it was surveyed and sold. The families that were chopping down trees and planting crops were squatters. They thought they had a moral claim to the land. They certainly had no legal claim. No matter: they were voters, and a series of laws gave piecemeal preference (pre-emption rights) to actual settlers, even illegal settlers, or recognized and ratified state policies on pre-emption.[12] Finally, in 1841, Congress passed a general pre-emption law. The head of a family who had settled "in person" on land and "improved" it had first choice or claim to buy the land, up to 160 acres, at the minimum government price.[13] Somewhat naive safeguards against abuse were written into the act. Big landowners were excluded from participation. No one was allowed to squat in the same state or territory as his former residence. The law removed the last shred of pretense that the squatters were acting either illegally or immorally. They still had to come up with the money; but widespread collusion (and sometimes violence) kept outsiders from bidding up the land, and the settlers quite generally got what they wanted, when they wanted it. A great tide of humanity swept over the central forests and plains.

[9] Hibbard, *op. cit.*, p. 75.
[10] 3 Stats. 300 (act of April 24, 1816).
[11] 3 Stats. 566 (act of April 24, 1820).
[12] E.g., 5 Stats. 412 (act of February 18, 1841) (Tennessee).
[13] 5 Stats. 453, 455 sec. 10 (act of September 4, 1841).

THE LAW OF PRIVATE LAND

Land-law reform was well under way even before the Revolution. After the Revolution, legislatures carried on the work of dismantling bits and pieces of land law that were tainted with the feudal past. In the popular mind, land was a commodity like everything else. It no longer carried its "premodern role as the foundation for social hierarchy and family position."[14] Millions of people—land speculators, big and small landowners, but also freeholders in general—stood to gain, or thought they did, from a free, mobile market in land. Primogeniture, dead in most of New England, vanished from the South by 1800. Gradually, the rules of inheritance of land were assimilated to rules of inheritance of money and goods. The statute makers swept feudal tenures—most of them were not living law in this country—clean off the books. "The title of our lands," wrote Jesse Root proudly in 1798, "is free, clear and absolute, and every proprietor of land is a prince in his own domains, and lord paramount of the fee."[15]

In the first generation, statutes and court cases brushed aside many obnoxious or ill-fitting English doctrines. One casualty, for example, was a common-law rule that when two or more persons held interests in land, they were presumed to be joint tenants, not tenants in common. The difference between the two forms of co-ownership was technical, but not unimportant. If two persons owned land in common, each had a separate, distinct, and undivided share. Each could sell, give away, or divide his interest. A joint tenancy carried with it the right of survivorship; if one tenant died, the other automatically succeeded to the property. A joint tenancy, then, was a sort of last-man club in land. It was suitable for family lands; less so, for lands of people dealing at arm's length with each other in the market. The change in presumption was defended in terms of the probable intention of the parties: "In ninety-nine cases out of a hundred, of persons purchasing land together, they would prefer not to be joint tenants, but tenants in common. The law ought therefore to follow what is the common wish of parties."[16] If this was in fact the "common wish," it was because partners who bought land bought it as a commodity, that is, as a marketable good.

Changes in land law were generally of this quality. They were in the first place empirical. They strove, to a marked degree, to follow the "common wish of the parties." But the common wish of parties reflected the rapid, volatile quality of dealings in land. Land not only could be traded on the market; it *was* traded, openly and often. In land lay the hope of national wealth; for countless families, it was their chance to make some money. The land, once it was cleared of the native peoples (by hook or by crook), and properly surveyed, was traded with speed and fury. Speculation in raw land was almost a

[14] Gregory S. Alexander, *Commodity and Propriety: Competing Visions of Property in American Legal Thought, 1776–1970* (1997), p. 114.

[15] Jesse Root, *Reports* (Conn., 1798), Intro, xxxix.

[16] 1 Am. Jurist 77 (1829). Another doomed doctrine was the doctrine of "tacking," in the law of mortgages. In English law, a third mortgagee might get the jump on a second mortgagee by buying the interest of a first mortgagee and "tacking" that interest to his own. This doctrine was "very generally exploded" in the United States. Chancellor Kent reported hearing Alexander Hamilton himself in 1804, "make a masterly attack upon the doctrine, which he insisted was founded on a system of artificial reasoning, and encouraged fraud." Kent, *Commentaries*, vol. IV (2nd ed., 1832), p. 178.

kind of national lottery. Even when genuine settlers arrived, built houses, and planted crops, the turnover was still exceedingly rapid. Farmers themselves were speculators who gambled on the rising price of land. Many farmers worked their land for a while, then eagerly sold out (at a profit) and moved on to a newer frontier.

The nineteenth century was full of talk about respect for property, for vested rights, and so on. But law, policy, and public opinion had most respect for productive property, property put to use, property that was dynamic rather than static. The very meaning of property changed—from a "static agrarian conception entitling an owner to undisturbed enjoyment, to a dynamic, instrumental . . . view."[17] The Virginia Declaration of Rights, in 1776, mentioned, as a fundamental right, "the means of acquiring and possessing property, and pursuing and obtaining happiness and safety." This, as Harry Scheiber has pointed out, was not a "defensive" concept of property rights, nor mere respect for "vested rights"; it implied that the process of getting and holding property had a "positive and dynamic character."[18] We have already seen the impact of this new view on the law of eminent domain. Now, in the nineteenth century, the preference for dynamic, active property—a conception which neatly fit the interests of the landowning mass—worked massive changes in the law of land and related areas of American law.

An active land market forced the law of conveyancing to undergo a sea change. In the United States, every man (and later, quite a few women) was or might be a conveyancer. The elaborate forms of English law were clearly unsuitable. Legal sophistication was a scarce resource. What was acceptable or tolerable to a small upper class of landlords was intolerable in the great American mass market. Vestigial modes of tenure and conveyancing survived in some parts of the country, particularly the plantation South. But even in South Carolina, a court of equity showed genuine surprise to learn that Alicia H. Middleton and Sarah Dehon of Charlestown had executed "deeds of feoffment, with livery of seisin," in 1836, instead of using more streamlined forms.[19] In the rest of the country, the enormous volume of land transactions meant that land documents had to become simple and standard. They had to be mass-produced at minimal cost for mass use. Conveyancing skills were rare. Yet, the country generated a huge volume of deeds and other instruments of land. There were plenty of lawyers. But there were not half enough *if* every land transfer needed careful counseling and delicate architecture. And the lawyers who practiced in small towns or on the frontier were unable to cope with the jigsaw puzzles of English land law.

In many ways, reform was clean and swift. The old conveyance of feoffment, with livery of seizin—the turf and twig—clearly had to go. It was little used; and the New York revised statutes of 1827–1828 expressly abolished it.[20] Deeds had to be in writing, but were valid if they followed simple, rational form. Out of the welter of available models, lawyers in the republic worked out two basic

---

[17] Morton J. Horwitz, *The Transformation of American Law, 1780–1860* (1977), p. 30.

[18] Harry N. Scheiber, "Economic Liberty and the Constitution," in *Essays in the History of Liberty: Seaver Institute Lectures at the Huntington Library* (1988), pp. 75, 81.

[19] See *Dehon v. Redfern,* Dudley's Eq. Rpts. (S. Car. 1838), 115.

[20] Kent, *Commentaries,* vol. IV (2nd ed., 1832), pp. 489–90.

types of deed. The *warranty deed* grew out of the old deed of bargain and sale, with covenants of warranty. The *quitclaim deed* developed from the common law release.[21] A warranty deed was used to make a full transfer of land from one owner to another. The seller guaranteed that he had and could transfer good title. The quitclaim deed made no such promises. It simply transferred whatever rights the transferor had, good or bad; and was so understood. People used quitclaim deeds to hand over or sell cloudy or contingent rights to land. In both kinds of deed, the wording and form still reflected their historical origins; but the instruments were drastically shortened and streamlined. It would be too much to say that the average layman could handle them. But they were accessible to lawyers of some training and experience, and to shrewd land dealers as well. They were available in popular form books, and in various versions of *Every Man His Own Lawyer,* or books with similar titles, which sold thousands of copies in America. Using these books, a businessman or lawyer could try to make deeds on his own. He could copy down the forms and fill in the blanks.

Both land practice and statutes worked toward simplicity in the law of real property. In old England, land actions (lawsuits over land) were a frightful jumble of technicality. There was plenty of American technicality, too, but it was a pale shadow at best of the English mess. Joseph Story grew almost ecstatic at the efficiencies of the action of ejectment, which tested title to land, "on the picturesque banks of the Hudson, the broad expanse of the Delaware and Chesapeake, the sunny regions of the South, and the fertile vales and majestic rivers of the West."[22] In fact, ejectment was most popular at the fringes of the country. In 1821, when Story wrote, Massachusetts, Maine, and New Hampshire still did not share the national passion for ejectment. These states, instead, used "writs of entry for the trial of land titles." The writs had been "disembarrassed . . . of some troublesome appendages and some artificial niceties," but were still, by comparison, archaic.[23]

A federal system is legally a decentralized system; and this was true of land law as well, except for the public domain. There was therefore a lot of local diversity. A state like Massachusetts could hold on to traditional methods; as long as these were not *too* irrational. A tradition could limp along, provided it did no great harm to the land market. The states also had different economic needs, different quantities of legal skill, and different geographical features. Land law moved, on the whole, in one general direction; still, the land law of no two states was identical. There was no authority that could impose a uniform pattern on the states. This meant that, for all the labor of simplification, land law was a complicated tangle.

Much of the English law of tenures and estates was nominally the law in the states as well; but much of it had little practical importance. American lawyers spoke of fee simple and life estates, terms of years, easements, covenants, and profits. The wonderland of executory devises, powers of appointment, contingent remainders, shifting and springing uses, was not formally abolished; it would be more accurate to say that these future interests were dormant. When,

[21] A. James Casner, ed., *American Law of Property,* vol. III (1952), p. 223.
[22] Joseph Story, "An Address Delivered Before the Members of the Suffolk Bar," Sept. 4, 1821, in 1 Am. Jurist 1, 17 (1829).
[23] *Ibid.,* p. 17.

in the 1820s, a movement arose to reform the law, reformers lopped away at doctrines and institutions that seemed positively harmful, then those which, whatever their impact, appeared to be "tyrannical" or "feudal." The urge to modernize was a crucial feature in the important revision of property law carried out in New York in 1827–1828.

Rules of *capacity* were among those most thoroughly revamped in the course of the nineteenth century. Ideally, every adult should be able to own and deal in land. Married women were a big exception; but this was cured, as we have seen, by the Married Women's Property Acts. In England, aliens could not, for reasons of policy, inherit land. The rule was out of place in America. The provisions against aliens "originated in ages of barbarism, out of the hatred and jealousy with which foreigners were regarded . . . [To] those [aliens] who are actually resident amongst us, the best policy" would be "to encourage their industry by giving them all reasonable facilities in the acquisition of property."[24] There was plenty of xenophobia in America—the Alien and Sedition laws; the Know-Nothing Party; the anti-Irish riots. But this was a country that was hungry for growth, including population growth. People played the land market the way their descendants played the stock market. More people meant rising land prices; an open-door policy for immigrants (of the right sort) was something devoutly to be wished.

As early as 1704, a South Carolina act, praising resident aliens for "their industry, frugality and sobriety," for their "loyal and peaceabl[e]" behavior, pointed out that they had acquired "such plentiful estates as hath given this Colony no small reputation abroad, tending to the encouragement of others to come and plant among us," and granted them full rights to acquire property by gift, inheritance, or purchase.[25] An Ohio law (1804) made it "lawful" for aliens who became "entitled to have" any "lands tenements or hereditaments" by "purchase, gift, devise or descent," to "hold, possess, and enjoy" their lands, "as fully and completely as any citizen of the United States or this state can do, subject to the same laws and regulations, and not otherwise."[26] Federal preemption and homestead laws also gave rights to resident aliens.

Against the "tyrannical" and "feudal," legislators slashed away with might and main. Primogeniture, as we noted, fell by the wayside. The fee tail was another casualty. When a man held land in fee tail, at his death, the land went to the heirs of his body, that is, to his lineal descendants (usually male), and so on for generations. No one could sell such a "fettered inheritanc[e]," as Kent called it,[27] because the land belonged to the tenant's children, and

---

[24] 1 Am. Jurist 87–88 (1829).

[25] *Statutes at Large of South Carolina,* vol. II (1837), pp. 251–52 (act of Nov. 4, 1704). To qualify, however, an alien had to take an oath to the crown "on the Holy Evangelists, or otherwise according to the form of his profession."

[26] Laws Ohio 1803–4, p. 123 (act of Feb. 3, 1804). The American experience brought about a redefinition of the very meaning of citizenship and allegiance. These were essentially a matter of free choice, not the result of an inborn, permanent, perpetual status. See James H. Kettner, *The Development of American Citizenship, 1608–1870* (1978). The usefulness of this idea of "volitional allegiance" in a country trying to build population and stimulate the land market is obvious.

[27] Kent, *Commentaries,* vol. IV (2nd ed., 1832), p. 12.

his children's children thereafter. As a matter of fact, as far back as the fifteenth century, tenants in tail had been able to sell their land, free of the claims of unborn generations, through tricks of conveyancing that "barred" the entail. But this was no job for an amateur. In a nation of amateurs, there was no point in preserving fee tail even if it was essentially toothless. The fee tail was formally abolished in Virginia in 1776, in New York in 1782. In some places, the fee tail survived in a weak and fossilized form; if a person tried to create a fee tail, the law treated this as an estate for life in the first grantee, followed by a plain fee simple (outright ownership). In any event, the fee tail had lost any and all meaning, everywhere.

In general, lawmakers reacted to the common fear and distrust of land monopoly and land dynasties. New York state was particularly sensitive on this score, perhaps because of the huge estates on the Hudson, a fertile source of unrest.[28] Even Chancellor Kent, certainly no radical, felt that free transfer of land was a core value of republican government:

> Entailments are recommended in monarchical governments, as a protection to the power and influence of the landed aristocracy; but such a policy has no application to republican establishments, where wealth does not form a permanent distinction, and under which every individual of every family has his equal rights, and is equally invited, by the genius of the institutions, to depend upon his own merit and exertions. Every family, stripped of artificial supports, is obliged, in this country, to repose upon the virtue of its descendants for the perpetuity of its fame.[29]

These general attitudes underlay the New York revision of property laws of 1827–1828. The revision can be properly called a code. It arranged, changed, and simplified large parts of the law of property. The English law of perpetuities was tightened. A more severe limit was placed on the time that land could be tied up within a family. Under the English rule, future interests in property became void, under a complicated formula, if there was excessive "remoteness of vesting." The New York rule made future interests invalid if they unduly "suspended" the "power of alienation." The difference between the two concepts was technical, and, in most cases, inconsequential. But the New York version of the rule expressed one dominant aim of land law reform: to keep the land market open and mobile. For the same reason, the code frowned on the creation of trusts of land. Trusts were only allowed for a few, specific purposes—for example, for the benefit of a minor. Here the dangers to the land market seemed slight, the usefulness of the trust was obvious, and the trust was likely to last only a few short years. In general, the revisions were meant to free property from its deadening past, and to stimulate "commodification" of land.[30]

The legislature watered down the more radical New York innovations in later years. Others were misconstrued or mishandled by the courts. The hostility of the judges was not simply blind reaction. There were flaws in the way the code was drafted. Some of its schemes were so novel that they caused confusion and

---

[28] See Charles W. McCurdy, *The Anti-Rent Era in New York Law and Politics, 1839–1865* (2001).

[29] *Ibid.*, p. 20.

[30] See Gregory S. Alexander, *Commodity and Propriety: Competing Visions of Property in American Legal Thought, 1776–1970* (1997), pp. 107–26.

encouraged litigation. Arguably, some of its provisions were simply wrong-headed. Chancellor Kent had been skeptical from the start; the trust provisions of the code, he felt, could not work. The desire to "preserve and perpetuate family influence and property," he noted, was "very prevalent with mankind," and was "deeply seated in the affections."[31] Trusts would probably not wither away. "We cannot hope," he wrote, to "check the enterprising spirit of gain, the pride of families, the anxieties of parents, the importunities of luxury, the fixedness of habits, the subtleties of intellect." The law, he predicted, would bring wholesale evasion: the "fairest and proudest models of legislation that can be matured in the closet" could not prevail against the "usages of a civilized people."[32] Time has proved Kent to be correct, on the whole, and a far better sociologist than his cohorts. Wealth grew; new fortunes were created; and among the super-rich, the dynastic urge soon reared its ugly head. The aristocracy of money usually got what it wanted. The land baronies, including the Hudson Valley estates, did not in fact survive for very long. But later in the century, the long-term trust became popular again among the very rich. It was a dynastic device, but one not necessarily tied to land. It grew to an extent even Kent would have found astounding; it is still growing today.

Land-law reform had, on the whole, turned the law of real property into a more usable tool. But as old problems were solved, new problems emerged. Title was a chronic problem. Government surveys, for all their defects, provided an accurate *physical* description of land. But title is more elusive than latitude and longitude, and cloudier than tree stumps and boundary markers. Land turned over rapidly; and chains of title often had weak or mysterious links. The beginning—the start of the chain of title—was often a problem. Did the claim go back to some vast, ambiguous grant—from the federal government, or the King of Spain, or some long-dead proprietor? Titles also had to take into account the patents (grants) of American state governments, sometimes ambiguous, and sometimes corrupt. There were types of claims and rights that were completely foreign to ancient practice. Georgia continued its headright system until past 1800.[33] Western lawyers got rich off all the raucous squabbles that arose under state and federal pre-emption laws, and the law and practice of local land offices. As a commodity, land was bought and sold and traded in ways that added to the general confusion. Federal and state governments floated land scrip and bounty warrants, to veterans, for example. Some issues were freely transferable; some fluctuated on the market, like modern stocks and bonds. These land certificates, passing from hand to hand, created a new body of land law—and a whole new body of disputes.

Especially in the West, local officials were weak and corrupt. This had a devastating effect on land titles. Forgery and fraud, if we can believe the stories, were epidemic. Land was the basis of wealth; bad titles made this wealth precarious. Public weakness and private greed were a formidable combination. Joseph Story remarked that the land law of Kentucky was a labyrinth, full of "subtle and refined distinctions." "Ages will probably elapse," he wrote in 1829, "before the

---

[31] *Ibid.*, p. 19.
[32] *Ibid.*, p. 313.
[33] Milton S. Heath, *Constructive Liberalism: The Role of the State in Economic Development in Georgia to 1860* (1954), pp. 84–92.

litigations founded on it will be closed." To outside lawyers, "it will forever remain an unknown code, with a peculiar dialect, to be explored and studied, like the jurisprudence of some foreign nation."[34] And Kentucky was not an old conservative society, but a new state at the legal periphery. It did not inherit its problems from the old common law. Rather, they came from the usual sources: greed and corruption. The same problem of tangled titles occurred time and time again: in Missouri, in Illinois, in California. With one hand, government labored to create a rational land system. It explored, surveyed, recorded, and worked toward orderly settlement. But at the same time, government would not and could not resist political pressures; would not and could not correct its weakness in the field. The result was constant tension between chaos and order.

The goals of policy in Kentucky were much the same as in other states: attracting people, giving them land, and clean, clear ways to register and keep track of their holdings. Kentucky also attempted to do justice to—or coddle—the "actual settler" (and voter). Disputes over claims were endless: Whose claim was valid? Hundreds of disputes ended up in court. Had A or B raised a crop of corn on the land or built a cabin? Had A gotten there ahead of B? Where were the boundaries between vague, overlapping claims, claims impossible to deal with rationally, even without human error—and barefaced lies? In one case, reported in 1799, a Kentucky court heard a witness say that a certain Berry "blazed a white ash or hickory" to mark his claim, "but which of them he can not be certain, and cut the two first letters of his name and blacked them with powder, and . . . sat down at the foot of a small sugar tree and chopped a hole with his tomahawk in the root of it. . . . [A]t the place where Berry made his improvement the branch [of a river] made a bend like a horse shoe." Where was the ash or hickory now? "Cut down, but the stump remained," in a "very decayed state." The sugar tree was still standing, and identifiable; the tomahawk mark was "still perceivable"; presumably the horseshoe bend could still be found. None of these was exactly an unambiguous sign.[35] This kind of evidence could be easily invented, or contradicted. In many of these cases, it was a struggle for the family home, the farm, the very livelihood. In some, the land was of baronial size, or a mighty city had grown up on top of it; hence, vast fortunes hung in the balance. Some of the greatest American trials, in terms of cost, time, and acrimony, have been trials over title to land.

The land law aimed to make land freely marketable. But this was not an end in itself. The goal was economic growth, a rising, spreading population, a healthy, aggressive middle class. Sometimes the market principle had to give way. Legal doctrines sometimes deviated from strict market principles, usually to protect a politically potent class—the small-holders. One example was the mechanic's lien. Essentially, the mechanic's lien gave special remedies and preferences to "mechanics," artisans who labored on buildings or made improvements to land. If the landowner failed to pay the "mechanic," the "mechanic" could enforce his claim directly against land and improvements.[36]

---

[34] Joseph Storey, in 1 Am. Jurist 20 (1829). On the Kentucky land title problem, see Mary K. Bonsteel Tachau, *Federal Courts in the Early Republic: Kentucky, 1789–1816* (1978), ch. 8.

[35] *McClanahan v. Berry*, Hughes' Ky. Rpts., vol. 1 (1799), pp. 323, 327–28.

[36] See Farnam, *op. cit.*, pp. 152–56.

The mechanic's lien was a purely American invention. It can be traced back to 1791. In that year, commissioners, in charge of building the new capital city of Washington, D.C., suggested a lien to "encourage master builders to contract for the erecting and finishing of houses." Maryland, the relevant state, passed the necessary legislation. Pennsylvania was the next state to enact a form of the lien. Its first law (1803) applied only to certain kinds of "mechanic," and only to certain sections of the city of Philadelphia. Gradually, more and more states adopted broader and broader versions of the lien. By the end of the period, the mechanic's lien was a sweeping security device. In Illinois, in 1845,

> any person who shall . . . furnish labor or materials for erecting or repairing any building, or the appurtenances of any building . . . shall have a lien upon the whole tract of land or town lot . . . for the amount due to him for such labor or materials.[37]

The mechanic's lien was a pro-labor statute, but not in the New Deal sense. The "mechanics" of the lien law were not poor urban workers; they were suppliers and artisans. The law protected labor, in the early nineteenth-century sense of the word: those who added tangible value to real assets. The law preferred their claims over those of general creditors. Not least of all, the lien was intended to *help* the landowner, in an age when cash, hard money, liquid capital was short. The law promised a safe and immovable form of collateral to those who supplied materials and labor. The lien was a kind of bootstrap finance (the phrase is Willard Hurst's), almost a subsidy, almost a kind of government credit to encourage building and improvement of land.

The small-holder's interests lay even more clearly at the root of another American innovation, the homestead exemption. The law made certain kinds of property (the "homestead") immune from the clutches of creditors. The homestead exemption first appeared in Texas, before Texas was admitted to the Union. The legislature expanded the doctrine steadily until, in 1839, up to fifty acres of land or one town lot—when these constituted a family's "homestead"—tools, books, livestock, feed, and some household furniture were immune from seizure for debt. The idea was attractive, and spread from the periphery toward the center. The first adoption was in Mississippi (1841). By 1848, Connecticut, Wisconsin, and Michigan, along with some of the Southern states, had enacted one form or other of the homestead exemption. By the time of the Civil War, all but a few states had done the same.[38]

The homestead exemption and the mechanic's lien seem, in a way, to contradict each other. One law made home and farm a sanctuary against creditors; the other gave creditors a sharp new legal tool to use against home and farm. In practice, there was little chance of collision between the two. A working farm was not usually exposed to the lien laws. And both laws were in a sense developmental. The homestead law, in Texas, was specifically meant to encourage immigration. It sought, indirectly, to mobilize labor and capital toward the

---

[37] Rev. Stats. Ill. 1845, p. 345.

[38] Farnam, *op. cit.*, pp. 148–52. The Texas constitution of 1845 specifically mentioned the right of the legislature to pass a homestead act. The Wisconsin constitution of 1848 also had a specific provision, which instructed the legislature to pass a "wholesome" exemption law.

prime job of the times: building population and enriching the land—precisely the aims of the mechanic's lien. To new settlers, the homestead exemption set up a kind of safety net, in a boom-and-bust world. The mechanic's lien got their homes built; and, if a crisis came, it gave a preference to productive laborers against mere lenders of money. Middlemen at the time were considered more or less parasitic. They did not produce goods or add to the nation's stock of wealth.

BOOM AND BUST: THE LAW OF MORTGAGES

Lien and exemption laws were enormously important because of the pervasive, ruinous force of the business cycle. Crisis struck the economy with shock waves at regular and irregular intervals. Volcanic eruptions and disruptions in prices caused deep insecurity among debtors, creditors, and merchants. The money system was disastrously weak; credit information was primitive. No one was safe unless he held silver and gold, and these metals were rare indeed. There was a desperate search for some kind of security—some way to protect your own assets; and to reach the assets of other people who might owe you money. Since land was so large a part of the national wealth, land law was very sensitive to the business cycle. Security devices in land were therefore of crucial importance.

The prime instrument of land security, then as now, was the mortgage. Mortgage means, literally, "dead pledge." A mortgage is "dead" to the creditors, since the landowner who borrows money stays in possession of the land, and keeps whatever it produces, over and above the debt; by contrast, a pawnbroker takes his pledges "live." The mortgage was an old, old legal device, but constantly readjusted to new realities.[39] Its development in modern times bears the scars of the never-ending struggle between debtor and creditor. In nineteenth-century America, there were definitely a debtor class and a creditor class, even though the groups overlapped—and many people were both borrowers and lenders. Normally, debtors outnumbered creditors; and this meant constant pressure to shape the law in such a way as to help debtors out—by abolishing imprisonment for debt, for example. There was also pressure for political change (widening of the suffrage), and for economic programs (inflation and easy money), in ways that favored debtors. Creditors also had considerable political influence. And it was not always clear whether a policy benefitted debtors or benefitted creditors. It could be argued that debtors needed laws giving lenders powerful rights, if only to encourage a flow of capital into real estate investment. In many states (Wisconsin, for example), the homestead exemption did not cover a purchase-money mortgage. This was a large hole in the law, but apparently vital for farmers and homeowners. Most people had no

---

[39] Much of mortgage law was developed in or through courts of equity. This made some technical adjustments necessary in those jurisdictions that had no chancery courts. Pennsylvania, for example, substituted, through the action of *scire facias sur mortgage* (1705), a common-law mode of foreclosure for the usual procedures in equity. *Scire facias sur mortgage* was a writ, used when the mortgagor lapsed into default, requiring him to "show cause" why the mills of the law should not begin to grind, foreclosing the mortgage.

capital security except the land itself; yet, only a fool would lend money to buy land without this security.

Debtors were, on the whole, inconsistent people, but for perfectly understandable reasons. They took one attitude during good times and another during bad. In good times they needed money to buy land and to build and raise crops; they were willing to promise the moon, hoping that land values would go up and lighten their debts. During bad times, promises turned sour, debts became mountainous, and debtors looked about for avenues of escape.

When legislatures found debtor relief politically irresistible, creditors sometimes turned to the courts for protection. The courts were free from the pressures of frequent election. They were therefore sometimes willing to take what struck creditors as a longer and sounder view of economic policy, compared to the legislature. Creditors were also expert at evading pro-debtor rules and statutes. In times of a credit shortage, the real demand for money and credit overpowered formal law. Players in the game were clever at inventing small-scale, half-visible ways of getting around rules that they felt were obstacles. The clash of interests also led to inconsistency and ambiguity in the living law, as both sides battled and maneuvered. The resulting complexity was particularly gross in a decentralized system, where the losers in one forum could often simply turn to another one. The outline history of mortgage law is instructive.[40] Over the years, a costly and complicated system of *equitable foreclosure* had evolved, partly to give the debtor some protection. Its essential feature was the debtor's "equity" or right to redeem his lost land. Draftsmen then invented clauses to get rid of this "equity." The debtor would agree, in advance, that if he defaulted, his creditor could sell the land without going to court. As early as 1774, a New York statute specifically ratified this practice, though with some procedural safeguards. In some Southern states, however, courts reached a different conclusion; they held that no one could legally grant such a power of sale to a mortgagee. Mortgages then began to name third persons ("trustees") to exercise the power of sale, in case of default. The "deed of trust," then, acted as the functional equivalent of the Northern mortgage with power of sale.

A mortgage armored with a power of sale was an effective instrument of credit. But while the courts accepted the power of sale, and the deed of trust (undercutting the old equity of redemption), other laws were passed that had the opposite effect. The year 1819 was a year of panic. New York, in 1820, passed a law giving hard-pressed land debtors a year of grace. It was not clear whether this type of law applied to mortgages at all. The question was decided one way by a court in New York, another way by Tennessee, which had adopted a similar law. The panic of 1837 produced a fresh crop of redemption statutes. Illinois's law (1841) specifically applied to "mortgaged lands." It gave the mortgagor, in essence, one year to redeem his property. It further provided that no mortgaged land could be sold at foreclosure sale, to any bidder, for less than two-thirds the appraised value of the land. This, too, was an attempt to salvage something from the land-debtor's equity. The *New York Journal of Commerce* spoke in disgust of this kind of law as "dishonest and knavish." "More than all defalcations of individual

---

[40] See Robert H. Skilton, "Developments in Mortgage Law and Practice," 17 Temple L.Q., 315 (1945). This excellent article is the source of much of the discussion of mortgage law in this chapter.

swindlers," it "attests the almost hopeless depravity and corruption of the age."[41] The law applied to existing, as well as to future, mortgages. Indeed, that was the point of it: to give relief to debtors in Illinois, who had been crushed by the fall in prices and values. In the famous case of *Bronson v. Kinzie*,[42] the U.S. Supreme Court struck down the Illinois statute. It was an "impairment" of the obligation of a contract, which the federal Constitution clearly forbade. A storm of protest arose in Illinois. But the burden of inertia had now shifted; creditors were once more in the saddle. *Bronson* precipitated a second crisis: a confrontation between the legislature, responsive to the debtors, and the courts, which were defending creditors' rights and the stability of the economy. Ultimately, it was conceded that the legislature could impose a right of redemption at least on all future mortgages. In the embattled field of mortgage laws, court decisions, while not totally decisive, had a definite impact. Courts could delay, obstruct, and, in the end, exact a compromise.

SUCCESSION: WILLS AND TRUSTS

In a market economy, property is freely bought and sold, and freely transferred by way of gift. Most gift transactions take place within the family. Most people with money do not, in fact, give it away during their lifetimes. But when you die, as the saying goes, you can't take it with you. Everything now passes to the living. Thus, almost the entire stock of private wealth turns over each generation. Either it passes through somebody's will, or through some other type of gift to take effect on death. In default, the state's intestacy laws take care of the distribution. Only public, corporate, and dynastic property is immune from this law of mortality.

Colonial probate law and practice had a certain flexibility. There were some early attempts to avoid probate since there were no hard and fast rules. Courts treated each estate case individually, looking at the particular family situation. Later, a rather tight network of rules grew up, more or less on English models. Flexibility was lost; but there was a gain in efficiency and certainty. A mass society, with mass ownership of wealth, could hardly afford to handle each estate individually, without fixed rules. American probate laws were never slavish imitations of the English laws.[43] To be sure, there was a good deal of copycatting in the law of wills. There were two key English statutes. Under the so-called statute of frauds (1677), a written, witnessed will was required for real estate. The Wills Act (1837) covered both realty and personalty. The two statutes differed, slightly, in other details. After 1837, American states tended to follow one or the other of these models, or a mixture of both. There were firm, formal rules

---

[41] Quoted in Charles Warren, *The Supreme Court in United States History* (rev. ed., 1935), vol. II, p. 102.

[42] 1 How. 310 (1843). For an attempt to measure the impact of the Illinois relief laws, see George L. Priest, "Law and Economic Distress: Sangamon County, Illinois, 1837–1844," 2 J. of Legal Studies 469 (1973).

[43] The Massachusetts double share for the eldest child was given up in 1789.

on how to execute a valid will. With few exceptions, American states imposed the same requirements on wills of land and on testaments of personal property.[44]

A standard, precise law of wills was vital to the property system. The Ordinance of 1787 authorized wills of land, "provided such wills be duly proved." This was a clear departure from English law. In England, a person could introduce a will into court, to prove a claim to ownership of land, even though the will had never gone through probate. And even if it had, that fact did not bind the court trying title to land. The Ordinance of 1787, and the practice that grew up under it, gave much more weight to the probate *process.*[45] There was colonial precedent for this practice.[46] But it is best understood in the context of post-Revolutionary land law. Land instruments had to be rational, simple, and standard; land procedures had to be objective and routine. The will, like the deed, was a fundamental instrument of transfer. Probate was to the will what recording was to the deed. Transitions were smoother, records were more exact, and title was less clouded, if all wills were funneled through probate.

Because of their importance to land titles, the wills themselves have been carefully preserved in many counties. They exist in an unbroken line from the beginnings of county history to the present day. An occasional title searcher disturbs their dust. An occasional genealogist tunnels into the caves, in search of a lost forefather. Historians have generally neglected them; but from these old wills, stiff and stereotyped as they are, the voice of social history speaks out. One finds in them an occasional flash of humanity, an insight into the era, or a fact of rare beauty, trapped in county archives as if in amber. John Randolph of Roanoke freed his slaves by will, "heartily regretting" that he ever owned slaves. He bequeathed to these "old and faithful servants, Essex and his wife Hetty . . . three-and-a-half barrels of corn, two hundred weight of pork, a pair of strong shoes, a suit of clothes, and a blanket each, to be paid them annually; also, an annual hat to Essex, and ten pounds of coffee and twenty of brown sugar." Benjamin Franklin left to his daughter "The King of France's picture, set with four hundred and eight diamonds." It was his wish that "she would not form any of those diamonds into ornaments, either for herself or daughters, and thereby introduce or countenance the expensive, vain and useless pastime of wearing jewels in this country."[47]

Wills are ambulatory, that is, the testator can revoke or replace his will up to the moment of death. In the nineteenth century, the deathbed will was more common than in later, more calculating times.[48] Perhaps partly for this reason,

[44] In a group of Southern and Western states, and states where civil law influence was strong (Texas, Louisiana), holographic wills were also valid. These wills, if entirely handwritten by the testator, required no witnesses.

[45] William W. Blume, "Probate and Administration on the American Frontier," 58 Mich. L. Rev. 209, 233 (1959).

[46] See Thomas E. Atkinson, "The Development of the Massachusetts Probate System," 42 Mich. L. Rev. 425, 448 (1943).

[47] Virgil M. Harris, *Ancient, Curious, and Famous Wills* (1911), pp. 370, 414.

[48] In earlier times and in England, wills were even more likely to be deathbed documents; see Wilbur K. Jordan, *Philanthropy in England, 1480–1660* (1959), p. 16, on sixteenth-century wills; for some colonial data, see James W. Deen Jr., "Patterns of Testation: Four Tidewater Counties in Colonial Virginia," 16 Am. J. Legal Hist. 154, 167–68 (1972).

many nineteenth-century wills seem more poignant and direct than twentieth-century wills tend to be. (The typical will, however, did little preaching and betrayed little sentiment.) Only the wealthy, by and large, made out wills. Even at the very end of the period, probably less than 5 percent of the persons who died in the typical county, in any one year, left wills that passed through probate.[49] Even fewer of those who died intestate, that is, without wills, left estates that were formally administered. All in all, more than 90 percent of the population passed on without benefit of probate.

Will-makers tended to be landowners, men (and some women) of substance. Their estate plans (to use a modern term) nearly always disposed of their land and other property within the family. It was not usual for men to give women actual control over land. Before the Married Women's Property Acts, property left to a woman might pass out of the testator's bloodline, might even fall prey to creditors of the woman's husband. Among the wealthy, then, there was a definite tendency not to make outright gifts of land in fee simple to women. Rather, property was *settled* on women; or left in trust; or given to women in the form of lesser "estates": life interests for daughters, estates during widowhood for surviving wives. Almost 40 percent of a group of New Jersey wills, in the period 1810–1813, which contained gifts to a widow, gave her rights to income, which ended if she had the gall to remarry.[50] In New York City, seven out of twelve wills probated, in the summer of 1843, contained some sort of disposition less than a full fee simple.[51] Similarly, in Bucks County, Pennsylvania, in 1790; nearly two-thirds of the testators provided essentially for a place to live, and provisions for life to a widow or, very often, only for so long as she remained a widow.[52]

One has the impression that more of the population stood outside the formal system of succession in New York in 1840 than in Massachusetts Bay two centuries before. In the early colonial period, probate was cheap, accessible, and relatively informal. In the eighteenth century, probate was more elaborate and costly; it was basically for people who were relatively well off. At some point, perhaps about 1800, the curve reached a peak and slowly changed direction. From then on participation in the probate process gradually increased, along with national literacy and wealth. In absolute terms, the number of dispositions that were not fee simple dispositions (trusts, settlements, chains of future interests) certainly increased, in the nineteenth century—at least as fast as the population and probably much faster. In Bucks County, in 1890, about 30 percent of the testators had trust provisions in their wills—and nearly 60 percent of married testators.[53]

Trust litigation was fairly sparse in the early nineteenth century. Except for marriage settlements, living trusts were probably not common. Most trusts were short-term, "caretaker" trusts, created to protect some weaker member of the family: married women, minors, incompetents. A man might set up a trust,

---

[49] Some probably wrote out a will, but left so small an estate it made no sense to probate the will.

[50] N. J. Archives, 1st ser., vol. XLI (vol. 12 [1949], Calendar of Wills, 1810–13).

[51] New York, Surr. N.Y. Cnty., Will Bk. No. 88, pp. 2–65 (July-Sept. 1843).

[52] Carole Shammas et al., *Inheritance in America* (1987), p. 112.

[53] Carole Shammas et al., *op. cit.*, p 186. In Los Angeles, however, in 1890, the percentages were far less: 12.5 percent of testators, nearly 21 percent of married testators.

to avoid passing property on to a bankrupt son or son-in-law. Thomas Jefferson left the residue of his estate to his grandson, Thomas J. Randolph, and two friends, in trust for Jefferson's daughter. Her husband, Thomas M. Randolph, was insolvent. The trustees were to hold the estate "in base fee, determinable on the death of my said son-in-law"; at that time, the estate would vest in the daughter and her heirs. This arrangement would "preclude the rights, powers and authorities" that would otherwise devolve on the son-in-law "by operation of law." In this way, the estate was guarded against the creditors of Jefferson's son-in-law.[54] In a Pennsylvania case, *Ashhurst v. Given* (1843),[55] the deceased left to his son Samuel Given, a kind of trusteeship over the estate, consisting of an "undivided half part of the Kidderminster estate, including the factory buildings, dwelling-house, water-powers . . . machinery and fixtures." Samuel was to manage the estate for the benefit of his children, paying himself a "reasonable support out of the trust fund." In this roundabout way, the testator hoped to provide for the family, without exposing the estate to "those debts which he [Samuel] contracted in an unfortunate business."

A second, rarer, use of the trust device might be called dynastic. Through trusts and settlements, a testator who wished could tie up his estate, within the family, for quite a long time. But not forever. There was a limiting doctrine, called the rule against perpetuities—a rule of incredible complexity. The rule, which had reached full flower in England by 1800, was at least nominally in force in the United States. The New York revision of 1827–1828 modified the rule, and made it even more stringent. The New York statutes on trusts were, as we have seen, anti-dynastic. Only caretaker trusts were intended to survive the onslaught of reform, although the point was blunted by later amendments. Neither in New York, nor in Michigan, Wisconsin, or Minnesota, which borrowed the code, were the rules to stamp out the dynastic trust ever fully carried out.

The draftsmen of the New York code had a specific image in mind, a specific type of dynasty. They were thinking of the great English landed estates. Under a settlement or long-term trust, such an estate was "tied up" in the family in two senses: No current member of the family had the right to sell his interest, nor could anybody, including the trustee, treat land and improvements as market commodities; land and family were bound tightly together. New York had some estates of this type; they were also known in the plantation South. But a new type of trust was developing, which was dynastic in a different sense. Some great merchant families were wealthy in capital assets other than land— factories, banking houses, ships, and stocks and bonds. Particularly in Boston, rich men in the early nineteenth century began planning dynastic trusts that were fundamentally different from the baronial land trusts. These long-term trusts needed flexible management. The assets were not meant to be preserved as such; it was taken for granted that the trustees would change the portfolio as their business sense dictated.

Massachusetts law proved quite permissive to this new form of dynastic wealth. In the famous *Harvard College* case (1830),[56] the court produced a standard of investment for trustees that came to be known as the "prudent investor"

---

[54] Harris, *op. cit.*, p. 398.
[55] 5 Watts & Serg. 323 (Pa., 1843).
[56] *Harvard College v. Amory*, 26 Mass. (9 Pick.) 446 (1830).

rule. It freed the trustee from rigid restrictions on trust investment. The rule in other jurisdictions was that a trustee could invest only in government bonds or first mortgages on land. From 1830 on, the trustee in Massachusetts could manage and invest more freely; he could shift assets about, buying whatever was "prudent"; he could, for example, buy sound corporate stocks. The rule was the Magna Carta for a Boston phenomenon, the private, professional trustee. This shrewd Yankee figure, manager of other people's fortunes, first appeared in Boston around 1820. For several decades, until the rise of trust companies, he managed the wealth of the Brahmins. The *Harvard College* case set him loose from restraints—restraints that made sense for caretaker trusts managed by nonprofessionals. Some old firms of private trustees, grown rich and indispensable, still survive on Boston's State Street, with a century or more of prudence in their files. They are still able to compete for a corner of the business which, in general, the trust companies captured after the Civil War.[57]

A certain amount of hostility to dynastic trusts is understandable. This was not so much envy and hatred of the rich, as suspicion of any arrangement that locked assets up and kept them off the market. The Massachusetts solution was to broaden the power of trustees, so that they too could trade in the market. Other states resisted the Massachusetts rule. But in Pennsylvania, for example, where the stricter investment rule prevailed, the legislature passed hundreds of private laws giving trustees and other fiduciaries power to sell land in specific instances. In *Norris v. Clymer*[58] it was argued that the legislature had no power to pass this kind of law. Chief Justice Gibson disagreed. He was impressed by a "list of nine hundred statutes" already passed, similar to the one at issue, and the possibility that "ten thousand titles" depended on acts of the type. Nineteenth-century policy strongly disfavored anything that would unsettle titles.

There is also a kind of dynastic trust that is not based on family: the long-term charitable trust. It has had a curiously checkered career in this country.[59] Charities, so goes the maxim, are favorites of the law. The favor was not always very obvious. In the early nineteenth century, charity was associated with privilege, with the dead hand, with established churches (especially the Roman Catholic church), with massive wealth held in perpetuity. None of these was particularly popular.

The key English statute was the statute of charitable uses, passed in the waning years of Queen Elizabeth I. In New York, this ancient statute was not in effect; and the revisions of 1827–1828 did not restore it. Virginia and Maryland did not recognize the charitable trust at all. Some states enacted "mortmain" laws. These laws, based on an English statute, tried to cut down on deathbed gifts to charity. A person could not leave money by will, unless the will was made at least a month before the person died. A faint odor of anti-Catholicism also hung over these laws—the fantasy of the evil priest, extorting ransom for the Church from a dying man, as the price of absolution.

---

[57] See Lawrence M. Friedman, "The Dynastic Trust," 73 Yale L.J. 547 (1964).

[58] 2 Pa. Stats. 277 (1845). The statute at issue was an act of March 2, 1842, authorizing trustees under the will of Joseph Parker Norris to sell lands from his estate, despite the provisions of the will.

[59] See, in general, Howard S. Miller, *The Legal Foundations of American Philanthropy, 1776–1844* (1961).

Hostility toward charitable trusts weakened, but only slowly. The trust in the *Harvard College* case was charitable. John McLean, the deceased, had left $50,000 to trustees; after the death of his wife, one half of the trust was to be paid to the Massachusetts General Hospital, the other half to Harvard College, to be "exclusively and forever appropriated to the support of a professor of ancient and modern history." A college endowment, consisting of stocks and bonds, and supporting a professor of history, was not as frightening as a barony or church. One sign of the turning tide was the great case of *Vidal v. Girard's Executors* (1844).[60] The banker Stephen Girard had died childless, leaving behind an enormous estate. His complex, quirky will called for creation of a school, Girard College, and provided American legal history with more than a century of litigation. The question in *Vidal* was whether charitable trusts were valid at all. Specifically, did courts of chancery have inherent powers to administer these trusts, without special permission in the form of a statute? This was a crucial question, since the English statute, or something like it, specifically authorizing such trusts, was lacking in many states. To uphold the charitable trust, which it did, the Supreme Court reversed a prior line of cases. New York, Virginia, Maryland, and a few other states, continued to limit the charitable trust. In other states, *Vidal* encouraged a fresh look at the social utility of nonprofit dynasties.

INTELLECTUAL PROPERTY: PATENTS AND COPYRIGHTS

The Constitution (art. 1, sec. 8) gave Congress power "to promote the progress of science and useful arts, by securing for limited times to authors and inventors the exclusive right to their respective writings and discoveries." This was the formal source of federal power over patents and copyrights.

In English law, a patent was a monopoly grant, an exclusive right to make and deal in some item of trade. The colonies here and there granted such a patent. For example, South Carolina passed an "Act for the due Encouragement of Dr. William Crook," who had devised a "Composition" of "Oyl or Spirit of Tar, which with other Ingredients will preserve the Bottoms of Vessels from the River-Worm, and also the Plank from rotting" (1716).[61] Monopoly was in bad odor by 1776, except for the special case of the patent, which was thought valuable, since it acted as an incentive to technical innovation. The first patent act (1790) gave the power to issue patents to the secretary of state, the attorney general, and the secretary of war, "or any two of them." A patent was to be awarded if "the invention or discovery [was] sufficiently useful and important."[62] Almost immediately, men began petitioning for patents, including a "method of slivering, preparing, and spinning flax and hemp," a "machine for making nails, screws, and gimblets by mill work," and "an improvement in the plough."[63] Procedures under this law were considered slow and unsatisfactory;

---

[60] 2 How. 127 (1844).

[61] Bruce W. Bugbee, *Genesis of American Patent and Copyright Law* (1967), p. 76.

[62] 1 Stats. 109–10 (act of April 10, 1790).

[63] Edward C. Walterscheid, *To Promote the Progress of Useful Arts: American Patent Law and Administration, 1789–1836* (1998), pp. 175–76.

and a new law was passed in 1793. Under the new act, the secretary of state, with the approval of the attorney general, had power to issue patents valid for fourteen years. The federal government did not independently investigate patents under this law. In the debates in Congress, members spoke of the "encouragement of genius," and about progress. It seems likely that most ordinary people were indifferent, and did not worship at the feet of the god of technology; but there was a scientific and technical elite that saw a bright, glowing future of massive invention.[64]

The number of patents grew steadily. By 1807, the United States was granting more patents than Great Britain. By 1836, 9,957 patents had been issued, and the rate was accelerating. An important handful of these were inventions of immense importance to business. A major patent act was passed in 1836. It established a Patent Office, headed by a commissioner of patents, within the Department of State. The commissioner was to grant patents only if the subject of the patent had not been previously "invented or discovered," the applicant was the actual inventor of the device, and the article was "sufficiently useful and important" to deserve a patent. In case of doubt, a board of "three disinterested persons," appointed by the secretary of state, would decide whether to issue the patent. One of the three was to be an expert in "the particular art, manufacture, or branch of science to which the alleged invention appertains."[65]

A fundamental question haunted patent law. To grant patents liberally might encourage innovation; but each patent was a little monopoly, and monopoly was in general undesirable. The liberal policy won some early victories in court. In *Earle v. Sawyer* (1825),[66] the question was whether a patent could be granted for a certain "new and useful improvement in the machinery for manufacturing shingles." The "improvement" consisted mostly of using a circular instead of a perpendicular saw. It was objected that "the combination itself is so simple, that, though new, it deserves not the name of an invention." Joseph Story, on circuit, brushed this objection aside. To be patentable, an object must simply be "new." That was the heart of the matter; a "flash of mind" or "genius" was not necessary.[67] The act of 1836, however, tightened the requirements for a patent grant. It rested, clearly, on a judgment that what was bad about patents (monopoly) could well outweigh what was good (its incentive effect).

Between 1783 and 1786, every state but Vermont passed a copyright law, partly at the urging of the Continental Congress, partly at the instance of authors like Noah Webster, who wanted protection from pirates. The first law was Connecticut's (1783)—a law "for the Encouragement of Literature and Genius." The first federal Copyright Act became law in 1790. An author might gain "sole right and liberty of printing, reprinting, publishing and vending" a "map, chart, book or books," for fourteen years, renewable for one additional term of fourteen years. The author had to deposit a printed copy of his work with the clerk of the federal court in his district, before publication. Another

---

[64] 1 Stats. 318 (act of Feb. 21, 1793); on the legislative history of the act, see Walterscheid, ch. 7.

[65] 5 Stats. 117, 119, 120 (act of July 4, 1836).

[66] 8 F. Cas. 254, No. 4247 (C. C. Mass., 1825).

[67] The "flash of mind" requirement did not stay permanently buried; it was resurrected later on in patent law. See Part III, ch. IV, p. 437.

copy had to be delivered within six months to the secretary of state as well.[68] In 1831, the original term was extended to 28 years. By this time, the act covered musical compositions, designs, engravings, and etchings as well as maps, charts, and books.[69] In the case law of copyright, *Wheaton v. Peters* (1834) was a landmark decision.[70] Curiously, this was a lawsuit by one reporter of Supreme Court decisions, Henry Wheaton, against another, Richard Peters. The Supreme Court here ruled on copyright aspects of its own opinions. Peters succeeded Wheaton as reporter. A go-getter, Peters published a condensed, six-volume edition of Wheaton's work, priced dramatically below Wheaton's price.[71]

Wheaton sued for copyright infringement. Wheaton did not, technically, have a copyright under the federal law; he had failed to comply exactly with the procedures and requirements of the law. But did he have a common law right—a right that existed independent of the federal law? No, said the Supreme Court; as soon as an author publishes a book, he comes under the Copyright Act, and the common law is displaced. This was a victory for the national (federal) power. There was to be only one source of copyright law, relatively uniform and simple. As in the law of patents, there was tension between the (monopoly) rights of creators and the free-market interests of the business public. In *Wheaton v. Peters*, the Supreme Court perhaps leaned away from the monopoly aspects of copyright, by confining copyright to the terms of the federal statute—a right that was, moreover, limited in time.

An allied field—trademark law—was relatively undeveloped in this period. A trademark is not a flash of genius, but a message: This product or business is mine, and you cannot steal its name or its logo. But no trademark infringement case was decided in the United States before 1825.[72] Joseph Story granted the first injunction for trademark infringement, in 1844, to protect the makers of "Taylor's Persian Thread." Congress provided neither guidance nor any machinery of registration. Legal protection for designers of trademarks had to be forged in the rough mills of the courts. As the country industrialized, as technology and mass marketing developed, the law of intellectual property became more significant. Most of the value of intellectual property, despite the name, was hardly intellectual; it was mercantile and industrial.

[68] 1 Stats. 124 (act of May 31, 1790).
[69] Lyman R. Patterson, *Copyright in Historical Perspective* (1968), pp. 180–212; Paul Goldstein, *Copyright's Highway: From Gutenberg to the Celestial Jukebox* (rev. ed., 2003), pp. 41–44.
[70] 8 Pet. 591 (1834).
[71] On the case, see Paul Goldstein, *Copyright's Highway*, pp. 41–44.
[72] *Two Centuries' Growth of American Law* (1901), p. 435.

CHAPTER 6

THE LAW OF COMMERCE AND TRADE

A FEDERAL QUESTION: ADMIRALTY
AND GENERAL COMMERCE

By all contemporary accounts, American commercial law was deeply and persistently in debt to England. New developments in English case law traveled across the Atlantic with almost the speed of the clipper ships. Theoretically, even national sovereignty was not a barrier. The laws of admiralty, marine insurance, commercial paper, and sale of goods, were not, supposedly, merely English law, but part of an international body of rules. "The marine law of the United States," wrote Chancellor Kent, "is the same as the marine law of Europe. It is not the law of a particular country, but the general law of nations."[1]

These words have to be taken with a grain of salt. But they did have a kernel of truth; and, what is more important, they reflected the opinion of leading American lawyers. Trade was international. The American population in 1776 was strung out narrowly along the coast. Commerce was, in large measure, ocean commerce; the customs and documents of trade were also those of ocean commerce. The laws and customs of admiralty, of ocean trade, were part of the standard equipment of a developing country with windows on the ocean. Law was a vital segment of the commercial infrastructure. It had, in fact, an international base; but it also soon developed, in the United States, its own substance and style.

The Constitution made admiralty jurisdiction a federal matter. It put an end to state admiralty courts, and to Congress's own creature, the "Court of Appeals in Cases of Capture," which had been set up under the Articles of Confederation. This Court heard appeals from state decisions in prize cases—mostly cases about British ships seized by American privateers.[2] The Constitutional text extended the judicial power of the United States to all "Cases of admiralty and maritime Jurisdiction" (art. III, sec. 2). But how broad was that grant of jurisdiction? What did the clause mean? What situations did it cover, and what areas of law?

---

[1] Kent, *Commentaries*, vol. III (2nd ed., 1832), p. 1.
[2] Henry J. Bourguignon, *The First Federal Court: The Federal Appellate Prize Court of the American Revolution, 1775–1787* (1977).

English precedent was not entirely unambiguous. In English tradition, admiralty had power only over matters within the "ebb and flow of the tide."[3] The "ebb and flow of the tide" was perhaps a good enough criterion in England, an island nation. England had no Great Lakes and no Mississippi River. This limit was more problematic in the United States.

Some people defended the tidewater concept. This was not blind imitation of the past; it was a useful argument for people who took a narrow view of admiralty power, who wanted to keep federal jurisdiction within narrow limits, and give the states more power and more scope. Chancellor Kent warned that a broad admiralty power would impair the right of trial by jury (admiralty courts used no jury). Expansion would also divest the state courts "at one stroke, of a vast field of commercial jurisdiction." Justice Story consistently defended the tidewater concept as "the prescribed limit," which courts were not "at liberty to transcend." Justice William Johnson spoke in 1827 of the "silent and stealing progress of the admiralty in acquiring jurisdiction to which it has no pretensions."

But as waves of human beings moved into the vast American interior, the lakes and rivers became arteries of commerce as important as turnpikes and roads. The tidewater concept now came in for serious reexamination. In 1833, in *Peyroux v. Howard,*[4] the Supreme Court discovered what one judge later called an "occult tide," invisible to the naked eye, but strong enough to bring the Mississippi at New Orleans into the nets of federal admiralty power. In 1845, Congress passed an act that gave district courts jurisdiction over "matters of contract and tort" concerning "steamboats and other vessels of twenty tons burden and upwards, enrolled and licensed for the coasting trade," and operating on "lakes and navigable waters." The act was vague, the wording clumsy. But this act, and a collision on Lake Ontario between the schooner *Cuba* and the propeller *Genesee Chief,* provided the occasion for the great case called by the name of one of the ships, the *Genesee Chief* (1851).[5] Here the Supreme Court, through Chief Justice Taney, finally got rid of the tidewater rule, as a limit on admiralty jurisdiction. Federal power extended to all public, navigable waters.

Admiralty cases were staples of the docket of all the federal courts. The federal judges became adept at handling matters of admiralty law, and Joseph Story, characteristically, was a master. His opinions swarmed with erudition (quotations from Latin sources, references to Richard Zouch, the laws of Oleron, and other mysteries of the maritime past). But admiralty law was not a game; it was, among other things, a branch of foreign policy. Decisions on prize law, neutrality, and the embargo were its meat and drink. The docket cast up cases like *Brig Short Staple and Cargo v. U.S.* decided by the Supreme Court in February 1815; the brig had been seized "for having violated the embargo laws

---

[3] On Admiralty power, see Milton Conover, "The Abandonment of the 'Tidewater' Concept of Admiralty Jurisdiction in the United States," 38 Oregon L. Rev. 34 (1958); Note, "From Judicial Grant to Legislative Power: The Admiralty Clause in the Nineteenth Century," 67 Harv. L. Rev. 1214 (1954).

[4] 7 Peters 324 (1833).

[5] *The Propeller Genesee Chief v. Fitzhugh,* 12 Howard 443 (1851).

of the United States, by sailing to a foreign port."[6] In an 1814 case, a vessel, the *Cordelia,* on its way to Surabaya, was boarded by a British officer, who warned the ship not to put in at any port in Java. The shipmaster obeyed, and sailed for Philadelphia. The ship was insured; its policy covered, among other risks, "unlawful arrests, restraints, and detainments." But the Supreme Court held that the policy did not reach the *Cordelia's* situation. "The right to blockade an enemy's port . . . is a right secured to every belligerent by the law of nations." The restraint therefore was not "unlawful."[7]

The federal courts also decided many cases of maritime commerce. In *De Lovio v. Boit* (1815), Joseph Story, on circuit, held that a policy of marine insurance was a "maritime contract."[8] This gave federal courts jurisdiction over the matter. But the jurisdiction was concurrent, not exclusive, that is, it was shared with state courts. The pages of New York's state reports, in the early nineteenth century, fairly bristle with cases on marine insurance.[9] Nonetheless, in the partnership between state and federal power, the federal presence was definitely growing, a process that led to the *Genesee Chief.* One goal of this trend was centralization of foreign policy. But there was also a strong domestic motive. The Supreme Court, and important segments of opinion, believed that the country should be governed as a single large free-trade area. Commerce should flow smoothly across state borders; no robber barons should be able to extract toll as the goods were on the way.

The issue came to the fore in the mighty case of *Gibbons v. Ogden,* decided by Marshall's court in 1824.[10] New York had given, to Robert R. Livingston and Robert Fulton, the exclusive right to navigate "all the waters within the jurisdiction of that State, with boats moved by fire or steam." Ogden operated a steamboat line between New York and New Jersey, under license from Livingston. Gibbons owned two steamboats, which he ran between New York and Elizabethtown, New Jersey. Ogden got an injunction against Gibbons, his competitor. The importance of the case went beyond the interests of these two conflicting companies. Other states had made similar grants; and there was an unseemly squabble among the states over the steamboat business. The result was a kind of commercial war.[11]

On appeal, the Marshall court voided the New York act and struck down the steamboat monopoly. The decision rested on two bases. In the first place, Congress had passed certain acts, licensing ships that plied the coasting trade. Arguably these laws "preempted" or shoved aside any state legislation that overlapped or conflicted. The second basis was the clause of the Constitution that gave Congress power to regulate interstate commerce. *Gibbons v. Ogden* did not flatly hold that the commerce power was exclusive, that is, that federal

---

[6] *Brig Short Staple and Cargo v. U.S.,* 9 Cranch 55 (1815). The shipowners admitted the fact, but claimed, in justification, that an armed British vessel had captured her and forced her into port.

[7] *M'Call v. Marine Insurance Co.,* 8 Cranch 59 (1814).

[8] 7 Fed. Cas. No. 3776 (C.C.D. Mass., 1815).

[9] On the law and practice of marine insurance, see Julius Goebel, ed., *The Law Practice of Alexander Hamilton,* vol. II (1969), pp. 391–778.

[10] 9 Wheat. 1 (1824)

[11] See Jean Edward Smith, *John Marshall, Definer of a Nation* (1996), p. 474.

power left the states no residual power over commerce that crossed state lines. And the federal license laws made the case a bit more ambiguous than otherwise, and blunted its thrust. Perhaps the court really wanted it that way. Federal power over interstate commerce was a sleeping giant, since the federal government did very little controlling or regulating. Still, to some unknown extent, federal power over commerce apparently cut down, by its very existence, the right and power of the states to have their own, independent policies about commerce and trade. In any event, the decision perhaps stimulated the growth of the steamboat business: Companies proliferated—by November 1824, the number of steamboats in New York waters went from six to forty-three, and transport became simpler and cheaper.[12]

The Supreme Court also moved to unify the commercial law of the country. It hoped that a single body of law would emerge under federal hegemony. *Swift v. Tyson* (1842)[13] decided that federal courts, in ordinary commercial cases, had the right to apply the "general" law of commerce, even if this was different from the law of the state in which the court was sitting, and even if no "federal question" was presented, and the case had come to a federal court solely because plaintiff and defendant were residents of different states. The actual question in the case came out of the law of negotiable instruments. If the holder of a bill of exchange endorsed the bill, and transferred it, what were the rights of the transferee? If he was a "holder in due course," his rights were fairly strong. Anybody who bought the bill with fresh money or goods was obviously a "holder in due course." But suppose he took the bill to satisfy an old debt which the endorser owed him. In that case, was he a "holder in due course"? The law of New York, where the bill had been accepted, at least arguably said no, he was not a holder; the general view, in commercial law, was yes he was. The law of commerce, Story said, speaking for the court, was and ought to be international—not the "law of a single country only, but of the commercial world." The parochial view of New York thus could not prevail. This view gave the federal courts the right to apply a national (and even international) legal standard in commercial cases. It thus took the side of the federal government—and the side of urban creditors—against the side of the states and the localities, with their prejudice in favor of the home-state debtors.[14]

---

[12] Smith, *John Marshall*, p. 481.

[13] 16 Pet. I (1842). The precise question was whether the Judiciary Act of 1789 required the court to follow state law. Section 34 of the Act directed federal trial courts to follow "the laws of the several states" except where the case presented a federal question. Did "laws" mean only statutes or did it include common law doctrines? Not the latter, said the court, at least in cases of "contracts and other instruments of a commercial nature." The doctrine of *Swift v. Tyson* later expanded to cover all sorts of diversity cases in federal court, not merely commercial cases; but the original holding was plainly influenced by the idea that commercial law had no room for strictly local doctrine. The *Swift* case has been treated in two monographs by Tony A. Freyer, *Forums of Order: The Federal Courts and Business in American History* (1979); and *Harmony and Dissonance: The Swift & Erie Cases in American Federalism* (1981).

[14] On this point, see Tony A. Freyer, *Producers versus Capitalists: Constitutional Conflict in Antebellum America* (1994), p. 86.

SALE OF GOODS

The law of sales of goods developed greatly in the first half of the nineteenth century. Many, if not most, of the leading cases were English. They were adopted in the United States with some rapidity. Two strains of law—contract and the law merchant—each with a somewhat different emphasis, were more or less godparents of the law of sales. What one might call the psychology of *market overt* (open market) suffused the law merchant. In market overt, goods were as freely transferable as bills, notes, and paper money. A buyer of goods in market overt acquired full rights to the goods. If he bought in good faith and for value, his claims were superior to those of any prior owner, even if the goods had been stolen. At one time, every shop in London was considered a market overt; but by the eighteenth century, the doctrine in the literal sense had gone into decline. Chancellor Kent condemned it as a barbarous survival; in any event, it never took root in the United States.[15] But the more general regime of contract flourished in the United States.

The law of sales grew up about the concept of *property* or *title* to goods. Title was an invisible rope that tied a chattel to its original owner until title legally "passed" to a buyer. Title was a concept of intention: In broad theory, title passed when the parties intended it to pass. But the rules of title were not as neutral as they appeared on the surface; they leaned in the direction of the rights of sellers, not buyers. English and American cases agreed that title could pass without either payment or delivery, if so intended. This meant that the risk of loss shifted to the buyer, at an early stage of the bargain. In a well-known English case, *Tarling v. Baxter* (1827),[16] the parties bought and sold a haystack. The buyer agreed not to remove the hay until he paid for it. The seller drew a bill of exchange on the buyer, payable in one month; the buyer accepted the bill. The bill was then negotiated to a good-faith purchaser. Meanwhile, a fire destroyed the haystack completely. The buyer was, naturally, unwilling to put out good money in exchange for some smoldering ashes; but the court held that he had to. Title to the haystack had passed; therefore, it was the *buyer's* haystack that had burned. On the other hand, if the buyer went bankrupt or failed to pay, so that the question was not, who had the risk of accident loss, but who had the right to repossess, here too the seller was favored. The courts invented a shadowy security interest that did not "pass" to the buyer quite so quickly.

These and other doctrines were gradually woven into a tight, logical fabric of rules. In operation, in the actual reported cases, courts applied these rules in a more flexible way than one might guess from the way they were formulated in the abstract. As a total package, they were rather too elegant (and too unknown except to lawyers) to have much effect on the real-life market. Whatever they meant in practice, it is worth asking why the rules and principles should have moved away from classic "mercantile" principles, even on paper, in the heyday of the market economy. The answer may lie in the difference between a market economy and a merchant's economy. Commercial law was once the province of a small in-group of merchants; in a typical transaction, both buyer and seller were middlemen, who understood the business background and

---

[15] *Wheelwright v. Depeyster*, 1 Johns. R. 471, 480 (N.Y. 1806).
[16] Barn & Co. 360 (1827).

were familiar with documents and customs. In the early nineteenth century, the law concerned itself more with the needs and activities of ultimate buyers and sellers. It shifted its emphasis to favor manufacturers and producers, a class vaguely correlated with sellers rather than buyers.

Even so, American commercial law, on paper, had a certain Adam Smith severity, a certain flavor of the rugged individual. American lawyers liked to contrast the stern simplicity (real or imagined) of the common law with the paternalism (real or imagined) of civil law. In California, just after statehood, a minority group of San Francisco lawyers petitioned the legislature, asking that "the Legislature . . . retain, in its substantial elements, the system of the Civil Law." The judiciary committee of the California Senate denied their request. The committee felt the common law was greatly superior to its rival, especially in commercial law. The common law doctrine, said the report, "is *caveat emptor*. . . . In other words, the Common Law allows parties to make their own bargains, and when they are made, holds them to a strict compliance"; the civil law, on the contrary, with its dangerous doctrine of implied warranty, "looks upon man as incapable of judging for himself, assumes the guardianship over him, and interpolates into a contract that which the parties never agreed to. The one is protective of trade, and a free and rapid interchange of commodities—the other is restrictive of both." The committee waxed eloquent over the almost mystical virtues of the common law. English and American commerce "whitens every sea, woos every breeze. . . . Its merchants are princes—its ships palaces. . . . The Commerce of Civil Law countries . . . creeps timidly along a few familiar shores . . . sluggish in its progress, and unprofitable in its results. It is not fostered by the quickening influence of English and American law . . . the spirit of life is not in it—it is dead."[17]

This, of course, is almost certainly nothing but patriotic self-delusion. Triumphant capitalism would not have smothered in its crib without the rule of *caveat emptor*.[18] It is doubtful whether actual doctrines of commercial law were cause, effect, or condition of American capitalism; or all or none of these. It is true that *caveat emptor* was loudly proclaimed in some American cases. In *McFarland v. Newman* (1839),[19] a Pennsylvania case, one Newman bought a horse from McFarland. The horse "had a defluxion from the nose at the time of the bargain," but McFarland "assured Newman it was no more than the ordinary distemper to which colts are subject." In fact, the horse had glanders. In a crisp, biting opinion, Pennsylvania's John Gibson reversed a lower court decision for the buyer. "He who is so simple as to contract without a specification of the terms, is not a fit subject of judicial guardianship." Under the civil law rule, the seller would have been liable; but this rule was (according to Gibson) obnoxious to the health of the economy. It "would put a stop to commerce itself in driving everyone out of it by the terror of endless litigation."

Not every reported opinion was so friendly to the rule of caveat emptor.[20] In South Carolina, at least one judge called *caveat emptor* a "disgrace to the law."

---

[17] Report of Feb. 27, 1850, reprinted in appendix to 1 Cal. Rpts. 588, pp. 595, 597.

[18] See Walton Hamilton, "The Ancient Maxim Caveat Emptor," 40 Yale L.J. 1133, 1178–82 (1931).

[19] 9 Watts 55 (Pa. 1839).

[20] *Barnard v. Yates*, 1 Nott & M'Cord 142 (S. Car. 1818).

In the case in question, decided in 1818, barrels of blubber were sold as "oil." The judge adopted the civil law rule: "A sound price requires a sound commodity."[21] This case, however, was regarded as exceptional. Most decisions in most states in the first half of the nineteenth century agreed with Gibson's formulation of the rule. But although common law courts refused to *imply* warranties, they showed a marked tendency to read *express* warranties into a seller's words, at the slightest provocation. Often, these "express" warranties were much the same as those that the namby-pamby civil law "implied."

In the twentieth century, warranty means a promise of quality, which is enforceable regardless of intention or fault. A supermarket is liable to its customer if adulterated soup makes her sick, even though the soup company sealed the soup can before it ever reached the supermarket shelf. In Gibson's day, warranty was still strongly colored with its historical meaning, which restricted recovery to open, blatant deceit. The civil law rule—that a sound price requires a sound commodity—arguably fits market systems better than *caveat emptor*, because it carries out the reasonable intention of honest parties. Gibson's language thus hid a paradox. *Caveat emptor* might be in fact a rule that ignores the actual intent of the parties to a contract. Yet perhaps, one might argue, it fits the conditions of a broadly based market. The Gibson rule on warranties favored sellers, to be sure. But more significantly, it enhanced the finality of bargains. It made it harder for parties to drag into court their harangues over warranty and quality. This is what Gibson had in mind when he spoke of the "terror of endless litigation." A clear, harsh rule, he felt, was necessary. Otherwise, the courts might be overburdened with cases, and this might choke the rivers of commerce.

Rules about bills, money, and notes made up the law of negotiable instruments, a somewhat different mix of law merchant and common law. The key concept in this field was negotiability. Paper money has this quality in the highest degree. Money is "bearer paper"; it can be transferred from hand to hand. A check is also negotiable, if you endorse it. A negotiable instrument, when validly transferred, cuts off "equities" between the original parties. In other fields of law, a buyer of rights or goods steps into his seller's shoes. A buyer of land is no better off than the seller. If there were claims, liens, or doubts about title that clouded the rights of the seller, they follow the land into the buyer's hands and haunt him there. But a good-faith buyer of a check takes fresh, clear, virginal title.

The colonies, as we have seen, had enacted liberal assignment statutes, so that the law of negotiable instruments was in some ways more advanced than in England. This liberality continued. A Georgia statute of 1799 declared that "All bonds, and other specialties, and promissory notes, and other liquidated demands . . . whether for money or other things . . . shall be negotiable by endorsement in such manner and under such restrictions as are prescribed in the case of promissory notes."[22]

---

[21] *Ibid.*

[22] Prince, *Digest of the Laws of Georgia* (2nd ed., 1837), p. 426 (act of Feb. 16, 1799, sec. 25); Frederick Beutel, "The Development of State Statutes on Negotiable Paper Prior to the Negotiable Instruments Law," 40 Columbia L. Rev. 836, 848 (1940).

The reference to "other things" was significant. Today, only instruments payable in money can claim to be negotiable. But the chattel note was widely used and recognized in colonial times. In the tobacco colonies and states, notes were commonly made payable in tobacco. After Independence, and well into the nineteenth century, chattel notes were common in the West, where hard money was in chronically short supply. In a Wisconsin case (1844), a note had been made payable in "five thousand three hundred and seventy-five lbs. of lead."[23] An Ohio case (1827) dealt with a note payable in "good merchantable whiskey." But this court refused to treat the note as negotiable.[24] Chattel notes were undesirable because they were hard to standardize. Negotiable instruments do their job best when they are as simple and formal as possible. A check is a bare, unvarying document. It is completely stereotyped in looks and in wording. Chattel notes were tolerated only because money was so scarce; or where (as in the tobacco states) a certain chattel, like wampum or cowrie shells in other cultures, was a recognized medium of exchange. These were transient conditions, however. By the end of the period, courts were regularly holding that no chattel note could be truly negotiable; only money instruments had that quality.

Throughout the first half of the nineteenth century, there was no satisfactory national currency. Gold and silver were rare. Private bank notes circulated as a kind of money. Credit depended on these bank notes and on personal promissory notes. For this reason, the law of bills and notes was important to the economy. As the pale of settlement moved west, the law of negotiable instruments went with it. Law reports were thick with cases on bills and notes. The bill of exchange was mostly used by merchants and bankers; it produced most of its case law in the East. The promissory note, on the other hand, was everywhere. Case law confirms the guess that basic aspects of the law of bills and notes were part of the living law. People were familiar with some of the simple, general rules about promissory notes, and the endorsement of promissory notes, just as they are more or less familiar with rules about checks today. Popular form books and how-to-do-it books showed people what bills and notes looked like and some of their basic legal characteristics.

In the nineteenth century, as in the twentieth century, the economy floated on a sea of credit. Credit, however, was a high-risk matter. This was an age of huge swings in the business cycle, an age without Dun and Bradstreet, without computerized credit services,[25] without deposit insurance or a firm and solid banking system. It was a life-and-death matter to know your debtor, and whether he was solvent. A circulating note, in proper form, was legally valid, and negotiable. Whether the people who signed it, as maker or endorser, were solvent was another matter. The more the note carried signatures or endorsements of sound, solid citizens, the more the note could be counted on. Endorsements were a form of credit guarantee. It was often the case that people signed notes as an "accommodation"—that is, for nothing—in order to lend their name or credit to someone else. An "accommodation" party, naturally,

---

[23] *Garrison v. Owens*, 1 Pin. 471 (1844).
[24] *Rhodes v. Lindly*, 3 Ohio Reports 51 (1827).
[25] By the 1840s, there was some rudimentary credit rating.

tended to lose enthusiasm for the transaction, if the maker of the note failed to pay, and the endorsers were called on to make good. These failures were all too frequent. The country was large, and there were many ways for a debtor to escape from his debts. In a great, young, runaway economy, subject to violent outbursts of boom and bust, fortunes were easily made and unmade. During the downswings, banks drowned in a sea of debt, leaving behind heaps of worthless paper. Makers and endorsers failed or dodged their obligation; and the sureties were sorely tempted to wriggle out of their obligations through tiny cracks in the law or the practice. Many cases, then, turned on the rights and obligations of sureties and accommodation endorsers. In general, the case law was lenient to them; unless the creditor swiftly and sternly pursued his rights, courts had a tendency to let the surety go. And if the creditor took any action that might be harmful to the surety—for example, if the creditor gave his debtor extra time to pay, without consulting the surety—then the surety was considered released.[26]

The *note* was paper of a thousand uses. It was a "courier without luggage": one scratch of the pen, and it moved swiftly and easily into the stream of commerce. Simplicity and ease of travel meant a great deal in a nation of continental size, with a population that moved restlessly from place to place. New types of negotiable instruments developed in the course of the century. Municipal and corporate bonds were drawn into the orbit of negotiability. Banks launched the negotiable certificate of deposit—so popular today—before 1850. The bank check had been in use for at least a century, but had never been of much consequence. Ultimately, it became the people's instrument of payment, just as the note was the people's instrument of credit. In Story's treatise on promissory notes and other commercial paper (1845), the check was important enough to merit a chapter of its own.[27] Some of these new developments came by way of England. Some changed radically in the United States. The bill of lading, in England, was a document of ocean freight. In the United States, the name and doctrine came to be used for railroad documents, too. A good deal of commercial law was, and always had been, judge made. But the judges did not make it up out of nothing. They took their guidance, often, from actual business practice, which they simply ratified. Statutes were an important, if secondary, source of law. Certain aspects of the law of commerce and trade, however, became issues of high public policy and led to fierce debate and controversy. This was especially true of questions of currency and banking. The rise and fall of the two banks of the United States has already been mentioned. There was always tremendous pressure for policies that would stimulate lending. Cash was in desperately short supply. Everybody—merchants, businessmen, mill owners, even farmers—needed credit. Much of the public debates over money and banks sounded high themes of political and economic principle; but underneath was brute economic and political interest. Policies that had the highest payoffs, or seemed to, for the loudest voices or the strongest interests tended to win out, regardless of abstract principle.

---

[26] See, for example, *Clippinger v. Creps*, 2 Watts 45 (Pa. 1833).
[27] Joseph Story, *Commentaries on the Law of Promissory Notes* (1st ed., 1845), pp. 614–45.

BANKRUPTCY AND INSOLVENCY

Bankruptcy law was another branch of commercial law with intense economic significance. The Constitution gave Congress the power "to establish uniform laws on the Subject of Bankruptcy throughout the United States." But Congress was slow to take up this clear invitation to create a national system. Before the Civil War, only two federal bankruptcy acts were passed. The first, in 1800, lasted two and a half years.[28] The second, in 1841, was repealed with even more haste.[29]

Charles Warren remarked that "desire for bankruptcy legislation" was always "coupled" with depressions in American history.[30] Panic and commercial failure were indeed the backdrop for the first act, the law of 1800. It followed closely the scheme of the contemporary English statute. Only creditors could initiate bankruptcy proceedings, and only "traders" (merchants) were liable to be put through bankruptcy. In fact, some merchants used the law to get rid of their debts, by inducing friendly creditors to push them into bankruptcy. Some members of Congress bitterly criticized the law. Thomas Newton Jr., of Virginia, denounced it as "partial, immoral . . . impolitic . . . anti-Republican."[31] The law was administratively inconvenient. In some parts of the country, it was awkward to travel long distances to reach the federal court. There may have been a certain amount of fraud; but this is difficult to prove. Critics complained that creditors got nothing for their pains; and, in fact, 40 percent of the estates in bankruptcy in Massachusetts yielded absolutely nothing. But this was only to be expected: there was no incentive, on either side, to seek the shelter of bankruptcy unless and until there was virtually nothing left.[32] Still, the arguments against the law led to its rather quick repeal.

In the second bankruptcy act, too, a creditor could force into bankruptcy only members of the commercial class: "all persons, being merchants, or using the trade of merchandise, all retailers of merchandise, and all bankers, factors, brokers, underwriters, or marine insurers, owing debts to the amount of not less than two thousand dollars." But the act, significantly, opened another door: "All persons whatsoever" might file a petition for voluntary bankruptcy. The act was passed, somewhat belatedly, in the wake of the shattering economic crisis of 1837. The act marked something of a shift in emphasis, as the debate over passage made clear. Earlier bankruptcy laws had been drafted primarily to protect the creditors of an insolvent person; the point was to make sure that everyone with cargo in a sinking ship was fairly and equitably treated. The act of 1841 was at least equally interested in another possible goal of bankruptcy: to wipe clean the debtor's slate. During debate, some in Congress denounced the proposed law as not a true bankruptcy law, but rather an "insolvency law." The term referred to state laws, which emphasized debtor relief rather than fair treatment of

---

[28] Act of Apr. 4, 1800, 2 Stats. 19, repealed Dec. 19, 1803, 2 Stats. 248.

[29] Act of Aug. 19, 1841, 5 Stats. 440, repealed Mar. 3, 1843, 5 Stats. 614.

[30] Charles Warren, *Bankruptcy in United States History* (1935), pp. 21–22; a modern study of the background of the law is Bruce H. Mann, *Republic of Debtors: Bankruptcy in the Age of American Independence* (2002).

[31] Quoted in Warren, *ibid.*

[32] Bruce Mann, *Republic of Debtors*, p. 252.

creditors. Debtor relief was certainly a major result of the act. Charles Warren, who studied its operation, reported that 33,739 persons took advantage of the law; $440,934,000 in debt was canceled; a mere $43,697,357 was surrendered by the debtors.[33] In most cases, the estates of bankrupts generated absolutely nothing for the creditors; in one district in New York, studied by Edward Balleisen, the creditors got, on average, 13 cents on the dollar; but this was exceptional; in many places, one cent on the dollar was more typical.[34] The law in fact did give debtors a good deal of leverage over creditors. They could demand settlements at favorable terms—or else. Yet, in a sense the law was a success; in any event, economic revival, and the rapid discharge of hundreds of debtors, removed some of the sense of urgency; the "reduction in the incidence of distress quickly eased the pressure for a permanent bankruptcy system."[35]

Bankruptcy and related laws were important in a dynamic economy, an economy of risk takers, an economy so dependent on credit. People take risks when the risks are not too overwhelming. More people will walk a tightrope when they see a net underneath. Bankruptcy laws are nets that catch falling merchants. They survive to work and take risks again. It may be precisely because law and society in this country encourage the taking of risks, that its bankruptcy laws, in the end, have been more generous and forgiving than in most other countries. From this standpoint, the collapse of the federal law was in many ways a misfortune. The law, for all its failings, might have led to a system of fair, uniform division of assets among creditors. But it was too much to hope for a long-lasting federal law, at this period at least, if only because of the "cankering jealousy of the general government with which some of the states are so deeply affected."[36] In between federal laws, the states did not leave the subject untouched. In the broadest sense, few legal relationships led to more ceaseless agitation and enactment than debtor-creditor relationships. The subject was rife with political passion. But it lost what had once been salient—its moral affect. Bankruptcy originally had a quite punitive ring. It was at one time a crime, later a disgrace. In the climate of a vibrant American economy, with so many men who risked so much on the toss of commercial dice, failure became more normal, more domesticated. Debt never lost its flavor of disgrace completely—there were still plenty of skeptics, plenty of what Balleisen has called "commercial moralists";[37] but in an age of business, its stigma lost much of its bite.

One symptom of changing attitudes was the abolition of imprisonment for debt. This was a humanitarian gesture; but it was particularly appealing in the new age. As William E. Nelson has pointed out, bankruptcy and insolvency laws are "sensible arrangements in an industrialized society"; a man does not lose his ability to work, to produce, when he goes bankrupt; but he does when he

---

[33] Warren, *ibid.*, p. 81.

[34] Edward J. Balleisen, *Navigating Failure: Bankruptcy and Commercial Society in Antebellum America* (2001), p. 120. This book is a careful study of the operation of the 1841 bankruptcy act.

[35] Peter J. Coleman, *Debtors and Creditors in America: Insolvency, Imprisonment for Debt, and Bankruptcy, 1607–1900* (1974), p. 24.

[36] 1 Am. Jurist 49 (1829).

[37] Balleisen, *Navigating Failure*, pp. 96–99.

sits in jail.[38] Bankruptcy and insolvency laws were alternatives to imprisonment for debt; and they eventually replaced it entirely.

Imprisonment for debt was thus both cruel and inefficient. It had long been under attack. By the end of the eighteenth century in New England, few debtors actually spent much time in prison—less than 2 percent spent a year or more; many were released after one day. The concept of a "prison" was also rather loose. Many debtors were only nominally in jail. Often they were allowed to roam about the city, or to work by day, and come back to the prison by night. Statutes, some of them dating from the colonial period, specifically authorized this practice. For example, a New Hampshire law of 1771, "for the Ease and Relief of Prisoners for Debt," gave imprisoned debtors the "liberty" of the prison yard, and established these limits at "within one hundred feet of the walls of the Prison," on posting of bond.[39] Statutes of this sort were helpful; but they did not do away with the abuses of the system; and there remained pathetic cases of people who did in fact rot in jail for trivial debts, well into the nineteenth century. In Rhode Island, in 1830, a widow from Providence was put in jail for a debt of sixty-eight cents; in 1827 and 1828, a sick, sixty-seven-year-old laborer named Freeborn Hazard was kept in prison for four months and later recommitted for a debt of one dollar and costs of $3.22. Nonetheless, abolition was, in part, a ratification of pre-existing social change. The very idea of imprisonment for debt became quite intolerable. It clashed with the growing ethos of second chances. It was inconsistent with the idea of the safety net. The mass basis of American law—and the American market—meant that imprisonment was a risk for thousands and thousands, not just a few misbehaving debtors. Hundreds of thousands, after all, played the land market, or dabbled in business. The business cycle, when it crashed, shook the economy with the primitive force of an earthquake, and brought down many small men, who did not seem like black-hearted villains. For these ordinary souls in financial trouble, even one day, and even in a jail that was loosely defined, seemed too much. The risk remained. In Boston in 1820, 1,442 debtors went to jail, and another 1,124 in 1830; in Springfield, one victim was a woman of nineteen, "with a child at her breast"; she owed six to eight dollars.[40]

Many state constitutions specifically addressed the issue of imprisonment for debt. The Pennsylvania Constitution of 1776 provided that "the person of a debtor . . . shall not be continued in prison after delivering up his Estate, for the benefit of his creditors, in such manner as shall be prescribed by law" (art. 9, sec. 16). This type of provision did not prevent debtors from going to prison in the first place. Abolishing imprisonment for debt altogether was a later step, and the states did not usually take it all at once. In New Hampshire, for example, a law passed before 1820 restricted imprisonment to those who owed more than $13.33. In 1831, the legislature ended the imprisonment of women debtors. Finally, in 1840, the whole institution of imprisonment for debt came to an end.[41] In other states, however, final, complete abolition did not become law until much deeper in the century.

[38] Nelson, *The Americanization of the Common Law,* p. 218.
[39] *Laws N.H. Province Period, 1745–1774* (1915), pp. 548, 549–50 (act of Jan. 17, 1771).
[40] Coleman, *op. cit.,* p. 42. The widow and Freeborn Hazard are discussed at p. 89.
[41] Coleman, *op. cit.,* pp. 62–63.

For most states, if not all, to ameliorate or abolish imprisonment for debt was only one aspect of debtor relief. The states quite generally had insolvency laws, which more or less substituted for the national bankruptcy law that Congress neglected to pass (except for the two brief episodes we mentioned). But these insolvency laws were patch works; they varied from state to state and from time to time. There were also stay laws and mortgage moratoria. The colonies had constantly tinkered with this or that law for the relief of debtors, and the Revolution did not interrupt the process; indeed, the dislocations of the war, and the economic misery that followed, gave a strong push to debtor relief. South Carolina passed an "installment" act in 1787. The act recited that "many inhabitants of this country before the revolution owed considerable sums of money," which they could not pay because of the "embarrassment of the war," and because of "very considerable importations of merchandise since the peace, and the loss of several crops." Under the act, debts contracted before January 2, 1787, might be paid in three installments, on March 1, 1788, 1789, and 1790. Ominously, a special section of the act imposed heavy penalties on "any person or persons [who] shall assault, beat, wound, or oppose" those who tried to carry the act into effect.[42]

The South Carolina law was a planters' relief law, on the face of it. Other states also tailored relief laws for groups of dominant debtors—farmers and landowners, typically. But the state laws were neither complete, nor uniform, nor fair. Insolvency laws and debtor-relief laws naturally followed the business cycle. Law making was most shrill and frenetic in the lean years following a crash. In some states (for example, Connecticut), insolvent debtors petitioned for private acts of relief, and these were frequently granted. The volume of these petitions added point to the demand for insolvency laws. The Rhode Island legislature received more than 2,300 petitions between 1758 and 1828.[43] Peter Coleman's research suggests that as many as one householder out of three may have been "hauled into court as a defaulting debtor" in the late eighteenth century, and that one out of five householders in the early nineteenth century would become insolvent during the course of a working lifetime.[44] The panic of 1819 stimulated a fresh burst of activity; everywhere there was agitation for stay laws and other forms of debtor relief; in some states, creditor interests blocked the legislation, but in others, particularly in the West, the agitation bore fruit.[45]

The typical state insolvency law gave the *debtor* the right to set the process of insolvency in motion. Some laws did, and some did not, provide for ratable division of assets among all creditors. Creditors complained long and loud about some of these laws—complaints about unfair preferences, fraud, and great inconveniences. So much smoke suggests at least a little fire. In most cases, the laws were probably badly administered. They sorely needed workable rules about priorities—which claims were to be preferred over others. They needed fair and efficient procedures. As it was, the elemental greed of creditors and

---

[42] *Statutes at Large, So. Car.*, vol. V (1838), pp. 36, 37 (act of Mar. 28, 1787).

[43] Coleman, *op. cit.*, p. 96.

[44] *Ibid.*, p. 207.

[45] See Murry N. Rothbard, *The Panic of 1819: Reactions and Policies* (1962), pp. 24–56.

debtors gutted these laws. A contemporary witness (in 1829) judged state insolvency laws very harshly:

> Instead of one uniform, unbending rule for dividing the estate of an insolvent among his creditors, it is left to be disposed of by accident or caprice. One man prefers his father, brothers, and uncles, because they are his relations; another prefers his endorsers and custom-house sureties, because that is the general practice; and the business of a third is often settled by the sheriff's seizing his stock, before he has time to complete his arrangements.[46]

Moreover, there were simply too many of these laws. There were businesses that crossed state lines. Insolvency law, however, stopped at the borders. "There should not be one law at New York and another at Philadelphia, one law at Charleston and another at New Orleans."[47] And yet there was. These were important laws; but they were almost continually under a legal cloud. They were often challenged in court. As a rule, state courts upheld their own insolvency laws. The judges knew the men who enacted these laws, and probably understood the reasons why. But insolvency laws raised a ticklish federal question. The Constitution gave Congress the power to enact a bankruptcy law: Did this mean the states were shut out? That they had no right to pass insolvency laws? In 1819, in *Sturges v. Crowninshield*,[48] the Supreme Court gave its answer, when it upheld a New York insolvency law (of 1811). The decision embodied a deft compromise, typical of John Marshall's skill. Insofar as it discharged contracts and debts that were older than the law itself, the law was unconstitutional, since it impaired the obligation of contracts, which the Constitution forbade. But the Court did not hold state insolvency laws illegal per se. Such laws could stand, if they met the Court's exacting standards. They must not be retroactive, and impair legitimate business expectations. They must not strangle instruments of credit.

State insolvency laws heavily favored debtors. There were usually more debtors than creditors, and that meant they had many more votes. Yet legislatures also enacted lien laws, which favored creditors. And they were careful to preserve some forms of creditors' rights, in lean years as well as in fat. State governments were poor and constricted. They did not indulge, in those days, in the lavish powers of subsidy and tax. But they did have power to bind and to loose, to create legal rights and impose legal duties. This power was often a substitute for direct intervention with money. Debtors desperately needed capital. This meant that the law had to be friendly to creditors too—only not too much. As a consequence, the law wobbled and vacillated; it often seemed to be of two minds at once. Similarly, in times of crisis, there was immense pressure to do something for debtors—but again, not too much, not in such a way as to do permanent damage to the economy. At every point, laws of insolvency and creditors' rights, reflected this push and pull of interests.

[46] 1 Am. Jurist 45 (1829).
[47] *Ibid.*, p. 36.
[48] 4 Wheat, 122 (1819).

CONTRACT

The nineteenth century was the golden age of the law of contract.[49] As late as Blackstone, contract law occupied only a tiny corner in the huge structure of common law. Blackstone devoted a whole volume to land law, but a few pages at most to informal, freely negotiated bargains.[50] In the nineteenth century, contract law, both in England and America, made up for lost time. This was a natural development. Contract law was that body of law that pertained to the growing market economy. It was the branch of law that made and applied rules for arm's-length bargains, in a free, impersonal market. Contract law grew up in the era when the last vestiges of feudalism vanished, and a capitalist order flourished. It became indispensable in the age of Adam Smith. After 1800, the domain of contract steadily expanded; it greedily swallowed up other parts of the law. Land law remained critically important, but land dealings were more and more treated contractually. Special rules still governed deeds, leases, and other kinds of conveyance; but these documents were now called *contracts* and many general doctrines of contract law now applied to them.

Contract also expanded as a constitutional concept. The Constitution forbade states from impairing the obligation of a contract. But what was a contract? The Supreme Court gave answers that were broad and surprising. A legislative land grant was a contract, and the state could not undo it; a college charter was a contract; so, too, was a legislative exemption from tax.[51] In part, these cases used the notion of contract as a metaphor. The state was duty-bound to support a broad, free market; to do so, business had to be able to rely on the stability of arrangements legally made, at least in the short and middle run. The contract clause guaranteed precisely that kind of stability, or tried to. The economic importance of the clause was particularly obvious in the *Dartmouth College* case, as we have seen. In any event, the root notion of the growing law of contract was basically the same as the root notion of the contracts clause. Freely made bargains should be honored, and, it necessary, enforced. Legislatures should not tinker, *ex post facto*, with bargains freely made.

Contract as a branch of law can best be called residual; it dealt with those areas of business life not otherwise regulated. Its cardinal principle was permissive: whatever the parties decide, that should be carried out. Of course, they had to agree, or else there was no contract—no meeting of the minds. This phrase, "meeting of the minds," should not be taken too literally. The law emphasized the document itself, if there was one, and the plain meaning of its words, just as it did in land law or the law of negotiable instruments, and probably for similar reasons. For example, a rule, which came to be called the *parol evidence rule*, shut off any evidence that might contradict the terms of a written

---

[49] On the meaning and role of contract law in the nineteenth century, see in general, Lawrence M. Friedman, *Contract Law in America* (1965); Morton J. Horwitz, *The Transformation of American Law, 1780–1860* (1977), ch. 6. For developments in England, see Patrick S. Atiyah, *The Rise and Fall of Freedom of Contract* (1979).

[50] He devoted somewhat more space to doctrines of commercial law, which were of course also concerned with economic exchange.

[51] Respectively, *Fletcher v. Peck*, 6 Cranch 87 (1810); *Dartmouth College v. Woodward*, 4 Wheat. 518 (1819), *Piqua Branch of the State Bank of Ohio v. Knoop*, 16 How. 369 (1853).

document (at any rate, a final document, as opposed to a draft or a preliminary version). As Theophilus Parsons explained, "the parties write the contract when they are ready to do so, for the very purpose of including all that they have finally agreed upon, and excluding everything else." If evidence of "previous intention" or earlier conversations were allowed, "it would obviously be of no use to reduce a contract to writing, or to attempt to give it certainty and fixedness in any way."[52] In *Mumford v. M'Pherson* (New York, 1806), the buyer of a ship claimed that the seller promised, orally, that "the ship was completely copper-fastened." The bill of sale contained no such promise. The parol-evidence rule prevented the buyer from winning his case; where a contract "is reduced to writing," said the court, "everything resting in parol" (that is, everything that was merely oral) "becomes thereby extinguished."[53]

Another major principle of contract law was its insistence on a true bargain between the parties. One party must have made an offer, which the other must have literally accepted. And offer and acceptance had to be glued together with a mysterious substance called *consideration*. Consideration was a term of many meanings; it signified, among other things, the *quid pro quo,* the exchange element of the contract. "The common law . . . gives effect only to contracts that are founded on the mutual exigencies of men, and does not compel the performance of any merely gratuitous engagements."[54] However, courts refused to measure the "adequacy" of consideration. If one man exchanged ten dollars in consideration for a tract of land worth (apparently) vastly more, the law was not supposed to interfere. For purposes of the law of contract, price as fixed by the parties was conclusive proof of value—it was proof at least of the value the parties themselves chose to put on their performances. As in sales law, where courts believed themselves bound by *caveat emptor,* contract courts insisted that no inquiry could be made into the price and the terms of the bargain. On the other hand, mere "moral" obligations, with no element of exchange, could not be enforced in court. When one part-owner of a brig, the *Sea Nymph,* promised to buy insurance for the brig, and forgot, and the ship was lost, he was not liable to the other owner. A father gave his note, as a gift, to one son who was "not so wealthy as his brothers," later the father "met with losses." The note could not be enforced.[55]

As is often true, the actual run of cases, as reported, presents a picture more complicated than theory would predict. In a broad-based market, not everyone who made a contract was a hard, shrewd businessman. Generally speaking, contract law rests on certain key assumptions. The parties to a contract were "assumed to be rational actors," who looked out for their interests; and they, as grown people who knew what they were doing, had to be held to their bargains. The courts were "responsible for seeing that agreements were kept." They were not to "interfere" in private bargains, unless they had an awfully good reason. But it was equally true that courts were sometimes "ingenious" in finding ways to modify and "soften the sharp edge of contract law" if too rigorous application of

---

[52] Theophilus Parsons, *The Law of Contracts,* vol. II (3rd ed., 1857), p. 57.
[53] *Mumford v. M'Pherson,* 1 Johns. R. 414 (N.Y. 1806).
[54] Theron Metcalf, *Principles of the Law of Contracts* (1874), p. 161.
[55] *Thorne v. Deas,* 4 Johns. R. 84 (N.Y. 1809); *Fink v. Cox,* 18 Johns. R. 145 (N.Y. 1820).

the principles offended the courts' sense of justice.[56] There were cases where unsophisticated people, amateurs, the weak—widows and orphans—sued on or defended claims in contract. Judges were only human. They sometimes bent the rules in hardship cases. In the long run, the slow drip-drip of life situations wore down the rules of consideration, and the other rules that insisted, in theory, that people had to be held to their bargains, rules that seemed to be made of the toughest stone.

Contract law was not as technical as land law or civil procedure. It had little jargon of its own. It had only a few, simple rules; and it departed less from ordinary common sense than other fields of law. Contract law asked for very little; agreements, to be enforced, had to have a definite shape, but the law of contract was itself relatively passive and amorphous. There was therefore not much room for trans-Atlantic differences. Of all the staple fields, contract was perhaps the most similar on both sides of the water. It was also to a large degree the province of the judges. Few statutes intruded upon it.

Of these few, the old statute of frauds (1677) was perhaps the most notable. The statute required certain types of contract to be in writing, and signed by the party "to be charged therewith," or his agent; otherwise, they were not enforceable in court. The contracts that had to be in writing included land contracts, contracts "to answer for the debt, default, or miscarriage" of another person; and contracts for the sale of goods above a minimum value (fifty dollars in New York). The states adopted the statute almost verbatim.[57] In one sense, the statute of frauds was hardly a statute at all. It was so heavily warped by "interpretation" that it had become little more than a set of common-law rules, worked out in detail by the common law courts.

The statute of frauds has been criticized as an anachronism. This venerable law is more than 330 years old, still under attack as empty formality. Formality it is, but not quite empty. To require land contracts, in 1800 or 1850, to be in writing, was not unreasonable; nor was it out of tune with the way land law was developing. An orderly land market (people thought) required orderly form: simple, standard deeds, duly recorded. In a market society, where land was essentially a commodity, oral land deals were an abomination. What was valued was not form for form's sake, but *useful* form. The statute of frauds survived; other formalities, which had no purpose or place, disappeared from the law of contract.

Among them was that ancient device, the seal. Early contract law paid great homage to the seal. Sealed documents were specially treated and favored in the law; the seal, for example, "imported" consideration, which meant that a sealed document needed no further proof of consideration. In the United States, few people actually owned and used a seal; and literacy was high enough to undercut the need for this device. Strictly speaking, a seal meant an impression in wax; but in some states, any scrawl or scroll on paper was good enough. In New

---

[56] Harry N. Scheiber, "Economic Liberty and the Modern State," in *The State and Freedom of Contract* (Harry N. Scheiber, ed., 1998), pp. 122, 149, 151.

[57] There were some local variations. In New York, contracts that offended the statute were "void" rather than (as in England) merely unenforceable. Rev. Stats. N.Y. 1836, vol. II, p. 70. This difference was not of much moment.

York, Chancellor Kent was insistent on the traditional method, wax and all.[58] But this was probably because he did not like the rules that required a seal and wanted to kill them with strictness.[59] Later, state statutes were passed that undercut the meaning of the seal. In New York, by the close of the period, a seal was "only . . . presumptive evidence of a sufficient consideration"; its effect could be "rebutted in the same manner, and to the same extent, as if [the] instrument were not sealed."[60] Ultimately, the seal vanished completely, except as an empty and unimportant form. In commercial law, sentiment and tradition had no role; the fit and the functional survived.

[58] *Warren v. Lynch,* 5 Johns. R. 239 (1810).
[59] Joseph Dorfman, "Chancellor Kent and the Developing American Economy," 61 Columbia L. Rev. 1290, 1305 (1961).
[60] Rev. Stats. N.Y. 1836, vol. II, p. 328.

CHAPTER 7

CRIME AND PUNISHMENT:
AND A FOOTNOTE ON TORT

PENAL LAW AND PENAL REFORM

The American Revolution, whatever else was at issue, fed on resentment against English oppression. Like all revolutions, it was a struggle for control of the reins of power. The criminal law is one of the levers that government uses to exercise its power over the individual, over the ordinary citizen. The leaders of the Revolution, as we know, felt that the British had abused criminal justice, and were impairing the rights of the colonists. The fundamental rights of man were closely identified, in their minds, with the basic rights to a fair criminal trial. The Bill of Rights, as we have seen, contained a minicode of criminal procedure. The late eighteenth century, moreover, was a period in which intellectuals began to rethink the premises on which criminal law rested. Great reformers—men like Cesare Beccaria, whose *Treatise on Crime and Punishment* was written in Italy in 1764—suggested that at least some of the premises were wrong and argued for a more enlightened criminal law.[1]

Reform ideas left an imprint on the early state constitutions. Section 38 of the liberal Pennsylvania Constitution of 1776 imposed on "the future legislature" a duty to "reform" the "penal laws." Punishment must be made "in some cases less sanguinary, and in general more proportionate to the crimes." Enlightened opinion was in revolt against bloodthirsty criminal codes. The Bill of Rights outlawed cruel and unusual punishment. "No wise legislature," said the New Hampshire constitution of 1784, "will affix the same punishment to the crimes of theft, forgery and the like, which they do to those of murder and treason. . . . [A] multitude of sanguinary laws is both impolitic and unjust. The true design of all punishments being to reform, not to exterminate, mankind" (art. I, sec. 18).

Of course, these were mere exhortations. Real penal reform was never easy to achieve. The legislature of Pennsylvania did not match action to words for ten full years. In 1786, the death penalty was abolished for robbery, burglary, and sodomy. In 1790, a new, more conservative constitution omitted the clause on penal reform, and the act of 1786 was repealed. But in 1794, Pennsylvania enacted an important, innovative law about murder. The statute stated that the "several offenses, which are included under the general denomination of murder, differ . . . greatly from each other in the degree of their atrociousness." The

[1] Marcello T. Maestro, *Voltaire and Beccaria as Reformers of Criminal Law* (1942), pp. 51–72.

statute then proceeded to distinguish between two different "degrees" of murder. Murder "in the first degree" was murder "perpetrated by means of poison, or by lying in wait, or by any other kind of willful, deliberate, or premeditated killing, or which shall be committed in the perpetration, or attempt to perpetrate, any arson, rape, robbery, or burglary." All other murder was murder in the second degree. Only murder in the first degree was punishable by death.[2] This idea of degrees was borrowed, first in Virginia, then in Ohio (1824), New York (1827), and Missouri (1835). Some states (for example, Missouri) also divided manslaughter into degrees.

The agitation in Pennsylvania was part of a wider movement to reduce the number of capital crimes, reform the penal code, and, if possible, get rid of the death penalty altogether.[3] According to the new penology, the proper goal of criminal law was to deter crime and rehabilitate the criminal. Crime was a social product: bad families, bad companions, plus poverty, idleness, and ignorance—these were the sources of crime.[4] Death did not seem a very good deterrent; and, of course, it was useless from the standpoint of rehabilitation. Death had no place, then, in a rational system of law. Some people made this argument with great vigor. They were never the majority. Many people (then as now) put the case strongly on the other side—people like the "citizens of Albany," who, by petition in 1842, asked the New York legislature not to do away with the death penalty for murder:

> The Penalties inflicted by human law, having their foundation in the intrinsick ill-desert of crime, are in their nature vindictive as well as corrective. . . . Beyond all question the murderer deserves to die. . . . Death is the fitting penalty for murder; fitting because, in addition to its correspondence with the enormity of the crime, it must needs be more efficacious than any other, in preventing its repetition . . . God has revealed to us His will, both through the laws of reason and conscience, and in his written word, that the murderer should be put to death.[5]

Judging by the results, neither side carried the day. The penal codes changed (quite dramatically in some instances), but most states never abolished the death penalty. In 1800, Kentucky restricted it to murder. Thomas Jefferson proposed, in 1779, that Virginia abolish the death penalty except for murder and treason. Rape was to be punished by castration; a woman guilty of sodomy was to have a hole bored through her nose; people who maimed or disfigured would be maimed and disfigured themselves, preferably in the "same part." Virginia never adopted this odd proposal; but the legislature did abolish the death penalty in 1796 for all crimes except murder (and crimes by slaves).[6]

[2] On the statute in general, see Edwin R. Keedy, "History of the Pennsylvania Statute Creating Degrees of Murder," 97 U. Pa. L. Rev. 759 (1949).

[3] See, in general, David B. Davis, "The Movement to Abolish Capital Punishment in America, 1787–1861," 63 Am. Hist. Rev. 23 (1957); Stuart Banner, *The Death Penalty in America* (2002), pp. 88–111.

[4] Roger Lane, *Murder in America: A History* (1997), p. 79.

[5] *Memorial to the Legislature*, N.Y. Senate Documents, vol. 4, 1842, Doc. No. 97, pp. 21–39.

[6] Kathryn Preyer, "Crime, the Criminal Law, and Reform in Post-Revolutionary Virginia," 1 Law and History Review 53, 58–59, 76 (1983). New Jersey also cut down on the death penalty in 1796; see John E. O'Connor, "Legal Reform in the Early Republic: The New Jersey Experience," 22 Am. J. Legal Hist. 95, 100 (1978).

Total abolition was another question. Edward Livingston omitted any provision for capital punishment in the penal code he wrote for Louisiana, but the code was never enacted. In 1837, Maine passed a statute that *almost* went the whole distance. A man under sentence of death would be placed in the state prison, in "solitary imprisonment and hard labor." The execution was put off for a year. The whole record of his case had to be certified to the governor, and the death sentence would be carried out only if the governor issued a warrant, under the great seal of the state, "directed to the Sheriff of the County wherein the State Prison shall or may be situated, commanding the said Sheriff to cause execution to be done."[7] In 1846, Michigan became the first state to abolish capital punishment completely, followed by Wisconsin. First-degree murder, in Michigan, was to be punished instead "by solitary confinement at hard labor in the state prison for life."[8] All other states kept the death penalty, but they drastically shortened their list of capital crimes. In South Carolina, 165 crimes carried the death penalty in 1813. By 1825, only fifty-one, by 1838, only thirty-two, and by 1850, only twenty-two crimes remained in this group.[9]

Most states did not overuse the death penalty, either before or after they reduced the number of crimes that nominally called for the hangman. There were important differences by race and by region. South Carolina hanged many more people than Massachusetts; and many more blacks than whites. Even though hangings were not everyday affairs, they did occur, and they were public events. When two slaves, Ephraim and Sam, killed their master in South Carolina, in 1820, Sam was burned, and Ephraim hung, with his "head severed from his body and publicly exposed." An onlooker, who described these events, expressed the hope that "this awful dispensation of justice" would have "salutary effects," and "preclude the necessity of its repetition."[10] In general, hangings took place in broad daylight, before morbid or festive crowds. A hanging was an occasion, a spectacle. People eagerly watched the trip to the gallows, and they listened eagerly to sermons preached on the occasion; or to the condemned man himself, when, as sometimes happened, he made a last speech in the shadow of the gallows.

In the nineteenth century, the spectacle began to appall polite society. Hangings were supposed to be vivid, palpable lessons on the wages of sin. That may

[7] Laws Maine 1837, ch. 292.

[8] This provision, it seems, was not literally carried out, and most of the prisoners convicted of first-degree murder were apparently not kept in solitary confinement. See James H. Lincoln, "The Everlasting Controversy: Michigan and the Death Penalty," 33 Wayne Law Review 1765, 1783 (1987); Eugene G. Wanger, "Historical Reflections on Michigan's Abolition of the Death Penalty," 13 Cooley Law Review 755 (1996).

[9] Jack K. Williams, *Vogues in Villainy: Crime and Retribution in Antebellum South Carolina* (1959), p. 100. In general, there were more capital crimes in the South than in the North. Some of the difference is accounted for by the special, severe laws relating to slaves and free blacks. Perhaps the special, archaic, patriarchal nature of the southern legal system accounts for more. For the thesis that finds the differences rooted, in part, in differences in legal culture, see Michael S. Hindus, *Prison and Plantation: Crime, Justice, and Authority in Massachusetts and South Carolina, 1767–1878* (1980); and Edward L. Ayers, *Vengeance and Justice: Crime and Punishment in the Nineteenth Century American South* (1984).

[10] Quoted in Thomas D. Morris, *Southern Slavery and the Law, 1619–1860* (1996), pp. 277–78.

have worked for small, theocratic colonial towns; but in big, bustling, raucous cities like Boston or New York, they seemed to have a different effect: They were vulgar, barbaric rituals that unleashed the "animal" instincts of the mob. There was a movement, then, to privatize the punishment of death. New York was a pioneer: Its law, of 1835, ordered executions to be held "within the walls of the prison . . . or within a yard or enclosure adjoining."[11] Other states followed suit, though by no means all.

Liberal reformers and humanitarians had led the movement to abolish the death penalty; but they also made a strong practical argument for squeezing the blood out of criminal law. The death penalty was a case of overkill, so to speak. Capital punishment was not effective, because it was not, and could not be, consistently applied. Its deadly severity distorted the working of criminal justice. A jury, trapped between two distasteful choices, death or acquittal, might choose to acquit the guilty, as the lesser of two evils. The New Hampshire constitution of 1784, criticizing "sanguinary laws," voiced a fear that "where the same undistinguishing severity is exerted against all offences, the people are led to forget the real distinction in the crimes themselves, and to commit the most flagrant with as little compunction as they do those of the lightest dye" (part I, art. 18). In South Carolina, the typical defendant in a homicide case was either acquitted or found guilty only of manslaughter. In one district, thirty-three men were tried on murder indictments between 1844 and 1858. Eighteen were acquitted, ten found guilty of manslaughter; only five were convicted of murder. In Philadelphia, between 1839 and 1845, there were sixty-eight indictments for first degree murder; forty defendants were tried; the jury found twenty-five of them guilty. Of those convicted, only a few were sentenced to death.[12]

This gap between indictment and conviction, and between conviction and sentence, probably prevailed in most parts of the country. The problem was not harsh punishment in itself, but formal harshness compared to what the moral sense of the community allowed. Severe penal codes are often instruments of repressive policy, imposed by the rulers on the ruled. In the United States, however, the rulers and the ruled overlapped to a greater degree than in England. This led to a certain looseness in the way penal measures were actually used.[13] Moreover, people tend to be less severe on themselves—on their own group— than on the crimes and misdemeanors of outsiders, particularly outsiders who are defined as different or inferior. Juries in America were more tolerant of violations of game laws than the king and his servants would have been; on the

[11] Lawrence M. Friedman, *Crime and Punishment in American History* (1993), pp. 75–76; Louis C. Masur, *Rites of Execution: Capital Punishment and the Transformation of American Culture, 1776–1865* (1989), pp. 96, 100.

[12] Williams, *op. cit.*, p. 38; Roger Lane, *Violent Death in the City: Suicide, Accident, and Murder in Nineteenth Century Philadelphia* (1979), pp. 68–69.

[13] This is not to say that the British system was not itself quite loose in certain regards. In eighteenth century England, there were many capital crimes; but justice was frequently tempered with a kind of mercy; and indeed it can be argued that a system of this sort, which is *potentially* extremely cruel and bloody, but which allows appeals for mercy, within the grace and favor of the rulers, makes for tight, efficient, repressive social control. Douglas Hay, "Property, Authority, and the Criminal Law," in Douglas Hay et al., eds., *Albion's Fatal Tree: Crime and Society in Eighteenth Century England* (1975), p. 17.

other hand, the slave codes were more bloody in theory and reality than criminal justice for white southerners. Juries may have been more willing to convict *after* the reform of the criminal codes, when capital punishment had been abolished for crimes that, in the public mind, did not deserve the supreme penalty.

A system of criminal justice is more than rules on paper. As a working system, it has to distribute power and function among judges, jurors, legislators, and other actors. In American legal theory, the jury had enormous power, and was subject to very few controls. There was a maxim of law that the jury was judge both of law and of fact in criminal cases. It is not entirely clear what this meant—except as an expression of almost unlimited power. This idea was particularly strong in the first, Revolutionary generation, when memories of royal justice or injustice were fresh. In Maryland, the slogan was actually imbedded in the constitution.[14] But the maxim came under savage attack from some judges and other authorities. There was fear that the rule, if taken seriously, would destroy the "chances of uniformity of adjudication." It also threatened the *power* of judges. By the end of the period, many states, by statute or decision, had repudiated the doctrine.[15]

It is not easy to say what this shift in doctrine meant in actual practice. Juries did not divide their verdicts into separate bundles of fact and of law. The maxim merely recognized, and celebrated, the supremacy of jury verdicts. Some juries were quite bold in asserting their power. In South Carolina, according to Jack K. Williams, "the same jury which would change a murderer's indictment to manslaughter would condemn a common thief to the gallows without hesitation," if so inclined.[16] On the other hand, the jury could be quite cavalier about the letter of the law, not to mention the facts of the world. This happened, notoriously, in capital cases. In one case, *State v. Bennet* (1815), a South Carolina jury had to decide the fate of a thief named John Bennet. Grand larceny would send him to the gallows. The jury "found" as a fact that the stolen goods were worth "less . . than twelve pence," even though all the witnesses had sworn they were "of much greater value." This "pious perjury" meant that Bennet was guilty only of petty larceny, and his life was spared. The appeal court affirmed the jury's right to do as it pleased.[17]

This same process had made some crimes on England's long list of capital crimes less fierce in practice than in theory. When juries behave this way, they are sometimes called "lawless"; but it is strange to pin the label of "lawless" on behavior that is so carefully and explicitly built into law. The jury deliberates in secret, gives no reasons, and is accountable to nobody. The jury's power meant that a certain amount of penal "reform" could take place without formal change in legal rules or institutions. Jerome Hall has suggested that, as social attitudes toward criminals and crime begin to change, these changes first appear in the

---

[14] Maryland Const., 1851, art. 10, sec. 5. It was a common provision that juries were judges of fact and law in "prosecutions or indictments for libel," for example, New Jersey Const., 1844, art. 1, sec. 5.

[15] See Francis Wharton, *A Treatise on the Criminal Law of the United States* (4th ed., 1857), pp. 1115–25; William Nelson, *Americanization of the Common Law* (1975), ch. 9.

[16] Williams, *op. cit.*, p. 39.

[17] *State v. Bennet,* 3 Brevard (S. Car.) 514 (1815).

administration of criminal justice; penal "reform"—enacted laws and new rules—follows as a "ratification of practices" already developed.[18]

But it is not easy to get an accurate picture of how the justice system worked in practice. The literature usually does not deal with the day-to-day, humdrum operations of trial courts. Only recently has there been much research that pushes aside the dust and muck and examines court records in the raw. The lower courts handled most offenders—and almost everybody charged with petty crimes—in a great rush, and without much fuss and bother. Only serious offenses went to the jury. Juries tended to convict: Michael S. Hindus's figures show that 71.5 percent of South Carolina defendants (1800—1860), and 85.9 percent of Massachusetts defendants (1833–1859) were found guilty. In South Carolina, there was much greater slippage at earlier stages. Of all cases presented to the grand jury, only 30.9 percent were eventually convicted; in Massachusetts, the figure was 65.8 percent.[19]

The criminal justice system was, on the whole, much less professional than it is today. Almost nobody involved in criminal justice was a full-time specialist. There were no detectives, probation officers, public defenders, or forensic scientists; even the district attorney worked at his job part-time. The jurors were of course total amateurs. Today, the system is highly professionalized; this means, among other things, that police and prosecutors can filter out the weakest cases, and toss them aside early in the process. Much less of this screening is left to judge and jury. In 1800 or 1850, no part of the system was particularly organized or bureaucratic. This even applied to what happened after conviction; the only way to get out of prison early (except through a break-out) was to appeal to the governor for a pardon. The governor in some states pardoned with a lavish hand. In any event, nothing formally guided his decisions. He did as he pleased and took advice from whomever he pleased.

Today, most people charged plead guilty to the charges brought against them, or to some lesser crime. The guilty plea accounts for as many as 90 percent of all convictions in some places, or even more. Ours is a system of plea bargaining, or "copping a plea." The beginnings of plea bargaining can be traced to the nineteenth century. The guilty plea was nothing as pervasive as it became; but it was already a significant factor. In New York State, in 1839, there were guilty pleas in a quarter of the cases, and this percentage rose to about half by the middle of the century.[20] A guilty plea puts an end to the proceedings; when a defendant pleads guilty, there is no trial, by jury or otherwise. Hence a rising rate of guilty pleas means a falling rate of trials.

[18] Jerome Hall, *Theft, Law, and Society* (2nd ed., 1952), p. 140.

[19] Hindus, *op. cit.*, p. 91. In Marion County, Indiana, in the period 1823 to1850, the ultimate conviction rate was more like South Carolina than like Massachusetts; for "all indictments, the prosecution secured convictions at a rate only slightly better than one of every three defendants." David J. Bodenhamer, "Law and Disorder on the Early Frontier: Marion County, Indiana, 1823–1850," 10 Western Hist. Q. 323, 335 (1979).

[20] Raymond Moley, *Politics and Criminal Prosecution* (1929), pp. 159–64. On the origins of plea bargaining, see George Fisher, *Plea Bargaining's Triumph: A History of Plea Bargaining in America* (2003).

WALKING THE BEAT

Law enforcement was one of the weakest links in the system of criminal justice. Public prosecution was mostly a part-time job. Private prosecution, more or less in the English style, apparently survived in Philadelphia well into the nineteenth century.[21] A step in the direction of professionalism came with the creation of city police forces. The model (imperfectly followed) was the metropolitan police of London, the recently established force of "bobbies" (1829). In Boston, the usual haphazard collection of constables and night watchmen was the standard until 1838, when Mayor Samuel Eliot founded a regular police force; the older system had been completely unable to cope with "the incendiary, burglar, and lawlessly violent."[22] New York's police force emerged in 1845.[23] Big cities soon began to build on these models. But in the South, and in rural areas, there was no professional enforcement at all in the first half of the century.

The development of police forces ultimately brought about dramatic changes in public crime fighting. But the early police were much different from the modern police. They were much less "professional." They took no exams and were not trained for the job. As in London, the main motive behind the creation of a police force was fear of urban disorders—riots, in short; and there were plenty of riots in the turbulent urban world of the early nineteenth century. In the 1830s and 1840s, there were vicious race riots and ethnic disorders; a city mob sacked the Ursuline Convent near Boston in 1834.[24] Baltimore had gained the nickname of "Mob-Town" in honor of its history of riots. Many of these riots, in Baltimore and some other cities, could be laid at the door of volunteer fire departments. When they were not fighting fires, they seemed to spend much of their time fighting each other.[25] To these problems of urban unrest and disorder, the police—a full time, paramilitary force, on duty twenty-four hours a day, with uniforms and badges—seemed like the answer.

Today, we accept, almost without thinking, the idea that the state has a monopoly of legitimate violence. But this was not always so, at least not literally. The state was weak and lax, for the most part; when it needed more muscle, it recruited private citizens to help it out. In the southern states, slave patrols, made up of local citizens, had authority to catch, and whip, slaves who were on the streets after curfew, or without a good reason or a pass from their owners.[26] The Western "posse," familiar to every movie fan, was a survival from the days when a sheriff or other officer rounded up able-bodied men to help him out.

[21] Allen R. Steinberg, *The Transformation of Criminal Justice: Philadelphia, 1800–1880* (1989).

[22] Roger Lane, *Policing the City: Boston, 1822–1885* (1967), p. 34.

[23] On the rise of the police, see Wilbur R. Miller, *Cops and Bobbies: Police Authority in New York and London, 1830–1870* (1977); Samuel Walker, *Popular Justice: A History of American Criminal Justice* (1980), pp. 55–64.

[24] Friedman, *Crime and Punishment*, p. 69; see Nancy L. Schultz, *Fire and Roses: The Burning of the Charlestown Convent, 1834* (2000), for this celebrated incident. Only one of the rioters was convicted, and none went to prison.

[25] See Amy S. Greenberg, *Cause for Alarm: The Volunteer Fire Department in the Nineteenth Century City* (1998), pp. 86–87.

[26] For a study of the patrols, see Sally E. Hadden, *Slave Patrols: Law and Violence in Virginia and the Carolinas* (2001).

The line, in short, between riot and disorder on the one hand and law enforcement on the other was at one time far from distinct.[27] Today the line is much sharper. One of the great master trends in the history of criminal justice is the creation of a wall of separation between public and private force.

In hindsight, we can see a clear, steady trend from the old days to the modern system. The road of history always seems to have the smooth, paved surface of inevitability—when we look back on it. Things were not that clear at the time. Amateurs, including members of the jury, were still extraordinarily important in the system. And the system reflected this fact. Outcomes were to say the least unpredictable. There were ways to control juries—the law of evidence, as we mentioned, was one. A system of checks and balances, in the trial process, grew almost cancerously. It reached its high point (or low) in criminal process. Here judge was played off against jury, state against citizen, county against state, state against federal government. Every master had to submit to another master. There was no overall control. No one was in charge. The system had benefits, of course. But it also had major defects: It reflected community sentiment, but also community prejudice. And one could never be sure that policies of criminal justice, however well formulated, would be actually carried out.

There was always tension between elite opinion, legal opinion, and what ordinary people wanted. The rise of the police did not put an end to the private use of force. On the contrary, it had ferocious powers of survival. There were periodic outbursts of lynching and vigilantes in almost every state. These cracks in law and order were no accidents. When judges, juries, the state, or any other authority reached a point where its effect on the system led to too much or too little vigor, sometimes "the people," or the self-appointed "people" took the law into their own hands. Vigilantes and lynch mobs were pathologies of a system with too many checks and balances to satisfy at least some members of the public. Vigilantes were especially vigorous in the South. Here the legal culture nurtured them. Lawlessness was a way of life; violent crime was common; men habitually walked the streets carrying guns; the elites placed heavier value on the code of honor (including the duel) than on resort to law. Vigilantes were the logical negative of the governor's power to pardon. The pardoning power was itself one kind of check and balance; the mob was another. In Montgomery, Alabama, for example, a vigilante group called the Regulating Horn sprang up in the 1820s. The men blew horns to summon the rest of the group. They gave suspects a hearing on the spot. If they found a man "guilty," they tarred and feathered him and rode him out of town on a rail. Violence can be an addictive habit; success sometimes breeds excess. The community that nurtured them began to turn against the Regulating Horn. At that point, they were doomed to fail.[28]

In South Carolina, the abolitionists were the prime target of vigilantes in the 1840s. Here, mob rule grew out of the gap between official, national doctrine and opinion in the local community. The abolitionists were arguably guilty of no crime. But they seemed dangerous to southern slave owners. The South, of

---

[27] On this point, see Pauline Maier, "Popular Uprisings and Civil Authority in Eighteenth Century America," 27 William and Mary Q. 3rd ser., 3 (1970).

[28] Jack K. Williams, "Crime and Punishment in Alabama, 1819–1840," 6 Ala. R. 1427 (1953).

course, was not the only region of bloodshed. Riots and mob violence were a dark stain on the whole country, crossing every border, entering every state. Between 1830 and 1860 "at least thirty-five major riots occurred in the four cities of Baltimore, Philadelphia, New York, and Boston."[29] It was out of a climate such as this that the demand had arisen for urban police.

The strength of the idea of checks and balances was also one of the factors that impelled penal law toward codification. The leaders of the Revolutionary generation felt strongly that there had to be safeguards against abuse of criminal justice, or the use of criminal process to crush political dissent—the offenses King George was blamed for. This was also an attitude underlying the Bill of Rights; and the attitude by no means died out in the Republic. The rules of criminal justice should be fair and balanced; they should also be open, transparent, and easy to know. Criminal law should not be scattered through hundreds of books, in obscure little pieces and fragments. It should be a single, clear-cut body of rules. Codification, as the Puritan magistrates found, can be an effective instrument to help keep authority under control. The same theory was behind codification of penal law in Europe, after the shock waves of the French Revolution.

The common law was supposed to rest on the moral consensus of the community, as it percolated through the collective mind of the judges. Many of the rules of law were judge made: they came out of the case reports. This was also true of criminal law. Judges worked out the definition of crimes, and sometimes even created new crimes. This seemed like an especially dangerous power. There was a reaction against the idea that judges could invent new crimes ("common law crimes"). Common-law decisions were in a sense retroactive, in so far as they made up new rules; and there was less control (it seemed) over judges than over members of the legislature. The people's chosen representatives made the laws in the legislature; and these laws were prospective—they applied only to future behavior. The behavior of the king's judges, both in England and in the colonies, suggested that common-law crimes were a very bad idea.

Occasionally, an American judge did in fact invent a new "common law" crime. In *Kanavan's case* (Maine, 1821), the defendant dropped the dead body of a child into the Kennebec River.[30] No statute covered the case explicitly; but the highest court in Maine affirmed the man's conviction. An appeal court in Tennessee sustained an indictment for "eaves-dropping" in 1808.[31] But on the whole, the concept of the common law crime was in retreat in the nineteenth century. And fear of a powerful central government made the common-law crime especially odious in the federal system. In *United States v. Hudson and Goodwin* (1812);[32] defendants were indicted for "a libel on the president and Congress of the United States." The libel, contained in the Connecticut Courant of May 7, 1806, charged them "with having in secret voted $2 million as a present to Bonaparte, for leave to make a treaty with Spain." No statute covered such an "offense" against the federal government. The Supreme Court

[29] Richard Maxwell Brown, "Historical Patterns of Violence in America," in Hugh D. Graham and Ted R. Gurr, eds., *Violence in America: Historical and Comparative Perspectives,* vol. I (1969), pp. 45, 54.

[30] 1 Greenl. (Me.) 226 (1821).

[31] *State v. Williams,* 2 Overton (Tenn.) 108 (1808).

[32] 7 Cranch 32 (1812).

rejected the idea of a federal common law crime. No federal court was "vested with jurisdiction over any particular act done by an individual in supposed violation of the peace and dignity of the sovereign power. The legislative authority of the Union must first make an act a crime, affix a punishment to it, and declare the court that shall have jurisdiction of the offense." If federal prosecutors and judges could define crimes for themselves and punish them, enormous (and in this instance, unwelcome) power would accrue to the central government.

Codification was something of a curb on the power of the judges; but it only went part of the way. Judges lost the power to invent new crimes; but they still had the job of defining the exact meaning of the laws that codified old crimes, like rape or theft. They still had the strong, sometimes freewheeling power to "interpret" the laws. The judges developed and used *canons of construction*—rules of interpretation—that maximized their discretion and authority. There was, for example, a canon that penal statutes should be narrowly construed, that is, limited to the smallest possible range of behaviors that the language would bear. Otherwise, retroactive, judge-made criminal law would enter the law through the back door, so to speak. Criminal behavior had to be plainly labeled as such—nothing beyond the unvarnished meaning of the words of the law:

> The law to bind (the prisoner) should first be *prescribed;* that is, not only willed by the legislature, but should also be announced, and clearly and plainly published, that every citizen, if he would, could learn its meaning and know the measure of its punishment.

This was said by counsel at the trial of one Timothy Heely of New York, charged with stealing a lottery ticket. The statute made it a crime to steal a "public security." Was a state lottery ticket a public security? The court, agreeing with counsel, said no; and set Heely free.[33] This canon, in theory, expressed the idea that judges were humble servants of the law, the people, and their elected representatives. But there was no short-run control over whether courts used the canon or avoided it. In fact, if not in theory, judges were free to use it or not, as they saw fit. Besides, it was not always clear which way of reading a statute was "strict" and which was not—a fact that gave still more discretion to the courts.

THE SUBSTANTIVE LAW OF CRIMES

In English law, treason had been a complex, protean concept, used to suppress all sorts of persons or groups defined as enemies of the state. It was treason to levy war on the kingdom; it was treason, too, to violate the king's (unmarried) eldest daughter. It was treason to alter or clip coins; or to color "any silver current coin . . . to make it resemble a gold one."[34] When war broke out, the colonists seized this terrible weapon for themselves. New York, for example, passed a fire-breathing law in 1781: anyone who preached, taught, spoke, wrote, or printed that the king had or ought to have dominion over New York

[33] *People v. Heely,* New York Judicial Repository, 277 (1819).
[34] 4 Blackstone, *Commentaries,* 90.

thereby committed a "Felony without Benefit of Clergy," punishable by death or by banishment.[35]

When the war ended, passions cooled. Maryland, Massachusetts, New York, Pennsylvania, and Vermont all provided, in their early constitutions, that the legislature had no power to attaint any person of treason.[36] The federal Constitution radically restricted this king of crimes. It defined its content, once and for all; and procedural safeguards hedged in treason trials. Treason against the United States "shall consist only in levying War against them, or in adhering to their Enemies, giving them Aid and Comfort. No Person shall be convicted of Treason unless on the testimony of two Witnesses to the same overt Act, or on Confession in Open Court" (U.S. Const., art. 3, sec. 3).

Treason was a special crime, with unusual political significance. It was important, in republican theory, to cut the law of treason down to size. A total state, even a semi-total state, has trouble distinguishing between treason and ordinary crime. During the heyday of the Soviet Union, for example, it was a crime against the state, severely punished, to deal in currency or to steal factory property (which was all state-owned). The United States took a strikingly different path. It shrank the concept of state crime to an almost irreducible minimum. The men who drafted penal codes were willing to accept a lot of slippage in enforcement, to protect the innocent and (even more) to keep the government in check. No doubt much of this liberality was only on paper. The Sedition Law of 1798, passed by a nervous, partisan federal government, was (to modern eyes) a shocking encroachment on the freedom of political speech; passage of this law showed, once again, that historical fears of central government were far from groundless.[37] Most people felt that it was important to restrain the government—especially the national government—in criminal matters.

By any measure, the *number* of acts defined as criminal grew steadily from 1776 to 1850, despite the decline in the use of the common law crime. The classic crimes (theft, murder, rape, arson) remained on the books. There were great numbers of economic crimes, and offenses against public morality; and new crimes were constantly added. The revised statutes of Indiana of 1831—a fair sample—made it a crime to allow epsom salts "to remain unenclosed and exposed to the stock, cattle, or horses of the neighborhood." It was a crime in Indiana to "alter the mark or brand" of domestic animals; to sell retail liquor without a license; to ferry a person across a creek or river for money, within two miles of any licensed ferry. It was a crime, too, to keep "either of the gaming tables called A.B.C., or E.O. Tables, billiard table, roulette, spanish needle, shuffle board, [and] faro bank." It was an offense, punishable by fine, to "vend any merchandize which may not be the product of the United States, without having a license." Profane swearing was a crime; so was "open and notorious adultery or fornication."

We usually think of crimes as acts that offend deep-seated moral sensibilities. But there is a blander definition: a crime is behavior that the state

---

[35] J. Willard Hurst, "Treason in the United States," 58 Harv. L. Rev. 226 (1944); see also Bradley Chapin, *The American Law of Treason: Revolutionary and Early National Origins* (1964).

[36] Hurst, *op. cit.*, p. 256.

[37] See, in general, James Morton Smith, *Freedom's Fetters: The Alien and Sedition Laws and American Civil Liberties* (1956).

can punish, at the state's own expense, though only if it uses the procedures defined as appropriate for *criminal* cases. If you have a contract to sell goods, and the buyer refuses to pay, or if you slip on the ice, you can sue the buyer or the landowner if you want to—and, if you choose to sue, it is at your own expense. But society as a whole bears the costs of bringing a murderer to justice, partly because violence is thought to be a danger to everyone, not just the victim's little circle of family and friends. Murder and other crimes were once privately enforced. But private justice is either too ineffective, or, conversely, *too* effective—it gives rise to feuds and leads to wholesale bloodshed. Public prosecution is supposed to do away with private vengeance.

The state enforces regulatory and economic laws at public expense and initiative, but for rather different reasons. If a man sells ten baskets of rotten strawberries to ten different people, no one buyer has an incentive to sue the seller. A lawsuit would eat up far more money than could possibly be recovered. If the sheriff and district attorney—public servants, paid by the state—have power to enforce the rules, this is likely to be a more effective deterrence. This is quite apart from whether selling rotten strawberries is considered especially immoral or not. Criminal process, then, can act as a kind of crude, undifferentiated administrative agency. This (largely inarticulate) conception was one of the reasons for the flowering of regulatory crimes. Economic crimes never gave trial courts much work. They never captured the imagination of the public. Criminal provisions in regulatory laws were not always even *meant* to be rigorously enforced. They were meant more as a last resort, as a club over the head of persistent and flagrant violators. When administrative justice developed in later generations, some of these "crimes" actually disappeared from the books.

The *relative* rise of the economic crime, on the statute books, was probably an external sign of a real change in the center of gravity of the criminal law. Crimes like fornication and blasphemy had been sins in colonial times (most notably in the seventeenth century). After the Revolution, the center of gravity seemed to shift to the protection of private property, and measures to make the economy grow. What little we know about actual enforcement suggests that as early as the eighteenth century, crimes against property took center stage, and prosecutions for sex and morals offenses dropped off drastically. This was, for example, decidedly the case in New England. William E. Nelson's research, in Massachusetts, provides some evidence. Nelson found that prosecutions for fornication, Sunday violation, and the like declined dramatically after the Revolution; prosecutions for theft, on the other hand, rose. By 1800, more than 40 percent of all prosecutions in seven counties studied were for theft, only 7 percent for offenses against morality.[38] In Philadelphia, a study of offenses punished in 1840 found that larceny accounted for 58.9 percent of the total, adultery 2.3 percent.[39] The behavior of the criminal justice system suggests a shift in the image of the criminal—less as a sinner against God, than as a danger to the

[38] William E. Nelson, "Emerging Notions of Modern Criminal Law in the Revolutionary Era: An Historical Perspective," 42 N.Y.U.L. Rev. 450 (1967); for some comparable English data, see Lawrence M. Friedman, "The Devil Is Not Dead: Exploring the History of Criminal Justice," 11 Ga. L. Rev. 257 (1977); on the date of the shift in the colonies, see Hendrik Hartog, "The Public Law of a County Court: Judicial Government in Eighteenth Century Massachusetts," 20 Am. J. Legal Hist. 282, 299–308 (1976).

[39] William Francis Kuntz, *Criminal Sentencing in Three Nineteenth Century Cities* (1988), p. 130.

social order. The penal code became less a guardian of sexual morality than a watchdog over property rights. Morals crimes remained on the books, to be sure. They were not vigorously enforced—except when they were blatant, "open and notorious." In some states the statutes were amended to read exactly that. The crime was not adultery or fornication as such, but open defiance of the moral code. The wheel would turn once more, but only later in the century.

THE CRIME OF PUNISHMENT: THE AMERICAN PRISON

The typical jail in 1776 was a corrupt, inefficient institution—a warehouse for the dregs of society. Men and women were thrown into common cell rooms. Administration was totally unprofessional. Everywhere was dirt and filth. Discipline was lax, yet brutality went unchecked. Oddly enough (to the modern mind), these jails were not primarily places where people were sent to be punished. Imprisonment was a rare sanction in the colonial period. Most people in jail were simply waiting for trial. Many others were debtors—men and women unable to pay their creditors.

The modern prison—the penitentiary—is a product of the nineteenth century. In part, it replaced the infliction of pain on the human body. Whipping declined in importance, and shaming punishments were given up. Shaming works best in small, homogeneous communities, and is out of place in the turmoil of big cities, full of strangers. Moreover, laws that cut down severely on the incidence of capital punishment created a vacuum that the prison now filled. People also came to believe that the "sources of corruption," as David Rothman has put it, "were external, not internal."[40] That is, society—bad company, the rot of cities, drinking and vice—were causes of crime. The community was not the solution, as in the colonial period, it was part of the problem. To rehabilitate a criminal would take a kind of radical surgery: He had to be removed from the context of evil. This meant imprisonment.

The old jails were obviously no good at this job. Radical new structures were needed. As early as 1767, Massachusetts law authorized imprisonment at hard labor. The Pennsylvania Constitution of 1776 mentioned "visible punishments of long duration," and called for construction of "houses" to punish "by hard labour, those who shall be convicted of crimes not capital." In 1790, the Walnut Street prison in Philadelphia, was remodeled as a showplace for enlightened penology. Its chief novelty was a "penitentiary House" (the name is significant) containing sixteen solitary or separate cells:

> Each cell was 8 feet long, 6 feet wide, and 10 feet high, had two doors, an outer wooden one, and an inside iron door.... Each cell had a large leaden pipe that led to the sewer, and thus formed a very primitive kind of a closet. The window of the cell was secured by blinds and wire, to prevent anything being passed in or out.[41]

[40] David Rothman, *The Discovery of the Asylum: Social Order and Disorder in the New Republic* (1971), p. 69.

[41] Orlando F. Lewis, *The Development of American Prisons and Prison Customs, 1776–1845* (1922), p. 27. The developments described in this section took place over time, and rather raggedly; more slowly, in general, in the South than in the North. So, for example, in a

Some convicts in the prison worked in shops during the day; but the convicts in the solitary cells did not work at all. This lonely asceticism, presumably, would give the prisoners of Walnut Street time to rethink their lives, and meditate on self-improvement. But isolation proved to be too inhuman. The prisoners had an unfortunate tendency to go insane under these brutal conditions. Labor was not so much a punishment as a necessity.

New York remodeled the north wing of Auburn prison in 1821 to conform to the new ideas about prisons and punishment. Under the Auburn system, the prisoners worked together during the day and slept in solitary cells at night. The Cherry Hill prison in Philadelphia (1829) was another innovation in prison styles.[42] Cherry Hill was built in the form of a grim fortress, surrounded by walls of medieval strength. Great stone arms radiated out of a central core. Each arm contained a number of individual cells connected to tiny walled courtyards, one to a cell. The prisoners spent their lives in their cell and courtyard, utterly alone, night and day. Sometimes they wore masks. Through peepholes, the prisoners could listen to religious services. In both Auburn and Cherry Hill, absolute silence was imposed on the prisoners—a punishment crueler perhaps than the flogging and branding that were, in theory, done away with.

Regimentation and uniformity were key planks of the new penology. Some of the state laws were remarkably detailed. When Massachusetts converted its state prison to the Auburn system in 1828, its statute carefully provided that:

> each convict shall be allowed, for his yearly clothing, one pair of thick pantaloons, one thick jacket, one pair of thin pantaloons, one thin jacket, two pairs of shoes, two pairs of socks, three shirts, and two blankets, all of a coarse kind.

The daily ration was part of the law, down to an allowance of "two ounces of black pepper" per hundred rations.[43] All this detail was part of the regimen, and was perhaps meant to symbolize careful administration and the meticulous care used in translating theory into practice.

Charles Dickens visited Cherry Hill on his American tour, and was completely horrified. "Those who devised this system of Prison Discipline," he remarked, "and those benevolent gentlemen who carry it into execution, do not know what it is that they are doing." This "dreadful punishment" inflicts "immense . . . torture and agony" on the prisoners. It was a "slow and daily tampering with the mysteries of the brain . . . immeasurably worse than any torture of the body." The silence, Dickens felt, was "awful. . . . Over the head and face of every prisoner who comes into this melancholy house, a black hood is drawn; and in this dark shroud . . . he is led to the cell. . . . He is a man buried alive."[44]

Tennessee County in the period before 1820 we find many examples of corporal punishment—whipping and branding—and even the pillory. See Cornelia Anne Clark, "Justice on the Tennessee Frontier: The Williamson County Circuit Court, 1810–1820," 32 Vanderbilt L. Rev. 413, 440 (1979).

[42] See, in general, Negley K. Teeters and John D. Shearer, *The Prison at Philadelphia: Cherry Hill* (1957); for New York, W. David Lewis, *From Newgate to Dannemora: The Rise of the Penitentiary in New York, 1796–1848* (1965); and, more comprehensively, Adam J. Hirsch, *The Rise of the Penitentiary: Prisons and Punishment in Early America* (1992).

[43] Mass. Laws 1828, ch. 118, secs. 14, 15.

[44] Charles Dickens, *American Notes* (1842), pp. 118, 121.

But not everybody agreed with Dickens. The states embraced the new penology with great enthusiasm. Visitors saw, perhaps, what they wanted to see. One of the ebullient visitors was no less than Alexis de Tocqueville, who, together with Gustave de Beaumont, published a book on the American system of punishment in the 1830s. Beaumont and de Tocqueville admired the rigor and discipline of the penitentiary. It was both "moral and just. The place which society has assigned for repentance, ought to present no scenes of pleasure and debauch." They praised the stark regimentation, the bare, unyielding routine—and even the food, which was "wholesome, abundant, but coarse": it supported the "strength" of prisoners, without unnecessary "gratification of the appetite." American prison life, they admitted, was "severe." But it was salutary. They did, however, point out a paradox: "While society in the United States gives the example of the most extended liberty, the prisons . . . offer the spectacle of the most complete despotism."[45]

But this was not, perhaps, a paradox at all. Here was a society embarked on what seemed at the time a radical experiment: popular government. All obvious forms of authority had been dethroned. There was no monarchy, no established church, no aristocracy. Instead there was only law. Essentially, people were supposed to govern themselves; the law entrusted them with power. Not everybody could handle the freedom, the power, the trust. Something had to be done about these people. One rotten apple spoils the barrel. Criminals, through their criminality, betrayed the American experiment. The strict regime of the penitentiary was what they needed—and deserved.

The modern reader is more likely to agree with Dickens than with Beaumont and de Tocqueville. The classic penitentiary seems indescribably cruel. Some prisoners, as we said, went insane in their solitary cells. Administration also quickly degenerated. The success of the penitentiary depended on absolute control, on total discipline, on keeping to the rule of one man, one cell. Honest guards and wardens were essential, too. But after a few years, straitjackets, iron gags, and savage beatings became a way of life at Cherry Hill. Even in the relatively well-run Massachusetts State Prison, the silent system was abandoned in the 1840s.[46]

What went wrong? Society in the nineteenth century, fearful of moral failure, committed to a dour theory of deterrence, intensely suspicious of power, stingy toward public enterprises, never had the will to carry its theories to their logical conclusion. What little vigor and talent were available expended themselves on theory, on legislation, on building the prisons, and, occasionally, on administration at the apex of the system. The central problem was administrative failure—not enough skill, money, and care to make the ideal a reality. This was the vice from top to bottom. Local jails—county and city—were also scandals, and what is more, archaic scandals. The great new prisons were victims of a war between the zeal of reformers and the anarchic indifference of everybody

---

[45] Gustave de Beaumont and Alexis de Tocqueville, *On the Penitentiary System in the United States and Its Application to France* (1964), pp. 66, 79.

[46] Hindus, *Prison and Plantation*, p. 169. In the prison, iron collars and leg irons were sometimes used to prevent escapes; and recidivists were tattooed with the letters "MSP." Also, anybody was entitled to visit the prison, after paying a twenty-five-cent admission fee. This practice, which brought in a fair amount of money, was not abolished until 1863. *Ibid.*, pp. 168–70.

else. The real power in the country did not belong to penal reformers. It belonged to the rest of the public, people whose main interest was to get criminals off the streets, and put them behind bars, out of sight. This interest explains why prison reform was possible at all. Before the Walnut Street reforms in Philadelphia in 1790, the good citizens of the city had to suffer the sight of shaven-headed men working the streets, heavily guarded, in "infamous dress . . . begging and insulting the inhabitants, collecting crowds of idle boys, and holding with them the most indecent and improper conversations."[47] The penitentiary reforms at least put these convicts where they were not an offense to the eyes and sensibilities of the public. The prisoners of Walnut Street lived like cloistered monks, out of sight and out of mind; but without the faith and the dignity of monastic life.

The new penitentiaries were expensive; they were big, strong buildings; and they needed enough cells to keep prisoners isolated and to make the silent system possible. The states never spent enough money. Some of the Southern states, indeed, tried to make a profit out of their penitentiaries by turning them into factories. When this failed to produce enough revenue, they leased the penitentiaries out to private businessmen. Kentucky did this as early as 1828; later, so did Alabama, Texas, Missouri, and Louisiana.[48]

In the end, prisons, like poorhouses, and insane asylums, continued to serve primarily as storage bins for deviants. Beatings and straitjackets, like the well-meant cruelty of solitary confinement, were visited on a class of men (and a handful of women) who had no reason to expect good treatment from the world, no hope of changing that world, and no power to do so. Their interests were represented by proxies in outside society; and their fate was determined by the strength and persistence—never great—of those proxies who had a sincere desire for reform and rehabilitation. Each failure merely paved the way for another wave of misguided and misplaced reform.

A FOOTNOTE ON TORT

A tort is a civil wrong, that is, something that is wrong, but not criminally wrong. It is any one of a miscellaneous collection of misdeeds that lay the basis for a suit for damages. If you sneeze and rear-end my car, it is a tort, and not a crime. One type of action, for negligence, came to outweigh all the others in importance. The lesser torts include assault and battery, trespass to land, and libel and slander.

All in all, tort law was not a highly developed field in 1776, or for a good many years thereafter. Not a single treatise on the law of torts was published before 1850, on either side of the Atlantic. Negligence was the merest dot on the law. Blackstone's *Commentaries* had almost nothing to say about the concept. Nathan Dane's *Abridgement,* in the 1820s, treated the subject quite casually. Negligence was a kind of residual category—those torts that could not "be brought conveniently under more particular heads." Only one or two of his examples of negligence had much empirical significance: "If the owner of a ship,

[47] Orlando F. Lewis, *op. cit.,* p. 18.
[48] Ayers, *Vengeance and Justice,* p. 68.

in the care of a pilot, through *negligence* and want of skill, sinks the ship of another, this owner is liable."[49] Indeed, well into the nineteenth century, Morton Horwitz has argued, negligence referred, by and large, to failures to perform a specific duty—often a contractual one.[50] It was not defined as a failure to measure up to a general standard of care, the behavior of the reasonable man—the standard familiar to generations of law students and jurists.

The explosion of tort law, and of negligence in particular, has to be laid at the door of the industrial revolution—the age of engines and machines. Tort law is concerned, above all, with personal injuries. In pre-industrial society, there are relatively few personal injuries, except as a result of assault and battery. Modern tools and machines, however, have a marvelous capacity to cripple and maim those who use them. From about 1840 on, one specific machine, the railroad locomotive, generated, on its own steam (so to speak), more tort law than any other in the nineteenth century. The railroad engine swept like a great roaring bull through the countryside, carrying out an economic and social revolution; but it exacted a tremendous toll—thousands of men, women, and children injured and dead. The development of tort law was, as James W. Ely Jr. has put it, "in large measure the result of railroading." The leading cases "invariably involved railroad accidents."[51] Another fertile source of accidents were steamboats. Their boilers had a distressing habit of blowing up in the middle of a journey, scalding and drowning passengers and crew.

Existing tort law was simply not designed to deal with collisions, derailments, exploding boilers, and similar calamities. It had been devised with other situations in mind. American law had to work out on its own schemes to distribute the burden of railroad and steamboat accidents among workers, citizens, companies, and state. Because the job was new, the resulting law was also new. There was some continuity in phrasing, but this was in a way misleading. Tort law was new law in the nineteenth century.

A lot has been written about the origins and functions of the developing law of torts. One view is that the new rules were rules with a single, distinct purpose: to encourage the growth of young businesses, or at least to remove obstacles in their way. Or, to be more accurate, the new rules were rules that judges and others might *think* of as pro-enterprise. To do so, the rules put limits on the liability of enterprises. This was the thrust of the developing law of negligence; and there were parallel developments in other branches of law—in nuisance law, for example; or in the law of eminent domain (the right of government to take—and pay for—property needed for some public purpose).[52]

The most famous (or infamous) new doctrine was the *fellow-servant rule*. This was the rule that a servant (employee) could not sue his or her master (employer) for damages for personal injuries, if the injuries were caused by the negligence of a "fellow-servant," that is another employee. Generally speaking,

[49] Nathan Dane, *A General Abridgement and Digest of American Law,* vol. III (1824), pp. 31–35.

[50] Morton J. Horwitz, *The Transformation of American Law, 1780–1860* (1977), p. 87.

[51] James W. Ely Jr., *Railroads and American Law* (2001), p. 211.

[52] This thesis is expounded by Horwitz, *op. cit., supra.* On the background and early history of negligence law, see also Robert L. Rabin, "The Historical Development of the Fault Principle: A Reinterpretation," 15 Ga. L. Rev. 925 (1981).

in the law of agency, the principal (an employer, for example) is liable for the negligent acts of his agent:

> If an inn-keeper's servants rob his guests, the master is bound to restitution. . . . So likewise if the drawer at a tavern sells a man bad wine, whereby his health is injured, he may bring an action against the master.[53]

But this general rule was never extended to the factory and to railroad workers. The reason was most notably expressed in the leading American case, *Farwell v. Boston & Worcester Railroad Corporation* (1842).[54] Farwell was a railroad engineer, working for a wage of $2 a day. A switchman carelessly allowed a train to run off the track. Farwell was thrown to the ground "with great violence"; and one of the wheels of the car crushed his right hand. He sued the railroad, claiming the switchman was negligent. Chief Justice Lemuel Shaw of Massachusetts wrote a brilliant opinion denying recovery. Shaw argued that the workman who takes on a dangerous job must be held to have assumed the ordinary risks of the job. In theory, the wage rate included an adjustment for the added danger. Since that was so, the risk must be left on the person who had, for a price, voluntarily taken it on. The injured workman was thus thrown back on his own resources, or, if he had none, left to the tender mercies of the poor laws. The economic impact of railroad accidents was thereby socialized (or ignored), relieving the roads of one possible heavy cost. Or so an enterprise-minded judge might have thought.

The fellow-servant rule, when we look back on it, seems particularly callous and unfair. Clearly, Shaw did not see it that way. Life itself was unfair. Accidents were inevitable; life was harsh, and full of uncompensated harms. A case like *Farwell* treated industrial injuries as "part of the social landscape—a routine, if regrettable occurrence"; and it was part of the price of a free and open society.[55]

In a world without social programs, without a "social safety net," a precarious world, full of calamities, plagues, catastrophes, it was not the normal course of events for "accidents" to give rise to claims for compensation. Also, in these early days of the industrial revolution, the ethos of the "dignity and importance of work" implied a degree of worker control over his own fate, his own work conditions. This perhaps made it easier, ideologically, to impose the safety burden on labor, not management.[56] But was Shaw also trying to

---

[53] 1 Blackstone, *Commentaries*, p. 430. On the rise of the fellow-servant rule, see Lawrence M. Friedman and Jack Ladinsky, "Social Change and the Law of Industrial Accidents," 67 Columbia L. Rev. 50, 51–58 (1967); an alternative view is in Comment, "The Creation of a Common Law Rule: The Fellow-Servant Rule, 1837–1860," 132 U. Pa. L. Rev. 579 (1984).

[54] 45 Mass. (4 Metc.) 49 (1842). The rule was first enunciated in *Priestley v. Fowler*, 3 M. & W. 1 (Ex. 1837), an English case, which did not, however, arise out of an industrial setting. *Murray v. South Carolina R.R.*, 26 So. Car. L. (1 McMul.) 385 (1841) was decided one year before *Farwell*, and reached the same result; but it was never so frequently cited as the opinion of Chief Justice Shaw.

[55] Christopher L. Tomlins, "A Mysterious Power: Industrial Accidents and the Legal Construction of Employment Relations in Massachusetts, 1800–1850," 6 Law and History Review 375, 421 (1988); see also Lawrence M. Friedman, *Total Justice* (1985). The railroad actually paid Farwell, after he lost his case, the sum of $720. Tomlins, loc. cit., p. 415.

[56] On this thesis, see John Fabian Witt, "The Transformation of Work and the Law of Workplace Accidents, 1842–1910," 107 Yale L.J. 1467 (1998).

subsidize the railroads? Perhaps not consciously. But he must have been aware how *popular* it was to encourage the development of railroads. Railroad building was popular, not only for people involved in what we would now call big business, but for the ordinary farmer or merchant, eager to get his goods to the market. It can hardly be a coincidence that so many emerging doctrines of tort law tilted toward railroads and other enterprises. There was no conspiracy. But there was, no doubt, a widespread consensus.

The fellow-servant rule had far-reaching consequences. An employee could not sue his employer for negligence unless his injuries were caused by the employer's own personal misconduct, not those of the fellow servants.[57] But in factories and mines and on railroads, any negligent conduct was likely to be conduct of a fellow servant. Factory and railroad owners and managers were not usually at the work site at all; and as the economy turned industrial, it was more and more the case that men and women worked for a "soulless corporation." In the years after *Farwell,* state after state adopted the fellow-servant rule. The doctrine of contributory negligence, which grew up in the first half of the nineteenth century, added another barrier to plaintiffs who sued in tort. If an injured party was negligent herself, however slightly, she could not sue a negligent defendant. Since most plaintiffs were individuals, and most defendants companies, the impact of the doctrine is quite obvious. Contributory negligence applied to passenger injuries as well as to injuries to workers. This made it doubly useful to the railroads.[58]

[57] The injured worker could also sue the negligent worker, of course; but this was a hollow right, because the fellow servant was almost certain not to have much money.

[58] The law of torts was never quite so harsh and unyielding as its formal rules may have made it appear. Almost from the very first, juries, judges, and legislatures took away with their left hand some of what had been built up with the right. The full sweep of this countertrend appeared most clearly only after 1850. See Part III, ch. VI.

CHAPTER 8

THE BAR AND ITS WORKS

THE BAR

The bar has always suffered from a certain degree of unpopularity. During the Revolution, it is said, lawyers became even more unpopular than before. If so, it was not for lack of heroes. Many lawyers were loyalists, to be sure; more than two hundred of these, perhaps, eventually left the country.[1] About 40 percent of the lawyers in Massachusetts were loyalists.[2] But, on the other side, almost half of the signers of the Declaration of Independence and more than half of the members of the federal Constitutional Convention were lawyers. Jefferson, Hamilton, and John Adams—patriots and heroes—were lawyers.

The two groups might have canceled each other out in the public mind. If they did not, the reasons why lawyers were unpopular must lie somewhat deeper. Some lawyers, not Tories themselves, defended the Tories against state confiscation laws Between 1780 and 1800. Alexander Hamilton built a career by working for these unpopular clients. Yet, even this fact does not carry us very far. Broader social forces were undoubtedly at work. Economic depression followed the end of the war. The clamor against lawyers rose and fell with the business cycle. In Massachusetts, during Shays's Rebellion, there were uprisings against courts and lawyers; the lawyers seemed too zealous in the oppression of debtors. It was a common lay opinion that the law was all tricks and technicalities, run by unscrupulous men who built legal careers "upon the ruins of the distressed."[3] "Lawyers," wrote St. John Crèvecoeur in 1782, "are plants that will grow in any soil that is cultivated by the hands of others; and when once they have taken root they will extinguish every other vegetable that grows around them. The fortunes they daily acquire in every province, from the misfortunes of their fellow citizens, are surprising! . . . They are here what the clergy were in past centuries. . . . A reformation equally useful is now wanted."[4]

---

[1] Charles Warren, *A History of the American Bar* (1911), p. 213. Some lawyers afterwards returned. For a case study of the career of a lawyer who wavered in his allegiance, left the country, lived in exile, and ultimately came back to a successful practice (Peter Van Schaack), see Maxwell Bloomfield, *American Lawyers in a Changing Society, 1776–1876* (1976), pp. 1–31.

[2] Gerald W. Gawalt, *The Promise of Power: The Emergence of the Legal Profession in Massachusetts, 1760–1840* (1979), p. 37.

[3] Quoted in Oscar Handlin and Mary Handlin, *Commonwealth: A Study of the Role of Government in the American Economy: Massachusetts, 1774–1861* (rev. ed., 1969), p. 41.

[4] *Letters from an American Farmer* (1904), pp. 196–97.

At various points in history, the lawyer has been labeled a Tory, parasite, usurer, land speculator, corrupter of the legislature, note shaver, panderer to corporations, tool of the trusts, shyster, ambulance chaser, and loan shark. Some of the lawyer's bad odor is due to the role of the lawyer as a hired gun. Rich and powerful people need lawyers and have the money to hire them. Also, lawyers in the United States were upwardly mobile men,[5] seizers of opportunities. The American lawyer was never primarily a learned doctor of laws; he was a man of action and cunning. He played a useful role, sometimes admired, but rarely loved.

Under the conditions of American society, it would have been surprising if a narrow, elitist profession grew up—a small, exclusive guild. No such profession developed. There were tendencies in this direction during the colonial period; but after the Revolution the dam burst, and the number of lawyers grew fantastically. It has never stopped growing. In Massachusetts, in 1740, there were only about fifteen lawyers (the population was about 150,000). A century later, in 1840, there were 640 lawyers in the state—ten times as many in proportion to the population. The big push came after the Revolution.[6]

This kind of growth would have been impossible if the established lawyers had been able to choke off entry into the profession. But the doors to the profession were at all times relatively open. Control over admission to the bar was loose, to say the least. The bar became a great avenue of social advancement. Young men flocked to the profession, for much the same reasons that young men and women flock to it today. It was a ladder to success, financially and politically. "Law," wrote young James Kent, "is a field which is uninteresting and boundless." It was "so encumbered with voluminous rubbish and the baggage of folios that it requires uncommon assiduity and patience to manage." Yet he pushed ahead, because law, despite its faults, "leads forward to the first stations in the State."[7]

Maxwell Bloomfield sampled death notices of lawyers, carried in the *Monthly Law Magazine*, around the end of the period. He found a rich diversity of family backgrounds. There were forty-eight in his sample. Among their fathers were three doctors, five merchants, eleven ministers, ten farmers, two mechanics, two soldiers, eleven lawyers, and four judges.[8] Some sons of poor men used careers in law as a means of upward mobility. Many failed, of course. The American dream was never that everyone succeeds, but that everyone had a fighting chance to succeed. There was enough truth in this—enough stories of

[5] All lawyers in this period were men.

[6] Gawalt, *op. cit.*, p. 14. In 1790, there were 112 lawyers; in 1800, 200; in 1810, 492. Some of these were practicing in what became the state of Maine; but nonetheless, the number of lawyers in the Massachusetts counties grew steadily and dramatically in ratio to the population. There were also substantial increases in the number of lawyers practicing in Virginia; see E. Lee Shepard, "Breaking into the Profession: Establishing a Law Practice in Antebellum Virginia," 48 J. Southern Hist. 393, 405 (1982).

[7] Quoted in William Kent, *Memoirs and Letters of James Kent, LlD.* (1898), p. 16. See, in general, E. Lee Shepard, "Lawyers Look at Themselves: Professional Consciousness and the Virginia Bar, 1770–1850," 25 Am. J. Legal Hist. 1 (1981).

[8] Maxwell Bloomfield, "Law vs. Politics: The Self-Image of the American Bar (1830–1860)," 12 Am. J. Legal Hist. 306, 313–14 (1968).

the trip from log cabin to wealth and distinction—to make law an attractive career for ambitious young men.

The bar was open to almost all men in the formal sense; but class and background did make a difference. Jackson ideology should not be taken at face value. The bar was, for one thing, quite stratified, even in the nineteenth century. At the beginning of the twenty-first century, there is a tremendous social distance between a Wall Street partner on the one hand, and on the other, the lawyers who scramble for a living at the bottom of the heap. Lawyers from wealthy or professional backgrounds are far more likely to reach the heights than lawyers from working-class homes. In 1800 or 1850, there were no large law firms; hardly any firms at all. But there were rich lawyers and poor lawyers in those years; there were lawyers who handled the business of well-to-do clients and rich merchants; and there were those who squeezed out a living scratching for petty claims in petty courts. Some of the best, most famous lawyers came up the hard way. But all in all, good social background was important in the eighteenth and nineteenth centuries also. A person with Jefferson's background got the right education and contacts more easily than a poor man's son. He was more likely to *become* a lawyer, more likely, too, to reach the top of the bar. Of 2,618 trained lawyers who practiced in Massachusetts and Maine between 1760 and 1840, 71.4 percent, or 1,859, had gone to college. Children of professionals, as compared to children of farmers or laborers, had better life chances. Between 1810 and 1840, it seems, more than half the lawyers, who were college graduates and were admitted to the bar in Massachusetts, were sons of lawyers and judges; before 1810, the figure was about 38 percent. The percentages of lawyers from a farming or laboring background declined slightly at the same time.[9]

Gerard Gawalt's figures for Massachusetts also show great variation in income and property holdings among lawyers. A typical income was apparently something less than $1,000 a year, in 1810 or 1820. But Lemuel Shaw probably grossed more than $15,000 in private practice in the late 1820s.[10] This was an enormous sum for the day—perhaps the equivalent of half a million dollars in purchasing power, in (say) the year 2000. Daniel Webster, who was one of the most famous lawyers of the period, usually earned over $10,000 a year after 1825; in 1835–1836, he earned over $21,000 in fees.[11] The leading lawyers of Guilford County, North Carolina, in the decades just before the Civil War, were rich men, who owned land and slaves and were powers in the local community.[12]

There were many styles and types of law practice. We have already mentioned that colorful subspecies, the frontier or western lawyer. No frontier town was too raw and muddy for lawyers. They were out to seek their fortunes in land and litigation, sometimes even in genteel larceny. Politics had an irresistible appeal for western lawyers, as one road to fame or to fortune, or both.

[9] Gerard W. Gawalt, *op. cit.*, pp. 140, 171–72.

[10] Leonard W. Levy, *The Law of the Commonwealth and Chief Justice Shaw* (1957), p. 17; Gawalt, *op. cit.*, pp. 109–15.

[11] Alfred F. Konefsky and Andrew J. King, eds., *The Papers of Daniel Webster, Legal Papers*, vol. 2, *The Boston Practice* (1983), pp. 122–23; see Robert V. Remini, *Daniel Webster: The Man and His Times* (1997), p. 228.

[12] Gail Williams O'Brien, *The Legal Fraternity and the Making of a New South Community, 1848–1882* (1986), p. 80.

Many began their careers in the West as politicians who had wangled a job in the territories. Some took up one public office after another. Lewis Cass, born in New Hampshire, in 1782, received a "classical education of a high order"; taught briefly in Wilmington, Delaware; and crossed the Alleghenies in 1799, at the age of seventeen, "on foot, carrying his knapsack and seeking, unaided, and without the help of wealth or power, a new home in the wilderness of Ohio."[13] In Marietta, Ohio, he learned law in a law office. Then he became a general, a politician, and governor of Michigan.

Some lawyers wandered from town to town, almost like itinerant peddlers, until they found the right opening for their talents. David Davis, Lincoln's friend, later a justice of the U.S. Supreme Court, was born in Maryland. He attended Yale, studied law in a Massachusetts office, and arrived in Pekin, Illinois, in 1835. A little while after, he moved to Bloomington, Illinois. George Grover Wright (1820–1896), who became president of the American Bar Association in 1887, was born in Indiana, in 1820, the "son of a poor man." He settled in Keosauqua, Iowa, in 1840, where, it is said, his stagecoach from Keokuk broke down.[14] Joseph G. Baldwin (1815–1864), whose vivid word-pictures of frontier justice have earned him a minor place in American literature, was born in Virginia, read Blackstone, settled in Dekalb, Mississippi, moved to Gainesville, Alabama, stayed there for eighteen years, then moved on to a newer frontier—San Francisco. He had been appointed to the supreme court of California before he died.[15]

A taste for the frontier was not limited to sons of the poor. Almost all of the thirty-six members of Harvard's law class of 1835 were natives of New England and the Middle Atlantic States, mostly middle class and above. One-third of them (twelve) ended their careers in another part of the country: Michigan, California (two), Ohio (two), Louisiana (two), South Carolina, Tennessee, Georgia, Illinois, and Missouri.[16] No doubt the idea of seeking a fortune in the West was romantically appealing; probably the main reason for all this shifting about, though, was ambition rather than wanderlust. It was not always easy to eke out a living in new soil. But for many young lawyers, the West seemed like a golden opportunity. In Fayette, Missouri, in 1841—a tiny little town—one resident complained that lawyers "spring up like mushrooms." In 1845, there were 131 lawyers in St. Louis, a town of about 35,000. As early as 1821, when the city had less than 5,000 people, there were thirty-one lawyers—a much higher ratio than in the cities of the East. The ratio of lawyers to population in St. Louis declined somewhat, later on. It is clear that lawyers were drawn to new places, however; they smelled an opportunity, and they took it.[17]

Some lawyers in these new places indeed found themselves a quick niche, and a lucrative one. Many stayed put, watched their rude villages grow up into cities, and became rich and respectable. If they lived long enough, they wrote

[13] William T. Young, *Sketch of Life and Public Services of General Lewis Cass* (1853), pp. 18–19.

[14] James G. Rogers, *American Bar Leaders* (1932), p. 47.

[15] William A. Owens, Introduction to Joseph G. Baldwin, *The Flush Times of Alabama and Mississippi* (1957).

[16] Charles Warren, *History of the Harvard Law School*, vol. III (1908), pp. 11–12.

[17] Stuart Banner, *Legal Systems in Conflict: Property and Sovereignty in Missouri, 1750–1860* (2000), pp. 103–4.

colorful "recollections" of bench and bar for local historical journals and lawyers' magazines. Their practice took patience, luck, and skill. They did not bother asking what was or was not fit work for a lawyer. Whatever earned a dollar was fair game. Some, indeed, had to leave the practice for a while, or for good, to make ends meet. John Dean Caton, later chief justice of Illinois, arrived in Chicago in 1833 with $14 in his pocket. He found a few lawyers there but little business. A "very good lawyer," Russell E. Heacock, who had practiced downstate, found the going so rough in Chicago that he "built a log carpenter's shop at the corner of State and South Water Street, where he worked at the trade which he had learned before he studied law. He also held the office of justice of the peace."[18]

Some lawyers came West as agents for eastern land speculators, then later struck out on their own. Their main legal business was the land—buying it and selling it for others, searching titles, making deeds. Land was the backbone of practice. It was also a medium of payment. Michael Stoner hired young Henry Clay, in 1801, to "prosecute a claim . . . to five hundred acres of Land." Clay would pay all the costs; if he won, he was to receive one fourth of the winnings.[19] Another staple of the lawyer's practice was collection work. Lawyers dunned and sued, both for local people and for easterners who held debts in the form of promissory notes. Clay, in Kentucky, got paid by claiming a percentage of the money he collected (5 percent or more); sometimes he warned debtors that he would go to law to seize their property if they failed to pay.[20] Hamilton Gamble, who practiced law in St. Louis, dealt with 163 matters in 1818 and 1819; 122 were actions to recover debts owed to plaintiff.[21] It was common for lawyers to pay themselves from the proceeds of actions for debt—provided they were able to get their hands on the money. Indiana attorney Rowland, collecting two notes in 1820 for E. Pollard, one "for 100 dollars in land-office money," the other for $100.37, "payable in leather to be delivered four miles from Bloomington," was to "receive the customary fees when the money is collected, and if it is never collected then a reasonable fee for [his] trouble."[22] Hard money was always scarce. A lawyer who had some cash would look around for profitable ways to invest it. So, some frontier lawyers, besides their collection work, and land speculation, added to their repertoire the high-risk venture of lending out money at interest. For nonresidents, the western lawyer searched titles, paid taxes, and in general handled the affairs of people who lived elsewhere. He might also scramble for a share of petty criminal work.

Courtroom clients were a shifting if not shiftless lot. House counsel was unknown, though in time successful lawyers and affluent clients did enter into occasional retainer agreements. Most lawyers were constantly hunting for new business and were in constant need of advertisements for themselves. There was no prohibition against advertising in the literal sense, and lawyers reached out

---

[18] John Caton, *Early Bench and Bar of Illinois* (1893), p. 2.

[19] James F. Hopkins, ed., *The Papers of Henry Clay*, vol. I (1959), pp. 59–60.

[20] Maurice G. Baxter, *Henry Clay the Lawyer* (2000), p. 20.

[21] Stuart Banner, *Legal Systems in Conflict*, p. 109.

[22] *Pollard v. Rowland*, 2 Blackf. 20 (Ind., 1826); see, for a general picture of western practice, William F. English, *The Pioneer Lawyer and Jurist in Missouri* (1947), pp. 65–80, 94–119.

for the public through notices ("cards") in the newspapers.[23] Word of mouth was probably the most effective way to attract good clients. The flamboyance, tricks, and courtroom antics of nineteenth century lawyers were more than a matter of personality; like the high-flown oratory of men like Daniel Webster, this kind of behavior created a reputation. A courtroom lawyer who seemed bland and dull would be hard pressed to survive.

Since most lawyers had no settled relations with definite clients, and since so much of practice was litigation, their lives were spent in close contact with other lawyers, as colleagues, friends, and friendly enemies. In some parts of the country, lawyers "rode circuit." This was a hard but rewarding school of experience. The most famous alumnus of this school was Abraham Lincoln. As John Dean Caton described it, in its Illinois version, lawyers traveled

> with the judge . . . on horseback in a cavalcade across the prairies from one county seat to another, over stretches from fifty to one hundred miles, swimming the streams when necessary. At night they would put up at log cabins in the borders of the groves, when they frequently made a jolly night of it. . . .
>
> This circuit practice required a quickness of thought and a rapidity of action nowhere else requisite in professional practice. The lawyer would, perhaps, scarcely alight from his horse when he would be surrounded by two or three clients requiring his services. . . . It is surprising how rapidly such practice qualifies one to meet . . . emergencies.[24]

Typically, the lawyer traveled light; he took with him a few personal effects, a change of linen, a handful of law books. In some cases, a young lawyer, too poor to buy a horse, trudged along the circuit on foot.[25]

Country lawyers were not the only ones who went on circuit. The Supreme Court bar, mainly recruited from Pennsylvania, Maryland, and Virginia, was also an itinerant group. Peter S. DuPonceau, of Pennsylvania, described the life of these lawyers:

> counsel . . . were in the habit of going together to Washington to argue their cases. . . . We hired a stage to ourselves in which we proceeded by easy journies . . . we had to travel in the depth of winter through bad roads in no very comfortable way. Nevertheless, as soon as we were out of the city, and felt the flush of air, we were like school boys in the playground on a holiday. . . .
>
> Our appearance at the Bar of the Supreme Court was always a scene of triumph.[26]

But any kind of settled practice—even debt collection—was an enemy of the personal, itinerant style. The circuit-riding era slowly passed on; it was colorful and romantic, but it was not the way to climb the professional ladder. Office

---

[23] Daniel H. Calhoun, *Professional Lives in America: Structure and Aspiration, 1750–1850* (1965), pp. 82–83.

[24] Caton, *op. cit.*, p. 51.

[25] John W. McNulty, "Sidney Breese, the Illinois Circuit Judge, 1835–1841," 62 J. Ill. State Historical Society 170 (1969).

[26] Charles Warren, *History of the American Bar*, p. 256.

work by lawyers who stayed put became the norm, even in outlying counties, before the Civil War.[27]

In any event, the eastern and southern statesman-lawyer was a far cry from the dusty rider of the plains. Some, like Jefferson, were great squires who studied law as a gentleman's pursuit. In the North, too, there were lawyers from elite backgrounds. They formed a small but sophisticated bar of commerce. They were joined by some upwardly mobile colleagues. Elite lawyers advised the great mercantile houses on matters of marine insurance and international trade. Yet they too were basically courtroom lawyers, in practice on their own, like their poor western cousins. Alexander Hamilton had a general practice in the late eighteenth century, and frequently appeared in court. He was "a very great favorite with the merchants of New York." Many questions of marine insurance went to court and Hamilton had an "overwhelming share" of this business.[28] According to one estimate, about five hundred lawyers practiced in New York City in 1830, when the city had a population of about 200,000.[29] Almost all of these men were solo practitioners. There was a handful of two-man partnerships, but no firms of any size. In a few of these partnerships, the partners began to specialize. George Washington Strong and John Wells formed a partnership in 1818; the two partners soon agreed on a rough division of labor. One was a good courtroom advocate; the other preferred to stay in the office, preparing the necessary papers and briefs.[30]

At least three embryo partnerships of old New York were ancestor firms of large "factories" of law on Wall Street. One of these, forefather of the Cravath firm of New York, has been carefully traced by Robert T. Swaine.[31] To Swaine we owe a valuable picture of the practice of R. M. Blatchford, one of the founding fathers, in the years 1826–1832, when he was still practicing alone. Blatchford's practice was exceptional but probably not unique. It was, in a way, far more like its Wall Street descendants than like the work of Blatchford's contemporaries in small towns, or out West, or in the petty criminal courts of New York. Blatchford in 1826 had become American financial agent and counsel for the Bank of England; this connection brought him "a great deal of business from English solicitors whose clients had American investments." He became counsel, too, to the second Bank of the United States. Blatchford went to court once in a while, but most of his work was as an advisor. When he formed a partnership with his brother in 1832, he again dropped out of litigation. The early years of this brotherly firm were spent in large measure on "office practice—advising on legal problems and drafting legal documents affecting industry, trade and finance. . . . There were many loan transactions, commercial and on real estate mortgages, much of the latter business coming from English clients, who also sent occasional marine insurance and other admiralty matters. There was also much collection business for City merchants and for English exporters."

[27] Daniel H. Calhoun, *Professional Lives in America* (1965), pp. 59–87.

[28] The quotations are from Chancellor Kent, in William Kent, *Memoirs and Letters of James Kent* (1898), p. 317. On Hamilton's career, there is abundant material in the various volumes of *The Law Practice of Alexander Hamilton*. vol. 1 (1964) and vol. II (1969) were edited by Julius Goebel; vols. III (1980), IV (1980), and V (1981) by Julius Goebel and Joseph H. Smith.

[29] Henry W. Taft, *A Century and a Half at the New York Bar* (1938), p. 7.

[30] Taft, *op. cit.*, p. 22.

[31] Robert T. Swaine, *The Cravath Firm and Its Predecessors, 1819–1948*, vol. 1 (1946).

Blatchford was also active as a professional trustee, and probated estates of wealthy clients. Later, as industry grew, there were cases where businesses needed loans "too large for a single lender." Here there developed a practice of pledging or conveying the security to a trustee,

> for the joint benefit of a group of lenders. Blatchford developed a business as trustee in such transactions—the forerunner of the modern corporate trust. In the 30's there also appeared a form of investment security as a means of attracting British capital to America of the same general nature as the modern investment trust. In this field, too, Blatchford was active, both as a trustee and as a lawyer. Out of that activity grew the North American Trust & Banking Company litigation which was in the New York courts from 1841 to 1858 and was one of the Blatchford firm's principal matters after . . . 1854.[32]

Blatchford was one kind of wave of the future. Few lawyers could afford to stray so far from litigation. Courtroom work, both East and West, was the main road to prestige, the main way to get recognized as a lawyer or a leader of the bar. It was practically the only way for a lawyer, as a lawyer, to become famous. Daniel Webster was a celebrity; Blatchford was not. Webster, the courtroom lawyer, lives on in literature and in folklore. Chancellor Kent, who was learned and influential, but whose courtroom delivery was "most shocking,"[33] is remembered only by specialists and scholars.

Eloquence in court gained attention, and attention gained clients. There was a ready audience. In the days before radio and television, the public appreciated a good trial and a good courtroom speech. In the provinces, when the court arrived at the county seat, court day was an occasion; trials and courtroom business broke up the monotony of life. In the rather dull society of Washington, ambassadors, congressmen, and the wives of politicians crowded into the Supreme Court galleries to hear the giants of the bar hold forth. "Scarcely a day passed in court," Story wrote in 1812, "in which parties of ladies do not occasionally come in and hear, for a while, the arguments of learned counsel. On two occasions, our room has been crowded with ladies to hear Mr. [William] Pinkney, the present Attorney General."[34] Speeches at the bar went on for hours, sometimes for days. Alexander Hamilton spoke for six hours before the New York Supreme Court in Albany, in a case of criminal libel in 1804.[35] The federal Supreme Court was described in 1824 as "not only one of the most dignified and enlightened tribunals in the world, but one of the most patient. Counsel are heard in silence for hours, without being stopped or interrupted."[36]

Some of these marathon speeches became famous. Daniel Webster argued for four hours in *Dartmouth College v. Woodward* (1818),

> with a statement so luminous, and a chain of reasoning so easy to be understood, and yet approaching so nearly to absolute demonstration, that he

---

[32] Swaine, *op. cit.*, pp. 14–15.

[33] Diary of George T. Strong, quoted in Taft, *op. cit.*, p. 102.

[34] Quoted in Charles Warren, *The Supreme Court in United States History*, vol. II, p. 467.

[35] Julius Goebel Jr., ed., *The Law Practice of Alexander Hamilton*, vol. 1 (1964), p. 793.

[36] Quoted in Charles Warren, *The Supreme Court in United States History*, vol. I, p. 467.

seemed to carry with him every man of his audience. . . . Now, and then, for a sentence or two, his eye flashed and his voice swelled into a bolder note. . . but he instantly fell back into [a] tone of earnest conversation.

The judges listened, we are told, with rapt attention. At the end of his formal argument, Webster supposedly added his famous peroration: "Sir, you may destroy this little institution; it is weak; it is in your hands. . ." At the words, "It is, sir, as I have said, a small college. And yet there are those who love it—"

the feelings which he has thus far succeeded in keeping down, broke forth. His lips quivered; his firm cheeks trembled with emotion; his eyes were filled with tears, his voice choked . . . he seemed struggling to . . . gain . . . mastery over himself.

At that point, according to one biographer, John Marshall's eyes were "suffused with tears"; and when Webster sat down, there was "a deathlike stillness" in the room; it lasted for "some moments; every one seemed to be slowly recovering."[37]

John Marshall's tears may be legendary; and even the text of Webster's famous speech is suspect. But there is no doubt about the oratorical athletics; and if not John Marshall, then certainly members of the audience were "dissolved in tears."[38] The great courtroom masters really poured it on. Rufus Choate, faced with an audience (in or out of court) "could work himself up into . . . a passion. . . . [H]is voice would rise to a shriek and the sweat pour from his head; he would sway back and forth on his heels." To fill his speeches with the necessary verbiage, he actually had the habit of reading the dictionary, mining it for a richer (and more pompous) vocabulary.[39] The style of men like Choate is too flowery, full of too much purple prose, for modern tastes; but it was a great hit in its day. Old Horace Binney, looking back at the bar of his youth (he wrote in 1866), saw the great lawyers in a romantic light: flamboyant, oratorical, anything but businesslike and gray. There was Theophilus Parsons, before the turn of the century: "Socratic in his subtlety," but "careless" of dress: "his purple Bandana handkerchief curled loosely over his neckcloth." William Lewis, born in 1745, appeared in court with a "full suit of black" and a "powdered head":

His first attitude was always as erect as he could make it, with one hand insinuated between his waistcoat and his shirt, and the other lying loose upon his loin; and in this position, without any action but that movement of his head, he would utter two or three of his first sentences. . . . Then, with a

[37] Quoted in George T. Curtis, *Life of Daniel Webster,* vol. 1 (1872), pp. 169–71. A lawyer who worked with Webster in New Hampshire described him as "a born actor . . . touring the courts with him . . . was like being on a caravan." Irving H. Bartlett, *Daniel Webster* (1978), p. 10; on the argument in the Dartmouth College case, see Robert Remini, *Daniel Webster* (1997), pp. 150–60.

[38] Jean Edward Smith, *John Marshall, Definer of a Nation,* p. 435n; the editor of Webster's papers feel that there is "strong evidence" that Webster did in fact say "something along the lines of this reported peroration." Alfred F. Konefsky and Andrew J. King, eds., *The Papers of Daniel Webster: Legal Papers,* vol. 3, *The Federal Practice,* Part 1 (1989), p. 154.

[39] Jean V. Matthews, *Rufus Choate: The Law and Civic Virtue* (1980), p. 45.

quick movement, and sometimes with a little jerk of his body, he would bring both his hands to his sides, and begin the action. And it was pretty vehement action from that time to the conclusion; his head dropping or rising, his body bending or straightening up, and his arms singly or together relieving his head. . . . His voice . . . was deep, sonorous, and clear to the last . . . not sweet, but . . . a fine working voice for a courtroom.[40]

Judges, too, were in a sense oratorical. Charges to the jury, in the early part of the period, sometimes ran on at enormous length. The judges expatiated on subjects far distant from the business at hand. Inflammatory speeches to grand juries, as we noted, helped bring on the crisis between Federalist judges and Republicans in office. In time, the free-flown speeches of the judges were curbed; and what one might call the oratorical style of law practice died down, though it never died out. The style was essentially suited for small elites and small communities, and for generalist, courtroom lawyers. The rise of big business and the Wall Street style of practice ruined the monopoly held by the oratorical style. Law office law implied a different relationship with clients, different ways of getting and keeping business. Then, too, the sheer mass of business had an effect; as dockets became swollen, there had to be an end to the leisurely pace of litigation. After the Webster days, hard-pressed courts, even had they wanted to, could not listen to long speeches and still get on with their work.

ORGANIZATION OF THE BAR

In England, there were distinctions between different grades and types of lawyer: between attorneys, counselors, barristers, and sergeants. The idea did not catch on in the United States. A few colonies had recognized a graded bar; some—New Jersey and Massachusetts—held on to a distinction between two classes of attorneys for a number of years after Independence. The statutes of the Northwest Territory also briefly distinguished between attorneys and counselors. Only "counselors," more exalted than ordinary attorneys, could appear before the highest court. This gradation (1799) lasted only a few years, even on paper.[41] New York distinguished between attorneys and counselors between 1829 and 1846; Virginia distinguished between solicitors, who practiced in equity, and the ordinary attorneys of the common-law courts. The distinction had no great significance; a common-law attorney could easily and quickly, with a few additional formalities, get for himself the solicitor's right to practice in equity court.[42] Soon Virginia did away with this small formal distinction, too.

The graded bar was thus a rather transient phenomenon. The established bar did struggle to keep their guild small and elite. Success eluded them. By the early nineteenth century, the bar was, formally speaking, an undifferentiated mass. There were rich and poor lawyers, high ones and low; but all were members of one vast sprawling profession. The few primitive bar clubs, associations,

[40] Horace Binney, *The Leaders of the Old Bar of Philadelphia* (1866), pp. 17, 38–40.
[41] Francis S. Philbrick, ed., *Laws of Indiana Territory, 1801–1809,* cxcii–cxciii.
[42] Alfred Z. Reed, *Training for the Public Profession of the Law* (1921), p. 80.

and "moots"[43] did nothing to provide real cohesion or self-control. The bar was very loose, very open. Nobody controlled it at the top, or from within. Requirements for admission to the bar were lax.[44] In New England and New York, during the late colonial period, the lawyers themselves had a great deal of power, formal or informal, over admission to the bar. But then the courts took over; they prescribed qualifications and handled applications. This meant a certain loss of professional control. The courts were bound to have a looser rein than the practicing bar; courts had less interest in keeping fee schedules high and the supply of lawyers low.

How did a young man get himself recognized as an actual lawyer? In Massachusetts, each county court admitted its own attorneys; the high court theoretically controlled all admissions in South Carolina; in Rhode Island, Delaware, and Connecticut local courts admitted lawyers; but admission to one bar gave an attorney the right to practice in all. After the Revolution, New York (1777) and the federal courts (1789) switched to the Massachusetts system, which became dominant in the Northeast. In the 1830s, the Delaware method became more popular. A lawyer admitted to any local court, no matter in how slipshod a process, was a fully licensed member of the state bar, and could practice before any court.

A few states were strict, with regard to prerequisites. In New Hampshire, between 1805 and 1833, the federated county bars required five years of preparation for admission to the lower courts, for applicants qualified to enter Dartmouth (but they did not have to know Greek). Three years was the term for college graduates. Two years further practice was required for admission to the superior court. New York, between 1829 and 1846, by rule of court, demanded seven years of preparation for the right to practice as an "attorney" before the supreme court, "toward which there might be counted up to four years of classical study pursued after the age of fourteen."[45] It took three years more of practice to become a "counselor." Most other states discarded these rigorous requirements. In 1800, fourteen out of the nineteen states or organized territories prescribed a definite period of preparation for the bar. In 1840, only eleven out of thirty jurisdictions did so. In Massachusetts, a statute was passed in 1836 that obliged the courts to admit anyone of good moral character who had studied law three years in an attorney's office. A person who did not meet this requirement could take his chances on an examination. In the 1840s, a few states eliminated *all* requirements for admission to the bar, except good moral character. One was Maine (1843); another was New Hampshire (1842),

[43] See Charles Warren, *A History of the American Bar* (1911), p. 203. In Massachusetts, the associations of the bar, under rules of court of 1810, gained significant power, which they had long desired. Recommendation from the county bar association became a prerequisite for admission to the court of common pleas and the Supreme Court. These rules lasted about one generation. Gerard W. Gawalt, *op. cit.*, pp. 116–17.

[44] The best treatment is Reed, *op. cit.*, pp. 67–103.

[45] Reed, *op. cit.*, p. 83. The New Hampshire rule was continued by order of court to 1838. On admission to the bar in Virginia, see Charles T. Cullen, "New Light on John Marshall's Legal Education and Admission to the Bar," 16 Am. J. Legal Hist. 345 (1972); a would-be lawyer would petition the governor; the governor would name two lawyers, and these lawyers would handle the examination. Jean E. Smith, *John Marshall*, p. 81.

reversing its former stringency. At this point, then, it was hard to make the case that law was a learned, difficult, exclusive profession.

These rules (or nonrules) should not be taken too literally. Laymen did not practice law, even in New Hampshire and Maine in the 1840s. Rules of admission and preparation were probably not very rigorous anywhere. In some states—particularly in the West—the "examination" of prospective lawyers was extremely slapdash, if we can believe a mass of anecdotes.[46] Gustave Koerner, who had immigrated from Germany, began to practice in the 1830s in Illinois; his examination, he said, was very informal, lasted about half an hour, and consisted of a few perfunctory questions; then everyone adjourned for brandy toddies.[47] Salmon P. Chase had almost as casual an examination in Maryland in 1829. The judge wanted him to "study another year"; but then Chase "begged for a favorable ruling," because he had "made all . . . arrangements to go to the western country and practice law"; the judge relented and swore him in.[48] John Dean Caton's experience was quite similar. Caton was admitted to the Illinois bar in 1833. He rode down to Pekin, Illinois, on horseback, one October day; there he introduced himself to Judge Samuel D. Lockwood. Caton told the judge he was practicing in Chicago, but needed a license. They went for a walk after supper; it was a "beautiful moonlit night." Suddenly, near a "large oak stump," Lockwood began asking questions. To Caton's surprise, this was the actual examination. There were some thirty minutes of questions; then the judge said he would grant the license, but that Caton still had "much to learn."[49]

Easy access to the bar was, perhaps, in line with the ideas of Jacksonian democracy. But basic social facts pushed in the same direction. There was essentially no government control over any sort of occupation; such controls came later. There was high geographical and social mobility. Government was fragmented into tiny jurisdictions. No one could really define standards for itself; and the weakness of one was the weakness of all.[50] Besides, a factotum profession, open to all sorts of ambitious men, was socially useful. The prime economic fact of American life, as we have said, was mass ownership of land and (some bits of) capital. It was a society where many people, not just the nobles or the lucky few, needed some forms or form books, some know-how about the mysterious ways of law, courts or governments, and some access to at least the rudiments of law. It was a society, in short, that needed a large, amorphous, open-ended profession.

In many ways, then, loose standards were almost inevitable. Perhaps they even enhanced the vigor of the bar. *Formal* restrictions tended to disappear; but the actual market for legal services was a harsh and perhaps efficient control. It pruned away deadwood; it rewarded the adaptive and the cunning. Jacksonian democracy did not make every man a lawyer. It did encourage a scrambling bar of shrewd entrepreneurs.

[46] On Missouri, see Stuart Banner, *Legal Systems in Conflict*, p. 108.

[47] Jack Nortrup, "The Education of a Western Lawyer," 12 Am. J. Legal Hist. 294, 301 (1968).

[48] J. W. Schuckers, *The Life and Public Services of Salmon Portland Chase* (1874), p. 30.

[49] John Dean Caton, *Early Bench and Bar of Illinois* (1893), pp. 170–71.

[50] Fragmentation and diversity were also traits of the substantive law—see the discussions of divorce law and corporation law, for example.

LEGAL EDUCATION

A lawyer was a man with legal training, or some legal training and some legal skill. Even at the low point of professional self-government, no one practiced law without at least some pretense of legal skill and some smattering of legal knowledge. Most lawyers gained their pretensions by spending some time in training, in the office of a member of the bar. The basic form of legal education, then (if you can call it that), was a kind of apprenticeship. For a fee, the lawyer-to-be hung around an office, read Blackstone and Coke and miscellaneous other books, and copied legal documents. If he was lucky, he benefited from watching the lawyer do his work, and do it well. If he was very lucky, the lawyer actually tried to teach him something.

Apprenticeship was useful to everybody: to the clerks, who picked up some knowledge of law, by osmosis if nothing else; and to the lawyers, who (in the days before telephones, typewriters, word processors, Xerox machines and the like) badly needed copyists and legmen. Young Henry Clay, in the office of George Wythe in Richmond, Virginia, acted as a secretary; Wythe was old and arthritic, and Clay took dictation; he also copied and filed documents.[51] Legal education, in the more literal sense of training in a school, grew out of the apprenticeship method. There were some lawyers who sincerely wanted to train their clerks properly. Some became in effect popular teachers. Theophilus Parsons, in Massachusetts, was so much in demand, shortly after 1800, that a special rule of court, aimed at him, restricted law offices to a maximum of three students at any one time.[52] Lemuel Shaw, too, was a popular and diligent teacher. He drew up rules to govern the conduct and training of his students. The students were to report each Monday on what they had read the previous week. They were also encouraged to "enter into free conversation" with Shaw "upon subjects connected with their studies, and especially in reference to those changes and alterations of the general law which may have been effected by the Statutes of the Commonwealth and by local usage, and in respect to which therefore little can be found in books."[53] Shaw's office became almost a small private school for lawyers. A few lawyers, with a flair for teaching, took the next logical step; they practiced less and less and spent more time with their clerks. Leonard Henderson of North Carolina, a future chief justice of the state, advertised in 1826 in the *Raleigh Register* that he had "four offices for the reception of Law Students" and was on the verge of opening a fifth. "I shall not," he promised, "deliver formal lectures, but will give explanations whenever requested, examinations will be frequent, and conversations held on law topics," most usually "at table after meals." Henderson fixed the fee for "instruction and boarding, exclusive of washing and candles," at $225 a year.[54]

---

[51] Maurice G. Baxter, *Henry Clay the Lawyer* (2000), p. 18.

[52] Frederic Hathaway Chase, *Lemuel Shaw, Chief Justice of the Supreme Judicial Court of Massachusetts* (1918), p. 37.

[53] *Ibid.*, p. 123.

[54] Quoted in Robert H. Wettach, ed., *A Century of Legal Education* (1947), p. 15.

The earliest actual law school was founded by Judge Tapping Reeve in Litchfield, Connecticut, probably in 1784.[55] At a few colleges or universities, there were professorships of law, as we shall see; but Reeve's was the first *law* school, that is a school to train lawyers. It was "established by a lawyer for lawyers, a place where a practical legal education could be obtained."[56] Reeve had been a successful lawyer, but he liked teaching students. Even before he actually started his school, he had prepared teaching materials, and was giving lectures to classes of students. Reeve's school was a great success. It grew rapidly in size. Eventually, it gained a national reputation, and attracted students from all over the country; three out of four of them came from outside Connecticut. The students sat at wooden desks, listening to the lectures, and diligently copying down or taking notes on what they heard.[57] In 1813, fifty-five students were in attendance. Reeve's partner in the school after 1798 was James Gould, himself a product of the school.[58] The fee was $100 for the first year; a second year would cost $60. Of course, there were other expenses, as a letter from a student explained in 1814: board and room, $13 for washing, $14 for wood, $6 for candles, and $5 for paper.[59] In the late 1820s, the school began to feel the keen effects of competition from other schools; it went into decline. Gould, who was the sole lecturer by this time, and in poor health, decided that it was time to put an end to the school. It closed its doors in 1833. More than a thousand students had been "graduated" from Litchfield by that time.

The Litchfield school taught law by the lecture method. Its lectures were never published; to publish would have meant to perish, since students would have lost most of their incentive for paying tuition and going to class. The lecture plan was modeled on Blackstone's *Commentaries,* but the Litchfield lectures paid more attention to commercial law, and little or none to criminal law. Daily lectures lasted about an hour and a quarter or an hour and a half. The full course took fourteen months, including two vacations of four weeks each. Students were required to write up their notes carefully, and to do collateral reading. Every Saturday there was a "strict examination" on the week's work. During the later years of the school, "optional moot courts and debating societies" were in operation.[60]

The Litchfield school spawned a number of imitators in other states. Some were popular; most lasted only a short time. Some students tried both law school and apprenticeship. Robert Reid Howison of Fredericksburg, Virginia, began to read law books on his own, at 18, in 1838. He began, naturally, with Blackstone, but plowed ahead through any number of texts. In fall, 1840, Howison took a course of lectures at a law school run by Judge John T. Lomax in the

---

[55] The fullest account of the rise of American legal education is Robert Stevens, *Law School: Legal Education in America from the 1850s to the 1980s* (1983), but, as the title suggests, it concentrates mostly on a later period.

[56] Marian C. McKenna, *Tapping Reeve and the Litchfield Law School* (1986), p. 59.

[57] Alfred Z. Reed, *Training for the Public Profession of the Law* (1921), p. 130; McKenna, p. 63.

[58] McKenna, p. 93.

[59] McKenna, p. 140.

[60] Reed, *op. cit.,* p. 131.

basement of his house in Fredericksburg. The next spring, Howison spent three weeks in the office of the clerk of court in Fredericksburg, copying documents. He was then examined and admitted to the bar.[61]

Ultimately, university law schools replaced the Litchfield type as the major alternative to office training. But legal training at universities was slow to get started, and well into the nineteenth century there were no "law schools" as such at universities. A few colleges taught law as part of their general curriculum. The first American chair of law was at William and Mary College. Here, at the behest of Thomas Jefferson, George Wythe was appointed professor of "Law and Police." St. George Tucker, who later held this chair, published an American edition of Blackstone in 1803, with copious notes and additions, to be used as a kind of textbook for students. Professorships were also established, in the late eighteenth and early nineteenth centuries, at the University of Virginia, the University of Pennsylvania, and the University of Maryland. These courses, unlike the Litchfield school, were not meant to train lawyers at all. James Wilson projected a series of lectures at Pennsylvania (1790) "to furnish a rational and useful entertainment to gentlemen of all professions." David Murray Hoffman's lectures at Maryland and James Kent's at Columbia produced works that enriched legal literature. But these early experiments were mostly in the tradition of Blackstone, that is, they were lectures on law for the general education of students, and not law training, strictly speaking.

The Harvard Law School was a somewhat different animal, and it proved more permanent than the lectureships at this or that college. Out of funds left to Harvard by Isaac Royall, a chair of law was set up in 1816. The first professor was Isaac Parker, chief justice of Massachusetts. Parker, in his inaugural address, spoke of law as a "science," one "worthy of a place in the University," and "worthy to be taught, for it cannot be understood without instruction."[62] At Harvard, there were already separate faculties in theology and medicine. Parker expected, or hoped for, a professional, independent law school as well. It would live with Harvard College but be clearly distinct from it. A major gift, from Nathan Dane, helped bring this hope to fulfillment. Dane had written a most successful law book, *A General Abridgement and Digest of American Law.* In England, in the eighteenth century, Charles Viner had written a popular abridgement of English law, and he used the proceeds to endow a chair in law, which Sir William Blackstone filled. Dane followed the Vinerian precedent; he gave $10,000 to support a professorship. Dane specifically urged that the professor's "residence at Cambridge shall never be required as a condition of his holding the office; believing the best professors will generally be found among judges and lawyers, eminent in practice in other places conveniently situated, and who, while professors, may continue their offices and practice generally; also thinking law lectures ought to increase no faster than there is a demand for them. Clearly, their great benefit will be in publishing them."[63] Dane himself suggested a candidate for the first Dane professor: Joseph Story. Story was indeed only a part-time professor, out of

---

[61] W. Hamilton Bryson, *Legal Education in Virginia, 1779–1979, A Biographical Approach* (1982), p. 10.

[62] Quoted in Charles Warren, *History of the Harvard Law School*, vol. I (1908), p. 301.

[63] Quoted in Warren, *op. cit.,* p. 420.

sheer necessity; when he accepted the post in 1829, he was a justice of the U.S. Supreme Court.[64]

The Harvard Law School, at least during the Story period, was extremely successful; by 1844, 163 students were in attendance, an unheard-of number.[65] Those who completed their course earned an LLB. The fame and skill of the professors undoubtedly acted as a drawing card. Students who could afford it must have preferred life at Cambridge to the typical sort of office apprenticeship, with its dreary routine. As the oldest and most successful law school, Harvard became the model for all newer schools. It was a pure and rigorous model, as Story wished it to be. It defined the province of law school and legal training severely. Politics and the study of government were put to one side;[66] the stress was on common law, rather than the study of statutes.

Within this narrow domain, the school produced a rich crop of scholarship. Ultimately, the law faculty turned into a veritable treatise-writing machine. Story wrote *Commentaries* on an amazing variety of subjects: promissory notes, equity jurisprudence, the conflict of laws, agency, bailments, bills of exchange, partnership. Simon Greenleaf wrote a popular treatise on evidence. The law school also began to amass a major law library. The catalogue for the academic year 1846–1847 claimed that the law-school library owned 12,000 books.[67] Harvard's success showed that training at a university could compete with the apprenticeship method in filling the wants and needs of young men who wanted to be lawyers. But, still, only a minority of prospective lawyers went to Harvard, or to law school in general. For most people, the path to practice still went through a clerkship at a lawyer's office. And, in this period, apprenticeship probably influenced Harvard more than Harvard influenced the general course of legal training.

THE LITERATURE OF THE LAW

The common law was judge-made law. It was embodied above all in the reported opinions of high court judges. What was not reported had no chance of becoming "law." In England, *reporters* (some skillful and accurate, others less so) privately prepared volumes of cases, for the benefit of the practicing bar. There were no American reports to speak of in the colonial period.[68] By and large, lawyers had to rely on English reports, or on secondhand knowledge of English

---

[64] Isaac Parker resigned as Royall professor in 1827. The subsequent holders of this chair—first John Ashmun, then Simon Greenleaf—were in regular full-time attendance.

[65] Reed, *op. cit.*, p. 143. On the later vicissitudes of Harvard, see Part III, ch. XI, pp. 612–18.

[66] By way of contrast, James Kent, in his *Introductory Lecture to a Course of Law Lectures* (1794), pp. 19–23, proposed to "begin with an Examination of the nature and duties of Government in general . . . The Political History of the United States . . . a summary review of the Law of Nations."

[67] *Centennial History of the Harvard Law School: 1817–1917* (1918), p. 94.

[68] Some colonial reports did get printed, but only later. Josiah Quincy's *Massachusetts Reports* (1761–1771), for example, was published in 1865. More recently, a fair number of volumes of colonial reports have been edited by scholars, sometimes with valuable introductory matter and notes.

cases, gleaned out of English treatises. Lawyers knew the local statutes, to be sure, and the local practice of their courts. Some lawyers prepared, for themselves, collections of local cases. Occasionally, manuscript volumes of cases circulated among lawyers. This practice was certainly followed in the Republican period. Eleven manuscript notebooks, covering the period 1792 to 1830, have been recovered and reprinted for the small state of Delaware alone.[69]

But manuscripts could not satisfy the hunger of lawyers for cases, in an expanding legal system. In 1789, Ephraim Kirby published a volume of *Connecticut Reports*. In the preface, Kirby voiced the hope that a "permanent system of common law," and an American one at that, would emerge in the country. This hope was quickly realized. It was more than a matter of patriotism and pride. After all, lawyers were eager for a supply of reported cases; and were willing to pay for such reports. In 1790, Alexander Dallas published a volume of "Reports of Cases Ruled and Adjudged in the Courts of Pennsylvania, Before and Since the Revolution." The earlier cases, from 1754 on, were "kindly furnished by Mr. Rawle"; sitting judges helped Dallas by giving him notes on their current cases. Dallas, like Kirby, professed a patriotic aim; he hoped that his reports would "tend to show the pure and uniform system of jurisprudence that prevails in Pennsylvania." In the second volume, Dallas added cases from the United States Supreme Court, which was then sitting at Philadelphia. In this volume, quietly and unobtrusively, began that magnificent series of reports, extending in an unbroken line down to the present, that chronicles the work of the world's most powerful court.

William Cranch, chief justice of the circuit court of the District of Columbia, was the Supreme Court's next reporter. Cranch's first volume appeared in 1804, bright with the hope (as a newspaper put it) that a "code of Common Law" would grow "out of our own Constitutions, laws, customs and state of society, independent of that servile recourse to the decisions of foreign Judicatures to which, since our revolution, we have been too much accustomed."[70] In his preface, Cranch added another theme, quite characteristic of the times. Reports, he said, were essential to "a government of laws." The "least possible range ought to be left to the discretion of the Judge. Whatever tends to render the laws certain, equally tends to limit that discretion; and perhaps nothing conduces more to that object than the publication of reports. Every case decided is a check upon the Judge." Cranch was succeeded by another able reporter, Henry Wheaton, later famous as a diplomat and legal scholar.[71]

More and more state reports were also issued. Nathaniel Chipman published *Reports and Dissertations* in Vermont, in 1793. Jesse Root published his *Connecticut Reports* in 1798. Bushrod Washington, soon to be a Supreme Court justice, published two volumes of *Reports of Cases Argued in the Court of Appeals of Virginia* in 1998.[72] By 1810, reports had appeared in New York, Massachusetts,

---

[69] Daniel J. Boorstin, ed., *Delaware Cases: 1792–1830* (3 vols., 1943).

[70] Quoted in Charles Warren, *The Supreme Court in United States History*, vol. I (rev. ed., 1935), p. 289n.

[71] See, in general, Elizabeth F. Baker, *Henry Wheaton, 1785–1848* (1937).

[72] James R. Stoner Jr., "Heir Apparent: Bushrod Washington and Federal Justice in the Early Republic," in Scott Douglas Gerber, ed., *Seriatim: The Supreme Court before John Marshall* (1998), pp. 322, 327.

and New Jersey as well. Some of these had official status—for example, George Caines's reports of the supreme court of New York, beginning in 1804. Many early reporters were judges who collected their own opinions and those of their colleagues. Other judges worked closely with their reporters, helping them bring out full, accurate work. Chancellor Kent had a close relationship with William Johnson, whose New York reports were very popular at the bar. Caines acknowledged his debt to "Their Honors on the bench [who] . . . have unreservedly given their written opinions . . . the whole bar has frankly and generously afforded their cases, and every other communication that was wished or desired. To these aids the clerk of the court has added an unlimited recurrence to the papers and pleadings his office contains."[73] Rhode Island was the last state to fall in line. The first volume of Rhode Island cases, reported by J. K. Angell, did not appear until 1847.

Among the early reports, some were far more than slavish accounts of the judges' words. Like the best of the English reports, they were guidebooks for the practitioner. Some reporters added little essays on the law to the oral and written courtroom materials they collected. Chipman filled out his book with "dissertations," including a "Dissertation on the Negotiability of Notes." The full title of Jesse Root's first volume of *Connecticut Reports* (1798) gives some indication of the contents:

> Reports of Cases adjudged in the Superior Court and Supreme Court of Errors. From July A.D. 1789 to June A.D. 1793; with a Variety of Cases anterior to that Period, Prefaced with Observations upon the Government and Laws of Connecticut. To Which Is Subjoined, Sundry Law Points Adjudged, and Rules of Practice Adopted in the Supreme Court.

But Root's "cases" were not full verbatim reports. Frequently, they were little more than brief notes recounting some point of interest in a trial or appellate case. The following is one "report," *Bacon v. Minor*, given in its entirety:

> Action of defamation; for saying that the plaintiff has forged a certain note. Issue to the jury. Daniel Minor was offered as a witness and objected to, on the ground that he was a joint promissor in said note, and is sued for speaking the same words. By the court—Not admitted being interested in the question.[74]

Eventually, appointed officials replaced private entrepreneurs as law reporters. Official reports tended to be fuller and more accurate than unofficial reports, but they were also much more standardized. Caines remarked that his "exertions have been reduced to little more than arranging the materials received, and giving, in a summary manner, the arguments adduced." What was lost in style was gained in authenticity.

The ultimate influence of the reports can hardly be measured. They enabled the states to put together their own common law, as independent of the common law of England, or of other states, as they liked. At the same time, the reports made it possible for states to borrow more freely from each other. Big states and famous judges carried more weight, and were cited more frequently

---

[73] George Caines, preface, *Reports* (1804).

[74] That is, the testimony was not allowed on the grounds that Minor had a financial stake in the matter litigated. The case is 1 Root 258 (1791).

than small states and small judges. New York's reports had high prestige, especially the opinions of Chancellor Kent. Lemuel Shaw in Massachusetts was another great name. At first, few state courts could rely entirely on local precedents. Nor, in practice, did appellate courts feel totally bound by local decisions. Judges felt that the common law was a single great language of law. No judge wanted to be completely out of step with the main body of the law, at least not without an awfully good reason. Many courts still had the habit of citing English cases, more or less frequently. In the first volume of Saxton's chancery reports (New Jersey, 1830–1832), well over half the citations were English—more than fifty years after Independence. A case that cited, followed, and digested an English doctrine obviously gave that doctrine, from then on, a local habitation and a name. Yet, basically, the case reports were building blocks for an indigenous system of law—actually, a system of systems, since each state was on its own.

With few exceptions, only *appellate* decisions and opinions were reported. Once in a while, newspapers covered important or lurid trials. A few trial transcripts appeared as pamphlets—this was especially true for juicy murder cases. A few especially succulent grand jury charges, by noted judges, were privately printed.[75] The best courtroom oratory was also published. In 1844, for example, an enterprising publisher brought forth the arguments by Horace Binney and Daniel Webster in the noted case of the will of Stephen Girard.[76]

A body of jurisprudential and practical literature also began to appear in the republic. Publishers brought out English works in "American editions"; often the editor added footnotes to bring these books up to date and to point out American innovations. A fourth American edition of Joseph Chitty's *Practical Treatise on the Law of Contracts* was published by J. C. Perkins in 1839, with "copious notes of American decisions to the present time." St. George Tucker, scholar and jurist of Virginia, published a five-volume Blackstone, in 1803. This was an important work in its own right; its thoughtful "Appendices" discussed government, law, and the jurisprudence of Virginia. John Reed published a *Pennsylvania Blackstone* in 1831, in three volumes. Reed retained the general plan of Blackstone (that "invaluable treasure of correct information, clothed in the most pure and classical style"),[77] and large chunks of the original (in quotation marks); but Reed also rewrote extensively and added much new material, in order to form "in a connected view, an elementary exposition of the entire law of Pennsylvania, common and statute." Gradually, more and more treatises were written that owed little or nothing to English models, except in the most general way.[78]

With some exceptions, American legal literature was (and is) rigorously practical. Books were written for the practicing lawyer. The goal was to help him earn a living, not to slake his intellectual curiosity. Most legal writers, and

---

[75] For example, Alexander Addison, *Charges to Grand Juries of the Counties of the Fifth Circuit in the State of Pennsylvania* (1800); an 1806 grand-jury charge of Chief Justice Parsons of Massachusetts is reprinted in 14 Am. Jurist 26 (1835).

[76] See *Entries, Catalogue of the Law School of Harvard University*, vol. II (1909), p. 1084.

[77] Preface, p. iv.

[78] See, in general, ch. xiii, "Early American Law Books," and ch. xx, "American Law Books, 1815–1910," in Charles Warren, *A History of the American Bar* (1911).

almost all members of the bar, studiously ignored systematic legal theory. Legal theory has never been a strong suit in common-law countries. There was a notable literature of political theory, and the law can lay some claim, not wholly farfetched, to the writings of Thomas Jefferson, James Wilson, and to the *Federalist Papers*. Some education in government was part of the general training of the better lawyers. Some general treatises on law did devote space to politics, natural law and the sources and aims of the law.[79] James Sullivan, in his *History of Land Titles in Massachusetts,* published in 1801 in Boston, saw fit to add to his book some "General Observations on the Nature of Laws in General, and those of the United States in particular."[80] The rest of the book was a conventional treatment of the American law of real property.

Even before 1800, some American lawyers struck out on their own. Zephaniah Swift published his *System of the Laws of Connecticut* in 1795–96. In 1810, he wrote a *Digest of the Law of Evidence in Civil and Criminal Cases* and a *Treatise on Bills of Exchange and Promissory Notes*. His books were informative and as readable as their subjects would allow. He propounded no grand theories; but was content, as he said in the *Evidence,* "to arrange the subject in a plain but systematic manner."[81] Swift was not afraid to criticize as well as arrange. For example, he attacked the American rule that the plaintiff (in discovery proceedings) was bound by the defendant's disclosures and might not contradict them. "This practice," he said, "must have been adopted at an early period, without due consideration."[82] Characteristically, Swift's criticism did not flow from any coherent ideology, or any theory of justice, clearly articulated. Criticism was always piecemeal and pragmatic. Later treatises had the same general features. Among the most popular or durable were the *Treatise on the Law of Private Corporations Aggregate* by Joseph K. Angell and Samuel Ames (1832); Simon Greenleaf's treatise on *Evidence* (1842); Henry Wheaton's *Elements of International Law* (1836); and Theodore Sedgwick's *Treatise on the Measure of Damages* (1847). A more general work was Timothy Walker's *Introduction to American Law* (1837). The book was designed for students, was enormously successful, and went through many editions. Nathan Dane's *General Abridgement and Digest of American Law* in eight volumes (1823–1824; a supplemental ninth volume was published in 1829), has already been mentioned. The "abridgement" was a loosely organized work; this had also been true of earlier "abridgements" published in England. As literature, Dane's work had little to recommend it. As one contemporary put it, Dane "had no graces of style, either native or borrowed; neither did he ever seek for any."[83] But lawyers bought the abridgement for their working libraries; and Dane made enough money to become a patron at Harvard.

---

[79] The first volume of Blackstone's *Commentaries* had also dealt with these general subjects.

[80] James Sullivan, *The History of Land Titles in Massachusetts* (1801), pp. 337–56, Emory Washburn (1800–1877), who became a judge, governor of Massachusetts, and then professor of law at Harvard, published a number of works in legal history, notably *Sketches of the Judicial History of Massachusetts, 1630–1775* (1840). On Washburn's career, see Robert M. Spector, "Emory Washburn: Conservator of the New England Legal Heritage," 22 Am. J. Legal Hist. 118 (1978).

[81] Zephaniah Swift, *Digest of the Law of Evidence in Civil and Criminal Cases* (1810), preface, p. x.

[82] *Ibid.,* p. 120.

[83] "Biographical Notice of the Honorable Nathan Dane," 14 Am. Jurist 62, 67–68 (1835).

Even less pretentious were works at the other end of the spectrum of generality—local practice manuals and helpful guides of one sort or another, for particular jurisdictions. William W. Henning's *The New Virginia Justice* (1795), a guide for justices of the peace, was one example of a common type of book, one that had many English and colonial ancestors. The book was vaguely designed for lay judges—perhaps for fledgling lawyers too. It quoted statutes, set out simple legal forms, and digested some relevant cases. Similar works appeared in other states. John E Grimké (1752–1819) wrote *The South Carolina Justice of the Peace* in 1788 and the *Duty of Executors and Administrators* in 1797. Esek Cowen wrote a *Treatise on the Civil Jurisdiction of Justices of the Peace in the State of New York* in 1821; this was a guide for the perplexed (lay) justice, perhaps also (Cowen hoped) "useful to the man of business," and even to Cowen's "brethren of the profession." Still lower on the literary scale were simple form books and guides for the laymen, works with the ubiquitous title *Every Man His Own Lawyer*, or books with names like the *Western Clerks' Assistant* or *The Business Man's Assistant*. This last was a compendium of "useful forms of legal instruments," together with tables of interest, currency information, "laws, instructions and forms necessary for obtaining a patent," and "agreements for constructing railroads." It claimed to have had sales well over 30,000 at the time it was reprinted in Boston in 1847 by one D. R. Butts, "assisted by an attorney." Richard Henry Dana (1815–1882), best known as the author of *Two Years Before the Mast* (1840), wrote a manual on the law of the sea called *The Seamen's Friend*, in 1841.

Legal periodicals were few, and even fewer had much of a life span.[84] Twelve periodicals were founded before 1830. *The American Law Journal and Miscellaneous Repository* was one of these, published in Philadelphia in 1808, but it expired within a decade. Most of its pages were devoted to case reports and digests of statutes; but there was also some secondary writing on legal subjects. Periodicals of this type competed weakly with the reports; they reprinted key decisions and other primary sources of law. Better reporting put most of them out of business. In 1810, only one periodical was actually in existence; this was also true in 1820. In 1830, there were five. *The American Jurist and Law Magazine* (1829–1842), founded by Willard Phillips, was one of the five. More pretentious and successful than most, it contained scholarly essays on points of law, case notes, historical notes, and question-and-answer materials. Prominent members of the Boston bar, including Joseph Story, often contributed to the journal.

By common consent, the two most significant figures in American legal literature in the first half of the nineteenth century were James Kent and Joseph Story. Both were erudite teachers and judges. Both had enormous reputations in their day. Both have since suffered a decline in prestige, and an irretrievable decline in their readership. In their day, they had greater reputations, at home and abroad, than any other legal scholars in America. No one on the Continent had ever heard of James Sullivan or Zephaniah Swift. But Joseph Story was a name that won respect even from continental jurists. And when Kent's *Commentaries* were published, George Bancroft said: "Now we know what American law is; we know it is a science."[85]

---

[84] On the periodicals of this period, see Maxwell Bloomfield, "Law vs. Politics: The Self-Image of the American Bar (1830–1860)," 12 Am. J. Legal Hist. 306, 309–19 (1968).

[85] Quoted in Warren, *op. cit.*, p. 543.

Joseph Story was born in 1779 and died in 1845.[86] In 1811, at the age of thirty-two, he was appointed to the United States Supreme Court. Contrary to expectations, since he was nominally a follower of Jefferson, he became John Marshall's strong right arm on the court. In 1829, he was named Dane professor at Harvard. He did not resign from the court (nor was he expected to). As Dane professor he wrote his series of *Commentaries,* published between 1831 and 1845—eleven volumes in all. He was a man of vast, almost ponderous erudition. According to his son,

> He was well versed in the classics of Greece and Rome. . . . He was a good historical scholar; and in the sciences and mechanic arts, he had attained to considerable proficiency. He was omnivorous of knowledge. . . . No legal work appeared, that he did not examine.[87]

Story was not one to wear his erudition lightly. His seminal work on the conflict of laws (1834) systematized a new field (at least new to the United States) out of virtually nothing. The work bristles with learned citations. One page (360) has three lines of French and six of Latin, and quotes from Louis Boullenois, Achille Rodemburg, P. Voet, J. Voet, C. d'Argentre, and U. Huberus, names that the typical American lawyer would find totally mysterious.

Story's erudition was not always so blatant. English-language jurists, in any event, had hardly touched the subject (conflict of laws). Learning did not interfere with the main line of Story's arguments, which usually proceeded clearly and stoutly, even gracefully at times. Story's erudition was organic; it involved his whole attitude toward law. He was a scholar and a traditionalist; he had reverence for the law and for the past. As he saw it, law was completely a product of history, of the historical dialectic of ideas. Without deep, total understanding of its history, it was foolhardy to try to interfere with the law and its modes of operation. Story fully agreed with Sir Edward Coke that the common law was reason personified; that it was not the parochial product of English or American experience, but a branch of the great, ancient tree of human wisdom. He was, in a sense, a legal pantheist. He saw divinity in Roman law as well as in common law. But for that very reason, he worshiped the law of his state and his nation; he saw them as connected with mighty currents of law that swept through human history. The precise development of one's own legal institutions was a specific adaptation of great general principles. In his treatise on *Equity Jurisprudence* (1835), Story asked:

> Whether it would or would not, be best to administer the whole of remedial justice in one Court, or in one class of Courts, without any separation or distinctions of suits, or of the form or modes of proceeding and granting relief.

We might have guessed that a lawyer from Massachusetts (which had no separate courts of equity), who had a profound knowledge of European law (where

[86] See Mortimer D. Schwartz and John C. Hogan, eds., *Joseph Story* (1959); Gerald T. Dunne, "Joseph Story: The Germinal Years," 75 Harv. L. Rev. 707 (1962); Gerald T. Dunne, *Justice Joseph Story and the Rise of the Supreme Court* (1970); R. Kent Newmyer, *Supreme Court Justice Joseph Story: Statesman of the Old Republic* (1985).

[87] Schwartz and Hogan, *op. cit.,* p. 202.

there was no distinction between law and equity) would have no trouble with the idea that law and equity should merge into a single whole.[88] But Story does not commit himself. He begins with a quote from Francis Bacon, to the effect that all nations have something more or less like equity, at least in the broad sense of the word. Bacon's view was that mixing law and equity in one and the same institution might be harmful. Six lines of Baconian Latin follow. Then Story refers to the civil law, where "the general, if not the universal, practice is the other way."

> But whether the one opinion, or the other, be most correct in theory, it is most probable, that the practical system, adopted by every nation, has been mainly influenced by the peculiarities of its own institutions, habits, and circumstances; and especially by the nature of its own jurisprudence, and the forms of its own remedial justice. . . . The question . . . never can be susceptible of any universal solution.[89]

James Kent, the second major figure of American legal literature, was born in New York in 1763. He went to Yale, then read law, and became a member of the New York bar in 1785. Like Story, Kent had a distinguished career on the bench. He served as chancellor of New York from 1814 to 1823. He was forced into premature retirement when the New York constitution of 1821 fixed a maximum age—sixty—for judges. In retirement, Kent wrote his masterpiece, *Commentaries on American Law,* in four volumes, published between 1826 and 1830. The bar received this work with enthusiasm from the moment it came out. Kent continued to bring out fresh editions until his death in 1847. The work was so popular that others prepared new editions, long after Kent's death. The twelfth edition (1873) was edited by young Oliver Wendell Holmes Jr.

Nobody reads Kent any more (or, for that matter, Story; or even Blackstone). Perry Miller found Kent a "bore"; he was repelled by Kent's "stiffly neoclassical rhetoric." Kent's "treatment of almost all areas" he thought "platitudinous."[90] But it is possible to read Kent and find him quite enjoyable. Kent intended his huge work to be the national Blackstone. To a considerable degree, he succeeded. Like Story, he was cautious and erudite. But he had little of Blackstone's smugness and self-satisfaction, and little of Story's stultifying pedantry. The style is at all points clear, the exposition transparent. Occasionally, Kent even turns a decent phrase or two. He had a sure and impressive grasp of the whole fabric of American law. His jurisprudential thought was not original or profound; but his attitude toward the living law was pragmatic, hard-boiled, and often shrewd.

Too much emphasis has been placed on Kent's conservatism. His biographer subtitled his book "A Study in Conservatism."[91] To be sure, Kent was not on the left, even in his day. He fought doggedly in New York against repeal of the property qualification for voters; he lost this fight. History is cruel to losers.

---

[88] Texas, too, had no separate court of equity; and the two forms were later merged in many states.

[89] Joseph Story, *Commentaries on Equity Jurisprudence,* vol. I (1836), pp. 34–36.

[90] Perry Miller, *The Legal Mind in America: From Independence to the Civil War* (1962), p. 92.

[91] John T. Horton, *James Kent, A Study in Conservatism, 1763–1847* (1939).

Kent was old-fashioned, in a sense, but he was never romantic or naive. He had no use for the obsolete, no aversion to productive change. In America, only a dyed-in-the-wool Tory would have been totally committed to the legal *status quo*. This would have meant denouncing American law in general, and defiling the American revolution. Kent was no Tory of this stamp. Throughout the text of his *Commentaries,* admiration for the American way of law emerges clearly. On dower, for example, he remarks that, "In this country, we are, happily, not very liable to be perplexed by such abstruse questions and artificial rules, which have encumbered the subject . . . in England to a grievous extent."[92] In general, he admired the common law: but he was not uncritical.[93]

Kent is often put in the camp of enemies of codification. He felt the law could not work, if it lost touch with living customs and habits, and codification, he feared, would be inflexible.[94] But he had praise for the American law of "crimes and punishments. . . . The law . . . has become quite simple in its principles, and concise and uniform in its details. Our criminal codes bear no kind of comparison with the complex and appalling catalogue of crimes and punishments . . . in England."[95] He had a deep respect for property rights, but a tremendous concern for enterprise as well. He loved law as an instrument both of security and of mobility. He had no sentimental attachment to tradition, if it interfered with the "stability and energy" of property. He wanted law to serve the cause of economic growth, to protect institutions that worked. What was conservative, perhaps, was his pessimism. He was profoundly skeptical about human nature. This made him suspicious of some kinds of reform; he often doubted whether mere tinkering with statutes could change entrenched patterns of human behavior. Many lawyers shared his belief. Many drew different political conclusions from similar premises. But there was no disputing Kent's clarity, his common sense, and his skill in expounding the law. The *Commentaries* deserved to be what they became from the moment of publication: a bestseller of American law.

[92] Kent, *Commentaries,* vol. IV (2nd ed., 1832), p. 52.
[93] See David W. Raack, " 'To Preserve the Best Fruits:' The Legal Thought of James Kent," 33 Am. J. Legal Hist. 320 (1989); see also Gregory Alexander, *Commodity and Propriety: Competing Visions of Property in American Legal Thought, 1776–1970* (1997), ch.5.
[94] David Raack, *op. cit.,* at 352–3.
[95] *Ibid.,* p. 544.

PART III

American Law to the
Close of the Nineteenth Century

CHAPTER 1

BLOOD AND GOLD: SOME MAIN THEMES
IN THE LAW IN THE LAST HALF OF
THE NINETEENTH CENTURY

THE NEW ERA

The years of the last half of the nineteenth century were crowded with events and evolutions. The most dramatic outer happening was the Civil War, when the country tore apart along the jagged line between North and South. Hundreds of thousands of soldiers died between 1861 and 1865, in this bloody, terrible war. The century also ended with a war—a "splendid little war," a war with little bloodshed, and no devastation; and when this war, with Spain, came to an end, the country, which had already swallowed up the Hawaiian islands, now owned an overseas empire.

In many ways, wars fundamentally disrupt the operation of the legal system. The Civil War was fought on American soil. It was an unusually violent episode, and it did unusual violence to the ordinary administration of justice. It was also a constitutional crisis: the Confederate states had declared themselves independent, and drafted their own constitution. The Civil War was followed by a period of martial law and domestic upheaval in the South. The war itself required enormous effort, both North and South—armies had to be raised and equipped; unprecedented problems had to be solved. This meant a dramatic escalation in the role of the central government. This, too, was reflected in many ways in every part of the law.

It is not hard to argue that American law, between 1850 and 1900, underwent revolutionary change. In many fields, the law or the practice looked entirely different at the end of this period, compared to the beginning. Change, then, was rapid and on a colossal scale; but it often came about because of the cumulative effect of tiny events, each one insignificant in itself. And some of these changes continued trends established earlier in the century.

Between 1850 and 1900, the population swelled; the cities grew enormously; the Far West was settled; the country became a major industrial power; there was a revolution in transportation and communication; overseas expansion began. The march of technology and science made life easier and healthier; at the same time, the social order became more complex, and the growing pains of modernity became more evident. New social cleavages developed. The North-South cleavage was bandaged over in the 1860s and 1870s. Whites took power again, and suppressed African Americans with a vengeance. When the blood of the Civil War dried, the Gilded Age began. This was the factory age, the age of money, the age of the robber barons, of capital and labor at war. And the frontier died. The pioneer, the frontier individualist, had been the American culture hero, free, self-reliant, unencumbered by the weakness and vices of city life. The frontier had been a symbol of an open society; opportunity was as unlimited as the sky. In 1893, Frederick Jackson Turner wrote his famous essay, "The Significance of the Frontier in American History." He argued for the powerful influence of the frontier on American character and institutions; but as he wrote the essay, Turner also announced that the frontier was no more—the frontier was dead.

What really passed was not the frontier, but the idea of the frontier. This inner sense, this *perception* of change, was perhaps one of the most important influences on American law in the late nineteenth century. Between 1776 and the Civil War, dominant public opinion believed in exuberant, never-ending growth, believed that resources were virtually unlimited, that there would be room and wealth for all. The theme of American law before 1850, in Willard Hurst's famous phrase, was the release of energy.[1] The ethos was: Develop the land; grow rich; a rising tide raises all boats. By 1900, if one can speak about so slippery a thing as dominant public opinion, that opinion saw a narrowing sky, a dead frontier, life as a struggle for position, competition as a zero-sum game, the economy as a pie to be divided, not a ladder stretching out beyond the horizon. By 1900 the theme was: Hold the line.[2]

Many trends, developments, and movements provide at least indirect evidence of some such basic change in legal culture. One piece of evidence was the increasing propensity of Americans to join together in organized interest groups. The United States became a "nation of joiners." De Tocqueville had already noted in his travels a magnificent flowering of clubs and societies in America. "Americans," he wrote, "of all ages, all stations in life, and all types of disposition are forever forming associations . . . religious, moral, serious, futile, very general and very limited, large and very minute."[3] But organizing, in the last half of the nineteenth century, was more than a matter of clubs and societies. Of key importance were groups that centered on economic interests—labor unions, industrial combines, farmers' organizations, occupational associations. These interest groups jockeyed for position and power in society. Their aspirations and their struggles shaped, molded, and dominated American law.

A group or association has two aspects: It defines some people in, and it defines some people out. People joined groups not simply for mutual help, but to

---

[1] J. Willard Hurst, *Law and the Conditions of Freedom in the Nineteenth-Century United States* (1956), ch. 1.

[2] We are speaking only of the United States, and only relatively. It was probably also true *after* 1870 that, compared to other societies and other periods, Americans were still a "people of plenty" and that the sense and reality of abundance profoundly shaped the national experience. David M. Potter, *People of Plenty* (1954). On the nature of law in this period in general, see Morton Keller, *Affairs of State: Public Life in Late 19th-Century America* (1977), ch. 9.

[3] Arthur Schlesinger, "Biography of a Nation of Joiners," 50 Am. Hist. Rev. 1 (1944); Alex de Tocqueville, *Democracy in America* (J. P. Mayer and M. Lerner, eds., 1966), p. 485.

exclude, to define an enemy, to make common cause against outsiders. Organization was a law of life, not merely because life was so complicated, but also because life seemed to be a competitive struggle, jungle warfare over limited resources, a game in which if railroads won, farmers lost; or if labor won, the bosses lost, and vice versa.

The consequences were fundamental. At first, this was a country wide open for immigration; by the end of the period, Congress had passed Chinese exclusion laws, and there were demands for literacy tests; importation of foreign workers was an issue; ultimately, in 1924, the country adopted a quota system, put limits on immigration, and controls on who could come.[4] Resources, in 1800, looked inexhaustible; by 1900, it seemed clear that natural resources could be chopped, burned, and eroded past recovery; the vast buffalo herds had been reduced to a pitiful remnant;[5] extinction threatened many of America's birds and animals; and a conservation movement was already under way. Government, in 1840, was boosting railroads, and farmers and merchants were desperate to have them; by the end of the century, railroads had become the octopus, the villains of industry, and there were frantic efforts to curb and control them. In general, before the Civil War, leaders of opinion looked at government, and law, as ways to unleash the capacity of the nation. After the war, the role of government began to change—slowly, and against great opposition—to a role more like that of regulator and trustee. Much of the opposition was couched in ideological terms. But the fundamental issues were not issues of ideology; they were issues of economic and political strength, issues of who gets what and when.

The Revolutionary generation had been suspicious of any governmental power. Government was necessary, but it had to be balanced and checked. Imbalance of power was still an issue in the Gilded Age. But now many people saw a power problem *outside* government, too: danger from the tyranny of trusts, or big business in general, or (conversely) from the "dangerous classes" or an angry urban proletariat. American optimism was balanced by a growing pessimism. America had been living a charmed life. But the charm was beginning to fade; and there was trouble ahead, unless people fought against moral and social decay.

None of the great changes in the last half of the century were sudden, none were quick, overnight shocks. There had been unions and farm groups and big companies before the Civil War. What changed was scope, scale, and intensity. The stakes were high. And in the economic struggle, law was an essential weapon. Classic English law was a law of and for an elite. In America, more and more people had a stake in the system. A broad and diverse middle class needed the law and used the law. They also had access to law. So did the rich and the powerful—even more so. There was a conscious struggle to control the law, to turn it to one's own uses. Each session of an American legislature was a cockpit of contention between interests. In the Midwest, in the early 1870s, the organized farmers had their day. Their legislation (the Granger laws) tried to restore

---

[4] Maldwyn A. Jones, *American Immigration* (1960), pp. 247–77; see Kitty Calavita, *U.S. Immigration Law and the Control of Labor, 1820–1924* (1984).

[5] Andrew C. Isenberg, *The Destruction of the Bison: an Environmental History, 1750–1920* (2000).

a balance, to take back power that the railroads and grain elevators had taken away when *they* were at the helm. Or so the farmers thought. Less dramatically, in the 1890s, there was a great rush to pass occupational licensing laws: for plumbers, barbers, horseshoers, lawyers, pharmacists, midwives, and nurses. These laws cemented (or tried to cement) the economic position of organized occupations. It is naive to think of these laws as hostile regulation, or as laws passed by legislators devoted to the "public interest."

Millions of people saw the struggle against industrial combines—the dreaded trusts—as part of a wider struggle for a "fair share" of the economy. It was not a struggle to keep free enterprise pure. It would be a mistake to read much economic theory into the passage of the Sherman Anti-Trust Act (1890). Small business, farmers, independent professionals, all feared the *power* of the trusts. Antitrust laws were an attempt to cut that power down to size. Regulation, trust-busting, licensing, labor legislation: all these were part of the same general battle of all against all, a battle for security, wealth, prestige, authority, for all the social goods. The power of the state—the law, in short—was both a means and an end in the battle: a way to achieve social goals, and a charter of the dominance of one set of norms and values. All these struggles, all these ideas and ideals, all these aspirations, were encoded in the growing volume of laws, rules, regulations, ordinances, and statutes. But underneath this mass of material, there was still an idea of individual autonomy. The farmer, for example, still valued his independence. But he sought help, subsidy, regulation, government intervention precisely for this reason: to counterbalance those mighty forces (railroads, for example) that held him in their grip and threatened that very independence.

The railroads were bound to fight back; and they had the money and the muscle to do so. Some sort of compromise was the typical outcome of contention in the halls of Congress and the state governments. No one group was ever absolute. Bargains were hammered out, some explicit, some not. Since power was not evenly distributed, some bargains were more one-sided than others. And some groups were so weak, so unorganized, or so oppressed that they never even got to the bargaining table. Among all the shouts and cries, there was hardly a whisper on behalf of black sharecroppers, or "tramps," or prisoners, or sexual minorities, or the desperately poor.

Different legal institutions were valuable in different ways and to different groups. Because there were so many power centers, so many little fiefdoms and bailiwicks, so much checking and balancing, groups could pick and choose among parts of the system for leverage and for veto power. In some states, labor had a relatively strong voice in the legislature; management, in reaction, might turn to the courts. Other groups and individuals also tried their hand at this game. Judicial review flowered in this period. It reached a stage—in the view of some critics—of bizarre excess. Some of the most prominent, or notorious, decisions had a conservative cast. Social Darwinism had its converts on the bench. This was also the period where courts ran railroads (in "equity receivership") and invented the labor injunction, a dreaded weapon against strikes and boycotts. Both of these showed how courts could flex their muscles. It was the period, too, in which lawyers themselves felt the urge to organize, to cement their positions, to move ahead. Lawyers and judges, like other social groups, invented fresh myths and disguises to protect their economic power—and their standing in society.

Since social change was so deep, legal culture changed along with it; the forces at work in society profoundly reworked every significant field of law. Some changes were big and overt. Other changes took place obscurely, in the dull brackish waters of the dockets. Each nugget of new doctrine had its point of origin in some concrete, living issue. However much judges liked to clothe doctrine in history and disguise it in the rhetoric of timeless values, doctrine was still at bottom flesh and blood, the flesh and blood of real arguments and struggles, over goods, positions, authority, and symbolic worth.

ORGANIC LAW

The Civil War was a profound constitutional crisis. The Union broke apart in 1861; but the Constitution survived. In fact, there was never really an attack on the *idea* of a Constitution. The Confederate states adopted their own constitution, suspiciously like the federal Constitution in many details. It provided for a Supreme Court; but this court in fact never sat, in fact was never organized.[6] The Confederate constitution itself died with the Confederacy. At the end of the war, only the old Constitution remained, bloody but unbowed.

The Constitution did not look much different, on paper, in 1900 from the way it looked in 1800. The major novelties were the three Civil War amendments—the thirteenth, fourteenth, and fifteenth. These were rammed down the throats of the Southern states. Ratification was so highhanded that well over a century later a few diehards still argued that the whole process was illegal, and even dreamed that these clauses might somehow go away. These amendments were important additions to the Constitution. They were meant to make victory in the Civil War a permanent feature of organic law. The Thirteenth Amendment abolished slavery. The Fifteenth Amendment guaranteed the right to vote to all citizens, regardless of "race, color, or previous condition of servitude." The Fourteenth Amendment has had the most marvelous career of the three. It was the longest of the amendments. Much of its language was tied to specific consequences of the Civil War. But some of the text was broad and sweeping. All persons born or naturalized in the United States were "citizens of the United States and of the State wherein they reside." No state could "abridge" their "privileges or immunities." No state could deprive any "person" of "life, liberty, or property, without due process of law"; nor could a state deny "to any person within its jurisdiction equal protection of the laws."

What was the "original understanding" of these clauses?[7] Were these clauses supposed to work some kind of fundamental change, in law, or in the balance of power between the states and the federal government? Were they meant to give Congress, or the courts, an (undefined) grant of power to supervise the social and economic activities of state and local governments? Were they intended to engraft some kind of laissez-faire theory onto the country's organic law? Or were they nothing more than expanded guarantees of rights for blacks who had

---

[6] William M. Robinson Jr., *Justice in Grey: A History of the Judicial System of the Confederate States of America* (1941), pp. 437–57; see, in general, Charles R. Lee Jr., *The Confederate Constitutions* (1963).

[7] See, in general, Harold M. Hyman and William M. Wiecek, *Equal Justice under Law: Constitutional Development, 1835–1875* (1982), ch. 11.

once been slaves? Whatever the draftsmen meant at the time, the words of the Fourteenth Amendment turned out to have marvelous powers of germination. The innocent words "due process" expanded—exploded might be a better word—into a whole cluster of consequences. "Equal protection of the laws" was another example of a handful of words that swelled in meaning almost magically. In the last two decades of the century, state courts, and some federal courts, used the due-process clause as a powerful weapon of policy. They used it as a textual hook, on which hung a sweeping assertion of authority: no less than the authority to strike down and decapitate offensive and unreasonable state laws. In some famous and infamous cases, the courts made the clause seem the very voice of economic reaction. If a state passes a regulatory law—a factory law, or a labor law of some sort—it does, in a sense, take away somebody's "liberty" or "property." They can no longer do something they could legally do before. If the law strikes a court as unfair or arbitrary or "unreasonable," the court can at least *say* that the statute deprived some people of a right without "due process of law."

The meaning of the Fourteenth Amendment was at issue in the famous *Slaughter-House* cases (1873).[8] Louisiana had passed a statute, in 1869, that gave a monopoly to the Crescent City Live-Stock Landing and Slaughter-House Company; Crescent City had the exclusive right to slaughter cattle in New Orleans. The law threatened the interests of other butchers, who wanted to do their own slaughtering; they attacked the law in court. A bare majority of the Supreme Court held what would have been self-evident two generations before: The Constitution said nothing that would prevent state regulation of slaughterhouses. (In reality, given the sanitary conditions of New Orleans, and the obnoxious nature of the regulated business, there was a lot to be said *for* the law.) Justice Bradley, however, dissented. He felt the law was "onerous, unreasonable, arbitrary and unjust." A law, he argued, that "prohibits a large class of citizens from . . . following a lawful employment previously adopted" deprives them of "liberty" and "property." Ergo, it violates the Fourteenth Amendment.

In time, Bradley's ideas won more converts on the Court. In *Chicago, Milwaukee, and St. Paul Railway Company v. Minnesota* (1890),[9] Minnesota had established a railroad and warehouse commission, and had given it power to fix freight rates. The commission ordered the railroad to reduce freight rates from three cents a gallon to not more than two and a half cents a gallon, on milk transported from Owatonna, Faribault, Dundas, Northfield, and Farmington, to St. Paul and Minneapolis. This half cent a gallon made legal history. The Supreme Court, speaking through Justice Samuel Blatchford, struck down the Minnesota statute that had set up the commission:

> The question of reasonableness of a rate of charge for transportation by a railroad company . . . is eminently a question for judicial investigation, requiring due process of law for its determination. If the company is deprived of the power of charging reasonable rates for the use of its property, and

[8] 16 Wall. 36 (1873); for a superb analysis of the background and meaning of this case, see Ronald M. Labbé and Jonathan Lurie, *The Slaughterhouse Cases: Reconstruction Politics and the 14th Amendment* (2003).

[9] 134 U.S. 418 (1890).

such deprivation takes place in the absence of an investigation by judicial machinery, it is deprived of the lawful use of its property, and thus, in substance and effect, of the property itself.[10]

Two aspects of the case are worth noting: first, the conservative tenor of the decision as far as the *economy* is concerned; second, its radical tenor as far as *judicial power* is concerned. Both aspects of the case drew fire from American progressives. Indeed, much of the American left was at war with the Supreme Court off and on until the later New Deal period. Undeniably, *some* major constitutional decisions, both state and federal, were both conservative in result and radical in method. It is easy to exaggerate the number of these decisions. On the whole, federal and state courts threw out only a small minority of the regulatory statutes that came before them. But this may not be an accurate measure of the impact of the courts. Fear of what the courts might do may possibly have had an effect on what legislatures passed and did not pass. The impact of doctrines of, say, liberty of contract, might have been more extensive than appears on the surface. It is impossible to say for sure.

Judicial review was a slow growth. After *Marbury v. Madison*, there was no clear-cut example of a case in which the Supreme Court dared to strike down an act of Congress until the *Dred Scott* case in 1857,[11] which overturned the Missouri Compromise. Northern opinion savaged this case. In the *Legal Tender* cases, the Court vacillated, now striking down a federal statute, then soon reversing itself.[12] In this affair, judicial review looked bad—it looked like nothing but politics. Still, the Melville W. Fuller court, between 1889 and 1899, did declare five federal acts unconstitutional, along with thirty-four state acts and four municipal ordinances.[13]

Heavy use of the Fourteenth Amendment made a mark only at the very end of the nineteenth century. In the first decade of the amendment, the U.S. Supreme Court decided only three cases, in the next decade, forty-six. After 1896, "the flood burst. Between that date and the end of the 1905 term of court, two hundred and ninety-seven cases were passed upon under the amendment. Substantially all of these were interpretations of the 'due process' and 'equal protection' clauses."[14] Whatever the impact of these cases, clearly the Supreme Court had developed a dangerous appetite for power. From then on,

[10] *Ibid.*, p. 458. Interestingly enough, Justice Bradley dissented in this case. One effect of the case was to weaken the authority of *Munn v. Illinois*, 94 U.S. 113 (1877), which had upheld an Illinois statute fixing maximum charges for grain elevators.

[11] *Dred Scott v. Sandford*, 60 U.S. 393 (1857). There is a huge literature on this case. See Stanley I. Kutler, ed., *The Dred Scott Decision: Law or Politics?* (1967); and Don Fehrenbacher, *The Dred Scott Case: Its Significance in American Law and Politics* (1978).

[12] *Hepburn v. Griswold*, 75 U.S. 603 (1870), which ruled that the Legal Tender Acts, passed during the Civil War, were invalid, was overruled in the *Legal Tender* cases, 79 U.S. 457 (1871).

[13] These figures are from William F. Swindler, *Court and Constitution in the 20th Century: The Old Legality, 1889–1932* (1969), p. 344. The worst was yet to come. The Edward D. White court invalidated twenty-two state statutes in a single year (1915); the William H. Taft court's finest hour was 1926, when twenty statutes fell. *Ibid.*, p. 345.

[14] Edward S. Corwin, *The Twilight of the Supreme Court: A History of Our Constitutional Theory* (1934), p. 77.

it was like a man-eating tiger; everyone in its vicinity had to cope with its awesome and lethal tastes.

STATE CONSTITUTIONS

The U.S. Constitution has been a steadfast rock—stable, rarely amended. The state constitutions were, on the whole, far more brittle. A few states have gone through their history with a single constitution (though usually with a great number of amendments). No state had a *coup d'etat*. But almost every state convened a constitutional convention, at least once in the period, to draft a new constitution. Sometimes, nothing came of all this effort. Illinois held a convention in Springfield, in 1862: Its proposal for a new constitution was massively rejected at the polls.[15] But particularly in the South, states constantly molted constitutions. Each Southern state typically had a Reconstruction constitution.[16] This came to be denounced as a carpetbag charter, when the worm turned, and a new constitution was then adopted. The Arkansas Constitution of 1868 restricted the right to vote or hold office of leaders of the "late rebellion." In 1874, the older elites were restored to power. A new constitution was adopted, which, among other things, dropped the elaborate franchise provisions of 1868. "[N]o power, civil or military," had the right "to prevent the free exercise of the right of suffrage"; and no law was to make the right to vote dependent on "previous registration of the elector's name" (Ark. Const. 1874, art. III, sec. 2; Ark. Const. 1868, art. VIII, secs. 3, 4, 5).

In constitution making, region differed from region, state from state; but some patterns did emerge. For one thing, state constitutions grew longer and longer. The constitutions also reflected deep distrust of legislatures. Even before 1850, there had been some restrictions and controls on the lawmaking branch. Now this trend grew stronger. Constitutions tried to prevent bad laws by enacting super laws, or, as it were, antilaws—that is, (constitutional) norms that precluded legislative norms.

Louisiana takes some sort of prize for fickleness and inflation. By 1847, it had already gone through two constitutions; before 1900 it added five more, in 1852, 1864, 1868, 1879, and 1898 (six, if one counts as a separate charter the revised constitution of 1861, which carried Louisiana out of the Union). The constitution of 1879 was already obese; that of 1898 was grotesque. It ran to 326 articles. It fixed the yearly salary of the governor at $5,000 and the lieutenant governor's pay at $1,500 (art. 68, art. 70). It put a limit on the "clerical expenses" of state officials; the state treasurer, for example, was not to spend more than $2,000 a year. Twenty-eight separate articles dealt with the government of the city and parish of New Orleans. The jurisdiction of state courts was specified to the last jot and tittle. One article created a "Railroad, Telephone, Telegraph, Steamboat

---

[15] Emil J. Verlie, ed., *Illinois Constitutions* (1919), p. xxvii.
[16] The Federal Reconstruction Acts—14 Stats. 428 (act of March 2, 1867), 15 Stats. 2 (act of March 23, 1867) and 15 Stats. 14 (act of July 19, 1867)—made restoration of civil government dependent on approval of the Fourteenth Amendment, and on adoption of a constitution, with full suffrage for blacks, ratified by Congress and by an electorate from which Confederate leaders were excluded.

and other Water Craft, and Sleeping Car Commission" (art. 283). This article then went on to enumerate the commission's powers, in elaborate detail. Buried in the mass of specifics were provisions of sharper bite—cutting off, in effect, the black man's right to vote. But the detail was so gross, and so stultifying, that the constitution was bound to fail, or, if it survived, to need constant bandaging through amendments. In fact, this constitution was amended twenty-six times before 1907. The Twenty-Fifth Amendment (1906) authorized, among other things, an appropriation for the Southern University at New Orleans, but of no more than $10,000 a year.

As before, the states freely borrowed constitutional clauses from each other. Important recent constitutions were popular models. In the West, the home state of most settlers was often used as a template. There were issues that always had to be thrashed out afresh. But settled matters, conventions, dead issues, and convenient ways of saying things were freely transferred from one place to another. A settled issue was not necessarily an unimportant one. For example, each new state copied a Bill of Rights from older states, in a fairly stereotyped form. More than half of the Oregon Constitution of 1859 can be traced to the Indiana Constitution of 1851. Other bits were based on clauses from the Iowa, Maine, Massachusetts, Michigan, Ohio, Illinois, Connecticut, Wisconsin, and Texas Constitutions. The Wisconsin Constitution of 1848 contained provisions against long-term agricultural leases and feudal tenures. These came from New York and reflected the Hudson Valley problem and the anti-rent disorders—problems that Wisconsin did not really have. The Nevada convention of 1864 was based on California patterns. This was no wonder, since all but two of the delegates had moved to Nevada from California.[17] The Colorado Constitution of 1876 was a model and a debating point for those Rocky Mountain states—Idaho, Wyoming, Montana—with similar problems of eminent domain, taxation of mining industries, and water rights.[18]

The trend toward curbing legislative power was strong in the 1850s. Rhode Island, by an amendment of 1854, took the pardoning power away from the legislature and gave it to the governor. State after state decided the legislature could meet less often and still get its business done. State after state put limits on legislative power—power to make law, or spend money, or both. Maryland, in 1851, increased the governor's term from one to four years. At the same time, the legislature—which met once every two years—was ordered not to establish lotteries, grant divorces, use the credit of the state for the special benefit of private persons or corporations, appropriate money for internal improvements, or contract debts for more than $100,000.[19] State constitutions became, on the whole, more rigid. The issue was fear of abuse, fear of corruption in the legislature, and the corrosive effects of great power.

Actual constitutional conventions were usually called to deal with major problems—railroad or bank regulation, or the issue of the suffrage. Another frequent bone of contention was reapportionment—an attempt to shift political

---

[17] *Official Report of the Debates and Proceedings in the Constitutional Convention of the State of Nevada, 1964* (1866), p. xvi.

[18] Gordon M. Bakken, "The Impact of the Colorado State Constitution on Rocky Mountain Constitution Making," 47 Colo. Magazine, No. 2, p. 152 (1970).

[19] Fletcher M. Green, *Constitutional Convention of the State of Iowa*, vol. I (1857), p. ii.

power from the east end of a state to the west, or from lowland to highland. The Iowa convention of 1857 was convened, after a referendum, partly because the "people of Iowa were anxious to repeal the restrictions upon banking."[20] Southern states held conventions after the Civil War to cement the results of the lost war. A decade later, southern states held conventions to undo *these* constitutions, and to make sure the white man won the peace. At the Nevada convention of 1864, there were furious debates about taxation of mines and mining enterprise. Some issues were so divisive that conventions turned them over to popular referendum. Wisconsin did this with a controversial banking provision in 1848; Colorado did so with the women's-suffrage issue, thirty years later.

The constitutions of the 1870s, in particular, stressed the idea of cutting down on the power of the legislature. The third Illinois Constitution, adopted in 1870, revamped the judiciary, increased the power of the governor, and put greater controls over legislative power. This constitution outlawed many kinds of "local or special laws":—no legislative divorces, no laws changing the rates of interest on money, no law providing for "the sale or mortgage of real estate belonging to minors or others under disability," no laws protecting fish or game, or granting "to any corporation, association, or individual the right to lay down railroad tracks," among other things. There were twenty-three of these prohibitions in all. Moreover, "in all other cases where a general law can be made applicable, no special law shall be enacted."[21] Later states copied this list, or similar lists, and often added new restrictions. In the 1889 constitution of North Dakota, the twenty-three specific prohibitions had grown to thirty-five.[22]

What was the point of these restrictions? Basically, it was fear of gross economic power, so gross it could buy and sell an upper and lower house. The Illinois Constitution of 1870 was the first of the midwestern Granger constitutions, and it reflected the fears and interests of Illinois' farmers. These constitutions typically called for tighter regulation of railroads and warehouses. The point was to set up some sort of countervailing force to balance the influence of the lobbies for industry. A special article (art. XIII) of the Illinois Constitution, seven sections long, dealt with regulation of grain elevators and warehouses. In another section, the general assembly was specifically told to "correct abuses and prevent unjust discrimination in the rates of freight and passenger tariffs on the different railroads in this State."[23] Nebraska, in 1875, was so bold as to empower its legislators to establish "maximum rates of charges" for railroads.[24] Legislatures were not to pass narrow, selfish laws, not to act as tools of railroads and banks. Constitutions in other parts of the country also mirrored this point of view. The Pennsylvania Constitution of 1873 took many a leaf from Illinois's book. It outlawed free passes on railroads, and attempted to work out a fair and rational way to tax these companies.[25]

---

[20] *Debates of the Constitutional Convention of the State of Iowa*, vol. I (1857), p. ii.

[21] Ill. Const., 1870, art. IV, sec. 22.

[22] N. Dak. Const., 1889, art. II, sec. 69.

[23] Ill. Const., 1870, art. XI, sec. 15.

[24] Neb. Const., 1875, art. XI, sec. 4.

[25] Rosalind L. Branning, *Pennsylvania Constitutional Development* (1960), pp. 101–5. Fear of the power of railroads lurked behind some apparently unrelated provisions of this constitution. One section, for example, denied to the legislature the power to authorize

Control of railroads was also an issue in California, in the brawling, bitter convention of 1878–1879.[26] A large and voluble bloc of radicals, the Kearneyites, whose leader was Dennis Kearney, clashed repeatedly with more moderate delegates. But the end result was not notably different from, say, the Illinois or Nebraska Constitution. One special feature, however, was the ruckus over Chinese labor and immigration. The debates were rabidly racist in tone. The Chinese, said one delegate, were "unfit for assimilation with people of our race"; to mix with them would produce a "despicable" hybrid, a "mongrel" of the most "detestable" sort "that has ever afflicted the earth." Fear of the Chinese impact on wage scales fueled the oratory. The Chinese

> have disorganized our labor system, brought thousands of our people to wretchedness and want, degraded labor to the standard of brute energy, poisoned the blood of our youth, and filled our streets with the rot of their decaying civilization. . . . [The Chinese] is a sinewy, shriveled human creature, whose muscles are as iron, whose sinews are like thongs, whose nerves are like steel wires, with a stomach case lined with brass; a creature who can toil sixteen hours of the twenty-four; who can live and grow fat on the refuse of any American laborer's table.[27]

A powerful, rotting sense of economic insecurity joined hands here with xenophobia and sexual paranoia. Only one or two delegates—spokesmen of industry—defended the Chinese. A proposed ban on "Asiatic coolieism" would have made it illegal for any corporation, or the state, to hire a Chinese to do any work whatsoever. That the convention showed any restraint at all was at least partly because the delegates were aware of the distant but powerful federal Constitution, which would have curbed the most extreme proposals.

New western states, in the late 1880s and the 1890s, drew up constitutions that in most regards fit the pattern of existing constitutions: bills of rights, two houses, a traditional judiciary. But they also reflected issues of the West including a suspicion of big business.[28] The Washington Constitution (1889) outlawed free railroad passes, and adjured the legislature to "pass laws establishing reasonable maximum rates of charge for the transportation of passengers and freight and to correct abuses." It prohibited corporations from issuing watered stock. Another provision of this constitution declared that "monopolies and trusts shall never be allowed in this state." Corporations were not to join together to fix prices, or limit output, or regulate "the transportation of any

"investment of trust funds by executors, administrators, guardians, or other trustees in the bonds or stock of any private corporation." The clause was proposed by George W. Biddle, a Philadelphia lawyer and delegate. Biddle charged that the legislature had once passed, in indecent haste, a law which in effect made it legal for fiduciaries to buy fourth mortgage bonds of the Pennsylvania Railroad. It was his desire—the convention agreed with him—that such things should never again be allowed to happen to the money of widows and orphans. See Lawrence M. Friedman, "The Dynastic Trust." 73 Yale L.J. 547, 562 (1964).

[26] Carl B. Swisher, *Motivation and Political Technique in the California Constitutional Convention, 1878–79* (1930).

[27] *Debates and Proceedings of the Constitutional Convention of the State of California*, vol. I (1880), pp. 632–33 (remarks of John F. Miller, December 9, 1878).

[28] On some of these constitutions, see Gordon Morris Bakken, *Rocky Mountain Constitution Making, 1850–1912* (1987).

product or commodity."[29] Particularly in the West, organized labor began to make a mark on fundamental law. Colorado, in 1876, ordered the general assembly to "provide by law for the proper ventilation of mines, the construction of escapement-shafts and other such appliances as may be necessary to protect the health and secure the safety of the workmen therein"; law was also to "prohibit the employment in the mines of children under twelve years of age."[30] Idaho, in 1889, also had a child labor provision in its Constitution: no child under fourteen was to work "in underground mines."[31] The New York Constitution of 1894 did not have clauses of this type. But it was forward-looking in other respects. For example, it called for a professional civil service. Appointments and promotions were to be made "according to merit and fitness to be ascertained, as far as practicable by [competitive] examinations." This constitution also showed an interest in conservation: the "forest preserve as now fixed by law . . . shall be forever kept as wild forest lands."[32]

A different kind of conservation pervaded southern constitutions in the last part of the century: conservation and preservation of white supremacy. The constitutions of the 1870s had taken away restraints on the right of "rebels" to vote. Later, when the North, the federal government, and the judiciary had lost any surviving taste for racial justice, the South proceeded to write white rule into their fundamental laws. As early as 1870, the Tennessee Constitution provided that no school aided by the state "shall allow white and negro children to be received as scholars together" (art. XI, sec. 12). This constitution also prohibited the "marriage of white persons with negroes, mulattoes, or persons of mixed blood, descended from a negro to the third generation" (art. XI, sec. 14). The South Carolina Constitution of 1895 had a similar clause. Ominously, this constitution contained a long paragraph on the penalties of lynching, including damages of "not less than two thousand dollars," assessed against the *county* in which the lynching took place (art. VI, sec. 6).[33] This provision, at least, was virtually a dead letter. Southern states also set out systematically to deprive the black man of his vote; and here they were effective indeed. The Mississippi Constitution of 1890 called for a poll tax of two dollars. It also required (after January 1, 1892) that "every elector shall . . . be able to read any section of the constitution of this State; or . . . be able to understand the same when read to him, or give a reasonable interpretation thereof" (art. 12, secs. 243, 244). Local officials would know how to make good use of these provisions. The Louisiana Constitution of 1898 contained a version of the famous grandfather clause: all males entitled to vote on January 21, 1867, their sons and grandsons, together with naturalized persons and their sons and grandsons, were excused from any onerous "educational or property qualification" in the constitution (art. 197, sec. 5). This meant that only blacks faced these hurdles, and local registrars knew exactly how to enforce these rules. The number of black

---

[29] Wash. Const., 1889, art. XII, secs. 18, 22. "The legislature shall pass laws," the text went on, "for the enforcement of this section," if necessary by declaring corporate charters forfeit.

[30] Colo. Const., 1876, art. XVI, sec. 2.

[31] Idaho Const., 1889, art. XIII, sec. 4.

[32] N.Y. Const., 1894, art. V, sec. 9; art. VII, sec. 7.

[33] The amount could be recovered by the county from those actually at fault.

voters declined in the Southern states, in some cases by 90 percent or more. Law and terror made a most effective combination.

The Utah Constitution of 1895, was, in a way, a summary of the state of the constitutional art toward the close of the century. It balanced the old and the borrowed against the particular and new. Bitter conflict between Mormon and gentile left its traces on provisions outlawing polygamy and plural marriages, in the emphasis placed on religious freedom and separation of church and state, in the abolition of the probate system through which, it was thought, Mormon elders helped perpetuate their power. Western radicalism was reflected in other provisions. The legislature was ordered to pass laws forbidding women and children from working in the mines, restricting convict labor, and preventing "political and commercial control of employees" by their masters (art. XVI, sec. 3). The new conservation motif was also present: "The legislature shall enact laws to prevent the destruction of and to preserve the forests on the lands of the State" (art. XVIII, sec. 1). Most of the rest of the constitution (bill of rights and all) was boiler plate. The constitution as a whole was long, detailed, and diffuse. It set out the salaries of seven state officials, headed by the governor at $2,000 a year.

All constitutions dragged along old matters from earlier versions, probably without giving the matter much thought. There was high turnover in constitutions; but many things did not change, or changed very little. Some constitutions (for example, Delaware's in 1897) went into great detail about the number, organization, and jurisdiction of courts, about civil procedure, and about appeal practice. Many provisions which seemed valuable when enacted became nuisances later on. In Michigan, for example, no general revision of the statute laws was constitutionally possible after 1850. Before 1850, a single man had revised the Michigan statutes; this struck many politicians in Michigan as too much concentration of power. Their solution to the problem lasted long after the problem had ended, and became a problem in its own right.[34] Michigan also found itself in acute political and financial embarrassment in the 1950s, partly because of a constitutional fossil—a provision left over from the nineteenth century that did not allow the state to contract any sizable debts.

Many of the new constitutions prohibited "local" legislation. At the time, this seemed like a good idea. It struck a blow at log-rolling, venality, inefficiency. Too many "local" laws, and the legal system might fragment into something like the Holy Roman Empire; every town and village would have its own rules. On the other hand, different parts of the state—and different cities—might *need* special legislation. Legislatures were not allowed to pass laws that applied to one town or city only; but they could put towns and cities into classes, and pass laws for all members of the class. This turned out to be an excellent loophole. The legislature could, and often did, set up classes that in fact had only a single member. In Wisconsin, under a law of 1893, cities with more than a population of 150,000 were cities of the first class. There was only one: Milwaukee.[35] More blatantly, Ohio passed an act in 1891, to authorize

---

[34] See W. L. Jenks, "History of Michigan Constitutional Provision Prohibiting a General Revision of the Laws," 19 Mich. L. Rev. 615 (1921).

[35] Laws Wis. 1893, ch. 312. See *State ex rel. Risch v. Board of Trustees of Policemen's Pension Fund*, 121 Wis. 44, 98 N.W. 954 (1904).

village councils to float improvement bonds; but the act was restricted to villages which, according to the 1880 or "any subsequent federal census," had a "population of not less than three thousand three hundred and nine nor greater than three thousand three hundred and twenty." Another act, of the same year, purported to "provide a more efficient government for cities having a population of not less than 33,000 and not more than 34,000 inhabitants." This kind of pinpointing, however, ran considerable risk in the courts.[36]

To say "big cities" (or "cities of the first class") rather than "Chicago" (a forbidden word) was hardly much of a burden to the states. But a constitutional limit on debt was not so easy to get around. Wisconsin could not float its own bonds; the constitution outlawed "public debts" except for "extra-ordinary expenditures," and even these could not exceed $100,000 (art. 8, sec. 6). Obviously, this limitation was hard to live with in the twentieth century. To get around the law, the state used various devices. Ultimately, it hit on the idea of the so-called "dummy corporation." Improvements, such as university dormitories, would be built by these corporations on state land; the corporation would lease the land from the state, then lease it right back to the state university. The university agreed to pay rent, including rent sufficient to retire the loan, which a bank had advanced for the purpose of financing the construction. The device was upheld in 1955 as valid, and not a violation of the state constitution.[37] But the debt probably carried higher than normal interest, because the state's own credit did not back it directly. The fact that these nuisance clauses survived meant that they had *some* lingering political strength or attractiveness—enough to allow a kind of veto power, since it took relatively little force to block any change in so rigid a structure as a state constitution. Moreover, legislators are sometimes shy about getting rid of some old or useless prohibition; they are afraid the public will misinterpret what they are doing. To repeal constitutional limits on debts might be like repealing the adultery laws; it looks like a vote in favor of sin. It was not until 1969 that Wisconsin pulled the teeth of this archaic limitation.[38] By this time, it was easier to vote in favor of sin as well.

Judicial review of state statutes was a rare, extraordinary event in 1850; it was a common occurrence in 1900. What happened in the state courts paralleled what happened in the federal courts. The taste for power was intoxicating to some state tribunals. The figures speak out loud and clear. In Virginia, for example, up to the outbreak of the Civil War, the state's high court had decided only thirty-five cases in which the constitutionality of a law or practice was questioned. Of these, the court declared only four unconstitutional. Between 1861 and 1875, "a dozen or more laws or practices were declared unconstitutional."[39] The Alabama supreme court went so far as to declare an entire

[36] Laws Ohio 1891, p. 74 (act of Mar. 4, 1891); Laws Ohio 1891, p. 77 (act of Mar. 5, 1891). A later version of this latter law, covering all cities with between 27,000 and 34,000 population, was upheld as sufficiently general in *State ex rel. Monnett v. Baker,* 55 Ohio St. 2, 44 N.E. 516 (1896).

[37] *State ex rel. Thomson v. Giesel,* 271 Wis. 15, 72 N.W. 2d 577 (1955).

[38] An amendment to art. 8, sec. 7, adopted in 1969, authorized the state to "contract public debt . . . to acquire, construct, develop . . . land, waters, property, highways, buildings . . . for public purposes," subject to certain limitations.

[39] Margaret V. Nelson, *A Study of Judicial Review in Virginia, 1789–1928* (1947), p. 54.

constitution, the constitution of 1865, null and void. But the real spurt in judicial review came at the end of the century. In Minnesota, the supreme court declared nineteen laws unconstitutional in the 1860s. Only thirteen statutes fell in the next fifteen years. But between 1885 and 1899, approximately seventy state statutes were struck down, with a decided bunching in the last few years of the century.[40] In Utah, between 1896 and 1899, twenty-two statutes were reviewed by the Utah supreme court. Exactly half of these were declared to be mere parchment and ink.[41]

It would be an exaggeration to call the state high court a third chamber of the legislature. But such a court was a force to be reckoned with. The explosion of judicial review did not rest on the due-process clause alone or on other clauses borrowed from federal law. Due-process cases grew voluminously; but many dramatic cases of judicial review turned on clauses with no federal counterpart at all. The wordy, excessive texts of the state constitutions were made to order for an aggressive judiciary. Technical controls over sloppy, corrupt, and selfish legislation were written into the constitutions; these too played into the hands of litigants and courts. In Indiana, for example, not a single statute in the nineteenth century failed because it violated the right of free speech. Eight statutes were void because they were *ex post facto* or because they were guilty of "impairing the obligation of contract." But eleven statutes could not meet the test of this clause: "No act shall ever be revised or amended by mere reference to its title, but the act revised, or section amended, shall be set forth and published at full length."[42]

Another fruitful clause for judicial review was the clause that provided that "Every act shall embrace but one subject . . . which subject shall be expressed in the title." The quoted version is from Indiana, and cost nine statutes their lives in the nineteenth century.[43] As early as 1798, as part of the backlash against the Yazoo shenanigans, the Georgia Constitution provided that no law might contain "any matter different from what is expressed in the title." The New Jersey Constitution of 1844 added to this a requirement that every law could "embrace but one object."[44] A year later, the Louisiana Constitution picked up the clause. It soon became quite common. It fit neatly into the general reform of legislative procedure. Reform of procedure went along with restrictions on the legislature's power that, as we saw, was a striking aspect of constitution-making in the last half of nineteenth century. The clause was by no means senseless. It was as Thomas Cooley explained,

> *first* to prevent *hodge-podge,* or "log-rolling" legislation; *second,* to prevent surprise or fraud upon the legislature by means of provisions in bills of which the titles gave no intimation, and which might therefore be overlooked and carelessly and unintentionally adopted; and *third,* to fairly

[40] These figures are from Oliver Field, "Unconstitutional Legislation in Minnesota," 35 Am. Pol. Science Rev. 898 (1941).

[41] Martin B. Hickman, "Judicial Review of Legislation in Utah," 4 Utah L. Rev. 50, 51 (1954).

[42] Ind. Const., 1851, art. IV, sec. 21. Oliver P. Field, "Unconstitutional Legislation in Indiana," 17 Ind. L.J. 101, 118, 121 (1941).

[43] Field, *op. cit*, p. 120.

[44] Ernst Freund, *Standards of American Legislation* (1917), pp. 154–55.

apprise the people . . . of the subjects of legislation that are being considered, in order that they may have the opportunity of being heard
thereon.[45]

Whether the clause actually had these effects is another question. It did give
the judiciary another meat ax to butcher legislation. It was general enough that
you could invoke it against almost *any* statute. In most instances, courts upheld
statutes attacked under the clause. But the power was there; it had to be reckoned with. Litigants could cite this text in hopes of delaying, thwarting, possibly even defeating legislation. Courts, too, could use the clause, in a number
of ways, to get at real abuses in the legislative process, or as a mere device to
further ends quite different from those that Cooley mentioned.

In *State v. Young*, an Indiana case of 1874, the legislature had passed an act
entitled, "An act to regulate the sale of intoxicating liquors, to provide against
evils resulting from any sale thereof, to furnish remedies for damages suffered
by any person in consequence of such sale, prescribing penalties, to repeal all
laws contravening the provisions of this act, and declaring an emergency." The
ninth section of the act imposed a five-dollar fine on any person "found in a
state of intoxication." This section, the court ruled, was unconstitutional. The
title "points to the sale of intoxicating liquors," not the "intemperate use of
such liquors." Hence, the punishment of drunks was a "matter not expressed in
the title," and the act was void.[46]

How courts made use of constitutional technicality is strikingly illustrated
by a bizarre West Virginia case, *Rachel Cutlip v. Sheriff of Calhoun County*.[47] The
county seat of Calhoun County had once been located at Arnoldsburg, West
Virginia. In 1867, the legislature passed "An Act locating the county seat of
Calhoun County." The first section of the act put the county seat "at the farm
of Simon P. Stump, on the Little Kanawha river." The third section of the act
authorized the board of supervisors "to sell any county property at Arnoldsburg." The next legislature unceremoniously repealed this act. Later, Rachel
Cutlip was indicted for murder in the circuit court of Calhoun County, sitting
at Arnoldsburg. She argued that she had been "unlawfully detained," that all
the proceedings were invalid, that there was in fact *no* county seat in Calhoun
County, and that the circuit court, meeting in what it imagined to be the
county seat, had no real power to indict her. It was not a frivolous argument.
The act of 1867 eliminated Arnoldsburg as county seat. The next statute got rid
of Simon Stump's farm as county seat. Through ignorance or inadvertence, it
failed to put the county seat back at Amoldsburg. The court had no wish to let
Rachel Cutlip go free. Nor did they want to leave Calhoun County in a state of
nature. They reached, in despair, for the West Virginia Constitution. The title
of the law in 1867 referred only to a change in the location of the county seat.
Another section authorized sale of county property at Arnoldsburg. This, said
the court, was a different "object" altogether, not expressed in the title of the
law. Hence, the statute of 1867 was never valid, and the county seat had never
really moved away from Arnoldsburg.

[45] Thomas M. Cooley, *A Treatise on Constitutional Limitations* (5th ed., 1883), p. 173.
[46] *State v. Young*, 47 Ind. 150 (1874).
[47] *Rachel Cutlip v. Sheriff of Calhoun County*, 3 W. Va. 588 (1869).

This can be described as crabbed, misbegotten, petty technicality. But it served, at least arguably, a useful purpose. It gave the court an excuse to intervene. The court patched up a job that the legislature had done badly; and sternly reminded the other branch that the court took standards of performance, as prescribed by the constitution, quite seriously.

This was perhaps a legitimate role. Far more controversial were cases that seemed to have a sinister goal: to "annex the principles of *laissez faire* capitalism to the Constitution and put them beyond reach of state legislative power."[48] An early and startling example, in which judicial review seemed to run wild, was *Wynehamer v. People* (New York, 1856).[49] New York had passed a prohibition law; *Wynehamer* declared it unconstitutional. The road to this surprising conclusion led through the due-process clause. The court pointed out that stocks of liquor had been, before the law was enacted, undeniably "property" in the "most absolute and unqualified sense." Afterward, "intoxicating liquors" were "laid under" the ban, "the right to sell them . . . denied, and their commercial value . . . thus annihilated." The law clearly took away some property rights; and it did it (said the court) without due process of law.

The precise holding of *Wynehamer* never won much of a following. Free enterprise in liquor, lottery tickets, gambling, and sex never appealed much to nineteenth-century judges. The case would be nothing more than a historical curiosity, except that its daring use of the due-process clause later became so popular. Activist courts fed on this kind of food, particularly after constitutional theorists made the idea intellectually respectable.[50] In *Matter of Jacobs* (1885),[51] New York had passed "An act to improve the public health, by prohibiting the manufacture of cigars and preparation of tobacco in any form, in tenement-houses." The law, said the New York Court of Appeals, in righteous indignation, "interferes with the profitable and free use of his property by the owner or lessee of a tenement-house who is a cigarmaker." It "trammels him in the application of his industry and the disposition of his labor, and thus, in a strictly legitimate sense, it arbitrarily deprives him of his property and of some portion of his personal liberty." Of course, the law claimed a valid purpose—to "improve the public health." But the court took it on itself to assess this claim; and was quite willing to dismiss it as a sham, even though the legislature, a coordinate branch of government, had in theory aired this question thoroughly and come to the opposite conclusion. The law had, in fact (said the court), "no relation whatever to the public health."

In *Godcharles v. Wigeman* (1886),[52] the Pennsylvania court confronted a statute, enacted in 1881, which required all businesses "engaged in mining coal, ore or other mineral . . . or manufacturing iron or steel . . . or any other kind of manufacturing," to pay their employees "at least once in each month," and to pay in cash or legal tender, not in "other paper." The law also aimed to

---

[48] Edwin Corwin, *The Twilight of the Supreme Court* (1934), p. 78. The quote actually referred to the work of the United States Supreme Court.

[49] 13 N.Y. 378 (1856).

[50] See, in general, Clyde Jacobs, *Law Writers and the Court* (1954); Arnold M. Paul, *Conservative Crisis and the Rule of Law: Attitudes of Bar and Bench, 1887–1895* (1960).

[51] 98 N.Y. 98 (1885).

[52] 113 Pa. St. 431, 6 Atl. 354 (1886).

prevent companies from overcharging in company stores.[53] Enraged, the court declared the statute "utterly unconstitutional and void." It was an attempt "to do what, in this country, cannot be done, that is, prevent persons who are *sui juris* from making their own contracts." The law was "an insulting attempt to put the laborer under a legislative tutelage, which is not only degrading to his manhood, but subversive of his rights as a citizen of the United States." The court did not bother to cite any clause, from either state or federal constitutions, in defense of its action. (Perhaps the "utterly void" was a self-evident category.) In *Ritchie v. People,* an emanation of the Illinois supreme court in 1895,[54] the law under attack limited the labor of women in "any factory or workshop" to eight hours a day and forty-eight hours a week. This, said the court, was a "purely arbitrary restriction upon the fundamental rights of the citizen to control his or her own time and faculties."

Perhaps the high-water mark of this mentality—certainly, the most famous example—was *Lochner v. New York,* decided by the Supreme Court in 1905.[55] New York had passed an elaborate labor law regulating work conditions in bakeries. Much of the law was concerned with sanitary conditions: bakeries had to be well ventilated; no animals (except cats) were allowed in any room where flour was stored, and so on. But the law also established maximum hours for bakery workers. No employee could be "required or permitted to work in a biscuit, bread or cake bakery or confectionery establishment more than sixty hours in any one week." This statute, said the court, in an opinion written by Justice Rufus Peckham, violated the due process clause of the Fourteenth Amendment. It interfered with the "liberty" of workers and their bosses. The case inspired Oliver Wendell Holmes Jr. to write one of his most famous dissents—the Constitution, he said, was "not intended to embody a particular economic theory." But the majority of the court either felt otherwise, or was unaware of the economic meaning of their decision.[56]

Cases such as these evoked, quite naturally, a good deal of liberal outrage. Labor groups and social reformers had struggled and lobbied for protective legislation. They learned soon enough that getting their programs enacted was winning a battle, not winning a war. Courts had the power to undo this legislation, sometimes on the flimsiest legal basis, sometimes, as in *Godcharles,* with apparently no basis at all. Out of these cases arose the reputation of courts as fortresses of dark and deep reaction. Conservatives took the opposite point of view; the courts were upholding the law, upholding the constitution, upholding liberty and justice for all. Conservatives felt that "unforeseen dangers" and hidden costs lurked in laws that may have seemed beneficial to some people,

[53] Laws Pa. 1881, No. 173, p. 147. One point of the law was to prevent companies from paying their workers in slips of paper redeemable only at the company store.

[54] 155 Ill. 98, 40 N.E. 454 (1895).

[55] 198 U.S. 45 (1905). See Paul Kens, *Judicial Power and Reform Politics: The Anatomy of Lochner v. New York* (1990). There is a large literature on Lochner; there is still a great deal of conflict over the meaning of the case, and its influence. See David E. Bernstein, "*Lochner* Era Revisionism, Revised: *Lochner* and the Origins of Fundamental Rights Constitutionalism," 92 Georgetown L.J. 1 (2003).

[56] John Marshall Harlan also dissented. He pointed out that bakery work was very unhealthy, that bakers died young, and that there was a genuine issue of health, which the majority had simply brushed aside.

but which actually ran "counter to the broad general basis of Anglo-Saxon civilization."[57] The court's reputation as a stronghold of reaction did not turn around decisively, among liberals, until the late 1930s, or perhaps even until the days of the Warren court, in the 1950s.

Neither the blame, nor the praise, for the courts in this period, and what they did, were entirely deserved. The cases mentioned, and some others, were indeed famous, horrible examples. But basically, the courts let the great wave of social legislation in the last two decades of the century pass undisturbed into law. A passion for "Lochnerism" was not evenly distributed across the country; the Illinois supreme court, for example, was exceptionally hostile to labor laws. Other state courts were more friendly. But what was general was the *threat*, the *possibility* of a contest in court. The test case became an accepted part of the life cycle of major legislation. This cloud, hanging over the fate of specific laws, or laws in general, was perhaps the main effect of judicial review.

What brought about this great increase in judicial activism? What aroused the sleeping dragon of judicial review? For one thing, the new constitutions almost invited judicial review. They were full of limitations on legislative power. Who would enforce these limitations? If not the courts, then nobody would. The high courts had reputations for integrity and craftsmanship. They had the technical skill to oversee legislation. They could criticize and correct draftsmanship and parliamentary process when these were shoddy or inconsistent. It was tempting for the courts to cross over from procedure to substance. Power invites the use of power. And the demand for it was there. When an interest group was thwarted in one branch of government, it naturally turned to another. If the legislatures were populist or Granger, there was always one last hope for a railroad or mining company: the courts. Much later, in the twentieth century, faced with hostile legislatures and city governments, entirely controlled by whites, the black civil rights movement turned once again to the courts.

Many nineteenth-century courts resisted the temptation to exercise their power. Other judges seemed to leap to the bait. Judges, after all, were members of the same society as the litigants. They shared the outlook that life was a zero-sum game. Their business was the rule of law, legal tradition, adjudication. Legislation, whatever its subject, was a threat to their primordial function, molding and declaring the law. Statutes were brute intrusions, local in scope, and often short-sighted in principle or effect. They interfered with a legal world that belonged, by right, to the judges. Particularly after 1870, judges may have seen themselves more and more as guardians of a precious and threatened tradition. The world about them seemed to be growing more turbulent and unsettled. The clash of interests, the warfare of classes, were threatening old and honored values. Barbarians were at the gates. The constitutions were instruments of caution, delay, and honest doubt, as the judges read them. They were texts that were meant to preserve reason and democratic society. They were, in the view of the judges, middle-class texts, embodying middle-class values, striving toward middle-class goals.

It oversimplifies matters to think of the courts as servants only of the rich and the powerful. In some blatant cases, to be sure, courts strengthened big

[57] Frederic J. Stimson, *Popular Law-Making* (1910), p. 238.

business at the expense of organized labor. Some judges believed that the unions were dangerous and un-American, and threatened the balance of society. But the judges were, by and large, also afraid of the sinister un-American trusts. The constitution, as they interpreted it, did not prevent the licensing of barbers, plumbers, doctors, and lawyers; did not prevent farmers, artisans, and professional men from uniting; and posed no obstacle to strong, solid middle-class groups. Some courts were suspicious of labor legislation. But they generally allowed legislatures to outlaw oleomargarine, in the interests of America's farmers, and they supported campaigns against prostitution, lottery tickets, alcohol, and vice. Their taste for power was general, but the prejudices of the judges—predominantly old-American, conservative, middle-class—determined where and how the effects of the power would fall.

The worst thing about this power was that it was randomly and irresponsibly exercised. It could be neither predicted nor controlled. Judges did not declare *all* social laws unconstitutional, only a small minority of them. Nor were *all* statutes challenged in court. The court had no way to pull cases onto its docket. A private litigant had to be willing to finance the case. Even then, the court might evade or avoid the constitutional issue. Judicial review was slow at best. One scholar studied 172 Indiana cases in which the court declared laws unconstitutional. On average, the statutes were slightly under five years old when they were voided. In fifty cases, the statutes had been on the books for more than five years. Seventeen statutes were struck down after ten years or more of apparent validity; in one case the elapsed time was forty-two years.[58] The impact, as we said, is unclear: perhaps more in blocking or preventing legislation, than in killing it. No doubt courts struck down some laws that were foolish or worse. On the whole, did judicial review do more harm than good? For the nineteenth century, many people would say, yes, more harm. But there were many, at the time, who would emphatically say, more good.

The West

At the end of the century, the frontier—according to Frederick Jackson Turner, and others—was officially dead. In 1850, by all accounts, it had been very much alive. After the Mexican War (1848), the United States extorted from Mexico another gigantic domain, sparsely settled, to add to a land area the Louisiana purchase had already enormously expanded. A steady stream of settlers made the dangerous crossing from East to West. Some were looking for land to farm in Oregon; some were Mormons making the trek to the promised land in Utah; many, after gold was discovered in California, were looking for wealth and adventure.

At the end of the rainbow was California, a beautiful land, mild and fertile, on the brink of the ocean. But California was not an easy destination. It was a kind of land island, sealed off from the rest of the country by a parched,

---

[58] Oliver P. Field, "Unconstitutional Legislation in Indiana," 17 Ind. L.J. 101, 108–9 (1941). The figures include cases up to 1935. But the conclusions hold reasonably well for the nineteenth century. Field cites a case in 1879, voiding a statute of 1861; a case in 1880 overturned a law of 1855. *Ibid.*, pp. 116–17.

blazing desert, and by a line of high, jagged mountains crowned with perpetual snow. The trek to the West, in the middle of the century, before the transcontinental railroad was completed, is one of the great sagas of American history. Thousands of settlers—men, women, children—made the slow crawl from the pale of society to the far off rim of the Pacific. Many died along the way.

For most of the distance, they were in a kind of legal no-man's land—outside the reach of law and order. Yet, the behavior of people on the wagon trains and in the emigration companies was surprisingly lawful in behavior. There are accounts of the way these travelers administered "crude but effective justice on their overland journeys"; in some cases, they had "courts," and conducted "trials," following procedures as regular as conditions permitted. Lafayette Tate, who murdered a man on the overland trail, in June 1852, just east of the Rockies, was caught, tried before a makeshift judge, with a makeshift prosecutor, defense counsel, and jury, convicted, sentenced, and quickly hanged.[59] Sometimes, the wagon trains used banishment as a punishment.[60] John Phillip Reid has shown the power and pervasiveness of ideas of due process and legitimacy on the overland trial. He has also shown that the pioneers had remarkable respect for certain postulates of living law in other areas as well. Out in the trackless wilderness, hundreds of miles from police, courts, and judges, they followed and honored fundamental rules of property and contract, almost as if they were still in Illinois or Massachusetts.[61]

This is no paradox. The travelers were transients; they were moving along a path they had never gone on before, and would never travel again. As Reid points out, under these circumstances, and in the midst of strangers, there was hardly an opportunity for new "customs" to develop. The "law" that prevailed was "the taught, learned, accepted customs" of the people; it was part of the baggage they brought with them.[62] Even more important, perhaps, was the influence of peers and of destinations. Behind them, in the East, were courts, judges, police; ahead of them, at the end of the road, more courts, judges and police. They were in an interlude, a halfway point, between two points of law. Under these conditions, old habits do not break; old fears of punishment and revenge do not snap in two.

When the pioneers reached the promised land, they confronted once more a kind of legal frontier. The United States had already absorbed millions of acres of land governed more or less by civil law—in Florida, Texas, and the Mississippi Valley. Now came California, New Mexico, Arizona, and the rest of the territory that had once been, at least nominally, under the civil law of Mexico. The struggle between the two legal systems was brief. The outcome was never much in doubt. American lawyers and judges poured in along with other American settlers. In some places, Utah, for example, Spanish-Mexican law

---

[59] David J. Langum, "Pioneer Justice on the Overland Trails," 5 Western Hist. Q. 420 (1974).

[60] A careful study of the criminal justice system of the overland travelers is John Phillip Reid, *Policing the Elephant: Crime, Punishment, and Social Behavior on the Overland Trail* (1997).

[61] John Phillip Reid, *Law for the Elephant: Property and Social Behavior on the Overland Trail* (1980).

[62] Reid, *Law for the Elephant*, p. 362; Reid, *Policing the Elephant*, p. 233.

never really had any force. The immigrants were Americans, who "tacitly" brought common law with them to an empty country.[63]

In California, however, and particularly in New Mexico, substantial numbers of Spanish-speaking residents lived and worked. In New Mexico, judges frequently cited civil law, sometimes approvingly.[64] California was not so close a case. The gold rush brought a cataclysmic inflow of population. The new residents were mostly Americans, all totally ignorant of civil law. Spanish-Mexican law had its spokesmen—members of the existing San Francisco bar vigorously defended it; but the more influential majority felt otherwise. The "Common Law of England" (insofar as not "repugnant" to the United States Constitution and the laws and constitution of California) was formally adopted in 1850 as the "rule of decision in all the Courts of this State."[65]

The civil law left some legacies behind. One was a muddled collection of land grants, which plagued the land law of California and New Mexico for decades. The civil law tradition influenced many specific doctrines and institutions—the community property system, for example.[66] Civil law background may have inclined western states to be hospitable to codes and procedural reform, but there were other, more cogent explanations. Idaho was a code state, too, without the slightest shadow of civil-law influence.

Many traits of the older frontier periods were repeated in the far West: the mixture of old and new in the substantive law; the code-making habit; a legal profession composed mostly of young hustlers. The nature of the land itself made legal change sometimes almost a necessity. Some western states—Texas and California—were rich in resources and had some excellent farmland. But most of the West was bleak, arid, and mountainous. Landscape strikingly affected water and resource law. The common law rule for water was the so-called doctrine of riparian rights. Every landowner, in other words, along the banks of a river, had an equal right to take water; and no one owner could take so much that the stock was depleted. This made sense in rainy England and in the rainy parts of the United States—the South, East, and Middle West. The West was desert or semi-desert. Western states quite generally discarded the doctrine of riparian rights. They replaced it with the prior appropriation doctrine, which was more or less first-come-first-served. There was never enough water to give every landowner who fronted on a river an equal shake. The western doctrine "encouraged entrepreneurs to scramble for water, quickly construct works, and apply the asset to the industry of the region." It "recognized the environmental limitations of the water supply" and "gave certainty to users in terms of title."[67] Significantly, only the wholly arid states bought the new

---

[63] See the remarks of Emerson, J., in *First National Bank of Utah v. Kinner*, 1 Utah 100, 106–7 (1873).

[64] In *Chavez v. McKnight*, 1 Gilsdersleeve (N.M.) 147, 150–51 (1857), the judge cited "Escriche" writing "under the head[ing] of Mujer Casada" (married woman), a reference to the work of Joaquin Escriche y Martin (1784–1847); the judge spoke of the "humane regard" and "wise and just policy" of the civil law toward married women.

[65] Laws Cal. 1850, ch. 95.

[66] On the civil law legacy, see also above, Part II, ch. 2.

[67] Gordon M. Bakken, *The Development of Law on the Rocky Mountain Frontier: Civil Law and Society, 1850–1912* (1983), p. 71.

doctrine completely. California and Texas, with their double climates, had mixed systems of water law, too.[68] As Donald Pisani has reminded us, landscape and climate do not make law; what made western land law was not rain or lack of rain, but concrete economic interests. And, as he points out, the prior appropriation doctrine was "one of the greatest nineteenth-century legal subsidies," since it allowed the water on public lands to be "taken for free."[69]

Two famous western institutions were the miners' codes and the vigilante movement. The miners' codes were little bodies of law adopted as binding customs in western mining camps. The miners' courts and codes resembled, in a way, the claim clubs of the Midwest. These were organizations of squatters who banded together to control the outcomes of public land auctions. The claim clubs also drew up rules and procedures, to govern, record, and document the land claims of their members. Such clubs flourished in Wisconsin in the late 1830s, in Iowa through the 1840s. There is some slight evidence of connection between the claim clubs, miners' groups in the Midwest (near Galena, Illinois, and in southwestern Wisconsin), and the miners' codes of the Far West. These miners' codes were at least as old as the California gold rush, and were also found in other parts of the West—in Gregory Diggings (Colorado) in 1859, in the Black Hills of Dakota Territory in the 1870s, and in Nevada. Many codes were reduced to written form. They set up rough but workable rules and processes for recording claims, for deciding whose claim was first, for settling disputes among claimants, and for enforcing decisions of miners' "courts." The Gregory Diggings ruled itself through its little legal system two years before Colorado Territory was formally organized. The mining code served the function, well known in American legal history, of a makeshift judicial and political order, in places that were settled before ordinary government institutions arrived. Other mining districts copied the Gregory code. As business increased, the "judges" handled a wide range of disputes. The Colorado territorial legislature in 1861 and 1862 ratified, with a broad sweep, the local claims and judgments these informal courts had rendered. A squatter, or his assignee, or any person whose title rested on a "decree or execution, of any of the so-called Provisional Government Courts, People's or Miners' Courts," could bring actions of trespass, ejectment, and forcible detainer (except against the U.S. government itself.)[70]

The vigilante movement was more flamboyant, and at times more sinister. This was not exclusively a western phenomenon; but the West was the vigilante heartland. The two San Francisco Vigilance Committees, of 1851 and 1856, were early and famous examples.[71] These committees were "businessmen's revolutions" directed against corrupt, inept local government. Those who supported the vigilantes considered themselves decent citizens, using self-help, taking the

---

[68] See Walter P. Webb, *The Great Plains* (1931), pp. 431–52; Betty E. Dobkins, *The Spanish Element in Texas Water Law* (1959).

[69] Donald J. Pisani, *Water, Land, and Law in the West* (1996), p. 36.

[70] Ovando J. Hollister, *The Mines of Colorado* (1867), pp. 75ff.; pp. 359–63; Laws Terr. Colo. 1861, p. 249; Laws Terr. Colo. 1862, p. 69.

[71] See Kevin J. Mullen, *Let Justice Be Done: Crime and Politics in Early San Francisco* (1989); Robert M. Senkewicz, *Vigilantes in Gold Rush San Francisco* (1985); Lawrence M. Friedman, *Crime and Punishment in American History* (1993), pp. 179–87.

law into their own hands, striking out against violence, corruption, and misrule in San Francisco. The city was turbulent, anarchic; gold-hungry hordes had swollen its population. The first committee began its work by arresting a "desperate character" named Jenkins. He was given a kind of trial, convicted and hanged from a heavy wooden beam on a small adobe house left over from the Mexican period.[72] Other bad characters were simply told to get out of town. The Second Vigilance Committee was more powerful than the first. It even presumed to seize and try David Terry, a justice of the California supreme court. The Committee hanged some unsavory local characters; it defied local, state, and national governments; in general, it held San Francisco in its despotic grip. "The safety of the people," said the *San Francisco Bulletin,* which spoke for the vigilantes, "is above all law."[73] The "trials" run by the Vigilance Committees were highly irregular; but they never quite descended to barbarism, and a lawyer would not have found them totally alien and unrecognizable. Best of all, the movement in San Francisco had the decency to die a natural death.

Vigilante justice was older than the gold rush; but San Francisco gave it new life and inspired imitation. There were twenty-seven vigilance committees in California in the 1850s. In 1858, there was a vigilance committee in Carson Valley, Nevada. There were vigilantes in Denver, Colorado, from 1854 to 1861. Wyoming had vigilantes too—beginning with "two lethal movements in the wild railroad boomtowns of Cheyenne and Laramie," in 1868–1869.[74]

In the 1860s, vigilantes flourished in Montana. In the words of their chronicler, Thomas Dimsdale, they brought "swift and terrible retribution" to the "ruffians and marauders" of the Territory. This included men like Captain J. A. Slade, a hell-raiser and disturber of the peace; the vigilantes of Virginia City seized him, condemned him to death, and strung him up on the gate posts of a corral while his wife raced madly on her horse from their ranch to try (in vain) to save him.[75] The Montana vigilantes were, in general, a rougher bunch than the boys of San Francisco. They had less regard for the niceties of trial. Sometimes they avenged crimes never committed or hanged the wrong man by mistake. For the sake of law and order, vigilantes were quite willing to put up with a bit of slippage in places where, as Dimsdale put it, regular justice was "powerless as well as blind."

The vigilantes, as this quotation makes clear, felt that formal justice was too slow; or, in other cases, formal justice was an invited guest who had not yet arrived. Willard Hurst has suggested that vigilantism was not really a "pre-law phenomenon," a "groping towards the creation of legal institutions," but more accurately a "reaction against the corruption, weakness, or delays"

---

[72] Alan Valentine, *Vigilante Justice* (1956), pp. 54–58. On American vigilante movements in general, see Richard Maxwell Brown, "The American Vigilante Tradition," in Hugh D. Graham and Ted R. Gurr, eds., *Violence in America: Historical and Comparative Perspectives* (1969), p. 154.

[73] Quoted in A. Russell Buchanan, *David S. Terry of California* (1956), p. 43.

[74] Brown, *op. cit.,* pp. 162–63.

[75] Thomas Dimsdale, *The Vigilantes of Montana, or Popular Justice in the Rocky Mountains* (1953), p. 13, 16, 194ff. The book was originally published in 1866. Dimsdale was an Englishman who arrived in Virginia City in 1863 and taught school. He was the first superintendent of public instruction in Montana Territory. *Ibid.,* intro., ix.

of the established legal order.[76] From one point of view, the vigilantes did no more than fill a vacuum. They put together a makeshift criminal justice system, just as the miners put together a makeshift property code, in accordance with their customs and needs. In Payette, Idaho, the Vigilance Committee drew up a constitution, and bylaws; it gave the accused the right to be tried by a jury of seven. In other cases, undesirables were strung up, or driven out of town, in a much less formal way.

There are two sides to the vigilante story. The vigilantes were often not really reacting to a legal vacuum; they were fighting against a legal order that was simply not to their liking. Not just weak justice, but justice that (in the eyes of elites) was reaching the wrong results. Dimsdale complains about juries who refused to convict, who showed too much "sympathy" for offenders; he whines about drunkenness, the use of "strong language on every occasion," about persistent Sabbath-breaking, and the pervasive presence of vice: "women of easy virtue" were seen "promenading" about, catering to the inordinate desire of the miners "for novelty and excitement."[77] Vigilante justice in Montana was not blind, neutral justice; it was the code of Montana's elites. It was "popular justice," in one sense, but deeply antipopular as well. This had also been true of the San Francisco vigilantes; and of many other western movements.

In any event, social control, like nature, abhors a vacuum. The "respectable" citizens—the majority, perhaps?—in western towns were not really lawless. Quite to the contrary, people were accustomed to the rule of law and order; these were the same people who, on the wagon trains described by Reid, paid scrupulous attention to property and contract. They were Americans; they were unwilling to tolerate too sharp a break in social continuity; they reacted against formal law that was too slow, or too corrupt, for their purposes, or that had fallen into the hands of people they did not trust or respect. Vigilantes were the products of a culture clash, in small communities; communities made up of transients and strangers, precarious, new, untried, and untested communities.

There may have been another, subtler factor at work. The men of the mob had the satisfaction, grim though it was, of a form of justice that was literally in their own hardened hands; they pulled on the ropes themselves; they were judges, juries, and executioners. Regular courts were not so swift, nor so dramatic. To many people, punishment is twice as satisfying when it works with white-hot immediacy, when the arguments, doubts, procedures, and technicalities of a trial do not disturb its naked emotions. Vigilante justice, in this sense, had affinities on the one hand to the public trials and executions of colonial justice; and in a darker, bloodier sense, to lynch law in the South.

Today, we see rather clearly that vigilante justice had its bloodthirsty side, and its antidemocratic side. But in its day, it evoked considerable enthusiasm. To men like Dimsdale, this was genuine folk justice; it was an Anglo-Saxon inheritance as old as Teutonic folkmoots, surviving in the new lands of the West. The historian H. H. Bancroft advanced this view, with great passion. Frederick Jackson Turner, too, pictured the westerner as nature's democrat, a noble breed, dying along with the buffalo, the Indian, the whooping crane.

[76] Willard Hurst, "The Uses of Law in Four 'Colonial' States of the American Union," 1945 Wis. L. Rev. 577, 585.

[77] Dimsdale, op. cit., pp. 9, 12.

Certainly, public opinion did not condemn vigilantes. William J. McConnell, "captain" of the Payette, Idaho, vigilantes, became a senator and a governor of that state. Dr. John E. Osborne, of Rawlins, Wyoming, who had skinned Big Nose George Parrott, an outlaw, and made a pair of shoes out of part of the skin, became governor of his state, too.[78]

Benjamin Shambaugh, writing in 1902, had romanticized, in a similar way, the Midwestern claim clubs. He saw them as "fountains of that spirit of western democracy which permeated the social and political life of America during the 19th century."[79] Modern scholarship has been more hardheaded, much less lyrical about the claim clubs.[80] It sees them not as fountains of western democracy, but as little cartels. They protected early claimants from later, more innocent arrivals; they used force and guile to keep down the price of government land. Miners' groups, too, were less like little democracies, than like little guilds; they were protectionist and exclusionary to the core. The drama of the landscape, the romance of the West, has a certain tendency to overwhelm the facts. The land was harsh and empty, to be sure. It opened up space for outlaws and rogues, and the occasional genuine free spirit. Some people slipped free of civilization, which they discarded somewhere in the vastness of the West. But many settlers wanted something quite different: security, law and order, traditional if transplanted values. Out West, people wanted freedom; but they also wanted subsidies for railroads; and since the sky was so unyielding, and drops of water so scarce, they wanted tax money and programs, to help them irrigate their lands. What traveled west, more important than form, was the general legal culture, the general ways of thinking about law. The West had its peculiarities; but it was, after all, America, not some primitive throwback to ancient democracy. Its root ideology was the same as in the rest of the country. Organize or die: This was a theme of American law, East and West, in the last half of the nineteenth century, in every area and arena of life.

[78] Brown, *Strain of Violence*, at 44.

[79] Benjamin F. Shambaugh, *History of the Constitution of Iowa* (1902), p. 65. He added that the members were men who "in the silent forest, in the broad prairies, in the deep blue sky, in the sentinels of the night, in the sunshine and in the storm, in the rosy dawn . . . must have seen and felt the Infinite," a rather florid way of saying that the pioneers rarely went to church. *Ibid.*, p. 24.

[80] See, for example, Allan G. Bogue, "The Iowa Claim Clubs: Symbol and Substance," 45 Miss. Valley Hist. Rev. 231 (1958).

CHAPTER 2

JUDGES AND COURTS: 1850–1900

THE JUDGES

After the middle of the century, the popular election of judges was more and more accepted as normal. Every state that entered the Union after 1846 provided that voters would elect some or all of their judges. The California Constitution of 1849 made the whole system elective, from the supreme court down to justices of the peace. In the year 1850 alone, seven states amended their laws to provide for more popular election of judges. In 1850, both the Michigan and Pennsylvania supreme courts turned elective.[1] In 1853, the voters of Tennessee approved a constitutional amendment; and from 1854 on, Tennessee abolished what one newspaper called a "relic of by-gone days," of "repressive monarchy"; the supreme court of Tennessee became an elective body.[2]

In only a few states were judges still appointed—Maine and Massachusetts, for example. Federal judges had life appointments. In Connecticut, the legislature chose judges, but, in 1856, the term of office was changed to eight years; before that, judges had served during "good behavior," which meant, in practice, for life. Traffic did not go entirely one way, that is, toward the elective principle. Some southern states returned to the appointive system during Reconstruction. Texas, between 1866 and 1876, went from an elective to an appointive supreme court and back. Mississippi abolished its elected high court of errors and appeals under the constitution of 1868. The new supreme court consisted of three judges appointed by the governor and confirmed by the senate. Not until 1910 did Mississippi return to an elective system.

What difference did the elective system make? It is hard to tell. Were elected judges more political than appointed ones? Were their decisions any different? In theory, yes. In practice, perhaps not. In the first place, elections were not as partisan as say, the election of governors. There had been fears that the elective principle would destroy the independence of judges. Hostile politicians could grub about in the law reports, find an unpopular decision, and use it to ruin a sitting judge. But as it turned out, most sitting judges who ran again won again,

---

[1] Evan Haynes, *The Selection and Tenure of Judges* (1944), pp. 100, 116, 127; Kermit L. Hall, "The Judiciary on Trial: State Constitutional Reform and the Rise of an Elected Judiciary, 1846–1860," 45 The Historian 337 (1983).

[2] Timothy S. Huebner, "Judicial Independence in an Age of Democracy: Sectionalism, and War, 1835–1865," in James W. Ely Jr., ed., *A History of the Tennessee Supreme Court* (2002), pp. 61, 85–88.

regardless of party. There were a few striking exceptions. Michigan's most illustrious judge, Thomas M. Cooley, lost his race for reelection in 1885. The main reason was a "Democratic Deluge" that "submerge[d] even the mountain tops"; labor was opposed to him, and his close connection with the railroads cost him dearly with some voters.[3] The wrath of the Grangers, in 1873, drove Chief Justice Charles B. Lawrence of Illinois out of office.[4] In 1861, in the court of appeals of Maryland, Chief Judge John C. Legrand and Judge William B. Tuck, two judges who ran on a ticket of stern loyalty to the Union, were defeated.[5]

The elective principle certainly helped undermine the idea that only law-trained people had the right to decide how cases should turn out; and that the only tools that belonged in the tool shed of judges were strictly legal tools. The elective principle at least seemed to give the public the power to assess decisions and decision making. The defeat of Chief Justice Lawrence looked like a case where "a herd of dissatisfied farmers have put an ignorant demagogue in the seat of an able and upright judge."[6] An editor of the *Albany Law Journal* wrote those words in 1873. At this time there was a new—futile—attempt to overturn the elective principle in New York. The writer added:

> The people are the worst possible judges of those qualifications essential to a good judge. They could select an orator, an advocate or a debater, as his qualities are palpable and salient; but the qualities of a judge are peculiar, and are seldom appreciated by cursory and general notice. That uncommon, recondite and difficult learning; that power and turn of mind and cast of character called the "judicial," are likely to go unremarked by the nonprofessional observer. To him the effective advocate seems best fitted to fill the judicial office; but experience has proved that the best advocate is not likely to prove the best judge, as the two functions exact diverse qualifications.
>
> But the chief objection to an elective judiciary is the effect it has upon the office; its dignity; its just weight; its hold upon the general confidence.
>
> While it may be true that the selection of candidates for judges is generally left to the legal members of the [party] conventions, it is equally true that these legal members are not usually such a class of lawyers as is competent to do anything so important as the making of a judge—young, ambitious men, more familiar with the management of ward caucuses or town meetings than with the conduct of a cause in court.

The claim, then, was that elections would debase the office of judgeship. People would elect hacks, not jurists. Certainly, there was no shortage of incompetent judges. Election, at least, helped in the withering away of impeachment. There were few removals after 1850, except for good and sufficient (that is, non-political) cause. Federal impeachment proceedings were exceedingly rare. The House judiciary committee recommended impeachment for John C. Watrous,

---

[3] Lewis G. Vander Velde, "Thomas McIntyre Cooley," in Earl D. Babst and Lewis G. Vander Velde, eds., *Michigan and the Cleveland Era* (1948), pp. 77, 92.

[4] James E. Babb, "The Supreme Court of Illinois," 3 Green Bag 217, 234 (1891).

[5] Carroll T. Bond, *The Court of Appeals of Maryland, A History* (1928), p. 159. This at least spared Maryland the embarrassment of fighting on the Union side with secessionist judges. To a certain extent, the federal government was in this fix. Chief Justice Taney, author of the *Dred Scott* decision, lived until 1864. His wartime conduct was a thorn in Lincoln's side.

[6] 8 Albany L.J. 18 (July 5, 1873).

district judge for Texas, in 1853. Supposedly, he practiced law while on the bench, and heard cases in which he had a financial stake. No action was taken against him. Between 1872 and 1875, four federal judges were investigated on grounds of irregular conduct; all of them resigned under fire.[7] Few state judges, too, were ever impeached. In 1852, Chief Justice Levi Hubbell of Wisconsin was accused of a wide range of offenses, partiality, improper conduct of trials, and bribe taking. Hubbell was irascible and partisan. There was evidence of "shoddy standards" in his work, but the senators seemed to demand (and did not get) extraordinary proofs of misconduct; Hubbell was not removed.[8]

In the Gilded Age, in the fetid atmosphere of the Tweed ring, scandal enveloped the lower New York bench, along with the rest of the government of New York City. "The stink of our state judiciary is growing too strongly ammoniac and hippuric for endurance," wrote George Templeton Strong in his diary. The courtroom stench was one of the reasons why New York lawyers formed the New York City Bar Association, in 1870—they were anxious to do something about the problem. George G. Barnard and Albert Cardozo, justices of the supreme court of New York were under suspicion.[9] Cardozo, whose son Benjamin ultimately redeemed the family name, handed out receiverships to relatives and friends. Strong wrote: "I think Nature meant Cardozo to sweep the court room, not to preside in it. . . . He would look more natural in the dock of the Sessions than on the Bench of the Supreme Court."[10] In 1872, charges of impeachment were drawn up against Barnard and Cardozo, accusing them of venality and "gross abuse of . . . powers." Cardozo resigned; Barnard was impeached and forever barred from public office.[11]

A more dubious use of the threat of impeachment drove "carpetbag" judges off the bench in the South, after the collapse of Reconstruction. In South Carolina, the one black supreme court justice, Jonathan Jasper Wright, was harassed from his post in 1877. Despite the smoke of propaganda, the charges against these southern judges have never been fully proven. The carpetbag judges, black and white, suffered the fate of history's losers. They were probably no more corrupt than southern white judges of the same time and culture. Moses Walker, from Ohio, served with some distinction on the Texas supreme court.[12] Albion W. Tourgée,[13] a carpetbag judge, was able and strong-minded. He drew on his experience to write a series of novels about race and the South. One of these books, A Fool's Errand (1879), was sensationally successful. Tourgée fought against, and wrote against, the Ku Klux Klan. His liberal views on black-white relationships were far ahead of his times. Late in his life,

---

[7] Joseph Borkin, The Corrupt Judge (1962), pp. 201, 253–54.

[8] Alfons J. Beitzinger, Edward G. Ryan, Lion of the Law (1960), pp. 32–39.

[9] The "supreme court" in New York, despite its name, is not very supreme: it is the basic trial court. The highest court in New York is called the Court of Appeals.

[10] A. Nevins and M. Thomas, eds., The Diary of George Templeton Strong, vol. 4 (1952), pp. 264–65.

[11] History of the Bench and Bar of New York, vol. I (1897), p. 199.

[12] James R. Norvell, "The Reconstruction Courts of Texas, 1867–1873," 62 Southwestern Historical Q. 141, 160–61 (1958).

[13] His career is described in Otto H. Olsen, Carpetbagger's Crusade: The Life of Albion Winegar Tourgée (1965); see also Richard Nelson Current, Those Terrible Carpetbaggers (1988), pp. 16–50, pp. 193–213.

he worked on the briefs in *Plessy v. Ferguson*, before the case went up to the Supreme Court. Tourgée was a truly exceptional person. But he demonstrates that we cannot condemn carpetbag judges wholesale, as stupid and corrupt.

Territorial judges were also at times controversial figures. Territorial jobs were strictly appointive; they were patronage jobs. Eager claimants badgered president after president for these positions. Some of these judges were hacks, ill-paid, ill-prepared for their jobs, almost invariably nonresidents, whose sole claim to office was success in finding a strong patron. There were judges who hardly had the decency to set foot in their jurisdictions; or who resigned after a short term in office, going after more lucrative game. Some, like the wandering frontier lawyers, took jobs in one territory after another. Samuel Chipman Parks of Illinois, for example, was a judge in three territories in a row: Idaho (1863), New Mexico (1878), and Wyoming (1882).[14]

A territorial judgeship was not a genteel post. It was worlds away from the dignity and tradition of the East. For good reasons or bad, local residents were often hostile to these judges. One hears about "sage-brush districting"—legislatures that carved up judicial districts in such a way as to exile an unpopular judge, sending him to the most barren wastelands. The legislature of New Mexico, according to the *Santa Fe Post,* sent Chief Justice Joseph G. Palen in 1872 "to the hottest locality over which they had jurisdiction," regretting only "that their jurisdiction is so limited."[15]

A few territorial judges became famous or notorious. Kirby Benedict served as chief justice of New Mexico Territory in the 1850s and 1860s. The territorial secretary of state complained, in a letter to President Lincoln, that Benedict "visits the gambling Hells and drinking saloons and with a swagger and bluster defiles his judicial robes." Perhaps he was driven to drink. As a new judge, in 1854, Benedict had to ride circuit through a vast desert country; hostile tribesmen hid in its arid canyons. Benedict gave as good as he got: he denounced his accuser as a "moronic maniac, an egotist, a general mischief-maker."[16] Lincoln reappointed Benedict; but President Johnson removed him from office as a drunkard. Benedict practiced law for a while, then was disbarred.

Most territorial judges were neither incompetent nor eccentric. Their worst sin, perhaps, was politics. Federal judges served for life; but justices of territorial supreme courts were appointed for four-year terms and could be fired at any time. This thrust territorial courts into "perhaps the wildest political scramble in American history." The phrase is from John Guice's study of these courts in three western states. But Guice's research led him to respect these Rocky Mountain judges: on the whole, they were "civilizers,

---

[14] Earl S. Pomeroy, *The Territories and the United States, 1861–1890* (1947), p. 136.

[15] *Ibid.,* p. 57. For other examples of "sage-brushing," see John D. W. Guice, *The Rocky Mountain Bench: The Territorial Supreme Courts of Colorado, Montana, and Wyoming, 1861–1890* (1972), pp. 59, 81.

[16] Letter of W. F. M. Arny to Lincoln, Dec. 19, 1863; letter of Benedict to Edward Bates, Jan. 3, 1864, printed in Aurora Hunt, *Kirby Benedict, Frontier Federal Judge* (1961), pp. 165, 166. On the administration of justice in New Mexico Territory, see Arie W. Poldervaart, *Black-Robed Justice* (1948).

builders, and makers of law who contributed substantially to the territories and to the nation as a whole."[17]

Western judges, at least in some locations, needed to be made of tougher stuff than eastern judges. The barren, empty lands bred or harbored a certain amount of lawlessness; the vast anonymity of the West attracted killers and thieves. This was the world of Judge Isaac Parker, the hanging judge, first appointed by President Grant, who ruled over the Western Arkansas District from his seat in Fort Smith. Parker's realm included Indian Territory. It was the "land of the six-shooter." Parker did not shrink from stern duty, as he saw it. He began his regime of law and order by condemning six men, who were hanged on September 3, 1875. Before his career was over, in 1896, seventy-nine men, many of them Native Americans or blacks, had put on the black hood and mounted the gallows. Superstitious men imagined that their restless ghosts haunted the gallows at night.[18]

The U.S. Supreme Court stood at the apex of the federal pyramid, at the farthest remove from Judge Parker.[19] The justices were all lawyers, and were on the whole, men of some stature. Justices in the late nineteenth-century were, on average, older men at the time of their appointment, than the justices earlier in the century. Young countries tend toward young leaders; older, more settled countries gravitate toward older leaders. Joseph Story was thirty-two when he was named to the Court; William Strong, of Pennsylvania, confirmed in 1870 at the age of sixty-two, was the first man over sixty ever appointed.[20] State courts were the main source of Supreme Court justices throughout the nineteenth century. Some justices, however, had some federal service in their background; Robert Trimble, appointed in 1826, was the first justice whose prior experience was in the lower federal courts.[21] David J. Brewer was a justice on the Kansas supreme court; he was appointed to the federal Eighth Circuit in 1884; and from there to the U.S. Supreme Court in 1889.[22]

Appointments to the U.S. Supreme Court were as political as those to any lower court. Presidents appointed old cronies, famous politicians, deserving members of the cabinet; they appointed men because they were southern or

[17] Guice, *The Rocky Mountain Bench*, pp. 48, 152. John Wunder's study of the justices of the peace in the Pacific Northwest in the late nineteenth century comes to a similar conclusion: "Justices have been regarded . . . as uneducated, illiterate personages with no legal training and no access to written law; in fact, local judges were sometimes learned in the law." They were a stable, established group; and Wunder feels they did a creditable job on the whole. John R. Wunder, *Inferior Courts, Superior Justice: A History of the Justices of the Peace on the Northwest Frontier, 1853–1889* (1979), p. 170; on the territorial justices of Nebraska, see Michael W. Homer, "The Territorial Judiciary: An Overview of the Nebraska Experience, 1854–1867," 63 Nebraska History 349 (1982).

[18] On Parker see Glenn Shirley, *Law West of Fort Smith: A History of Frontier Justice in the Indian Territory, 1834–1896* (1957); J. Gladston Emery, *Court of the Damned* (1959).

[19] The literature on the justices is, quite naturally, much richer than the literature on other judges. See, in general, Melvin Urofsky, ed., *The Supreme Court Justices: a Biographical Dictionary* (1994).

[20] Cortez A. M. Ewing, *The Judges of the Supreme Court, 1789–1937* (1938), pp. 66ff.

[21] *Ibid.*, p. 100.

[22] His career is recounted in Michael J. Brodhead, *David J. Brewer: The Life of a Supreme Court Justice, 1837–1910* (1994).

because they were not southern, as the case might be. The Senate occasionally rejected nominees. President Grant nominated Attorney General E. R. Hoar. He had made many enemies in the Senate, and in the end, he was turned down.[23] Most nominations, however, went through Congress unopposed or with little opposition. Judges of the Supreme Court, almost always men with political backgrounds, occasionally kept their taste for politics. David Davis, for example, was a serious contender for the presidential nomination in 1872; he was elected to the Senate from Illinois in 1877. Chief Justice Chase lusted after the Democratic nomination for president in 1872. Joseph P. Bradley cast the deciding vote on the Electoral Commission that made Rutherford B. Hayes president in 1877.[24]

Despite the politics of the appointment process, the judges' own nose for politics, and numerous errors of ambition and prejudice, the Supreme Court had an unblemished record of honesty; and it crafted its decisions with care. The prestige of the Court ebbed and flowed, but the long-range trend, as far as one can tell, rose fairly steadily. The judges had tremendous responsibilities—and life tenure. They were totally independent of regime changes, and this may have enhanced their prestige. The justices survived the *Dred Scott* case, the *Civil Rights* cases, the *Slaughterhouse* case, the *Income Tax* case, and the thousand crises, large and small, that rained in upon their heads. Their written opinions were always sleekly professional. Increasingly, people who never read a single opinion—the general public—seemed to accept the Court as powerful and legitimate. The Supreme Court by 1900 was more than a century old. It was a fixed and traditional part of an accepted system of government.

The canonization of the Supreme Court, or at least its beatification, was not a fast or automatic process. *Dred Scott* brought about relatively dark days. Yet, at some point—roughly, in the last half of the century—the prestige of the Court reached a high, perhaps unassailable, point.[25] In some ways, the Court was an accurate mirror of upper middle-class thought. The Court vacillated between nationalism and localism; so did the country. And the Court fulfilled a valuable function, or seemed to: it was the forum for sober second thoughts. The

[23] Grant next tried Edwin Stanton, who had been a member of Lincoln's cabinet. Stanton was confirmed but dropped dead before assuming office. Two other Grant nominees were withdrawn because of newspaper outcry or senatorial reluctance.

[24] The election of 1876 was inconclusive. Both parties claimed victory. Samuel Tilden, the Democratic candidate, was one electoral vote short of a majority; but electoral votes from Florida, Louisiana, South Carolina, and Oregon were in dispute. To settle the matter, Congress established an Electoral Commission of fifteen, five Senators, five Representatives, and five judges. Seven of these were Democrats, seven Republicans; the fifth judge was to be chosen by the other four judges. Bradley was named as this fifth judge. The Commission gave Rutherford Hayes all the disputed electoral votes, 8–7. Bradley cast the deciding vote, and Hayes was elected. Bradley always claimed his work on the Electoral Commission was as pure as the driven snow: "So far as I am capable of judging my own motives, I did not allow political, that is, party, considerations to have any weight whatever in forming my conclusions." Quoted in Charles Fairman, "Mr. Justice Bradley," in Allison Dunham and Philip Kurland, eds., *Mr. Justice* (1956), pp. 69, 83.

[25] On the parallel (and related) deification of the Constitution, see Michael Kammen, *A Machine that Would Go of Itself: The Constitution in American Culture* (1986).

Supreme Court (and many of the state high courts) could smooth over the wide swings of public opinion. At least this was a plausible claim.

The size of the Court fluctuated until the 1870s. Lincoln and Grant were not above a genteel sort of court packing. Lincoln did some unpacking, too; he allowed three seats to stay empty. John A. Campbell, of Alabama, had resigned at the outbreak of the Civil War; two other justices had died, one a southerner. Lincoln held the seats open until it was clear that the South would not voluntarily return.[26] During the Civil War, Congress by law gave the Court its largest size: ten members. Congress played with these numbers during Reconstruction, at the time of its tug of war with President Andrew Johnson. A law of 1866 provided that no vacancy should be filled until the membership of the Court sank to seven. This looked suspiciously like a plan to keep Andrew Johnson from making any appointments.[27] During the Grant administration, finally, Congress settled on what has since become the sacred number—nine.

The Court was, in general, blessed by a number of long tenures. This gave the Court great stability, perhaps too much. Unionists considered Taney's long life a great curse (he was eighty-seven when he died in 1864). Robert C. Grier stayed on the Court three years after a stroke had left him somewhat befuddled. It is not certain that he understood, in late 1869, which side he was voting for in the *Legal Tender* cases. A delegation from the Court, including Stephen Field, asked him gently to resign. Field's own career was the longest in the nineteenth century. He was appointed in 1863, at the age of forty-six, and he served for thirty-four years, eight months, and twenty days. In his last year on the Court, in 1897, his mind failed noticeably; at times he lapsed into a "dull stupor." He wrote no majority opinions at all in the 1890s; all he wrote were cranky concurrences and dissents. Justice John Marshall Harlan was sent to talk to Field, and persuade him to resign. Harlan reminded Field of his mission to Grier; but Field, his eyes "blazing with the old fire of youth,   burst out; . . . 'a dirtier day's work I never did in my life.'"[28]

When Taney finally died, in 1864, Lincoln appointed a new chief justice, Salmon P. Chase, once Lincoln's secretary of the treasury. But Chase disappointed the administration. In 1870, in the first *Legal Tender* case, the Court held that paper-money laws, passed during the Civil War, were beyond the power of Congress. Ironically, Chief Justice Chase repudiated, as part of the majority, a policy that Secretary Chase had devised. But Secretary Chase was a Republican in the midst of a war; Chief Justice Chase in 1870 was a Democrat, confronting problems of peacetime finance. One year later, after two new appointments by President Grant, the decision was reversed. This incident shows how much control a president could exercise over the Supreme Court—and also how little. The power to appoint was balanced by the fact that a justice, once confirmed, was free to go his own way, and often did.

[26] Carl B. Swisher, *Stephen J. Field, Craftsman of the Law* (1930), p. 113.

[27] See Stanley I. Kutler, *Judicial Power and Reconstruction Politics* (1968), pp. 48ff.

[28] Quoted in Swisher, *op. cit.*, p. 444; see also John S. Goff, "Old Age and the Supreme Court," 4 Am. J. Legal Hist. 95 (1960); Owen M. Fiss, *Troubled Beginnings of the Modern State, 1888–1910* (History of the Supreme Court of the United States, Volume VIII, 1993), pp. 29–30.

No chief justice in the later nineteenth century had the stature of Marshall or Taney; but there were outstanding men on the Court: Samuel Miller, Stephen Field (in his better days), Joseph Bradley, and John Marshall Harlan. They served during the first golden age of judicial review. It was a period in which high court judges seized a share of the power of government. They found the basis for this power in the Constitution, especially in the new Fourteenth Amendment. In this period, open disagreement on the Court became more visible. Dissenting opinions had been rare on the Marshall court. Peter V. Daniel (1841–1860) was a persistent dissenter. He wrote almost as many dissents and special concurrences as majority opinions.[29] Samuel F. Miller dissented 159 times, and Stephen Field 233 times, in the course of their careers. John Marshall Harlan (1877–1911) entered no less than 380 dissents.[30]

Still, most cases were unanimous—unlike cases on the Warren, Burger, and Rehnquist courts. In Volume 71 of the *United States Reports,* there are more than seventy cases from the December term 1866. All except five were unanimous. In one of these five, the famous case of *Ex parte Milligan,* there was a separate opinion; but it was a concurrence, that is, it agreed with the *result* of the others, though not with their reasons. In four cases, there were dissents; but in two of these, the dissenters merely recorded the fact that they dissented; they did not file a written disagreement. On the other hand, the famous test oath cases, *Cummings v. Missouri* and *Ex parte Garland,* elicited a long dissent.[31]

It was the difficult, controversial cases that drew blood, in other words. Most of the work of the Supreme Court did not consist of such cases. A slowly increasing minority turned on constitutional issues. A growing number arose under important federal statutes. But the Supreme Court still decided many cases about commercial contracts, or land titles, or the like. These were often "diversity" cases—that is, cases that were in the federal system because the parties were citizens of different states. Typically, there was no federal issue in them at all. The sheer burden of work rose constantly. Between 1862 and 1866, the Court handed down 240 decisions; between 1886 and 1890, 1,125—and this without relief from the arduous burden of traveling on circuit.[32] The leisurely days of long oral argument were over. They could allocate only so much time to each case—even to important cases.

By common consent, by 1870 some sort of golden age of state judges had ended. A golden age is a tricky concept. Lemuel Shaw, John Bannister Gibson, John Marshall, and others, were great judges: builders of institutions and molders of doctrine; moreover, they had style.

The next generation of judges approached their craft somewhat differently. Ironically, in this age of silver or brass, there was a lot of controversy about

---

[29] John P. Frank, *Justice Daniel Dissenting* (1964), p. 181; on Brewer, see n. 22 supra; on Harlan, see Linda Przybyszewski, *The Republic According to John Marshall Harlan* (1999).

[30] Karl ZoBell, "Division of Opinion in the Supreme Court: A History of Judicial Disintegration," 44 Cornell L.Q. 186, 199 (1959).

[31] Dissents and concurrences rose with the years; but rather slowly. Volume 168, reporting cases from October term, 1897, contained forty-three unanimous opinions, five dissents and two concurrences without opinion; and only three dissents and one concurrence with separate written opinion.

[32] Charles Fairman, *Mr. Justice Miller and the Supreme Court, 1862–1890* (1939), p. 62.

judicial activism. There were, to be sure, state judges after 1860 who were famous men in their day, men of vigor and imagination: Edward Ryan of Wisconsin, Oliver Wendell Holmes Jr., of Massachusetts, Thomas Cooley of Michigan. Holmes was perhaps the greatest master of the English language ever to sit on an American court. But his fame rests mostly on his later career, as a justice of the U.S. Supreme Court. Of the state-court judges of the period, Roscoe Pound thought that only one stood out "as a builder of the law since the Civil War"— Charles Doe.[33] Doe was chief justice of New Hampshire from 1876 to 1896. He was a man who, in the words of his biographer, believed that "judicial power was grounded upon the logic of necessity and the function of the court [was] to furnish a remedy for every right."[34] In a number of important cases, Doe disregarded formalities, ignored niceties of pleading, and shrugged off the burden of precedent. Judges, he thought, had a duty to make law, at least sometimes; and should do so openly.

What most marked Doe from his contemporaries was not so much substance as style. Doe stood out because he denied the dominant theory on which the legitimacy of judges was supposed to rest. Of course, judges *did* make law. The judges who first used the labor injunction were obviously making law. Each time a judge reworked doctrine, and knew it, he was making law. The judge made law even if he was unaware of what he was doing. Yet, judges of the late nineteenth-century insisted they never made law. Precedent, the Constitution, principles of common law—these were what decisions rested on. The judge was an instrument, a vessel. A judge should not be or even *seem* to be creative. There were good reasons for this posture. It was great camouflage. It denied responsibility for unpopular opinions. It was one reason why judges, even elected judges, were not as naked before the public as, say, governors and congressmen. Technicality and impersonality were not necessarily signs of humility. A doctor is not humble when he invokes medical science. The judges insisted they were professionals. They claimed an expert's privilege: monopoly control of their business. What they did, like the work of other experts, was value-free. This claim was a great tool of self-defense.

Judges and courts varied greatly. Styles of decision, literary merit, and craftsmanship were not uniform. Nor did judges always agree with each other. Dissents, in general, increased on state high courts in the later part of the century. Dissent rates themselves were quite variable. In the Missouri reports of 1885, there were 275 unanimous opinions and 57 cases with dissents or concurring opinions (mostly dissents). But the Vermont supreme court, in 1890, decided seventy cases unanimously; there was only one dissent, and that one lacked a written opinion. In New York's Court of Appeals, in 1888, about one case in ten had a dissenting opinion.[35]

[33] Roscoe Pound, "The Place of Judge Story in the Making of American Law," 18 Am. L. Rev. 676, 690 (1914).

[34] John P. Reid, *Chief Justice: The Judicial World of Charles Doe* (1967), p. 300.

[35] Dissents and concurrences were not the rule in any court. A study of sixteen state supreme courts, for the period 1870–1900, found that over 90 percent of the reported decisions were unanimous; there were concurring opinions in 2.7 percent of the cases, and dissents in 6 percent. Lawrence M. Friedman, Robert Kagan, Bliss Cartwright, and Stanton Wheeler, "State Supreme Courts: A Century of Style and Citation," 33 Stan. L. Rev. 773, 787 (1981).

Karl Llewellyn has called the late nineteenth century the period of "formal" style, in contrast to the "grand" style of Marshall, Gibson, and Shaw.[36] Crispness and flair had gone out of most printed reports. Many high court opinions, in the late nineteenth century, were bombastic, diffuse, labored, drearily logical, crammed with unnecessary citations. Reports were fuller, and were not carefully edited. The workload was too great to allow time for pruning and polishing. But style also reflected the training and philosophy of judges.

Who were these judges? On the whole, they were fairly conservative men, educated in traditional ways, who lived and worked in an environment that exalted the values of American business (though not necessarily *big* business). They tended to be jealous of their judicial and economic prerogatives. High-court judges were hardly a cross section of the country. They represented old America. The bench was lily-white and mostly Protestant. All of them were men. There were a few dynasties of judges—the Tuckers in Virginia, for example. In New Jersey, every chief justice from 1776 to 1891, except one, was Presbyterian. Most associate justices were also Presbyterians, many of them elders in their churches. Nearly all of the judges with a college education had gone to Princeton.[37] As of 1893, of forty-eight judges elected to Virginia's highest court, only three had been "born outside of the . . . limits of Virginia."[38] From 1860 to 1900, virtually every Vermont judge was a native; only occasionally did a son of Connecticut or New Hampshire creep in. The fifteen supreme court judges of Minnesota between 1858 and 1890 were all Protestants, and primarily from good, solid middle-class backgrounds.[39]

For these judges, formalism was a protective device. They were middle-of-the-road conservatives, holding off the vulgar rich on one hand, the revolutionary masses on the other. The legal tradition represented balance, sound values, a commitment to orderly process. The judges, by habit and training, preferred to work within the confines of legal tradition. The judges of the "golden age" invented whole areas of law with a few majestic brushstrokes. In an age of bulging law libraries, creativity took different forms. There were still great opinions (great in the sense of consequential), but they did not *look* so great. "Formalism" flourished; probably less as a habit of mind than as a habit of style, less a way of thinking than a way of disguising thought.

---

[36] Karl N. Llewellyn, "Remarks on the Theory of Appellate Decision and the Rules or Canons About How Statutes Are to Be Construed," 3 Vanderbilt L.R. 395, 396 (1950); *The Common Law Tradition: Deciding Appeals* (1960), pp. 35–39. See below, ch. 11, pp. 623–24.

[37] John Whitehead, "The Supreme Court of New Jersey," 3 Green Bag 493, 512 (1891). Whitehead adds that, except for Chief Justice Hornblower, "a small, delicate slender man," the judges were "of good size, well-proportioned, strong, and vigorous." The trial bench of Boston 1880–1900, was equally monolithic: there were 14 judges, all men, every one born and raised in New England. Six were Harvard alumni. Robert A. Silverman, *Law and Urban Growth: Civil Litigation in the Boston Trial Courts, 1880–1900* (1981), p. 38.

[38] S. S. P. Patteson, "The Supreme Court of Appeals of Virginia," 5 Green Bag 407, 419 (1893).

[39] Robert A. Heiberg, "Social Backgrounds of the Minnesota Supreme Court Justices: 1858–1968," 53 Minn. L. Rev. 901 (1969). In the West, the situation was the reverse. In states like Washington, or Wyoming, few judges were (or could have been) natives. Of the 21 justices of the Oregon Supreme Court between 1854 and 1883, all but one was born outside the state. Ralph J. Mooney and Raymond H. Warns Jr., "Governing a New State: Public Law Decisions by the Early Oregon Supreme Court," 6 Law and History Review 25, 29 (1988).

Still, it is probably true that the judges *were,* by and large, lesser men than the judges of older generations. They were elected, not elite. America of 1880 was an ambitious, industrial society, run by businessmen and politicians. High court judges were simply successful or ambitious lawyers. Few were educated gentleman like John Marshall; few had a sense of style and *noblesse oblige.* Their background and values showed in their craft, if not necessarily in doctrines and results.

JUDICIAL ORGANIZATION

There was no radical innovation in court systems in the late nineteenth century; but there were important changes of a more gradual nature. State systems were still pyramids of courts, imperfectly manned and badly paid at the bottom.[40] No administrator ran, controlled, or coordinated the judicial system. No one could shift judges about as needed from a crowded to an empty docket or monitor the flow of litigation or set up rules to tell the courts how to behave. Higher courts controlled lower courts—weakly—through the power to reverse decisions, but only if someone appealed. At one time, almost all high court judges did some trial work; and almost all high courts were trial courts to some degree. In the late nineteenth century, this was less and less the case. The lines between court levels became more rigid.

As the population grew, state courts, like the U.S. Supreme Court, had to scramble to keep up with their load. The Illinois supreme court wrote 150 opinions in 1854 and 295 in 1889–1890.[41] The federal courts, too, increased their business. In 1871, the U.S. district courts disposed of 8,187 criminal cases; in 1900, 17,033. In 1873, these courts disposed of 14,527 civil cases; in 1900, 22,520. There were 52,477 civil cases pending in the district courts in 1900.[42]

To solve the problem of overload, the states tried various devices. Some states added another tier to the pyramid of courts. They set up intermediate appellate courts. Illinois, for example, divided the state in 1877 into four districts, each with a three-judge court (two of these in crowded Cook County). Texas established a court of criminal appeals in 1891. Under the Missouri Constitution of 1875, a special appellate court was created for the city of St. Louis; another court of appeals, for Kansas City, was established in 1884, and the two courts then handled appeals from lower courts in the rest of the state as well.[43]

[40] Where the fee system was in effect, some lower court judges had been paid only too well. The Pennsylvania Constitution of 1873 (art. V, sec 12) specifically provided that Philadelphia magistrates "shall be compensated only by fixed salaries."

[41] James E. Babb, "The Supreme Court of Illinois," 3 Green Bag 217, 237 (1891).

[42] American Law Institute, *A Study of the Business of the Federal Courts* (1934), Part 1, Criminal Cases, p. 107; Part 2, Civil Cases, p. 111.

[43] Roscoe Pound, *Organization of Courts* (1940), pp. 227–31. At the time of the Civil War, in eleven states the highest court was still a wanderer—required or expected to sit at least once a year in various parts of the state. Before 1900, five of these—Maryland, Michigan, Missouri, Georgia, and Illinois—had settled down permanently at the state capital. Pound, *op. cit.,* p. 199. On the creation of intermediate appellate courts, and other devices to solve the problem of overload at the level of the highest court, see Robert Kagan, Bliss Cartwright, Lawrence Friedman, and Stanton Wheeler, "The Evolution of State Supreme Courts," 76 Michigan L. Rev. 961 (1978).

Many states increased the number of high court judges—Minnesota, for example, went from three to four, then to five. California, in 1879, tried an interesting and productive experiment; it allowed its supreme court to divide itself, like an amoeba, into separate segments ("departments"); only especially difficult or important cases would be decided *en banc,* that is, by the whole court. In some states the supreme court could farm out cases to "commissioners," whose decisions could be (and usually were) accepted by the court as its own. Kansas, in 1887, authorized the governor, "by and with the consent of the senate," to appoint three citizens of Kansas, "of high character for legal learning and personal worth," to be "commissioners of the supreme court." They would "aid and assist the [supreme] court . . . in the disposition of the numerous cases pending in said court" (Laws 1887, ch. 148). In 1895, Kansas created two "courts of appeal," one for the northern and one for the southern part of the state, "inferior to the supreme court and superior to other courts in the state" (Laws 1895, ch. 96). And a constitutional amendment of 1900 (to art. III, sec. 2) increased the size of the supreme court from three to seven; the court could "sit separately in two divisions."[44]

In some states, the legislature lightened the burden of the supreme courts, to some degree, by trying to cut down the flow of cases into the court. The West Virginia Constitution of 1872 (art. VIII, sec. 3) confined the appellate jurisdiction of the Supreme Court of Appeals to criminal cases, constitutional cases, "controversies concerning the title or boundaries of land," or the "probate of wills," civil cases "where the matter in controversy, exclusive of costs," was "of greater value, or amount than one hundred dollars," and a miscellaneous category, included cases "concerning a mill, roadway, ferry, or landing." In Illinois, in 1877, the appellate (intermediate) courts became last-stop courts of appeal for contract and damage cases where the amount in controversy was less than one thousand dollars, exclusive of costs. The supreme court still heard criminal cases, and "cases involving a franchise or freehold."[45]

Congress came to the rescue of the federal system in 1869, by providing a circuit judge for each of the nine circuits. Supreme Court justices were each still assigned to a circuit; but it was recognized that the justice could not and would not do much of the circuit's work. The Civil War, Reconstruction, and the post-Civil War amendments added to the importance of the federal system. The Removal Act of 1875 gave more power to the federal courts. Any action asserting a federal right could begin in a federal court; or, if begun in a state court, could be removed to the federal courts. The act "opened wide a flood of totally new business for the federal courts."[46] Finally, Congress enacted major reform in 1891. Each circuit was to have a circuit court of appeals, acting as an appellate court. This act provided for an extra circuit judge. Supreme Court justices could still sit in their circuits, but almost none ever did.[47]

Beyond these changes, political leaders showed little desire to make court organization more rational. Lay politicians did not want to appoint a czar for

---

[44] The courts of appeal were abolished in 1901.
[45] Laws Ill. 1877, pp. 70–71.
[46] Felix Frankfurter and James M. Landis, *The Business of the Supreme Court: A Study in the Federal Judicial System* (1928), p. 65.
[47] 26 Stats. 826 (act of March 3,1891).

the courts of their states. Muddled and overlapping jurisdiction was perfectly acceptable; the alternative—a strong chief justice with power to run his system—was not. In some states, to prevent any chance of this kind of leadership, the legislature downgraded the office of chief justice. In Ohio, in 1852, the chief justice was nothing more than "Judge of the Supreme Court having the shortest time to serve."[48] Many state constitutions had similar provisions.[49] Obviously, this system resulted in "a periodical rotation" in office, and precluded "any continuity of development of the administrative side of the court's work." In 1900, however, no less than seventeen of the thirty-eight states with an elected supreme court had this or a similar provision.[50] In some states, even clerks of court were elected—an absurdity from the standpoint of administrative coherence.[51]

The high courts were busy institutions. About a third of their decided cases, in the period 1870–1900, were cases of debt and contract; another 21 percent dealt with issues of real property law. About 10 percent were tort cases; another 10 percent criminal cases; 12.4 percent were on questions of public law (tax, regulation of business, eminent domain, and similar matters); 7.7 percent on issues of family law and family property (divorce, inheritance, administration of estates).[52] There were among all these cases some that involved great issues or huge sums of money. Yet, most ordinary business and nonbusiness disputes avoided the courts. The courts were too slow, too expensive. Perhaps society, in a sense, had decided to allow the price of a full trial or a complete day in court to rise, in order to encourage the development of alternatives. In this sense, the history of the great American courts is also a history of events that passed them by. This was true of the trial courts as well as appellate courts, perhaps even more so. The economy was booming; industry and commerce were growing. There was a vast army of middle-class consumers of law. Slow, expensive, relatively technical, courts could not possibly meet the needs of economy and society.

Courts were fixed in size and limited in staff; legislatures never added enough new judges and courts to fill the need. Delays piled up. Routine commercial disputes stayed away. Even filed cases did not, as a rule, go to trial. Most were settled along the way. The legal business of business mostly avoided the courts. Aside from the expense and the delays, there was the problem of the law itself, and the judges who expounded it. They were men trained in the law; they did not necessarily understand what business people wanted or needed.

Trial courts did make a contribution, low-key but real. For one thing, the judicial system *worked*. It provided stability and certainty. Creditors knew, in general, that they could collect debts without bribery or incompetence. Courts would be open and functioning, in every season. Some courts were corrupt, but

---

[48] Laws Ohio 1852, p. 67 (act of Feb. 29, 1852).

[49] Neb. Const. 1875, art. VI, sec. 6. In Wisconsin (const. 1848, art. VII, sec. 4, as amended, 1889) the judge longest in service would become chief justice.

[50] Pound, *op. cit.*, p. 169.

[51] For example, Va. Const. 1850, art. VI, sec. 19: "The Voters of each county . . . in which a circuit is held shall elect a clerk of such court, whose term of office shall be six years."

[52] Robert A. Kagan, Bliss Cartwright, Lawrence M. Friedman, and Stanton Wheeler, "The Business of State Supreme Courts, 1870–1970," 30 Stan. L. Rev. 121, 133–35 (1977).

not so many as to spoil the whole system. At the lower levels, courts processed huge numbers of small cases. Divorces were granted, mortgages foreclosed. The courts acted as debt collection agencies. All this they did quickly and without much fuss or bother. In Chippewa County, Wisconsin, courts handled hundreds of cases of domestic relations, unpaid debts, insurance, mortgage foreclosure, petty criminal actions, and the like.[53] Big city courts also took care of a staggering volume of matters. The municipal courts of Boston, at the very end of the century, "entertained the problems of about 20,000 plaintiffs a year."[54] Almost all the "cases" were utterly cut-and-dried. Debt collection was the main theme: grocers, clothing stores, doctors, using the courts to force clients and customers to pay.

This great volume of cases called for radical routinization. In probate, mortgage, divorce, and commercial law, courts developed or used standardized procedures, almost as perfunctory—and essential—as parking-ticket procedures in the twenty-first century. This was assembly-line justice. The losers, overwhelmingly, were little people: men and women who owed money on a piano or a sewing machine; tenants who could not pay their rent; patients who fumbled on the doctor bill. On the surface, it looks as if the law "responded to the cold-blooded interests of merchants whose poor customers could not pay."[55] But perhaps the courts made it easier and cheaper to extend credit to great masses of people. Thus, "millions had a chance to buy goods and services they could not have obtained otherwise."[56] This chance came, of course, at a price.

[53] Francis Laurent, *The Business of a Trial Court: One Hundred Years of Cases* (1959). On the flow of business through the courts of St. Louis, see Wayne V. McIntosh, *The Appeal of Civil Law: A Political-Economic Analysis of Litigation* (1990); and for a picture of the courts at work in a rural California county toward the end of the century, Lawrence M. Friedman, "San Benito 1890: Legal Snapshot of a County," 27 Stan. L. Rev. 687 (1975).

[54] Robert A. Silverman, *Law and Urban Growth: Civil Litigation in the Boston Trial Courts, 1880–1900* (1981), p. 144.

[55] Lawrence M. Friedman, "Law and Small Business in the United States: One Hundred Years of Struggle and Accommodation," in Stuart W. Bruchey, ed., *Small Business in American Life* (1980), pp. 304, 314.

[56] *Ibid.*

CHAPTER 3

PROCEDURE AND PRACTICE:
AN AGE OF REFORM

MR. FIELD'S CODE

1848 was a year of revolution in Europe. In the United States it was the year in which New York passed an "act to simplify and abridge the Practice, Pleadings, and Proceedings of the Courts."[1] This was a full-blown Code of Civil Procedure, radically new in appearance at least. The Code is often called the Field Code, after David Dudley Field, who did more than anyone else to devise it and get it enacted. The Field Code also served as a kind of catalytic agent for procedural reform elsewhere in the United States.[2]

New York had adopted a new constitution in 1846. One clause called for the "appointment of three commissioners, to revise, reform, simplify, and abridge the rules and practice, pleadings, forms and proceedings of the courts of record of this State" (art. VI, sec. 24). Perhaps the state got more than it bargained for. One of the original commissioners, Nicholas Hill Jr., resigned in 1847, horrified that his colleagues were willing to recommend changes "so purely experimental, so sudden and general, and so perilous." David Dudley Field (1805–1894) was appointed in his place. From his early days at the bar, Field had been seized with the vision of codification and law reform. In 1839, he wrote an open letter on reform of the judicial system. He later harangued a legislative committee on the subject. From 1847 on, he was the heart and soul of the movement.[3]

Stylistically, the 1848 Code was a colossal affront to the common-law tradition. It was couched in brief, gnomic, Napoleonic sections, tightly worded and skeletal; there was no trace of the elaborate redundancy, the voluptuous heaping on of synonyms, so characteristic of Anglo-American statutes. It was, in short, a code in the French sense, not a statute. It was a lattice of reasoned principles, scientifically arranged, not a thick thumb stuck into the dikes of common law. It meant to get rid of the archaic matters that encrusted common pleading like so many barnacles—including the jargon and the Latin. It was even suggested that the Code should substitute "writ of deliverance from

---

[1] Laws N.Y. 1848, ch 379.

[2] See Daun van Ee, *David Dudley Field and the Reconstruction of the Law* (1986).

[3] Henry M. Field, *The Life of David Dudley Field* (1898), pp. 42–56. Mildred V. Coe and Lewis W. Morse, "Chronology of the Development of the David Dudley Field Code," 27 Cornell L.Q. 238 (1941).

prison" for "habeas corpus"; but this heresy was too much for one of the commissioners, and it never came to pass.[4]

In substance, the Field Code was almost as daring as in style. Section 62, the heart of the Code, boldly stated that:

> The distinction between actions at law and suits in equity, and the forms of all such actions and suits heretofore existing, are abolished; and, there shall be in this state, hereafter, but one form of action, for the enforcement or protection of private rights and the redress or prevention of private wrongs, which shall be denominated a civil action.

Taken literally, this was a death sentence for common-law pleading. It was meant to end all special pleading, forms of actions and writs, and to close the chasm between equity and law. It was meant, in other words, to revolutionize the most recondite, most crabbed, most lawyerly area of law. The goal was law that was clear, predictable, simple in operation, simple in application.[5]

Like many other revolutions, the upheaval of 1848, in the legal communes of New York, was not a complete bolt from the blue. The Field Code had its share of intellectual forefathers. In England, Jeremy Bentham, who died in 1832, had savagely attacked the "ancestor-worship" of the common law. Bentham used his vigorous pen in the service of legal rationality. Benthamite lawyers preached reform of the common law, especially its procedure. In 1828, Henry Brougham spoke for six hours in the House of Commons, eating a "hatful of oranges as he went, calling for law reform," and ending with a dramatic plea: "It was the boast of Augustus . . . that he found Rome of brick, and left it of marble; a praise not unworthy of a great prince. . . . But how much nobler will be the Sovereign's boast . . . that he found law dear, and left it cheap; found it a sealed book—left it a living letter; found it a patrimony of the rich—left it the inheritance of the poor; found it a two-edged sword of craft and oppression—left it the staff of honesty and the shield of innocence."[6] Parliament appointed a commission to consider procedural reform, and actually passed some reform statutes in the early 1830s. In the United States, the Field Code had a precedent of sorts in the codes drawn up by Edward Livingston in Louisiana; and there is evidence that Field was influenced by the Louisiana codes.[7] Louisiana was, as we saw, more or less a civil-law state; law and equity in Texas were fused, too, but this could be explained on the grounds of civil-law contamination. In some states—Massachusetts, for example, commissions had called for improved and simplified procedure. Colonial practice had been simpler than English practice, and colonial

[4] Van Ee, at p. 42.

[5] See Stephen N. Subrin, "David Dudley Field and the Field Code: A Historical Analysis of an Earlier Procedural Vision," 6 Law and History Review 311 (1988).

[6] Quoted in Brian Abel-Smith and Robert Stevens, *Lawyers and the Courts: A Sociological Study of the English Legal System 1750–1965* (1967), p. 19; see also Robert W. Millar, *Civil Procedure of the Trial Court in Historical Perspective* (1952), p. 43. Millar's book is a richly detailed, if technical, account of American civil procedure. Also useful is Charles M. Hepburn, *The Historical Development of Code Pleading in America and England* (1897). On the general background, see Charles M. Cook, *The American Codification Movement: A Study of Antebellum Legal Reform* (1981).

[7] David S. Clark, "The Civil Law Influence on David Dudley Field's Code of Civil Procedure," in Mathias Reimann, ed., *The Reception of Continental Ideas in the Common Law World, 1820–1920* (1993), p. 63.

habits never wholly died. As we saw, a number of states took up procedural reform. Georgia's experiment was quite radical for its day.

No doubt, those precedents were important. Also, Field had spent a year traveling abroad; he was familiar with Continental law; he was an intelligent, broadly educated man. Basically, however, code pleading was an idea whose time had come. Not that code pleading was an immediate, unqualified success. Ironically, the Code had particular trouble in New York itself. In 1849, New York reenacted the Field Code, but in a version much impaired by amendments and supplements. This Code had 473 sections. An act of July 10, 1851, again made major changes. Later came still more amendments. In 1870, the legislature appointed a new commission to revise the Code; its version, reported out in 1876, was monstrously inflated—"reactionary in spirit . . . a figure of Falstaffian proportions among the other codes," its principles "smothered in details."[8] By 1880, the New York procedural codes (including the code of criminal procedure) contained no less than 3,356 sections.[9] This was a long way from Field's dream of simplicity. In the 1890s, New York's procedure was still considered so flawed that many leaders of the bar wanted new and better reforms.

Once passed, the Code had to face the judges. Some of them manhandled the Code. Judge Samuel Selden, for example, was convinced that law and equity were categories of the real world. The idea of merging the two was totally beyond him: "It is possible to abolish one or the other," he wrote, in 1856, "but it certainly is not possible to abolish the distinction between them."[10] Chief Justice John Bradley Winslow of Wisconsin in 1910 referred to the "cold, not to say inhuman, treatment which the infant Code received from the New York judges."[11] Actually, very little is known about the behavior of trial court judges. But of course, their behavior would decide the fate of the Code. Probably the Code was unable to destroy the habits of a lifetime. Nor could it, by itself, transform legal culture. But stubborn judges were probably only a passing phase. The real vice of the Code was probably its weak empirical base. The draftsmen never made a careful study of what actually happened in American courts, or considered what functions and interests courts and their lawsuits served.

The Field Code did not make much headway in the East. Even in New York, the draftsmen thought of it as a draft; the final, full text, when it was finished, was too much for the legislature to swallow. The West was different. The ink was hardly dry on Field's Code when Missouri adopted it (1849); so did California, a new state at the edge of the continent, in 1851. Before the Civil War, Iowa, Minnesota, Indiana, Ohio, Washington Territory, Nebraska, Wisconsin, and Kansas had all adopted the Code; then Nevada in 1861, and by the turn of the century, so had the Dakotas, Idaho, Arizona, Montana, North Carolina, Wyoming, South Carolina, Utah, Colorado, Oklahoma, and New Mexico.[12]

---

[8] Hepburn, op. cit., p. 130.

[9] Alison Reppy, "The Field Codification Concept," in Alison Reppy, ed., David Dudley Field Centenary Essays (1949), pp. 17, 34–36.

[10] J. Selden, in Reubens v. Joel, 13 N.Y. 488, 493 (1856); see Charles E. Clark, "The Union of Law and Equity," 25 Columbia L. Rev. 1 (1925).

[11] Quoted in Clark, op. cit., p. 3.

[12] Kentucky and Oregon also adopted the code, but maintained the separation of law and equity. Iowa reintroduced the distinction in 1860. Millar, op. cit., p. 54. Later, Arkansas adopted the Kentucky model.

Why the West? Perhaps because the Western bar was young and open-minded; or because common-law pleading was a lost art among these lawyers. Stephen Field, David Dudley Field's brother, a prominent California lawyer, may have helped advance the cause. In Missouri, David Wells for years had been working to get rid of the distinction between law and equity. Both states had bits of civil law in their background; both entered the Union with a history of land controversies and a full deck of land-grant problems. Land claims were hard to analyze in terms of "legal" and "equitable" titles; for these claims, the distinction was both meaningless and disruptive.

Western states were also more eclectic in general than states of the older East. Some Eastern states (Massachusetts, for example) were working toward procedural reform in their own way. Some states rejected the Field Code as unsuitable, or too advanced, or as the product of a different culture. Dean Henry Ingersoll of the University of Tennessee, writing in the *Yale Law Journal* in 1891, was against the "attempt of one State to adapt a Code of Procedure prepared for an entirely different social and business condition." In North Carolina, one of the few Eastern states to adopt the Code, he felt the experiment (which he blamed on blacks and carpetbaggers) had been a disaster:

> During . . . Reconstruction . . . the legal practice of the State was recon-structed by the adoption of the New York Code of Civil Procedure, with all its penalties and high-pressure machinery adapted to the conditions of an alert, eager, pushing commercial community. Rip Van Winkle was not more surprised on returning to his native village after his long sleep than were the lawyers of the old "Tar-heel State." . . . This new-fangled commercial machine . . . was as well adapted to their condition as were the light driving buggies of the Riverside Park to the rough roads of the Black mountains, or the garb of the Broadway dandy to the turpentine stiller. . . . North Car-olina had about as much use for the system as she had for a clearing-house, a Central Park or a Stock Exchange. The clamors of the bar soon brought about . . . amendment . . . and left [the code] . . . a great cumbrous piece of machinery without driving-wheels, steam-chest or boiler, propelled along by the typical slow oxteam.[13]

Ingersoll attacked code pleading as the product of an alien, hated culture. His diatribe may harbor a grain of truth: procedural reform was most needed, or at least most desirable, in commercial states. Business likes its legal process to be rational and predictable. Business likes swift, nontechnical, decisions, based on facts, not writs and forms of action. Common law pleading was chaos. It was a kind of slow ritual dance. Its aim was to isolate pure "issues" of law or fact. But these issues were often simply artifacts of the pleading, hence, in a sense, hypothetical.

The trial of a murderer is a unique event, the exact opposite of a parking ticket. Routine business claims also need routine. For these claims, procedure was radically and successfully simplified. The development was quiet, almost invisible. Just as a mass market led to mass production of commodities, so a mass market led to mass production of law. The system stamped out, like so many paper clips, its tiny but numberless outputs—grocery and doctor bills, sewing machines repossessed, wages garnished, documents recorded. In the

---

[13] Henry H. Ingersoll, "Some Anomalies of Practice," 1 Yale L.J. 89, 91, 92 (1891).

aggregate, they were more important than murder trials—perhaps vastly more important. They were fuel for the engine of a market economy. They depended, too, on the validity of forms and documents that businessmen and business lawyers invented. The courts usually accepted and validated such documents and forms. Business could then safely ignore the grand debate over codes and procedure, debates about the esthetic shape of the legal system, that raged in upper circles of the bar.

In the earlier part of the nineteenth century, law reform probably did command wide support from businessmen or merchants.[14] They felt law was cumbersome and unfeeling; they wanted to redirect the law, to strip it of excesses and make it more efficient. David Dudley Field promised the world of business that law would become a willing tool of the economy. And law did do so—only not in the way that Field imagined. Business did not use law and lawsuits to solve ordinary disputes—if they could help it. They used law to collect and record. There were grander struggles, to be sure—lawyers who worked for the robber barons, battling each other in court, pelting each other with a blizzard of writs and injunctions, in order to win some advantage in the struggle to control some prostrate railroad net, or a giant corporation. There were also, from time to time, constitutional cases. But it is important not to overlook the vital drudgery of the living law.

The reformers never realized their dream of a simple, rational system of law. This was not a technical failure. What frustrated their hopes were the activities of concrete interest groups, with concrete demands on law for instrumental purposes. In some states, the bar opposed code pleading with great passion. But in the long run code pleading was probably good for the lawyers. One of its root ideas was *fact pleading,* so simple and rational that the average citizen could do it on her own. This was Utopian. Yet, procedure did become, on the whole, less technical. In a small way, this helped free lawyers to concentrate on what their clients' wanted. And the rise of a business bar, a bar that rarely set foot in a courtroom, meant that traditional rules and skills of pleading became less useful and less in demand.

By 1900, the Field Code was widely adopted, copied, and modified. Field's reforms had earned, moreover, one supreme compliment: close study in England. Field's work influenced the English Judicature Act of 1873. English reforms, in turn, had American consequences. The Connecticut Practice Act of 1879, for example, drew "in considerable measure upon the English reforms," and was, on the whole, "a distinct advance over the codes which had emanated from . . . New York."[15]

Before the nineteenth century was over, almost all states had reformed their procedures, at least somewhat. Only a minority—New Jersey, Delaware, Illinois—clung tenaciously to old-style pleading. No state went as far as Field would have liked. In every state, law and equity were only imperfectly merged. For one thing, the federal Constitution, and state constitutions, made trial by jury a constitutional right. Since "equity" cases never had a jury, the historical

---

[14] See, in general, Lawrence M. Friedman, "Law Reform in Historical Perspective," 13 St. Louis U.L.J. 351 (1969); Maxwell Bloomfield, *American Lawyers in a Changing Society, 1776–1876* (1976), ch. 3 (on William Sampson).

[15] Robert W. Millar, *Civil Procedure of the Trial Court in Historical Perspective* (1952), p. 55.

distinction between law and equity was important; it marked the boundary line of the right to trial by jury.

Insofar as the two were joined, it was in many ways equity that came out on top. Greater freedom in joinder of parties, a liberal attitude toward counter-claims, more suppleness in judicial remedies—all this was due to equity. Even those New England states that had never given their courts full equity powers—Maine, New Hampshire, Massachusetts—expanded equitable remedies after the Civil War. In fact, many striking legal developments, between 1850 and 1900, depended on creative use of tools of equity. Courts put bankrupt railroads into (equity) receivership and virtually ran them; they forged out of the injunction a terrible sword to use in industrial disputes. Injunction and receivership were both old tricks of equity, rapidly and vigorously reshaped. Equity, free from the whims of a jury, was made to order for a judge with a taste for power.

APPELLATE COURTS

Despite the Field Code, appellate courts spent an astonishing amount of time and effort on questions of procedure. In the common-law system, upper courts never retried a case; "appeal" simply meant reviewing the formal record of the work of the trial court. Between 1870 and 1900, there were persistent complaints about the tendency of some state supreme courts to reverse decisions of their lower courts for all sorts of minor technical errors. The Texas Court of Appeals, according to one writer in 1887, "seems to have been organized to overrule and reverse. At least, since its organization that has been its chief employment." As evidence, the article cited an amazing fact: During the twelve years of the court's existence, it had reversed 1,604 criminal cases, and affirmed only 882— a margin of almost two to one. In one volume of reports, there were five reversals to every single affirmance.[16]

This was Roscoe Pound's "hypertrophy," at its most extreme in criminal cases. At least on paper, there were tight rules about trial that were meant to curb the power of trial court judges. They had once been in the habit of giving oral instructions to the jury. They taught the jury about the relevant rules, in frank, natural language. But this practice died out—or was driven out. Instructions became formal written documents, drafted by lawyers. Each side drew up its own version of the applicable legal doctrines. Then the judge picked out those that were (in his judgment) legally "correct." These instructions were in any event, technical, legalistic, utterly opaque. They were almost useless as a way to instruct, that is, to explain to juries what the law actually was; the medium conveyed no message.[17] Instructions had to be framed with great care, so as not to give an upper court a chance to find reversible "error." At one time, too, it was standard for a judge to comment on the evidence, to tell the jury quite frankly what he thought about the witnesses, and what their

---

[16] Note, "Overruled Their Judicial Superiors," 21 Am. L. Rev. 610 (1887).

[17] See, for examples in criminal cases, Lawrence M. Friedman and Robert V. Percival, *The Roots of Justice: Crime and Punishment in Alameda County, California, 1870–1910* (1981), pp. 186–87.

testimony was worth. In Missouri, for example, this practice was stamped out by 1859.[18]

Appellate procedure itself was highly technical, throughout the nineteenth century. After reading cases in the last part of the century, Roscoe Pound was "tempted to think that appellate procedure existed as a system of preventing the disposition of cases themselves upon their merits."[19] Here, too, the Field Code tried to bring in a radical new order; it swept away a flock of cumbersome rules. It got rid of the technical distinctions between writs of error and appeals in equity, and created a single form of review, which it called an "appeal." Some noncode jurisdictions (Alabama in 1853, Pennsylvania in 1889) also abolished the writ of error, and brought in a simpler form, which they too called an *appeal*.[20]

But in general, "record worship" did not die out. It seemed to keep its stranglehold on appellate review. Some upper courts were sticklers for technicality; some tended to overturn trial courts on the basis of warped and unreal distinctions. Again, the problem was most acute in criminal appeals. Harwell, the defendant in a Texas case decided in 1886,[21] had been arrested and convicted for receiving stolen cattle. The Texas court reversed, because, among other things, the jury found the defendant "guity" instead of "guilty." In 1877, the same court reversed a conviction because the jury carelessly wrote, "We, the jury, the defendant guilty," leaving out the word "find."[22] The same court, however, magnanimously upheld a conviction of "guily" in 1879,[23] proving that a "t" was less crucial than an "l" in the law of Texas.

It is not easy to account for this behavior. Appeal courts were busy; they relied less on long oral arguments than on written briefs. They spent their lives looking at formal records, and may have come to believe in them too much. Again, the profession took itself (as always) very seriously. A judge may consider an error significant that an outsider would find trivial at best. Stylistically, this was a period of conceptualism, of dry legal logic. The bench, as we have suggested, was less talented than earlier in the century. Formalism was a source of power for judges of small talent. Procedural excess was in some ways a good idea gone bad: a fumbling attempt to govern, standardize, and rationalize trials, appeals, and written arguments. Appellate judges sometimes complained that the work of the lawyers, and the lower-court judges, was sloppy or misguided. This was particularly true in the early years of a state or territory. An appeal judge who took seriously the job of riding herd on lower courts, lawyers, and juries, might set a high value on regularity in procedure.[24] Also, it

---

[18] Henry F. Luepke Jr., "Comments on the Evidence in Missouri," 6 St. Louis U.L.J. 424 (1959); on the role of the jury in nineteenth century law in general, see Note, "The Changing Role of the Jury in the Nineteenth Century," 74 Yale L.J. 170 (1964).

[19] Roscoe Pound, *Appellate Procedure in Civil Cases* (1941), p. 320.

[20] Pound, *op. cit.*, PS, pp. 260–61.

[21] *Harwell v. State*, 22 Tex. App. 251, 2 S.W. 606 (1886); see also *Taylor v. State*, 5 Tex. App. 569 (1877); *Wilson v. State*, 12 Tex. App. 481 (1882).

[22] *Shaw v. State*, 2 Tex. App. 487 (1877).

[23] *Curry v. State*, 7 Tex. App. 91 (1879).

[24] Litigants who lost in municipal courts or justice-of-the-peace courts could take their cases up to the regular trial courts. There the litigant would get a trial *de novo* (that is, the court would do the whole trial over, including the evidence and the finding of facts). See,

is easy to exaggerate record worship. The literature is full of horror stories, but short on facts and figures. Consistently, more cases were affirmed than reversed: 60 percent or more, in most jurisdictions. How many *deserved* to be affirmed is something we simply do not know.

Criminal procedure was harder to reform than civil procedure. There was, for example, no way the federal government could abolish the grand jury for serious criminal cases; the grand jury system was enshrined in the Constitution, with regard to federal cases.[25] To relax rules of criminal procedure was to unleash the full power of government; and this was in some regards unpopular. Criminal procedure seemed highly technical, even over-technical; but this was, to a large degree, simply an illusion. Legal guarantees of fair trial hardly worked at all for ignorant, timid, or unpopular defendants. Kangaroo court justice, the blackjack, police harassment, the Ku Klux Klan, vigilante justice, lynch law in the late nineteenth-century South—these were more a part of the normal, everyday, living law of criminal procedure than record worship was. The two phenomena may even be connected. Vigilantes and lynch mobs demanded quick, certain law and order (as they defined them); they did not trust the regular courts. Vigilantes and lynch mobs were a kind of devilish counterbalance to the formal law. Lynch law in particular was an excuse to use torture, savagery, and animal brutality, in ways that the formal law could never openly espouse.

The law of evidence remained complex. Simon Greenleaf, in his treatise on evidence (first published in 1842), had once praised the "symmetry and beauty" of this branch of law. A student, he felt, "would rise from the study of its principles convinced, with Lord Erskine, that they are founded in the charities of religion, in the philosophy of nature, in the truths of history, and in the experience of common life." A more realistic critic, James Bradley Thayer, of Harvard, writing in 1898, felt, on the other hand, that the law of evidence was "a piece of illogical . . . patchwork; not at all to be admired, or easily to be found intelligible."[26] Its amazing bulk, its jungle of rules and doctrine—John H. Wigmore spun ten volumes out of the law of evidence in the twentieth century—had no counterpart outside of the common law. Indeed, Thayer reported that even English lawyers were surprised "to see our lively quarrels over points of evidence." In the United States, objections to evidence were presented as "exceptions, a method never common in England and now abolished there, which presents only a dry question of law—not leaving to the upper court that power to heed the general justice of the case which the more elastic procedure of the English courts so commonly allows; and tending thus to foster delay and chicane."[27]

---

for example, *Hurtgen v. Kantrowitz*, 15 Colo. 442, 24 Pac. 872 (1890). This shows a certain lack of respect for the craftsmanship of these lowest courts.

[25] By the Fifth Amendment: "No person shall be held to answer for a capital, or otherwise infamous crime, unless on a presentment or indictment of a Grand Jury." On this institution in general, see Richard D. Younger, *The People's Panel: The Grand Jury in the United States, 1634–1941* (1963).

[26] The Greenleaf quote, and Thayer's comment, are in James B. Thayer, *A Preliminary Treatise on Evidence at the Common Law* (1898), pp. 508–9.

[27] Thayer, *op. cit.*, pp. 528–29.

The law of evidence grew like mushrooms grow: in a dark cellar world of mistrust and suspicion; a world of checks and balances run riot. The jury was the key to the law of evidence. The whole point of all these rules was to regulate what the jury could and could not hear. The jury had enormous power—even life and death—and yet it was not to be trusted—at least not completely. Evidence had to be censored, filtered, bowdlerized, before it reached the tender ears of the jury. Everything even remotely prejudicial or irrelevant had to be kept out of the courtroom.

A few of the more restrictive rules of evidence were, to be sure, relaxed. At one time, as we noted, nobody who was an interested party was allowed to testify at trial. England abolished this rule in 1843, Michigan in 1846, and other states followed over the next thirty years. The rule that disqualified the *parties* to a lawsuit was only a special case of the rule; it too was abolished. Connecticut did this in 1848; and the Field Code, in New York, in the same year, did the same. Other states gradually joined in the trend, Illinois, for example, in 1867.[28] But the states then backtracked slightly; they passed laws to prevent a surviving party from testifying about transactions with a dead person: "If death has closed the lips of the one party, the policy of the law is to close the lips of the other."[29]

In general, "hearsay" was not allowed in evidence. The "hearsay" rule was at the very core of the law of evidence. But the rule had a long list of exceptions, and exceptions to exceptions. There were more and more doctrines and strictures and rules as time went on—exceptions to the hearsay rule, rules about privilege, rules about relevance, and so forth and so on. The rules, dry and technical, were nonetheless deeply consequential. There was controversy over the rule about party testimony, after the Civil War, in so far as it concerned the right of African Americans to testify. The rules were related, too, to the rise of the jury as (in George Fisher's term) a "lie detector." In a criminal trial, for example, when both the state and its witnesses, and the defendant, could testify under oath—and obviously, the two sides contradicted each other—it was left to the jury to sift truth from falsity, which it did in a particularly decisive and dramatic way.[30] The rule that disqualified parties from testifying had a real impact, too, in personal injury cases. It had been a serious obstacle to plaintiffs who were trying to sue. Now this rule was gone. But nothing in legal history is simple. When this rule disappeared, and the plaintiff was free to talk under oath, other rules of evidence—hearsay, *res gestae*—took its place, sometimes with almost equally damaging results.[31]

---

[28] Rev. Stats. Conn. 1849, Title 1, ch. 10, sec. 141: "No person shall be disqualified as a witness . . . by reason of his interest . . . *as a party* or otherwise" (emphasis added); Laws Ill. 1867, p. 183.

[29] *Louis's Adm'r v. Easton*, 50 Ala. 470, 471 (1874); see John H. Wigmore, *A Treatise on the Anglo-American System of Evidence*, vol. 1 (2nd ed., 1923), pp. 1004–5.

[30] See the discussion in George Fisher, "The Jury's Rise as Lie Detector," 107 Yale L.J. 575 (1997).

[31] See John Fabian Witt, "Toward a New History of American Accident Law: Classical Tort Law and the Cooperative First-Party Insurance Movement," 114 Harv. L. Rev. 690, 754–758 (2001).

CODIFICATION AND REFORM

Field's Code of procedure was only part of a larger, bolder plan: to codify the whole common law. The smell of feudalism still seemed to ooze from the pores of the common law. To men like Jeremy Bentham in England, and David Dudley Field, Edward Livingston, and others in America, the common law was totally unsuited for an Age of Reason. It was huge and shapeless. Common-law principles had to be painfully extracted from a jungle of words. "The law" was an amorphous entity, a ghost, scattered in little bits and pieces among hundreds of case reports, in hundreds of different books. Nobody knew what was and was not law. Why not gather the basic rules of law, put them together, and build a simple, complete, and sensible code? The French had shown the way with the Code Napoleon. Louisiana had a Civil Code, based on European models. Why not try something similar? In 1865, Field published a general Civil Code, divided into four parts. The first three dealt with persons, property, and obligations; the fourth part contained general provisions. The scheme of organization ran parallel to the great French code; like that code, Field's Code tried to set out principles of law exhaustively, concisely, and with great clarity of language. But New York would have none of it. Till the end of his long life, Field continued to press for adoption in his state. He never succeeded. New York did enact a penal code, which went into effect in 1881; but the civil code was repeatedly turned down, the latest snub occurring in 1885.

The codification movement is one of the set pieces of American legal history. It has its hero, Field; its villain is James C. Carter of New York,[32] who fought the idea of codification with as much vigor as Field fought for it. Codification was wrong, Carter felt, because it removed the center of gravity from the courts. The legislature—the code-enacting body—was comparatively untrustworthy; it was too passionately addicted to the short run. "The question is," he wrote, whether "growth, development and improvement of the law" should "remain under the guidance of men selected by the people on account of their special qualifications for the work," or "be transferred to a numerous legislative body, disqualified by the nature of their duties for the discharge of this supreme function?"[33] Codes impaired the orderly development of the law. They froze the law into semipermanent form; they prevented natural evolution. Carter was impressed by the so-called historical school of jurisprudence, founded by German jurists in the early nineteenth century. They taught that laws were and ought to be derived from the folk wisdom of a people. A statute drafted by a group of so-called experts, Carter thought, could not be as good as law that had evolved over centuries of self-correcting growth. The courts apply to private disputes a "social standard of justice" which is "the product of the combined operation of the thought, the morality, the intellectual and moral culture of the time." The judges know and feel this, because "they are a part of the community." The "social standard of justice grows and develops with the moral and intellectual

---

[32] On Carter (1827–1905), see the essay by George A. Miller in *Great American Lawyers*, vol. 8 (1909), pp. 3–41; on Carter's thought, Lewis Grossman, "James Coolidge Carter and Mugwump Jurisprudence," 20 Law and History Review 577 (2002).

[33] James C. Carter, *The Proposed Codification of Our Common Law* (1884), p. 87.

growth of society. . . . Hence a gradual change unperceived and unfelt in its advance is continually going on in the jurisprudence of every progressive State."[34] Judges could decide cases on a "moral" basis; this was of course impossible for politicians.[35] Carter's point of view was useful not only in fighting codification; it was also a handy club to use against much of the social and economic legislation of the late nineteenth century. These laws, it could be argued, were also doomed to failure; they were hasty and ill-advised, and they contradicted the deeper genius of the law, and its inner commitment to justice.

Field saw codification in a different light. The laws were "now in sealed books, and the lawyers object to the opening of these books." Lawyers "as a body never did begin a reform of the law, and, judging from experience, they never will."[36] The closed books had to be opened. Progress demanded no less. Yet the two great antagonists were in agreement in certain basic points. A legislative hodge-podge was as offensive to Field as to Carter. The codes Field had in mind would be the work of experts—jurists like Field himself. The legislature would simply take the codes and give them its stamp of validity. The codes, then, would come from a legal elite; they would be clear and definite, progressive and reliable. The common law had become a prisoner of its own history. It was tied to the narrow self-interest of old-fashioned men. Carter and Field agreed about ends, but disagreed about means. They both wanted rationality. They both wanted a workable system of law, a system that business could rely on. Both distrusted the role of laymen, in the making of law. Carter preferred common-law judges, as philosopher-kings, and looked on codes as straitjackets. Field took the opposite view.

In the last third of the century, ideas like those of Carter and Field were, so to speak, in the air. They were similar, in some respects, to the ideas of Christopher Columbus Langdell, who reformed legal education at Harvard, from 1870 on. Langdell felt strongly that law should be taught as a science, as a set of basic principles. Langdell, however, was suspicious of statutes; unlike Field, he valued the pure and "scientific" common law. Langdell shared with Carter his love of the common law; yet his idea of a legal principle was much like that of Field, only implicit, evolutionary, and more subtly dynamic.

The Civil Code—and Field's Codes on other branches of law—were not total failures. Like the Code of Civil Procedure, they found greater acceptance far from home. Dakota Territory enacted a civil code in 1866; Idaho and Montana also made a code part of their law. The chief victory, however, was California, which enacted a civil code in 1872. This was no blanket adoption of Field's Code. California thoroughly revised the code to make it conform to California's own statutes and cases. California also adopted a penal and a political code. In California, too, codification was not meant to empower the legislature; here too it was meant to be clear, clean, and scientific: an important step in human (and legal) progress.[37]

[34] James C. Carter, *The Provinces of the Written and the Unwritten Law* (1889), pp. 48–49.

[35] Grossman, "James Coolidge Carter," at 604.

[36] Titus M. Coan, ed., *Speeches, Arguments, and Miscellaneous Papers of David Dudley Field*, vol. III (1890), pp. 238, 239.

[37] Lewis Grossman, "Codification and the California Mentality," 45 Hastings L.J. 617 (1994).

Codification found a home in Georgia as well. The legislature appointed three commissioners in 1858 to prepare a code "which should, as near as practicable, embrace in a condensed form, the Laws of Georgia." The Code was to embody the "great fundamental principles" of Georgia's jurisprudence, and "furnish all the information, on the subject of law, required either by the citizen or the subordinate Magistrate." The Code was divided into four parts— "the Political and Public Organization of the State," then a civil code ("Which treats of rights, wrongs, and remedies"), a code of practice, and a penal code. The Georgia Code was not intended to make new law, or to "graft upon our system any new features extracted from others, and unharmonious with our own." The goal was to clarify and restate, to "cut and unravel Gordian knots," to "give shape and order, system and efficiency, to the sometimes crude, and often ill-expressed, sovereign will of the State." The Code ran to some 4,700 sections. It was adopted in 1860 as the law of Georgia.[38]

Codes were successful in the West for reasons that by now are familiar. These were sparsely settled states in a hurry to absorb a legal system. A few had something of a civil-law tradition. In none of the Western states did the bar have a vested interest in old rules, especially rules of pleading. Codes were a handy way to get new law, a way of buying clothes off the rack, so to speak. But once the codes were on the books, the results fell far short of the hopes of the draftsmen. What happened afterward would have disgusted Field. Courts and lawyers were not used to codes. They tended to treat the Code provisions in accordance with their common-law habits and prejudices. In some cases, the Codes' provisions were construed away; more often, they were simply ignored. Nor did the legislature keep its hands off the Codes; they tended to let stand broad statements of principles (these made little difference anyway), while adding all sorts of accretions. It is hard to resist the conclusion that the Codes had almost no impact on behavior, either in court or out. The living law of California did not seem much different from the living law in noncode states, at least not in any way that the Codes would help to explain.

The Codes did focus attention on some drawbacks of the common law. The Codes are spiritual parents of the *Restatements of the Law*—black-letter codes of the twentieth century, sponsored by the American Law Institute. The restatements are supposed to do nothing more than restate the law, though in a mildly progressive way; and to persuade judges to adopt the Restatement view of doctrine. Both codes and restatements were reforms that did not reform. In the nineteenth century, law was constantly changing; every new statute was in a sense a reform; so was every new doctrine and ruling. The drafters of the codes were interested in reform in a special sense. They wanted to perfect an existing system. They wanted to make it more knowable, harmonious, and certain. Drastic shifts in political or economic power were no element of their plan.

A theory of sorts lay behind their work: a legal system is best, and works best, and does the most for society, if it conforms closely to the ideal of legal rationality. A legal order which is clear, orderly, systematic (in its formal parts), which has the most structural beauty, which most appeals to the modern,

---

[38] *The Code of the State of Georgia,* prepared by R. H. Clark, T. R. R. Cobb, and D. Irwin (1861), pp. iii, iv, vii, viii.

well-educated jurist, is also the best and the most efficient. This theory was rarely made explicit, and naturally never put to empirical test. It was in all probability wrong, since it exaggerated the impact of technical changes, and the value of rules on paper. One child labor act or one homestead act can have more potential impact than volumes of codes.

Paper changes were in a way the main point of law reform: law reform was, basically, changes in law that the leaders of the bar could agree on, and which were not socially or politically sensitive. Anything else was too controversial. A uniform wage-and-hour law, or a tax code, could never be presented as if it was blandly, incontrovertibly good. Law reform was a prominent part of the public-service work of the profession. It was useful for the lawyer's tarnished image. Law reform masqueraded as a socially important movement. It helped lawyers justify their monopoly of practice. It could pass for a service to society.[39] But service to the whole public is sometimes the same as service to nobody.

Late nineteenth-century law reform was a program of the upper or organized bar. The bar association movement began in the 1870s; and by the 1890s, the American Bar Association, and the local organizations, were pushing vigorously for reform and unification of American law. But the "law reform" that came out of these efforts was fairly meager, at least up to the end of the nineteenth century. Uniformity was tough to achieve in a federal union. As far as most branches of law were concerned, each state from Maine to the Pacific was a petty sovereignty, with its own brand of law. The American Bar Association left most of the law alone; it concerned itself with fields of law whose implications crossed state lines: the law of migratory divorce, for example, and commercial law, both of which were notoriously diverse.

On the surface, the most solid achievements were in commercial law. Arguably, the need was great. The United States was, or had become, a gigantic free-trade area. Businessmen could see the need for fair, uniform laws of commerce, in a huge, rich, and national market. Many differences in detail, among the state laws, had no particular point; the laws were functionally the same, with little quirks here and there, and small technical differences. This could be and often was a nuisance. The courts obviously could do little or nothing to make commercial law more uniform; there was no guiding hand, no ministry of justice, no overall control and coordination.[40] The job demanded legislation. In the last decade of the century, the American Bar Association encouraged states to appoint commissioners to meet and consider the problem of uniformity. A Negotiable Instruments Law (NIL), modeled after the English Bills-of-Exchange Act (1882), and with something of a nod to the California Code, was the first major effort of the commissioners on uniform state laws. The NIL became one of the most successful of the so-called uniform laws. By 1900, many states had

---

[39] See, in general, Lawrence M. Friedman, "Law Reform in Historical Perspective," 13 St. Louis U.L.J. 351 (1969).

[40] The federal courts, under the doctrine of *Swift v. Tyson* were supposed to apply general law, not the law of particular states, in cases between citizens of different states. See above, pp. 261–62; Tony A. Freyer, *Harmony and Dissonance: The Swift & Erie Cases in American Federalism* (1981); on other efforts by the federal courts in this direction, see Tony A. Freyer, "The Federal Courts, Localism, and the National Economy, 1865–1900," 53 Bus. Hist. Rev. 343 (1979).

adopted it; and it won almost universal acceptance before it was swept away by the Uniform Commercial Code in the 1950s and 1960s.

There were other triumphs of uniformity, however, that are easy to overlook, because they did not come out of the formal movement for uniform laws. The Interstate Commerce Act of 1887, the Sherman Act of 1890, the Bankruptcy Act of 1898, were all in a real sense responses to demands, commercial or political, for a single national authority. The "national" scope of legal education and legal literature was another factor, at least as far as legal culture is concerned, and particularly after Langdell purged Harvard of the lecture method and launched the case method of instruction. Not that all members of the legal profession were trained and socialized in the same way; but the profession was stratified more by social class and training than along geographical lines.

Publishers continued to spew forth an incredible profusion of legal materials: cases by the thousands; statutes in every state, every year or every other year; regulations, rulings, ordinances, and local customs on a scale that dwarfed the imagination. Tricks of research made this fabulous diversity somewhat more tractable. In the last quarter of the century, West Publishing Company, of St. Paul, Minnesota, began a profitable business, which promised to tame the dragons of case law. States tended to publish their high court decisions very slowly; West published them fast, and bound them into regional reports (Atlantic, Northeast, Northwest, Southern, Southeast, Southwest, and Pacific). *The Northwest Reporter,* which included Minnesota, was the first; it began to appear in 1879. West ultimately indexed the cases with a naive but effective "key-number" system. Keyed headnotes told the reader what the case decided; and put it into its appropriate legal category. Very soon, the little pop-art key of this private company became an indispensable tool of the lawyers. *The Century Edition of the American Digest,* which West published beginning in 1897, gathered together every reported case (it claimed there were more than 500,000 of them) indexed, classified, and bound into fifty volumes, from "Abandonment" through "Work and Labor." Each ten-year period since then, West has published a *Decennial Digest,* harvesting the cases for that decade; in between, it markets advance sheets and temporary volumes. The Citator system also began in the late nineteenth century. The Citator, published for individual states, then for regional groupings, helped the lawyer find the later history of a reported case. This was expressed in dry numbers and letters; but these told the reader *who* cited the case, on what point, and whether the case was approved, disapproved, or "distinguished." The Citator began as gummed labels for lawyers to paste in their personal or office copies of reports. Then it graduated to bound volumes. These red books, thick and thin, useful but unloved, became as familiar to lawyers as West's little keys.

Nothing remotely comparable was ever done, unfortunately, for the even more chaotic problem of statute law; Frederic Stimson published *American Statute Law* in 1881, a thick volume that gave a summary of the statutes of the states. This was nothing but a palliative. Until very recently, enacted law was still a jungle, fifty times over; trapped in complexity, it was waiting for some hero with an index. Nothing, until the computer came to the rescue, proved up to the task.

In a federal system, the diversity of American law was deep-seated and hard to eradicate, despite a common economy, a common legal tradition, despite the tools (telephone, telegraph) that bridged the distances, despite the West system of reporters and digests. The older the state, the more volumes of reports bulged on its shelves. Each state built up its own body of laws, and, as time went on, had less and less need to grub around elsewhere for precedent, or pay attention to its neighbors, and hardly any need at all to look to mother England. The West system did not cure these local diseases. The same was true of statutes; borrowing was common, but each state had its own codes and revisions. There were regional groupings, to be sure. "Legislative precedents" traveled across the country. California acted as a focal point for Western legislation and case law; Nevada, its desert satellite, drew on it heavily. The Southern states looked to each other for ways of getting rid of black voters; the smaller New England states modeled their railroad commissions on that of Massachusetts; states of the great plains had common problems of agriculture, freight rates, grain storage, railroad regulation; they all borrowed solutions from each other. In general, what kept the dialects of law from becoming separate languages was their community of experience. The states were moving in similar social and economic directions, and the law went along.

That people and goods flowed freely across state lines was the most important fact of American law. It meant that a competitive market of laws existed in the country. If a New Yorker had money, and wanted a divorce, she went to another state. If the corporation laws of his state were too harsh for an entrepreneur, there were friendlier laws in New Jersey, and later on, in Delaware. The states could act as "laboratories" of social legislation, to use a later euphemism; but this was only half the story. The states were sellers of competing laws in a vast federal bazaar. A kind of Gresham's law was in operation: easy laws drove out the harsh ones. Experiments in the "laboratories" would not work so long as neighbor states refused to go along. New York's hard divorce laws remained on the books, but the divorce mills made a mockery of these laws, especially (in the twentieth century) the great divorce mill in the desert, Nevada.[41] Legislators in the North and Middle West hesitated to pass progressive labor laws, because other states (often in the South) were eager to attract businesses with low-wages and easy laws. No one state could control big national companies; the national railroad nets laughed at the efforts of little Rhode Island or Connecticut. The only solutions were voluntary moves toward uniformity—or strong federal control. The first had no real muscle behind it. The second was the ultimate solution.

As of 1900, the American legal system was, as it had been, a system of astonishing complexity. Much had been streamlined and simplified; but the sheer number meant that there was plenty of complexity (useful and useless) left to complain about. Diversities as old as the seventeenth century still survived here and there. Local circumstances, local economic needs, local turns of

---

[41] In the twentieth century, Nevada made a career, so to speak, out of legalizing what was illegal elsewhere, especially in its big neighbor, California. Gambling was and is the most egregious example

events, local legal cultures—these helped preserve some diversities, and worked to create new ones. Each state had its own set of statutes. English influence was down to a trickle. No two states had the same economy, society, or history; no two had the same mix of peoples. These differences account for most of the variation. But not all of it. Why civil procedure in Illinois should have been more backward than civil procedure in Missouri is not easy to explain in terms of concrete social forces.

On the other hand, procedure and jurisdiction, those most lawyerly of subjects, were never merely neutral instruments. They made a difference. The choice between state and federal courts, for example, was not value-free. The big corporate interests much preferred the federal courts, in personal injury cases. They bent every muscle to shift cases to that forum.[42] Centrifugal and centripetal forces were both strong currents—and complex currents—running through American law.

---

[42] See Edward A. Purcell Jr., *Litigation and Inequality: Federal Diversity Jurisdiction in Industrial America, 1870–1958* (1992).

CHAPTER 4

THE LAND AND OTHER PROPERTY

THE TRANSFORMATION OF LAND LAW

The dominant theme of American land law was that land should be freely bought and sold. For this reason, lawyers, judges, and legislatures—and the landowning public—had gone to great pains, in the years after Independence, to untie the Gordian knots of English land law. Law had to fit the needs of those in a big, open country, who thought they lived in a land of abundance, a land with huge tracts of vacant land. (That there were native people living on some of this land was either ignored or ruthlessly dealt with.) For the settlers, land was the basis of wealth, the mother of resources and development. As the frontier moved farther west, land law followed at a respectable distance. The land itself was transformed from wilderness to farm or industrial land; from vacant sites to towns to cities. The land law, too, passed through phases of development. A state like New York had conditions different from Wyoming, and its land law reacted accordingly. Some of these differences in land and resource law, though never eliminated, tended to weaken over time. Colonial history in a way repeated itself; relatively rude, relatively simple land law, in the new settlements, changed to more complex, more sophisticated law, chiefly because more sophisticated law became more relevant to conditions.

For example, there was never much question that American law would absorb the concept of the fixture, with its attendant rules. A *fixture* is an object attached to the land. It is legally treated as part of the land. This means that sale of the land is automatically sale of its fixtures. A building is par excellence something attached to the land. Yet, in Wisconsin in the 1850s, a court decided in one case that a barn in Janesville, in another, the practice hall of the "Palmyra Brass Band," were not fixtures at all, but chattels, that could be detached from the land.[1] These were flimsy, temporary buildings; the cases simply recognized what was a local and transient condition.

Older doctrines did not last if they seemed not to fit the American ethos. The law of property became vigorously pro-enterprise: for example, the doctrine of nuisance in the late nineteenth century was bent to the needs of entrepreneurs who were using the land; private homeowners suffered.[2] In England,

---

[1] Lawrence M. Friedman, *Contract Law in America: A Social and Economic Case Study* (1965), p. 34.

[2] Paul M. Kurtz, "Nineteenth Century Anti-Entrepreneurial Nuisance Injunctions—Avoiding the Chancellor," 17 William & Mary L. Rev. 621 (1976).

"uninterrupted enjoyment" could give a landowner an *easement* of light and air. In other words, a landowner whose land had a pleasant, open view had a right to keep things that way; he could block his neighbor from putting up a building that would block his view and impair this easement. Especially in towns and cities, this doctrine was out of place—or so the courts thought. America was bent on economic growth—on trying to promote, not curb, the intensive use of land. Chancellor Kent thought the rule did not "reasonably or equitably apply . . . to buildings on narrow lots in the rapidly growing cities in this country." "Mere continuance of . . . windows," according to a Massachusetts law (1852), did not give an easement "of light and air" so as to keep an adjoining landowner from building on his land.[3] By the late nineteenth century, virtually every state had rejected this easement.[4]

In contrast, the states eagerly embraced the doctrine of adverse possession. Under this doctrine, if a person occupied land that belonged to somebody else, and did it openly and notoriously, and for a certain number of years, the actual title to the land shifted to the person in possession. The old owner lost his rights.[5] Western states, in particular, passed laws that made it easier to get title through adverse possession. They shortened the "adverse" period of time. Traditionally, the period had been twenty years; this shrank to five under the Nevada territorial laws of 1861.[6] To get the benefit of the doctrine, the settler had to show a house, a fence, a pastoral or pasturage use, or some other sign that he had actually used the land. Quite a few court cases turned on the question of what was enough possession to constitute "adverse possession."

On the surface, the doctrine of adverse possession seemed to favor settlers against absentee owners. Western land law seems to support this explanation. On the other hand, some evidence points in a different direction. In some states, starting with Illinois in 1872, an adverse claimant could not gain good title unless he paid taxes on the land while the period of possession was running. This requirement too was most common in Western states. An adverse claimant was not supposed to be a mere squatter. He was supposed to be someone who honestly thought he had a claim to the land. Such a person would naturally pay his taxes. This rule suggests that the doctrine was yet another response to chaotic land titles. Title was sometimes so murky and conflicted that many times a person might think he had good title, when in fact he did not. If he stayed in possession long enough, the doctrine cured the mistake. The statute, said Chief Justice Gibson of Pennsylvania, in 1845, "protects the occupant, not for his merit, for he has none, but for the demerit of his antagonist in delaying the contest beyond the period assigned for it, when papers may be lost, facts forgotten, or witnesses dead."[7] Yet, the doctrine itself was a cloud on titles; you could search county records till kingdom come—adverse possession left no records behind.

[3] Kent, *Commentaries*, vol. III (2nd ed., 1832) p. 446n; Laws Mass. 1852, ch. 144.

[4] Christopher G. Tiedeman, *An Elementary Treatise on the American Law of Real Property* (1885), sec. 613, pp. 475–76.

[5] Possession also had to be "hostile," that is, inconsistent with the true owner's claims. A tenant, for example, who leases land and pays rent, is in possession, but his possession is not "hostile," and does not threaten the landlord's title.

[6] Laws Terr. Nev. 1861, ch. 12, sec. 5.

[7] *Sailor v. Hertzogg*, 2 Pa. St. 182, 185 (1845).

THE PUBLIC LAND

Public lands were still a major topic of debate in the second half of the century. The idea that this great federal treasure should be used to raise money was all but dead. The demand for cheap land reached its climax in the famous Homestead Act of 1862, which actually gave it away for nothing, at least to settlers. The government continued to use land heavily as a kind of subsidy. The Morrill Act of 1862 handed over to the states a vast tract of land. Each state was entitled to 30,000 acres for each Senator and Representative, using the 1860 census as a base. Each state was to use the land (chiefly by selling it for cash) for the purpose of setting up "Colleges for the Benefit of Agriculture and Mechanic Arts."[8] In 1850, after much debate, the federal government also began to make land grants to help build railroads. The economic advantages, for most sections of the country, outweighed any lingering doubts about whether the national government could or should support internal improvements.

A proposed railroad from Chicago to Mobile was the subject of the first major land grant. This ultimately became the Illinois Central Railroad. The law, passed in 1850,[9] gave to the states of Illinois, Alabama, and Mississippi alternate sections of land for six miles on either side of the future line of tracks; the state could sell off the land and use the proceeds to build the road. Ungranted sections of land were to be sold by the U.S. government at not less than $2.50 an acre ("double the minimum price of the public lands").[10] Later acts— for example, the law of 1862 in aid of the Union Pacific—short-cut the process by giving the alternate sections directly to the railroad instead of to the states.[11]

In theory, the government lost nothing and got a railroad free, that is, without spending any cash. Government land, sandwiched between sections of railroad land, would fetch a double price, because the presence of a railroad would surely drive up its value. But even this notion was abandoned in the 1860s. The railroads of the 1860s had to run through the Far West—through endless grasslands, over great mountains, past deep forests, and across huge deserts. This domain was almost empty of settlers. The government price, understandably, had to be lowered. Moreover, the railroad grants conflicted with the spirit of the Homestead Act. After 1871, for a variety of reasons, the government made no more land grants to railroads. By this time, the harm or good had mostly been done. The exact amount of land granted to the railroads is in some dispute; even a conservative estimate would put it at more than 130 million acres.[12]

The Homestead Act was itself the climax of a long political struggle. It was a logical extension of trends in public-land policy. A vocal, sharply focused interest group worked (on the whole successfully) to defeat the policy of using

---

[8] 12 Stats. 503 (act of July 2, 1862); Paul W. Gates, *History of Public Land Law Development* (1968), pp. 335–36.

[9] 9 Stats. 466 (act of Sept. 20, 1850); see Gates, *op. cit.*, pp. 341–86.

[10] 9 Stats. 466 (act of Sept. 20, 1850). The government retained the right to transport its property and troops "free from toll." Since some land on either side of the road might be already occupied or taken, the statute made provision for substitute lands in such cases.

[11] 12 Stats. 489 (act of July 1, 1862).

[12] Robert S. Henry, "The Railroad Land Grant Legend In American History Texts," 32 Miss. Valley Hist. Rev. 171 (1945).

the land to raise cash for the government. As this policy faded, the land-grant principle was the only rival of the homestead policy.

Until 1861, the homestead idea was entangled in sectional disputes and the slavery crisis. There were strong champions of a homestead bill in Congress, like Galusha Grow of Pennsylvania, but there was also bitter opposition; President Buchanan vetoed a homestead bill in 1860. The outbreak of the Civil War removed many of the opponents from Congress. In 1862, the bill became law, and the government was now formally committed to the policy of granting land, free, to the pioneers, described by Grow as the "soldiers of peace," the "grand army of the sons of toil," people who struggled against the "merciless barbarities of savage life," and who had "borne [the] eagles in triumph from ocean to ocean."[13]

The provisions of the act were simple. Heads of families, persons over twenty-one, and veterans (but not those who had "borne arms against the United States or given aid and comfort to its enemies") were eligible, subject to certain exceptions, to "enter one quarter section or a less quantity of unappropriated public lands." Claimants had to certify that they wanted the land for their own "exclusive use and benefit" and "for the purpose of actual settlement." After five years of settlement, the government would issue a patent for the land. An actual settler who qualified could, however, buy up the land at the minimum price (generally $1.25 an acre) before the end of the five-year period.[14]

The Homestead Act assumed that there was productive land in the West, waiting for settlers. Special laws provided for the disposal of less desirable land—swamp land (1850), and desert lands (1877). These lands were commercially useless, and the government threw in extra inducements for reclamation. The swamp lands went free to the states, which, however, could sell them off to be drained. The desert land laws allowed individual claimants more acres than they could acquire through the Homestead Act; but the claimant had to irrigate his holdings. In addition, the federal government gave each new state a dowry of land as it entered the union. The states, therefore, held a considerable stock of land—swamp land; land under land-grant college laws; dowry lands at statehood. The states sold these lands on the open market. Wisconsin, for example, when it was admitted to the union, received public land from the federal government to be sold to raise "a separate fund to be called 'the school fund.'" The state disposed of its school lands at cheap prices and very favorable terms. It used the proceeds to lend money at interest to farmers who needed money, thus (it was thought) killing two birds with one stone. The panic of 1857, however, wrecked the farm-loan system. As debtors went into default, it became clear that the program had been fearfully mismanaged. The state lost heavily on its investments.[15] Many states in the 1860s similarly frittered away land they got under the Morrill Act. In some states, the "school lands" generated a tangled, almost forgotten mass of law about claims, terms, and priorities, a wonderland

[13] Galusha Grow, quoted in Benjamin Hibbard, *A History of the Public Land Policies* (1924), p. 384.

[14] 12 Stats. 392 (act of May 20, 1862).

[15] On the operation of the Wisconsin School Land Act, see Joseph Schafer, "Wisconsin's Farm Loan Law, 1849–1863," in *Proceedings, State Historical Society of Wisconsin, 68th Ann. Meeting (1920)*, p. 156.

of complexity which demonstrated the weakness of public-land law and the greed and dishonesty of some of its customers.

The public-land laws were hopelessly inconsistent. Some land was free for settlers; other land was for sale. The government proposed to sell some land to the highest bidder; proposed using other land to induce private enterprise to build railroads; gave other land to the states to fund their colleges. Administration was extremely feeble. The homestead principle, if that meant giving land free to the landless poor, was perhaps the most feeble. The government continued to sell land for cash; and the best land was "snapped up" by speculators. As Paul Wallace Gates describes it, settlers arriving in Kansas between 1868 and 1872 were greeted with advertisements announcing that the choicest lands in the state had been selected by the State Agricultural College, which was now offering 90,000 acres for sale on long-term credits. The Central Branch of the Union Pacific Railroad offered 1,200,000 acres for prices ranging from $1 to $15 per acre; the Kansas Pacific Railroad offered 5,000,000 acres for $1 to $6 per acre; the Kansas and Neosho Valley Railroad offered 1,500,000 acres for sale at $2 to $8 per acre; the Capital Land Agency of Topeka offered 1,000,000 acres of Kansas land for sale; Van Doren and Havens offered 200,000 acres for $3 to $10 per acre; T. H. Walker offered 10,000 (or 100,000) acres for $5 to $10 per acre; Hendry and Noyes offered 50,000 acres, and even the U.S. government was advertising for bids of approximately 6,000 acres of Sac and Fox Indian lands.[16]

All of this choice land, in government or private hands, was unavailable to the homesteader. In addition, those who drafted the act were apparently thinking of the rich and well-watered land of the Middle West. Immense tracts of land in the Far West were simply not fit for family farms; they were more suited to grazing and ranching.[17] Particularly after 1880, many people made use of the commutation privilege of the Homestead Act—the right to short-cut the homestead period by paying the regular price for the land. From 1881 to 1904, 22 million acres were commuted, 23 percent of the total number of homestead entries for this period. This was the "means whereby large land holdings were built up through a perverted use of the Homestead Act." A Senate document later recorded that "not one in a hundred" of these commuted lands was "ever occupied as a home. . . . They became part of some large timber holding or a parcel of a cattle or sheep ranch." The commuters were "usually merchants, professional people, school teachers, clerks, journeymen working at trades, cow punchers, or sheep herders." Typically, these commuters sold their land immediately after title vested.[18]

So complete a failure casts doubt on the idea that aid to the actual settler was ever really the guiding principle of public land law. Land law used the

[16] Paul W. Gates, "The Homestead Law in an Incongruous Land System," in Vernon Carstensen, ed., *The Public Lands* (1963), pp. 315, 323–24.

[17] Similarly, the Southern Homestead Act of 1866, which aimed to open public land in the South to freedmen and refugees, "turned out to be a resounding failure, partly because the lands set aside under it were the poorest quality, and partly because the freedmen lacked the necessary means to support themselves while working to clear the land and cultivate a crop." Martin Abbott, *The Freedmen's Bureau in South Carolina, 1865—1872* (1967), pp. 63–64.

[18] Hibbard, *op. cit.,* pp. 386–89; Paul W. Gates, *History of Public Land Law Development* (1968), pp. 387ff.

image of the sturdy farmer for slogans and propaganda. The law itself served more complicated interests: farmers and settlers, yes, but also businessmen, speculators, merchants, and lawyers. The Homestead Act itself, and public-land law in general, were complex and contradictory because so many interests had a voice in enactment and administration. The maze of case law, legislation, regulations, public-land-office rulings, and decrees owe their confusion to the same basic fact.

Toward the end of the century, there was a lot of talk about the death of the frontier. This conception made something of a mark on public-land law. In the beginning, a kind of roaring optimism underlay policy. The public domain was seen as an inexhaustible treasure. Whether land was to be sold or given away, used to create new centers of population or fund a school system, government's function was to move the land onto the market as soon as possible.[19] In the last years of the nineteenth century, the psychological horizon darkened. The national domain was visibly vanishing. There grew up a sense of scarcity and a kind of muted pessimism. Out of this grew the seeds of a conservation movement. Yellowstone National Park was established in 1872 "as a public park or pleasuring-ground for the benefit and enjoyment of the people."[20] A law of 1891 gave the president authority to "set apart and reserve . . . public lands wholly or in part covered with timber or undergrowth, whether of commercial value or not, as public reservations." President Harrison set aside, by proclamation, about 13,053,440 acres. President Cleveland added a vast new area—over the protests of Western Congressmen and Senators who valued the land for its mines and timber.[21]

Parallel developments took place in the states. A law of New York State, in 1892, established "the Adirondack Park," to be "forever reserved, maintained and cared for as ground open to the free use of all the people for their health or pleasure, and as forest lands necessary to the preservation of the headwaters of the chief rivers of the state, and a future timber supply."[22] The New York Constitution of 1897 declared the preserves "forever" wild. Conservationists made halting attempts to stop the slaughter of wildlife. Fish and game laws, too, were passed in increasing numbers. New Hampshire, for example, created "a board of commissioners on fisheries" in 1869. This later became a full-fledged fish and game commission, with power, for example, to close any restocked waters against fishing "for a period not exceeding three years." As of 1900, New Hampshire statutes forbade anyone to "hunt, kill, destroy, or capture any moose, caribou, or deer," except between September 15 and November 30. It was illegal to use dogs to hunt these animals. There was a season, too, for sable, otter, fishers, gray squirrels and raccoons, and an absolute prohibition on killing beaver. There were protective laws for many birds, too, including a ban on killing any "American or bald eagle."[23] After 1900, Americans could not foul their nest with quite so much impunity or legitimacy. But the growth of industry, cities, and

---

[19] The chief exception—mineral lands—merely underscores this point: it was recognized much earlier that these resources were finite and irreplaceable.

[20] 17 Stats. 32 (act of Mar. 1, 1872).

[21] Gates, *op. cit.*, pp. 567–69.

[22] Laws N.Y. 1892, vol. 1, ch. 707.

[23] N.H. Stats. 1901, chs. 130–32.

population, and the insatiable hunger for profit and consumption, meant that conservation efforts would never be easy or automatic.

In the cities, too, there was an upsurge of interest in beautification, parks, and boulevards. The first great public park was Philadelphia's Fairmount Park (from about 1855), followed soon afterward by New York's Central Park. The "green boulevard" soon became a feature of city landscapes. Illinois passed an elaborate statute on parks in 1871.[24] Cities and states began to use their powers of eminent domain as a way to *expand* the public sector, as a means of preserving natural beauty, and for parks and boulevards, not simply as a tool of economic growth.[25] Some towns and cities began to regulate, or even prohibit, billboards.[26]

A conservation mentality of another variety colored the growth of new tools of land-use control. Fashionable neighborhoods, with "good" addresses, developed in Eastern cities. Enclaves of wealth generated a demand for legal devices to protect property values and to maintain patterns of segregation by income and class. A leading English case, *Tulk v. Moxhay* (1848),[27] launched the doctrine of the equitable servitude or covenant. This was a doctrine that could be used to protect new subdivisions or neighborhoods. *Parker v. Nightingale* (Massachusetts, 1863)[28] brought the doctrine to America. The heirs of Lemuel Hayward had sold lots in Hayward Place, Boston, but with the express condition that only buildings "of brick or stone, of not less than three stories in height, and for a dwelling house only could be built." Forty years later, in 1862, James Nightingale, who owned one of the lots, leased his land to Frederick Loeber, who opened a "restaurant or eating-house." Crowds of "noisy and boisterous persons" disturbed the peace of Hayward Place. The neighbors brought an action to try to stop this. But what right did they have to interfere? They had an agreement, to be sure, but it ran to Hayward and his heirs, not to Nightingale or Loeber. The court, as in *Tulk v. Moxhay*, leaped right over this objection. The original covenant "ran with the land," as the phrase went. It was binding, in equity, on behalf of the "parties aggrieved." By the original scheme, "a right or privilege or amenity in each lot was permanently secured to the owners of all the other lots." As one writer put it, in 1901, allowing "free changing of property" and "shifting of titles" could sometimes work "hardship"; the "continued use of property in a particular locality for the same purpose was a very important element in the value and desirability of an investment . . . in the building of new towns of great promise, and in the building of great houses in old

---

[24] Christopher Tunnard and Henry H. Reed, *American Skyline* (1956), pp. 108–10; Rev. Stats. Ill., 1877, ch. 105.

[25] Generally speaking, too, the courts (and legislatures) in the years after the Civil War changed their general attitude toward eminent domain doctrines; in the early period (see above, Part II, ch. 3), doctrines tilted toward the taker of the lands; now protection leaned more toward the landowner whose lands were taken. See *Pumpelly v. Green Bay Company*, 80 U.S. 166 (1871).

[26] At first, these ordinances did not always find a friendly reception in the courts. In *Crawford v. City of Topeka*, 51 Kan. 756, 33 Pac. 476 (1893), a billboard ordinance was voided as "unreasonable." The court could not see how "the mere posting of a harmless paper upon a structure changes it from a lawful to an unlawful one."

[27] 2 Phil. 774, 41 Eng. Rep. 1143 (Ch., 1848).

[28] 6 Allen (88 Mass.) 341 (1863).

towns."[29] Long before any zoning laws (these did not arrive until the twentieth century) the equitable covenant was a kind of functional equivalent—a legal tool to protect neighborhood values against the risks of urban change. Yes, land was a commodity; but it was also somebody's asset and somebody's home; and the middle class rarely let ideology stand in the way of its interests.

PROPERTY LAW AND THE DYNASTS

The New York property codes, from the late 1820s, were adopted, as we have seen, by Michigan, Wisconsin, and Minnesota. Later Western states—the Dakotas, Arizona—also swallowed chunks of property law whose ultimate source was New York. New York had abolished a lot of dead wood and revised many aspects of property law. This includes the law of *future interests*—interests in property that were not present and possessory. The old law of future interests had served the great landed estates. With a slight twist, the law served the needs of new dynasts, whose money was tied up not in landed estates, but in trusts.

The details of the law of future interests are not important and, in any event, are almost beyond the layman's patience or comprehension. Essentially, what happened was this: in some rare but important cases, rich men established trusts (by will or deed), to be held for their children, and later distributed to grandchildren (or collateral relatives). Meantime, the principal was safe, and the estate remained intact. The law of future interests regulated relationships among remote beneficiaries, determined what kinds of dynastic arrangements were permissible, and how long these arrangements might last. Now the New York reforms, in the end, themselves had to be reformed. And the ghosts of old English doctrines of contingent remainders, springing uses, determinable fees, and other mysteries, began to haunt the law courts. A person could "tie up" his or her estate after he or she was dead.

A law and practice of trust administration grew up to handle and manage dynastic wealth. Most trustees were amateurs—relatives or friends named in a will, or appointed trustees in a trust agreement. A few (almost exclusively in Boston) were professional managers. After the Civil War, a new institution appeared: the corporate trust company. In 1871, for example, a charter was issued in New York to the Westchester County Trust Company. The company had power to invest trust money "in public stocks of the United States," in securities of New York State, in "bonds or stocks of any incorporated city," and in corporate securities up to $10,000.[30] Toward the end of the century, some states began to formalize the law of trust investment by enacting "legal lists"—lists of investments trustees could put trust funds in, without running the risk of lawsuits by beneficiaries. Massachusetts, and a few other states, gave their trustees more autonomy. The leading decision in Massachusetts was the famous *Harvard College* case (1830), which we mentioned in an earlier chapter.[31]

---

[29] Henry U. Sims, *A Treatise on Covenants Which Run with Land* (1901), preface v.

[30] Laws N.Y. 1871, ch. 341 See James G. Smith, *The Development of Trust Companies in the United States* (1928); Lawrence M. Friedman, "The Dynastic Trust," 73 Yale L.J. 547 (1964).

[31] *Harvard College v. Amory,* 26 Mass. (9 Pick.) 446 (1830); see above p. 253.

The *Harvard College* rule—the rule of the prudent investor—was a rule that was suitable to long-term, dynastic trusts. This kind of trust was relatively rare, and the Massachusetts doctrine did not spread very far in the nineteenth century. The other line of authority, the more restrictive line, aimed to protect people who were legally or factually helpless—the proverbial widows and orphans. This was almost the only type of trust outside the major commercial centers; and even in the East it was the dominant form. The Pennsylvania Constitution of 1873 forbade the legislature from authorizing the investment of trust funds "in the bonds or stocks of any private corporation."[32]

There were a number of quite startling developments in the law of trusts. One was the so-called spendthrift trust doctrine. A spendthrift trust was a trust that tried to lock up the beneficiary's interests as tightly as possible. No beneficiary could give away or mortgage the beneficiary's rights in the trust; and no creditor of a beneficiary could reach or attach that interest, before money actually passed into the beneficiary's hands. There was no such thing, in other words, as the right to garnish an interest in a spendthrift trust, or put a lien on it. John Chipman Gray, a Bostonian and a law teacher, in the first edition of his tedious little book, *Restraints on the Alienation of Property,* attacked this extraordinary doctrine; it was, he said, both illogical and against the weight of precedent. Yet Massachusetts, Gray's home state, ignored logic and precedent and baldly adopted the doctrine, in *Broadway Bank v. Adams* (1882).[33] Gray wrote an angry preface to his second edition: the spirit of "paternalism," he said darkly, was abroad in the land. This was the "fundamental essence alike of spendthrift trusts and of socialism." But the spendthrift trust certainly had nothing to do with socialism; and its paternalism was the dynastic urge of rich people, whose doctrinal capital was Boston, Massachusetts.

The *rule against perpetuities* was a doctrine that put a limit on dynastic dreams of financial immortality. The rule developed over the course of two centuries. It reached the form that tortured generations of suffering law students by about 1800. John Chipman Gray made a specialty of this rule, too. His treatise on the subject was first published in 1888. The rule dealt with long-term trusts or chains of future interests. A future right to income or property was no good, unless it "vested" no later than within twenty-one years of some "lives in being." You could postpone "vesting" during the lifetimes of people born before the will or trust went into effect, with another twenty-one years tacked on. The details were horrendously complicated, mind-bending, treacherous. They were so convolute, that it is easy to lose sight of the point, which is this: How long can the dead hand rule? How long can a person "tie up" his estate, after he dies? The practical effect of the rule was to limit dynasties to a period of no more than seventy-five or one hundred years, at the outer limit. New York, in the late 1820s, had adopted a more ruthless and restrictive rule, copied later in California, Michigan, and Wisconsin, among other states. The ordinary, common law rule was in effect in most other places.

For much of the nineteenth century, the law had not shown much favor to the *charitable trust.* The problem here was fear of the dead hand, particularly

---

[32] Pa. Const. 1873, art. III, sec. 22. A similar provision appears in Alabama (1875), Colorado (1876), Montana (1889), and Wyoming (1889).

[33] 133 Mass. 170 (1882).

the dead hand of the Church. New York's property laws severely limited the charitable trust. When Samuel Tilden, lawyer and almost-president, died, he left millions of dollars to fund a public library in New York City. But the New York courts (1891) struck down the Tilden trust, and gave the money to his heirs. This galvanized the legislature into action. In 1893, New York changed its laws, and removed the shadow of invalidity from charitable trusts.[34]

Charitable trusts were also invalid or restricted in Midwestern states which borrowed New York's property laws (Michigan, Minnesota, Wisconsin), and in a cluster of Southern states centering on Virginia. Here there were, perhaps, long memories and old hatreds going all the way back to the Reformation. Some states also enacted so-called "mortmain" statutes, as we have seen (Part II, p. 207). These outlawed death-bed gifts to charity. The Pennsylvania version was passed in 1855.[35] Behind these laws, as we pointed out, was the fantasy of the evil priest, who preyed on the fears of the dying.

The changing nature of American wealth was what finally weakened restrictions on charitable gifts and charitable trusts. The great foundations were still far in the future; but the barons of finance, oil, and steel were beginning to give away conscience money. When the Tilden trust failed in New York, it was not a defeat for the "dead hand," but for the city of New York, and the people who lived in it.

New York was late in embracing the charitable trust. Some states were more hospitable. Massachusetts, in fact, had put new life in the doctrine of *cy pres* (law-French for "so near")—a doctrine essential to the long-term charity. Suppose the original purpose of a charitable trust has failed or become impossible. Instead of giving the money back to the heirs, a court of equity could modify it, and apply it to a purpose as close as possible to the original. In *Jackson v. Phillips* (1867),[36] Francis Jackson of Boston had died in 1861, leaving money to be used to "create a public sentiment that will put an end to Negro slavery," and also for the benefit of fugitive slaves. By 1867, slavery had been legally ended. Jackson's relatives came into court and said, quite naturally, the purpose cannot be carried out. Give the money back to us. But the court refused. Instead, it directed a "so near" use of the fund—for welfare and educational work among New England blacks, and among freed slaves. The court did not invent the doctrine—it was old in England—but the case did give it a new and vigorous lease on life. The doctrine helped the long-term, dynastic charity, just as the Massachusetts rule on trust investment helped dynastic trusts in general.

The law of *wills* had always been receptive to doctrines imported from England. Some American statutes, for example, remodeled themselves in the light of the English Wills Act (1837). The general trend was toward more formality in the execution of wills, for the sake of property records if nothing else. Informal, oral wills ceased to count, practically speaking.[37] This does not mean that the law of wills remained implacably formal and rigid. In general, courts loosened

---

[34] *Tilden v. Green*, 130 N.Y. 29, 28 N.E. 880 (1891); James B. Ames, "The Failure of the 'Tilden Trust,'" 5 Harv. L. Rev. 389 (1892); Laws N.Y. 1893, ch. 701.

[35] Laws Pa. 1855, ch. 347, sec. 11.

[36] 96 Mass. 539 (1867).

[37] In the West and South, the holographic will—handwritten, but needing no witnesses— was allowed.

their rules of interpretation of wills. They moved away from fixed canons of construction, and put more stress on what the testator actually meant to say. His intention was the "pole star," the "sovereign guide" of interpretation.[38] This attitude was appropriate in a country of general, though hardly sensational, literacy, where millions owned property, and standards of legal (and lay) draftsmanship were low. The cases reflected a certain tension: courts wanted to carry out the testator's wishes, but they also recognized the need for certainty, sound routine, and rough predictability.

Between 1850 and 1900, more ordinary people developed the habit of making wills; and more estates went through probate. One study of wills compared a sample of wills in Essex County, New Jersey, in 1850, 1875, and 1900. In 1850, less than 5 percent of those who died left wills; only about 8 percent had estates of any sort. By 1900, roughly 14 percent of the dying population left estates that went through probate; 8 percent were testate. Fewer probated wills were "deathbed" or last-illness wills in 1900. In 1850, at least a quarter of the wills were executed less than a month before death; in 1900 less than a fifth. The wealthier testators were more sophisticated about the draftsmanship of their wills in 1900 compared to 1850. They were more likely to cover such simple contingencies as what to do if a beneficiary died before the testator did.

The earlier the will in Essex County, the more likely it was to leave property in trust or in the form of a legal life estate. This was especially true of gifts to or for women: 73.3 percent of the 1850 wills made this kind of gift, but only 40 percent of the 1900 wills. Does this mean that women had become more independent, socially, or that more middle-class people made out wills, or does it reflect the fact that the legal status of married women had changed? It is hard to know, because so little research has been done on the subject. A study of Bucks County, Pennsylvania, which compared wills at the beginning and near the end of the nineteenth century, had rather different results. About 12 percent of the testators around 1800 created trusts, and about 30 percent in the 1890s—half of these were trusts for the surviving spouse (usually a widow). Many 1900 testators were themselves women, in both Essex and Bucks County. In fact, in Bucks County, in the 1890s, some 38 percent of the testators were women. Some of the women testators may have been women in simple circumstances—Mrs. Mary Duffy, who signed her will by mark and left everything to her husband in Essex County; or Grace Creamer, also of Essex County, whose pathetic will, executed on her dying day, left everything to her newborn, illegitimate child. The earlier Essex County wills, by and large, directed the executors to sell off the property; in the 1850s, the safest course seemed to be to turn the estate into cash. Later the more sophisticated wills set up estates that would continue, under careful management, retaining its assets until market conditions dictated otherwise.[39]

---

[38] James Schouler, *A Treatise on the Law of Wills* (2nd ed., 1892), p. 500.
[39] The data from Essex County comes from Lawrence M. Friedman, "Patterns of Testation in the 19th Century: A Study of Essex County (New Jersey) Wills," 8 Am. J. Legal Hist. 34 (1964); the material on Bucks County is from Carole Shammas, Marylynn Salmon, and Michel Dahlin, *Inheritance in America: From Colonial Times to the Present* (1987), pp. 107, 119.

LANDLORD AND TENANT

A *tenant* can mean different things, depending on whether the tenant holds farm land, commercial property, or a city apartment, and on what terms. The American lease was, in general, no longer purely a document of land tenure. Even for agricultural lands, it was basically a commercial contract.

In New York, pitched battles in the 1840s marked the beginning of the end for one of the last remnants of one kind of feudal tenancy in America. The New York landed estates were an anachronism. The American dream was to hold land in fee simple. It seemed inconsistent with American ideals to have a permanent class of tenants with no right ever to own their land. The New York Constitution of 1846, after the downfall of the patroons, outlawed feudal tenures and long-term agricultural leases. Meanwhile, exemption and homestead laws, in almost all the states, protected the farmer's basic holdings of land, animals, and tools from seizure for debt. Distress for rent—the landlord's right to extract delinquent rent directly from the land—was, in many states, abolished.[40]

Most farm families were freeholders; but there were in fact tenant farmers, absentee landlords, and sizable leaseholds, even in the North. Large "frontier landlords" in Illinois had tenants who paid in shares of crops or, more rarely, cash. One of the most notorious was William Scully, of Ireland, an alien and absentee landlord; there was considerable unrest on his vast prairie holdings in the 1880s.[41] On the other hand, the leasehold, protean and flexible, was for many young farmers the first step up the ladder of farm success; and for old farmers, it was a way to transfer land to sons to manage, without giving up complete control.

That characteristic Southern arrangement, the cropping contract, was quite different. There had been cropping contracts in the North and South before the Civil War. But only after the war did the cropping system become a cardinal feature of the economic system in the South. Along with the changing social meaning of the sharecropping contract went changes in its legal attributes, as developed by the courts. In 1839, the North Carolina supreme court held that a landlord had no rights in the crop before the tenant actually gave the landlord his share. There was no statutory lien, and the right to distress for rent had been done away with; creditors of the tenant were free to levy on the crop, without interference from the landlord.[42]

In 1874, the legal relationship looked different to the court. A cropper was now said to have "no estate in the land"; the estate "remains in the landlord." The cropper was only a "laborer receiving pay in a share of the crop."[43] There was room for dispute about who was or was not a "cropper." In the case that inspired the words quoted, the tenant was held *not* to be a cropper, even though he received his horses, his corn and bacon, his farming utensils and his feed from the landlord. Some farmers in fact *were* like ordinary tenants, paying

---

[40] Laws N.Y. 1846, ch. 274; see, in general, Charles W. McCurdy, *The Anti-Rent Era in New York Law and Politics, 1831–1865* (2001).

[41] Paul W. Gates, *Frontier Landlords and Pioneer Tenants* (1945).

[42] *Deaver v. Rice*, 20 N. Car. 431 (1839).

[43] *Harrison v. Ricks*, 71 N.H. Car. 7 (1874).

"rent" with a share of the crop; there were also farm workers who were paid in crop shares.[44]

But much more common than either of these arrangements was true share-cropping. It obtained in over 50 percent of the small farms in the South. The cropper (usually black, usually illiterate) signed (or marked) a contract. One typical contract—it was executed in 1886, in North Carolina—gave the cropper half the crop, in exchange for a promise to work "faithfully and diligently," and to be "respectful in manners and deportment" to the owner. The owner provided "mule and feed for the same and all plantation tools and Seed to plant the crop," and advanced "fifty pound of bacon and two sacks of meal per month and occasionally Some flour," to be paid for out of the cropper's share.[45]

The cropper was thus a worker, not an owner; he was not a partner of the landlord, but an "employee"—one that was paid in a share of the crop, rather than in money.[46] North Carolina (1876) made clear the landlord's rights. All crops at all times were "deemed and held to be vested in possession" by the landlord, or his assigns. The sharecropper himself owned nothing, until his share was actually turned over to him.[47] The landlord's rights were para-mount—against the village merchant and outside creditors, as well as against the tenant. The land tenure system reflected and reinforced the real world of power relationships in the South. And race relations, as well.

MORTGAGES

The mortgage was (and is) a primary mode of financing the buying and selling of land. The buyer would, very often, execute a promissory note, secured by a mortgage on the property. Since land was the most valuable asset of most people who owned anything, the mortgage was a major instrument of credit and finance, and a major subject of the law. West's *Century Digest,* covering all cases reported to 1896, has more than 2,750 pages of cases on mortgages. Farmers used the mortgage to raise money for more land, to buy agricultural machinery, even to cover personal expenses. In some parts of the country, farmers tended to borrow to the limit of their equity; in good years, when land prices were rising, they simply borrowed more. One swarm of locusts, one drought, one "panic" was enough to wipe out the security, sweep the farm into court, and replace an economic problem with a legal one. No wonder, then, that mortgage law tended to swing with the business cycle. Legislatures expanded or contracted the redemption period, according to whether times were good or bad. In 1886, Washington state changed a six-month period to a full year; in a period of upswing (1899), Michigan, perhaps as an incentive to investment, passed a statute that gave the

[44] Roger L. Ransom and Richard Sutch, *One Kind of Freedom: The Economic Consequences of Emancipation* (1977), pp. 90–91.

[45] *Ibid.,* p. 91.

[46] Harold D. Woodman, *New South—New Law: The Legal Foundations of Credit and Labor Relations in the Postbellum Agricultural South* (1995), ch. 3.

[47] Laws N. Car. 1876–77, ch. 283, sec. 1.

debtor six months after sale to redeem; the period had previously been two years and three months.[48]

No wonder, too, that voters in agricultural states constantly agitated for government loans, cheap mortgage money, tough rules on foreclosure, easy rules on redemption. One incident may give some idea of the politics of mortgage law. In the early 1850s, many Wisconsin farmers bought stock in railroad companies. Since they had no ready money, they pledged their lands as security. The railroad's future dividends were supposed to pay the interest due on the mortgage—usually 8 percent. The railroads then used, or misused, the farmers' notes and mortgages to seduce Eastern investors into investing in railroad finance. In the panic of 1857, the Wisconsin railroads collapsed. The farmers were left high and dry, holding worthless stock. Meanwhile, their mortgages were in the hands of Eastern interests.

The farmers put pressure on the legislature. The legislature responded by passing a series of laws, trying every which way to prevent a wave of foreclosures. The laws used various techniques. One law stripped the notes and mortgages of negotiability. This meant that the farmers could raise the defense of fraud in foreclosure suits before friendly local juries. In a line of cases, beginning in 1858, the Wisconsin supreme court declared this and every single one of the relief statutes unconstitutional, citing the *Dartmouth College* doctrine and the court's own sense of justice and sound economics.[49] Foreclosure was a bitter pill, but not half so bitter as a policy that would dry up the money market and choke off investment in the state. At least this is what the court must have thought. It was an idea that, in the long run, preserved the tensile strength and flexibility of the law. The need for a source of mortgage money, in any event, acted as a brake on runaway mortgage and foreclosure law.

THE DECLINE OF DOWER

Common law dower had once been the chief way to provide for a widow's twilight years. Dower was a peculiar kind of estate. For one thing, it attached to land only. For another, dower was a mere life estate (in one-third of the late husband's real estate). The widow had no right to sell; and she had no rights over the "remainder," that is, no right to dispose of the land after her death, by will or otherwise. The land remained, in short, in the husband's bloodline. Dower had one rather remarkable feature: a husband could not defeat the right by selling his land or giving it away. Over all land he owned, or had owned, hung the ghostly threat of "inchoate dower." This potential claim followed the land through the whole chain of title, until the wife died and extinguished the claim.

As a protection device, dower had severe limitations. It perhaps made sense for the landed gentry of England; or for plantation owners. But if the husband's wealth consisted of stocks and bonds, or a business, dower did the wife

---

[48] Robert H. Skilton, "Developments in Mortgage Law and Practice," 17 Temple L.Q. 315, 329–30 (1943).

[49] The story is told in Robert S. Hunt's fine study, *Law and Locomotives: The Impact of the Railroad on Wisconsin Law in the Nineteenth Century* (1958).

little good. Dower had another fault, too. It was superior to the claims of the husband's creditors, which was good for wives but bad for the creditors. And dower was an annoying cloud on titles. Long years after some piece of land had been sold, the widow of some prior owner could rise up like a ghost to haunt a buyer. This was perhaps the real fly in the ointment. The Midwest, poor in everything *but* land, showed early impatience with dower. Indiana abolished it, at least in name, in 1852. In its place, Indiana gave the widow a cut from her husband's personal property, and one-third of his real estate "in fee simple, free from all demands of creditors."[50] The same statute abolished "tenancies by the courtesy" (usually spelled *curtesy*). This was the corresponding estate for widowers—which had, however, this peculiarity: It vested only if the couple ever had a child born alive. Under the new law, the husband gained symmetrical rights in his wife's estate. Kansas, in the Civil War period, gave the widow the right to elect her dower, or, "as she may prefer," to choose an absolute share (one-half) of her husband's estate, both real and personal.[51] The absolute share was always to her advantage, unless her husband died insolvent, in which case dower was better.

A TANGLE OF TITLES

As before, so also after 1850, the traumatic weakness of land titles had a pervasive effect on land law. It played a role, for example, in the decline of dower. It hastened the decline of the common-law marriage, and stimulated formality in the law of wills. As fast as the law developed ways to make land more marketable, and to improve the quality of titles, other events seemed to pop up to make the situation worse. Railroad, school, and land grants, for example, created problems of vague and overlapping titles in some of the Western states. California and New Mexico inherited a legacy of confusion from the Mexican period. Congress established for California a three-man commission to unsnarl titles flowing from Mexican grants (1851). Every claimant whose "right or title" to land "derived from the Spanish or Mexican government" was to present the claim to the commissioners, together "with such documentary evidence and testimony of witnesses as the said claimant relies upon."[52] The board completed its work by 1856; but litigation continued for years in the federal courts. The board handled something over 800 cases; 604 claims were confirmed, 190 rejected, 19 withdrawn. But landowners in California had to wait, on average, seventeen years after filing a petition before title was finally confirmed.[53] The course of events in New Mexico was even more protracted. As late as 1891, Congress passed an act "to establish a Court of Private Land Claims," to untangle Mexican land grants in New Mexico, Arizona, Utah, Nevada, Colorado, and Wyoming.[54]

[50] Rev. Stats. Ind. 1852, ch. 27, secs. 16, 17. If the land was worth more than $10,000, the widow could have only one quarter of it, as against the husband's creditors; and if the land was worth more than $20,000, one fifth.

[51] Kans. Stats. 1862, ch. 83. For these and other early developments, see Charles H. Scribner, *Treatise on the Law of Dower*, vol. 1 (2nd ed., 1883), p. 48.

[52] 9 Stats. 631 (act of March 3, 1851).

[53] W. W. Robinson, *Land in California* (1948), p. 106.

[54] 26 Stats. 854 (act of March 3, 1891).

Floating land scrip was another source of confusion. Scrip had been issued for a number of purposes: under the Morrill Act, for example, the scrip stood as evidence that the state was entitled to land, to be used to raise money for colleges. A miscellaneous group of statutes created other scraps of scrip. One Thomas Valentine, a land claimant from California, lost his fight for a three-square-league ranch near Petaluma, but got Congress to pass a private relief act in 1872. In exchange for a release of his claims to the ranch, Valentine received scrip for 13,316 acres of public land. Some he used, and some he sold:

> Speculators got some, hiking the price, to peddle along with other types of scrip. In time Valentine scrip became too high-priced to be used on admittedly public lands, and scrip owners had to look for forgotten islands—"sleepers"—areas overlooked by government surveyors and with questionably held titles.[55]

Land law itself contributed to the weakness of titles. Adverse possession was one problem. Poor administration of land laws was another chronic cause of doubtful titles. "Tax-titles" were notoriously weak. A "tax title" came about when local government sold off property for delinquent taxes and issued a deed to the purchaser. The laws on the subject were complicated, and so difficult to comply with that, in the words of a contemporary treatise, "the investigator of titles always looks with suspicion upon a title that depends upon a tax-deed."[56] Legislatures constantly had to intervene to make good the faulty work of local officials. Iowa, for example, passed fifty-nine separate acts in 1880 to legalize defective actions of officials. Many of these were land actions. One law, for example, recited that some swamp lands had been sold without the county seal, as the law required, and without the clerk's signature; since "doubts" had "arisen" about these deeds, the deeds were "hereby legalized and made valid" (ch. 180).

The sheer volume of land transactions made the situation worse. There were deeds, mortgages, transfers, in the thousands, then in the hundreds of thousands. The crude system of land registration could barely cope with the volume. Title companies sprang up to check titles for a fee, and to insure landowners against mysterious "clouds" that might arise to befuddle their interests. The Real Estate Title Insurance Company of Philadelphia, chartered in 1876, seems to have been the pioneer. The predecessor of New York's Title Guaranty & Trust Company was chartered in 1883.[57] The great fire of 1871 destroyed the public records in Chicago. Four private abstract companies saved their records: indexes, abstracts, maps, and plats. These companies later formed a title-guarantee company; a merger in 1901 created the Chicago Title & Trust Company, which came to dominate the business in Chicago.[58]

An Australian system, called *Torrens* after its inventor, Sir Robert R. Torrens, held out hope for a way to cure diseases of title once and for all. The standard practice was for land documents—deeds, mortgages, land contracts—to be

---

[55] Robinson, *op. cit.*, p. 179.

[56] Christopher G. Tiedeman, *An Elementary Treatise on the American Law of Real Property* (1885), p. 580.

[57] Laws N. Y. 1883, ch. 367.

[58] Pearl J. Davies, *Real Estate in American History* (1958), pp. 35–36.

deposited and noted in a public-record office. The office acted as little more than a warehouse with indexes. But when land went into the Torrens system, the state of the title was examined, and a certificate of title issued. Land brought into Torrens underwent a scathing, one-time baptism of law; in the process, it was cleansed of its sins, all those "faint blemishes" and "mysterious 'clouds'" which "so darkly and portentously" hung over real estate, even when "hitherto not visible to the naked eye."[59] After this initial trauma, the land emerged as fresh and free of taint as a newborn baby. From that point on, title was in effect insured by the state. A contract, not a deed, became the instrument of transfer; and title and guaranty were at all times kept up to date simply and efficiently.

Illinois was the first state to pass a title-registration statute, in 1895; Massachusetts. Ohio, and California had statutes before 1900. The state bar association and the Chicago real-estate board supported a Torrens system for Illinois; but there was bitter opposition, too; and the title guarantee companies were not happy to see a governmental competitor. The Illinois law called for a referendum in any county that wanted to embark on Torrens; Cook County (Chicago) complied, and after one false start—the Illinois supreme court declared the first Torrens act unconstitutional—a valid act was passed, in 1897, and put into effect.[60] The system was optional, however, even in Cook County. The public, legal and lay, was torpid and indifferent. Besides, Torrens had a serious drawback: the first land registration for any parcel of land was expensive. In 1899, there were only 155 applications to register land under the Torrens system in all of Cook County.[61] As of 1900, then, title registration was at best a hope, at worst a missed opportunity.

INTELLECTUAL PROPERTY. PATENTS, COPYRIGHTS, AND TRADEMARKS

After the act of 1836, which established the Patent Office, Congress made few major changes in the administration of patent law. Patents themselves multiplied like weeds. The number increased each year. Between 1836 and 1890, 431,541 patents were granted.[62]

The volume of patent litigation increased along with the number of patents. The patent office refused many applications; but even when it granted a patent, this was no guarantee that the patent was valid. Getting a patent did not mean, in itself, that the patent would stand up in court. Patent litigation was complex, and fruitful of doctrine and controversy. In an infringement suit, it was a good defense to claim that the patent should never have been granted. A few law firms and lawyers built their fortunes on patent cases, especially after the Civil War, when a specialized patent bar began to develop. George

[59] John T. Hassam, "Land Transfer Reform," 4 Harv. L. Rev. 271, 275 (1891).

[60] Theodore Sheldon, *Land Registration in Illinois* (1901), pp. 1–3.

[61] Richard R. Powell, *Registration of the Title to Land in the State of New York* (1938), p. 145.

[62] Chauncey Smith, "A Century of Patent Law," 5 Quarterly J. of Economics 44, 56 (1890).

Harding (1827–1902) became rich and prominent arguing patent cases in federal court.[63]

The path of a patent could be rocky. According to one authority, between 1891 and 1904, 30 percent of the patents in the circuit courts of appeal were declared invalid; another 41 percent were held not to be infringed. Only 19 percent were declared both valid and infringed.[64] In effect, the federal courts sat as a kind of many-headed commissioner of patents.

An industrial society rests on pillars of fresh technology. In an expansive, free-market economy, the patent monopoly was in a way anomalous. But, like corporate franchises, land grants, and high tariffs, the patent was also a kind of subsidy, an incentive to inventors and to innovation. Public opinion was of two minds about it. The original law no doubt had in mind the small inventor, working through the night in his study or laboratory. There were such people. But they came to be a minority of American inventors. In general, they were precisely the ones who could not afford patent litigation, or the expense of fighting off patent pirates.

Toward the end of the century, the courts seemed to become keenly aware that a patent could be used to stifle competition. They grew quite stingy about granting preliminary injunctions against infringement. The only foolproof way to protect a patent, then, was to engage in long, costly litigation. This policy was hard on the small inventor; on the other hand, it made patents harder to use in restraint of trade. Some courts apparently felt that there were too many patents; no "standing room for an inventor" was left, no "pathway open for forward progress."[65] Patents were, potentially, a tool of the trusts. This attitude, this fear, was part of the feeling of economic constriction, the general terror of small horizons, which was so salient in the late nineteenth century.

An important Supreme Court case, in 1850, turned on whether a patent for a new doorknob was valid. The only novelty, it seemed, was that the doorknob was made out of porcelain. A patent, said Justice Samuel Nelson, required "more ingenuity" than that of "an ordinary mechanic acquainted with the business."[66] This was a doctrine that cut down, severely, the number of valid new patents. In 1875, the Court confronted a patent for preserving fish "in a close chamber by means of a freezing mixture, having no contact with the atmosphere of the preserving chamber." The Court held the patent void. There was nothing novel here; the scheme made no advance over prior art. It reminded Justice Noah H. Swayne of a technique used by undertakers (though not for fish) and of things about ice cream that were common knowledge.[67] In 1880, Swayne used a striking phrase—"a flash of thought"—to describe what a valid patent needed.[68] The "ordinary mechanic"—a kind of blue-collar version of the "reasonable man" in the law of torts—was the negative model; only a "flash of genius," gave merit to a patent. In general, the courts steered a cautious,

---

[63] See Albert H. Walker, "George Harding," in *Great American Lawyers,* vol. VIII (1909), pp. 45–87.

[64] Floyd K, Vaughan, *The United States Patent System* (1956), p. 199.

[65] *Two Centuries' Growth of American Law,* p. 396.

[66] *Hotchkiss v. Greenwood,* 52 U.S. (11 How.) 248, 267 (1850).

[67] *Brown v. Piper,* 91 U.S. 37 (1875).

[68] *Densmore v. Scofield,* 102 U.S. 375, 378 (1880).

middle-of-the-road course in patent law. Patents were for genuine novelty, for rewarding skill and insight, and nothing else. Courts were suspicious of small improvements, mass-produced by big companies.

Entrepreneurs, for their part, were hardly fond of the chaos of patent law. As early as 1856, manufacturers of sewing machines formed a patent pool.[69] Large companies learned how to manipulate patents to stretch out their monopoly. Bell Telephone bought a German patent, vital to the technology of long-distance telephoning. It waited until *its* telephone patent had almost expired, then pressed ahead with the German device. This gave it control of the telephone industry even after its first basic patent passed into the public domain. Under the umbrella of the patent monopoly, companies divided up markets, chopped up the country into segments, parceled these out in licenses, and chained whole counties or states to particular vendors of a patented good.

The law of intellectual property shows the tendency of the law to expand the concept of property—to protect whatever had a real market, including intangibles. This was true of patent rights; and also of copyright. In 1856, the copyright statute was amended to include dramatic productions; in 1865, to cover photographs and negatives.[70] In 1870, the copyright (and patent) laws were substantially revised. Copyright law now covered any "painting, drawing, chromo, statue, statuary, or model or design for a work of the fine arts" as well as the usual material. The law also, for the first time, protected authors with regard to translations of their work. Copyright registration was moved from the federal courts to the Library of Congress. Each author had to deposit two copies of the work with the Library. One of the copies went to the library's own collection; in this way, the Library become the largest in the country.[71]

The law also protected photographs—which did not exist when the Constitution was adopted. Was protection of photography within the power of Congress? A photo, after all, is not a "writing." The issue came in a case turning on a photograph of Oscar Wilde. Napoleon Sarony, a New York photographer, had taken the picture; a lithographic company sold 85,000 copies of this photo. Sarony sued. The Supreme Court upheld his claim. A photograph was a work of art; the photographer did the work of posing, arranging, "disposing the light and shade"; and was thus entitled to protection. Later, in 1903, in an opinion by Oliver Wendell Holmes Jr., the court extended copyright protection to advertising—in the precise case, circus posters.[72]

Developed countries are more interested in copyright protection than the underdeveloped. When Americans wrote few books, it was in their interest to treat copyright quite narrowly, since copyright protection mostly went to foreigners. By the late nineteenth century, America was a big country, with a substantial literature of its own. The expansion of copyright, and the strengthening of copyright, thus seemed to be in the national interest. Books and pictures were also commodities. Extending copyright protection to photos and advertisements recognized this fact and underscored the role of copyright in a market economy.

---

[69] Vaughan, *op. cit.,* p. 41.

[70] 13 Stats. 540 (act of March 3, 1865).

[71] 16 Stats. 198, 213 (act of July 8, 1870); Paul Goldstein, *Copyright's Highway: From Gutenberg to the Celestial Jukebox* (rev. ed., 2003), pp. 44–46.

[72] Paul Goldstein, *op. cit.,* pp. 47–49.

The expansion of *trademark* law was also remarkable. This branch of law was cobbled together from a few scattered judicial opinions, all of them after 1825. The first injunction in a trademark or trade-name case was granted in 1844, as we saw, to protect the makers of "Taylor's Persian Thread."[73] From this acorn grew a mighty oak. Trademark has a vital role to play in a consumer society, a free-enterprise society, a society with mass production of standard goods. Products compete jealously for the consumer's dollars. Many products pour out of factories identical except for package and name. The 1870 law that codified patent and copyright law applied to trademarks, too. But the Supreme Court, in 1879, thought that the patent power did not extend to trademarks. They saw no way to justify the law under the commerce clause as well. They declared the law unconstitutional as to trademarks.[74] State statutes partly filled the gap. And the courts continued to rework and define the trademark laws of the states.

Trademark litigation was acrimonious and, like patent litigation, relatively frequent. Business ethics in the nineteenth century were not simon-pure, to put it mildly. Many jackals of commerce tried to steal the values inherent in somebody else's product. An independent concept of unfair competition arose, as a kind of supplement to the protective armor of a trademark. A man named Baker, for example, who made chocolate, could not behave in such a way as to make people think his product was the famous Baker's Chocolate. He could not imitate the shape, label, and wording of Baker's Chocolate, whether or not he was technically "infringing" a trademark.[75]

Toward the end of the century, unions encouraged use of union labels on union-made goods, and tried to get laws passed to protect these labels. A Minnesota statute (1889) made it "lawful for unions to adopt labels, trademarks and advertisements," announcing that the goods were union-made; and it was unlawful to imitate such a label.[76] Illinois had a similar law. The Cigar Makers' International Union, for example, put a "small blue plaster" in each box of cigars, certifying that the cigars were union-made, and not the product of "inferior, rat-shop, coolie, prison or filthy tenement-house workmanship." The state court upheld the law in a case against a cigar-dealer who had blithely copied the label.[77] Businesses, unions, and trade groups were all battling for their share of the economy, and looking for ways, legally or otherwise, to protect their claims and their positions in a tough competitive world.

[73] *Two Centuries' Growth of American Law,* p. 436.
[74] Trade-Mark Cases, 100 U.S. 82 (1879).
[75] *Walter Baker and Co. v. Sanders,* 80 Fed. Rep. 889 (C.C.A. 2nd 1897).
[76] Laws Minn. 1889, ch. 9.
[77] *Cohn v. Illinois,* 149 Ill. 486 (1894).

CHAPTER 5

ADMINISTRATIVE LAW AND REGULATION OF BUSINESS

THE COMING OF THE BUREAUCRATS

In hindsight, the development of administrative law seems mostly a contribution of the twentieth century. American historiography has always been biased toward the big federal agencies. The creation of the Interstate Commerce Commission (ICC), in 1887, was taken as some sort of starting point. The ICC, to be sure, was the first great independent regulatory commission—on the federal level. But there was a great deal of administration, and administrative law, in the nineteenth century in a wider sense. The U.S. Post Office, to take an obvious example, was a large, functioning, federal bureaucracy. There were agencies attached to the office of the commissioner of patents, the General Land Office, and the Pension Office of the Department of Interior. This last, the Pension Office, handled massive amounts of work (often badly). It made many small decisions that affected the lives of many people every day of its official life. In 1891, the Pension Office was reported to be the "largest executive bureau in the world." It had an office force of over 2,000; and there were 18 pension agents, "with a clerical force of 419, and 3,795 examining surgeons stationed in various parts of the country." In 1898, 635,000 cases were pending for adjudication.[1]

Before 1887, also, there were many administrative agencies attached to state and local government. State railroad commissions preceded the ICC by many years. Agencies regulating warehousing, grain elevators, and railroad freight rates were a regular feature in the Midwest during the Granger period. Most states had some sort of functioning insurance or banking commission before 1870. Locally, there were boards of health and bodies to administer school affairs.

The administrative agency was the child of necessity. Big government and positive government meant a government which divided its labor among specialists and specialized bodies. The period between 1850 and 1900 is considered the climax of *laissez-faire*—the age of Social Darwinism, the businessman's earthly kingdom in the United States. Obviously, there is some truth to this idea. It was a period in which businessmen made the loudest noise, some of it defensive. The

---

[1] Leonard D. White, *The Republican Era: 1869–1901* (1958), pp. 211, 214; Theda Skocpol, *Protecting Soldiers and Mothers: The Political Origins of Social Policy in the United States* (1992), p. 120.

legal culture had been for some time a culture of modern rationalism, a culture of instrumentalism. The ultimate tests of law and government were pragmatic. Traditional authority had always been weak in the United States.

The legal system was both strong and legitimate. Its main strength was its instrumental power. There was a certain aura of natural law or natural rights that hovered about the Constitution and the Bill of Rights, and powerful religious traditions supported laws against, say, sexual misbehavior. But as far as the economy was concerned, levers of power were fair game for anybody who could grab them and make them do his bidding. Ideas and ideologies, of course, were weapons in the social struggle. The rich and powerful invoked Social Darwinism and *laissez-faire* to justify the status quo. They argued that their policies worked for the ultimate good of society. The argument had a certain impact. But never totally.

Meanwhile, there was power, too, located in the huge, uneasy, middle-class, people looking for security and a decent standard of living. The country was enormous; production was enormous; technology was advanced and advancing. Slowly, too, the government became enormous, as well. The many publics had a rich menu of demands. Interest groups grew in size. The new technology—railroads, telephone, and telegraph—gave rise to giant industries. Control over these monsters seemed more and more necessary to millions of people—and it also seemed possible.

Control was the key. In a society of mass markets, mass production, and big business, the lonely individual seems to shrink into insignificance. What she eats and wears is made in some distant factory; there is no *personal* control over safety, over quality. When she rides in a train, or even walks along crowded city streets, she puts her very body in the hands of strangers. Moreover, the great aggregations—in business, for example—visibly exercise more and more power. To the general public, the only source of control is that system called law. And, more and more, this control is in the hands of administrative agencies—institututions of civil servants charged with the duty of continuous, steady, monitoring.[2]

There was (and is) no real alternative. Courts are not good regulators. They are passive, reactive, and usually lack the skill and knowledge good regulation requires. Kansas created a "court of visitation" in 1898 to regulate railroads, fix freight rates, classify freight, "require the construction and maintenance of depots, switches, side-tracks, stock-yards, cars"; regulate crossings and intersections; require safety appliances; and in general ride herd on railroads. The law was declared unconstitutional, which prevents us from knowing whether such a plan would have succeeded, or was a dead end.[3] Ordinary

[2] Jonathan Lurie points out, too, that there developed what might be called "the field of nonpublic administrative action undertaken by private voluntary associations, wielding considerable power in the name of public policy." His example: commodity exchanges, like the Chicago Board of Trade. Public administrative regulation, when it ultimately came, was imposed on this preexisting body of administrative practice and behavior. Jonathan Lurie, "Commodities Exchanges as Self-Regulating Organizations in the Late 19th Century: Some Parameters in the History of American Administrative Law," 28 Rutgers L. Rev. 1107 (1975).

[3] Laws Kans. Spec. Sess. 1898, ch. 28; the statute was voided in *State ex rel. Godard v. Johnson* 61 Kans. 803, 60 Pac. 1068 (1900).

courts, as we said, are poorly equipped to manage businesses.[4] In an age of national railroad nets, an age of the telegraph and telephone—that is, communication and coordination across great distances—town and county authorities were particularly futile and ineffective. The cure was, at first, statewide control. But the states too could not deal with *national* businesses, legally or factually. The only remedy, then, was *federal* control. The process was repeated in many areas of law. In welfare, for example, first came local poor laws, run by local overseers of the poor. Then came statewide systems. When the states could no longer handle the job (much later, to be sure), the federal government stepped in. This did not take place until the great depression of the 1930s. Railroad regulation reached its federal stage in 1887. Elementary education, on the other hand, only crossed the federal threshold in the 1960s, and rather timidly at that.

REGULATING THE INFRASTRUCTURE: BANKS, INSURANCE, AND RAILROADS

These differences in pace were not accidental, of course. The most vital (and most threatening) sectors of the economy came on to be regulated first: transport and money—railroads, banks, insurance companies. It was not merely the fact that these were essential services; transport and money represented power, or the danger of power. In the United States, there had always been a strong element of fear and distrust toward concentrations of power. And in the case of the railroads, for example, there were specific, powerful interest groups that considered themselves aggrieved.

The national currency had been in a chronic state of disrepair before the Civil War. After Andrew Jackson's time, there was no national banking at all. The states regulated currency and banking; but regulation was confused, halting, and in general ineffective. During the Civil War, there was a desperate wartime need for central control of fiscal and monetary systems. The Legal Tender Act was a wartime measure; after the war, it provoked one of the Supreme Court's most spectacular flip-flops, first a decision that the law was invalid, then a quick change of mind (following a change in personnel).[5] In 1863, during the war, Congress established a national banking system; in 1865 Congress placed a 10 percent tax on the notes of state banks. The national bank notes provided far more uniformity, certainty, and stability than the prior system. But state banks, as banks, did not by any means fade from the picture. They remained—and so did state banking regulation.

---

[4] But, through the device of equity "receiverships," the courts did in fact run bankrupt railroads—with a lot of help, to be sure.

[5] The cases were *Hepburn v. Griswold*, 75 U.S. 603 (1869), overturned by the *Legal Tender* cases, 79 U.S. 457 (1870). The backgrounds of the Legal Tender act and the national banking law are exhaustively treated in Bray Hammond, *Sovereignty and an Empty Purse: Banks and Politics in the Civil War* (1970); see also David M. Gische, "The New York City Banks and the Development of the National Banking System, 1860–1870," 23 Am. J. Legal Hist. 21 (1979).

Insurance companies, too, were an early subject of regulation.[6] Fire insurance, after the Civil War, became more and more accepted as a business necessity. Life insurance spread more slowly. There were even, at one time, moral objections: life insurance was a kind of bet on life and death, which seemed distasteful. Moreover, insurance cost money; millions of families could not afford it. Still, by the end of the century, a great many families had embraced life insurance, and thousands of policies were sold.[7] Insurance was a rich source of litigation, and of dissatisfaction. Some companies tried every trick in the book to weasel out of claims. And no doubt, some claims were fraudulent.

Hardly any subject was more often the subject of statute than insurance. Insurance commissions were established in many states. Their development followed a well-marked path. The first commissions were not independent bodies; commissioners were state officers who held down other jobs as well. The Massachusetts commission of 1852 consisted of the secretary, treasurer, and auditor of the state. The commission's job was to receive statements from the companies, abstract the data, and present the results to the legislature. Wisconsin established an Insurance Department in the office of the secretary of state; in 1878, an independent Insurance Department was created, headed by an appointed insurance commissioner. In New York, the comptroller had some powers over insurance companies before 1859, at that point, an Insurance Department was established along the lines of the Banking Department. In almost all states, then, separate "commissions" or "departments" grew out of embryonic boards, which piled new labors onto old officers. At first, state government was too poor, weak, or listless to support strong, well-financed, independent regulation. An "independent" commission, in most states, was not even independent in the financial sense; typically, fees extracted from the companies paid for the commission.

The urge to regulate, however, was cumulative and persistent. In 1873, twelve states had "some form of institutionalized insurance regulation"; in 1890, seventeen states; in 1905, twenty-two.[8] Early commissions were usually advisory or exhortatory; they built up their bureaucratic traditions, and gained power and skill, unevenly but definitely. The power came from a steady inflation of insurance laws. The states passed laws that outlawed discrimination in rates, curbed "unfair" marketing practices, tried to safeguard the solvency of the companies, harnessed foreign insurance companies, and insisted on financial reserves. The volume and scope of this legislation grew to fantastic proportions. The Massachusetts law to "Amend and Codify the Statutes Relating to Insurance," passed in 1887, contained 112 closely packed sections of text.[9]

Rococo excess in size does not mean that a statute succeeds in controlling its subject. Bulk may mean almost the opposite: frantic, hopeless flailing about, ceaseless tinkering, constant dissatisfaction and frustration. Complexity may mean that interest groups, at war with each other, stake all sorts of claims on the subject matter, many of them conflicting and inconsistent. A long, complex law

---

[6] A comprehensive study of insurance law in one state is Spencer L. Kimball, *Insurance and Public Policy: A Study in the Legal Implementation of Social and Economic Public Policy, Based on Wisconsin Records 1835–1959* (1960).

[7] See Viviana A. Rotman Zelizer, *The Development of Life Insurance in the United States* (1979).

[8] Morton Keller, *The Life Insurance Enterprise, 1885–1910* (1963), pp. 194, 197.

[9] Laws Mass. 1887, ch. 214.

is the text, then, of an elaborate treaty, full of loopholes, special benefits, and compromises. Interest groups were in general eager to resort to legislation. Competition was never confined to the market; groups competed for legal advantage as well, in the courts, in the legislatures. Insurance regulation, in this period, was not exactly a triumphal success. In New York, for example, corruption ate at the heart of the Insurance Commission. The legislature investigated insurance regulation in 1870, 1872, 1877, 1882, and 1885. Some administrators were halfhearted and ineffectual. James F. Pierce, appointed commissioner in 1890, did not believe (he said) that his department should "erect over the lawfully appointed custodians of the people's funds another custodian who should intermeddle in their corporate administration."[10] This creed, or something like it, so delighted some companies that they were willing to buy it for cash. On the whole then, despite progress in tightening the reins, the state had by no means made itself master over insurance companies, at least not before 1900.

Partly this was because they had no coherent theory of regulation. Regulations were reactions—to public fear and mistrust of the financial power of the companies; reactions, too, to the sense that the companies were fleecing the public. The demand for regulation was diffuse and shallow; the companies, which had vital interests at stake, were able to gain leverage over the texts of the law and over everyday administration. Morton Keller points out that "the structure of supervision was at its friendliest when dealing with the technical details of the business"—taxation, investment, reserves, dividend policy. The public hardly understood such things, at least not in any detail. On the other hand, policyholders had a stake in the policy itself—the contract of insurance. They also knew whether claims were paid or not, or paid promptly or not. This was therefore "a subject of fruitful and alert legislative concern." States passed nonforfeiture laws, mitigated the rules and clauses that made policies void if an applicant made false or misleading statements, and even controlled the methods of marketing insurance.[11]

Despite the volume of insurance regulation, the *railroad* still dominated administrative law, between 1850 and 1900, just as the railroad dominated tort and corporation law. By 1850, states had turned to general statutes regulating railroads, and had given up the effort to slip special clauses into individual charters. In any event, in much of the country the first, promotional phase was over; from this point on, railroads consolidated their lines and extended existing nets of track. In the boom years, the years of railroad infancy, the promoters and their supporters in the community spoke with the loudest voices. The public wanted railroads built, almost at any cost. Once the roads were in place and running, public opinion shifted dramatically. Railroads created markets, made towns bloom in the wilderness, lured farmers into planting particular crops, drew settlers from one place to another. People invested their lives and their future in the farms, towns, and markets that grew up along the lines. The railroads held power of life and death, power of prosperity or ruin, over those who lived along the way. The farmers, who had mortgaged themselves to buy railroads, had created a monster in their midst. They were prisoners of freight rates over which they had no control. Also, the railroads were corrupt, excessively

[10] Quoted in Keller, *op. cit.*, p. 203.
[11] Keller, *op. cit.*, p. 200.

capitalized, overloaded with debt, controlled by out-of-state interests, monopolistic. Among themselves they were vicious and quarrelsome. They manipulated state governments; they practiced the black arts of lobbying, and the seduction of men in public office. They cheated each other, their contractors, their stockholders, and their customers. They floated great balloons of debt that burst during panics and crashes, ruining the greedy, hopeful people who sank money into stocks and bonds. They were deeply immersed in local politics; they were at the mercy of the business cycle, and also of the prices of cotton, coal, wheat, tobacco, and corn. In the space of one short generation, engines of hope and prosperity turned into roaring, smoking black devils.

The state of public opinion about railroads wrote the script for railroad regulation. Regulatory statutes ranged from severe to toothless, even on paper. Usually, the early stages were the toothless ones. Rhode Island set up the country's first railroad commission in 1839; it "stemmed from the necessity of imposing upon rival and warring railroads convenient connections and reasonable joint fares, freights, and services."[12] A New Hampshire commission was created in 1844.[13] Its main function, however, was to help railroads buy needed land along their routes. The statute gave the commissioners roughly the same powers and functions as those of the old commissioners of roads and highways. But the commissioners did have the duty to look over the railroads once a year, check their condition and management, and inspect "all books, papers, notes, records, bonds, and other evidences of debt, and all property, deeds and bills of sale," to see if the railroads were obeying all relevant laws. Connecticut established a commission which, in the 1850s, had the right to inspect the physical equipment of the railroads and to recommend needed repairs; safety on the roads was one of the major aims of this law.[14] Maine's commission of 1858 was very much like Rhode Island's.

A new era began in 1869. In that year, Massachusetts established its own, and stronger, commission. There were three commissioners, one of them Charles Francis Adams Jr. The commission had "general supervision of all railroads," with the right to examine them and monitor their obedience to law. Whenever the commissioners felt that a company was derelict in this regard, or needed to make repairs, or if the commission felt that a "change in its rate of fares for transporting freight or passengers," or in its "mode of operating its road and conducting its business" was "reasonable and expedient," the commissioners were to so inform the company. They were also to make annual reports to the legislature.[15] The other New England commissions were gradually remolded to fit the Massachusetts pattern, and the influence of the Massachusetts law was felt as far away as California.[16] The New England railroad commissions gained power and influence under the benevolent guidance of Massachusetts. But they were still able only to suggest and persuade; they had

[12] Edward G. Kirkland, *Men, Cities and Transportation: A Study in New England History, 1820–1900,* vol. II (1948), p. 233.

[13] Laws N.H. 1844, ch. 93.

[14] Conn. Stats. 1854, pp. 759–60.

[15] Laws Mass. 1869, ch. 408.

[16] Gerald D. Nash, *State Government and Economic Development: A History of Administrative Policies in California, 1849–1933* (1964), p. 160.

no power to fix rates or make major changes on their own. Even under later commissions, the distribution of function between court, legislature, and commission was never completely unscrambled; neither the legislatures nor the courts abdicated their right to tinker with railroad law. And the railroads remained at all times influential. An extreme case was New York, which created a commission in 1855; the commissioners, paid off by the railroads, recommended that their office be abolished, and this was done in 1857.

In the Midwest, the so-called Granger laws, passed in the 1870s, took a far more radical approach to railroad regulation than anything attempted in New England. In the 1870s, the demand for regulation had grown louder. Merchants complained about freight rates that were, they felt, too high—and discriminatory. Actually, rates were declining; but every shipper "was convinced that someone else was getting a better rate."[17] The railroads priced freight the way airline tickets were priced in 2004: Where there was competition, the rates were low; for towns served by only one railroad, the rates were high. Also, big shippers got big discounts. The market was responsible for some of these anomalies; but, as James Ely has pointed out, "economic arguments" do not count for much "in the political arena."[18] An Illinois law of 1871 established a Railroad and Warehouse Commission. It had the authority to find out whether railroads and warehouses complied with the laws of the state. If the laws had been violated, the Commission had power to "prosecute . . . all corporations or persons guilty of such violation."[19] By an act of April 15, 1871, the legislature flatly laid down maximum railroad rates. Class A roads—railroads whose gross annual earnings, per mile, were ten thousand dollars or more—could charge no more than two and one-half cents a mile for passengers (half fare to children under twelve).[20]

The Granger movement was a farmers' revolt. It aimed to bring under control the farmers' symbiotic enemies—railroads, warehouses, and grain elevators. But the legislation actually passed in Illinois, Iowa, Wisconsin, and Minnesota probably owed more to merchants and businessmen than to the farmers themselves. The Illinois law, it has been said, was "not so much the product of spontaneous indignation on the prairies as a monument to the strategic talents of the Chicago Board of Trade."[21]

The Grangers, in fact, came in on the tail end of a whirlwind that was already blowing full storm. In Wisconsin, in 1864, Milwaukee merchants pressed successfully for a statute to force the railroads to deliver bulk grain to any elevator designated by the shippers, as long as it had adequate sidetracks.[22] Wisconsin farmers had been badly burnt in ill-advised schemes in promotion of railroads; it "was to be a long time before they regarded railroad men as anything but scoundrels. They prepared the ground for the growth of the Grange."[23] In Iowa,

---

[17] James W. Ely Jr., *Railroads and American Law* (2001), p. 81.

[18] Ibid., p. 82.

[19] Laws Ill. 1871, pp. 618, 622 (act of Apr. 13, 1871, secs 1, 11).

[20] Laws Ill. 1871, p. 640 (act of Apr. 15, 1871).

[21] Lee Benson, *Merchants, Farmers, and Railroads: Railroad Regulation and New York Politics, 1850–1887* (1955), p. 25; see also George H. Miller, *Railroads and the Granger Laws* (1971).

[22] Frederick Merk, *Economic History of Wisconsin during the Civil War Decade* (1916), p. 371.

[23] Robert S. Hunt, *Law and Locomotives* (1958), p. 64.

in the 1860s, railroad regulation bills were introduced in almost every session—and this was before there ever was a Granger movement. Iowa laws of 1868, granting lands to the railroads, carried with them a poisonous rider, reserving to the legislature the right to prescribe "rates of tariff."[24]

In the world of decentralized legal power, so characteristic of America, struggle for and against important laws does not end with enactment. Often enough, there was a second round, in the courts. Here the Grangers and their commissions won some famous victories, capped by the great (if transient) case of *Munn v. Illinois* (1876).[25] In *Munn*, the Supreme Court broadly upheld Illinois's package of Granger laws; specifically, the power of commissioners to regulate railroads, warehouses, and grain elevators. These businesses, said the court, were "clothed with a public interest." Hence they could not claim immunity from public supervision. But, quite typically, there was also a third round: actual administration. The Granger commissions were something of a failure in operation. The right of legislatures to make rates was a famous victory; but the process itself was stiff and arbitrary. The roads were congenitally prone to financial troubles; it was easy for them to blame their troubles on mismanagement by commissions. The railroads and their friends turned their talents and money once more to legislative action. Wisconsin's proud and famous "Potter Law," of 1874, one of the most radical of the laws to tame the railroads, lasted a mere two years; with a turn of the political wheel, and the election of a legislature more sympathetic to the roads, the Potter Law was cast into outer darkness.[26]

Regulation by commission did not die. Farmers and merchants did not lose their voice. The naked strength of the railroads was not to be tolerated. In the South, freight and passenger rates were higher than those in the North. The behavior of the Southern Railway and Steamship Association, dominated by Albert Fink, was odious to farmers and shippers. Virginia established an advisory railroad commission in 1877, similar to the Massachusetts commission; so did South Carolina in 1878; in 1879, Georgia established a three-man commission, with power to fix rates. In New York, railroad rate wars in the 1870s ended in a trunkline pool of 1877; the New York railroads set up their own private administrative agency, and imported Albert Fink from the South to run it. Under the pooling arrangement, rate differentials favored Philadelphia and Baltimore; the New York Chamber of Commerce, outraged, turned Granger, and exacted from the legislature the right to investigate the railroads. The result was the Special Committee on Railroads to Investigate Alleged Abuses in the Management of Railroads Chartered by the State of New York, commonly known as the Hepburn Committee. It reported its findings in a blaze of publicity in 1880. The Hepburn Committee helped crystallize opinion to the point where the legislature, in 1882, established a railroad commission, though with many compromises.[27]

Did the railroad commissions accomplish anything? Some were venal and impotent, like the first New York commission or the second California commission.

---

[24] See Earl S. Beard, "The Background of State Railroad Regulation in Iowa," 51 Iowa J. of Hist. 1, 17–22 (1953).

[25] 94 U.S. 113 (1876).

[26] Robert S. Hunt, *Law and Locomotives* (1958), pp. 98–103, 140–42.

[27] See Lee Benson, *Merchants, Farmers, and Railroads: Railroad Regulation and New York Politics, 1850–1887* (1955), chs. 6–8.

This commission was born in a burst of indignation; yet in 1895, a gloomy critic summed up its work as follows:

> The curious fact remains that a body created sixteen years ago for the sole purpose of curbing a single railroad corporation with a strong hand, was found to be uniformly, without a break, during all that period, its apologist and defender.[28]

Even the clean commissions, of the New England type, disappointed the hopes of farmers and small shippers. As was true of insurance commissions, the problem was partly one of political leverage. Farmers and shippers were a large, diffuse group. The railroads were few and powerful. When farmers and shippers organized, and made a lot of noise, they got some results in the legislatures. But these campaigns depended on wobbly, transient coalitions. All the passion went toward *passage* of these laws. After enactment, passion died down. Commissions had to live with their railroads every day. They had to chastise them but not kill them. In practice, this meant that commissions learned—if not already so disposed—to be gentle and sympathetic with their railroads. This habit, once acquired, was hard to break. On each daily decision, the railroad exerted its moral and economic pressures; farmers and shippers were unaware, unrepresented, apathetic. Moreover, not all farmers and shippers had the same interests. There was no coherent program on the demand side; thus, no coherent outcome was supplied.

The state commissioners were, in any event, bound to fail in a federal system. Their power extended only to the boundaries of their state. After the Civil War, railroad entrepreneurs sewed together small railroads into big, interstate nets. How much control could Rhode Island ever hope to exert over railroads that passed through its tiny area? The Supreme Court drove home the point that state commissions were powerless, in *Wabash Railway v. Illinois* (1886).[29] States could not regulate commerce, if it came from or was destined for a point outside the boundaries of the state. They could have an "indirect" effect on interstate railroads, but no "direct" effect. Only the federal government had this power.[30] The decision overturned an Illinois statute aimed at discriminatory freight and passenger rates. The decision gave an added push to the campaign for a federal railroad commission. This was the Interstate Commerce Commission, enacted into law in 1887.[31]

This famous statute was controversial in its day and has produced a rather considerable historical literature. One point is fairly clear: It would be naïve to consider the ICC as the triumph of Grangerism on the federal level. The law paid lip service to the principle of strict control over railroads. And antirailroad agitation was indeed a vital part of the political background. But at least one scholar has argued that the railroads themselves were "anxious to have federal railroad legislation—on their terms." For some railroad men, this was simply a

---

[28] S. E. Moffet, "The Railroad Commission of California: A Study In Irresponsible Government," 6 Annals 469, 476 (1895). The "single railroad corporation" was the Central Pacific, later part of the Southern Pacific.

[29] 118 U.S. 557 (1886).

[30] See I. L. Sharfman, *The Interstate Commerce Commission*, vol. 2 (1931).

[31] 24 Stats. 379 (act of Feb. 4, 1887).

way of bowing to the inevitable. Others felt the government could help them against cut-throat competition and price wars. John P. Green, a vice-president of the Pennsylvania Railroad, stated in 1884 that "a large majority of the railroads in the United States would be delighted if a railroad commission or any other power could make rates upon their traffic which would insure them six per cent dividends, and I have no doubt, with such a guarantee, they would be very glad to come under the direct supervision and operation of the National Government."[32] One of the first commissioners of the ICC was no less a figure than Judge Thomas M. Cooley of Michigan, a conservative, and a high priest of theories of constitutional limits on regulation. Cooley was by no means as simple and one-sided as pictured;[33] still the commission was not at all radical—it never intended to ride herd over the roads in the way that a fire-eating Granger might have liked.

Nor was the text of the act particularly fierce. The law gave the ICC no express power to set railroad rates, though it did declare (sec. 1) that "All charges . . . shall be reasonable and just." The commission, however, took a rate-making function upon itself, until the Supreme Court in the late 1890s stripped away this power, saying that "there is nothing in the act fixing rates. Congress did not attempt to exercise that power. . . . The grant of such a power is never to be implied."[34] This left the commission relatively naked. It could do little more than punish past transgressions against the Commerce Act. The Supreme Court in 1897 also emasculated the fourth section of the act, the long-and-short haul section, which prohibited railroads from charging more for short hauls than long hauls. The case concerned the Alabama Midland Railway. The road charged $3.22 per ton "on phosphate rock shipped from the South Carolina and Florida field" to Troy, Alabama, for example, but only $3.00 per ton to carry this product to Montgomery, Alabama, a longer distance—in fact, the route to Montgomery ran through Troy. Troy suffered too on shipments of cotton and other goods. No matter; there was more competition in shipping to Montgomery than to Troy; hence, the railroad had an adequate reason to lower prices to Montgomery. The railroad's traffic managers were not "incompetent," nor were they "under the bias of any personal preference for Montgomery." The market set their rates. This made their pricing legal, despite what the statute said.[35]

But was this reasoning sound? Was it really the intent of Congress (and the country) to write this brand of economics into the Commerce Act? Justice John M. Harlan, who dissented, argued the decision made the commission "a useless

---

[32] Quoted in Gabriel Kolko, *Railroads and Regulation, 1877–1916* (1965), p. 35, an important revisionist history of the ICC.

[33] See Alan Jones, "Thomas M. Cooley and the Interstate Commerce Commission: Continuity and Change in the Doctrine of Equal Rights," 81 Political Science Q. 602 (1966).

[34] J. Brewer, in *ICC v. Cincinnati, New Orleans and Texas Pacific Rr. Co.*, 167 U.S. 479, 494 (1897). In *Smyth v. Ames*, 169 U.S. 466 (1898), the Court reviewed a Nebraska statute, in which the legislature imposed rate cuts of almost 30 percent on railroad charges within the state. The Court struck down the law. See James Ely, *Railroads and American Law*, pp. 97–98; Stephen A. Siegel, "Understanding the *Lochner* Era: Lessons from the Controversy over Railroad and Utility Rate Regulation," 70 Va. L. Rev. 187, 224ff. (1984); Eric Monkkonen, "Can Nebraska or Any State Regulate Railroads? *Smyth v. Ames*, 1898," 54 Nebraska History 365 (1973).

[35] *Interstate Commerce Commission v. Alabama Midland Railway Co.*, 168 U.S. 144 (1897). The ICC had found the railroad in violation of the statute.

body for all practical purposes." Those purposes were political purposes; and the shippers who fought for the law had not intended a pristine free market. But what the Supreme Court held *became* the law, at least unless and until Congress chose to do otherwise. In these cases, the Supreme Court asserted its own point of view, exercised its own brand of power, and, in effect, threw down the gauntlet to Congress.

Still, it would be wrong to claim that the Court had crippled the act. In some respects, the act was born to be crippled. Congress was only half-serious about taming the railroads; it was in deadly earnest only about public opinion. The act was "a bargain in which no one interest predominated except perhaps the legislators' interest in finally getting the conflict . . . off their backs and shifting it to a commission and the courts." And the real flaw in the act was not that it leaned toward this interest or that; but that its policy was inconsistent, incoherent, inherently ambiguous.[36] Moreover, once the movement for enactment had run its course, Congress showed no great enthusiasm for putting back in the act any teeth that the Court pulled out. As Mr. Dooley said about Theodore Roosevelt and the trusts, the ICC was supposed to stamp the "heejoous monsthers" under foot, but "not so fast" or so much.[37]

The regulatory history of other public utilities ran parallel to the history of railroad regulation. The same kinds of compromise took place. In 1855, for example, Massachusetts passed a general incorporation law for gaslight companies. Under the law, if a city already had a gas company, no new one could be incorporated unless the established company had earned an annual dividend of seven percent on its capital stock for a number of years. This invitation to monopoly was withdrawn in 1870, and, during the 1880s, gas companies began to feel the bite of competition. It was not to their liking. A law of 1885 established a Board of Gas Commissioners; under this law, the companies submitted to the yoke of regulation, but the law also protected their monopoly position.[38]

Public-utility law in general had this nature: regulation in exchange for a sheltered market. Competition was the "life of trade," but only for other people. Businesses actually welcomed state control, so long as the control was not unfriendly, protected their little citadels of privilege, and guaranteed them a return on their investment. This is one reason why some forms of government intervention, chiefly on the state level, grew phenomenally during the last half of the nineteenth century. The statute books swelled like balloons, despite all the sound and fury about individualism, the free market, the glories of enterprise, Horatio Alger, and the like, from pulpit, press, and bench. Every group wanted, and often got, its own exception to the supposed iron laws of trade.

It is misleading to think in terms of strict *laissez-faire* ideology. Before the Civil War, as Charles McCurdy has argued, state and private enterprise often cooperated—in building roads, canals, and railroads, most notably. In the postwar period, consensus about state aid broke down; and groups disagreed about where to draw the line between the spheres of government and free enterprise.

---

[36] Stephen Skowronek, *Building a New American State: The Expansion of National Administrative Capacities, 1877–1920* (1982), pp. 148–49.

[37] Quoted in William Letwin, *Law and Economic Policy in America: The Evolution of the Sherman Antitrust Act* (1965), p. 205.

[38] I. R. Barnes, *Public Utility Control in Massachusetts* (1930), pp. 14–15.

Everybody drew a different line; each group fixed the boundaries according to its own private interests. Ideology came afterward, as rhetoric or icing on the cake.[39] This is one way of looking at the temper of the times. Of course, the ideology was real enough; and some scholars feel that the role of ideology should be stressed, rather than the role of "material self-interest."[40] Jurists did weave together a fabric of concepts and principles, coherent, subtle, and complex. It appeared somewhat value-neutral—free from crass bias against any level of society. But the actual *impact* of this tower of ideology must be left an open question.

OCCUPATIONAL LICENSING: AND THE PULL OF PUBLIC HEALTH

Occupational licensing, which absolutely burgeoned in this period, can be seen as a test case. The basic idea was not entirely new. Colonials had licensed auctioneers and peddlers. Lawyers had to be admitted to the bar. Some licensing laws were frankly and solely passed to raise money. Some, too, were harsh and discriminatory—tools against outsiders. Wisconsin's statutes, as of 1898, required every prospective peddler to make a "written application . . . to the secretary of state," revealing whether he intended to travel on foot, or with "one or more horses or other beasts of burden." The peddler who intended to peddle by bicycle paid a thirty dollar fee; to use a vehicle drawn by two or more horses cost seventy-five dollars. The peddler could not sell in any town without this license, plus whatever fees the local community chose to levy, up to fifty dollars a day.[41] These were stiff amounts—almost prohibitive. The point was to protect local merchants and drive away these pesty competitors. It is significant that such laws flourished during this age of (alleged) *laissez faire*. Small-town merchants were protectionist to the core.

The more familiar kind of occupational licensing blossomed in the late nineteenth century and reached some sort of climax in the period from 1890 to 1910. The health professions led the way. In Illinois, for example, a law of 1877 required a license for the practice of medicine. In 1881, the state created a board of pharmacy; no one was to "retail, compound or dispense drugs, medicines or poisons," or "open or conduct any pharmacy," except a registered pharmacist. In the same year, the state brought "the practice of dentistry" under regulation. A board, consisting of "five practising dentists," was charged with enforcement of the dentist's law. By this time, the idea had become quite popular. In 1897, Illinois created a State Board of Examiners of Architects. In 1899, the statutes added midwives, coal miners, and veterinarians, and also chiropractors and osteopaths ("those who desire to practice any . . . system or science of treating human ailments who do not use medicines internally or

---

[39] Charles W. McCurdy, "Justice Field and the Jurisprudence of Government-Business Relations: Some Parameters of Laissez Faire Constitutionalism, 1863–1897," 61 J. Am. Hist. 970 (1975); see also David M. Gold, "Redfield, Railroads, and the Roots of 'Laissez Faire Constitutionalism,'" 27 Am. J. Legal Hist. 254 (1983).

[40] See the discussion in Stephen A. Siegel, "The Revision Thickens," 20 Law & History Review 631 (2002).

[41] Wis. Stats. 1898, secs. 1571, 1572.

externally").[42] Most of the licensed occupations were, by common consent, "professions" or subprofessions, and not just trades; but by no means all. Many states in the 1890s licensed plumbers, barbers, and horseshoers. A New York law licensing transportation ticket agents was passed, only to be declared unconstitutional in 1898.[43]

These laws were backed by the professions and occupations themselves. Undertakers, embalmers, and funeral directors also heard the siren song of licensing. They were struggling to define for themselves, and protect, their own little monopoly. They had many rivals. Doctors embalmed the dead. Clergymen controlled funerals. Many undertakers were part-time funeral directors whose main business was the sale of coffins and caskets. In the late 1880s, Hudson Samson, president of the Funeral Directors' National Association of the United States, prepared a model legislative act for licensing embalmers. At the same time, Samson tried to uplift the artifacts of professional funerals. (In 1889, he designed a "special eight poster, oval-decked funeral car"; in 1898, a magnificent hand-carved, wooden draped hearse.) It was all part of a movement, to give tone and economic strength to the occupation, in short, to "professionalize" these doctors of the dead. Samson wanted the law to regulate "the care and burial of the dead," just as it regulated "the practice of medicine." In 1894, Virginia passed the first licensing law. The statute set up a "state board of embalming," consisting of five members, to be appointed by the governor. Each member of the board had to have at least "five years' experience in the practice of embalming and the care of and disposition of dead human bodies." The board would control the profession and grant licenses. Thereafter, only registered embalmers could practice the "science of embalming." By 1900, some twenty-four states had passed similar laws.[44]

These new licensing laws had certain traits in common. Legally, they rested on the developing concept of the state's police power—its power to pass laws to protect the health and safety of the public. But powerful economic motives were at the root of these laws. Many of these licensed occupations had strong unions or strong trade associations; but they had nobody to strike against. Barbers, for example, were highly unionized; but their "bosses" were the millions of people who needed a haircut. Licensed occupations, in short, were in a different position from ordinary industrial labor, or the farmer, or the businessman. Their goals were the same; but their tactics had to be somewhat different.

Among occupational licensing laws, the Virginia embalmers' law was typical—the "board," with power to decide who was fit to be a doctor, barber, nurse, plumber, or undertaker, was effectively a private group, a clique of insiders. Its goal was to drive out marginal competition, to raise the prestige of the trade. It aimed at the status of a self-perpetuating guild, made up of respectable professionals or tradesmen. By and large, the courts had no problem with these laws. Few licensing statutes were challenged in court; fewer still

---

[42] Laws Ill. 1877, p. 154; 1881, pp. 77, 120; 1897, p. 81; 1899, pp. 273, 277. The licensing of coal miners—always anomalous—did not last long.

[43] *People ex rel. Tyroler v. Warden,* 157 N.Y. 116, 51 N.E. 1006 (1898).

[44] The material on the embalmers is from Robert W. Habenstein and William M. Lamers, *History of American Funeral Directing* (1955), pp. 365, 369, 457–501; the Virginia law was Laws Va. 1893–1894, ch. 625.

were overturned. In the midst of a period when some courts were hard on unions of factory workers, middle-class professionals and artisans gained monopoly power with hardly a murmur of protest from the courts. This helps us understand the inner meaning of "freedom of contract" and other constitutional shibboleths, which courts sometimes used to overthrow social or labor legislation. The judges, middle-class, conservative men, could empathize easily with professionals and artisans. They were rather less understanding when they sensed class struggle or proletarian revolt, things which they barely understood and desperately feared.[45]

Most licensing laws had an easy time at the capital, too. The lobby of plumbers, or pharmacists, or architects, was small but vocal, and no one spoke for the consumer. The justification was the same for almost all of the occupations: safeguarding public health. This was a simple, obvious argument in the case of doctors. For barbers, the argument was a trifle strained; for horseshoers, fairly desperate. The Illinois law of 1897, "to insure the better education of practitioners of horseshoeing, and to regulate the practice of horseshoers in the State of Illinois,"[46] put a veterinary surgeon on the horseshoers' board—immunized, no doubt, by his four blacksmith colleagues—and also provided that apprentices must attend lectures on the anatomy of horses' feet. The Illinois court was not impressed; but a Minnesota court, upholding a statute on barbers, spoke of the threat of "diseases spread . . . by unclean and incompetent barbers."[47]

Health was a powerful argument, in any case—even in the days of (so-called) *laissez-faire*. Public health was a legitimate reason to regulate; this was conceded.[48] Laws on public health and sanitation increased spectacularly toward the end of the century. Again, motivations were mixed. No one, or almost no one, could object to a law against rancid cheese and watered milk. On the other hand, quality control of food products meant a lot to the more respectable dairies and cheesemakers. They stood to gain if the state drove out marginal producers and raised public confidence in their products. Farmers and dairymen conducted a vendetta against "butterine" or oleomargarine, both on the state and national levels. Many states enacted laws against oleo. In some states there were stringent laws against passing the product off as butter. In 1885, Pennsylvania outlawed oleo altogether. In the 1880s, too, the federal government slapped a tax on the sale of oleomargarine. This was probably a purely economic battle; other campaigns against the sour, the putrid, the diseased seem to us far more justified. But the tremendous volume of "health" laws, snowballing between 1850 and 1900, was something of a failure for pure free-enterprise theory. Good goods should, ultimately, drive out bad ones in the market, or batter down their price. But many people—not to mention those who produced high-quality products—were not willing to wait so long.

---

[45] See, in general, Lawrence M. Friedman, "Freedom of Contract and Occupational Licensing 1890–1910: A Legal and Social Study," 53 Cal. L. Rev. 487 (1965).

[46] Laws Ill. 1897, p. 233.

[47] These cases are, respectively, *Bessette v. People*, 193 Ill. 354, 62 N.E. 215 (1901); *State v. Zeno*, 79 Minn. 80, 81 N.W. 748 (1900).

[48] See William Novak, *The People's Welfare: Law and Regulation in Nineteenth-Century America* (1996), p. 194ff; Wendy E. Parmet, "From Slaughter-House to Lochner:: The Rise and Fall of Constitutionalization of Public Health," 40 Am. J. Legal Hist. 476 (1996).

Times, too, had changed. Science made a contribution. People became aware that danger lurked in bad food and bad water. The discovery of germs—invisible, insidious, hidden in every spot of filth—had a profound effect on the legal system. Moreover, goods (including food) were now packaged and sent long distances. And they were marketed impersonally, in bulk, rather than felt, handled, and squeezed at the point of purchase. The consumer was thus dependent on others, on strangers, on far-off corporations, for necessities of life; society was more than ever a complex cellular organism; these strangers, these distant others, had the capacity to inflict catastrophic, irreparable harm. Science, which revealed hidden dangers, also gave promise, or hope, of making the dangerous safe. Water and food could be sterilized; dirty streets could be scrubbed; light and air could be let into factories. In the Gilded Age, there was not much moral or economic force left in the excuse that industry needed total protection, from seedling to tree. A look into the Massachusetts session laws of 1887 shows how much issues of public health concerned the legislatures. One law required sellers of arsenic, strychnine, and other poisons to keep records of their sales, open to inspection by the police. Another act stated that killed poultry could not be sold unless "properly dressed, by the removal of the crop and entrails when containing food." City boards of health were to enforce this law. A few pages on, factories with five or more employees were ordered to be kept free "from effluvia arising from any drain, privy or other nuisance," and told to provide "water-closets, earth-closets, or privies" for employees. Another law created a State Board of Registration in Dentistry. Another law required factories to be ventilated, and still another was "an Act to Secure Uniform and Proper Meal Times for Children, Young Persons and Women Employed in Factories and Workshops."[49]

This was an industrial state, and its health laws reflected the strength of organized labor and its allies. There were no factory acts in the Arkansas session laws of 1881. But one act regulated "the Practice of Medicine and Surgery"; another made the sale of poisons unlawful, unless labeled as such, and required the keeping of records; another established a State Board of Health.[50] The crush of health laws was earlier and heavier in the Northeast, slower and later in the South; but the overall direction was unmistakable.

Older protective laws, largely economic—lien laws and homestead provisions—were still in force. The new legislation simply added to the bulk. Homestead exemptions were primarily for the benefit of the farmer. The new laws reflected the rise of the cities, the growth of heavy industry, the slow passing of rural America. Iowa, for example, passed a coal-mine inspection law in 1880; the governor was to appoint an inspector, who would check ventilation and safety conditions in mines, among other things.[51] John F. Dillon, reporting as president of the American Bar Association in 1892, was struck by how much of "recent legislation" related to "matters concerning the public health and safety, and particularly the safety of operatives and laborers."[52] He noted that Ohio now required guardrails or handrails on bridges, viaducts, culverts, and

[49] Laws Mass. 1887, chs. 38, 94, 103, 137, 173, 215.
[50] Laws Ark. 1881, pp. 41, 107, 177.
[51] Laws Iowa 1880, ch. 202.
[52] *Report, 15th Ann. Meeting A.B.A.* (1892), pp. 167, 177–8, 183.

handrails for stairways in hotels and factories; Ohio and New York regulated scaffolding, ropes, blocks, pulleys, and tackles used in building. Georgia compelled seaside hotel keepers to maintain lifeboats. Rhode Island, in an "Act for the Prevention of Blindness," required midwives and nurses to report to health officers any inflamed or reddened eyes among newborn babies. Ohio strengthened its laws on factory inspection, and regulated the manufacture of explosives. Rhode Island and Colorado "joined the long list of other states in prohibiting the sale or gift of cigarettes to minors" and forbidding minors "to smoke or chew tobacco in public places." And so it went.

Most of the health laws were, in form, criminal statutes. But they were not necessarily the product of moral outrage. Private initiative simply did not work as a means of enforcement. In theory, the courts could have strengthened the law of warranty. After all, anybody could sue a seller whose goods were shoddy, or whose food product made you sick. There could have been a strict, expansive law of products liability—something that actually happened in the twentieth century. Yet, who would or could go to court over a single can of rotten peas? As we have pointed out, if the laws are in form criminal laws, then the state assumes the cost and the burden of enforcement; another method of socializing the remedy is through administrative action.

There is no doubt about the number of laws passed. Actual impact is another question. Constant tinkering indicates something less than full enforcement. In most cases, the state did little more than place people's interests or passions on record. The record suggests little real control over the quality of products, even food. Quack medicines, some consisting mostly of alcohol, or hideously dangerous drugs, mislabeled, or underlabeled, were brazenly peddled; the patent-medicine industry wielded enormous power over newspapers, which depended on revenues from ads. During the Spanish-American War, there was a scandal over "embalmed beef"—rotten meat allegedly served to the troops who were fighting in Cuba. At the end of the period, there was intense agitation for stronger food laws. Existing legislation was almost useless. To be sure, it was obviously a crime to sell bad or rotten food knowingly; and there were statutes, like that of Pennsylvania (1860), which made it a misdemeanor to "sell . . . the flesh of any diseased animal, or any other unwholesome flesh, knowing the same to be diseased or unwholesome." But no real machinery backed up these laws. The demands for consumer protection outstripped mechanisms of enforcement.

Consumers were unorganized; but not powerless. Their voices grew in strength. In a mass market, high-technology society, consumers were, as we saw, more and more vulnerable. But the key factor in the rise of health laws was cultural: the willingness to demand collective, legal action. It was the idea that calamities had human causes. Disaster was not simply destiny. There were people and institutions to blame; and there were remedies to be had. Parts of the public exerted direct pressure on government. There was also indirect pressure: Sales resistance, after repeated food scandals, hurt companies in their pocketbooks and frightened them into accepting or actually asking for control. In 1883, Congress passed a law forbidding the importation of adulterated tea. In 1890, a federal statute authorized inspection of "salted pork and bacon intended for exportation"; the law also forbade the import of diseased meat and adulterated food products. The next year, Congress passed a meat inspection law, covering "all cattle, sheep, and hogs which are subjects of interstate commerce, and which are about to be slaughtered at slaughter-houses, canning, salting, packing or rendering establishments."[53] New state food laws were also passed toward the end of the century. By 1889, twenty-three states had laws against the adulteration of drugs. Massachusetts, Michigan, New Jersey, and New York had more general statutes. Each year there was fresh legislation. In Minnesota, in 1889, laws were passed forbidding the sale of adulterated baking powder; regulating the manufacture of vinegar; requiring local boards of health to appoint inspectors to "inspect all cattle, sheep, and swine slaughtered for human food"; preventing the sale of cigarettes or tobacco to children under sixteen; and regulating the quality and purity of milk, butter, and cheese.[54]

State laws were ineffective, however, against bad products that were marketed across state lines. In Congress, 190 food bills were introduced between 1879 and 1906, when the Pure Food Act finally became law.[55] A few succeeded—as we have seen, mainly those that protected export markets. There were elements of the bureaucracy that became powerful allies of the consumer. Dr. Harvey W. Wiley, chief chemist of the U.S. Department of Agriculture, later one of the guiding lights behind the Pure Food law, exposed food fraud and poisonous food products in the late 1880s and 1890s. USDA bulletins, published from 1887 to 1893, documented the national disgrace: wines were made of alcohol, sugar, and water; lard was adulterated; coffee was fabricated out of wheat flour and sawdust; canned vegetables sometimes contained sulfurous acid.[56] The Senate Committee on Manufactures, in 1899–1900, conducted a massive investigation of adulteration; it turned a glaring spotlight on the sorry state of at least some of the country's food.

Wiley's work showed that the bureaucracy was at least potentially an agent of reform. It could teach the public where its interest lay, and this could increase the *political* strength of reform. As the civil service professionalized, this factor became more important. Cities had long since had boards of health, though not necessarily very active ones. State boards proved to be more potent. Wisconsin created a State Board of Health in 1876. It tested the state's major rivers and found them polluted. Water supplies were "discolored, odorous, and nauseous-flavored"; it was for this reason, ironically, that some people believed the water had medicinal qualities. Sewage, oil-refinery filth, sawdust, and industrial wastes poured into the water. Underpaid and feebly buttressed by law, the board acted as an "eternal lobbyist," begging and cajoling legislatures and local government. The board's first president stated in 1876: "The people need facts: facts fortified and made cogent by figures; facts demonstrated from persistent and ever active causes." For many years, the board could do little *except* give out facts. But in the long run this may have been a potent contribution.[57]

---

[53] 26 Stats. 414 (act of Aug. 30, 1890); 26 Stats. 1089 (act of Mar. 3, 1891).

[54] Laws Minn. 1889, chs. 7, 8, 14, 247.

[55] Thomas A. Bailey, "Congressional Opposition to Pure Food Legislation, 1879–1906," 36 Am. J. Sociol. 52 (1930).

[56] Oscar E. Anderson, *The Health of a Nation: Harvey W. Wiley and the Fight for Pure Food* (1958), pp. 72–74.

[57] Earl F. Murphy, *Water Purity: A Study in Legal Control of Natural Resources* (1961), pp. 41, 74–78.

Tenement-house laws, too, owed a great deal to public commissions and committees, which made use of their power to scandalize the articulate public. New York had had a tenement-house law since 1867. It seemed to have little impact. Then the horrors of the tenements were brought forcibly to the eyes, ears, and noses of the public. A ponderous federal report was issued in 1894; in 1900, Laurence Veiller, one of the tireless reformers of the late nineteenth century, held a tenement-house exhibition. He played on the fear and heartstrings of the public, as Jacob Riis had done in his famous book, *How the Other Half Lives* (1890). In 1900, after the exhibit, the legislature appointed a new commission to investigate; and a major law was passed in 1901.[58]

THE GREAT ANTITRUST ACT

The Sherman Antitrust Act, of 1890, was another crucial—and permanent— entry of the federal government into the world of business regulation. The Sherman Act was cut from quite different cloth than the Commerce Act. That act had created an administrative agency; whatever its defects, it had a certain hard edge of concreteness. It spoke of particular abuses and particular remedies, dealt with a particular industry. The Sherman Act was broader, vaguer, cloudier. It responded to no specific program, except the widespread, somewhat hysterical cry from the countryside to "do something" about the trusts. Some state antitrust acts preceded it. The Act also built on the basis of a common-law rule, never very precise, that "restraints of trade" were against public policy and could not be enforced.

Fear of monopoly was an old theme in the United States. "Monopoly" meant exclusive franchises or land speculation that kept good farms off the market. Then it came to mean big and biggest business. The astonishing growth of major corporations after the Civil War fed fear of monopoly among farmers, workers and small businessmen. After 1880, the specific bugbear was the giant combinations that came to be called "trusts." Standard Oil was apparently the first to use the trust device, in 1882, as means of gathering together a whole flock of companies into a single cohesive unit, controlled by one man or corporation. A Cotton Oil Trust was organized in 1884; Linseed Oil followed in 1885. In 1887, came the Sugar Trust: a merger of fourteen companies, controlling 70 percent of the country's sugar refining; and, in the same year, Whiskey, Envelope, Cordage, Oil-Cloth, Paving-Pitch, School-Slate, Chicago Gas, St. Louis Gas, and New York Meat trusts.

The actual trust device was not used very long. After 1890, men like Rockefeller used holding companies to put their monopolies together. The name *trust* survived, however, for agglomerations that monopolized some field of business, and the branch of law that governed them is still known as "anti-trust law." Whatever their name, the public feared and hated them. In the late 1880s, attorneys general in some states tried to break up some of the more egregious trusts. Michigan, Kansas, and Nebraska passed antitrust laws in 1889. The Nebraska act

---

[58] Lawrence M. Friedman, *Government and Slum Housing: A Century of Frustration* (1968), ch. 2; Roy Lubove, *The Progressives and the Slums: Tenement House Reform in New York City, 1890–1917* (1962).

outlawed "any contract, agreement, or combination" to fix "a common price" for a product, or to limit the "amount, extent or number of such product to be sold or manufactured," or to divide up the profits in "a common fund." Also forbidden was "pooling" between companies and "the formation of combinations or common understanding between . . . companies . . . in the nature of what are commonly called trusts."[59]

The Sherman Act,[60] in comparison with the ICC act, or with some of the state laws, was brief and gnomic. Under the first section of the act, "Every contract, combination in the form of trust or otherwise, or conspiracy, in restraint of trade," was illegal. The second section made it a crime to "monopolize or attempt to monopolize, or combine or conspire . . . to monopolize any part of the trade or commerce among the several states." The fate of the Oil Trust, the Sugar Trust, the Whiskey Trust, and the Linseed Oil Trust hung on these general words, on the zeal of the federal government in bringing suit, on the temper of the federal courts in putting some flesh on the bare bones of the statute.[61] In a sense, then, the act was something of a fraud. Even its proponents thought of it as "experimental." In itself it did nothing and solved nothing, except to satisfy the political needs of Congress, which felt it had to answer the call for action—some action, *any* action—against the trusts. Like the ICC Act, too, it was a recognition that the states by themselves, in a national free trade area, were powerless to control these mighty beasts.

Vague language in a statute is, in effect, a delegation by Congress to lower agencies, or to the executive and the courts; it passes the problem along to these others. Such a law often buys time; it postpones resolution of a problem; it acts as a compromise between those who want sharp, specific action and those who want to stand pat. The Sherman Act did not, as some have thought, mechanically reflect a commitment to pure, free trade and free enterprise. The United States, in the late nineteenth and early twentieth centuries, was a high tariff country. Theory did not prevent building these tariff walls.[62] In fact, the Sherman Act was the product of a Babel of voices. It hardly reflected any coherent economic theory at all. What the solid middle class wanted, insofar as one can speak of a dominant desire, was not pure, unrestricted competition; but a giant killer, a law to cut down to size the monstrous combinations that had too much power for the good of the country.

A flurry of satellite statutes followed the Sherman Act in the states. By the turn of the century, there were some 27 state antitrust laws. Ohio and Texas had tried (unsuccessfully) to use law to break up Standard Oil.[63] But the main

[59] Laws Neb. 1889, ch. 69, p. 516.

[60] 26 Stats. 209 (act of July 2, 1890); on the history of the Sherman Act, see William Letwin, "Congress and the Sherman Antitrust Law, 1887–1890," 23 U. Chi. L. Rev. 221 (1956); and William Letwin, *Law and Economic Policy in America: The Evolution of the Sherman Antitrust Act* (1965).

[61] And on the initiative of private persons; under the seventh section of the act, a person "injured in his business or property" by "a person or corporation" which did "anything forbidden or declared to be unlawful by this Act," had the right to sue for treble damages.

[62] See, for this point, Tony Freyer, *Regulating Big Business: Antitrust in Great Britain and America, 1880–1990* (1992).

[63] Bruce Bringhurst, *Antitrust and the Oil Monopoly: The Standard Oil Cases, 1890–1911* (1979), chs. 1 and 2.

event had to be in the federal ring. Here enforcement was fairly wobbly and unpredictable. Attorneys general of the late nineteenth century were hardly a trust-busting lot. Nor did they have the money and staff to smash the combinations. Nor did the Supreme Court give them much encouragement at first. The government did try to break up the American Sugar Refining Company; this company dominated its industry and had begun reaching out its claws to acquire the stock of four Pennsylvania refiners, the only important surviving competitors. But in *United States v. E. C. Knight Co.* (1895),[64] the Supreme Court refused to find a violation of the Sherman Act. Chief Justice Fuller drew a distinction between attempts to monopolize "manufacture" and attempts to monopolize "commerce." Control of "manufacture" was no part of the task of the Sherman Act, according to Fuller: to apply the act to "manufacture" might affect the "autonomy" of the states. Justice John Marshall Harlan dissented. In his view, the Court had "defeated" the "main object" of the Sherman Act. He shuddered at the power and size of the great "overshadowing combinations." There was no "limit" to their "financial" resources; their "audacity" recognized "none of the restraints of moral obligations controlling the action of individuals"; they were "governed entirely by the law of greed and selfishness."

The conventional view is that the *Knight* case gutted the Sherman Act, that the court spoke for big business, and that Harlan's was probably the authentic voice of small businessmen, farmers, middle-class professionals. *Knight* can be read as an attempt to keep alive the power of states to control corporations, including out-of-state corporations, provided they did business inside a state's borders.[65] But as things turned out, state regulation was not exactly a roaring success and could not be. The Harlan view soon gained the upper hand in the Supreme Court. *United States v. Trans-Missouri Freight Association*[66] was decided in 1897. Here the Court, speaking through Justice Rufus W. Peckham, confronted that ancient enemy of the people, the railroads. By a bare majority, the Court rejected the view that the Sherman Act proscribed only "unreasonable" restraints of trade. The majority now spoke of how trusts ruthlessly drove out of business the worthy "small but independent dealers," and how these men were transformed into economic robots, each "a mere servant or agent of a corporation," with "no voice in shaping the business policy of the company and bound to obey orders issued by others." In *Addyston Pipe and Steel Co. v. United States.*[67] (1899), the Court continued along this road. The government had proceeded against six corporations that made and sold cast-iron pipe. The Supreme Court essentially upheld the government's position. The *Knight* case was distinguished to the point where it was meaningless. It was clear by 1900 that the courts would be an important battleground and that companies would resist the government's moves, with all the legal resources at their command.

[64] 156 U.S. 2 (1895).

[65] Charles W. McCurdy, "The *Knight* Sugar Decision of 1895 and the Modernization of American Corporation Law, 1869–1903," 53 Bus. Hist. Rev. 304 (1979).

[66] 166 U.S. 290 (1897).

[67] 175 U.S. 211 (1899); an important turning point, in the twentieth-century, was the Northern Securities case, 193 U.S. 197 (1904); on the antitrust laws in this period, see Martin J. Sklar, *The Corporate Reconstruction of American Capitalism, 1890–1916: the Market, the Law, and Politics* (1988); and Herbert Hovenkamp, *Enterprise and American Law, 1836–1937* (1991).

The Court was split down the middle on many issues of policy and interpretation, so that minor shifts in personnel could switch the Court from one track to another. In 1900, then, the future of the Sherman Act was quite uncertain.

In the twentieth century, administrations vacillated between genuine trustbusters, and those who merely made noises. The Court, too, went from one side to another. Big cases sometimes succeeded (AT&T), and sometimes failed (IBM). But an antitrust division in the Justice Department, more laws, and a burst of private suits, made antitrust law a force to be reckoned with, ultimately. John D. Rockefeller could swallow up competitors at will; the modern merger barons must humbly beg permission.

CHAPTER 6

TORTS

For the nineteenth century, it is hard to think of a body of new judge-made law more striking than tort law. As we have seen, the law of torts was totally insignificant before 1800, a twig on the great tree of law. The old common law had very little to say about personal injuries caused by careless behavior. A good many basic doctrines of tort law first appeared before 1850; but it was in the late nineteenth century that this area of law (and life) experienced its biggest spurt of growth.

The legal world began to sit up and pay attention. The very first English-language treatise on torts appeared in 1859: Francis Hilliard's book, *The Law of Torts, Or Private Wrongs*. Then came Charles G. Addison, *Wrongs and Their Remedies* in 1860, in England; a second edition of Hilliard came out in 1861, and a third in 1866. By 1900, there was an immense literature on the law of torts; Joel Bishop and Thomas M. Cooley had written imposing treatises on the subject; the case law had swollen to heroic proportions.

Superficially, the new law was built up out of old bricks from the common-law brickyard. And there was also a certain amount of transatlantic traffic. English influence on American law was dying fast, but an unusual number of leading torts cases were English: *Priestly v. Fowler* (1837) (the fellow servant rule); *Davies v. Mann* (1842) (last clear chance); *Rylands v. Fletcher* (1868) (liability for extra hazardous activities).[1] Crosscurrents of this kind were perhaps understandable in a field left largely to the judges. Besides, it is not quite accurate to speak of English *influence*. The Industrial Revolution had a head start in England; problems emerged there first, and so did their tentative legal solutions.

Every legal system tries to redress harm done by one person to another. The Industrial Revolution added an appalling increase in dimension. The new machines had a marvelous, unprecedented capacity for smashing the human body. Factories manufactured injury and sudden death as well as their ordinary products. Businesses were making money; this was a tempting and logical fund out of which the dead and the injured, and their families, might be compensated. Moreover, the industrial relationship was impersonal. No ties of blood or love prevented one cog in the machine from suing the machine and its owners. But precisely here lay the danger. Lawsuits and damages might injure the health of precarious enterprise. Industry—and especially the railroads—seemed to be the foundation on which economic growth, national

---

[1] These cases are, respectively, 3 M. & W. 1 (1837); 10 M. & W. 546 (1842); L.R. 3 H.D. 330 (1868), affirming L.R, 2 Ex. 265 (1866).

wealth, and the greater good of society rested; and thus industry had to be protected from harm.

The railroad, in general, was crucial to tort law. Almost every leading case in tort law was connected, mediately or immediately, with the iron horse. In the first generation of tort law, the railroad was the prince of machines, both as symbol and as fact. It was a vital necessity. It cleared an iron path through the wilderness. It bound cities together, and tied the farms to the cities and the seaports. It carried the farmer's crops to his markets. Yet, trains were also wild beasts; they roared through the countryside, killing livestock, setting fires to houses and crops, smashing wagons at grade crossings, mangling passengers and freight. Boilers exploded; trains hurtled off tracks; bridges collapsed; locomotives collided in a grinding scream of steel. There was a rich harvest of death, injury—and potential lawsuits.

The basic concept of the growing field of tort law was negligence: it was a law about carelessness, about not living up to standards. It was about those who inflicted harm—but not on purpose. It was about lapses in judgment. Liability for negligence was not absolute; it was based on fault. What was expected was not perfection, but the vague, subtle standard of the "reasonable man." Fault meant a breach of duty to the public, meant that the defendant had not done what a reasonable person should do. Absolute liability was rejected; more accurately, it was never considered. In the mind of the nineteenth century, absolute liability might have been too dangerous; it might have strangled the economy altogether. If railroads, and enterprise generally, had to pay for all damage done "by accident," perhaps they would not survive, or would not thrive. Ordinary caution became the standard.[2] The judges worked to limit damages to some moderate measure. Capital had to be spared for its necessary work.

Not that this underlying policy jumps out from the pages of reported cases. The cases, on the whole, did not talk policy. They used the dry, dreary language of law, in the main. Occasionally, judges let down the veil and discussed policy issues more openly. In the well-known case of *Ryan v. New York Central Rr. Co.*, decided in New York in 1866,[3] a fire broke out in the city of Syracuse, New York, in the railroad's woodshed, because of the "careless management" of an engine. Plaintiff's house, "situated at a distance of one hundred and thirty feet from the shed, soon took fire from the heat and sparks, and was entirely consumed." Other houses, too, were burned. There was no question that the railroad was at fault. The fire was the product of negligence. But how much should the railroad pay? There had to be a limit. Liability could not go so far as the plaintiff wanted:

> To sustain such a claim . . . would subject [the railroad] to a liability against
> which no prudence could guard, and to meet which no private fortune

---

[2] See Charles O. Gregory, "Trespass to Negligence to Absolute Liability," 37 Va. L. Rev. 359 (1951). Was there a "reasonable woman" as well as a "reasonable man"? In fact, as Barbara Welke has pointed out in an important study, tort law was extremely "gendered"; and to take gender "out of the law was something like taking the bounce out of a rabbit. . . . Men's and women's accidents were patterned by gender." Even such matters as the kind of skirts women wore had an impact on whether they were careless or not in getting on or off trains. Barbara Young Welke, *Recasting American Liberty: Gender, Race, Law, and the Railroad Revolution, 1865–1920* (2001), pp. 96, 98.

[3] 35 N.Y. 210 (1866).

would be adequate. . . . In a country . . . where men are crowded into cities and villages . . . it is impossible [to] . . . guard against the occurrence of accidental or negligent fires. A man may insure his own house . . . but he cannot insure his neighbor's. . . . To hold that the owner . . . must guarantee the security of his neighbors on both sides, and to an unlimited extent . . . would be the destruction of all civilized society. . . . In a commercial country, each man, to some extent, runs the hazard of his neighbor's conduct, and each, by insurance against such hazards, is enabled to obtain a reasonable security against loss.

The railroad in *Ryan* was not liable, precisely because the harm it caused was so great, and even though the damage could clearly be laid at the railroad's door. The words of the court were revealing. The opinion referred explicitly to the railroad's capacity to buy and carry insurance. Insurability was important, because an insurable risk was one that could be spread, that *would* be spread by a careful businessperson, and thus would not ruin the finances of a well-run enterprise.

The *Ryan* case also reminds us that fault was only one blade of the scissors that cut away enterprise liability; the doctrine of proximate cause was another. As late as the 1870s, it was barely mentioned in the treatises; by the end of the century, it was worth a whole chapter on its own.[4] In theory, proximate cause was a concept of physical fact: did Mr. X, by his actions, cause the injury to Mr. Y, and were his actions the "proximate" cause, with no other person, event, or situation intervening? For enterprise-minded courts, proximate cause and fault were strong and supple doctrines, useful in confining liability to what the judges considered socially reasonable bounds. Courts invented others doctrines, too. This is not to say that there was a conscious attempt to cut liability down to size, a conspiracy against injured workers, passengers, and pedestrians. Some judges—men like Lemuel Shaw—were indeed quite sophisticated; they were aware of the need to craft what they considered rules that made economic sense. Most judges simply followed what they thought was the law; but their own value system, and the value system of their period, subconsciously pushed them in a particular direction.

In any event, the spirit of the age was a spirit of limits on recovery. People lived with calamity; they had no sense (as would be true in the twentieth century) that *somebody* was always responsible—either the state or some private party; that somebody or something was going to pay.[5] In the novel by Mark Twain and Charles Dudley Warren, *The Gilded Age,* written in the 1870s, there is a description of a terrible steamboat disaster. Twenty-two people died; scores more were injured. But after an investigation, the "verdict" was the "familiar" one, heard "all the days of our lives—'NOBODY TO BLAME.'"

The traps for unwary plaintiffs were mostly in place by the middle of the century. Prominent among these were the doctrine of contributory negligence, the fellow servant rule, and its fellow traveler, the doctrine of assumption of risk. The basic idea of contributory negligence was extremely simple: If the plaintiff was negligent himself, ever so slightly, he had no right to recover from

---

[4] Herbert Hovenkamp, "Pragmatic Realism and Proximate Cause in America," 3 J. Legal History 3, 7 (1982).

[5] Lawrence M. Friedman, *Total Justice* (1985).

the defendant. This was a harsh doctrine, but extraordinarily useful. It became a favorite method through which judges kept tort claims away from the jury. The trouble with the jury (people thought) was they always decided for the plaintiff, in pitiful cases where crippled men sued big corporations. Even people who respect general rules find it hard to resist bending them once in a while, especially if the victim hauls his battered body into the courtroom, or a widow and orphans stare into the jury box. For jurors—amateurs all—every case was a one-time cause. Business and business lawyers were convinced that juries were incorrigibly plaintiff-minded; that they played fast and loose with other people's money; that they had a deep-dyed tendency to stretch facts to favor the poor suffering plaintiff. But if plaintiff was clearly negligent himself, there could be no recovery; there were no facts to be found, and a judge might take the case from the jury and dismiss it.

Contributory negligence can be traced, as a doctrine, to an English case decided in 1809. But it was rarely used before the 1850s.[6] What happened in between was the rise of the railroads. In 1840, there were less than 3,000 miles of track in the United States; by 1850, 9,000; by 1860, 30,000; by 1870, 52,000. Personal injury cases grew as fast as the trackage. Most cases were crossing accidents. The air brake was not invented until 1868; and it was not in general use until much later than that. Before the air brake, trains could not slow down very quickly. They sped through the countryside, clanging their bells; all too often, with a sickening noise, they crashed into cattle, other trains, or the bodies of human beings.

In crossing accidents, a plaintiff had to prove two things: first, that the railroad was negligent; second, that he was faultless himself. But if he was injured at a crossing, in relatively open country, with a clear view of the train, he *must* have been careless; and a court could, if it wished, take the case away from the jury and dismiss it. Contributory negligence was a common issue in reported cases. Professor Malone has counted the appellate cases—and these, it must be recalled, were probably only a small fraction of the cases that began and ended in the lower courts. Between 1850 and 1860, there were only twelve reported cases on the doctrine. Between 1860 and 1870, there were thirty-one. Between 1870 and 1880, there were fifty-eight.

Typical of these cases was *Haring v. New York and Erie Rr. Co.,* decided in 1852.[7] John J. Haring was "struck by the engine of the defendants, while he, with another person, was crossing the railroad in a sleigh." The railroad was plainly negligent; but the judge refused to let the case go to the jury. "A man who rushed headlong against a locomotive engine, without using the ordinary means of discovering his danger, cannot be said to exercise ordinary care." "We can not shut our eyes," added the judge, "that in certain controversies between the weak and the strong—between a humble individual and a gigantic corporation, the sympathies of the human mind naturally, honestly and generously, run to the assistance and support of the feeble. . . . [C]ompassion will sometimes exercise over the . . . jury, an influence which, however honorable

---

[6] For the story, see Wex S. Malone, "The Formative Era of Contributory Negligence," 41 Ill. L. Rev. 151 (1946).

[7] 13 Barb. 2 (N.Y. 1852).

to them as philanthropists, is wholly inconsistent with the principles of law and the ends of justice."

The doctrine of assumption of risk was almost as great a hurdle as contributory negligence. A plaintiff could not recover if she assumed the risk, that is, put herself voluntarily in a position of danger. Put that way, the doctrine seems to express a simple, harmless, even self-evident idea. In practice, it had a more sinister case. It was easy to say that a miner, railroad worker, or factory hand assumed the ordinary risks of employment, just by taking the job. If the job was dangerous, they could be expected to know this; if so, the risk was theirs, not the company's. This doctrine could easily be carried to extremes, and courts sometimes did so. In any event, in the last half of the century, cases that invoked this doctrine increased quite strikingly.[8]

Assumption of risk developed along with the fellow servant rule. Under this rule, as we have seen, a servant (employee) could not sue his master (employer), for injuries caused by the negligence of another employee. He could sue his employer for injuries if the employer was personally negligent. This meant very little in a factory or railroad yard. The employer was a businessman, or an abstraction—a corporation. In a crossing accident, or an accident in a textile mill, if anyone was negligent, it was most likely a fellow servant. Of course, the injured worker could always try to sue the negligent worker. But this was usually pointless; workers were poor and uninsured. The fellow-servant rule, then, meant that an injured workman had no real recourse at law.

The doctrine, as we saw, began with an English case, *Priestley v. Fowler* (1837),[9] and quickly crossed the Atlantic. "Lord Abinger planted it, Baron Alderson watered it, and the devil gave it increase," said the secretary for Ireland, in a famous remark in the House of Commons in 1897.[10] The American Abinger or Alderson was Lemuel Shaw, who wrote the opinion in *Farwell v. Boston & Worcester Rr. Corp.* (1842).[11] And the devil, on both sides of the Atlantic, was the concept of spoon-feeding enterprise, the blind desire for economic growth, responsible for a good deal of nineteenth-century callousness.

The doctrine did not look like the devil's work to Shaw's contemporaries. Within a few years of *Farwell*, the issue came up in state after state. Courts eagerly swallowed the doctrine. When the Wisconsin supreme court considered the doctrine in 1861, it treated it as part of the American common law, as if it had been handed down from the medieval Year Books. The fellow servant rule, said the court (and accurately), had been "sustained by the almost unanimous judgments of all the courts both of England and this country . . . [an] unbroken current of judicial opinion."[12] The rule had at least this advantage, in its early stages: It was clear-cut and brutally simple. It seemed to shift the cost of industrial accidents from entrepreneurs—the most productive members of society—to the workers themselves.

---

[8] See G. Edward White, *Tort Law in America: An Intellectual History* (1980), pp. 41–45.
[9] 3 M. & W. 1 (1837); see above, part II, ch. VII, p. 301.
[10] Quoted in Walter F. Dodd, *Administration of Workmen's Compensation* (1936), p. 5, n. 7. Sir Edward Hall Alderson was an English judge who further developed the doctrine.
[11] 45 Mass. (4 Met.) 49 (1842).
[12] *Mosley v. Chamberlain*, 18 Wis. 700, 705 (1861).

Another restrictive device was found by rummaging about in the toolsheds of the old common law. At common law, when a person died, he carried to the grave all of his claims in tort. Tort actions were "personal," it was said, and so rights to sue in tort died with the victim. In the old common law, it was a felony to kill another person. Felons forfeited all their property; and the victim's family might claim a share in the forfeiture. Since this was the case, an action in tort was arguably unnecessary. Meanwhile, the criminal law changed over the years, capital punishment was used less frequently, and the rule about forfeiture in felony cases vanished. The rule that tort actions died with the victim no longer made sense by the early nineteenth century. Yet, the English courts dredged it up again. The leading case arose out of a stagecoach accident. Courts then applied the rule in railroad cases, and the courts wove it once more into the fabric of tort law.[13]

The American experience is equally enlightening. There were signs in the early nineteenth century that American courts had never really accepted the rule.[14] Then, lo and behold, the rule sprang to life, in a Massachusetts case, *Carey v. Berkshire Rr.* (1848).[15] A railroad worker was killed in an accident, and his widow ("who was poor," she alleged, and "left to provide for herself and the support of three small children") sued the railroad. The court cited the English cases and denied recovery; actions for personal injuries, said the court, died with the person. Ten years later, in New York, Eliza Green, whose husband's life was snuffed out "by a collision of the cars" of the Hudson River Rail Company, filed a claim against the railroad. The court slammed the door on this claim. "The question," said the judge, "has been too long settled, both in England and in this country, to be disturbed." It would "savor somewhat more of judicial knight errantry, than of legal prudence, to attempt to unsettle what has been deemed at rest for more than two hundred and fifty years."[16]

The irony was that the matter had been settled, not for 250 years, but for ten years at most in the United States. The appeal to the past was disingenuous. Courts were, however, quite leery about measuring death damages. And it was a horrifying prospect, apparently, to make railroads and business, in general, take on the role of pensioners for widows and orphans. But as a result, in the words of one commentator, it became "more profitable for the defendant to kill the plaintiff than to scratch him."[17] Not that defendants habitually made such calculations—locomotives and their engineers did not engage in cost-benefit analysis before bearing down on potential plaintiffs in tort.

The courts also invented, and insisted upon, another doctrine that today seems somewhat outrageous: A charity was immune from any action in tort. This doctrine, too, could be traced to an English case, *Heriot's Hospital v. Ross,*

---

[13] See the perceptive article by Wex S. Malone, "The Genesis of Wrongful Death," 17 Stan. L. Rev. 1043 (1965).

[14] See *Cross v. Guthery,* 2 Root 90 (Conn., 1794); *Ford v. Monroe,* 20 Wend. 210 (N.Y., 1838); see also *Shields v. Yonge,* 15 Ga. 349 (1854), where the fellow-servant rule was applied, but at the same time the court rejected the common-law doctrine that personal injury actions did not survive.

[15] 55 Mass. (1 Cush.) 475 (1848).

[16] Bacon, J., in *Green v. Hudson River Rr. Co.,* 28 Barb. 9, 15 (N.Y. 1858).

[17] William Prosser, *Handbook of the Law of Torts* (3rd ed., 1964), p. 924.

decided in 1846.[18] At home in England, the case only lasted twenty years. But after its death, surprisingly enough, it rose from the grave in America. Its first important victim was James McDonald of Massachusetts, who entered Massachusetts General Hospital with a broken thighbone.[19] He later claimed that a third-year student at Harvard Medical School, who worked on him in the hospital, did not properly set the bone. The hospital, said the court, makes no profits, pays no dividends. It had a duty to its patients to select agents and employees with reasonable care. Having done so, it had no further responsibility for what these employees actually did.

This was in 1876; in Maryland, in 1884, a court reached a similar result. The case was brought against the Baltimore House of Refuge, on behalf of a boy who claimed he was "maliciously assaulted and beaten" there.[20] Both of these cases cited the English decision, without bothering to mention that it had been overruled. Apparently that hardly mattered. There is a suspicious parallel between these cases and the early cases on the fellow servant rule. In both instances, the court seemed concerned with distribution of costs. In both cases, they seemed fearful that liability would damage defendants and hurt their desirable work. These courts also had the idea that some plaintiffs—and some juries, and perhaps some lower courts—looked on corporations, including charities, as a cat looks on a canary. These appellate courts felt constrained to fight the impulse to give away other people's money. Charities, like the infant railroads of the past generation, were working for the public good; and they were financially precarious. Caring for destitute victims was a task for society in general, if it was a task for anybody. The loss was not to fall on hospitals and other charities.

By the beginnings of the Gilded Age, the general contours of nineteenth-century tort law were crystal clear. The leading concepts—fault, assumption of risk, contributory negligence, proximate cause—had been all firmly launched. All had either been invented or refined by the judges themselves. What they added up to was also crystal clear. Enterprise was favored over workers, slightly less so over passengers and members of the public. Juries were suspected—on thin evidence—of lavishness in awarding damages; they had to be kept under firm control. The thrust of the rules, taken as a whole, came close to the position that businesses, enterprises, and corporations should be flatly immune from actions for personal injury.

Courts never went this far; and never wanted to. They had no wish to encourage carelessness. They were never entirely heartless. In fact, the pull in the opposite direction—toward making business pay—was always there, subdued but there. It seemed to grow stronger with time. Almost as soon as a restrictive doctrine was born, shaped, and perfected, a reaction was seen and felt in the case law. In their nagging, fuzzy way, each rule bred its counter rule. The bench was not monolithic; as time went on, some high court judges showed tendencies much like those that juries were accused of having. Sympathy eroded firm, tough rules; hard cases, pitiful cases, tended to snag and rip at the fabric. Politically, too, the rage of the victims counted for very little in 1840, not

---

[18] 12 C. & F. 507 (1846).

[19] *McDonald v. Massachusetts General Hospital*, 120 Mass. 432 (1876).

[20] *Perry v. House of Refuge*, 63 Md. 20 (1884).

much in 1860; by 1890, it was a roaring force. Labor found a voice and agitated in every forum for safety, and for some way of getting compensation. The awful toll of deaths and injuries in factories, mines, and railroad yards came to be seen as a major social problem. A stream of statutes chipped away at the doctrines. The rules were pawns in a political chess game; as the balance of power shifted, so did the rules. The law of torts was therefore never a perfect engine of oppression. It was an imperfect instrument from the start. From birth, it showed symptoms of mortality. Just as there was never a perfect free market, the classic nineteenth-century law of torts held such brief sway that in a sense it never was.

Gradually, too, the "nobody to blame" notion began to erode. Toward the very end of the century, personal injury cases in the courts grew in number.[21] Not enough is known about the actual operation of the tort system, at the trial court level; there are only a few, scattered studies.[22] Even appellate cases have rarely been studied systematically. About the rest of the system—settlements and claims adjustment, for example—even less is known. Legal scholars tend to look mostly at reported cases. These can be quite misleading. A study of reported cases, in the last quarter of the century, found about a nine to one ratio in favor of plaintiff—in cases that were actually appealed. But we know that actual trials were not so lopsided; a small sample of Illinois trials showed plaintiff winning nineteen jury cases, and defendant winning thirteen.[23] Recoveries, too, were often extremely small. The vast majority of cases never got to court—they were dropped, or settled. Not much is known about the process; but what evidence there is suggests that most victims got little or nothing from the tort system. Thomas Russell studied the claims department of the Oakland Traction Company, which ran a street railway (a fertile source of accidents). Between 1903 and 1905, 3,843 passengers were injured; only 581 received any compensation at all; most received amounts between $10 and $35. In a ten-year period (1896–1906), there were thirty-five deaths. In no cases, did the company pay more than $300; in twenty cases, they paid nothing at all. The average amount paid out was $169.[24]

The rise of personal injury cases meant also the rise of a personal injury bar. It was not a branch of the profession that enjoyed high prestige. The lawyers (or their agents) were labeled as "ambulance chasers"; vile men who

[21] For facts and figures, see Randolph Bergstrom, *Courting Danger: Injury and Law in New York City, 1870–1910* (1992).

[22] See Bergstrom, n. 21 *supra;* Lawrence M. Friedman, "Civil Wrongs: Personal Injury Law in the Late 19th Century," 1987 American Bar Association Research J. 351.

[23] Richard A. Posner, "A Theory of Negligence," 1 J. Legal Studies No. 1, pp. 29, 92 (1972). The volume of personal injury cases in the appellate courts grew tremendously in the last quarter of the century, according to Posner's study. Almost half of these were railroad accident cases. *Ibid.*, 63, 85. See also Robert Kagan, Bliss Cartwright, Lawrence M. Friedman, and Stanton Wheeler, "The Business of State Supreme Courts, 1870–1970," 30 Stan. L. Rev. 121, 142 (1977). Lawrence M. Friedman, "Civil Wrongs," n. 22 above, was a study of tort cases in Alameda County, California, in the late nineteenth century; here, too, plaintiffs won most but by no means all of their cases.

[24] Thomas D. Russell, "Blood on the Tracks: Turn-of-the-Century Streetcar Injuries, Claims, and Litigation in Alameda County, California" (unpublished mss) referred to in John Fabian Witt, "Toward a New History of American Accident Law: Classical Tort Law and the Cooperative First-Party Insurance Movement," 114 Harv. L. Rev. 690, 769n (2001).

rushed to the scene of an accident, or to the home or hospital, to sign victims up as soon as possible. But these notorious ambulance chasers were racing against the company's claims adjusters, who were also in a big hurry, trying to get the victim to sign a release, perhaps for some sort of (low) payment. These adjusters were often ruthless and deceitful. They used "high-pressure" methods; they took advantage of victims who were sick, drugged, in pain; or who knew little or no English; sometimes they made threats, sometimes they used empty promises of money or jobs.[25] Only a few cases got as far as court. Once there, plaintiffs did tend to win, but not overwhelmingly. It was (and still is) a myth that juries *always* favor the victim over a corporate defendant; that they cannot resist dipping into the defendant's deep pockets.[26] Defendants, as we saw, won a significant number of cases.

Doctrine by the end of the century was ambiguous and tottering. The judges made many inroads on classical doctrine; they thus disinvented their own inventions. The doctrine of imputed negligence was one of the most offensive rules, and one of the first to go. This rule "imputed" the negligence of a driver to his passenger, and the negligence of a parent to his child, so as to prevent passenger or child from recovering in personal-injury actions.[27] Even so conservative a judge as Stephen Field thought this rule was unfair, and should be abandoned.[28] Some courts even experimented with ways to pull the teeth of the doctrine of contributory negligence. In a railroad case, in 1858, the supreme court of Illinois expressed the idea that the "more gross the negligence" of defendant, "the less degree of care" would be "required of the plaintiff." So, if plaintiff's negligence was "comparatively slight," and "that of the defendant gross," plaintiff might still recover.[29] The notion of comparative negligence found an echo in the courts of Kansas, but nowhere else. Both Illinois and Kansas courts were backtracking by the 1880s, and their doctrine disappeared, only to reemerge with greater force in the twentieth century. But these decisions showed a certain impulse to soften the roughest edges of contributory negligence.

Two new doctrines—last clear chance and *res ipsa loquitur* (the thing speaks for itself)—eased the burden of proving a negligence case, at least slightly. Both doctrines were English in origin; both were somewhat ingenious. In *Davies v. Mann*,[30] an English case of 1842, plaintiff "fettered the forefeet of an ass belonging to him" and "turned it into a public highway." Defendant's wagon, "with a team of three horses," came along "at a smartish pace," smashed into the animal and

---

[25] Edward A. Purcell Jr., "The Action Was Outside the Courts: Consumer Injuries and the Uses of Contract in the United States, 1875–1945," in Willibald Steinmetz, ed., *Private Law and Social Inequality in the Industrial Age* (2000), p. 505.

[26] Lawrence M. Friedman, "Civil Wrongs," n. 22 supra.

[27] The rule applied to this situation: B hired a carriage; and was riding in it; C was the driver. The carriage collided with a carriage driven by D. Both C and D were at fault. Can B, who was injured, sue D? The doctrine of imputed negligence denied him this right.

[28] Field, J., in *Little v. Hackett*, 116 U.S. 366 (1885). See also *Bunting v. Hagsett*, 139 Pa. St. 363, 21 Atl. 31 (1891).

[29] *Galena and Chicago Union Rr. Co. v. Jacobs*, 20 Ill. 478 (1858); see, on this and other Illinois cases, Howard Schweber, *The Creation of American Common Law, 1850–1880* (2004), pp. 90–111.

[30] 10 M. & W. 546 (1842).

killed it. The plaintiff was obviously negligent, and strictly speaking should not
have recovered for his donkey. But defendant, zooming along the road, had the
"last clear chance" to avoid the accident. The court felt this fact ought to cancel
out, in effect, plaintiff's early bit of fault. The plaintiff won his case, and a doctrine was launched. The "groan, ineffably and mournfully sad, of Davies' dying
donkey," as one judge later put it, "resounded around the earth."[31] Dead donkeys
were not a significant element in nineteenth century law, but railroads were. The
doctrine had rich possibilities in railroad cases—for plaintiffs who wandered
onto the tracks or otherwise got themselves in trouble and had no way to get out.
Last clear chance did not get very far in the courts before 1900; still, it made a
small, clean wound in the body of contributory negligence.

Baron Pollock in *Byrne v. Boadle*, an English case of 1863,[32] launched the
phrase *res ipsa loquitur*—the thing speaks for itself. The plaintiff was walking
past the defendant's warehouse. A barrel of flour fell on his head and injured
him. The plaintiff had no way to prove who was negligent, and how; all he knew
was that a barrel fell and hit him on his head. To the court, this mysterious
falling barrel was as inspirational as Newton's apple. "A barrel," said Pollock,
"could not roll out of a warehouse without some negligence." The mere fact of
the incident "spoke for itself." It made out a prima-facie case of negligence. The
burden thus shifted to the defendant; he had to prove that he was *not* at fault.
Otherwise, the plaintiff had to win. This rule, too, seemed helpful in railroad
cases—in an 1868 Illinois case, for example, where the boiler of an engine mysteriously exploded.[33] The scope and limit of the doctrine were never quite clear;
but it was definitely useful to victims of wrecks, crashes, explosions, and those
pursued by all manner of falling and flying objects. It was the middle twentieth
century, however, the period of the "liability explosion," that really made this
doctrine its own.

Changes in tort law imposed by statute were also significant. In some legislatures, labor's voice, and the voice of passengers, sounded quite loudly. Some
laws raised the standard of care imposed on tortfeasors. In Kansas, a dry, flat
state, anyone who started a prairie fire had to bear the resulting costs, whether
negligent or not. The firestarter was liable "to the party injured for the full
amount of such damage."[34] Statutes as early as the 1850s imposed safety pre-
cautions on railroads; if they failed to obey, they had to take the consequences.
A New York statute of 1850 made it the duty of locomotives to ring a bell when
approaching a crossing. Any railroad company that failed to comply was "liable

---

[31] McLean, J., in *Fuller v. Illinois Central Rr. Co.*, 100 Miss. 705, 56 So. 783 (1911).

[32] 2 H. & C. 722 (1863).

[33] *Illinois Central Rr. v. Phillips*, 49 Ill. 234 (1868). But the upper court reversed. The explosion did not raise a presumption of negligence. The trial court should have given an instruction about the type of evidence that would rebut this presumption.

[34] Kans. Stats. 1868, ch. 118, sec. 2. The doctrine of the *Ryan* case (pp. 373–74, above)
was also not universally accepted by the courts. In most states, wrote Thomas M. Cooley in
1879, a "negligent fire is regarded as a unity; it reaches the last building as a direct and
proximate result of the original negligence, just as a rolling stone put in motion down a
hill, injuring several persons in succession, inflicts the last injury as a proximate result of
the original force as directly as it does the first." Thomas M. Cooley, *A Treatise on the Law of
Torts* (1879), p. 77.

for all damages . . . sustained by any person by reason of such neglect."[35] A Rhode Island law of the same decade ordered "a bell of at least thirty-two pounds in weight" to be hung on every locomotive, and sounded "at the distance of at least eighty rods" from a crossing; the bell had to keep on ringing until the engine crossed the road. Railroads had to post warning signs, too, at every crossing, "of such height as shall be easily seen," and on each side of the signboard an "inscription . . . painted in capital letters, of at least the size of nine inches each, 'Railroad Crossing—Look out for the Engine while the Bell Rings.'" If a train failed to comply, the company would be liable "for all damages sustained by any person."[36] Other statutes required railroads to build fences, and made them liable for fires caused by engine sparks. Frequently, railroads were forced to pay for any livestock that their locomotives killed. A Colorado statute of 1872 imposed liability for the death of all domestic animals; the law included a schedule of damages, ranging from $1.50 for Mexican sheep to $37.50 for "American Work Cattle"; thoroughbred cattle and sheep, and horses, mules and asses had to be paid for "at two-thirds of their cash value." Not a word was said in the statute about negligence.[37] An interesting New Hampshire statute, dating from before the Civil War, imposed liability on railroads for any fires they caused; to soften the blow, the law gave every railroad corporation "an insurable interest in all property situated on the line of such road." In theory, then, the railroad could limit its financial risk by buying fire-insurance policies for the land along its right of way.[38]

As these statutes show, big corporations, particularly the railroads, spoiled children of land grants and subsidies, darlings of public opinion in the middle of the century, began to feel the rod of regulation. Their immunities melted away. Toward the end of the century, the pace of safety legislation quickened. The Interstate Commerce Commission called a conference of state regulatory authorities in 1889. Safety was on the agenda; many participants urged the ICC to look into the problem of slaughter on the railroads and recommend some positive remedies. The plight of the railroad workman was extremely pressing. Between June 30, 1888, and June 30, 1889, 1,972 railwaymen were killed on the job; 20,028 workers were injured. One worker died for every 357 employees; one in thirty-five was injured in this single year. Tort law, thanks in good measure to the fellow servant rule, did almost nothing for these workmen and their families. In 1876, in Illinois, hundreds of workmen were killed and injured; but only twenty-four workers recovered damages, and fifty-three railroad companies paid out a grand total of $3,654.70. Human lives were worth less than the life of cows; the same companies paid $119,288.24 in damages for the death of livestock.[39]

---

[35] Laws N.Y. 1850, ch. 140, sec. 39.

[36] R.I. Stats. 1857, ch. 130, secs. 3–5.

[37] Laws Colo. 1872, p. 185.

[38] N.H. Stats. 1851, ch. 142, secs. 8–9; see *Hooksett v. Concord Rr.*, 38 N.H. 242, 244 (1859).

[39] Walter Licht, *Working for the Railroad: The Organization of Work in the Nineteenth Century* (1983), pp. 181–208. Some railroads took care of certain medical expenses, and gave charity to injured workmen and their families, on a voluntary basis. But the process was "arbitrary," and done in such a way as to avoid even the appearance of "fixed rules and procedures." *Ibid.*, p. 205. Some railroads had "relief associations," mostly voluntary, to help injured or disabled workers. Usually, a member who accepted benefits had to release any legal claim against the road. James W. Ely Jr., *Railroads and American Law* (2001), pp. 216–17.

There were, however, signs of change. Eighteen-ninety was not 1850; labor agitation, strikes, and union activity were national political facts. In 1893, Congress imposed a clutch of safety regulations on interstate railroads: "power driving-wheel brakes," "couplers coupling automatically by impact," and "secure grab irons or handholds in the ends and sides of each car."[40] Employees injured "by any locomotive, car, or train in use contrary to the provisions" of the act were not to be "deemed . . . to have assumed the risk."

There were safety regulations for other forms of transport, too. If anything was more dangerous than riding the rails, it was steamboat travel. Boilers had the distressing habit of blowing up, and thousands were scalded and drowned. A federal statute as early as 1838 tried to regulate boilers on steamboats; and an elaborate act "for the better Security of the lives of Passengers on board of Vessels propelled in whole or in part by Steam" was passed in 1852.[41] Whether these did much good is another question. On April 27, 1865, the boilers exploded on the steamboat *Sultana*, on the Mississippi River; the *Sultana* was jammed with 2,300 Union soldiers, just released from southern prison camps, plus crew and passengers; the boat sank, and 1,700 people died.[42] Late in the century, the states began to pass laws regulating safety conditions in mines and factories. These related specially to dangerous machines, hoistways, and elevators, and often had provisions for guarding or belting machinery; other provisions imposed broader but vaguer standards, requiring factories and mines to provide comfort and good ventilation. Administration of safety regulations was spotty at best. But they had an effect, in the long run, on civil litigation. "Statutory negligence" became an important concept in the cases. That is, the plaintiff could make out his case for negligence by showing that the defendant had violated a safety statute. In a leading case, *Osborne v. McMasters* (1889),[43] a drugstore clerk sold a woman "a deadly poison without labeling it 'Poison.'" This was a criminal offense. The woman took the poison by mistake, and died. Her survivors sued, in tort. Negligence, said the court, "is the breach of legal duty." The duty can be defined just as well by statute as by common law. The fact that the statute spoke only of *criminal* penalties was immaterial.

The life of the rule about wrongful death was also mercifully short. Lord Campbell's Act in England (1846)[44] gave a cause of action on behalf of a "wife, husband, parent, and child" who died by virtue of a "wrongful act, neglect, or default." The action lay against the person who would have been liable "if death had not ensued." Many American states copied this statute. Indeed, Massachusetts had such a law as early as 1840, in favor of the next of kin of passengers who died on boats and railways.[45] The first Kentucky statute (1854) applied only to victims of railroad accidents; it specifically excluded employees. Another section

---

[40] 27 Stats. 531 (act of Mar. 2, 1895). The roads were given until Jan. 1, 1898, to comply, and the ICC was authorized to grant extensions.

[41] 10 Stats. 61 (act of Aug. 30, 1852).

[42] Gene E. Salecker, *Disaster on the Mississippi: The Sultana Explosion, April 27, 1865* (1996).

[43] 40 Minn. 103, 41 N.W. 543 (1889).

[44] 9 and 10 Vict., ch. 93 (1846).

[45] Wex S. Malone, "The Genesis of Wrongful Death," 17 Stan. L. Rev. 1043, 1070 (1965). Note that this law was passed eight years before Massachusetts, in the *Carey* case (discussed earlier), denied that wrongful death actions survived at common law. The dead man in *Carey* was, alas, a worker, not a passenger.

of this same law gave a general action for wrongful death, but only in cases where the defendant was guilty of "wilful neglect."[46] Many courts clung to their homemade wrongful death rules, except insofar as these were modified by statute. The statutes tended to become more general, however; or they filled in gaps in older laws. Massachusetts, in 1883, finally extended protection to the families of dead railroad workers. The typical statute restricted recovery to widows and next of kin of the dead man; and they often put a ceiling on the amount that could be recovered—for example, ten thousand dollars in Kansas in 1859. The legislatures seemed to agree with the courts that it was hard to measure death damages. The statutory figures represented a rough sort of compromise, between giving the companies what they would have liked (no recovery at all) and giving the plaintiff an unlimited go at the jury. Ten thousand dollars, however, was quite a substantial amount in the nineteenth century. Very few plaintiffs in tort ever recovered this much from a jury, or anything even close to it.

The fellow servant rule was strong medicine. It was meant to be firm and clear-cut. It demanded unswerving legal loyalty. But that is precisely what it did not get. Shaw wrote his *Farwell* opinion in 1842. Later in the century, some judges wavered, or actually showed dissatisfaction with the rule. In "nearly all jurisdictions," said a Connecticut court in 1885, the "tendency" was to "limit rather than enlarge" the fellow servant doctrine.[47] A Missouri judge, in 1891, candidly spoke of the "hardship and injustice" that the rule had brought about. In the "progress of society," "ideal and invisible masters and employers" (the corporations) had replaced "the actual and visible ones of former times." The "tendency of the more modem authorities" was to mitigate the rules, and to place on the employer "a due and just share of the responsibility for the lives and limbs of the persons in [its] employ."[48]

There was more here than judges who changed their minds. The accident rate kept increasing at a rate completely unforeseen by Shaw's generation. The railway injury rate, always high, doubled between 1889 and 1906. At the turn of the century, industrial accidents were claiming about thirty-five thousand lives a year, and inflicting close to two million injuries. One quarter of these were serious enough to disable the victim for a solid week or more. These accidents were the raw material of possible lawsuits. Litigation was costly, but lawyers took cases on contingent fees. If the case was lost, the lawyer charged nothing; if he won, he took a huge slice of the gain. The upper part of the bar looked with beady eyes at this practice, "most often met with in suits for alleged negligent injuries." Thomas Cooley thought they were beneath contempt: "mere ventures," no better than "a lottery ticket." They debased the bar, brought "the jury system into contempt," and horror of horrors, helped create "a feeling of antagonism between aggregated capital on the one side and the community in general on the other."[49] But the contingent fee had its merits. A poor man could sue a rich

---

[46] Laws Ky. 1854, ch. 964, secs. 1, 3.

[47] *Zeigler v. Danbury and Norwalk Railroad Co.*, 52 Conn. 543, 556 (1885).

[48] Thomas, J., in a separate opinion in *Parker v. Hannibal & St. Joseph Railroad Co.*, 109 Mo. 362, 390, 397–98, 19 S. W. 1119 (1891), quoting from *Gilmore v. Northern Pacific Railroad Co.*, 18 Fed. Rep. 866 (C.C.D. Ore., 1884).

[49] Quoted in 24 Albany L.J. 26 (1881).

corporation. By 1881, the contingent fee was said to be an "all but universal custom of the profession."[50]

Neither the number of accidents nor the contingent fee system, in itself, can completely explain the rise in litigation. To justify taking risks, and to make a living, the lawyer had to win at least some of his cases. The erosion of the fellow servant rule was a kind of conspiracy in which juries, judges made of less stern stuff than Lemuel Shaw, and legislatures all joined in. The evolution of the rule followed a common pattern. The courts had laid down a simple, flat rule, in a form intended to be the final formulation. But workers and their lawyers tried to get around the rule, or modify it, through one means or another. In a sense, strict tort rules simply did not work. The rules choked off thousands of lawsuits, no doubt. In countless cases, a worker or his family gave up the idea of suing; or settled their claim for a piddling sum. Still, thousands of cases descended on the courts, toward the end of the century. Plaintiffs won some of these cases—not by any means all; but some. The more plaintiffs won, the more lawyers were encouraged to try again. Juries, contrary to legend, did not (as we said) automatically hand out money to plaintiffs; on the other hand, neither were juries and lower-court judges totally committed to stern general principles. In Wisconsin, workers in the trial courts won nearly two-thirds of the 307 personal-injury cases appealed to the state supreme court up to 1907. The supreme court, however, decided only two-fifths for the worker.[51] These appellate cases were merely the tip of a huge iceberg of cases, or potential cases. Most worker cases went nowhere. Evidence from the early twentieth century suggests that injured employees workers received little or no compensation.[52] Still, cases that did make it to court had a decent chance of success. Trial judges and juries were not playing the *Farwell* game as strictly as they could.

Doctrine, too, was wobbling. The cases opened up exceptions to the rule. One of these was the vice-principal doctrine. An employee could sue if the careless fellow servant was a supervisor or a boss, a "vice-principal," that is, more like the employer than a fellow servant. In one case, a railroad worker, injured by a collapsing roundhouse door, succeeded in winning by showing negligence on the part of a "master mechanic in charge of the roundhouse, foreman of the workmen, having the power to employ and discharge the hands."[53] The vice-principal concept was potentially a large hole in *Farwell*. Some states never adopted the rule, however; some states never carried it very far. In some there were exceptions to this exception; and the exceptions in turn had their own exceptions.

Other counterrules had even greater importance. There was a doctrine that the master had a duty to furnish a safe place of work, and safe tools and appliances. This duty was not "delegable." Failure in this regard opened the employer to liability. Many cases turned on this point. In one case, *Wedgwood v. Chicago & Northwestern Rr. Co.*,[54] the plaintiff was a brakeman. He went to "couple the cars,"

---

[50] 13 Central L.J. 381 (1881).

[51] [1907–1908] *Wis. Bureau of Labor and Industrial Statistics, 13th Bienn. Rep.*, pp. 85–86 (1909).

[52] Price V. Fishback and Shawn Everett Kantor, *Prelude to the Welfare State: The Origins of Workers' Compensation* (2000), pp. 30–42.

[53] *Missouri Pac. Ry Co. v. Sasse,* 22 S.W. 187 (Ct. of Civ. Appeals, Texas, 1893).

[54] 11 Wis. 478 (1877).

and was hurt by a "large and long bolt, out of place," which "unnecessarily, carelessly and unskillfully projected beyond the frame, beam or brakehead, in the way of the brakeman going to couple the cars." The trial court threw the plaintiff's case out; but the supreme court of Wisconsin disagreed: The railroad had a "duty . . . to provide safe and suitable machinery." Truly, this was an exception that could have swallowed up the rule, if courts had been so inclined. They never were, not quite. So the safe-tool rule grew its own exceptions—the "simple tool" rule, for example. A defective hammer or ax did not result in employer liability—another exception to an exception to an exception.

Then there were modifications by statute. The rule first arose in railroad cases, and for the benefit of railroads. As the railroads became bogeymen rather than heroes, legislatures sometimes changed the rule in ways that applied *only* to railroads. A Georgia statute, in the 1850s, gave railroad employees the right to recover damages for injuries caused by fellow servants, as long as they themselves had not been negligent. Similar laws were passed in Iowa (1862), Wyoming (1869), and Kansas (1874).[55]

Small wonder, then, that the law of industrial accidents grew monstrously large. In 1894, William F. Bailey published a treatise on "The Law of the Master's Liability for Injuries to Servants"; the text ran to 543 pages. "No branch of the law," Bailey wrote in the preface, was "so fraught with perplexities to the practitioner." There was no uniformity; indeed, the law was full of "unpardonable differences and distinctions." By 1900, then, the rule had lost some of its reason for being. It was no longer an efficient way to choke off accident claims. It did not have the courage of its conviction. It vacillated between harshness and humanity, never making up its mind. It satisfied neither capital nor labor. It siphoned millions of dollars into the hands of lawyers, court systems, administrators, insurers, and claims adjusters. Companies spent and spent; but their money did not buy industrial harmony—and not enough of the dollars flowed to the injured workmen. At the turn of the century, rumblings were already heard of the movement that led ultimately, to workers' compensation. England had already passed a compensation law. In the United States, no state enacted a compensation statute until 1911. By that time, more than half the states had abolished the fellow servant rule, at least for railroads; and the Federal Employers Liability Act of 1908 (FELA) had done away with the rule for interstate railways.

By 1900, then, tort law had gone through a marvelous series of changes. It stood in what might seem a state of indecision. The courts, by and large, still upheld the rights of enterprise; but they were creatures of their time, and their faith had been shaken. The doctrinal structure, the stiff bony skeleton on which the system rested, was weakening; perhaps even tottering. Judges were becoming more "humane,"[56] at least in selected cases. One symptom of change was the way American courts reacted to the great English case of *Rylands v. Fletcher*, decided in the 1860s.[57] The defendants in this case had owned a mill. They built a reservoir on their land. Some old, unused mining shafts lay

---

[55] Laws Ga. 1855–56, p. 155; Laws Iowa 1862, ch. 169, sec. 7; Laws Wyo. Terr. 1869, ch. 65; Laws Kans. 1874, ch. 93.

[56] Gary Schwartz, "Tort Law and the Economy in Nineteenth-Century America: A Reinterpretation," 90 Yale L.J. 1717 (1981).

[57] L.R. 1 Ex. 265 (1866); upheld in the House of Lords, L.R. 3 H.L. 330 (1868).

underneath their land. The water broke through these and flooded the plaintiff's coal mine, which lay under land close by. The English court imposed liability on the defendants, even though the plaintiff could not prove any negligence. The principle of the case—somewhat fuzzy to be sure—seemed to be that a person who sets in motion some extraordinary or dangerous process must take the consequences. It was no excuse to show he was as careful as he could be, or as careful as the reasonable man.

This was the germ of a notion far more pregnant with consequences, at least potentially, than Davies's donkey or the falling barrel. Out of it, the courts could have fashioned a doctrine of absolute liability for industrial hazards. There were piecemeal statutes on strict liability; but no general principle—as yet. *Rylands v. Fletcher* had a mixed reception in America. A few courts eagerly accepted the principle. It was mentioned, approved, and applied in an Ohio case in 1899, where nitroglycerin stored on defendant's land blew up "from some cause unknown" and shattered the glass in plaintiff's factory.[58] Other courts reacted in utter panic at this alien intruder. The doctrine was too much, too soon. Oliver Wendell Holmes Jr., writing in 1873, did admit that it might be "politic" to put risks on those who engaged in "extra-hazardous employments"; but Holmes thought strict liability—liability without fault—was primitive, a throwback to those ancient times before the concept of fault had evolved, when an "accidental blow was as good a cause of action as an intentional one."[59] Chief Justice Charles Doe of New Hampshire, who had a firm reputation as a liberal judge, also found the doctrine indefensible, and stoutly rejected it. Horses owned by a certain Lester Collins had been frightened by a railroad engine; they bolted, and broke "a stone post on which was a street lamp," on Albert Brown's land in front of his store in Tilton, New Hampshire. Brown sued Collins for damages. Doe took the trouble to write a long essay attacking *Rylands v. Fletcher*. The case would "impose a penalty upon efforts, made in a reasonable, skilful, and careful manner, to rise above a condition of barbarism. It is impossible that legal principle can throw so serious an obstacle in the way of progress and improvement." He refused to "put a clog" on "natural and reasonably necessary uses of matter."[60] This seems rather heavy freight for a case of a damaged post. But Doe was clinging to the ethos of the earlier nineteenth century: social progress depended on the vigor and prosperity of risk takers, entrepreneurs. To burden them with strict liability—as *Rylands* might—would slow down the journey toward civilization and economic growth, and out of barbarism.[61]

But what *was* barbarism, after all? The American landscape had subtly altered since the 1850s. Smokestacks were as dense as trees in the forest. In row on row of mean houses, in crowded cities, lived hundreds of poorly paid, landless workers. Each year, accident tore through these *barrios*, extracting its tax of dead and shattered bodies, ruined lives, destitute widows and children. A finger of shame pointed at industry. Dissatisfaction was in the air. Labor denounced the system of tort law as cruel and inefficient. It *was* inefficient, if

---

[58] *Bradford Glycerine Co. v. St. Mary's Woolen Mfg. Co.*, 60 Ohio St. 560, 54 N.E. 528 (1899).
[59] 7 Am. Law. Rev. 652, 653 (1873).
[60] *Brown v. Collins*, 53 N.H. 442, 448 (1873).
[61] See the essay of Francis H. Bohlen, "The Rule in *Rylands v. Fletcher*," 59 U. Pa. L. Rev. 298, 373, 423 (1911) on the meaning of the case; and on the judicial reaction to the decision.

only because it no longer worked, because too many people had lost or were losing their faith in a harsh, simple system; they no longer saw it as a necessary evil. Change was clearly on the way. Insurance and risk-spreading techniques were ready; cushions of capital reserves were ready; most important, perhaps, an organized and restless working class pressed against the law with voices and votes. The rules of tort law, in twilight by 1900, were like some great but transient beast, born, spawning, and dying in the shortest of time. The most stringent rules lasted, in their glory, two generations at most. Was that interlude worthwhile? Would the economy have done less well under some other arrangement? It is impossible to know. That short, bitter life may have had a point. The lives and fortunes that were sacrificed might have gone toward a greater cause. Or, again, it might all have been in vain.

CHAPTER 7

THE UNDERDOGS: 1850–1900

THE DEPENDENT POOR

The American system provided a voice and a share in the economy to many more people than most of the old world societies. But decisively not everybody. For blacks, for Native Americans, for the Chinese, and for the unorganized and the powerless in general, the share was skimpy and begrudging. In a relatively open society, interest groups made politics, and politics made law. The squeaky wheels got the oil. Power led to privilege. Old people, transients, the feeble minded, dirt-poor and crippled families—all of these people stayed, by and large, at the bottom of the social pit. Tort law blossomed, corporation law swelled in pride, contract expanded; but the poor laws remained obscure, local, haphazard, backward, and cruel. But there were certain changes in the late nineteenth century; perhaps even a measure of improvement.

There was a great deal to improve. In some counties of some states, the poor, in the age of the railroad and the telegraph, were still bound out "like cattle at so much per head, leaving the keeper to make his profit out of their petty needs."[1] Or they might be sold at auction to the lowest bidder. Sometimes, there was no real alternative. Trempealeau County, Wisconsin, in the 1870s and 1880s, boarded out its handful of "permanently demented" people; the state's asylum could not or would not hold them.[2] Many people found the auction system abusive; it would eventually die out. "Indoor" relief, that is, relief inside the walls of institutions, was clearly, by 1850, in the ascendancy; "outdoor" relief was declining. The trend meant poor farms and poorhouses, if not more specialized institutions. One reason for the change in policy was ideology. Outdoor relief was just not stigmatic enough. "Men who before had eaten the bread of industry saw their fellows receiving sustenance from the overseer of the poor. . . . The pauper came to look upon the aid given as his by right."[3] Many people sincerely believed that poorhouses were a good idea. Moral training, medical treatment, rehabilitation—all this was hard to do under a system of "outdoor" relief. A well-run institution could improve the lot of the poor.

---

[1] Quoted in Grace A. Browning, *The Development of Poor Relief Legislation in Kansas* (1935), p. 59 n. 7. The statement quoted, from an 1899 report, actually referred to the treatment of the insane in Kansas, who were indeed were farmed out to the counties at so much a head.

[2] Merle Curti, *The Making of an American Community* (1959), p. 285.

[3] 10th Ann. Rpt., *Bd. of State Charities*, Indiana (1900), p. 154.

In 1850, Rhode Island made a study of its poor-law system at work. The results were harrowing. There were fifteen almshouses. They spent, on average, $51.50 per inmate per year. Some of the poor were still "vendued" to keepers who competed with low bids. There was testimony about one keeper who beat and abused his charges: "He used to drag John Davis, an old man as much as sixty years old up stairs with a rope and kept him there in the cold for days and nights together until he died, having one of his legs frozen. . . . [H]e died before midnight, with no person watching with him & he lay until the sun was 2 or 3 hours high in the morning, & on a very cold morning before they came to him."[4]

But was the poorhouse, or poorfarm, any better? Poorfarms too were run on the cheap; and sometimes callously. In the words of one observer, they housed "the most sodden driftwood from the social wreckage of the time. . . . In some of the country almshouses, no clergyman comes the year round; and no friendly visitor appears to encourage the superintendent to be faithful, or to bring to light abuses that may exist."[5] The Ulster County poorhouse (New York) in 1868 was an "old, dilapidated two-story wooden structure." The rooms were small, "ceilings low, ventilation imperfect"; there were no "suitable bathing conveniences." The little wooden house for the insane contained "twenty-five small unventilated cells." The inmates were all "noisy and filthy"; several were "nearly nude." The beds were disordered and torn, and the halls littered with straw and bits of clothing. The bathroom, used by both sexes, was out of repair; and the air in the room was "foul and impure." In the Schoharie County poorhouse, "an insane woman was chained to the floor, and a man to a block of wood in the yard." Twenty years later, some of these hovels had been improved; some had not.[6] The poor got almost no medical care in many counties. In Michigan, in 1894, a former county physician reported the auction system still at work; many counties awarded medical contracts this way. The local doctor who bid the lowest got the contract to supply medicine, give medical care, and perform surgery for the poor.[7]

Who were the people who went to the poorhouse? Obviously, only those who had no choice—the most desperate; men and women at the bottom of the barrel. Very few studies take a worm's-eye view of these dismal, obscure institutions. Not surprisingly, the poorhouses drew on unwed mothers with small children, widows, old folks with no place to turn, and, in great numbers, the mentally ill.[8] Some contemporaries described the poorhouses as homes for the "unworthy poor." Dr. Charles S. Hoyt, who surveyed poorhouse inmates for New York in 1874–1875, talked about "idleness, improvidence, drunkenness . . . vicious indulgence"; he talked about "hereditary" tendencies. Paupers were paupers because of their own inadequacy. The number who were "reduced to poverty by

---

[4] Margaret Creech, *Three Centuries of Poor Law Administration: A Study of Legislation in Rhode Island* (1936), pp. 195–97, 325.

[5] Amos G. Warner, *American Charities* (3rd ed., 1919), p. 179.

[6] 22nd Ann. Rpt., *State Bd. of Charities*, N.Y. (1889), pp. 505–11.

[7] Isabel C. Bruce and Edith Eickhoff, *The Michigan Poor Law* (1936), p. 77.

[8] Elizabeth G. Brown, "Poor Relief in a Wisconsin County, 1846–1866; Administration and Recipients," 20 Am. J. Legal Hist. 79 (1976). Another study of a poorhouse, also from the Middle West, is Eric H. Monkkonen, *The Dangerous Class: Crime and Poverty in Columbus, Ohio, 1860–1885* (1975), chs. 5, 6.

causes outside of their own acts is . . . surprisingly small."[9] But the good doctor was quite wrong. The inmates were, by and large, the detritus of capitalism, victims of the decay of traditional society. They were men who had been thrown out of work, accident victims, widows, old people, ill people; in fact, almost all the people in the poorhouse had "lived their lives in the most vulnerable sectors of the working class."[10] Now they were dumped into the poorhouse or poorfarm. Here they got at least some food, shelter, a bit of clothing, some rudimentary health care—though apparently very little empathy. No doubt some poorhouses were better than others. Whether all, or most, of the hundreds of such places were as bad as the Rhode Island or New York examples is hard to tell.

After the Civil War, some states began to experiment with more centralized administration. Massachusetts created a State Board of Charities in 1863, Illinois in 1869.[11] A Connecticut law of 1873 set up a five-member board of charities—"three gentlemen and two ladies"—appointed by the governor. The board was to visit and inspect "all institutions in the state, both public and private, in which persons are detained by compulsion for penal, reformatory, sanitary, or humanitarian purposes." The board had the duty to see whether inmates were "properly treated," and whether they were "unjustly placed" or "improperly held" in the institution. The board had some vague powers to "correct any abuses that shall be found to exist," but were told to work, "so far as practicable, through the persons in charge of such institutions."[12] This was something less than iron discipline over charitable institutions. But the boards had the power of publicity. They could, if they wished, evoke scandal. In the late nineteenth century, a small but enthusiastic band of people, inside and outside of government—men and women like Florence Kelley, Lawrence Veiller, and others—worked hard to improve the lot of the poor, and the institutions that served them. The reformers used words, charts, and pictures as their weapons. They tried to enlist the sympathy of the wider public, or, more tellingly, appeal to the self-interest of the public. They tried to show that callousness, in the long run, did not pay.

This social-cost argument probably had some effect. In the 1890s, Amos G. Warner and associates noted that ten American cities, with an aggregate population of 3,327,323, spent $1,034,576.50 in one year on medical relief. Warner mentioned "three strong motives" at work: "the desire to aid the destitute, the desire to educate students and build up medical reputations, and the desire to protect the public health. The latter has often been the leading cause of public appropriations for medical charities."[13] Poverty bred crime, plague, and social disorder. Fighting poverty was therefore a fight against crime, plague, and social disorder.

---

[9] Quoted in Michael B. Katz, *In the Shadow of the Poorhouse: A Social History of Welfare in America* (rev. ed., 1996), p. 89.

[10] Katz, *op. cit.*, p. 90.

[11] Sophonisba P. Breckenridge, *The Illinois Poor Law and Its Administration* (1939).

[12] Edward W. Capen, *The Historical Development of the Poor Law of Connecticut* (1905), pp. 213–14; Laws Conn. 1873, ch. 45. The power to investigate whether persons were "unjustly placed" or "improperly held" did not extend to "cases of detention for crime."

[13] Amos G. Warner, Stuart A. Queen, and Ernest B. Harper, *American Charities and Social Work* (4th ed. 1930), pp. 143–44.

Still, reformers had to struggle against other strongly held attitudes—attitudes less friendly to relief. The Illinois board of charities, in 1886, voiced a common fear: the "inevitable consequences of substituting the machinery of state for the spontaneous impulses of private benevolence," would be to "paralyze" the "charitable activity" of the private sector.[14] Josephine Shaw Lowell, writing in 1890, thought that public relief was justified only when "starvation is imminent." How could one tell when this was the case? "Only by putting such conditions upon the giving of public relief that, presumably, persons not in danger of starvation will not consent to receive it. The less that is given, the better for everyone, the giver and the receiver."[15]

Nobody asked the poor *their* opinion in this matter. The poor were victimized by stereotypes and assumptions. If you paid people who did not "earn" their pay, you were encouraging laziness and social disorganization. On the other hand, most people did not want to let other Americans starve to death. The usual solution was to make relief available to people who needed it; but relief had to be stingy, painful, and stigmatic. It had to be so degrading and obnoxious that no one with any possible alternative, and with an ounce of pride, would choose it. Mostly, in fact, family and friends had to sustain the urban poor; private charity took care of some others; the public sector lagged behind. In times of depression, however, there were soup kitchens in the major cities. Some relief agencies protested that these kitchens were too indiscriminate; it was "impossible" to tell the "worthy" from the "unworthy poor."[16] Soup presumably corrupted the one but not the other. The big city machines had no such qualms. Boss Tweed of New York City personally donated $50,000 to provide the poor with Christmas dinners in the harsh winter of 1870. He used his position in the state legislature to squeeze out appropriations for charities in his city; city funds, too, were distributed to welfare institutions. Some of this money, to be sure, had been extorted from the public, rich and poor. Caustically, the *New York Times* compared Tweed to a medieval baron, "who swept a man's land of his crops, and then gave him a crust of dry bread."[17] Hard times returned in the nineties; and with it, more poor and destitute people. Mayor Hazen Pingree of Detroit produced a garden plan; the poor would grow vegetables on vacant lots. San Francisco spent $3,000 a month in 1893 to help the unemployed. Some of these jobless men were put to work cleaning streets and building roads.[18]

Many states reformed the law of settlement and removal, getting rid of some of the worst features. But the obsession with drawing a line between worthy and unworthy poor continued. Unworthy were drunks, transients, tramps, and the proverbial sturdy beggars. Worthy meant, in essence, guiltless. These were the blind, children, veterans, the deaf and dumb, the epileptic. Legislatures were particularly likely to show sympathy for temporary sufferers who had

---

[14] Quoted in Breckenridge, *op. cit.,* p. 76.
[15] Quoted in Ralph E. and Muriel W. Pumphrey, eds., *The Heritage of American Social Work* (1961), p. 223. See also, in general, Walter I. Trattner, *From Poor Law to Welfare State: A History of Social Welfare in America* (6th ed., 1999), pp. 95–96.
[16] Leah H. Feder, *Unemployment Relief in Periods of Depression, 1857–1922* (1936).
[17] Quoted in Alexander B. Callow Jr., *The Tweed Ring* (1966), p. 159.
[18] Frances Cahn and Valeska Bary, *Welfare Activities of Federal, State, and Local Governments in California, 1850–1934* (1936), pp. 201–2.

fallen out of the middle class (and who were voters). Kansas, for example, was as stingy as any toward its destitute poor. But in 1869, it appropriated $15,000 to buy seed wheat for impoverished settlers on the Western frontier; more money was appropriated in 1871 and 1872. Grasshoppers scourged the western plains in 1874; in 1875, the state passed a "seed and feed" law. Townships could float bonds to provide "destitute citizens . . . with grain for seed and feed." Another law authorized counties to sell bonds for relief purposes. (The farmers were expected to pay the money back.) In the 1890s, Kansas gave away seed wheat, and sold grain and coal to farmers hurt by drought and crop failures.[19]

There was, indeed, a tradition of federal welfare—despite the states' right arguments. But it was confined to victims of wars and disasters. In general, war veterans were a meritorious class. There had been both state and federal pensions for veterans of every American war, including the Civil War. Thousands of Revolutionary War veterans received pensions. The Civil War produced a much larger crop of veterans. Wounded war veterans and their families were singled out for special benefits in a federal pension law of 1862. The law gave pensions to disabled veterans; and to their widows and orphans. The government also offered soldiers who lost arms and legs free prostheses; by 1966, the government had subsidized 3,981 legs, 2,240 arms, 9 feet, and 55 hands. Veterans also got preferential treatment with regard to government jobs.[20] In the 1850s, Congress established a U.S. Soldiers' Home, in the District of Columbia, for veterans; but after the Civil War, Congress vastly expanded the scope of institutional care for veterans, creating what was known after 1873 as the National Home for Disabled Volunteer Soldiers. The home was originally open only to disabled veterans; but by the 1880s, it was admitting veterans who were simply old and worn out, and there was a whole network of branches.[21]

Over time, the Civil War pension laws became more generous—the veterans were, after all, a potent political lobby. In 1890, Congress passed the Dependent Pension Law, which expanded coverage greatly. Anybody who served three months and was honorably discharged from service could get a pension if they suffered from a "mental or physical disability of a permanent character" (provided it was not the "result of their own vicious habits"). The "disability" no longer had to be connected to the service at all. A 1906 law made old age a "disability" in itself: Anybody over sixty was disabled enough to get a pension. In 1910, of people over sixty-five, no less than 30 percent in Kansas were getting this pension, although in some states the percentage was far less (3 percent in Georgia).[22] The veterans were a potent lobby in the states, too; and various states provided a mixed bag of benefits. Connecticut, for example, granted former soldiers some tax relief (1869), established a home for

[19] Grace A. Browning, *The Development of Poor Relief Legislation in Kansas* (1935), pp. 77–81.

[20] Patrick J. Kelly, *Creating a National Home: Building the Veterans' Welfare State, 1860–1900* (1997), p. 56.

[21] The story of the National Home is told in Kelly, *op. cit., supra*. On the history of federal disaster relief, see Michele Landis: " 'Let me Next Time be "Tried by Fire" ': Disaster Relief and the Origins of the American Welfare State, 1789–1874," 92 Northwestern U.L. Rev. 967 (1998).

[22] Theda Skocpol, *Protecting Soldiers and Mothers: The Political Origins of Social Policy in the United States* (1992), Part 1, ch. 2; and Appendix I, p. 541.

orphans of soldiers (1864), gave veterans preferences in applying for state jobs (1889), and exempted veterans from the need to obtain a peddlers' license (1895).[23]

There were many categorical programs—programs taking care of special classes of the unfortunate. States granted charters to private charities; and also donated money to these agencies.[24] States ran many institutions themselves. In Massachusetts, the state lunatic hospital at Worcester was founded in the 1830s.[25] In the 1840s, Dorothea Dix bravely roamed the country, pleading for more to be done for the mentally ill. In New Jersey, she talked the legislature into creating an insane asylum at Trenton; it opened its doors in 1848. Kansas set up a hospital for the insane at Osawatomie in 1863; later, four more such hospitals were created, and in 1881, a state home for the feeble minded. But even in states with statewide institutions, most of the insane were either at home, or at the tender mercies of county officials of the poor. The state institutions themselves were a mixed bag. Taxpayers hated to spend money; and their attention span was short. Hence, many institutions were shortchanged and neglected. Some of them turned into snake pits. Centralized abuse was no better than the decentralized kind.

Children are favorites of law and society; and there were special efforts to do something for unfortunate children. Pennsylvania, in 1860, donated $5,000 to the "Northern Home for friendless children," a typical act of largess.[26] Children win sympathy more easily than adults; moreover, people were afraid that, if nothing was done for homeless or abandoned children, they would be altogether lost to decency; and would grow up to be recruits for the army of the "dangerous classes." In the age of cities and factories, the old apprenticeship system was dead. In New York, the Children's Aid Society, founded by Charles Loring Brace in 1853, gathered up homeless children from the streets and sent them into the country—many to the Midwest—to work and build character on clean, honest, Protestant farms. This was not a program that worked perfectly. Some of the new foster parents were cruel and exploitative; some Catholics (and many of the children were Catholic) objected to the program as a threat to their religion. No doubt, some orphans found decent homes and a way to earn an honest living. Western farm life was in any event better than street life, hunger, and an early, violent death. Up to 1892, the Children's Aid Society had "emigrated" 84,318 children; most of these (51,427) were boys.[27]

---

[23] Capen, *op. cit.*, pp. 249–55, 387–89.

[24] There were innumerable instances. See, for many examples in a general appropriation law, Laws N.Y. 1850, ch. 365. See also Jacobus ten Broek, "California's Dual System of Family Law: Its Origin, Development and Present Status," Part II, 16 Stan. L. Rev. 900, 944–49 (1964).

[25] The story of this institution is told in Gerald N. Grob, *The State and the Mentally Ill* (1966).

[26] Laws Pa. 1860, ch. 551, sec. 38.

[27] Amos Warner et al., *American Charities and Social Work* (4th ed., 1930), p. 136; Miriam Z. Langsam, *Children West: A History of the Placing-Out System of the New York Children's Aid Society, 1853–1890* (1964); Marilyn Irvin Holt, *The Orphan Trains: Placing Out in America* (1992). In Boston, too, there was a Children's Aid Society (1864), which "maintained a home to discipline children before placing them out." Robert M. Mennell, *Thorns & Thistles: Juvenile Delinquents in the United States, 1825–1940* (1973), p. 43.

On the whole, the categorical approach was the only one that had much political appeal. Only the guiltless or worthy poor had a fair chance at arousing
human sympathy. No programs dealt with the leftovers, the unworthy poor (so-
called) in any meaningful way. The dregs of humanity, or what was defined as
the dregs, got nothing but the dregs of support. It was a story that would be
often repeated. In the 1950s, it was the fate of AFDC and public housing. These
became more and more controversial and degraded, the more they became last-
stop programs for the most problem-ridden, dependent, and needy. President
Reagan demonized "welfare queens"; and President Clinton ended "welfare as
we know it." Tough love turned out to be mostly tough and very little love.

FAMILY LAW AND THE STATUS OF WOMEN[28]

The second half of the nineteenth century was a period of great change in the
legal position of women. Most middle-class men believed that women had their
own special and limited sphere. Women were highly moral but delicate creatures, who belonged in the home, which was their exclusive empire. Railroads
had separate "ladies' cars"; and in one case, in 1874, when a man tried to get
into one of these (he was tired of standing up in the smoking car), he was removed by force. He sued for damages. The supreme court of Wisconsin turned
him down: Women traveling without men need "protection"; they had to be
"sheltered . . . from annoyance and insult."[29]
As we shall see, a few women successfully stormed the citadel of the legal profession—though against great opposition.[30] They were at the top end of a vast
army of working women. The factory revolution drew thousands of women from
their farms and homes into textile mills or shops. They may have exchanged one
master for another; but in some ways work led to the legal liberation of women.
A woman who earned a living was not as totally dependent on men. Women did
not get the right to vote until the twentieth century;[31] but in the nineteenth century, there were a set of partial, but important, emancipations.
For the sake of free enterprise, if for no other reason, the law presumed that
adults were fully capable of buying, selling, and acting in the marketplace.
Married women's property laws, already discussed, were extended, broadened,

---

[28] There is a growing literature on the history of family law. See especially Michael
Grossberg, *Governing the Hearth: Law and the Family in Nineteenth-Century America* (1985);
Nancy F. Cott, *Public Vows: A History of Marriage and the Nation* (2000); Hendrik Hartog, *Man
and Wife in America: A History* (2000); Lawrence M. Friedman, *Private Lives: Families, Individuals, and the Law* (2004).
[29] Quoted in James W. Ely Jr., *Railroads and American Law* (2001), p. 146. On the ladies'
cars, see Barbara Young Welke, *Recasting American Liberty: Gender, Race, Law, and the Railroad
Revolution, 1865–1920* (2001), pp. 253–54.
[30] See below, ch. 12.
[31] There was a woman's suffrage movement in the nineteenth century; and it made some
progress. The territories of Wyoming and Utah granted women voting rights around 1870.
Congress eliminated voting rights for women in Utah, in 1887; but when Utah was admitted
to the union, these rights were reinstated. By 1890, some nineteen states gave women the
right to vote in elections for local school boards. Eleanor Flexner, *Century of Struggle* (1972),
pp. 159–63, 176–77.

and generalized after 1850. No doubt some men felt that these laws went too far "towards clothing one class of females with strange and manly attributes," as a Wisconsin judge put it.[32] But the market and creditor's rights ultimately won out over these faintly archaic sentiments. In New York, statutes of 1860 and 1862 extended the rights of married women. A married woman now had rights, not only with regard to property she owned or acquired, but also with regard to whatever she acquired "by her trade, business, labor or services." The courts at first interpreted this statute quite narrowly. A case in 1878 held that the husband still had the right to sue for his wife's wages.[33] But the trend in the law—as in society—was clear. Women were empowered in the marketplace, at least, if not at home, or in public life.

Dower, too, had been substantially revised and revamped, as we have seen. This, too, was generally in the interest of women—though also, and perhaps more crucially, it was in the interests of those who traded in the market. In community-property states (California, Texas, Louisiana, and others), although husband and wife "owned" the community property equally, the husband was totally in charge. He had the right of management and control. This situation would change, but slowly. As far as inheritance was concerned, community property states were ahead of the other states. The wife's inheritance rights were rather firm. She automatically owned one half of the "community." A widow came into possession of this half, no matter what her husband's will said; after all, it was already legally hers.[34]

In the last half of the century, the doctrine of the common-law marriage went into decline. The doctrine, as we pointed out, had been highly favored in the earlier part of the century. But the new urban, industrial world was more bureaucratic; it was a world of records and documents. When records were sparse and poor, the common-law marriage helped regularize property rights. By the end of the century, it had become something of a nuisance. Most states made provision for marriage licenses, and for civil and religious ceremonies. A few states abolished the common law marriage; or construed their statutes as killing the doctrine.[35] In other states, the common law marriage did remain valid. Courts sometimes construed marriage license laws as optional only; a couple could have a formal marriage, if they so chose, but there was no obligation. The actual incidence of common law marriage was no doubt declining. Common law marriage was now an anachronism. It created problems in inheritance cases, and later, in the twentieth century, in cases of workers' compensation, state pensions, and social security,[36] among other situations. The common law marriage had another failing: it frustrated state control over marriage. Marriage was, after all, the gateway to reproduction. Common law marriage allowed anybody, including the insane and the diseased, to marry. A

---

[32] Crawford, J., in *Norval v. Rice*, 2 Wis. 22, 31 (1853).

[33] *Birbeck v. Ackroyd*, 74 N.Y. 356 (1878); Norma Basch, *In the Eyes of the Law: Women, Marriage, and Property in Nineteenth-Century New York* (1982), pp. 217–18.

[34] See Peter T. Conmy, *The Historic Spanish Origin of California's Community Property Law and Its Development and Adaptation* (1957).

[35] See *Beverlin v. Beverlin*, 29 W. Va. 732, 3 S.E. 36 (1877).

[36] Thomas Clifford Billig and James Phillip Lynch, "Common-Law Marriage in Minnesota: A Problem in Social Security," 22 Minn. L. Rev. 177 (1937).

Connecticut state of 1895 provided that no man or woman who was "epileptic, imbecile, or feeble-minded," could marry, or live together, if the woman was "under forty-five years of age"; it was also a crime for an epileptic, or a feeble-minded man to "carnally know" a woman under forty-five. An Indiana law (1905) barred any man from marriage if he had been in the poor house within the prior five years, unless he could show he could support a family; no license was to issue if either party had an infectious disease.[37] These statutes show the influence, too, of the eugenics movement, and to a heightened state concern for control of reproduction.

Marriage, in other words, was becoming more formal; and the state was taking a more active interest in the subject. The law concerned itself with the proper age of marriage. At common law, the age of consent (to marriage) had been fourteen for boys, twelve for girls. This common law rule allowed very young marriages; Joel Bishop thought it unsuitable to the "northern latitudes"; it must have "originated in the warm climate of Italy."[38] American statutes generally redefined the age of marital consent, raising it to more fitting levels. In Illinois, in 1827, the ages were seventeen for men, fourteen for women. In Idaho, in 1887, the ages were eighteen and sixteen. As we will see, the age of consent for sex, and not just marriage, was also in the process of going up.

One special case of informal marriage has to be mentioned. No slave had been allowed to marry. Slave "marriages" were not even common law marriages. But when slavery ended, the states had to validate those stable unions which had been, functionally speaking, marriages. An Alabama law of 1868 declared that "freedmen and women . . . living together as man and wife, shall be regarded in law as man and wife"; their children were "declared . . . entitled to all the rights, benefits and immunities of children of any other class."[39]

Ex-slaves were thus allowed to marry—each other. But they were certainly not allowed to marry white folks. Interracial marriage was against the law in the Southern states; and in general, interracial sex was a crime. In 1881, Tony Pace, a black man, and Mary J. Cox, a white woman, were indicted, convicted, and sentenced to prison in Alabama for "living together in a state of adultery or fornication." The U.S. Supreme Court upheld their conviction.[40] But laws that made it an offense for whites and blacks to marry were not only found in the South.[41] They were also on the books in some Western and Northern states: a California statute of 1850 declared "illegal and void" all "marriages of white

---

[37] Laws Conn. 1895, ch. 365, p. 667; Edward W. Spencer, "Some Phases of Marriage Law and Legislation from a Sanitary and Eugenic Standpoint," 25 Yale L.J. 58 (1915).

[38] Joel P. Bishop, *Commentaries on the Law of Marriage and Divorce*, vol. I (4th ed., 1864) p. 127. See, in general, on state control over marriage, Michael Grossberg, "Guarding the Altar: Physiological Restrictions and the Rise of State Intervention in Matrimony," 26 Am. J. Legal Hist. 197 (1982).

[39] Laws Ala. 1868, ord. no. 23, p. 175.

[40] *Pace v. Alabama*, 106 U.S. 583 (1882). See Julie Novkov, "Racial Constructions: The Legal Regulation of Miscegenation in Alabama, 1890–1934," 20 Law and History Review 225 (2002). Despite severe taboos, there *were* instances in the South of stable, long-term black and white relationships. See Martha Hodes, *White Women, Black Men: Illicit Sex in the Nineteenth-Century South* (1997).

[41] See, for example, Peter Wallenstein, *Tell the Court I Love My Wife. Race, Marriage, and Law—An American History* (2002).

persons with Negroes and mulattoes." In 1913, thirty of the forty-eight states had some sort of law against miscegenation.

Bigamy had always been a crime; but never one that loomed very large in the criminal justice system. Bigamy became somewhat more significant in the nineteenth century. A mobile society, a society full of immigrants and strangers—and one which no longer has arranged marriages—is a society where dishonest men can easily slip from one identity to another, abandon an old wife, and marry a new one without the bother of divorce.[42] Bigamy was not, however, a serious social issue—except in one regard: plural marriages among the Latter-Day Saints. The Mormon practice of polygamy evoked a storm of rage, horror, and disgust; it was denounced vehemently from pulpit, legislature, and press, to a degree hard to understand today. Polygamy somehow threatened the very basis of society. Society was a huge organic compound; the molecules that composed it were made up of traditional families, husbands and wives, bound together in "Christian monogamy." Anything else threatened to lead to perdition.[43] The Christian monogamists took action. In the Morrill Act (1862), Congress moved "to punish and prevent the practice of polygamy in the territories." *Reynolds v. United States* (1878),[44] was a test case, involving George Reynolds, who was Brigham Young's secretary. George Reynolds was tried and convicted of polygamy. Reynolds argued that the anti-polygamy laws went beyond the power of Congress to govern the territories and infringed his freedom to practice his religion. The government's lawyer argued that allowing polygamy would open the door to unspeakable horrors: "Hindu widows" throwing themselves on their husband's funeral pyres, "East Islanders" exposing their "new-born babes," and "Thugs," committing murder.[45] The Court seemed to agree. They upheld the laws, and Reynolds' conviction. They repeated the horror stories about Hindu widows and human sacrifice. Moreover, polygamy was "patriarchal" and had always been confined to "Asiatic and . . . African peoples." Apparently the Court felt that it belonged only in such uncivilized places. Clearly, to the Court, polygamy was not just out of place in America; it represented a profound social danger.

Many Mormons were arrested and convicted; but Mormons in Utah continued their hated practice. In the 1880s, the Gentiles returned to the battle. President Arthur in 1881 called plural marriages an "odious crime"; James G. Blaine warned against abominations disguised as religious practices; he repeated the line about "the claim of certain heathen tribes, if they should come among us, to continue the rite of human sacrifice."[46] The vicious and punitive Edmunds Law,

---

[42] On bigamy in the nineteenth century, see Lawrence M. Friedman, *Crime and Punishment in American History,* pp. 197–201.

[43] Sarah B. Gordon, *The Mormon Question: Polygamy and Constitutional Conflict in Nineteenth Century America* (2002), p. 33. A general study of the relationship between the Mormon church and the law is Edwin Brown Firmage and Richard Collin Mangrum, *Zion in the Courts* (1988).

[44] 98 U.S. 145 (1878).

[45] Quoted in Sarah Gordon, *op. cit.,* at 126.

[46] Quoted in Thomas F. O'Dea, *The Mormons* (1957), p. 110. See also Ray Jay Davis, "The Polygamous Prelude," 6 Am. J. Legal Hist. 1 (1962). In Idaho Territory, anti-Mormons were in control; and an act of 1885 required all voters to swear they were not polygamists, and that they did not belong to an "order" that taught bigamy.

of 1882, put more teeth into the laws against polygamy; it also attempted to smash the political power of Mormon leaders. Under the Edmunds Law, great numbers of Mormons were arrested for "unlawful cohabitation," fined, and jailed.[47] Mormon leaders went underground. The Edmunds-Tucker Law, of 1887, was even more stringent. It aimed to destroy the power of the Mormon Church, seizing its property, and dissolving it as an entity. In 1890, Wilford Woodruff, president of the Mormon Church, in defeat, threw in the towel. The Church renounced polygamy. The Mormon rebellion against America was over. Plural marriages faded into history, even though a few deviant offshoots of the main Mormon branch secretly kept this practice alive. No doubt, thousands of good Americans sighed with relief at the downfall of Satan, and the triumph of American morality.

Divorce

The law of divorce was always more complex and controversial than the law of marriage. It changed greatly in the last half of the century, both on the official level, and even more significantly in its subterranean life. The first great change was the extinction of the legislative divorce. State after state abolished it, usually by constitutional provision. By about 1880, it was virtually gone. The last holdout was Delaware, where it survived until 1897. A new constitution in Delaware then put an end to the practice. In the last year of this noble institution, the legislature of Delaware granted no less than 100 divorces.

After the era of the legislative divorce, all suits for divorce had to go through the court system, as had been true in the Northern states for a long period of time. The divorce statutes varied from state to state. At one end of the spectrum was South Carolina, the only state where absolute divorce was simply not available.[48] From about 1850 to 1870, a few states adopted rather loose divorce laws. Connecticut at one point made any "misconduct" grounds for divorce, if it "permanently destroys the happiness of the petitioner and defeats the purposes of the marriage relation." In Maine, a supreme court justice could grant a divorce if he deemed it "reasonable and proper, conducive to peace and harmony, and consistent with the peace and morality of society." Divorce laws in states as different as North Carolina, Indiana, and Rhode Island were also quite permissive. Some states that did not go as far as Maine or Connecticut broadened their statutes considerably; they added to the traditional list of grounds for divorce (adultery, desertion, and impotence, for example) new and vaguer ones such as "cruelty." In the Tennessee Code of 1858, for example, divorce was available on grounds of impotence, bigamy, adultery, desertion, felony conviction, plus the following: attempting to take a spouse's life by poison; concealing a pregnancy by another man at the time of marriage; and nonsupport. In addition, the court might, in its "discretion," free a woman from the bonds of matrimony if her husband had "abandoned her, or turned her out

---

[47] Sarah Gordon, *op. cit.*, is a careful study of this campaign.

[48] It says something that, under South Carolina law, a man was not allowed to leave more than one quarter of his estate to his mistress. Glenda Riley, *Divorce: an American Tradition* (1991), p. 70.

of doors," if he was guilty of cruel and inhuman treatment, or if he had "offered such indignities to her person as to render her condition intolerable and force her to withdraw."[49]

After 1870, the tide began to turn. Influential moral leaders had never stopped attacking loose divorce laws. Horace Greeley thought that "easy divorce" had made the Roman Empire rot. America could suffer a similar fate, "blasted by the mildew of unchaste mothers and dissolute homes."[50] Theodore D. Woolsey, president of Yale University, wrote a book in 1869 denouncing the divorce laws of Connecticut as immoral and unscriptural. If laws against adultery were not vigorously enforced, the public sense of sin would be dulled.[51] Moreover, adultery should be the only legal grounds for divorce. In Woolsey's view, "petitions for divorce become more numerous with the ease of obtaining them". Lax divorce laws could disintegrate the family, the backbone of American life. In 1881, a New England Divorce Reform League was formed. Dr. Woolsey was its president. Out of this grew a National Divorce Reform League in 1885.[52] A second edition of Woolsey's book appeared in 1882. By this time, the Connecticut law had been repealed. Maine's law fell in 1883. A more rigorous divorce law replaced it, with tougher grounds, a six-month wait before decrees became "absolute," and a two-year ban on remarriage of the plaintiff without court permission; the guilty defendant could *never* remarry, without leave of the court.[53]

Militant feminists, on the other hand, took up the cudgels for permissive divorce. A furious debate raged in New York. Robert Dale Owen, son of the Utopian reformer, went into battle against Horace Greeley. Owen, like Joel Bishop, felt that strict divorce laws, not lax ones, led to adultery. New York, rather than permissive Indiana, Owen said, was the "paradise of free-lovers."[54] Bishop bitterly condemned divorce *a mensa et thoro* (legal separation): "in almost every place where Marriage is known, this Folly walks with her—the queen and the slut, the pure and the foul, the bright and the dark, dwell together!"[55] Both men agreed, in other words, that divorce laws had a direct impact on sexual morality and sexual behavior—a questionable assumption. One thing was certain: The divorce rate was rising. In the period 1867–1871, 53,574 divorces were granted; in 1877–1881, 89,284. In every part of the country, but especially in the West, divorce rates rose faster than the population: By 1900, there were 39 divorces per 100,000 population in the North Atlantic states, and 131 per 100,000 in the Western states.[56]

What accounts for the rising demand for divorce? There are various possibilities. One is that dry rot had affected family life. This is what people who prattled about Babylon and chastity believed. But perhaps a larger number of people simply wanted *formal* acceptance of the fact that their marriages were dead. Just as more of the middle class wanted, and needed, their deeds recorded, their wills

[49] Tenn. Stats. 1858, secs. 2448–49.
[50] Quoted in Nelson Blake, *The Road to Reno* (1962), p. 91.
[51] Theodore D. Woolsey, *Divorce and Divorce Legislation* (2nd ed., 1882), p. 221.
[52] Blake, *op. cit.,* p. 132.
[53] Laws Me. 1883, ch. 212.
[54] Blake, *op. cit.,* p. 90.
[55] Bishop, *Commentaries on the Law of Marriage and Divorce,* vol. I (4th ed., 1864), p. 26.
[56] Glenda Riley, *op. cit.,* pp. 79, 86.

made out, their marriages solemnized, so they wanted the honesty and convenience of divorce, the right to remarry in bourgeois style, to have legitimate children with their second wife (or husband), and the right to decent, honest disposition of their worldly goods. Only divorce could provide this.

This was the middle class need for divorce. But divorce began to spread throughout the population. A study of divorce, in two California counties, 1850 to 1890, examined the class and income status of litigants. Almost a quarter of the husbands were laborers, another 9 percent were unskilled tradesmen; 19 percent were skilled workers, 14 percent farmers, 17 percent "middle class," 15 percent upper class.[57] But why would a ditch-digger, or his wife, want a divorce? Why would they be willing to put up with the cost and the fuss? Here, pure economic analysis breaks down. Divorce had a moral aspect, too. Living in sin was not respectable. And, thanks to divorce, not always necessary. Victorian morality was for everybody. This was the paradox of the moral attack on divorce: Divorce was immoral because marriage was holy. But the holiness of marriage only increased the demand for divorce. It was divorce that paved the way, for many people, to the sanctuary of respectable remarriage.

Divorce law, and divorce practice, reflected changes in the family that went beyond either of the factors mentioned. When divorce was a matter mostly for the well-to-do, men asked for, and got, custody of their children; the general rule was preference for the father. As divorce percolated downward, it became the custom for the woman to file for divorce; this meant she was the "innocent" party, entitled to custody, alimony, and the like. And small children, especially children of "tender years," belonged with their mothers. In addition, it was much less damaging to accuse a man of adultery, desertion, or cruelty than to accuse a woman. Divorce became much more a woman's remedy, at least in form. This was especially pronounced in the Northern states. In the period 1887–1906, women were plaintiffs in exactly two-thirds of the divorce cases; but there was great variation among states. In Mississippi most plaintiffs were men (almost 60 percent); in Rhode Island, 78 percent of the plaintiffs were women. Western plaintiffs were overwhelmingly female, too.[58]

Divorce, as we said, became a woman's remedy; but what did it remedy? Did the state of the law (and practice) improve the lot of the deserted or mistreated wife? There is no reason to believe that it did. The women in divorce cases were victims, not partners, dependents, not independent women—by and large. Often, they wanted divorce only because it was forced on them by a brutal, absent, or philandering husband. Also, the nature of marriage itself was changing. Men were still in charge—often overwhelmingly so. But slowly, almost imperceptibly, some marriages were becoming more of a partnership—at least emotionally. The more demands people (men and women) put on marriage, however, the more they expected out of marriage, the more they wanted the other partner to be lover, friend, confidant, someone who shared all of

---

[57] Robert L. Griswold, *Family and Divorce in California, 1850–1890: Victorian Illusions and Everyday Realities* (1980), p. 25; another study which uses divorce records is Elaine T. May, *Great Expectations: Marriage and Divorce in Post-Victorian America* (1980).

[58] Lawrence M. Friedman and Robert V. Percival, "Who Sues for Divorce? From Fault through Fiction to Freedom," 5 J. Legal Studies 61 (1976).

life—then the more likely it was that a marriage would fail these awesome tests. This is a key aspect, no doubt, in the rising demand for divorce.[59]

Did strict divorce laws have any effect on family solidarity? Doubtful. Did they lower the divorce rate? Perhaps. But only by encouraging desertion and adultery. In Maine and Connecticut, there were short-term "improvements" when permissive laws were abolished; but between 1850 and 1900, the divorce rate skyrocketed everywhere. Yet the laws were not reformed. Those who wanted a divorce found ways to get around the laws. Divorce became what we might call a dual system: a system in which the law on the books differed radically from the law in action.

In theory, divorce came at the end of an ordinary lawsuit. Plaintiff attacked; defendant resisted. This did happen—sometimes; there were some unedifying battles in which bitter spouses aired their dirty linen in public. But by the end of the century, the vast majority of divorce cases were empty charades. Both parties wanted the divorce; or were at least willing to concede it to the other party. Even in states with rigid statutes, collusion was a way of life in divorce court. Divorce in New York was a scandal. Lawyers openly advertised their skill at arranging divorce. Reed's "American Law Agency," at 317 Broadway, advertised in 1882 in the *New York Sun:*

DIVORCES quietly; desertion, drunkenness; any cause, advice free.[60]

"Divorce rings" operated practically in the open. Manufactured adultery was a New York specialty. Henry Zeimer and W. Waldo Mason, arrested in 1900, had hired young secretaries and other enterprising girls for this business. The girls would admit on the witness stand that they knew the plaintiff's husband, then blush, shed a few tears, and leave the rest to the judge. Annulments, too, were more common in New York than elsewhere. In most states, annulment was rare and hard to get, but not in New York. In New York, they were a prominent loophole in the divorce laws. Judges passed out annulments like candy. Friendly divorces were easier in states where "cruelty" as grounds for divorce. It is hard to know exactly how much collusion there was, and when it began. Francis Laurent's figures for Chippewa County, Wisconsin, suggest a dramatic rise in friendly divorce (so to speak), in this nonurban county from the 1870s on.[61]

The migratory divorce, for people with money and the urge to travel, was another detour around strict enforcement of divorce law. To attract the "tourist trade," a state needed easy laws and a short residence period. Indiana was one of these states, before the 1870s. The moral opponents of easy divorce fought these divorce colonies as hard as they could. Notoriety and bad publicity helped their campaign in Indiana; in 1873, the legislature passed a stricter law that shut the divorce mill down. South and North Dakota, too, had their day. Finally, in the twentieth century, Nevada became *the* place. Earl Russell was one of the birds of passage who looked for divorce in this desert haven; he was granted a divorce in Nevada in 1900, and immediately remarried in Nevada. The new Countess Russell had herself gotten a quick divorce in Nevada. The

[59] On this point, see William O'Neill, *Divorce in the Progressive Era* (1967).
[60] Blake, *op. cit.,* p. 190.
[61] Francis W. Laurent, *The Business of a Trial Court* (1959), pp. 176–77.

Earl was later indicted for bigamy in England; he was charged with "feloniously marrying Mollie Cooke in America," while his wife Mabel was still alive.[62] Publicity only helped Nevada's business. The moral arguments that eventually destroyed the divorce mills in Indiana and other states had little or no effect in Nevada, a state quite impervious to moral arguments. Its career as national divorce mill proved to be quite durable.

The rising divorce rate, and the rising *demand* for divorce scandalized pious people all the more. The last part of the nineteenth century was an era of national panic over morality, eugenics, the purity of the bloodline, and the future of old-fashioned white America. Whores and divorce had to be contained. An irresistible force (the demand) met an immovable object (the resistance to divorce). The result was a stalemate. It became almost impossible to change the law—or the practice. State statutes were like weird ice formations, frozen into absurd shapes at whatever point in time forces had been more or less evenly balanced. South Carolina still allowed no divorces at all.[63] New York allowed divorce, practically speaking, only for adultery. Most states had a broader list. In a few jurisdictions, the innocent party might remarry, the guilty party not.[64] In some jurisdictions, the grounds were very broad—in Wyoming, for example, divorce was available for "indignities" that rendered the marriage "intolerable."[65] In most states, compromise took the form of the dual system we described. The moralists had their symbolic victory, a stringent law strutting proudly on the books. But nobody enforced these laws, least of all judges. A cynical traffic in runaway and underground divorce flourished in the shadows.[66] Divorce law was an egregious example of a branch of law tortured by contradictions in public opinion, trapped between contending forces of perhaps roughly equal strength; trapped, too, in a federal system with freedom of movement back and forth, and beyond the power and grasp of any single state.

THE RACES

The war, the Emancipation Proclamation, and the Thirteenth, Fourteenth, and Fifteenth Amendments ended American slavery and gave the blacks the right to vote. The Fourteenth Amendment also gave them (ostensibly) the equal protection of the laws. The basic promises of Reconstruction, however,

[62] New York Times, Jan. 18, 1901; New York Times, April 21, 1900.

[63] South Carolina did, however, grant alimony under some circumstances to separated wives, even though no divorce was possible. See Michael S. Hindus and Lynne E. Withey, "The Law of Husband and Wife in Nineteenth-Century America: Changing View of Divorce," in D. Kelly Weisberg, ed., *Women and the Law*, vol. II (1982), pp. 133, 140–45.

[64] In Tennessee, a divorced adulterer or adulteress could not marry the "person with whom the crime was committed during the life of the former husband or wife," Tenn. Stats. 1858, sec. 2475.

[65] Wyo. Stats. 1899, sec. 2988; conduct by a husband that would "constitute him a vagrant" was also grounds for divorce.

[66] As early as 1882, a committee of the American Bar Association went to work drafting uniform legislature to get rid of fake domicile and the runaway divorce. They succeeded in inducing some states to pass their statute, but the problem did not go away. See Amasa Eaton, "Proposed Reforms in Marriage and Divorce Laws," 4 Columbia L. Rev. 243 (1904).

were never kept. Until well into the twentieth century, historians who wrote about Reconstruction were mostly white Southerners; they heaped scorn on Reconstruction, on the radical Republicans, on the carpetbaggers and scalawags—and on the blacks themselves. Popular literature—and movies like *Birth of a Nation* and even *Gone With the Wind*—made much the same point. The Civil War had destroyed a rich and beautiful way of life; and the post-war era was a time of corruption and black misrule. But during and after the age of the civil rights movement, historians have peeled away all of these misconceptions; and reconstructed Reconstruction in a more generous, balanced way. Even the carpetbaggers have been rehabilitated.[67]

Leaders of the old South who survived the war were in no mood for racial equality. The end of slavery was a bitter enough pill to swallow. The white South wanted to change things as little as possible. Almost all the states of the old Confederacy passed laws in 1865, the so-called Black Codes, which aimed to replace slavery with a kind of caste system. The point was to preserve, in general, the prewar way of life. The 1865 laws of Mississippi, for example, plainly intended that blacks would work as laborers, on farms and plantations owned by whites. No freed slave could own any farm land. As laborers, blacks would work under written contracts. Any black laborer who quit "without good cause" could be arrested and dragged back to his employer. In Mississippi, blacks still could not testify in cases where plaintiff and defendant were white. Intermarriage between the races was strictly forbidden. Blacks could not sit on juries. There were also stringent vagrancy laws, in Mississippi and other states, which could be, and were, used to keep blacks under strict social control.[68]

The North—at least the radicals—found this kind of law totally unacceptable. The Black Codes were erased; Congress enacted a strong Civil Rights Act (1866), anticipating the Fourteenth Amendment (1868). The South was put under military government. The Freedmen's Bureaus, established by Congress, were an experiment in social planning; they were supposed to help blacks adapt to the white man's society and economy. Blacks were elected to Congress and held state offices. But Reconstruction did not last. The Freedmen's Bureaus practically ceased operation by 1869; they were at all times understaffed and underfinanced; and their boldest moves—for example, land redistribution on the Sea Islands of South Carolina—were frustrated by the policies of the Johnson administration.[69] By 1875, the North's passion for equality, never very profound, had all but dribbled away. The North lost interest in black welfare. Northern racism, briefly and thinly covered over, came to the surface once more. The South would be left to solve the "Negro problem" on its own. As for the white South, it eagerly embraced the new situation. The Ku Klux Klan terrorized the blacks. Blacks who offended against their code—or even blacks who were too successful for their own good—were beaten and sometimes murdered. Educating blacks was a dangerous occupation. The Klan attacked a teacher in North Carolina, flogged him, cut off his hair, and left him unconscious in the woods. His offense, they told him, was "Teaching niggers."

---

[67] Richard Nelson Current, *Those Terrible Carpetbaggers: A Reinterpretation* (1988).

[68] See Laws Miss. 1865, ch. 4, 6.

[69] Martin Abbott, *The Freedmen's Bureau in South Carolina, 1865–1872* (1967).

The first black school that opened in Selma, Alabama, in the 1890s, was burned down by whites.[70]

During Reconstruction, blacks had voted and held office. The new white regimes were determined to end this situation. Blacks were relegated to a kind of peonage, bound laborers on the white man's land. Rural blacks were desperately poor and largely illiterate. Around them a tight network of law and practice tied them to the soil. The network consisted of lien laws for landlords, vagrancy laws, enticement laws (which made it a crime to lure workers from their jobs, even by offering them better wages and conditions), laws against "emigrant agents," who were more or less labor brokers, and even laws that made it a crime to quit work "fraudulently." None of these laws specifically mentioned race; but they were practically speaking directed against black workers only. Blacks were not much better off than under slavery—except that the worker now could also be fired.[71] In Florida, a statute of 1891 made it a crime to take money on a promise to do work, and then quit. Owners of turpentine camps used the law to tie their workers to the job. Black workers could also be rounded up as "vagrants," and offered a choice of work or jail. There were some prosecutions under federal laws against "peonage"; and the U.S. Supreme Court in 1911 struck down the Alabama statute that made quitting work, in effect, a crime; but the net result of all this activity was zero.[72] There was no follow-up, and the black system of virtual peonage remained stubbornly in place.

The caste-and-class system that replaced slavery included a system of legal and social apartheid. It developed inexorably in area after area of southern life. C. Vann Woodward has described the strange career of Jim Crow.[73] Woodward has argued that the end of Radical Reconstruction did not mean a complete, immediate system of segregation in the South. Many of the most blatant Jim Crow laws, on the contrary, belonged to the very end of the nineteenth century. Not that race relations were smooth before that, or that the black was ever welcomed into white society. But there was a certain period of trial and error, of ambiguity and complexity, before the decisive instruments of segregation were nailed into law. "Custom" preceded law. In South Carolina, according to Joel Williamson, blacks could technically make use of all public facilities between 1868 and 1889; but few blacks actually dared to do so. In some ways, formal segregation replaced a system, not of integration, but of outright exclusion.[74] Segregated schools replaced a system of *no* schools for blacks. And in

---

[70] Leon F. Litwak, *Trouble in Mind: Black Southerners in the Age of Jim Crow* (1998), pp. 87–88. These were extreme cases. Most Southerners, perhaps, believed in educating black people—up to a point; and teaching them deference and devotion to manual labor. Ibid., pp. 90–91.

[71] William Cohen, "Negro Involuntary Servitude in the South, 1865–1940: A Preliminary Analysis," 42 J. Southern Hist. 31 (1976); Daniel A. Novak, *The Wheel of Servitude: Black Forced Labor after Slavery* (1978).

[72] Kermit L. Hall and Eric W. Rise, *From Local Courts to National Tribunals: The Federal District Courts of Florida, 1821–1990* (1991), pp. 51–54; Laws Fla. 1891, ch. 4032 [No. 23], pp. 57–58; *Bailey v. Alabama*, 219 U.S. 219 (1911).

[73] C. Vann Woodward, *The Strange Career of Jim Crow* (2nd rev. ed., 1966).

[74] Joel Williamson, *After Slavery: The Negro in South Carolina during Reconstruction, 1861–1877* (1965), p. 287; John William Graves, "The Arkansas Separate Coach Law of 1891," 7 Journal of the West 531 (1968); on the exclusion thesis, see Howard N. Rabinowitz, "From Exclusion to Segregation: Southern Race Relations, 1865–1890," 63 J. Am. Hist. 325 (1976).

some parts of the South, Jim Crow tightened its grip at the point where blacks showed signs of protesting against their position in society; it was a reaction, in short, to "uppity" blacks.[75]

What is beyond dispute is the eruption of segregation laws near the end of the century. Georgia required separate railroad cars for blacks and whites in 1891; the state even separated white and black prisoners in chain gangs. The laws and ordinances came thick and fast. In Arkansas, by 1903, the statutes required separate "apartments" for whites and blacks in all jails and penitentiaries, and "separate bunks, beds, bedding, separate dining tables and all other furnishings" (sec. 5901); even voting was segregated—voting officials were to "conduct admittance to the voting place [so] as to permit persons of the white and colored races to cast their votes alternately" (sec. 2822). Whites insisted on strict separation of the races, in every walk of life—even separate telephone booths and elevators, separate Bibles to swear on in a courtroom. Segregation even persisted after death. Cemeteries were white or black, not both; and Leon Litwack records the "bizarre" fact that a white man named Will Mathis, condemned to die, demanded segregation in execution. He objected to the use of the same gallows as a black man who was also sentenced to death.[76]

All of these legal and social arrangements carried a message, a strong message. They proclaimed a rigid social code, a rigid "way of life." Those who violated the code were severely punished. Major infractions could mean death. Four blacks were lynched in South Carolina in 1876 for killing an old white couple. The Columbia *Daily Register* approved: "Civilization" was "in banishment . . . a thing apart, cowering in a corner"; there was a need for the "equity" of "Judge Lynch." Later the bloodletting increased. Between 1888 and 1903, 241 blacks died at the hands of lynch mobs.[77] Lynching was at times incredibly brutal and barbaric. Sam Hose, accused of killing a white man, was lynched in 1899, before a huge crowd near Newman, Georgia. His ears, fingers, and genitals were cut off; his face was skinned; he was soaked with kerosene, and set on fire while still alive; afterward, his body was cut to pieces and his bones crushed; some bits were sold as souvenirs. Nobody in the crowd was masked, and leading citizens took part in this horrible ritual.[78]

White supremacy in the deep South was total. Blacks had zero political power. The U.S. Constitution guaranteed the right to vote. But these were empty words. In fact, black southerners were unceremoniously stripped of this right, though one device or another. Black officeholders were driven from office. Southern laws and constitutions were amended to make sure blacks did not vote. Under the constitution of South Carolina (1895), a voter had to be able to read and understand the state constitution or have $300 in real property. Not many blacks could qualify. Southern states used a variety of devices: poll taxes, literacy tests, and residence requirements, for example. Then there

---

[75] Litwack, *op. cit.*, p. 230.

[76] Litwack, *op. cit.*, p. 236.

[77] Clarence A. Bacote, "Negro Proscriptions, Protests, and Proposed Solutions in Georgia, 1880–1908," 25 J. Southern Hist. 471 (1959); on South Carolina, George B. Tindall, *South Carolina Negroes, 1877–1900* (1952), pp. 236–37.

[78] Litwack, *Trouble in Mind*, pp. 280–82.

was the infamous "grandfather clause." First used in South Carolina in 1890, it excused voters from literacy tests, poll taxes, and the like, if they or their ancestors had voted in the 1860s (or were foreign). This let in all whites and no blacks.[79] In Louisiana, the number of blacks registered to vote fell from 127,000 in 1896 to 3,300 in 1900, after the imposition of the "grandfather clause."[80] The North essentially did nothing, said nothing. In the Senate, in 1900, Ben Tillman of South Carolina told the North, "You do not love them any better than we do. You used to pretend that you did, but you no longer pretend it." He defended what the South had done: "We took the government away. We stuffed ballot boxes. We shot them. . . . With that system . . . we got tired ourselves. So we called a constitutional convention, and we eliminated . . . all of the colored people whom we could."[81]

Tillman was blunt, but probably accurate, in his assessment of Northern opinion. In 1860, there were only five states, all in New England, that permitted blacks to vote. Massachusetts was the only state to allow black men on juries. The post-Civil War amendments gave Northern blacks the vote, but did not change the climate of opinion very much. In such an atmosphere, one could hardly expect the federal courts to stand in the way of Jim Crow, or prevent the murder and oppression of America's untouchables. But in truth these courts hardly tried. Even the Supreme Court had a dismal record in its race cases. In 1878, the Court faced a Louisiana statute (1869) that forbade "discrimination on account of race or color" in common carriers. The Court felt this law was an unconstitutional "burden" on interstate commerce. The case arose when the owner of a steamboat, bound for Vicksburg from New Orleans, refused plaintiff, "a person of color," a place "in the cabin specially set apart for white persons."[82] In 1883, the Court declared the Civil Rights Act of 1875—a public accommodations law—unconstitutional.[83] The Constitution, the Court said, applied only to state discrimination; private parties, including hotels, inns, and other public accommodations, were free to discriminate if they wanted to. And they did. Nothing much happened to alter this situation until the civil rights movement and the civil rights laws of the 1960s.

Plessy v. Ferguson (1896) was an especially dark decision. It put the Supreme Court's stamp of approval on apartheid.[84] This was another case from Louisiana.

---

[79] Alexander Keyssar, *The Right to Vote: The Contested History of Democracy in the United States* (2000), pp. 111–13. The restrictions also, as a kind of side effect, discriminated against poor whites.

[80] Thomas E. Gossett, *Race: The History of an Idea in America* (1963), p. 266.

[81] Quoted in Harold U. Faulkner, *Politics, Reform and Expansion, 1890–1900* (1959), pp. 7–8.

[82] *Hall v. DeCuir*, 95 U.S. 485 (1878).

[83] *The Civil Rights Cases*, 109 U.S.3 (1883). One exception to the otherwise bleak record of the Supreme Court was *Strauder v. West Virginia*, 100 U.S. 303 (1880). The state of West Virginia allowed only "white male persons who are twenty-one years of age" to serve on juries. The Supreme Court struck down this provision.

[84] 163 U.S. 537 (1896). Interestingly, Plessy argued also that he was not really "colored," since he had only "one-eighth African blood" and "the mixture of colored blood was not discernible to him." But the Supreme Court left to the states the power to define membership in the races. For a full treatment, see Charles A. Lofgren, *The Plessy Case. A Legal-Historical Interpretation* (1987).

The Court confronted a law that called for "equal but separate accommodation for the white, and colored races" in railway carriages. Of course this law did not create a system of segregation; it merely ratified and formalized it. Steamboats were rigidly segregated. On trains, blacks were generally relegated to the smoking car, which was hardly de luxe; usually it was dirty, full of men drinking and spitting, and, of course, full of smoke.[85] In the *Plessy* case, Homer Plessy, a light-skinned black, brought a test case on behalf of a New Orleans group that wanted to fight the segregation law. Plessy bought a ticket and refused to move from the white section of the car to the "colored" section. He was arrested; and the case went up to the Supreme Court of the United States. The Court turned down Plessy's complaint and upheld the statute. The decision, which was eight to one, showed a studied ignorance (or disregard) of the realities of life in the South; according to the Court, if blacks thought such a law imposed "a badge of inferiority," that was "not by reason of anything found in the act, but solely because the colored race chooses to put that construction on it." In any event (said the Court), laws are "powerless to eradicate racial instincts or to abolish distinctions based upon physical differences." In reply, Justice John Marshall Harlan wrote a lonely but powerful dissent: "Our Constitution is color-blind, and neither knows nor tolerates classes among citizens." Harlan had also dissented in the *Civil Rights Cases*. He was a former slave-owner himself. His ideas on race were complicated, and sometimes less than consistent.[86] But he saw clearly the iniquity of the *Plessy* decision; and he spoke out forcefully against it. In any event, segregation became the norm in the South and in some of the border states.

First Nations

The blacks were not the only race to feel the lash of white hatred. The shock-word "genocide" is often used loosely. But it comes embarrassingly close to reality when we consider how the white man treated Native Americans. The tribes were driven from their lands; they were hounded and sometimes slaughtered. They had to give way constantly to land-hungry armies of white settlers. Both treaties and conquest were used to dispossess the tribes. In *Johnson v. McIntosh* (1823),[87] the Supreme Court, through John Marshall, held that the Indians enjoyed only a right of "occupancy"; sovereignty rested with the United States. The tribes could sell lands to the government, but not to private citizens (this was the issue in the case). In theory, this doctrine might have protected the tribes from white settlers and their crafty ways. But the loss of sovereignty was more significant than the right of "occupancy." The discovery of gold on lands of the Cherokee nation, in Georgia, set off a crisis. Georgia, in essence, seized the land and declared all the laws of the Cherokees null and void. A long period of legal wrangling followed. Ultimately, in 1832, in *Worcester v. Georgia*,[88] the Supreme Court, still under John Marshall, held that Georgia had no right to

---

[85] Barbara Welke, *Recasting American Liberty*, pp. 257–62.
[86] On Harlan and his views, see Linda Przybyszewski, *The Republic According to John Marshall Harlan* (1999), ch. 4.
[87] 8 Wheat (21 U.S.) 543 (1823).
[88] 6 Pet. (31 U.S.) 515 (1832).

dispossess the tribe; and their laws on the subject were unconstitutional. Justice Story wrote that the Court had "done its duty"; the country should "now do theirs." But the country did not.[89] Georgia paid no attention to the decision. In the end, the Cherokees were expelled, and sent on the infamous "trail of tears" to what is now Oklahoma.[90]

By 1880, the tribes were no longer a military threat. They had been thoroughly defeated. The remnants were herded onto reservations, usually on land the white man did not want. As Red Cloud, a Sioux Indian, put it, in 1870: whites "had surrounded me and left me nothing but an island. When we first had this land we were strong, now we are melting like snow on a hillside."[91] The United States and the individual states constantly broke faith, violated treaties, and trampled on ancient rights. The dominant culture had no respect for native religion, language, or way of life. The dominant culture looked on itself as superior—indeed, as the climax of human evolution. The Indians were "savages," primitive and with at best a kind of childlike nobility. Cultural relativity was not a strong point of the nineteenth century.

In some ways, policy toward the native tribes was the opposite of Southern policy toward the blacks: not segregation, but assimilation. The Dawes Act of 1887[92] aimed at turning the natives into true Americans; it attacked traditional systems of land tenure. The land would be split into individually owned family farms; no more tribal or common ownership. Natives who conformed to the act could detribalize and become American citizens. On the surface, the point of the Dawes Act was protection of the property of the natives and their absorption into the American mainstream. The (not so hidden) agenda was destruction of native culture; moreover, through fraud and imposition, the Dawes Act resulted in another vast hemorrhaging of land from natives to whites. Sovereignty was largely a myth. In *Lone Wolf v. Hitchcock* (1903), the Supreme Court held that Congress had plenary power over the native tribes. Indian rights were thus inherently precarious.[93]

Asian Americans

In California (and in the West generally), the arrival of Chinese workers and immigrants touched off another epidemic of race hatred. The virulent feeling against Asians showed itself in a blizzard of ordinances and laws. Whites and "Mongolians" were not allowed to marry. Local laws openly or covertly aimed to harass the Chinese, in large ways and small. A San Francisco ordinance of 1880

[89] Jean Edward Smith, *John Marshall, Definer of a Nation* (1996) p. 518.

[90] Georgia was not the only culprit. On the removal of the Choctaws from Mississippi, roughly in the same period, see James Taylor Carson, "State Rights and Indian Removal in Mississippi, 1817–1835," 57 Journal of Mississippi History 25 (1995).

[91] Quoted in Edward Lazarus, *Black Hills, White Justice: The Sioux Nation versus the United States, 1774 to the Present* (1991), p. 60.

[92] 24 Stat. 388 (act of Feb. 8, 1887). See Wilcomb E. Washburn, *The Assault on Indian Tribalism: The General Allotment Law (Dawes Act) of 1887* (1975).

[93] *Lone Wolf v. Hitchcock* is 187 U.S. 553 (1903); see Blue Clark, *Lone Wolf v. Hitchcock: Treaty Rights and Indian Law at the End of the Nineteenth Century* (1994); and Edward Lazarus, *Black Hills, White Justice* (1991), pp. 168ff, on the impact of the case on the claims of the Sioux.

made it unlawful to carry on a laundry in the city without the "consent of the board of supervisors," unless the laundry was "located in a building constructed either of brick and stone." Almost every San Francisco laundry was in fact in a wooden building. The Board turned down all applications from Chinese people; and granted every one that came from a Caucasian. In the much-cited case of *Yick Wo v. Hopkins* (1886),[94] Yick Wo had applied for permission to run his laundry in a wooden building; the supervisors said no, he kept on working, and was arrested and fined. The Supreme Court overturned Yick Wo's conviction. The way the ordinance had been enforced was "a denial of the equal protection of the laws and a violation of the Fourteenth Amendment."

But such victories were rare. Anti-Chinese feeling ran very deep. One cause was fear of the competition from Chinese labor. The hostility, wrote John R. Commons, "is not primarily racial in character. It is the competitive struggle for standards of living."[95] It was, however, racist to the core. Organized labor in the West was almost as anti-Chinese as Southern populists were anti-black. Dennis Kearney, in California, rabble-rousing leader of the Workingmen's Party, ranted and raved against the Chinese, the "Asiatic leper," the "parasites from China," who ate "rice and rats," and were "used as a weapon by the grinding, grasping capitalists" to "oppress the poor laboring man."[96] Labor leaders, indeed, supported restrictions on Chinese immigration. In 1879, Congress passed the "Fifteen Passenger Bill"; on any ship arriving in the United States, there could be no more than fifteen Chinese passengers; the president vetoed it.

But cutting off the flow of Chinese laborers was a popular policy. Debate in Congress, on this issue, often sounded as racist and radical as Kearney: Senator John Miller of California denounced the "dwarfed, leathery little man of the Orient." American civilization had to be saved from the "gangrene of oriental civilization."[97] The Chinese, moreover, could survive on less food (and less money) than the American worker. Congress acted. The law Congress passed in 1882 announced that the "coming of Chinese laborers to this country . . . endangers the good order of certain localities."[98] Everyone knew which localities were meant. This law suspended the immigration of Chinese laborers. It also provided that no state or federal court "shall admit Chinese to citizenship." The Scott Act of 1888 prohibited some 20,000 Chinese (who had temporarily left the country) from coming back. An act of 1892, "to prohibit the coming of Chinese persons into the United States," suspended immigration for another ten years, and provided that Chinese laborers were to be deported unless they applied for and obtained a "certificate of residence." A statute of 1902 made the ban on Chinese entry and Chinese citizenship permanent.[99]

---

[94] 118 U.S. 356 (1886).

[95] John R. Commons, *Races and Immigrants in America* (1907), p. 115.

[96] Quoted in Andrew Gyory, *Closing the Gate: Race, Politics, and the Chinese Exclusion Act* (1998), p. 116; Gyory's book is the source for the material on the Fifteen Passenger Law and the Chinese exclusion act.

[97] Andrew Gyory, *Closing the Gate*, p. 224.

[98] 22 Stats. 58 (act of May 6, 1882).

[99] Ronald Segal, *The Race War* (1966), pp. 205–7; 25 Stats. 476 (act of Sept. 13, 1888); 27 Stats. 25 (act of May 5, 1892); 32 Stats. 176 (act of April 29, 1902). On the administration of the law, see Lucy E. Salyer, *Laws Harsh as Tigers: Chinese Immigrants and the Shaping of Modern American Immigration Law* (1995).

Race thus was an essential part of the story—race, xenophobia, fear of the "yellow peril." Hatred sometimes led to outright violence. In the 1880s, riots in Rock Springs, Wyoming, ended with twenty-eight dead Chinese; then the whites in Tacoma, Washington, put their Chinatown to the torch. In Oregon, in 1887, a group of whites murdered thirty-one Chinese miners, and stole their gold dust. A careful and conservative estimate found 153 incidents of violence against Chinese in the West, between 1852 and 1908. In these outbreaks, 143 Chinese died, and over 10,000 Chinese were driven from homes or places of work.[100] Hatred also left its mark on the statute books. The formal law discriminated against Asians. A California law, of 1880, prohibited any corporation from employing "in any capacity any Chinese or Mongolian"; in 1882, the state authorized segregated schools for Asians (there were already segregated schools for blacks).[101] The racial minorities—blacks, Chinese, native Americans, and Mexican Americans in the Southwest and in California—were dealt with in different ways, and had different fates in America. But all were either voteless or powerless. They were strangers at the pluralist table.

[100] John R. Wunder, "Anti-Chinese Violence in the American West, 1850–1910," in John McLaren et al., eds, *Law for the Elephant, Law for the Beaver: Essays in the Legal History of the North American West* (1992), pp. 211, 214–15.

[101] Robert F. Heizer and Alan J. Almquist, *The Other Californians* (1971), ch. 7; on the treatment of Chinese Americans in the courts, see John R. Wunder, "The Chinese and the Courts in the Pacific Northwest: Justice Denied?" 52 Pac. Hist. Rev. 191 (1983).

CHAPTER 8

THE LAW OF CORPORATIONS

CORPORATION LAW: FREEDOMS AND RESTRAINTS

Law is often thought of as unfolding in slow patterns, at least before it "exploded" in the twentieth century. Yet, nothing could be more startling than the difference one century made in the law of the business corporation. In 1800, corporation law was a torpid backwater of law, mostly a matter of municipalities, charities, and churches. Only a bridge or two, a handful of manufacturing enterprises, a few banks, or insurance companies, disturbed its quiet. The business corporation, in the nineteenth century, gave rise to a great deal of controversy. By 1870, corporations had a commanding position in the economy. They never lost it. In the 1880s, there was a great outcry against the big, bad "trusts," like Standard Oil. And Congress enacted the Sherman Anti-trust Act in 1890. In between, and afterward, there was constant argument and change. Much of this revolved about particular kinds of corporations: banks, railroads, and insurance companies. Some of it, however, concerned the corporation in general. Of the original law of corporations—from Blackstone's day—hardly a stone was left unturned. Even Chancellor Kent's law of corporations was basically transformed by 1900.

Private practice and legislation made the law of corporations. The courts played a minor role. No constitutional convention met, between 1860 and 1900, without considering the problem of the corporation. This was a nineteenth-century constant; it changed form, format, and its cast of characters; but there was a numbing sameness of theme. Meanwhile, businessmen and their lawyers built up corporate practice (and malpractice). Courts usually turned practice into law. Sometimes the courts were ahead of the other lawmakers, sometimes behind. The general trend in the law was clear: corporations could do as they wished, arrange their affairs as they pleased, exercise any power desired, unless some positive rule outside of "corporation law" made the action plainly illegal. In short, the trend was toward giving free rein to management. In a kind of counterattack, statutes were passed regulating corporations in specific industries. These were nationwide trends, though with regional variations. Western legislatures were still inviting, bribing, and cajoling railroads at a time when disenchantment had plainly set in in the East.

Perhaps the biggest event in corporation law, between 1850 and 1900, was the decline and fall of the special charter. This was, if nothing else, an advance in legal technology. It was cheap and easy to incorporate under general laws—a few papers filed, a few forms and signatures, and that was all. Under a general corporation law, anybody who wanted to could incorporate, and without wasting the time of the legislators. For a generation or so, a number of states (New York, Illinois, Wisconsin, Maryland, and North Carolina) still maintained a dual system of incorporations. Special charters were possible, but only if the object of the corporation could not be attained under the general laws.[1] The dual system was not a particular success. In Wisconsin, for example, between 1848 and 1871, almost ten times as many incorporators went the special-charter route.[2] The Louisiana Constitution of 1845 took the more radical step of forbidding the special charter altogether. One by one, other states adopted similar provisions. Alabama, in 1867, was a Southern convert: "Corporations may be formed under general laws, but shall not be created by special act" (art. XIII, sec. 1). And Congress in 1867 prohibited all incorporation laws in the territories except for general ones.[3]

In the same period, the states, burned by experience, and distrustful of their own legislatures, began to forbid direct investment in enterprise. Cities, counties, and the states themselves had rashly piled up mountains of worthless bonds, discredited paper, and high tax liabilities. By 1874, sixteen state constitutions provided that the state could not own stock in private corporations. In twenty states, the state was forbidden to lend its credit to any corporation.

Corporations, then, had to rely solely on private investors for investment money. The investment market was totally unregulated; no SEC kept it honest, and the level of morality among promoters was painfully low, to put it mildly. It was a generation of vultures. In the 1860s and 1870s, men like Vanderbilt, Jay Gould, and Jim Fisk fought tawdry battles over the stock market, the economy, and the corpses of railroad corporations. The investing public was unmercifully fleeced. Not all the investors were the proverbial widows and orphans; many were men with a taste for easy money. They had as much larceny in their hearts as the Fisks and the Goulds, but their scale of operation was smaller, their cunning infinitely less.

The pillaging of the Erie Railroad by the robber barons, in the late 1860s, was a classic case of financial mismanagement and public corruption. The story was coldly recounted by Charles Francis Adams in his essay, "A Chapter of Erie." Adams was alarmed at what was happening—not just to a railroad, or to the stock market, but to all of America. The best that could be said was that society was "passing through a period of ugly transition." Adams suspected far worse; the signs for the future were "ominous." The offices of the "great corporations," he wrote, were "secret chambers in which trustees plotted the spoliation of their wards"; the stock exchange was "a haunt of gamblers and a den of thieves." Modern society had "created a class of artificial beings who bid fair soon to be the masters of their creator"; they were "establishing despotisms which no spasmodic popular effort will be able to shake off. Everywhere . . . they illustrate the truth of the old maxim of the common law, that corporations have no souls."[4]

---

[1] John W. Cadman, *The Corporation in New Jersey: Business and Politics, 1791–1875* (1949), p. 187.

[2] George J. Kuehnl, *The Wisconsin Business Corporation* (1959), p. 143.

[3] Gordon M. Bakken, *The Development of Law on the Rocky Mountain Frontier: Civil Law and Society, 1850–1912* (1983), p. 118.

[4] Frederick C. Hicks, ed., *High Finance in the Sixties* (1929), pp. 114–16.

In the face of this threat, legislatures seemed supine, powerless. Men like Gould or Fisk seemed able to buy and sell legislators; they controlled the law. "The halls of legislation were transformed into a mart in which the price of votes was niggled over, and laws, made to order, were bought and sold." The courts were corrupted, too. Justice was at times a whore of the rich. In New York, judges like George Barnard and Albert Cardozo did what the robber barons wished; they issued injunctions for a price, and sold the public interest down the river out of ignorance or greed.

Inevitably, there were reactions. Many middle-class Americans no doubt agreed with Adams; corporations had to be brought under control, and kept there. Railroad regulation was a leading public issue in the 1870s. The Midwest states established agencies to control warehouses and grain elevators as well. Still later came the Sherman Act. These developments have already been discussed.

The law of corporations, as such, deals less with the economic power of corporations than with their everyday behavior. The two are connected, to be sure. The rules as they developed were supposed to promote honest dealings between the corporation, its managers and promoters, on the one hand, and investors, stockholders, and creditors, on the other; but to do so in such a way as not to interfere with business efficiency. The corporation should have a free hand to conduct its business; but be ruggedly honesty in its internal affairs. As we have seen, the courts had begun to develop a tool kit of doctrines, even before the Civil War. One issue was watered stock. This was stock given to insiders, who did not pay full value. The promoters or subscribers then threw the stock on the market. This cheated investors who thought they were buying shares backed solidly by assets or cash. Under the New York corporation law of 1848—on "corporations for manufacturing, mining, mechanical, or chemical purposes"— "Nothing but money shall be considered as payment of any part of the capital stock"; this was amended, however, in 1853, to allow a company to issue stock in exchange for "mines, manufactories, and other property necessary for . . . business."[5] Other states adopted similar rules. The Illinois Constitution of 1870 stated that "no railroad corporation shall issue any stock or bonds, except for money, labor or property actually received and applied to the purposes for which such corporation was created." Outlawed too were "all stock dividends, and other fictitious increase of capital stocks or indebtedness" (Const. Illinois 1870, art. XII, sec. 13).

Such laws did make the grossest frauds at least nominally illegal; and did outlaw the most clearly watered stock. There remained gray areas of doubt. If a promoter exchanged his land, or a coal mine, or a building, for $100,000 in stock, how could one tell if the promoter had transferred full value? The only *safe* rule was to require all subscriptions in cash. But this rule seemed too restrictive. Courts tended to accept what promoters did so long as they acted in "good faith." Par value of stock was once a meaningful concept. But when shares changed hands in the open market, the face value meant little or nothing. Stock was worth what a buyer would pay for it. Par meant nothing at all to a going concern. Corporate capital, then, was not some fixed fund of assets. "Par

---

[5] Laws N.Y. 1848, ch. 40, sec. 14; Laws N.Y. 1853, ch. 333, sec. 2.

value" was not something basic, like the gold reserves of a bank. The corporation as a going concern was worth what it did and what its prospects were.

Management was a critical aspect of value. Managers owed a duty to stockholders. In the Gilded Age, this often seemed like the right to cheat. Technically, it was the corporation itself that had the right to sue an officer who cheated the corporation. But officers controlled the corporation; men who were milking the company could hardly be expected to sue themselves. The *stockholders' suit* was a class action, brought on behalf of a stockholder plaintiff and all others in his position. The device was foreshadowed as early as the 1830s, but the Supreme Court gave it a further push in *Dodge v. Woolsey,* decided in 1856.[6] *Dodge* did not come out of one of the grand postwar piracies. The corporation had paid a tax, which the stockholder insisted was unconstitutional. In *Morgan v. Skiddy* (1875),[7] a New York case, the defendants, directors of the "Central Mining Company of Colorado," had dangled in front of the gullible public glittering prospects of endless money from "the celebrated 'Bates lode.'" Here, the stockholder's suit attacked plain, unvarnished corporate fraud.

What was the standard of conduct for officers and directors? They had a *fiduciary duty.* Officers and directors were trustees for the corporation. This meant that they could not self-deal, could not buy from or sell to the company, they were strictly accountable for any profits they made in transactions with the company. Fiduciary law was austere and demanding. Courts of chancery used it to monitor trustees who managed money for widows and orphans. They now applied it, in essence, to promoters, officers, and directors. These persons had "a sacred trust"—a phrase with moral overtones. But the point was less about morality than convenience; here was a ready-made body of doctrines that seemed to fit the problem before the courts.

The "trust fund" doctrine, even before the Civil War, meant that creditors had first claims on the assets of a corporate corpse, at least as opposed to stockholders.[8] The doctrine grew steadily in importance. One notable series of cases rose out of the wreckage of the Great Western Insurance Company of Illinois. The Chicago fire of 1871 had scorched the company into bankruptcy. In one case, decided in 1875,[9] a certain Tribilcock had subscribed for stock with a face value of $10,000. He paid in a mere $2,000. The company's agent, he claimed, told him that was all he had to pay. When the company went under, its assignee, on behalf of the creditors, demanded the rest of the money. Justice Ward Hunt, speaking for the U.S. Supreme Court, wasted little sympathy on Tribilcock. The capital stock "is a trust fund . . . to be managed for the benefit of . . . shareholders"; if the corporation dissolves, this fund belongs to the creditors. Capital was not "a football to be thrown into the market for the purposes of speculation." Subscribers had a duty to pay in all of the money they owed; managers had no power to excuse them. This "fund" belonged to the company and its creditors; no one had the right to "squander" it or give it away.

The tone of Justice Hunt's language was severely moral. In practice, however, the cases did not pose clear questions of good against evil. The doctrine,

---

[6] 59 U.S. 331 (1856).
[7] 62 N.Y. 319 (1875).
[8] See part II ch, III, p. 199, above.
[9] *Upton v. Tribilcock,* 91 U.S. 45 (1875).

with its emphasis on par value as a measure of "capital," was already archaic. But it protected corporate creditors, in their injured innocence, against small stockholders like Tribilcock—who themselves were often gulled by promoters and salesmen. Also adverse to stockholders was the common provision that, until *all* of the capital (as measured by par value) was paid in, stockholders were doubly liable on their stock. This was a New York idea of 1848, widely copied elsewhere. Commonly, too, stockholders were liable for debts that the corporation owed to employees. These rules lasted through the end of the century in many of the states. In other states, however, legislatures loosened the law, partly to attract the business of roving companies, looking for easy states in which to incorporate.

The trust fund doctrine, as metaphor, was logically weak. The corporate assets, as some courts and some writers acknowledged, were in no "true sense, held in trust" for the creditors.[10] It was also something of a metaphor to call officers and directors "trustees." This was the rather pious hope: that robber barons, big and small, might be brought to account. Charles Francis Adams Jr., surveying the Erie scandals, expressed the idea that the corporate officer ought to be a "trustee—a guardian . . . [E]very shareholder . . . is his ward"; in the case of a railroad, "the community itself is his *cestui que trust*."[11] The acts of corporate plunder in the Gilded Age, in Adams's view, "strike at the very foundation of existing society. . . . Our whole system rests upon the sanctity of the fiduciary relation."[12]

The courts sometimes did what they could. Directors and officers of the Arkansas Valley Agricultural Society, in Kansas, sold stock in the company to themselves, at par ($5 a share), after selling off thirty-six acres of fairgrounds near Wichita at a price that made each share worth ten times as much. The court made them disgorge their profits. Fiduciaries could not serve two masters. They could not "secure to themselves an advantage not common to all the stockholders."[13] Gross negligence, too, laid directors or officers open to liability. A Virginia case, decided in 1889, turned on the affairs of a "broken bank," the Farmers' and Mechanics' Savings Bank of Virginia. The president of the bank had pillaged it mercilessly, and had foolishly lent large sums of money to the Washington & Ohio Railroad. The directors rarely met, and never audited the books. They did nothing, while notes payable to the bank were allowed to "sleep unprotested, unsecured, unrenewed, uncollected, and unsued on." For their negligence, they were held personally liable to make up the bank's large losses.[14]

A treatise could distill out of such cases a high-minded body of law to display. But we can well ask whether corporation law—reported cases and their doctrines—exerted any real control over the affairs of corporations. Victories were expensive; lawsuits cost money; many cases arose in the context of bankruptcy; and the worst thieves, like the president of the raped Virginia bank, were penniless, or had run away. Lawsuits were a clumsy way to protect the innocent. Most lawsuits probably did too little and came too late; or were useful only in arranging the affairs of a dead or plundered corporation.

---

[10] William L. Clark, *Handbook of the Law of Private Corporations* (1897), p. 540.
[11] A *cestui que trust* (the s and u in *cestui* are silent) is the beneficiary of a trust.
[12] Hicks, *op. cit.*, pp. 26–27.
[13] *Arkansas Valley Agricultural Society v. Eichholtz*, 45 Kan. 164, 25 Pac. 613 (1891).
[14] *Marshall v. Farmers' and Mechanics' Savings Bank*, 85 Va. 676, 8 S.E. 586 (1889).

At the same time, the corporation was shaking loose legal chains that once bound it rather tightly. Business wanted freedom to raise, and use, capital assets. There were more and more corporations; and the big ones got bigger and bigger. In the last half of the nineteenth century, some corporations had become diversified "entities," dealing with many aspects of one business, or with many businesses. The old idea of a one-purpose charter was totally dead. Like a natural person, a corporation could mobilize its power now for this purpose, now for that. A corporation could start as a railroad, gobble up a steamship line, buy timber lands, build houses, manufacture dolls, or weave clothing. The largest corporations were like huge investment trusts. They were ancestral forms of modern conglomerates, creatures with many heads and hundreds of legs.

The old restrictions on what corporations could or could not do were abolished or relaxed. Once, nothing was so central to the corporation law as the doctrine of *ultra vires*. The phrase means "beyond the powers"; it stood for the proposition that the corporation was a creature of limited authority. "All corporate acts which the legislature has not authorized remain prohibited."[15] The powers of a corporation had to be expressed in the charter. Officials and courts were supposed to construe these charters narrowly, and jealously. As late as 1856, Jeremiah Sullivan Black, chief justice of Pennsylvania, put it this way: "A doubtful charter does not exist; because whatever is doubtful is decisively certain against the corporation."[16] Borderline corporate acts were *ultra vires*. And *ultra vires* acts, under the original version of the doctrine, were null and void. No one could enforce an *ultra vires* act against another party; the state could object to the act; so could any stockholder. This meant that a person entered into contracts with corporations at some risk. If the contract was *ultra vires*, it was unenforceable. In a Maryland case, in 1850, a company had been incorporated to conduct "a line of steamboats . . . between Baltimore and Fredericksburg, and the several parts and places on the Rappahannock." A certain Alexander Marshall pressed a claim against the company; he based his claim on improvements on the Rappahannock River. These improvements were made on waters beyond Baltimore, hence, not within the limits of the statutory route. The corporate undertaking (said the court) was therefore void; Marshall was turned away without a dime.[17]

But the courts soon backed off from this extreme form of *ultra vires*. They began to "imply" powers much more freely. In 1896, the Supreme Court held that a Florida railroad company had not exceeded its power when it leased and operated the San Diego hotel, in Duval County, Florida. A summer hotel at this seaside terminus might increase the railroad's business; to "maintain cheap hotels or eating houses . . . at the end of a railroad on a barren, unsettled beach . . . not for the purpose of making money out of such business, but to furnish reasonable and necessary accommodations to its passengers and employees, would not be . . . an act [such as] . . . to compel a court to sustain the defense of *ultra vires*."[18] At any rate, corporations were becoming indispensable. And they were also larger, more flexible. No longer specially created for

---

[15] Victor Morawetz, *A Treatise on the Law of Private Corporations*, vol. II (2nd ed., 1886), p. 617.

[16] *Commonwealth v. Erie & No. East Rr. Co.*, 27 Pa. St. 339, 351 (1856).

[17] *Abbott v. Baltimore and Rappahannock Steam Packet Company*, 1 Md. Ch. 542, 549–50 (1850).

[18] *Jacksonville, Mayport, Pablo Railway & Navigation Co. v. Hooper*, 160 U.S. 514, 526 (1896).

some special, public task, the corporation was now "simply an alternative form of business organization"; and as such, "should presumptively be able to do what any business firm can lawfully do."[19] *Ultra vires* was a nuisance. It was an obstacle to corporate credit. The doctrine had to go.

Moreover, it became irrelevant. Corporate charters could be framed so broadly that nothing was beyond the power or reach of the company. This made diversified businesses legally possible, regardless of doctrine. Skillful lawyers improved the art of drafting corporate charters and other documents. The charter contained a statement of purpose; but this was now a mere form, which covered anything and everything. The more "liberal" statutes ratified this change. Under the key New Jersey Act of 1896, a corporation could be formed for "any lawful business or purpose whatever."[20] Even in such sensitive areas as railroad consolidations, the law did not stand in the way of business practice and the growth of enterprise. A New York law, for example, in 1883, allowed the Poughkeepsie, Hartford, and Boston Railroad to consolidate with a connecting line in New England (ch. 514). Then, to save everybody time and trouble, some states passed statutes giving blanket approval to railroad consolidation.[21]

The same story occurred in the development of holding companies. Originally, corporations were not supposed to own stock in other corporations. But companies wanted this privilege, especially banks and insurance companies. In nineteenth century law, where there was a corporate will, there was generally a corporate way, at least eventually. As early as the 1850s, legislatures began to grant special charters in which they allowed companies to own stock in other corporations. For example, Alabama (1851–1852) gave the Wetumpka Bridge Company the right to own stock in other internal improvement companies; Florida (1866) gave the Pensacola and Mobile Railroad and Manufacturing Company the right to own stock in the Perdido Junction Railroad Company. Pennsylvania, in 1861, authorized railroads chartered in the state to "purchase and hold the stocks and bonds" of other railroads, if they were also chartered in Pennsylvania, or if the roads ran into the state. In 1888, New Jersey issued a general *nihil obstat;* its law gave all corporations the privilege of owning stock in any other corporation.[22]

What came to be called the business-judgment rule was also an important development. Essentially, this was a rule that let management run its own show. So long as a decision was made in good faith, and in the ordinary course of business, no stockholder could complain, even if the decision turned out badly.[23] The doctrine of "corporate personality" was also a significant boon to American corporate enterprise. This was the doctrine that corporations, legally speaking, were entities—"persons," for almost all legitimate purposes. The corporation had the right to sue and be sued, just like any other "person." And—very significantly—the corporation was a "person" under the protection of the Fourteenth Amendment, the same as flesh-and-blood people, if not more

---

[19] Herbert Hovenkamp, *Enterprise and American Law, 1837–1937* (1991), p. 59.

[20] Laws N.J. 1896, ch. 185, sec. 6, p. 279.

[21] For example, Ohio Stats. 1880, secs. 3379–92.

[22] See William R. Compton, "Early History of Stock Ownership by Corporations," 9 Geo. Wash. L. Rev. 125 (1940); Laws N.J. 1888, ch. 269.

[23] Hovenkamp, *op. cit.,* pp. 62–64.

so.[24] This idea was first hinted at in the 1880s.[25] From 1890 on, it became solid constitutional doctrine. In the late nineteenth century, a striking series of cases turned the due-process clause into a kind of mighty wall of protection for business. The wall of the Fourteenth Amendment had been built, or so it seemed, to protect black people; by irony or design, it became a way to protect a quite different minority: corporations. Some of the critical cases have been mentioned elsewhere: for example, cases on state power to fix utility rates. In a few key cases, courts struck down statutes that corporations objected to, on the grounds that such laws violated the due-process clause of the Fourteenth Amendment.

Other cases turned on the commerce clause—the power of Congress to regulate commerce "among the several states." Doctrine here was a mighty but sometime force. Under the clause, the federal government clearly had power to regulate interstate commerce. But throughout the nineteenth century, it made only sparing use of this power. If federal law was silent, could the states regulate interstate commerce, or was the federal power "exclusive"? There was never a complete, general answer. In some areas, the states were supposed to have concurrent power over commerce; but state regulation was unlawful if it "burdened" that commerce. These general notions did not have, to say the least, any razorlike precision. This much was clear: cases which held federal power exclusive often wiped out the only regulation—state regulation—that was in vigorous effect. So, in *Western Union Telegraph Company v. Pendleton* (1887),[26] William Pendleton, of Shelbyville, Indiana, sued Western Union for damages, claiming the company had failed to deliver a telegram on time, which he had sent to Ottumwa, Iowa. He based his claim on an Indiana statute, which required companies to deliver telegrams promptly, if the addressee lived "within one mile of the telegraphic station or within the city or town in which such station is." But the Indiana statute, the Supreme Court thought, was an encroachment on the (unused) federal power; only Congress had authority to regulate "telegraphic communications between citizens of different states." The Court, in short, helped establish and protect a giant free-trade area within the United States. It made the country safe for big business. But the Court acted in cases that businesses had pressed; generally, speaking, only businesses had the money and nerve and legal talent to fight these cases all the way to the top.[27]

The main thread of the story of the commerce clause lies outside the boundaries of the corporations; it is part of constitutional history. But the law of corporations was no longer a true measure of the rights and powers of corporations. Corporations confronted law at every point; they were the litigants in a larger and larger share of reported cases; they hired lawyers and made use of whole law firms; they bought and sold governments; other governments came to power as reactions against corporate mismanagement or fraud. Every state constitution after 1850 had some provision about corporations. The rights and liabilities of corporations were, more and more, what constitutional cases turned

[24] Hovenkamp, *op. cit.*, ch. 4.

[25] *Santa Clara County v. Southern Pacific Railroad*, 118 U.S. 394 (1886).

[26] 122 U.S. 347 (1887).

[27] See Charles W. McCurdy, "American Law and the Marketing Structure of the Large Corporation, 1875–1890," 38 J. Econ. Hist. 631 (1978).

out. Even questions of individual rights emerged in cases with corporate liti- gants. *Plessy v. Ferguson,*[28] the 1896 segregation case, was a case about a common carrier. In the great cases on rate making, labor relations, and social welfare, corporations were litigants, bystanders, or protagonists.

Big business spilled over state lines. Multistate business was keenly con- cerned with the relationship between federal and local law. Each state created its own body of corporation law. But the lines between states were almost meaningless, economically speaking. Only a cornfield, a bridge, a short ride on a ferry, an invisible line, separated one jurisdiction from another. A corpo- ration could be chartered in one state, and do business in six others, or thirty others. This was both a danger and an opportunity for the interstate corpora- tion. The opportunity consisted of playing one state off against another; or mi- grating, like a divorce-hunting wife, to the laxest of states. For this reason, it made little difference to big companies that some states had strict corporation laws. In Massachusetts, for example, no "mechanical, mining and manufactur- ing" corporations could have large capitalization; the limit was $500,000 until 1871, $1 million until 1899. (In New York, too, there was a limit on capitaliza- tion: $2 million until 1881, $5 million until 1890.) Massachusetts law also made no provision for different classes of stock. Any change in the nature of the cor- poration's business had to be approved unanimously by the stockholders. Mass- achusetts directors had no power to increase the stock without stockholder permission; any new stock had to be offered to old stockholders, at par. These statutes "plainly envisaged" the corporation as an enterprise of limited scope, "simple in its capital structure," and incapable of "changing its general charac- ter" against the opposition of a single shareholder.[29]

Massachusetts law was plainly out of step; and the same was true of the other tough states. But these laws were toothless. They were victims of the national free market in laws. Some states passed looser laws, to compete for corporate business. A cynic might even argue that these easy states helped tough states stay tough. There was a kind of moral division of labor, similar to what was hap- pening in divorce law. Massachusetts kept an attitude of rectitude, without *ac- tually* interfering with interstate business. Business simply went elsewhere to be chartered. Such companies then did business as "foreign corporations" in Mass- achusetts. The federal constitution protected them against the worst forms of discrimination.

The law set up few real barriers to the migration of headquarters. A few early cases held that a corporation could not be chartered in one state if it in- tended to do all of its business in another. But from an equally early date, pre- cisely this was done, and successfully. Hence, the burden of strict statutes only fell on small companies that could not afford to incorporate far away. Tough and easy states coexisted. Pennsylvania and Ohio were places to steer clear of in the 1890s. Connecticut, in 1891, "drove from her borders not only foreign enterprises but also her own industries"; under a law that William W. Cook called "ill-advised," a majority of the board of directors of Connecticut com- panies had to be residents of the state, and 20 percent of the capital stock had

---

[28] 163 U.S. 537 (1896).

[29] For this analysis of the Massachusetts statutes, see E. Merrick Dodd, "Statutory Devel- opments in Business Corporation Law, 1886–1936," 50 Harv. L. Rev. 27, 31–33 (1936).

to be paid in cash. New Jersey, a poor but convenient neighbor of New York, became the "favorite state for incorporations." It succeeded in attracting big New York businesses with low taxes and easy laws. West Virginia, too, became a "Snug Harbor for roaming and piratical corporations," the "tramp and bubble companies of the country." The reason was simple: her laws were loose, and she was extremely cheap. Incorporation cost $6; the annual corporation tax was $50. These prices made West Virginia "the Mecca of irresponsible corporations."[30]

New Jersey's laws obviously threatened the power of other states to control corporations, foreign or domestic. There was talk in some states of ways to retaliate against New Jersey, and to reinstate a strict regime of corporation law through controls over corporations chartered elsewhere. There was talk—but no action.[31] Instead, still more states were lured by the idea of easy money from the chartering business. They cut prices and vied with each other in passing liberal laws. They allowed nonresident directors; corporate meetings could be held outside their borders. After all, a state could make a profit even from *low* taxes, if the volume was great enough. In the late nineteenth century, then, a group of hungry states openly competed for corporate business. Hundreds of corporations flew these flags of convenience. Fashions changed. Maine lost its popularity as a result of a dangerous court decision. New Jersey's corporation law of 1896 outbid all the others; it made New Jersey the "Mother of Trusts." In the first seven months of 1899, 1,336 corporations were "organized under the laws of New Jersey . . . with an authorized capital of over two thousand million dollars." These included the "notorious Whiskey Trust"—the Distilling Company of America—and 61 out of 121 "in a list of the existing industrial corporations having stock and bonds exceeding ten million dollars."[32] In 1899, another eager contender, the tiny, sleepy state of Delaware, passed its own act of welcome. It, too, was vastly successful. Corporations flocked to Delaware, and the phrase "Delaware corporation" passed into the English language.

No wonder that thoughtful but gloomy observers saw no real chance to control these creatures, favored by chance, by the iron laws of trade, and by the Constitution itself. Corporations were obviously going to swallow up more and more of the nation's economy. The fight against corporations became a dim, feeble rear-guard action. Basically, the corporation had torn free of its past— it could be formed almost at will, could do business as it wished, could expand, contract, dissolve. Legal emphasis changed: first, to regulation, as we have seen; and, second, to countervailing power. The big corporation was here to stay. Perhaps this was not a bad thing. "A great consolidated corporation," said Charles Francis Adams in 1888, "can be held to a far stricter responsibility" than "numerous smaller and conflicting corporations."[33]

[30] William W. Cook, *A Treatise on Stock and Stockholders, Bonds, Mortgages, and General Corporation Law*, vol. II (3rd ed., 1894), pp. 1603–5.

[31] Charles W. McCurdy, "The *Knight Sugar* Decision of 1895 and the Modernization of American Corporation Law, 1869–1903," 53 Bus. Hist. Rev. 304, 336–340 (1979).

[32] Edward Q. Keasbey, "New Jersey and the Great Corporations," 13 Harv. L. Rev. 198, 201 (1899); see also Melvin I. Urofsky, "Proposed Federal Incorporation in the Progressive Era," 26 Am. J. Legal Hist. 160, 163–64 (1982).

[33] Quoted in William W. Cook, *A Treatise on the Law of Corporations*, vol. III (5th ed., 1903), p. 2543.

This was the period, however, when John D. Rockefeller's lawyers put a voting trust together to consolidate his holdings in a flock of oil companies. The *trust* became a household word. Trusts were the bogeymen of the late 1880s; but it was power, not form, that was at issue. Corporations carved up markets; they made treaties with each other; and they formed huge and menacing agglomerations. The business frontier seemed as dead as the Western land frontier. America no longer seemed to be a society of individuals, fighting to get ahead. Everything now was groups, entities, and institutions. Society was a seamless web. The time had come for reallocation. It was time to fight back. Farmers, workers, and small business—all of these formed their own "trusts," massed their own forces, demanded a larger or better share of the economic product, or at least tried to hold on to their own. Business aggregations inspired counteraggregations.

A DISCORDANT ADDENDUM:
THE MUNICIPAL CORPORATION

Before Blackstone's day, there was a "law of corporations" which covered all entities with charters. Public and private, profit and nonprofit companies—towns, churches, and businesses—all fit in one legal bag. The various branches of "corporation law" split off and grew, in different directions. The private corporation became freer and more flexible. Towns and cities never got this much freedom. They remained closely regulated, and extensively controlled.

Like businesses, cities, towns, and villages were at first incorporated, one by one, by special charter. These charters were amended, recast, revised, and tinkered with piecemeal. City charters tended to be much alike, but rarely *exactly* the same, even in a single state. The powers and duties of one city differed from others in small, irritating, and confusing ways. Also, the charter business became an appalling legislative burden. To mend the matter, legislatures passed general laws about cities, just as they passed general corporation laws. An important English act of 1835 was a model. Ohio, in 1852, had an important early statute.[34] The Iowa Constitution (1846) barred the legislature from incorporating cities and towns through special acts. Most states had a more or less similar provision by 1900. Constitutions, late in the century, often divided municipalities into classes, depending on population size. Legislatures could pass laws that applied to an entire class, even though they were not allowed to pass laws for individual cities or towns. The Kentucky Constitution of 1891, for example, set out six municipal categories. Cities with more than 100,000 population made up the first class; towns with less than 1,000 souls made up the sixth (Const. Kentucky 1891, sec. 156). Often, the state's one big city stood all alone in its class. The set of first-class cities in Wisconsin, for example, had only one member in 1893: Milwaukee. This made it possible, as we have seen, for legislatures to pass laws meant only for their big or biggest city.

Early charters contained a quaint collection of municipal "powers"; early general statutes often did nothing more than copy those common clauses.

[34] Laws Ohio, 1852, p. 223. John F. Dillon, *The Law of Municipal Corporations*, vol. I (2nd ed., 1873), sec. 20, pp. 121–24. The English statute was "An act to provide for the Regulation of Municipal Corporations in England and Wales," 5 & 6 Wm. IV, ch. 76 (1835).

Wisconsin cities, for example, were given the right to control the "assize of bread." This meant something to a fifteenth-century borough, but was Greek to Midwestern America. The "assize of bread" even showed up in some charters as the "size of bread"; no one seemed to notice the mistake. Municipal powers in the 1850s seem strangely inadequate for mushrooming cities and towns. The Ohio statute (1852) gave cities power to abate nuisances; to regulate "the transportation and keeping of gunpowder or other combustibles"; to "prevent and punish fast or immoderate riding of horses or driving or propelling of vehicles through the streets"; to establish markets; to provide for the measuring or weighing of "hay, wood, coal, or any other article for sale"; to prevent overloading of streets; to suppress riots, gambling, "houses of ill fame, billiard tables, nine or ten pin alleys or tables, and ball alleys." There were also powers to "regulate the burial of the dead," provide a water supply, restrain animals from running at large (including dogs), make and maintain streets and sewers, wharves, "landing places, and market spaces"; regulate vehicles for hire, taverns, and theatrical exhibitions; provide for "the regular building of houses," and make "regulations for the purpose of guarding against dangers by fire." This was a long and not unimportant list of powers; but it was a curious hodge-podge; obviously, too, it fell far short of a general grant of authority to govern. No one really wanted to govern the cities of the American plains the way medieval boroughs were governed. Indeed, nobody expected much in the way of city government. It was boom-town law that was wanted. The Ohio statute of 1852 is once more instructive. Many sections of the law concern annexation of surrounding land. The cities of Ohio were not expected to rule their citizens with an iron hand; cities and towns were expected, above all else, to grow.

General statutes were passed not simply to help out busy legislatures. These statutes marked a change in the whole idea of the municipal corporation. New York and other cities and towns had had one of a kind charters. Each city was indeed a corporation, a separate entity—it functioned as a property owner, as an association, a community, more or less autonomous. The new law of municipal corporations was really not a law of "corporations" at all; but a law about cities and towns; a law about places that were, basically, merely parts of a whole (the state), and were under its ultimate control. This was the main theme of the growing law of "municipal corporations."[35] How much the state actually controlled was another matter. Even in the period of general laws, legislatures usually deferred to the locals. For example, in 1892, Baltimore's representatives in the Maryland House of Delegates made forty-seven recommendations—all were accepted, thirty-eight of them unanimously.[36]

Cities became big, complex organisms, and city finance generated huge amounts of living law. During the age of railroad optimism, cities indulged in an orgy of aid. They wanted the roads, they wanted land values to skyrocket, and only growth, growth, growth could do the trick. Short-run results were often

---

[35] See Hendrik Hartog, *Public Property and Private Power: The Corporation of the City of New York in American Law, 1730–1870* (1983), ch. 14.

[36] Jon C. Teaford, "Special Legislation and the Cities, 1865–1900," 23 Am. J. Legal Hist 189, 200 (1979). But *potentially*, the power to tax, control, and even destroy was lodged in the state.

disastrous. Many cities spent trough periods of the business cycle in a bankrupt condition, just like their railroads and banks. But still the debts grew; still more bond issues were floated. The indebtedness of cities with a population of 7,500 and more was $51 million in 1860; the debt of all other local governments came to about $100 million. By 1890, local government owed $900 million.[37] No wonder that a reaction set in against boom-town psychology. Restrictions on municipal debt began to appear in state constitutions. Under the Illinois Constitution (1870), for example, no municipal corporation could become indebted "in the aggregate exceeding 5 percent on the value of the taxable property therein" (Const. 1870, art. 9, sec. 12). Provisions like this were very much in the mainstream of American legal culture: first, insofar as they reacted to power, and abuse of power, by heaping on more checks and balances; second, in the typical cycle, first, of incentives, then, second, laws punishing those who rose too eagerly to the bait. The restrictions did not reach another problem: corruption in government. The shame of the cities was a byword by 1900. The Tweed ring in New York, in the decade after the Civil War, was only one of many notorious examples. William M. Tweed made an art of graft and corruption; he and his henchmen, it is said, stole more than $60 million. Tweed's influence reached up into Albany, into the legislature, and into the governor's office itself.[38] Tweed was overthrown; but this did not end the problems of New York City. Reform movements came and went; at the end of the century Boss Richard Croker, a latter-day Tweed, ruled over a city that, since 1897, had been expanded to include Brooklyn, Queens, and the Bronx.

Along with the struggle for municipal reform went a quieter struggle for municipal self-rule. State control seemed *too* tight for efficiency and for local problem solving. The major legal innovation, for the cities, in the last quarter of the century, was an idea usually called *home rule*. This appeared first in the Missouri Constitution of 1875. Cities of more than 100,000 population had the right to frame their own charters, so long as these charters did not contradict state law. California adopted a home-rule provision in its 1879 constitution; as amended in 1890, home rule was available (if the legislature approved) to cities of more than 3,500 population.

One reason home rule became popular was similar to the reason why general laws were passed; it eased the legislature burden. The (nonhome-rule) New York statutes of 1873 show many examples of time-consuming trivia: "An act to provide for the regulation and licensing of scavengers in the City of New York," "An Act in relation to a sidewalk from the Village of Albion to Mount Albion Cemetery" and "An act to amend an act entitled 'An Act to authorize the construction of sewers in the village and town of Saratoga Springs'" (chs. 251, 667, 670). It did not make much sense for legislatures to spend their energy on this kind of law. Nevertheless, legislatures proved surprisingly jealous of their power. They nowhere abdicated final authority to decide what cities could and could not do. Even a century later, home rule was more an ideal than a working reality.

Courts, too, played something of a role in running the cities. Then, as now, courts were the last resort of interests and power groups politically frustrated

---

[37] *Two Centuries' Growth of American Laws*, p. 241.
[38] See, in general, Alexander B. Callow Jr., *The Tweed Ring* (1966).

in local affairs. In the last half of the century, cities grew enormously. So, too, did their demands on the time and attention of higher courts; and the demands of villages, counties, and towns. John F. Dillon, in 1872, wrote the first treatise on local government law, *The Law of Municipal Corporations*. Dillon had served on the supreme court of Iowa, and had seen that "questions relating to the powers, duties and liabilities of municipalities were presented at almost every term." By 1890, a fourth edition, in two bulky volumes, appeared, reflecting, in its hundreds of pages, the vast ocean of decided cases. The expansion of judicial review had touched the law of municipal government, too. Many of the cases in Dillon were cases in which citizens or businesses attacked some action of local government—as unconstitutional or as beyond the powers of the municipal corporation.

The law of municipal corporations went its own way, along paths quite different from the law of business corporations. *Ultra vires* never died for municipalities. Charles Beach, in his treatise on public corporations, published in 1893, flatly declared that "Acts of municipal corporations which are done without power expressly granted, or fairly to be implied from the powers granted or incident to the purposes of their creation, are *ultra vires*." So, too, were acts of city officials that fell outside the precise literal limits of their authority.[39] Cities and villages had only those powers that were given them from above. In literally scores of cases, taxpayers and others tested in court the power and authority of cities, villages, and their officers. Appellate courts decided dozens of issues like that of "the validity of a sewer assessment under the sixty-fourth section of the charter of the city of Bayonne [New Jersey]."[40] The late nineteenth century was not known for the bashfulness of courts. Municipalities probably won most of their cases, especially in the lower courts; but they had to spend time and money in court; and the danger of losing hung over them like a black cloud. Often, judicial review had a healthy impact. It perhaps forced a bit more honesty and efficiency. But the costs were also high. Litigants were only interested in themselves, their taxes, their use of land. They couched their lawsuits in general terms. But one disgruntled landowner who attacked a sewer assessment might, if he won, shatter a whole scheme of urban sanitation.

---

[39] Charles F. Beach, *Commentaries on the Law of Public Corporations*, vol. I (1893).
[40] *Central N.J. Land Co. v. Mayor of Bayonne*, 56 N.J. L. 297, 28 Atl. 713 (1894).

CHAPTER 9

COMMERCE, LABOR, AND TAXATION

CONTRACT

The law of contract occupies a special place in American law in the nineteenth century. In theory, this was the century of the contract. Contract was the hallmark of modern law. Progressive societies, wrote Sir Henry Maine in his pathbreaking book, *Ancient Law* (1861), had evolved from status to contract. These societies organized social relations through free voluntary agreement; individuals, pursuing their own ends, made their own "law," perfected their own arrangements. The dominance of contract was one of the sovereign notions of the nineteenth century. By constitutional mandate, no state could "impair" the obligation of contracts. Many crucial constitutional cases, before the Civil War, pivoted on this clause. In the late nineteenth century, liberty of contract became another constitutional slogan. The Fourteenth Amendment, as the Supreme Court and some state courts read it, protected the right to enter freely into contracts. The boundaries of this right, to be sure, were vague. But the principle—that contract deserved this kind of privilege—was significant nonetheless.

Contract law was also one of the basic building blocks of legal study. (It is to this day.) C. C. Langdell's first casebook (1871), a milestone in the history of legal education, was a casebook on contracts. To constitutional theorists, free contract was an essential idea, a pillar of the palace of liberty; to students and teachers of law, it was the great gate to entry in the palace.

The *idea* of contract, and the *fact* of contract, were probably as fundamental as everybody said. The concrete body of law called "contract law" was another matter. In a way, it hardly seemed worthy of the fuss. The law of contract was essentially negative. Its doctrines gave more or less free play to individual choice. What people freely agreed on, courts would freely enforce. Beyond this simple principle, there were certain rules of thumb: on the formation of contracts, on the interpretation of contracts, and on remedies for breach of contract. Not much of this body of law changed fundamentally between 1850 and 1900—nothing compared to the transformation of tort law, or the law of corporations. Old technicalities had been dismantled long before 1850. What remained was more or less to tidy up doctrine and to express its principles as general rules.

If we look, not to treatises, but to the actual business of the courts, it could be argued that contract law, after 1850, was beginning a long slide into marginality. Courts were not equipped to handle business disputes as rapidly and efficiently as a brawling capitalist economy demanded. The doctrines were attractive and necessary; the rules were flexible enough; but judges were judges, not mediators.

They named winners and losers. Where parties stood in continuing business relations with each other, they preferred not to litigate at all. They worked their problems out by themselves, or went to arbitration. Moreover, judges simply lacked the right degree of business sense. They were trained in law, not in business; certainly not in the details and jargon of a thousand fields and trades. Of 206 contract cases decided by the Wisconsin supreme court, roughly in the decade before 1861, fifty-four dealt with land. Thirty-one were cases of sale; most concerned horses, sheep, oxen, and the cash crop, wheat, rather than manufactured goods. The thirty labor cases also arose out of simple situations. There were thirty-one cases on credit and finance, mostly about bills and notes, and the sureties who signed them.[1]

So far, an intelligent judge could manage very well. He was probably a landowner himself, so that the cases that came before him were part of his common experience. As the country industrialized, this was less and less the case. By 1905, the contract docket of the Wisconsin supreme court looked very different. A few types of transaction were overrepresented—real estate brokers suing for their commissions, for example. Manufacturers and major merchants had virtually disappeared from the docket, and indeed, they had never been there in any quantity. It is risky to infer the business of lower courts from upper courts; but big companies were surely more likely to appeal a commercial case than small businesses or individuals. It is a plausible guess that large businesses did not litigate contract issues in any regular way.

Between 1750 and 1850, the domain of contract law had expanded to include most of the universe of economic transactions. Even leases and deeds were treated, basically, as contracts, or as contractual in nature. Businesses became associations, working groups, rather than holders of little monopolies—grants from the state. All law seemed to take on a contractual flavor. Yet, like the golden age of tort law, the golden age of contract was marvelously brief. The most familiar rules—on damages, offer and acceptance, parol evidence, interpretation of contracts—frayed noticeably between 1850 and 1900. Since business stayed out of court, what came into court tended to be marginal: special situations, unusual cases. These tempted the judge to do justice in the particular case, for the unique facts before him. Contract law—that is, the doctrines applied by appeal courts in actual cases, rather than the basic *regime* of contracts—was not a vital prop of the economy. The cases were one-of-a-kind. Why not warp the rules to do the right thing for *this* litigant? Most appealed cases, in any event, turned only on their facts or on questions of interpretation. Each case stood on its own merit. Moreover, statute law, after 1850, shrank the kingdom of contract significantly. Every new law on the statute books, if it dealt with the economy at all, was a cup of water withdrawn from the pool or puddle of contract.

A few new doctrines were invented or extended after 1850 that, on the surface, helped fill in gaps in classical, free-market contract law. *Lawrence v. Fox* (New York, 1859)[2] was a leading case on the so-called third-party beneficiary contract. The doctrine of Lawrence v. Fox allowed a person to enforce a contract, even if

---

[1] This discussion is based on Lawrence M. Friedman, *Contract Law in America* (1965). Wisconsin was an agricultural state, first settled in the 1830s. Some of the trends discussed no doubt appeared earlier in New England, later in the prairie states, and in the West.

[2] 20 N.Y. 268 (1859).

that person was not actually a party to the contract, provided the contract was meant for his benefit. So, if A sold a horse to B, and told B, "Pay the money to my creditor, C," creditor C could sue B for the money if B refused or neglected to pay. The common law had been very reluctant to allow anybody to transfer abstract rights (including rights to collect and to sue); transferees were not allowed to sue on the original claim or right. This was inconsistent with the worldview of nineteenth-century contract. In the market, all interests or values should in principle be subject to sale or to transfer.[3]

During this period, too, a specific body of law about damages for breach of contract developed out of almost nothing. Courts developed systematic rules for calculating damages at a surprisingly late date. They had before simply thrown the whole matter to the jury. A crucial case, out of England, was *Hadley v. Baxendale* (1854).[4] A mill had stopped working because of a broken crankshaft. The millowner sent for a new shaft. The shaft was delivered by "well-known carriers trading under the name of Pickford &: Co." These "well-known carriers," however, delivered the crankshaft late. The mill was shut down longer than expected, and the plaintiffs, the millowners, lost some of their profits. They felt the carriers should pay. But the court disagreed. The carriers had breached their contract to deliver on time—no question. But the plaintiff could only recover for the "natural consequences" of this breach; and the lost profits, said the court, did not fit in this box. The rule of Hadley *v.* Baxendale fit neatly the ethos of the developing law of contract. It was a law that assumed impersonal markets. No special, personal, idiosyncratic factors ought to influence the calculus of damages. Damages had to be objective. Some mills—perhaps the more prudent ones—might have had a spare shaft.[5] The case also limited the risks of carriers. They were liable only for "natural" consequences of misdelivery—damage they could foresee and take account of. The rule was therefore a way to standardize costs and rationalize enterprise. In this regard, it can be compared with many of the newer tort rules. Tort law and contract law were both in tune with the economic thinking of the day, at least as the judges saw this. The rule of *Hadley v. Baxendale* was eagerly adopted in the states. Indeed, it was anticipated there; in *Brayton v. Chase,*[6] for example, decided in Wisconsin in the same year (1854). A farmer ordered a "New York reaper," to be delivered before the first of July. The reaper came late. Brayton, the farmer, claimed he lost thereby his "large crops of winter and spring grain." But he collected no damages. Crop losses, said the court, were "too

---

[3] The old rule was, moreover, a rule of procedure. It seemed particularly out of date in the period of the Field Code, which allowed lawsuits to be freely brought by those who had a real interest in the outcome.

[4] 9 Ex. 341 (1854). For the background and meaning of the case, see Richard Danzig, "*Hadley v. Baxendale:* A Study in the Industrialization of the Law," 4 J. Legal Studies 249 (1975).

[5] Another rule of damages allowed the plaintiff in a contract case to recover only the difference between the contract and market prices. "It follows from this rule, that, if, at the time fixed for the delivery, the article has not risen in value, the vendee having lost nothing can recover nothing." Theodore Sedgwick, *A Treatise on the Measure of Damages* (2nd ed., 1852), p. 260. Only economic damages—never punitive damages—were recoverable. Breach of contract was not a wrong, not a tort.

[6] 3 Wis. 456 (1854).

remote" a consequence of Chase's delay. They resulted "rather from the particular situation of the plaintiff than from the breach of the contract."

These doctrines aimed at objectivity; but the way they were phrased made them tents rather than cages. Application was all. *Hadley v. Baxendale,* for example, spoke of "natural consequences." Only the courts could say what was natural and what was not. By 1900, cases were shifting subtly away from the hard line of the 1850s. The ideal remained: rational, calculable damages, limited to the natural, foreseeable results of a breach. In general, the market was the measure of loss. But actual decisions warped the logic of doctrine, for reasons already mentioned. Judges were people, human beings; and occasional cases that struck them as harsh tempted them to alter or modify doctrines—though usually without admitting what they were doing. The temple stood firm: its architects still worked on decoration, but the termites worked busily underneath.

NEGOTIABLE INSTRUMENTS

The law of bills, notes, checks, and certificates of deposit came from the law merchant by way of England, was modified in America, and was stabilized and somewhat Anglified by decisions and scholarly writings before 1850. This branch of law was of tremendous importance in the nineteenth century. Before 1864, bank notes were the chief circulating currency. Both before and after the 1860s, personal promissory notes were a crucial American instrument of debt and credit. Because of its key position, the note opened up endless possibilities for disputes and ultimately lawsuits. As we have seen, lawyers, particularly in the West, spent much of their time collecting debts in the form of personal paper. The machinery of business could not run without the law of bills and notes to oil it. This was indeed living law. The *Century Edition of the American Digest,* covering reported cases up to 1896, gave over almost an entire volume to the subject of "Bills and Notes" about 2,700 pages, a tremendous bulk few other topics could match.

It was living law, moreover, with flexible ideology. The law was supposed to follow the custom of the business public. And in truth, the law was often supple and inventive. The bill of lading was originally used for ocean shipping; by the 1850s, it had become a railroad document. The certified check, barely mentioned in treatises in the 1860s, had become an important type of negotiable instrument by 1870. Business practice created it. Justice Swayne, in a Supreme Court case in 1871, had this to say: "By the law merchant of this country the certificate of the bank that a check is good is equivalent to acceptance. . . . The practice of certifying checks has grown out of the business needs of the country. . . . [T]he average daily amount of such checks in use in the city of New York, throughout the year, is not less than one-hundred millions of dollars. We could hardly inflict a severer blow upon the commerce and business of the country than by throwing a doubt on their validity."[7]

Courts had more trouble with municipal and corporate bonds. Should these be treated as negotiable, like ordinary bills and notes? And how strictly should

---

[7] *Merchants' National Bank of Boston v. State National Bank of Boston,* 77 U.S. 604, 647–48 (1871).

courts look them over before deciding whether they were valid? These were important policy questions. If negotiable, a transferred bond cut off any defects in the original transaction. The interests of the issuer, the original investors, and later investors who came to hold the bonds were sometimes in conflict. The later investors were, quite often, banks and financial interests, who had perhaps invested in the Eastern money markets. The original holders were, sometimes, farmer speculators, townspeople, small-scale gullibles. In some states, statutes settled the issue in favor of negotiability. In general, the courts, too, with some vacillation, cloaked these bonds with the magic mantle of negotiability. In so doing, they disregarded—in the words of Justice Robert C. Grier—the "epidemic insanity of the people, the folly of county officers, the knavery of railroad 'speculators.'" They favored, rather, the "malleability" of the bonds, in order to "suit the necessities and usages of the mercantile and commercial world." The need for a free, open capital market, with no second thoughts about the validity of bond issues, was a paramount consideration. "Mere technical dogma . . . cannot prohibit the commercial world from inventing or using any species of security not known in the last century."[8]

The case that evoked Grier's eloquence turned on the status of bonds of Mercer County, Pennsylvania. The county issued the bonds in order to subscribe for stock in a thievish railroad, the Pittsburgh and Erie. Some of the bonds came into the hands of a certain Hacket, "a citizen of New Hampshire," and a purchaser (in law at least) in good faith. The county wanted to renege; the issue, it claimed, had irregularities. The Supreme Court refused to go along. This case illustrates the tendency of courts to favor the good-faith purchaser for value, as much as possible, ignoring blemishes in the bonds themselves.

Occasionally, the swindle or scandal was so great that the legislature adopted a different posture. The farm-mortgage crisis of Wisconsin, which we have mentioned, was one of these occasions, in the 1850s and 1860s. Farmers had given notes in exchange for railroad stock. The notes were secured by mortgages on their farms. The stock became worthless after the crash of 1857. Meanwhile, the notes and mortgages had been sold to Eastern interests. If the notes were *not* negotiable, despite appearances, then the farmer's "equities" survived; and the farmers could defend themselves in a foreclosure action by claiming fraud or mistake. A Wisconsin law of 1858 prohibited the holder of the note from claiming to be a (legally) innocent purchaser. The point was obvious. The farmers were voters; the noteholders were not. The law might save Wisconsin's farms. The Wisconsin supreme court, however, defied popular pressure, struck down the statute; it treated later attempts by the legislature to intervene with equal disdain.[9]

In almost all states, crisis or no, statutes aided, hindered, or muddled commercial law, by tinkering with some of the rules of commercial paper.[10] The statutes ranged from a few trifling, standard provisions—postponing the maturity date of an instrument to Monday if it fell due on Sunday, for example— to sizable codes. California, for example, adopted a whole code on negotiable

[8] Grier, J. in *Mercer County v. Hacket,* 68 U.S. 83, 95–96 (1864).

[9] See Robert S. Hunt, *Law and Locomotives; the Impact of the Railroad on Wisconsin Law in the Nineteenth Century* (1958), pp. 48–50; and see also p. 344, supra.

[10] See, in general, Frederick Beutel, "The Development of State Statutes on Negotiable Paper Prior to the Negotiable Instruments Law," 40 Columbia L. Rev. 836 (1940).

instruments in 1872. It consisted of 117 sections, and was copied from a code that David Dudley Field had proposed for New York. Six Western states later followed California's example. Almost every state abolished the antiquated custom of days of grace. Of the harvest of laws, some were for the benefit of commercial interests; others for even narrower groups. Some states made usurious notes totally void, and did the same with regard to notes given for gambling debts. No one, not even a good-faith holder, could collect on a note that suffered from these original sins. Other states protected the good-faith purchaser despite these taints.[11] In a few states, for example Ohio, a note given for "the right to make, use, or vend a patent invention" had to bear on its face the words "given for a patent right"; and any holder of the note was "subject to the same defenses as . . . the original owner"[12]—all this to help stamp out a common rural swindle.[13]

Commercial law was a field where people in business saw value in uniformity among the states. Law reformers, too, had a taste for technical change, in the direction of innocuous consistency. The law of commercial paper was in theory, international. But states were free to develop variations, and they did. A report of the American Bar Association, in 1891, complained that there were "fifty different languages" of business law. A business person had a right to ask why "the meaning and effect of a promissory note" should not be "as certain and definite" in all states "as the meaning of words in an American dictionary." "Variance, dissonance, contradiction" caused "perplexity, uncertainty and damage."[14]

No wonder, then, that the general movement for uniformity in law focused first and foremost on commercial matters. On instructions from the Conference of Commissioners on Uniformity of Laws, which met in Detroit in 1895, John J. Crawford drafted a Negotiable Instruments Law.[15] Crawford relied heavily on the British Bills of Exchange Act (1882) and, as Professor Beutel has shown, on the California Code of 1872.[16] The NIL was the first of the "uniform laws." It was one of the most successful. The act, in general, did not try to make changes in the general thrust of the law. It was a restatement of existing rules. The NIL consisted of short, clean, polished sections. The rules it codified were already generally accepted, either as business norms or as courtroom doctrine. The NIL tidied up the facade of the law of commercial paper; it was not a reform law. Still, no one had asked for anything else.

THE LAW OF SALES

Commercial law in general was sensitive to business needs. Courts were willing to let business practice take the lead and show the way—so long as no oversensitive nerve of politics or legal tradition was touched. There was very little

[11] John Daniel, *A Treatise on the Law of Negotiable Instruments,* vol. 1 (5th ed., 1903), pp. 223–25, sec. 197.

[12] Rev. Stats. Ohio 1880, sec. 3178.

[13] See "State Interference with Patent Rights," 16 Albany L.J. 360 (1877). These statutes were passed in the 1870s, for example, Laws N.Y. 1877, ch. 65.

[14] "Report of the Committee on Uniform State Laws," *Report, 14th Ann. Meeting ABA* (1891), pp. 365, 371.

[15] John J. Crawford, *Negotiable Instruments Law* (1897), pref.

[16] Beutel, *op. cit.,* p. 851.

regard for what we would now consider consumer interests. But, toward the end of the century, arguments along such lines began to be heard more often in court decisions.

A case in point was the law of sales. It was well developed by mid-century. It had the dignity of a separate "field" of law, thanks in part to a series of classic English cases. One key concept was "title"; title determined who bore the risk of loss. But subtle nuances of doctrine allowed sellers to keep their security interest in goods, even when the risk (and the "title") had shifted.

Overall, the case law showed a certain bias in favor of the seller—manufacturer or merchant. The maxim *caveat emptor* flattered the manhood and pride of the judges. In California, in 1850, as we saw, the maxim was considered one of the glories of the common law, in contrast to the flabby solicitude of civil law. But by 1888, Edmund Bennett, in his treatise on sales, was admitting that the rule had "many limitations." These were cast in the form of "exceptions," but really amounted to "independent rules and principles."[17] Courts after all decided cases individually. The rule of *caveat emptor* was clean, abstract, general, but harsh. It was, moreover, one thing to tell the buyer to beware; in a mass-production market, there were limits to what the buyer could realistically beware of. It was one thing to examine a horse's mouth and hoofs before buying it, quite another to assess goods made by machines, sealed by machines, and packaged by machines.

The concept of *implied warranty* was one way to sap the vitality of *caveat emptor*. Sales by sample "implied" a warranty that the bulk would conform to the sample. When goods were sold "by description," without inspection, courts implied a warranty of "merchantability." The goods were not to be "so inferior as to be unsalable" among merchants who dealt in the article. Also, if a buyer bought for a "particular use made known to the seller," and relied on the seller's judgment to select the goods, there was an implied warranty that the goods were "reasonably fit and suitable for that purpose." When a seller, for example, sold "Wilcox's Superphosphate," a fertilizer or guano, to a farmer, the guano had to be "merchantable"; and it had to fertilize at least reasonably well. If not, the buyer had a cause of action, for breach of implied warranty.[18]

These implied warranties were especially suited to manufactured goods. For manufacturers, at least, implied warranties almost nullified the rule of *caveat emptor*. By 1900, the *results* of the cases were probably not much different from the results in civil law countries. Law was tilting more toward the consumer. But "the consumer" was not the man or woman in the street. The consumer of 1890 or 1900 was the small merchant or farmer. Courts were avidly middle class in their outlook. Their shift in emphasis meant that they catered less to big business and paid more attention to small business.[19]

---

[17] Edmund H. Bennett, American edition of Judah P. Benjamin's *A Treatise on the Law of Sale of Personal Property* (1888), p. 623.

[18] See *Gammell v. Gunby & Co.*, 52 Ga. 504 (1874).

[19] The actual history of warranty law was quite complex. For example, breach of warranty, whether express or implied, is a kind of absolute liability. Fault or negligence has nothing to do with the matter. But one line of cases—*Hoe v. Sanborn*, 21 N.Y. 552 (1860) was an example— seemed to veer off in another direction. The goods in that case were circular saws; the "alleged defect" was due in part to the fact that the saws were made out of unsuitable material. The

Mass production was the key fact of life in the new economy. Some manufactured goods were as small and mundane as the nails Adam Smith used as examples. Others were expensive hard goods. Unless the goods were sold for cash, the seller wanted some kind of security. Sellers needed devices that would do for reapers, pianos, and sewing machines what the mortgage did for land. The conditional sale was one such device. Under a conditional-sale contract, title to the goods did not pass to the buyer until he paid in full. In a New Jersey case, Gustave Wetzel bought (in 1876) "one Domestic sewing machine," for fifty-five dollars. He paid fifteen dollars down, and gave a note "payable in installments of five dollars a month." The machine was to remain the "property" of the seller until "actually paid for in cash."[20] In some states, local doctrines were unfriendly to the conditional-sale contract. In these states, sellers used chattel mortgages—mortgages specially adapted for sales of personal property. In Pennsylvania, where conditional sales were void, still another device was used— the bailment lease.[21] Goods were "leased" to the buyer, who agreed to pay on installments; after he paid "rent" for so many months, he gained full ownership.

These devices became standardized, routine. They appeared in form contracts, used in marketing soda fountains, pianos, and reapers. They foreshadowed the sale "on time" of automobiles, television sets, computers, washing machines, and golf clubs in the twentieth century. After a while, the three security devices became almost indistinguishable. It was another example of the nineteenth century principle that nothing—neither small technicalities nor large doses of legal logic and jargon—interfered in the end with what judges or the dominant public saw as the highroad to progress and wealth. Economic conditions, trends, and business practices molded decisions and laws. There *were* differences in statutes and doctrines. Hence, security devices had different names, different blanks for buyers to fill out, different dotted lines to sign. But basically they all came out the same in the end. The pressures to buy and sell on credit were very strong. Resistance was absent or transient or weak.

THE USURY LAWS

Installment sales were a triumph of marketing over small qualms and slight technicalities. The usury laws responded to other pressures. They were barometers of shifts in the demand for credit and money.

Usury laws were part of the legal inheritance; they were of medieval origin, and fraught with moral and religious overtones. Almost every state had some kind of law putting a ceiling on interest rates. In the late eighteenth and early nineteenth centuries, almost for the first time, some thinkers began to question these laws. Jeremy Bentham attacked them as economically unwise, as an interference with liberty. "No man of ripe years and of sound mind, acting freely,

---

judge, Samuel L. Selden, in the course of a thoughtful opinion, seemed to make the manufacturer's *negligence* an issue. Some cases followed this hint. This might have been a way out for those who thought *caveat emptor* was too harsh, and *caveat venditor* unwise. Tort and warranty law might have merged. But the courts never went this far.

[20] *Cole v. Berry*, 42 N.J.L. 308 (1880).

[21] See "Bailments and Conditional Sales," 44 Am. Law Reg. 335, 336 (1896); *Goss Printing Press Co. v. Jordan* 171 Pa, St 474, 32 Atl. 1091 (1895).

and with his eyes open, ought to be hindered . . . from making such bargain, in the way of obtaining money, as he thinks fit."[22] There were no good reasons, he thought, why government should fix the price of money, any more than it should fix the price of bread. On both sides of the Atlantic, this argument for free trade in money was heard; and it seemed to be fairly persuasive. A number of states—first Alabama, then Indiana, then Wisconsin and California—repealed their usury laws before 1860, and experimented with interest rates fixed solely by the market. The question led to vigorous debate. Much of the rhetoric in the debate was on a high theoretical plane. Typically, a chorus on one side quoted Jeremy Bentham and the slogans of free trade; the chorus on the other side used the Bible (condemning usury) as its basic handbook.

When one peels away the layers of rhetoric, a number of striking facts emerge. By and large it was economic interest, not ideology, that called the tune. In the first place, statutory interest rates varied tremendously from state to state. In the West, where hard money was scarce, statutes allowed far higher rates than in the East; and penalties for usury tended to be milder. This suggests that states raised their rates to a point where they would not interfere *too* much with the flow of credit to farmers and dealers in land. States that abolished usury laws generally did so at the end of their territorial period, or at the very beginning of statehood. At this point in a state's career, the government dumped public lands on the market, at a relatively favorable price. Squatters and speculators needed money for cash downpayments. The land was a bargain; the money was not. It was vital to relax interest rates, and attract money from the East, even at high rates, to cash in on the bargain price of land. Some usury laws were repealed precisely in response to this kind of settler pressure. In 1849, for example, there were, in Wisconsin, a great many settlers who were actually squatters on government land. They needed cash desperately, to buy the land as it came on the market. The state, not surprisingly, repealed its usury laws. The following year, California, another new state, did the same. Typically, too, the free-trade period was short. At the next downswing of the business cycle (when land values fell, debts became burdensome, and foreclosures threatened), the same people who had begged for money at any price sang a different tune. Now, they denounced the men who came with their satchels of money as evil, blood-sucking usurers. New, stringent usury laws were passed.[23] Usury laws, in short, were as volatile as prices and credit; the high-minded Benthamite debate was largely, though not wholly, a facade. In 1851, when the great need for money was over, Wisconsin repealed its repeal. And depressions, in general, caused states to toughen their usury laws, because of the clamor of debtors.

In the 1870s, a movement to repeal the usury laws appeared in the industrial East. The movement made some inroads. On the whole, though, usury was the farmer's problem for most of the century. He needed mortgage money. Later, attention shifted to the urban wage earner, borrowing small amounts to live on, or to buy some goods. The labor unions took up the battle cries of the

---

[22] Jeremy Bentham, *Defence of Usury* (3rd ed., 1816), p. 2.
[23] See, in general, Lawrence M. Friedman, "The Usury Laws of Wisconsin: A Study in Legal and Social History," 1963 Wis. L. Rev. 515.

Granger movement about high interest rates; they demanded stringent laws, low rates, and government regulation of "loan sharks." But the law hardly changed before 1900.

INSURANCE

No business was subject to as much legal regulation as insurance. The courts took second place to the legislature here. Even litigation about claims was not very frequent, it seems, until late in the century. There were perhaps as few as one hundred reported cases on life insurance down to 1870.[24] The number of appellate cases is not a reliable guide to what happened at the trial level; but the figures do suggest that trial litigation was not as dense as it would become in the next generation. The early cases were mostly about fire and marine insurance. By the 1890s, appellate decisions on insurance law had mushroomed. In the *Century Digest* (1896), there were 2,808 pages densely packed with brief summaries of insurance cases. The middle class was buying more insurance, including life and accident insurance. The great number of cases suggests an absolute increase in lawsuits on all levels. It also suggests that the companies, engaged in aggressive marketing, were also aggressively contesting a certain number of claims.

Insurance litigation developed along interesting lines. Lawyers for the companies drafted stiff clauses to protect company interests; yet courts and juries often found ways to "interpret" the language of policies against company interests. They did this to help a widow trying to collect on her husband's policy, or to help out a family whose house or store had burned down. Company lawyers may have done *too* good a job in drafting the typical policy, adding clauses that were unfair, or that did only too well for their clients. Strict, unfair clauses, clauses strict beyond the general norms of fairness, clauses that exaggerated warranties "to the point where they were almost one hundred percent protection against claims"—these helped create a "public atmosphere" against the companies. Decisions and laws tended to go against these unpopular companies, so that they fared "worse . . . than . . . any other contracting party."[25]

In claims cases, courts faced concrete human situations, and sometimes their sympathies showed. In many trials, the legal issue turned on whether what the insured stated in his application, or his policy, constituted a "warranty" or not. If the statements were "warranties," and were wrong—lies or mistakes—the policy was a mere scrap of paper. But suppose the insured had been just a teeny bit larcenous, foolish, or mendacious. Should his grieving family, say, pay the consequences? Or if the home or business had burnt to the ground, should the owners get nothing at all? This seemed a high price to pay for some slight misstatement (or fib). Chief Justice Ryan of Wisconsin spoke of the "crafty conditions with which fire insurance companies fence in the rights of the assured, and the subtle arguments which their counsel found upon them." The companies, he felt, acted almost as if their "single function" was to collect premiums, and not to pay

[24] Morton Keller, *The Life Insurance Enterprise, 1885–1910* (1963), pp. 187ff., is the source of this statement and much of the following paragraph.

[25] Thomas I. Parkinson, law professor and insurance executive, quoted in Keller, *op. cit.*, p. 190.

claims at all.[26] The concept of warranty was never allowed to dominate the cases. Courts went to great lengths to hold that misstatements were only "representations," even when the policy said in plain English that all statements were "warranties." A typical case was *Rogers v. Phoenix Ins. Co.* (1890),[27] where a "one-story, shingle-roof, frame building," owned by Edward and Mary Rogers, burnt down. When they applied for insurance, they said the house was fifteen years old. The policy stated that "every statement . . . is a warranty . . . and if any false statements are made, this policy shall be void." The company argued (among other things) that the house was twenty years old, not fifteen; the policy was therefore void. But the court disagreed; the statement was a mere "representation." Since it did not "render the risk more hazardous," the policy was good, and the company would have to pay.[28]

Not that the companies always lost. Some of their customers *did* lie badly, some *did* conceal facts that increased the risk. And some litigants were blocked by language drawn so clear and so tight that it left no room to escape. Judges were willing to twist the sense of English words, but only up to a point. The case law was complex and chaotic. The outcome of lawsuits was not easy to predict. Uncertainty invited litigation. The insurance contract, especially insurance on lives, is not a pact between people in continuing, multiple relations. It is drawn up for a single end. No one claim is worth the company's while to pay. On the other side, no widow had an incentive to give up her claim, merely to please the company, or keep its good will. The companies usually settled or paid; but they also sometimes fought; and so, too, did survivors and insured people.

Meanwhile, states passed a torrent of statutes. The law touched every aspect of the insurance business. Some statutes plainly tried to benefit the companies, some the policyholders; some compromised the interests of the two. On balance, however, regulation was unfriendly to the companies. Wisconsin, for example, passed a law in 1870 requiring fire and marine insurance companies to keep strong reserves. The companies could not distribute profits until they had set aside "a sum equal to 100 percent of the premiums on unexpired policies."[29] A Nebraska law (1889) required companies to pay off fire, tornado, and lightning insurance, at the value asserted by the policy, which was to be "taken conclusively to be the true value," whenever the property was "wholly destroyed." In Nebraska, brokers and agents had to be licensed. Pages of closely knit prose in the statute books, before 1900, described the duties and obligations of insurance companies. Insurance companies were identified with two major devils: aggregated capital and foreign (that is, out-of-state) corporations (which most of them were, in any given state). This made the companies all the more vulnerable, and contributed to the dense texture of regulation.

---

[26] Quoted in Spencer Kimball, *Insurance and Public Policy* (1960), p. 211.

[27] 121 Ind. 570, 23 N.E. 498 (1890).

[28] Similar results were reached by statute, for example, in Missouri: "No misrepresentation made in [a life-insurance policy] . . . shall be deemed material, or render the policy void, unless the matter misrepresented . . . actually contributed to the contingency or event on which the policy is to become due and payable, and whether it so contributed in any case, shall be a question for the jury." Rev. Stats. Mo. 1879, sec. 5976.

[29] Kimball, *op. cit.*, p. 150.

The companies fought in court against some of these laws. They did not win very often. One estimate is that the courts, between 1890 and 1908, found only 1 percent of some two thousand statutes unconstitutional. *Paul v. Virginia* (1869)[30] was a famous earlier defeat. A Virginia law (of 1866) licensed "foreign" insurance companies. To get a license, the company had to deposit bonds with the treasurer of Virginia. Paul was agent for various New York companies (New York was "foreign" from the Virginia standpoint). This was a test case, challenging the Virginia law, and financed by the National Board of Fire Underwriters. The argument was that states had no power to regulate this business; it was interstate commerce, and exclusively the domain of the federal government. But the Supreme Court disagreed. Insurance, the Court said, was not "commerce." This seems to modern readers a rather strange idea (it was repudiated by the Supreme Court some 80 years later). But in context it made sense. The federal government had never shown the slightest inclination to regulate insurance. A decision for the companies would destroy the whole vast body of state laws on insurance. The Court was unwilling to do this; and its holding threw the companies back to the howling wolves in the states.

These wolves, to be sure, could often be tamed through judicious lobbying. But insurance companies were, like railroads, unusually subject to hostile, local legislation. Sometimes it took the form of laws favoring mutuals and fraternals over stock companies. Out-of-state companies had a particular cross to bear. State laws discriminated against them, taxed them more heavily than locals, sometimes tried to drive them out altogether. There was some merit to the argument that out-of-state companies were irresponsible, hard to police. But the zeal of in-state companies, eager to get rid of competition, was the real force, no doubt, behind many such laws.

The Standard Fire Insurance Policy of Wisconsin, enacted in 1895, can be taken as a symbol of how far the state was willing to go to regulate insurance. Here was a whole policy, in the form of a law, down to very small details—no more than 25 pounds of gunpowder could be kept on premises insured against fire; and no "benzine, benzole, dynamite, ether, fireworks, gasoline, greekfire . . . naptha, nitro-glycerine."[31] One insurance man saw in this standard policy the dragon of "socialism," which had "upreared its head" in the quiet precincts of Madison, Wisconsin. But if so, it was a strange sort of socialism. Before the policy was enacted, the insurance commissioner had talked the matter over with merchants; he had looked at and made use of a form current among companies in New York. The standard policy was a compromise. In many regards, it was quite strict with buyers of insurance. The company had the right to cancel, with five days' notice; the insured had to file burdensome proofs of loss within sixty days of his fire. The freedom of the companies was narrowed; but the law was about standardization (which business tended to like) as much as it was about regulation; moreover, the companies had a voice in the regulatory process. The law was no total victory or defeat for either side, but a typical example of American legislation, where the strength or weakness of contending interests determined the shape of the final (compromise) product.[32]

[30] 75 U.S. 168 (1869).
[31] Laws Wis. 1895, ch. 387.
[32] On the history of the standard policy, see Kimball, *op. cit.*, pp. 230–32.

BANKRUPTCY

Between 1841 and 1867, there was no federal bankruptcy law. The states filled in with insolvency laws, stay laws, and exemption laws. In 1867, Congress passed a bankruptcy act, though by a tiny margin, and over bitter opposition. This law allowed both voluntary and involuntary bankruptcy. Anyone (not merely a "trader") could be forced into bankruptcy. The opposition railed at this notion: "Farmers and merchants" could, under the law, be "squeezed" into a "straitjacket" more "befitting the madmen of Wall Street." But arguably small debtors could benefit from this way of getting rid of their burden of debt. There was a sectional angle to the law. Some Northern creditors hoped to use the law to reclaim at least a pittance from ruined debtors in the South. A federal law, they felt, federally administered, would avoid state laws granting stays and exemptions, and keep at bay the prejudices of Southern juries.[33]

Conventional wisdom has it that the law of 1867 was a failure. It was cumbersome, badly administered, corruptly applied. The costs of proceedings consumed immense amounts of money; after lawyers and administrators took their bite, creditors were left with crumbs. It was an age of shaky credit. The act was a sword of Damocles over the heads of merchants. A coldhearted creditor could push them into bankruptcy. This fear was not irrational. The Supreme Court (1871) construed "insolvency" broadly. It meant not only lack of assets to pay debts, but also inability to pay debts as they came due in the ordinary course of business.[34] The panic of 1873 and hard times brought on a mad urge to repeal. The House killed the act in a frantic hurry (1874). The Senate, however, gave the law a reprieve. They added, too, a provision for "composition." Debtors might propose a plan for gradually settling their debts, over a period of years. If a "majority in number and three-fourths in value" of the creditors accepted the plan at a composition meeting, it would go into effect and be enforceable.[35] Other provisions, too, were designed to ease the problems of debtors. The 1874 amendments did not end criticism, however. The law lasted four more years; in 1878, it was finally repealed. Once more there was no national bankruptcy act.

But the federal law was scarcely cold in its grave when a movement began to revive it. This time, revival was helped along by business interests that favored uniform, national laws of commerce and trade. Politically, the influence of farmers was waning; and commercial influence was growing.[36] Samuel Wagner, in a report (1881) to the American Bar Association, called for a "National Bankrupt Law." The worst fault of the prior laws had been their impermanence, he thought. The laws had been "like so many sponges"; they "wiped off a vast amount of hopeless debts," and gave everybody "a clean slate with which to start afresh"; they were temporary "physic." administered in one large dose, "brief and spasmodic efforts," quickly repealed. What was needed was a permanent, national law, "in the nature of a regimen of diet and exercise." Partly "restrictive and partly remedial," such a law might "tend to prevent rather than to cure

[33] See Charles Warren, *Bankruptcy in United States History* (1935), pp. 104ff.
[34] Warren, *op. cit.*, pp. 113–14.
[35] 18 Stats., Part III, 178, 182 (act of June 22, 1874, sec. 17).
[36] David A. Skeel Jr., *Debt's Dominion: A History of Bankruptcy Law in America* (2001) p. 38.

disease," through its "even and continuous operation."[37] A young St. Louis lawyer, Jay L. Torrey, drafted a bankruptcy bill in 1890, stimulated by conventions of national commercial organizations, held in St. Louis and Minneapolis in 1889.[38] The Torrey bill met bitter opposition—by Southern and Western debtors, for example. These debtors preferred to trust in their own legislatures, which might enact sweeping delay laws, or debt cancellation measures. One Southern orator called the proposed law a "crushing and damnable instrumentality," an "infernal engine of ruin," the "last screw in the coffin of liberty," a plot to deliver "farmers, laborers, debtors, or small dealers" into the "soulless cupidity of a Shylock."[39] But even the South was generally in favor of *voluntary* bankruptcy.

The panic of 1893 lent arguments to both sides. Debate in Congress was sharp and prolonged. On the whole, Democrats sided with debtors and opposed the law; Republicans were pro-creditor, and favored the law. Finally, in 1898, the law was passed: "to establish a uniform system of bankruptcy throughout the United States."[40] This act was long, detailed, carefully drawn. Under the law (sec. 4a), "any person who owes debts, except a corporation," was "entitled to the benefits of this Act as a voluntary bankrupt." Involuntary bankruptcy could not be forced upon "a wage-earner or a person engaged chiefly in farming or the tillage of the soil" (sec. 4b). The act did not disturb state exemptions "in force at the time of the filing of the petition" in the state of the bankrupt's domicile (sec. 6). The law granted special priority, over other debts, to "wages due to workmen, clerks, or servants" if "earned within three months before the date of the commencement of proceedings, not to exceed three hundred dollars to each claimant"; the law also recognized priorities granted under state law, though these priorities ranked lower than federal priorities (sec. 64). In the course of passage many compromises were made. The act as it emerged was much more favorable to debtors than the creditors would have wanted. Administration was turned over to "referees," but they were given only limited powers.[41] Though no one could know it at the time, this bankruptcy act was not destined to suffer the fate of its predecessors. It had survival power. It is still in force (though with major changes). Repeal of the federal bankruptcy law became, in the twentieth century, inconceivable. The era of "temporary physic" ended in 1898.

ADMIRALTY

Admiralty was a fairly pure body of merchant's law. The Constitution gave admiralty to the federal courts. After the *Genessee Chief* (1851),[42] federal admiralty law, as we saw, governed on the Great Lakes as well as on coastal and international waters. For rules on navigation and maritime collisions, Congress still

---

[37] Samuel Wagner, "The Advantages of a National Bankrupt Law," *Report, 4th Ann. Meeting ABA* (1881), pp. 223, 227–28.

[38] Warren, *op. cit.*, p. 134.

[39] Quoted in Warren, p. 136.

[40] 30 Stats. 544 (act of July 1, 1898).

[41] Skeel, *op. cit.*, at 42–43.

[42] 53 U.S. (12 How.) 443 (1851).

looked overseas. In 1864, Congress adopted, practically verbatim, the English code (1863) of navigational rules.[43] In 1890, Congress adopted into law the International Rules, "Regulations for preventing collisions at sea," for "all public and private vessels . . . upon the high seas and in all waters connected therewith, navigable by seagoing vessels." These were rules about lights, sound signals for fog, steering and sailing rules, and distress signals. The Inland Rules (1897), which also dealt with lights, signals, steering, and sailing, applied to "harbors, rivers, and inland waters of the United States."[44]

Rules of admiralty law, in general, seemed to reflect merchants' ideas about splitting and compromising loss. In case of accident, where both sides, or neither side, was at fault, both were to share in the loss. If, for example, a ship and its cargo stood "in a common imminent peril," and the captain had to sacrifice some cargo to save the ship and the rest of the cargo, the owner of the lost goods had the right to make ship and cargo share in his loss; this ancient principle was called *general average.* The classic case was jettison—throwing cargo overboard to lighten the load. But general average was widely applied in the nineteenth century. In one case, fire broke out in the hold; the crew doused it, but damaged part of the cargo with water. General average applied.[45] The rules of general average thus seemed, on the surface, quite different from rules of tort law, which tilted heavily toward one side of the scale.

Admiralty law was also framed in terms that looked kinder to the sailor than tort law looked to the miner, brakeman, or machinist. A sailor was entitled to "maintenance" and "cure." That is, if he fell sick or was injured in service, he had a right to living expenses, wages, and medical care, at least to the end of the voyage. Was he entitled to more—to damages for negligence? The chief cook on a steamship, sailing to Vera Cruz from New York, by way of Havana, in 1879, was ordered to fetch some ice from the ice closets, to pack the corpse of a person who died on board. On his way, in the dark, he fell "through the hatch into the hold below, and received considerable personal injury." He was "cared for at the expense of the ship," and got his full wages. But he also claimed "additional compensation"—$10,000—"for his permanent injuries and consequential damages, on the ground of the negligence of the officers in leaving the hatch open through which he fell." The federal court denied this claim. They found no warrant for the cook's claim under the "sea laws" and in "recognized authorities on maritime law." The ship's liability was absolute, but it was also limited; negligence and contributory negligence had no impact on results, either by inflating or deflating the rights of an injured sailor.[46] This was a kind of compromise strikingly similar to the one that factory workers ultimately settled for, some thirty years later, in the form of workers' compensation.

Meanwhile, the Harter Act, passed by Congress in 1893, excused the "owner of any vessel transporting merchandise or property" from "damage or loss resulting from faults or errors in navigation, or in the management" of the ship, or for "losses arising from dangers of the sea . . . acts of God, or public

---

[43] See Robert M. Hughes, *Handbook of Admiralty Law* (1901), p. 212.
[44] 26 Stats. 320 (act of Aug. 19, 1890); 30 Stats. 96 (act of June 7, 1897).
[45] *The Roanoke,* 59 Fed. 161 (7th Cir., 1893).
[46] *The City of Alexandria,* 17 Fed. 390 (D.C.S.D. N.Y., 1883).

enemies," so long as the owner had exercised "due diligence" in making his ship "in all respects seaworthy and properly manned, equipped, and supplied."[47] The concept of "seaworthiness" was to prove as plastic as that of "negligence." But this long voyage lay ahead. There were strong parallels between admiralty and tort law, despite their traditional differences. Even the loss-splitting concept, so foreign to the common law, was perhaps more a difference in style than in substance. Admiralty, after all, had no jury. What the jury did secretly, in the holds and fastnesses of its chamber, admiralty judges had to do aboveboard, on open deck.

LABOR AND LAW

The labor problem—the problem of industrial relations—became an issue of major legal importance after the Civil War. The basic ingredients were the factory system and the mass of landless, class-conscious urban workers. Unrest began earlier in Europe and perhaps went deeper (though this is arguable). In 1848, Europe was in upheaval; the antirent agitations of New York were at best feeble copies of European-style revolution, and involved farmers at that.[48] Communism, the specter that haunted Europe, did not trouble America very much—at first. This country had to wait a while for its own version of class struggle. After 1860, the rich got richer and expanded their mines, factories, and banks. The poor had children; and in addition, their relatives came over from the old country. The new industrial system created or exploited a huge pool of workers. Many were immigrants. About half a million entered the country in 1880 alone. Most late nineteenth-century immigrants were peasants from southeastern Europe. They "provided an apparently inexhaustible reserve of cheap labor for mines, mills, and factories."[49]

These workers in industry were poor; work and life were hard. In 1840, the average workday was 11.4 hours; in 1890 it had fallen to 10 hours, but in some industries—paper manufacturing, for example—the average workday was still 12 hours.[50] Conditions in many factories and mines were appalling. Employers hired and fired at will; there was little or no job security. The worker was trapped in a web of company rules.[51] The business cycle added special miseries. Social services were weak; sickness, broken bones, or a downturn in business could bring disaster to the worker and his family. Many employers were callous in fact; others adopted the detached, studied callousness of social Darwinism. That the workers should remain unorganized, that business should be free from control, that enterprise was the way, the truth, the consummate social good: this was the faith of the class that owned the factories and shops. But there were also, in time, intellectuals and leaders of quite another stamp—men who got drunk on European radical thought or concocted a native version.

[47] 27 Stats. 445 (act of Feb. 13, 1893, sec. 3).
[48] On this situation, see Charles W. McCurdy, *The Anti-Rent Era in New York Law and Politics, 1839–1865* (2001).
[49] Foster R. Dulles, *Labor in America* (2nd rev. ed., 1960), p. 98.
[50] W. S. Woytinsky *et al.*, *Employment and Wages in the United States* (1953), p. 47.
[51] See Walter Licht, *Working for the Railroad* (1983), ch. 3.

"Closed resources and freedom with insecurity," said John R. Commons, "produce in time a permanent class of wage earners."[52] He might have added: they produce disaffection. Labor problems multiplied because it seemed to both sides that the game of life was zero-sum. Inexhaustible growth had come to an end. This was a world of finite possibilities. Everybody had to scramble for his share; what one person added to *his*, had to be subtracted from somebody else's. This attitude affected every aspect of living law. It also rubbed social relations raw. The rich resisted anything that smacked of "socialism" (from nationalized steel mills to unemployment compensation); the poor made war on the rich. In the postwar years, a trade-union movement grew rapidly—as rapidly perhaps as industrial combination. By the 1870s, mass labor confronted big business. In some ways, the labor history of the United States was as bloody and violent as in any industrial nation, even though there was never an actual revolution. In 1877, strikes and riots "swept across the United States . . . with almost cyclonic force."[53] The major rail centers, from Baltimore west, were struck. Nineteen died and one hundred were wounded in a skirmish on July 26, in Chicago, between police, National Guardsmen, and a mob. At the Carnegie Steel plant in Homestead, Pennsylvania, in the early 1890s, strikers fought against Pinkerton guards. In Coeur d'Alene, Idaho, in 1892, metal miners attacked the barracks where strikebreakers lived. In the disorders that followed, five miners died, and troops were called out. Most of the violence was unplanned; it simply erupted. It was not formally the policy of unions. Sometimes violence achieved results; sometimes—perhaps more often—it stiffened the backs of employers, and frightened the neutral middle class.

Forced to choose sides, legal institutions necessarily reflected their basic constituencies. Money talked; and so did voting power. Legislatures swung back and forth, depending on the strength of interests, blocs, parties, and lobbies; or tried to compromise. The courts were less subject to short-run swings of opinion. Partly for this reason, courts could indulge in principles and ideologies. These were usually on the conservative side; the judges, after all, were solid, independent men of the middle class. They were terrified of class struggle, mob rule, the anarchists and their bombs, railroad strikers, and the collapse of the social system as they knew it. When the left raged against decisions that seemed antilabor, the judges took refuge in the temple of the federal Constitution, in its regional chapels, the state constitutions, and in the half-ruined forums of the common law. These were sanctuaries where the mob (they felt) dared not enter. Their decisions were not biases, they insisted—not their personal opinions—but rather decisions under law; and law was impersonal, classless, and neutral. Perhaps they even believed this.

The battle for labor reform was fought, first in the streets, then in the legislative halls, and then, less successfully but inevitably, in the courts. In each arena, the rhetoric was different, but the stakes were more or less the same. Early cases on strikes, picketing, and boycotts have evoked a good deal of

[52] John R. Commons and John B. Andrews, *Principles of Labor Legislation* (rev. ed., 1927), p. 4.

[53] Philip Taft and Philip Ross, "American Labor Violence: Its Causes, Character, and Outcome," in Hugh D. Graham and Ted R. Gurr, eds., *Violence in America: Historical and Comparative Perspectives*, vol. I (1969), pp. 226–28, 230–32.

historical interest. The cases are few, the literature fairly large. Were strikes illegal? Did they amount to a criminal conspiracy? This was an issue in the trial of the Philadelphia cordwainers, in 1806. The case—and some later cases—did hold that striking workers could be charged with conspiracy. But in *Commonwealth v. Hunt* (1842), Lemuel Shaw, chief justice of Massachusetts, held to the contrary.[54] Prosecutions for conspiracy slowed down to a walk in the 1850s and 1860s. Conspiracy trials were major criminal prosecutions; they were inevitably slow and tortuous. They were embarrassed by a multitude of defendants, and subject to all the safeguards of trial by jury. Strikes were, in the abstract, perfectly legal—this was the view of most courts. Some strikes amounted to illegal conspiracies; but this was hard to prove. Each case stood on its own private facts. Conspiracy law, then, was not an effective strike-breaking tool. It fell out of use in the later nineteenth century.

More effective weapons took its place. A judge with a will could find a way. Many railroads in the 1870s, and later, were in receivership, after financial collapse. Technically, then, they were wards of the federal courts. This gave judges the chance to meddle in railroad labor disputes. Some judges did so, with a strong and mighty arm. Thomas S. Drummond, judge of the seventh circuit, made virtuoso use of contempt power to combat the strikes of 1877, against railroads that happened to be in receivership.[55] Later the judges invented, or discovered, the labor injunction, a stronger and more powerful piece of artillery. The injunction was an ancient and honorable tool of courts of chancery. It had infinite possibilities and uses. Its suppleness and strength made it a deadly threat to labor. During a strike, a company might ask for a restraining order (a temporary injunction). Courts of chancery had power to grant these orders quickly, without notice or hearing, if the court was persuaded that delay might harm the company irreparably. There was no need for trial by jury. If a union defied the order, or the injunction itself, it stood in contempt of court. Its officers and members could be summarily punished, even thrown into jail.

It is not clear where the labor injunction was first used. The Johnston Harvester Company asked a New York court to issue one in 1880; the defendants, claimed the company, had "combined" and "enticed" workers from the factory "by means of arguments, persuasion and personal appeals." The judge denied this request; but injunctions apparently did issue in Baltimore and at Kent, Ohio, in 1883, in Iowa in 1884, and during the railroad strikes of 1886. Between then and 1900, the cases "grew in volume like a rolling snowball."[56] In 1895, a unanimous decision of the U.S. Supreme Court sanctioned the labor injunction. This was the famous case of *In re Debs.*[57] It grew out of the Pullman strike of 1894. This major strike paralyzed the railroad lines; and President Cleveland in alarm, called out the troops. The attorney general also asked for an injunction against Eugene V. Debs, the union leader, calling on him to "desist . . . from

---

[54] *Commonwealth v. Hunt,* 4 Metc. (45 Mass.) 111 (1842); see Leonard W. Levy, *The Law of the Commonwealth and Chief Justice Shaw* (1957), pp. 183–206; Christopher L. Tomlins, *Law, Labor, and Ideology in the Early American Republic* (1993), pp. 199–216.

[55] See, in general, Gerald G. Eggert, *Railroad Labor Disputes: The Beginnings of Federal Strike Policy* (1967).

[56] Felix Frankfurter and Nathan Greene, *The Labor Injunction* (1930), p. 21.

[57] 158 U.S. 564 (1895).

. . . interfering with . . . the business of . . . the . . . railroads." Debs refused to desist; he was charged with contempt, convicted, and sentenced to six months in jail. The Supreme Court affirmed the conviction. The opinion, by Justice David Brewer, emphasized the sovereign power of the government, its right to protect its commerce, and its duty to deliver the mail.[58] From this point on, organized labor had to reckon with the crushing power of the injunction. The injunction was swift, and it could be murderously inclusive—broad enough to cover a total situation, outlawing every aspect of a strike and effectively destroying it. Few courts opposed the use of injunctions in industrial cases; but labor and its allies were outraged. The Democratic platform of 1896 denounced "government by injunction." It was a new and dangerous kind of "oppression"; the federal judges were acting as "legislators, judges and executioners," at one and the same time. Labor lobbied hard to get laws against the injunction passed. But the injunction had strong friends, too; and the attempt came to nothing—at that time.

An injunction did not issue as a matter of course. There had to be a threat of irreparable harm. Courts accepted the proposition that a strike was not illegal *per se,* as we mentioned. To warrant an injunction, the strike had to fall on the illegal side of this line. Even before the Civil War, some scattered, rather inconclusive, cases had tried to explain what made a strike legal or illegal, and also dealt with the legal status of other aggressive union tactics. Between 1870 and 1900, there were many more decisions. Some tactics were clearly proscribed— the boycott, for example. "It is difficult," said Frederic J. Stimson, writing in 1896, "to conceive of a boycott conducted solely by lawful acts."[59] Picketing, too, had a rocky course. A few judges thought it was always illegal: "There is and can be no such thing as peaceful picketing, any more than there can be chaste vulgarity, or peaceful robbing, or lawful lynching."[60] Most courts disagreed; they saw a clear distinction between peaceful picketing and intimidation. But it was hard to know where the boundaries were. Thus, a union that threw up a picket line always ran a certain risk of illegality. On the other side, management tactics rarely ran afoul of the law. Companies fired workers who were active in unions; they blacklisted union leaders. Few cases challenged the blacklist; and courts failed to find any trace of conspiracy or illegality in this behavior.

Still, the labor movement made great headway in the last decades of the century. Its power was greatest in the industrial states, and its grievances were most clearly formulated there. Not all their victories were won by sheer muscle. Labor showed strength in the legislatures, too. States enacted an increasing volume of protective laws. Some states forbade the blacklist. Some outlawed the "yellow dog" contract, which forced employees to promise not to join a union.[61] Other statutes made companies pay workers in cash (as a weapon against the company store); and to pay employees weekly or fortnightly. Still others punished infringement of the union label. These protective statutes, taken together, probably

[58] See Michael J. Brodhead, *David J. Brewer: The Life of a Supreme Court Justice, 1837–1910* (1994), pp. 108–9.

[59] Frederic J. Stimson, *Handbook to the Labor Law of the United States* (1896), p. 223.

[60] McPherson, J., in *Atcheson, Topeka and Santa Fe Rr. Co. v. Gee,* 139 Fed. 582, 584 (C.C.S.D. Iowa, 1905).

[61] For example, Laws Minn. 1895, ch. 174. The Utah constitution of 1895 outlawed the blacklist; art. 12, sec. 19.

had some effect on labor relations. But they were often poorly drafted, poorly administered, and poorly enforced. Most grievous of all, a certain number of these laws had to run the terrible gauntlet of constitutionality. It was a test some failed to pass. The results of these cases varied from state to state. The more spectacular (and reactionary) cases have been most apt to catch the historian's eye. On the whole, labor laws were upheld; most were never even questioned. Maine, for example, passed a law in 1887, of a common type, requiring employers to "pay fortnightly each and every employee . . . the wages earned by such employee to within eight days of the date of such payment." The Maine act, perhaps because of a favorable Massachusetts case, was never challenged in court before 1900. In the whole period from 1873 to 1937, a study of some ninety-four cases involving "protective labor legislation" found that 60 percent or so of them upheld the statute; and there was no significant difference between state and federal courts.[62]

But there was considerable local variation. The Illinois supreme court, for one, was politically conservative, judicially activist, and intoxicated with constitutionality. For a while, labor laws fell like tenpins in Illinois. In 1886, a coal-weighing act—the weight of the coal fixed the wages of the miners—was held unconstitutional; in March 1892, the court struck down a law forbidding mine owners and manufacturers from running company stores; in the same year, a new coal-weighing law failed to pass muster; in 1893, a law requiring weekly wages for workers was voided; in 1895, the court voided a law restricting the hours worked by "females" in "any factory or workshop."[63] These decisions in Illinois and like-minded states rested on various doctrines. Sometimes courts said laws were bad because they were "class legislation." Sometimes they were bad because they violated the cloudy concept of "liberty," in the due-process clause of the Fourteenth Amendment. "Liberty" included, it seemed, a doctrine of liberty of contract. In some extreme cases, statutes were overthrown for apparently no good reason. We have already cited one horrible example: *Godcharles & Co. v. Wigeman* (1886),[64] a Pennsylvania case. Here the court threw out a statute which, among other things, required laborers to be paid at regular intervals, and in cash. This law, said the court, was "utterly unconstitutional and void." It was an "insulting attempt to put the laborer under a legislature tutelage," "degrading to his manhood," and "subversive of his rights." No clause of any constitution was cited.

In 1884, New York, ostensibly "to improve the public health," prohibited the "manufacture of cigars and preparation of tobacco in any form in tenement-houses." *In re Jacobs*, decided a year later, held the statute void.[65] A person had the right, said the court, to earn a living "in any lawful calling." If the state interfered with the economy, it might "disturb the normal adjustments of the

---

[62] For the Maine situation, see E. S. Whitin, *Faculty Legislation in Maine* (1908), pp. 60–61; the figures on the outcomes of cases is in Julie Novkov, *Gender, Law, and Labor in the Progressive Era and New Deal Years* (2001), p. 31.

[63] The cases are respectively *Millett v. People*, 117 Ill. 294, 7 N.E. 631 (1886); *Frorer v. People*, 141 Ill. 171, 31 N.E. 395 (1892); *Ramsey v. People*, 142 Ill. 380, 32 N.E. 364 (1892); *Braceville Coal v. People*, 147 Ill. 66, 35 N.E. 62 (1893); *Richie v. People*, 155 Ill. 98, 40 N.E. 454 (1895).

[64] 113 Pa. St. 431, 6 Atl. 354 (1886); see above, Part III, ch. I, pp. 359–60.

[65] *In re Jacobs*, 98 N.Y. 98 (1885).

social fabric . . . derange the delicate and complicated machinery of industry and cause a score of ills while attempting the removal of one." A California law, fairly typical, required corporations to pay workmen their wages at frequent intervals and in cash. A quartz mine, brought to task for violation, defended itself on constitutional grounds. The California court (1899) declared the statute an abomination: "the working man of intelligence is treated as an imbecile. . . . [h]e is deprived of the right to make a contract as to the time when his wages will come due." Why should he not be allowed to "make an agreement with the corporation that he will work 60 days" and take a "horse in payment" instead of cash? The laborer might be "interested in the corporation, or for some reason willing to wait until the corporation could pay him." The statute was unreasonable because it did not allow these (unrealistic) arrangements; and the "infirmities" of the law were "sufficient to destroy it."[66] One wonders how many workers were in fact "interested in the corporation," or "willing to wait," or anxious to take a "horse in payment."

Opinions like this one in California rang false even in their day. The rhetoric of these cases is interesting. Government meddling would treat the worker as an "imbecile"; they would impair his "manhood," or put him under "tutelage."[67] The image of labor relations in these cases had an air of complete unreality. But, as we noted, these cases were not in the majority. In the long run, did the will of a few judges who stood in the doorway, trying to block bad laws (as they saw it), prevail? Perhaps not. The judges could call a short truce; they could try to hold problems at bay until the country came to its senses. This never happened. The madness got worse; history—that is, the ultimate lines of force—seemed to be on the side of more moderate measures. There was more litigation, and more "liberal" laws. Unions, their allies, and legislatures refused to give up. They may have modified their behavior—a point we will come back to. Indeed, there may have been a significant, even decisive, impact on the shape of American social legislation and social behavior. But in the end, social legislation had too many branches and heads to be killed; when one law was chopped off, ten more seemed to grow in its place.

In the late nineteenth century, labor law advanced along the lines where employer defenses, and conservative opinion, were at their weakest. Unions and workingmen in general struggled against convict labor, which they considered (quite naturally) a form of unfair competition. Convicts made shoes, chairs, and other items. Southern states frequently leased out gangs of convicts to private businesses. Convicts mined coal in Tennessee; and in that state, in the late nineteenth century, "free" coal miners rose up, and even resorted to arms against the system of convict labor.[68] Here was a situation where the general public tended to be somewhat sympathetic (though violence, on the whole, turned the general public off).

[66] *Johnson v. Goodyear Mining Co.,* 127 Cal. 4, 11–12, 59 Pac. 304 (1899).

[67] See Aviam Soifer, "The Paradox of Paternalism and Laissez-Faire Constitutionalism: The United States Supreme Court, 1888–1921," 5 Law and History Review 249 (1987).

[68] The story is told in Karin A. Shapiro, *A New South Rebellion: The Battle Against Convict Labor in the Tennessee Coalfields, 1871–1896* (1998).

Child labor was an important issue. Child labor came to be considered a terrible abuse. Small children were working long, hard hours under miserable conditions in factories and mines. The "bitter cry of the children" touched even hearts of stone. The movement to abolish child labor drew strength from changing social conceptions of childhood. Children were precious, sacred, jewels beyond price; their sufferings touched a chord that the sufferings of adults never could.[69] A movement arose to abolish child labor. This was more than a child-saving movement. Unions that fought against child labor had mixed motives, part "humanitarian," part "protectionist."[70] Child workers depressed wage rates. They inflated the supply of cheap labor. Adult male workers had good reason to oppose the labor of children in factories. Children also did hard, brutal, dangerous work on farms; but *this* kind of work was, if anything, romanticized.[71]

Organized labor felt the same way about women in the factories. Unions strongly supported wage and hours laws for women, and other forms of protective legislation. Of course, many women badly needed jobs; and many widows and single women toiled away in shops and factories. "Protective" legislation was not always protective; sometimes it could protect women clean out of their jobs. What organized labor wanted, above all, was good solid jobs, and good solid wages for *men*. This was probably what most married women wanted as well.

It was all of a piece: campaigns against child labor, the labor of women, against contract workers flooding in from outside, against convicts who worked for little or nothing. All this makes it easy to understand why organized labor strongly supported laws against Asians on the West Coast. Such radical groups as the Workingmen's Party led the agitation in California in the 1870s against Chinese labor, the "yellow peril." No one was as stridently in favor for restrictions on immigration of Asians as the workmen's champions in the labor movement.

Social-welfare programs were successful, in the main, if conscience and passion could form an alliance with strong self-interest. These programs also needed an efficient civil service, well-drafted statutes, and money for enforcement. Protective labor legislation—on child labor, women workers, factory safety, and the hours of work—grew from very little before the Civil War to an impressive web of legislation in 1900. But the trend proceeded very unevenly. The rich, highly unionized, and heavily industrialized states led the way. The South lagged badly behind. Connecticut had a primitive wage-and-hour law for children in 1842. Vermont was the last New England state to adopt some sort of child labor law; that was in 1867.[72] Yet in 1896, Mississippi, Kentucky, Arkansas, and North Carolina, among others, still lacked any law that even purported to outlaw child labor.[73]

Child-labor laws on the books were not the same as child labor laws enforced. New Jersey's law of 1851 outlawed factory work for children under ten;

[69] On this point, see Viviana A. Zelizer, *Pricing the Priceless Child: The Changing Social Value of Children* (1985), ch. 1.

[70] Hugh Hindman, *Child Labor: an American History* (2002), pp. 49–50.

[71] Zelizer, *op. cit.*, pp. 77–79.

[72] Lorenzo D'Agostino, *History of Public Welfare in Vermont* (1948), p. 181.

[73] Frederic J. Stimson, *Handbook to the Laabor Law of the United States* (1896), pp. 74–75.

older children could work no more than ten hours a day, sixty a week.[74] Punishment for violation was a fine of $50, to be sued for "in an action of debt, in the name of the overseer of the poor." This law was probably a pious nullity. It expressed official policy; but that was all. Compulsory-education laws put life into laws against child labor. An act of 1883 raised the minimum working age to twelve for New Jersey boys, fourteen for girls; employers of young people needed a certificate, showing the minor's age, the name of his parents, and a statement, signed by the teacher, that the child had attended school. This law, too, was weak; but it at least gave the governor the power to appoint an "inspector," who, at the modest salary of $1,200 a year, had the duty of inspecting factories (there were more than 7,000 in New Jersey) as best he could, in order to enforce the law.[75] In 1884, the inspector got two assistants; by 1889, he had six. In 1892, the act was amended to include provisions about women workers; the work week was set at fifty-five hours for women and persons under eighteen; fruit-canning plants and glass factories were exempted.[76] At the end of the century, children still slaved in New Jersey factories; but not so many, and not so young. A similar story could be told for other Northern states.

Constitutionally, child labor laws had less to fear than other welfare laws. It was difficult to stretch freedom of contract, the new sacred cow of constitutional law, to cover minors, who even at common law had no power to make contracts. Married women, too, had had contractual disabilities. This fact gave some color to arguments that the law should be able to control the labor of women. There were other, stronger arguments: women were different from men, they were more delicate, and (above all) they were mothers. There was a dash of Victorian sentimentality in the campaign, coupled with the fear that women who were wage slaves would break down physically and produce inferior children. *Muller v. Oregon* (1908)—a Supreme Court case—decisively settled the point. A state could set valid limits on the hours that women might work.[77] "The future well-being of the race" required as much: Women had to be protected "from the greed as well as the passion of man." To readers in the early years of the twenty-first century, the decision has a patronizing, sexist ring. But in its day most social activists, women as well as men, approved of it. Before *Muller v. Oregon*, state cases on this question of women and labor had gone both ways. An ordinance of San Francisco made it a misdemeanor to hire any "female" to work, "wait" or "in any manner attend on any person" in any "dance-cellar, bar-room, or in any place where malt, vinous, or spirituous liquors are used or sold." The supreme court of California struck the ordinance down.[78] A Massachusetts case (1876) upheld a law of 1874 that put a ten-hour limit on the working day of women, and a sixty-hour limit on their work week, in "any

---

[74] This discussion of New Jersey is taken from Arthur S. Field, *The Child Labor Policy of New Jersey* (1910).

[75] Laws N.J. 1883, ch. 57.

[76] Laws N.J. 1892, ch. 92.

[77] 208 U.S. 412 (1908). See Nancy S. Erickson, "Historical Background of 'Protective' Labor Legislation: *Muller v. Oregon*," in D. Kelly Weisberg, ed., *Women and the Law*, vol. II (1982), p. 155; see also July Novkov, *op. cit. supra*, n. 62, pp. 149–164.

[78] *In the Matter of Mary Maguire*, 57 Cal. 604 (1881).

manufacturing establishment."[79] The well-known Illinois case, *Ritchie v. People*, decided in 1895, reached the opposite conclusion.[80]

These cases were about women. A mandatory ten- (or eight-) hour day for all workers, men as well as women, was thought to be beyond the pale, even where it was politically acceptable. The state could, in fact, regulate the labor contract. But regulation was limited by the vague concept of "police power," the right to pass laws in the interests of health, safety, or morality. Of course, the state, as an employer, could itself make any contract it wished with its workers, and adopt any rule about these contracts. So New York, in 1870, restricted the hours of state employees. Federal eight-hour laws were passed in 1868, in 1888 (for employees of the Public Printer and the Post Office), and in 1892 for all "laborers and mechanics" employed by the government, the District of Columbia, or by "any contractor or subcontractor upon any of the public works of the United States." But even these laws were fitfully and reluctantly enforced.[81]

Limitations on the hours of some workers could be justified on grounds of public safety. New York, in 1888, adopted a law forbidding street-railway workers from working more than twelve hours at a stretch. This was followed, in 1892, by a ceiling on the hours of all railroad workers. The argument (or excuse) was that an exhausted trainman or engineer endangered the public. On this basis, enough outside support could be mustered for passage—support that the ordinary factory laborer lacked. That further step—maximum hour laws for adult male workers—was not possible in the nineteenth century. *Holden v. Hardy* (1898)[82] upheld, in the Supreme Court, a Utah law, of 1896, which limited, to eight hours a day, the workday of "workingmen in all underground mines or workings," in "smelters and in all other institutions for the reduction or refining of ores or metals." These were particularly onerous, dangerous, and unhealthy occupations; this case, as the century ended, stood perilously close to the legal frontier.

As we have seen, a few courts stubbornly resisted some of the country's labor laws—in some instances, the Supreme Court itself. Did this behavior have an impact on the course of labor history? This is impossible to measure. Probably fear of what courts could do, or the expectation of what they might do, influenced the legislative program in a number of states. It has also been powerfully argued that judicial review, and the awesome power of American courts, was a decisive influence on American social history.[83] It helps to explain why nothing like the British Labor Party ever developed in the United States; or why American unions seemed to lack the militant edge of their European counterparts.[84] American labor history, like American history in general, is extremely complicated; it defies easy explanations. No doubt the Constitutional system, and the work of the courts, had some impact. But we cannot

[79] *Commonwealth v. Hamilton Mfg. Co.*, 120 Mass. 383 (1876).

[80] 155 Ill. 98 N.E. 454 (1895).

[81] Marion C. Cahill, *Shorter Hours* (1932), pp. 69–73.

[82] 169 U.S. 366 (1898).

[83] William E. Forbath, *Law and the Shaping of the American Labor Movement* (1991).

[84] William E. Forbath, "Courts, Constitutions, and Labor Politics in England and the United States: A Study of the Constitutive Power of Law," 16 Law and Social Inquiry 1 (1991). Forbath also stresses the lack, in the United States, of a centralized government and a strong, centralized civil service.

rewind the tape to see what would have happened if there had been no Four-teenth Amendment, no labor injunction, no judicial review.

FEDERAL TAXATION

For most of the nineteenth century, the tariff, protective or otherwise, served two functions. It was a controversial element of economic policy; and it brought in revenue for the federal government. Congress was reluctant to expand the government's taxing authority. That would increase federal power, and state sovereignty was a mighty counterforce. Even the costs of the Civil War did not at first inspire new forms of tax. Initially, the government tried to fight the war by floating bonds; Jay Cooke took up residence in Washington and lent a hand to Salmon P. Chase, who presided over Lincoln's treasury. Bond financing and greenback money did raise revenue, after a fashion. But the North lost too many battles; costs mounted; the war dragged on; the struggle, it became clear, would be long and hard. Events forced the government's hand. Lincoln turned to an income tax. The tax, first imposed in 1862, and amended in 1864, was mildly progressive; in its later version, the top bracket was 10 percent. The government also imposed a death tax, and new or bigger excises on all sorts of services and goods: beer, public utilities, advertisements, perfumes, playing cards, slaughtered cattle, and railroads, for example. Despite some unfairness and some bungling, these taxes brought in a good deal of money. In fiscal 1866, more than $300 million dollars was collected.

The Confederate government, on the other hand, mismanaged its finances. The Provisional Congress, in August 1861, imposed a direct tax of one-half of one percent on all property (except Confederate bonds and money). The various states, however, were allowed to pay the tax themselves. This concession proved to be a disaster; rather than collect the money from their publics, the states simply issued treasury notes or required local banks to furnish the money. The Confederate treasury became "the greatest money factory in the world." It created "wealth out of nothing" by "magic revolutions of the printing press." The natural result was wild inflation. The notes "drove prices to fantastic heights. Counterfeiting . . . ran riot. Faith in the government vanished." The Confederacy never really undid this early mistake. Its later tax laws were inept or ill-timed; the major law of April 1863 was complex and, in part, unpopular; one feature called for payment of one-tenth of the produce of farm land as a tax in kind. The revenue question was never solved; soon Grant and Sherman made the question academic.[85]

The victorious North was anxious to return to normalcy, at least in money matters. Congress let the wartime taxes die. Indeed, the small scale of the federal government did not seem to call for severe and exotic taxes. Excise taxes, on liquor and tobacco, produced nearly ninety percent of the government's internal revenue from 1868 to 1913. Internal revenue receipts were $113,500,000 in 1873, $161,000,000 in 1893—pennies in today's world of billions and trillions.[86] But government was gradually becoming more active; and that meant

---

[85] For the above, see Randolph E. Paul, *Taxation in the United States* (1954), pp. 7–22.
[86] Lillian Doris, ed., *The American Way in Taxation: Internal Revenue, 1862–1963* (1963), p. 34.

money. The obscenely rich evoked jealousy and fear; and so did the powerful trusts and the robber barons east and west. Political and ideological arguments, coupled with a real need for cash, won recruits for the idea of a progressive income tax—a tax that would serve as a brake on the power of the rich. Between 1873 and 1879, fourteen different income-tax bills were introduced into Congress.

The movement reached its climax in the 1890s. The 1890s had no war for an excuse, except the Spanish-American War, which was short and profitable. But there was another war: for control of America's economy, not to mention its soul. The super-rich naturally fought the very idea of an income tax: this was the archenemy, the entering wedge of socialism, the beginning of the end for America. In 1893, Grover Cleveland suggested a "small tax" on incomes "derived from certain corporate investment"; when a tax bill passed in 1894, however, he let it become law without signing. The law taxed incomes (and gains) over and above an exemption of $4,000 at the flat rate of 2 percent.[87] Ward McAllister, "leader of the Four Hundred," threatened to leave the country if the law was passed. William Jennings Bryan, rushing to the barricades, cried out that he had "never known one so mean that I was willing to say of him that his patriotism was less than 2 percent deep."

In the 1890s, it was not enough to pass an important law; the Supreme Court also had to be convinced. William D. Guthrie of New York, who rose from office boy to lion of Wall Street, was bound and determined to kill this 2 percent dragon. He raised money for the lawsuit among his clients, found a willing litigant named Pollock, and launched an attack that he carried all the way to the highest court.[88] Here, an epic struggle took place. On one side, a battery of prominent Wall Street lawyers—Guthrie, Joseph H. Choate, and others—on the other, Attorney General Olney, his assistant, Edward B. Whitney, and James C. Carter. There were great flights of oratory, and some dubious essays in pseudo-history, concerning the historic powers of the federal government to tax. In *Pollock v. Farmers' Loan and Trust Co.* (1895),[89] the Court at first held the tax unconstitutional, but only as it applied to income derived from real estate. On the big question, whether the *whole* law was unconstitutional as a "direct Tax," the Court was evenly divided, four against four.[90] The ninth judge, Howell Jackson, was sick. The case was then reargued—with Jackson present—and this time the Court threw out the entire statute, by a bare majority, 5 to 4.[91]

---

[87] 28 Stats. 553 (act of August 27, 1894, sec. 27).

[88] Randolph Paul, *Taxation in the United States,* pp. 30ff; Arnold M. Paul, *Conservative Crisis and the Rule of Law* (1960), chs. 8, 9. On Guthrie's role, see Robert T. Swaine, *The Cravath Firm and its Predecessors,* vol. 1, *The Predecessor Fiarms* (1946), pp. 518–36; Henry James, *Richard Olney and His Public Service* (1923), pp. 70–76.

[89] 157 U.S. 429, 158 U.S. 601 (1895).

[90] The Constitution, art. 1, sec. 2, required "direct taxes" to be apportioned among the states by population. For a century or more, it had been understood that poll taxes and property taxes, and only these, were "direct."

[91] When the Court is evenly divided, by custom it does not reveal who voted on which side. When the case was reargued, Jackson, the missing judge, voted to uphold the act. This should have given the law a 5–4 majority; in fact it lost by 5–4. There is a minor historical mystery here, since one of the other four judges in the majority must have changed his mind between the time of the two votes. No one is quite sure which judge is the guilty one. See A. M. Paul, *op. cit.,* pp. 214–17. On the Pollock case, see Owen M. Fiss, *Troubled Beginnings*

History has not been kind to *Pollock*. Professor Edward S. Corwin called it a case of "bad history and bad logic";[92] it was surely both of these. He might have added bad law, bad politics, and bad form. The case has had one rare distinction: a constitutional amendment, adopted in the twentieth century, specifically undid it. At the time, of course, this could not be foreseen. Defenders and detractors alike agreed on the point of the decision: it was meant to make the world safe for that brand of democracy which Guthrie believed in, and Justice Field, and the rest of the "sound" and wealthy people of the country. Perhaps *Pollock* deserves a bit better than it has gotten from historians. Its logic and history were weak; but its instincts were rather shrewd. The income tax *was* the opening wedge for the transformation of American society. A journey of a thousand miles begins with a single step; and a tax whose brackets once rose as high as seven dollars out of ten may begin with a mere 2 percent.

STATE AND LOCAL TAX

In the nineteenth century, local government relied primarily on the general property tax. In 1890, this tax produced 72 percent of state revenues, 92 percent of local revenues. It is still a prime source of local revenue, but state governments later tended to abandon this tax[93] and turn to other sources.

The general property tax, as its name implies, was a tax on all types of property. Essentially, it was the old real-property tax, with a tax on intangibles and personal property added. Most states at some time in the century had some sort of constitutional provision mandating fairness and uniformity in such taxes. "All taxes," said the Pennsylvania Constitution of 1873, "shall be uniform, upon the same class of subjects within the territorial limits of the authority levying the tax, and shall be levied and collected under general laws" (art. IX, sec. 1). Again: "Laws shall be passed taxing by uniform rule all property according to its true value in money" (North Dakota Const. 1889, art. XI, sec. 176).

The tax was not easy to administer. It is hard enough to assess land and houses fairly; at least real estate is visible, and there are records of title. Chattels are easy to hide, and intangibles most furtive of all. Rich taxpayers could easily evade taxes on invisible assets. The general property tax essentially reduced itself to a tax on land and buildings. Meanwhile, a lot of the property of the less well-off was exempt from tax. Landowners, who wanted to share the burden, often called for passage of more general taxes. But in the end, they had to bear most of the burden themselves.

Assessment and collection of the property tax was a constant problem. Assessment was local, chaotic, and frequently unfair. Assessors were greatly tempted to undervalue property in their own counties: why not pass the problem

---

of the Modern State, 1888–1910 (History of the United States Supreme Court, vol. VIII, 1993, ch. 4).

[92] Edward S. Corwin, *Court over Constitution* (1938), p. 188.

[93] George C. S. Benson *et al.*, *The American Property Tax: Its History, Administration and Economic Impact* (1965), p. 83. On city use of the tax, see Jon C. Teaford, *The Unheralded Triumph: City Government in America, 1870–1900* (1984), pp. 293–304.

on to other parts of the state? Hence, on top of the layers of local officials, states began to impose "boards of equalization," first countywide, then statewide. An early state board was Iowa's: by the Iowa code of 1851 the board was "authorized and required to examine the various assessments . . . and equalize the rate of assessment of real estate in the different counties," in the name of uniformity. The board could equalize "either by changing any of the assessments or by varying the rate of taxation in any of the counties."[94]

But the boards did not, in general, have adequate power to control local assessors. Indiana took the next step, in 1891: creation of a board of state tax commissioners. The board had general supervision over the tax system; but its power was "chiefly advisory," and it did not succeed in curbing all the abuses that had grown up under the older system. Still, Indiana's law was "the beginning of a new administrative policy," and ultimately led to more efficient ways to assess and collect this tax.[95]

Even on paper the general property tax was never completely general. There were many exceptions and exemptions. The exemptions list was similar to, but less extensive than, the list of property that creditors could not touch. In the Iowa code of 1851, tax-exempt property included poultry, wool shorn from sheep, one year's crop, private libraries up to $100 in value, family pictures, kitchen furniture, food, one bed and bedding for each member of the family, and clothes "actually used for wearing."[96] In the Iowa code of 1897, much the same exemptions appeared, but with additions: "the farming utensils of any person who makes his livelihood by farming, the team, wagon and harness of the teamster or drayman who makes his living by their use in hauling for others, and the tools of any mechanic, not in any case to exceed three hundred dollars in actual value."[97] The property of charities, schools, and churches was also free from tax.

During the promotional years, railroads and other favored corporations were often granted tax exemptions. When these companies fell from grace, they had to pay their own way—in theory. In legislatures between 1870 and 1900, there were constant battles over taxation. Smallholders and organized labor wanted vengeance on the large corporations; they wanted the power of big money kept under control. But revenue needs were real enough, too. To lay the foundation for more active government, states needed a broad based, productive tax system. Where was the money to come from? State constitutions often hamstrung legislatures in their search for money. They were not allowed to float bonds at whim or will. The lower orders of government were also squeezed. Some governmental services could be supported by fees; but this method was regressive and liable to abuse. On the other hand, business was rich and getting richer; and it had long escaped paying what looked like its reasonable share. Some states competed for incorporations with *low* taxes; but railroad tracks once laid could not run away, and it was tempting to try to get all one could from these captive giants.

---

[94] Iowa Stats. 1851, secs. 481, 482. See, in general, Harley L. Lutz, *The State Tax Commission* (1918).

[95] Lutz, *op. cit.*, p. 152.

[96] Iowa Stats. 1851, sec. 455.

[97] Iowa Stats. 1897, sec. 1304, sec. 1304(5).

Taxation of business proved enormously difficult. First of all, there were political difficulties. Wealth excited the lust of tax collectors; but wealth was also power, and power spoke loudly in the halls of the legislatures. Volumes could be written about the struggles over railroad taxation alone. State governments rose and fell on the issue. Second, there were the special complexities of a federal system. Before 1850, the railroads, when they were taxed, paid the local property tax. Afterward, more and more states added taxes based on capitalization or gross receipts. Thus, interstate businesses—railroads and telegraph companies, for example—ran the risk of taxation all along their lines, as if by so many Rhenish baronies.

How much taxation of "commerce" across state lines was actually valid? How could the property of some giant firm, sprawled across the states like a Gulliver among Lilliputians, be sliced into rational pieces and taxed? There was no uniform plan. In 1899, railroads in some parts of the country paid 17 percent of net earnings; in others, only 8.4 percent.[98] Fundamental questions of constitutional law, and of conflicts of law, were often at issue. But the real issue was politics. The solutions made for very intricate law. When all concerned—legislatures, state courts, and federal courts—had had their say, there was still no definitive answer, still no one definite limit to the taxes that a state could lawfully impose on an interstate tiger with one paw in the taxing *situs*. Formulas, of more or less sophistication, determined what part of the tiger "belonged" (for tax purposes) to Rhode Island or Texas or Washington state. Massachusetts, for example, taxed railroads and telegraph companies on that portion of their capital that bore the same ratio to total capital as tracks and lines inside the state bore to total tracks and lines. The Supreme Court, in a test case (1888), held that this method was fair.[99] But taxation of multistate commerce was one of the high court's most persistent and bothersome issues.

DEATH TAXES

The idea of death taxes grew out of fear of dynasties and the enormous power of their money. Even before the Civil War, there had been some state and federal attempts to tax estates and inheritances. A death tax was part of the Civil War package. But the real upsurge in demand came after 1885. Economists like Richard T. Ely and Edwin R. Seligman, along with such strange bedfellows as Andrew Carnegie, argued that great fortunes should be heavily taxed when the founder died. About half the states adopted some form of death tax by 1900. Generally, these taxes were not steeply progressive. Almost always, they were biased against collateral heirs and strangers to the blood: they gave spouses and children of the dead more favorable treatment. In Michigan's law of 1893, for example, the tax (on "transfers . . . by will or by the intestate laws," or "in contemplation of the death of the grantor," or "intended to take effect . . . at . . . death"), was a flat 5 percent of the market value of these transfers. But the rate was only 1 percent on gifts to "father, mother, husband, wife, child,

---

[98] Emory R. Johnson, *American Railway Transportation* (rev. ed., 1907), p. 416.

[99] *Western Union Telegraph Co. v. Mass.*, 125 U.S. 530 (1888); Mass. Stats. 1882, ch. 13, sec. 40.

brother, sister, wife or widow of a son or the husband of a daughter," adopted children, and "any lineal descendants"; and the first $5,000 for these heirs was exempt.[100]

In 1898, the federal government re-entered the field, with a modified form of estate tax.[101] Its top rate was 15 percent, a rate that applied only to gifts from estates of more than $1 million, and that passed from the decedent to distant relatives, nonrelatives, or "bodies politic or corporate." The law was part of the revenue package for the Spanish-American War, and it was repealed in 1902. All told, it brought in $22,500,000. This paltry sum was hardly enough to make a dent on American's great fortunes. Like the Civil War taxes, however, the death tax passed its constitutional test; and so did the state taxes on estates, to the horror and disgust of Guthrie and the Cassandras of Wall Street. Again, these rich and conservative men were not wholly wrong. In the future, some of their worst nightmares would come true. Tax laws would be enacted that took a substantial chunk of some large estates. But steep and progressive rates would come only in the century ahead.

[100] Laws Mich. 1893, ch. 205; see Edwin R. Seligman, *Essays in Taxation* (6th ed., 1909), pp. 133ff.

[101] Randolph Paul, *op. cit.*, pp. 65–70.

CHAPTER 10

CRIME AND PUNISHMENT

THE MANY FACES OF CRIMINAL LAW

At one time, most lawyers were generalists, and handled criminal matters along with civil suits. Even Alexander Hamilton, a prestigious and prominent business lawyer, did criminal work. In the West, and in small towns generally, criminal law was a staple of the practice. Later in the century, the bar in major cities became more specialized. There were professional criminals—and also a professional criminal bar. This segment of the bar never had the prestige of the lawyers for big business. Some small-scale lawyers eked out a living by gathering crumbs of practice in the lower criminal courts. A few big-city lawyers made a more handsome, and sometimes less honorable, living. In New York, the "magnificent shyster," William E. Howe, flourished between 1875 and 1900. He was a member of the infamous firm of Howe and Hummel; he defended hundreds of madams, pickpockets, and forgers, as well as the most notorious murderers of his day. Howe's specialty was gilded courtroom oratory, judiciously backed up by perjury, bribery, and blackmail.[1]

The leaders and moneymakers of the criminal bar were always flamboyant, though not always unscrupulous. Howe and Hummel were not afraid to advertise their wares. Over their "shabby but conspicuous offices . . . hung not the modest shingle of a firm of counsellors-at-law but a sign thirty or forty feet long and three or four feet high . . . illuminated at night."[2] The organized bar, dominated by elite business lawyers, and jealous of professional prestige, stamped out the practice of openly asking for business through advertisements and illuminated signs. A criminal lawyer had no retainer business, and few repeats. Word of mouth was one of the few ways he could build a practice. A criminal lawyer, unlike the Wall Street lawyer, *wanted* publicity, wanted his name in the paper. It was for this reason that these lawyers (to this day) like to call attention to themselves. Flamboyance was good for business. It was publicize or die. The good gray lawyers of Wall Street would have starved in the criminal practice.

Howe and Hummel were seamy caricatures; but in their own way they illustrate a trait that is particularly marked in the criminal justice system: the huge gulf between the open, public, floodlit aspects of the system, and its grubby underbelly. The public thinks of criminal justice in terms of show trials, publicity, high drama, lawyers' tricks, and newspaper stories. But there was also the

---

[1] The story of Howe and Hummel has been entertainingly recounted by Richard Rovere, in *The Magnificent Shysters* (1947).

[2] Rovere, *op. cit.*, p. 34.

darker, underground tale of corruption and routine; of hasty, slap-dash "trials," and, toward the end of the century, the steady rise of plea bargaining.

The formal criminal law itself changed a good deal in the later nineteenth century. It was by and large a matter of statute. The concept of the common law crime, as we have seen, had been wiped out in federal law. The concept decayed on the state level, too. As of 1900, most states still *technically* recognized the possibility of a common law crime. But other states, by statute, had specifically abolished the concept. These statutes stated bluntly that only acts listed in the penal code were crimes, and nothing else. In some states, the courts *construed* their penal codes as (silently) abolishing common law crime. Where the concept survived, it was hardly ever used; the penal codes were as a practical matter complete and exclusive—the total catalog of crime.

The living law was rather more complicated. The New York penal code (enacted in 1881) provided that "no act . . . shall be deemed criminal or punishable, except as prescribed or authorized by this Code, or by some statute of this state not repealed by it." This was plain abolition. Yet, the penal code had a sweeping catchall clause: "A person, who willfully and wrongfully commits any act, which seriously injures the person or property of another, or which seriously disturbs or endangers the public peace or health, or which openly outrages public decency or is injurious to public morals . . . is guilty of a misdemeanor."[3] Prosecutors and courts conceivably had almost as much power under this language as under the reign of common law crime. In fact, the section was not used very much. Nor did the states that kept the concept of common law crime in theory actually use it much in practice.

There was, perhaps, more to the death of the common law crime than meets the eye. What died was the overt, unabashed power of courts to pull out new crimes from the folkways. It was killed by that pervasive feature in American legal culture, horror of uncontrolled power. Lawmakers believed that courts should be guided—ruled—by the words of objective law, enacted by the people's representatives; nobody else should have the power to make behavior criminal, or define some behavior as a crime. But the judges had the power to construe, to "interpret" the penal codes. This was no small power. There was an old maxim that courts had a duty to construe penal statutes narrowly. Courts constantly referred to this maxim. But it was the judges who decided, after all, what was narrow and what was wide.

Criminal justice was particularly rich in countervailing power. Police, prosecutors, trial judges, appellate judges, juries, legislatures, and prison officials, all had the power to frustrate the work of all the others. At best, they had some sort of uneasy equilibrium. The Constitution, the Bill of Rights, and the Fourteenth Amendment tried to strike a kind of balance between federal and state power. At least in legal theory, criminal trials had to be scrupulously fair. Rights of defendants were carefully safeguarded. A stern law of evidence kept juries honest; juries kept judges and the government in check; meticulous attention to procedure protected the life and liberty of citizens from injustice. Indeed, many people—legal scholars and ordinary people—thought the safeguards went too far; people worried about the coddling of criminals, and some scholars (like Roscoe

---

[3] N.Y. Penal Code 1881, secs. 2, 675.

Pound) thought they saw a "hypertrophy" of procedure—technical niceties went from the meticulous to the ridiculous.

The picture that emerged was one of precision, rigidity, and care. Nothing was a crime unless it was clearly engraved, labeled, and pasted in the statute books. Courts had a duty to construe criminal statutes as narrowly as possible. Trials had to be free of legal error. Probably no field of law, however, was quite so two-faced. The real criminal law, in part at least, was blunt, merciless, and swift; in other regards, it was sloppy and inefficient and slapdash. On the appellate level, it was true enough that high courts often reversed lower court verdicts; but only a tiny percentage of criminal cases were appealed in the first place— one half of one percent of the total prosecutions in Chippewa County, Wisconsin; about 1 percent of the felony prosecutions in Alameda County, California (1870—1910). In this period, only about 5 percent of the cases before the Wisconsin supreme court were criminal appeals.[4]

In the living law, the safeguards did not safeguard everybody—not "tramps," not the poor, not blacks in the south; it was also living law that the real criminal justice system was made up of many overlapping layers, none of which resembled very closely the ideal picture of criminal justice. There were at least three of these layers: the bottom layer, where courts handled tens of thousands of petty cases rather roughly and informally; a middle layer, for serious but ordinary cases—many thousands of assaults, burglaries, robberies, and embezzlements; and a top layer, made up of a few dramatic cases—cases where the crime was especially lurid or the defendant a prominent or unusual person, or both of these. It was a sensation when Professor John W. Webster of the Harvard Medical School went on trial, in 1850, for killing another professor, Dr. George Parkman, and chopping his body into pieces.[5] Even more sensational was the Lizzie Borden case, in the 1890s. Did Lizzie Borden, spinster, daughter of a prominent family in Fall River, Massachusetts, hack her father and stepmother to death with an axe on a stifling morning in August? The jury said no; most observers today think yes. In some ways, the Borden case was sensational because it put bourgeois respectability on trial; and the jury acquitted it. That a woman like Lizzie Borden could be guilty of such a hideous crime was simply unthinkable.[6] Whatever the ultimate meaning of the case, it attracted newspaper reporters like flies, it dominated the headlines, and the public devoured every detail. Cases of this sort were, in essence, great theater.

Everybody loves a mystery; everybody loves a courtroom drama. The great cases were also the ones in which all the stops were pulled out: juries were carefully and laboriously chosen; trials were long and crammed with detail; both

---

[4] For the Wisconsin figures: Edward L. Kimball, "Criminal Cases in a State Appellate Court: Wisconsin, 1839–1959," 9 Am. J. Legal Hist. 95, 99–100 (1965). For Alameda County: Lawrence M. Friedman and Robert V. Percival, *The Roots of Justice: Crime and Punishment in Alameda County, California, 1870–1910* (1981), p. 262. After 1880, about 5 percent of the felony convictions were appealed, and roughly one out of seven cases in which there was a jury verdict of guilty.

[5] Webster was convicted and executed, after a long trial conducted by Lemuel Shaw, Chief Justice of Massachusetts.

[6] See Cara Robertson, "Representing 'Miss Lizzie': Cultural Conviction in the Trial of Lizzie Borden," 8 Yale J. of Law and the Humanities 351 (1996).

sides marshaled evidence, introduced experts, battled and sparred on cross-examination; and due process was meticulously observed. These trials were replete with sensational events, witnesses who wept or fainted, grisly evidence and exhibits, and vast flights of purple oratory. They served, perhaps, important functions. They were "propaganda plays, plays of morality, cautionary tales." They were also the vehicle for teaching the public about law. But the public learned a curious, double message. They learned that America was scrupulous about the rights of people accused of crime. They saw that justice was real; but they also saw that it was absurd. They saw careful meticulous justice; but they also saw justice "as a ham, a mountebank, a fool."[7]

The picture was also profoundly misleading. Underneath, in the second layer, a different kind of system operated. Here, ordinary cases of assault, theft, burglary, and similar crimes were prosecuted. The trial courts, as far as we can tell, were by no means kangaroo courts; but there were no long, drawn-out trials. The "hypertrophy" of due process had no role in these courts. For many defendants, there was no trial at all. The beginnings of plea bargaining can be clearly traced to this period. Defendants in increasing numbers pleaded guilty; in some cases, there was an obvious "deal"; in others, defendants simply entered such a plea, in hopes of getting better treatment. Plea bargaining, in fact, goes back to the earlier part of the century: patient researchers have found evidence for it in Massachusetts, for example.[8] By the turn of the century, less than half of all felony defendants went to trial in some communities; in others, they were "tried," but in slapdash and routine ways, in trials that lasted a few hours or a few minutes at best. And most were convicted. In Greene County, Georgia, in the 1870s, eight out of ten blacks were found guilty; six whites out of ten.[9]

Plea bargaining did not represent some sort of decline from the golden age of trials (no such age ever existed). Rather, it was a sign of the increasing professionalization of criminal justice. During the nineteenth century, the system shifted away from its almost total reliance on amateurs and part-timers. It came to be dominated more and more by full-time crime handlers: police, detectives, prosecuting attorneys, and defense attorneys who did defense work almost exclusively, judges who mostly sat for criminal cases, and forensic experts of one sort or another. Later would come social workers, probation officers, and still more professionals. The system became more administrative, less adjudicative. In a system of this sort, the jury of amateurs had less place. *Routine* was not new; but the personnel who ran it, and the way it was run, altered dramatically.

---

[7] Lawrence M. Friedman and Robert V. Percival, *The Roots of Justice* (1981), p. 259–60.

[8] See, for example, Theodore Ferdinand, *Boston's Lower Criminal Courts, 1814–1850* (1992), pp. 89–97; George Fisher, *Plea Bargaining's Triumph: A History of Plea Bargaining in America* (2003)

[9] Edward L. Ayers, *Vengeance and Justice: Crime and Punishment in the 19th-Century American South* (1984), p. 176; Friedman and Percival, *op. cit.*, p. 173. Forty percent of the felony defendants in Alameda County pleaded guilty, in the period 1880–1910; about a fifth of the cases were dismissed or continued indefinitely; in 23 percent the jury convicted the defendant; in 16 percent the jury acquitted. On the origins of plea bargaining, see Friedman and Percival, *op. cit.*, pp. 175–81; George Fisher, *op. cit.*, n. 8; Lawrence M. Friedman, "Plea Bargaining in Historical Perspective," 13 Law & Society Rev. 247 (1979); on implicit bargaining, Milton Heumann, "A Note on Plea Bargaining and Case Pressure," 9 Law & Society Rev. 515 (1975).

Perhaps the key to the new system was the expanded role of the police. Police departments had been organized in New York and a few other large cities before the Civil War; but it was only in the period after the war that the police became a universal feature of urban criminal justice. In 1880, New York City had a force of 202 officers and 2,336 patrolmen; but even Keokuk, Iowa, population 12,117, had a police force: two officers and four patrolmen (who made 1,276 arrests between them).[10] The police were divided into ranks that had military names (captains, sergeants); and, more and more, they wore uniforms and badges. Compared to the old constables and night watchmen, the police were indeed professionals—they had a full-time job as police; but they were hardly professional in a more modern sense, at least not in most cities.[11] Almost anybody could be a policeman—there were no requirements of training or education; police departments were often often; the jobs were patronage jobs, and politics always reared its ugly head. In Cincinnati, after an election in 1880, 219 out of 295 officers were dismissed.[13] But commissioners of police also issued rule books and manuals, and there was at least some attempt at discipline—and decorum: The police commissioners of Chicago, in 1861, issued orders that "prohibited mustaches," regulated beards, and "required that all patrolmen eat with forks."[13]

By the end of the century, police were a familiar and ubiquitous feature of city life; criminal justice was unthinkable without them. They made thousands of arrests, not only for major crimes, but also for those petty offenses that jammed the dockets of the municipal courts, justice courts, and police courts—the third, bottom layer of the criminal justice system. Here justice was quick and informal. An endless stream of drunks, prostitutes, and hoboes paraded before bored judges; there were also innumerable cases of barroom brawls, domestic quarrels, and disturbances of the peace. The police patrolled the public spaces of the cities, symbolizing and maintaining order and regularity, which a modern, industrial society needed, or thought it needed. This was a period in which states passed stringent laws against beggars and "vagrants"; in the south, these laws were aimed mostly at blacks, but northern states too made it a crime to beg, or, indeed, to be homeless and unemployed.[14] In this and other regards, the police acted as a kind of civilian army; they exerted control in the interests of the respectable and the comfortable against the "dangerous classes." This included those who were actually dangerous to the established order and those (like tramps and vagrants) whose threat was largely symbolic. During periods of labor unrest, in many cities the police were enlisted to take the side of management, which they often did with great vigor—protecting "scabs," breaking up picket lines, and interfering with union activities. They practically acted as

---

[10] Lawrence M. Friedman, *Crime and Punishment in American History (1993)* p. 149.

[11] The San Francisco police were, apparently, somewhat more elite and professional than most departments, see Philip J. Ethington, "Vigilantes and the Police: the Creation of a Professional Police Bureaucracy in San Francisco, 1847–1900," 21 J. Social History 197 (1987).

[12] Samuel Walker, *Popular Justice: A History of American Criminal Justice* (1980), p. 61.

[13] David R. Johnson, *Policing the Urban Underworld: The Impact of Crime on the Development of American Police, 1800–1887* (1979), p. 94.

[14] See Amy Dru Stanley, "Beggars Can't be Choosers: Compulsion and Contract in Postbellum America," 78 J. American History 1265 (1992).

municipal strikebreakers. In Buffalo, in 1892, in a strike on the streetcar lines, the police were even accused of scabbing themselves. The union claimed that police officers acted as switchmen and helped move the trains.[15]

Police violence and irregularity formed part of what was virtually a fourth, unofficial layer of the criminal justice system. This force and violence was, strictly speaking, illegal. In the slums and tenderloins of big cities, street gangs, prostitutes, and thieves ran their American underworld, enforced their own rules, and governed their own society. Police violence was the only kind of law that ever penetrated that jungle. Alexander S. Williams, of the New York police force, became famous in the 1870s because he "invoked the gospel of the night-stick" and organized "a strong arm squad." Patrolling the Gas House District, Williams battered "thugs," "with or without provocation." Charges were preferred against Williams no less than eighteen times; but the board of police commissioners "invariably acquitted" him. He justified his "furious" drubbing with the observation that "there is more law in the end of a policeman's nightstick than in a decision of the Supreme Court."[16] As a matter of living law, he had a point.

Policing was, in any event, often a dirty business. Corruption was epidemic. The famous Lexow Committee, investigating police corruption in 1894, found massive amounts of it: payoffs from gamblers, prostitutes, poolhalls, and even pushcart vendors. This was the first of a long series of investigations: but somehow the situation never improved. Payoffs continued, because they paid off. There was a tremendous subterranean demand for illegal sex, gambling, and fringe amusements—the clergy and the respectable bourgeoisie could influence law on the books, but the streets (and the police) controlled the living law. As for police brutality, it too was widely popular. Meticulous attention to civil liberties has never been a majority view. If the police cracked a few heads, so be it. "Thugs" deserved nothing better from society.

The history of the police is, however, not all a history of darkness. They were on call twenty-four hours a day, unlike other agencies of government. Hence they acted as a kind of catch-all social agency—breaking up fights, patrolling, answering anguished calls for help. Police departments also often ran a kind of rough and ready welfare program. In many cities, police stations took in the homeless; until cities built municipal lodging houses, in the 1890s, the cold and hungry often converged on the neighborhood station house.[17]

Lawless Law

The regular criminal law had, indeed, many irregular helpers. Police brutality was not an isolated phenomenon. The Ku Klux Klan rode in the South, from 1867 to the early 1870s; it burned and pillaged and punished blacks and whites

[15] Sidney L. Harring, *Policing a Class Society: The Experience of American Cities, 1865–1915* (1983), pp. 117–18. On the work of the police in the "basement" courts, see Friedman and Percival, ch. 4; there is also material on the criminal work of justices in John R. Wunder, *Inferior Courts, Superior Justice: A History of the Justices of the Peace on the Northwest Frontier, 1853–1889* (1979).

[16] Herbert Asbury, *The Gangs of New York* (1928), pp. 235–37; in general, see Marilynn S. Johnson, *Street Justice: A History of Police Violence in New York City* (2003).

[17] Friedman, *Crime and Punishment*, p. 152.

who violated the Klan's notion of the proper social order. The vigilantes of the West, with their brand of do-it-yourself criminal justice, were in some ways following an old American tradition. The first American vigilantes, the South Carolina regulators, appeared in 1767.[18] But the movement really flourished after 1850. As we have seen, the most famous, and the models for the rest, were the two Vigilance Committees of San Francisco (1851 and 1856). Vigilante justice cropped up throughout California; in Colorado, Nevada, Oregon, Texas, and Montana; and generally in the West. "Swift and terrible retribution is the only preventive of crime, while society is organizing in the far West," wrote Thomas J. Dimsdale, chronicler of the Montana vigilantes, in 1865.[19] All told, there were hundreds of vigilante movements. One hundred and forty-one of them took at least one human life. The total death toll has been put at 729. Virtually all of this took place before 1900, and in the West. Texas was the bloodiest vigilante state; and the peak decade was the 1860s.[20]

The vigilantes were not alone in running a private system of criminal justice. Claims clubs in the Middle West, and miners' courts in the sparse, bleak reaches of the far West, constructed their own version of property law and punished offenders. Later in the century, "Judge Lynch" presided at an all-too-frequent court in the South and the border states. Mobs, in the 1890s, tortured, hanged, and sometimes burned alive black men accused of assault, murder, or rape. They sometimes snatched their victims from jail, furious at any hint of delay. Lynch mobs and vigilantes had their own sense of mission. Some vigilante groups, hungry for legitimacy, parodied the regular written law; they had their own "judges" and "juries," their own quick and summary trials. They punished crimes without names or without remedies, and enforced public policy as they saw it. They were responses to what some elites felt was an absence of law and order in parts of the West, or to the feebleness or venality of regular government. The Klan grew out of the disorganization of a defeated society. Their forms of "popular justice" were much cheaper, too, than tax-fed trials and long prison sentences. A newspaper writer, after a vigilante lynching in Golden, Colorado, in 1879, reported that "the popular verdict seemed to be that the hanging was not only well merited, but a positive gain for the county, saving at least five or six thousand dollars."[21]

The Southern lynch mobs were the most savage and the least excusable of all the self-help groups. Their law and order was naked racism, no more. Their real complaint against law was that courts were too careful and too slow; that some guilty prisoners went free; and that they did not make a sharp enough example of black criminals. The lynch mobs enforced a code that no court could be expected to enforce, not even a white-supremacist court in the rural South.

---

[18] See Joe B. Frantz, "The Frontier Tradition: An Invitation to Violence," and Richard Maxwell Brown, "The American Vigilante Tradition," in Hugh D. Graham and Ted. R. Gurr, eds., *Violence in America: Historical and Comparative Perspectives* (1969), pp. 101ff., 121ff.; Richard Maxwell Brown, *Strain of Violence: Historical Studies of American Violence and Vigilantism* (1975).

[19] Thomas J. Dimsdale, *The Vigilantes of Montana* (new edition, 1953), p. 13.

[20] Richard Maxwell Brown, "The American Vigilante Tradition," pp. 128, 130.

[21] Quoted in Richard M. Brown, *op. cit.*, p. 143.

There were instances of appalling savagery—we have referred already to the lynching of Sam House, in 1899, tortured, mutilated, and then burned.[22] Nobody today defends the lynch mobs. Western vigilantes, on the other hand, have had a more mixed press. They are still regarded with a certain sympathy, or as a necessary evil, or even as a form of popular democracy. The historian Hubert H. Bancroft heaped praises on the vigilance committees. Indeed, he loved all forms of Western justice. Vigilance, he wrote, is an "expression of power on the part of the people in the absence or impotence of law." It is "the exercise informally of their rightful power by a people wholly in sympathy with existing forms of law." It is "the keen knife in the hands of a skillful surgeon, removing the putrefaction with the least possible injury to the body politic." The San Francisco Committee of 1856, for example, was just such a surgeon: "Never before in the history of human progress have we seen, under a popular form of government, a city-full rise as one man, summoned by almighty conscience, attend at the bedside of sick law . . . and perform a speedy and almost bloodless cure."[23] Indeed, public opinion tended not to condemn the "beloved rough-necks" at all; quite the contrary. Many vigilantes were community leaders, or became community leaders. Thomas Dimsdale, the Englishman who chronicled the vigilantes of Montana— and praised them—served as the state superintendent of public instruction. Two governors of New Mexico had vigilante episodes in their past. A vigilante past was obviously no disgrace, no impediment to success.[24]

Under some conditions, self-help law can make a persuasive case. The Donner party, in 1846, tried, convicted, and banished a man named James Reed, who had killed John Snyder in a fight. The travelers were months away from Missouri—in Mexican territory, in fact—and hundreds of miles from any court, or judge, or arm of any state.[25] The ideology of self-help was strong, too, in the nineteenth century; and government was stingy. A Wisconsin law of 1861 authorized the "organization of societies for mutual protection against larcenies of live stock." The societies were given power to choose "riders" who might "exercise all the powers of constables in the arrest and detention of criminals."[26] A similar law in Pennsylvania in 1869 incorporated the "Spring Valley Police Company of Crawford County," a "company for the recovery of stolen horses and other property." Its members were to have the same powers of arrest and detention as policemen of Philadelphia.[27] The antihorsethief movement arose "spontaneously" after the Revolutionary War. From the 1850s on, the societies sought, and got, legislative authorization. They lasted until better public police and the automobile put them out of business. In their heyday, they had more than 100,000 members.[28]

Private law enforcement has often been an attractive idea, and still is: think of the tens of thousands of security guards. A statute of 1865, in Pennsylvania, gave railroads the power to employ their own police. An act of 1866 extended

[22] Leon F. Litwack, *Trouble in Mind: Black Southerners in the Age of Jim Crow* (1998), pp. 280–81.
[23] Hubert H. Bancroft, *Popular Tribunals,* vol. 1 (1887), pp. 10, 11, 16.
[24] Richard M. Brown, *op. cit.,* p. 150.
[25] John W, Caughey, *Their Majesties the Mob* (1960), p. 6.
[26] Laws Wis. 1861, ch. 222.
[27] Laws Pa. 1869, ch. 991.
[28] Richard M. Brown, "The American Vigilante Tradition," p. 148.

this law to any "colliery, furnace or rolling-mill," thus creating the "coal and iron police." The state here authorized "a veritable private army," at the request of "powerful interests." These private police—they existed in other states as well—were deadly enemies of the unions. They were "toughs," strikebreakers, inimical to organized labor.[29] The companies nominated members of the coal and iron police. The governor then appointed them. They had the same authority as city police officers.[30] It was not until the 1930s that they were finally abolished in Pennsylvania.

THE STATUTE LAW OF CRIMES

Over the years, the criminal codes, like the dollar, became markedly inflated. Traditional crimes—treason, murder, burglary, arson, and rape—stayed on the books; new crimes were constantly added. Roscoe Pound counted fifty crimes in 1822 in the Rhode Island penal code. The number had grown to 128 crimes by 1872.[31] The revised statutes of Indiana of 1881 contained more than three hundred sections under the general heading of crimes. Instead of one section about embezzlement, there were many: embezzlement of public funds, embezzlement by officers (the crime committed when "any County Treasurer, County Auditor, Sheriff, Clerk, or Receiver of any Court, Township Trustee, Justice of the Peace, Mayor of a city, Constable, Marshal of any city or incorporated town," or any other officers and agents of local government, failed to turn over or account for funds in their trust), embezzlement by employees, by "lawyers and collectors," by railroad employees, by "innkeepers and carriers," by bailees (a "storage, forwarding, or commission merchant, carrier, warehouseman, factor, auctioneer, or his clerk, agent or employee"), by agricultural tenants, by treasurers (of state or local government), by city officials, or by fiduciaries (secs. 1942–52).

The list of crimes was long; one wonders why certain acts were singled out for separate treatment—why, for example, there needed to be a specific section directed against anyone who "maliciously or mischievously" injured "any telegraph-pole or telephone-pole" (sec. 1956). There were great numbers of new economic or regulatory crimes, of a quite miscellaneous sort: shooting prairie hens or prairie chickens out of season, selling grain seed that harbored seeds of Canada thistle, swindling an underwriter, selling coal by false weight (secs. 2107, 2121, 2138, 2202). Anyone who "stretches or places any net . . . across any creek emptying into the Ohio river in this State . . . in order to prevent the ingress of fish . . . or their egress," was guilty of a crime, and liable to pay between $5 and $20 for each day the obstruction continued (sec. 2118). It was a crime to sell skimmed milk in Indiana; to dam up a stream and produce stagnant water; to sell "diseased or corrupted or unwholesome provisions" (secs. 2067, 2069, 2071).

There were also many sections concerned with public morality: sections against gambling, "bunko-steering," selling liquor on Sunday, pimping,

---

[29] J. R Shalloo, *Private Police, with Special Reference to Pennsylvania* (1933), pp 60, 62, 88.

[30] Harold W. Aurand, "Early Mine Workers' Organizations in the Anthracite Region," 58 *Pennsylvania History* 298, 301 (1991).

[31] Roscoe Pound, *Criminal Justice in America* (1930), p. 16.

adultery, and public indecency. It was a crime to "entice" any "female of pre-vious chaste character . . . to a house of ill-fame," for the "purpose of prosti-tution" (sec. 1993); it was also forbidden to deal in obscene literature. The statutes reflected a new, heightened interest in morals crimes, an interest that, as we will see, was characteristic of the late nineteenth century. It was also a crime to sell or advertise "any secret drug or nostrum purporting to be for the exclusive use of females, or which cautions females against their use when in a condition of pregnancy; or . . . any drug for preventing conception or for procuring abortion or miscarriage" (sec. 1998).[32] In addition, the code referred, in the section on crimes, to more than ninety other statutory sec-tions scattered elsewhere in the revised statutes, provisions that also imposed criminal sanctions for this or that conduct. These were tacked on to a wide variety of statutes—on maliciously killing or injuring a "registered and tagged dog" (sec. 2649), on selling intoxicating liquors to inmates of the Sol-diers' Home (sec. 2834), on violations of provisions of the "Dentistry Act" (sec. 4254), on sale of commercial fertilizers not "labeled with the State Chemist's analysis . . . or . . . labeled with a false or inaccurate analysis" (sec. 4897), and on violations of the Public Warehouse Act (sec. 6549).

What was true in Indiana was true in the other states as well. The list of crimes grew steadily. Few were ever repealed; fresh ones were constantly added. In 1891, it became a misdemeanor in Indiana to "wilfully wear the badges or buttonaire [sic] of the Grand Army of the Republic" or other veter-ans' groups unless one was "entitled to use or wear the same" under the rules and regulations of the organization. Another law required road supervisors or "Gravel Road Superintendents" to cut hedges along the highways; failure to do so was an offense, and was punishable by fine. It became a felony in that year for officers of public institutions to "purchase, sell, barter or give away to any other officer . . . or to appropriate to his or their own use any of the slops or offal of any of the said public institutions." Railroads had to employ flagmen at railroad crossings; for failure to comply, money penalties were prescribed.[33] About a dozen more distinct items of behavior became criminal, in 1891, and other, older crime laws were amended.

In every state, each extension of governmental power, each new form of reg-ulation, brought in a new batch of criminal law. Any important statute—on railroads, banks, and corporations; or the marketing of milk, cheese, fruit, or coal; or concerning taxation, elections and voting, or licensing an occupa-tion—included at the end a sentence or two imposing criminal sanctions on vi-olators. No doubt the criminal parts of these laws were never enforced at all. These statutes are really part of the history of regulation of business, rather than the history of criminal justice.

But these regulatory crimes should not be completely written off. Not that people looked on some of these forbidden forms of business behavior with a sense of moral outrage. These laws, rather, were decisions to socialize respon-sibility for enforcing certain aspects of law. This process began long before the Civil War (see above, Part II, ch. VII, pp. 239–42). Criminal law was a kind of

[32] On the development in this period of laws against abortion, see James C. Mohr, *Abor-tion in America: The Origins and Evolution of National Policy, 1800–1900* (1978).

[33] Laws Ind. 1891, ch. 33, 39, 146, 150.

low-level, low-paid administrative aid. New York, in 1898, amended its penal code to make it a misdemeanor to sell articles as "sterling silver" unless they consisted of 925/1000ths of pure silver.[34] The buyer still had his action for fraud; the criminal sanction was simply added on. Criminal sanctions, of course, were no substitute for sustained, efficient bureaucratic control; rather, they were a small step in that direction. These statutes are part of the obscure but important history of nineteenth-century regulation in the states.[35]

VICTIMLESS CRIMES

The Indiana statutes, as we have seen, contained many provisions on morality and vice. Not much in general is known about whether and how these laws were enforced. Some of them may have almost been dead letters. In the late nineteenth century, however, there was a strong resurgence of laws about sex, morality, and so-called victimless crimes.

Colonial law, as we saw, was much concerned with sexual conduct, especially fornication. The early nineteenth century was a kind of dead point, a lull in the war against vice. The major concern of criminal justice was property offenses, especially theft. Adultery (for example) remained a crime; but its nature was subtly redefined. In some states it was illegal only if it was "open and notorious"; this was true of California, for example.[36] What was illegal, then, was not sin itself—and certainly not secret sin—but sin that offended *public* morality. This was what we might call the Victorian compromise: a certain toleration for vice, or at least a resigned acceptance, so long as it remained in an underground state.[37] If the crime was fornication, rather than adultery, the criminal law was even sometimes willing to forgive, if the miscreants did the right thing and got married. In Florida, for example, a "marriage legally solemnized" might bring about a suspension of prosecution. In 1851, one Lewis Sparkman got out of custody when it "appeared to the court that the defendant had intermarried with the female with whom he is charged."[38]

The strange status of prostitution was another case in point of the Victorian compromise. Curiously enough, prostitution itself was not always criminalized, though owning or running a brothel almost always was. In many cities, so-called brothel riots took place—another example of self-help—as respectable citizens tried to take the law into their own hands and stamp out these cesspools of

[34] Laws N.Y. 1898, ch. 330.

[35] See, in general, William J. Novak, *The People's Welfare: Law and Regulation in Nineteenth-Century America* (1996).

[36] Cal. Penal Code, 1872, sec. 266a; Ill. Crim. Code 1874, ch. 38, sec. 11 used the phrase "open state of adultery or fornication." On the history of victimless crime, see Lawrence M. Friedman, *Crime and Punishment in American History* (1993), ch. 6.

[37] Mark M. Carroll, writing about Texas in the middle of the nineteenth century, expresses a rather different notion. Open and notorious adultery inevitably meant desertion. Thus, the statute worked to discourage desertion. Mark M. Carroll, *Homesteads Ungovernable: Families, Sex, Race, and the Law in Frontier Texas, 1823–1860* (2001), p. 151.

[38] James M. Denham, *"A Rogue's Paradise": Crime and Punishment in Antebellum Florida, 1821–1861* (1997), p. 105.

vice.[39] Yet the "social evil" was a flourishing business; one contemporary in New York claimed that the city in 1866 had ninety-nine "houses of assignation" and 2,690 prostitutes, along with "waiter girls" of "bad character" by the hundreds, and "vile" barmaids to boot. A bishop of the Methodist church, in a speech at the Cooper Union, claimed that there were as many prostitutes as Methodists in the City.[40] The police did not, as a rule, interfere; instead, they collected payoffs or "protection fees." As early as 1839, it was possible for potential customers and out-of-towners to buy published guidebooks to New York's houses of prostitution. The first one, hypocritically entitled "Prostitution Exposed," and claiming to be a "moral reform directory, laying bare the lives, histories, residences, seductions of the most celebrated courtezans and ladies of pleasure," was written by someone who took the wonderful alias of "A. Butt Ender."[41] New York was not unique. Indeed, in most American cities, prostitution was tacitly accepted, at least so long as it stayed in its place. Its place was the so-called red-light district. Some cities—New Orleans was one—even passed ordinances that defined the boundaries of these districts, districts in which illegal vice was, if not legal, at least immune from destructive raids.[42] San Antonio, Texas, even tried to collect license fees from "bawdy-houses," although the ordinance failed a court test. Licensing an illegal business was too much for the judges to swallow.[43] But "protection money" paid to the police, in many cities, functioned as a kind of license fee. Or the "license" consisted of a monthly fine: This was the case in the 1890s in Sioux City, Iowa—madams, prostitutes, gambling house operators, and saloon keepers paid these "fines," each month, in exchange for an (unspoken) promise by the authorities not to shut them down.[44] Bills to regulate prostitution, particularly to control the spread of venereal disease, were discussed in New York in the 1870s; nothing came of it. St. Louis tried a licensing and regulation system; but this was only a brief experiment. Cries of horror resounded throughout the state, and the legislation shut the experiment down.[45]

Nobody planned or intended what we have called the Victorian compromise. It simply happened. It happened because many men (and some women) were unable or unwilling to live the life of respectable bourgeois society every day and every hour. There was a tremendous underground demand for gambling, drink, risque theater, and all forms of nonmarital sex. Yet, outright legalization was impossible. High-minded people opposed it. And even many low-minded people preferred a system of don't ask don't tell. Officially abandoning traditional morality was unthinkable. Vice in the nineteenth century was a little bit like speeding on the highway today: most everybody violates,

[39] On brothel riots, see John C. Schneider, *Detroit and the Problem of Order; 1830–1880* (1980).

[40] Matthew Hale Smith, *Sunshine and Shadow in New York* (1880), pp. 371–72.

[41] Timothy J. Gilfoyle, *City of Eros: New York City, Prostitution, and the Commercialization of Sex, 1790–1920* (1992), p. 131.

[42] The New Orleans ordinance even reached the attention of the U.S. Supreme Court, *L'Hote v. New Orleans*, 177 U.S. 587 (1900).

[43] See *Ex parte* Garza, 28 Tex. App. 381, 13 S.W 779 (1890).

[44] William L. Hewitt, "Wicked Traffic in Girls: Prostitution and Reform in Sioux City, 1885–1910," 51 Annals of Iowa 123, 131 (1991).

[45] Marilynn Wood Hill, *Their Sisters' Keepers: Prostitution in New York City, 1830–1870* (1993), p. 138; on the short-lived attempt, in St. Louis, to institute medical inspection, see Mark T. Connelly, *The Response to Prostitution in the Progressive Era* (1980), p. 5.

from time to time; but even the violators are mostly strong believers in the laws against speeding. Without these laws, there would be chaos on the highways.

By the late nineteenth century, the Victorian compromise began to break down. A new, intense concern with victimless crime developed. In the 1870s, societies "for the suppression of vice" sprang up everywhere. The Boston group, later called the Watch and Ward Society, was particularly vigorous.[46] In 1873, Congress passed the so-called Comstock Law. The law made it a crime to send any "obscene, lewd, or lascivious" book in the mail—or any "article or thing designed or intended for the prevention of conception or procuring of abortion."[47] The law gets its nickname from Anthony Comstock, a private citizen who waged an unending battle against smut and vice. Many states passed their own versions of the Comstock law.[48] Gambling was the target of other moral reformers. Mostly, these gambling wars were local struggles; on the national scene there was a furious battle over lotteries. At one time, state governments used the lottery freely to raise money for new courthouses, internal improvements, and the like. But moral leaders constantly railed against the lotteries. By the time of the Civil War, legal lotteries existed only in Delaware and Kentucky. In 1868, however, Louisiana chartered a lottery company, as a state monopoly. The Kentucky lottery was a national success; the winning numbers were picked by blindfolded orphan boys, escorted by nuns. This was not enough to guarantee respectability. Kentucky got rid of its lottery in 1890.[49] In the 1890s, too, Congress prohibited the sale of lottery tickets across state lines; this was the final, decisive blow against the lottery.[50]

After 1870, the purity campaign led to a demand for more control over sexual behavior in general. One sign of success was change in the statutory age of consent. The age of consent determined whether a crime called "statutory rape" had taken place. All sexual intercourse below the age of consent was legally rape, whether the girl was willing or not. The age of consent, at common law, was ten—which strikes us as absurdly low. On the other hand, in the late nineteenth century, the states began to raise the age. In California, for example, the age of consent was fourteen in 1889, sixteen in 1897; ultimately, the age was fixed at eighteen, which strikes us as a bit on the high side. As a result, teenage sex was, for the male, a serious crime, at least on the books. Even if he, too, was (say) sixteen, and the sex was completely consensual, she was officially labeled a victim, and he was guilty of a serious crime.[51] This was a nationwide development. In 1885, no state had an age of consent above twelve—in the vast majority, the age was still ten (seven in Delaware!); by 1920, it was eighteen in twenty states, and sixteen in all the rest (except Georgia's fourteen).[52]

One vice, however, dominated public agitation: the curse of drink. Liquor sale had been regulated continuously. Every state had laws about the who, how,

---

[46] See David J. Pivar, *Purity Crusade: Sexual Morality and Social Control, 1868–1900* (1973).

[47] 17 Stats. 598 (act of March 3, 1873).

[48] Andrea Tone, *Devices and Desires: A History of Contraceptives in America* (2001), pp. 23–24.

[49] James C. Klotter, "Two Centuries of the Lottery in Kentucky," 87 Register of the Kentucky Historical Society 405 (1989).

[50] John S. Ezell, *Fortune's Merry Wheel: The Lottery in America* (1960).

[51] Laws Cal. 1889, ch. 191, p. 223; Laws Cal. 1897, ch. 139, p. 201.

[52] Mary E. Odem, *Delinquent Daughters, Protecting and Policing Adolescent Female Sexuality in the United States, 1885–1920* (1995), pp. 14–15.

and when of liquor consumption, and about the business of running a tavern and selling liquor. There were periodic temperance outbursts. In 1887, six states were legally dry: Iowa, Kansas, Maine, New Hampshire, Rhode Island, and Vermont.[53] The temperance movement never gave up fighting against the evils of drink. The movement endured many defeats, had many triumphs, and ultimately won a stunning victory, national prohibition, in 1920.[54] Joseph Gusfield has argued that the crusade against liquor was a "symbolic crusade." The point lay less in whether people drank or not, than in making temperance official policy and the official standard of morality. The issue was: whose norms were dominant, whose norms should be labeled right and true: those of old-line, middle-class, Protestant America, or those of Catholics, immigrants, the working class, and city folk, all of whom drank without shame.[55]

Much about this thesis is attractive: It turns the struggle into a kind of Kulturkampf, in a time of rapid social change, a time in which new immigration was changing the demographic face of America. It was also a period of urbanization—the threat to old American values came not only from immigrants, but from the children of the solid yeoman farmers, who moved to the cities and rejected the norms of the American gothic. Neat parallels can be drawn to other areas of struggle over law. Divorce, for example, comes to mind.

To be sure, in many of the struggles, the moral side also had a clear instrumental value as well. The sleepy old Sunday laws, for example, received new vigor in part because unions wanted them enforced; they wanted a shorter work week, and Sunday laws were a useful tool toward this end. Ministers and preachers acted as willing accomplices; labor and religion formed an odd but understandable coalition. In Philadelphia, for example, the barber's union formed a Sunday closing committee. The committee ran a campaign against barbers who would not cooperate; 239 of these were arrested in the two-year period starting December 1898.[56] In New York City, in the 1890s, when Theodore Roosevelt was president of the police board, he vigorously enforced the laws that made saloons close their doors on Sundays; bakers and barbers demanded enforcement for *their* trades, too, though with mediocre results.[57] Connecticut passed a tightened Sunday law in 1897; the statute increased the fines that could be imposed for violation, and lengthened the hours of the ban. Between twelve o'clock Saturday night and twelve o'clock Sunday night all shops, warehouses, and factories had to stay closed.

Even laws about sex and vice had a strong practical base; people understood more about venereal diseases than they had at the beginning of the century. Prostitution was a public health problem, as well as a matter of morals. But it would be wrong to dismiss the symbolic, ideological element of these laws. If, in regard to Sunday laws, the ministers were tools of the unions, so too were the

[53] Livingston Hall, "The Substantive Law of Crimes, 1887–1936," 50 Harv. L. Rev. 616, 633 (1937).

[54] On the background, see Richard F. Hamm, *Shaping the 18th Amendment: Temperance Reform, Legal Culture, and the Polity, 1880–1920* (1995).

[55] See Joseph Gusfield, *Symbolic Crusade: Status Politics and the American Temperance Movement* (1963).

[56] 12 Barbers' Journal 28 (1902).

[57] Howard L. Hurwitz, *Theodore Roosevelt and Labor in New York State, 1880–1900* (1943), pp. 149–54.

unions tools of the ministers. The laws were never purely instrumental. The Connecticut Sunday law, for example, also outlawed sports on Sunday, which was hardly an economic matter.[58] The culture clash that Gusfield saw seems real enough. And perhaps there was something more. Criminal justice over the years had become, in a way, more democratic. The social base of power had broadened. Power flowed to a large, compact, middle-class mass; this class, by the end of the century, had moral as well as economic strength. High-minded people believed in one society, one community, one universal moral code—a code which applied to *everybody,* even the poor, even the *lumpenproletariat.* Elites—aristocrats–tend to react to the behavior of the lower orders with a kind of bored tolerance. The triumphant middle-class expected and demanded more.

It was one thing to pass laws about morality; enforcement was quite another. The reader in the twenty-first century does not have to be told that crusades against vice never quite succeed; all the Prohibitions, of whatever stamp, have had to taste the bitter fruit of failure and obloquy. Comstock, fresh from his statutory triumph, arranged for the arrest of one George Brinckerhoff in 1873, who sold contraceptives by mail (under the name of "Ladies Rubber Goods"). Brinckerhoff pleaded not guilty (although he obviously *was* guilty); and to Comstock's disgust, the prosecutor dropped the charges.[59] Contraceptives continued to be sold—and more or less openly. In general, forbidden acts managed to survive. Often they flourished. Still, even "unenforceable" laws were never uniformly unenforced. A symbol loses power when it is only a symbol and nothing more. The evidence suggests that blue laws and liquor laws had meaning, and some bite, at particular times and places. Even in New York, Boston, and Philadelphia, there were occasional arrests and prosecutions for adultery, in the middle of the nineteenth century.[60] Francis Laurent collected figures for the flow of court business in the lower courts of Chippewa County, Wisconsin. Between 1855 and 1894, sex-law prosecutions were extremely rare, but they never fell to zero. There were five cases of incest, nine of adultery, four of fornication, one of lewd and lascivious behavior. Fifteen accusations of prostitution were brought, all within one decade. There were sixty-one prosecutions for violation of liquor-control laws; fifty occurred in one year, 1871.[61] Perhaps laws against immorality were useful ways to "get" somebody or were invoked against some unusually flagrant or unlucky offender. One wonders about the one man who, alone in a forty-year period, was officially lewd and lascivious. What had he done, and how was he caught? Laws came to life during the occasional crackdowns—on gambling, liquor, or prostitution. And crackdowns were most likely to occur after some scandal or when a strong organization, like the Women's Christian Temperance Union, with a firm political base, exerted its pressure. Arrests for drunkenness were high in the nineteenth

---

[58] Laws Conn. 1897, ch. 188. The statute excepted, as was usual, "works of necessity or mercy."

[59] Andrea Tone, *Devices and Desires,* p. 25.

[60] For the figures, see William Francis Kuntz II, *Criminal Sentencing in Three Nineteenth-Century Cities* (1988).

[61] Francis Laurent, *The Business of a Trial Court,* pp. 37, 122, 125.

century, and rose dramatically between 1860 and 1900, at least in one jurisdiction, Massachusetts, where the matter has been carefully studied.[62]

CRIME, CRIME RATES, INSANITY, THE GUILTY MIND

Each society defines for itself what behaviors it will label as crimes. Obviously, in one sense, society chooses how much crime it wants. If its code declares some act to be criminal, then the actors are themselves criminals. In 1900, there was vastly more criminal law on the books than in 1850 or 1800, hence in this narrow sense more crime. But people who worry about the crime rate are thinking not of economic crime, or even morals crimes, but about the classic crimes of violence and social disruption, murder, rape, robbery, burglary, assault. These are enforced more systematically and with greater use of public resources than other kinds of crime. The definitions of these crimes remained more or less constant during the century, or at least constant enough for meaningful comparisons, if only the figures were at hand.

Some facts are known about crime in the real world in the nineteenth century. What evidence there is suggests that the crime rate for serious crimes, at least after 1860, gradually declined.[63] Violence, murder, and assaults were less of a problem in the late nineteenth century, and well into the twentieth, than they had been before. Roger Lane's research, for Massachusetts, found a marked falling-off in jail commitments, from 333 per 100,000 population to 163, between 1860 and 1900. There are pitfalls and traps in the data; but studies in other places tend to confirm Lane's conclusions.[64] Erik Monkkonen's figures for New York City show that the murder rate spiked upward in the 1850s. Then came a rapid decline. There was a relatively low rate of homicide in the rest of the nineteenth century.[65] The social investment in crime fighting increased; so, too, did the worry and the tumult over crime. Violent crime, particularly in the cities, is intolerable in an interdependent, industrial society, at least above a certain minimum. The city is the heart of modern society; society is governed from the city; the economy depends on city life. The city is the place where people confront strangers most continuously, where their lives, property, and health are

---

[62] Roger Lane, "Urbanization and Criminal Violence in the 19th Century: Massachusetts as a Test Case," in Hugh D. Graham and Ted R. Gurr, eds., *Violence in America: Historical and Comparative Perspectives* (1969), pp. 361–62; see also Eric H. Monkkonen, "A Disorderly People? Urban Order in the Nineteenth and Twentieth Centuries," 68 J. Am. Hist. 539 (1981).

[63] Roger Lane, "Urbanization and Criminal Violence in the 19th Century, p. 361.

[64] This is, to be sure, a vexed and difficult subject. It is discussed in Eric H. Monkkonen, *Police in Urban America, 1860–1920* (1981), ch. 2; see also Lawrence M. Friedman and Robert V. Percival, *The Roots of Justice*, pp. 27–35; Elwin H. Powell, "Crime as a Function of Anomie," 57 J. Crim. Law, Criminology, & Police Sci. 161 (1966) (Buffalo, 1854–1956); Eric H. Monkkonen, "A Disorderly People? Urban Order in the Nineteenth and Twentieth Centuries," 68 J. Am. Hist. 539 (1981); and, for cities outside the United States, Ted R. Gurr and Peter N. Grabosky, *Rogues, Rebels and Reformers: A Political History of Urban Crime and Conflict* (1976).

[65] Eric H. Monkkonen, *Murder in New York City* (2001), p. 19.

most at hazard. A society that is heavily urban and industrial, with extreme division of labor, must invest in controlling violent crime. Crime is bad for business, and bad for the social order. The city civilizes and tames, to a certain extent; for this reason violence apparently diminished in the course of the nineteenth century. But crime did not go down fast enough for some people; the public demand for law and order, perhaps, more than kept pace with supply.[66]

Violent crimes were also the stuff of mystery and drama; these were the crimes that provided raw material for novels, poems, and plays; the crimes par excellence, in the public conception of crime. Pamphlets, trial transcripts, last words of condemned men, were part of American popular culture. There were hundreds of these fugitive writings: John Erpenstein, who gave his wife a bread-and butter sandwich liberally sprinkled with arsenic, was credited with writing the "Life, Trial, Execution and Dying Confession of John Erpenstein, Convicted of Poisoning His Wife, and Executed in Newark, N.J., on March 30, 1852. Written by himself and translated from the German." The great Harvard murder mystery, the Parkman-Webster case, was notorious (and commercially significant); publishers rushed into print with transcripts and other material to satisfy the public's hunger for sensation. The Fall River tragedy—the murder of Lizzie Borden's parents in 1892—has enlivened American literature ever since.[67] The penny press, the mass-circulation newspapers, fed the appetites of the public.[68]

It was this type of crime, too, which evoked the raw hatred that could mold a mob and lead a man to be lynched. It was this type of crime in which trial by jury was frequent, and in which the jury was free to apply its "unwritten laws," in which justice was, in theory, tailored to the individual case. These were also the cases that invoked the insanity defense. Criminal law assumes a *mens rea*—a guilty mind. If the mind is deranged, or gone, there can be no criminal responsibility. This was the official law. Juries, to be sure, mostly went their own way; they excused men for insanity, or did not excuse them, in accordance with their own moral code and common sense, rather than the science of their time. But those scientific notions had at least a marginal and indirect effect. And in the nineteenth century, almost for the first time, lawyers and doctors engaged in a grand and continuing debate about the meaning of criminal responsibility and the scope of the insanity defense.

The dominant definition of legal insanity was the so-called M'Naghten rule, named after a mad Englishman; the rule was first announced in 1843, in M'Naghten's case.[69] Simply put, a defendant was not criminally responsible if he was "labouring under such a defect of reason . . . as not to know the nature and

---

[66] Interestingly, the same study by Lane which suggests a decline in arrests for major offenses in Massachusetts suggests an equally striking increase in arrests for minor offenses, mainly drunkenness. This suggests a certain diminished tolerance for what is defined as antisocial behavior; Eric Monkkonen, on the other hand, in "A Disorderly People?" *supra*, found a decline in drunkenness and disorderly conduct arrests after 1860.

[67] The examples above are drawn from Thomas M. McDade, *The Annals of Murder, A Bibliography of Books and Pamphlets on American Murders from Colonial Times to 1900* (1961), pp. 35–37, 87, 311–16.

[68] See Andie Tucher, *Froth and Scum: Truth, Beauty, Goodness, and the Ax Murder in America's First Mass Medium* (1994); Karen Halttunen, *Murder Most Foul: The Killer and the American Gothic Imagination* (1998).

[69] *M'Naghten's Case*, 10 Cl. & F. 200 (1843).

quality of the act he was doing; or . . . that he did not know what he was doing was wrong." This "right or wrong" test was a kind of pleasing platitude; but in any event, it won rapid acceptance in the United States. In a few states, this "right or wrong" test was supplemented by another, the "irresistible impulse" or "wild beast" test. If a man, said Chief Justice John F. Dillon of Iowa in 1868, knew that his act was wrong, but "was driven to it by an uncontrollable and irresistible impulse, arising, not from natural passion, but from an insane condition of the mind," he was not to be held responsible.[70] The idea of irresistible impulse strikes the modern ear as somewhat romantic, not to say medically absurd; but the wild-beast test allowed a broader definition of insanity than the M'Naghten test alone; and some of the best psychiatrists of the day believed in irresistible impulse.[71] A third rule stood all by itself in New Hampshire. This was Chief Justice Charles Doe's rule, enunciated in *State v. Pike* (1869). Here the test was no test at all: the question in each case was whether the criminal act was the "offspring or product of mental disease." In Doe's view, neither delusion, nor knowledge of right and wrong, as a matter of law, should be the test of mental disease. Rather, all symptoms and "all tests of mental disease" were "purely questions of fact," within the province and power of the jury, to determine and decide.[72]

Arguments over these various "tests" were really arguments over the form of stereotyped instructions that the judge read to or told to the jury. The tests seemed to vary the degree of power they gave to the jury, and the extent to which they deferred to the "science" of psychiatry, then in its infancy. Whether the jury listened, or cared, or understood the rather subtle differences in wording is another question. In a few great cases, the tests acted as a dark and bloody battle ground for struggles between contending schools of psychiatry. Most notable was the weird trial of Charles Guiteau, who murdered President Garfield in 1881. Guiteau's behavior, before and after (and during) the trial, was bizarre, to say the least; but probably no test, however worded, could have persuaded the jury not to send to the gallows a man who had murdered the president.[73]

The debates in some ways were signs of a heightened moral sensitivity among professionals in the criminal law system. At least they implied that mentally incompetent people were not to be locked up in prison or put to death. But psychiatry was hardly an exact science. And some of its fashionable concepts seemed to threaten the very foundations of criminal law. One such concept was "moral insanity"—insanity that affected, not the reason, but the subject's emotional and moral life. This concept, carried to its ultimate logic, might have destroyed the bases on which popular ideas of criminal responsibility rested.[74] Then as now people found it hard to accept any doctrine that seemed to give people an excuse for gross, hateful, or heinous behavior.

[70] *State v. Felter*, 25 Iowa, 67, 82 (1868).

[71] On contemporary tests of insanity see, in general, Joel P Bishop, *Commentaries on the Criminal Law*, vol. 1 (6th ed., 1877), pp. 213—29.

[72] John P. Reid, *Chief Justice: The Judicial World of Charles Doe* (1967), pp. 114–21; *State v. Pike*, 49 N.H. 399, 442 (1869).

[73] The story of this trial has been beautifully recreated in Charles Rosenberg's *Trial of the Assassin Guiteau* (1968).

[74] See Janet A. Tighe, "Francis Wharton and the Nineteenth-Century Insanity Defense: The Origins of a Reform Tradition," 27 Am. J. Legal Hist. 223 (1983).

On the other hand, juries were inclined to be lenient to people whose crimes seemed justified—even when the letter of the law seemed to admit of no exceptions. In a few notorious cases, juries applied the "unwritten law"—excusing men who (for example) killed their wife's lover. They sometimes covered this up with the figleaf of "temporary insanity." One of the earliest, and most dramatic of these instances, was the trial of Daniel Sickles, a Congressman, for murder, in 1859. Sickles had a young wife; and she took a lover, Philip Barton Key (his father had written the Star-Spangled Banner). Sickles got his gun and shot Key dead on the streets of Washington. Yet a jury acquitted Sickles, in almost indecent haste.[75]

We have already talked about the use of criminal law in the policing of regulatory offenses. These crimes lacked the passion of ordinary criminal law. For normal crimes, the prosecution had to show a specific intent to act illegally. There had to be "a definite motive of hatred, revenge, or cruelty, as well as an intent to cause the injury." But this requirement of a *mens rea* was inappropriate for some regulatory crimes. It was the behavior itself that had to be controlled; the state of the actor's mind was much less relevant or downright irrelevant. Take, for example, the question whether a corporation could be guilty of a crime. Could a corporation form an "intent" to commit a crime? At one time, a corporation could not be indicted at all; and as late as the 1850s, scattered cases held that corporations were criminally liable only for acts or omissions that did not require a criminal "intent."[76] Of course, corporations did not commit rape or treason; but corporations (and other businesses) could be tried and convicted under statutes that punished economic or regulatory crimes—creating a nuisance, charging too much interest, breaking the Sabbath, or, as in one case, "permitting gaming upon its fairgrounds."[77]

For ordinary crimes, there is (in theory at least) a presumption of innocence. The state must prove guilt, and beyond a reasonable doubt. But for some crimes, the presumption of innocence or regularity was turned topsy-turvy by statute. The object was to toughen the regulatory blade of the criminal law. In the New York penal code, the "insolvency of a moneyed corporation" was "deemed fraudulent" unless "its affairs appear, upon investigation, to have been administered fairly, legally, and with care and diligence" (sec. 604). In Indiana, under a law of 1891, when a bank failed or suspended within thirty days of accepting a deposit, there was a prima-facie case of "intent to defraud" the depositor.[78] There was some no-nonsense toughness in liquor statutes, too. Dry states outlawed the sale of hard liquor; but it was not easy to catch violators red-handed. So, in New Hampshire it was "*prima facie* evidence" of violation of liquor laws if the defendant "exposed" any bottles with liquor labels "in the windows of, or upon the shelves within his place of business," or if his store had a "sign, placard, or other advertisement" for liquor, or if he possessed coupon receipts showing he had paid his federal tax as a dealer or wholesaler in liquor, or if a person delivered liquor "in or from any store, shop, warehouse, steamboat . . . or any

---

[75] See Nat Brandt, *The Congressman Who Got Away With Murder* (1991).

[76] Livingston Hall, *op. cit.*, p. 647.

[77] *Commonwealth v. Pulaski County Agricultural & Mechanical Assn.*, 92 Ky. 197, 17 S.W. 442 (1891).

[78] See *State v. Beach*, 147 Ind. 74, 46 N.E. 145 (1897).

shanty or tent . . . or any dwellinghouse . . . if any part . . . be used as a public eating-house, grocery, or other place of common resort." In Iowa, possession of liquor, "except in a private dwelling house," created a presumption of guilt.[79] These laws were attempts to get at crimes that were in practice very hard to prove. For this reason, the state can and does outlaw ownership of burglary tools, or skeleton keys, or under modern laws, "drug paraphernalia."

PUNISHMENT AND CORRECTION

A movement to humanize punishment, to make it less barbarous, might seem ironic in the age of the nightstick— and of lynch law. But social behavior is rarely even or consistent. Police, prison guards, and racist mobs could act with callous indifference to suffering and pain; while another cohort, of jurists, penal experts, and respectable citizens, were working to soften the treatment of criminals, before and after jail.

The official use of capital punishment declined in the last half of the nineteenth century. Wisconsin entered statehood without any death penalty at all. Michigan abolished it in 1882, except for treason; Maine eliminated the death penalty completely in 1887, and practically speaking, it was absent in Rhode Island, too.[80] Corporal punishment (whipping and flogging) survived in a few states—in Delaware for example —as a kind of abominable relic. Elsewhere, even in the South, its legitimacy was slowly sapped. Though whipping was still legal in South Carolina up to the Civil War, a "cloud of disapproval" made public whipping of whites a rare event (black slaves, on the other hand, were routinely whipped).[81] By 1900, except for convicts, whipping was almost extinct in the South, at least as a legitimate punishment; in fact, prisoners, especially on the chain gang, were commonly brutalized and whipped.

Death itself was brought somewhat up to date when the so-called "electrical chair" appeared in New York in 1888, to replace the hangman's noose. This was in a way the end point of the process that had started earlier in the century as a reaction against public executions. Polite opinion no longer thought a nice hanging in the public square was morally uplifting and downright educational; in the hurly-burly of nineteenth century cities, with fear of "the mob" running high, these spectacles were condemned as brutal, atavistic, mere catering to the blood lust of the lower orders. Executions were moved into the prison yard, walled off from the public. But not walled off enough. Each county hung its own prisoners; crowds of visitors sometimes climbed trees and tall buildings to peek in on the show in the yard of the local jail. The electric chair made real privacy possible. In California, for example, in 1891, county executions were banned; all executions were to be carried out within the gloomy walls of San Quentin before the warden, a doctor, the attorney general, twelve "respectable

[79] William C. Osborn, "Liquor Statutes in the United States," 2 Harv. L. Rev. 125, 126 (1888). Stats. N.H. 1878, ch. 109, secs. 24, 25; Iowa Code 1873, sec. 1542.

[80] On capital punishment in this period, and in general, see Stuart Banner, *The Death Penalty: An American History* (2002).

[81] Jack K. Williams, *Vogues in Villainy: Crime and Retribution in Ante-Bellum South Carolina* (1959), p. 110.

citizens," a few relatives and friends, peace officers—and nobody else.[82] In many states, executions took place at night. A Minnesota law of 1889 not only insisted on night-time executions; it banned reporters as well; and newspapers were allowed to print only the fact of the execution, but none of the details.[83] So much for freedom of the press.

The death penalty was a rare and dreadful punishment. Most convicted criminals either paid a fine or went to prison. By and large, fines were for petty offenses and economic crimes. In the justice and municipal courts, thousands of men and women paid a few dollars for the privilege of being drunk or disorderly or for violating some municipal ordinance. If they could not pay, to be sure, they worked off the fine with days or weeks or months in the local jail. For more serious crimes—manslaughter, assault with a deadly weapon, burglary, rape—the basic punishment everywhere was prison. The penitentiary system had carried the day. Sentences for particular crimes—say, burglary—varied from state to state; and perhaps from judge to judge; but the basic idea was the same—incarceration within the gloomy walls of the penitentiary.

The New Penology[84]

Solitary confinement, hard labor, strict discipline, regimentation, and total silence: These were at the very heart of penal theory, as it developed in the first half of the nineteenth century. All of these, acting together, were supposed to have a marvelous effect on the criminal's psyche and character. The results, however, were distinctly disappointing. In any event, the states had great trouble keeping to the strict recipe that penologists prescribed. Massachusetts dropped the silent system as early as the 1840s.[85] Penitentiaries were expensive to build and maintain; the states never provided enough cells; and as soon as more than one prisoner was put in a cell, the silent system was doomed. The original scheme was losing its grip. Something new was needed.

The old penology had treated all prisoners alike. The new theories tailored (or tried to tailor) punishment and correction to the individual case. The aim was to make criminal justice perhaps more humane; but certainly more precise and effective. Some men and women were beyond reformation; they were rotten to the core. Others might yet be saved. The new techniques and institutions tried to distinguish between these two crucial categories.

A key device of the new penology was probation. In 1841, a bootmaker named John Augustus began to frequent the Boston criminal courts. In August 1841, his heart was touched by the case of a "ragged and wretched looking" drunk. This man, Augustus felt, was "not yet past all hope of reformation." The man swore he would not touch another drop if he could only be "saved from the House of Correction." Augustus stepped up, went bail for the man, and

---

[82] Friedman and Percival, *The Roots of Justice*, pp. 304–6.

[83] Laws Minn. 1889, ch. 20; John D. Bessler, *Death in the Dark: Midnight Executions in America* (1997), pp. 98–99.

[84] See Lawrence M. Friedman, *Crime and Punishment*, pp. 159–166.

[85] Michael S. Hindus, *Prison and Plantation: Crime, Justice, and Authority in Massachusetts and South Carolina, 1767–1878* (1980), p. 169.

brought him back to court three weeks later, "a sober man." The judge, impressed as always by repentance, waived imprisonment. From this point on, Augustus began to act as a private angel and guardian for men convicted of crime. He bailed almost two thousand convicts until his death in 1859. Other Bostonians had helped him out or had given him money; some of these carried on his work after his death. In 1878, a Massachusetts statute provided for the appointment of a paid probation officer for the Boston criminal courts. A further law in 1891 authorized a statewide system. Between 1897 and 1900, Missouri, Vermont, Rhode Island, and New Jersey also enacted probation laws; Illinois and Minnesota provided for juvenile probation. Probation only came into its own in the twentieth century; but the seeds had been planted by 1900.[86]

Probation was an alternative to prison. The key notion was to sift through the facts, to examine the life of a man or women convicted of crime, and to decide whether he or she was sound enough human material to deserve another chance. It focused, in short, on the offender, rather than simply on the offense. Punishment was to fit the criminal, and not only the crime. The same ethos underlay a number of other reforms: the suspended sentence, indeterminate sentence, and parole. These served, too, as more professionalized substitutes for that older method of grace, the governor's pardon. (The pardon, to be sure, did not by any means die out.) A judge had always had power to suspend a sentence if he felt that the trial had miscarried. But could judges suspend a sentence, after a trial that was scrupulously fair, simply to give the defendant a second chance? The question was litigated in a New York case in 1894.[87] The defendant, John Attridge, a "clerk in a mercantile firm," had helped himself to his employer's money. He pleaded guilty at the trial. Attridge was young and well liked; and there were a number of "mitigating circumstances." "Numerous respectable citizens" of Monroe County petitioned the court for a suspended sentence. Two out of three of the judges agreed to suspend; and the highest court in the state affirmed their decision, on appeal. The power to suspend sentence, said the appeal court, was "inherent" in criminal courts.[88]

Indeterminate sentence and parole were more significant, more institutionalized reforms. An American Prison Association was formed after the Civil War; and the so-called "Cincinnati Declaration" came out of the first meeting of this group; it called for sentencing reform. The earliest practical applications were in New York, in the 1870s, at the Elmira "reformatory." By law, Elmira received only young offenders, between the ages of sixteen and thirty, "not known to have been previously sentenced to a State prison," in New York or elsewhere.[89] Prisoners at Elmira were given indeterminate sentences, that is, sentences of variable (and unpredictable) length. In Elmira, the prisoners were supposed to learn trades; the prison furnished programs of religious and moral uplift. The prisoners were divided into several "classes"; those who behaved and showed progress could move into a higher class; bad prisoners moved down. The best prisoners, in the highest class, were eligible for parole.

[86] David Dressler, *Practice and Theory of Probation and Parole* (1959), pp. 13–21.
[87] *People ex rel. Forsyth v. Court of Sessions of Monroe County,* 141 N.Y. 288, 36 N.E. 386(1894).
[88] Legal doubts about the power of courts to suspend sentence continued in the early twentieth century and were only laid to rest in some states by statute.
[89] Laws N.Y. 1870, ch. 427, sec. 9.

A few states copied the idea; and in 1901, New York made it mandatory for first offenders. Meanwhile, a number of states experimented with parole systems— California, for example, authorized parole in 1893.[90]

The indeterminate sentence was based on a simple theory. Judges were not, and could not be, wise enough to tell when and if a prisoner was "cured," or if he was curable at all. Prison officials, on the other hand, had the prisoner in their sights every day. A criminal should be locked up only as long as he was "unfit to be free." The criminal in an indeterminate sentencing system was the "arbiter of his own fate"; he carried "the key of his prison in his own pocket." His background and character, and the way he behaved in prison, would determine his fate. The Illinois statute, passed in 1899, directed the warden to pay attention to "early social influences" that affected the prisoner's "constitutional and acquired defects and tendencies," among other things. Both parole and the indeterminate sentence were further moves along the road to professionalization in criminal justice. They shifted power from amateurs to full-time workers in the criminal justice "field."[91]

The Elmira experiment was by no means an unqualified success. Originally, this had been a maximum-security prison, surrounded by a grim high wall. Despite remodeling and good intentions, Elmira was essentially "founded on custody and security, not on rehabilitation." Within ten years, "it was just another prison." The other systems based on the Elmira plan tended to share its defects. They suffered from neglect and "legislative starvation"; the theory of the graded system won only "perfunctory obedience." Money was a key issue. Prisons were supposed to pay their own way through prison industry; but it was hard to reconcile this goal with the goal of reform and reformation. The general public had little enthusiasm for prison experiments, and an inveterate capacity for grumbling about prisons as "country clubs," "military academies" or "private schools."[92] We will return to this point.

The Elmira idea, it was thought, was especially right for young offenders. Many people thought it was shocking to treat juveniles the same as adult offenders, to lock them up together in a single school for vice. Legislatures came to share this view. As early as 1825, New York set up a "House of Refuge" for juveniles. A few states tried modified forms of probation for young people in trouble. A New York law of 1884 provided that when a person under sixteen was convicted of a crime, the judge might, in his discretion, put him in care of some suitable person or institution, instead of sending the boy or girl to jail. Laws in Massachusetts, and later in Rhode Island (1898), authorized separate trials of children's cases. Indiana, in a series of statutes beginning in 1889, established a Board of Children's Guardians for densely populated townships. The board had the right to petition the circuit court for custody and control of a child under fifteen. Custody could last until the child came of age. The board was empowered to act when it had "probable cause to believe" that the

[90] On the California experience, see Sheldon Messinger et al., "The Foundations of Parole in California," 19 Law and Society Review 69 (1985).

[91] Laws Ill. 1899, P. 142; Lawrence M. Friedman, "History, Social Policy, and Criminal Justice." in David J. Rothman and Stanton Wheeler, eds., *Social History and Social Policy* (1981), pp. 203, 207–9.

[92] Miriam Allen deFord, *Stone Walls* (1962), p. 85.

child was "abandoned, neglected or cruelly treated" at home, or had been sent out to beg on the streets, or was truant, or "in idle and vicious association," if the parents of the child were "in constant habits of drunkenness and blasphemy, or of low and gross debauchery," or if the child was "known by language and life to be vicious or incorrigible."[93]

Despite these halting moves, it was still true, in the nineteenth century, that children could be arrested, detained, tried, and sent to prison or reformatory. There were 2,029 minors in jail in Massachusetts in 1870; 231 of these were under fifteen.[94] The first true juvenile court was established in 1899 in Cook County, Illinois (Chicago). Under the governing statute, circuit-court judges of Cook County would designate one judge to hear all juvenile cases. He would sit in a separate courtroom, and keep separate records; his court was to be called "the juvenile court."[95] The court had jurisdiction over "dependent and neglected" children as well as over delinquents—children, for example, whose home was "unfit" by reason of "neglect, cruelty or depravity"; or children "found living in any house of ill fame or with any vicious or disreputable person." The theory was to save children, delinquents or not, who needed saving. The impulse was humane. But the law was also, through this development, extending its power over young people, mostly lower class children, who had been beyond the reach of prior law, and who had committed no actual crimes.

The juvenile court idea, however, had enormous appeal; from its small beginnings in Cook County, Illinois, it spread so fast and so far that within twenty years or so almost every state had some version of a juvenile court. The juvenile court was an example of the new professionalism: no jury, but (ultimately) a flock of social workers and other experts. The whole baggage of rights and rules was gotten rid of; and the emphasis was on the offender, not the offense: the individual child. (Some, indeed, had committed no offense at all.) Juvenile justice was to the minor what probation was to the adult, only more so.

Juvenile court was a reform hatched by the "child-savers" of the nineteenth century. Its paternalism, middle-class bias, and absence of due process make it seem less progressive a century or so later than it seemed to the good people of its day.[96] There were real abuses from the start; and more abuses developed over time. The double standard was in full operation; teenage girls who were sexually active were adjudged "delinquent" by the hundreds. But the oppressors were *not* exclusively the police, or upper-class reformers and do-gooders; they were also the parents themselves of lower-class children. At least, this is the evidence from the early California records (1903–1910). In case after case, mothers and

[93] See Laws Ind. 1891, ch. 151

[94] Anthony Platt, *The Child Savers: The Invention of Delinquency* (1969), p. 120. On the development of separate prisons for women, see Estelle B. Freedman, *Their Sisters' Keepers: Women's Prison Reform in America, 1830–1930* (1981).

[95] Herbert H. Lou, *Juvenile Courts in the United States* (1927), pp. 19–20; Laws 111, 1899, p. 131; see also Michael Willrich, *City of Courts: Socializing Justice in Progressive Era Chicago* (2003).

[96] On the background of the juvenile court: movement, see Platt, *op. cit., supra;* David J. Rothman, *Conscience and Convenience: The Asylum and Its Alternatives in Progressive America* (1980), ch. 6; Peter D. Garlock, "'Wayward' Children and the Law, 1820–1900: The Genesis of the Status Offense Jurisdiction of the Juvenile Court," 13 Ga. L. Rev. 341 (1979); Robert M. Mennel, *Thorns and Thistles: Juvenile Delinquents in the United States, 1825–1940* (1973).

fathers—often of immigrant stock—threw up their hands at their unruly or incorrigible children and turned them over to the state. What these parents wanted was tradition, middle-class morality, obedience, and old-country ways. But America provided them with a raging generation gap. Juvenile justice gave them access to state power to curb unruly children or, if necessary, get them off their parents' backs.[97]

The Crime of Imprisonment

The period was rich in institutional experiment. There were new theories and new applications of theory. But the landmark places, like Elmira, were not typical of the everyday world of corrections. Elmira, though a failure, at least had high aspirations. Ordinary prisons, state and local, were starved for funds, filthy, sometimes debauched. Many prison jobs were held by ward heelers, appointed to pay off political debts. With dreary regularity, commissions reported bad news about prisons and local jails—a dark chorus of complaints. Prisoners were whipped, starved, and tortured in prisons and jails all over the country, though not in all prisons and jails at all times. Local jails were probably, on the whole, even worse than the big state prisons.[98] The county jails of New Jersey were described as a disgrace in 1867. Young and old men and women were heaped together, under conditions of "dirt, vermin, offensive air and darkness." At the state prison, on the other hand, in a perversion of the penitentiary idea, the prisoner lived in a cell measuring seven by twelve feet—with one to four cellmates; or alone in a newer cell only four feet wide and seven feet long. In this case, he lived and ate "in a room the size of a small bathroom, with a noisome bucket for a toilet and a cot narrower than a bathtub." To bathe "occasionally," there was a "bathhouse in the yard, which was closed in bad weather."[99] In Illinois, the Cook County jail, inspected in 1869, was also "filthy and full of vermin." The county jails were "moral plague spots"; they made "great criminals out of little ones."[100]

The prisons had become, in many ways, much more lax than in the first days of the penitentiary system; in the 1870s, at Sing Sing, investigators found incredible corruption: Guards sold forbidden items to prisoners; convicts were allowed to lounge about idly, or play games; the prison yard "had something of the atmosphere of a village." Yet, at the same time, there was incredible brutality in some prisons: Prisoners were whipped and beaten; or they were tortured with pulleys, iron caps, or "cages," or afflicted with the lash, the paddle, or (in the Kansas prison) a fiendish form of water torture.[101] In Sing Sing, an investigation in 1882 found deplorable conditions: The prison stank from the night tubs filled with excrement; men cleaned themselves in a bathing barrel filled with water—after a few men had used the barrel, the water was dirtier than the men who tried to clean themselves. In summer, swarms of bedbugs passed

[97] Friedman and Percival, *Roots of Justicet,* pp. 223-24.
[98] Lawrence M. Friedman, *Crime and Punishment,* pp. 166–68.
[99] James Leiby, *Charity and Correction in New Jersey* (1967), pp. 126–28.
[100] Platt, *op. cit.,* pp. 118–19.
[101] David J. Rothman, *Conscience and Convenience,* pp. 17–21.

through the ventilators and infested every cell; disease and sexual abuse were epidemic.[102]

The story was always the same: charges of brutality and corruption, investigations, recommendations. But somehow reforms never took hold, or were perverted in practice. The fact is that convicts, like paupers, were at the very bottom of American society; powerless, their wants and needs had no American priority. If the convicts were black, they were double pariahs. The middle-class public feared and detested crime. People wanted criminals punished, and severely; even more, they wanted bad people kept out of sight and out of circulation. The evidence of what legislatures did, and what was accomplished and not accomplished, shows that the main point of imprisonment, for society as a whole, was to warehouse, quarantine, and guard the "criminal class"; curing them of their criminal habits was a lesser goal. People were inclined to be skeptical, moreover, about the chances of reforming criminals at all. Were criminals simply born that way? Criminal anthropologists and others explored the idea that men and women *inherited* their evil inclinations. The criminal, in other words, was a definite physical or mental type. "Intellectually and morally, criminals are for the most part weak," wrote Frederick Howard Wines, in 1895. This showed itself in "inattention, lack of imagination or the power of representation, defective memory, lack of foresight, and general aversion to mental exertion." A rich literature–a leading figure was the Italian penologist, Cesare Lombroso—insisted that there were physical signs of criminal personality: "The prominence of the criminal ear," wrote Frederick Wines, "has been especially noted. Prisoners are said to have wrinkled faces; male prisoners have often scanty beards; many hairy women are found in prison. Redhaired men and women do not seem to be given to the commission of crime. . . . Convicts have long arms, pigeon-breasts and stooping shoulders." Criminals, it was commonly observed, did not blush.[103] Richard Dugdale, in his famous book about the "Juke" family, traced a whole gaggle of misfits, criminals, and prostitutes, to the descendants of a single bastard; the "Jukes" of the world, "breeding like rats in their alleys," threatened to "overwhelm the well-bred classes."[104]

The average person did not know these "facts"; but people had their own common sense, no doubt, to guide them. They probably often felt that the criminal was another breed. For the sake of public safety, such people should be removed from society. In the late nineteenth century, too, the question of eugenics was widely debated. Concern for purity of morals joined hands with concern for purity of the blood. Attitudes toward "born criminals" surely reinforced the central tendency of the law of corrections, which was to quarantine bad people and get them off the streets. What went on inside prison walls hardly mattered, so long as these walls were impermeable. If most convicts were rotten from the day

---

[102] Roger Panetta, *Up the River: A History of Sing Sing in the Nineteenth Century* (Ph.D. diss., City University of New York, 1999), pp. 298–99, 326.

[103] Frederick H. Wines, *Punishment and Reformation: A Study of the Penitentiary System* (2nd ed., 1910), pp. 234–35.

[104] The book was R. L. Dugdale, *"The Jukes": A Study in Crime, Pauperism, Disease, and Heredity* (1877); see Ysabel Rennie, *The Search for Criminal Man: A Conceptual History of the Dangerous Offender* (1978).

they were born, there was no point in letting them loose. Better to let them vegetate behind prison walls.[105]

Public attitudes no doubt made a bad situation worse. Legislatures tended to starve the prisons for funds. Jails were jammed with prisoners, far beyond their capacity.[106] The misery of prison life may have caused some men to go straight; but it embittered others, and frustrated any hopes of rehabilitating them. In the end, it is likely that the misery of prisons and jail led to still more crime; or at the least, more social disorder.

On one point there was a general consensus: Prisoners ought to do useful work. Reformers, who wanted prisoners to improve themselves, certainly thought so; but so did stingy officials, who wanted to cut costs and raise the income of the prison. Convicts labored away on a wide range of products, including brushes, brooms, chairs, boots, and shoes. At one time, New York tried to turn Sing Sing into a silk factory; this failed, but the search for profit continued. In the 1870s, Sing Sing gave a contract to John S. Perry, an Albany businessman, who put almost the whole prison to work making stoves.[107] Organized labor was the sworn enemy of convict labor. Unions saw prisons as gigantic scab workplaces. In this case, they had some employers on their side—those who paid higher wages than prisoners got and made products that competed with prison-made goods. Labor and management united to fight against convict industry. The threat was real. Moundsville Penitentiary, in the late 1870s, in West Virginia, was turning out 280,000 cigars a month, at half the price of other cigars, arousing (of course) enormous anger among cigarmakers and their union.[108]

The unions and their allies did achieve a certain success. Pressure in New York forced the legislature to end the contract with John Perry. The Illinois Constitution was amended in 1886 to make it "unlawful . . . to let by contract . . . the labor of any convict." Michigan provided that "no mechanical trade shall hereafter be taught to convicts in the State prison . . . except the manufacture of those articles of which the chief supply for home consumption is imported from other States or countries." Some states ruled that convict-made goods had to be specially marked. A Pennsylvania statute, passed in 1883, required these goods to disclose that they were "convict made," in "plain English lettering . . . by casting, burning, pressing or other such process," and in such a way that the brand could not be "defaced." In every case, the brand had to be put "upon the most conspicuous place upon such article, or the box . . . containing the same."[109] For political reasons, some states tried to divert prison labor into channels that did not offend major interest groups. In Minnesota, beginning in 1892, statutes directed the state prison to acquire equipment and machinery "for

[105] See Mark H. Haller, *Eugenics: Hereditarian Attitudes in American Thought* (1963); Ysabel Rennie, *op. cit.*, n. 104.

[106] Sometimes, too, prisons were so crowded that the state felt obliged to make wholesale use of pardon and parole. This happened in New Jersey in the late nineteenth century; the ordinary outflow of prisoners "did not clear the prison fast enough." Leiby, *op. cit.*, p. 133.

[107] Panetta, *op. cit.*, p. 292.

[108] Glen A. Gildemeister, *Prison Labor and Convict Competition with Free Workers in Industrializing America, 1840–1890* (1987), p. 148.

[109] Laws Pa. 1883, ch. 110, sec. 2. Interestingly, "goods . . . shipped to points outside of the State shall not be so branded."

the manufacture of twines known as hardfiber twines." Prison-made binding twine would be sold to farmers, "in quantities necessary for their own use." In this way, prison power would help farmers fight the National Cordage Company, which farmers felt was a vicious and domineering trust.[110]

Southern prisons were particularly disgraceful; and the campaign against prison labor made less headway there. In the South, too, convicts were still hired out on the contract system. Florida statutes specifically authorized the commissioner of agriculture (with the approval of the board of commissioners of state institutions) to "enter into contracts . . . for the labor, maintenance and custody of . . . prisoners." No labor was to be done on Sunday, or "before sunrise or after sunset on any day." The contracts could provide for "surrendering the control and custody of the prisoners to the person . . . contracting for their labor."[111] In Georgia, under the code of 1895, a person convicted of a misdemeanor could be sentenced "to work in the chain-gang."[112] These infamous gangs worked for counties and cities, often on the public roads. The law empowered the "authorities of any county or municipal corporation" using the gang to "appoint a whipping-boss for such convicts"; the boss was not to use his whip except "in cases where it is reasonably necessary to enforce discipline or compel work or labor by the convict."[113]

Bad as the system was in the North, the situation in the South was much worse.[114] Most of the convicts leased out in the South, and almost all of the prisoners on chain-gangs were black; and indeed, as Edward L. Ayers has put it, the lease system was merely "part of a continuum of forced labor in the New South," a continuum that ran from the "monopolistic company store," through share-cropping and the peonage system, all the way to the "complete subjugation of convict labor."[115] Before the Civil War, almost all Southern prisoners had been white—slaves were punished in other ways. After the Civil War, the situation reversed itself: Now, almost all prisoners were black.[116] White Southerners, in general, would have laughed at the notion of using prisons as places of reform and character building. In many ways, the southern correctional system, in the last half of the century, was simply a pool of black slave labor.

Farming out criminals brought revenue to the state. In some places, large lessees subleased convicts in small or large gangs. The prisons of the South were "great rolling cages that followed construction camps and railroad building, hastily built stockades deep in forest or swamp or mining fields, or windowless log forts in turpentine flats."[117] The system was highly profitable. Alabama and Tennessee made over $100,000 a year from their convict-leasing

[110] See, in general, *20th Ann. Rpt. U.S. Commr. Labor, Convict Labor* (1905).

[111] Fla. Rev. Stats. 1892, sec. 3065.

[112] Georgia Code 1895, vol 111, sec. 1039. The statute did go on to recite that the gangs were not to be employed "in such mechanical pursuits as will bring the products of their labor into competition with the products of free labor."

[113] *Ibid.*, secs. 1146, 1147.

[114] See, in general, Mark Colvin, *Penitentiaries, Reformatories, and Chain Gangs: Social Theory and the History of Punishment in Nineteenth-Century America* (1997), chs. 9–11.

[115] Edward L. Ayers, *Vengeance and Justice: Crime and Punishment in the Nineteenth Century American South* (1984), p. 191.

[116] Colvin, *Penitentiaries*, p. 220.

[117] C. Vann Woodward, *Origins of the New South, 1877–1913* (1951), p. 213.

system in the late 1880s; and there were respectable profits in Georgia, Mississippi, Arkansas, North Carolina, and Kentucky. For the convicts themselves, the picture was quite different. The dry statistical evidence suggests a system of almost unbelievable brutality. The prisoners were overwhelmingly young, healthy men when they were leased out; yet in 1888, when the death rate in Virginia's prison was 1.5 percent, in contractors' camps on the Richmond and Allegheny Railroad the death rate was an alarming 11 percent.[118] But this was positively mild compared to the situation in other southern states. In 1870, 41 percent of 180 convicts in Alabama, leased out for railroad work, died during the year; in the prior two years, there had been death rates of 18 and 17 percent; the death rate in Mississippi in the 1880s was nine times as great as in the prisons of the Northern states.[119] Alabama prisoners later worked in coal mines, where conditions were if anything even more inhuman. Every day, a prisoner said, "we looked Death in the face & was afraid to speak." One black prisoner, who had escaped, was stripped naked and beaten until he died. In one privately run prison camp, 150 black prisoners lived in a cabin with no windows; they slept on straw-filled bunks, on bedding that was "revoltingly filthy"; all convicts, black and white, wore shackles.[120]

The Southern lease system, racist and brutal, was in a way only an exaggerated form of the pathologies of the national system of corrections. The prison system, despite the reformers, in essence had no heart. It was expected, above all, either to earn a profit or at least leave the tax burden light. The leasing system persisted, despite countless reform plans, and countless scandals and exposes. The only protests that seemed to do any good came from organized labor. In 1883, the Tennessee Coal, Iron, and Railroad Company hired the thirteen hundred convicts of the Tennessee penitentiary. They used the convicts partly as a lever to force free workers to agree to stiff terms of employment. In 1891, free miners set the convicts loose at the Tennessee Coal Mine Company and burned down the stockades. The next year, miners in Anderson County battled the militia over the issue of convict labor. The lease system was finally abolished, in Tennessee, after this period of lobbying with fire and with blood.[121] Other Southern states abandoned or modified their leasing system in the 1890s. The new plan was to use centralized state prison farms; by 1898, though nine states still made some use of leasing, the prison farm system had made enormous headway. The chain gang survived, however; and so did brutality and abuse.[122]

[118] Paul W. Keve, *The History of Corrections in Virginia* (1986), p. 74.

[119] Ayers, *op. cit.*, pp. 196–201. The regular branch prisons in Tennessee were described as "hell holes of rage, cruelty, despair, and vice." Young boys thrown into the cells were common victims of sexual assault. Ibid., at 200.

[120] Mary Ellen Curtin, *Black Prisoners and Their World, Alabama, 1865–1900* (2000), pp. 63–64, 69–70.

[121] Woodward, *op. cit.*, pp. 232ff.

[122] Ayers, *op. cit.*, pp. 221–22.

CHAPTER 11

THE LEGAL PROFESSION: THE
TRAINING AND LITERATURE OF LAW

THE RISE OF THE LAW SCHOOL

Of the lawyers practicing in the United States in 1848, the overwhelming majority had been trained in a private law office or had educated themselves by a course of reading. This was particularly true in the West. In 1858, Abraham Lincoln wrote in a letter that "the cheapest, quickest and best way" into the legal world was to "read Blackstone's *Commentaries,* Chitty's *Pleadings,* Greenleaf's *Evidence,* Story's *Equity* and Story's *Equity Pleading,* get a license, and go to the practice and still keep reading."[1] Thousands of the lawyers practicing in 1900 still had come from this rough school of experience. But slowly the gap between law school and clerkship was closing. Fewer would-be lawyers studied or clerked in law offices, doing service while learning through practical experience. Some combined clerkship with halfhearted or short attendance at a law school. A growing number simply went to school.

No state in the nineteenth century made a law degree, or a college degree, a prerequisite for admission to the bar. Many lawyers, however, even in the 1850s, did go to college,[2] and more and more students who could afford it chose law school as well. Indeed, by 1900 it was quite clear that the law schools would come to dominate legal education. It was clear, too, what kind of school: a law school affiliated with a university, public or private. Only a handful of private schools were founded after 1860; one was "Col. G. N. Folk's school, at Boone, North Carolina," established in 1867, which lasted some twenty-odd years.[3] Schools of the Litchfield type were almost extinct by 1900. On the other hand, after the Civil War, an increasing number of law schools formed some sort of tie with a college or university. More than three quarters of the schools open and running in the 1890s were of this type.

Particularly in the East, law school gave the student a kind of prestige law-office training could not match. In the better schools, too, the student probably

---

[1] Quoted in Jack Nortrup, "The Education of a Western Lawyer," 12 Am. J. Legal Hist. 294 (1968).

[2] Even Western lawyers. See Nortrup, *op. cit.,* n. 1. Nortrup's article describes the education of Richard Yates, who combined law-office training with a course in the law department of Transylvania (1836).

[3] Alfred Z. Reed, *Training for the Public Profession of the Law* (1921), p. 433.

learned more than the typical student learned as a clerk, and perhaps in less time. Whatever the facts, the law schools sold themselves, slowly but surely, to the student public, as better or more efficient, or an easier road to success. There is some evidence, too, that a change in the demographics of the bar influenced the rise of the law schools. The old established lawyers in Philadelphia had blocked the formation of a law department at the University of Pennsylvania in the 1830s. They wished, apparently, to preserve their private prerogative of training the bar. The revolt came from the law students themselves, "restive in the confinement of law offices," and eager for a "less inbred program of legal studies"; and one "less dominated by the old elites." In 1850, George Sharswood, in response to student demands, reopened the department of law at the University of Pennsylvania.[4]

There was another factor, too. The day of the clerk was fading. Typewriters and other office machines spelled his doom. The law office of 1900 no longer needed copyists, gophers, and drones. It needed secretaries, stenographers, and typists. Typically, young women were trained in these skills. They worked at jobs that were dead-end jobs. Unlike the clerks, they were permanently sealed off from the ladder to professional success. But in any event, the old-style clerk was obsolete.

The figures plainly show the triumph of the law school. In 1850, fifteen law schools were in operation; in 1860, twenty-one; in 1870, thirty-one; 1880, fifty-one; 1890, sixty-one. In the last ten years of the century, the number of schools grew even more rapidly. By 1900, 102 were open for business. In 1850, there were one or more law schools in twelve of the states; in nineteen states there were no law schools at all. In 1900, thirty-three states had law schools; only thirteen had to import school-trained lawyers from outside.[5] These were small or sparsely populated states—like New Hampshire and Nevada—or satellite states like New Jersey.[6] In the academic year 1849–1850, Harvard, the country's largest law school, had a total attendance of ninety-four. Ten years later, Harvard's enrollment had risen to 166; 180 students were enrolled at Cumberland University Law School, in Lebanon, Tennessee. In the academic year 1869–1870, Michigan, the country's largest law school, had 308 students; at the close of the century, Michigan again led all other law schools, with 883 students.[7] This was probably more than the total enrollment in the country's law schools in 1850. In 1870, law schools had a total student population of 1,611; in 1894, the number had risen to 7,600.[8]

Many major universities, public and private, opened a law school between 1850 and 1900. The University of Michigan, a public university, established a "law department" in 1859. The regents, at the very outset, voted to spend up to $100 to place advertisements for the "law department" in newspapers in

---

[4] Gary B. Nash, "The Philadelphia Bench and Bar, 1800–1861," in *Comparative Studies in Society and History*, vol. VII, No. 2 (1965), pp. 203, 207–8.

[5] Reed, *op. cit.,* pp. 444, 446.

[6] In 1970, seven states—New Hampshire, Nevada, Delaware, Vermont, Rhode Island, Alaska, and Hawaii—had no law school. By 1984 the list was down to three: New Hampshire, Rhode Island and Alaska; in 2004, Alaska was the sole survivor.

[7] Reed, *op. cit.,* pp. 451–52. On the University of Michigan Law School, see Elizabeth G. Brown, *Legal Education at Michigan, 1859–1959* (1959).

[8] Albert J. Harno, *Legal Education in the United States* (1953), p. 82.

Detroit, Chicago, New York, Cincinnati, St. Louis, and Washington, D.C.,[9] St. Louis University, in the 1840s, was the first Roman Catholic university to establish a law school. This was a short-lived venture; but other Catholic universities followed in due course. Notre Dame law school was founded in 1869; and Georgetown, in 1890, was one of the four largest law schools in the country. The law department of Howard University, in Washington, D.C., was the first, most successful, and most permanent of the dozen or so black law schools. It opened in January 1869 under the leadership of John Mercer Langston.[10] The law school of the University of Georgia began life as the Lumpkin Law School, which opened its doors in 1859. There were daily lectures, and moot court on Sundays. Classes met in a small wooden building—the law office of two of the founders, Joseph Lumpkin and Thomas Cobb. The school closed during the Civil War. After the war, the school revived; now, however, it was known as the Law Department of the University of Georgia.[11]

The relationship of law schools to their universities was, in general, a far cry from what it became in the twentieth century. The usual law degree, the L.L.B., was certainly not a postgraduate degree. Law schools did not usually require *any* college work to get in. The more pretentious law schools tightened their entrance requirements toward the end of the century; none required a full college education. Many "university" law schools were rather loosely connected to their parent institutions. They were by no means an organic part of world of higher education. Yale Law School in the 1870s supported itself, as best it could, from tuition payments; it got nothing from the University; at least Yale, unlike most law schools, did make an attempt to form relationships with academic departments, a "striking departure from the trend of the times."[12] At Columbia, from 1858, until he retired in 1891, Theodore W. Dwight was the dominant figure in the law school. He ran his own show. Under arrangements solemnized in 1864, Dwight, as, "Professor of Municipal Law," collected the students' tuition (fixed at $100 a year for new students). Out of these fees, Dwight paid expenses, and gave himself a salary of $6,000 a year. Any surplus was to be split fifty-fifty between Dwight and the university.[13] It was decidedly a novelty when Michigan decided to pay the salaries of its faculty—$1,000 a year—out of general university funds.[14] Other "university" law schools were private schools annexed by, swallowed by, or federated with a university, which had varying degrees of success in digesting them. There are even cases of law schools that shifted allegiance from one university to another. What is now the law school of Northwestern University began as a department of law of the old

[9] E. G. Brown, *Legal Education at Michigan* (1959), p. 14.

[10] Maxwell Bloomfield, *American Lawyers in a Changing Society, 1776–1876* (1976), p. 328.

[11] Gwen Y. Wood, *A Unique and Fortuitous Combination: An Administrative History of the University of Georgia School of Law* (1998), pp. 12–13.

[12] See Mark Bartholomew, "Legal Separation: The Relationship between the Law School and the Central University in the Late Nineteenth Century," 53 Journal of Legal Education 368 (2003); John H. Langbein, "Law School in a University: Yale's Distinctive Path in the Later Nineteenth Century," in Anthony T. Kronman, ed., *History of the Yale Law School: The Tercentennial Lectures* (2004), p. 52.

[13] Julius Goebel Jr., ed., *A History of the School of Law, Columbia University* (1955), pp. 57–58.

[14] On Michigan, see Elizabeth G. Brown, "The Law School of the University of Michigan; 1859–1959," 38 Mich. St. Bar J., No. 8, p. 16 (1959).

Chicago University; in 1873, it became the Union College of Law, connected both with Chicago and Northwestern; in 1886, Chicago University went out of business; but the law school was not formally integrated into Northwestern University until 1891.[15]

Today, law school training takes, almost universally, three years. In 1850, the standard course in many law schools ran for one year only. Later in the century, a two-year program became more popular. The three-year L.L.B. was a late innovation, which began at Harvard, during the deanship of Christopher Columbus Langdell; Boston University then adopted this program as well. Prominent judges and lawyers constituted the faculty at most law schools. Full-time teachers were rare before the 1880s. The full-time teacher, too, was one of Langdell's innovations. Judges and lawyers were not necessarily bad teachers. Story and Greenleaf at Harvard lectured to a student body made up mostly of college graduates; and they worked up their lectures into books that were real contributions to U.S. legal literature. Other law schools also offered fairly rigorous training before the Civil War.[16] But it was not the rigor of the twentieth century. The Cumberland Law School, for example, in Lebanon, Tennessee, had basically no admission requirements; there were no course examinations, and no grades. The students, instead, had daily quizzes.[17]

Even Harvard, the standard-bearer, seemed to regress toward the mean. The number of law students who were college graduates declined at Harvard after 1845. The school entered what seemed to be a period of stagnation.

> Everything about the School was stereotyped. For twenty years the language of the Catalogue as to entrance, course of study, and degree was not changed by a letter. There was no recorded faculty meeting during the entire period. . . . Library rules were made in theory by the Corporation, in practice by the janitor. . . .[18]

During Harvard's dark age, which lasted until 1870, the prevailing mode of instruction was not the lecture, but the "text-book method."

> from recitation period to recitation period, the students are assigned a specified portion of a regulation text-book to study, and for the most part

[15] James A. Rahl and Kurt Schwerin, "Northwestern University School of Law; A Short History," 55 Northwestern U.L. Rev. 131 (1960); Reed, *op. cit.*, p. 185.

[16] In the late 1840s, the University of North Carolina established a professorship of law, under the direction of a high court judge, William Horn Battle. According to the university catalogue, the "department for the study of municipal law" was divided into two "classes." One, "the Independent Class," consisted of "such Students of Law as have no connection with any of the College Classes"; the "College Class" consisted of "such irregular members of College as, with the permission of the Faculty, may be desirous of joining it." The Independent Class was a two-year program, with "recitations three times a week"; the "College Class" recited once a week, and its recitations were "so arranged as not to interfere with the ordinary studies of College." The College Class took two and a half years to earn its L.L.B. "The Professor of Law and the members of the Independent Class" were not "subject to any of the ordinary College regulations." This system lasted until 1868, when the whole university closed its doors during Reconstruction. Albert Coates, "The Story of the Law School at the University of North Carolina," N. Car. L. Rev., Special Issue, Oct. 1968, pp. 1, 13, 14.

[17] David J. Langum and Howard P. Walthall, *From Maverick to Mainstream: Cumberland School of Law, 1847–1997* (1997), pp. 75–76.

[18] *Centennial History of the Harvard Law School, 1817–1917* (1918), pp. 22–23.

to memorize; this is then explained by the teacher and recited on at the next period.

Part of the hour was taken up by "quizzing." This was the "more or less purely mechanical testing of the knowledge learned by the students."[19]

Neither the textbook nor the lecture method was an unmitigated evil; much depended on the man in front of the class. By all accounts, Theodore W. Dwight of Columbia was a brilliant teacher; observers such as Lord Bryce and Albert Dicey thought his school the very best imaginable. Richmond M. Pearson of North Carolina, a judge and then chief justice of the North Carolina high court, ran a private law school that lasted into the 1870s; Pearson "adopted the methods of Socrates, Plato, and Aristotle"; students read their books, then came to his office twice a week, where he "would examine them upon what they read by asking them questions." Pearson also lectured, after coming in from a "walk around the hillside," chewing "a little twig from some favorite tree." At least one student thought he was "the greatest teacher that ever lived on the earth."[20]

Lawyers often remember their school days romantically and nostalgically. Law school teaching was dogmatic and uncritical, except from the standpoint of the law's internal logic; or simply dogmatic from any standpoint. Law schools never conveyed a sense of connection between law and life; or even of the evolution of the common law. Even the most brilliant lectures were fundamentally hollow. The basic aim of the schools was to cram young lawyers with rote learning, of a more or less practical nature, as quickly and efficiently as possible.

At one time, the Blackstone model had been strong in legal education—peppering legal education with some notions of government, politics, and ethics. This tradition never completely died. In Dwight's Columbia, Francis Lieber gave lectures "upon the State, embracing the origin, development, objects, and history of Political Society, on the Laws and usages of War, on the history of Political Literature, on Political Ethics, on Punishments, including Statistics, etc." As part of the curriculum, Professor Charles Nairne delivered a "course of lectures on the Ethics of Jurisprudence." Lieber attracted only a few students; nonetheless, Dwight became jealous and hostile. Lieber handed in his resignation shortly before he died, in 1872. His successor was John W. Burgess. Burgess, too, eventually left the law school; he then founded, at Columbia, a "School designed to prepare young men for the duties of Public Life," to be "entitled a School of Political Science."[21] This new social science ultimately produced a rich scholarship about the living law. But its first effect was to impoverish legal education, which was already thin and ailing.

The stage was ripe for reform or revolution. The first shot was fired in 1870. Charles W. Eliot had become president of Harvard the year before. He appointed Christopher Columbus Langdell to a professorship in the law school; in September 1870, Langdell was made dean, a position new to the school. The duties of the dean, on paper, were not very awesome; he was to "keep the Records of the Faculty," prepare "its business," and "preside at its meetings in the absence of the

[19] Josef Redlich, *The Common Law and the Case Method in American University Law Schools* (1914), pp. 7–8.

[20] Quoted in Coates, *op. cit.*, n. 16, pp. 9–10.

[21] Goebel, *op. cit.*, n. 15, pp. 60, 89.

President."[22] But Langdell, with Eliot's backing, turned Harvard Law School upside down. First, he made it harder for students to get in. An applicant without a college degree had to pass an entrance test. He had to show his knowledge of Latin, translating from Virgil, or Cicero, or from Caesar; he was also tested on Blackstone's *Commentaries*. Skill in French was acceptable as a substitute for Latin.

Next, Langdell made it harder for a student to get out. The L.L.B. course was raised to two years in 1871 and to three years in 1876 (though the third year did not have to be spent in residence). By 1899, the school had adopted a straight three-year requirement. The old curriculum had taken up matters subject by subject, as time allowed; it paid little attention to the relationship between courses; students entered and left according to their own rhythm. Under Langdell, the curriculum was divided into "courses," each of so many hours or units apiece. Courses were arranged in a definite order; some were treated as basic, some as advanced. In 1872, Langdell instituted final examinations. The student had to pass his first-year exams before he went on to the second-year courses.

Langdell also introduced the case method of teaching law. This was his most far-reaching reform, the one for which he is most remembered. Langdell drove the textbooks out of the temple, and brought in casebooks instead. These were collections of reports of actual cases, carefully selected and arranged to illustrate the principles of law, what they meant, and how they developed. At Langdell's Harvard, the classroom tone was profoundly altered. There was no lecturer up front, expounding "the law" from received texts. Now the teacher was a Socratic guide, taking the student by the hand and leading him to understand the concepts and principles hidden inside the cases.[23] The teacher, through study of a series of "correct" cases over time, showed how these concepts developed, how they grew and unfolded, like a rose from its bud.

There was a theory behind Langdell's method. He believed that law was a "science"; it had to be studied scientifically, that is, inductively, through primary sources.[24] These sources were the printed cases; they expressed, in manifold dress, the few, ever-evolving and fructifying principles that were the foundations and the genius of the common law. Law, Langdell wrote,

> considered as a science, consists of certain principles or doctrines. To have such a mastery of these as to be able to apply them with constant facility and certainty to the ever-tangled skein of human affairs, is what constitutes a true lawyer; and hence to acquire that mastery should be the

[22] Quoted in Arthur E. Sutherland, *The Law at Harvard: A History of Ideas and Men, 1817–1967* (1967), p. 166. There is a large literature on the Langdell revolution. In addition to Sutherland, see especially Robert Stevens, *Law School: Legal Education in America from the 1830s to the 1980s* (1984); and Thomas C. Grey, "Langdell's Orthodoxy," 45 U. Pitt. L. Rev. 1 (1983).

[23] Langdell was not the first to teach through cases. John Norton Pomeroy used a case method at New York University Law School, in the 1860s. But Pomeroy did not "shape the whole program of a leading school" with this technique. J. Willard Hurst, *The Growth of American Law* (1950), p. 261.

[24] On the intellectual background, see Howard Schweber, "The 'Science' of Legal Science: The Model of the Natural Sciences in Nineteenth-Century American Legal Education," 17 Law and History Review 421 (1999).

business of every earnest student of law. Each of these doctrines has arrived at its present state by slow degrees; in other words, it is a growth, extending in many cases through centuries. This growth is to be traced in the main through a series of cases; and much the shortest and best, if not the only way of mastering the doctrine effectually is by studying the cases in which it is embodied. But the cases which are useful and necessary for this purpose at the present day bear an exceedingly small proportion to all that have been reported. The vast majority are useless, and worse than useless, for any purpose of systematic study. Moreover the number of fundamental legal doctrines is much less than is commonly supposed; the many different guises in which the same doctrine is constantly making its appearance, and the great extent to which legal treatises are a repetition of each other, being the cause of much misapprehension. If these doctrines could be so classified and arranged that each should be found in its proper place, and nowhere else, they would cease to be formidable from their number. It seemed to me, therefore, to be possible to take such a branch of the law as Contracts, for example, and, without exceeding comparatively moderate limits, to select, classify, and arrange all the cases which had contributed in any important degree to the growth, development, or establishment of any of its essential doctrines; and that such a work could not fail to be of material service to all who desire to study that branch of law systematically and in its original sources.

These words appeared in the preface to Langdell's first casebook, on *Contracts,* which came out in 1871. Unlike twentieth-century casebooks, it was totally barren of any aids to the student—it had no notes, comments, or explanations. It consisted exclusively of those cases which Langdell had culled from the mass. Most of these were English cases; a smaller number were American, chiefly from Massachusetts and New York. The West and the South, it seemed, had added nothing to the law. The material was arranged by topics; within topics, cases were in chronological order, showing the evolution of principles from darkness to light. Practically speaking, no statute was permitted to enter the harem of common law, not even the Statute of Frauds, which was so old and barnacled with doctrine that it was almost not a statute at all.

Langdell claimed he was interested in the growth or evolution of law; but new-fangled reforms, when they were not the work of judges, did not concern him in the least. In his *Summary of Equity Pleading* (1877), he asked the reader to "bear in mind that it is the object of these sheets to aid the student in acquiring a knowledge of the equity system as such; and with this view the writer confines himself to the system as it existed in England from the earliest times to the end of Lord Eldon's chancellorship." At least one reviewer wondered why "the study of equity pleading at Harvard University in 1877 should be limited to the system as it existed prior to 1827."[25] But from the strict Langdell standpoint, these recent changes—many of them statutory—were not part of the science of law. Even constitutional law was not part of this science—it was too textual, and was therefore an excrescence. The three-year curriculum, starting in 1876–1877, did not include constitutional law at all, not even as an elective.[26] Harvard soon drew back from this extreme position, and brought constitutional law back into

[25] 3 So. Law Rev. (N.S.), 316, 317 (1877).
[26] Charles Warren, *History of the Harvard Law School,* vol. II (1908), pp. 405–6.

the fold. But even this brief interlude shows how far Langdell was willing to carry his logic. Besides, he needed every scrap of time. The dialogues in Langdell's classes went slowly, and covered very little ground, compared to the lecture method.

The Langdell plan burst like a bombshell in the world of legal education. "To most of the students, as well as to Langdell's colleagues, it was abomination."[27] The students were bewildered; they cut Langdell's classes in droves; only a few remained to hear him out. Before the end of the first term, his course, it was said, had dwindled to "seven devoted men . . . who went by the name of 'Kit's Freshmen' or 'Langdell's Freshmen.' "[28] Enrollment at Harvard fell precipitously. Langdell's colleagues, who included the remarkable Emory Washburn, continued to teach the old way. The Boston University Law School was founded in 1872 as an alternative to Harvard's insanity. But Langdell persisted, and Eliot backed him up. The few students who stayed to listen found the method exciting. Among the faithful of "Kit's Freshmen" was a young man named James Barr Ames. Soon after graduation, Ames was taken onto the Harvard faculty. Here was another insult to pedagogical tradition. Young Ames was scholarly and intelligent, but he had no practical experience. He had no stature at the bench or bar. No matter: to teach a science, scientists were needed, not practitioners of law. Thus the law professor, in its modern sense, was another of Langdell's inventions.

This radical break with the past evoked strong opposition. Ephraim Gurney, dean of the faculty of Harvard College, was dismayed. Langdell, he wrote to President Eliot in 1883, had given him insomnia. At night he found his mind "revolving about the Law School problem." What caused his sleepless nights was Langdell's proposal to appoint William A. Keener to the faculty. Keener was young, a rather recent graduate, with a marked academic bent. The appointment meant, Gurney thought, that the "School commits itself to the theory of breeding within itself its Corps of instructors and thus severs itself from the great current of legal life which flows through the courts and the bar." Langdell's idea seemed to be to "breed professors of Law not practitioners"; his school would divorce the study of law from "its actual administration." Both Langdell and Ames, Gurney felt, were "contemptuous" of judges, because judges did not treat "this or that question as a philosophical professor, building up a coherent system as they would have done." Langdell had an "extreme unwillingness to have anything furnished by the School except the pure science of the law." Students at the end of three years, Gurney thought, would enter a law office feeling "helpless," at least "on the practical side."[29]

Eliot never answered this letter; Keener got his appointment; Langdell and his followers stayed in command. Langdell must have been a charismatic teacher. At any rate, he carried the day. The casebooks got written; the students trickled back to Harvard and back to class; the method spread to other schools. At first it was Langdell's disciples who carried the message to the Gentiles. James Bradley Thayer and John Chipman Gray, inside Harvard's own walls, were converted to the cause. John H. Wigmore took the case method to

[27] *Centennial History of the Harvard Law School*, p. 35.
[28] Charles Warren, *op. cit.*, vol. II, p. 373.
[29] Quoted in Sutherland, *op. cit.*, pp. 187–90.

Northwestern; Eugene Wambaugh, to the State University of Iowa. William Keener stormed the citadel at Columbia, and carried that prize from the aging Dwight, who resigned in 1891. Indeed, at Columbia, too, it was the president of the University, Seth Low, who sensed the need for change, and recruited Keener. The old guard at Columbia retired; and the case-method carried the day.[30] In 1892, the law school of Western Reserve was founded; it was planned to be a school run along the Harvard lines. The dean of the University of Cincinnati law school—a judge named William Howard Taft, of whom more would be heard—reported in 1896 that his "Faculty [had] decided that its wisest course would be to follow . . . the course and methods of study prevailing at the Harvard Law School," especially "the Case System." Cincinnati would use the "same books of select cases" that Harvard used for contracts, property, and torts.[31] The new law school of the University of Chicago sent to Harvard for a dean, in order to get themselves properly started; in 1902, Joseph Beale arrived on the Midway, with the mandate to use the "ideals and methods" of Harvard.[32] By the early twentieth century, the method was well on its way to its ultimate success. In 1902, Professor Ernest Huffcutt of Cornell reported to the American Bar Association that twelve law schools had adopted the method root and branch; thirty-four others "unequivocally" clung to the "text-book system or the text-book and lecture system"; forty-eight schools professed some sort of mixture.[33] Ultimately, every major and most minor law schools converted to case-books and the Socratic method.

Like most revolutions, Langdell's was not an unmixed blessing. There were worms in the apple. Gurney's opinion was not unique. Many lawyers and teachers thought the method too theoretical—a poor way to train good lawyers. In actual practice and in the hands of good teachers, the method worked fairly well. It did imbue students with a craftsman-like skill in handling the materials of case law. But the vices of the method lay deep. In the most radical sense, the new method severed the cords, already tenuous, that tied legal study to American scholarship, and American life. Perhaps it was part of a trend: Howard Schweber feels that Langdell's "legal science" helped along a development that was already underway, a certain inward turning of the professions. Lawyers "became less and less identified as public intellectuals and more and more as professional specialists."[34] In any event, Langdell purged from the curriculum whatever touched directly on economic and political questions, whatever was argued, voted on, or

---

[30] On the spread of the Harvard method, see Stevens, *op. cit.*, pp. 60–64; on the revolution at Columbia, see William P. LaPiana, *Logic and Experience: The Origin of Modern American Legal Education* (1994), pp. 92–99.

[31] Quoted in Warren, *op. cit.*, vol. II, p. 500.

[32] Frank L. Ellsworth, *Law on the Midway: The Founding of the University of Chicago Law School* (1977), pp. 61ff; this represented a defeat for those forces led by Ernst Freund, who had been interested in infusing law training at Chicago with study of administrative law as well as traditional subjects. See also William C. Chase, *The American Law School and the Rise of Administrative Government* (1982), pp. 46–59. On the struggle over the introduction of the case method at Wisconsin, see William R. Johnson, *Schooled Lawyers: A Study in the Clash of Professional Cultures* (1978), ch. V.

[33] Ernest W. Huffcutt, "A Decade of Progress in Legal Education," *Report, 25th Ann. Meeting ABA* (1902), pp. 529, 541.

[34] Schweber, *op. cit.*, at 463.

fought over. He brought into the classroom a worship of common law and of the best and the brightest among common law judges. He ignored legislation; he despised any decisions that were, in his view, illogical or contrary to fundamental common law principles. He cloaked his views with a mantle of science. He equated law absolutely with judges' law; and judges' law, to Langdell, was formal, narrow, and abstract. The textbook method had been bad enough. It, too, was divorced from living law and apathetic toward issues of social policy. Langdell did not correct these evils. Instead, he purified and perpetuated them. Though many old textbook-and-lecture teachers probably had trouble retooling, others perhaps simply adapted old materials to new methods. After Langdell, they taught from the cases that had been lurking in the footnotes of their texts, and simply ignored the texts.

Langdell's proudest boast was that law was a science, and that his method was highly scientific. But his model of science was not experimental, or experiential; his model was Euclid's geometry, not physics or biology. Langdell considered law a pure, independent science; it was, he conceded, empirical; but the only data he allowed were reported cases. If law is at all the product of society, then Langdell's science of law was a geology without rocks, an astronomy without stars. Lawyers and judges raised on the method, if they took their training at all seriously, came to speak of law mainly in terms of a dry, arid logic, divorced from society and life. To understand Langdell's method and, more important, to understand why it triumphed, one must see it in long-term context. In the history of legal education, two paired sets of principles were constantly in battle. A principle of vocational training struggled against a principle of scientific training. At the same time, a principle of integration with general liberal education struggled against a principle of segregation. University law schools had been weakly integrationist, and weakly and reluctantly vocational. Langdell's new method was antivocational, but strongly segregationist within the university and in the context of scholarship.

Why was Langdell's method so attractive in the long run? In some way, it suited the needs of the legal profession. It exalted the prestige of law and legal learning. At the same time it affirmed that law stood on its own two feet. It was an independent entity, a separate science; it was distinct from politics, legislation, and the opinions of lay people. This was a period in which interest and occupational groups fought for their places in the sun. Langdell concocted a theory that strengthened the claims of the legal profession. Law, he insisted, was a branch of higher learning, and it called for rigorous formal training. There was good reason, then, why only trained lawyers should practice law. They deserved their monopoly of practice. The bar-association movement began at roughly the same point in time. Langdell's new method and the bar-association movement had a kind of ideological and political partnership.

Langdell's method also promised to solve the problem of teaching law in a federal union. He handled local diversity by ignoring it entirely. There was only one common law; Langdell was its prophet. More than half of the cases in his first casebook were English. Oceans could not sever the unity of common law; it was one and indivisible, like higher mathematics.

In this regard, Langdell's method was by no means novel. The ideal had always been "national" law schools. There was a good deal of traffic across state lines; even vocational Litchfield had attracted students from all over the country.

Harvard prided itself on its national scope; it even advertised in far-off places. A notice in the *St. Louis Republican,* for example, in 1848, invited law students to Harvard; the advertisement mentioned the tuition fees ($50 a term, including books), and added that "neither expediency nor the usages of society" required a large "amount of pocket-money."[35] When Michigan opened its school, too, as we have seen, it advertised in a number of cities.

A varied student body was probably a real advantage to a school. Moreover, even local boys did not always stay put. Some lawyers were rolling stones like the rest of the population. A Bostonian might go to Harvard and end up in Ohio or California. But ignoring local law was a mixed blessing at best. The unity of some parts of the common law was a fact. Langdell's abstractions, however, ignored the nature of law as a living system, rooted in time, place, and circumstance. To be sure, few schools that taught local law taught it as anything better than tricks of the trade, nuts and bolts, nuggets of practical information. In one sense, Langdell's method—austere, abstract—helped save legal education from degeneration. Two contradictory influences pressed against legal education. There was a constant demand for rising standards for lawyers. But there was an insistent push in the opposite direction, too—toward loosening the reins, toward opening the practice to more and more people. The first pressure came from leaders of the bar, worried about income and prestige. The second pressure came from the open market.

Elite lawyers were alarmed by the lax standards, by the pressures of the market. A law school required little capital to open. As demand rose, so did supply. Purists may have been shocked when the so-called Iowa Law School, in 1866, had the presumption to award twelve L.L.B. degrees. This was a mere night school, started the year before at Des Moines, by two justices of the Iowa supreme court.[36] The idea of a nighttime law school was appalling to many lawyers; but appealing to its customers. Many potential students worked for a living by day, as clerks in law offices, or in factories, offices, or shops. The Columbian College of Washington, D.C., was in operation in the late 1860s. The college was deliberately set up to "reach employees in the government departments, released from their labors at three o'clock in the afternoon."[37] The movement spread to other cities. The University of Minnesota, in 1888, offered parallel day and evening sessions. In 1889–1890, there were nine pure night schools, as against fifty-one day schools. In the 1890s, the number of night schools doubled. In 1900, there were twenty, as against seventy-seven schools that operated only during daytime, and five schools which, like Minnesota, mixed day and night.[38]

The night schools, by and large, were rigorously "practical." They had neither the patience nor the inclination to serve a rich intellectual feast. They emphasized local practice far more than the national day schools. Their main vice was that they were totally and exclusively trade schools. Their main merit was to open the door of legal training to poor, immigrant, or working-class students. They were breeding grounds for the ethnic bar. Night schools turned

---

[35] *St. Louis Republican,* Oct. 7, 1848, p. 3.

[36] Reed, *op. cit.,* pp. 396–97.

[37] Reed, *op. cit.,* p. 396; Stevens, *op. cit.,* p. 74.

[38] There was also the opportunity to study law by mail. The Sprague Correspondence School of Law, in Detroit, claimed 1,172 students in 1893. 1 Law Student's Helper 143 (1893).

out Polish, Italian, Jewish, and Irish lawyers. Many of these men went back to their neighborhoods and worked with their own communities. Lower-court judges and local politicians were drawn heavily from the graduates of these schools. Few found their way to Wall Street or La Salle Street. Naturally enough, these schools were resented on Wall Street and La Salle Street. For their part, these schools fought valiantly for students, money, legitimacy, and recognition from the bar.

One dearly sought prize was the so-called diploma privilege. If a school had the diploma privilege, its graduates were automatically admitted to the bar, without any further exam. Between 1855 and 1870, Louisiana, Mississippi, Georgia, New York, Tennessee, Michigan, and Wisconsin gave the privilege to graduates of home-state law schools. In 1870, Oregon, which had no law school of its own, went so far as to give the privilege to graduates of *any* school that had this boon at home.[39] Politically, it was difficult for a state to discriminate among its law schools, even though, arguably, some state law schools did and some did not deserve the privilege.

The bar examination was one way to dam the flood of lawyers into the profession. As apprenticeship declined and law schools became more important, supply could also be controlled, in theory, by controlling the schools. Bar associations began taking an interest in legal education. The schools themselves formed a trade group, the Association of American Law Schools, around the turn of the century. Both AALS and the American Bar Association went into the accreditation business. A school that lacked the approval of either or both was at a disadvantage in competing for students. But the standards set were a kind of lowest common denominator. Substandard legal education did not die; like stale bread or used cars, there was demand for it, and it prevailed despite attempts to drive it off the market.

THE LITERATURE OF THE LAW

By all counts, the basic literature of law, the most prolific form, was reported case law. Hundreds of volumes of reports were in print. Year by year, month by month, day by day, more reports appeared. This fabulous collection of law was so bulky by 1900 that the Babylonian Talmud or the medieval Year Books seemed inconsequentially small by comparison. One could not, to be sure, get a complete or balanced picture of American life from their collective pages; but they touched on an amazing variety of topics. Every state published reports for at least its highest court; many states, like New York and Illinois, published reports of intermediate courts; Pennsylvania even published reports of some county courts. Every new state after 1850, out of a sense of legal independence, or merely out of habit, began to issue reports promptly after statehood. In most instances, territorial reports had also been published.

Under the California Constitution, it was the duty of the state supreme court to put its decisions "in writing" and to state "the grounds of the decision."[40] The

---

[39] On the diploma privilege, see Reed, *op. cit.*, pp. 248–53.
[40] Cal. Const. 1879, art. VI, sec. 4.

states hardly needed such a mandate. As a matter of course, each state high court published decisions and opinions. Lawyers often complained that the case law was impossible to handle, that the production of reports was out of control. "What Shall be Done with the Reports?" was the title of a plaintive essay published in 1882. The author, J. L. High, was troubled by the "pernicious" effects of the "vast accumulation of reported cases." It weakened the law; the lawyer, groping his way through this "labyrinth," was bound to neglect the "underlying principle" of law, "in the search for a precedent exactly in point."[41] Alas, no reform was forthcoming. Indeed, these moans and groans now seem as naive as complaints that twenty miles an hour was too fast for the human body to bear. Each generation taught the older one a lesson in sheer voluminousness. In 1810, there were only eighteen published volumes of American reports; in 1848, about eight hundred; by 1885, about 3,798; by 1910, over 8,000.[42] The end is by no means in sight. The National Reporter System, which began in 1879, and the digests of the West Publishing Company, helped lawyers cope a little. Even so, lawyers could hardly keep up with their own jurisdictions, let alone handle the others. Typical lawyers simply gave up any attempt to grasp the whole of the law or stay abreast of it. They concentrated on problems at hand, on the corners of law they dealt with day by day; they grumbled about the expense and the confusion of law reports. Yet, basically it was the lawyers' own hunger for precedent, for case law, that kept the system going as it was.

State and federal reports are important historical documents. In some ways, however, they are as hard to read as hieroglyphics. The language is stilted and formal. The "facts" are what a lower court "found," not necessarily what happened. Only the *legally* relevant is systematically reported. Even as law, reports are a strange and unreliable guide. Most cases were unimportant or ephemeral. But cases never came neatly labeled wheat or chaff. The trouble with the common law was not only the *number* of cases, but the fact that books could never be safely thrown away.

Judges wrote more poorly, it seems, after 1850, though these are very difficult matters to deal with rigorously. Karl Llewellyn called the style of Gibson, Marshall, and Shaw the "grand style"—the style that looked for "wisdom-in-result." It was based on broad principle; it was sweeping, magisterial, and creative. This style was all but dead by 1900. It was replaced by what Llewellyn called the "formal style," which stressed order and logic in the law.[43] Opinions tended to be bombastic and repetitious. Strings of useless citations filled the pages of the reports. There was bad logic and worse English. At least this was Llewellyn's impression; and he might have been right. As the Marshalls, Shaws, and Gibsons died, or retired, comparable men did not replace them. Few high court or federal judges wrote opinions with power and persuasion. The picture

[41] J. H. High, "What Shall Be Done with the Reports?" 16 Am. L. Rev. 429, 439 (1822).

[42] Charles Warren, *A History of the American Bar* (1911), p. 557.

[43] Karl N. Llewellyn, "Remarks on the Theory of Appellate Decision and the Rules or Canons about How Statutes are to be Construed," 3 Vanderbilt L. Rev. 395, 396 (1950); *The Common Law Tradition: Deciding Appeals* (1960), pp. 35–39. For Llewellyn, period-style was "a way of thought and work, not . . . a way of writing." But his analysis fits matters of style rather better than it fits the actual work of the courts; and of course what judges actually thought remains a mystery.

was never completely dark, the work never completely drab. From 1882 on, a master stylist, Oliver Wendell Holmes Jr., sat on the highest court of Massachusetts. But the work of the average judge in 1870 or 1900 *seems* plainly weaker than the average work of 1830.

Talent and style are not historical accidents. There were social reasons why the art declined. Judges were rushed, dockets were crowded; there was less time to polish and rework the opinions. The leisurely style of oral argument led to a leisurely style of writing opinions. All that had ended. Marshall's court had perhaps more time to ponder, to compose, to discuss, and to polish its work than the court of Chief Justice Fuller. Judges in a hurry were tempted to dish up, as the opinion of the court, a scissors and paste job taken mostly from the winning lawyer's brief. Conditions of judicial life may have plugged the heady sense of creativity of earlier days, the ability to work with broad, sweeping principle.

And perhaps the judges were not the men they used to be. The judges represented—or overrepresented—old-American, conservative values. Yet, on the whole, judges of 1900 were much less likely than judges of 1800 to be men of high general culture, less likely to have esthetic command of the English language. Local politicians were not likely to become great stylists on the bench. Besides, the theory of judicial decision making had subtly altered. Formality was not only form, it was also a concept. Judges were not builders of law now; they were protectors of the existing law. That, at least, was their mask or disguise. Judges as before wielded power, sometimes great power; but they hid the power of the bench behind the cloak of legalism; they concealed their thought processes in jargon. This had two definite advantages. First, it provided a screen of legitimacy against attack from left and right. The *judges* were not responsible for unpopular decisions—it was the law and only the law that determined results.[44] The long list of cited cases—"precedents" strung out row after row in the judge's written opinion—drove this position home. Second, formalism reinforced one of the judges' primarily claims: that they had the sole and exclusive right to expound the law. The law, as the judge laid it out in his opinion, seemed impossibly technical, erudite. Everyman or everywoman could not be a lawyer or judge; the lay person was too ignorant of legal science. Langdell's theory made the same point and was therefore most welcome to the judges.

Langdell drove the textbooks and treatises out of the temple of legal education. They lost face, but not importance. As the population of cases exploded, treatises were needed more desperately than ever. No single writer dared to restate all of American law any more. But texts and treatises of all types poured

---

[44] See, further, on this point, Morton J. Horwitz, "The Rise of Legal Formalism," 19 Am. J. Legal Hist. 251 (1975); Duncan Kennedy, "Form and Substance in Private Law Adjudication," 89 Harv. L. Rev. 1685 (1976). "Formalism" is hard to measure; and there is always a nagging doubt whether or not this is a useful way to characterize the work of the judges. Harry N. Scheiber has argued forcefully that "instrumentalism" survived and flourished in the late nineteenth century, despite the supposed triumph of "formalism." "Instrumentalism and Property Rights: A Reconsideration of American 'Styles of Judicial Reasoning' in the 19th Century," 1975 Wis. L. Rev. 1; see also Walter E Pratt, "Rhetorical Styles on the Fuller Court," 24 Am. J. Legal Hist. 189 (1980). On legal thought generally in this period, see Morton J. Horwitz, *The Transformation of American Law, 1870–1960: The Crisis of Legal Orthodoxy* (1992).

off the presses, on specific subjects, to turn a profit and help lawyers in their work. It has been estimated (perhaps conservatively) that a thousand treatises or so were published in the last half of the nineteenth century. Overwhelmingly now, these were American treatises, rather than American editions of British books. Blackstone by now was hopelessly out of date. There were new old favorites now—Simon Greenleaf's *Evidence,* Theophilus Parsons's *Contracts,* for example. Parsons (1797–1882) first published his treatise in 1853; supposedly, it sold more copies than any other American treatise. One admirer spoke of Parsons's "pleasing" style, his "sugar coated pills of legal lore," so easily "swallowed and assimilated."[45] When a work was popular, as Parsons's was, it was repeatedly revised, even after the author died or withdrew from the stage. Publishers hired other men to carry on under the valuable name. Samuel Williston edited the eighth edition of Parsons's *Contracts* in 1893; Oliver Wendell Holmes Jr., edited the twelfth edition of Kent's *Commentaries* in 1873.[46]

Most nineteenth-century treatises were barren enough reading when they first appeared and would be sheer torture for the reader today. Charles Warren listed some thirty-seven works, written between 1870 and 1900, which he considered of prime importance.[47] There was clearly a market for lawbooks that lawyers could use. The books were practical books on practical subjects. The busy lawyer had a voracious appetite for helpful texts, texts that wove the authorities into neat, indexed packages. Some treatises dealt with strictly American developments in new and emerging fields of law: railroads, business corporations, and torts. John Forrest Dillon's *Law of Municipal Corporations,* first published in 1872, was a pioneering book, written over a period of nine years, in moments snatched in the "interstices" of this judge's busy life. The book was needed; it was an immediate success. Victor Morawetz threw himself into the work of writing a treatise on corporations. It appeared in 1882, and made his reputation; later he earned a fortune at the bar. John Chipman Gray (1839–1915), on the other hand, a distinguished Boston lawyer, one of the founders of the firm of Ropes and Gray, professor of law at Harvard, dipped into the older cellars of the common law and exhausted the subject of *The Rule Against Perpetuities* (1886) in a dark and dreary book that (according to tradition) no one has ever really read, though countless lawyers and students have skimmed through its pages in search of light. Gray also wrote a little treatise on *Restraints on the Alienation of Property* (1883).

Not surprisingly, law professors were among the most prolific and successful writers of treatises. Emory Washburn of Harvard wrote a treatise on *Real Property* (two volumes, 1860–1862); it was a great success. Theophilus Parsons's *Contracts* was, as we noted, a huge bestseller; and Parsons wrote seven other treatises. One of them reportedly brought him $40,000, an enormous fortune for the day. Christopher Tiedeman, professor at the University of Missouri, wrote another

---

[45] Charles Warren, *History of the Harvard Law School,* vol. II, p. 312.

[46] Mark DeWolfe Howe, *Justice Oliver Wendell Holmes: The Proving Years, 1870–1882* (1963), pp. 10–17; see G. Edward White, *Justice Oliver Wendell Holmes: Law and the Inner Self* (1993), pp. 124–27. There is an enormous literature on Holmes. See, for example, Robert W. Gordon, ed., *The Legacy of Oliver Wendell Holmes, Jr.* (1992); Thomas C. Grey, "Holmes and Legal Pragmatism," 41 Stanford Law Review 787 (1989).

[47] Charles Warren, *A History of the American Bar* (1912) pp. 551–62.

popular treatise on real property (1884). Langdell's daring practice of hiring young full-time teachers and scholars, rather than elderly judges and lawyers, created a new occupation, the legal academic; at least in theory, these men could devote most of their lives to the literature of law. Some of their creative energy went into casebooks rather than textbooks or treatises. Langdell himself wrote very little besides his casebooks. But on the whole the academics did produce a substantial body of literature.

The most famous treatises were those that treated large, basic blocks of law, such as torts or property. But there were many highly specialized books, for example, Edward Keasbey's *Law of Electric Wires in Streets and Highways*, published in 1892. It is dangerous to generalize, but the treatises after 1870 seemed somewhat drier and less imaginative than the best work of the prior generation. Late nineteenth-century treatises tended to be humorless, impersonal, less concerned with praise and blame than with bare exposition of law. James Schouler, himself a treatise writer (Volume I of his *Personal Property* appeared in 1873), pleaded for more skill in synthesizing cases and other legal materials; in his view, even this talent was frequently lacking. The standard editions of texts were becoming so "honeycombed with this insect annotation that the text seems to belong to the footnotes, not the footnotes to the text."[48] In this kind of book, there was no place for critique or for culture.

Not much could be expected from books written strictly for the lawyer's market. But in truth not much could be expected from legal literature in general. Common law thought, in and out of universities, was isolated and inbred. The dominant culture of legal scholarship was infected by Langdell's ideas of legal science, or converged on the same state, for similar reasons. Few text writers indulged in social commentary, or any commentary at all. John Forrest Dillon, a man of high intelligence, explained, in the preface to the fourth edition of his treatise on local government: "No writer on our jurisprudence is authorized to speak oracularly, to excogitate a system, or to give to his views any authoritative sanction. To this rule the most eminent are no exception." Dillon saw a role for the author's "reflections, criticisms, and conclusions"; but it was a limited role, and most of his colleagues did without these "reflections, criticisms, and conclusions."[49] After 1870, the tone of John Chipman Gray was more representative of the better treatises—logical, pseudoscientific, frankly jejune. Authors tended to confine personal opinions about social worth and social impact to the preface, if anywhere. There were exceptions. Joel Bishop, who wrote on a number of subjects—family law, criminal law most notably—wrote lively, mordant comments throughout his treatises. Even he was proud to assert that "nothing merely theoretical" was "admitted" into his pages. And he was convinced that the "student, the practitioner, and the judge" all needed "the same learning," and therefore the same kind of book.[50] Thomas Cogley wrote a cranky, obstreperous book on the *Law of Strikes, Lock-outs and Labor Organizations* (1894), more a tract than

[48] James Schouler, "Text and Citations," 22 Am. L. Rev. 66, 73 (1888).

[49] John F. Dillon, *Commentaries on the Law of Municipal Corporations* (4th ed., 1890), preface, pp. vii–viii.

[50] Joel P. Bishop, *Commentaries on the Criminal Law* (7th ed., 1882), xiv; on Bishop's intellectual world, see Stephen A. Siegel, "Joel Bishop's Orthodoxy," 13 Law and History Review 215 (1995).

a treatise. But there was nothing before 1900 to match the magnificent treatise on evidence (1904–1905) by John H. Wigmore, scholarly, yet critical, the product of a glowing intelligence. Gray's style led directly to Samuel Williston, whose treatise on contracts in the 1920s was, from the standpoint of legal or social thought, volume after volume of a heavy void.

Basically, legal literature was pragmatic; the differences between the famous treatises and strictly local manuals—and even such subliminal stuff as layman's guides and the many versions of *Every Man His Own Lawyer*—was a difference not of kind but of degree. Legal literature, with some exceptions, was empty of philosophy or social science. European jurisprudence was occasionally studied; the German historical school influenced the writing of James Carter, Field's great antagonist. John Chipman Gray's early twentieth-century book *The Nature and Sources of the Law* (1909), well written and well balanced, is still worth reading. A school of legal history did develop in the latter part of the nineteenth century. It was not concerned with how the legal system developed; its subject was the history of common law doctrine, rather narrowly defined. Hence it was mostly English legal history, and fairly ancient history at that. The essays of James Barr Ames were among the best of these works.

Oliver Wendell Holmes's exploration of origins, *The Common Law* (1881), an authentic classic, was easily the most distinguished book on law, by an American, published between 1850 and 1900.[51] "The life of the law," wrote Holmes at the beginning of this book, in a famous passage, "has not been logic; it has been experience." This line, endlessly quoted, served almost as a slogan or motto for the legal realists of the 1920s and 1930s. It has been an important, even revolutionary, maxim for jurisprudence and legal research. To Langdell, and his disciple Ames, conceptual clarity and logic were at the very heart of law, or at any rate at the heart of legal science. Holmes understood that aspect of their thought; he called Langdell "the greatest living legal theologian." But Holmes saw logic as an "evening dress which the newcomer puts on to make it self presentable"; the "important phenomenon is the man underneath it, not the coat."[52] Yet, despite their difference in viewpoint, Holmes was not so distant in historical technique from Langdell's disciple Ames. The "experience" that most fascinated Holmes was a common law experience. He was as eager as Ames to look into the *Year Books;* and he groped for an understanding of common law roots among Norman and Germanic materials. At times he seemed to care more for these origins than for the way law fulfilled itself in his own generation.

Outside the academy, there was hardly any literature on legal history worthy of the name. Most "Histories of Bench and Bar"—there were scores of these—were trivial, bombastic, and maddeningly repetitious. One of the best of a bad lot was John Belton O'Neall's *Biographical Sketches of the Bench and Bar of South Carolina,* a two-volume work published in 1859. The prose was execrable:

> William Henry Drayton is a name not to be forgotten while liberty is appreciated. I turn to it with the delight with which the awakened sleeper witnesses the Aurora of a bright day.[53]

---

[51] On the nature and contents of this book, see G. Edward White, *op. cit.,* ch. 5.
[52] Quoted in Howe, *op. cit.,* pp. 155–57.
[53] Vol. I. p. 13.

Many later histories were a hodgepodge, cobbled together from the reminiscences of aging lawyers. When the upstarts of the "flush times" grew gray and respectable, they delighted in telling tall tales of their youth. Their memory was not to be trusted. Occasionally, though, these books preserved traditions and sources that have some historical value. Court histories were only a little better; they tended to be strings of anecdotes, punctuated with cameo descriptions of judges. In this wilderness, any careful and balanced study stood out dramatically. Such a book was Judge Charles P. Daly's *History of the Court of Common Pleas* (New York), a slim but valuable work that appeared in 1855.

More lasting and important work was written by constitutional theorists. If Holmes's *Common Law* was the most important nineteenth-century book, from the twentieth-century standpoint, Thomas M. Cooley's *Constitutional Limitations*, written in 1868, was the most important book in its own time. Its full title was: *A Treatise on the Constitutional Limitations Which Rest Upon the Legislative Power of the States of the American Union.* Benjamin Twiss has claimed that Cooley's book supplied "capitalism . . . with a legal ideology . . . almost a direct counter to the appearance a year earlier of Karl Marx's *Das Kapital*."[54] This was a wild exaggeration. But the sentiment is understandable. The book was ahead of its time; it appeared before the full flowering of the due-process clause. It anticipated these developments. Ultimately, Cooley's book ran through several editions, and some prophecies of the first edition were fulfilled by the courts in time to appear as settled law in the later ones. Cooley's treatise was useful; it provided a beautiful constitutional theory for those who wanted limited government, who were frightened of impulsive and radical lawmaking, who wanted no more hostile regulation of business, no laws on the side of organized labor and the mob. This, the *laissez-faire* or social Darwinist point of view, found expression in some passages in Cooley's text. Cooley himself was much less of a cardboard reactionary than he has been pictured.[55] The book was solidly written, well thought out, the product of an inventive mind. Its actual influence is a matter of some dispute. As we have seen, there were important cases, toward the end of the century, which took a conservative point of view much like Cooley's. The judges in these cases often cited Cooley. Thus he seemed like the true source of a lot of constitutional doctrine. He did supply authority and text for those who needed and wanted these. But the Supreme Court was not hypnotized by Cooley. Rather, both Cooley and the judges were hypnotized by similar ideas. One wrote a book, the others decided cases, from similar impulses. Cooley was architect, prophet, and publicist, of a theory of social order, at a time when the specter of "socialism" sent waves of panic through the upper stories of society. For the solid citizen, who saw with dismay huge hordes of immigrants pouring into the country, and who worried about traditional American values, the Supreme Court was a mighty shield, protecting the country from moral and political collapse. In the next generation, Christopher Tiedeman's book, *A Treatise* on *the Limitations of Police Power in the United States* (1889), took a position further to the right than Cooley. Tiedeman's idea of limited government gave the courts another text to

---

[54] Benjamin R. Twiss, *Lawyers and the Constitution* (1942), p. 18.

[55] See Alan Jones, "Thomas M. Cooley and the Michigan Supreme Court: 1865–1885," 10 Am. J. Legal Hist. 97 (1966).

refer to; once again, then, the constitutional theorists like Tiedeman could cite, in the next edition of their book, the courts who cited their earlier editions.[56]

LEGAL PERIODICALS AND CASEBOOKS

When West began to publish the *National Reporter System,* it undercut the reason for being of many law magazines. These periodicals were full of little essays and comments about the law; they also brought the profession news about recent, interesting cases. The *Albany Law Journal,* the *Central Law Journal* and the *American Law Review* of St. Louis, the *American Law Register* of Philadelphia, and the *Virginia Law Journal* of Richmond still appeared in the 1880s.[57] But their day was almost done. A few journals specialized in insurance, or patents, or corporation law. Thomas B. Paton launched a *Banking Law Journal* in New York in 1889. *Green Bag,* begun in 1889, was an uninhibited potpourri of interesting articles and comments on the law.

A more significant event was the birth of the university law review. The first issue of the *Harvard Law Review* appeared on April 15, 1887. It was (and is) edited by students at the law school; every issue contained some of their work, along with the work of professors, lawyers, and judges. The first issues included lawschool news, and notes "taken by students from lectures delivered as part of the regular course of instruction in the school."[58] The *Review* proposed to appear monthly "during the academic year," at a subscription price of $2.50 a year, or $0.35 per number. (The price in 2004 was $55 for individuals per year; $200 for institutions.) The *Review* did not intend "to enter into competition with established law journals," but rather to "give . . . some idea of what is done under the Harvard system of instruction." Yet the staff did hope that its work might "be serviceable to the profession at large."[59] Most articles discussed points of laws doctrinally, and more or less in the Langdell mode of thought. But there were other kinds of articles as well. William H. Dunbar, in the first volume, contributed an essay on "The Anarchists' Case before the Supreme Court of the United States"; and Samuel B. Clarke produced "Criticisms upon Henry George, Reviewed from the Stand-point of Justice."[60]

The *Yale Law Journal* was launched four years later, in October 1891; its first article was on "Voting-Trusts," by Simeon Baldwin. Other law reviews followed—Columbia in 1900, for example. The university law review proved an apt vehicle for speculative writing on law. It was the perfect outlet for shorter

---

[56] John Forrest Dillon, in his treatise on local government (1872), was also responsible for a few notions which became important in conservative decision making. See Clyde Jacobs, *Law Writers and the Courts* (1954), for a good assessment of the work and importance of Cooley, Tiedeman, and Dillon.

[57] For a list of periodicals, see 21 Am. L. Rev. 150 (1887). Some of the reviews did not print cases, and were more strictly scholarly, like the later university reviews. One of these was the Southern Law Review, New Series, which Seymour D. Thompson began to edit at St. Louis in 1875. Thompson discontinued case digests, and promised to present instead "the *best legal thought* in America and Europe."

[58] See, for example, 1 Harv. L. Rev. 103 (1887).

[59] 1 Harv. L. Rev. 35 (1887).

[60] 1 Harv. L. Rev. 205, 307 (1888).

works by the new class of teaching scholars. The law review could justify itself as a training device for students, and as a scholarly journal; it did not have to meet the immediate demands of the marketplace. The writing in the early reviews was not uniformly good; but the reviews did publish some distinguished articles. A striking example was the article by Samuel D. Warren and Louis D. Brandeis in 1890, in the *Harvard Law Review,* on "The Right to Privacy."[61] Out of a few scraps of precedent, the article proposed a brand-new tort, invasion of privacy. With the curious modesty of the common lawyer, the authors never claimed this new tort was their personal discovery. They preferred to pass it off as a foundling. Citing this or that principle or case, they claimed it already existed; only the courts and the public were simply not aware of what was there, underneath the surface. The question was "whether the existing law affords a principle which can properly be invoked to protect the privacy of the individual?" Their answer was yes. The response of courts to this suggestion was not overwhelming; but when a more sympathetic time rolled around, Warren and Brandeis's child, like Cooley's theories in *their* realm, was available for adoption and support.

One final form of legal literature should also be mentioned: the casebook. This was a by-product of Langdell's reforms; and Langdell himself published the first teaching casebook, on contracts, in 1871. His disciples and converts followed with casebooks of their own.[62] James Barr Ames edited cases on *Bills and Notes* in 1881. John Chipman Gray brought out a six-volume casebook on *Property* (1888–1892).[63] The early casebooks were pure and austere; there was nothing in them but cases. They were totally devoid of any commentary. Finding, pasting, and stitching cases together was not so simple as it might appear. The best casebooks required a great deal of creative imagination. But these bare, spare books carried to its extreme a most striking characteristic of the teaching style they were reflecting. This was the Socratic masquerade: the art of saying everything while appearing to say nothing at all.

---

[61] 4 Harv. L. Rev. 193 (1890).

[62] Collections of cases were not entirely new. For example, Edmund Bennet and Franklin Heard published *A Selection of Leading Cases in Criminal Law* in two volumes, in 1856. In the preface they noted that the "selection of important Cases on different branches of the Law, and the elucidation and development of the principles involved in them, in the form of Notes," had become an "acceptable mode of presenting legal subjects to the Profession." Langdell's was the first collection, however, arranged systematically, in accordance with his theory of legal education.

[63] Interestingly, Gray arranged his materials to follow the organization of Emory Washburn's textbook on property, which had been published in 1860. See Sutherland, *op. cit.,* p. 152.

CHAPTER 12

THE LEGAL PROFESSION: AT WORK

THE NIMBLE PROFESSION

In 1850, there were, according to one estimate, 21,979 lawyers in the country.[1] The number of lawyers grew very rapidly after the Revolution. In the last half of the century, there was even greater increase. The transformation of the American economy after the Civil War profoundly affected the demand for lawyers, and hence the supply. By 1880, there were perhaps 60,000 lawyers; by 1900, about 114,000. (In the twentieth-century, growth would be even greater—in 2000, there were approximately one million lawyers.)

The functions of the profession changed along with its numbers. The New York Code of Civil Procedure, of 1848, symbolized one kind of change. The code did not end the lawyer's monopoly of courtroom work. It did not abolish the bag of jargon and artifice that was as much a part of his equipment as the doctor's black bag with stethoscope and tools. But the code symbolized, in a way, the end of the hegemony of the courtroom. One reason why procedural codes had become necessary in the first place was because lawyers had less skill and talent in the art of pleading. They were less sure-footed in matters of procedure. The work of the lawyer became less centered on litigation and courtroom work. This was an outstanding fact about the practice of law in the second half of the century. Most lawyers still went to court; but the Wall Street lawyer, who perhaps never spoke to a judge except socially, made more money and had more prestige than any courtroom lawyer could hope for.

The law itself was changing. Life and the economy were more complicated; there was more, then, to be done, in the business world especially; and the lawyers proved able to do it. There was nothing inevitable in the process. It did not happen, for example, in Japan. The legal profession might have become smaller and narrower; lawyers might have become highly specialized, like the English barrister, or confined themselves, like the brain surgeon, to a few rare, complex, and lucrative tasks. Automation and technological change were challenges for lawyers, just as they were challenges to other occupations. Social invention constantly threatened to displace lawyers from some of their functions. It was adapt or die. Lawyers in the first half of the century made money searching titles. After the Civil War, title companies and trust companies were efficient competitors. By 1900, well-organized companies nibbled away at other staples of the practice, too: debt collection and estate work, for example.

---

[1] [John] *Livingston's Law Register* (1851), preface, p. iv.

Still, lawyers prospered. The profession was exceedingly nimble at finding new kinds of work and new ways to do it. Its nimbleness was no doubt due to the character of the bar: open-ended, unrestricted, uninhibited, and attractive to sharp, ambitious men. In so amorphous a profession, lawyers drifted in and out; many went into business or politics because they could not earn a living at their trade. Others reached out for new sorts of practice. At any rate, the profession did not shrink to (or rise to) the status of a small, exclusive elite. Even in 1860, the profession was bigger, wider, more diverse than it had been in years gone by. In 1800, lawyers in Philadelphia came "predominantly from families of wealth, status, and importance." In 1860, a much higher percentage came from the middle class—sons of shopkeepers, clerks, and small businessmen.[2] In Massachusetts, too, in the period 1870–1900, there was an increase in the percentage of lawyers who were recruited from business and white-collar backgrounds, rather than professional or elite backgrounds, compared to the prewar period.[3]

The external relations of the bar were always vitally important. After 1870, there was another line of defense against competition: the lawyers' unions (never called by that name), which fought vigorously to protect the boundaries of the calling. The organized profession raised (or tried to raise) its "standards"; tried to limit entry into the field, and (above all) tried to resist conversion of the profession into a "mere" business or trade. In fact, lawyers did not incorporate during this period; and did not become fully bureaucratized. The bar was able to prevent the corporate practice of law. Large private law firms were able to compete with captive legal departments and house counsel staffs of large corporations. For the time being, at least, the private lawyer kept his independent status as a middle-class craftsman and entrepreneur. The lawyer's role in American life had never been very clearly defined. What lawyers actually did constituted the definition of legal practice. This was a tautology; but it also expressed a truth. The upper echelons of the profession never succeeded in closing the doors against newcomers and outsiders. They dreamt of a close-knit, guildlike bar. They envied the honor and security of the English barrister. But they could not have their dream; it was too easy to pass in and out of the profession.

The corporation lawyer, on Wall Street and its sister streets in other cities, was a dramatic new figure at the bar. But he did not put the other kinds of lawyer out of business. He supplemented them. He superimposed another layer on a profession already made up of many layers and strata. Before the Civil War, the most prominent, famous lawyers were lawyer-statesmen, who argued great cases before great courts, who went into politics, and, above all, were skilled in the arts of advocacy. Daniel Webster was the prototype. There was no Daniel Webster in the Gilded Age. But the orator-statesman was not quite extinct. Jeremiah Sullivan Black, one of the most colorful nineteenth-century lawyers, was a well-known survivor.[4]

---

[2] Gary B. Nash, "The Philadelphia Bench and Bar, 1800–1861," in *Comparative Studies in Society and History,* vol. VII, No. 2 (1965), p. 203.

[3] Gerard W. Gawalt, "The Impact of Industrialization on the Legal Profession in Massachusetts, 1870–1900," in Gerard W. Gawalt, ed., *The New High Priests: Lawyers in Post-Civil War America* (1984), pp. 97, 102.

[4] His biography has been written by William N. Brigance, *Jeremiah Sullivan Black* (1934).

Black was born in 1810. He read law in the office of Chauncey Forward and formed his distinctive style of speech and writing from close study of Shakespeare, Milton, and the Bible. He served on the Pennsylvania supreme court in the 1850s, where his pungent prose spices the otherwise dry, brittle pages of these law reports. Later, Black served in Buchanan's cabinet, as attorney general (1857). Still later, Black got rich off the fat of California land cases, which he sometimes argued before the U.S. Supreme Court. He fought the good fight in two great cases after the Civil War, *Ex parte Milligan* and *Ex parte McCardle*.[5] He figured on the Democratic side of the Tilden-Hayes controversy, and died in 1883. Black was a fiery lawyer and a superb orator. His oral arguments were flawless; he could speak for hours on end, without referring to his notes, and without misciting a single case. He was a lone wolf who never really maintained an office, never had a partner for any length of time. Nor did Black have any permanent clients; he was always hired for one particular case. His income, it was said, was enormous. But he kept no records, and, indeed, rarely fixed a fee. However, for one case alone, in 1879, he was paid the princely sum of $28,000.

Lawyers like Black were rare. One direct descendant was Clarence Darrow, also a loner, also a dramatic courtroom warrior, whose amazing career began toward the end of the century.[6] Other modern examples are the great civil rights lawyers, and the famous tort and criminal lawyers; men and women who do not have a fixed clientele, and whose livelihood depends on publicity and word of mouth. Howe and Hummel were not entirely aberrations. It is possible to be shy and bookish and make a fortune as a tax lawyer. But to be a king of torts, like Melvin Belli, or a great criminal lawyer, like Samuel Leibowitz or (the fictional) Perry Mason, an attorney has to be made of more sensational stuff. Great careers were made by these lawyers; and by prosecutors. There was, for example, the New York career of William Travers Jerome (1859–1934), the enemy of Tammany Hall; and prosecutors could make their way into high politics, as the career of Thomas E. Dewey would later demonstrate.[7] But the big money was mainly elsewhere on Wall Street. The Wall Street lawyer of the late nineteenth century was self-effacing. He had no hunger, or need, for publicity. What he wanted was a steady and permanent group of well-paying clients.

The rise of the Wall Street lawyer was the most important event in the life of the profession during this period. First-hand accounts of the upper levels of the bar are not common. Robert T. Swaine, the historian of the Cravath firm of New York, has provided a detailed account of the rise of one Wall Street office.[8] For most of the nineteenth century, the firm was extremely small, a two-man partnership. Members of the Seward and Blatchford families were dominant figures in the early history of the firm. The firm was originally based in Auburn, New York. When William H. Seward became a U.S. senator in 1849, he loosened his ties to the office. But he never gave up the business of law, even though his career led him into Lincoln's cabinet, as secretary of state. In the 1850s, the firm did a great deal of debt collection, real estate, and title

5 71 U.S. 2 (1866); 74 U.S. 506 (1869).

6 Darrow's career is described in Kevin Tierney, *Darrow: A Biography* (1979).

7 On Dewey's career, see Mary M. Stolberg, *Fighting Organized Crime: Politics, Justice, and the Legacy of Thomas E. Dewey* (1995).

8 *The Cravath Firm and Its Predecessors*, vol. I (1946).

business; its lawyers drafted wills and trusts. Cyrus McCormick retained the firm for a patent matter in 1850. In 1854, the firm moved to New York City. It was by then already active in patent litigation. The Bank of North America and the Girard Trust Company were among its clients.

After the Civil War, the booming express companies took over as the firm's biggest clients. Corporate business expanded; patent litigation gradually diminished. The firm added new members. In 1869, Charles M. Da Costa joined the firm. He was an expert on admiralty matters, but he soon gravitated toward work on corporate reorganization. In 1880, the firm became involved with Kuhn, Loeb & Co., and hence with corporate securities and finance. William D. Guthrie became a partner in 1883; Victor Morawetz, the author of a treatise on corporations, joined in 1887. Between 1880 and 1900, the career of the firm was intimately bound up with Wall Street finance; it drew up papers merging businesses, it advised railroads on their legal affairs, handled stockholders' suits, and floated bond issues. In 1896, Morawetz withdrew, to become general counsel for the Santa Fe Railroad; Charles Steele, a partner in the 1890s, went over to the house of Morgan. The junior partners and clerks still handled small litigation for big clients; and the firm still argued cases before the Supreme Court (Guthrie's role in the income tax case has been mentioned), but the partnership had become the very model of a Wall Street firm. It was a servant and advisor to big business, an architect of financial structures; it did not feed on lawsuits, rather it avoided them.

The Cravath story is one of continuous success. It is also a survivor. Nobody chronicles extinct firms. Many firms formed, reformed, split up, and disappeared from history.[9] Yet, there were others, established in this period, that have had histories as long as the Cravath firm. These histories in the main run parallel to the history of Cravath—for example, the story of the firm of Thomas G. Shearman and John W. Sterling, which handled many of Jay Gould's tangled affairs, and later those of William Rockefeller.[10] There is also Coudert Brothers, founded by three brothers in the 1850s. A fourth partner joined the firm in 1877. This was Paul Fuller. His was a real rags to riches story. Fuller, an orphan, cared for by a Mexican family in California, somehow traveled back to the East Coast at the age of 9, became a homeless street child; the father of the Coudert brothers noticed him, because the lad spoke fluent Spanish. Coudert brought the boy into his home. He later became an office boy, then married a Coudert daughter, and finally became a partner. By 1883, the Coudert firm had at least eight lawyers in the firm—three partners (one of the founding brothers was dead) and five associates, plus clerks, scriveners, and others. The Coudert firm was also a pioneer in opening a foreign branch—the brothers were totally bilingual, and they established an office in Paris in 1879.[11]

New York did not have a monopoly of legal practice. There were little Wall Streets in other cities, too. Each major city had a corporate bar, at least on a lesser scale. In Milwaukee, Wisconsin, Finches, Lynde & Miller was the leading

[9] Wayne K. Hobson, "Symbol of the New Profession: Emergence of the Large Law Firm, 1870–1915," in Gawalt, ed., *The New High Priests*, pp. 3, 5.

[10] The firm has been chronicled by Walter K. Earle, *Mr. Shearman and Mr. Sterling and How They Grew* (1963).

[11] Virginia Kays Veenswijk, *Coudert Brothers: A Legacy in Law* (1994), pp. 1–58.

firm, with four lawyers. In 1879, they also had four paid clerks, at a salary of $1,100 each. The firm had been active in real estate matters, in estates and trust work, and it also represented many of the city's major businesses. Like the great Wall Street houses, this firm grew steadily, and in somewhat similar ways.[12] The house chronicle of O'Melveny and Meyers, a giant Los Angeles firm, recounts how the founding father of the firm shifted his talents to municipal bonds when the title business threatened to dry up.[13] When the firm of Munford, Hunton, Williams & Anderson was formed, in 1902, it was the largest in Richmond, Virginia—with four lawyers and a part-time stenographer.[14] In Philadelphia, the predecessor to Morgan, Lewis, and Bockius dates back to 1873. Randal Morgan, the younger brother of a founding partner, "read law" at the firm; then became a partner in 1885. He left to become general counsel to the United Gas Improvement Company (UGI); and, no surprise, UGI retained the firm as its outside counsel (the relationship lasted more than a century).[15] This kind of symbiosis was not at all uncommon. It was a great source of strength to the growing law firms.

By and large, the leading lawyers of the big Wall Street firms, and their equivalents in other cities, were solid Republican, conservative in outlook, standard Protestant in faith, old English in heritage. These men were also the leaders of the bar associations. They were the men who spoke for and about "professional ethics."[16] But the firms were never wholly monolithic. Morawetz was a Southern Democrat. Guthrie, Seward's most militant and reactionary partner, was Roman Catholic; he began his career as an office boy. Da Costa, another partner, was descended from West Indian Jews. Charles O'Connor (1804–1884), a dominant figure in the New York trial bar, was born in New York of Irish parents. There were many others at the bar of Irish descent, like Charles P. Daly (1816–1899), author, lawyer, and chief judge of the New York court of common pleas.[17] It did help a rising lawyer, of course, to have a good background—and cultural compatibility. Old-line lawyers were never too happy about the influx of "Celts," Jews, and other undesirables. George T. Strong, writing in his diary in 1874, hailed the idea that the Columbia Law School should institute an admission test: "either a college diploma, or an *examination including Latin*. This will keep out the little scrubs (German Jew boys mostly) whom the School now promotes from the grocery-counters . . . to be 'gentlemen of the Bar.' "[18] Meritorious outsiders once in a while reached the celestial heights of Wall Street or the equivalent—

---

[12] This firm was the predecessor of the modern firm of Foley & Lardner. Ellen D. Langill, *Foley & Lardner, Attorneys at Law, 1842–1992* (1992), p. 80; see also Emily P. Dodge, "Evolution of a City Law Office, Part II," 1956 Wis. L. Rev. 35, 41.

[13] William W. Clary, *History of the Law Firm of O'Melveny and Myers, 1885–1965*, vol. 1 (1966), p. 102.

[14] Anne Hobson Freeman, *The Style of a Law Firm: Eight Gentlemen from Virginia* (1989), p. 1.

[15] Park B. Dilks Jr., *Morgan, Lewis & Bockius: A Law Firm and its Times, 1873–1933* (1994), pp. 14–15.

[16] E.g., the leadership of the New York City Bar Association, see Michael J. Powell, *From Patrician to Professional Elite: The Transformation of the New York City Bar Association* (1988).

[17] Harold E. Hammond, *A Commoner's Judge: The Life and Times of Charles Patrick Daly* (1954).

[18] Quoted in Henry W. Taft, *A Century and a Half at the New York Bar* (1938), p. 146.

Louis Dembitz Brandeis, from a Jewish family in Louisville, Kentucky, was an extremely prominent Boston lawyer in the 1890s. But men like Brandeis and O'Connor generally succeeded by adopting, to a greater or lesser extent, the protective coloration of the dominant culture.

Women and blacks were truly outsiders. No woman practiced law before the 1870s. Mrs. Myra Bradwell, born in 1831, married a lawyer in 1852, studied law, and passed her examination. She tried to get admitted to the Illinois bar in 1869; but she was turned down. She appealed and lost her case. The legislature relented a few years later. Another state where the legislature came to the rescue was Massachusetts. In 1881, the Supreme Judicial Court turned down the application of Lelia J. Robinson. But six months later, the legislature gave women the right to practice law; and Ms. Robinson was duly admitted to the bar.[19] Earlier, Mrs. Arabella Mansfield had been admitted to the Iowa Bar about the time that Myra Bradwell lost her case.[20] Clara Foltz was the first woman lawyer in California. A California statute restricted the practice of law to "any white male citizen"; Mrs. Foltz had to struggle to get the law changed, in addition to all the other obstacles that stood in her way; but her vigorous lobbying paid off, in 1878, when California passed a law allowing women to be admitted to the bar.[21] It is hard to understand, in this day and age, the horror and disgust evoked by these few brave, stubborn women. Women who could fight a system so prejudiced against them, and so stacked against them, were truly rare. At the turn of the century, about fifty women practiced in Massachusetts. In 1905, there were exactly three women lawyers practicing in Philadelphia.[22] Black lawyers, too, were unknown on Wall Street, and rare everywhere. The 1870 census listed only three in Massachusetts; there were fourteen listed for North Carolina in 1890, and something slightly above two dozen in Texas in 1900.[23]

---

[19] Douglas Lamar Jones, "*Lelia J. Robinson's Case* and the Entry of Women into the Legal Profession in Massachusetts," in Russell K. Osgood, ed., *The History of the Law in Massachusetts: The Supreme Judicial Court 1692–1992* (1992), p. 241.

[20] On Myra Bradwell, see 49 Albany L.J. 136 (1894); Nancy T. Gilliam, "A Professional Pioneer: Myra Bradwell's Fight to Practice Law," 5 Law & Hist. Rev. 105 (1987); on Arabella Mansfield, 4 Am. L. Rev. 397 (1870). Myra Bradwell's case was *Bradwell v. Illinois*, 16 Wall. (83 U.S.) 130 (1873). She based her claim on the Fourteenth Amendment. The Court, 8 to 1, denied her claim. In this notorious decision, Justice Joseph P. Bradley pontificated against the very idea of a woman lawyer: a woman's "paramount destiny and mission" was to "fulfill the noble and benign offices of wife and mother." This was God's will, apparently.

The resistance to women lawyers diminished only gradually. Even at the beginning of the twenty-first century, we hear about the "glass ceiling" in law firms; how hard it is for women to move up the ladder in the firms; and about the conflict between family life and professional life.

[21] On the career of Clara Foltz, see Barbara Allen Babcock, "Clara Shortridge Foltz, 'First Woman,'" 28 Valparaiso U.L. Rev. 1231 (1994).

[22] Gerard W. Gawalt, "The Impact of Industrialization on the Legal Profession in Massachusetts, 1870–1900," in Gawalt, ed., *The New High Priests* (1984), pp. 97, 104–105. Robert R. Bell, *The Philadelphia Lawyer: A History, 1735–1945* (1992), p. 206.

[23] Gawalt, *op. cit.*, p. 104; Frenise A. Logan, *The Negro in North Carolina, 1876–1894* (1964), p. 108; Maxwell Bloomfield, "From Deference to Confrontation: The Early Black Lawyers of Galveston, Texas, 1895–1920," in Gawalt, *op. cit.*, pp. 151, 152–53.

Two charges have been leveled against the Wall Street firm: that it served its rich and perhaps ruthless clients rather than the public; and that it perverted the legal profession, turning free, independent craftsmen into workers in law factories. Both charges were already heard in the late nineteenth century and have never completely subsided. The first charge is hard to evaluate. Most lawyers always served, mainly themselves, next their clients, last of all their conception of that diffuse, nebulous thing, the public interest. No doubt the Wall Street lawyer sincerely felt he served God by serving Mammon and Morgan.[24] Lawyers, after all, have to make a living. They go where the money and the practice are. As for the second charge, the rise of the big law firm, and the rise of big business were bound to change the myths and the outlook of the legal profession. A lawyer in a large law firm, who rarely set foot in court, who did preventive-law work with big business clients, had a different work life, and perhaps a different view of his profession, than a courtroom virtuoso, who worked alone. To help float a bond issue worth millions, or to reorganize a railroad, lawyers needed staff and specialists, and a certain amount of investment in legal plant.

Indeed, the growth of law firms—large by standards of the day, though small by the standards of the twentieth century—was one of the most striking developments of the late nineteenth century. Firms of more than three partners were rare before the Civil War. By 1900, they were more common on Wall Street and in some of the other large cities. The largest firm in 1872 had six members; and only one firm was that large. The largest firm at the turn of the century had about ten members; there were about seventy firms with five or more lawyers. More than half the big firms were in New York; Chicago was a distant second. Altogether, firms of this size made up a tiny percentage of the total practice; but they had a significance and influence beyond their mere numbers.[25]

The big firms were also more highly organized than the lawyer in solo practice could be or needed to be. The Wall Street firms hired clerks and associates. In the 1870s, three or four law students, on the average, took up space in the firm headed by Clarence A. Seward. Besides clerks and stenographers, the firm had about six associates. Student lawyers came, clerked, learned, and did service, partly on their own, partly for the firm's benefit. But as late as 1879, Seward wrote that it was "not the custom of my office, nor of any other with which I am acquainted, to give any compensation to students." At the end of the century, the system began to change. Under the "Cravath system," all lawyers who worked in the office were paid. Beginners received $30 a month. They were hired right out of law school. The "associates" worked on an up-or-out system. After some years, they either "made partner," or had to go elsewhere. Later, virtually all big firms operated on this system.[26] Law offices also took up use of the

---

[24] Though not without a great deal of role strain, and even self-doubt. On the way in which lawyers in the period tried to reconcile their activities with their idealized conception of the legal order, see Robert W. Gordon, "'The Ideal and the Actual in the Law': Fantasies and Practices of New York City Lawyers, 1870–1910," in Gawalt, *op. cit.*, p. 51.

[25] The figures in this paragraph are from Wayne K. Hobson, "Symbol of the New Profession: Emergence of the Large Law Firm, 1870–1915," in Gawalt, *op. cit.*, p. 3.

[26] Robert T. Swaine, *op. cit.*, vol. 2 (1948), pp. 1–13.

telephone and the typewriter. The firms began to hire office workers skilled in the use of business machines. In 1899, Cravath's firm started a filing system and took on a file clerk. In 1885, young Editha Phelps, daughter of a clergyman, applied to the Chicago firm of Williams and Thompson. She was, she said, "a first class stenographer and typewriter of two years experience . . . Salary about $50 per month." She was hired and stayed ten years.[27] Like Editha Phelps, the first women to appear in law offices did not come to practice law; they came to type and take shorthand.

The salaried lawyer became more common in the late nineteenth century. The big firms, as we noted, hired lawyers who were not immediately made partners; some never reached this rank at all. House counsel—lawyers on the full-time payroll of a company—were unheard of in 1800, exceedingly rare in 1850; by 1900 this was a well-worn groove of practice. The corporate giants hired their own law firms and had lawyers on their staffs as captives or collaborators. Other big corporations needed whole armies of lawyers to do their legal chores, big and small. In 1885, the Prudential Insurance Company "began to require the exclusive attention of its attorneys; the Mutual and the New York Life established their first full-time solicitors in 1893; the Metropolitan had a claim and law division by 1897."[28] To be general counsel of a major railroad, after the Civil War, was to occupy a position of great prestige and enormous salary. William Joseph Robertson left the Virginia supreme court to become general counsel for two railroads; Judge G. W. McCrary left the federal bench in the 1880s to take such a post on the Santa Fe; the chief justice of Kansas, Albert H. Horton, resigned and became attorney for the Missouri Pacific, in 1895.[29] Then as now, business attorneys sometimes moved up to top management. Thomas C. Cochran studied railroad leaders between 1845 and 1890; he found that many railroad presidents had begun as lawyers—for example, Frederick Billings (1823–1890) of the Northern Pacific. Chauncey Depew (1834–1928) began his career as a lawyer, acted as a railroad attorney, then executive of the New York Central, and became a U.S. senator in 1899.[30] Most railroad lawyers did not reach such heights. As the railroads extended their tentacles throughout the country, they needed, and hired, scores of local lawyers—to buy land, to handle personal injury suits, and, in general, to represent the road in their community.[31]

Small-town and small-city practice changed less in this period than big-city practice. The gap between Wall Street and Main Street was quite wide. There

---

[27] Herman Kogan, *Traditions and Challenges: The Story of Sidley & Austin* (1983), p. 48. Williams and Thompson was a predecessor firm to Sidley & Austin. Theron Strong, looking back over a long career, praised the work of the women office workers; he felt that "the presence of a right-thinking and dignified young woman in an office tends to elevate its tone"; such women had a "restraining influence . . . upon the clerks and students, preventing the use of language which might otherwise escape, and actions which might be open to criticism." Theron G. Strong, *Landmarks of a Lawyer's Lifetime* (1914), pp. 395–96. In Milwaukee, the first female employee of Finches, Lynde & Miller was one Daisy F. Wright, hired in 1899. Ellen Langill, *Foley & Lardner*, p. 104.

[28] Morton Keller, *The Life Insurance Enterprise, 1885–1910* (1963), p. 187.

[29] J. Willard Hurst, *The Growth of American Law* (1950), pp. 297–98.

[30] Thomas C. Cochran, *Railroad Leaders, 1845–1890* (1953), pp. 249, 309.

[31] William G. Thomas, *Lawyering for the Railroad: Business, Law, and Power in the New South* (1999).

were 143 items of business on the office docket, for 1874, of a "leading law firm" in a small Illinois city. They included three partition proceedings, one divorce, one petition for a writ of mandamus, three cases for specific performance, three attachments, one arbitration award, and a petition to sell real estate to pay debts. All the rest were collection matters, requiring either negotiation, or legal action before a justice of the peace or in county or circuit courts; twenty-two of these were foreclosures of mortgages on land. During the entire year, the firm appeared frequently in court, but in only the three lower courts just mentioned.[32] An Indiana lawyer later recalled life in the 1850s, in the fifth judicial circuit of Indiana. The firm of Fletcher, Butler, and Yandes had the most extensive practice in the circuit. But its work consisted largely of "the making of collections for eastern merchants."[33]

One instructive career was that of James Carr. He came to Missouri about 1850 from Pennsylvania. First he taught for some years at a country school in Monroe County, where he assumed a Virginia accent (the locals were not friendly to Yankees). Carr read law, and set up shop in Paris, Missouri, in a "small 14 × by 14 office room." Since he could not afford a table, "he put a board on the arm of a split-bottom rocking chair, and on that he for some time did his studying and writing." Carr was, in the judgment of his peers, a fairly learned man, but nothing to write home about as a courtroom lawyer. He was not "a good judge of human nature," and "found it a difficult task to compete with the average country lawyer." So far, Carr's story was not much different from that of many other country lawyers, who eked out a bare living at the law. But Carr "continued to fill his head with what the books said," especially books about the law of corporations. In 1865, he got work as attorney for the Hannibal & St. Joe Railroad, and moved to Hannibal, Missouri. Later, he transferred to St. Louis, where he practiced corporation law. When he died, late in the century, he "left a good estate for his family."[34] Other small-town lawyers were as successful as Carr, and some even more so. Some could make their fortune without life in the big city. They became rich country lawyers, like rich country doctors. Often they owed only part of their success to the practice of law. Law was a lever or an opening wedge: Real estate, or local business, or political achievement were the spokes on their wheel of success.

By 1900, circuit riding was only a memory, part of the golden past. Even Abraham Lincoln, before he entered the White House, could have used the railroad to do all the traveling he needed, from county seat to county seat. Some of the romance of the practice was still alive, however, in the more remote parts of the country: the plains states, the Far West, the mountain and desert country. There were differences between the buckskin lawyer of the 1800s, in the Northwest Territory, and the lawyers of the Far West, in the cattle towns and mining camps. But there were also striking similarities—commonalities of frontier legal culture, whatever the period and place. These far-off

[32] R. Allan Stephens, "The 'Experienced Lawyer Service' in Illinois," 20 Amer. Bar Ass'n. J. 716 (1934).

[33] W. W. Woollen, "Reminiscences of the Early Marion County Bar," *Publications, Indiana Hist. Soc.,* vol. VII (1923), pp. 185, 192.

[34] W. O. L. Jewett, "Early Bar of Northeast Missouri," in A. J. D. Stewart, ed., *History of the Bench and Bar of Missouri* (1898), pp. 54, 59.

spots still attracted adventurous young men: ambitious, variously educated, looking for a fortune in law, business, or politics, or simply interested in raising hell. David Dudley Field, in the East, fought for his codes, and made money as lawyer for the robber barons; his younger brother Stephen went to California during the gold rush days. He became alcalde of Marysville, California; here he built a frame house and "dispensed justice for the community, holding court behind a dry goods box, with tallow candles for lights." He also made money in land speculation, fought or almost fought duels, rose to become justice of the California supreme court and from there was appointed to the U.S. Supreme Court.[35] Field practiced in a rough community, during rough times. If we can believe what a Kansas lawyer (trained in New England) said, his colleagues at the bar were an "ignorant, detestable set of addle-headed numbskulls."[36] But the man who said these words was not himself of this sort. Stephen Field, too, was a person of education, culture, and great legal acumen. He was not the only one of this stamp in California. Joseph G. Baldwin, fresh from the "flush times" of the old Southwest, arrived in California in 1854: he, too, served on the state supreme court. Many territorial lawyers had been educated back East. Luther Dixon was born in Vermont, studied law under a Virginia judge, practiced for a while in Wisconsin, then settled in Colorado. Another Colorado attorney, Joseph N. Baxter, advertised himself in 1892 as "formerly of the Boston Bar." A Texas lawyer in the same year proudly proclaimed himself a "Graduate of Columbia College Law School, New York City, Class of 1884."[37]

The practice of the frontier lawyer was like frontier practice in earlier places and times. James M. Mathers, in Indian Territory, stated that "our practice . . . was by necessity a criminal practice . . . and the great bulk of cases were murder cases."[38] This was probably exceptional. Land law, claim law, real-estate brokerage and speculation, money brokerage, collection work, mortgage work—these were staples of practice in the more lightly settled territories. The letterhead of E. P. Caldwell, an attorney in Huron, Dakota Territory, in the 1860s, stated his business as follows: "Money Loaned for Eastern Capitalists. Taxes Paid for Nonresidents. Investments Carefully Made for Eastern Capitalists. General Law, Land and Collection Business Transacted. Buy and Sell Real Estate. U.S. Land Business promptly Attended to. Contests a Specialty."[39] An attorney in Waco, Texas, advertised in 1892: "Have splendid facilities for lending money on first-class real estate security." In Utah, in the same year (1892), the American Collecting Agency, an association of attorneys, reported that:

A prosperous business year has enabled us to enlarge our offices and put in them an immense fireproof safe to protect our clientage. We have added to our home force, secured detectives in all parts of Utah, and engaged first-class correspondents. . . . We make no charge unless we collect.

[35] The most recent biography is Paul Kens, *Justice Stephen Field: Shaping Liberty from the Gold Rush to the Gilded Age* (1997).
[36] Quoted in Everett Dick, *The Sod House Frontier, 1854–1890* (1954), p. 450.
[37] *Hubbell's Legal Directory* (1892), Appendix, pp. 14, 197.
[38] Quoted in Marshall Houts, *From Gun to Gavel* (1954), p. 33.
[39] Howard R. Lamar, *Dakota Territory, 1861–1889: A Study of Frontier Politics* (1956), p. 127.

Our charges are reasonable. We remit promptly. We are a godsend to honest creditors—a holy terror to delinquents.[40]

Not every lawyer was a glorified collection agent. But no Wall Street or Wall Street practice was possible in these dry and far-off places. One novelty was railroad work. As the railroads pushed west, they constantly needed local attorneys, to handle affairs along the route. In Dakota Territory, in 1889, the "assistant solicitor" of the Milwaukee Road heard young Thomas J. Walsh argue a case before the supreme court of the Territory. The man was impressed, and the future Montana senator was appointed "local attorney" for the railroad in Redfield, Dakota Territory. This entitled him to a free pass on the railroad, as a "retainer."[41] Mining companies needed skilled lawyers, too; and so did the big landowners, merchants, and ranchers.

Some Western lawyers were almost as peripatetic as prospectors, who wandered from mining camp to mining camp, looking for gold. Homebodies stayed home in the East; and most lawyers, it seems, were homebodies.[42] The West was the place for rolling stones. Thomas Fitch, once an editor in Milwaukee, a member of the Nevada Constitutional Convention, practiced law in Nevada (1869), Salt Lake City (1871), San Francisco (1875), Prescott, Arizona (1877), Minneapolis (1880), and then Tucson, Arizona (1881).[43] James Clagett, born in Maryland, migrated with his parents to Iowa in 1850. He was admitted to the Iowa bar in 1858. In 1861, he moved to Carson City, Nevada, and, in 1862, served as a member of the territorial house. The discovery of gold drew him to Montana in 1867; here he became territorial delegate to Congress. In 1873, he turned up in Denver, Colorado. Later, he shifted his base of operations to Deadwood, Dakota Territory, where he "thrived on the intrigues and law suits brought by the large mining companies against one another." In 1882, he moved to Butte, Montana, to engage in the mining business. Next, Clagett was president of the Idaho Constitutional Convention, in 1889. Unsuccessful in Idaho politics, he moved to Spokane, Washington. He died there in 1901. Clagett was "an excellent example of the mobility which was a primary feature of political life in the West. . . . It was the Clagetts . . . who wrote the codes, and who were elected to such offices as register of deeds, county commissioner, or territorial delegate. They were the men who organized political parties in the wild lawless towns situated in some narrow gulch where a shallow creek ran, with a fortune hidden in its wet sands."[44]

In the far Western states, legal systems had to be borrowed or invented in a hurry; lawyers were the only ones who could do this job. J. Warner Mills of

[40] Hubbell, op. cit., Appendix, pp. 206, 208.

[41] Walsh to Elinor C. McClements, Feb. 13, 1889, in J. Leonard Bates, ed., Tom Walsh in Dakota Territory (1966), p. 218.

[42] On this point, Gawalt's figures for Massachusetts are enlightening. Nearly 90 percent of the lawyers admitted to the bar in the state between 1870 and 1890 practiced in one town or city for their entire career; less than 5 percent moved out of state. Lawyers admitted before 1840 were much more mobile, geographically; only 70 percent practiced in a single town; nearly18 percent left the state. Gawalt, "The Impact of Industrialization on the Legal Profession in Massachusetts, 1870–1900," in Gawalt, ed., The New High Priests, pp. 97, 102.

[43] Gordon Morris Bakken, Practicing Law in Frontier California (1991), pp. 13–14.

[44] Howard R. Lamar, Dakota Territory, 1861–1889: A Study of Frontier Politics (1956), pp. 68–69.

Colorado lent his name to the annotated Colorado Statutes. Matthew Deady (1824–1893) did the same service in Oregon. But he was also a maker of laws. He drew up many of the Oregon codes, played a crucial role in revising Oregon's statutes between 1859 and 1872 and drafted much legislation himself.[45] Many Western lawyers rose to eminent positions, and not only in the West. Few of them were born in the West. James Mills Woolworth, born in New York, settled in Omaha in 1856, two years after the area had been wrested from the native tribes. In 1896, he was elected president of the American Bar Association. Charles E. Manderson, president of the Association in 1899, was born in Pennsylvania, practiced in Ohio, rose to the rank of brigadier general during the Civil War, moved to Omaha, Nebraska, in 1869, served as U.S. senator, and became general solicitor for the western portion of the trackage of the Burlington Railroad in 1895.[46] These careers were not typical; but neither were they unique. Lawyers came early to the frontier boomtowns, eager to turn a quick dollar. Lawyers who placed money and collected on notes often turned to banking and merchandising to earn a better living. Some lawyers needed some other source of income to make ends meet. A lawyer in Placer County, California, J. P. C. Morgan, began his practice from a hotel room, and, besides law, offered to give "lessons in bookkeeping, penmanship, and German."[47] For many lawyers, politics was the best way to scramble up the greasy pole. In these small communities, one of the biggest businesses was government. Politics was bread-and-butter work. For lawyers, county, state, territorial, and federal jobs were sources of income and, in addition, advertisements for themselves. Politics, law-making, and law administration, were as much a part of the practice as collection work and lawsuits over land. The frontier attorney "was always a politician. Law and politics went hand in hand. . . . The lawyer filled all the 'respectable government offices.' "[48]

The lawyer-politician was not only a Western phenomenon. Lawyers were in the midst of politics everywhere. They were always an influential bloc in state legislatures, sometimes an absolute majority. Many presidents after 1850 were lawyers: Buchanan, Lincoln, Chester A. Arthur, James Garfield, Grover Cleveland. From 1790 to 1930, two-thirds of the senators and about half of the members of the House of Representatives were lawyers; the percentage seems to have stayed fairly stable. Between half and two-thirds of the state governors were also lawyers. Lawyers were especially numerous in Southern legislatures. Lawyers in the North tended to represent metropolitan areas in state legislatures.[49] Lawyers were also prominent at constitutional conventions. Of 133 delegates to the 1872 Pennsylvania Constitutional Convention, 103 were lawyers.[50] This was, perhaps, an unusual percentage; but lawyers swarmed in thick

---

[45] Harrison Gray Platt, "Matthew P. Deady," in *Great American Lawyers*, vol. VII (1909), p. 357.

[46] James G. Rogers, *American Bar Leaders* (1932), pp. 90, 104.

[47] Gordon Bakken, *Practicing Law in Frontier California*, p. 12.

[48] Raymond T. Zillmer, "The Lawyer on the Frontier," 50 Am. L. Rev. 27, 35 (1916); for a similar point about California lawyers of the nineteenth century, see Gordon Bakken, *Practicing Law in Frontier California*, pp. 9–12.

[49] J. Willard Hurst, *The Growth of American Law* (1950), p. 352.

[50] Rosalind L. Branning, *Pennsylvania Constitutional Development* (1960), p. 61.

numbers at other conventions, too. In Ohio, 43 out of 108 delegates at the constitutional convention of 1850–1851 were lawyers; in the 1872–1874 convention, 62 out of 105.[51]

It was not that public office required legal skill; rather, the lawyers were skillful at getting and holding these offices. They were by instinct political; political animals gravitated toward the practice of law. A public career was helpful to private practice, which cannot be easily said for doctors, bankers, or farmers. After 1850, too, the civil-servant lawyer became more common. Lawyers had always worked in Washington, at state capitals, in city hall, and in the county seats. As government grew, so did the number of government lawyers. In 1853, the attorney general of the United States, Caleb Cushing, performed all his duties with the help of two clerks and a messenger. In 1897, Attorney General Joseph McKenna was the head of a respectable staff, including a solicitor general, four assistant attorneys general, seven "assistant attorneys," and one "attorney in charge of pardons," not to mention three law clerks, forty-four general clerks, and miscellaneous other employees, among them eight charwomen. The "Office of Solicitor of the Treasury" had sixteen employees.[52] Lawyers were scattered about other government departments as well. The same growth occurred at the state and city level. In the last third of the century, the job of corporation counsel for big cities took on considerable importance. By 1895, the Law Department of New York City "was the largest law office in the country"; twenty-eight lawyers worked there, with sixty-four clerical assistants.[53]

ORGANIZATION OF THE BAR

For most of the nineteenth century, no organization even pretended to speak for the bar as a whole, or any substantial part, or to govern the conduct of lawyers. Lawyers formed associations, mainly social, from time to time; but there was no general bar group until the last third of the century. On February 15, 1870, a group of lawyers, responding to a call that had gone out in December 1869, with eighty-five signatures, met, formed the Association of the Bar of the City of New York, and acquired a house at 20 W. 27th Street as headquarters. In the first year, about 450 lawyers joined the organization, representing the "decent part" of the profession, that is, primarily well-to-do business lawyers, predominantly of old-American stock.[54]

---

[51] See Isaac F. Patterson, *The Constitutions of Ohio* (1912), pp. 109, 176.

[52] *Official Register of the United States*, 1853, p. 154; 1897, vol. I, pp. 827–29.

[53] On these city lawyers, see Jon C. Teaford, *The Unheralded Triumph: City Government in America, 1870–1900* (1984), p. 61–64. Corporation counsel jobs were good stepping stones to success, talented young men held positions in these offices—men like Francis L. Stetson, in New York, who later became J. P. Morgan's attorney; Clarence Darrow was acting corporation counsel in Chicago in the early 1890s.

[54] On the formation of the Association, see George Martin, *Causes and Conflicts: The Centennial History of the Association of the Bar of the City of New York, 1870–1970* (1970); Michael Powell, *From Patrician to Professional Elite: The Transformation of the New York City Bar Association* (1988); see also John A. Matzko, " 'The Best Men of the Bar': The Founding of the American Bar Association," in Gawalt, *op. cit.*, p. 75; see also the remarks of George T. Strong, quoted in Henry W. Taft, *A Century and a Half at the New York Bar* (1938), p. 148; other details are in Theron G. Strong, *Landmarks of a Lawyer's Lifetime* (1914), ch. 6.

In the immediate background was the stench of corruption in Tweed's New York; corruption even seemed to have enveloped the courtrooms of New York City. Justice appeared to be blatantly for sale. The robber barons fought each other with injunctions and writs; some of the judges—Barnard and Cardozo, for example—were believed to be plainly corrupt. On February 13, 1870, Dorman B. Eaton, a lawyer who had taken part in some of the Erie litigation, was savagely beaten. The "decent part" of the bar was appalled; this incident quickened their interest in action. The new Association, like any other club, aimed to "cultivate social relations among its members." But it also promised to promote "the due administration of justice"; and the articles of incorporation stated as one of the Association's purposes "maintaining the honour and dignity of the profession of the law."

The crisis in the profession was more than a crisis in decency. There was also a real sense of business crisis. The bar felt the hot breath of competition. In the late nineteenth century, the response of any trade group to a business threat was to organize and fight back. At the meeting of the New York bar, "for the purpose of forming an Association," James Emott complained that the profession had lost its independence. "We have become simply a multitude of individuals, engaged in the same business. And the objects and the methods of those engaged in that business are very much dictated by those who employ them. [Lawyers] . . . are and do simply what their employers desire."[55] In union, it was hoped, there would be strength against the outside world. The bar-association movement began and spread at a time when farmers and workers were also organizing, and shortly before the great outburst of occupational licensing laws.

The movement soon spread beyond New York. The bar of New Hampshire organized in 1873. An Iowa state bar association was formed in 1874. During its brief span of life, the Iowa State Bar Association discussed ways to raise standards for admission to the bar, and the need for laws to punish and disbar attorneys "guilty of shystering and unprofessional conduct." The Association also discussed problems of judicial organization and whether it was desirable or not to enact a statutory "fee-bill, or system of costs." The Association was also a club and a social organization. The Hon. Edward H. Stiles, of Ottumwa, in 1876, regaled the membership with a talk on "the relation which law and its administration sustain to general literature," and Judge James M. Love, before a "very fine audience assembled in the Opera House," gave out "one of the most scholarly efforts ever delivered in Des Moines, rich in historic lore, beautiful in diction, and philosophical in style." A "bountifully laden table" in 1881 inspired a toast to "Good Digestion: its compatibility with a lawyer's conscience."[56] There were also city bar associations, first in Cincinnati (1872), then in Cleveland (1873).[57] Chicago lawyers formed a bar association, in 1874, prodded into life

---

[55] Quoted in 1 Albany L. J. 219 (1870). Somewhat naïvely, Emott blamed the degeneracy of the profession on the New York Constitution of 1846, which brought in an elective judiciary and "broke down the bar."

[56] A. J. Small, comp., *Proceedings of the Early Iowa State Bar Association, 1874–1881* (1912), pp. 36, 37, 42, 83, 84, 141.

[57] An even older organization, of sorts, existed in Milwaukee, first organized in 1858 as the Milwaukee Law Institute. J. Gordon Hylton, "The Bar Association Movement in Nineteenth Century Wisconsin," 81 Marquette L. Rev. 1029 (1998).

by the "activities of a notorious fringe of unlicensed practitioners." Between 1870 and 1878, eight city and eight state bar associations were founded in twelve different states. Most of them, like the groups in Chicago and New York, had a reform ideology, and were anxious to improve the image and performance of the bar.[58] But their successes were probably mostly social. The New York City group moved very slowly and cautiously against Tweed and other malefactors; it moved smartly on other fronts, buying a nice brownstone in which the association installed a librarian, old books, busts of lawyers, and a punch bowl filled with a drink made "according to a special recipe furnished by the nearby Century club."[59]

With few exceptions, state and city bar associations were not open to everybody; they did not invite the bar as a whole, but sent out feelers to a select group, the "decent part" of the bar. The same was true of the American Bar Association, founded in 1878. "Seventy-five gentlemen from twenty-one jurisdictions" (out of the country's roughly 60,000 lawyers) got together in Saratoga, New York.[60] Simeon E. Baldwin, of Connecticut, was prime mover. The purpose of the Association was to "advance the science of jurisprudence, promote the administration of justice and uniformity of legislation . . . uphold the honor of the profession . . . and encourage cordial intercourse among the members of the American Bar." During the Saratoga years, the American Bar Association (ABA) paid a great deal of attention to the "cordial intercourse" part of its mandate; but Simeon Baldwin was a good organizer, and a man of conviction; he put his stamp on the ABA in these early years. The ABA grew only slowly in size. In 1902, there were 1,718 members. But as a reform group, it was far from inert.[61]

From the outset, the ABA did much of its work through committees. Early on, a number of standing committees were appointed—on jurisprudence and law reform, judicial administration and remedial procedure, legal education and admission to the bar, commercial law and international law. The committee on obituaries, established in 1881, reported names and achievements of dead members, to be duly published in the annual reports. A flock of special committees, however, worked on law reform issues (for example, on the problem of the low salaries of federal judges, 1888), or issues of interest to the working profession (on trademarks, 1898). The ABA never really clarified its relationship to local bar associations during the Saratoga period. In 1887, a group of lawyers formed a rival organization, the National Bar Association, expressly to serve as the apex of the pyramid of local and state associations. It proved ephemeral. The ABA encouraged state and local bar groups to send delegates to its Saratoga meetings. At first, few came—two lonely delegates from South Carolina were the only ones at the third annual meeting, in 1880. By the end of the century, there was a more respectable turnout; eighty delegates,

---

[58] J. Willard Hurst, *The Growth of American Law*, (1950) p. 286.

[59] John A. Matzko, " 'The Best Men of the Bar': The Founding of the American Bar Association," in Gawalt, *op. cit.*, pp. 75, 79.

[60] Alfred Z. Reed, *Training for the Public Profession of the Law* (1921), p. 208. Material on the early history of the ABA comes from Reed, Matzko, *op. cit.*, *supra*, n. 45; for the number of lawyers in 1880, see John M. Shirley, *The Future of Our Profession*, 17 Am. L. Rev. 645, 650 (1883).

[61] On Baldwin's work, and the early history of the ABA, see Matzko, *op. cit.*, *supra*, n. 45.

from twenty-nine states, were accredited to the annual meeting in 1902; and forty-one actually attended.

Still, the ABA before 1900, despite its efforts, never proved to be much more than a gathering of dignified, well-to-do lawyers enjoying the comfort and elegance of Saratoga. Its prime significance, perhaps, was the way in which it expressed, in concrete form, the ambitions of the "best men" of the bar for status and organization. Speeches and reports to the meetings voiced conventional sentiments about law reform—ways and means to keep the profession decent, well-liked, and well paid. The lowlifes of the bar—the ambulance chasers, the sleazy lawyers who hung around the rear of criminal courtrooms, the small-time debt collectors—were not represented, and not welcome. Speeches also voiced the fear that too warm an embrace from big business might be a threat to the independence of the bar. The ABA aspired to a moderate, middling role, a role of mild, beneficial reform.

Uniformity in the law was frequently discussed. The jumble of laws in the various states might strangle interstate business. Easy laws in some states could corrode wholesome, tougher laws in other states. All this was deplorable. In 1889, the Association, by resolution, directed its president to appoint a committee, consisting of one member from each state, to "compare and consider" the laws on marriage and divorce, inheritance, and "acknowledgment of deeds" and to report measures that would promote the uniformity of law. Shortly thereafter, New York State created a board of three "Commissioners for the Promotion of Uniformity of Legislation in the United States." The ABA seized on this law, touted it to its members, and recommended it for other states as well. A National Conference of Commissioners on Uniform State Laws was organized in 1892, in Saratoga, and began to hold annual meetings in close connection with those of the ABA. Out of the work of the conference ultimately came a series of recommendations for uniform laws, endorsed by the ABA as well, and proposed to the states.

ADMISSION TO THE BAR

Nothing so dissatisfied the "decent part" of the bar as the fact that it was easy to set up as a lawyer. They felt that the country was flooded with lawyers, and that many of these lawyers were mediocre or worse. Few states controlled admission to the bar through a single agency or court. In 1860, ten out of thirty-nine jurisdictions did so; in 1890, sixteen out of forty-nine. In Wisconsin, before 1885, a prospective lawyer had to be twenty-one, and of good moral character (whatever that meant); there were no educational requirements at all. The bar exam consisted of a few questions in open court by any circuit judge, or a lawyer examiner appointed by the judge. Graduates of the law department of the University of Wisconsin, and lawyers admitted in other states, were admitted with no examination at all.[62] "Control," in other words, was slight, even in those states that in theory exercised control; and the standards of admission were vacuous. Where local courts each passed on admission to

[62] J. Gordon Hylton, "The Bar Association Movement in Nineteenth Century Wisconsin," 81 Marquette L. Rev. 1029, 1039–1040 (1998).

their bar, they usually gave oral exams—exams so cursory as to be almost a joke. Recommendations from well-known lawyers weighed more heavily than actual answers to questions. Before 1890, only four states had boards of bar examiners; only a few required a written examination. Nothing in the way Oliver Wendell Holmes Jr., entered the ranks of the Massachusetts bar would inspire confidence that the state could select a Holmes and reject the unqualified. Judge Otis P. Lord of the superior court appointed two examiners; they separately asked Holmes a few questions; Holmes answered the questions, paid his $5, and was admitted to the bar.[63] Charles Francis Adams, after "about twenty months of desultory reading" in a law office, went to his friend and neighbor, Justice George T. Bigelow of Massachusetts, and asked for an examination. Bigelow invited him "into the Supreme Court room, where he was then holding court." A clerk handed him "a list of questions, covering perhaps, one sheet of letter paper." Adams "wrote out answers to such of them as I could. . . . On several . . . subjects . . . I knew absolutely nothing. A few days later I met the Judge on the platform of the Quincy station, and he told me I might come up to the court room and be sworn in. . . . I was no more fit to be admitted than a child."[64] This was in the late 1850s.

In other parts of the country, admission to the bar was even more perfunctory. L. E. Chittenden, in Vermont in the 1850s, was chairman of the committee to examine candidates for admission. Two young men came before him: "Of any branch of the law, they were as ignorant as so many Hottentots. I frankly told them that for them to attempt to practice law would be wicked, dangerous, and would subject them to suits for malpractice. They begged, they prayed, they cried." Anyway, they wanted to go west: "I, with much self-reproach, consented to sign their certificates, on condition that each would buy a copy of Blackstone, Kent's Commentaries, and Chitty's Pleadings, and immediately emigrate to some Western town."[65] James Mathers, born in 1877, took a two year course at Cumberland; this made him automatically a member of the Tennessee bar. Immediately, he moved to Indian country, in what is now Oklahoma, around the turn of the century:

> We went over to the courthouse and I shook hands with Judge Kilgore. . . . He examined my diploma from Cumberland, which was about a yard square and had to be rolled up for easy carrying, and then he looked at my license from Tennessee. That was all I needed to get his permission to practice in his court.

Kilgore asked Mathers the next day to become a law examiner, with two others, and screen applicants to the bar in Indian Territory. Mathers used no written examination or set questions. In his view, two or three hours at a dinner table or relaxing over coffee or a drink was enough; this told him all he needed to know. He did not expect applicants to have "a great knowledge of case law since none of us did; but . . . good, reasonable common sense."[66]

[63] Mark deWolfe Howe, *Justice Oliver Wendell Holmes: The Shaping Years, 1841–1870* (1957), pp. 263–64.

[64] *Charles Francis Adams (1835–1915), An Autobiography* (1916), pp. 41–42; for a similar account, from 1861, see George A. Torrey, *A Lawyer's Recollections* (1910), p. 81.

[65] L. E. Chittenden, "Legal Reminiscenses," 5 *Green Bag* 307, 309 (1893).

[66] Marshall Houts, *From Gun to Gavel* (1954), pp. 28, 31.

At one time, there had been rather stringent educational requirements for admission to the bar, at least on paper. Before the Civil War, these requirements had considerably eroded. Four states actually abolished educational or training requirements altogether: Maine (1843–1859), New Hampshire (1842–1872), Wisconsin (1849–1859), and Indiana (from 1851).[67] After the Civil War, the trend toward laxity was reversed, particularly in the East. In 1860, only nine out of thirty-nine states and territories prescribed some minimum preparation for the practice. In 1890, twenty-three jurisdictions asked for some formal period of study, or apprenticeship. In 1878, New Hampshire set up a permanent committee to examine potential lawyers. A written bar exam became increasingly the norm.[68] In much of this development, the bar lobbied hard for more rigor. The motives were, as usual, mixed. Many lawyers sincerely wanted to upgrade the profession. This mingled with a more selfish desire to control the supply of lawyers, and keep out price cutters and undesirables. Control was, arguably, in the public interest. To keep out bad lawyers was as beneficial as to getting rid of quacks, or policing how midwives or pharmacists were trained; as defensible, too, as license laws for barbers, plumbers, and embalmers of the dead.

[67] Reed, *op. cit.*, pp. 87–88.
[68] Robert Stevens, *Law School* (1983), p. 2.

PART IV

The Twentieth Century

CHAPTER 1

LEVIATHAN COMES OF AGE

Most of this book has been concerned with the growth and development of American law in the period between the Revolution and the end of the nineteenth century. But more than a hundred years has gone by since then. During the nineteenth century, revolutionary changes took place in society—and revolutionary changes in law as well. A country of three million or so, clustered mostly along the Eastern seaboard, turned into a mighty nation of some seventy-six million. The United States had also become an empire: by 1900, it had not only swept across the continent, it had annexed Hawaii, and acquired at least a modest collection of overseas territories—chiefly Puerto Rico and the Philippines. What had once been a nation of farmers, was now an industrial power. The biggest cities at the time of the Revolution would have been classified as smallish towns in 1900: New York was a megalopolis in 1900, and the second city, Chicago, had not even existed at the time of George Washington. There were, in 1776, slaves in every state. By 1900, slavery was gone, but a kind of black serfdom remained. Issues of immigration were on the agenda, which had never been there before. Demographically, the country was changing dramatically. Technology also made an enormous difference to American life. The railroad, the telegraph, and the telephone: These were not even dreamt of in the days of Bunker Hill and Saratoga.

Change in the twentieth century was, in some ways less dramatic; in other ways more so. The country was still much the same size at the end of the century; indeed, its empire shrank when the Philippines gained independence, after the Second World War. The population grew enormously, to be sure—to more than two hundred and fifty million; and there were, as we will see, decisive demographic changes. The main engines of revolution were social and technological. The technological revolution was, perhaps, one of the chief *causes* of the social revolution. This was the century of the automobile and the airplane; the century of radio, the movies, and television; the century of the computer and the Internet; the century of antibiotics and the birth control pill. Each of these great advances in science and technology eventually had a deep impact on society; and a deep impact on law.

The main political events of the century are familiar enough. In the twentieth century, the United States emerged, without question, as a major world power. It played a decisive role in both of the century's great world wars. After the end of the Second World War, it was without doubt the richest, strongest country in the world. It was the only country with an atom bomb. Europe lay in ruins; the Soviet Union was a huge, powerful beast, wounded but dangerous; Japan was an occupied power, its empire in shreds. Then came the cold war—the war against Communism; in Korea and Vietnam, the cold war turned into a hot war. The United States lost its monopoly on atomic power; the Soviet Union, which had atom bombs and hydrogen bombs, and sent men into space, was a rival in most of the inhabited world. The Soviet Union had occupied and then dominated most of Eastern Europe. It had a powerful ally in Mao Tse Tung's China, although the relationship eventually turned cold. Meanwhile, the great empires of the West collapsed: the British, French, Dutch, and Portuguese colonies turned into a collection of sovereign nations, and the two great superpowers vied for their affections.

But suddenly, toward the end of the century, the Soviet Union imploded. Its satellites in Eastern Europe burst the ropes that tied them down. The Union itself went out of business. Fifteen independent countries rose out of the ruins. The Russian Federation was the largest of these countries; but it seemed to be sinking into poverty and corruption, ravaged by crime and besotted with vodka. By 1990, then, the United States had emerged as the one and only super power, the sole, undisputed king of the mountain. No other country came close to it in terms of military and economic power. There were smaller countries that were richer, in per capita income; but the United States was enormous as well as rich; and its economic muscle dwarfed that of any other single nation. How long this will remain true, nobody can tell. Certainly, not forever. But for the time being this meant that American power, American influence, American culture, and the American economy, had a special, dominant place in the world; and that implied, too, a special role for American law.

CENTER AND PERIPHERY

Internally, the twentieth century was a century in which the central, national power grew and grew and grew. On paper, the United States is still a federal republic. In the twentieth century, the last territories—Oklahoma, Arizona, New Mexico, Hawaii, and Alaska—became states, on a par with the others. (The status of Puerto Rico remains anomalous.) The United States has been, for half a century, a federation of fifty states. The states, in fact, are far from unimportant, even in this age when the federal government has enormous power. In theory, each state is sovereign. Each one has its own legal system. This is not unimportant. At the end of the century, just as in the beginning, most lawsuits were state lawsuits; most law was state law. To get a divorce, you go to a state court; and you go there too to collect damages for whiplash injury, or to ask for a zoning variance; rapists, drunk drivers, murderers, and embezzlers are tried in state courts. Ordinary commercial law is state law. So is basic property law. States and cities make up and enforce thousands of rules that affect the daily life of the average person. They make speed limits and decide where you can park your car. They draft building codes, plumbing codes, and electrical codes for cities and towns. They regulate dry cleaners, license nurses, and dictate the open season on pheasants and oysters and white-tailed deer. They control the right to marry, to own a dog, to sell vegetables from an open-air stall, or to run a saloon. They collect property taxes. They run the schools. Some money comes from the federal government; but most school money is state and local money. Local school boards and schools systems perform what is perhaps the single biggest, and most important function of government, at any level. The states also are in the business of higher education. There is a University of California and a University of Idaho; there are no federal universities. The states also license lawyers and doctors and architects and morticians. A person can be a member of the New Hampshire bar or the Arizona bar; but there is no national bar. Indeed, there really is no such thing as an "American" lawyer; there are only California lawyers and Vermont lawyers, and so on. There is also no national auto license. The states test drivers; and each state gives out its own license. States and cities also do the heavy lifting and the dirty work in running the welfare system; they supervise foster care, and (with federal money, to be sure) provide for the mentally ill and the disabled. Thus, the states, in 2000, still made a great deal of difference. Indeed, they taxed more, spent more, regulated more, and controlled more than was true in 1900—by orders of magnitude. Local government, too, enjoys its share of authority and jurisdiction. The sheer increase in law and government has affected the cities, countries, sewer districts, and other small powers as well as the states and the national government. From New York City to Wichita and Jackson, Mississippi, there is much more activity, more employees, more taxing and spending, than in 1900. The states have lost power *relative* to the federal government; but they have gained in absolute terms. They are themselves bigger than ever; and state law remains vigorous and essential.

All this is true: but the more dramatic story is the story of the growth of the federal government. The federal budget in 1900 was $567 million; in 2000, it was almost $2 trillion. The dollar is worth a lot less than it was in 1900; but still, this represents a fantastic increase. The number of federal employees in 1900 was approximately 200,000; in 2000, there were on the order of 2,800,000 civilian employees. Before Franklin D. Roosevelt, a federal budget of $80 billion a year was inconceivable, astronomical, a matter of science fiction. Now the federal government spends, each year, an amount that Roosevelt—or Kennedy, or Nixon would find absolutely staggering. The sums spent on war and national defense, by 2000, and the sums spent on major entitlement programs, add up to more than $1 trillion. The federal Caesar fed on the meat of social upheaval, the two great wars and the cold war, a vast depression and, above all, a revolution in science and technology. The word Caesar is not much out of place. The main beneficiary of power at the center was the President, and the executive branch of government—not Congress; and not even the Supreme Court, though the Supreme Court, too, gained enormously in the century, as we will see. The man who holds the office of president has become, as presidents like to think, the most important, the most powerful person in the world. Theodore Roosevelt and Woodrow Wilson already sensed this role; Franklin D. Roosevelt glorified in it and magnified it. Harding and Coolidge, small men with small conceptions of their job, were detours, anomalies. Weak presidents—narrow men with narrow ideas—are still possible (if not probable), but a weak Presidency is not.

Every event of the century has seemed to conspire to make the central government stronger. Prohibition, the "noble experiment" (1919 to 1933)—the national ban on liquor—fed the federal colossus. In some ways, this was the last stand of a dying order, but in any event, Prohibition had no chance to succeed except on a federal basis. The states were powerless to stamp out the curse of liquor. In the event, the federal government turned out to be almost equally powerless; but it was the only entity strong enough to try. Goods, people, and ideas flowed freely across state lines. The railroad, then the automobile and the airplane, made these lines even more irrelevant—culturally and economically, if not legally. If you cross from North Dakota to South Dakota, nothing in the landscape or the culture changes. You have gone from one "jurisdiction" to another; but most people hardly notice.

The states were too feeble to stamp out the saloon; they were also too feeble to control the airwaves, or the railroads, or to stop the trusts, or to uplift the quality of food products made in one state and sold in all the others. Moreover, because the country was a gigantic free trade area, because there were no border guards, customs officials, and inspections, at state lines; and because a factory could relocate at will from one place to another, the states in a real sense competed with each other. If the Northern states wanted to get rid of child labor, they needed federal help; otherwise, the textile mills could flee to the South, where the law was much less finicky about children in factories. The only solution to the problem, from the Northern point of view, was a national law, which would bring the southern states into line. That legislation, in fact, got passed—closing interstate commerce to products made with the blood and sweat of the children; but the Supreme Court declared it void, in 1918, in *Hammer v. Dagenhart*.[1] Congress tried again: it passed a law in 1919 that put an "excise tax" (10 percent) on the net profits of any factory or mine that hired children. But the Supreme Court interposed another veto. This was not really a "tax," but another misguided attempt to get rid of child labor through a national law.[2]

Hammer v. Dagenhart was one of the cases that gave the U.S. Supreme Court a bad name with social progressives. In *Hammer,* the Court impeded the passage of *national* legislation on social issues; in a number of notorious cases, the Court obstructed *state* laws that represented what was thought to be advanced social policy. One of the most famous of these cases was *Lochner v. New York* (1905), which we have already mentioned.[3] This was the case where the Supreme Court struck down a law that, restricted the hours of bakery workers. The law, thought the Court, violated the federal Constitution. It "interfered" with the freedom of workers and employers to strike their own bargain; that was an impairment of their "liberty." In cases like this, the Supreme Court in fact promoted its own version of central control: it imposed a national standard on the states, however negative and retrograde.

Not all Supreme Court decisions can be put in the same box as these two: In *Muller v. Oregon* (1908), as we have seen,[4] the Supreme Court upheld an Oregon law that set a maximum of ten hours work, per day, for women in factories and laundries. When Joe Haselbock, who worked in the Grand Laundry of Portland, Oregon, asked a Mrs. Gotcher to work a longer day, he ran afoul of the law, and the laundry was fined. The famous "Brandeis brief" (compiled under the direction of Louis D. Brandeis) piled up evidence of the effect of

---

[1] 247 U.S. 251 (1918).

[2] *Bailey v. Drexel Furniture Co.*, 259 U.S. 20 (1922).

[3] 198 U.S. 45 (1905). On the *Lochner* case, see above, Part III, ch. 9. See Howard Gillman, *The Constitution Besieged: The Rise and Demose of Lochner Era Police Powers Jurisprudence* (1993).

[4] 208 U.S. 412 (1908); see above, Part III, ch. 9.

long hours on women's health. There were other cases, too, that were less extreme than *Lochner.* There was, in fact, no consistency at the level of the Supreme Court—or of the state courts. Yet, the narrow, laissez faire decisions, represented at least one strong strand of American opinion.

In any event, in the decade of the 1930s, cases of the *Lochner* sort were swept away. The Great Depression brought to power Franklin D. Roosevelt, and his New Deal, about which more later. The two World Wars, the cold war, the Vietnam War—all these cataclysmic events funneled power into Washington, and away from the states and localities. The atomic age only reinforced the trend. After all, it is the president's finger that rests on the fateful button, and not the finger of the governor of Idaho. It is the president who is the "leader of the free world," and not the mayor of Tampa. Arkansas has no stealth bombers; Ohio no nuclear submarines.

But the stampede to the center is more than a matter of armies. The federal government has a presence in every field today—even fields where it had no role at all in the nineteenth century. Welfare law is one example: the federal role before the twentieth century was distinctly limited—disaster relief, veteran's pensions. The states were in charge of welfare, and welfare institutions. In the 1910s and 1920s many states passed mothers' pension laws, to help poor but respectable women who had children to raise. A modest federal bill, the Sheppard-Towner Act of 1921, aimed to further "the welfare and hygiene of maternity and infancy"; it parceled out some money to the states to help them finance their own programs. Women had just gotten the right to vote; and women's organizations backed Sheppard-Towner, over tremendous opposition. It was denounced as socialistic and worse; one representative warned that it was only the first step on the road downward; soon would come "Government supervision of mothers," and even worse horrors, such as "insurance against unemployment."[5] Somehow, the bill got through. But even this modest effort did not last very long. Sheppard-Towner went out of business in 1929.[6]

But 1929 was also the year of the great stock market crash, followed by the worst depression in U.S. history. The Great Depression brought in a tidal wave of votes for Franklin Delano Roosevelt and the Democratic Party; the political situation changed radically. The states were prostrate and out of cash. Unemployment was epidemic. The federal government stepped into the vacuum. Program after program poured out of Washington. What seemed unthinkable in 1921—insurance against unemployment—became a reality. And one of the high points of the New Deal was the Social Security Act (1935).[7] It promised pensions for the elderly. It also gave the old folks an incentive to retire from their jobs. And making jobs was one of the great goals of the New Deal. The army of the unemployed had to be put to work. Among the first fruits of the New Deal were massive public works programs. The Social Security law, thus, served a number of purposes. Not the least of these was to dampen the ardor of the nation for even more radical schemes—like the Townsend plan, the brainchild

[5] Quoted in Theda Skocpol, *Protecting Soldiers and Mothers: The Political Origins of Social Policy in the United States* (1992), pp. 500–501.

[6] On Sheppard-Towner, see Molly Ladd-Taylor, *Mother-Work: Women, Child Welfare, and the State, 1890–1930* (1994); Skocpol, n. 5 *supra,* ch. 9.

[7] 49 Stat. 620 (act of Aug. 14, 1935).

of Dr. Francis E. Townsend, which promised everybody 60 and over a monthly pension of $200. The Social Security Act was a complex piece of legislation. It was more than a pension plan for old folks; it included many other forms of welfare—grants to the states to help "needy individuals who are blind"; and Aid to Dependent Children. The Act was wildly popular, and has continued to be. It is the cornerstone of the modern American welfare state.

From this federal program there was no turning back. There were mainly additions. In the 1960s, under the presidency of Lyndon Johnson, there was a new burst of welfare energy. Johnson began a "war on poverty," which included such programs as Head Start. But his most notable achievements were Medicare, a health care program for men and women over sixty-five; and Medicaid, a program for the medically indigent. Medicare joined Social Security in the pantheon of totally popular, almost untouchable programs. Medicare had many constituencies: the gray lobby, more and more important as people lived longer; and the children of senior citizens, who no longer had to pay for mother's hospital bills, and father's hip replacement, at a time when the extended family was growing weaker anyway.

The federal government began to have more of a say in criminal justice, too. Prohibition focused attention on Washington. Under J. Edgar Hoover, a federal agency, the Federal Bureau of Investigation, took on the job of fighting crime that crossed state lines. Hoover was a master of publicity, and a genius at assembling power. President Herbert Hoover appointed a federal commission (the chair was George W. Wickersham, a former attorney general) to examine the problem of crime. The Wickersham Commission published fourteen volumes of reports in 1931. A massive increase in violent crime, after the Second World War, put the issue once more on center stage. Center stage meant Washington. But the federal role chiefly took the form of shoveling out money to the states. The Law Enforcement Assistance Act (LEAA), passed in 1965, did precisely this. It made grants to local governments and police forces. State crime-fighting dwarfs the federal effort, which is fairly anemic; but people look nonetheless to Washington at least for guidance; and candidates for federal office posture and brag about how tough they are or will be with regard to crime.

Education too was once entirely a local matter. The center of gravity still remains in the states and even lower—in local school districts. There are very dense, detailed state laws: on finances, on curriculum, on teachers and students. But the federal government has entered this area, too. In 1946, a federal law gave money to the states to support school lunches for poor kids. Millions of veterans went to college under the terms of the "GI Bill of Rights" of 1944. When the Soviets put a satellite ("sputnik") in space, there was a kind of national panic— the United States simply must be number one in everything—and the federal government began to pour money into science education. Other programs siphoned money into local education. A Department of Education became part of the cabinet in 1979. Presidential candidates began to talk education as well as crime control. A recent emanation from Congress, the "No Child Left Behind Act of 2001" (the title reflects a growing trend toward double-speak and propaganda in naming statutes) runs to hundreds of pages of detailed provisions. The federal government, in other words, has become a partner—big or little, "silent" or active—in every aspect of social control.

Wars and depressions may be aberrations; but even without these, the central government would have continued its remorseless process of growth. How could it be otherwise? Even in the late nineteenth century, or earlier, it was obvious to educated people that industrial development was changing the world. The industrial revolution had let loose, like a jinni out of its bottle, enormous social and economic forces. It created wealth; and it created problems. No single state, no Rhode Island or Alabama or Oregon, had the muscle to handle the problems. The primitive conception of a country of yeoman, a federalism of smallholders, no longer fit reality, not even remotely. The population continued to swell; but it was more and more a metropolitan population. Fewer people lived on the land or in small towns. Most people worked in factories, offices, and shops. They owned no land, except perhaps their own little house; they depended for their daily bread on an employer. Later, particularly after the Second World War, millions of people moved to the suburbs, the rings of houses and towns and developments that surrounded, and sometimes strangled, the central cities. The federal government played a part in this development, of course. For one thing, it lent money to veterans to buy houses in the suburbs. Government programs changed the *physical* face of America in the twentieth century, just as surely as the surveys and land grants of the nineteenth century had done so.

City life is interdependent life. But this is not the interdependence of small, face-to-face groups—not the interdependence of colonial Salem or Williamsburg. Rather it is the interdependence of strangers—buyers who never see their sellers, sellers who do not know their buyers; patients in the hands of "specialists," instead of the old family doctor; passengers dependent on a driver or a pilot they never see and whose name they do not know. And all the millions and millions who live in the United States form a single unit. They are part of one huge nation, and, perhaps more significantly, one huge economy, and one huge culture. Technology created new ways to travel and to communicate. It took months, in 1800, for a human being or a message to get from one end of the country to another. In 1900, thanks to the telephone and telegraph, messages sped across the country in almost no time at all. Actual bodies took somewhat longer, but fast continental trains tied East and West, North and South. The automobile was a rarity, a toy, in 1900, a novelty on the streets. It took less than twenty years to turn this country into an automotive society. The automobile made travel something individual, personal; a matter of choice. Trains have schedules; cars do not. The Wright brothers flew their tiny little airplane, at Kitty Hawk, in 1903. Within a few decades, people were flying commercially, and at enormous speed. Then came the jets. Air traffic drove the passenger railroad into virtual extinction, except in a few crowded urban corridors. In 2000, for passengers sitting in a wide-bodied jet, New York and Los Angeles were closer in time than Baltimore and Washington had been when Jefferson sat in the White house. A yawn, a drink, a bad meal, a movie, and you had crossed the entire continent—at a discounted fare, at that. Television and the Internet meant that images and messages could be transported from one end of the country to the other in no time at all—and indeed, could be transported all over the world. And television and the Internet completed a job that radio and the movies began: a homogenized mass culture: the culture of rock-and-roll, blue jeans, and hamburgers; of action movies, television sitcoms, and broadcasts of major league baseball.

Moreover, Americans have always been a restless lot. They moved from house to house, from city to city, from state to state. Mobility, however, is the deadly enemy of local customs, foods, speech habits, ways of life. Politically, America seems fragmented into interest groups and identity groups. But culturally, it has become more or less homogeneous, everywhere. All airports look the same. All highways look the same. More and more, all shopping centers look the same. The American market was now truly national in scope. The century began with mass-produced goods. It ended with mass-produced stores: Chains that make shopping malls in Anchorage and Key West look suspiciously alike. The small merchants fought the chains—between 1927 and 1941, most of the states passed laws trying to curb them, tax them, attack them, in the interests of small merchants. In the end all of this was a dismal failure. Nothing now is more American than MacDonald's, Holiday Inn, The Gap, Victoria's Secret, Starbucks, Wal-Mart, and other missionaries of similitude. Geographically, the United States is amazingly varied. The weather outside may be a blizzard or a tropical rainshower; the topography may be desert, mountain, forest, or swamp; but all this gets flattened out in the realm of consumption and entertainment. When people in Wichita watch the same programs as the people in Juneau and Fort Lauderdale, when you can buy sushi in Denver and bagels in Bangor, Maine, when small towns in Vermont are full of New York exurbanites, and the Mormon church seeks converts in Alabama—it is futile to think of states as anything but convenient political subdivisions. As "sovereigns," as bearers of some unique history or culture, they never had much meaning; and whatever it was, now it is lost. There is a lot of talk about states' rights; but the original meaning of states' rights is forever dead. To try to resurrect it is to try to bring life back to a corpse. At times, one must admit, it is a fairly lively corpse.

In complex ways, the national culture and the national economy led to an ever rising level of demands on government. When we write about history, it is easy and tempting to use impersonal phrases and the dreaded passive voice. It is easy to write that government got bigger, that federal power was extended over more and more areas, as if one was talking about a natural process, like a chemical reaction, or some sort of progress that was biologically programmed, like the way an egg turns into a chicken or a bud turns into a rose. Politicians love to talk, too, about bloated government, as if the administration were some sort of fat man with an uncontrollable appetite, something that grew all by itself. There is a grain of truth in all of this, but only a grain. Parkinson's law and the greed of bureaucrats do explain some of the growth of government. People who run organizations (and not just governments) are often ambitious and grasping; they want their agency, company, hospital, university, or whatever, to get bigger and stronger. There are empire-builders within government. But even the timid souls, and there are many of these among the bureaucrats, contribute to the size of the government. Cautious civil servants like to cover themselves with rules, forms, and red tape. Yet the monstrous size of modern government does not come, on the whole, from pathologies of the civil service. All modern governments are big and bureaucratic. They are all built, too, on a foundation of concrete demands, which come from concrete groups, groups that clamor for public, that is, governmental response.

And the growth of big government also has a kind of snowball effect. The more government does, the more money it needs to finance itself; and the more men and women to run its affairs. Big government, then, becomes a major employer, which gives it yet another lever of control over the economy.

It also develops an enormous appetite for taxes, and the apparatus to feed that appetite. In the late nineteenth century, the Supreme Court struck down a federal income tax law, which Congress had passed in 1894, as we saw.[8] But Congress did not take this lying down. In 1909, both houses endorsed an amendment to the Constitution—in the Senate, by a unanimous vote—and sent the amendment to the states. It went over the top in 1913, when enough states had ratified it. Congress then passed an income tax law in 1913. The rates were modest—the top bracket was 6 percent, and it applied only to truly enormous incomes, incomes over half a million dollars a year (almost nobody had an income that large). In fact, only about 2 percent of the country's families had to file any sort of return under this early law.[9] The rates crept up, but not alarmingly: The top rate, in 1916, was 13 percent; and this applied only to incomes of $2 million or more. Taxes rise, however, in wartime: a War Revenue Act was passed in 1917, during the First World War; and the income tax became the most significant source of federal money.

The Second World war was an even greater turning point. It soaked up money like a sponge. The war brought the income tax home to the masses. Under the pay-as-you-go system, tax money was withheld from the paychecks of the workers. The rates skyrocketed; the top wartime rate was over 80 percent of net income. Tax planning, tax avoidance (and outright tax fraud) became national pastimes. The Internal Revenue Code grew into a kind of monster—the longest, most complicated law of the land. Since the 1960s, income tax rates have gone down considerably; and the Republican Party would like them to go down even more. The administration of George W. Bush pushed through a very sizeable tax cut law. But the government needs its trillions, and they have to come from somewhere.

Despite the flight of power to the central government, the warlord system in American politics refuses to die. The system continues to reject any hint of absolute power (except *perhaps* the president's control over foreign policy, and perhaps, too, some aspects of the executive's "war on terror" at the beginning of the twenty-first century). In general, American government is a patchwork, a rug made of rags. Fragmentation is as American as apple pie. There are all sorts of checks and balances. Everybody checks and balances and vetoes everybody else. The checkers and balancers include voters, members of juries, police and prosecutors, judges exercising judicial review, ombudsmen, political parties, members of the bureaucracy, and many other actors. Some of these have a formal duty to check and balance; some do not, but in practice checking and balancing is exactly what they do. The formal structure itself is mightily fragmented. There is the state level and the federal level. The counties have some (limited) powers. The cities and towns, with or without "home rule," overlap the larger jurisdictions. In some cases, they deal directly with the federal government, as its special client. Besides all these, there are little zones of power, almost limitless in number: sewer districts, school districts, mosquito abatement districts, air-pollution districts; and such mighty vassals as the New York Port

---

[8] *Pollock v. Farmers' Loan and Trust Co.*, 157 U.S. 429 (1895); 158 U.S. 601 (1985).
[9] The law was 38 Stat. 166 (act of Oct. 3, 1913); on the scope of the act, see John F. Witte, *The Politics and Development of the Federal Income Tax* (1985).

Authority. Some of these districts and authorities are accountable, it seems, to no one in particular; some have gigantic mouths to feed on the plankton of nickels, dimes, quarters, and dollars thrown into the hopper by motorists; some have expanded to monstrous size.

Since 1900, too, local government has become steadily *less* rational in at least one important sense. In the nineteenth century, as a rule, a city gobbled up more land as its population grew; its boundaries swelled and stretched as it became an urban center. This process ground to a halt around 1900. Since 1930, the older big cities have been, on the whole, trapped inside old borders, like prisoners in a tiny cell. Many have actually lost population, in some cases, quite dramatically. The population of St. Louis was 856,000 in 1950—and 334,000 in 1999. The newer cities in the South and the West had more power to "annex." Places like Houston, Texas, and San Jose, California, were able to swallow huge tracts of outlying land. For most of the older cities, on the other hand, city limits were fixed and frozen. The boundaries had no relationship to the realities of urban life—no sensible connection with problems of crime, garbage collection, transportation, education, or tax bases. When the populations of St. Louis and Detroit began to shrink, this was not a sign that people were going back to their farms. Quite the opposite: Rural America lost ground steadily throughout the century. People from small towns and rural areas fled to the cities as if a pack of wild dogs was after them. Or rather, they ran to the metropolitan areas. These are now gigantic conurbations, endless sprawling growths, some of them, like Los Angeles, almost headless wonders, without any central core, or with a whole congeries of central cores. The metropolitan areas are made up of a mixture of jurisdictions: central cities, old suburbs, new suburbs, towns, villages, exurban areas. Some of these fragments of government are little more than incorporated neighborhoods, but as autonomous (in theory) as Boston or New York City. These little fragments stoutly resist the large agglomerations that might want to engulf them. They expect to rule their own roost. In particular, they want to resist the influx of blacks and low-income people. There are hundreds and thousands of villages that are little more than restrictive covenants, or zoning ordinances, in corporate form, with a lofty name, and a show of undeserved power. The fear of crime adds to this impulse to retreat behind the invisible walls and barriers of these little enclaves. And, more and more, people with money retreat behind visible walls and gates: into "privatopias" ruled (and rather autocratically) by homeowner associations.[10]

The struggle between centralism and localism thus goes on. It never ends. And perhaps there is no reason for it to end. The balance between Washington and the communities is not a "problem," to be resolved once and for all. It is silly to think that uniformity or lack of uniformity is a problem in itself; or that centralization or decentralization is either a problem or a solution. In real life, problems are specific: poverty, or air pollution, or terrorism, or crime, or low economic growth, or the balance of trade, or juvenile delinquency, or whatever society defines as a situation gone wrong. Structural features are tools or effects. Each situation might call for a different kind of legal architecture. It

---

[10] See Evan McKenzie, *Privatopia: Homeowner Associations and the Rise of Residential Private Government* (1994).

would be ridiculous to let Wichita, Kansas, decide whether there should be a free trade treaty with Chile; but it would be just as ridiculous for Washington to decide if Wichita should have speed bumps in residential neighborhoods.

Yet, tools or effects are not unimportant. The basic issue is power: Where does it sit, and who exercises it? The structural features of the legal system reflect the distribution of power and, at the same time, influence or perpetuate power. A good distribution for one purpose is a bad one for another purpose. Institutions work in different ways. Juries are usually quite good, sometimes very good—at blocking an overreaching government. Government cannot punish draft dodgers if juries refuse to convict. On the other hand, white juries in the prejudiced South refused to apply the law to whites who committed crimes against blacks, or to blacks who were falsely accused of crimes against whites. Juries in tort cases are running amok, robbing from deep pockets; or voices of ordinary people, punishing rogue companies and disciplining the market—depending on how you look at it. Presidential power is good for some things, and bad for others. Legislative power is good and bad. Judicial review is good and bad. The bureaucracy is good and bad. There is no generalization that holds true for all cases, all times.

Decentralization continues to be part of the legal culture, as we said. People seem to cherish their localism: local school boards, local sewer districts, tiny suburbs and enclaves that choke the decaying central cities. Fragmentation is politically useful, and politically appealing. When people or groups demand central control, they do not want big government as such. Few people care (and why should they?) whether government is big or small or at what level. They care about results. They care about whether they feel free or stifled. Arguments about centralism, or decentralism, are surrogates for something else. Southerners who preached states' rights, before (and after) the civil rights revolution, were not really professing a political theory. They had a shopping list of things they wanted, and they knew which stores carried the goods. White supremacy was high on the list. Conservatives still talk about states' rights: but when it comes to something like gay marriage or medical malpractice or the question of how much money a plaintiff can squeeze from a business defendant, they plead frantically with Washington to rescue them from local insanity.

Moreover, when local people and local government ask for federal intervention, they are not really interested in federal *control*. They want money, and Washington is the place to get it from. Many so-called federal programs are not really programs of central control; they are merely statutory pots of cash to be distributed among local interests and power groups. Sometimes these programs develop a thick texture of federal regulation, but nonetheless they are, at heart, simply devices for siphoning funds. Efficient federal tax machines collect the money and pass it out to states, cities, and local authorities. Often, under the law, the locals can do more or less as they please with the money, subject to fairly loose, general limits and controls.

Both centralization and fragmentation, then, were facts of life in the twentieth century. But, if one had to choose, the more dramatic change was the roaring engine of the central government, especially during and after the New Deal. Nothing seemed beyond the power of Congress and the executive—in theory, although in practice so many things were left to the states and the cities. A very conservative Supreme Court, at the end of the twentieth century, let it be known that it felt the centralization had gone too far. The Supreme Court had, since the late 1930s, more or less given up on controlling the actions of Congress, in the economic sphere. Congress could regulate interstate commerce. It could also regulate anything that affected interstate commerce. That meant, basically, almost anything that had even a potential impact on people, goods, or whatever, that crossed or might cross a state line. Even before the New Deal era, the Court, though tough on such things as child labor, was willing to expand the reach of the commerce clause, when this was for something it liked. Thus, the Mann Act, which made it a crime to transport women across state lines for prostitution or other "immoral purposes" was perfectly okay.[11] *Wickard v. Filburn* (1942) came up under a law that was part of the New Deal agricultural program.[12] The law aimed to prop up the price of farm products by controlling production. Roscoe Filburn, an Ohio farmer, produced more bushels of wheat than he was allowed to. He became subject to a penalty. But Filburn sold no wheat in interstate commerce; in fact, he sold no wheat at all. It was all consumed on his own personal farm. How could Congress tell Filburn, under the commerce clause, how much wheat he could raise on his local farm, for local consumption? But the Supreme Court sided with the government. Filburn himself was not important; but multiply him by dozens of other Filburns, and there was an impact on interstate commerce—at least arguably.

And in the 1960s, Congress passed the great Civil Rights Act. Hotels and restaurants, for example, could not discriminate against African Americans. Was this something Congress could order—could they tell purely private businesses, like Ollie's Barbecue in Birmingham, what to do? Yes, said the Court, because the hotels and restaurants might serve interstate travelers; or use products that came across state lines.[13] It seemed as if nothing, now, was beyond the power of Congress to control, under the rubric of "interstate commerce."

But apparently there were limits. In 1990, Congress passed the "Gun-Free School Zones Act." It was now a federal offense to bring a gun into a school zone. Guns, after all, crossed state lines by the thousands, so why not a federal law? A senior in a high school in San Antonio, Texas, Alfonso Lopez, brought a .38 caliber handgun to school; he was indicted and convicted. The Supreme Court, in a narrow 5–4 decision, struck down the law in 1995.[14] The connection to interstate commerce was too tenuous. The commerce clause was not a "blank check." If the government won its case, there would be no "limitation on federal power," even in "areas . . . where States historically had been sovereign."

This case set off alarm bells in the academy: Was this the opening shot of a new war, or a passing fancy? The Court's conservative majority was quite serious about putting on the brakes, as a handful of cases afterwards made clear. But nobody, not even the U.S. Supreme Court, can revive the dead. Eighteenth-century federalism is gone. It was not Roosevelt that killed it, or the New Deal, or a liberal Supreme Court. It was killed by powerful social, economic, and political forces. It was killed by the railroad, the telegraph, movies, automobiles,

---

[11] *Hoke v. United States,* 227 U.S. 308 (1913).

[12] 317 U.S. 111 (1942).

[13] *Katzenbach* v. *McClung,* 279 U.S. 294 (1964); this was the case coming out of Ollie's Barbecue. On hotels, see *Heart of Atlanta Motel* v. *United States,* 279 U.S. 241 (1964).

[14] *United States* v. *Lopez,* 514 U.S. 549 (1995).

television, the Internet—the list could be extended. There can be no going back. Great oceans ebb, but they never shrink and dry.

The Court's move here should not, however, be dismissed as a quirk—a pet doctrine of four oldish men and one oldish women, who made up a (bare) majority of the Court. These commerce clause cases are (probably) not going anywhere. But they are interesting at least symbolically. They express the abiding faith of Americans in layers and layers of countervailing power. This faith manifests itself in all sorts of ways, some of which we have discussed. What comes out of the process is a delicately balanced system, incredibly complicated, but with tremendous tensile strength. Its flaws are also massive. It is tremendously hard to unravel or reform. And, at times, because of its complexity, because of the existence of so many veto groups, and because of its obsession with checks and balances, it can be monstrously inefficient.[15]

Yet oddly enough, localism does not mean that the average American pays a great deal of attention to what goes on in his or her community. The average American can hardly bring himself or herself to vote for president; but at least they know who the president is. They see him every day on television. Ask the same person who their local representative is in Springfield or Albany, and you get a blank stare. The local alderman or city council member? No idea at all. Politics, thanks to the media, has become as national as shopping malls and chain stores.

---

[15] For a brilliant critique and explication, see Robert A. Kagan, *Adversarial Legalism: The American Way of Law* (2001).

CHAPTER 2

THE GROWTH OF THE LAW

THE LIABILITY EXPLOSION: WORKERS' COMPENSATION

One of the most striking developments in the twentieth century was the so-called liability explosion: the vast increase in liability in tort, mostly for personal injuries. The nineteenth century—particularly the early part—had built up the law of torts, almost from nothing, as we have seen; courts (and it was mainly courts) created a huge, complicated structure, a system with many rooms, chambers, corridors, and an ethos of limited liability. The twentieth century worked just as busily to tear the whole thing down. The process had started much earlier, as we noted. One of the first doctrines to go was the fellow-servant rule. By 1900, it no longer worked very well. It was still heartless, it still cut off most lawsuits and claims by workers; but it no longer had the virtue of simplicity or efficiency. Lawyer's fees, insurance, litigation costs: the system was costly and slow, and the middlemen took much or most of the money; the system was like a body infested with tapeworms. Congress swept the rule away for railroad workers, in the Federal Employers' Liability Act, in the first decade of the century.[1] Many states also abolished the rule, or limited it severely. Between 1900 and 1910, there was vigorous debate and discussion about alternatives—notably, some sort of compensation scheme. Industry on the whole was opposed to the idea; but business resistance gradually tapered off. Perhaps a compensation scheme would make sense, even for employers. It might buy a measure of industrial peace. England and Germany already had compensation schemes, which seemed to work. New York passed a compensation statute in 1910. It was declared unconstitutional.[2] Next came Wisconsin (1911), this time successfully. Other states now passed their own versions, trying to avoid the pitfalls of the New York law. The Supreme Court later held the most common types of plan constitutional. By 1920, almost all states had adopted a workers' compensation law, of one sort or another. The last holdout, Mississippi, joined the chorus in 1948.

---

[1] 34 Stats. 232 (act of June 11, 1906). The Supreme Court, in the Employers' Liability Cases, 207 U.S. 463 (1908), struck down the law by a narrow 5 to 4 margin. But Congress passed a new law, 35 Stats. 65 (act of April 22, 1908), which successfully met the Court's objections.

[2] *Ives* v. *South Buffalo Railway Co.*, 201 N.Y. 271, 94 N. E. 431 (1911).

Workers' compensation did not come out of nowhere.[3] Besides the foreign models, there were also domestic models: schemes of insurance, including co-operative insurance plans for workmen.[4] In any event, workers' compensation, when it emerged, was something of a compromise system. Each side gave a little, got a little. The worker got compensation. If you were injured on the job, you collected; you no longer had to show that somebody else was at fault. Nor was contributory negligence an issue: even a foolish, careless worker had a right to claim compensation. In *Karlslyst v. Industrial Commission* (1943),[5] a Wisconsin case, the worker, a truck driver's assistant, urinated off the side of a moving truck, fell off, and was injured. This was stupid behavior, to say the least. His case would have been doubly hopeless in the nineteenth century: the fellow-servant rule, plus contributory negligence, would have robbed him of any chance at a claim. But this was now, not then, and the worker recovered: He was injured on the job; his own carelessness was completely irrelevant.

Compensation laws did away with the fellow-servant rule and also with the doctrine of assumption of risk. Unless the worker was drunk, or deliberately try-ing to hurt herself, she was entitled to her compensation. On the other hand, the statute set up a formula that would determine what the employer had to pay: medical expenses and a fixed percentage of the wages she lost; but with a defi-nite ceiling. In Wisconsin, for example, under the 1911 law, a totally disabled worker could collect, as long as her disability lasted, 65 percent of her average weekly wage, up to four times her average annual earnings. But this was as high as she could go.[6] The statutes also commonly set a definite price for "permanent partial disability"; and also fixed a price for damaged or missing body parts—an arm, a leg, a finger, a foot, an eye, or an ear. The employee could get no less, but also no more. No more jury trials. No more chance at the litigation lottery. No big recoveries. No money for pain and suffering. For all this the employers were grateful. Both sides, in other words, won and lost.

Only the middlemen—this was the theory—would be the losers. Workers' compensation would do away with the plague of accident cases. It would elimi-nate the need for lawyers, claims adjusters, insurance brokers, and so on. In the main, it did exactly what it was supposed to do. Most work accidents—the over-whelming majority, in fact—were, from the start, handled smoothly, and with-out great fuss, by boards and commissions. But the new statutes did generate enough case law to surprise, and disappoint, some people who had champi-oned the system. The case law—and later, the statutes—also began to push the system into new areas, in directions that would have amazed reformers in the early part of the century. What fueled the movement for workers' compensa-tion was the classic industrial accident: the thousands of workers mangled, maimed, killed, crippled, destroyed, in mines, factories, railroad yards—the dead and wounded victims of the industrial revolution. Indeed, one early statute, in Oklahoma, was specifically limited to "hazardous occupations," and

---

[3] On the rise of workers' compensation, see Price V. Fishback and Shawn Everett Kantor, *A Prelude to the Welfare State: The Origins of Workers' Compensation* (2000).

[4] See John Fabian Witt, "Toward a New History of American Accident Law: Classical Tort Law and the Cooperative First-Party Insurance Movement," 114 Harv. L. Rev. 692 (2001).

[5] 243 Wis. 612, 11 N.W. 2d 179 (1943).

[6] Laws Wis. 1911, ch. 50, pp. 46–47.

even listed what these were: factories, blast furnaces, and so on. There was to
be no coverage for "clerical workers."[7] Nor did the early statutes, typically,
cover occupational diseases—if the job poisoned the worker, or just slowly wore
him out, the worker could not recover. These harms were not "injuries" and
they did not come from "accidents." The "radium girls," who painted dials on
watches that would glow in the dark, and who began to die of cancer, in the
1920s, collected almost nothing.[8]

But over time, the system evolved toward more and more liability—case law
and statutes alike. The statutes, as originally worded, covered injuries "arising
out of" (caused by) and "in the course of" (during) employment. These words,
or their equivalent, appeared in most of the statutes. The courts gradually
stretched the meaning of these words as if they were made out of rubber. If a
secretary strains her neck at the office, turning to talk to her girlfriend, she
collects compensation. Dozens of cases dealt with accidents at company parties
or picnics. Often these were held to be injuries "in the course of" employment.
A crazed killer storms into a restaurant, firing at random; bullets hit a bus boy.
He collects workers' compensation.[9] Some states began to cover occupational
diseases; and this coverage expanded over the years; indeed, in New Jersey, the
plight of the "radium girls" helped spur reform of this sort. The courts even
began upholding or mandating awards in cases where workers had heart attacks on the job. Sometimes they required evidence of an unusual strain; but as
time went on, this doctrine became more and more tenuous, and more and
more workers who had heart attacks at work were able to recover.[10]

How rational is a system where a man who has a heart attack on Sunday,
watching football on television, gets nothing; while a man who has a heart attack
on Monday, sitting at his desk reading a report, gets coverage under workers'
compensation? In a country without a system of cradle-to-grave security, and in
particular without national health insurance, piecemeal bits of what would be a
full welfare system start sticking like burrs to existing institutions. In any event,
the compensation explosion marched on through the last half of the century.
Courts began upholding awards for psychological injury—people who said the
job had stressed them to the point of illness, or that the trauma of getting fired,
or of losing a promotion, drove them into deep depression, or triggered mental
illness, or the like.[11] Awards of this type, in the 1980s and onward, drove up the
costs of the system. These added costs alarmed and enraged the business community. Business brought its lobbying muscle to bear on the issue. A number of
states cut back sharply. In California, for example, from 1989 on, no worker
could recover compensation for "psychiatric injury" brought about by a "lawful,
nondiscriminatory, good faith personnel action."[12] No longer was it possible to
claim that a layoff had driven the worker crazy.

[7] Okla Comp. Stats. 1926, sections 7283–4, pp. 662–63.
[8] On this incident, see Claudia Clark, *Radium Girls: Women and Industrial Health Reform,
1910–1935* (1997).
[9] *Louie v. Bamboo Gardens,* 67 Ida. 469, 185 P. 2d 712 (1947).
[10] See *Workmen's Compensation Appeal Board v. Bernard S. Pincus Co.,* 479 Pa. 286, 388 A. 2d
659 (1978).
[11] For an example, see *Helen J. Kelly's Case,* 394 Mass. 684, 477 N. E. 2d 582 (1985).
[12] Cal. Labor Code, sec. 3208.3; Laws Cal. 1989, ch. 892, sec. 25.

MORE EXPLOSIONS: TORT LAW

These developments in workers' compensation ran parallel to, and were dwarfed by, changes in the tort law system in general. These changes did not happen overnight. Early in the century, the tort system was still stingy and withholding; procedural and legal obstacles kept most victims of accident out of court. When a Seaboard Air Line train was wrecked in 1911, carrying 912 black passengers on an excursion, ten blacks were killed and eighty-six injured. Liability was obvious; but the company sent out agents, and settled for tiny amounts—from $1 to $1000.[13] These were blacks, in the South, and they settled out of court. But Northern whites were not much better off. The famous Triangle Shirtwaist Disaster, in the same year, in which scores of young women died—needlessly—created a furor, influenced the course of legislation, but resulted in almost nothing at all for the victims. The wrongful death claims settled for about $75 each.[14] Here the fellow-servant rule was one of the villains. In general, the culture of total justice did not develop overnight. What produced it was a combination of factors—the development of insurance, the timid but real beginnings of a genuine welfare state; factors which led people to want, and expect, some kind of system of compensation, for disasters that were not their own personal fault.[15]

The automobile was one of the great innovations of the twentieth century. At the beginning of the century, automobiles were, in essence, curiosities, expensive gadgets. By the 1920s, as we said, this was fast on the way to becoming a society of people with cars. There were forty million cars registered by 1950; by 1990, 123 million cars. The automobile remade America. Its social (and legal) implications are endless. The automobile helped create suburbia. It revolutionized tourism. It led to a demand for roads, more roads, highways, more highways; a federal Road Aid Act was passed in 1916, and another in 1921; and the interstate highway system was created after the Second World War. The automobile transformed the cities. First, it helped them, by getting rid of the horse. Horses at one time dumped two and half million pounds of manure, sixty thousand gallons of urine, day in and day out, in New York City alone. Cities had to dispose of thousands and thousands of dead horses a year—not to mention the stench, the flies, the dirty straw, and the thousands of stables.[16] By the end of the century, the tables were turned: now the automobile was choking the city; and creating its own forms of pollution.

The automobile also created a whole new field of traffic law. There were rules of the road before the automobile, but they were of minor legal importance. By the middle of the century, traffic law touched everybody's life: drivers' licenses, stoplights, parking regulations, speed limits, auto insurance—no branch of the law was more familiar (or more commonly avoided and violated). Speed limits

---

[13] Edward A. Purcell Jr., "The Action Was Outside the Courts: Consumer Injuries and the Uses of Contract in the United States, 1875–1945," in Willibald Steinmetz, ed., *Private Law and Social Inequality in the Industrial Age* (2000), pp. 505, 524.

[14] See Arthur F. McEvoy, "The Triangle Shirtwaist Factory Fire of 1911: Social Change, Industrial Accidents, and the Evolution of Common-Sense Causality," 20 Law and Social Inquiry 621 (1995).

[15] Lawrence M. Friedman, *Total Justice* (1985).

[16] Ruth Schwartz Cowan, *A Social History of Technology* (1997), pp. 233–34.

and drivers' licenses came in early in the century. Traffic violations run into the millions every year; they are the plankton, the krill, of criminal justice. Most of these violations are trivial. But drunk driving is taken seriously—indeed, since the 1970s, very seriously, helped along by organizations such as Mothers Against Drunk Driving (MADD). And the automobile accident replaced the train accident as the staple of personal injury law, the bread and butter of the tort lawyer. Here was a machine, tons of metal and rubber, racing along streets and roads, in the millions, and at high speeds. To be sure, the overwhelming majority of accident cases, the fender-benders, the smashed rear ends, and the whiplash injuries, were settled out of court, "adjusted," compromised, or simply handled with a phone call and a check.[17] The real parties in interest were the insurance companies. But a residue of serious and contested cases remained for the personal injury bar to handle. These lawyers, and tort lawyers in general, worked (as we have seen) on the basis of the contingent fee—they earned nothing if they lost the case; but if they won, they took a healthy cut (a quarter, a third, perhaps even a half). The elite bar hated the contingent fee, and looked down on "p.i." lawyers. But the practice flourished.

Even more dramatic changes took place in aspects of tort law that hardly existed before 1900. One of these was products liability. In 1916, in a decision clearly written for posterity, Benjamin Cardozo, of the New York Court of Appeals, seized an opportunity, and helped change the direction of liability law. The case was *MacPherson v. Buick Motor Co.*[18] MacPherson bought a Buick from a dealer. The wheel was "made of defective wood." Its spokes "crumbled into fragments." MacPherson was seriously injured. He sued the car company. There was a long-standing technical barrier to MacPherson's claim. No "privity," no direct relationship, connected plaintiff and defendant. MacPherson never dealt directly with the Buick Motor Company; he dealt only with an auto dealer. In the past, that would have made his lawsuit dubious if not impossible. But Cardozo cut through this technicality. When a manufacturer makes a product that is or can be dangerous, and knows that the product will end up, not with a dealer or a middleman, but with a consumer, the manufacturer must suffer the consequences. And the injured party can sue him directly.

This was the core of the decision, cleverly disguised in cautious and craftsman-like language. Within a generation or so, other states had followed Cardozo's lead; and products liability law had taken a giant step forward (or backward, if you will). "Followed" may be the wrong word. Other courts did cite Cardozo, and refer to his famous decision. His written opinion was seductive, persuasive. But the doctrine spread, not because of Cardozo's reputation and skill, but because it struck judges as intuitively correct. This was an age of mass production, an age of advertising, of brand names. People associated products with their makers—with Buick, not with an auto dealer. If a can of tainted soup poisoned someone, did it make sense to hold the grocer liable, and only the grocer? Why not sue the manufacturer, the company that made the soup, put it in a can, and sealed the can airtight? It was easy for people in the twentieth century—including judges—to accept the basic idea

---

[17] See the classic study by H. Laurence Ross, *Settled Out of Court: The Social Process of Insurance Claims Adjustment* (rev. 2d ed., 1980).
[18] 217 N.Y. 382, 111 N.E. 1050 (1916).

of products liability. Companies that make a product must bear the responsibility, if the product hurt the ultimate consumer. In later times, courts have carried products liability further than Cardozo ever dreamt of. The original standard was the usual one: negligence. But the courts have come closer and closer to a kind of absolute liability. There is a tendency to make the company pay for what a defective product does, whether or not the plaintiff can prove there was negligence in its manufacture. In a few dramatic cases, recoveries have soared into millions of dollars. Companies that mass-produce goods obviously cannot guarantee absolute safety. They cannot guarantee that one widget out of millions made won't be defective and cause harm. The court put it this way, in a case involving a glass jar of peanuts that shattered, "a seller . . . is liable for defects in his product even if those defects were introduced, without the slightest fault of his own."[19]

The liability explosion was not confined to manufactured products. Particularly in the last half of the twentieth century, more people began to sue their doctors, their lawyers, and their accountants; they sued cities, hospitals, businesses, and labor unions; occasionally, they even sued ministers and priests. Old doctrines that stood in the way were swept ruthlessly aside. Suing a (nonprofit) hospital was at one time impossible: Charities were not liable in tort. But in the second half of the twentieth century state after state abandoned charitable immunity. By 1964, only nine states still were clinging to the doctrine.[20] Later, these nine also gave up the ghost. Now nothing stands in the way of lawsuits against hospitals, universities, or other nonprofits.

Medical malpractice—suing your doctor for careless treatment—in a way broke no new ground, doctrinally speaking. A negligent doctor, like anybody else who was negligent, had to take the consequences. But dragging the friendly family doctor into court had been uncommon and somewhat disreputable; moreover, doctors (at least so it was said) were reluctant to testify against each other. Their instinct was to stick together against the lay public. Malpractice cases were rare in the first part of the century. But in the late twentieth century, medicine had become much more impersonal (and more high-tech). Malpractice suits also became more common. In a study of New York city cases (1910), only a little more than 1.1 percent of the tort cases were malpractice cases; in San Francisco, between 1959 and 1980, 7 percent of the civil jury trials came under this heading.[21] In one regard, too, the standard did shift: it was also malpractice if a doctor filed to tell his patient about risks and dangers in medicines or procedures. The doctor had to get what came to be called "informed consent." If not, the doctor might be liable if something went wrong—regardless of fault. This doctrine appeared in the late 1950s, and later spread and became more general. The doctrine of "informed consent" reflected two social norms that were dominant in the late twentieth century: a kind of free-wheeling individualism, which stressed the right to choose; and, a related norm, a suspicion of experts and elites. Contrary to what most people believed, juries in malpractice

---

[19] *Welge v. Planters Lifesavers Co.*, 17 F. 3d 209 (7th Cir. 1994).

[20] William Prosser, *The Law of Torts* (3rd ed., 1964), pp. 1023–24.

[21] Randolph Bergstrom, *Courting Danger: Injury and Law in New York City, 1870–1910*, (1992), p. 20; Michael G. Shanley and Mark A. Peterson, *Comparative Justice: Civil Jury Verdicts in San Francisco and Cook Counties, 1959–1980* (1983).

cases were not pushovers: most plaintiffs lost their cases. Some plaintiffs won only small recoveries. A tiny minority collected huge amounts. But this was enough, apparently, to send insurance premiums through the roof; and to frighten and enrage thousands of doctors.

The liability explosion is real and powerful. But it has not gone unchallenged. Money for plaintiffs and for their lawyers did not grow on trees. The money came from insurance companies and from the coffers of corporations. There was backlash and counterrevolution in the 1980s. Doctors threatened to stop delivering babies. Companies claimed plaintiffs were driving them into bankruptcy. Urban legends spread like wildfire: the burglar who sued a landlord for defective premises; the foolish old woman who won millions because she spilled hot coffee. The Republicans denounced the hungry, parasitic army of lawyers. All this had some results. Some states cut back: on recoveries for pain and suffering, on punitive damages. But the core of the system remained solid.

One particular type of tort case, statistically insignificant but socially and economically important, was the so-called mass toxic tort. The paradigm case is asbestos. Clarence Borel, dying of lung cancer at the end of the 1960s, had been an "industrial insulation worker." He sued the asbestos companies; he blamed them for the illness that was killing him. By the time he won his case (1973), he was already dead.[22] But there were armies of the living that followed him. By the mid-1980s, there were 30,000 claims against asbestos companies. The number rose to over 100,000, and the cases drove every asbestos company into bankruptcy. There were other mega-cases, huge affairs with hundreds or thousands of plaintiffs: about the Dalkon Shield, a birth control device; about Agent Orange, a pesticide used in Vietnam; about diethylstilbestrol (DES), a drug used to prevent miscarriages. These cases lumbered through the courts for years. At the end of the century, cancer victims and states were suing tobacco companies, for sums that would dwarf the gross national product of most small countries. On the horizon were mass lawsuits against gun companies; and even against companies that sold junk food and made people fat.

The mass toxic tort cases accentuate a peculiarity of the American tort system. No other common law country—and probably no other country at all—makes such heavy use of the tort system, such heavy use of private lawsuits. The big awards—rare though they are—are unheard of in other countries. Part of this is due to the fragmentary nature of American government; and to the deep streak of stubborn resistance to government. In other countries, the welfare system carries more of the burden. The point we made about worker's compensation, applies to the whole tort system. People are much less likely to sue a doctor in a country with a national health system. America regulates business, sometimes quite effectively; but the country still relies on tort cases to do work and carry out policies that have a more central, comprehensive solution in other countries. The tort system creaks and lumbers under the burden; it is a costly, inefficient way to do the heavy lifting.

The faults of the tort system have led, as we saw, to a major backlash. The pathologies of litigation are a campaign issue; and the trial lawyers are, in some circles, convenient scapegoats. Nobody could really argue that the tort

---

[22] *Borel v. Fibreboard Paper Products Corp.*, 493 Fed. 2d 1076 (C.A. 45, 1973).

system is perfect or even half way to perfect. But it is, perhaps, better than nothing.

THE CONSTITUTION, RIGHTS, AND CIVIL LIBERTIES IN THE TWENTIETH CENTURY

The rush of power to the center meant not only that the president and the executive gained power; so too did the federal courts. The Supreme Court had always been important, always been in the eye of the storm. But it was even more so in the twentieth century. The twentieth century, from start to finish, was a golden age for constitutional law.

Just as state governments gained in absolute power, even as they lost relative to the federal power, so too did state courts. And state constitutional law. This is, to be sure, a rather obscure subject. The state high courts have the final word on the meaning of their own constitutions; and they decide many important, even vital, cases. The public largely ignores them. In one survey, in 1991, only about half the population even knew they *had* a state constitution.[23] The state constitutions, as in the past, were much more brittle than the federal constitution. They were constantly tinkered with. Actually constitution-making—adopting whole constitutions—slowed to a crawl in the twentieth century. Only twelve states adopted new constitutions in the twentieth century. (Five new states—Oklahoma, Arizona, New Mexico, Hawaii, and Alaska—adopted their first constitution.) The amending process, however, ran wild. The federal constitution is hard to amend, and is rarely amended (the failure, in 2004, of a proposed amendment to ban gay marriages is only the latest example). But this reticence does not apply to the states at all. In New York, between 1895 and 1937, there were 76 amendments to the constitution, between 1938 and 1967, there were 106, between 1968 and 1995, 46.[24] In some states (Georgia, for example) there were literally hundreds of amendments—654, by one count, by the end of the 1960s. The result was an incredible amount of constitutional bloat. The Louisiana Constitution contains 254,000 words—it rivals *War and Peace,* though is nowhere near as readable. In short, there was nothing fixed and sacred about the state constitutions. Nonetheless, these were significant documents—on most issues, they were the highest law of the state.

The first part of the century was a low point, in many ways, for race relations in the United States. It was a period extremely conscious of race—and not only with regard to what we would now consider racial minorities. There was a sense of crisis among old-line Americans—white Protestants living on farms or in small towns. The poem on the Statue of Liberty talked about welcoming the tired, the poor, the huddled masses; but most old-line Americans wanted nothing to do with huddled masses. Immigration control had begun, as we saw, with laws directed against the Chinese. Now agitation for limits on who came in, and how many, resulted in a series of restrictive laws. Paupers, contract laborers, polygamists, people who advocated "the overthrow by force and

---

[23] G. Alan Tarr, *Understanding State Constitutions* (1998), p. 21.

[24] Peter J. Galie, *Ordered Liberty: A Constitutional History of New York* (1996), pp. 228, 306, 357.

violence of the Government," people with any "loathsome . . . disease": all these were excluded. A kind of climax was reached in the immigration law of 1924. This statute limited the sheer numbers of immigrants, and strongly favored people from the British Isles and northern Europe. It did this through a system of quotas. The results were dramatic. About 17,000 Greeks and more than 150,000 Italians had streamed into the country each year; under the 1924 law, Greece was allowed 307 immigrants, Italy a little under 6,000.[25]

In the South, where most African Americans lived, the early part of the century was the high noon of white supremacy. Blacks had no political power. They had no vote. True, the Constitution supposedly guaranteed the right to vote. The Thirteenth Amendment had abolished slavery; and the Fifteenth Amendment provided that the right to vote was not to be abridged on account of race or color. But the Constitution was, insofar as black voting was concerned, nothing but a piece of paper on display in a museum. Southern whites did not want blacks to vote; and they used every trick in the book to keep black people away from to the polls. We have already seen how this was done. Anybody who wanted to vote in Mississippi or South Carolina had to show that they could read and interpret the state constitution. No blacks ever seemed able to pass this test. Some state constitutions embodied the famous "grandfather" clause, as we have seen. In the new state of Oklahoma, for example, prospective voters were supposed to demonstrate their knowledge of the state constitution; but a voter was excused from this awkward test if he was a "lineal descendant" of someone entitled to vote in 1866, or of some foreigner. This covered just about everyone who happened to be white; and just about nobody who was not. The Supreme Court struck down the "grandfather clause" in 1915;[26] but this made little or no difference. There were other ways to stop blacks from voting; and the South used all of them to good effect. In Alabama, in 1906, 85 percent of the adult white males of the state were registered to vote—and 2 percent of the adult black males. By 1910, effectively, blacks had been totally shut out of the voting process.[27] Southern Democrats had "executed a series of offensives" with the aim of "the elimination of black voting and the emasculation of their political opponents." For decades to come, the South was a one-party and a one-race region, politically speaking.[28]

No blacks in the South held office. No office-holder had any need to show sympathy or understanding for the needs and wants of blacks. And since there were no black judges, and no blacks on juries, the whole criminal justice system—the whole weight of state power—could come crashing down on the helpless black population. The criminal justice system was grossly unfair to blacks. When a black man or woman was accused, and the accusers were white, the black had little chance of justice in the white man's court.

Yet, for much of the white population, criminal justice was not unfair *enough*: it was too slow and uncertain. Lynch mobs made sure that the message of white

---

[25] The law was 43 Stat. 153 (act of May 26, 1924); see Elliott Robert Barkan, *And Still They Come: Immigrants and American Society, 1920 to the 1990s* (1996), pp. 11, 14.

[26] *Guinn v. United States*, 238 U.S. 347 (1915).

[27] Leon F. Litwack, *Trouble in Mind: Black Southerners in the Age of Jim Crow* (1998), pp. 225–26.

[28] Michael Perman, *Struggle for Mastery: Disfranchisement in the South, 1888–1908* (2001), p. 328.

supremacy rang through loud and clear. A black who dared to transgress the southern code—or was accused of it—risked swift, brutal death. This savagery had begun its reign of terror in the nineteenth century; and it continued, unabated, in the twentieth. Luther Holbert was seized in Doddsville, Mississippi, in 1904, accused of killing his employer. As a thousand people watched, Holbert and his wife were tied to trees; their fingers were chopped off one at a time; their ears were cut off; they were tortured with corkscrews in their flesh, beaten, and then burned to death. The wife, at least, was completely innocent of this or any crime.[29]

Some Southerners, to be sure, were appalled by lynching; and organizations of blacks protested and lobbied to get federal legislation. Southern members of Congress blocked any movement in this direction. The federal government showed little or no interest in civil rights, and indeed, Woodrow Wilson, a Southerner by birth, was only too eager to promote segregation in Washington, D.C. Almost in desperation, black America turned to the federal courts. The National Association for the Advancement of Colored People (NAACP) was founded in 1909. Almost from the start, the NAACP used litigation as one of its weapons of choice. They had, after all, nowhere else to turn. This strategy soon began to show some results. In 1915, as we noted, the Supreme Court held the "grandfather clause" unconstitutional. In *Buchanan v. Warley*,[30] in 1917, the Supreme Court struck down a Louisville segregation ordinance. Louisville had enacted an ordinance, ostensibly "to prevent conflict and ill-feeling between the white and colored races," by making segregation the norm. If a block had a white majority, no black family could move onto the street; and no white could move into a residential block where most of the families were black. But this case, like the case on the grandfather clause, was a victory mostly at the symbolic level. The cities remained rigidly segregated. There were black neighborhoods and white neighborhoods, and very few areas where the races ever mixed.

The cases did suggest, however, that litigation had at least some potential. The Supreme Court, and perhaps the federal courts generally, showed a willingness at least to listen to the claims of black citizens. This seemed to be true of no other institution, no other branch of government. The constitutional war on racism continued. The results were slow and incremental. In a series of cases after the Second World War, the Supreme Court declared this or that situation or practice (segregated law schools, for example), unconstitutional. Still, the Court shied away from the broader issue: whether segregation, under the fig leaf of "separate but equal" had any warrant in law and morality at all. The NAACP pushed and pulled. The Court was a reluctant bridegroom. The plaintiffs won most of their cases, but on narrow grounds. As early as 1938, the Supreme Court ordered the University of Missouri to admit Lloyd Gaines, an African American, to its law school.[31] Gaines never attended—in fact he disappeared, somewhat mysteriously; and Missouri hastily created a law school for

---

[29] Litwack, *Trouble in Mind,* p. 289.

[30] 245 U.S. 60 (1917).

[31] *Missouri ex rel. Gaines v. Canada,* 305 U.S. 337 (1938).

[32] On this, and the integration of Missouri's law schools in general, see Robert C. Downs et al., "A Partial History of UMKC School of Law: The 'Minority Report,'" 68 UMKC Law Review 508 (2000).

blacks.[32] Would this technique—quickly providing some sort of school for black students—satisfy the Supreme Court? The answer came in *Sweatt v. Painter* (1950).[33] Heman Sweatt, a mail carrier in Houston, Texas, had ambitions of becoming a lawyer. The University of Texas Law School was open only to whites. Texas, to avoid integration, set up a new law school for blacks. But the Supreme Court would have none of this. The University of Texas was a powerful, unique institution, famous, rich in tradition; a feeble new school could not be in any sense its "equal." In Oklahoma, George W. McLaurin, an African American, wanted to earn a doctorate in education at Oklahoma's university, in Norman, Oklahoma. The University said no; but a federal court ordered him admitted. Once in, he was treated as an outcast: he ate at a separate table in the cafeteria, and studied at a segregated desk in the library. The Supreme Court ordered the school to give him the same "treatment . . . as students of other races."[34]

These decisions were unanimous—but nonetheless, quite cautious. Caution was, in a way, understandable. The Court had no power to force states to follow through. Every step of the way was bitterly contested. In general, the house of white supremacy stood strong and fast. The United States fought racist Germany with an army, navy, and air force that was rigidly segregated by race. It fought Japan in the same way; and, after an outburst of hysteria on the West Coast, fueled by greed and paranoia as well, the Japanese of the Western states were shipped to dismal internment camps in the blistering deserts of eastern California. The Supreme Court supinely upheld this action of the government, in *Korematsu v. U.S.*[35] The government defended its actions vigorously: we were at war with Japan, and "properly constituted military authorities" had raised the spectre of a Japanese invasion of the West Coast; the measures were tough but necessary wartime medicine. A majority of the court went along with these arguments More than forty years later, in 1988, Congress officially apologized, and even awarded some compensation to the men and women who survived the camps.

Korematsu was a kind of low point. The times were changing, however. American apartheid was an embarrassment in the postwar period. It handed the Soviet Union, during the cold war, a priceless weapon of propaganda.[36] The colonial empires of Africa were dissolving; and black sovereign nations appeared all over that continent. President Harry S. Truman, after the end of the Second World War, issued an order, as commander-in-chief, desegregating the armed forces. Blacks had migrated in great numbers to the northern states. In the North, they voted, and exerted, directly or indirectly, more influence on national politics than was possible in the South. And the battle in the courts continued. The Supreme Court had come a bit closer to the heart of segregation, in *Shelley v. Kraemer* (1948).[37] The issue was a restrictive covenant—a

[33] 339 U.S. 629 (1950).

[34] *McLaurin v. Oklahoma State Regents for Higher Education*, 336 U.S. 637 (1950).

[35] 323 U.S. 214 (1944). For an exhaustive—and depressing—treatment of this case, see Peter Irons, *Justice at War: The Story of the Japanese-American Internment Cases* (1983).

[36] See Mary L. Dudziak, *Cold War Civil Rights: Race and the Image of American Democracy* (2000).

[37] 334 U.S. 1 (1948). On this case, see Clement E. Vose, *Caucasians Only: The Supreme Court, the NAACP, and the Restrictive Covenant Cases* (1959).

clause in a real estate deed, which made landowners promise never to sell or rent the property to blacks. These covenants were extremely common, especially in suburban developments. And they "ran with the land," that is, they bound all later owners as well as the original buyers. In *Shelley,* the Supreme Court refused to enforce the covenant. Under the Fourteenth Amendment, states could not deny to their citizens the "equal protection of the laws." Courts are a vital part of the state government. Race discrimination was a violation of equal protection; and if a court enforced such a covenant, this was state action, and consequently unlawful. *Shelley v. Kraemer* certainly did not put an end to housing segregation—nothing has—but it did make it easier for blacks to break out of some of the very narrowest of urban ghettos. And a genuine, crucial climax in the long struggle for equality came in 1954, when the Supreme Court handed down its decision in *Brown v. Board of Education.*[38]

This was surely one of the most momentous of all Supreme Court decisions. To find a case comparable in importance, and fame, one has to reach as far back as the *Income Tax* cases, or even *Dred Scott;* or perhaps forward to *Roe v. Wade.* The new Chief Justice, Earl Warren, wrote the Court's opinion in *Brown;* It was short, and unanimous. In *Brown,* the Court faced an issue it had dodged before: even assuming facilities—schools for example—were equal yet continued to be separated, is this situation allowed under the Constitution? No, said the Court, it is not. Segregation is inherently unequal; and inherently unlawful. It is a violation of the federal Constitution. The dual school system had to be ended.

The Court did not order the system to end immediately; it did not tell the schools to open their doors, at once, to all races indiscriminately. The Court left the question of a remedy open. It asked for arguments from all parties, on how to implement its decision. In the second *Brown* decision,[39] the Court dumped the problem into the laps of the local district courts. They were to see to it that schools were desegregated, "with all deliberate speed." In the event, there was very little sign of speed, especially in the deep South. In fact, the white South reacted to *Brown* with fury and dismay. At best, Southern states tried delaying tactics; at worst, they resorted to violence. For at least a decade, almost nothing changed in the deep South; and there are those who think that *Brown,* like so many other of the Court's decisions on race in the twentieth century, ended up accomplishing nothing.[40] Some federal judges—at great personal cost—tried honestly to enforce what was now the official law of the land.[41] Others were themselves segregationists, who did what they could to obfuscate and delay. In any event, every attempt to integrate, even at the university level, touched off riots, mob action, and a blizzard of federal writs and orders. In 1956, Autherine Lucy, a young black woman, tried to enroll in the University of Alabama. A mob "roamed Tuscaloosa for several days, burning crosses, waving

---

[38] 347 U.S. 483 (1954).

[39] 349 U.S. 294 (1955).

[40] This view was advanced, very notably, by Gerald Rosenberg in *The Hollow Hope: Can Courts Bring about Social Change?* (1991).

[41] One clear example was Alabama federal judge Frank M. Johnson Jr., See Tony Freyer and Timothy Dixon, *Democracy and Judicial Independence: A History of the Federal Courts of Alabama, 1820–1994* (1995), pp. 215–55.

Confederate flags, and attacking cars driven by blacks." Lucy was expelled from the university.[42]

Still, most scholars are not ready to write off *Brown* as a failure. *Brown* ended segregation in the border states (the named defendant, one must recall, was the school system of Topeka, Kansas, not Jackson, Mississippi). And the case, and the events and litigation that followed, certainly catalyzed the civil rights movement. Brown did not specifically overrule *Plessy v. Ferguson*. But in fact, "separate but equal" was dead. Even though the *Brown* case talked only about education, the Supreme Court soon made it crystal clear that their principle went far beyond the schools. The Fourteenth Amendment meant there could be no segregation by race at all—anywhere, in any aspect of public life. American apartheid was a violation of fundamental rights. Vilification and "massive resistance" in the South did not move the Court. Chief Justice Warren and his colleagues refused to budge. The segregation case, and the cases that followed, also forced the hand of the federal government. President Dwight D. Eisenhower was no fan of the *Brown* decision. But when states openly defied the federal courts, and federal authority, he was forced to act. Eisenhower sent paratroopers into Little Rock, Arkansas, to enforce a segregation order directed at Central High School.[43]

With enormous effort and cost, and great personal humiliation and pain, in the decade after *Brown,* a handful of black students did manage to force their way into segregated schools and universities—guarded at times by battalions of federal troops. The civil rights movement, and its leaders, including Martin Luther King Jr., struggled to break the stranglehold of white supremacy on the South. It was the age of TV; and the whole country watched as southern sheriffs broke up crowds of peaceful black citizens, hounded and harassed people demanding their rights in a dignified way and sprayed them with hoses; and let loose dogs on small children. A bomb in Birmingham, in 1963, killed four little black girls at Sunday school. This, and other horrors, helped turn public opinion around, in the North. Under President Lyndon Johnson, Congress passed two historic civil rights laws. There was ferocious opposition from Southern die-hards; they hoisted the banner of states' rights, but everybody knew what they really had in mind. The great Civil Rights Law of 1964 banned discrimination in education, housing, public accommodations, and on the job.[44] It was a strong law; and it created a federal agency with power to make rules and regulations, and turn principle into working reality. The Voting Rights Law, in 1965, was if anything even more significant. This was a law that aimed to end the white monopoly on voting and political power. It too was a strong law, with real teeth. It got rid of all those legal tricks of the trade that had kept blacks from voting: poll taxes, literacy tests, and so on. It also contained a unique, and powerful, "trigger": Any county (or state) where less than half the potential voters

[42] Michal R. Belknap, *Federal Law and Southern Order: Racial Violence and Constitutional Conflict in the Post-Brown South* (1987), p. 29.

[43] Belknap, *Federal Law and Southern Order* (1987), pp. 44–52. The Supreme Court weighed in on the Little Rock issue in *Cooper v. Aaron,* 358 U.S. 1 (1958). In *Loving v. Virginia,* 388 U.S. 1 (1967), the Supreme Court struck down one of the last remnants of the old order: the miscegenation laws. The decision was unanimous. Any law that prevented blacks and whites from intermarrying was a violation of the Fourteenth Amendment.

[44] 78 Stat. 241 (act of July 2, 1964).

were registered or voted, had to reform itself; and any changes in voting rules and regulations had to be submitted to federal authorities for clearance.[45]

These laws were more sweeping than any passed since the false dawn of radical reconstruction. And they made a difference. Segregation is almost completely dead in hotels, public facilities, and restaurants. It is almost dead in higher education. It is still alive, but less virulent than before, in housing and employment. Blacks vote freely all over the South, and in substantial numbers. The black vote matters. Blacks serve as mayors and city councilors; they sit in state legislatures; they represent black districts in Congress. There are black judges on state and federal benches. Virginia, the capital of the confederacy, went so far as to elect a black man as governor. Even the most conservative Southern Senators feel the need to have some black people on their staffs. They may still play the race card—and some do—but they have to play it much more cautiously.

The North had its own brand of apartheid, more subtle than the southern form, but also quite real. Here too the last decades of the twentieth century brought about enormous change. The Civil Rights Act opened many doors for blacks. They were able to get jobs and positions that excluded them in the past. Black salespeople appeared in department stores; black secretaries in offices. Black police appeared on the streets. Blacks increased their role in political life. The civil rights movement, and the civil rights laws, led to profound changes in American culture. Overt discrimination went underground. The black middle class suddenly found itself in demand. Blacks now sing with the Metropolitan Opera, play baseball, run school districts, and work at trades that were once in essence lily-white. A few blacks have become big business executives; or partners in law firms. Blacks appear in TV ads, and in the movies; and interracial love and interracial marriage are no longer subjects of taboo on big and little screens. At the national level, presidents began to feel pressure for "diversity" in judgeships and high federal positions. President Lyndon Johnson, in 1967, appointed Thurgood Marshall, veteran of the civil rights movement, to be the first black justice on the U.S. Supreme Court.[46] When Marshall retired, in 1991, President George Bush appointed a conservative black, Clarence Thomas. By the end of the century, black cabinet members were no longer a novelty. President George W. Bush, elected in 2000, appointed the first black Secretary of State, Colin Powell. There were parallel developments at the state level. Black mayors of big cities, by 2000, were no novelty. One or more blacks had been mayors in New York, Chicago, Los Angeles, San Francisco, Detroit, Atlanta, and many other cities. In part, this was because white flight to the suburbs left the cities with black majorities; but in some cities—San Francisco is a prime example—it took generous amounts of white votes to put a black mayor in office.

In many regards, then, there has been enormous progress in race relations. But racism remains a powerful force. It is a source of strong white backlash. The vigor of this backlash should not be underestimated. Also, there are still vast numbers of poor blacks who live in squalid ghettos. For whatever reason, black men and woman sit in prison in numbers far out of proportion to their share of

---

[45] 79 Stat. 437 (act of Aug. 6, 1965).

[46] On Marshall's life and career see Howard Ball, *A Defiant Life: Thurgood Marshall and the Persistence of Racism in America* (1998).

the population. White fear of black violence and the social disorder of black ghettos helped trigger white flight. Black poverty and misery in turn feed black anger and alienation.

Within the legal world, no issue touching race has been so divisive and disputed as the issue of *affirmative action* or *reverse discrimination*. In the famous *Bakke* case in 1978,[47] the University of California at Davis turned down a white student, Alan Bakke, who had applied for admission to the medical school. Bakke went to court, claiming that the school had discriminated against him. Out of one hundred spots in the entering class, the school had set aside sixteen for minority students. Students who got these sixteen spots had, on average, lower grades and scores than the whites—and lower than Bakke. He won his case; but the Court was badly fractured, and it was not at all clear exactly what the case had decided. It was read to mean this: Outright quotas (which Davis had) were unacceptable, but apparently a state university *could* take race somehow into account, in the interests of promoting diversity.[48] In 1980, the Court also upheld a law of Congress that set aside a percentage of government contracts for businesses owned or controlled by minorities.[49] But a more conservative court began to backtrack. *Adarand Constructors, Inc. v. Pena* (1995)[50] was one of a series of cases that gutted the affirmative action doctrine. A federal court in Texas, in 1996, struck down race-conscious admissions to state colleges and graduate schools; the Supreme Court, somewhat surprisingly, refused to review the case.[51] Whenever affirmative action comes to a vote, or a referendum, as it did in California ("Proposition 209") in 1996, it loses, usually badly. Yet in 2003, in a case that came out of the University of Michigan,[52] the U.S. Supreme Court did not take the opportunity (as some people had expected) to kill off affirmative action once and for all. Rather, it stuck, more or less, to its *Bakke* idea: Quotas were bad, wrong, and illegal; but taking race into account—somehow—was all right. Universities and other institutions read this case to mean that affirmative action, provided it was subtle and measured, had the Court's seal of approval. At least for the time being.

Affirmative action has had its ups and downs; but the civil rights revolution is, in essence, irreversible. Whites have, on the whole, accepted large chunks of it, and have abandoned any thought of segregation, except perhaps for a lunatic fringe holed up in compounds in Idaho or elsewhere. But some—many—whites have never come to terms with other aspects of a multicultural society. They vote for the likes of Proposition 209; and through "white flight," they vote with their feet. Race feeling lies at the root of some aspects of the law-and-order

---

[47] *Regents of the University of California v. Bakke*, 438 U.S. 265 (1978).

[48] In fact, there was no "majority" opinion. There were six separate opinions. This was a 5 to 4 decision. Justice Powell provided the crucial fifth vote to let Bakke into the school. But he agreed with the four dissenters that the state could, under some circumstances, and in some ways, take race into account.

[49] 448 U.S. 448 (1980).

[50] 515 U.S. 200 (1995).

[51] *Hopwood v. Texas*, 84 Fed. 3d 96 (C.A. 5, 1996); the Supreme Court denied certiorari, *Texas v. Hopwood*, 518 U.S. 1033 (1996).

[52] In *Grutter v. Bollinger*, 539 U.S. 306 (2003) the Court approved of the law school's program of affirmative action, though in *Gratz v. Bollinger*, 539 U.S. 244 (2003), they disapproved of the undergraduate plan, which was more rigid.

movement; and contributes to the deep unpopularity of welfare programs. The gap between black and white in America has not been eradicated by any means—not economically, not socially, not culturally. Prejudice is more deeply rooted than Brotherhood Week or Black History Month.

FIRST NATIONS

The civil rights movement was about black liberation; but it accomplished, in the end, a great deal more. It helped influence the feminist movement, and the liberation movements of Native Americans, Asians, Hispanics, the so-called sexual minorities, old people, and the handicapped—almost everybody with a grievance against what they considered the majority force in society. Perhaps "influence" is not the right word. Rather, the same social forces that created the civil rights movement and led to *Brown v. Board of Education* were at work on other identity groups.

The legal story of the Native American peoples in the twentieth century is extremely complex. For them, too, the first part of the century was a kind of low point. The native tribes had been defeated militarily, robbed of most of their land, and relegated to "reservations" under the thumb of the Bureau of Indian Affairs. The Dawes Act (1887) set in motion a process of turning native lands into individual allotments. The underlying motive, supposedly, was assimilation—turning "savages" into real honest-to-goodness Americans. The effect, however, was more loss of land. In the early twentieth century, Native Americans were among the poorest of the poor; and the Depression made matters even worse. Navajo income in 1930 was $150 a year, per capita; in 1935, on the Sioux reservations, annual income was a pathetic $67. This was misery with a vengeance.[53]

But during the New Deal, almost for the first time, the Bureau of Indian Affairs put on a different face, under the leadership of John Collier. Collier, Roosevelt's choice for the job, was unusual among bureaucrats of Indian Affairs. He admired Indian culture and felt that it was worth preserving—languages, customs, religions, and all. He rejected the idea of assimilation. He did not favor the idea that the natives were doomed or destined to melt into the great American melting pot. The Indian Reorganization Act (1934)[54] allowed native peoples to draw up constitutions. Many of them did so—constitutions, and also tribal codes of law. This was an important step toward autonomy. In the 1950s, however, there was another turn of the wheel, and Congress took steps to "terminate" many of the tribes—another attempt to turn the native peoples into just plain Americans. All sort of benefits were also "terminated" along with tribal status. The results, for many native peoples, were nothing short of disastrous.

But then came yet another turn of the wheel. Lessons of the civil rights movement were not lost on tribal leaders. In 1968, the American Indian Movement was founded; in 1969, the Movement made headlines by seizing Alcatraz Island, in San Francisco Bay. In the 1970s, Congress put an end to "termination." More and more, under pressure from activists, public policy moved away

[53] John R. Wunder, *Retained by the People: A History of American Indians and the Bill of Rights* (1994), pp. 62–63.
[54] 48 Stat. 984 (act of June 18, 1934).

from assimilation. This was the period of "roots," a period in which minority after minority began to celebrate whatever remained of their uniqueness. Hence, society accepted more and more the right of the native peoples to their own languages, culture, and way of life—even the right to reclaim old bones from museums. The Indian Self-Determination and Education Assistance Act of 1975 declared that federal domination had "served to retard rather than enhance the progress of Indian people."[55] The Indian Child Welfare Act (1978) gave tribes jurisdiction over cases of child custody.[56] On the whole, too, Indian populations were now growing, not shrinking. "Affirmative action" extended to the native peoples as well as to blacks. Some tribes have struck it rich with minerals; some run lucrative casinos, or sell fireworks to the Anglos. There are quite a number of such stories. Yet, on the whole, poverty still stalks many of the reservations—in some cases extreme, grinding poverty, together with all the troubles that poverty brings in its wake, alcoholism, crime, social disorganization.

Moreover, plural equality has arrived too late to save the cultural heritage of many of the native peoples. A good proportion of the native languages are totally extinct. Others survive only in the mouths of a handful of very old people; in twenty years, most of these languages will be totally gone. Navajo and a few others languages seem, for the moment, secure—they are taught in schools, and there are kids who speak them on the playground and in their homes. Assimilation is no longer *official* policy. But it marches on, nevertheless. The villain now is not the Bureau of Indian Affairs; it is, rather, the overwhelming dominance of American television and American mass culture.

ASIAN AMERICANS

Asian American history has many parallels to the history of other minority races. The Chinese were hated and vilified in the nineteenth century, particularly in California. The Chinese exclusion laws made it almost impossible for Chinese to enter the country, and denied them the right to become naturalized citizens.[57] On the West Coast, laws were passed to keep Asians—especially the Japanese—from owning land. And, during the Second World War, as we saw, in a shameful episode, the West Coast Japanese were rounded up and sent to camps in dreary and remote desert areas.[58] But the racist immigration laws died in the 1960s, and with them, the restrictions on Asians. In the 1980s and 1990s, far more Asians than Europeans entered the country as immigrants. The Chinese have been, on the whole, an economic success story. The same is true for the Japanese, the Vietnamese, and people from the Indian subcontinent—motel-owners, engineers, and on the whole upwardly mobile. The Korean grocery store is as familiar as the Chinese laundry once was. America—and especially such states as California—is more and more a rainbow of racial colors.

---

[55] 88 Stat. 2203 (act of Jan. 4, 1975).

[56] 92 Stat. 469 (act of Aug. 11, 1978).

[57] See Lucy E. Salyer, *Laws Harsh as Tigers: Chinese Immigrants and the Shaping of Modern Immigration Law* (1995); Bill Ong Hing, *Making and Remaking Asian America Through Immigration Policy, 1830–1900* (1993).

[58] *Korematsu v. United States*, 323 U.S. 214 (1944); Peter Irons, *Justice at War* (1983).

HISPANICS

After the Mexican War, the United States absorbed a substantial Hispanic population, especially in California and New Mexico. Thousands of Hispanics, mostly Mexicans, also crossed the border, or were imported, to do tough, dirty jobs that most Americans did not want—picking crops, washing dishes, scrubbing floors. The numbers of Spanish speakers swelled even more in the last half of the twentieth century—millions of Porto Ricans (American citizens by birth), who moved to the mainland, Cubans running away from Fidel Castro, Central Americans, and Caribbeans, and, again, a flood of Mexicans, fleeing from poverty and overpopulation in their homeland. Most of the millions of illegal immigrants are Hispanic. Mexicans have met with hostility and race discrimination in many parts of the country. In certain California towns, there was outright apartheid: the city of San Bernardino refused to allow people of "Mexican or Latin descent" to use the city's precious swimming pools and parks. A federal court declared these practices unconstitutional in 1944, ten years before *Brown v. Board of Education*.[59] There were segregated schools as well: in Orange County, in El Modena, poor Mexicans went to one high school, the Anglos went to another. The two schools were basically in the same place, separated by a playing field and an invisible social wall. In the 1940s, federal courts declared this arrangement was a violation of the Constitution.[60]

Overt discrimination lost any claims to legitimacy in these cases; and then came *Brown* and the various civil rights laws. But Hispanic issues did not go away. By 2000, immigration politics was dominated by issues of legal and illegal immigration, mostly Hispanic. Questions of bilingual education and the like were also mainly Hispanic issues. The public dutifully voted against bilingual education in California. Apparently, the language of Cervantes and Garcia Marquez posed some kind of awful threat to the polity or to the survival of the English language. California also voted, in 1986, to make English the official language. What that means is unclear. Instructions for voters in California are sent out in both English and Spanish; in California, drivers can take their written driving tests in Spanish, if they wish, and many do so. By 2000, Hispanics were the largest of America's minorities, and their numbers continued to grow. They were, on the whole, less active politically than blacks, but their voice and vote were bound to be felt in the future.

THE REVOLT OF OTHERNESS

We have mentioned the ripple effect of the civil rights movement—or, as we were careful to add, the effect of the social forces that gave rise to the civil rights movement. At least some members of every group that considered itself an "other" rose up, in their own way, to ask for rights, and for a place at the bargaining table. Some won significant constitutional victories; some won victories in the halls of Congress; some won both. Hardly any got everything they wanted; but all got some. There was a students' rights movement, and a prisoners'

---

[59] *Lopez v. Seccombe*, 71 F. Supp. 769 (D.C.S.D., Cal., 1944).
[60] *Westminster School District of Orange County v. Mendez*, 161 Fed. 2d. 774 (C.A. 9, 1947).

rights movement. Gays and other so-called sexual minorities, against passionate resistance, won substantial victories. Most states wiped the "infamous crime against nature" off their books; and the Supreme Court, in 2003, finished the job. In some places, "domestic partners" had rights to benefits. Some cities and states had laws or ordinances banning discrimination. At the beginning of the twenty-first century, gay marriage became a fact in Massachusetts.

The gray lobby too had considerable success. This was a matter of both ideology and demographics: People were living longer, and voting longer, too. Social norms changed along with demographic facts. People talk about a "youth culture"; but this means not only worshiping youth, it also means the right to *act* young, regardless of age. In any event, people over forty got themselves a law forbidding discrimination in hiring and firing in the 1960s. Somewhat later, Congress banned mandatory retirement.[61] Congress also passed a strong law to protect the handicapped in 1990. The Americans with Disabilities Act prohibits discrimination against people who are blind or deaf or sick or in a wheelchair, in places of public accommodation or, more significantly, in the job market (the act carefully excepted people with "gender identity disorders," compulsive gamblers, pedophiles, pyromaniacs, and kleptomaniacs.[62] These groups, apparently, will have to wait, perhaps forever.)

By far the most important "minority" was in fact a majority: American women. Here too, the results have been both legally and socially revolutionary. The Civil Rights Act of 1964 prohibited discrimination against women, as well as against racial and religious minorities. In 1971, the Supreme Court made one of its periodic discoveries: the Fourteenth Amendment turned out to ban discrimination on the basis of gender. This would probably have been a great surprise to the men who drafted the Amendment; but, whatever the Justices say, their actions show that they believe in an evolutionary Constitution, a living, breathing, changing Constitution. Whether the Court was leading society or following it in this area is a difficult question to answer. The courts, in general, read the Civil Rights law broadly; and the Equal Employment Opportunity Commission did the same. Women won cases that gave them access to jobs that had been reserved for men; and men won access to jobs (as flight attendants, for example) that had been reserved for women. There were to be no more employment ghettos. Women, like blacks, began to appear on the bench, in high positions in industry, in the professorate, and in the president's cabinet. Here too there was a long way to go, at the end of the twentieth century; but gender relations had clearly changed as dramatically as race relations, if not more so.[63]

---

[61] The Age Discrimination in Employment Act was passed in 1967, 81 Stat. 602 (act of Dec. 15, 1967); on the background, see Lawrence M. Friedman, *Your Time Will Come: The Law of Age Discrimination and Mandatory Retirement* (1984); on the subsequent history of this law, see Lawrence M. Friedman, "Age Discrimination Law: Some Remarks on the American Experience," in Sandra Fredman and Sarah Spencer, eds., *Age as an Equality Issue* (2003), p. 175.

[62] 104 Stat. 327 (act of July 26, 1990).

[63] The breakthrough case was *Reed v. Reed*, 404 U.S. 72 (1971). See, in general, Deborah L. Rhode, *Justice and Gender: Sex Discrimination and the Law* (1989).

FREEDOM OF SPEECH

A serious body of law on the subject of free speech hardly existed, at the level of the U.S. Supreme Court, until around the time of the First World War. The war set a whole caldron of chauvinism boiling. Congress passed wildly expansive laws about espionage and sedition. A great witch hunt began, against disloyalists, Bolsheviks, and the like, which lasted into the 1920s.[64] The courts were not as heroic in defense of free speech as modern civil libertarians would have liked them to be. In *Schenck v. United States* (1919),[65] a unanimous court upheld the Espionage act, and the conviction of Charles Schenck, a Socialist, who had distributed leaflets denouncing the draft and the war in Europe. Oliver Wendell Holmes Jr., writing for the Court, argued that Congress could suppress words "used in such circumstances and . . . of such a nature as to create a clear and present danger that they will bring about the substantive evils that Congress has a right to prevent." Fine words, and later famous words. They were little comfort to Schenck. In *Abrams v. United States* (1919),[66] decided shortly afterward, Jewish radicals had written pamphlets, in Yiddish and English, condemning President Wilson for sending soldiers to fight in Soviet Russia. The United States was not at war with Soviet Russia; and yet these pamphlets struck the Court as a clear and present danger (they were written and distributed while the war with Germany was still going on). This time Holmes dissented.

In general, the courts were not much help during the waves of repression and deportation that came right after the First World War—the famous "Red scare." As we saw, the Supreme Court, during the Second World War, allowed the internment of Japanese Americans. After the Second World War came the Cold War. State and federal committees hunted everywhere for "un-American" activities. During the feverish, paranoid days of McCarthyism, in the 1950s, the Supreme Court was, at first, exceedingly timid; the Court, for example, upheld the Smith Act, in *Dennis v. United States* (1951).[67] Under the Smith Act, it was a crime to "knowingly or willfully advocate, abet, advice, or teach the . . . desirability . . . of overthrowing . . . government in the United States by force or violence." In *Dennis*, eleven leaders of the American Communist Party were indicted, and convicted, of this crime. The Communist Party was a danger to the nation, in the view of the Court. The Supreme Court also upheld loyalty oaths and, in general, bent with the winds. The campaign against "reds," "dupes," and "fellow-travelers," was more virulent in the United States than, for example, in Great Britain. In part, it was a reaction against the New Deal, and against liberals in general; anti-Communism was a convenient weapon against socialized medicine, civil rights, and whatever else offended the right wing of the political spectrum. To be sure, the Soviet Union *was* dangerous; and there *were* Soviet spies in the country; perhaps some had infiltrated the government itself. The most dramatic of the spy trials ended with a death sentence, in 1951, for Julius and Ethel Rosenberg. They were executed in 1953.

---

[64] See Harry N. Scheiber, *The Wilson Administration and Civil Liberties, 1917–1921* (1960); Richard Polenberg, *Fighting Faiths: The Abrams Case, the Supreme Court, and Free Speech* (1987).

[65] 249 U.S. 47 (1919).

[66] 250 U.S. 616 (1919).

[67] 341 U.S. 494 (1951).

Another sensation was the trial of Alger Hiss, who had been a high official of the state department. Hiss was ultimately convicted of perjury, in 1950, and went to prison.[68] In later years, as the McCarthy era subsided, the Supreme Court's played a somewhat more ambivalent role. It accepted some Cold War outrages, but others it turned aside. In 1957, for example, the Supreme Court overturned the conviction of another group of Communists, who were charged with conspiracy to evade the Smith Act.[69]

In general, the *concept* of free speech was expanding; and the Court ultimately accepted and reflected changes in the social meaning of free speech. The war in Vietnam raged on without benefit of new sedition and espionage acts. The Court also, in its own fumbling way, wrestled with the issue of obscenity and pornography—a free speech issue that the court had never confronted before the second half of the century. Nor did it ever really work out a coherent constitutional theory. The Court never held, flatly, that states had no power to ban pornography or censor obscenity. Here too what happened in society at large really rewrote the law. The sexual revolution (so-called) was sweeping over most of the country. The courts came to accept books, movies, and plays that would have horrified and scandalized the Victorians, or even Americans of the early twentieth century. In theory, local communities can regulate or even ban hard-core pornography; but at least in most big cities, anything goes.

RELIGION AND THE LAW

The Supreme Court has also wrestled with another almost intractable problem: church and state. Church and state are constitutionally separate in the United States: but what exactly does this mean? In the nineteenth and early twentieth centuries, public education had a distinctively sectarian, Protestant cast; Bible-reading and prayers were common in many schools in many states. In the 1960s, the Supreme Court exercised one of its most dramatic vetoes. The Court held that prayer in public school was a violation of the Establishment Clause of the First Amendment. Bible-reading suffered the same fate.[70] These decisions were wildly unpopular, and continue to be; but the Supreme Court has stuck to its guns. On other issues—aid to parochial schools, vouchers, creches on city hall lawns—the decisions have been more mixed, and the problems of state involvement with religion remain alive and deeply controversial. This is perhaps inevitable. Of all the developed countries, the United States is the most fervently

---

[68] See Sam Tanenhaus, *Whittaker Chambers: A Biography* (1997); Chambers was the former Soviet agent who accused Hiss.

[69] *Yates v. United States,* 354 U.S. 298 (1957); Arthur L. Sabin, *In Calmer Times: The Supreme Court and Red Monday* (1999).

[70] The cases were *Engel v. Vitale,* 370 U.S. 421 (1962), and *Abington School District v. Schempp,* 374 U.S. 203 (1963); religion had long been an issue—for example, in the famous Scopes trial, in the 1920s, where the issue was whether the state could prohibit the teaching of evolution in the schools. See Edward J. Larson, *Summer for the Gods: The Scopes Trial and America's Continuing Debate over Science and Religion* (1997); Lawrence M. Friedman, *American Law in the Twentieth Century* (2002), pp. 506–16.

and deeply religious. Yet, of all the developed countries, it is the most reli-
giously diverse. No single religion commands more than a quarter of the population. There is every conceivable denomination of Christian, plus millions of
Jews, Muslims, Hindus, and Buddhists, to mention only a few of the minority religions. There are Mormons and Christian Scientists and Jehovah's Witnesses
and dozens of small splinter religions. Under these circumstances, it is not easy
to disentangle government from religion—while at the same time recognizing
the massive role of religious feeling and religious faith in the United States.

CHAPTER 3

INTERNAL LEGAL CULTURE IN THE TWENTIETH CENTURY: LAWYERS, JUDGES, AND LAW BOOKS

If the theme of the twentieth century was growth, nowhere was this more evident than in the legal profession itself. At the beginning of the century, there were some one hundred thousand lawyers in the country. At the end of the century, there were about a million—the population had more or less doubled, but the number of lawyers had increased by a factor of ten. This growth process had accelerated in the last part of the century; in the early 1980s, there were about six hundred thousand lawyers—four hundred thousand more joined them in the next generation.

The profession was transformed in other ways as well. At the beginning of the century, the bar was basically a white male preserve. There were women lawyers and minority lawyers; but freakishly few. In Philadelphia, for example, as we noted, exactly three out of some 1,900 lawyers in 1905 were women.[1] In fact, women continued to be rare beasts in the bar until the 1960s. Then the tide turned, and dramatically. By the end of the century, about a quarter of the bar was made up of women, most of them rather young; and there were so many women in the pipeline—half or more of the law students in many schools—that the percentage of women lawyers was bound to rise, perhaps to majority status, in the twenty-first century. The number of black lawyers was extremely small in the first half of the century; and black women were even rarer—they were "doubly marginalized."[2] But black lawyers were in the forefront of the battle for civil rights, and the cadre of minority lawyers (men and women) grew in the last third of the century. In that period, black, Hispanic, and Asian faces began to appear in the offices of law firms, on the bench, and on the law faculties of schools all over the country as well.

What does this army of a million lawyers do? Not all of them practice law. Some, as has always been the case, drift away from the practice—they go into business, or politics, or quit doing anything even remotely resembling law

---

[1] Robert B. Bell, *The Philadelphia Lawyer: A History, 1735–1945* (1992), p. 206.

[2] The phrase is from Kenneth W. Mack, "A Social History of Everyday Practice: Sadie T. M. Alexander and the Incorporation of Black Women into the American Legal Profession, 1925–1960," 87 Cornell L. Rev. 1405, 1409 (2002). This is a study of the career of Ms Alexander, who, in 1939, was the "first and only black woman lawyer" in Pennsylvania.

practice. The majority, however, do make use of their training. More and more, they practice with other lawyers: in a firm, or partnership (or professional corporation). The firms have been steadily growing in size.[3] In 1900, a firm with twenty lawyers was a giant. In 1935, the largest Chicago firm, Winston, Strawn & Shaw, had forty-three lawyers. In 1950, the largest Chicago firm, Kirkland, Fleming, Green, Martin, & Ellis, had fifty-four lawyers. At that date, a firm of one hundred lawyers would have been a super-giant, and such hulking creatures were found only in New York City. But by the 1980s, the situation was dramatically different. Baker and McKenzie had 697 lawyers in 1984.[4] The best (or worst) was yet to come. The giant firms grew like weeds. In 2001, it was reported that Baker & McKenzie had grown to a truly mammoth size: 3,117 lawyers. No other firm had reached the 2000 mark; but the number two firm, Skadden Arps, had well over 1,000. Nor was this only a phenomenon of Wall Street. There were large firms in every major city, and even minor ones. The largest firm in Richmond, Virginia, at the beginning of the twenty-first century had 584 lawyers, the largest firm in Kansas City, Missouri, had 568. The 250th largest firm in the country had no less than 158 lawyers.[5]

In the old days, a New York firm was a New York firm, a Houston firm was a Houston firm, and that was that. Slowly, a few firms began to branch out. At the end of the twentieth century, the biggest law firms all had branch offices. Sometimes, a firm acquired a branch by swallowing up a local firm; sometimes a firm colonized distant cities. It is unlikely that law firms will match the record of Motel 6, or Kentucky Fried Chicken, let alone McDonald's; but the big firms by 2000 had a toehold in all sorts of domestic and foreign sites, either far away, or as close as the flashier suburbs. Coudert Brothers, the firm founded in the nineteenth century by three brothers, had 650 lawyers, in thirty offices and in eighteen countries. Hunton and Williams, a big firm in Atlanta (over 700 lawyers), had offices in Miami, Washington, D.C., New York, Raleigh and Charlotte, North Carolina, Norfolk and Richmond, Virginia. It also had branches in Brussels, Hong Kong, Bangkok, Warsaw, and London. Skadden, Arps, aside from its many American branches, had offices in Paris, Brussels, Hong Kong, Beijing, Frankfurt, Toronto, Moscow, and Sydney, Australia.[6] Coudert Brothers had an office in Almaty, one of eight Asian branches (the others were in less offbeat places—Singapore, for example).

Not all lawyers by any means worked for firms. There were also solo practitioners; "in-house" counsel, and government lawyers. In 1952, about 10 percent of the lawyers worked for government, about 9 percent for private companies. The percentages did not go up appreciably; but by the end of the century, the

[3] On the large law firms, see Robert L. Nelson, *Partners with Power: The Social Transformation of the Large Law Firm* (1988); Marc Galanter and Thomas Palay, *Tournament of Lawyers: The Transformation of the Big Law Firm* (1991).

[4] This figure, and those on Chicago firms, are from Nelson, *Partners with Power,* p. 41.

[5] Source: National Law Journal, Annual Survey of the Nation's Largest Law Firms, Nov. 19–26, 2001.

[6] Source, National Law Journal, *supra.*

absolute numbers were impressive: 80,000 house counsel in 1995, 65,000 government lawyers.[7]

By the end of the century, too, lawyers seemed to be everywhere in government and in society. They busied themselves with every conceivable kind of work: merging giant corporations, suing the government, handling cases of child custody, drawing up wills, or handling a real estate deal. They gave advice to people who wanted to open a pizza parlor, or set up a private foundation. A few were even traditional courtroom warriors. The most elaborate study of what lawyers actually do, the study of Chicago lawyers in the 1970s, by John Heinz and Edward Laumann, classified lawyers into two big groups (the authors called these "hemispheres"). The larger "hemisphere" was made up of business lawyers. This was the "corporate client sector." The second, somewhat smaller "hemisphere" did half of its work on business law, but for little businesses, not big ones; and this "hemisphere" devoted about a fifth of its total legal effort to nonbusiness matters—divorces, personal injury work, and criminal defense.[8] Relatively few lawyers ever crossed over from one "hemisphere" to the other, or worked in both at the same time.

LEGAL ETHICS

In 1908, the American Bar Association adopted a canon of professional ethics. Most states accepted it, or a similar code, as the official rules on the conduct of lawyers. State bar associations, or state judges, had nominal or real power to enforce these canons, and discipline black sheep in the profession. Many of the canons were rules of plain common sense, or ordinary morality. No lawyer was supposed to steal his client's money. But other rules reflected the norms and ambitions of the elite members of the bar. No lawyer, for example, was allowed to use "circulars or advertisements" (Canon 27). Wall Street lawyers never advertised; big firms had no need to. They had old, stable clients on retainer; and they got new business through informal networks. On the other hand, store-front lawyers, who represented people run over by streetcars, or who wanted a divorce, needed a constant stream of new business; they had "one-shot" clients, and no retainers. Other canons of "ethics" were simply anticompetitive. The rules basically outlawed price-cutting. Bar associations set minimum fees, and they fought against "unauthorized practice," that is, they defended their turf against other professionals. They wanted to keep others off their turf. They wanted a monopoly over all activities that could reasonably be defined as the practice of law.

The bar never gave up the fight against "unauthorized practice"; but in some regards the canons of ethics have been democratized. The Supreme Court gave the trend a big push when it struck down the ban on advertising in 1977. The case involved two Arizona lawyers who put an ad in the newspapers,

[7] Survey of the Legal Profession, *The Second Statistical Report on the Lawyers of the United States* (1952), p. 2; Clara N. Carson, *The Lawyer Statistical Report: The U.S. Legal Profession in 1995* (1999), p. 10.

[8] John P. Heinz and Edward O. Laumann, *Chicago Lawyers: The Social Structure of the Bar* (1982).

offering "legal services at very reasonable fees."[9] The Supreme Court saw this as an issue of free speech; the public had a right to hear what lawyers who advertise wanted to say. At the top levels of the profession, this decision made very little difference. Wall Street lawyers still do not advertise; why should they? But it is now common to see lawyers on television, selling themselves like pizza parlors and used-car dealers, scrambling for low-income clients facing drunk driving charges, or people with whiplash injuries, or aliens in trouble with immigration authorities. The lawyers of the old days, the old Wall Street bar, would turn over in their graves.

THE ORGANIZED BAR

The bar associations began as organizations of elite and high-toned lawyers, as we have seen—they were a reaction to the muck and the scandal of city politics. The bar associations were exclusive in more ways than that. The American Bar Association (ABA), for example, was for white lawyers only. In 1912, the ABA admitted three black lawyers—by mistake. The executive committee, when it discovered this dreadful error, tried to rescind their admission. The three lawyers remained members, in the end; but future applicants were screened by race.[10] In response, black lawyers felt compelled to found their own organization, the National Bar Association, in 1925. No women were admitted to the ABA until 1918. Only gradually did the ABA mend its ways, and become more inclusive. By the end of the twentieth century, the situation had changed radically. The ABA was open to any lawyer of any race or sex. Roberta Cooper Ramo became the first woman president of the ABA in 1995–1996.

From about the middle of the century, many state bar associations became "integrated." This had nothing to do with race; it simply meant that all lawyers in the state had to belong to a single (state) bar association, which collected dues, and claimed the power, at least in theory, to police the bar and discipline members who strayed from the straight and narrow path. By 1960, more than half of the states had integrated their bars. Illinois integrated its bar in the 1970s. Still, compared to the hold of the American Medical Association over doctors (largely through control of hospitals), the legal profession has been fairly loose and free-wheeling. Despite furious membership campaigns, at the end of the twentieth century only a little more than a third of the country's lawyers even bothered to join their national association. And although the bar tried to speak with one voice, it never quite persuaded the outside world to listen.

This was not necessarily a bad thing. The behavior of the organized bar, compared to its ballyhoo, has been weak and retrograde. It does not take much courage to thunder invective against shysters and ambulance chasers. But when justice or civil liberties were in genuine crisis, the organized bar was not always on the side of the angels. During the McCarthy period, the ABA was eager for loyalty oaths and purges; the House of Delegates recommended disciplinary

---

[9] *Bates v. State Bar of Arizona*, 433 U.S. 350 (1977).

[10] Jerold S. Auerbach, *Unequal Justice: Lawyers and Social Change in Modern America* (1976), p. 66.

action, and even expulsion, for lawyers who were Communists, or who advocated Marxism-Leninism.[11] But as the bar expanded and took in a more diverse mix of lawyers, its began to change its general orientation. Indeed, toward the end of the twentieth century, the ABA came out in favor of a moratorium on the death penalty, which no doubt startled many people on the right. The bar has also, since the 1950s, played a role in vetting lawyers nominated to the federal courts. Judges are still appointed for political reasons. But the ABA does screen nominees for minimal competence. It has helped keep some egregiously unqualified lawyers off the bench.

LEGAL EDUCATION

In 1900, the apprenticeship system was in retreat; by 2000, it was virtually dead. Practically speaking, the law schools now have a virtual monopoly on access to the bar. The sheer number of schools—and students—has grown tremendously, which is not surprising, since the number of lawyers (and of people who wanted to be lawyers) was also growing rapidly. There were about one hundred law schools in 1910 (some of them night schools). In 1980, there were more like two hundred. Most states had one or more law schools; and the states that had done without lawyers now mended their ways. Hawaii and Vermont joined the list of states with law schools. Nevada joined them at the very end of the century. In 2000, Alaska was the only state without a law school inside its borders. Most big states had not one but many law schools. California, the biggest state, had the most law schools—more than 35—including a flock of unaccredited ones.

The Langdell method had, as we saw, struggled to stay alive even in its mother church in Cambridge during its early years. By 1900, it was clearly on the move and conquering new territory.[12] The armies of Langdell eventually swept the field, spreading the gospel of casebooks and Socratic dialogue throughout the country. Yale was a convert in 1903. Other holdouts gave up and fell into line somewhat later. Schools that switched to the Harvard method also tended to hire Harvard men as their teachers: Harvard, in the first part of the century, supplied almost a quarter of all the country's law school teachers. All over the country, in 1930 or 1950, small, poorly financed schools, some with night divisions as well as day-time students, pathetically tried to imitate Harvard, buying its methods and its casebooks, rather than searching for their own mission and soul, or asking how they could better serve their own community. A good law school was (and is) supposed to be "national," that is, to ignore whatever state it happens to be located in, pretending instead to teach more general truths and more national skills.

Meanwhile, it became harder to get into law school. At the beginning of the century, Harvard already required a bachelor's degree for admittance. Other schools gradually fell into line—Stanford, for example, in 1924; George Washington in 1935. In the 1960s, the ABA and the AALS required four years

[11] Jerold S. Auerbach, *Unequal Justice* (1976), p. 238.
[12] On the rise and spread of the Langdell system, see William P. LaPiana, *Logic and Experience: The Origin of Modern American Legal Education* (1994).

of college for everybody. The requirement, in short, became universal. After the Second World War, the GI Bill of Rights allowed thousands of bright young veterans to go to any school that accepted them. The government would pay for it all—tuition, books, and living expenses. Elite schools were no longer only for elite people. Any veteran with brains could go to Harvard or Yale. Veterans made up over 90 percent of the Harvard class of 1947.

Applications now flooded the schools. Social background and money no longer did an adequate job of filtering students. What replaced these, in part, was the Law School Admission Test (LSAT). The LSAT and other requirements were meant to eliminate unqualified students. The LSAT was launched in 1948; 3,500 applicants, in sixty-three cities, took the test. In 1952, forty-five law schools required it; the rest eventually followed suit. The University of Georgia adopted the test in 1962.[13] The LSAT led to a drastic reduction in flunk-out rates. Schools as late as the 1950s admitted great numbers of students, and flushed out as many as a third of them after their first-year exams. According to a famous story, Professor Edward Warren of Harvard (the notorious "Bull" Warren) used to tell the entering students, "Look to the right of you. Look to the left of you. One of the three of you will be gone within a year."[14] Similar grim warnings—and predictions—were made at other schools as well. In the LSAT era, schools became very selective; it was much harder to get in to the top schools. But there was an end to the slaughter of the innocents. In 2000, and for many years before, it was almost impossible—short of outright cheating or plagiarism or, more commonly, a nervous breakdown—to flunk out of Harvard, or most other law schools for that matter.

LEGAL LITERATURE

During most of the twentieth century, Langdell and his way of thinking had the upper hand in literature as well as in legal education. This was the age of huge, elephantine treatises. Samuel Williston built a monumental structure (1920–1922) out of the law of contracts, volume after volume, closely knit, richly footnoted, and fully armored against the intrusion of any ethical, economic, or social ideas whatsoever.[15] On the model of Williston was the ponderous treatise of Austin Wakeman Scott (on trusts); and indeed, each branch or field of law had at least one example of an arid and exhaustive treatise. Arthur Corbin, at Yale, published his own treatise on contracts. It reflected the influence of the legal realist movement (about which more later). Corbin served as a kind of counterpoise to the old man of Harvard. Wigmore's monumental treatise on the law of evidence also deviated considerably from the Williston model.

Changing times—and the legal realist movement—had a certain impact on the law school curriculum. There was some attempt to change content in older

---

[13] Gwen Y. Wood, *A Unique and Fortuitous Combination: an Administrative History of the University of Georgia School of Law* (1998), p. 86.

[14] Arthur E. Sutherland, *The Law at Harvard: A History of Men and Ideas, 1816–1967* (1967), p. 322.

[15] Williston was born in 1861, and died in 1963 at the age of 101.

courses; and new courses, like administrative law and taxation, made their way into the ranks. Thus, a professor of 1900, come back to life, would have found the law school curriculum familiar in some ways, strange in other ways. The classroom culture, too, was the same only different. The classic "Paper Chase" professors, hectoring and badgering their students, terrorizing the classroom, had gone to their eternal rewards; many professors in the late twentieth century still used the Socratic method, but in a modified way—much milder and more humane. After the 1960s, it was unfashionable to mock and humiliate students. But many aspects of the core curriculum would be quite familiar to our professor of 1900. The list of first-year courses, in 2000, would not have been *that* surprising to Langdell. The center seemed to hold, for better or for worse. Many upper level courses, on the other hand, would have struck Langdell, or for that matter, Samuel Williston, as rather odd. Many schools have added "enrichment" courses; some have tinkered with clinical courses and clinical training; a few have gone further and made clinical training a key aspect of legal education. While most students stick to "the basics" (corporations, taxation, and similar courses), those who want to stray off the beaten track can now do so, at least to some extent. The catalog of Cornell's law school, for 1995–1996, for example, offered courses in Comparative and Transnational Litigation, Economics for the Lawyer, Feminist Jurisprudence, Law and Medicine, and Organized-Crime Control, plus a flock of seminars, clinical courses, and externships.

In part, this reflects the recurrent attempts to bring law closer to the university, that is, to the larger world of theory and scholarship. There were experiments in integrating law and social science in the 1920s and 1930s, at Columbia and Yale.[16] The Johns Hopkins Institute of Law, in Baltimore, was established as a research institution, devoted to the empirical study of legal institutions. After publishing a few studies, the Institute died of financial starvation during the Depression. After the Second World War, more serious efforts were made to integrate law and the social sciences. Government and foundation money began to trickle into the law schools. One notable result was *The American Jury* (1964), by Harry Kalven Jr., and Hans Zeisel, of the University of Chicago Law School, a monumental study of a major institution. Kalven and Zeisel showed that collaboration between legal scholars and social science colleagues was a real possibility.[17] But mostly, law and social science remained only a promise. In most schools, it was not even a promise. Only a few schools— notably Wisconsin, Denver, and Berkeley—did anything more than pay lip service to the interdisciplinary ideal.[18] In the 1960s, law study did broaden to include more social issues—courses on welfare law, for example, a reflection of President Lyndon Johnson's "war on poverty"; a few schools initiated a richer, more varied dose of foreign law. The social sciences, basically, made hardly a

[16] See John Henry Schlegel, *American Legal Realism and Empirical Social Science* (1995); Laura Kalman, *Legal Realism at Yale, 1927–1960* (1986).

[17] In 1941, in the preface, Kalven and Zeisel stated that the study meant to "bring together into a working partnership the lawyer and the social scientist. . . . To marry the research skills and fresh perspectives of the one to the socially significant problems of the other." Harry Kalven Jr., and Hans Zeisel, *The American Jury* (1966), p. v.

[18] However, the social study of law *outside* the law schools continued, and grew, throughout the last decades of the twentieth century.

dent. The one exception was economics. Here the University of Chicago was a leader; and Richard Posner, later a federal judge, was a key contributor to the field. His *Economic Analysis of Law* went through many editions, and made a major splash in the world of legal education. Many law professors, especially those who were politically liberal, resisted and resented the "law and economics" school, which they considered right-wing, and excessively narrow. They also accused it, with some justice, of disguising ideology in the Halloween costume of hard science. Still, by the 1980s, the law and economics movement had won a significant place in legal teaching, thought, and research, and not only in the more obvious fields (antitrust law), but in other courses as well—torts, property, contract. It retained its strong position for the rest of the century.

Of the making of books, quality aside, there was truly no end. The few university law reviews of the nineteenth century multiplied like rabbits over the years. By 1950, there were about seventy; and by the late 1990s, more than four hundred. Virtually every law school, no matter how small or marginal, published a law review, as a matter of local pride. The classier schools had more than one—perhaps as many as ten. One of these was the flagship journal—the *Yale Law Journal;* the *Harvard Law Review;* the *University of Chicago Law Review.* This was the most general (and the most prestigious). The others were more specialized. One of these others was, almost certainly, some sort of journal with an international or global bent. The law journals had also become extremely fat; and fatter and fatter over the years. Volume 15 of the *Yale Law Journal,* for 1905–1906, ran to 446 pages; by Volume 40 (1930–1931), the journal had swollen to 1,346 pages, and Volume 109 (1999–2000) had no less than 2,024 pages. Many schools could beat this dubious record. Volume 74 of the *Tulane Law Review* (1999–2000) was 2,268 pages long (Volume 15, for 1940–1941 had been a mere 652).

By law school tradition, it is the students, not the professors, who run these journals. They choose the articles, they edit them, they mangle the prose (when it has not arrived pre-mangled), they check the footnotes and make sure every jot and tittle is correct. Traditionally, too, these law review students formed the student elite of their schools. They were the ones with the best grades, the best (or only) rapport with the faculty; and when they graduated, they were rewarded with the best clerkships and the best jobs with the best of the law firms. Some schools, in a burst of democracy in the 1960s, opened law-review competition to all students who wished to try out, regardless of grades. The law reviews also began to worry about "diversity." Many of them actively tried to recruit more women and minorities. By the end of the century, the law reviews had lost a little of their glamour—they were less of a club of the chosen, the crème de la crème; and they no longer had a total monopoly on top jobs and top clerkships.

They remained powerful in the world of scholarly publishing, but here too they did not keep their total stranglehold. In the early 1930s, in a pioneering and daring move, Duke University began to publish a journal called *Law and Contemporary Problems.* Each issue was a symposium on some topical subject; the journal did not set aside any section for student work. Later, more specialized scholarly journals—*Law and History Review,* for example—began to appear; and journals devoted to law and economics. The first issue of *The Law and Society Review* appeared in 1966—an outlet for the social scientific study of law. The American Bar Foundation published a research journal, later renamed *Law and*

Social Inquiry. Many of these are peer-review journals; the students do not have the dominant role in these journal, rather the professors do.

Conceptualism long retained its baleful and persistent influence; and this influence has never died out. Nonetheless, the twentieth century managed to produce a rich legal literature. One of the most notable scholars was Roscoe Pound (1870–1964), a Nebraska native, who began his scholarly career studying fungus, and then switched to law. Pound became dean of the Harvard Law School, and poured a lot of his energy into legal philosophy. He founded a school of "sociological jurisprudence," although there was precious little about it that was truly sociological. Karl Llewellyn (1893–1962), was a key figure in the realist movement of the 1920s and 1930s. He was clever and iconoclastic, despite a dense and Teutonic writing style. Others in that movement included Jerome Frank and Thurman Arnold. Realism was, in fact, less a philosophy than an attitude. It rejected the mind-set of judges and scholars of the late nineteenth century, who had emphasized legal logic and the purity of concepts. It rejected, in other words, the philosophy of Langdell. The realists had no great reverence for legal tradition as such. They were skeptical about rules—skeptical whether they worked in practice. They doubted that judges could or should decide cases according to the dictates of legal logic. They had little or no tolerance of artifice, fictions, real and apparent irrationalities. Law was a working tool, an instrument of social policy; and it had to be *seen* in that light. Jerome Frank's book, *Law and the Modern Mind* (1930) was one of the key documents of the realist movement. Frank denounced legal formalism, the "illusion" of "certainty" in the law. Rules were only the "formal clothes" in which judges dressed up their actual thoughts. The search for certainty (Frank said) was nothing more than the vain search for a father-figure, something to believe in implicitly. Another leading realist was Thurman Arnold. His books, *The Symbols of Government* (1935) and *The Folklore of Capitalism* (1937), written in a witty and sarcastic style, hammered away at the "myths" and "folklore" of legal thought.

These attitudes were not entirely new; and they never captured the minds of all judges and lawyers. But they did affect an important elite. Realism made a difference in the way a small but important group of judges wrote, and perhaps (though here we are on thinner ice) in the way they thought and the way they decided their cases. And a notion of law as instrumental, as a tool of policy, rather than the dry bones of classical legal thought, the ideas of men like Langdell, was a natural fit for the lawyers who flocked to Washington in the early 1930s, who inhabited Franklin Roosevelt's New Deal, and who were eager to reform the world (or at least the country) through law. These were the lawyers who drafted New Deal legislation, who devised the bold new programs that came out of Roosevelt's administration, and who then argued and fought for these programs during the long battles in New Deal courts.[19]

Llewellyn was also a leading figure behind the drafting of the Uniform Commercial Code, of which more later. He coauthored a book on the

---

[19] Peter H. Irons, *The New Deal Lawyers* (1982); Ronen Shamir, *Managing Legal Uncertainty: Elite Lawyers in the New Deal* (1995). On the legal realists and their movement, see the sources cited in n. 16, *supra;* see also Robert W. Gordon, "Professors and Policymakers: Yale Law School Faculty in the New Deal and After," in Anthony Kronman, ed., *History of the Yale Law School: The Tercentennial Essays* (2004), p. 75.

Cheyenne Indians with the anthropologist, E. Adamson Hoebel (*The Cheyenne Way*, 1941). Between the two world wars, Charles Warren wrote a number of seminal studies of the American legal past. Legal history emerged once more from the shadows after the Second World War. The outstanding practitioner was J. Willard Hurst, who spent almost his entire career at the University of Wisconsin. Hurst and his followers—the so-called Wisconsin school—moved sharply away from case-centered, formalistic, doctrinal history. Hurst placed his attention squarely on the relationship between law and society—in particular, between law and the economy.[20] In the 1970s, a group of younger historians, somewhat more radical, began questioning some aspects of the work of Hurst and his school; but this too was, in a way, a mark of its permanent influence.[21] The law and society movement gathered scholars from various disciplines—psychology, sociology, political science—who were looking at law with a fresh and sometimes illuminating eye, and (importantly) an empirical eye. Many of these scholars—a majority, in fact—were not lawyers or members of law faculties at all.

In the late 1960s, volcanic rumblings began to disturb the peace of the law schools. Students led the way: they marched under banners of civil rights and civil liberties; then they flew the flag of the war against poverty; then they embraced a more general radicalism, a more general revulsion against the established order. The richest and most famous schools were the most affected; and within the schools, on the whole, it was the most intellectually active students who made the most stir and the most noise. When the Office of Economic Opportunity put money into neighborhood law offices, young lawyers eagerly turned out to work in the ghettos. Wall Street had to raise its prices, to keep its pool of talent from drying up. Things (it appeared) would never be the same. Classical legal education looked like Humpty Dumpty, teetering on the wall. Would it bounce, or would it break?

In the event, it bounced. But this was not obvious at the time. Law seemed caught up in crisis. To some, on the right, the welfare state seemed to be dangerously overextended; most government programs seemed foolish, counter-productive, and in violation of basic economic laws. The left condemned the system as rotten, racist, and unjust. The war in Vietnam was another massive irritant. And many people, left, right, and center, complained about a litigation explosion (largely mythical, perhaps).[22] Society seemed to be choking to death on its own secretions.

Yet, when the war in Vietnam ended, the student movement seemed to deflate, like a balloon when the air is let out. In the 1980s, the country seemed remarkably quiescent; there was a hunger for old-fashioned verities; the most conservative president in decades (Ronald Reagan) smiled soothingly from the

---

[20] Among Hurst's many important works were *The Growth of American Law: the Law Makers* (1950); *Law and the Conditions of Freedom in the Nineteenth Century United States* (1956); and *Law and Economic Growth: The Legal History of the Lumber History of the Lumber History in Wisconsin, 1836–1915* (1964).

[21] See the discussion of various schools of thought in the world of legal history, in Robert W. Gordon, "Critical Legal Histories," 36 Stanford Law Review 57 (1984).

[22] For a discussion, see Marc Galanter, "Reading the Landscape of Disputes: What We Know and Don't Know (and Think We Know) about our Allegedly Contentious and Litigious Society," 31 UCLA Law Review 4 (1983); Lawrence M. Friedman, "Are We a Litigious People?" in Lawrence M. Friedman and Harry N. Scheiber, eds., *Legal Culture and the Legal Profession* (1996), p. 53.

White House and on TV screens. In many law schools, professors began to complain that their students were boring, complacent, and vocational. New radical movements sprang up among the professorate—Critical Legal Studies, and its black and Latino branches—but the student body (and the bar) hardly blinked. The professors, left, right, and center, continued churning out pages, and filling the law reviews. The students, on the whole, seemed mostly absorbed in finding and keeping a job.

THE TWENTIETH CENTURY BENCH

At the beginning of the century, the reputation of the U.S. Supreme Court was low among labor leaders and, generally, those who identified themselves as progressives. A few of the Supreme Court's decisions seemed incredibly retrograde, cases like *Lochner v. New York* (1905), and *Hammer v. Dagenhart* (1918), the child labor case, which we have already discussed. During the early years of the New Deal, in the 1930s, the Supreme Court—the "nine old men"—hacked away at New Deal programs. The National Industrial Recovery Act was one of the keystones of the early New Deal; but the Supreme Court struck it down in the so-called "sick chicken" case, *Schechter Poultry Corp. v. United States* (1935).[23] The next year, in *United States v. Butler* (1936),[24] the Supreme Court consigned the Agricultural Adjustment Act to the ash heap.

To be sure, even liberals on the Supreme Court did not like some aspects of the early New Deal, which struck them as too much in the direction of corporatism. Moreover, the Supreme Court did sustain many notable labor and social laws, state and federal. *Home Building and Loan Association v. Blaisdell* (1934),[25] was one of these cases. The Court, by a narrow margin, sustained a Minnesota law that tried to delay and avoid foreclosures of houses and farms. This seemed to be in flat contradiction to the contracts clause of the constitution, but the Supreme Court was only too aware of the country's economic crisis.[26] There was real anger against the Court for blocking much of the New Deal program. President Franklin D. Roosevelt, immensely popular, swept into a second term in 1936 in a landslide. He then made a clumsy attempt at reform and revenge. This was the infamous court-packing plan: a plan to give him the right to appoint extra justices, one for each justice who was older than seventy and a half. The plan would have allowed him to appoint as many as six new justices. But a storm of protest arose, and the plan was shipwrecked from the start.[27] He had, in a way, attacked something holy; even his political allies deserted him. Congress scuttled the plan; it was one of Roosevelt's worst defeats.

[23] 295 U.S. 495 (1935).
[24] 297 U.S. 1 (1936).
[25] 290 U.S. 398 (1934).
[26] The decision was 5 to 4. Chief Justice Charles Evans Hughes, who wrote the majority opinion, realized quite well the highly charged nature of the issue. An "emergency," he said, "does not create power"; but he argued that the Contracts clause was not absolute; and that the law in this case was a "reasonable means to safeguard the economic structure" of the country.
[27] See William E. Leuchtenberg, *The Supreme Court Reborn: The Constitutional Revolution in the Age of Roosevelt* (1995).

But in the event, the plan proved to be unnecessary—even in the short run. In 1937, the Supreme Court, by a 5 to 4 vote, upheld the National Labor Relations Act.[28] In this, and a number of other cases, one Justice—Owen Roberts—apparently changed sides. This was the famous "switch in time that saved the nine." Was there really a "switch" at all? Did Roberts have a genuine change of heart? Was he motivated by political events? Or was the decision, and what followed, unrelated to the court-packing plan—and to Roosevelt's reelection? The question has been much debated; and is much disputed.[29] G. Edward White takes the position that the court-packing crisis did not produce the "constitutional revolution of the New Deal"; rather, the crisis itself was the "product of a constitutional revolution." The crisis grew out of a growing recognition that the Court was, and had to be, deeply political—a "modernist" theory of constitutional law and constitutional interpretation, and "of the nature of legal authority."[30] Indeed, there is no question that the Court is (and always has been) a political institution, though of a rather special kind. The Court is not, to be sure, autonomous—that is, merely applying "law," in ways that are detached from the swirling, vibrant forces working away in society. Social norms and values are at the heart of the work of the Court. But the Court *is* independent, that is, the government cannot control it; and, unlike the legislature, it has no irate constituents on whose votes it depends. Nobody can fire a Justice. Nobody can throw him out of office. The Justices serve for life. And they tend to live a long, long time.

Still, Roosevelt had the last laugh, switch or no switch. He was elected four times. In short, he outlasted the "nine old men"; ultimately, he was able to fill the Court with men who were friendlier to the New Deal, and had a less jaundiced view of government regulation in general. The Supreme Court virtually abdicated its role as an economic watchdog; it accepted, basically, whatever the states and the federal government wanted to do, provided the program had any hint of a rational motive behind it. But the Court did not skulk off the stage and hide behind the scenes. It assumed an equally powerful and controversial role, as we have seen: champion of the underdog, the voice of the voiceless, the protector of human rights, the *inventor* of new human rights. This was the role of the Warren court; and the Courts that followed it—the Burger and Rehnquist courts—though much more conservative, never really abandoned this role.

The prestige of the Supreme Court in the late twentieth century continued to be great. What the Court did about segregation, the death penalty, rights of criminal defendants, voting rights, contraception, abortion, and gay rights—all these were hotly debated and hotly contested. The Court—a deeply secretive body, allergic to press conferences and spin doctors—was nonetheless often front page news.[31] At times, the Court did seem timid and deferential (during

---

[28] *National Labor Relations Board v. Jones & Laughlin Steel Corp.*, 301 U.S. 1 (1937).

[29] One view—which Leuchtenberg, n. 27 *supra* represents—makes the court-packing plan extremely significant in explaining the "switch." On the other side, see Barry Cushman, *Rethinking the New Deal Court* (1998).

[30] G. Edward White, *The Constitution and the New Deal* (2000), pp. 235–36.

[31] Bob Woodward and Scott Armstrong, *The Brethren: Inside the Supreme Court* (1979) became a best-seller, by promising to tell inside secrets of the Court, and to rip aside its curtain of secrecy.

the McCarthy period, for example); at times, so bold it seemed almost breathtaking (school segregation, voting rights, abortion, sodomy laws). Scholars sometimes worried about the Court's "legitimacy." If the Court seems too political, will this kill it in the minds and hearts of the public? Won't people stop supporting and respecting the Court? But the evidence suggests that not even the most controversial decisions damage the Court.[32] "Legitimacy" adheres to the institution, not to individual justices, or individual decisions. This is not surprising. Even people who feel the police in their town are brutal and corrupt want better, more honest policemen; they do not withdraw their support from the *idea* of police.

The power of the Court is obvious; and more and more so over the years. Appointments to the Court had always been at least somewhat controversial. Controversy did not end in the twentieth century; on the contrary, it probably increased. There was a major tumult over the appointment of Louis Brandeis, the first Jewish Justice, in 1916, and, more recently, over the appointment of Robert Bork in 1987 (Bork was defeated). Another contested appointment was Clarence Thomas, a conservative black lawyer, in 1991 (Thomas got the job, after a bitter struggle).[33] The public seems acutely aware that appointments matter—on issues such as abortion, for example. A single vote may make all the difference. In the election campaign of 2000, for example, whether George W. Bush or Al Gore would have power to name justices was a significant talking point. Ironically, events during and after the election showed that this was far from foolish. The Supreme Court, in *Bush v. Gore*,[34] took a decisive step in determining the outcome of this disputed election; George W. Bush won by a single vote in the Supreme Court—and this guaranteed his victory in the electoral college as well.

The Supreme Court is an exceptional court. The federal judiciary, in general, gained power in the twentieth century—an inevitable result of the flow of authority to the center. But the Supreme Court rarely had to share the limelight with the lower federal courts. And few federal judges, below the Supreme Court, ever achieved much fame. They were crucial, however, to judicial policy and to social policy in general. The district court judges in the South bore the brunt of the furor over desegregation. Learned Hand (1872–1961), an appeals court judge, though he never made it to the Supreme Court, was perhaps the most respected federal judge of his day.[35] State courts and state court judges were relatively less powerful and significant than they had been in the nineteenth century, compared to the federal judges. But they almost surely *gained* power in absolute terms. Like federal judges, few state court judges could expect to become famous. They were rarely celebrities. Yet, there are a handful that are at least familiar to legal scholars and law students. Benjamin Cardozo (1870–1938) of New York served on the U.S. Supreme Court, from 1932 on,

---

[32] See, for example, James L. Gibson, Gregory A. Caldeira, Lester Kenyatta Spence, "The Supreme Court and the US Presidential Election of 2000: Wounds, Self-Inflicted or Otherwise?" 33 British Journal of Political Science 535 (2003).

[33] See George L. Watson and John A. Stookey, *Shaping America: The Politics of Supreme Court Appointments* (1995).

[34] 531 U.S. 98 (2000).

[35] See Gerald Gunther, *Learned Hand: The Man and the Judge* (1994).

but is best known for his work on the New York Court of Appeals.[36] In the 1950s and 1960s, Roger Traynor of California had perhaps the largest reputation of any state court judge; few nonlawyers, probably, had ever heard of him. An occasional state court judge was famous or notorious for one reason or another. Rose Bird, first woman chief justice of California, and the storm center of continual controversy, was unceremoniously dumped by the voters in 1987. But in general, state court judges remained obscure and unsung.

The differences between Cardozo and Traynor were, in one respect, highly revealing. The two men lived a generation apart. Both were considered bold, innovative judges. Cardozo, however, was subtle and crafty; he preferred to disguise change in old-fashioned, common law clothes; he liked to show continuity in the midst of change, to argue that the genius or spirit of the common law required him to move as he did. He was an artisan molding traditional clay. At least that is how he liked to position himself. Traynor was more likely to break sharply with the past. He was willing, at times, to say quite openly that times had changed, and the law must change with it. He spoke a different, franker language than Cardozo.

Both judges may have been influenced by the legal realist school, or, perhaps more accurately, by those social forces and currents of thought that created the realist school to begin with. On the surface, decisions of 1970 or 1990 or 2000 were more likely to contain explicit or implicit appeals to "public policy," compared to decisions written by judges of the late nineteenth century. Judges also seemed more willing to overrule cases they considered outmoded. Overruling had always been possible in America; but the power was, on the whole, rarely used. It became, most probably, more frequent over time. The Supreme Court uses it sparingly, but it is a powerful weapon, nonetheless, even if exercised only once or twice a year.[37] Far more often, courts "distinguish" away or simply ignore prior cases they do not care for. Modern high court judges also tend to write more dissenting opinions than their predecessors, and more concurring but separate opinions. In Michigan, in the 1870s, about 95 percent of all high court cases were unanimous; in the 1960s, there were dissents or concurrences in 44 percent of the published opinions.[38]

The trend toward more dissents and concurrences was most marked in the U.S. Supreme Court. Oliver Wendell Holmes and Louis Brandeis were "great dissenters" in the first third of the century. In their day, however, most of the Court's decisions were unanimous. In the last half of the century, unanimous decisions were becoming unusual, at least in cases of first importance. The school segregation case, *Brown v. Board of Education*, was unanimous. This was, however,

---

[36] On Cardozo, see Richard Polenberg, *The World of Benjamin Cardozo: Personal Values and the Judicial Process* (1997).

[37] See Christopher P. Banks, "Reversals of Precedent and Judicial Policy-Making: How Judicial Conceptions of Stare Decisis in the U.S. Supreme Court Influence Social Change," 32 Akron L. Rev. 233 (1999).

[38] Lawrence M. Friedman et al., "State Supreme Courts: A Century of Style and Citation," 33 Stan. L. Rev. 773, 790 (1981). Michigan was one of 16 state supreme courts studied; there was tremendous variation among states. Dissent rates actually *fell* in West Virginia between 1870 and 1970; in the decade of the 1960s, more than 98 percent of the West Virginia high court cases were unanimous. But the number of nonunanimous decisions, in general, doubled in the 16 states during the century between 1870 and 1970.

the result of considerable maneuvering behind the scenes. In the 1973 term, there were 157 full opinions; 33 of them (21 percent) were unanimous; in 79 percent (124 cases) somebody dissented. The Court at the end of the century *seemed* a bit less conflicted, but probably only because it took so few cases. There were 77 full opinions in the 1999 term, and 58 percent of them had one or more dissenting opinions.[39]

The Court has often been fractured and splintered—during the New Deal decade, for example, and even at times in the nineteenth century. In the 1990s, the Court again frequently split down the middle. There were 18 cases in the 1999 term that were decided 5 to 4. The Justices seem to feel no particular need to agree with each other—even with those on the same side of the issue. In some cases, the Justices wrote three, four, five, even nine separate opinions. In *Furman v. Georgia,* the 1972 death penalty case, every single Justice wrote an opinion of his own. Political scientists (and journalists) amuse themselves analyzing blocs on the Court, trying to figure out the games that Justices play. It is not always possible to pigeonhole a particular Justice. But because the Court's cases are so often deeply political, commentators are able to label Justices as liberal or conservative or in between; and to predict how they will vote in a particular case. Often they have it exactly right.

To say that Justices "write" opinions is not quite accurate. John Marshall certainly wrote his own opinions, and so did Oliver Wendell Holmes Jr. But after the 1920s, the Justices began to rely more on their law clerks—bright young men (later bright young women too) who had just emerged from the cocoon of law school. Clerks typically served a year, then went on to greener pastures. William Rehnquist, later Chief Justice, was a law clerk to Justice Robert Jackson, in 1952–1953.[40] In the 1950s, each justice had two clerks, for the most part; the Chief Justice had three. In the 1940s, most Justices were still writing their own opinions; the clerks did legal research. But by 2000, it was the clerks who wrote at least the first drafts of opinions.[41] How much actual influence they had is hard to say; and no doubt varied from Justice to Justice. The Justices, and their clerks, of course, also had access to the latest, most up-to-date online services. One result of all this was judicial bloat. Opinions became longer, wordier. Some of them seem to go on forever. For a decided case to take up a hundred pages—majority, concurrences, dissents—is nothing at all unusual.

The Justices also seem less interested in presenting a united front. Collegiality is not gone, but it is not the collegiality of the nineteenth century. The proliferation of concurrences is one sign of this: Justices agreeing with the result but not with the reasoning, or agreeing with this or that bit or section of the

[39] For these figures, see 88 Harvard Law Review 376 (1974); 114 Harvard Law Review, 394–395 (2000).

[40] A few years later, Rehnquist wrote an article in which he accused the clerks as a whole of "liberal" bias. He warned that they could bias the Court by presenting material in a slanted way. William R. Rehnquist, "Who Writes Decisions of the Supreme Court?" *U.S. News and World Report,* Dec. 13, 1957, p. 74.

[41] This was also true of the whole federal system. District judges have had clerks since 1936, appeals court judges even earlier. Only a handful of federal judges—Richard Posner of the Seventh Circuit is perhaps the most prominent—actually write their own opinions from start to finish.

majority opinion, disagreeing with this or that; accepting (say) Part IIB and Part IIIC of the majority, withholding acceptance from everything else. If the Justices all insist on their own particular take, it becomes very hard to decide what if anything the Court actually decided. It makes the decisions fragmented, unwieldy. The Supreme Court, more and more, consists of nine little law offices, each one to a degree independent of all of the rest.

In the twentieth century, the bench had become fully professional. In most states, lay judges—even lay justices of the peace—had gone the way of the heath hen and the Carolina parakeet. To be sure, judges were still elected in most states; they were, in this sense, more like politicians than like civil servants. But in most states, most of the time, the election of judges tended to be a dull, routine affair—an electoral rubber stamp. Most often, a judge got the seat on the bench through appointment, when an old judge died or resigned. After serving for years as a judge, the new judge would run for reelection, but typically without serious opposition.

The Missouri plan (1940) made "elections" even more of a sham. Under this plan, a panel made up of lawyers (chosen by the local bar), a sitting judge, and laymen appointed by the governor, would nominate judges. The panel would put forward three names; the governor would pick one of the three. This judge would then serve one a year on the bench. At that point he or she would run for re-election, but unopposed. In the 1960s, a number of states adopted the Missouri plan, or something similar. Since it is hard to defeat somebody with nobody, the unopposed judge was supposed to win; and almost always did. There were, however, a few glaring exceptions: in 1987, as we mentioned before, Rose Bird, chief justice of the California Supreme Court, and a very controversial figure, was buried in an avalanche of "no" votes; two other liberal judges went down to defeat along with her.

In states without the Missouri plan, or something like it, judges run for election, just like any other candidate. But not quite the same. Most of these elections are quiet and uneventful. The public is profoundly uninterested. There are few real contests. In some states, the parties divide up the slots. The judges typically serve for long terms. Mostly, they are unopposed. Even when there is opposition, judges can hardly campaign as vigorously as candidates for, say, Congress; or even a local school board. They can hardly make promises, or announce how they intend to decide cases, except in the vaguest, and most general way. This adds to the bloodless character of judicial elections. There are occasional nasty battles; but they are the exception, not the rule. In 1998, not one sitting judge was defeated; and between 1964 and 1999, only fifty-two judges out of some 4,588.[42]

[42] Larry Aspin, "Trends in Judicial Retention Elections, 1964–1998," 83 Judicature 79 (1999).

CHAPTER 4

REGULATION, WELFARE, AND THE
RISE OF ENVIRONMENTAL LAW

LAND USE

The twentieth century was a century of land-use controls. The nineteenth century had its share of devices to protect property rights and monitor the use of law. These included the restrictive covenant and common law nuisance law. But in the twentieth century, many people considered these old tricks to be too weak to contain and control the forces of change, especially in big cities. *Zoning* was one of the legal inventions of the twentieth century.[1] The central idea of zoning is to regulate what kinds of land use are allowed, in particular areas or zones of a city or town. Some zones will be limited to one-family houses, some will be open to apartment buildings, some to stores and offices, some will even be open to factories. New York City was a pioneer in the zoning movement. After the state passed an enabling act, New York City adopted the first comprehensive zoning ordinance (1916). The powerful merchants of Fifth Avenue were among the enthusiastic backers of the ordinance. They wanted to keep the sweatshops and grime of the garment industry from creeping north and polluting their elegant precincts. Zoning soon became genuinely popular, in city after city. By 1930, it was pretty much the rule in both large and small cities; and in the suburbs. Over a thousand cities had zoning ordinances. These cities relied on zoning to preserve the character of neighborhoods, to stop any downward slide of land values, and to counterbalance the iron laws of the market. Zoning served the interests of the middle-class homeowner, and (to some extent) the businessperson, too. The Supreme Court, in *Euclid v. Ambler* (1926)[2] enthusiastically upheld the principle of zoning. The argument against zoning was that it took rights away from property owners. It destroyed some of the potential value of their land; for this, they were paid nothing, in violation (it was argued) of the Constitution. But the Supreme Court disagreed. To the Justices, zoning was useful, benign, and important. Keeping up land values, keeping residential neighborhoods firmly residential—this struck them as definitely in the public interest. Zoning was a tool

---

[1] See John Delafons, *Land-Use Controls in the United States* (1962); on the background and the ideology of the movement for zoning, see Martha A. Lees, "Preserving Property Values? Preserving Proper Homes? Preserving Privilege? The Pre-*Euclid* Debate over Zoning for Exclusively Private Residential Areas, 1916–1926," 56 U. Pitt. L. Rev. 367 (1994).
[2] 272 U.S. 365 (1926).

of orderly planning. It put things in their rightful place. Commercial buildings, apartment houses, and factories—all these were fine in their place. But if they encroached on the homes of the middle class, they were a nuisance, the "right thing in the wrong place—like a pig in the parlor instead of the barnyard."

The American passion for income segregation made land-use controls popular. Zoning ordinances are the norm; Houston, Texas, is probably the only city of any size that does without one. The ordinances are administered by zoning boards; and are often quite complex. Zoning was followed by a host of other land-use measures, including building permits, control over "development," and, in some places, restrictions on lot sizes and architectural controls. All this was in the interests of the middle-class mass, the homeowners, the people in suburbia and exurbia, with their little houses, yards, and fences.

Problems tended to arise at the borders of land-use areas; or in enclaves. Income segregation often overlapped race segregation. Suburban developments after the Second World War were usually reserved, initially at least, for white people only. But from the period of the First World War on, the black rural masses had been moving North and into the cities in search of jobs. This movement became a flood after the Second World War. White fear was one of the dominant pillars of support for land-use controls. Federal programs—Urban Renewal and Redevelopment from 1949, Modern Cities in the late 1960s— hardly made a dent in urban segregation; indeed, these programs were not really intended to. These programs took the form, by and large, of grants made to local warlords, and they depended on the approval of the locals as well. Cities and neighborhoods crafted the policies; and the white majority never favored any plan that smacked of large-scale integration—or any integration at all. *Shelley v. Kraemer*, as we saw, outlawed the racial restrictive covenant in 1948;[3] in 1949, Urban Redevelopment popped out of the legislative box. Not that the two events were directly connected. But the energy released by one act flowed into the other. Urban Renewal acquired the sardonic nickname of Negro Removal. Those who wanted to keep blacks and poor people out of a neighborhood could not do this directly. But now they found that the job could be done indirectly, through some sort of campaign to fight "blight."

In the background of Urban Renewal, and its various recensions, was the dream of the city beautiful: the dream of rational, clean, civilized life in a beautiful and pleasing location. The actual impact of the programs was different. Urban Renewal sometimes disrupted and destroyed old and established neighborhoods. It had nothing to replace them with. The New Deal had begun a public housing program, which was quite popular at first. The real estate lobby became its implacable enemy. There was never enough public housing to fill the needs of the poor. As slums were torn down, the poor were simply shunted about elsewhere in the city, forming new slums. Not surprisingly, a backlash developed against urban renewal. Blacks were part of the backlash, along with radicals and (sometimes) also white smallholders: those who suspected the bulldozers were about to crash through their own backyards. At first, the courts were not very sympathetic to people who protested against Urban Renewal and other forms of

---

[3] See Part IV, ch. 9, *Shelley* v. *Kraemer* was 334 U.S. 1 (1948).

redevelopment and land-use planning. Stripped of jargon, the cases said, first, that papa knew best; second, that judges could not interfere with orderly decisions by respectable authorities.

In the 1960s, a few judges had second thoughts; a few housewives chained themselves to trees for publicity; and there was much handwringing and pamphlet-writing from Washington. Planners now had to contend with a growing conservation movement. Not many people still saw "blight" as *the* social problem of the cities. It became harder to gash out the heart of a city to build a new highway, or simply to get rid of "blight." Many old buildings that once might have been torn down now found themselves spared on the grounds of beauty or historic value. As early as 1931, Charleston, South Carolina, established a "historic district." A few years later, New Orleans followed suit, with regard to the old Latin Quarter. Such districts were created in other cities, too, along with landmark commissions that had the job of finding, labeling, and protecting beautiful and historic buildings. Congress established a National Trust for Historic Preservation in 1949; a National Historic Preservation Act (1966) set up a program of matching grants to the states.[4] By the end of the century, there were perhaps thousands of landmark commissions or the like, dedicated to protecting architectural beauty and the historical heritage. Land prices and economic considerations had once consigned great buildings to the wrecker's ball—buildings like Louis Sullivan's Stock Exchange Building in Chicago. By 2000, this was almost impossible. The architectural heritage of the United States was, relatively speaking, safe.

ENVIRONMENTAL LAW AND THE ENVIRONMENTAL MOVEMENT

Meanwhile, a newer social problem moved to center stage: the problem of the physical environment. Problems of air and water pollution, and other symptoms of distress, caught the attention of the public, and quite dramatically, from the late 1940s on. Los Angeles was famous or notorious for its smog. A tragedy, the "Donora death fog," helped focus national attention. Lethal fumes from industrial plants enveloped Donora, Pennsylvania, at the end of October 1948. These fumes literally created darkness at noon; people were choking, gasping for air. Before the Donora death fog dissipated, it made hundreds of men, women, and children sick; and claimed twenty victims, dead from asphyxiation.[5] Government entered the picture, but quite slowly. In the 1950s, there were grants to state and local government, for research on problems of air pollution. Congress passed a Clean Air Act in 1963; a Motor Vehicle Air Pollution Control Act, in 1965; an Air Quality Act in 1967; and a Clean Air Act in 1990. These laws were progressively tighter; they began to set up actual standards of air quality, and put some muscle behind pollution control. President Richard Nixon, by

---

[4] These laws were 63 Stat. 927 (act of Oct. 29, 1949); and 80 Stat. 915 (act of Oct. 15, 1966).

[5] Lynn Page Snyder, " 'The Death-Dealing Smog over Donora, Pennsylvania:' Industrial Air Pollution, Public Health Policy, and the Politics of Expertise, 1948–1949," 18 Environmental History Review 117 (1994).

executive order, created an Environmental Protection Agency in the 1970s, and the EPA soon became an important player in the battle to fight pollution.

Water quality control traveled a path somewhat similar to air quality control: a Water Quality Act in 1965, a Clean Water Act in 1972, and a Safe Drinking Water Act in 1974. This last law gave EPA the task of setting standards to make sure that when Americans turned on their faucets, something clean and ready to drink would come flowing out. In 1962, Rachel Carson published her book, *Silent Spring*. She warned about the dangers from pesticides and other poisons. Congress (and the public) began to take notice. A Toxic Substances Control Act became law in 1976. This law gave EPA strong new powers to control pesticides and other chemicals. EPA could require warning labels, and could even remove risky substances from the market.[6] The public had gotten the message. By the end of the century, many Americans recycled paper and glass; and many also shopped for organic lettuce and free-range chickens at markets that catered to these tastes.

Environmentalism has always been more than esthetics. It has a strong admixture of self-interest. After all, nobody wants to be poisoned. At the end of the nineteenth century, Frederick Jackson Turner lamented the closing of the geographical frontier; now, by the end of the twentieth, the environmental movement mourned the death of another kind of frontier: the end of an era of limitless possibilities. More than a century before, people began to realize that the great herds of bison were no more. They sensed that the wilderness was disappearing. Later in the twentieth century, the world seemed very small, and very much at risk. There was a sense of cosmic doom. Atomic and hydrogen bombs threatened the earth with mass destruction. There were other kinds of doomsday threats as well: holes in the ozone, global warming, runaway population growth. Resources seemed terribly finite. Big business was poisoning the rivers and darkening the air; lumber companies were chopping down beautiful and irreplaceable trees; cities were pouring tons of muck into lakes and oceans; the corps of Engineers was putting a dam on every wild river; the hearts of the cities were dying; shopping malls were gobbling up open space. Nothing could justify such reckless policies—except, perhaps, blind faith in the invisible hand of the market, or in "progress." But this faith was itself becoming scarce. More and more people came to feel that the villain was not Adam Smith's market; rather, it was the greed and abuses of a form of crony capitalism. If they had thought more deeply, they might have come to the conclusion that they themselves were part of the problem; that we were wasteful, profligate people; and that for millions of us, consumption was the ultimate good.

On the other hand, this was a rich country, and it was getting richer all the time. Economic growth no longer satisfied everyone, particularly people with time and money to spare, and still no inner peace. Millions of people wanted a chance to escape from their humdrum lives, to camp in a national forest, or hike in one of the great national parks. Wilderness was a dirty word in the nineteenth century, but not in the twentieth century. Health was, as we saw, one motivation behind the National Environmental Protection Act, and the EPA; but esthetics and preservation did play a role. Mother earth and its creatures had to

[6] Lawrence M. Friedman, *American Law in the Twentieth Century* (2002), pp. 196–99.

be protected. Laws were passed to keep native plants and animals from going the way of the bison. Marine mammals got their bill of rights in 1972; and a general Endangered Species Act was passed in 1973. The public was all in favor. Nobody wants to see wilderness paved over, nobody wants the whooping crane or the California condor to fly into the black night of extinction.[7]

But there are limits. The general idea of the endangered species law was popular. But particular projects, particular preservation or wilderness plans, always have winners and losers. The losers do not give in easily. There have been monumental battles over the environment, and over the uses of public lands. If a tiny fish threatens a mighty dam, if lumber workers stand to lose jobs because a rare owl lives in their trees, the result can be a massive legal conflict. These cases end up in the courts—or in Congress. Often, neither side is able to deliver a knockout blow. Many people are convinced the environmental movement has "gone too far." At the beginning of the twenty-first century, under President George W. Bush, the administration's energy policy turned sharply away from the goals of the environmental movement. The administration, if it had its way, would drill for more oil in Alaska, and open up big chunks of the public domain to energy and timber companies. This brought the administration in direct conflict with passionate environmentalists. In a battle between lovers of the caribou and giant oil companies, or between snowmobile companies and lovers of pristine forests, it is by no means clear which side will win.

INTELLECTUAL PROPERTY

There were many other changes in the law relating to land, property, and property rights in the twentieth century. One branch of the law that became more and more significant was intellectual property—the law of patents and copyright. America had become a gigantic industrial power. Its might was based on science and technology, basic and applied. Particularly toward the end of the century, it seemed critically important to preserve and extend the monopoly protection that patents and copyrights afforded. As jobs and factories fled to cheaper labor markets, only the American edge in science and technology could keep the economy afloat, or so it seemed. It was and is not easy to work out sensible schemes to protect intellectual property just enough and not too much—how long, for example, should a copyright last? Can computer software be copyrighted?

There were questions, too, about the scope of patent law: can you, for example, patent a new hybrid plant? Yes, according to the Plant Patent Act of 1930; and in 1980, the Supreme Court allowed a microbiologist and his employer, General Electric, to patent a genetically altered bacterium.[8] Patent law was overhauled in 1952; and in 1982, a new law took patent cases out of the regular federal courts, and gave them to a new court, the Court of Appeals for the

---

[7] See Shannon Peterson, "Congress and Charismatic Megafauna: A Legislative History of the Endangered Species Act," 29 Environmental Law 463 (1999).

[8] The act is 46 Stat. 1376 (act of May 23, 1930); the case, *Diamond v. Chakrabarty*, 447 U.S. 303 (1980). On copyright in general, see Paul Goldstein, *Copyright's Highway: The Law and Lore of Copyright from Gutenberg to the Celestial Jukebox* (rev. ed., 2003).

Federal Circuit. Earlier in the century, courts had been somewhat reluctant to enforce patents, in infringement suits. The new Court was much more apt to protect patents. Perhaps this was because the patent no longer seemed like a noxious monopoly; it seemed, rather, like the key to American prosperity.

Trademarks, too, in an era of intense competition for the consumer's money, took on even greater significance than before. The Lanham Act (1946) codified and strengthened the law of trademarks. The chief value of many products lies in their brand name, even more than in the product itself. This was an age of national markets, chain stores, and huge franchises like McDonald's. Malls all over the country had what seemed to be the same clusters of shops—all with familiar names. In a mobile, restless society, the power of the trademark, or brand name was an essential aspect of any successful business.

REGULATION OF BUSINESS

A national economy creates national brands and brand names; it also generates a demand for national regulation. This was already evident in the nineteenth century, as the Interstate Commerce Commission Act, and the Sherman Act clearly demonstrated. The trend continued into the twentieth century. One of the first manifestations was the federal food and drug law, passed in 1906. A bizarre episode of struggle preceded it. There had been, for a generation, a genuine pure food movement. It had very little to show for itself, at the federal level. State laws were as ineffective against nationally marketed food products as they were against national railroad nets. Then came Upton Sinclair's shocking novel, *The Jungle*. It told the story of an immigrant family, who arrived in Chicago from Lithuania, eager to start a new life. The American dream becomes, for them, a nightmare. They lived and worked under terrible conditions; raw, naked capitalism (as Sinclair described it) crushed them, body and soul. In the course of the book, there were vivid, appalling descriptions of conditions in the meat-packing plants of Chicago, where the young hero, Jurgis Rudkis, had gone to work. The reading public nearly retched at the thought that moldy and disgusting matter made up the meat products they ate; that pieces of rat ended up inside their sausages; worst of all was one passage in the book, describing how a worker fell into a vat and was processed into lard. The helpless consumer saw himself now as an unwitting cannibal. Sinclair wrote the book to advance the cause of socialism; he wanted to expose the plight of "the wage-slaves of the beef trust."[9] He said, in a famous sentence, "I aimed at the public's heart," but "I hit . . . the stomach." Indeed, he had. Scandal cut the sale of meat products almost in half. This made a point the food industry understood all too well. The public demanded action. Pure food laws and meat inspection laws sailed through Congress. If such laws could restore public confidence, people would begin spending money again on meat and food products. If so, then regulation was well worth the price.

The food and drug act is a dramatic example of the role played by scandals and the media in law-making—a role which only got stronger and more powerful

[9] Upton Sinclair, *American Outpost, A Book of Reminiscences* (1932), p. 154.

in the course of the twentieth century, the century of radio, then television, then the Internet. Almost a hundred years later, in 2003, the "mad cow" panic cut sales of beef dramatically—and again, the government had to respond. Scandal also continued to play a role in the evolution of food and drug law. In the 1930s, the first antibiotics, the sulfa drugs, came on the market. A drug company, in 1937, had the happy thought of marketing the new wonder drug in liquid form, instead of in the form of pills. There was one slight problem: the solvent was diethylene glycol, which was in fact a deadly poison. Over 100 people, a third of them small children, died after they swallowed "Elixir Sulfanil-imide."[10] The Food and Drug Administration pulled the elixir off the market; but this clearly seemed too little and too late. The furor led Congress to pass new laws, strengthening the FDA, giving it new and more powerful weapons. Before, the FDA had authority to pull a drug off the market; but now, no drug could be marketed at all, unless it had FDA approval—and this approval depended on elaborate and careful tests.

The twentieth century was a century with more and more laws that were passed in the name of health and safety. Because markets were national, the federal government came to play a major role in health and safety legislation. We have already mentioned air and water pollution; there were also laws about consumer safety; and OSHA (the Occupational Safety and Health Administration) laid down rules to protect workers on the job.

The federal government also became more and more active in the general regulation of business. There was a burst of activity after the election of Franklin D. Roosevelt. Roosevelt's New Deal, from 1933 on, was perhaps not quite so drastic a break from the past as has sometimes been pictured. But it was drastic enough. The country was bleeding from a thousand wounds. Banks were failing, businesses had gone belly-up, the stock market had collapsed, millions were out of work, people were losing their homes and their farms, families were going hungry. The New Deal wanted above all to make jobs—it sponsored massive public works programs for this reason. But it also wanted to regulate: to control the banks, the corporations, the big enterprises, and the stock exchanges. The stock market in particular was seen as part of the problem. Some New Dealers were downright antibusiness in their outlook. Business itself was stunned, and shattered in morale, after the great crash of 1929. Politically, business had never been more feeble than it was in the early 1930s, in the years of the Great Depression. As enterprise cowered or took flight, like a deposed monarch, unions, workers, and the man and woman in the street swarmed into the burned and deserted palaces. The political and economic situation gave the New Deal, with its huge majorities in Congress, chances to pass laws that would have been almost unthinkable before.

The New Deal was nothing if not hyperactive. The New Deal brought in deposit insurance and the Securities and Exchange Commission. It enacted a tremendous number of new regulatory laws; many of them, like the SEC Act, created new administrative agencies. The New Deal brought electricity to the Tennessee Valley; and it began (as we said) a program to build cheap public

---

[10] Charles O. Jackson, *Food and Drug Legislation in the New Deal* (1970), ch. 8.

housing. The National Labor Relations Act (1935)[11] guaranteed the right to unionize, and regulated union elections. Under this law, it was an "unfair labor practice" for an employer to interfere with efforts to organize workers. The law set up an agency, the National Labor Relations Board, to enforce the Act. The New Deal also launched the first meaningful programs of unemployment insurance, old-age pensions, and public housing. These pensions—embodied in the great Social Security Act—had a double purpose, as many laws do. The Act provided money for older people—but to get the money, at 65, they had to leave their jobs. These would presumably go to younger workers, hungry for employment.

There had been administrative agencies, and administrative law, long before the New Deal. But, despite the Interstate Commerce Commission, the Federal Trade Commission, and such older federal bureaucracies as the postal service, the administrative state, on the national level, was underdeveloped until the advent of the New Deal, and perhaps even afterwards, as compared with the democracies of Western Europe. It was an administrative state in bits and snatches.[12] And the field of administrative law was hardly recognized as a field before the New Deal. The courts were, at first, rather hostile to administrative agencies, and looked askance at their powers. Judicial review of administrative agencies has had its ups and downs; it has vacillated between poles of hostility and super scrutiny, on the one hand, and supine deference on the other.[13] In 1935, Congress created a Federal Register, a huge book (in normal years, it runs to tens of thousands of pages) in which every executive order, every rule and proposed rule of every administrative agency, gets published.[14] In 1946, Congress passed an Administrative Procedure Act, after many years of struggle and argument over the issue; President Roosevelt had vetoed an earlier version. The APA tried to set up orderly and fair procedures that every agency had to follow. If an agency proposed new rules, it had to give the public notice; and "interested parties" had to have the right to express their views on the subject.[15]

The Social Security Act nationalized welfare law. It replaced the mean-spirited and chaotic programs of the states. It was meant to put the poorhouse out of business. Politically, the Social Security Act was both potent and successful. Part of its success comes from the fact that pensions under the act were not "welfare." They were social insurance. The workers paid part, the employers paid part. Rich or poor—everybody collected, at the age of retirement, which was fixed at 65. Nobody who gets a monthly check thinks of herself as on

[11] 49 Stats. 449 (act of July 5, 1935); the Norris-LaGuardia Act, passed in 1932, when Herbert Hoover was still the president, did away with the labor injunction. 47 Stats. 70 (act of March 23, 1932).

[12] See Stephen Skowronek, *Building a New American State: The Expansion of National Administrative Capacities, 1877–1920* (1982).

[13] For a discussion of some of the ins and outs of administrative law, see Reuel E. Schiller, "Enlarging the Administrative Polity: Administrative Law and the Changing Definition of Pluralism, 1945–1970," 53 Vanderbilt L. Rev. 1389 (2000).

[14] 49 Stat. 500 (act of July 26, 1935)

[15] 60 Stat. 237 (act of July 11, 1946); on the background, see George B. Shepherd, "Fierce Compromise: The Administrative Procedure Act Emerges from New Deal Politics," 90 Northwestern University L. Rev. 1557 (1996).

the dole, or compares herself with an unwed mother getting a welfare check. Pensioners felt and feel that they had earned their money. Hence the program was popular in a way that "welfare" never was; and never could be.

The Second World War finally ended the Great Depression, and brought back a kind of prosperity. Millions of men and some women served in the armed forces. There were millions of jobs in the booming war industries. The long lines of the unemployed disappeared overnight. Prosperity probably meant more to the average American, in the long run, than all the reforms and programs of the New Deal. But in fact, people wanted both: a booming, free economy; and their share of a social safety net. Prosperity in the 1950s also revived the strength and power of business. As memories of depression faded, conservatives scrambled to recover influence they had lost during the bleak days of the 1930s. Franklin D. Roosevelt, the charismatic charmer who was elected four times, was dead. The New Deal was not overturned, to be sure. But people stopped talking about "economic royalists," or "malefactors of great wealth." Labor and business shared in the economic product. A rising tide raises all the boats; it also makes passengers happy, ship owners rich, and crews docile and content.

Active government, however, did not end with the end of the war. The government set out, even before 1945, to help the masses of veterans, on a scale never before attempted. This seemed like simple justice; members of the armed services had put their lives on hold, and many had risked their lives. But it was also a conscious effort to smooth the transition from a war to a peace economy. Under the "GI Bill of Rights" millions of soldiers, sailors, and airmen went to college (instead of glutting the labor market). The government gave loans to veterans who wanted to start a business. Veterans and their families also got money to buy a house. The dream of a little house in the suburbs, a yard, rosebushes, a lawn, a garage, a kitchen filled with gleaming new appliances—this became a reality. These programs also made jobs for bricklayers and plumbers; they put money in the pockets of contractors and mortgage bankers, not to mention manufacturers of plaster, glass, pipe, refrigerators, and toilet bowls.

In the 1950s, the Republicans regained the White House, under a popular military leader, Dwight D. Eisenhower. But Eisenhower's government made no attempt to repeal the Social Security Act, no attempt to abolish the Securities and Exchange Commission. They did not add to the house of the New Deal; but the structure remained standing, almost intact. And so it has remained, to this day. Indeed, under the presidency of Lyndon Johnson, in the 1960s, the welfare state zoomed forward, with a dramatic burst of new legislation. The most important innovations were Medicare and Medicaid. Medicare covered hospital expenses for everybody over 65. It was financed, like Social Security, by payroll taxes. Medicaid provided matching funds for state programs of medical care for the blind and disabled; and the states could take the money they used for the elderly poor (who were now under Medicare) and use it for the rest of the needy population. Medicare, like Social Security, was a social insurance program. It was and is enormously popular—and not only with the old folks. After all, it took the burden of grandma's hip replacement, and grandpa's cataract operation, off the back of their families. Medicare is now almost as unassailable as Social Security itself. In the early years of the twenty-first century, the air is full of talk of reform, talk of partial privatization, talk of financial problems plaguing these programs; but nobody dares mention, or even think about, outright repeal or anything that would seriously impair the program or its benefits.

BUSINESS LAW AND THE LAW OF BUSINESS

There are divorce lawyers and personal injury lawyers, civil rights lawyers and lawyers who specialize in all sorts of subjects. But the main business of lawyers is business. The economy is locked into a world of law, rules, forms, and formalities. This is a free market society; but a free market does not mean a market without law, laws, and lawyers. The free market—as many countries have discovered, to their grief—may work through an invisible hand; but the invisible hand needs very visible help. It needs a firm foundation, a bedrock of institutions, customs, habits, norms, and, not least of all, a foundation of laws. The market rests on rules of contract, property, and business associations; it rests on a body of commercial law. It also more and more requires laws about patents, trademarks, and copyright; and rules about fair and unfair competition.

And that market was, and had been for some time, a national market. National markets call for national controls, and national institutions. This is, as we pointed out, one of the central facts of twentieth century law and life. Clearly, for antitrust law, railroad regulation, and the like, this had been recognized even in the nineteenth century. But the same may be true for basic contract and commercial law. In our federal system, these fields were and remain stubbornly local. Many legal scholars, and some business people, have called for uniformity, or harmonization. It seemed wrong, and inefficient, to have as many different laws of commerce as there were states. One possible remedy was to persuade the states to pass "uniform" laws—to march to the same legal drummer. A Conference of Commissioners on Uniform State Laws was formed toward the end of the nineteenth century. Law reform and, incidentally, the interests and good name of the legal profession were very much on the minds of the members. The American Law Institute, encouraged by the organized bar, began drafting "uniform laws"—prepackaged model laws, which the states, it was hoped, would adopt on their own. The Negotiable Instruments Law, as we saw, was widely adopted in the late nineteenth century. Another important law was the Uniform Sales Act (1906). There were also uniform laws on bills of lading, warehouse receipts, and other commercial subjects. Not every state adopted these laws; but some of the uniform laws were adopted by *most* states.[16]

This was all rather piecemeal; and some scholars felt there should be one grand, national body of commercial law. The idea was to replace chaotic state laws, and also the various "uniform" laws, with a single, comprehensive, up-to-date code of commercial law. The chief intellectual parent of the Code was

[16] The uniform laws movement went beyond drafting commercial laws. A Uniform Flag Act of 1917 dealt with the weighty problem of defacing, defiling, or trampling on old glory; and the Uniform Simultaneous Death Act of 1940 was an attempt to clean up the tangled inheritance mess that sometimes happened when a husband and wife, say, died together in an accident.

Professor Karl Llewellyn; but along the way many others played a role—members of the bar, bankers, and other legal scholars. The first drafts appeared in the 1940s. There were many concessions and compromises, and about a decade of wrangling and redrafting, before a final version was presented to the world, in 1950.[17] This version summed all of the statute law of commerce, improved it (in theory at least), and replaced the old laws, uniform or not, on sales, bills and notes, bulk sales, warehouse receipts, bills of lading, and secured transactions.

But this was only the beginning. The drafters now had the job of selling their beloved Code to the various states. It was not an easy sell. Pennsylvania (1953) was the first to bite; then came Massachusetts (1957). These were the pioneers. Other states seemed reluctant to follow. But, after years of agitation, a bandwagon effect set in; fourteen states had the Code by 1962; and by 1967, every state except Louisiana, with its civil law tradition. Even Louisiana fell into line, ingesting the bulk of the Code in 1974. Formally, at least, the country now had a single, uniform law on commercial transactions. In size and scale, the Code was a clear break with the past. No more bits and pieces and patches. This much was revolutionary. The content was much less so. In some ways, it was curiously old-fashioned. Many of the problems it attacked were strictly "legal"; that is, they were problems of disorder in doctrine, clashing case law, unlovely, unsympathetic arrangements of statutes. Llewellyn also believed that courts, and legislatures, did not understand the world and the mind of businesspeople. In his view, the norms and customs of the mercantile world ought to be what commercial law was based on. Originally, he wanted to set up a "merchant jury," a panel of businesspeople, who would have important decision-making power. But during the long process of haggling that led to the final text, the merchant jury dropped out of sight.

The Code was, perhaps, a mixture of two ideologies. One was the ideology of codes themselves, stressing system, order, logic, and uniformity. The other was the ideology of the classical law merchant. The Code flew the banner of service to the business community. But on the whole, the Code's devotion to business practice was mere window dressing. The drafters of the Code did not fund or carry out empirical studies. They had no way of knowing what businesspeople actually wanted, or how business actually behaved. Some Wall Street lawyers and some businesspeople were asked their opinions. But there were no real explorations of what was wrong (if anything) with the way the system worked before the Code. This was never researched systematically. The Code, moreover, was ruthless with regard to regional variation. Any deviation was forbidden, or at least massively discouraged. To suggest that some state just *might* have a policy of its own, something which called for an exception to the broad generalizations in the Code, was heresy; and no heresy was tolerated. Nor did the drafters pay any attention to people who were outside the business community—workers or consumers. It may be somewhat unfair to stress this point. Academic interest in poor people, or in consumer problems, was not in fashion

---

[17] On the background, drafting, and early history of the Code, see Allen R. Kamp, "Uptown Act: A History of the Uniform Commercial Code, 1940–1949," 51 Southern Methodist Law Review 275 (1998); "Downtown Act: A History of the Uniform Commercial Code, 1949–1954," 49 Buffalo Law Review 359 (2001).

until the 1960s. Any nod in the direction of consumer interests was slashed and burned from the text along the way. The Code was the product of legal scholars, and some voices from Wall Street. The dissenters came from the right, not from the left: old fogies at the bar who were against any change.

But even as the Code was sweeping the country, the consumer movement was getting underway. Congress enacted a Truth-in-Lending Act in 1968. In 1975, Congress enacted the Magnuson-Moss Warranty Improvement Act. Under this law, the Federal Trade Commission (FTC) could fix standards for written warranties covering consumer products.[18] The states, too, got into the act. California, in 1970, passed a so-called "lemon" law.[19] The "lemons" in question were mostly cars: if a dealer sold a "lemon," he would have to take it back; and it would be forever labeled, on its ownership certificate, "Lemon Law Buyback." A Consumer Product Safety Act became law, too, in 1972.

The modern corporation developed in the nineteenth century; in the twentieth century, corporations utterly dominated the economy. The corporation had become a flexible, malleable tool. Corporate charters were typically so broad that they allowed a company to do pretty much anything it wanted, go into any business, pursue any opportunity. The "business judgment" rule gave managers enormous discretion. Some states, to be sure, had more stringent laws than other states. But in a federal system, a company could incorporate wherever it chose. Hundreds of corporations, as we have seen, chose to incorporate in little Delaware—a state that deliberately made its laws as permissive and attractive as possible. It is a kind of irony of modern corporation law that so much of it consists of the case-law of the Delaware Chancery Court. Doctrines that concern billions and billions of assets are forged in the crucible of one of the smallest, least populated states, and in a court of an archaic type, that has been abolished almost everywhere else.

Corporation law was essentially open-ended and permissive; but this did not mean corporations had an utterly free hand. Corporations were hemmed in by all the federal regulatory laws. They were subject to securities laws (after the New Deal), to labor laws, to anti-discrimination laws (after the 1960s), and to dozens and dozens of others. And they were still subject to the anti-trust laws. The Sherman Act (1890) is still in force, supplemented by later laws; and there are periodic waves of "trust-busting."[20] Early in the century, the government

---

[18] Truth-in-Lending is title one of the Consumer Credit Protection Act, 82 Stat. 146 (act of May 29, 1968); the second act cited is 88 Stat. 2183 (act of Jan. 4, 1975).

[19] Laws Cal. 1970, ch. 1333, p. 2481. More and more, general contract law itself was irrelevant; it was special laws of this sort that actually governed market transactions. Business, too, tended to follow its own normative path. Stewart Macaulay's famous study (1963) of business behavior in Wisconsin demonstrated this in a significant way; and a follow-up study of corporate counsel, in 1992, confirmed Macaulay's insights. Stewart Macaulay, "Non-Contractual Relations in Business: A Preliminary Study," 28 Am. Sociological Review 55 (1963); Russell J. Weintraub, "A Survey of Contract Practice and Policy," 1992 Wisconsin L. Rev. 1 (1992).

[20] On anti-trust law and policy, see Tony Freyer, *Regulating Big Business: Antitrust in Great Britain and America, 1880–1990* (1992); Rudolph J. R. Peritz, *Competition Policy in America, 1888–1992: History, Rhetoric, Law* (1996).

moved to break up Standard Oil; and it was successful in doing so.[21] Later came IBM (unsuccessful), and AT&T (successful); at the end of the century, the most notable battle was over Microsoft—litigation which, at this writing, is still going on. Anti-trust law is complex, and quite variable from administration to administration. Nonetheless, it is a fact of corporate life. Giant corporations, eager to merge with other giant corporations, cannot simply go ahead with their plans; they have to reckon with the Anti-Trust Division of the Justice Department.[22] Corporate capitalism was a mighty economic, political, and social force; but the law at least attempted, sometimes feebly, sometimes not, to teach it to behave.

---

[21] *Standard Oil v. United States*, 221 U.S. 1 (1911). This was a somewhat mixed victory for the government. The Court held that the Sherman Act prohibited only "unreasonable" restraints of trade. This "rule of reason" came back to haunt the government in later cases.

[22] On merger policy, see Herbert Hovenkamp, *Enterprise and American Law, 1836–1937* (1991), chs. 20 and 21.

CHAPTER 5

CRIME AND PUNISHMENT IN THE
TWENTIETH CENTURY

In the nineteenth century, criminal justice was as local as local could be. It was primarily a matter for the cities and towns, secondarily for the states, hardly at all for the federal government. There were federal crimes—a murder on an army post; smuggling; making moonshine liquor—but basically, it was the states and local governments that caught and prosecuted people who broke the law, who committed arson, or robbery, forged checks, or assaulted somebody with a deadly weapon. Until the 1890s, the federal government did not even have a prison it could call its own; it lodged the few federal prisoners in state prisons, and paid their room and board.

The situation changed in the twentieth century. As the federal government grew in size, and as the federal statute book grew along with it, a whole new array of federal crimes came into existence. Income tax evasion or fraud was one of these—a crime that obviously did not exist before the income tax law was passed. Every regulatory law created a new federal crime: violating the food and drug law, or stock fraud under the SEC law, or killing a black-footed ferret, under the Endangered Species Act. Earlier in the century, the Prohibition Amendment and the Volstead Act (1919) filled the jails with bootleggers and other violators. People often sneer at Prohibition, and call it a dead letter; but it was a most lively dead letter in many ways. In 1924, 22,000 prohibition cases were pending in the federal courts.[1] The Dyer Act (1919) made it a crime to transport a stolen car across state lines. This, too, led to a great number of federal arrests. It also underscored the point that crime itself had become less local; that it too had much more mobility.

In the age of radio, and then television, people's attention focused more and more on Washington, on the national government. Particularly after the New Deal era (the 1930s), people expected Washington, not the states, to solve big problems. Crime control remained local, but politically it became more federalized. An early sign of this was the so-called Lindbergh Act. In March 1932, a terrible crime horrified the country: the kidnap and murder of Charles Lindbergh's baby—the child of one of the greatest national heroes. Bruno Hauptmann paid with his life for this crime. And Congress passed a law making it a federal crime to cross state lines with anybody "unlawfully seized . . . decoyed, kidnapped, abducted, or carried away . . . and held for

---

[1] Lawrence M. Friedman, *Crime and Punishment in American History* (1993), p. 266.

ransom."[2] We have mentioned before the Wickersham Committee. From the 1950s on, crime and crime policy became more and more of a national issue. First, there was great national alarm over juvenile delinquency. Then came a panic over crime in the streets. In 1965, Congress passed a Law Enforcement Assistance Act, and launched a federal war on crime. Under President Richard Nixon, there was the Omnibus Crime Control and Safe Streets Act. Essentially, these were laws that made grants to local police forces, and in other ways simply supported crime control at the level of the states and cities. These federal programs did not, in fact, federalize crime control. But they did focus attention on the central government. Candidates for president, like candidates for the office of sheriff of some county in Texas or Pennsylvania, have argued for the last thirty years or so that they could do better than their rival in fighting the epidemic of crime.

The drug laws were an especially fertile source of federal criminals; unlike Prohibition, which died in the early 1930s, the drug laws are still actively filling the federal prisons. The Narcotic Control Act of 1956 was a very stringent law. Congress established a Drug Enforcement Administration in 1973; its budget was well over $1 billion in the late 1990s. By the end of the century, there were tens of thousands of men and women in federal prisons for crimes of this nature—63,898, to be exact, at the end of the year 2000 (56.9 percent of all federal prisoners).[3] The states were equally eager to punish users and pushers. In the state courts, in 1996, there were almost 350,000 felony convictions for drug offenses.[4] The federal government was also spending billions fighting drugs in other countries—persuading Bolivians to stop growing coca leaves, working with Mexican drug authorities, patrolling the seas to keep out smugglers of drugs.

DECRIMINALIZING SEX AND VICE

The drug laws are a major factor in the criminal justice system. But in one sense they are a great exception to one massive social trend of the late twentieth century—the trend toward wiping "victimless" crimes off the books. This was an amazing reversal of the trend in the first half of the century. There the movement was exactly the opposite. The movement started in the late nineteenth century, as we have seen—breaking down the Victorian compromise, and getting serious about vice and other forms of victimless crime. Perhaps the outstanding example of the effects of this crusade was national Prohibition, the "noble experiment," which went into effect in 1919. The Mann Act of 1910 made it a crime to transport a woman across state lines for purposes of prostitution, debauchery, or other "immoral" purposes.[5] The laws against fornication and adultery were still part of state penal codes. Undoubted, millions of people fornicated away without legal consequences. Nonetheless, these laws were far

[2] 47 Stats. 326 (act of June 22, 1932).

[3] *Sourcebook of Criminal Justice Statistics 2001*, p. 512.

[4] Bureau of Justice Statistics Bulletin, *Felony Sentences in the United States, 1996*, pp. 2, 5.

[5] On the Mann Act, see David J. Langum, *Crossing Over the Line: Legislating Morality and the Mann Act* (1994).

from inert. In 1913, Chicago established a special "Morals Court" to deal with morals offenses. In 1914, no less than five hundred fornication and adultery cases were handled in Morals Court.[6] One wonders why Stanley Butkas, a Lithuanian laborer, twenty-seven years old, had the bad luck to fall into the hands of the Morals Court, charged with fornication, while no doubt so many others got away with this offense.[7]

Many states also tightened their sex laws considerably. Many of them raised the "age of consent"—in some states to eighteen. This meant that sex with a girl or a young woman was a serious crime—the crime of rape. If two seventeen year olds had sex, then the male was by definition a rapist, and the female by definition a victim, even if she consented, indeed, even if she was ready, willing, and eager for the sex.[8] Around the time of the First World War, city after city became alarmed about the problem of vice, vice districts, prostitution, and venereal disease. Many cities commissioned reports on the "social evil." These vice commission reports generally called for serious action. They called for efforts to stamp out the red light districts, and to do as much as possible to end the regime of vice. As the Hartford, Connecticut, report put it, the "sexual impulse," which is "especially strong in the male," cannot be "eliminated"; but it was not an "entirely uncontrollable force." It could be "discouraged" by "social disapproval," but also by "obstacles placed in the way of its satisfaction," as well as by "removing . . . open allurements to vice," and by "education in self-control."[9] Most of the reports—there were some forty-three of them—agreed that vice had to go; and that it was possible to get rid of it, at least in its worst and most obvious forms. And indeed, states and cities paid attention to these commission reports. Many states passed stringent new laws against vice and vice districts; they mounted serious campaigns to get rid of brothels and whores. By 1917, some thirty-one states had passed strict "abatement" laws. Michigan's, for example, in 1915, gave any citizen the right to bring an action to "abate" a house of prostitution. Masses of upright citizens put pressure on the police to follow through. Some of the country's most famous vice districts—Storyville in New Orleans, for example—had to shut down. Vice, to be sure, always found ways to come back.[10]

There was a strong moral and religious element in the campaign. But it also had secular roots. One was a fear of venereal disease, and what it could do to the lives and bodies of innocent women and children (and even not-so-innocent men). There was also a strong belief that as human beings advanced toward civilization, they needed to control and suppress the animal side of their nature. But after the 1920s, the tide began to turn. The ideology that sustained the war on vice slowly but surely decayed. Prohibition was the first casualty. In the last decades of the twentieth century, law and society did almost a complete about face. Permissiveness, not repression or suppression, was the watchword. The

---

[6] Michael Willrich, *City of Courts: Socializing Justice in Progressive Era Chicago* (2003), p. 189.

[7] Ibid., p. 191.

[8] On the age of consent laws, see Mary Odem, *Delinquent Daughters: Protecting and Policing Adolescent Female Sexuality in the United States, 1885–1920* (1995).

[9] *Report of the Hartford Vice Commission* (July, 1913), p. 67.

[10] Lawrence M. Friedman, *Crime and Punishment in American History* (1993), pp. 328–32.

animal side won battle after battle. Pornography was, essentially, decriminalized, especially in big cities. Many states, like Illinois and California, reformed
their criminal codes; whatever consenting adults chose to do to and with each
other, was more or less okay. The laws against fornication and adultery disappeared in most states. The Mann act was amended to the point where it was
toothless and irrelevant. Most states, too, ended their laws against same-sex behavior—the "infamous crime against nature." The police were still, in some
cities, arresting people for homosexual behavior in the 1950s and 1960s; but in
the age of civil rights and the gay rights movement, this kind of police action
could not be sustained. Most of the sodomy laws were repealed. In a few states,
they were declared unconstitutional. At the end of the century, only about a
dozen states still had sodomy laws—which the Supreme Court (2003) finally
swept away.[11] The age of consent laws became unisex, and were modified in such
a way as to make teenage sex perfectly legal. Meanwhile, taboos against gambling all but vanished. At one time, casinos were open for business only in
Nevada—the barren desert state that specialized in legalizing sin (even prostitution was legal in most Nevada counties). Then gambling began to spread all
over the country. Now there are casinos on Indian reservations, gambling halls
in Atlantic City, and legal state lotteries pretty much everywhere.

The Supreme Court also, and very dramatically, decriminalized abortion in
the famous case of *Roe v. Wade* (1973).[12] Politically, this was—and remains—a
bombshell. Legally speaking, the case rested on the constitutional right to privacy—a concept (one must admit) that has only the flimsiest connection with
the actual text of the Constitution. The constitutional right to privacy made its
debut, basically, in 1965, in *Griswold v. Connecticut*.[13] Connecticut was a state
that still made contraception essentially illegal. It was a crime to use any drug
or device to prevent a pregnancy; or to aid or abet anybody in committing this
crime. The Supreme Court overthrew the statute. William O. Douglas, who
wrote the majority opinion (or one of them) argued that the Constitution implied certain "zones of privacy." The Bill of Rights, he said, had "penumbras"
and "emanations"—mysterious but liberating smoke. *Griswold,* despite its shaky
legal basis, led to a line of cases that expanded on the notion of a constitutional
right of privacy. Douglas' emanations and penumbras proved to be quite powerful. The case itself is firmly fixed in the canon. After all, very few people in
the twenty-first century still feel the state should or could ban condoms or the
use of birth control pills. *Roe v. Wade,* on the other hand, has been a bone of
contention since the day it was born.

It has, however, survived. And so has the war on drugs, despite the rampant
permissiveness and the overthrow of most laws against "victimless crimes." If
anything, the war on drugs has gotten even fiercer. Perhaps one element that
sustained it was parents' fear of pushers who preyed on their children. People
felt that addiction was a one-way trip, a journey into a realm like Dante's

---

[11] *Lawrence v. Texas,* 539 U.S. (2003). The defendant had been caught in the act, having
sex with another man. The Supreme Court reversed the conviction, 6 to 3. There was no
state interest, said the Court, that justified the "intrusion" into the defendant's private life.
[12] 410 U.S. 113 (1973). On the background of this case, and its predecessors, see David J.
Garrow, *Liberty and Sexuality: The Right to Privacy and the Making of Roe v. Wade* (1994).
[13] 381 U.S. 479 (1965).

Inferno, where all hope had to be abandoned, and there was never a good way out. As adults gained the right to do *anything*, sexually speaking, so long as they had consent, panic over children grew if anything more severe. Child molesting, child pornography, and incest: these remained crimes, severely punished crimes; and the laws became perhaps even more stringent at the end of the century.[14]

DEFENDANTS' RIGHTS

The Supreme Court, in the nineteenth century, decided very few cases on the constitutional rights of criminal defendants. But these rights became a major concern in the twentieth century, and most especially when Earl Warren was Chief Justice (1953–1969). In case after case, the Supreme Court boldly extended legal doctrine; it insisted on strict adherence to principles of fair search, arrest, interrogation, and trial. These were principles that the Court read into the Constitution. One of the legal tools for doing this was the so-called incorporation doctrine—the idea that the Fourteenth Amendment, adopted after the Civil War, "incorporated" (swallowed up) most of the Bill of Rights, and imposed them on the states. The incorporation doctrine got off to a slow start. Not all of these rights, the Court said, were incorporated, only those that were truly "fundamental." Which ones were truly "fundamental"? The Supreme Court began to define the term more expansively in the second half of the century. In *Wolf v. Colorado* (1949),[15] for example, the issue was: could a state court convict Wolf, using evidence they seized without a warrant? The Supreme Court allowed the conviction. But only twelve years later the Court reversed itself. In *Mapp v. Ohio* (1961),[16] the police had raided the home of Dolly Mapp; they never produced a warrant. They did not find what they were looking for, but they did find dirty books. Dolly Mapp was convicted of possessing obscene literature. The search was admittedly unlawful; but the Ohio court let the evidence in nonetheless. The Supreme Court reversed. Tainted evidence had to be excluded, under the Fourteenth Amendment.

This was only one of a series of dramatic cases during the Warren era, which expanded the rights of criminal defendants, on constitutional grounds. In these cases, the power of the state dramatically confronted a single individual: sometimes a broken figure of a man or woman, shuffling into court, a drunk, a gambler, a dope addict, a prostitute, a four-time loser, a petty thief—in any event, someone at the bottom of the ladder. Yet time and again, the Supreme Court sided with this underdog. In perhaps the most famous case, the Supreme Court took the side of a pool-hall drifter, Clarence Gideon. Gideon was accused of breaking into a poolroom. He was a man of stubborn persistence. He had no money, but he demanded a lawyer; he said the state (of Florida), had to provide him with legal counsel, free of charge. He had no such right under Florida law. Gideon tried to appeal all the way up to the Supreme Court. The Court

---

[14] See Philip Jenkins, *Moral Panic: Changing Concepts of the Child Molester in Modern America* (1998).

[15] 338 U.S. 25 (1949).

[16] 367 U.S. 643 (1961).

appointed Abe Fortas (later a member of the Court) to argue for Gideon. The Court reversed his conviction in 1963. The right to counsel, enshrined in the Bill of Rights, would be meaningless for a poor man accused of a felony (said the Court), unless he had a lawyer; and if the defendant had no money the state had to provide. Gideon got a new trial—and won his case.[17] Almost as notable was the *Miranda* case, decided in 1966.[18] Ernesto Miranda, arrested for rape in Arizona, was taken to an "interrogation room" and questioned. After a couple of hours of grilling, he signed a confession of guilt. The confession was admitted into evidence at Miranda's trial; and he was convicted. The Supreme Court set aside his conviction; and in so doing, they laid down a set of rules for the police to follow. Whenever the police arrest someone, the Court insisted, they cannot question that person until they advise him of his rights—the right to remain silent, the right to talk to a lawyer, and have the lawyer present when he is questioned. This is the famous "Miranda warning," familiar to everybody who watches television cop shows.

Cases of this sort drew cries of pain and dismay from the temples of law and order. There were howls of protest: the Warren court was taking the side of criminals and thugs, it was hamstringing the police, and it was working against the interests of the public. But Warren and his justices stood their ground. Earl Warren was replaced by Warren Burger as Chief Justice (1969–1986), a much more conservative judge. The Court drew back a bit, retreated a bit here and there, threw a sop or two to the law-and-order crowd, but despite its right-wing reputation, the Burger Court kept most of the law it inherited. It did not, however, strike out in bold and new directions, as Warren's Court had.[19] The next chief justice, William Rehnquist, was even more conservative. His hand was strengthened when two conservative presidents, Reagan and Bush, put their stamp on the Court. The Rehnquist Court was even more reluctant to add to the rights of defendants. But the hottest items on the wish list of conservatives—overruling *Miranda* was one of these—never came to pass.[20]

The complaint about *Miranda* had been that it hobbled the police. The same complaint was made against the "exclusionary rule," the rule in the *Mapp* case. Dangerous criminals are set free on technicalities. The hard empirical evidence suggests that these fears are exaggerated. Perhaps the benefits are also exaggerated. What impact did all these decisions have on police behavior, on procedural fairness, or on the crime rate? There is little or no agreement on the answers. Some scholars feel that the decisions accomplished very little. *Miranda*, for example, simply degenerated into "empty formalism." The exclusionary rule, on the other hand, perhaps had "positive long-term effects on policing." The new rules in general might have raised public consciousness. They may have focused attention on the way the police behave. And they may have "stimulated

---

[17] *Gideon v. Wainwright*, 372 U.S. 335 (1963); for an account of this case, see Anthony Lewis, *Gideon's Trumpet* (1964).

[18] *Miranda v. Arizona*, 384 U.S. 436 (1966).

[19] See Earl M. Maltz, *The Chief Justiceship of Warren Burger, 1969–1986* (2000), pp. 151–65.

[20] The Supreme Court reaffirmed *Miranda* in *United States v. Dickerson*, 530 U.S. 428 (2000).

wide-ranging reforms in the education, training, and supervision of police offi-cers."[21] In any event, it is hard to disentangle the complex knot of causality. Po-lice brutality and dirty tricks fell most heavily on the poor, on minorities, on the disenfranchised: but precisely during this period, these were groups that were making noise, demanding to be heard, calling for a place at the tables of power and control. The civil rights movement, and its ethos, were powerful sources of pressure on police, and on criminal justice in general. The critics of *Miranda* probably make too much of a point about Supreme Court interference with po-lice behavior. Decades after the Warren Court handed down its decision, scan-dals about police behavior continued to erupt: the beating of Rodney King, in Los Angeles, and the torturing of Abner Louima in New York City are only two of the most egregious examples.

THE DEATH PENALTY

Nothing the Supreme Court did was more dramatic than its actions with re-gard to capital punishment. In the early twentieth century, the rate of execu-tions had gone into a long and fairly sharp decline. Then the numbers rose again, until, in 1935, there were 199 executions. Afterward, executions began to drop off again. In 1961, there were forty-two executions, in 1963, twenty-one; in 1968, none at all.[22] Nine states abolished the death penalty between 1907 and 1917 (although seven of these had second thoughts and brought it back). Civil liberties organizations, and the NAACP, worked and argued and lobbied to get rid of capital punishment. They also took their fight to the courts. Then, in 1972, in *Furman v. Georgia*,[23] the Supreme Court handed down a dramatic decision. By a bare majority, the Court decided that the death penalty, in every version, in every state, was unconstitutional—was, in fact, "cruel and unusual punishment" forbidden by the Eighth Amendment. Every statute on the subject was wiped off the books. The life of every man and woman on death row was spared.

Furman lasted exactly four years. It was, to begin with, a highly fractured opinion. Four of the nine Justices were in dissent; and each of the five in the so-called majority wrote his own opinion. Some Justices thought the death penalty was unconstitutional—period. *Any* form of capital punishment. But they were a minority. Others, who joined them, did not condemn the death penalty ab-solutely—only the death penalty as it then existed. Most of the states began to comb the text of the *Furman* opinions for clues, looking for ways to salvage the death penalty. They passed new statutes, hoping for better luck. The Supreme Court had said the death penalty was just too random, too arbitrary had com-pared it to being struck by lightning. Very well, thought North Carolina; we will take away the guesswork and the randomness: *all* first-degree murderers, and

[21] Samuel Walker, *Taming the System: The Control of Discretion in Criminal Justice, 1950–1990* (1993), pp. 46–53.

[22] Stuart Banner, *The Death Penalty: An American History* (2002), pp. 208, 221–23. The Ban-ner book is the source of much of the information in the following paragraphs.

[23] 408 U.S. 328 (1972).

aggravated rapists, will get the death penalty. Other states took a different tack: they set up a two-stage process. The first stage would be the "guilt" stage. Once the defendant is found guilty, a second "trial" occurs—the trial of life or death. To impose the death penalty, the jury (or in some cases, the judge) would have to find one or more "aggravating circumstances." Both types of statute came before the Supreme Court. The Court, in 1976, struck down the North Carolina type of statute. But it approved of the other type, which was the Georgia version. The death penalty was in business again.[24]

At the end of the century, the situation remained quite complex. About a dozen states had no death penalty at all. The rest of them did: but in some, it was rarely or never used. New Jersey, for example, had not executed anybody since the death penalty was reinstated in 1976. Most Northern and Western states used the death penalty quite sparingly. California, with its population of over thirty million (and five hundred or more men and women on death row), had executed less than a dozen before 2000. Most executions were in the South, in Florida, Virginia, Alabama (though, surprisingly, Tennessee and Mississippi had few executions). Texas was in a class by itself. It alone accounted for about a third of the executions in the country. This angel of death wore cowboy boots and a Texas hat.

In most states, the death penalty was not only rare, it was painfully slow. Everywhere, it was entangled in a maze of procedures. Giuseppe Zangara tried to kill Franklin D. Roosevelt, the president-elect, on February 15, 1933. He missed, but his bullet hit the mayor of Chicago, Anton Cermak. Cermak died on March 6. Zangara was executed less than three weeks later. In the late twentieth century, speedy execution had become completely impossible. There were too many procedures, appeals, hearings, and writs, federal and state. Men grew old on death row. Ten years was no time at all for the condemned. Some convicts were put to death only after fifteen or even twenty years of waiting, and after a long and torturous procedural path.

All this seems to suggest elaborate caution and extreme care and solicitude for the rights of the accused. And, indeed, there were skillful and dedicated lawyers who worked hard on appeals, writs of habeas corpus, petitions, and the whole corpus of higher legal remedies. Yet at the trial court level, the situation was much grimmer: hasty, poorly handled trials, with slap-dash defense, and untrained, unqualified lawyers. At the very end of the century, there were some second thoughts about the death penalty—not in Texas, perhaps, but elsewhere. DNA came to the rescue and saved the lives of some of the men on death row. People began to ask themselves: how many innocent men have actually gone to their death? The governor of Illinois called for a moratorium. So did the American Bar Association. But the machinery of death, slow and creaky as it was, ground on.

[24] Stuart Banner, *The Death Penalty*, pp. 267–75. The North Carolina case was *Woodson v. North Carolina*, 428 U.S. 280 (1976); the two-stage process was approved in *Gregg v. Georgia*, 428 U.S. 153 (1976).

CRIME WAVES AND THE NATIONAL RESPONSE

The great Supreme Court decisions were an attempt to reform, and humanize, criminal process. There were also notable attempts to control police brutality— and to hire more women and minorities and make the police responsive to their communities. Yet the central fact of the last half of the twentieth century, in many ways, was exactly the opposite trend: the criminal justice system became harsher and harsher. At the end of the period, about two million men and women were in prison or jail. The savagery of the American system stood in stark contrast to most other countries of the "civilized" or at least the developed world.[25]

Why does this democratic, pluralistic country have so brutal a system? The answers are far from clear. One factor, surely, was the crime rate itself. America is a violent place, compared to any of the Western European nations. It has always been more violent; but homicide rates went through the roof in the 1950s and 1960s—for reasons that remain somewhat mysterious. The homicide rate in 1987 was seven times as great as in Canada, more than twenty times as great as in Germany, more than forty times as great as in Japan.[26] The public reaction was to demand tougher and tougher measures. They got these measures. Parole was abolished in some states. "Sentencing guidelines" took discretion away from judges, and mandated (or tried to mandate) strict, long sentences. California's notorious "three-strikes law" was meant to put repeat criminals behind bars for long, long periods, perhaps for life. States went on an orgy of prison building, and as fast as they built them, they filled them up. The prisoners were disproportionately black and Hispanic. In the 1990s, the crime rate, including the murder rate, began to fall—again for mysterious reasons—but there were few signs of a let up in the war on crime. But this is in many ways a guerrilla war; and it cannot be won by harsh and conventional means.

---

[25] See James Q. Whitman, *Harsh Justice: Criminal Punishment and the Widening Divide between America and Europe* (2003).

[26] *New York Times,* June 27, 1990, p. A12.

CHAPTER 6

FAMILY LAW IN THE TWENTIETH CENTURY

Law is a mirror of life, although sometimes a cracked and distorted mirror; and family law is a mirror, too, of family life. In the twentieth century, family life changed in many ways, some quite dramatic. More and more women entered the workforce. Women won the vote just after the First World War. Women entered the jury box. Women became lawyers and judges. This was also the century of the birth-control pill, and the century of the so-called sexual revolution. People lived longer, and had more money. Millions moved from the city to the suburbs. Radio and then television and then the Internet invaded the home. All the events, crises, and developments of the twentieth century had a deep impact on family life and family law.

The common law marriage was already in decline toward the end of the nineteenth century; this change accelerated in the twentieth century. At the end of the century, only a handful of states still allowed it. In those states, too, it is probably the case that most people knew nothing about it; and that few people made any use of the doctrine. Ceremonial marriage—a license, witnesses, usually a wedding party, too—was the norm. In a bureaucratic age, the common law marriage had become an anomaly. In the early years of the century, there was an additional reason to be against common law marriage. This was a period in which the "science" of eugenics was extremely popular. The state was anxious to control marriage—to make sure that only the right people got married. Marriage, after all, opened the door to reproduction. It was sound policy, people believed, to take steps to prevent inferior people from marrying and having children. Low intelligence, and even criminality, were passed down from generation to generation. Common law marriage was difficult to control—impossible, in fact.

Many states not only abolished common law marriage, they followed through and took the logical next step: rules about who could, and who could not, marry. Washington State, in 1909, passed a law that prohibited the marriage of any "common drunkard, habitual criminal, epileptic, imbecile, feeble-minded person, idiot or insane person"; or people "afflicted with hereditary insanity," or "pulmonary tuberculosis in its advanced stages, or any contagious venereal disease." A Wisconsin statute of 1913 provided that all "male persons" who wanted a marriage license had to have a physical examination; and procure a document from a doctor, certifying that they were free from "acquired venereal disease."[1] These strictures, however, did not last very long. As of 1930 or so, only a handful

---

[1] On these statutes, see Lawrence M. Friedman, *Private Lives: Families, Individuals, and the Law* (2004), pp. 51–54; Laws Wisc. 1913, ch. 738; Laws Wash. 1909, ch. 174, p. 633.

of states required a medical certificate, although about half still had laws that purported to keep unfit people from marrying. There were also, in many states, laws against miscegenation (these lasted, in the south at least, until the 1960s). By the end of the century, there were few controls over marriage left. Almost anybody of age could get a marriage license. The common law marriage was virtually gone. It was replaced, in part, by cohabitation, of which more later.

The Law of Divorce

None of the changes in family law were quite so dramatic as the changes in the law of divorce.[2] At the beginning of the century, divorce was available in every state except South Carolina—a haven, apparently, of sound and eternal marriages. (South Carolina gave in to the inevitable with a law that went into effect in 1949.) Each state had its own divorce law, with its own peculiarities, but in all of them, a person could, in theory, only get a divorce through a lawsuit, an action in court; and an action of a particular sort. Divorce was a reward, to be granted to an innocent spouse, who had sued a spouse guilty of spoiling the marriage by committing some serious offense. These offenses were the statutory "grounds" for divorce. What these grounds were varied from state to state. In New York, essentially, adultery was the only grounds for divorce. Most other states added desertion and cruelty, to name the two most popular. Cruelty, in 1950, was the grounds in more than half of all divorce cases. In many states, there were other grounds, usually not very significant. In Hawaii, leprosy was grounds for divorce. A Virginia man could divorce a woman if he found out she had once been a prostitute.[3]

All states agreed that a divorce was not supposed to be the product of "collusion." That is, no court was supposed to grant a divorce simply because both parties wanted it. In theory, if neither party was guilty of adultery, desertion, cruelty, or some other statutory grounds, then they were married for life. The fact that both of them desperately wanted to end the relationship, in a friendly way, was of absolutely no legal force or concern. The fact that the marriage was dead, that it had broken down completely, was also in itself of no importance.

That was theory. Practice was otherwise. Most divorces in fact *were* collusive. The wife filed a lawsuit, told her sad story of abuse, neglect, desertion, or philandering; and the husband said nothing, did nothing, filed no papers, made no defense. The judge then granted the divorce, by default. In most states, the sad story was about cruelty or desertion. In New York, the sad story had to be a story about adultery. Here a cottage industry of imitation adultery sprang up. There were women who made a living pretending to be "the other woman." A man checked into a hotel, and went to his room. The woman appeared. The two of them got partly or totally undressed. Suddenly, and miraculously, a photographer appeared, and took their picture. The man then handed over cash to the woman; she thanked him and left. The damning photograph somehow found its

[2] See Lawrence M. Friedman, "A Dead Language: Divorce Law and Practice Before No-Fault," 86 Virginia Law Review 1497 (2000).

[3] Chester G. Vernier, *American Family Laws* (Vol. 2, 1932), pp. 67–69; Paul H. Jacobson, *American Marriage and Divorce* (1959), p. 122.

way into court, as "evidence" of adultery. The judges, of course, were not fools. They knew what was going on. They rarely bothered to ask how a photographer just happened to barge into the love nest and take pictures. Usually, they said nothing and did nothing. The title of a magazine article from 1934 tells the story in a nutshell: "I Was the Unknown Blonde in 100 New York Divorces."[4]

There were other ways around strict divorce laws. One was to visit a "divorce mill," that is, a state that had loose and easy divorce laws. There were divorce mills in the nineteenth century, as we saw. They tended not to last—respectable people complained, and the legislature put an end to them. In the twentieth century, as we saw, Nevada became the divorce mill *par excellence*. This arid, barren stretch of Western desert made a living legalizing things that were illegal in California. The chief business was gambling. But Nevada also provided easy marriage and easy divorce, with a short "residence" period. Wealthy New York women would head to Reno, spend the minimum time there, and end up with a bona fide divorce—or what they hoped was a bona fide divorce.[5] The whole divorce system, in other words, was rotten and corrupt; a fraud and a deception. Yet it stayed in place, without fundamental reform, for much of the twentieth century.

Why was this the case? Perhaps because the law was caught in a trap: because it was stalemated. On the one hand, modern life placed enormous stresses and strains on the family. The nature of marriage was changing. The role of women, in particular, was changing. The rise of companionate marriage meant that people expected a great deal out of marriage. Often, they expected more than they were getting. More men, and more women, wanted an escape from their marriages. The divorce rate went steadily upward. Hollywood stars were notorious patrons of the divorce courts; but ordinary folks also clamored for divorce. This meant a kind of vast, subterranean pressure for change; a vast, subterranean pressure for cheap, easy divorce. This pressure was not, however, enough. Powerful church groups and their allies were adamant in their opposition to easy divorce. Divorce was wrong. For Catholics, it was an absolute wrong; for Protestants, it was not forbidden, but it was also not to be encouraged. Divorce was a threat to the American family. These anti-divorce forces were strong enough to prevent real change—real change, that is, in the formal law. Though even here, only up to a point.

[4] This is cited in Note, "Collusive and Consensual Divorce and the New York Anomaly," 36 Columbia L. Rev. 1121, 1131n (1936).

[5] See Frank W. Ingram and G. A. Ballard, "The Business of Migratory Divorce in Nevada," 2 Law and Contemporary Problems 302 (1935); see above, pp. 402–03. Another way around divorce, in New York state, was to get an annulment. An annulment is a declaration that a marriage was void from the very beginning—because, for example, it was based on fraud. Annulments were uncommon in most states. They were exceedingly common in New York, where the courts stretched traditional annulment doctrine like taffy. On annulment in California, see Joanna Grossman and Chris Guthrie, "The Road Less Taken: Annulment at the Turn of the Century," 40 Am. J. Legal History 307 (1996).

Most divorces were uncontested, and this applied to Nevada divorces as well. If, however, there was a contest, the validity of the Nevada divorce was by no means assured. In the 1940s, the Supreme Court considered this issue in two cases involving one O. B. Williams of North Carolina, his new wife, Mrs. Hendrix, and the divorces they got in Nevada before marrying each other—and before they were charged with bigamy in North Carolina. *Williams v. North Carolina*, 317 U.S., 287 (1942); *Williams v. North Carolina*, 325 U.S., 226 (1944).

Cracks in the facade began to appear after the 1950s. In some states, it became possible to get a divorce, without "grounds," if the man and the woman lived apart long enough; in this period, about nineteen or twenty states had provisions of this sort. The period of separation ranged from two years (North Carolina) to ten (Rhode Island).[6] Most couples were unwilling to wait that long; after all, a little white lie could bring them a divorce much more quickly. But these statutes did convey a message. They recognized that not all marriages work out, that some are dead bones, the empty shell of relationships, devoid of feeling or meaning. More and more people no doubt thought it would do no harm to admit this fact frankly, and give these marriages a decent burial. *And* give the partners a chance to start over again.

Nobody could have liked the existing system, with its lies, its pretense, its corruption. Even divorce lawyers loathed it. The forces that kept the system alive—traditional values and old-time religion—were getting weaker, especially in big urban areas. The sexual revolution put an end to the divorce charade, perhaps for good. New York finally reformed its laws in 1966; now, in addition to adultery, a spouse could get a divorce for desertion, or for "cruel and inhuman treatment." The old system was on the verge of collapse. The beginning of the end came in 1970, when California passed the first "no-fault" divorce law. Under this statute, "grounds" for divorce were no longer needed. The very word "divorce" was banned: the statute spoke of "dissolution of marriage." So long as there were "irreconcilable differences," and an "irremediable breakdown," the judge was authorized to put an end to the marriage, and grant a "dissolution."[7] Under the statute—if you read it literally—"dissolution" was an issue of fact. Had the marriage really broken down irremediably? Were the differences between him and her truly "irreconcilable?" Presumably a judge would decide this question. But in fact, almost immediately, no fault came to mean something quite different. It meant no hearing, no fact-finding, no judging at all. It meant automatic divorce. The judge was a rubber stamp.

No-fault spread like wildfire—within a few years, most states had their own version of this statute. And no-fault went way beyond the old dream of reformers—the dream of legalizing consensual divorce. No-fault was unilateral divorce. It meant that either party, whatever the other one felt, could get out of the marriage. People talked about marriage as a partnership. Partnership implies cooperation, mutuality, and sharing, which is what good marriages are. But under a no-fault system, there is no partnership at the end of a marriage. Each partner, in an intensely personal way, chooses to stay in the marriage or go. The other partner has no veto power, not even a power to delay.

Was no-fault a good idea? Many people had their doubts. Some women thought it made women worse off than before. Clearly, divorce put many women in a bad position. They were saddled with the children. They struggled

---

[6] On these statutes, see Lawrence M. Friedman, "A Dead Language," n. 2 *supra;* J. Herbie DiFonzo, *Beneath the Fault Line: The Popular and Legal Culture of Divorce in Twentieth-Century America* (1997), pp. 69–70, 75–80.

[7] On the history and background of no-fault, see Herbert Jacob, *Silent Revolution: The Transformation of Divorce Law in the United States* (1988); on divorce and popular culture, see J. Herbie DiFonzo, *Beneath the Fault Line,* n. 6 *supra.*

economically. Husbands frequently paid too little, or not at all, for child support. Alimony virtually disappeared. But old-fashioned divorce had not been much better. It too left most women badly off. No-fault did not solve problems of custody or property division; these hung on, and perhaps got worse. No-fault did not put divorce lawyers out of business. They had plenty to do on issues of children, houses, stocks, and bonds. Then there was the policy issue. Many people thought no-fault made marriage much too fragile. Divorce should always be a last resort. Cheap, easy divorce was in itself a cause of dry rot in the family.

In 1997, Louisiana amended its family laws to create a new kind of marriage: "covenant marriage." Covenant marriage was supposed to be a "lifelong arrangement." Couples could choose an ordinary marriage; or, after some counseling, and after hearing about the provisions of the law, they could opt for this "lifelong arrangement." Arizona and Arkansas also have versions of covenant marriage.[8] Spouses with a covenant marriage are not prevented from getting a divorce, if the marriage goes sour. But they cannot get a no-fault divorce; they must have grounds—in Louisiana, these include the usual: adultery, desertion, physical or sexual abuse. In the early years in Louisiana, it seemed that very few couples were choosing to go down the road of covenant marriage; but it is perhaps too early to tell what impact the law will have in the long run.

"Covenant marriage" appealed to tradition-minded people. To these people, the whole institution of marriage, bedrock of society, seemed endangered. (Gay marriage, which became a reality in Massachusetts in the early twenty-first century, horrified social conservatives, and struck them as an even more deadly threat to marriage.) Marriage, to be sure, seems to have lost some of its glamour, and a good deal of its popularity. The divorce rate, which rose throughout the century, seemed to hit a plateau at the very end; but it was still extremely high. At least divorced people were people that went through the bother of actually getting married. Millions of people, in the last third of the century, "cohabited," that is, lived together, without troubling themselves about the ceremony of marriage. Some of them even had children together.

Cohabitation was once "living in sin"; and it scandalized respectable society. More than that: it constituted a crime, the crime of adultery (and even open and notorious adultery). In the late twentieth century, it lost its power to scandalize almost completely. In the famous case of *Marvin v. Marvin* (1976),[9] the defendant was a famous movie star, Lee Marvin. The plaintiff, Michelle Triola Marvin, had lived with him for years. She claimed they had an "oral agreement"; under this agreement, they would share his earnings, she would be his "companion" and "homemaker," and would give up her career. Obviously, they also had a sexual arrangement. When they broke up, she sued him for her share of his wealth. Courts had in the past consistently refused to enforce contracts that were based on "immoral" consideration, contracts to render "meretricious sexual services." The lower court therefore dismissed the case. Michelle appealed. The California Supreme Court ordered the case to be heard. They distinguished the earlier cases: an agreement was not illegal, even if it had a sexual

---

[8] La. Rev. Stat. Ann. sec. 272, 273 (West 2000); Ariz. Rev. Stats. sec. 25-901; Ark. Code sec. 9-11-801, to 9-11-811. See Laura Sanchez et al., "The Implementation of Covenant Marriage in Louisiana," 9 Virginia J. of Social Policy and the Law 192 (2001).

[9] 18 Cal. 2d 660, 557 P. 2d 106; 134 Cal. R. 815 (1976).

element, so long as sex was not the only object of the contract. The court was also frank: the "mores of the society" had changed, and sex without marriage was no longer taboo. The court did not want to impose on people a standard that had been "widely abandoned." The case made headlines. Dozens of cases followed, in other states; some followed the lead of the *Marvin* case, others did not. It is still a complex issue—what rights accrue to "cohabiters," and under what conditions? But courts have had to face the fact that "living in sin" is now a recognized legal category.

The Marvin case was not, as some people thought, a revival of the old doctrine of the common law marriage. A common law marriage was, after all, a completely valid marriage, with all the legal consequences of a marriage. The case was, however, yet another sign that the sexual revolution has had an enormous impact on society, and on the legal system. In the age of the sexual revolution, and the age of cohabitation, old taboos about illegitimacy also could not survive. State after state removed the legal disabilities of children whose parents were not married.[10] The illegitimate child was once called "filius nullius," that is nobody's child. Such a child had no rights of inheritance—originally, even from its mother. By 2000, the child of unmarried parents, whose father acknowledged the child, stood almost on a par with children whose parents were married in church in front of a crowd of guests. The word "bastard" was virtually obsolete. The stigma of illegitimacy had weakened enormously.

Cohabitation had an effect, too, on the law and practice of adoption. In the first half of the century, the teenage, unmarried girl who became pregnant was a key source of babies for adoption. When this became much less of a shame and a scandal, more unmarried mothers kept their babies, and the supply of such babies shrank. In the late twentieth century, too, many adopted children began to demand the right to find their "roots," to discover their "real mother" and "real father."

At the end of the century, the family seemed in many ways to be in crisis. More and more children were born to unmarried parents. This was most alarming in black families and in Hispanic families; but it was common in white families too. For those children whose parents were unmarried, but who lived in a stable union, whether or not mom and dad had a certificate made little real difference in their lives. But children raised by poor, unmarried, single mothers began life with two strikes against them.

Conservatives were also dismayed at new and strange variations on marriage and parenthood: surrogate parenting, children who had both egg mothers and womb mothers, children born through in vitro fertilization, gay couples who adopted children, and domestic partnerships. The administration of George W. Bush asked Congress in 2002 for money to help shore up marriage and cut down on illegitimacy. West Virginia began to pay welfare families a bonus, when the children were raised by married parents, and "Utah was showing a free video to couples who applied for marriage licenses,

[10] The Supreme Court gave this idea constitutional recognition in *Levy v. Louisiana,* 391 U.S. 68 (1968). Louise Levy was the unmarried mother of five children. When she died, her children tried to bring an action for wrongful death. Louisiana gave the right to sue only to legitimate children. This, said the Court, was a violation of the equal protection clause of the Fourteenth Amendment.

stressing the 'three C's,' commitment, communication, and conflict-resolving skills."[11] In Louisiana, as we saw, there was the new institution of covenant marriage. Not many people thought these devices would make much difference. This was a culture of consumption, of expressive individualism. It was a culture that saw repression (of sexual desires, among other things) as an evil. "Traditional values" faced an uphill battle.

And in some regards, they are fighting the wrong battle. Marriage and family have changed enormously; but they have also survived, and will continue to survive. They are simply in the process of changing their definitions. Some sort of essential core of marriage remains—and remains vital. This core is commitment. Even the idea of gay marriage, which so horrifies traditional people, is a kind of homage to commitment, to stability, monogamy, and to a kind of old-fashioned nuclear family. Traditional marriage has lost its monopoly of legitimacy. But one of its key ideas: long-lasting, unselfish love, is very much still alive.

[11] Amy Goldstein, "Tying Marriage Vows to Welfare Reform; White House Push for State Strategies to Promote Family Ignites Dispute," *Washington Post,* April 1, 2002, p. A1.

EPILOGUE

A FINAL WORD

The twentieth century has ended, and the twenty-first century has begun. At this writing, a conservative president, George W. Bush, is once more in the White House. He was, in a sense, put there by the legal system, or rather the court system. The election of 2000 was bitterly contested, and the results were actually in doubt. A handful of votes in Florida would decide the issue. The Supreme Court made the decisive move to end the wrangling; by a slim, 5 to 4 majority, it put an end to the recounting and the squabbling—and gave the presidency to George W. Bush.[1] At the beginning of 2004, Republicans controlled both houses, the presidency, and the Supreme Court. Conservatives talk about a return to older traditions: states' rights, a smaller, more feeble welfare state, a cap on tort recoveries, an end to "judicial activism." But nobody, conservative or liberal, Republican or Democrat, southerner or northerner, can turn back the clock. Much can change; much will change; change can go in many directions, none of them predictable. What is absolutely certain is that the past is dead.

People grumble that there are too many lawyers; that taxes are too high; that the government is the problem not the solution; that Americans are too litigious; that society is obsessed with rights, laws, too much of it for our own good; and that something has to be done. But nothing dramatic is likely to happen, at least not soon—nothing, at least, that will make the legal system shrink. A massive, powerful, active legal system is here to stay, for the foreseeable future. The reasons lie deep in the culture, in the economy, and in the political system. They lie deep in the psyche of the American people—and of all modern peoples. They lie deep, too, in American institutions. The Supreme Court, as of 2004, is a conservative Supreme Court, in some ways *very* conservative. Yet, this same court, in 2003, overruled *Bowers v. Hardwick,* a case from 1986 which upheld sodomy laws, and struck down every state sodomy law that still survived. It gave its approval (somewhat gingerly, to be sure) to affirmative action.[2] It shows no sign of crawling into the cave of "original intent," shutting down the machine of judicial review, and adopting a stance of humbleness and passivity. The same is true of the supreme courts of the various states.

A legal system is an organized system of social control. It is the skeleton, the bony structure, the musculature that holds a modern society together. Complex societies cannot live without law, in the broadest sense. Higher organisms

---

[1] *Bush* v. *Gore,* 531 U.S. 98 (2000).
[2] *Lawrence* v. *Texas,* 539 U.S. (2003) was the sodomy case; the case that upheld the affirmative action program of the University of Michigan Law School was *Grutter* v. *Bollinger,* 120 S. Ct. 2325 (2003). *Bowers v. Hardwick* was 478 U.S. 186 (1986).

cannot survive without structure and program. As long as the country lasts, in this complicated, technological, multiplex world, its legal system will be a vital part of its body, the brains and the heart of its institutions. The legal system is coextensive with society. It reflects the wants, wishes, hopes, and demands of society, in all their irrationality, ambiguity, and inconsistency. It follows every twist and turn of their development. The catastrophic attack on America, on September 11, 2001, which destroyed the World Trade Center, has already had a deep impact on politics and on the legal system as well. The "war on terror" is very much a legal war: the Patriot Act, tighter controls on immigration, federalization of air traffic control, and so on. Every crisis and incident in American history leaves its mark, and will continue to leave its mark, on the legal system, as well as on society. The Enron Corporation scandal, and other business scandals, led to calls for more laws, new laws, and changes in old laws. Scandals, tragedies, and incidents reverberate in the legal system. Even more important are and will be the slow, hidden, invisible, underground movements that in the long run shape and mold every society.

The law will reflect, as well, the yearnings of people for justice and fairness: the sense of right, and the sense of wrong. It will also reflect other, less laudable motives: prejudice, a lust for revenge, the thirst for power. It has reflected the strong push toward social and political equality—the civil rights movement, feminism, and so many other movements—but it has reflected, too, and will continue to reflect the deep inequality built into the structure of society. The law, after all, is a mirror held up against life. It is whatever results from the scheming, plotting, striving, hoping, and dreaming, of people and groups, with and for and against and athwart each other. A full history of American law would be nothing more or less than a full history of American life. The future of one is the future of the other. Exactly *how* the game will play out, in the future, is beyond our capacity to say. But the game will be played, rain or shine.

BIBLIOGRAPHICAL ESSAY

The literature on American legal history is large and getting larger all the time. In the 30 years or so since the first edition, dozens and dozens of books and articles have poured out of the presses. In this brief essay, I am trying to compile a short, selective list, mostly of books. These are exceptionally cogent, or comprehensive, or well-written, or in some other way worthy of special notice.

There is a profound shortage of *general* books on American legal history, other than this one. Another book that tries to deal with the whole history of American law, or most of it, is Kermit Hall's *The Magic Mirror: Law in American History* (1989); I also published a short text, *Law in America: A Brief History* (2002). I should also mention another book of mine, *American Law in the Twentieth Century* (2002). Kermit Hall has produced a five-volume bibliography of American legal and constitutional history, published in late 1984 under the title *A Comprehensive Bibliography of American Constitutional and Legal History, 1896–1979*. Also, Borzoi Books/Knopf has brought out a series of short paperbacks, which together cover the main periods of American legal history. Each of these books—there are five—contains an introductory essay (usually about 50 or 60 pages long), followed by some representative documents. The books are: Stephen Botein, *Early American Law and Society* (1983); George Dargo, *Law in the New Republic: Private Law and the Public Estate* (1983); Jamil Zainaldin, *Law in Antebellum Society: Legal Change and Economic Expansion* (1983); Jonathan Lurie, *Law and the Nation, 1865–1912* (1983); and Gerald L. Fetner, *Ordered Liberty: Legal Reform in the Twentieth Century* (1982). A very broad and inclusive constitutional history—at times close to a general history of the whole legal system—is Melvin I. Urofsky and Paul Finkelman, *A March of Liberty: A Constitutional History of the United States* (2 volumes, and 2 volumes of documents, 2002). There are also a number of collections of materials, for students, notably Stephen B. Presser and Jamil S. Zainaldin, *Law and Jurisprudence in American History: Cases and Materials* (5th ed., 2003). There are surprisingly few general books that try to tell the history of the law of a particular state. A rare exception is Joseph A. Ranney, *Trusting Nothing to Providence: A History of Wisconsin's Legal System* (1999); one of the broader studies of law in a particular state is William E. Nelson, *The Legalist Reformation: Law, Politics, and Ideology in New York, 1920–1980* (2001).

No student of American legal history can ignore the seminal work of J. Willard Hurst. Of his many books, *The Growth of American Law: The Law Makers* (1950), is the most general and accessible; it treats the work of certain "principal agencies of law" (the bar, the bench, the legislatures, the constitution makers), between 1790 and 1940, all with great clarity and insight. *Law and the Conditions of Freedom in the Nineteenth Century United States* (1956) is a short but brilliant essay that digs below the surface of American legal culture in the nineteenth century. Perhaps the most ambitious of Hurst's books is *Law and Economic Growth: The Legal History of the Lumber Industry in Wisconsin, 1836–1915* (1964). This is a case study, tied to a concrete time, place, and industry, but it deserves close attention for its thoughtfulness, care, and detail. Among Hurst's other works are *Law and Social Order in the United States* (1977), and *Law and Markets in United States History: Different Modes of Bargaining among Interests* (1982).

There are not many other books that present a general theory or a broad, wide-ranging approach to our legal history, or even a substantial portion of it. Two books about the transition between the colonial period and the period of the Republic, or rather between a less and a more modern phase of legal history, have evoked considerable discussion. One is Morton J. Horwitz's *The Transformation of American Law, 1780–1860* (1977); the other is William Nelson's *Americanization of the Common Law: The Impact of Legal Change on Massachusetts Society, 1760–1830* (1975).

The reader interested in the *colonial period* will want to begin with George L. Haskins's *Law and Authority in Early Massachusetts* (1960), a seminal book. A short, but well-done overview of the period is Peter C. Hoffer, *Law and People in Colonial America* (rev. ed., 1998). There are a number of collections of essays, notable David H. Flaherty, ed., *Essays in the History of Early American Law* (1969); and see also Richard B. Morris, *Studies in the History of American Law, with Special Reference to the Seventeenth and Eighteenth Centuries* (2nd ed., 1959), which is still valuable, though it has been superseded on many points by more recent work; and Christopher L. Tomlins and Bruce H. Mann, eds., *the Many Legalities of Early America* (2001). There are also collections of essays on the legal history of particular colonies, for example, Herbert A. Johnson, *Essays on New York Colonial Legal History* (1981). There are some well-crafted recent monographs on particular places and subjects. There is, to begin with, William E. Nelson's study, *Dispute and Conflict Resolution in Plymouth County, Massachusetts, 1725–1825* (1981), which, as the name suggests, laps over into the Republican period. David L. Konig, *Law and Society in Puritan Massachusetts, Essex County, 1629–1692* (1979), is one of the most insightful attempts to make sense of the colonial tapestry. The transition from English to American ways is dealt with in David G. Allen's book, *In English Ways* (1981); another important book is Marylynn Salmon, *Women and the Law of Property in Early America* (1986). There is quite a bit of work on criminal justice, for example, Julius Goebel Jr. and T. Raymond Naughton, *Law Enforcement in Colonial New York: A Study in Criminal Procedure* (1944); Douglas Greenberg, *Crime and Law Enforcement in the Colony of New York, 1691–1776* (1974). Edgar J. McManus, *Law and Liberty in Early New England: Criminal Justice and Due Process, 1620–1692* (1993), N. E. H. Hull, *Female Felons: Women and Serious Crime in Colonial Massachusetts* (1987); Donna J. Spindel, *Crime and Society in North Carolina, 1663–1776* (1989). For a rich treatment of the work of the county courts, there is Hendrik Hartog's "The Public Law of a County Court: Judicial Government in Eighteenth-Century Massachusetts," 20 Am. J. Legal Hist. 282 (1976). The literature is mostly about Massachusetts, with a bit of Virginia and New York thrown in; it would be useful if there was more work on other colonies.

The reader interested in the colonial period has another advantage: There are quite a few good modern editions of colonial court records. Joseph H. Smith's *Colonial Justice in Western Massachusetts (1639–1702), The Pynchon Court Record* (1961) is particularly noteworthy, because of its long and informative introduction. Studies of particular aspects of colonial law are not, to say the least, overabundant; but Richard B. Morris, *Government and Labor in Early America* (1946) covers this important subject in fine detail. Joseph H. Smith's *Appeal to the Privy Council from the American Plantations* (1950) is the definitive study of its subject.

The Revolution itself, and the period immediately following, have been somewhat neglected in legal history. Hendrik Hartog edited a collection of review essays, *Law in the American Revolution and the Revolution in the Law* (1981). John Phillip Reid has written extensively on the legal events leading up to the Revolution, see, for example, *In Defiance of the Law: The Standing-Army Controversy, the Two Constitutions, and the Coming of the American Revolution* (1981), and on the legal and constitutional ideology of the Revolution, see, for example, *Constitutional History of the American Revolution: the Authority of Rights* (1986). On the other hand, constitutional history, and the history of various aspects of constitutional law, has produced a gigantic literature. A good place to start is Urofsky and Finkelman, mentioned previously.

There is also an enormous literature on the drafting of the Constitution, and the "original understanding." Particularly noteworthy are Jack Rakove, *Original Meanings: Politics and Ideas in the Making of the Constitution* (1996), and Larry D. Kramer, *The People Themselves: Popular Constitututionalism and Judicial Review* (2004). There is a considerable literature on institutional history. Legal historians, to no one's surprise, are particularly interested in courts. Unlike the colonial period, certain of the nineteenth-century sources are to a degree readily available; reported appellate cases, and the state and federal statutes, can be found in any decent law library. The trial courts, alas, are if anything more obscure than in the colonial period. On court history, the U.S. Supreme Court, naturally, has garnered the lion's share of attention. Charles Warren's *The Supreme Court in United States History* (3 vols., 1922) is a genuine classic—engrossing, richly detailed, superbly easy to read. Warren had a point of view—or bias, if you will—and did not hide it; but nothing before or after provides so generous a look at the Court at work, or is so studiously attentive to the political context in which the Court does its labors. Still, eighty years of research and thought have passed since Warren's work came out. A new history of the Court, in many volumes, has been in process for what seems like forever—over 30 years, in fact. Most of the volumes by now have actually appeared. They include Volume I, *Antecedents and Beginnings to 1801*, by Julius Goebel Jr. (1971); Volume II, *Foundations of Power: John Marshall, 1801–1815* (1981), by George L. Haskins and Herbert A. Johnson; Volume V, *The Taney Period, 1836–1864* (1974), by Carl B. Swisher; Volume VI, Part One, *Reconstruction and Reunion, 1864–1888*, by Charles Fairman (1971); G. Edward White, Vol's III and IV, *The Marshall Court and Cultural Change, 1815–1835* (1988), is especially fine. These are all big books, in the physical sense, and extremely detailed. A good short treatment is William M. Wiecek, *Liberty Under Law: The Supreme Court in American Life* (1988). For specific periods, the reader can choose among a number of other books; for example, Scott Douglas Gerber, ed., *Seriatim: The Supreme Court before John Marshall* (1998); Stanley I. Kutler, *Judicial Power and Reconstruction Politics* (1968); Harold M. Hyman and William M. Wiecek, *Equal Justice under Law: Constitutional Development, 1835–1875* (1982); William F. Swindler, *Court and Constitution in the Twentieth Century: The Old Legality, 1889–1932* (1969); Arnold M. Paul, *Conservative Crisis and the Rule of Law: Attitudes of Bar and Bench, 1887–1895* (1960). There are also many books on particular doctrines or rights—for example, James W. Ely Jr., *The Guardian of Every Other Right: A Constitutional History of Property Rights* (2d ed., 1998). There are also some interesting studies of particular decisions—for example, C. Peter Magrath, *Yazoo: Law and Politics in the New Republic: The Case of Fletcher v. Peck* (1966); Stanley I. Kutler, *Privilege and Creative Destruction: The Charles River Bridge Case* (1971); Charles A. Lofgren, *The Plessy Case: A Legal-Historical Interpretation* (1987). Don E. Fehrenbacher's *The Dred Scott Case: Its Significance in American Law and Politics* (1978) is a massive and definitive study, not only of the case itself, but of many salient features in the legal and constitutional background. A shorter version, *Slavery, Law, and Politics: The Dred Scott Case in Historical Perspective*, appeared in 1981. Tony Freyer's book, *Harmony and Dissonance: The Swift and Erie Cases in American Federalism* (1981), follows the career of one important case through time. Ronald M. Labbé and Jonathan Lurie, *The Slaughterhouse Cases: Regulation, Reconstruction and the Fourteenth Amendment* (2003), is an exceptionally good and rich study of the background of these crucial cases. On the technical growth of the jurisdiction of the Supreme Court, Felix Frankfurter and James M. Landis, *The Business of the Supreme Court: A Study in the Federal Judicial System* (1928), still has value.

Some of the best work on the Supreme Court lurks in judicial biographies. Three older but excellent examples are Charles Fairman, *Mr. Justice Miller and the Supreme Court, 1862–1890* (1939), and two studies by Carl B. Swisher, *Stephen J. Field. Craftsman of the Law* (1930) and *Roger B. Taney* (1935). The old biography of John Marshall, by Albert Beveridge, is long-winded and biased, but the writing is sprightly. A more recent biography is Jean Edward Smith, *John Marshall: Definer of a Nation* (1996). Gerald T. Dunne has published a biography of Joseph Story, *Joseph Story and the Rise of the Supreme Court* (1970);

another biography is R. Kent Newmyer, *Supreme Court Justice Joseph Story: Statesman of the Old Republic* (1985). For the same period, there is Donald G. Morgan's *Justice William Johnson: The First Dissenter* (1945). For the late nineteenth century, see Linda Przybyszewski, *The Republic According to John Marshall Harlan* (1999). Paul Kens has written a new biography of Stephen Field, *Justice Stephen Field: Shaping Liberty from the Gold Rush to the Gilded Age* (1997). Mark DeWolfe Howe's study of the life of Oliver Wendell Holmes Jr., was cut short by Howe's death. Two volumes had appeared: *Justice Oliver Wendell Holmes: The Shaping Years, 1841–1870* (1957); and *Justice Oliver Wendell Holmes: The Proving Years, 1870–1882* (1963). The whole life is well covered in G. Edward White, *Justice Oliver Wendell Holmes: Law and the Inner Self* (1993). Leon Friedman and Fred L. Israel have edited *The Justices of the United States Supreme Court, 1789–1969* (1969), in four volumes. An extremely useful reference book is Kermit L. Hall, ed., *The Oxford Guide to United States Supreme Court Decisions* (1999).

The lower federal courts, and the state courts, have done much more poorly in legal scholarship. Richard E. Ellis, *The Jeffersonian Crisis: Courts and Politics in the Young Republic* (1971), is exceptional, in that it looks at courts in selected states, as well as on the federal level. A rare study of a lower federal court is Mary K. Bonsteel Tachau, *Federal Courts in the Early Republic: Kentucky, 1789–1816* (1978); others include Christian G. Fritz, *Federal Justice in California: The Court of Ogden Hoffman, 1851–1891* (1991), and Tony Freyer and Timothy Dixon, *Democracy and Judicial Independence: A History of the Federal Courts of Alabama, 1820–1994* (1995). See also Kermit L. Hall, *The Politics of Justice: Lower Federal Judicial Selection and the Second Party System, 1829–1861* (1979). Studies of state courts—one older example is Carroll T. Bond, *The Court of Appeals of Maryland: A History* (1928)—are rare, and leave a lot to be desired. Russell K. Osgood has edited *The History of the Law in Massachusetts: The Supreme Judicial Court, 1692–1992* (1992); and James W. Ely Jr., has edited *A History of the Tennessee Supreme Court* (2002). There are also a few biographies of state judges that have merit, for example, John Philip Reid, *Chief Justice, the Judicial World of Charles Doe* (1967), and Leonard Levy, *The Law of the Commonwealth and Chief Justice Shaw* (1957). For the twentieth century, there is Gerald Gunther, *Learned Hand: the Man and the Judge* (1994), an important study of a federal judge who never made it to the U.S. Supreme Court.

Historical studies of the actual work of American courts—the flow of business through them; the kinds of disputes they handle—are also not common. For a long time, the only book that could be cited here was Francis W. Laurent's *The Business of a Trial Court: 100 Years of Cases* (1959), an intriguing but somewhat unsatisfying study of the work of the trial courts of general jurisdiction in Chippewa County, Wisconsin. The literature has grown; it now includes Lawrence M. Friedman and Robert V. Percival, "A Tale of Two Courts: Litigation in Alameda and San Benito Counties," 10 Law & Society Review 267 (1976), Robert Silverman, *Law and Urban Growth: Civil Litigation in the Boston Trial Courts, 1880–1900* (1981); and Wayne V. McIntosh, *The Appeal of Civil Law: A Political-Economic Analysis of Litigation* (1990), a quantitative history of litigation in St. Louis. The very lowest courts never get much of a break in research, but justice courts were the subject of John R. Wunder, *Inferior Courts, Superior Justice: A History of the Justices of the Peace on the Northwest Frontier, 1853–1889* (1979).

For those interested in the history of the legal profession, there is Gerard W. Gawalt's book, *The Promise of Power: The Emergence of the Legal Profession in Massachusetts, 1760–1840* (1979); Maxwell Bloomfield's essays on the profession are collected in *American Lawyers in a Changing Society* (1976); and Gerard W. Gawalt has edited an (uneven) group of essays in *The New High Priests: Lawyers in Post-Civil War America* (1984). A general study of lawyers, which has a great deal of historical material is Richard L. Abel, *American Lawyers* (1989). William F. English, *The Pioneer Lawyer and Jurist in Missouri* (1947), makes lively reading. There are a few more specialized studies, for example, William G. Thomas, *Lawyering for the Railroad: Business, Law, and Power in the New South* (1999).

Another good read is William F. Keller, *The Nation's Advocate, Henry Marie Bracken-ridge and Young America* (1956). This book also represents a large and very mixed litera-ture: biographies of lawyers. If the "lawyer" has made his mark in another field, too, the material tends to balloon—for example, Abraham Lincoln, treated in John P. Frank, *Lincoln as a Lawyer* (1961); and John J. Duff, *A. Lincoln, Prairie Lawyer* (1960). Thus, there are many biographies of Daniel Webster; the most comprehensive is Robert V. Remini, *Daniel Webster: The Man and His Time* (1997). But rare indeed are books that open the door to the lawyer's office, so to speak.

The monumental edition of *The Law Practice of Alexander Hamilton: Documents and Commentary,* in five volumes (Vol. I, 1964, and Vol. II, 1969, edited by Julius Goebel Jr.; Vol. III, 1980, Vol. IV, 1980, and Vol. V, 1981, edited by Goebel and Joseph Smith), does nobly for the period around 1800; Webster's legal papers, too, are in the process of getting themselves edited; a number of volumes, edited by Alfred S. Konefsky and Andrew J. King, have so far appeared. One wishes a similar job could be done for the Wall Street lawyer of the late nineteenth century; but there is at least some raw mate-rial in the law-office histories that have appeared, notably, Robert T. Swaine, *The Cra-vath Firm and Its Predecessors, 1819–1947,* Vol. I, *The Predecessor Firms, 1819–1906* (1946). Henry W. Taft's book, *A Century and a Half at the New York Bar* (1938), is entertaining reading. Harold Hyman's *Craftsmanship and Character: A History of the Vinson and Elkins Law Firm of Houston, 1917–1997* (1998) is a rare example of a law-firm history done by a first-rate historian.

On legal education, Alfred Z. Reed, *Training for the Public Profession of the Law* (1921), is old but useful. Robert B. Stevens, *Law School: Legal Education in America from the 1850s to the 1980s* (1983), is the most comprehensive treatment of the subject; there is also William P. LaPiana, *Logic and Experience: The Origin of Modern American Legal Education* (1994). In addition, a number of law schools, most notably Harvard, have had their chroniclers; Arthur E. Sutherland's *The Law at Harvard: A History of Ideas and Men, 1817–1967* (1967) is quite readable; see also David J. Langum and Howard P. Walthall, *From Maverick to Mainstream: Cumberland School of Law, 1847–1997* (1997). Frank L. Ellsworth, *Law on the Midway: The Founding of the University of Chicago Law School* (1977), is particularly interesting for the light it sheds on the spread of the influence of Har-vard. Elizabeth G. Brown, *Legal Education in Michigan, 1859–1959* (1959), covers the first century of this important school.

The literature on legal literature and on legal thought is not entirely satisfactory. Perry Miller collected some snippets and edited them under the title *The Legal Mind in America: From Independence to the Civil War* (1962). Miller's own treatment of the subject in *The Life of the Mind in America: From the Revolution to the Civil War* (1965), is, to me at least, not very enlightening. On lawyers and general culture, see Robert A. Ferguson, *Law and Literature in American Culture* (1987). There is also Charles M. Cook, *The Amer-ican Codification Movement: A Study of Antebellum Legal Reform* (1981). For the end of the century, one can cite Clyde Jacobs, *Law Writers and the Courts: The Influence of Thomas M. Cooley, Christopher G. Tiedeman, and John F. Dillon upon American Constitutional Law* (1954). Legal thought is covered also in Morton Horwitz, *The Transformation of Ameri-can Law, 1870–1960: The Crisis of Legal Orthodoxy* (1992). On civil procedure, there is a rather ponderous but carefully executed book by Robert W. Millar, *Civil Procedure of the Trial Court in Historical Perspective* (1952); federal jurisdiction, which seems like a dry and uninviting subject, is skillfully illuminated—and its social importance deci-phered—in Edward A. Purcell Jr., *Litigation and Inequality: Federal Diversity Jurisdiction in Industrial America, 1870–1958* (1992).

A number of monographs have appeared on the subject of state constitution-making; of special interest are Willi P. Adams, *The First American Constitutions: Republican Ideology and the Making of the State Constitutions in the Revolutionary Era* (1980); Fletcher M. Green, *Constitutional Development in the South Atlantic States, 1776–1860* (1966); and Carl B.

Swisher, *Motivation and Political Technique in the California Constitutional Convention, 1878–1879* (1930). One interesting side show in American legal history is treated in William M. Robinson Jr., *Justice in Grey: A History of the Judicial System of the Confederate States of America* (1941); another is considered in Carol Weisbrod, *The Boundaries of Utopia* (1980), which deals with the internal affairs of "self-contained communities" in the United States (the Oneida community, for example). Frontier law has generated far more heat and romance than light. A careful glimpse of an early period is in William Baskerville Hamilton, *Anglo-American Law on the Frontier: Thomas Rodney and His Territorial Cases* (1953); for later periods, it is hard to resist a book as lively as Glenn Shirley's *Law West of Fort Smith: A History of Frontier Justice in the Indian Territory, 1834–1896* (1957). Two books by John Phillip Reid are important studies of legal culture in the West: *Law for the Elephant: Property and Social Behavior on the Overland Trail* (1980), and *Policing the Elephant: Crime, Punishment, and Social Behavior on the Overland Trail* (1997), both of which deal with the living law of the pioneers who followed the trails to Oregon and California in the middle of the nineteenth century.

The *substantive* law is a mixed bag. Many areas have never gotten their due. No one seriously interested in American legal history should ignore the series of books that emerged from the workshops of the University of Wisconsin law school, under the direct or indirect influence of J. Willard Hurst, all dealing with one or another aspect of law in Wisconsin, chiefly in the nineteenth century. Taken as a whole, these books provide the fullest available picture of the law in action in a single state. Some are better or more readable than others. Robert S. Hunt's *Law and Locomotives: The Impact of the Railroad on Wisconsin Law in the Nineteenth Century* (1958) is particularly fascinating. Others in the series include Lawrence M. Friedman, *Contract Law in America: A Social and Economic Case Study* (1965); Spencer Kimball, *Insurance and Public Policy: A Study in the Legal Implementation of Social and Economic Public Policy* (1960); and George J. Kuehnl, *The Wisconsin Business Corporation* (1959).

The Wisconsin school of legal history has had a special interest in the relationship between law and the economic system, and between law and business. This aspect of law has been treated rather better than certain other aspects of law in the nineteenth century, though no one would say that anywhere near enough work had been done. The area, too, is much illuminated by the literature on government's role in the economy— works such as Oscar and Mary Handlin, *Commonwealth: A Study of the Role of Government in the American Economy: Massachusetts, 1774–1861* (rev. ed., 1969); and Louis Hartz, *Economic Policy and Democratic Thought: Pennsylvania, 1776–1860* (1948); Harry N. Scheiber, *Ohio Canal Era: A Case Study of Government and the Economy, 1820–1861* (1969); William J. Novak, *The People's Welfare: Law and Regulation in Nineteenth-Century America* (1996). Harry N. Scheiber has edited *The State and Freedom of Contract* (1998). On banking and the law, there is Bray Hammond, *Banks and Politics in America from the Revolution to the Civil War* (1957); he also published *Sovereignty and an Empty Purse, Banks and Politics in the Civil War* (1970). On railroad regulation, there is the Hunt study, mentioned previously, for Wisconsin; Edward C. Kirkland, *Men, Cities and Transportation: A Study in New England History, 1820–1900* (2 vols., 1948); George H. Miller, *Railroads and the Granger Laws* (1971); and the iconoclastic study by Gabriel Kolko, *Railroads and Regulation, 1877–1916* (1965). James W. Ely Jr., *Railroads and American Law* (2001), is an important recent study; and so too is Barbara Young Welke's book, *Recasting American Liberty: Gender, Race, Law, and the Railroad Revolution, 1865–1920* (2001). On the ICC Act, and administrative development in general, see Stephen Skowronek, *Building a New American State: The Expansion of National Administrative Capacities, 1877–1920* (1982). For the background and early history of the antitrust laws, see William R. Letwin, *Law and Economic Policy in America: The Evolution of the Sherman Antitrust Act* (1965); on antitrust and other aspects of business and corporation law, see Herbert Hovenkamp, *Enterprise and American Law, 1836–1937* (1991); see also Morton Keller, *Regulating a New Economy: Public*

Policy and Economic Change in America, 1900–1933 (1990). There has been some excellent work on bankruptcy: Peter Coleman, *Debtors and Creditors in America: Insolvency, Imprisonment for Debt, and Bankruptcy, 1607–1900* (1974); David A. Skeel Jr., *Debt's Dominion: A History of Bankruptcy Law in America* (2002), Edward Balleisen, *Navigating Failure: Bankruptcy and Commercial Society in Antebellum America* (2001); Bruce Mann., *Republic of Debtors: Bankruptcy in the Age of American Independence* (2002). On tort law, see Randolph E. Bergstrom, *Courting Danger: Injury and Law in New York City, 1870–1910* (1992); John Fabian Witt, *The Accidental Republic: Crippled Workmen, Destitute Widows, and the Remaking of American Law* (2004). On corporation law, there is John William Cadman, *The Corporation in New Jersey: Business and Politics* (1949); and Ronald E. Seavoy, *The Origins of the American Business Corporation, 1784–1855* (1982); also Herbert Hovenkamp's book, cited earlier. On taxation, there is Randolph E. Paul, *Taxation in the United States* (1954); on the development of the law of municipal corporations, Hendrik Hartog, *Public Property and Private Power: The Corporation of the City of New York in American Law, 1730–1870* (1983), and Jon C. Teaford, *The Unheralded Triumph: City Government in America, 1870–1900* (1984). The literature on labor law is quite rich. I want to mention two books by Christopher L. Tomlins, *Law, Labor, and Ideology in the Early American Republic* (1993); and *The State and the Unions: Labor Relations, Law, and the Organized Labor Movement in America, 1880–1960* (1985). Another important study is William E. Forbath, *Law and the Shaping of the American Labor Movement* (1991).

In general, the law of property is still waiting for its prince to come and rouse it from the long sleep of obscurity. Public land law has done a bit better than the rest of this field. A comprehensive, early account is Benjamin H. Hibbard, *A History of the Public Land Policies* (1924); another treatment is Paul Gates, *History of Public Land Law Development* (1968). Vernon Carstensen collected important essays and edited them under the title of *The Public Lands: Studies in the History of the Public Domain* (1963). A key essay on eminent domain law is Harry N. Scheiber's "The Road to *Munn:* Eminent Domain and the Concept of Public Purpose in the State Courts," in Donald Fleming and Bernard Bailyn, eds., *Law in American History* (1971), p. 329. Carole Shammas, Marylynn Salmon, and Michel Dahlin's *Inheritance in America: From Colonial Times to the Present* (1987) fills in a very glaring gap in the historical record; and so does Paul Goldstein, *Copyright's Highway: From Gutenberg to the Celestial Jukebox* (rev. ed , 2003). On the concept and ideology of property, see Gregory S. Alexander, *Commodity and Propriety: Competing Visions of Property in American Legal Thought, 1776–1970* (1997); on land and water law, see Donald J. Pisani, *Water, Land, and Law in the West: The Limits of Public Policy, 1850–1920* (1996).

For a long time, criminal law and criminal justice were surprisingly neglected. But the situation has much improved. A general treatment is Lawrence M. Friedman, *Crime and Punishment in American History* (1993). See, for specific states or topics, Jack K. Williams, *Vogues in Villainy: Crime and Retribution in Ante-Bellum South Carolina* (1959); Michael S. Hindus, *Prison and Plantation: Crime, Justice, and Authority in Massachusetts and South Carolina, 1767–1878* (1980); Lawrence M. Friedman and Robert V. Percival, *The Roots of Justice: Crime and Punishment in Alameda County, California, 1870–1910* (1981); Edward L. Ayers, *Vengeance and Justice, Crime and Punishment in the 19th-Century American South* (1984); James M. Denham, *A Rogue's Paradise: Crime and Punishment in Antebellum Florida* (1997). Samuel Walker, *Popular Justice: A History of American Criminal Justice* (1980) is a readable general survey. On the police, see Roger Lane, *Policing the City: Boston, 1822–1885* (1967); and Wilbur R. Miller, *Cops and Bobbies: Police Authority in New York and London, 1830–1870* (1977). There are useful essays in *Violence in America: Historical and Comparative Perspectives*, edited by Hugh D. Graham and Ted R. Gurr (1969), a report submitted to the National Commission on the Causes and Prevention of Violence. Other relevant studies include Richard Maxwell Brown, *Strain of Violence: Historical Studies of American Violence and Vigilantism* (1975); Roger Lane, *Violent Death in the City: Suicide, Accident and Murder in 19th Century Philadelphia* (1979); and *Murder in America: A History* (1997); see also Eric H. Monkkonen, *Murder in New York City* (2001). For the death penalty, see Stuart Banner, *The Death Penalty: An American History* (2002); on plea bargaining, George Fisher, *Plea Bargaining's Triumph: A History of Plea Bargaining in America* (2003).

David J. Rothman's provocative book, *The Discovery of the Asylum, Social Order and Disorder in the New Republic* (1971), illuminates many areas of legal and social history. The theme of the book is the shift to institutional treatment of deviants in the nineteenth century—the rise to prominence of the penitentiary, poorhouse, insane asylum, and the juvenile house of refuge. Rothman continued the story in *Conscience and Convenience: The Asylum and Its Alternatives in Progressive America* (1980). A later treatment of the rise of the penitentiary is Adam J. Hirsch, *The Rise of the Penitentiary: Prisons and Punishment in Early America* (1992). Rothman's work straddles welfare history and the history of criminal justice; this double treatment is found also in Eric H. Monkkonen's book, *The Dangerous Class: Crime and Poverty in Columbus, Ohio, 1860–1885* (1975). This is perhaps also the best place to mention Joseph Gusfield's stimulating study of the liquor laws, *Symbolic Crusade: Status Politics and the American Temperance Movement* (1963).

Welfare law itself is another field that is developing a significant literature. In the 1930s, a series of studies of the poor laws came out of the University of Chicago, under the sponsorship of the School of Social Service Administration. A typical example was Alice Shaffer, Mary W. Keefer, and Sophonisba P. Breckinridge, *The Indiana Poor Law* (1936). The overall quality of these publications left something to be desired. Henry Farnam, *Chapters in the History of Social Legislation in the United States to 1860* (1938), is still of value; another monograph is James Leiby, *Charity and Correction in New Jersey* (1967). Joel Handler has edited *Family Law and the Poor: Essays by Jacobus ten Broek* (1971), and has written a number of books on welfare policy, including *The Poverty of Welfare Reform* (1995). A good overall study is Michael Katz, *In the Shadow of the Poorhouse: A Social History of Welfare in America* (rev. ed., 1996). On the early history of housing law, see Lawrence M. Friedman, *Government and Slum Housing: A Century of Frustration* (1968); on environmental law, Earl F. Murphy, *Water Purity: A Study in Legal Control of Natural Resources* (1961).

There has been rapid progress, too, in family law, once a stepchild of research. Michael Grossberg, *Governing the Hearth: Law and the Family in Nineteenth-Century America* (1985) was the beginning of a boom in studies of marriage, divorce, and family law in general. A notable book is Nancy F. Cott, *Public Vows: A History of Marriage and the Nation* (2000). On divorce, Nelson M. Blake, *The Road to Reno: A History of Divorce in the United States* (1962), is good reading; see also Richard H. Chused, *Private Acts in Public Places: A Social History of Divorce in the Formative Era of American Family Law* (1994); Norma Basch, *Framing American Divorce: From the Revolutionary Generation to the Victorians* (1999); Lawrence M. Friedman, *Private Lives: Families, Individuals, and the Law* (2004). William L. O'Neill's book, *Divorce in the Progressive Era* (1967), is provocative and important. Another study of the same period is Elaine Tyler May, *Great Expectations: Marriage and Divorce in Post-Victorian America* (1980). On married women's property laws, see Norma Basch, *In the Eyes of the Law: Women, Marriage, and Property in Nineteenth-Century New York* (1982). D. Kelly Weisberg has edited two volumes on *Women and the Law: The Social Historical Perspective* (1982); the essays collected here vary in quality and theme, but they gave a good overview of women's legal history.

The law of slavery and race relations is often treated in general books on these subjects, for example, in some of the classics in the field: Kenneth Stampp's *The Peculiar Institution: Slavery in the Ante-Bellum South* (1956); or C. Vann Woodward's *The Strange Career of Jim Crow* (rev. ed., 1966); John Hope Franklin and Alfred A. Moss Jr., *From Slavery to Freedom: A History of African Americans* (8th ed., 2002), is a standard text. There is also a developing literature on the subject that stresses the legal side; very notably,

Thomas D. Morris, *Southern Slavery and the Law, 1619–1860* (1996). Criminal justice is treated in Hindus and Ayers's books, cited previously; and there is also Robert M. Cover, *Justice Accused: Antislavery and the Judicial Process* (1975); Philip J. Schwarz, *Twice Condemned: Slaves and the Criminal Laws of Virginia, 1705–1865* (1988). On slavery and federalism, see Paul Finkelman, *An Imperfect Union: Slavery, Federalism, and Comity* (1981). See also Paul Finkelman, ed., *Slavery and the Law* (1996); and A. E. Keir Nash's long essay, "Reason of Slavery: Understanding the Judicial Role in the Peculiar Institution," in 32 Vanderbilt Law Review 7 (1979). On the period afterwards, see Leon F. Litwack, *Trouble in Mind: Black Southerners in the Age of Jim Crow* (1998). There is a growing literature, too, on native Americans and the law. See, for example, Edward Lazarus, *Black Hills, White Justice: The Sioux Nation versus the United States, 1775 to the Present* (1991). On the Chinese, see Lucy Salyer, *Laws Harsh as Tigers: Chinese Immigrants and the Shaping of Modern Immigration Law* (1995); on the treatment of the Latter Day Saints, see Sarah Barringer Gordon, *The Mormon Question: Polygamy and Constitutional Conflict in Nineteenth Century America* (2002); Edwin B. Firmage and Richard C. Mangrum, *Zion in the Courts: A Legal History of the Church of Jesus Christ of Latter-Day Saints* (1988).

The literature on the twentieth century has also become enormous, and I will content myself with the barest of minima. General books that include the twentieth century have already been mentioned. On the Supreme Court, as usual, the literature is particularly vast. See, for example, Melvin Urofsky, *Division and Discord: The Supreme Court under Stone and Vinson, 1941–1953* (1997). The Warren Court is treated in Morton J. Horwitz, *The Warren Court and the Pursuit of Justice* (1998); and Lucas A. Powe Jr., *The Warren Court and American Politics* (2000); see also Bernard Schwartz ed., *The Warren Court: A Retrospective* (1996). On civil liberties, a useful summary is Samuel Walker, *The Rights Revolution: Rights and Community in Modern America* (1998). There is a particularly rich literature on *Brown v. Board of Education* and the rights revolution. See, in particular, Richard Kluger, *Simple Justice* (1976); Austin Sarat, ed., *Race, Law, and Culture: Reflections on Brown v. Board of Education* (1997); Mary L. Dudziak, *Cold War Civil Rights: Race and the Image of American Democracy* (2000). The bibliography in my own book, *American Law in the Twentieth Century*, is, I hope, a useful guide to some of the literature, and can supplement the works listed here.

INDEX

600INDEX